I0741353

# LAST TO KNOW

## MICALEA SMELTZER

- A WILLOW CREEK NOVEL -

Music gives a soul to the universe,
Wings to the mind,
Flight to the imagination,
And
Life to everything.
—Plato

# CHAPTER ONE

The grass crunched beneath my feet as I followed Sadie through the fair entrance. I hadn't even wanted to come. I would rather be home reading or playing the piano, but Sadie, who'd been my best friend since we were in diapers, was relentless.

It was the first official day of summer vacation and she didn't want me to lock myself in my house until school started in August and I was forced to emerge.

She called this fun.

I called it hell.

"Isn't this nice, Emma?" She chimed, clapping her hands together. Her brown eyes were bright and happy.

"Uh… *nice* isn't the word I'd choose." I wrinkled my nose at the trash littering the grass. Some guy bumped into me, knocking me to the side. I reached up to keep my hat from falling off. It was one of those large black round hats that helped to shade my face from the sun. Sadie said it looked ridiculous, but I liked it. I'd never been one to take another person's opinion to heart. My mom raised me to be a free spirit like her, so I always did my own thing.

"Emma!" Sadie groaned when she saw I'd been separated from her. "Taking you places is like having a child. I take my eyes off of you for two seconds and you're gone." She grabbed my arm, dragging me through the crowd. "Willow Creek is playing and I won't miss this! I had to give Adam Carson a lap dance to get these tickets at the last minute."

"Ew! Sadie! You gave him a lap dance?!"

People turned to stare at us with my exclamation.

"A girl's gotta do what a girl's gotta do." She gave me a look like I'd know exactly what she meant.

"I don't even want to go!" I complained. "I don't know who they are, and I won't like their music anyway!"

"Well, we can't all be freaks that listen to classical music, like Beethoven," she argued.

"Why don't you go on without me," I pleaded, semi impressed that she knew who Beethoven was. "Look, food!" I pointed to a stand. "I'll get something to eat while you go listen to them play and we'll meet up afterwards."

"You *really* don't want to go, do you?" She frowned, her brows drawing together. Sadie wasn't used to me balking at her plans.

"Not really," I shrugged. "I'll probably just get a headache and want to go home afterwards."

She sighed. "Fine, you get something to eat, I'll go to the concert, and then we'll walk around for a while."

"Great," I said, prying my arm from her hold.

"I'll see you in a little bit!" She grinned, skipping off towards the bleachers in front of the stage. Her wavy brown hair swished around her shoulders.

I headed for the area with the food vendors, thankful that I'd gotten out of going to the concert. Willow Creek was the star act this year at the fair. Some local band that was making it big. I didn't know who they were or what they sang, and I didn't care to find out.

I grabbed a hotdog and fries before finding a vacant picnic table.

I heard the music start up a few minutes later with a clash of drums.

I sighed. Yep, so not my thing.

After I finished eating, I grabbed my purse—a large messenger bag with tie-dye strings of fabric hanging off of it—and pulled out the book I was reading. I never left home without something to read.

I got sucked into the fictional world of fairies and completely lost track of time.

I was shocked when I looked up and realized the sun was setting and people were clearing off the bleachers.

Where was Sadie?

I looked around, scanning the crowd of people for her.

I started to panic when I couldn't find her.

It wouldn't be the first time Sadie had ditched me, usually for a guy.

Some people might think she was a crappy friend, but Sadie was just… Sadie. And when I really needed her she was always there for me.

I tucked my book back into the bag, grabbed my trash, and dropped it in the nearest trashcan.

All the while I kept looking for Sadie.

I grabbed my phone sending her a text asking where she was.

Unfortunately, if she was with a guy I wouldn't get a reply—and cell service was spotty on the fairgrounds anyway. I was *so* giving her a piece of my mind for this. I hadn't even wanted to come! And *of course* I'd gotten a ride with her, so I was trapped at the frigging Clarke County fair twenty to thirty minutes from home. In other words, there was no way I could walk. And since my mom didn't even own a cellphone it wasn't like I could call her—and she'd be working in her studio at this time, which meant she wouldn't even hear the home phone ring.

"Are you lost?"

I squeaked at the sound of the voice and took a few steps back. I almost fell in a hole and the guy reached out to steady me.

"Whoa, are you okay?" He asked, flicking dark hair from his eyes. It was slightly damp with sweat, as was his whole body. I wondered what he'd been doing to get that sweaty, but then decided I'd rather not know. While I watched him he pulled a baseball cap out of his back pocket and fixed it onto his head, pulling the brim down low so that half his face was shadowed.

"I'm fine." I straightened my cardigan and squared my shoulders. "I'm… I'm waiting for someone." I didn't want to give this guy the impression he could take advantage of me.

He grinned crookedly, tilting his head. "Something tells me you're lying." He scratched his stubbled chin. He couldn't be more than two years older than me, maybe nineteen or twenty at the most, but something in his silvery gray eyes made him seem so much older. Like he'd had a rough life or something. It made me a little more trusting of him. I could relate to rough. My dad was an alcoholic and before he walked out on us things had been bad. "I promise I don't bite."

"I can't find my friend," I shrugged. "I'm sure she'll show up eventually." I looked around—for the thousandth time—hoping Sadie was about to jump out from behind one of the stands and scream, "Gotcha!" But she didn't, of course.

"Would you like me to wait with you?" He asked, tapping his fingers along his jean clad leg.

I looked around at all the people milling around and decided there wasn't much this guy could do to me in public.

"That would be great," I smiled. "Thank you for offering."

His lips twisted, almost as if he was trying not to laugh at me. "I'm going to grab a bottle of water and then we can find a table."

"Okay." I fell into step beside him. I checked my phone and wasn't surprised to find nothing from Sadie.

He bought a bottle of water from one of the vendors and cheese fries—the kind with the liquid cheese that grossed me out.

"Come on," he tilted his head towards a free picnic table. "Let's just sit down for a while and look for your friend. What exactly does she look like?"

"Tall, brown hair, pretty," I shrugged.

He laughed. "You just described half of the girls here. Although, none of them are as pretty as you," he winked.

My cheeks heated and I looked down. I wasn't used to being called pretty. Most of the people that I went to school with, guys and girls, thought I was weird. I was *different*, and people didn't seem to understand different. It was all too easy to pass me up as odd.

"Surely you know you're pretty," the guy added. "I think I might be developing a crush on your freckles."

When I was little I hated my freckles. None of the other kids had them and I'd been embarrassed, but as I got older I learned to love them because they were a part of me. My mom always told me there was no point in not loving yourself, because you can't change who you are and might as well embrace it.

"What's your name?" I asked him, wanting to steer the topic of conversation away from myself.

"Maddox." He answered, wiping his cheese covered fingers on a napkin. "Yours?"

"Emma."

"Emma," he repeated. "I like that."

"Um… thank you?" It came out as a question.

He chuckled, like my awkwardness was cute or something. "Are you from around here, Emma?"

"About twenty or so minutes from here," I shrugged.

"Winchester?" He asked.

"Uh… yeah… how'd you know?"

"Don't worry," he laughed, "I'm not a creep, it's just where I'm from."

"Oh," I relaxed.

"We have a lot in common," he continued, eating another heart attack inducing cheese fry.

"We do?"

"Yeah," he nodded.

"I don't see how we have much in common except where we live…"

"Really?" He quirked a brow. "You look like you don't want to be here and I don't want to be here either. That's another thing we have in common."

"I don't like crowds," I mumbled.

"What a coincidence," he grinned widely. "I don't either!"

I narrowed my eyes at him.

"What?" He frowned. "You don't believe me?"

"I don't know you," I countered. "How could I tell if you were being serious or sarcastic?"

"Then why don't you get to know me," he suggested. "Go on a date with me."

I gaped at him, unable to form a coherent sentence. "You're very presumptuous."

"I'm not asking you to go to bed with me, *that* would be presumptuous. A date allows two people to get to know each other in a no stress environment."

"No stress?" I laughed. "I hardly consider a date as no stress."

He tapped his fingers against the top of the table. I was beginning to wonder if it was a nervous habit or something.

"So… are you saying no the date?"

"Yes. No. I don't know," I stammered. "You're making me nervous." My hands wrung together beneath the table where he couldn't see.

He chuckled, taking off the hat and running his fingers through his hair before replacing it. "I make lots of people nervous."

"I'm only seventeen," I warned, the words tumbling out of my mouth before I could stop them, "so if you're like twenty-five you might want to give up now."

"Do I looked twenty-five to you?" He laughed.

"No," I squirmed.

"I just turned nineteen," he supplied. "Is that too old for you?"

"I don't date," I mumbled, hoping he'd get tired of me and just leave.

"I find it hard to believe that a girl as beautiful as you doesn't date." He flicked the plastic top to the water bottle into the grass and I almost felt like scolding him for it, but I couldn't find the words. "And I hardly think one date is that dangerous."

"You're annoyingly persistent," I mumbled.

He grinned widely, his teeth perfectly straight and white. "I guess I just don't want to get old and look back on my life and wonder what would've happened if I asked the pretty girl with freckles that I met at the fair out on a date," he rambled.

This guy? Was he for real? And yet I found myself succumbing to his charms. "Fine, I'll go on a date with you," I mumbled, agreeing mostly to get him to shut up. As soon as I finished speaking I realized I'd just agreed to go on a date with a virtual stranger.

"Excellent," he grinned, and I couldn't stop my smile, "and wear that hat, I like it."

Wait until I told Sadie that one.

"Any word from your friend?" He asked, eyeing my phone that lay on the table.

I checked it even though I knew there was no message. "Nothing," I mumbled.

"You need to find a better friend," he joked.

"I think you might be right," I frowned.

He stood up and held his hand out for me. "Well, we're already here, we might as well have fun."

I eyed his hand like it was a live grenade that might detonate at any second. He wiggled his fingers, trying to coax me. Instead of accepting his hand I stood up to follow him. He let his hand drop to his side and smiled to show that he wasn't offended.

He started to walk away, assuming I would follow, and I called, "Maddox!"

"Yeah?" He turned around.

"Your trash… are you just going to leave it?" I frowned.

He narrowed his eyes at me. "Are you one of those girls that's always preaching about saving the environment and won't eat meat?"

"No," I scoffed. "I'll have you know that I can devour a cheeseburger in three seconds flat."

He laughed. "Good." He came back and picked up his trash, discarding it. "Coming?" He called over his shoulder.

I hurried after him.

"Nice boots." He pointed to my flowery Doc Martens styled shoes.

"Thanks," I smiled.

"What do you want to do? There's pretty much everything." He shoved his hands in his pockets. "There's the carnival setup over there," he nodded his head, "or the track… although it's probably too late for that. Or we could take a look at the different booths—we might find something interesting there."

I found Maddox's rambling endearing.

"I don't know, this isn't exactly my scene," I shrugged.

He chuckled, grinning crookedly. He peered down at me and I realized now how much taller he was than me. His white t-shirt stretched taut across his muscular chest, making his tanned skin seem even darker. My eyes ventured further down and I saw that he wore black jeans with a studded belt and boots.

"Are you checking me out, Emma?"

"What? No! Of course not!" I flailed.

He chuckled, rubbing his jaw to hide his widening smile. "You definitely were. It's okay. You can look, but no touching below the belt… yet."

I gaped at him. He did *not* just say that.

He laughed, continuing to play with me. "I like to know girls a little better before I unleash the beast. It might scare them."

I didn't know what to say and I kind of felt like running away.

He reached out, wrapping his arms around my shoulders, drawing me against his muscular body. "If you're going to go on a date with me, you better get used to my sense of humor."

"I'm not sure I want to," I mumbled.

"Oh come on, I'm delightful."

I wasn't sure delightful was the word I'd use to describe Maddox. Then again, I'd only met him thirty minutes ago.

"You say delightful, I say crude."

"Oh, you wound me." He grasped his heart with his free hand.

"I doubt your ego is bruised." I couldn't help smiling at him. There was something about him that was infectious and easy to like.

"Don't doubt my affection for you, Emma. I promise you it's more than bruised. It's downright shattered."

I couldn't contain my laughter.

"You know what, forget this madness," he waved his arm to encompass all the roaming people. His other was still slung around my shoulder, a heavy and warm reminder of his presence. "You wanna just talk for a while?"

"Talk?"

"Yeah, you know, where you move your mouth like this," he mimed with his hand, "and words come out."

"Uh… isn't that what we've been doing?" I asked, confused.

"Yes, but I think it's imperative that we get to know each other better before our date so that we can avoid the obligatory awkward first date and get to the fun stuff."

"The fun stuff?" I repeated. "This isn't the below the belt stuff is it?"

"Of course not, Emma. What kind of man do you take me for? I'm offended."

"Hey, you were the one that brought that up before," I defended.

He steered me away from the crowd and towards the now empty bleachers. A crew was packing up the stage equipment and loading it onto a truck with the Willow Creek logo—a willow tree with a tire swing.

"Anyway," he continued, leading me up to the very top of the bleachers and sitting down, "I figure if we know each other a little better tonight, then the hard part is out of the way for our date."

I was still shocked that I'd actually agreed to go on a date with him, but he had a point.

He stretched his legs out on the bleachers in front of him. "So, tell me a little bit about yourself."

"There's not much to tell," I shrugged, playing with a strand of my wavy blonde hair.

"You really suck at this whole getting to know each other thing." He grinned.

"You're right," I frowned. I guessed I'd spent too much time avoiding people that now I didn't really know what to do. I took a deep breath and tried to think of something to tell him that wouldn't be too personal or exposing. "I play piano. Does that suffice?"

"It does," he grinned. "I happen to play the drums."

"Really?" I asked, surprised. "You're not just telling me that so that I'll think you're cool, are you?"

He laughed, ducking his head so that the brim of the baseball cap hid his face. "Not at all. Scoot over."

I slid away from him and he leaned over, plucking drumsticks from his back pocket and hit them against the bleachers—creating a beat. "Believe me now?" He quirked a brow.

"I believe you."

He continued to drum, spinning one of the sticks around his fingers in a fancy trick. "I can keep going if you don't believe me," he grinned boyishly.

"I said I believed you," I laughed.

He smiled, and the drumming ceased. "Ah, that's what I wanted."

"What?" I asked confused.

"To hear your laugh. It's beautiful, just like you."

"You're full of all kinds of cheesy lines," I laughed.

"Cheesy?" He faked that he was offended. Removing the baseball cap he said, "Most girls eat that stuff up."

"I'm not most girls," I stated. I wasn't like most people my age and I was fine with that. I was happy to be a free spirit like my mom.

"I'm beginning to see that." He smiled, closing the space between us so that our legs touched.

I hadn't even wanted to come to the stupid fair, and I'd been pissed at Sadie for abandoning me, but sitting here with Maddox made me glad I had come. Even if he was a bit cocky, I liked him for some reason.

Looking out at the dark sky, I frowned. "I better call for a taxi," I mumbled. Since apparently Sadie had left I had no choice. She was getting a mouthful later.

"Taxi?" Maddox's eyebrows furrowed together and he looked at me with a perplexed expression. "Why would you call for a taxi?"

"Uh…" Now it was my turn to look at him weird. "Because I need to go home. It's getting late."

"I can take you home," he offered.

"No, that's not necessary." I waved away his concern.

"Don't be silly," he stood up. "I'm heading that way anyway. We'll go together."

"I don't know," I frowned.

I might like Maddox, but I didn't *know* him. Getting in a car alone with him could be dangerous.

"Come on," he coaxed, "I'll find my brother and we'll head out. What do you think?"

Brother? So we wouldn't be alone. I guessed that made it better. "Yeah, sure."

"Great," he grinned. "Here, let me help you," he held a hand out to me.

"Uh…"

"It's just my hand and these steps can be shaky, plus it's getting dark. Just let me help you," he pleaded.

He was right and I was being stupid. He just… he made me nervous.

I placed my hand in his and he helped me off the bleachers. There'd still been enough light when we climbed up them that I hadn't had a problem, but now I was glad for the security his hand provided.

When we were on solid ground again he released my hand. For some reason I missed the feel of it.

He pulled his phone out of his pocket, texting his brother I assumed. A few seconds later his phone vibrated with a response.

"He says he's at the entrance."

"Cool," I said for lack of anything else to say.

"So, you said you were seventeen?" When I nodded, he added, "Does that mean this is your last summer before you're a senior?"

"It is," I nodded.

"Have you decided what you're going to do after school?"

"No," I admitted, wincing. "Are you in college or working?" I asked, tilting my head back to look up at him.

"…I guess you could say I'm working."

"You guess?" I questioned, confused.

"It's complicated," he shrugged.

I wondered exactly what he meant by complicated, but I didn't think he was likely to answer if I asked.

"I see him," Maddox pointed up ahead.

I squinted, not sure if I was seeing right.

"Uh…" I paused, looking from his brother to him. What the actual fuck? Were they clones or something? I guessed the more plausible explanation would be that they were twins, but a Maddox clone sounded a hell of a lot cooler.

We stopped in front of his brother and Maddox introduced us. "Emma, this is my twin brother Mathias."

"Hi, nice to meet you," I smiled.

"Whatever." Mathias rolled his eyes, and strolled off towards the parking lot.

"Sorry," Maddox frowned. "He doesn't like people… or animals… or living."

I laughed. "Is there anything he likes?"

"Sex."

"Of course," I sighed. I should've known that would be his reply.

"Just ignore him. It's what I do," he shrugged, and we followed after his brother.

Mathias stopped in front of a gray Nissan sports car I'd never seen before. "What kind of car is that?" I asked, pointing. It looked futuristic, like it could take flight to outer space or something.

"Nissan GT-R," Maddox answered, "isn't she gorgeous?"

What was it with guys and cars? Honestly.

"Looks nice to me," I shrugged. In my humble opinion a car was a car and nothing more.

Maddox looked at me like my simple statement was downright murderous. "Nice? *Nice?* This car," he reached out and lovingly stroked the hood of the car, "is what dreams are made of."

"If you say so."

"Can we get in the fucking car?" Mathias asked, sticking a cigarette between his lips and lighting the tip.

"No smoking in the car," Maddox warned with a raised finger.

"Fucking killjoy," Mathias rolled his eyes, tossed the cigarette on the ground, and opened the car door. I was surprised when he slid the seat forward and climbed in the back.

"Milady," Maddox extended his hand towards the car, "get in."

I gave him a smile and got in the car. Even though I wasn't that tall I had to practically sit on the ground to get in the low vehicle. Who the hell wanted a car like this? Well, obviously Maddox.

He started the car and caressed the steering wheel, making a sound that could only be described as a moan. "Do you hear that purr?"

Was it too late to run away?

"You're scaring the poor girl," Mathias said from the backseat. "Shut up and drive or I will light a cigarette in here and good luck ever getting the scent out of the leather."

"Asshole," Maddox groaned, turning on the headlights and speeding out of the parking lot.

"Whoa," I grabbed onto the door.

"Sorry," Maddox gave me a sheepish smile. "I should've warned you about the power she has."

I'd never been in a car like this before. I drove an old 1972 Volkswagen Beetle that didn't start half the time, and it sounded like the engine was going to go up in flames anytime I actually drove it. This one sounded nothing like that. Maddox was right, it did purr.

Since Mathias was in the car we didn't really talk. Maddox turned on the radio and let that fill the silence.

When we got close to Winchester I started giving him directions, leading him to the simple brick one-story house that I called home.

To someone else it might've seemed like a dump, but I loved it.

My mom and I did our best to keep it up and decent looking. The front windows had white shutters and flower boxes overflowing with purple petunias. The grass was freshly mowed and green, instead of brown like the other houses on the street.

"Thanks for the ride," I reached for the door.

"Wait!" His warm hand wrapped around my arm and I turned back to look at him. "I don't have your phone number."

"Oh, right," I mumbled, rattling off the numbers so he could enter them into his phone. "I'll call you."

"Call?"

"Yeah, call. Is that a problem?" A single dark brow rose.

"No, not at all," I stammered nervously, "I just assumed you'd text."

He chuckled. "If I text you I wouldn't be able to hear your voice and that would be a damn shame. Texting is so impersonal."

"Oh," was all I said.

I'd never met a guy like Maddox before and I hadn't decided yet if that was a good or bad thing.

"I'll see you soon," I smiled at him. "Nice meeting you Mathias."

I heard a grunt in reply from the back of the car. Mathias was clearly a guy of few words. Besides their looks the twins were clearly polar opposites.

I was surprised when I closed the car door and heard another one close.

I looked over the top of the car and saw Maddox.

"What are you doing?" I asked, perplexed.

"Giving you a proper goodnight," he shrugged. "Did you really think I'd just drive off without knowing you got inside okay?"

"I-I don't know," I stuttered. Maddox had left me flustered.

We walked up the pathway together and stopped outside the front door while I fumbled for my house key. Once I got the door opened I expected him to leave, but he didn't.

Instead, he lowered his head and whispered, "Thank you for making tonight worth remembering. Goodnight, Emma." He pressed his lips to my cheek and walked away, leaving me standing there flabbergasted.

I forced myself to move and stepped into the house.

I leaned my back against the closed door, my mouth parted with surprise. I raised my shaking fingers to press them against my cheek and closed my eyes. A part of me was convinced that tonight had been a dream and I'd wake up in the morning and find that Maddox didn't exist. And that, surprisingly, left me feeling heartbroken.

# CHAPTER TWO

I didn't dream it.

How'd I know?

Because at seven in the morning the next day the sound of my phone ringing woke me up.

"What the hell?" I groaned sleepily, slapping my hand against my nightstand for my phone.

I looked at the unknown number flashing across the screen. Who would call me at this time of the morning on summer-freakin'-vacation.

"Hello?" I asked, smacking a hand over my mouth to stifle a yawn.

"Emma!" A cheery voice chirped.

"Who is this?" I asked.

"Maddox," the person answered.

"Maddox?"

"Do you know more than one Maddox?" He chuckled.

"No, I'm just wondering why the Maddox I know is calling me so early?" I rolled onto my back and covered my eyes with the crook of my arm.

"Early? The sun is out, therefore it's not early."

"It's seven," I mumbled. "That's early."

He tsked. "Someone is clearly not a morning person."

"Nope, not at all," I agreed.

"Do you think you'll be feeling more chipper this evening?"

"Uh…"

"Great, I'll pick you up at six-thirty."

"Maddox, I didn't—"

He hung up.

I stared at my phone and the blinking screen that declared *call ended*.

I shook my head and set the phone back on the nightstand. Something told me I'd bitten off more than I could chew when it came to Maddox.

I rolled over and closed my eyes in the hopes of going back to sleep, but when I saw that it wasn't going to happen I pushed the covers back with a groan.

I padded down the hall and into the kitchen.

I wasn't surprised to find my mom sitting at the table reading the newspaper with a mug of hot tea.

She looked up when she heard me approach and smiled, her eyes crinkling at the corners. Her blonde hair, the same shade as mine, flared around her head in wild untamable curls.

"What are you doing up so early, Emmie? Are you sick?"

I waved away her concern with a flick of my hand. "No. I…" I couldn't exactly tell her that Maddox had called or she'd ask me a bunch of questions, particularly about who Maddox was, and I'd have enough explaining to do later before he showed up for our—gulp—date. "I had a bad dream," I lied.

"Let me fix you some tea then."

My mom thought tea could fix everything.

Your dog died? Drink some tea.

Your bike got stolen? Drink some tea.

The world is ending? Let's all drink some tea!

"No, thanks." I pulled a chair out and sat down, but she was already making the tea.

"How was the fair?" She asked. When I'd gotten home I'd showered and went straight to bed. I hadn't even bothered saying goodnight to my mom. She was working in her studio—the garage—and I knew she hated when I disturbed her cosmic energy or some shit like that.

"It was okay," I shrugged, taking a deep breath. I figured since she brought it up now would be as good a time as any to tell her about Maddox. "I met a guy while we were there." I purposely left out the part about Sadie ditching me.

"A guy?" She handed me the cup of tea, her eyes wide.

"Yeah," I nodded, blowing on the steaming liquid to cool it.

"Tell me about him," she smiled, sitting down once more. "He must be worth knowing if he's caught your interest."

"Uh… he's…" How did one possibly describe Maddox? "He's kind of a jokester," I supplied. "Very nice." I figured it was best to keep the details to a minimum.

"Is he cute? He must be cute."

"*Mom!*" I groaned, and felt my cheeks flush with color.

"Oh, he's definitely cute," she pointed at me, rolling her finger in a circle.

"Yeah, he's hot," I finally agreed.

"Oooh, do I get to meet him?" She asked excitedly. "Your first boyfriend! This is so exciting!"

"He's not my boyfriend," I snapped. "I just met him, so let's not go putting labels on it yet. And you'll get to meet him… soon."

"Soon?" She repeated.

"Yeah, like tonight… at six-thirty." I mumbled, staring into the cup of tea to avoid her eyes.

"Are you going on your first date, Emmie?" She started clapping her hands. It was safe to say that my mom was more excited about this than I was. Maybe she'd been worried that she'd be eighty and I'd still be living at home, unmarried, with a bunch of cats. But what was wrong with that? Sounded pretty peaceful to me.

"I guess I am," I sipped at the tea.

Despite his phone call this morning I still couldn't quite wrap my head around the fact that I was going on a date and that last night had been real. The whole thing seemed too good to be true. Guys like Maddox didn't have anything to do with girls like me. I was too quiet and different. I didn't go out and party, I stayed home and read a book. I didn't listen to popular music, read magazines, or even watch many movies. I was, as my mom liked to say, "an old soul", just like her. I couldn't figure out what Maddox saw in me that made him think I was worth his time.

"Emma," my mom said, jolting me out of my thoughts, "stop it."

"Sorry," I frowned. "I can't help it."

"You're a beautiful, sweet girl and this boy can obviously see that. Don't let your doubts hold you back."

I nodded, she was right. But it was more than my… quirkiness, that made me nervous. Ever since my dad walked out, I'd feared that if I met a guy he'd only do to me what my dad did to my mom, and I wasn't sure I could survive the pain of it happening again.

"Drink your tea and go back to bed," she picked up her newspaper once more, but her eyes remained on me. "We'll go out for lunch and do a little shopping. Get a new dress for your date. Does that sound good?" She smiled.

"It does. Thanks mom." I stood up and wrapped my arms around her shoulders. "I love you." My mom was all I had and the greatest person I knew. I didn't know what I'd do without her.

"I love you too, Emmie."

I picked up the cup of tea and went back to my room. Maybe it was the tea, or maybe I was just really tired, but this time I did manage to fall back to sleep—and

I dreamt of a dark haired boy with a smile that stole my breath.

"Wake up!" Sadie bounced on my bed, jostling me from my dream.

"Sadie," I groaned, rolling over to see that the clock on my nightstand said it was after ten in the morning. "Get off my bed."

"Your mom let me in."

"I don't care who let you in," I mumbled.

She ignored my grumbling and settled onto the bed beside me. "What happened to you last night? You just disappeared."

I snorted. "*I* didn't disappear. You did. I couldn't find you and you didn't answer my texts."

"My phone died," she defended. "Josh and I spent at least an hour looking for you."

"Who's Josh?" I asked even though I didn't care.

"I met him at the concert. Anyway," she babbled, and I wondered if she ever stopped to breathe when she talked, "we ran into Kayla—you remember her from school right?"

"Uh… yeah." School had ended a few days ago for the summer and we attended school with the same kids we'd known since kindergarten, so did she really think I'd forget who Kayla was?

"Good, well Kayla said she saw you leave with some guy. She didn't get a look at his face but she said he had a great ass. I can't believe you didn't call and tell me. This is newsworthy information Emma, and as your best friend I should've known immediately. I've been waiting since eighth grade for you to get that cherry popped."

I gaped at her. "Well I'm sorry I can't be a slut like you."

She laughed, completely unaffected by my words, since we both knew it wasn't true. "So, tell me about him!"

"He's just a guy," I shrugged, rolling out of bed.

"Ugh, Emma!" She shrieked. "I need more than that!"

"He's hot! Does that suffice?" I growled, getting frustrated. "You *ditched* me, Sadie, so excuse me if I feel like I don't really owe you an explanation!" I snapped, anger lacing my tone. I didn't get mad at Sadie often, so my explosion was unusual.

Her face flashed with hurt and I instantly felt bad for my harsh words. "I'm sorry, I didn't mean that."

She stood up, straightening her clothes. "Yeah, you did. I'll see you later." She walked towards my bedroom door, her head bowed sadly.

When the door closed behind her I stood there staring at it. Maybe it was silly, but a part of me expected her to open the door and laugh it off. Sadie and I had never fought before—or when we did we made up before the other person left. This time felt different, and maybe it was because we were older, or maybe it was because I didn't really want to share Maddox with her. Right now I wanted to keep him to myself. Things were still so new and we hadn't even gone on a date yet— and what if after tonight he decided I wasn't worth his time? I didn't want to gush to Sadie only to have it blow up in my face. I wasn't like her, I didn't have a crush on a new guy every week. The fact that I actually liked Maddox was a big deal, and until I wrapped my head around my own feelings I didn't want to talk about it with her. I'd have to call her later to explain, but right now I knew I needed to give her a chance to cool down.

I knew my mom would want to leave soon, so I showered and dried my hair, letting it hang with its natural curl. I dressed in a plain white t-shirt, a pair of high-waisted jean shorts, and a pair of converse. I grabbed the black hat I'd worn yesterday and instantly thought of Maddox as I put it on.

I found my mom in the kitchen drinking a fresh cup of tea. "Is everything okay?" She asked. "Sadie looked upset when she left."

I shrugged. "I don't really know."

"Oh," she frowned. "Well, if you'd rather go to Sadie's house and talk to her we can do lunch another day."

"No, mom," I protested. "It'll be fine. I think we both just need to cool off."

She appraised me carefully and finally said, "Alright." She tossed me the keys to her car. "You drive."

While she finished her tea I headed outside and got into her teal colored Nissan Cube. It was a weird looking car, kind of reminded me of a bubble, but at least it was reliable unlike my old Volkswagen Beetle which had been a hand-me-down from my mom. Once I got my license she decided it was time that she upgraded her car—about thirty years too late, might I add. I wasn't sure how much longer the Beetle was going to last. Luckily it had never let me down when I needed it the most.

I had finished adjusting the mirrors when my mom walked out the door and slipped into the car. "Where do you want to eat?" She asked.

"Marigold's?" I suggested. Marigold's was a small restaurant on main street that offered the best sandwich's around, not to mention their sweets, which were all unique flavorings—my personal favorite being lavender cupcakes with lemon icing.

"That sounds perfect," she smiled, buckling her seatbelt, "we can check out the thrift store across the street after we're done."

Most girls probably would balk at the thought of spending the afternoon with their mom, but my mom was my rock. She'd always been there for me and I liked spending time with her. We didn't fight like other kids did with their parents. Sadie's mom and dad were constantly mad at her for something, although she usually deserved it.

With traffic it took ten minutes to get to Marigold's. Luckily there was a free parking space right in front. My mom grabbed a quarter from her purse and put it in the parking meter.

I watched for traffic and once no one was coming I slipped out of the car and followed her into the restaurant.

Marigold's was a small café with only three tables. The walls were painted bright yellow and the tables were mismatched. The counter that housed the sweets and sandwiches was green.

Marigold's was in fact, not owned by someone named Marigold. Her name was actually Betty and I had no idea why she named the place Marigold's, but I guessed she liked the name, or maybe the flower.

A lone woman sat in the corner eating a cupcake and Betty wasn't at the counter. My mom reached out, dinging the bell. A moment later we heard a call of, "Just a minute!"

"Why don't you grab a table before someone else comes in?" My mom suggested.

"Sure."

I sat down at the table in the corner by the windows so we could look out. Little pots shaped like a watering can sat on the center of the tables with various flowers planted in them.

While I waited for my mom to order the food I checked my phone, thinking Sadie might have sent a text. Nothing. She really was mad at me. Maybe I was wrong to snap at her, but she was also wrong to leave me alone yesterday without a ride. If I hadn't met Maddox I would've been screwed.

"Are you sure everything is okay?"

I startled at the sound of my mom's voice as she sat our bag of food down and two cupcakes.

"Yeah, everything is fine," I assured her, putting my phone away.

"You look sad."

"I just hate having Sadie mad at me," I mumbled, reaching for the bag and pulling the sandwiches and chips out.

Betty approached our table then with two water bottles. "You left these on the counter," she smiled, setting them on the table. "Let me know if you need anything else."

"Why is Sadie mad at you?" My mom asked, unwrapping her sandwich.

"I wouldn't tell her about Maddox," I supplied.

"Oh," she said.

"Yeah, oh," I sighed. "Do you think it was wrong of me not to talk to her about it?" I wiggled nervously in my seat.

She shrugged. "I don't know. I thought you two told each other everything."

"I messed up, didn't I?" I asked, but didn't wait for her to give me a reply. "I was so mad at her for ditching me at the fair and I really don't even know what to think of this whole Maddox thing, so I didn't know what to say." I rambled, only realizing too late that I'd let it slip about the fair. My mom might've liked Sadie, but she wouldn't be pleased to know she'd abandoned me.

"She ditched you at the fair?" My mom's eyes widened.

Oops.

"Yeah…" I said slowly.

"I cannot believe she left you alone at the fair. Why didn't you call me, Emmie?" She frowned.

"You were working, I knew you wouldn't answer."

She shook her head and I wished I hadn't let that tidbit of information out. "Now I can see why you're fighting. I love Sadie, I do," she eyed me, "but sometimes she can be so irresponsible that I just want to shake her."

It wasn't funny, but I started laughing anyway. "I'm pretty sure Mr. and Mrs. Westbrook want to shake her too." And my poor mom didn't even know some of the more outlandish stunts Sadie had pulled—like skinny-dipping in the neighbor's pool with a random guy.

"Enough Sadie talk," she waved her hand in dismissal. "We're going to enjoy today."

I finished my sandwich and wadded up my trash, putting it in the bag. "I'm nervous," I admitted.

"Aw, honey, I'd be worried about you if you weren't nervous."

I reached for my lavender and lemon cupcake. "I… I'm scared that after tonight he might think I'm weird and never want to see me again."

"Emma," she scoffed, "you're a wonderful girl, who's smart, beautiful, kind… the whole package. Any boy would be lucky to have you in his life. Remember that."

Sometimes it was all too easy to compare myself to others and feel like I wasn't good enough. But the fact of the matter was, every person on the planet was different from everyone else and it was stupid for me, or anyone else, to try to compare to another person. We were all different for a reason and we needed to learn to embrace our uniqueness. Too many people acted like 'unique' was a disease, when it was the only thing that made you, *you*.

"Thanks mom. You're right." I needed to stop doubting myself and Maddox's motives.

We finished eating and headed across the street, exploring the thrift shop.

"What do you think of this?" My mom held up a simple red dress with small black buttons running down the front with a black belt.

"Um…" I was scared that it might be a bit too bold for me. "I don't really like that."

"Okay," she put it back, "what about this one?"

She held up a navy dress with short sleeves and different colored flowers all over it.

I reached over the clothing rack and rubbed my fingers against the material.

"This is perfect," I smiled, feeling my excitement build.

"I like this one the best too," she agreed.

I ended up getting a few more dresses and other clothing items before we headed home. It had been too long since I'd spent a day with my mom and I realized now how much I'd missed her company. No matter how old I got I always wanted my mom to be one of the first people I went to for everything. She'd always been there for me and I never wanted to be like those other kids that 'hated' their parents. I'd already lost my dad and the last thing I wanted was to lose her too.

I dumped the bags of new-to-me clothes on the bed and looked at the time.

Maddox would be showing up in a few hours and I felt completely unprepared. What did I do? What did I say?

I picked up the phone and called Sadie.

It rang and rang. Just when I thought she wasn't going to answer she did. "What?" She sounded sad.

"I need your help," was all I said.

"I'll be there in five minutes."

Sadie might've been a lot of things, but I always knew that when I needed her most she'd be there.

# CHAPTER THREE

"What do you think?" Sadie turned me around to look in the mirror. She'd done my eyes in a smoky gray color and my lips were a bright red. The red was far more daring than I was used to, but with my blonde hair and the navy dress it worked.

"It's perfect, thank you," I hugged her.

I'd spent the last few hours picking her brain on all things boys and makeup. I think Sadie had been pleased. At one point she'd even said I was, 'a real girl now,' which had made me laugh.

"You look great and you'll be fine," she assured me. "I'm going to head out."

"You're not going to stay and meet him?" I asked.

"No," she smiled, "Josh and I are going to the movies. He's at my house waiting on me."

"Oh, right. Of course," I mumbled. "Thanks for coming over and I'm sorry about earlier."

"You don't need to apologize," she assured me, grabbing her purse. "You were right, I did ditch you, and I guess I got mad because you made me realize what a shitty friend I am. I mean, I did try to look for you, but not very well. I suck. Why do you even like me?"

"Because you're my best friend," I laughed, sitting on the end of my bed, lacing my converse.

"I think you have bad taste in friends," she started towards the door.

"You would know," I laughed. Once I had my shoes tied I walked her to the front door, thanking her again.

"Don't forget to call me to tell me all about your date," She waggled her eyebrows.

"Ew! Sadie! Nothing like *that* is going to happen!"

"Whatever," she laughed, "but seriously, you better call me." She narrowed her eyes.

"I will," I assured her. "Now hurry before you miss your movie!"

"Later, bitch!"

"Takes one to know one!" I shot back, laughing.

When I turned around from closing the door my mom stood behind me, suppressing a laugh. "I can see you two made up."

"We did," I smiled.

"I'm glad. I don't like to see you two fight, even if it's justified. So, what time is Maddox getting here?" She asked, perching on the arm of the couch.

"Six-thirty."

My heart started to race and not because it was almost time for him to arrive.

"Mom," my voice shook, "what if he doesn't show up?"

"Oh, Emma, don't be silly." She dismissed my concern.

"Sorry," I frowned, wringing my hands together. "I'm nervous."

"It'll be fine, Emmie. As long as he comes to the door and introduces himself to me," she warned. "If he stays in his car you're not going. Introducing himself is a sign of respect and if he can't do that then he's not good enough for you," she rambled.

"Okay, mom," I laughed.

I jumped when my phone chimed with a text message. My heart stopped when I saw Maddox's name flash on the screen. I was sure he was telling me he couldn't come now. I forced myself to read the text and breathed a sigh of relief when it simply said he was on his way.

I hadn't planned on meeting Maddox, or going on a date, but one night with him and I'd already turned into a giddy schoolgirl. Pretty soon I'd be sitting in my yard picking petals off of flowers chanting, "He loves me. He loves me not."

"He'll be here soon," I told my mom. I felt like this was my prom night and she was about to whip out her camera and start taking a million pictures.

"I can't wait to meet him. He must be a nice boy for you to like him."

I stood near the front door, watching for the car. When I saw it coming up the street I jumped in surprise.

He was here.

He was actually here.

Oh my God.

I'd been so focused on wondering if he'd actually show that I'd forgotten to think about being alone with him in the car and what on earth we'd talk about. All the information Sadie had given me went flying out of my panicking brain.

"I'll be right back," I squeaked, running to my room.

My mom gave me a peculiar look and started to say something, but then the doorbell rang and she let it go.

I closed my bedroom door behind me and paced the length of the small room.

I couldn't get enough air into my oxygen starved lungs. I was going to be alone with Maddox for hours and I had no idea what to do, or say, or even where we were going.

"What have I gotten myself into?" I mumbled to myself.

"Emma!" My mom called and I knew my time was up. "Maddox is here!"

"You can do this, Emma. Take a deep breath and calm down."

I grabbed my hat and a gray cardigan, and put them both on.

I walked as slow as humanly possible to the front room. Maddox sat on one couch and my mom sat across from him. I wasn't sure what they were talking about. My ears seemed to have stopped working and I felt dizzy. Was I going to pass out? Oh God, that would be beyond embarrassing.

"Emma," Maddox grinned, standing up. "I got these for you." He held out a bouquet of sunflowers. "I wasn't sure what you would like but these reminded me of you."

"Thanks," I took them from him. At least I could speak and didn't stutter. "I'll put them in a vase," I pointed over my shoulder towards the kitchen area.

"I'll come with you," Maddox stepped forward. He was dressed simply, much like he was yesterday only this time his shirt was black instead of white.

I opened the cabinet where we kept the vases and stood on my tiptoes trying to reach the nearest one.

"Here I've got it," Maddox stepped up behind me, his tall lean body pressing up against mine. While one of his hand reached for a vase the other was pressed against the counter near my waist. I held my breath, scared to move. My body was reacting in ways I didn't even know it could.

Maddox seemed to notice so once he had the vase in his hand he cleared his throat and took two steps back. I instantly missed the heat of his body against mine.

"Thank you," I whispered, filling the vase with water and emptying the packet of powered stuff into it.

"You're welcome," he grinned.

Once the flowers were fixed in the vase I pointed towards the back of the one-story house. "I'm going to go put these in my room. Wait here."

I hoped he didn't think I was rude by not inviting him to my room, but it would be my luck that I'd left a bra sitting on the floor and then I'd end up mortified. My cheeks were already coloring at the thought alone.

He chuckled. "Okay. I'll be here. Talking to your mom." I started to walk away and then he called, "I think she mentioned some naked baby pictures."

I dropped the vase and it shattered everywhere. At the feel of the cold water on my feet I screamed and jumped back.

Maddox started laughing uncontrollably. "Oh my God, I hate you!" I shrieked, chucking off my now drenched shoes. I slipped into a pair of flip-flops that sat in the hallway.

My mom poked her head around the corner. "What happened? Oh," she drew out the word when she saw what happened. "You two get out of here. I'll clean this up." She shooed us out the door.

"It was nice meeting you, Dawn," Maddox called over his shoulder. "I'll have her back by ten."

He placed is hand on my waist as we started towards the car. "You're on a first name basis with my mom?"

"Why does that surprise you? I'm quite charming and she clearly likes me. But what's not to like? I'm wonderful."

"You think very highly of yourself," I commented.

He chuckled, the sound warm and husky. "Should I not?"

I had no comment for that.

"Let me get that." He jumped in front of me and opened the car door.

"Thanks," I smiled, once again wondering why anyone liked having a car so low to the ground. I was surprised I didn't fall on my butt.

He got in the car, turning the music down so that we could speak. "Where are we going?" I asked. I hoped he planned for us to eat. I was starving. I probably should've asked him if this was a dinner date, because if he didn't plan to feed me I was going to turn into the kraken.

"The park. I thought we could feed the ducks, walk around, that sort of thing," he shrugged. "I want this to be casual and comfortable."

My stomach rumbled and he chuckled when he heard it.

"And I packed a picnic. I wouldn't let you starve," he glanced over at me, grinning.

"That actually sounds… really nice," I admitted.

His smile was so genuine when he asked, "Really?"

"Yeah. It's perfect."

He breathed a sigh of relief. "I was worried you might wonder why I wasn't taking you to a nice restaurant, but this felt like something you'd enjoy."

I was surprised that he admitted to putting so much thought into this date.

"How was your day?" He asked and I was surprised at the change of subject.

"It was nice," I told him, "I spent it with my mom. We got lunch and went to a couple of stores."

"You're close with your mom," he stated.

"I am," I confirmed, even though it was unnecessary. "After my dad left, she was all I had."

"It's nice that you have a mom like that," he whispered, and his eyes were sad when he looked at me.

"You don't?"

"Not biological."

"You're adopted?" I asked, shocked.

"No," he frowned, "my brother and I were foster kids. Luckily the family that took us in is great, and not like those horror stories you hear on the news. Why'd your dad leave?"

I wanted to question him further, but we were still in the getting to know each other phase and I didn't want to push him too far, too fast.

"My dad was an alcoholic," I spoke, "so I guess he chose the bottle over us. I think the worst part is, I was relieved when he left. He was always yelling at my mom and me. I felt like I had to tiptoe around the house and couldn't make a sound. I was afraid of him," I confessed.

"Living in fear is one of the worst things we can experience as a human being. It sucks the life out of you." His face darkened with shadows.

"You sound like you know."

"I do," he replied, but didn't elaborate.

"He wasn't always bad," I continued. Normally I wouldn't have said a word about this but I felt a sense of comfort with Maddox and it was nice to talk to someone about it. My mom never liked to talk about it and Sadie would rather talk about boys. "I remember times that were great, like when he taught me to ride my bike."

"It's nice that you have some memories like that," he commented.

"It is," I agreed. "And even though I'm relieved that he's gone there's a part of me that wonders if I'll ever see him again… there's so much I'd like to say to him."

"Maybe you should write him a letter," Maddox suggested, pulling into the parking lot.

"I don't know where he is." I looked at him like he was crazy.

Maddox chuckled. "You don't have to know. You just have to write what's in your heart." I jumped when he pressed his finger against my chest where my heart beat.

He startled, and jerked his hand away, as if he'd been unaware as to what he'd done.

"Sorry," he mumbled, ducking his head in embarrassment. In the short time I'd known him I'd never seen him uncomfortable and I felt like it wasn't something he experienced often. Maddox oozed confidence and charm, even if I didn't want to admit it, so it was nice to see a more vulnerable side to him.

"It's okay," I replied, as he parked the car, but he wouldn't meet my eyes.

He reached into the back of the car and handed me a blanket. "Can you carry that? I'll get the rest."

"Sure." I cradled the blanket against my chest and got out of the car.

When Maddox emerged he gave me a stern look. "I would've gotten the door for you."

"Your hands are full," I reasoned.

He chuckled, smiling, back to his carefree ways. "Have you been here before?" He asked.

"Of course," I replied. "I think I was little though. I spend most of my time at home," I admitted.

"Really? Doing what?" He asked as we walked over to the picnic tables.

"Reading. Writing songs. That kind of thing."

"You write songs?" His eyes widened in surprise.

"Yeah," I said slowly. "Why?"

"I do too," he grinned. "I told you we had a lot in common, Emma."

I shivered at the sound of my name rolling off his lips. I'd never known that someone could make your name sound so… so… I didn't have words for it, I just knew it felt amazing.

"What kind of songs do you write?" I asked, sitting down at the table and placing the blanket beside me.

Maddox sat down across from me and placed the picnic basket in front of us. Peering over the top of it, he answered, "Songs about life."

"Life… do you know a lot about life?"

His lips twisted in thought. "I might be young, but yeah, I'd say I know a lot about life. The rougher parts at least." Opening the picnic basket, he grinned. "And now I'd like to see you devour this in three seconds, I mean you did say you could," he winked.

I laughed when he pulled out a to-go bag from Five Guys.

"What?" He quirked a brow, that boyish smile still tugging his lips. "You didn't really think I'd slave over a home-cooked meal for you? I don't know you well enough for that."

I'd never met a guy like Maddox and I found that refreshing. "At least your honest," I reached for one of the foil wrapped burgers, "and for the record, I never said I'd eat anything you made."

He winced, his hand darting to his heart. "You wound me. Bullet straight to the heart." Dropping his hand, he leaned forward and waved me closer, like he was going to tell me a secret. "Just so you know, I make some wicked good mac n' cheese and maybe if you're nice to me one of these days I will bestow you with a delectable bowl of powdered cheese goodness."

"Powdered cheese? As opposed to real cheese?"

"Powered cheese as in the Kraft kind. You know, in the little blue box that contains everything childhood dreams are made of," he chuckled, grabbing a handful of fries.

"I can see why you write songs," I grinned. "You don't by any chance have any drinks in there do you?" I tried to peer into the basket.

"I hope you like water or Diet Pepsi. That's all I've got."

"I'll take the Diet Pepsi," I held my hand out for the bottle.

He handed it over, his eyes sparkling with laughter. "I think I love you."

"And I think it's a bit too soon for you to say that. I mean, you haven't even seen me in the mornings. My hair is a mess and my breath smells awful." I wasn't normally one to joke, but with Maddox it was effortless.

"Well, I guess you'll have to let me stay over so I can be the judge of that," he winked and I blushed. "But seriously, you play piano, write songs, you're not afraid to eat meat, *and* you like Diet Pepsi, you're my dream girl."

I snorted. "You don't have very high standards then."

"If my standards are here," he held his hand up as high as he could reach, "then you are here." He stood up, lifting his hand even higher. "Don't ever doubt yourself."

I bowed my head. "Thank you."

"Don't thank me for being honest." He shook his head. "But you can thank me for this food, this stuff wasn't cheap," he grinned, and I knew he was only trying to make me laugh.

"Thank you for the food, Maddox." I reached for a fry, dipping it into one of the containers of vinegar. "This was a great idea," I waved my hand to encompass the park. Pointing to the food I added, "And this is way better than mac n' cheese."

"I'm glad you approve," he chuckled. Sobering, he added, "I hope your burger is okay. I didn't know what to put on it since we haven't progressed to the state in our relationship where we share personal details such as which condiments we put on our food."

"I didn't know condiments were such an important thing to share." I twisted the cap off the Diet Pepsi and took a sip.

"It is. It's right up there with birthday's, blood type, and social security numbers."

Wiping my hands on a napkin, I joked, "It sounds like you're trying to steal my identity."

"That, my dear Emma, would require a sex change," he pointed a finger at me, "and I'm quite happy with my member. It's impressive, I assure you."

I snorted.

"Too far?" He sobered. "Sometimes my mouth has a mind of its own."

"I've noticed," I laughed. "I actually find it entertaining."

"Oh good," he breathed a sigh of relief. "I'll let the crazy run free then. But first, I'll ask you a normal question."

"What's your normal question?" I raised a brow.

"How's your summer so far?"

I thought about it for a moment before I replied. "Interesting."

"A good interesting?" He questioned.

"Yeah," I nodded, my lips quirking into a smile.

"Why is it interesting?" He rattled.

"You ask a lot of questions," I laughed. "But if you must know, it's interesting because…"

"Because?" He prompted when I trailed off.

I raised my eyes to meet his. "Because I met this really crazy guy at a fair last night and something tells me this summer isn't going to go at all how I had planned."

His grin was infectious. "And what was it you had planned, sweet Emma?"

"Nothing much," I shrugged. "Just sitting at home reading or whatever. I thought I might try to get a job."

"Well, you're right Emma, because this summer is not going to be at all like you thought if I have anything to say about it. In fact, I think it just might end up being the best summer of your life," he spread his arms wide.

"And why is that?" I questioned, wadding up the foil.

"Because I'm going to make sure it's one to remember."

He said the words with a laugh, but there was a seriousness in his eyes, so I believed him. Something told me that while Maddox might be a jokester, he wasn't one to make idle declarations. I might've only met him last night, but I already knew there was something special about him. I'd never had this kind of connection with anyone. My mom would say we must be soul mates, but I wasn't sure if I could buy into that. I did believe that we met people for a reason and that each of them could impact our lives in some way if we let them. When I'd agreed to go on a date with Maddox my mind had already decided to go on a journey with him—whatever it may be. I knew that I couldn't pass off the opportunity to let him into my life, even if it was only for a short time. I wasn't even dreaming of a summer fling or anything like that. I just wanted to do something that pushed me out of my comfort zone, and being around Maddox certainly did that. He brought out a part of me in the extremely short time I'd known him that I hadn't even been aware existed. He showed me an Emma that was warm and fun, who laughed and joked, and wasn't afraid of getting hurt. When you met someone who did that for you, you didn't just walk away.

"I don't doubt you," I finally whispered, a shiver running down my spine.

"You shouldn't. Prepare for the most epic summer of your life," he rambled. "Nothing will ever top this."

"You're very confident in that fact," I laughed, finishing the last of the Diet Pepsi and dropping the empty bottle in the basket.

"I know how to have a good time," he grinned, tapping a finger against his lips.

And now my eyes were focused on his lips. My throat closed up and my heart raced as I thought about how his lips would feel pressed against mine. I wanted to smack myself for thinking about kissing him. I'd only known him *one day* and I was already turning into a swoony mess. By tomorrow I might name our children if I didn't snap out of it. I needed to think of Maddox as my friend and nothing more. I wasn't going to be one of those girls that had a summer fling that ended in heartbreak.

Maddox smacked the palms of his hands against the top of the table, effectively snapping me out of my thoughts.

"It's time to feed the ducks!" He chanted, throwing in a fist pump. "We'll just leave this here." He pointed to the basket and blanket I'd picked up to take with us.

"Oh, okay," I set the blanket back down. "You're very trusting of people, aren't you?"

"I've seen a lot of bad," he admitted, all joking gone, "but I still choose to see the good in the people around me. Once you lose trust in your surroundings, you've lost everything."

"Wise words," I whispered.

"I'm a wise guy," he quipped, pulling a bag of bread out of the picnic basket.

"Are you sure we're not going to get in trouble for feeding the ducks?" I asked, suddenly nervous.

"Don't you know, the first rule to having fun is *don't* follow the rules." He headed towards the water and I hurried to catch up with him.

"My mom will kill you if I end up in jail," I warned him.

"Your mom loves me, she'd never harm a hair on my perfect head. Besides, we're not going to get arrested. Now here, take a piece of bread and we'll play a game."

"What kind of game?" I asked suspiciously.

"One where we give each duck that comes up to us the weirdest name we can think of," he grinned.

"How do you win this game?" I started picking apart the bread he'd handed me, the ducks already waddling towards us.

"If you're having fun then you've already won," he replied, tossing a piece of bread to one of the ducks. "That one's Casper."

"Casper?" I laughed, my hair blowing around me from the wind. "That's not a weird name."

"I think it is," he countered, his gray eyes lightening with laughter, "you've got a better one?"

"I've got lots of better ones," I grinned. I dropped a piece of bread to the ground for the duck by my feet. "That's Pipin."

"Myrtle," he tossed another piece.

"Trixie."

"Leviathan," Maddox chuckled as the ducks swarmed us.

"Uh…" I backed away from a duck that looked like it was ready to attack me. "Miggy." I threw the piece at the duck and it squawked, flapping its wings.

I let out a scream and Maddox hurried to my side.

"I think this was a bad idea," I hissed. "That duck looks like it wants to kill me."

It let out another loud bellow and more ducks started for us. "M-Maddox?" I stammered. "I think they're cornering us."

We became surrounded by ducks on all three sides as they herded us towards the small manmade pond.

"Throw all of the bread at them," he told me, tossing his own bread. I did as he said and felt his hand close around mine. "Emma, do you trust me?"

I glanced over at him, mulling over his words. Did I trust him? No, not the way I trusted my mom or Sadie—people I'd known my whole life. But I did trust him in a different way or I wouldn't be here right now.

"Yes," I answered, my voice nothing but a whisper.

"Then we're about to have some real fun," he grinned, pushing his hair out of his eyes.

"Huh?" Then I shrieked when he wrapped his arms around my waist and hauled me into the water. "Maddox!" I screamed. "Put me down!"

"Okay."

I shouldn't have said that. The jerk let me go and I went straight into the water. It was chilly and murky—I couldn't see the bottom *at all*. I'd probably end up with some flesh eating disease from being in it.

I came up sputtering, wiping water from my eyes.

Maddox stood in the water, wet up to his knees, laughing hysterically at me.

My hat had come off my head and I grabbed it, tossing it onto the grass.

The water wasn't very deep, but it was deep enough to soak a person, and that's exactly what I intended to do with Maddox. He was too busy laughing to pay much attention to me.

I grabbed his arm and jerked. I was small compared to him, but it was enough to throw him off balance. He stumbled and tipped fully into the water. When he stood up his black t-shirt was drenched and clung to his chest.

"Oh, that wasn't nice, Em."

He surged forward, dragging me into the deeper part of the water. I wrapped my legs around his waist. If I was going down then so was he.

"I can't believe this is your idea of fun," I scolded.

He chuckled, kicking his legs to keep us both afloat in the deeper area. "But you're having fun, aren't you?"

"Yes," I admitted, wrapping my arms around his neck.

Water clung to his long lashes and his lips parted with a breath. I found myself imagining what it would be like to lean forward that last little bit and kiss him. I knew I would never actually do it, but a girl could dream.

"This isn't something I would normally do," I admitted, lowering my legs from his waist. I kicked against the water, but kept my arms around his neck.

"What? A date?"

I laughed, looking down bashfully. "Well, that part too. I just mean… this… makes me feel kind of fearless. Like I can do anything."

"You can do anything, Emma." His fingers tangled in my wet hair. "We're all capable of great things if we allow ourselves."

"I don't know what my great thing is," I confessed.

His voice lowered and he pressed his forehead against mine. His damp hair brushed my skin and I shivered. "Then we're just going to have to find that great thing."

"Hey!" An unfamiliar voice called. "What do you two think you're doing?"

Maddox and I turned to look for the sound of the voice.

"You can't swim in there!"

"Oh, shit," Maddox mumbled. "Come on, swim. Faster, faster," he coaxed me, as we swam to the other side away from the police officer.

Once were in the grass he grabbed my hand.

With a smirk, he cried, "Run!"

And so I ran.

# CHAPTER FOUR

Only I would get arrested on my first date. And not even for something cool like smoking pot or indecent exposure. Nope, we got arrested for fleeing the scene—which somehow turned into resisting arrest—and were being charged a fine for trespassing.

"This is unbelievable." I grasped the metal bars of the holding cell in my hands. "You told me we wouldn't get arrested for feeding the ducks," I hissed.

"Hey, at least it will be a nice story to tell your grandchildren one day," Maddox reasoned. "And we *didn't* get arrested for feeding the ducks." I guess he was right about that—but feeding the ducks, did lead to the reason for our arrest, so it still counted in my mind.

I turned around to glare at him where he sat on the thin metal bench. "You think this is real funny, don't you?" I shivered, because my clothes were still wet.

"I think it's hysterical," he grinned. "I mean, who knew swimming in a pond could get you arrested?"

"Apparently when there are signs telling you not to swim," I glared at him. He wasn't taking this seriously at all.

"Admit you were having fun," he challenged. "Sometimes a little fun is worth the consequences."

"And sometimes a little fun leads to getting arrested!" I shrieked. "And other times it leads to babies!"

He laughed, leaning his head against the cinderblock wall. "Boy, that escalated quickly. From arrests to babies—does this mean the next time we want to have some fun we try for the baby part?" He grinned crookedly, waggling his brows.

My mouth fell open. "You are unbelievable!"

"And you're adorable when you're angry," he smirked.

"Oh, if you think this is angry then you haven't seen anything yet." I put my hands on my hips and leaned forward, leveling him with a glare.

"I see your boobs, does that count?"

With a squeak I threw my arms over my chest and turned around. Maddox's chuckle echoed around the small space. He might've been driving me nuts, but I was secretly glad they hadn't separated us.

An officer passed by and I implored, "When's my mom coming?"

He stopped, looking at the two of us, and shrugged. "If they'll do the right thing then they'll leave you in jail tonight to teach you a lesson."

He walked off, leaving me standing there in shock.

I turned to Maddox. "All night?! I won't last a night in jail! I want to go home! I want my bed!"

"Yeah, well I want my bed too, Em. And Sonic."

Why the fuck was he talking about Sonic right now? Food was the last thing on my mind.

"You are so infuriating."

"And yet you like me," he countered, leaning his head back and closing his eyes. "Just sit down and relax. I'm sure your mom will be here soon. There's no way she'd leave you here."

I sat down beside him, but not because he told me to. It came from the fact that my body was no longer strong enough to hold me up. I sniffled, wiping the tears off my face.

I felt his body turn towards me. "Are you crying?"

"Y-yes," I stuttered, wiping away more tears.

"Please don't cry, Emma, it'll be okay." He wrapped an arm around my shoulders and pulled me close. I let him, simply because I needed the comfort. "I know I didn't say it, but I'm so sorry. I didn't mean for this to happen."

"I k-know."

"Oh, Em." He swiped his thumb under my eyes. "I didn't mean to make you cry. I just wanted us to have a good time."

"I d-don't even k-know w-why I'm c-crying," I stammered, clinging to his shirt for support—and I might've purposely wiped some snot on it because he deserved it.

He smoothed my hair away from my face. "We're going to get out of here any minute, you'll see."

"My mom's never coming to get me! She's going to let me rot here in jail for the rest of m-my l-life!" Sobs overtook my body. I sat on the floor with my back against the wall. We'd been at the police station for over an hour and Maddox's foster mom had just shown up to release him. My mom was MIA. Actually, she was probably at home in her studio slaving away over her latest piece and wouldn't know I was in jail until tomorrow.

Yep, I was going to end up spending the night in jail.

Maddox stood outside the jail cell with his mom by his side. "Don't worry, Em. We'll get you out of here."

"B-b-but y-you're n-not m-m-my m-mom."

I was having a full on breakdown like a five year old, but I didn't care. I'd been *arrested*—there had seriously been handcuffs involved—and I was in *jail*. I was pretty sure that was worth a breakdown.

"I'm very aware that I'm not your mom," he chuckled, staring at me through the bars. "But I promise I'm going to get you out."

"H-how?" I questioned, raising tear-rimmed eyes to meet his.

"I have my ways," he winked. To his foster mom he said, "Stay with her, please." I watched him leave and I started to cry harder.

"Hey, sweetie," his mom said through the bars. "I know this isn't exactly the best way for us to meet, but I'm Karen."

I took several deep breaths, trying to stifle my sobs. "I-I'm Emma."

"Emma," she repeated. "That's a lovely name. I always wanted a daughter named Emma, but I ended up with three sons."

"T-three?" I asked, trying to distract myself from the fact that she would no doubt abandon me within minutes, because there was no way Maddox could sweet talk me out of here.

"Yes," she smiled, squatting down so we were eyelevel. "Ezra, Maddox, and Mathias."

"I t-thought M-Maddox and Mathias were f-foster kids?"

"He told you?" Her voice squeaked with surprise and then she smiled. "You must be special. To answer your question, yes, they're my foster sons—but they've felt like real sons from the moment I met them as little boys."

"I d-don't like Maddox v-very much r-right now." I hiccupped, drying the last of my tears. Crying was going to solve nothing and I had to toughen up if I was going to spend the night in jail.

Karen laughed and it was a light twinkling sound. "No, I don't imagine you do." She looked down the hallway and stood up. "Here he comes."

I gathered myself to my feet, prepared for him to tell me that I was staying here.

His head was bowed and his shoulders were slumped.

My stomach rolled and I thought I might throw up. I knew there was no way he could pull it off.

I almost started crying again when the fucker held up a set of keys and jangled them.

"They gave you the keys?!" I shrieked, jumping around excitedly. "I'm free! I'm free! I'm free!"

He chuckled, unlocking the door to the holding cell. "Yes, they were really quite accommodating once I explained things." Once I was out he closed the door and removed the keys.

"For the record," I stared him down, "I hate you." I slapped his cheek—not hard, but enough to leave a sting. "And that's for getting me arrested." Kissing the spot I'd just slapped I whispered in his ear, "*That* is for getting me out."

I walked off and behind me I heard Karen say to Maddox, "I like her."

"Yeah, me too," he agreed.

Karen was kind enough to drive us back to the park for Maddox's car. I thanked her profusely and might've promised her my firstborn child for coming to get Maddox since he was able to bust me out.

Maddox and I walked back to his car in silence. He unlocked it and opened the door for me. He handed me the keys. "Start the car, I'll be right back."

I gave him a peculiar look, but did as he asked—mostly because I was still cold and wanted to turn the heater on despite the fact that it was summer.

I pulled my phone out of the pocket of my cardigan and cringed. The cop that arrested us had confiscated it, but I'd gotten it back once we were discharged— although that was kind of pointless since the thing was now ruined.

The night had started out great and then turned into one big ball of disaster. I didn't regret going out with Maddox, but I wasn't jumping up and down to go on a second date with him either. Maybe that was unfair of me, after all it's not like he planned for us to be arrested, but I was still mad.

The car door opened and he slipped inside. He tossed the picnic basket into the back and held out my hat. "Here you go," he grinned.

"I forgot about this," I mumbled, taking it from his hand.

"Well, I didn't," he boasted.

I rolled my eyes. I didn't know how he could be so happy considering all the crap we'd been through tonight. I wanted to mouth off at him, but it wasn't in my nature. Besides, without him I would still be sitting in a holding cell crying my eyes out. So, I guess he was good for some things… like getting you arrested and then breaking you out of jail.

I set the hat on top of my head and went back to fiddling with my phone—basically willing it to live. I didn't have the money to buy a new one.

Maddox looked over and saw what I was messing with. "Is your phone okay?"

"No," I sighed, pinching the bridge of my nose. I was tempted to throw the thing out the window, but I thought maybe I could still salvage it.

"Aw, Emma, I'm so sorry. I'll get you a new one," he promised, his voice ringing with sincerity.

I winced. "I'm not a charity case. You don't owe me a phone."

He snorted, driving through town towards my home. "I never said you were a charity case, but it's my fault your phone's ruined, so the least I could do is get you a new one."

"You got me out of jail, so I think you've repented enough," I mumbled, propping my elbow on the edge of the window and my head in my hand.

"I also got you into jail." His fingers danced along the steering wheel.

"Don't remind me," I grumbled.

"Does this mean you don't want to go on another date?" He rambled. "Because that whole getting arrested thing was a total fluke, I swear. I mean, it's not like I make a habit of getting arrested," he shrugged his strong shoulders, "that was actually a first for me. I'd like to promise that it'll never happen again, but hey, you never know."

"Do you ever stop talking?" I interrupted him. My words might've been harsh, but I didn't mean them that way. "You're like a toddler that's just learned to talk and won't shut up for five seconds."

Ignoring me, he added, "Basically, I think I deserve a second chance."

"Oh, you think so," I snorted. "And why is that?"

"I'm hot, you're hot, together we can make magic happen."

I pressed my lips together, trying to contain my laughter but it eventually burst forth. "I think it's safe to say I've never met anyone quite like you."

"I strive to be like no one else," he winked. "It keeps things interesting."

"Mhmm," I hummed, looking out the window.

"So…" He started. "You never gave me an answer about a second date…"

"I need to think about it and unfortunately," I held up my phone and gave it a shake, "I won't be able to let you know what I decide."

"Bummer," he winced. "But I stand by what I said about getting you a new phone, so there's hope for me yet!" He cried like a man about to go to battle. I was learning quickly that Maddox was the dramatic type. I wondered if he'd ever tried acting.

My house came into view and I breathed a sigh of relief. I was exhausted, my eyes hurt from crying, and all I wanted to do was shower off the nasty pond water from my body and climb into my bed.

Maddox parked in the driveway and I reached for the door handle. "Thank you for a… uh… interesting evening. I can assure you it's one I'll never forget… like ever."

Maddox chuckled and leaned towards me. I scooted away from him so that my back was pressed firmly against the car door.

He ducked his head and lifted his eyes to peer at me through the veil of his dark hair. "Oh, Emma, you're like a little bird the way you quiver around me. I might have sharp teeth," his eyes lowered to my throat, where my heart fluttered erratically, "but it doesn't mean I *bite*." His voice dropped to a low, throaty octave.

My body heated all over. I'd never felt the sensation before—but I'd heard about it plenty from Sadie.

If I didn't get away—and stay away—from Maddox, I was going to end up in big trouble.

"I-I-I have to go," I stammered, clawing at the door handle. I tumbled from the car, falling onto the gravel driveway. "Shit," I cursed, when the sharp rocks dug into my knees.

"Emma!"

A moment later Maddox was out of the car and in front of me. He grasped my elbows and lifted me from the ground.

"Are you okay?" He looked me up and down. "You're bleeding." His eyes zeroed in on my knees and he frowned.

"It's just a scrape," I mumbled, backing out of his hold. I went to walk around him, but squeaked when my legs went out from under me.

He cradled me against his chest and strode up to the front door.

"What do you think you're doing?" I shrieked.

"I'm carrying you inside, cleaning your wounds, and slapping a Band-Aid on these suckers," he explained. "Now give me your keys before I'm forced to breakdown the door and don't doubt my ability, because I'll do it."

"Oh. My. God." I rolled my eyes.

"Emma," he groaned. "Key."

"There's one under the mat, I didn't bring mine with me. It looks like you'll have to put me down," I smiled triumphantly.

Maddox noticed my smile and returned it with one of his own. I let out another shriek when he tossed me onto his shoulder so he could grab the key.

He carried me inside and straight back to the bathroom. He flipped the light switch on and set me on the counter.

"This is… cute." He commented, looking around at the outdated décor.

"We haven't had the money to update," I mumbled, ducking my head in embarrassment.

I'd never been ashamed of being poor, but it didn't mean I wanted to show it off to the masses… or Maddox.

"I like it," he smiled. "It's old-fashioned."

I snorted. "Yeah, I don't think it's been updated since the seventies." I nodded towards the pea green bathtub. "But this place… it's home," I shrugged.

I startled when his warm hand cupped my cheek. "Shh," he hushed, rubbing his thumb against my bottom lip. "You don't need to explain anything to me." He tilted my head back and pressed his forehead against mine. His voice lowered to a whisper. "I know I literally just met you yesterday, but it feels like I've known you forever. I've only ever had this feeling of… of *belonging* with my foster family, and I know this sounds crazy, but I feel like we're supposed to get to know each other."

"Maddox—" I started.

"Let me finish," he hushed. He shook his head so his dark brown hair brushed against my forehead. "I'm not asking for anything romantic—although I'll admit to really wanting to kiss you," he grinned. "But it's summer vacation for both of us and I think we should make this the best summer of our lives."

"H-how?" My voice shook with nerves. Maddox affected me in a way that one minute I was mouthing off to him and the next I was a nervous and shaking mess.

His smile widened. "I guess we'll have to find out together."

Without another word he opened the medicine cabinet and set about cleaning my scraped knees, slathering them with Neosporin, and sticking Band-Aids— Hello Kitty ones—on top.

He lifted me off the counter and kissed my forehead.

"Get some rest. The most epic summer of your life begins tomorrow."

I opened my mouth to reply, but he already had his back turned and walked out the bathroom door. A moment later I heard the front door close.

What the hell had I gotten myself into?

# CHAPTER FIVE

After deleting the messages from the police station off the voicemail I'd gotten into bed and fallen right to sleep. I'd been exhausted, but this morning I felt refreshed and ready to conquer the day.

"Mom," I called, stifling a yawn as I headed into the kitchen.

I stopped when I found a note sitting on the kitchen table explaining that she was gone for the day, restocking her supplies.

I grabbed an apple and sat down to eat.

Since I was currently phoneless and had no plans it looked like I'd spend the day doing what I typically did—playing piano and reading. I wasn't complaining, though. I enjoyed spending time by myself.

I finished the apple and tossed the core in the trashcan.

I got dressed for the day and sat down at the piano. I picked a random song, placed the sheets of music in front of me, and let my mind empty.

I'd started playing piano at an early age. My talent had been a source of conflict for my parents. Many said I was a prodigy and early on my dad had wanted to push me to make a name for myself. I'd been so young, though, and my mom had been firmly against it. She felt that talent was meant to be enjoyed, not forced, and she didn't want to see me learn to hate something I loved so much. I was thankful that I had a mom like her. While my dad had ended up a drunk asshole that abandoned us, at least I had one parent that was amazing when a lot of people had none.

I was so lost in the music and the way the keys felt against my fingertips that when the doorbell rang I squeaked and fell off the bench.

Gathering myself I straightened my clothes and pushed my hair out of my eyes.

I was sure it was Maddox at the door, but I was surprised to find that no one was there. Instead a plain brown box sat on the Welcome mat. I picked it up and gave it a little shake. The rustle of sound didn't give any indication of what might be inside.

I kicked the front door closed and headed to the kitchen for a knife.

I cut the tape around the corners and burst into laughter when I found what was inside.

"Really, Maddox?" I laughed out loud. Inside was a white box containing a shiny new iPhone. What made me laugh though, was the cartoonish drawing of, what I assumed was Maddox himself, asking for forgiveness. I peeled the drawing off, careful not to tear it. I carried it and the small box back to my room. I don't know what possessed me, but I stuck the drawing to the mirror above my dresser. I didn't want to get rid of it.

Once the piece of paper was stuck to my mirror I sat down on my bed and removed the lid off the small box.

Inside the phone lay nestled. I'd never owned anything so… so *shiny*. Or new.

I picked the phone up out of the box and pressed the round button to light up the screen. Since Sadie owned one I already knew how to work it.

I snorted when I saw the wallpaper. It was a photo of Maddox pouting with a little comic bubble added, asking, "Am I forgiven *yet?*"

I jumped when the phone started ringing in my hand. Maddox's face popped up again, but this time it was a different photo—a normal one where he wore an easy smile and seemed to be laughing at something in the distance.

"Hello?" I answered.

"How about now?"

I laughed, ducking my head. "You are relentless."

"So…?"

"You're forgiven," I sighed. I decided then that it was impossible to stay mad at Maddox.

"Excellent," he said, and I knew he was grinning. "Don't forget, adventure number one starts today."

"When?" I asked.

"Right about… now."

He hung up and a moment later a text popped up on the screen.

**Go out your front door. Walk down to the stop sign and take a right. I'll be waiting.**

I shook my head and muttered, "Maddox."

I hoped my shorts and t-shirt were appropriate since I didn't seem to have time to change.

Stuffing the phone in my back pocket I followed his directions.

When I rounded the street corner and saw him I laughed.

"You were mighty confident I'd show up, weren't you?" I pointed to where he stood leaning against a shiny red motorcycle. It shimmered like a candied apple in the sunlight.

He shrugged sheepishly. "I hoped."

"So," I waved a hand at the motorcycle, "is this our first adventure?"

"It is," he grinned. "Have you ever been on one?"

"No," I admitted.

His smile widened. "Does it scare you? You can hold on tight, my abs won't mind." He rubbed a hand over his smooth stomach concealed behind a tight gray t-shirt.

I rolled my eyes. "I'm not scared."

"Maybe you should be, because when Mathias finds this thing gone he's going to try to kill us," he frowned, rubbing his chin.

"Or we might end up arrested again, this time for stealing a motorcycle," I pointed out.

"Well, at least we'll be mixing things up," he shrugged.

"Why would you take Mathias' motorcycle?" I asked.

He held out a leather jacket for me. It was the perfect size and I noticed a price tag still dangled from the sleeve so I ripped it off. Maddox seemed to have a lot of money and I wondered momentarily where it came from.

As I shrugged into the jacket he began to explain. "Well, I had one…"

"You had one?" I repeated. "What happened to it?"

"Uh…" He ducked his head, scrubbing his hand against the back of it. "It's kind of a long story."

I crossed my arms over my chest. "I have time."

He peered at me with hesitant gray eyes. "It's really not worth telling."

"Mhmm," I harrumphed. "I'm waiting."

He let out a sigh and looked up towards the sky like he was trying to gather his strength. "I… uh… I… crashed it."

"You crashed your motorcycle and now you want me to get on your brother's with you? That sounds like a sure way to land myself in the ER."

"I only broke my arm!" He defended. "Besides, I'd protect you!"

"You'd protect me while crashing the motorcycle? That makes a whole lot of sense," I snorted.

He mumbled unintelligibly. "You know what I meant."

"So, despite the fact that you crashed your own motorcycle, and we might get arrested for stealing your brother's, you still think this is a great idea?" I raised a brow, waiting for his reply.

His face crinkled. "It's an excellent idea," he corrected.

Of course he thought it was.

I was a smart girl. I never did anything I wasn't supposed to do.

I was normal, and some may say boring.

I was plain.

Ordinary.

Nothing special.

Unmemorable.

And that's why, even though I knew going home and pretending this encounter never happened would be the best thing to do, I said, "Okay, let's do this."

Maddox's grin split his whole face.

"I thought you were going to tell me to take a hike there for a second," he chuckled.

"I considered it," I admitted. "But only for like a second," I confessed, when his head fell. He grinned at that. "You're right Maddox. This is a summer for adventures."

His smile was blinding. "I'm glad you agree." He reached behind him and held out a helmet. I tried to take it from him, but he refused. He set it on top of my head and secured it. "Look at you," he chuckled, rapping his knuckles against the hard surface. It felt heavy and uncomfortable on my head—like my small frame might topple over from the weight. "You make for a very sexy biker babe."

"Thanks… I guess," I laughed.

He put his own helmet on and straddled the motorcycle.

"Come on, Em." He reached out a hand, waving me over.

My whole body shook. I couldn't believe I was actually doing this. Despite my previous confidence I was terrified. Motorcycles had two wheels and an engine that was fast—that was enough to send me running the other way.

But I refused to be the girl that shied away from everything—so I squared my shoulders, pretending my fear didn't exist.

I grasped Maddox's shoulder and swung my leg over the side. I wiggled my body against his until I was seated and didn't feel like I was going to fall off.

"Comfortable?" He chuckled warmly, reaching back so his hand grasped my thigh.

I bucked against him and made a choking sound.

"You okay?"

"Mhmm, yeah. I'm good." I tried to gather my breath. He hadn't meant anything by touching me and I was making a big deal out of nothing. "Where exactly are we going?"

"I have no idea," he answered truthfully, "and that's where the fun lies."

Before I could respond we were speeding down the road. I let out a small scream and wrapped my arms tightly around his chest. I felt him chuckle rather than heard it. I squished my eyes closed and laid my head against his back. He was going so fast that I was scared to look around.

When we were stopped by a red-light he said, "Emma, you're holding me so tight that I'm going to have bruises from your fingers."

"Then don't go so fast!" I defended.

"Fine," he chuckled. "I'll slow it down… a little bit."

I gulped.

The light turned green and he kicked off again.

"Maddox!" I shrieked. If this was his idea of fun, then I wanted off of this ride.

"Open your eyes, Emma!" How the hell did he know I'd closed my eyes? "The world is passing you by!"

I wrapped my arms tighter around his body and slowly peeled my eyes open.

Everything was a blur around us—like we were going so fast that time had come to a halt.

It wasn't as scary as I thought it might be.

Our small town soon disappeared as he headed towards the city.

An hour later he pulled into the parking lot of a restaurant. My arms shook and I couldn't move if I wanted to.

He reached up and removed his helmet, musing his hair with his fingers. "Em? Emma?" He probed, when I didn't move.

I was frozen.

"I can't move." I mumbled against his back.

He chuckled huskily. "Of course you can."

I tried to wiggle my fingers. "Nope."

"Aw, I didn't scare you *that* bad, did I?" He asked, grasping my arms and removing them from the stranglehold around his torso.

"I'll be okay," I assured him. "Just give me a minute… or five."

He kept still, waiting for me to muster the energy to get off the motorcycle. When I finally got brave enough I nearly fell thanks to how bad my legs were shaking.

"Whoa." Maddox's hand shot out to grab me before I could fall.

"Thanks," I replied, steadying myself. When he was sure that I was okay he let me go and climbed off as well.

He reached up and removed the helmet from my head and stowed it away.

I smoothed my fingers through my hair, hoping he couldn't see how bad my hands were shaking. The ride hadn't been terrible after he slowed down, but I'd still been scared that if I didn't hold on tight enough I might fall off.

"M-maybe it won't be so bad on the way back?" I reasoned.

Maddox laughed, slinging his arm around my shoulders as he towed me towards the restaurant. "Maybe."

"You sound like you don't think so?"

He pulled me closer. "Well, you seemed pretty scared. I have the scratches on my stomach to prove it. Would you like to see?" He winked, reaching for his shirt with his free hand.

"Nope. No. I'm good," I stuttered.

He chuckled, shaking his head.

"What?" I prompted.

He shrugged as we started up the steps to the restaurant. "I think it's cute how embarrassed you get about certain things I say."

"That's because you have no filter," I countered.

"True," he agreed with a laugh. Opening the door to the restaurant, he added, "I hope you like pizza."

"Pizza is my life," I stated. "It's more important than showering and breathing."

He laughed, his lips twisting into a smile. "You really love pizza, then."

The inside of the restaurant was fancy for a pizza place. I looked around at the shiny wood floors and rich wood accents. I could see the kitchen where a wood fire burned.

"That's how they cook the pizza. Wood-fired. They're delicious." Maddox commented when he saw me staring at the fireplace.

"Two?" A hostess spoke up.

The pizza place had a freaking hostess?

"Yes," Maddox answered, "and could we be seated outside?"

"Certainly," she smiled, grabbing the menus. "Follow me."

Once we were seated and she had disappeared I hissed at Maddox, "I thought you said this was a pizza place?"

He arched a brow as he looked at me over the top of the menu. "It is."

"I was picturing like… Pizza Hut with red and white checkered tablecloths and paper plates," I mumbled. "This place is too fancy."

Maddox chuckled and set aside his menu. "Well, the way I see it, I kind of owe you after last night. So I thought a nice lunch would suffice."

"After you nearly killed me on the motorcycle?"

He rolled his eyes. "I did not nearly kill you. Don't be dramatic."

"I'm pretty sure I was holding on for dear life."

A playful smirk lifted his lips. "Maybe on the way back I can do some tricks."

"Don't even think about it," I narrowed my eyes.

He chuckled and picked up the menu once more. "I'd never really do that to you."

"I would hope not," I mumbled just as the waiter appeared at our table.

"I'm Tyler, I'll be your waiter. Can I start you off with something to drink?"

"Water, please," I smiled at the waiter.

"Diet Pepsi."

The waiter winced. "I'm sorry, we only have Coke products from the vending machine right now. Our machine is down."

"Fucking Coke," Maddox grumbled, "it's a conspiracy, I tell you."

I snorted and then tried to cover it with a cough.

"Water for me too, then," Maddox mumbled.

"I'll be right back." The waiter turned and disappeared inside the building.

I looked at the menu once more.

"Order whatever you want," Maddox stood up. "And if he comes back before I do, order me a large pepperoni pizza… and no, I'm not sharing. I'm eating that sucker all by myself."

"Where are you going?" I asked, puzzled.

"To get a Diet Pepsi, of course." He looked at me like I was the crazy one.

"Well, okay then," I laughed.

I watched him walk away and shook my head

"Are you ready to order?" The waiter asked, sitting the glasses down.

"Oh, uh… yeah. A large pepperoni pizza for him and cheese for me. Ooh, and some of these pepperoni rolls." I pointed at the picture on the menu. "Those sound good."

"Sure thing." He took the menus. "I'll put that right in."

While I waited for Maddox to return I studied the nearby buildings. Most seemed to be occupied by lawyers and other professionals, but I did see a pet store and ice cream shop.

"Found one!" Maddox chimed, breaking me out of my thoughts. He flopped into the seat and held the bottle of Diet Pepsi up proudly.

"I take it you really like Diet Pepsi," I laughed, sipping my water.

"I love Diet Pepsi the way you love pizza, with all my heart." He slapped a hand dramatically against his chest before unscrewing the lid.

"That's a lot then," I commented.

Maddox opened his mouth to say something, but the waiter appeared at the table with the pepperoni rolls. "Here's your starter," he smiled at me. His gaze flicked towards Maddox and he startled. I thought maybe he was about to scold Maddox for the Diet Pepsi, but that didn't happen. Instead, the guy stared at Maddox with a puzzled expression. Finally, he said, "You look really familiar."

Maddox squirmed uncomfortably in his seat. He covered his mouth with his hand and mumbled, "Nope, don't think so. You must be confusing me with someone else."

The waiter lingered for a moment longer, before shaking his head. "Yeah, I guess so, my bad." He smiled awkwardly at me and backed away from our table.

"That was weird," I wrinkled my nose, and looked across the table at Maddox.

He stared off into the distance. "Mhmm, weird… I'll be right back."

He stood up once more to leave and was gone before I could say anything else.

What the hell?

I watched him leave with a mystified look on my face.

He wasn't gone long, but returned with a black baseball cap perched on top of his head. He kept the brim low so that his eyes were bathed in shadows.

When he sat down I glared at him. "You're really bad at this whole date thing."

He grinned. "What? Are you kidding? I excel at everything." He reached once more for a Diet Pepsi.

"What's up with the hat?" I asked, reaching for one of the pepperoni rolls and dipping it in marinara sauce.

He reached up and touched the brim. "The sun was in my eyes."

I stared at him for a moment. "Maddox?"

"Emma?" He grinned.

"If the sun was in your eyes why didn't you put on your sunglasses?" I pointed the fancy pair dangling from the collar of his shirt.

He looked down and smiled sheepishly. "I forgot about them."

For some reason I didn't believe him. I had a gut feeling that his sudden desire to wear a hat came from what the waiter said.

"Do you really know that guy and not want him to remember you?" I asked.

"What? No. I don't know him." He scoffed. "Like I told you, the hat was for the sun."

I sighed heavily and decided to let it drop. "These are really good," I said instead, pointing to the appetizer.

Maddox reached for one. "Yeah, I love this place. Good food and good atmosphere."

"But no Diet Pepsi," I jested.

He chuckled and I noticed that some marinara sauce sat adorably in the corner of his mouth. "And that's a shame."

Maddox polished off the rest of the pepperoni rolls just as the waiter brought out our pizzas. My stomach rumbled as I eyed the delicious cheesy goodness. I hadn't been lying when I told Maddox I loved pizza.

After the exhausting drive here I was starving.

I grabbed a piece and took a bite. "Oh my God." I had to suppress a moan. "This is the best pizza I've ever had."

Maddox stared at me for a moment and cleared his throat.

"What?" I asked.

"You… uh… might not want to make noises like that in public." He nodded his head in the direction of a table occupied by three men old enough to be my grandpa. They all stared at me with an open mouthed expression.

"Oh." I blushed, and set my pizza down, suddenly embarrassed.

"Now behind closed doors with me on top… yeah, I could go for that," he winked.

"Maddox," I hissed, my cheeks flaming red.

"Sorry, I couldn't resist." He chuckled.

I'd like to say that I lost my appetite, but that would be a lie. This was pizza and nothing, not even my embarrassment, would stop me from enjoying it.

We finished eating and Maddox paid for our meal. Normally I would've protested, but after getting arrested last night and the scary motorcycle ride this morning I figured he owed me.

As we walked through the parking lot my stomach twisted.

I had to get back on the motorcycle.

Oh, God.

I stood frozen and Maddox turned back to look at me when he noticed I was no longer beside him. "Emma?" He prompted. "Are you okay?"

"Uh…"

"Aw, Em," he strode up to me and reached for my hand. "It'll be okay. I won't go fast this time, I swear."

I closed my eyes and took a deep breath. It was only a motorcycle. I could do this. This was all about having an adventure and pushing myself outside my comfort zone.

"Slow?" I asked.

"So slow a baby turtle could pass us," he chuckled. Sobering, he added, "I'm sorry I scared you earlier."

"You're forgiven," I mumbled. "But seriously, if you scare the crap out of me again on this thing you better sleep with one eye open."

His lips quirked into a smile. "I'm intrigued by the idea of you sneaking into my room at night. This has possibilities."

I rolled my eyes. "You are…" There were no words for what Maddox was.

"Amazing?" He supplied with a grin.

"More like unbelievable," I countered. "But you can go with amazing if that makes you feel better."

He chuckled, rubbing his fingers through his hair. We reached the motorcycle and he grabbed the helmet I'd worn on the way here. Before placing it on my head he said, "I think I've met my match with you."

He cut off my retort by shoving the helmet onto my head. I wobbled with the extra weight and he grasped my hips in his hands, drawing me against his body. Our bodies lined up perfectly. In fact, mine curled against him—like my brain had completely shut down and my body had taken over. I swallowed thickly and was silently glad for the protection the helmet provided.

"I'm not quite ready for our first adventure to end." His hands flexed against my hips.

"You're not?" If this adventure continued on the motorcycle I'd have to put a stop to it. I might have a heart attack if I was stuck on the thing a second longer than necessary.

"No." He shook his head and his unique gray eyes darkened to the color of rain clouds before a storm.

"Oh… what do you have planned? Because this motorcycle and I aren't very good friends."

He chuckled and his hands skimmed higher up my back. I shivered from his touch, despite the fact that it was well over eighty degrees outside.

"I thought you could come to my house." As if he sensed my distress he hastened to add, "My mom will be there, so you have nothing to worry about. I just… you said you liked music and there's something I want to show you."

Behind the safety of the helmet I took a deep breath to steady myself. I knew I would agree, because there was something about Maddox that was impossible to resist, but a part of me was screaming that I was insane. After all, I'd only met him a few days ago. But I didn't want to be that same girl I'd been my whole life— spending the summer locked in my house playing piano and reading all the time… and occasionally getting dragged to the mall by Sadie. I wanted to *live* and with Maddox I… well… I felt *alive*.

"That sounds okay," I squeaked.

His hands disappeared from my waist. "Excellent." He rapped his knuckles against the helmet. "Let's get out of here."

My body broke out in a sweat at the thought of the ride back.

He climbed on the motorcycle and put his helmet on. "It'll be okay, Emma." He reached out a hand to me.

I nodded and forced myself to get on behind him. Since I had no experience with guys whatsoever it was a bit awkward being pressed so close to him, but I had little choice.

"Hold on tight—" He warned, revving the bike. I wrapped my arms around his torso and felt him chuckle. He reached back and put his hand on my upper thigh. My gasp was so loud I swore he had to have heard it over the roar of the engine. "—And don't let go."

# CHAPTER SIX

The ride to Maddox's home wasn't nearly as bad as the first time. In fact, I kind of enjoyed it.

Despite that by the time we arrived at his house I was ready to get off the thing.

Removing the helmet I gaped at the massive house. "Holy crap, you live here?"

He chuckled. "Yes. Mathias and I actually live in the guesthouse out back, but we have rooms in the house as well. We just prefer our privacy."

"Guesthouse? You have a freaking guesthouse?" I gasped. Due to the large size of the home I should have suspected as much, but still…

Maddox chuckled and removed the leather jacket he wore. Heading towards the back of the house he nodded for me to follow him. "The guesthouse is actually where we're headed." He pushed open a wrought iron gate and we stepped into a nice backyard. It was flat with bright green grass and a shimmery blue pool. I'd only ever seen homes like this in a magazine. It definitely didn't compare to the shabby ranch-style home I lived in.

"I'd say for foster kids you and Mathias really lucked out with Karen," I commented, still looking around at the palatial house. It really was gorgeous. While it was large it wasn't overly intimidating. In fact, there was something rather homey to it, and I thought that was thanks to the cape cod style. It looked like a home you'd see by a lake somewhere. "This place is beautiful."

"Yeah, we did get lucky." Maddox's smile was small and his eyes darkened. "But after all the shit we went through as kids with our parents, I think we deserve every little bit of happiness that's thrown our way."

I nodded. I knew Maddox didn't know me well enough to spill the secrets of what life was like with his biological parents, and the details behind his foster parents, but I was curious. Normally I didn't care to get to know anyone. I was happy to bury my nose in a book and forget the real world existed, but I felt connected to Maddox. I *wanted* to get to know him. I *wanted* to spend time with him. I was drawn to him in a way that even at seventeen years old I knew it was different. *He* was different.

"Emma?"

I stumbled and realized I'd been completely lost in my thoughts. Maddox stood by the door of the two-story guesthouse. It looked like a small version of the main house.

"Are you coming?" He prompted.

"Oh, uh, yeah." I scurried over to his side.

He smiled down at me before swinging the door open. "Home sweet home."

Inside the downstairs area was decorated sparsely, a small kitchenette lay to my right, and a rug was scattered over the wood floors. The back and sidewalls were painted white and brick. I didn't think I'd ever seen brick used inside a room before.

"This is what I wanted you to see." Maddox swept his arm to the side and his smile was almost shy.

In the living room, the only pieces of furniture were a futon laid flat like a bed covered in random pillows and blankets and a desk covered in scattered papers.

I knew the futon wasn't what he was talking about though.

"Wow," I gasped at the full instrument set up. There was a mic, drum kit, guitar, bass, and a piano.

Maddox ducked his head. "You said you liked music and could play the piano… so I was hoping you might want to do a song with me."

I stood in shock. I couldn't get over how unsure Maddox seemed all of a sudden, since he was always so cocky. This was a side to him that was very much boyish.

I opened my mouth to tell him that I would love to when I heard a scuffling sound behind me. I let out a shrill scream and grabbed his arm. "What the hell was that?" I gasped.

He pressed his lips together, trying to hold in his laughter. He grabbed me by the shoulders and turned me around. Against the wall sat a small cage and I could see some sort of creature scurrying around. I stepped forward, peering inside. I expected to see a hamster, but it wasn't. It lifted its head slightly to look at me and wiggled its little black nose.

"Is that—?"

"A hedgehog," Maddox supplied with a grin. He opened the cage and reached inside to grab the little guy. "Emma, meet Sonic."

"Sonic?" I questioned, remembering last night at the police station. I'd thought he'd been talking about the fast food restaurant. "Why would you name him Sonic?"

Maddox gasped, clutching the hedgehog against his neck. "You don't know who Sonic the Hedgehog is?"

"Uh…" I looked at him like he'd lost his mind. "Isn't he right there?" I pointed to his pet.

He shook his head rapidly back and forth. "Sonic the Hedgehog… the videogame? Ringing any bells?"

I thought. "No. Sorry."

He gasped. "This. Is. A. Tragedy." He pulled his phone out of his back pocket and typed something in. He proceeded to shove it in my face. "*This* is Sonic the Hedgehog."

I stared at the cartoon drawing of a blue hedgehog. "That doesn't really look like a hedgehog, but if you say so."

Maddox sighed and put his phone away. "Well, when you get a hedgehog it's only appropriate to name it Sonic. Although, I did have a weak moment where I considered Aquilla the Hun."

I snorted. "Like a pun on Attila the Hun?"

Maddox gaped at me. "The fact that you know who Attila the Hun is, but not Sonic the Hedgehog, is appalling, Emma. It's downright blasphemy."

"You feel very passionately about this hedgehog," I laughed.

"I'm going to get a Sonic the Hedgehog videogame and make you play it. Just you wait and see," he mumbled. "Here, do you want to hold him?"

The spiky creature was shoved unceremoniously into my face. "Uh…" I eyed the hedgehog. "How do I hold him?"

"Just like I am," he chuckled, "but be mindful of the quills."

I held my hands out and he placed the hedgehog in them. Sonic sniffed at my hands, and I guess he decided he liked me, because he promptly fell asleep in my hands. I giggled. "I think he likes me."

I looked up in time to see something flash in Maddox's eyes. "What's not to like?" He murmured.

I startled at his words and warmth flooded my body.

Clearing his throat, he crossed his arms over his chest. The gesture pulled his shirt taut over the muscles in his chest and stomach. I swallowed thickly at the sight. "Maybe I should get you a hedgehog," he chuckled, "since Sonic likes you so much."

"Sonic and Aquilla the Hun?" I joked with a raised brow.

He laughed and took the hedgehog from my hands, putting him back in the cage. I watched the little guy burrow his way beneath the bedding.

Maddox put a guiding hand on my waist and led me over to the piano. I sat on the bench and he took the spot beside me. Since the bench was so small our bodies were squished together.

"What should I play?" I asked, my voice shaking with nerves. Normally I only played when I was alone. The most audience I had anymore was my mom. I was terrified that I might mess up with Maddox watching me.

"Whatever you want." His voice was soft and close to my ear. I jumped when his fingers touched my neck, pushing my hair over my shoulder. "I wanted to see your face." He whispered the words, looking at me with an intensity that left me breathless.

I gave him a shy look in return, my heart thumping madly behind my ribcage. I was mystified by this boy.

This crazy, cocky, insanely good-looking boy, that I had only just met, but managed to jumble my insides.

Even though I was nervous, I had truly never been so immediately comfortable with someone like I was with Maddox. There was something so infectious about him and impossible not to like.

"Okay," I finally replied.

I closed my eyes and my tongue flicked out to wet my lips.

I didn't think about any particular song. I just let my fingers guide me.

Typically I played with sheet music, even though I didn't have to. I'd always had an ear for music and could pick up on almost any song after hearing it once. It would take me a few tries to get it right, but I'd always been able to master even the most complicated of pieces.

This piano was much nicer than my one at home.

The keys were smooth and soft—almost as if it was brand new and had never been used.

When the song finished I opened my eyes to find a mystified Maddox staring at me.

"You're amazing," he whispered.

I ducked my head. "Hardly."

Shaking his head, he smiled. "Do you think we could do one together?"

"Sure," I agreed.

His smile was blindingly bright, causing my stomach to flip and flop.

"What instruments do you play… besides the drums, of course?" I asked.

"A little of everything. Drums is my favorite. I love the feel of the beat thrumming though my body and vibrating in my bones." He spoke with passion. "I can play the guitar decently, a little piano—nothing like you can, I assure you," he chuckled. "I sing… but not in front of people, only when I'm alone writing songs."

"You're such an overachiever." I joked with a smile, lightly bumping his shoulder with mine.

He smiled down at me. "It's only because I love music so much. It's my life."

I could see the love he spoke of shining in his eyes. I envied him for that. I was going to be a senior in high school and I was clueless about what I wanted to do. That scared me.

"What do you want to do for the rest of your life?" I asked Maddox, the words tumbling out of my mouth.

He grew quiet and his eyes were serious. "Music, of course."

I bowed my head.

"What do you want to do?"

I took a deep breath and forced myself to look at him once more. "That's the thing. I don't know and it scares me. I have to get it figured out, but I don't know if I'm as passionate about anything the way you are with music." I frowned. "I want… I want to have that sparkle in my eye that you have."

He reached up and smoothed the hair away from my forehead. "You do have a sparkle in your eye, Em. One for *life*."

"Somehow, I'm not feeling better."

He chuckled and bowed his head. His dark hair tumbled forward into his eyes. I itched to push it away from his eyes like he had done with me, but I wasn't nearly as bold as Maddox.

Finally he rested his fingers on the keys of the piano and began to play. "Do you know this one?" He asked when I didn't immediately join him.

"I don't… keep playing."

He did, and I closed my eyes, listening to the sound.

"It's Counting Stars by One Republic," he said.

"Never heard of them," I replied, still listening.

The music cut off and I opened my eyes.

"You don't know who One Republic is?" He gaped at me "That's like… impossible."

"Uh… sorry?" I laughed. "I don't really listen to anything but classical."

He looked like I'd just broken his heart. "Emma, I must introduce you to the amazing awesomeness that is One Republic… and The Fray, because they're fucking amazing too." He slid off the bench and said, "I'll be right back."

I watched as he headed to the upstairs part of the guesthouse.

He wasn't gone long and he returned with a black iPod. "Here," he held it out to me. "You can keep it."

"I don't want to keep it. I'll just borrow it for a little while," I slid it into my pocket.

"No, no. Just keep it. I don't even use it anymore. I've got everything right here." He pulled his phone from his pocket and waved it around. "Which reminds me, you can put music on the phone I got you. We'll do that another time though. Mathias is still sleeping and if I take you upstairs and we wake him up he'll be even more pissed than he would've been if he saw his motorcycle gone."

"Still sleeping? It's like two in the afternoon?"

"He was out all night," he shrugged, sitting down beside me once more. He started to play the song again and glanced at me. "If I play it once, then do you think we can play it together?"

I nodded. "Yeah."

He smiled and I closed my eyes again so that I could focus on the music. It didn't take me long to pick up on the song and by the time it finished I was ready to play.

A shy smile graced my lips as we started to play together.

I gasped in surprise when Maddox started to sing along. His voice was soft and husky. He became completely lost in the song and it was a sight to see. I wondered if I looked the same way when I was absorbed in a song. Or even a book. There was a look of such pure satisfaction on his face. If he looked this way singing and playing piano I longed to see him on the drums.

The last note lingered in the air and I dropped my hands into my lap.

Maddox glanced at me. His eyes were a light and happy gray. "Thank you."

I ducked my head, a few strands of hair falling forward to hide my face. Maddox made me feel things I hadn't believed possible.

When I lifted my gaze he still stared at me intensely, with those unique silvery gray eyes.

"Do you want to do something crazy?" He asked, his voice no more than a whisper—like he was afraid if he said the words in a normal voice I might go running.

"What?" I asked, my brows furrowing together.

"Anything we want." His eyes darted to my lips. My heart jolted in my chest at the look of longing in his eyes. "I want more adventures with you like we had today. I don't want it to stop here."

I stared at him, puzzled. I didn't understand his sudden train of thought, but I rolled with it.

"Yes," I grinned. "Let's do it." I heard what he said last night echoing through my head, *Prepare for the most epic summer of your life. Nothing will ever top this.*

I *wanted* that epic summer he spoke of. I wanted to do the craziest things I could think of and finally allow myself the chance to live and stop fearing getting hurt by opening myself up.

His smile was blindingly bright and I squealed in surprise when he wrapped his strong arms around me in a hug. Mine hung limply at my side for a moment before I lifted them slowly to wrap around his torso. I could feel his muscles flex at my touch and the warmth of his body heat wrapped around me.

He let me go and I let my arms drop—hoping it hadn't seemed like I was feeling him up.

I swept my hair out of my eyes, hoping he didn't notice the way my hand shook.

"So," he started, and his lips turned up crookedly, "what's the second adventure you'd like to do this summer? —Because the motorcycle was number one. In case you didn't know." He winked, his smile playful.

"Knitting." The word fell out of my mouth before I could stop it. I slapped a hand over my mouth, like I thought the gesture alone could put the word back in there. Yes, I wanted to learn to knit—I was a dork like that—but I felt silly to have admitted that to Maddox.

"Knitting?" A brow quirked. "You want to sit around and knit sweaters and baby blankets like old ladies do?"

"Yes," I winced. "We don't have to do that, though. I don't know why I said it."

"No, no," he rushed to assure me, "it's okay. Knitting could be fun. Maybe I can make a Christmas present for Mathias," he grinned impishly. "I think he needs some new socks. What else?" He asked. "The craziest thing you can think of."

"I've always wanted to jump into a massive pool of those plastic ball things," I admitted with a shrug. "I never got to do that as a kid."

"Done. What do you think about skydiving?"

"Like jumping out of a plane?" I asked and he nodded. "I would do it.'"

"I think I love you, Emma," he chuckled.

I hated the way my body warmed at his words. I should *not* be thinking about the words *love* and *Maddox* in the same sentence. I'd just met him—and I'd vowed to never fall in love, anyway. Love made people weak. It made you do stupid things because you cared too much.

"Ooh!" He clapped his hands together. "Let's go to the aquarium in Baltimore."

I shook my head free of its previous thoughts, dismissing them from my mind.

"I've never been to the aquarium so that sounds fun to me," I grinned.

He gaped at me, his eyes bugging out. "You've never been to the aquarium? Even as a child?" I shook my head at his question. "That's just wrong, Em." He tapped a finger against his full bottom lip as he thought. "How about hiking?" He asked. "There's supposed to be an amazing view from the mountain not too far from here."

"I'm in," I agreed. Hiking really wasn't my thing, but this summer was meant for going outside my comfort zone. "I'll do it, but I won't be happy about it." I stuck my tongue out at him. "So when I get blisters on my feet I expect you to carry me the rest of the way up the mountain," I jested.

He chuckled. "I can do that." He proceeded to flex his arm muscles. Sobering, he said, "This sounds like one epic summer to me, Em."

I stared into his silvery eyes, getting lost for a moment. "Yeah, epic." I agreed, and I wasn't being the least bit sarcastic.

# CHAPTER SEVEN

"Rise and shine! We're going to the mall!"

I peeked my eyes open and hastily slapped a hand over them, wincing at the sunlight streaming through my now open windows.

"Sadie," I groaned. "I was sleeping."

"And now you're awake." I felt her hand slap against my feet. "Get out of bed, get dressed, and drink some of this lovely tea your mother made. I actually like this one, it doesn't taste like mud like the last one she gave me."

"I don't want to go anywhere," I pleaded. "Let me sleep."

"No can do. It's summer and we're going to have *fuuuuun*," she sing-songed.

"I was having fun… sleeping."

"Emma Rayne Burke, I will drag you from this bed if I have to. I need best friend time."

"Fine," I groaned.

"I'm glad you could see things my way," she clapped her hands together.

A moment later I heard my bedroom door close.

I forced my tired body from my bed and pulled on a pair of shorts, a white tank top, and the black hat Maddox loved so much—simply because there was no time to tame the beast. The beast being my hair, of course.

I found my mom and Sadie in the kitchen.

"Here you go, Emmie." My mom handed me a plate with an egg sandwich. "I'm glad you girls are spending some time together." With that she headed into her studio and I knew I'd be lucky if I saw her the rest of the day.

I sat down at the table beside Sadie and took a bite of my sandwich.

"Do we really have to go to the mall?" I whined. Our mall was the bane of my existence. It was a crappy mall—but even if it had been a nice mall I still would've hated it—with stores that charged too much and burnt food smelling up the place.

"Yes, we really do," she laughed, finishing her sandwich. "I need a dress for my parent's barbeque this weekend. You better come." She eyed me, daring me to say no.

"Of course," I agreed. "I'm there every year."

Sadie's family held a barbeque the week after school ended every year to celebrate the start of summer. It had been a tradition in my life as long as I'd been friends with Sadie—which was my whole life.

"I know," she frowned. "But you've been weird since the fair."

I knew this was the perfect opportunity to tell her more about Maddox, but I couldn't seem to open my mouth and get it to work. I thought a part of me was afraid that if I didn't keep Maddox a secret, he'd suddenly disappear—or become a figment of my imagination.

"Yeah, I know," I sighed.

"You were really mad at me, weren't you?" She frowned.

I shrugged. "You've done it before. I should be used to it."

"God," she smacked her hand against the top of the table, "I'm such a shitty friend. You should really fire me and find a replacement."

I cracked a smile at that. "You know there's no one else quite like you."

She laughed, the tension bleeding out of her body. "You've got that right. I'm one of a kind."

I finished my sandwich and washed our plates. "Okay," I sighed heavily. "I'm ready to be tortured."

She rolled her eyes and grabbed her purse. "You are so fucking dramatic, Emma. You should really consider joining the drama club." She started towards the front door, leaving me in the kitchen.

"Yes, because I like people so much." I dead-panned.

She stopped in her tracks, laughing. "Oh yes, I forget, I'm your only human friend. The rest are fictional."

"At least they don't piss me off like you do," I jested.

"Whatever, Emma." Her tone was light. "Get your ass out here before I leave you!" She called, going out the door.

"Yes, because I would be heart broken if you left without me!"

The glass storm door swung closed but she turned around, giving me the finger.

A lot of people probably didn't understand our friendship, but when you'd known each other for forever you stopped caring what you said to one another.

I grabbed my purse and followed her outside. I slid into the passenger seat of her old Hyundai Elantra. "I better get some pretzels out of this with that yummy mustard sauce, it's the only good thing that ever comes out of the mall."

She laughed, backing out of the driveway. "Don't worry. I'll make sure you get your pretzels. Maybe, if you're a good girl and don't complain too much I'll even get you Cinnabon." She patted me on top of my head.

I clapped my hand over my heart. "I think you love me."

"Only a little." She held her thumb and index finger apart slightly.

In many ways Sadie was like the annoying sister I'd always wanted but never had. Sadie had her own little sister, Abby, and an older brother named Sam. When I was younger I used to be jealous of the fact that she had a brother and sister—even when they argued I wanted that. Now that I was older, and had grown up with my dad being such an asshole, I was glad that I didn't have any siblings.

As my thoughts turned to my dad I frowned.

There was a part of me that missed him. He was my dad after all.

And I knew I was still angry at him for abandoning us the way he had. My mom didn't deserve to be walked out on with a house and bills to pay for—not to mention a kid.

My dad was probably—okay, *definitely*—the reason I preferred the company of books and stayed away from guys.

Except for Maddox.

He was different.

But I didn't quite understand *how* he was different.

I didn't trust him, though. I couldn't. And he'd never get my heart. I wouldn't give it to him. But we could be friends.

Friends—wasn't that a joke with the way I was attracted to him.

I would be better off staying away, but I *couldn't*.

He was the sun and I couldn't help but be drawn to his warmth.

"Emma? Emmmmma?"

"What?" I shook my head free of my thoughts.

"We're here." Sadie pointed to the mall.

"Oh." I looked up at its brick exterior. When did we get here? I couldn't remember.

She shut the car off and climbed out, slinging her purse over her shoulder and fluffing her hair.

Sadie always looked like she was ready to pose for a picture—and not of the selfie variety.

Sadie was always put together—hair done, makeup impeccable, and her clothes stylish.

I followed her into the mall, praying that we didn't run into too many people we went to school with.

Small talk was the bane of my existence.

Sadie seemed to be on a mission, though. She power walked through the crowds and I hurried to catch up.

"They better still have this dress," she muttered. "It's on sale and it's perfect."

I had no idea what dress she was talking about, but if I knew Sadie it was probably short and would have her boobs practically spilling out of the top.

When she looked back and saw me dragging behind her she grabbed my arm and pulled me along. "Come on," she groaned.

She didn't let go of me as she practically ran into the store.

She scanned the racks and squealed. "Cross your fingers that they have my size!" She finally let go of me and went through the dresses. "Yes!" She exclaimed, holding up a strapless dress. The top was a corset design with flowers while the skirt was aqua colored. "It was meant to be." She clutched it to her chest.

I thought she was seconds away from kissing it and offering to have its children.

"Now we have to find a dress for you!" She jumped up and down.

"Uh, no." Clothes like this weren't my thing. They were too fancy and far too pricey for what I could afford. Sadie was always trying to buy me clothes and other things—even her parents tried to spoil me, since they all knew things were hard on my mom since my dad left.

She rolled her eyes and clutched the top of the metal rack. "Yes, you're getting a dress. I owe you for the fair and all the other shit I put you through. Pretzels and Cinnabon is not enough to make up for it. Please don't fight me on this." Her bottom lip curled down.

I was powerless to the pout and she knew it. It was how she'd gotten me to do many things over the years—usually to go to parties.

"Fine," I agreed. "But nothing over fifty dollars. I mean it." I pointed a finger at her warningly.

She didn't say anything in response. Instead she started darting around to the different racks like a demented fairy on crack.

"And nothing too revealing!" I yelled after her, causing several people to look my way.

I hurried after Sadie, lest she get too carried away.

She pulled a dress off a rack and held it out to me as I approached. "This one is perfect!"

I had to admit, she actually chose well for me. The dress was cream colored with pink, red, orange, and blue flowers embroidered on it. It had thicker straps and didn't dip down low in the front.

"You like it," she stated, smiling like the Cheshire cat. "Say it, Emma."

"You did good," I groaned. "I really like it." In fact, I might've even loved it.

I reached out, rubbing the fabric between my fingers.

"See, you should trust me more often." She beamed, her light brown hair swishing around her shoulders. She carried the items towards the checkout area, stopping at one of the spinning displays of jewelry. She grabbed a set of simple silver bangles and then placed her items on the counter by the register.

I nibbled my bottom lip nervously. "Sadie, you really don't have to get me that dress."

"Shut up. You deserve it and I'm getting it for you. End of discussion." She nodded her head firmly.

"Thank you," I said, knowing I'd end up thanking her a hundred more times before the day was over.

Once she'd paid she grabbed the bag and we headed towards the food court.

As promised she got me those pretzels I loved so much and Cinnabon. We sat in the food court eating and laughing. I was glad that I wasn't fighting with her anymore. I hated being mad at Sadie.

After hitting a few more stores we left and she dropped me off at home.

"Thank you again for the dress," I told her, clutching the bag in my hand. I was thinking about asking Maddox if he'd want to go to the barbeque with me. I was still scared to introduce him to Sadie—that was my insecurity showing—but I wanted him to come. I was already imagining his reaction to seeing me in the dress.

She rolled her eyes. "And for the thousandth time, Emma, you're welcome."

We both laughed and I got out of the car. I waved briefly before heading inside.

"Emmie, is that you?" My mom called from the kitchen when I closed the front door.

"Yes," I answered, wondering whom else it would be.

I found her sitting at the kitchen table with a cup of tea. Clay was caked underneath her fingernails and her light hair was pulled back messily and secured with a clip.

She looked up from the notepad where she was making a grocery list and smiled. "There's some more tea if you want some."

I poured a cup and sat down beside her. "I'm going back into my studio tonight. While I've got this…" She paused, searching for the right words, "… creative mojo going on I want to keep going. I thought maybe you could order Chinese or something."

"Sounds good," I agreed.

My mom rarely ever cooked dinner. It wasn't for a lack of care, she was just scatterbrained and often lost track of time. I didn't mind fending for myself, though. Especially since on the rare occasions when she did cook she liked to experiment—and all of her experiments ended badly.

She set the pen down and stared at me.

I gave her a peculiar look and asked, "Why are you looking at me like that?"

She shook her head and a sad smile turned her lips. "I was just thinking about what a beautiful young woman you've turned into. You're going to be a senior in high school, and then off too college. I know whatever you want to do with your life you'll excel at it. You've always been a brilliant girl. How'd I get so lucky?"

I didn't get emotional over much, but I felt tears well in my eyes.

My mom always went out of her way to tell me how smart and pretty I was. She was constantly telling me she was proud of me, and praising my accomplishments.

But sometimes I felt… almost worthless.

I wasn't an idiot, I knew where those feelings came from.

Having my dad treat me like crap and then abandon us had left a sour taste in my mouth.

If I wasn't good enough for him, then how would I ever be good enough for something or someone else?

I forced a smile. "Thanks, mom." I took a sip of my tea to mask the quake in my voice. I set the mug down and traced my finger over the design of the skeletal T-Rex, smiling at the words painted on the mug: Tea Rex. It always made me smile.

She gave my hand a pat and stood up from the table, finishing the last of her tea. She set the empty cup in the sink. "I'll see you later, Emmie." She bent down and kissed the top of my head as she passed.

I picked up my cup of tea and headed back to my room.

Since the last few days had been… weird—that was the only word I could think to describe it—I hadn't been reading. But I was going to change that tonight.

I scanned my bookshelves for something new to read.

I read all genres, and even the occasional non-fiction book. I got bored easily if I read the same thing all the time.

When I couldn't decide I finally closed my eyes and picked a random book off the shelf.

I sat on my bed and turned the TV on for background noise while I flipped through the pages of the book.

I got lost in the imaginary world—picturing myself as the heroine. After all, wasn't that why people read? So they could live someone else's life for a little while?

Several hours passed and I was finally pulled from my fictional world by the rumbling of my stomach.

Clearly, it was time to order takeout.

And since I was starving I ordered enough food to feed five people.

My mom was going to kill me—but at least I remembered to order her chicken fried rice for later, so hopefully that counted as bonus points.

I settled on the couch in the living room, with my book in my lap, and listened to Maddox's iPod. I twirled one of the wire headphones around my finger, bobbing my head along to the song playing. It actually wasn't bad, and I found myself putting it on repeat. Maybe I was missing out on something by only listening to classical.

When the doorbell rang I set my book aside, but kept the iPod clasped in my hand. I grabbed the cash off the kitchen table and opened the door.

I stared at the guy standing there.

"You're not the Chinese guy." I eyed his empty hands.

"No," he chuckled.

"Who are you?" I asked, starting to ease the door closed. I'd seen *48 Hours*, so I knew a strange guy showing up on your doorstep was never a good thing.

"Ezra," he replied, sweeping curly black hair from his dark almond shaped eyes. "I'm Maddox's friend."

"Best friend and foster brother!" Another voice called from near the driveway.

I stepped outside and eyed Maddox, who strode towards me with confidence clear in the way he held himself. "Why are you here?" I asked.

"Are you not happy to see me?" He feigned a gasp.

"I'm confused," I countered.

"We were nearby," he shrugged, "and I needed to ask you a favor. Can we come inside?" He pointed towards the house.

"Sure," I shook my head, moving out of the way. Once they were inside I closed the door and pulled the iPod out of my pocket, sitting it on a side table. "So, if you had a favor to ask why didn't you text me? Or call?"

"And miss the chance to see your pretty face? I don't think so," he jested, sitting down on the couch. "Now, for the introductions, Emma, this is Ezra. He's Karen's real son."

Ezra rolled his eyes. "Please, I might be the biological son but you know she loves you more."

Maddox chuckled. "True, I mean, what's not to love?" He motioned to himself.

"Can we get to the point as to why you're here?" I interrupted. I wasn't normally so snappy, but I was hungry, and when I was hungry… watch out.

"Someone's grouchy," Maddox muttered under his breath to Ezra.

"I'm hungry," I defended, crossing my arms over my chest.

"Anyway," Maddox continued, rubbing his hands together, "We, and by *we* I mean my whole family, have to go out of town through the weekend. We leave tomorrow morning and I need someone to watch Sonic."

"Are you seriously asking me to babysit your hedgehog?" I resisted the urge to laugh. "I don't know the first thing about taking care of one."

"It's easy. You feed it, give it water, and shower it with love and affection. What's so difficult about that?" He countered.

"My mom's never let me have a pet. She's not going to let me," I warned him. The truth was my mom wouldn't care—it had always been my dad that was the real animal hater—but Maddox didn't need to know that.

"It's not like you're keeping Sonic. The moment we get back I'll pick the little guy up. It's only a few days."

"What if he dies?" I hissed. "I will not be responsible for the death of your hedgehog." I'd once killed a fish just by staring at it. True story.

Maddox looked at Ezra and back at me. "You're not going to kill him, Em. You're going to take care of him."

"What if by taking care of him I send him to an early grave!" I shrieked.

"You'll do fine," he continued. "I have the utmost faith in your hedgehog babysitting abilities."

I knew then that I wasn't getting out of this.

"Please, Em?" He begged, his gray eyes were wide and pleading. "You're the only one I trust with him."

I sighed in defeat. "Fine, I'll watch the hedgehog."

"Thank you!" He jumped up from the couch and wrapped his arms around me, planting a wet kiss on my cheek.

"Um… you're welcome," I mumbled.

The doorbell rang and before I could move Maddox was striding across the room to the door. He opened it wide, screamed, "Ooh! Food!" and pulled his wallet out his back pocket. He handed the guy a wad of cash and closed the door with his booted foot.

I stood there, shell-shocked at Maddox's take-charge attitude.

"I had money for that, you know."

"And I beat you to it," he winked, sitting the bags down on the coffee table. "It's like you knew we were coming. You ordered enough food for all of us, which is great since I'm *starving*."

He proceeded to sit on the floor and start pulling out the white boxes.

"Just help yourself," I muttered with a shake of my head.

I headed into the kitchen to grab plates and forks—I'd never been able to master the art of using chopsticks.

I set the stuff on the kitchen table and called, "Why don't you bring it in here?"

After a moment of shuffling the guys appeared in the kitchen doorway. Half of an egg roll stuck out of Maddox's mouth.

"I hope it's good," I stuck a hand on my hip, "because that was mine."

He chewed and swallowed. "There are like six in here."

"And I was going to cat all of them," I joked.

"Well you can have the other five then," he chuckled.

The three of us emptied out portions of everything onto our plates. "Seriously, why'd you get so much food?" Ezra asked, looking around like he expected a group of people to pop out from behind a hidden doorway.

"I was hungry, and I like this stuff left over," I shrugged. "And since you two showed up and want to steal all my food, I guess it's a good thing I ordered so much."

Ezra had the good graces to look ashamed, but it was clear Maddox didn't care. He was the kind of guy that was used to doing what he wanted, when he wanted. I wasn't annoyed, though. I liked that about him—that he wasn't afraid to be himself.

"Maddox said you guys met at the fair?" Ezra questioned.

I nodded, but before I could say anything Maddox spoke up. "She was overcome by how hot I am and fainted right at my feet. But just like Sleeping Beauty, my kiss awakened her. It's a very romantic story, one I'm sure we'll tell our grandchildren."

I looked at Ezra and we both started to laugh.

"You're so full of shit." Ezra pushed Maddox's shoulder.

"Excuse me if the truth was boring and I saw fit to stretch it," Maddox harrumphed. Maddox looked around and asked me, "Where's your mom?"

"In her studio, oblivious to the rest of the world." I wasn't angry about that fact. After all, I was very much like my mom. I got lost in my own little world all too easy where the passage of time ceased to matter.

"Well, then I think we should eat until we burst and then go for some ice cream," Maddox suggested.

"Yes, because gorging myself until I want to throw up and then eating ice cream sounds like such a good idea," I laughed.

"Fine," he chuckled, ducking his head, "maybe we should watch a movie?"

Ezra cleared his throat. "I feel like you've completely forgotten I'm here."

"Aw, sorry, sweet pea," Maddox feigned a high voice, "please forgive me?" He leaned towards Ezra, making kissy lips.

Ezra pushed him away. "We can't stay late," Ezra warned. "We still have to pack."

"I'll throw some clothes in a bag in the morning," countered Maddox.

Ezra rolled his eyes. "Yes, but our flight is at nine in the morning and we have to drop Sonic off here. Plus, you know what a delight Mathias is in the mornings."

Maddox frowned. "I wish we could just leave him."

"Yeah, well, we can't," Ezra muttered.

"Just one movie?" Maddox pleaded, looking between Ezra and me.

"Uh..." I started.

"As long as it's not a three hour movie I'm okay with it."

"It's settled then," Maddox grinned at me. "Movie time!"

The guys helped me clean up our mess and put away the leftovers before we settled in the living room. Ezra removed some cushions from the one couch and put them on the floor. That left the loveseat for Maddox and I.

I couldn't help wondering if Ezra had done that on purpose.

Maddox scanned the DVDs we owned. "You don't have anything recent," he muttered. "What's with that?"

"We don't really watch movies," I shrugged, "so we stopped buying them."

"Looks like we're going with *Air Bud.*"

A moment later the movie started to play and Maddox sat down beside me.

I didn't know why, but I desperately wanted to close the space between us and curl my body around his.

It was silly.

Stupid even.

He wasn't my boyfriend, and I wasn't even sure we were *friends*.

My mind and body were fighting a battle of reason and attraction.

I didn't want a boyfriend—after all, I couldn't trust that a guy wouldn't abandon me just like my dad.

But my body… oh, my body wanted Maddox.

I'd never experienced this kind of attraction.

Sure, I'd had crushes here and there, but nothing compared to this.

It was like the moment I decided to close my heart off forever Maddox came along.

I kept telling myself that I'd only just met him and my feelings would fade, but somehow I didn't believe it.

I startled when I felt Maddox's arm fall around my shoulders. "Come here," he coaxed, pulling me against his side. He reached behind us on the back of the couch and grabbed the blanket, draping it over my body.

He made me feel protected and cared for.

I was totally screwed.

But I guessed there were worse things than crushing on the hot guy you met at the fair, right?

At least I hoped so.

# CHAPTER EIGHT

I woke up sometime after midnight and blinked my eyes open.

"What?" I asked blearily.

"Shh," Maddox crooned. "We fell asleep."

I startled.

Oh my God.

He was carrying me to bed.

He laid me down gently on my bed and pulled away. "I'll see you in the morning." His voice was soft. "Goodnight."

His lips pressed tenderly against my forehead and my eyes closed at the touch.

"Goodnight, Maddox," I whispered as he walked out of the room.

Once I knew he was gone I changed out of my clothes and into pajamas.

I snuggled beneath the covers, and soon dreams floated behind my closed lids—all of them starring a gray-eyed boy.

I sat up and threw the covers off my body.

Why was the doorbell ringing at—I searched for my alarm clock—six in the morning?

"Oh crap," I muttered, suddenly remembering my hedgehog babysitting duties.

I ran out of my room and down the hall, throwing open the front door.

My poor mom didn't even know I'd agreed to take care of the little creature. I knew she wouldn't care, but I still felt bad for not letting her know.

"Morning," Maddox grinned, standing with a grumpy looking Mathias who held Sonic's cage. Sonic, himself, was clasped in Maddox's hands.

I stepped aside and waved the twins into my house, while stifling a yawn.

"You can put him in my room."

Mathias grumbled something unintelligible, and I figured it translated to how much he hated the world and life itself. He just seemed like the type of guy to bitch about everything.

"This way." I guided the grumpy twin to my room.

He set the cage on top of my dresser, muttered, "Bye," and left the room.

"He hates mornings," Maddox shrugged.

"Your brother and I have that in common." I pushed my messy hair out of my eyes.

He chuckled. "Here, I made you a list." He pulled a piece of paper out of his pocket and shoved it in my hands.

I opened it up, squinting to make out what he'd scrawled.

He began to recite everything he'd written. Telling me how much food to give Sonic, bath time instructions, and even how often a day Sonic liked to play.

"I thought Hedgehogs were nocturnal," I muttered.

"They mostly are, but Sonic is special." Maddox grinned proudly at the hedgehog. Maddox reminded me of some of the crazy people I saw with dogs. You know the ones that talk to them all the time and kiss them? Yeah, that was Maddox, but with a hedgehog.

"Of course he is," I sighed.

Maddox frowned at the spiky creature. "I don't want to leave him."

"When will you be back?" I asked.

"Sunday night." He shoved his fingers through his messy hair.

I frowned. I remembered him saying yesterday they'd be gone through the weekend—so that meant he couldn't come to the barbeque.

A car horn honked and Maddox cursed. "I really have to go." He handed the hedgehog over to me and said, "Thanks, Em." He started to pass by me and stopped, lowering his head to kiss my cheek. "I'll miss you," he whispered. "But when I get back it's time for another adventure."

"Sounds good," I smiled. Clutching Sonic to my chest I followed Maddox to the door. I didn't understand why my chest ached at watching him leave. We hadn't even known each other a week yet. It made no sense, but in the back of my mind I remembered my mom telling me once that the greatest things in our lives have no explanation, they just are.

"Bye," I called, when he started to get in the car.

He smiled and my stomach stirred with butterflies.

As the SUV—one of those big black Suburban's—backed out of the driveway I lifted my hand to wave. Then, feeling silly, I even lifted Sonic's little hand—or whatever it was called—so he could wave too.

Once the SUV was out of sight I looked down at the hedgehog.

"Well, it's just you and me now, buddy."

He sniffed my hand and then proceeded to pee.

"Oh, gross," I gagged. I ran back to my room and put him in his cage, before washing my hands five times.

When I returned to my room Sonic was snoozing peacefully in his cage. I climbed in bed once more and promptly fell asleep.

This time I woke up to the smell of tea and my mother standing over me.

"Emma," she eyed me with a stern expression, "what on Earth is this?" She moved out of the way to nod her head at the cage where Sonic was currently drinking some water.

"That's Sonic," I sat up, rubbing my eyes, "Maddox's hedgehog."

"Well, if this thing belongs to him why is it in our house?" She raised a brow, giving me her stern 'mom' look.

"Uh… I said I would watch him. Maddox and his family are out of town until Sunday and he needed someone to take care of him," I explained.

She sighed. "Well, he is kind of cute."

"The hedgehog or Maddox?" I laughed.

She rolled her eyes. "I was talking about the hedgehog, but Maddox is cute too." She sat down on the end of my bed and her eyes grew serious. "He's a nice boy too. Sweet… I like him."

"Do you want to date him?" I giggled.

She swatted lightly at my leg. "Emmie, I'm being serious. He seems like a good guy. I know you've never dated before and I'm not stupid, I know it's because of your dad, and I guess I don't want to see you push him away because of that."

"We're not dating, mom," I groaned. "We just met."

She smiled. "I see the way he looks at you. I might be old, but I still know what that look means."

"You're not old," I told her, "and he doesn't look at me in any certain way."

"I know what I saw last night." Her smile widened.

"Last night?" My brows furrowed together.

She nodded. "Mhmm," she took a sip of her tea. "I came in last night for some water and found the three of you in the living room. You'd already fallen asleep and the way he looked at you…" She smiled wistfully. "It reminded me of a boy I loved one summer, just like this, before my sixteenth birthday. He used to look at me like that and I've never forgotten it. It was so… pure."

I'd never heard my mom talk about any man besides my dad. "What happened to that guy?" I asked.

She frowned. "I don't know," she shrugged. "He was only visiting family for the summer, and I never saw him again. Then I met your father."

"And we know how that ended," I grumbled, rolling my eyes.

"Emmie," she clutched my hand, "you have to stop hating him. I know things were bad there for a while before he left, but it wasn't always that way."

"Why don't you hate him?" I asked, my lower lip trembling with the threat of tears.

"Because, he gave me you. How can I hate the man that gave me such a precious gift?"

I wished I could be more like my mom—so kind and forgiving.

I held my arms out and she enveloped me in a hug.

I didn't care how old you were, you were *never* too old to hug your mom.

She smoothed her fingers through my hair. "I love you so much, Emma."

"I love you too, mom." I wiped my tears away with a swipe of my hands. "What was that guy's name?" I asked.

"Matthew," she replied.

Were Maddox and I doomed to be like Matthew and my mother? Nothing more than a carefree summer fling?

I shook my head forcefully.

What was I thinking? This wasn't a fling.

This was nothing.

Okay, that was wrong.

It was an adventure.

And an adventure had nothing to do with love.

But if I never saw Maddox again after this summer would I be okay with that?

I knew, without a doubt, that the answer was no.

I wouldn't be okay.

Not at all.

# CHAPTER NINE

The week passed by at an obnoxiously slow rate and was rather boring without Maddox around.

I'd planned to read books and basically do nothing all summer—but now that held no appeal to me.

Staying in the house day in and day out was getting annoying.

At least it was Sunday, which meant I had Sadie's barbeque to attend this afternoon and Maddox would be home tonight.

I'd heard from him several times every day—and he got antsy if I didn't give him regular updates on Sonic.

It was cute how much he worried about the hedgehog.

As if he was triggered by my thoughts alone, my phone flashed with a text.

**Maddox:** See you tonight. Give Sonic a kiss for me.

I laughed.

**EMMA:** What time are you getting in? And, no, I'm not kissing him.

**MADDOX:** Pls? 4 me? And we should be in by 10pm but u know how flights can be.

**EMMA:** Actually, I don't.

**MADDOX:** Don't what?

**EMMA:** Know how flights are. I've never been on a plane.

**MADDOX:** I guess it's a good thing we're jumping from one. ;)

**EMMA:** I forgot about that.

**MADDOX:** Don't chicken out on me.

**EMMA:** I won't.

**MADDOX:** Hey, sorry, I have to go.

**EMMA:** K. See you later.

I set my phone aside and looked at Sonic. "He'll be back soon."

His little head perked up, like he knew what I said.

I opened the cage and reached in to take him out. After giving him a brief cuddle—which was hard with the quills—I proceeded to coo and tell him how cute he was per Maddox's instructions. Seriously, he put it in writing.

I set Sonic on my bed while I got ready. I changed into the pretty dress Sadie got me, fixed my hair in a messy bun, and applied some makeup. I didn't normally wear much—only mascara and lip-gloss—but I decided to do a little more today. I rubbed the foundation on my face watching my freckles nearly disappear.

When I finished with my hair and makeup I went in search of my mom. "Are you ready?" I knocked on her door.

"Almost!" She called.

I went back into my room to put my shoes on and gasped. "Sonic?" I looked all over my bed. "Sonic?" I moved some pillows around, thinking he was hiding behind them. "Sonic!"

Oh no! I'd lost Maddox's hedgehog!

I dropped to my knees on the floor, looking under the bed. "Sonic?" I couldn't see him, but then again it was so dark under there that I couldn't see anything… and I was pretty sure I'd hidden some Cheez-It crackers down there. Maybe Sonic found them and was having a little hedgehog feast. Did hedgehogs even like cheese crackers? What if cheese was bad for them?

Oh my God, I was going to end up inadvertently killing Maddox's hedgehog with Cheez-Its!

I grabbed my fancy new phone and turned on the flashlight—and seriously, how cool was it that this thing had a flashlight?

I shined it under the bed, but Sonic wasn't there.

The Cheez-Its were though.

"Mom!" I called. "Mom! Come here!"

I was really starting to panic now.

"What?" She stumbled into my room, her hair half done.

"I can't find Sonic."

"What do you mean you can't find Sonic?" She practically screeched. "Isn't he in his cage?"

"I took him out and put him on my bed while I got ready. I felt bad for him cooped up in that cage and I didn't think he'd wander." I clutched at my chest, gasping for air. "Maddox is going to kill me."

"Don't panic," my mom warned, "he couldn't have gone far."

She moved the pillows around, just like I had, but Sonic definitely wasn't there.

"Oh God," I muttered. "This is bad. So bad."

"Calm down, Emma," she grumbled. "Wait… what's that?" She pointed to the pillow I slept on which contained a mysterious lump.

"Sonic!" I cried. I lifted the pillowcase and reached inside to grab him. "You scared me!" And then I proceeded to kiss the hedgehog, just like Maddox had wanted me to. I guessed he always got his way in the end. I put Sonic back in his cage and made sure everything was secure. "You're not going anywhere now."

"I'm going to finish getting ready," my mom said as she backed out of the room. "Try not to lose the hedgehog again."

"Don't tell Maddox!" I called after her.

Her only response was to laugh at me, and even I had to admit that it was pretty funny.

"Emma!" Sadie shrieked, running towards me. I only had a moment to brace myself when her thin arms wound around my shoulders as she crashed into me. "I'm so glad you're here. I can't handle all these old people," she muttered, looking around at her various family members that were gathered in the backyard. "Grandpa keeps asking for potato salad, and every time we give it to him he bangs his fists against the table and says, 'I did not ask for this! Bring me potato salad!' And then he doesn't believe us that it is, indeed, potato salad."

"Wow."

"Yeah, I know."

I looked around. "I thought you invited some people from school."

She shrugged. "I did, but it seems like everyone is having a more fun summer vacation than we are." She threw an arm around my shoulders, guiding me to one of the tables covered in food. My mom had brought a cake and tea… iced tea this time, and not her traditional hot tea. "Whatever happened to that guy you went on a date with?"

I'd always shared everything with Sadie, but suddenly I just… didn't want to. Maddox seemed like a fairytale to me and I was afraid if I started telling her about him it would break the spell.

I was kind of shocked that she was just now asking me about him, since I'd promised—and failed—to call her the night of our first date.

"Uh, we've just hung out a few times," I shrugged casually. "No big deal."

She gave me a doubtful look. "Sure. Let me know when the wedding is."

I laughed. "You're crazy."

"And *you've* never even batted your eyes at a guy before. This is a big deal."

I picked up one of the paper plates and started piling food on it. "Hardly."

Sadie settled into line behind me. "We should see a movie tomorrow," she suggested.

I frowned. "I don't think I can."

She snorted. "What could you possibly be doing? Reading? Come on, Emma. Wait…" She paused. "Are you going to be with *him?* Mystery boy?"

I blushed.

"You are!"

"I don't know that," I mumbled. "And he's not a mystery."

"But you hope," she countered, "and he is to me. I know nothing about him."

"He's amazing," I finally muttered. "I really like him, okay? We're just friends, though."

"You went on a date," she reasoned as we headed to one of the tables to sit down, "so that means you're more than friends."

"It does not," I grumbled. I searched for any topic that didn't have anything to do with my own life. "So, who do you have your eyes set on this summer?"

Sadie never stayed with one guy very long, but she usually picked one guy for the summer and then when it was time for school to start she cut ties. "Meh," she shrugged. "Everyone hot is gone for the summer. Figures." Smiling, she added, "I'm trying to get my dad to let me spend the summer at my aunt and uncle's beach house." She licked her lips like she was already imagining the guys she'd find there.

"I'm sure your dad is being really agreeable about that," I laughed.

Mr. Westbrook was one of the strictest parents I knew, but it was only because he cared so much about his kids. He wasn't an asshole like my dad. In fact, growing up, I'd often wished I could have Sadie's dad. The kind of dad that would've thrown me up on his shoulders, taken me to the zoo, and just spent time with me.

She huffed. "He's being an ass about it. But I'm going to be eighteen in a few months, so I don't see what the big deal is. I'm an adult."

Calling Sadie an adult was laughable.

"At least your dad is looking out for you," I commented. "He cares."

She flipped her brown hair over one shoulder and peered at me with searching honey colored eyes. "Your dad cares about you, Emma. You're his daughter after all."

I eyed her. "He has a funny way of showing it."

"It's been two years," she said softly.

"I know," I sighed. "I'm over it, I am. But sometimes it's all too easy to get mad."

She smiled sadly. "Maybe when you get mad you should think about how much better off you are with him gone."

Sadie could be crazy. She could be loud. She could even be annoying.

But at the end of the day, we were best friends for a reason and sometimes she was wiser than me.

"You're right."

"You say that like you're surprised," she laughed. She stood and came around the table to hug me. "I love you, Emma, like a sister and I hate it when you get sad."

"I know… where do you think he is?" I whispered.

She pulled away and gave a small shrug. "I don't know anymore than you do, but wherever he is, I hope he's getting the help he needs."

"Yeah," I agreed.

My emotions were always a rollercoaster when it came to my dad.

I was so angry at him for leaving us—for not being the dad I needed—that if he showed up at our home today I'd probably slap him.

But another part of me was sad and missed him. He might not have been a great dad, but he was my dad.

And then, like Sadie said, I also hoped he'd decided to get help.

I might've hated his guts most days, but I still didn't want him to suffer.

Sadie sat down once more and changed the conversation to lighter things.

Soon thoughts of my dad disappeared, along with the light from the sky.

Once it started to get dark was when the true party started.

Mr. and Mrs. Westbrook had twinkling lights strung up around the yard, and music pumped from a set of Bose speakers.

"Come on," Sadie grabbed my hands, "let's dance."

I let her drag me into the middle of the yard, where her older brother, Sam, danced with one of her baby cousins.

Sadie started to dance crazily and I mimed her movements. We looked like goofballs, but I didn't care. I was having fun.

My mom laughed at us from the table where she sat with Sadie's parents. I waved her over to join us.

"No!" She laughed. "Y'all keep going."

I smiled and reached up to pull the elastic from my hair. I let the blonde strands flow around my shoulders as I danced and sang.

I felt like a butterfly breaking free of its cocoon.

And even though Maddox wasn't here, I couldn't help thinking that he was responsible for my metamorphosis.

# CHAPTER TEN

Maddox called me last night and told me that their flight had been delayed and he'd be home too late to pick up Sonic. I assured him that it was fine, and that I'd even grown fond of the hedgehog. I left out the part about losing him.

Since I knew Maddox would probably arrive early to pick up his beloved pet I made myself get up and ready. Last night when we spoke on the phone he told me to be ready to cross off another adventure today. I was excited and scared, all at the same time, to see what he had planned. I mean, I might've known what the possibilities were, but I had no idea which one he'd picked.

I stared at my reflection in the mirror.

The girl I saw there almost looked like a stranger.

Yeah, it was definitely me—the same wild and untamable hair, full lips, and freckles—but what I saw reflected in my eyes was where the difference lay. My eyes sparkled with happiness. Even my skin glowed and my cheeks had a natural and pretty flush.

Maddox was bringing back the carefree Emma that had rolled down hills and sang songs without abandon—the girl who'd been unaware of the world's cruel punishments.

It was strange to see her reflected back at me again.

She'd been gone so long I thought she was lost forever.

In fact, I'd stopped looking for her.

I had accepted that this melancholy way was how my life was meant to be—but I'd been wrong.

I smiled and smoothed my hands down my cardigan.

This excitement I felt at seeing him was foreign, but exhilarating.

I wasn't supposed to like him—or any guy—to avoid getting hurt, but I knew without a doubt that Maddox was impossible to ignore.

The doorbell rang through the house and I stepped out of the bathroom. My cheeks lifted in a permanent smile as I headed towards the door. I tried to tone it down, but I couldn't. I was just that happy to see him.

It hadn't even been a week since the last time I saw him, but the moment I opened the door and saw him standing there it felt like forever.

I couldn't control my reaction to seeing him, even if I had wanted to.

I jumped into his arms, wrapping mine around his neck. "I missed you," I admitted against his shoulder.

His chuckle was warm and pleased sounding. His hands rubbed against my back and he didn't seem to want to let go either.

I forced my arms to fall and took a step back. Now, the embarrassment came. "Sorry about that," I mumbled, toeing the ground with my shoe.

He chuckled and I felt his fingers connect with my chin. He slowly lifted my chin until he could look fully at my face. "Don't apologize. I enjoyed it." His eyes were serious for once, with no laughter sparkling in the gray depths.

I didn't know what to say, and since I was quite possibly one of the most awkward people on the planet I stuttered, "Uh… you should… uh… get Sonic."

His lips twisted into a smile. "Really?" His brows rose. "Because I think there's something else I should do first."

"Really? Wha—"

My reply was cut off by his soft lips connecting with mine. I was shocked and didn't know what to do at first.

My brain was all like, *"Oh my God! He's kissing you!"*

And then a moment later it yelled at me, *"Do something! Don't just stand there and make him do all the work!"*

With my heart skipping a beat in my chest, I wrapped my hands around his neck. My fingers played with the silky strands of his hair. His hair was so soft and the feel of his stubble brushing against my face was actually quite pleasant. His fingers dug into my hips and I gasped at the pressure.

Suddenly I found my back against the wall—the breeze from the open doorway tickled my face.

He slanted his lips over mine.

Claiming me.

Devouring me.

*Owning* me.

And I let him.

His lips fell away from mine and his breath fanned across my face. Both of us were breathing heavily. His hands flexed against my hips and I'd yet to drop my hands from his hair.

"I wasn't expecting that," I panted.

He chuckled, brushing his lips lightly over mine. My eyes closed at the feel of the feather light touch.

"That's exactly why I did it." He nuzzled my neck. "I've been wanting to kiss you since the moment I saw you, but I wanted to wait until I knew."

"Knew what?" I croaked, my voice suddenly hoarse.

"I wanted to know that you felt it too," he whispered in my ear and I shivered, "this crazy connection we have."

"C-connection?" I stuttered, my fingers now digging into the tops of his shoulders for support.

"Mhmm," he hummed. "I don't normally pick up girls at fairs," he laughed, "and then plan a whole summer of adventures with them." His voice lowered, "But I knew you were different, and I selfishly wanted to keep you around."

My whole body shook.

"What are we doing, Maddox?"

"What do you mean?" He asked.

"Are we a couple?" I said before I could decide against it.

"If you're asking me if I want you to be my girlfriend, the answer to that question is very much… *yes*." He murmured the last word lowly in my ear.

I shivered, grasping his arms so that I didn't fall.

"I-I don't know if I can do this," I admitted.

His eyes filled with sadness and his lips thinned. "I was afraid you might say that."

"It's t-too soon," I stuttered, my throat closing up. Did I really believe that? I felt like I knew Maddox better in a week than I knew most of the people I'd went to school with since Kindergarten. But I didn't feel like I was ready to take that leap yet.

His forehead touched mine and his eyes closed as if he was in pain. "It's okay." His tongue swept out to moisten his lips and his hands came up to form a cage beside my head. His eyes darkened with a promise. "Just so you know, I don't regret kissing you, and one day you're going to ask me to, and I'm going to kiss you until you forget who you are."

My breath shook. I believed him.

He stepped back and with a wink he headed down the hall to my room.

I still stood stunned. I couldn't move if I wanted to.

I tentatively reached up and touched shaking fingers to my lips.

The last—and only—time I had kissed a guy had been before my dad walked out, and that kiss was in no way comparable to this one. If a kiss could set off fireworks it would be Maddox's.

"Wow," I whispered, lowering my hand.

I did my best to compose myself before Maddox returned with the cage clutched in his hands and Sonic sitting on his shoulder.

"Aren't you afraid he'll fall?" I asked.

"No," he tilted his head to peer at the hedgehog, "Sonic knows to hang on. He's used to it. Would you mind holding the door?" He asked.

"Oh, yeah, sure." I bumbled over my words and hastily opened the door so he could head to the car.

I hurried after him and helped him get the cage in the backseat—which wasn't an easy feat since the car was a coupe.

"Are you ready to go?" He smiled down at me and my stomach flip-flopped. I hated the way my body reacted to him—how he was impossible to resist.

"Let me say goodbye to my mom."

My mom already knew I was spending the day with Maddox, so there was really no need for me to go back inside, but I had to get away from him and his hypnotizing gaze before I did something stupid. Like, ask him to kiss me again and prove him right.

I left Maddox standing by his car and walked swiftly into the house and straight to my mom's studio.

She looked up when I entered and stopped what she was doing. "Are you okay?"

"Yeah, I just wanted to say bye… so, bye." I stood awkwardly in the doorway.

She laughed, her smile bright and happy. "Bye, Emma. Have fun with Maddox, but don't get pregnant."

"Mom!" I groaned, my cheeks flaming.

She laughed. "Sorry, I felt like it was the responsible parent thing to say. Although, I know I don't have to worry with you."

"Thanks, mom." I whispered, suddenly overcome by an emotion I couldn't begin to describe.

She tilted her head, still smiling. "Why are you thanking me?"

"For being there for me… for always being the best mom you could be."

"Oh, Emma," her hands fell to her sides and some of the clay got on her jeans, "you never need to thank me for that—though it is nice to hear. It's my job as your mother to always be what you need. Whether it's a shoulder to cry on, or a disciplinary figure."

"I just want you to know that I think you're a pretty amazing mom," I shrugged. "You deserve to know."

"Well, thank you. I love you, Emmie."

"Love you too, mom." I took a step back and started to close the door. "I better go before Maddox comes to find me."

She chuckled. "Yes. Go on, and have fun."

I smiled one last time before closing the door.

I slipped into the sleek sports car and laughed when I saw that Maddox had Sonic balanced on the wheel.

"Is everything okay?" He asked, worry wrinkling his brow.

"Yeah, everything is great," I assured him.

"Okay," he said, "here, hold Sonic while I drive."

I took the hedgehog and placed him on my lap while I buckled my seatbelt.

"Ready?" He asked.

I wasn't sure if he was asking if I was ready to leave, or ready for another adventure. I guessed it didn't matter since the answer was the same.

"Yes."

"Oh my God." I gaped at the swimming pool that had once been filled with glimmering blue colored water. Now, all the water was gone and replaced by plastic balls. "You know, when I suggested this, I didn't quite expect... *this*."

Maddox smiled proudly with his hands on his hips. "Isn't it wonderful?"

"Aren't your mom and dad mad?" I countered.

He waved a hand dismissively. "They don't care as long as I fill it up with water again."

"Uh-huh," I nodded.

"What are you waiting for?" He asked.

I shrugged. "You go first."

He chuckled, his eyes squinting from the sun. "I can do that right after I put Sonic away."

"Oh, right." I'd been so overcome by the site of the ball pit—or I guess *pool* was the better term—that I'd forgotten about Sonic.

"Wait here," he said, like he was afraid I might run away.

I wasn't scared though—just stunned. I hadn't expected this at all.

A slow smile began to spread across my face.

This was going to be fun.

Maddox returned and took in my expression. "I take it you're not stunned anymore?"

"No," I shook my head. "But I am wondering how you got all of these."

"I know people," he shrugged. "You still want me to go first?"

I nodded.

He grasped the bottom of his white t-shirt and started to pull it over his head.

"Whoa, whoa, whoa! What are you doing?" I cried.

He threw the shirt over his shoulder into the grass. "Taking my shirt off, isn't that obvious?"

"Why do you need to take your shirt off to jump in there?" I hissed.

"It's a pool, Emma."

"Yes," I agreed, "but that's not water!"

He smiled impishly and reached up to ruffle his brown hair. The movement caused my eyes to zero in on the way the muscles in his arms flexed, which then led my eyes to wander down over his sculpted chest and stomach. His body was filled out and not at all scrawny. I'd never blatantly checked out a guy before, but I couldn't tear my eyes away from Maddox.

"Like what you see?"

I squeaked and covered my face, embarrassed at being caught.

Maddox's laugh echoed around me and I startled when I felt his hand close around my arm. He pried my hands away from my face. "Don't get shy on me now, Em. We're about to jump into a pool of balls."

I snorted and he grinned.

"How about we go together?" He suggested, peering into my eyes.

I nodded. "Yeah, that would be good."

His smile was blinding. Reaching into his back pocket he plucked out a pair of drumsticks that I hadn't noticed earlier and set them down. He then reached for my hand—his larger one nearly swallowing mine whole.

Excitement pulsed through my body. I felt giddy like a little kid, where you were too young for the bad things to touch you and things like ball pits seemed like the coolest thing ever.

"Ready?" Maddox asked, and when I nodded he counted, "One, two, three!"

We ran forward together and jumped into the pool of plastic balls. I giggled as my body began to sink into the multi-colored balls.

"This is kind of amazing," I grinned.

Maddox smiled at me. "It is."

I moved through the ball pool laughing and smiling.

I was pretty certain that no one could be mad when doing something like this.

I didn't know how much time passed, but suddenly I heard an exclamation of, "What the fuck is going on?"

I turned to find Ezra and Mathias standing by the edge of the pool. Ezra was grinning and Mathias wore a scowl on his face.

"Having fun," Maddox responded to his grumpy brother.

"This is so cool," Ezra clapped his hands together. "Cannonball!" He yelled, jumping in with us.

Mathias rolled his eyes. "Y'all have lost your fucking minds."

"Come on, Mathias! Have some fun!"

Mathias wrinkled his nose at us like we were all disgusting.

"No."

"Mathias." Maddox growled.

"Oh, fine." Mathias huffed. He turned around and fell back into the pool like a crowd surfer at a concert.

"Way to go Mattie boy!" Ezra cheered.

"Oh, shut up," Mathias mumbled. His voice lightening he said, "This is actually kind of cool, but may I ask why you filled our swimming pool with balls?"

"It was Emma's idea," Maddox responded.

Mathias turned to look at me. "Why?"

"I thought it would be fun. I certainly didn't expect Maddox to go to this extreme to make it happen, though." I smiled, lifting a blue ball and throwing it towards Maddox. He wasn't paying attention and it bounced off his head, making all of us laugh.

After a while Mathias and Ezra left and it was just the two of us once more.

The excitement was wearing off so we climbed out and headed to the guesthouse.

Maddox called someone to come remove the balls and fill up the pool once more. I sat perched on the couch, not sure what I should do. I felt a bit out of place. I still wasn't familiar enough with Maddox to make myself at home.

*You sure were familiar enough to let him kiss you*, my conscience spoke up.

My cheeks started to heat at just the thought of the way his lips moved so effortlessly against mine.

After hanging up the phone Maddox strode past me and sat behind his drum kit. He'd put his shirt back on so I could no longer embarrass myself by staring at his bare chest.

"Do you mind if I play?" He asked, grabbing his drumsticks from his back pocket and raising a brow at me.

"No, not at all. I'd love to hear you play." I sat forward, intent not to miss a moment of this.

He lowered his eyes, trying to fight a smile.

Flicking his wrists he began to beat out a rhythm. At first it was slow, like he was almost hesitant to play in front of me, but soon his passion overrode his fear. His eyes closed and his head fell back as the speed picked up. The symbols clashed and the beat of the drum flowed through my body.

I had figured he'd be good, but I hadn't expected him to be *this* good.

I sat in awe as he played.

I was quite certain that Maddox might've been the most amazing person I'd ever met—and I didn't even know his last name.

Ten minutes passed before he stopped. He reached out, silencing the symbol and grinned at me.

"What did you think?"

I shook my head, unable to form words.

"Good? Bad?" He prompted.

"You're incredible," I finally gasped.

He grinned, standing up so he could put the drumsticks in his pocket once more.

"You know," I started, "I only just realized that I don't even know your last name."

He chuckled and sat down beside me on the couch. "It's Wade."

"Mine's Burke," I responded.

His lips twisted into a smile and he held out his hand. "Nice to meet you, Emma Burke."

"Back at ya, Maddox Wade."

It grew quiet between us and the way he stared at me had me squirming.

"What's your middle name?" I asked, hating the silence between us. Besides, I itched to get to know him better.

"Carson," he replied with a chuckle, draping his arm over the back of the couch. His fingers hovered dangerously close to my upper arm and Goosebumps broke out across my skin at his nearness. "What's yours?" He asked. "Wait… let me guess…" He tapped a finger against his chin. "Tallulah."

I snorted. "Tallulah? How the hell did you come up with that?"

He grinned crookedly. "Your mom seems like the type to give you an off the wall middle name," he shrugged, "and that was the first one to pop into my head."

"It is kind of different," I admitted.

"It's not Moon, is it?" He asked.

"No!" I laughed. Sobering, I added, "Although it's close."

"Oh God," he tilted his head back, his Adam's apple bobbing with his laughter.

"It's Rayne," I finally told him. "But spelled R. A. Y. N. E. instead of rain."

"Well, thank God for that," he chuckled.

"My mom is a bit of a hippy," I shrugged. "I guess it could've been a lot worse."

"Yeah, you could've been Emma Moon… which sounds like a stripper name." His eyes sparkled with barely contained laughter.

I snorted, laughing so hard that tears streamed down my cheeks.

He started to laugh too and I smiled at how easy it was being in his presence. I didn't feel the need to try to be someone else. I was just… Emma.

"Well, I'm definitely not a stripper," I continued to laugh.

"I don't know," he eyed my chest, "with those curves I think you could pull it off."

"Maddox!" I shrieked, playfully swatting at his arm.

He pretended to wince. "That hurt."

"Oh, I'm sure the injury is life threatening." I turned towards him, studying his face carefully.

"Why are you looking at me like that?" He asked with wonder.

I shrugged. "You've lived here for a while, right?" I asked.

"Yeah, my whole life." He answered with a tone that suggested he was curious as to what I was getting at.

"How have we lived in the same place for all these years and only just met?"

"Because," his voice lowered and he leaned towards me so that there was little space between us, "we weren't meant to meet then. This is our now."

My eyes fluttered closed and his words felt like a tender caress against my skin.

He sat back once more and the spell was broken.

I opened my eyes and scooted away from him a bit, hoping to dispel the energy buzzing around us.

He stared at me intensely and I found myself squirming. "Are we friends, Emma?" His question startled me since I hadn't been expecting it.

"Yeah… I believe so?" It came out sounding like a question.

"Do you like me?" He continued.

"Yeah," I said again, "Why? What are you getting at?" I was extremely confused by this sudden turn in the conversation.

He shrugged. "What is it specifically that you like about me?"

"Maddox," I started, my brows furrowing together, "I'm confused."

"Just answer the question, please," he growled desperately.

I stared at him for a moment, extremely puzzled. His question wasn't harsh, just curious, but I still found it an odd thing to ask. "I like that you make me laugh," I shrugged. "I like that we have things in common—like music. I like that when I'm with you I'm *me*."

He bowed his head and he seemed almost relieved.

His eyes rose to meet mine, and his playfulness returned. "I thought you were going to tell me that you only liked me because I'm hot."

I rolled my eyes. "Maddox," I groaned.

"Sorry," he apologized, but his smile told me he wasn't sorry at all. He reached out, startling me, and grabbed a strand of my blonde hair. He began to wrap it around his finger.

"Maddox?" I questioned. "What are you doing?"

He jumped, looking at his hand and released my hair. He smiled sheepishly, like he'd only just realized what he was doing. "I couldn't resist. Something about you," his voice lowered to a whisper and he looked away, almost as if he wished I wouldn't hear his next words, "draws me in and I'm powerless to what I feel."

I sat silently, unsure of what to say, but luckily Maddox saved me from having to reply.

"Would you mind playing the piano again?" He asked, his eyes glimmering with hope.

"I'd love to," I smiled, my hands already itching at the thought of running my fingers along the smooth keys of the shiny black upright. My piano at home was old, out of tune, and falling apart. This one was perfect. In fact, it was so pristine that I had a feeling it was practically brand new. "Is there anything you'd like me to play?"

He shook his head. "Just whatever you want."

I stood up and walked over to the piano.

I sat down and ran the tips of my fingers along the keys. My body instantly began to hum with happiness.

I heard shuffling behind me and I turned to find Maddox lying down on the couch with his arms crossed behind his head. He smiled crookedly when he saw me watching him.

"Go on. Play."

I turned around, pretending I didn't feel his eyes perusing my body. Goosebumps broke out across my skin and I shivered.

I closed my eyes and began to play the first song that came to mind.

The music flowed from my fingertips, through the piano, and out into the room. My body swayed with it—feeling it, living it.

I played song after song, never wanting to stop.

The music made me feel alive, much in the same way Maddox did when I was around him.

Not just alive, but *free*—like nothing that happened to me mattered anymore. Something told me that finding someone that made me feel the way music did was a rare thing.

The music ceased as my hands fell to my lap. I turned around on the bench and giggled when I found Maddox fast asleep on the couch, snoring lightly.

I was sure after his late night travels he was exhausted.

The angular curves of his face were softened in his sleep, somehow making him even more handsome. There was a blanket sitting on the arm of the couch and I picked it up. Shaking it out I draped it over his body.

He blinked his eyes open halfway and yawned. "Lay down with me?" He asked in a sleepy voice that made my insides hum and dance.

"Uh-I-uh," I floundered.

He grasped my arm, opening his eyes a little wider so I saw a sliver of gray peeking through. "Please?"

How could I resist him?

"Okay, but only for a little while," I agreed.

He scooted over, trying to make room for me, but the couch was small.

He wrapped one arm around my body and pulled me against his chest. I was pretty sure this was called spooning—I was also pretty sure that my heart had stopped.

"Is this okay?" He whispered, brushing my hair away from my neck.

"Yes," I squeaked.

"Good," he murmured, and I swore he pressed his lips to the skin just below my ear in a kiss, but the touch was so quick and light that I couldn't be positive.

He grew quiet and a few minutes later his breath grew heavy when it tickled my neck, so I knew he'd fallen asleep.

I felt like an intruder curled up against him—like I was playing a role in someone else's life, but selfishly I did want this life to be mine.

I wanted to have the starring role in Maddox's life, and that scared me more than anything else ever could.

# CHAPTER ELEVEN

"Well, this is interesting," someone laughed.

I blinked my eyes open and rubbed the sleep from them. Maddox groaned, tightening his arms around me and squeezing…

"Did you just squeeze my boob?" I shrieked, sitting up.

"Sorry," he grinned, "it was a reflex."

"Uh-huh, I'm sure," I mumbled, standing up from the couch. I avoided eye contact with a smiling Ezra and brooding Mathias. My shirt had ridden up and I hastened to pull it down. I wrapped my arms around my chest, like that could protect me from the penetrating stare of Mathias. There was something about him that set me on edge. I wasn't afraid of him, but something about him told me to keep a safe distance. I wondered what could've happened in his life to make him so unhappy.

Ezra smiled at me, pushing dark colored curls from his eyes. Looking from me to Maddox he said, "Hayes wants to hang out."

"Who's Hayes?" I asked.

Maddox spoke before either of the other guys could say anything. "He's a friend." He eyed the other two, like he was daring them to dispute him.

I couldn't understand what was going on. "Ooookay," I drew out the word. "I'll head home then," I mumbled, then realized I didn't have a car.

"Nonsense," Ezra grinned, glancing over at Maddox with a victorious smile, "you'll come with us."

"Come with you?" I repeated. "To do what?"

"Bowling," Matthias answered in a lazy drawl. "Fucking bowling, because there's nothing else to do in this stupid little town."

"Hey," Maddox pointed towards the door, "we currently have a ball pit in our yard. I'd say there's plenty to do."

Mathias rolled his eyes. "Whatever. I'm going to smoke." He stormed outside, pulling a pack of cigarettes from his back pocket.

"He's such a joy," Ezra deadpanned. "Sometimes I can't believe you guys are twins. Hell, if you weren't identical I wouldn't know."

Maddox chuckled. "I'm pretty sure he came out of the womb with a chimp on his shoulder."

"Chimp?" I laughed. "I'm pretty sure it's, 'chip on your shoulder.'"

"In Mathias' case it's a chimp," he chuckled, "a very large, very hairy, very smelly, chimp."

Ezra and I both laughed. I couldn't help picturing the tall, brooding, Mathias with a chimp on his shoulder. Yeah, it was a pretty funny sight.

Maddox stood up from the couch and stretched his arms above his head. "Alright, let's go, but we're taking your car. No way am I going to listen to Mathias bitch about sitting in the back of mine."

Ezra chuckled. "Mathias bitches about everything."

"It's true," he shrugged. "I'll be right back." He ran up the steps and I looked questioningly at Ezra, who simply shrugged in reply to my questioning gaze.

Maddox wasn't gone long, and when he returned he wore a black beanie. Strands of his brown hair stuck up in the front. "Alright, let's go."

We headed towards the door, with me lagging behind. I smiled at the sight of the drumsticks in Maddox's back pocket. He almost always had a pair with him— like it was an important extension of himself.

I followed the three guys into the garage and stared at the row of vehicles. Normal people didn't have this many nice cars. Their parents must have made a lot of money.

I tried not to gawk too much when Maddox held open the door to a shiny black SUV. The thing was huge—more like a tank than a vehicle.

The leather was cool against my bare legs and buttery smooth.

Maddox closed the door and jogged around to climb in on the other side. Ezra was driving, obviously, and Mathias joined him in the front.

"What kind of car is this?" I asked—once again showing my lack of knowledge when it came to cars.

"A GMC Yukon," Ezra answered, glancing at me in the rearview mirror as the garage door rolled up.

Ezra reached over and turned on the radio. The volume was blasting and he hastily turned it down to a decibel that wasn't deafening.

I didn't recognize the song, but I did recognize the name of the band flashing on the fancy touch screen display.

"Hey, this is Willow Creek," I commented. "They're from here. I've never heard any of their music before."

Maddox coughed beside me, and when I turned to look at him he was glaring at Ezra.

Mathias huffed and reached for the dial. "No one wants to listen to this garbage."

Ezra didn't reply, he was still looking at Maddox—with the car idling in the garage. I didn't understand the silent battle that seemed to be taking place between the two. I wished now I hadn't said anything.

The drive to the bowling alley was distressingly silent.

The silence made me nervous, because I felt like I'd done something wrong.

I was glad when Ezra parked the car and I could leave the tension behind—hopefully.

I walked ahead of the guys and straight into the building.

They came in and I looked over my shoulder, gaping at them. Ezra now wore a baseball cap that pushed down his curls and Mathias was wearing a beanie similar to Maddox's but his was gray. What was up with the hats?

We grabbed our shoes from the lady working at the front and Ezra pointed to one side of the alley. "Hayes is supposed to be over here."

We followed him into to the darkened room. The chairs and tables glowed purple and green so you could see where you were going and some kind of country song blared from the speakers.

A tall guy waved to us from the last alley.

"Someone remind me, why the fuck are we bowling again?" Mathias grumbled, but Hayes heard him.

"Because bowling is great and I really wanted a hotdog," Hayes smiled.

I reared my head back, taking in his monstrous height. The guy was a giant—probably six foot five. Sandy blond hair fell into his blue eyes and a light dusting of stubble dotted his jaw. He was handsome in an all-American sort of way.

"Hi," he smiled at me, and Maddox's hand fell possessively on my waist. "I'm Hayes, and you are?"

"Emma," I smiled.

"Nice to meet you, Emma." My name rolled off his tongue like it was an exotic wine. Maddox growled at my side and Hayes chuckled. "I'm not hitting on your girl, so calm down."

Maddox's hand fell away and he grumbled, "I knew that."

I didn't bother correcting Hayes on the fact that I wasn't Maddox's girl, because it kinda felt like I was.

Mathias sat at one of the chairs with his legs kicked up on the table while Ezra entered our names into the computer. "Are we going to play or have a pissing contest, boys?"

Hayes smiled, shaking his head. "Welcome to the family," he shrugged in a *what-*

*are-you-going-to-do* kind of way.

It took us a few minutes to get everything set up.

The guys went first, all of them getting a strike except for Mathias who ended up getting a spare. He kept bitching about it too and I was really tempted to tell him to shut up. His negativity was giving me heartburn.

It was my turn and I was terrified that I was about to make a fool of myself in front of the four guys.

I grabbed my bowling ball—a swirly purple one that Maddox picked for me—and walked up to the lane.

I squared my shoulders and breathed out, acting like I knew what I was doing.

I swung my arm back and let the ball go… only it didn't go the way it was supposed to.

It flung off my fingers and rolled back towards the guys.

My cheeks flamed and I wanted to crawl into the nearest hole and die.

Mathias was the first to start laughing, which shocked me, but the others were quick to join in.

The other people near us started to stare, and my mortification grew.

Maddox grabbed the ball and stalked towards me. I gulped.

Something told me I was in trouble—of the sexy and dangerous kind, because Maddox knew how to play with me.

He handed me the ball.

"Like this." His voice was a gruff whisper in my ear. With a hand on my waist he positioned me, and then used the other to move my arm. I felt like a puppet on a marionettes strings, willing to let him do whatever he wanted to me.

When had I become so pathetic? It was like my backbone had snapped.

"And then," his lips brushed my cheek and I swore he had to be doing this on purpose, trying to break my resolve, "you let it go."

He'd said something before this spiel but I had missed it.

I hoped it wasn't important.

He released me and my body felt icy without his touch to warm me.

I took a deep breath, staring at the pins and trying not to think about the way his eyes felt perusing my body.

I swung my arm back and let the ball go.

It went into the gutter.

"Dammit," I cursed, pissed at myself.

Maddox chuckled. "Don't worry, I'll help you again."

I hated to inform him, but I was pretty sure it was his 'help' that messed me up this time.

We waited for the slow progression of the ball and Mathias made obnoxious snoring sounds. One of these days I was going to go off on him for his rude ways.

"How about I help this time?" I startled at the sound of the new voice and turned to find Hayes standing behind me with the ball clasped in his hands. I hadn't even realized the ball had come back.

"I was helping her," Maddox growled.

"That looked like flirting, not helping," Hayes grinned at me and not Maddox. "Why don't you let an unbiased third party help Emma out?" This time he did look at Maddox.

Maddox's eyes shifted to me and he grunted, "Okay." I guess he realized that he really had no claim to me and was being ridiculous anyway.

Hayes gave me some basic instructions and helped position me. There was nothing flirty in the way he touched me and his touch didn't set my body aflame like Maddox's had. Hayes was truly just trying to help me.

This time when I let the ball go it roared down the lane, knocking over all but two pins.

"Yes!" I screamed, jumping up and down. "I did it!" I jumped into Hayes' arms, giving him a hug. "Thank you."

"You're welcome," he chuckled warmly.

At the sound of a crash Hayes set me down and we turned to see a fallen chair and Maddox stalking off. I frowned, looking from Hayes to the other two guys. "I-I didn't mean to—"

"We know," Ezra interrupted, "Maddox is just being…"

"Possessive," Mathias supplied with a sly smile.

"I should go apologize," I mumbled.

I turned to leave but Hayes' hand wrapped around my arm, urging me to stay. I looked up into his eyes and he said, "Give him a few minutes to cool off and realize what an ass he was."

"Are you sure?" I frowned, picking at the hem of my shirt. "I feel bad."

"Positive." He nodded his head towards the table. "Sit tight for a bit."

The three guys took their turns, but when Maddox's name popped up he still hadn't returned. I felt horrible knowing that this was my fault.

Ignoring Hayes' pleas to stay I went in search of Maddox.

It didn't take me long to find him near the front entrance playing with one of those claw machines.

I stepped up behind him and the way his body stiffened told me he knew it was me.

"Maddox," I whispered hesitantly.

"What?" He grumbled, his eyes briefly connecting with the reflection of mine in the glass case.

"I'm sorry," I said. "It was just a hug. I didn't mean to make you mad."

"I know," his head lowered with shame, "and that's why I'm upset. I *shouldn't* be mad, but I am. You're not mine, but it feels that way, and seeing his arms around you… I didn't like it."

"I'm sorry," I said again, "I should've thought of your feelings."

"No," he shook his head, glaring at my reflection, "you shouldn't have. I was being stupid."

"Maddox," I started, at a loss for words.

He whipped around, the stuffed teddy bear he'd won falling into the chamber. "I get it, okay. You don't like me the way I like you and I need to get over it. I have to… I have to stop *wanting* you." He let out a weighty sigh and his eyes shifted to look at the wall.

"I do like you!" I screamed, for once not caring how much attention I attracted. His head whipped back so he could look at me. "It scares me how much I like you as *way* more than a friend. I don't want to have these feelings, but I do. I'm just scared." My eyes lowered to the ground, and I kicked the toe of my converse against a ripped patch in the carpeted floor. "I'm scared of what I feel for you. I only just met you," I raised my arms, meeting his eyes once more. "I'm not ready for more. Give me time."

Silence stretched between us like an endless sea and my chest heaved with each breath I took.

"I can do that," he finally said.

My breath rushed out of my lungs like the air from a deflating balloon.

He smiled slowly and I smiled in return.

"We're good?" I asked.

"Yeah," he chuckled, ducking his head in embarrassment. "Sorry for being an asshole."

"You're forgiven, but only if you get me a drink," I jested.

He laughed, reaching down to grab his prize. "I can do that, and here."

He handed me the teddy bear. It was small and wore a blue shirt with the name of the bowling alley on it. "Now every time you look at it you can think of me."

"I most definitely will," I assured him, clutching the bear to my chest. "But he needs a name."

Maddox tilted his head, looking closely at the bear. "Harold."

"Harold?" I laughed.

He shrugged. "It's a very distinguished name."

"Okay then, Harold it is," I giggled, inhaling the buttery smell of the teddy bear. I guessed the smells of the bowling alley had seeped into it.

"Shall we get some drinks and food then?" He nodded his head towards the small café.

My stomach rumbled at the mention of food.

"Yes," I agreed, following him to the line.

The line moved slowly so we waited a good ten minutes before we could place our order. Maddox ordered enough food for him and the guys and I ordered what I wanted… plus a Coke.

Maddox gasped. "Emma, you can't get a Coke."

"Why?" I asked.

"Because I love Diet Pepsi, and Pepsi and Coke are not friends."

I raised my brows at him. "I'm getting Coke."

He mumbled something and the lady manning the register looked at us like we were crazy. She rattled off the total and he pulled his wallet out of his back pocket—the one without the drumsticks.

She swiped his credit card and handed him the slip to sign. She did all of this with a scowl on her face, like we were pesky teenagers ruining her day. We might've been teenagers, but I didn't think we were pesky. Maybe I was wrong.

After signing the slip we stood off to the side to wait for our drinks and food—which took another fifteen minutes. I was shocked the other guys hadn't come looking for us. Maybe they didn't miss us yet… or maybe they thought we were otherwise occupied.

Oh God.

Now I was going to be scared to look them in the eyes and I hadn't even done anything wrong!

Before I could really start freaking out they called our number and Maddox grabbed the two trays of food and I grabbed the one with our drinks on it. We stopped off at a condiment station, grabbing everything we'd need.

When we finally returned to the guys they'd grown tired of waiting for us and had finished the game. They were already halfway through a second one.

"Food," Hayes grinned, rubbing his flat stomach, "y'all are saviors."

"So," Ezra looked between the two of us, "all is forgiven?"

"There was nothing to forgive," Maddox shrugged, ripping open a packet of ketchup with his teeth. "I overreacted."

The other three guys exchanged looks and then their gazes rose to me. They all looked at me curiously, like I was some exotic animal.

Mathias spoke first. "I think you've bewitched my brother."

Maddox chuckled. "Maybe she has. Look at her, she's enchanting."

I shook my head, ignoring their conversation.

I grabbed a hot dog and fries. "Maddox, can you hand me my Coke?" I asked, since that tray was closer to him and too far for me too reach.

He gasped dramatically. "That's right, guys, Emma has gone to the dark side and ordered Coke."

"What is wrong with Coke?" I laughed, taking the cup when he handed it to me.

"Pepsi is so much better," he shrugged, eating a fry.

I opened a pack of ketchup and squirted it on my hotdog. "In my defense, I don't drink a lot of soda, but if I have the choice I prefer Coke. I mean, it's not that Pepsi is bad," I rambled, "it's just not my favorite."

Maddox pretended to wince. "You wound me. I thought you were the most perfect girl ever when you chose Diet Pepsi on our date, and now I feel like I've been betrayed."

I laughed, unable to hide my smile.

When I looked up Ezra was watching me closely. He hastily lowered his gaze, like he was embarrassed at getting caught.

"Was there something on my face?" I reached for a napkin.

Ezra looked up and shook his head, his black curls bouncing from beneath the baseball cap. "No…"

"Oh," I replied. "Why were you looking at me like that then?"

His smile grew shy, almost embarrassed. He looked between Maddox and me, and replied, "You make him happy."

I choked on a piece of hotdog—like full on coughing until I cried, struggling for air.

Maddox reached over, beating my back.

I finally managed to get the hotdog down and took a large sip of Coke.

"Sorry," I said breathlessly, "that caught me off guard."

Luckily, neither of the four guys said anything. Maddox's hand didn't fall from my back, though, and now he rubbed soothing circles in an effort to calm me.

We finished eating and played a new game—Hayes won.

When we left the bowling alley, Maddox and I hung back from the other guys.

"Did you have fun?" He asked me.

I nodded enthusiastically. Besides the choking fit today had been great, one of the best ever. "I did. I like your friends… and Mathias."

"Don't lie, no one likes Mathias," he chuckled, rubbing his jaw.

"Okay, so maybe I'm not his number one fan," I admitted sheepishly, "but I do like him… somewhat."

"Well, that's more than most people," he shrugged.

"The way I figure, every single person has a reason for acting a certain way."

"True," he agreed, "but Mathias and I have shared many of the same hardships and I don't act like an asshole."

I stopped walking and tilted my head to look at him. "Yes, but Mathias is also a different person from you. He would process things differently. I guess you can cope better." And then I reached up and stroked the side of his face in a gesture that was all too loving for the kind of relationship we had. "I'm sorry," I stuttered awkwardly, my hand falling, and my eyes darting to the ground, "I shouldn't have done that."

What was wrong with me?

"It's okay," he replied, his gray eyes searing me.

I nodded, reading so much in his eyes that I didn't—*couldn't*—want to see.

"Hurry the fuck up!" Mathias called with this hands cupped around his mouth.

Maddox gave me a small smile. "Come on, I'll have Ezra drop you off at home."

We started forward again, my arms hanging limply at my sides.

I itched to reach out and hold his hand.

What the hell had he done to me?

# CHAPTER TWELVE

The next day passed slowly.

Oh, so, slowly.

In fact, it wasn't even over yet.

Darkness was only just now beginning to settle in the sky.

Maddox hadn't called or texted me at all today, which was unusual. I figured he was busy, and that was fine. I wasn't his girlfriend. He didn't owe me an explanation, but I hated how lost I felt without him. It wasn't normal. You shouldn't have such intense feelings for someone you just met, but I did, and I couldn't stop them. I was beginning to think I didn't *want* to stop them.

I pressed the heels of my hands into my eyes, blocking out the sight of my bedroom ceiling above me. I wished this simple act alone could erase the foreign feelings invading my body, but I knew nothing could do that.

I rolled over, clutching my pillow to my chest.

Sadie had been busy today—she went into the city with her mom—and unable to distract me from my thoughts that were consumed by Maddox.

"Emmie?"

I startled and looked over to find my mom standing in the doorway—two cups of hot tea clutched in her hands.

"Are you okay?" She asked, stepping inside and sitting down on my bed. "You look like you don't feel good. Do you think you're sick?"

Yes, I was sick if Love-Sick-Fool counted.

"I'm fine, mom," I forced a smile, "I'm just really tired."

Her lips thinned as she looked at me, almost like she didn't believe me.

"Well, drink this and if you are coming down with something it will help."

She held the cup out to me and I took it. Once the cup was in my hand hers flitted out to touch my forehead.

"You don't feel warm," she mused.

"See?" I quirked a brow. "Just tired."

She sighed and looked up at a poster taped to my wall—one of a Broadway show, no boy bands for me.

"Is this about Maddox?" She asked, her gaze falling to me. "Did something happen between you two? He didn't hurt you, did he? I swear to God, if he hurt you—"

"No, mom," I laughed, smiling for the first time that day. "I'm just being a typical surly teenager. Don't worry about me, please," I begged, reaching out to grasp her hand.

She sighed heavily, like the weight of the world was on her shoulders. "I'm your mother, Emma. I worry. I will *always* worry about you."

I set my cup of tea on the table beside my bed. I reached forward and wrapped my arms around her. "I know that, mom, but I promise there's nothing to worry about right now."

"Okay," she sighed, running her fingers through my tangled hair. "How about we order something to eat and have a movie night? Sound good?" She asked, pulling away.

"It sounds great," I smiled.

"Good." She stood up and headed for the door. "Oh, and Emma?"

"Yeah?" I asked.

"Brush your hair."

I rolled my eyes. "Okay, mom."

She smiled and disappeared down the hall. I brushed my hair like she asked, but didn't bother to change out of my sweats and tank top. After all, she hadn't said anything about that and I wanted to be a bum today.

"I ordered steak and cheese subs," she said when I walked into the kitchen. With a smile, she added, "I'm sorry I'm not one of those moms that cooks you a fancy meal all the time and makes brownies for school functions."

I laughed, sitting down at the table with my cup of tea. "Don't worry, I think you're a great mom even if you don't cook. Plus, you do make me tea." I played with the string on the tea bag.

She finished her tea and pointed towards the living room. "Should we pick a movie?"

"Oh, yeah," I shook my head, following her.

We ended up settling on *Bride Wars* and it had just started when our food arrived.

Besides the subs she'd also ordered cheese fries and mozzarella sticks. It was heaven.

We laughed and talked through the movie, and I reveled in how nice it was to spend some time with my mom. Since she worked all the time it was rare that we did anything.

The movie ended and by the time we cleaned up it was after nine—which was really still early, but I figured I could go to bed and read for a while.

I said goodnight to my mom and headed to my room.

The twinkling lights I'd hung up on the wall lit the now darkened room.

I grabbed my book and Maddox's iPod. I put the buds in my ears and pressed play, listening while I read.

I hadn't read more than two chapters when my phone began to vibrate. I pulled the ear buds out and set my book aside as I searched for my phone, which was currently lost beneath the sea of blankets.

I finally located it and answered, "Hello," sounding breathless.

"Come outside."

"Maddox?"

"Yeah," he answered slowly. "Didn't my name come up on the caller ID?"

"I didn't look," I mumbled. "So, you're here?" I asked, sneaking over to my bedroom window and peeking through the blinds.

"Yeah, I can see you Emma."

I squeaked and jumped away from the window, dropping the phone in the process. While I scrambled to retrieve it his boisterous laughter echoed over the line.

"You're mean," I hissed when the phone was back in my possession.

My declaration didn't faze him. He kept laughing.

"I'm hanging up now," I swore.

"Wait!" He sobered. "Come outside, please?" He begged. "Let's go get ice cream?"

Did he say ice cream?

"I'll be out there in a minute."

✗

"Oh my God, this is so good," I moaned. "I love ice cream."

Maddox watched me with a wide-eyed expression. "I can tell." His eyes zeroed in on my tongue on the spoon and my cheeks began to heat.

"But I'm curious, why the ice cream?" I asked, taking another bite of its raspberry chocolate swirl goodness.

"I wanted to apologize for today," he shrugged, taking a bite of his own vanilla ice cream.

I might've been upset earlier about not hearing from him, but I didn't want him to know that. The last thing I wanted was for him to start thinking I was dependent on him.

"Why?" I asked, sounding indifferent.

"I felt bad for not calling you."

"You don't need to call me," I told him. And it was true. Even if I had been upset, I didn't have a claim to him. He didn't have to share every part of his life with me.

He tilted his head. "Anyway," he continued, "I wanted to see you and I wanted ice cream so this seemed like a win-win. I also wanted to tell you that I've cleared my schedule for tomorrow and we're going to do something fun."

The way he said it made 'fun' sound super scary.

"Cleared your schedule?" I asked, my lips turning up into a smile. "You're nineteen and unemployed, what kind of schedule could you possibly have to clear?"

He chuckled, wiping ice cream from his lip. "A very busy one full of awesomely amazing things that would blow your mind."

"Let me guess," I held up a finger, "cleaning Sonic's cage?"

"That's on Thursday's," he replied with a chuckle.

"So, are you going to tell me what this fun thing is that we're doing tomorrow?"

"No," He looked at me like he was crazy. "The surprise is part of the adventure." And then he flicked his ice cream at me, some of it landing in my hair. "See? Suuurprise!"

"Oh, you asshole!" I laughed, flicking my own ice cream at him. It landed in a blob on his forehead.

And then a full on ice cream war broke out between us. I guessed it was a good thing that the ice cream place was one of those little stands and we were sitting outside.

"Mommy!" A kid called. "I want to do that!" The kid pointed at the two of us flicking ice cream at each other.

"No, don't even think about it," she groaned, probably cursing our existence for giving her kid ideas.

Our laughter filled the air in a raucous roar.

I couldn't remember the last time I had this much fun.

We didn't stop our fight until all the ice cream was gone and we were both covered in its stickiness. Random giggles kept escaping my mouth as Maddox took my hand and we ran back to his car. People looked at us strangely, but I didn't care.

I was happy and when you're happy you don't care what other people think. Their thoughts and opinions cease to matter.

"Where are we going?" I asked, when Maddox drove in the opposite direction of my house.

"The park," he answered.

"The same park we got arrested in?" I questioned, my voice sounding stern.

He laughed heartily. "Yes, the very same one, but I promise that no one will get arrested tonight."

"Mhmm," I mumbled, fighting a smile, "that sounds like a promise you might not be able to keep."

He shrugged. "I guess there's always the small possibility… but I doubt stargazing can lead to an arrest."

"Stargazing?" I asked, tilting my head.

He chuckled, pulling into the parking lot.

"Yes, stargazing. You know, where you lay on the ground and look up at the sky."

I wanted to tell him that sounded romantic, but then I worried he'd interpret my words in the wrong way, so I kept quiet.

He grabbed a sweatshirt from the back of his car and handed it to me. "Here, you might need this. It's getting cold out."

"I have ice cream on me," I told him. "I don't want to get your sweatshirt dirty."

He shrugged. "I'll wash it. It's no big deal."

Since the temperature was dropping I took the sweatshirt he offered me and fitted my arms through the large sleeves. The thing nearly swallowed me whole.

Maddox's hand reached for mine, but he let it fall before our hands connected. He cleared his throat and looked away, like he was hoping I had missed the gesture.

Maddox strolled through the park, looking for a spot where we could look up at the sky and not have our sight shielded by the tops of the trees. After five minutes of walking he finally picked a spot he believed to be good enough.

He lay down on the ground and I followed his lead, stretching my body out.

My hand itched to reach for his, much the way he had for mine.

I finally clasped my hands together on top of my chest in the hopes that the urge would disappear.

It didn't.

"There's the North Star," Maddox pointed.

I squinted my eyes, trying to see what he saw. "Uh-huh," I nodded, pretending I saw.

He rattled off a few more and I was shocked by his knowledge of astronomy. I'd never been interested in the skies or the stars. I'd always been more focused on fictional worlds and music, and maybe that was my problem. Life had been passing me by until I met Maddox. Now I actually felt like I was living it—an active participant in my destiny and future.

"It's pretty," I whispered. My words felt like such an inadequate description of the beauty above me, but I was at a loss for words.

"It's extraordinary," he supplied.

"Yeah," I agreed.

"Emma?" He whispered into the darkness.

I sat up a bit and looked at him. "What?"

He stared at me for a moment, his silvery gaze making me shiver with the intensity. He swallowed thickly and his Adam's apple bobbed. "Never mind." He looked away.

"Say it," I pleaded, my voice no more than a whisper.

His face contorted like he was in pain. "No."

"Maddox," I urged. "Now you have me worried thinking it's something bad."

"I just… I wanted to know if I could hold your hand." He looked away. Mumbling, he added, "It's stupid."

I bowed my head, trying to hide my pleased smile.

I lay down and said, "You can hold my hand. I wouldn't mind."

"Are you sure?" He asked, sounding young.

And at nineteen he *was* young. Maddox seemed to know so much more than me—to have so much life experience—that I kept forgetting that he was nearly as young as me. In some people's eyes we were still very much children, and not the adults we pretended to be.

"Positive." I smiled up at the twinkling stars and laid my hand within his reach.

His fingers intertwined with mine and my body zinged with an electricity only Maddox could produce.

I scooted closer to him until our legs touched. He cradled our joined hands on his chest and I wondered if his smile matched mine.

Suddenly, the starry sky above us didn't hold my attention anymore.

I turned my head to look at him, studying the elegant arch of his nose and his pouty lips. He sensed my eyes on him and turned too.

Our eyes connected and he reached out with his free hand to caress my face with the backs of his fingers.

There was nowhere else I'd rather be than right here with him.

It was scary and exhilarating all at the same time.

I knew I was falling, and falling hard. I only hoped Maddox would be there to catch me.

# CHAPTER THIRTEEN

Maddox's sleek sports car wound around the windy road. Rocks jutted out to our right and on the left side of the road was a straight drop down to the river.

I wasn't scared. Not at all.

That was a lie. I was totally freaking out—especially since he was driving like we were in a race, then he pulled off on the side of the road where several other cars were parked. Dust floated up around the car when it came to a stop.

"What are you doing?" I asked, holding onto the seatbelt strap like it was my last hold on humanity.

"Parking the car," he said like I was stupid.

"I can see that, but *why?*"

"Because we're going zip lining." He stated with a proud smile.

My body suddenly buzzed with excitement and I forgot all about the scary road I'd been bothered by.

It was kind of funny that I'd been terrified of this stupid road and Maddox's crazy driving, but not the thought of zip lining. Clearly, I was weird.

I hurried out of the car and together we crossed the road. I followed him down a narrow path, wondering how he ever found this place.

The gravel path soon turned to dirt and I spotted people up ahead.

"We're really doing this?" I asked.

He glanced down at me and a small chuckle escaped his lips. "Yes, Em."

Maddox introduced himself to one of the men and I figured this must be the guy in charge.

I rubbed my hands together and Goosebumps broke out across my skin and my whole body bubbled with an excited energy.

It was mostly guys standing around—some clearly working the zip lining rig and others getting strapped into harnesses. There was a lone woman and she seemed to be working here.

"I'm Brad," the guy reached out a hand to me.

"Oh, I'm Emma." I hoped he hadn't been waiting long for me to respond. Oftentimes I got too lost in my thoughts to notice what was going on in the real world.

"Nice to meet you," he said, smiling pleasantly. If I'd had any fears about doing this his smile would've put me at ease. "Let's head over here and fill out some paperwork."

It took us about ten minutes to fill out the paperwork and sign a waiver. Once that was complete and Brad was satisfied, he and another guy that introduced himself as Jim helped to harness us.

My heart thundered in my chest.

Fear was beginning to settle in my body, but I wasn't going to back out. The thrill would be worth it.

The harness cut into my hips and thighs, but at least I didn't have to worry about it falling off of me. The people working this clearly knew what they were doing.

"Who's going first?" Stan asked the two of us.

Maddox raised his hand to volunteer. "No chickening out," he warned me.

"I won't," I assured him, grinning. My legs began to shake with adrenaline. We were going to fly—at least that's the way I looked at it.

They fixed a helmet onto both of our heads and then lined up Maddox to strap him on.

"See you on the other side." He grinned at me and gave me a thumb's up before taking off. He let out a cry of joy as he flew down the line, over the river, and onto the other side.

I watched in awe.

Maddox reached the end and the people working that side unhooked him from the line and helped him out of the harness.

"Your turn," Stan told me. He went over some instructions and I listened carefully even though I already knew this information from when he told Maddox.

My heart skipped a beat when they strapped me onto the line.

"One, two, three," Stan counted.

And then I was falling, only I wasn't falling, I was *flying* just like I thought I would.

I spread my arms out like I was a bird, and let out a scream of delight. This was amazing. The world zipped by me in a swirl of green, blue, and gray. Within seconds I reached the other end and it was over all too soon.

I felt high, or maybe drunk was a better term for it.

Yes, drunk on life.

On the possibilities.

A man unhooked me from the rig and helped me out of the harness.

Maddox stood off to the side, watching me closely while grinning like a fool.

Once I was free I ran into his arms, crashing into him. He stumbled back a step and tightened his arms around my upper body.

"That was amazing," I breathed into his neck.

"I'm glad you liked it."

I tilted my head back to look at him. His eyes were a stormy gray filled with longing.

"Kiss me."

The words were no more than a whisper on my tongue, barely audible.

He startled, looking at me like he couldn't believe he heard me right.

"Kiss me," I said again, my voice stronger this time. "Please kiss me, and don't stop."

"Never," he vowed, taking my face in his large hands and angling my head back to kiss me.

Oh, boy.

This kiss was nothing like the first.

He'd been right—he did make me forget who I was. Heck, he made me forget where we were or that an entire world existed outside of our lips.

Not even the hoots and hollers from the zip-lining guys could break through the fortress.

His tongue swiped against my lips and my mouth parted on a breath.

Maddox was devouring me. There was no other word for it.

My fingers tangled in the soft, short strands of his dark hair. I felt lost in him, in *us*.

My hands moved down to his shoulders, holding onto him. I needed the support, because his kiss was leaving me dizzy.

"I told you," he whispered, smoothing my hair back off my forehead.

"Told me what?" I asked, confused. He'd left me breathless and with my world spinning.

"That you'd ask me to kiss you."

And then he kissed me again.

I was pretty sure I'd be content to let him kiss me for the rest of my life.

A few minutes ago I thought the most exhilarating thing I had ever done was go zip lining.

But I'd been wrong.

This, right here, was it.

Admitting my feelings—asking for what I wanted—*that* was the most exhilarating thing I had ever done.

Maddox and I sat in a little diner, on the same side of the booth holding hands.

I laid my head on his solid shoulder, unable to wipe the smile from my face.

I felt giddy—on top of the world.

Nothing could touch me or ruin this day.

Who knew something like this could make me so immeasurably happy?

I looked up at Maddox and he grinned down at me with a crooked smile.

I could've missed out on something great if I'd been stupid.

I guess all it took was me zip lining into the unknown to finally gain some clarity.

"What are you thinking about?" He asked, his eyes scanning my face.

"You. Us." I admitted.

He twisted a piece of my dirty-blonde hair around his finger. "Good things I hope." He lowered his head to brush his lips lightly against mine.

I got the impression that now that I'd asked him to kiss me he was never going to stop, and I was perfectly okay with that.

"Mhmm," I hummed, "of course." I stiffened a bit and looked up into his gray eyes. "Does this mean I'm your girlfriend?"

"Well," he slung an arm around my shoulders and played with the saltshaker with his free hand, "I want you to be, but that's really up to you." He wouldn't look at me and I knew it was because he didn't want me to feel pressured into anything.

"I want to be." I probably said the words too quickly, but let's face it, I had no experience when it came to this sort of thing.

"Then you are." He grinned and kissed me again, just a light quick peck.

"Here you go," the waitress said, setting down our plates of food. We'd both ordered burgers—and of course Maddox got a Diet Pepsi.

"God, I'm starving." Maddox's arm fell from my body as he basically dove for the burger.

I couldn't blame him, though. I was hungry too.

As if zip lining hadn't been enough of an adventure today, we were also headed to the aquarium. Since the location of the zip-line was well on the way to the aquarium he figured this was easiest.

But we'd both grown hungry and somehow ended up stopping at this diner.

I reached for my own burger. All I'd had for breakfast was a protein bar, so to say I was hungry was an understatement.

Since we were both so hungry it didn't take us long to finish and leave—Maddox left with a to-go cup of Diet Pepsi and I left with a boyfriend.

Holy shit.

Maddox was my boyfriend.

I had a boyfriend.

I was pretty sure this was the craziest thing to ever happen in my life—even crazier than meeting Maddox in the first place.

It took another hour drive to get to Baltimore, but I didn't mind. We chatted easily about random things. I learned that when he was five he fell out of a tree and broke his ankle. And that he had a scar on his shoulder from crashing his BMX bike at seventeen.

They were little things, but it made me happy to find out more personal bits and pieces about his life.

I knew we both still had a lot more to open up about. Me with my dad, and him with his real parents, but that stuff was harder and would come with time.

Maddox found a parking garage that claimed to have some available spaces and pulled inside. We wound around and around, looking for one of those so-called empty spaces.

We finally found one. On the roof. And there wasn't an elevator.

"Dammit," he cursed. "Figures."

"It's okay," I assured him. "There's nothing wrong with walking."

He slipped out of the car and I followed. It took us forever to go down the six flights of steps. But Maddox made it fun by singing a song. I would've sang with him, but I didn't know the words to the song.

We burst outside and the summer heat burned down on us. It was nearly scalding.

Maddox pulled his dark sunglasses from the V-neck of his shirt and slipped them on along with a beanie. "It's this way." He nodded to our right, reaching for my hand.

I fit mine inside his larger one, my body humming pleasantly.

The harbor, shops, and nearby restaurants was all crowded to the point that we had to elbow our way through. People roamed the water in some kind of dragon looking paddleboat. "We should do that," I pointed.

Maddox looked in the direction I pointed and laughed. "Whatever you want, Em."

We walked up to the line for the aquarium. It wasn't as busy as I anticipated and soon we were headed inside with tickets clasped in our hands.

I was awed by the bright colors of the fish and coral. I'd never seen anything so stunning before. We often forgot to stop and appreciate the simple things in life—the bits of beauty nature afforded us on a daily basis.

"This is incredible." I looked around in awe. I gasped when a blacktip shark swam overhead. "Wow."

Maddox chuckled. "You look like a kid in a candy store."

"I feel like one." My head was on a swivel, trying to see everything at once.

"Come on, let's go to Shark Alley." He took my hand, dragging me away. I guess he'd decided I had gawked long enough.

"There are more sharks?" I asked, my voice spiking with excitement.

"Yes," he chuckled, leading me through the building.

"This is the best day of my life!" I exclaimed, like an over-excited little kid jacked up on sugar.

Maddox's laugh grew louder, echoing around us and causing more than a few people to turn and look at us.

Shark Alley turned out to be relatively boring. We sat in the middle of a ring-shaped aquarium and the sharks, and other creatures, swam around us. I wanted some action.

From there we headed to the jellyfish exhibit. I became enamored with the strange orb like creatures.

"I want one as a pet," I declared to Maddox.

He laughed. "Really? A jellyfish as a pet? That sounds dangerous."

"Says hedgehog boy."

He snorted at my new nickname for him. "Hedgehogs aren't dangerous, though."

"But they are an uncommon pet," I countered.

"And a jellyfish is a non-existent pet." He laughed, rubbing his stubbled jaw.

He had me there so I didn't bother arguing with him.

"Wanna go see the dolphins now?" He asked, leaning against one of the jellyfish tanks and appearing bored.

"Dolphins!" I squeaked. "They have dolphins?! Why didn't you tell me sooner?!"

Maddox's eyes widened in surprise at my exuberance. "I didn't know I should tell you."

"Dolphins are my favorite animal!" I resisted the urge to clap my hands and dance around. I was going to see a dolphin! A real, live, dolphin. I was pulsating with excitement.

Maddox began to laugh. "I'm never bringing you to the aquarium ever again. You turn into a crazy person."

It was true.

I tried to tone down my excitement as we headed to the dolphin cove.

When I finally saw the dolphins I let out a shriek that had Maddox covering his ears. "You have got to stop doing that," he winced. "I think you busted my eardrum."

"Sorry," I shrugged sheepishly, "I couldn't control it."

"Uh-huh," he muttered like he didn't believe me.

An employee stood by the tank explaining different facts about dolphins. I joined in with the group that was already there, listening carefully.

"Any questions?" The staff member asked.

My hand shot up and she pointed at me. "Can I pet one?" I asked, dancing on the balls of my feet.

She laughed. "Of course. They're very playful."

I walked over to the tank and listened to her instructions. When one swam up I extended my arm slowly and let my finger glide over its thick blubber.

"It's so soft," I whispered in awe. It was nothing like I had expected.

Another dolphin swam up and I petted that one too.

Maddox was going to have to drag me out of here. I never wanted to leave.

Maddox came to stand beside me and petted one of the dolphins as well. "Whoa," he gasped. He laughed when the dolphin then rolled over to get his belly rubbed. "He likes me."

"Actually that one is a female," the staff member said.

"She *likes* you," I bumped his shoulder playfully. "The dolphin is totally flirting with you."

He laughed, glancing at me and smiling adorably. "Everyone flirts with me. Have you seen my face? I'm irresistible."

"Uh-huh, sure you are," I nodded.

"You *are* my girlfriend, so that means you couldn't resist me," he winked.

I smiled, ducking my head.

The dolphin nearest me splashed some water at me like she was mad I'd stopped petting her. "Sorry," I told her. "He's distracting me."

Maddox laughed beside me and I joined in with him.

We played with the dolphins for a little while longer before heading out. I hated to leave them, but I knew we couldn't monopolize their time since other people wanted to play with them too.

"Still want to do the paddle boat?" Maddox pointed.

"Of course…" I paused, looking at the prices. "Are they for real? That's way too expensive. Forget it, we're not doing this." I started to walk off towards the shopping area.

Maddox grabbed my arm and pulled me back against his solid chest. "You want to, so we will."

"Maddox—" I pleaded, but he wasn't listening.

He shook his head and basically carried me over to the guy who manned the boats. He paid and we walked down the steps to the little dock.

"You pick." He pointed to the different colored dragon boats.

"Yellow," I said.

"Thank God you didn't pick the pink one," he laughed.

"Now you just make me want to pick that one." I warned him, with my hands on my hips.

"Too late, I'm already in this one." He said, slipping into the yellow boat and onto the far side. He reached a hand up to help me down.

The boat wobbled with our combined weight, but we both managed to hold our balance and sit down. I reached over and untied it from the dock and we began to paddle.

"This is fun," I smiled, letting my fingers skim the water and the sun warm my face.

"I'm glad you think so."

"Thank you for today," I smiled, reaching over to touch my fingers to his cheek. "It's seriously been one of the best."

Still peddling, he leaned over and kissed me. "I think we can both agree on that."

I smiled at his words—the kind of smile that hurt your cheeks—and I knew that with Maddox I would never stop smiling like this.

He was different.

# CHAPTER FOURTEEN

Two weeks passed and the stifling July heat rolled in. Even in Maddox's air-conditioned guesthouse my tank top still stuck to my body with a fine sheen of sweat.

"It's too hot," I whined, crooking my arm over my eyes where I laid on the cool floor.

Either he ignored me or he couldn't hear me over the drums.

I had no idea what he was playing, it didn't sound like any song I knew but I quite liked it.

A moment later the banging of the drums ceased.

"We could always go swimming. You know, that's what the pool is for when it isn't filled with balls."

"You did hear me," I mumbled, turning my head towards the area where the drum kit sat. I still couldn't really see him, just his sneaker-covered feet, since I was lying on the floor.

He chuckled. "Yes, I did. But I wanted to finish the song. Now, do you want to go swimming or not?"

"I don't have a bathing suit," I argued.

I heard him stand up from the stool and his boots clomped across the floor before stopping in front of me. He lowered to a squat and stared down at me. "Unless you're naked under there," he eyed my clothes, "then I think you'll be just fine."

I wrinkled my nose. The idea of stripping down to my unflattering grandmaish underwear in front of Maddox was not appealing.

"I was lying, I'm not that hot."

He threw his hands in the air, exasperated. "Women," he muttered. His eyes softening, he said, "I'll take you to Target for a swimsuit then."

"No, it's okay." I stretched my arms out on the cool hardwood floor. "This floor has accepted me as one of it's own. We're family now."

He stared at me for a moment, his lips twitching with the threat of a smile.

Instead of saying anything he reached down and grabbed me up into his arms.

"Maddox," I groaned, "this is silly."

"You're the one that's claiming my floor is now your family, so who's the silly one again?"

I groaned. "Just put me down."

"Nope," he said, and I knew he had to be grinning, "we're going to Target and getting you a bikini… a really slutty one." I swatted at his behind and he chuckled in response. "And then we're getting Slurpee's."

"Slurpee's?" I confirmed as he carried me outside and to his car.

"Yep. On hot days like this it's absolutely necessary to have a Slurpee."

He set me down then and opened the car door.

The heat rolled out from the vehicle and I nearly fell down. "I think I'm going back to the floor."

"Don't even think about it." He blocked my way.

I grumbled and slid into the car, the hot leather nearly burning my bare legs.

"Let's go somewhere cold," I told Maddox when we got in, "like Antarctica."

"Sorry, but we're not cuddling penguins today," he chuckled, cranking up the AC. "Target will have to do."

"Look, Emma!" Maddox called. "I found the perfect one!"

I glanced over to find him grinning and holding up the skimpiest bikini I had ever seen. I looked down at my ample chest and then at him. "That wouldn't even cover my nipples," I blurted.

He laughed heartily and returned the skimpy garment to where it belonged.

I grabbed a simple navy top and bottom with sunflowers on it. I liked it and it wouldn't be overly revealing. I also wouldn't look like a nun either.

Since we were already in Target Maddox wanted to go look at the pool things. He ended up adding five of those noodle things to the cart, along with squirt guns, floaties, and a few other items.

"Do you think you got enough stuff?" I joked, pushing the car towards the checkout area.

"I think so," he said, completely serious.

After checking out he stopped at 7-Eleven for Slurpee's just like he said he was going to.

When we got back to his house Ezra was lounging by the pool. "Did you get me one?" He asked, pointing at the Slurpee in Maddox's hand.

"No," he shook his head, "sorry. But I did get pool stuff."

Ezra lowered his sunglasses and his eyes lit up at the sight of all the bags.

I left the guys alone and headed inside the guesthouse to change into my bikini. I swung the plastic bag around and around, nearly whacking Mathias with it when I walked inside and ran into him.

"Sorry," I apologized, putting a hand to my racing heart. I was glad that I'd managed not to spill my red Slurpee on his crisp white shirt. "I didn't know you were here."

He grunted in response and moved around me to head outside.

He was so weird.

I shook my head and locked myself in the small bathroom to change.

I hadn't been in there long when I heard the door to the guesthouse open and close.

"I'm going to change," Maddox called, and I heard the sound of his feet on the steps.

Once I was in my bikini I slipped my shorts on. I knew it was silly since I'd be taking them off to get in the pool, but I hated the idea of walking outside and facing Mathias and Ezra without them. I headed out of the bathroom and threw away the plastic bag.

My hand was on the knob to head outside when I heard Maddox coming down the steps.

I turned to look at him and all coherent thought went out the window. His body was a work of art. I mean, I had no idea abs could be like that—so defined, sculpted, and perfect.

He chuckled, his lips turning up in a crooked smile.

I floundered and hurried to turn back around, but the door opened at the same time and slammed into my face.

My hand shot up to my nose and I felt the sticky warmth of blood on my fingers.

"Oh God." My voice was muffled sounding.

Maddox rushed forward and grabbed me by the shoulders, turning me around.

Ezra stood there apologizing profusely.

"Let me see it," Maddox pleaded, trying to pry my hands from my face.

I shook my head.

"Emma," he warned, his eyes flashing silver. Growing exasperated with me he grabbed me by the arm and towed me towards the small kitchen area. Ezra hovered behind us, still mumbling that he was so sorry.

Maddox lifted me by my hips up onto the counter.

"No, no." I pleaded when he tried to pry my hands from my face again.

"Silly girl," he muttered, smoothing my hair behind my ears, "let me see."

With tears pooling in my eyes I let my hands drop. My face hurt—like I'd walked face first into a concrete wall… which I guessed was kind of what happened. Only it was a door… not a wall.

Maddox winced when he saw my face.

"Is it that bad?" I asked. "Do you think my nose is broken?"

"Oh, God! Did I break her nose?" Ezra exclaimed, echoing my question.

Maddox shook his head. "I don't think so. There doesn't seem to be enough blood for that and it doesn't look crooked. Go get me a cloth," he told Ezra.

Ezra disappeared, clearly happy to be assigned with a task.

"Be honest," I pleaded, resisting the urge to cover my face again, "how bad is it?"

"I think it might bruise," he shrugged, inspecting my face. He took my chin between his fingers and tilted my head in different directions. "You're definitely going to be sore for a little while."

"Great," I huffed. I was going to have a bruise and puffy nose all because I'd been drooling over Maddox. It was like the universe was trying to punish me for being happy.

**Universe:** *Oh, look! Emma is ogling her smoking hot boyfriend! Let's ram a door in her face!*

Ezra returned with a dampened washcloth and handed it to Maddox, who then gently dabbed at the blood on my face.

"I'm so sorry, Emma." Ezra started in again.

"It was an accident," I told him. "You didn't know I was standing there. I'm not mad," I promised.

The door to the guesthouse opened again and I looked to see Mathias stroll in.

"What happened to your face?" He asked, looking between the three of us. "Did you try to kill her or something? Should I get the shovel?"

Maddox shook his head at his twin brother. "No, she had a very unfortunate encounter with a door."

Mathias winced. "Looks like it hurts."

"It does," I muttered.

Mathias came over to stand beside his brother in front of me where I sat on the counter. He inspected my face much the way Maddox had.

"Get her some ice you idiot." He finally told Maddox.

Maddox balked like he couldn't believe his brother was bossing him around. He handed the cloth to Mathias and said, "Finish cleaning her face off, please. I'll have to go into the main house, I know we don't have anything in the freezer here."

I was surprised when Mathias didn't argue about tending to me. I'd gotten the impression that Mathias didn't like me—or anyone for that matter. It shocked me even more when he tenderly wiped away the last of the blood from my face.

Ezra hopped up on the counter beside me, but seemed to have stopped apologizing—at least for the moment.

"Can you breathe through your nose?" Mathias asked.

I tried. "Yeah," I answered.

"Good." He gave me a small smile and I figured that was a lot coming from him. Up this close I noticed his eyes were a bit different than Maddox's. While Maddox's gray eyes usually looked silver, Mathias' were darker like the stormy gray clouds you saw before a storm. With a nod of his head, like he was agreeing to a thought he'd had, he walked off and out the door.

Maddox came busting in only a few seconds later with an icepack wrapped in a cloth. I tried to take it from him, but he insisted on holding it to my face.

"I don't need you to be my nurse," I mumbled.

"Well, I'm going to be," he stood his ground.

Ezra sighed. "I'm so sorry, Emma."

"It's okay," I assured him, for what felt like the thousandth time. "Go swim or something. You don't need to stay here."

He nodded and jumped off the counter. "Holler if you need me."

Once he was gone Maddox lowered the icepack and frowned.

"What's wrong?" I asked. "Is it getting worse?"

He shook his head. "No, it's not that… I just… I feel weird inside."

"Huh?" I looked at him like he'd lost his mind.

"What I mean is, I've never felt so terrified in my entire life. I don't like seeing you hurt." He reached up and tenderly stroked the side of my face. I relaxed into his touch, closing my eyes. I never thought being with a guy could be like this—so easy and happy. My dad had always been a jerk, even when the alcohol hadn't been a problem. I'd never had a good male figure in my life, and I guess along the way I'd come to believe all guys would be like my dad.

I wrapped my arms around his neck. "I'm not as breakable as I look. Don't worry about me, please."

He chuckled, giving me a small smile. "I don't think I could stop worrying about you if I tried." The look he gave me was so intense that I felt it all the way down to my toes. He pressed the icepack to my nose once more. "I think if you keep icing it the swelling will go down quickly."

"Well," I grinned, putting my hand overtop his, "at least I'm not hot anymore."

His laugh boomed around us. "Yes, at least there's that," he agreed.

"The swelling has gone down a lot," Maddox commented. "It doesn't even look that bad anymore."

I peered up at him where I was lying with my head in his lap. "You're such a liar."

The movie continued to play on the large TV in the basement of the main house, but neither of us was currently paying any attention to it.

"I would never lie to you, Em. I promise it's better. I should probably get you another icepack though." I sat up from his lap and he stood. "I'll be right back," he promised.

I gave him a small smile. It was all I could muster. The day's events had really knocked me down.

While he was gone I went to use the bathroom. I'd only seen part of the main house when he brought me down here but everything looked so pretty and shiny. But you could tell it was lived in. It wasn't one of those places that looked so pristine that you were scared to sit down on a couch for fear of leaving behind a miniscule stain. I was also quite taken with the cape cod style of the home. Most homes in this area didn't look like this, and I liked it. It made me feel like I was vacationing by a beach up north.

I washed my hands and inspected my appearance. Maddox hadn't been lying. The swelling had gone down some—but in its place a bruise was forming.

I had just sat back down on the large sectional couch when Maddox returned with the fresh icepack and popcorn.

The buttery smell invaded my senses and my mouth watered.

He handed me the icepack and sat down, draping a blanket over our bodies.

I curled against him, soaking in his warmth. I still couldn't believe that I was with Maddox—that he was my boyfriend. I hadn't been planning on him, but I was discovering that it's the unexpected things in life that make it so great.

He placed the popcorn bowl in his lap and I reached for a handful.

I popped a piece in my mouth and moaned. "This is so good." It tasted like the kind of popcorn you got from the movie theater, not from the grocery store in a box.

"If you think I make fantastic popcorn, wait until you see my cooking skills," he boasted with a proud smile.

I narrowed my eyes. "I thought you said your freezer was empty?"

He chuckled. "That's only because mom likes to make dinner for us," he shrugged. "She likes to make sure she sees all of us at least once a day."

"I think it's nice that you call Karen mom," I commented, laying my head on his shoulder.

I felt, rather than saw, him smile. "She is my mom. Just because we don't share blood doesn't make her any less of a mom to me, and I always want her to know that."

I tried to resist the urge to sigh dreamily. "You're a good guy, Maddox."

"No, I'm not," he answered quickly, glancing down at me. "I'm selfish."

"Why do you say that?" I questioned, my brows furrowing together with curiosity.

He looked away with his jaw clenched tightly. I noticed his hands start to shake where he held the bowl in his lap.

"Maddox?" I prompted. "What's wrong?"

The shaking stopped and he schooled his features. "Nothing. Never mind."

I stared at him, puzzled. I couldn't figure out what was going on, but I felt like it was important.

"You can tell me anything, Maddox. I hope you know that."

"I do, Em," he winced.

"Then what's the problem?"

He took a deep breath and looked down at me. "There's no problem, I swear."

I stared at him for a moment, contemplating his words. I finally nodded, and said, "Okay." If I was going to make this relationship work I had to learn to trust him. If he was keeping a secret from me, which it felt like he was, then I had to believe he had a good reason for keeping it.

*He's not like your dad.* I repeated the mantra over and over again in my head. But somehow I didn't feel any better, because another voice kept piping in with, *What if he is?*

# CHAPTER FIFTEEN

"I thought we'd take it easy today, but still do something… fun." Maddox smiled, standing on my front porch.

I rubbed the sleep from my eyes. "I just woke up. Fun is not on my agenda for a few more hours." It was already after noon, but I'd been up late reading.

"You're going to have to put it on your schedule then, because we need to be there in thirty minutes."

"Where is there?" I whined, blocking the sun from my eyes with my hand.

He snorted. "Did you really think I'd tell you?" Pushing his way inside he waved a hand at me. "Go get ready. You have ten minutes before I come after you and dress you myself."

"You wouldn't." I glared at him as I shut the door.

"I would," he replied with a grin.

"Ugh." I shoved my fingers through my messy hair and stomped back to my room. Thank God I'd showered last night and didn't have to worry about that. I grabbed a pair of shorts, a tank top, and a cardigan with an Aztec design. I tried my best to tame my hair, but it was sort of a lost cause. At least the swelling in my nose was practically gone, and a little bit of concealer and foundation hid the bruise.

Grabbing my bag I darted out into the living room and ran smack into Maddox's hard chest. His hands clasped around my arms to steady me.

"Oh you're ready," he frowned. "How disappointing for me. I was quite looking forward to dressing you myself." He winked, causing my cheeks to heat with color. He held me at arms length, appraising my nose. "Looks good today. Ezra's still torn up about it."

I laughed. "He's not even the one hurt and I feel like I need to get him a Get Well balloon."

"We should," Maddox agreed. "It would only make him feel even sorrier."

I winced. "It was an accident. I really hate that he feels so bad."

Maddox let go of me and started towards the door. "He should feel bad," he mumbled.

I let the subject drop, because I didn't want to deal with the teasing I'd get if I told him the only reason it happened in the first place was because I was gawking at him.

I followed Maddox to the car, which was still running, and busted out laughing when I saw Sonic sitting on the dashboard.

"The hedgehog is coming with us?"

"Of course," Maddox gasped. "He's like our team mascot."

I snorted. "But you don't bring him everywhere with you."

"Well, zip lining was not hedgehog appropriate. Today's activities are."

"Good to know," I nodded, sliding into the car.

Maddox got behind the wheel and placed Sonic in his lap.

He drove through the neighborhood where his house was, so I assumed we were going there.

I was shocked when he pulled into the driveway of a different home. Several other cars were parked in the driveway and on the street.

"Why are we here?" I asked, unbuckling my seatbelt.

"You'll see," he sing-songed.

I followed him to the front door where he rang the bell. I heard the sounds of several voices on the other side and the door opened to reveal a little old lady standing there. Her gray hair was bushed around her head, and she was hunched over. Her blue eyes were kind and sweet and her smile was blindingly happy.

"Are you here for the knitting party? Karen said one of her sons was coming with his girlfriend."

I smiled, pleased that Karen had called me his girlfriend. I immediately scolded myself for being a lovesick fool, though.

"That would be us," Maddox grinned, and I looked up noticing for the first time that he had Sonic perched on his shoulder. "I'm Maddox, this is Sonic, and—"

"I'm Emma," I interrupted him, holding my hand out to the woman.

She ignored my hand and reached her thin arms out to hug me. She smelled like peppermint.

"I'm Maise," she replied. "I'll introduce you to the rest of the ladies."

She led us through her beautiful home and to a back porch, where five more ladies sat, plus Karen. I smiled at Karen, giving her a small wave.

"You both already know Karen, obviously," Maise spoke, "this is Alice, Margaret, Beth, Jane, and Mary."

Hellos echoed around us, and Maddox and I responded.

"This is Maddox, Karen's son, and his girlfriend Emma." She introduced us to the group.

Maddox and I took a seat on one of the couches and Maise handed each of us a ball of yarn and knitting needles.

"I can't believe I'm doing this," Maddox muttered, grabbing Sonic and putting him back on his shoulder—the hedgehog had been trying to climb on his head.

I pointed to the knitting needles. "Just pretend they're drumsticks."

He wrinkled his nose and tapped them against his knees. "Yeah, that isn't working for me."

I laughed. "It was worth a try."

Maise cleared her throat, and we both looked up.

She guided us through instructions on how to fix the yarn around the needle and make our first stitches. It seemed easy enough.

A little while later Maddox cursed, "Fuck."

The room had been filled with the quiet chatter of the ladies voices but everyone shut up at Maddox's exclamation. He looked up, his eyes wide like a deer caught in headlights.

"Oops." He mumbled. "It fell off." He pointed to the crumpled pile of yarn in his lap.

Masie sighed. "Then start again and try to keep the cursing to a minimum."

"Sorry," he bowed his head, looking truly ashamed of himself. It was cute.

He started again, going slower this time.

I smiled proudly at my neat rows of stitches. I might actually manage to make a scarf.

"It's too quiet in here," Maddox mumbled, from beside me. His face brightened. "I know…" He set his scarf—or whatever the lopsided thing was that he was attempting to make—aside. He steadied Sonic with one hand and grabbed his phone and some earbuds from his pocket. He handed me one and put the other in his ear, turning on the music.

"Ah!" I cried, when it blasted.

"Sorry," he mumbled, quickly lowering the volume.

He picked the knitting needles back up and went to work once more.

I knew it sounded crazy, but Maddox made knitting look hot.

A few minutes later he poked my shoulder and I turned to look. He had Sonic in his lap with the small piece of fabric he'd knit lying across the hedgehog's back. "Look, Emma, I made him a cape! He's Super Sonic!"

I snorted, slapping a hand over my mouth to stifle my laughter. It was no use, though. Pretty soon the both of us had dissolved into laughter and tears ran down my cheeks.

"Super Sonic? You couldn't come up with something better?" I wiped the tears from beneath my eyes.

He shrugged, his grin huge. "It was the first thing that popped into my head."

I shook my head at him, fighting a smile. "Maybe you can start a trend of hedgehog capes."

Maddox picked up Sonic, cradling him to his chest. "What do you think Sonic? Do you want to be my model?"

The hedgehog wiggled his nose. I wasn't sure if that was meant to be a yes or no.

"Sonic says he'll be my model." He returned the hedgehog to his shoulder once more.

I looked up to find all the old ladies watching us and staring at Sonic like he was some kind of rodent.

"What is that creature?" One of the ladies asked. I was pretty sure it was Alice.

"He's a hedgehog," Maddox replied.

"Huh," she muttered, and returned to knitting.

I looked up at Maddox and smiled.

Only Maddox Wade would sit in a room with a bunch of old ladies and knit a scarf with a hedgehog on his shoulder for me.

He went out of his way to make me happy—to make me feel special.

He was remarkable, and I might've been young, but I knew enough to know that most guys weren't like him.

I swallowed past the lump in my throat and looked down at the colorful yarn in my lap.

What was he doing to me?

I breathed deeply, fighting the panic that threatened to choke me.

I knew what I felt for him was too much, too soon. I was turning into one of those girls I made fun of for claiming they loved a guy after one date.

"Emma," Maddox's voice sounded concerned. "Are you okay?"

"Yeah, I'm fine. Just a little thirsty." My voice came out sounding breathless.

"I'll go get you some water, dear." Maise smiled, tapping my knee kindly as she left the room.

"Are you sure that's it?" Maddox asked, his silvery eyes radiating with concern.

"Positive," I assured him.

He still looked at me doubtfully, but let it drop.

My panic was beginning to ebb when Maise returned with a bottle of water. I took it from her and drank it greedily.

"Better?" Maddox asked.

"Yes," I replied, sitting the bottle on the floor.

He stared at me a moment longer before turning his attention to Maise. "What do I do if I want to end this here?" He asked, holding up the small piece of fabric.

"Why would you want to do that?" She asked. "That's nowhere near being a scarf, sweetheart."

"I know, but I want it to be a hedgehog cape."

Maise turned her gaze towards Karen, as if to say she couldn't believe Maddox would dare ask such a thing. Karen shrugged with a small smile.

"Alright," Maise sighed, coming over to show him how to finish it off.

Once it was done Maddox stuck it to Sonic's quills and smiled proudly.

While I finished my scarf Maddox stayed beside me with Sonic sleeping in his lap, humming along to the song he was listening to. I'd long ago tuned the music out.

Maise helped me finish my scarf, like she had Maddox. I knew my scarf was hardly the prettiest thing anyone had ever made, but I was quite proud of it. I knew I'd always cherish it, and this day. And it was all thanks to Maddox.

As we walked outside to his car, I stood on my tiptoes and quickly kissed his stubbled cheek.

"What was that for?" He asked.

"For being you."

He grinned at my words and started to say something, but was interrupted by Karen coming outside and calling for us. We paused, waiting for her.

She came hurrying towards us. "I'm glad I caught you. I was afraid you were already gone."

"What do you need, mom?" Maddox asked. He didn't say the words rudely, he sounded genuinely concerned.

"I was wondering if Emma would like to come to dinner?" She looked at me, smiling kindly as she waited for my reply.

"I'd love to," I answered honestly.

"Great," she clapped her hands together. "I'll see you for dinner then."

She waved goodbye and headed to her own car.

"You okay to hang out at the guesthouse?" Maddox asked.

"Yeah, of course," I replied.

It didn't take us long to get to his house.

He placed Sonic in his cage—and the hedgehog immediately burrowed his way under his igloo to sleep.

"I have something I want you to take a look at," Maddox said, bowing his head. He seemed unusually shy.

"Okay," I replied, following him over to the desk that was always covered in paper. I'd never inspected them before, but now that I was up close I could see that they were covered in song lyrics and music.

He grabbed a few papers up and nodded for me to follow him to the piano.

He lined up the papers and looked at me rather bashfully. "Will you play it while I sing?"

I started. "Of course… you wrote this, didn't you?" I asked.

He nodded. "I've been working on a few different songs for a while, but I got the idea for this one a few weeks ago and I haven't been able to get it out of my head since. I think I finally have it right, though. If you hate it, tell me. I trust your opinion."

"I'm not going to hate it." I looked at him like he was crazy.

He shrugged. "It's possible."

He then waved his hand for me to start playing. It didn't take me long to recognize the song—he'd been playing the same one on the drums yesterday.

He sang softly at first and I could taste his fear in the air. He truly thought I was going to hate the song. But it was beautiful, absolutely amazing, and in my (un) biased opinion the greatest thing I had ever heard.

His voice, just like the song, grew with more strength.

Unable to help myself I started to sing with him—a song about love, hope, and forgiveness.

My voice was quiet and high compared to his low gravel, but somehow our voices blended beautifully together.

I wanted so desperately to look at him, but I kept my eyes on the sheets of music in front of me. I could feel his eyes on my face though, and it was nerve-wracking.

The song ended, the last note still lingering in the air.

I turned to look at him and found passion burning in his eyes. I wasn't prepared when he grasped my face and tugged me impossibly closer.

He slanted his mouth over mine, kissing me deeply—with his heart and soul.

I kissed him back, grasping the collar of his white t-shirt.

Our lips moved together to a song of our own making.

One of his hands lowered to the nape of my neck and he hummed happily in the back of his throat. I pressed my chest against him and let out a small sound when his other hand grabbed me by the hip, pulling me onto his lap. I rocked against him—kissing him with all the passion I possessed.

He pushed against me and my elbow hit several of the keys on the piano. Neither of us was bothered by the clamor.

He pulled back, just a breath, and whispered, "What are you doing to me?"

He didn't give me a chance to respond. His kiss was electrifying. It burned me straight down to the core—branding me forever.

I grasped his stubbled cheeks in my hands and from this position I hovered above him.

The piano stool teetered and I squealed when we lost our balance. We fell, and Maddox wrapped his arms around me. He tucked me against his chest so he took the brunt of the short fall.

We looked at each other for a brief second before bursting out in laughter.

"That was some kiss," he chuckled, reaching up to tuck my hair behind my ear. I was still lying on his chest and had no intention of moving.

"Who said it was over?" I said boldly, closing the short distance between us.

Our lips connected once more and my body flooded with electricity. One spark could set me on fire.

He rolled us over so he was now on top with my back against the floor. His strong arms caged me in and my legs wound around his waist. I tugged his hips down to mine and we both let out soft moan.

I'd never experienced these types of feelings before, and it was scary how intense they were with Maddox.

"Emma," he murmured against our lips.

I panted, unable to respond.

His tongue ghosted against mine and I tugged at the short strands of dark hair near his neck, urging him on.

"What the fuck?" The door slammed. "Thank God your fucking clothes are on. I live here you know and I don't need to see this stuff."

Maddox's lips left mine and he rolled off me. His chest rose and fell in soft pants. He reached a hand down to me and pulled me up.

"Good to see you too, Mathias." Maddox groaned, clearly irritated by his brother interrupting us.

"Whatever," Mathias mumbled, walking to the refrigerator and grabbing a bottle of orange juice. He poured himself a glass and stared at us. "Neither of you are even sorry, are you?"

We both shook our heads.

"Don't act like you weren't the same way with Remy," Maddox challenged.

Mathias' face morphed from mildly irritated to full on livid. His face turned red and a vein threatened to burst on his forehead. He threw the glass of orange juice and it shattered on the floor near our feet. I let out a small scream and grasped tightly onto Maddox's arm.

"Do not fucking say her name ever again!" Mathias roared, pointing an accusing finger at Maddox. "She is none of your fucking business!"

He grasped the countertop so tightly that his knuckles turned white.

With another roar he stormed up the steps and I jumped when the door to his bedroom slammed.

Maddox and I both stood silently, neither of us knowing what to make of the what went down.

When a minute passed I finally had to do something. "I'll get a rag to clean this up," I mumbled, skirting around the broken glass.

My words seemed to get Maddox moving. "I'll get the dustpan," he muttered.

Together we managed to clean up the mess. Both of us were quiet, lost in our thoughts.

When the last of the orange juice was wiped away I looked at Maddox. "What was that about?"

He sighed, dumping some of the glass he'd brushed up into a trashcan. "That's Mathias."

"He's quite explosive, isn't he?" I asked hesitantly.

Maddox nodded. "He doesn't handle much well." His jaw clenched and he looked away. I wanted so desperately to ask him to elaborate, but I kept my mouth shut. When he was ready to tell me he would.

"What do you want me to do with this?" I asked, holding up the soiled rag.

He took it from my hand, holding the small trashcan in his other. "I'll take it inside and put it in the washer. What time is it?" He asked me.

I pulled out my phone and looked at the time. "Four."

He nodded. "Mom will have dinner ready soon. She likes for us to eat early."

He started towards the door and I said, "Is Mathias coming?"

He looked towards the stairs. "Not likely."

"Oh," I frowned.

"Don't worry about him," Maddox mumbled. "Trust me, he doesn't deserve your sympathy."

"But he's your brother," I said, confused.

"And he's also an asshole," he replied. "I might love the guy, but even I know better than to go near him when he's like this."

I sighed, following him out of the guesthouse.

We entered the main house through a set of French doors that opened into a cozy living room. Maddox turned down a hall and I followed him. He opened the door to a laundry room that was larger than the bathrooms in my house. I couldn't believe that people lived in homes this large—and I knew this home wasn't even as large as some.

He tossed the soiled rag in the washer and headed to the kitchen, getting rid of the trash bag full of glass and fixing a new one in place.

Karen was cooking away, but didn't question anything. To her it just looked like he was changing the trash. She had no idea why, and I wondered what she'd think of Mathias' outburst if she'd been there. I got the impression that she wouldn't put up with that kind of behavior.

"Is there anything I can do to help?" I asked her. I hated standing around feeling useless.

She smiled at me over her shoulder. "It would be wonderful if the two of you could set the table."

"No problem, mom," Maddox chimed.

He showed me the silverware drawer while he gathered the plates.

Despite the fact that he said Mathias wouldn't bother joining us I noticed he still set a place for him.

Ezra came sauntering into the kitchen just as we finished with the table.

"Hey," he greeted me, slinging his arm around my shoulders, "I didn't know you were joining us for dinner."

"Your mom invited me," I told him.

"Mom's thrilled to have a girl hanging around the house," Ezra joked.

"Stop it." She scolded her son.

He chuckled and took a seat. "Dad called and said he'd be a little late."

Her brows furrowed together. "He didn't call me."

Ezra propped his elbow on the table and his head in his hand. "He said he did. You know how you get absorbed in cooking. You probably just didn't hear it."

She reached into the front pocket on her apron and pulled out a sleek phone that looked identical to the one Maddox had gotten me. "Oh, you're right," she laughed.

Ezra shook his head. To me he said, "I don't know why she doubts me."

"Maybe because when you were ten you lied about *everything*," Maddox chuckled, pulling out a chair for me. I sat down and he took the spot beside me.

"That was nine years ago," Ezra defended. "She should have restored her faith in me."

"*She* is standing right here," his mom scolded, placing a dish filled with some sort of casserole on the table.

"Sorry." Ezra bowed his head. Even though he was nineteen, he clearly respected his mom and still acted very much like a little boy in her presence.

She finished placing the various dishes on the table and by the time she sat down a man's booming voice called through the house, "I'm sorry I'm late!"

I looked over to see a tall, handsome man enter the room. He wore a nice suit— and when I said nice, I meant *nice*. His dark hair was trimmed short, sprinkled with a few gray hairs, and his face was clean-shaven.

The man startled when he saw me, placing his briefcase on the floor by the archway. Loosening his tie he smiled. "I didn't know we had company. I'm Paul," he held a hand out for me to shake.

"Emma," I replied, taking his offered hand.

He smiled kindly and his eyes turned to Maddox.

Maddox squirmed in his chair, but didn't say anything.

"I'm assuming she didn't just wander in off the streets…" Paul paused, waiting for Maddox to elaborate.

I swore there was a slight tinge of pink to his cheeks, but as quickly as I saw it, it was gone. "She's my girlfriend."

"And here I thought you told us everything." Paul tapped Maddox on the shoulder as he strolled towards his wife who sat at one of the heads of the table. He lowered and kissed her cheek, whispering something in her ear. Heading to the empty seat across from her, he said to Maddox, "I always knew you'd be the first to go down."

Ezra snorted.

And Maddox tried to fight a smile.

I felt like I was missing something.

"Excuse me?" I asked, looking between Paul, Ezra, and Maddox.

"I always knew Maddox would be the first to fall in love," Paul answered simply.

If there had been water in my mouth I would've spit it out. "What?" I gasped.

Paul shrugged. "Just callin' it like I see it."

I'm pretty sure I turned as pale as Casper the Friendly Ghost.

Love?

Maddox didn't *love* me.

It wasn't possible.

We'd only known each other a month. That was not enough time to fall in love.

I sat there, shaking my head. My appetite was suddenly gone.

Maddox groaned beside me and growled, "Thanks dad, now you've gone and scared her to death." To me he said, "Breathe, Emma."

Breathe? What was breathing?

Oh, right, that thing where you inhaled oxygen.

"She's not going to pass out, is she?" Ezra voiced. "Should we splash water on her? I think that's what they always do in the movies with these sorts of situations."

"Shut up," Maddox snapped. "Emma," he took me by the shoulders and turned me towards him. "Please, stop freaking out."

"Freaking out?" I panted. "I'm not freaking out."

He raised an eyebrow in disbelief.

"Okay, fine," I relented. "I'm freaking out."

"Here," he grabbed my water glass, "drink some of this. It'll help."

I really didn't see how it would, but I was willing to try anything to calm my racing heart. I took slow sips of the cold liquid and it did somehow manage to help alleviate my nerves.

Once I was calmed down, Karen cleared her throat and asked, "Where's Mathias? Is he not joining us?" She eyed the empty place setting beside Ezra.

Maddox grumbled, "He's in one of his moods sulking in his room."

"Oh." Karen mumbled. "I'll save him a plate then." Changing the subject once more, she asked me, "So, Emma, will you be attending college in the fall?"

"No," I shook my head, "I'll be a senior in high school."

She smiled. "That's wonderful. Senior year was the only year of school I actually liked. It was also the year I met Paul." She pointed her fork at her husband.

"Really?" I asked, suppressing the urge to laugh as Maddox piled food on both of our plates. "So, you're high school sweethearts?"

"Yes," she smiled wistfully.

I looked between the two. You could see how in love they were, even this many years later. It gave me hope that some loves could last.

Shaking her head, Karen addressed me once more, "What do your parent's do?"

"Oh, uh, my mom's an artist," I stuttered. "She mostly does pottery and things like that. And my dad is gone."

"Oh, I'm so sorry to hear that," she frowned. "Dealing with the death of a parent at such a young age is a difficult thing. My mom died of breast cancer when I was a sophomore in college and it was devastating."

I winced. "He didn't die," I frowned, huffing out a breath, "he left us. He *chose* to leave us." I looked down at the table when I felt the familiar burn of tears prick my eyes.

Karen let out a startled gasp, floundering for something to say.

"Would you mind if I used your bathroom?" I asked, not meeting anyone's eyes. I might've told Maddox about my dad leaving, but it was something I *hated* talking about.

"Not at all," Paul replied, clearing his throat. "It's just down the hall. Second door on your right."

I pushed away from the table and scurried into the bathroom.

I closed and locked the door behind me, leaning my back against its surface.

I breathed in and out deeply for a moment.

Sometimes the fact that my dad was gone hit me hard. I liked to pretend I didn't care, but deep down I *did*. What girl didn't need her father in her life? And mine was just gone. Not because he was dead and had no choice in leaving, but because he couldn't stand my mother or me. I *knew* we were better off without him. He wasn't a good man, but he was still my dad. Fuck, my feelings were so messed up. One minute I hated him, and the next I missed him. It was all so stupid.

I moved over to the sink, running some cool water. I splashed some on my face to refresh me. It helped, but I was still upset.

I took a deep breath, focusing on the silvery damask design of the wallpaper.

"Emma," a fist rapped against the door, "can I come in, please?"

"I'm fine," I muttered, hoping he'd go away.

"Emma," he pleaded again. "Let me in."

For some reason I felt his words of *let me in* were referring to much more than just letting him into the bathroom.

"Fine," I sighed, turning the lock and opening the door.

He slipped inside and the door closed.

The bathroom was one of those small powder rooms and much too tiny to contain the two of us. His chest pressed against mine and his hands came up to cup my cheeks.

He swiped his thumbs underneath my eyes, his normally silver eyes nearly black. "I hate seeing you cry."

"I didn't know I was." But he was right, silent tears fell down my cheeks.

He swallowed thickly. "Your dad is an asshole for leaving you. You're wonderful and so is your mom. Some people don't know how to cherish what they have, so instead they destroy it." His tongue flicked out to wet his lips and he looked at me with a serious expression. Normally Maddox was all carefree smiles, so this was a new side of him. "Sometimes I'm thankful that I had such a rough start to life, because it makes me appreciate every good thing I have in my life. Like getting to have dinner with my family, and you, I didn't have that growing up. *Please*," he begged, "don't let that man make you bitter. Don't let him win, Em. You deserve to be happy and you can't do that if you don't let him go."

My face crumpled and I began to sob. "I hate him so much, Maddox. I hate how mean he was to my mom and me. But I think I hate him even more because I love him and that makes me angry. It's this vicious cycle that never stops."

"Shh," he hushed, wrapping his arms around me. "Let it out, Em. Let it all out."

"He chose to leave me," I cried against his chest, soaking his shirt with my tears. "I wasn't good enough for him."

"That's not true." He shook his head, his chin brushing against the top of my head as I clung to him. "He wasn't good enough for *you*."

He smoothed his fingers through my hair as I clung to him like he was a life preserver and the only thing keeping me afloat.

I felt his lips press lightly against the top of my head.

"You know," I choked, "it's like that day at the fair you knew I needed you to save me." I whispered the last part, like I was scared to breathe life into the words.

"No, Emma, it was me that needed you. Never forget that."

And then he just held me, and I knew that everything was going to be okay.

# CHAPTER SIXTEEN

**MADDOX:** I have to go out of town for a few days.

The text message flashed on the screen of my phone. I currently sat on my bed with a book in my lap, the afternoon sunlight streaming in through the open blinds.

**EMMA:** Did something bad happen? I couldn't stop myself from asking.

**MADDOX:** No. Nothing like that. I'll be back in two days… tomorrow evening if I'm lucky.

**EMMA:** I'll see you soon then.

**MADDOX:** I'll miss you.

I'd be lying if I said I wasn't going to miss him too, but he wasn't my whole life. Besides, this was a good thing. Sadie had been bitching at me the last few days for not hanging out with her. I couldn't blame her for being irritated with me, and I felt bad for blowing her off. Things had been so new and exciting with Maddox that I'd started neglecting my best friend.

After telling Maddox I'd miss him too I sent a text to Sadie, asking if that girl's day she'd talked about was still open. She was quick to reply.

**Sadie:** How about you come over tonight? Sleepover? Pizza? And then we can go shopping tomorrow.

**Emma:** Sounds good.

"He is so hot," Sadie sighed dreamily, drooling over the half-naked guy on her TV. I think he was supposed to be a werewolf or something. I wasn't sure, since I didn't watch much TV. Shows made me bored for some reason, which was why I stuck to music and books. "Don't you think he's hot?" She asked me.

"Sure," I agreed. I was currently too busy devouring a slice of pizza to check out the guy.

"Ugh, you're no fun," she groaned, pushing my shoulder in jest.

I smiled. "Hey, look at it this way, at least we don't have to fight over who gets him."

"Bitch, he's mine," she narrowed her eyes, fighting a smile. "You know how those dark-haired, dark-eyed boys make me."

I giggled. "Yeah, they make you throw your underwear across the room."

She rolled onto her back laughing. "It's true." Sobering, she said, "I'm putting myself on a strict no dating policy for senior year."

I snorted.

"What?" Her eyes widened. "You don't think I can do it?"

"Nope."

"I'm going to prove you wrong." She jutted out her chin defiantly.

"You'll last a day," I grinned, taking another bite of pizza.

"You have such little faith in me," she shook her head. "You're my best friend, you should be cheering me on."

"I think you have some pom poms in your closet if you need me to cheer," I joked. Sobering, I added, "Seriously, I think it's good for you to focus on something other than boys for a change."

She reached for a slice of pizza. "I don't want to be that girl anymore. You know," she shrugged, "the slut."

I rolled my eyes. "You're not a slut, Sadie." I knew for a fact that she'd only had sex with one guy. She might've been provocative, but she didn't jump into bed with every guy she batted her eyes at.

"That's not what the people at school think," she sighed. "I want to show people, and myself, that I can stand on my own two feet and do something for me. No, not just that," she frowned. "I want to prove that I can *be* someone."

"What do you mean?" I asked.

She shrugged and dropped pizza crust into the box. Rolling onto her back she stared up at the fan as it went around and around. "This is senior year, Emma. Then it's the real world. It's scary. I have to figure out what the hell I'm going to do with my life."

"I'm in the same boat, you know," I told her.

"I know."

"So," I ventured to ask, "what do you think you're going to do after we graduate?" Wasn't that the million-dollar question?

"I don't know," tears pricked her eyes, "and that scares the shit out of me. I need a plan, and I don't have one beyond buckling down."

"Well," I smiled, hoping the gesture offered her a small amount of reassurance, "at least that's a start."

"Enough serious talk," she dabbed at the moisture pooling beneath her eyes, "I'm missing my show."

I laughed gathering up our trash into a small smile.

One of the things I loved most about Sadie was that one-minute we could discuss something serious, and the next she could make me laugh.

I tried to pay attention to the show, but I honestly had no idea what was going on. All I knew was there were a lot of half-naked guys on it—and that was clearly why it appealed to Sadie.

"I hope you're ready for a long day of shopping," Sadie warned, as I fixed to go to sleep in the pull out trundle. Her parents had insisted on having one, since Sadie and I had many sleepovers over the years.

"Ugh," I groaned. "Shopping."

"Hey," she pouted, "brighten up that attitude and maybe I'll suck it up and let you browse through the flea market for a little while."

"You have yourself a deal."

"I'm pretty sure my sweat is sweating," Sadie complained, pulling her long brown hair off her neck and fanning herself.

"Don't be dramatic," I warned her, focusing on the jewelry stand I was browsing.

"I think I'm going to die," she panted.

I pulled a bottle of water out of my purse and handed it to her. "Here, drink this."

She took it and chugged it down greedily. "Why does it have to be so hot?" She whined.

I turned and glared at her. "I spent five hours at the mall with you, and we've only been here thirty minutes. Stop bitching."

She frowned. "How are you not hot?"

"I am hot," I told her, "but I'm not complaining."

"Fine," she relented, "I'll keep my mouth shut."

Something told me I'd be lucky if she was quiet for five minutes.

I browsed through a few more of the stands, picking up a few necklaces, a cardigan, a pair of worn chestnut colored cowboy boots, and a handmade metal drummer and drum set made out of nuts, bolts, and other odds and ends. I just couldn't resist getting it for Maddox. I was lucky that when I found it Sadie had abandoned me to go sit underneath a shaded tree.

"I'm done," I called as I approached her.

"Thank God," she wiped sweat from her brow. "Can we get some dinner now? I need a cool place to lay down and a table sounds like it would be pretty perfect."

I snickered. "Whatever you want."

I waited a moment for her to get up, but she didn't move. "I think I've lost the function of my legs." Pouting her glossed pink lips, she poked one of her legs. "Move," she demanded. Looking up at me, she said, "They're not moving."

"Such a baby," I laughed, reaching out a hand to haul her up.

"I hate this heat," she whined. "And my hair keeps frizzing." She reached up to bat it away.

I shook my head, walking back to the parking lot.

I put my bag in the trunk—trying not to laugh at the other fifty bags that belonged to Sadie.

"Where do you want to eat?" She asked, cranking up the AC.

"Wherever you want. I honestly don't care."

"TGI Friday's it is, then," she chirped. "I want some of those green bean things so I can trick myself into thinking I'm eating healthy."

I snorted. "Sounds like a plan."

By the time we got there the restaurant was packed and we ended up having to wait thirty minutes to be seated.

When we were finally seated at a booth in the back I was ready to go to bed. Shopping was exhausting.

Sadie seemed to agree since she immediately flopped her head on the table and groaned. "My feet hurt."

"You shouldn't have worn those shoes." I wiggled my own toes, encased in a pair of comfy converse.

"Uh, you're right." She sat up, propping her head in her hand. "I would take these off right now if I didn't think I might kill everyone in a five foot radius with the smell of my feet."

I laughed as I pictured the people around us falling to the floor from the fumes. "Yeah, you better leave them on."

The waitress came by for our drink order and before she left Sadie demanded her green bean appetizer thing. It didn't sound that good to me, but she swore it was the greatest thing ever.

"We haven't talked about lover boy in a while," she mused, looking down at her nails, trying to pretend that she wasn't curious.

"There's nothing to talk about," I shrugged. Since I hadn't been able to bring Maddox to the barbeque I'd decided it was fate intervening and saying that I needed to keep him to myself for a little while longer. It wasn't that I thought Sadie would try to steal him from me—she certainly wasn't like that—or that I thought Maddox would choose her over me. It came from a place of, for once in my life, wanting something that was just for me. I felt like I had a whole separate life—no, world— with Maddox and I'd grown to love it. I wasn't ready to share yet, but if things got more serious I would introduce her to him. But for right now, I liked things the way they were.

The waitress set our drinks on the table and Sadie began to peel the paper away from the straw. "I'm starting to think he isn't even real."

"He's real," I assured her. Being honest, I added, "I just don't know where this is going between us, and I'd like to keep things low-key for now."

"So, basically you're saying that you won't introduce him to your best friend?" She raised an elegant brow.

"Basically," I confirmed.

"This hardly seems fair," she pouted. "As your best friend I should know all the details of your life. Keeping secrets is wrong, Emma." She smiled so I'd know she was only joking. "It's okay, though. I won't bring him up anymore. I'm just glad you've finally gotten yourself a boy. But," she leaned towards me, "if you turn in your V-card to him, I better be the first one to know."

"Sadie," I groaned, rolling my eyes.

She laughed, sitting back in the booth, and turned the conversation away from Maddox.

I was glad I'd gotten to spend the day with her, and yesterday evening too. I hadn't realized how much I was missing girl time.

Despite that, by the time she dropped me off at home I was ready for bed. I was completely exhausted and my feet hurt from so much walking. Clearly, I was out of shape.

I tossed my purse on the couch, placed my bag on the floor, and was kicking off my shoes when the doorbell rang. I sighed. Had I left something in Sadie's car?

I opened the door and took a prompt step back. "Maddox," I gasped, "what are you doing here?"

"Surprise," he grinned, holding out a bouquet of pale pink tulips. "For you," he handed them to me.

"I-I thought you weren't getting in until tomorrow." I stepped back, waving him inside.

"I told you I might get back early," he shrugged, smiling down at me, "so I wanted to stop by and see you."

"You're incredible," I whispered.

His lips pulled into a grin. "I try."

"Let me put these in a vase." I nodded my head towards the kitchen and he followed. I grabbed a clear vase and filled it with water. "I'm just going to tell my mom you stopped by." I pointed to the door that led to the garage that served as her workshop.

He nodded, preoccupied by looking at the framed family photos on the wall beside the kitchen table.

I stepped into her studio and she looked up from the pot she was painting. "Did you have fun with Sadie?"

"Mhmm," I nodded, "it was nice to hang out with her."

"Good." She stared intensely at the pot, working on some sort of intricate circular design.

"I just wanted to tell you Maddox stopped by." I tossed a thumb over my shoulder. Normally, I wouldn't bother my mom while she was working, but I didn't want her to think I was hiding things by not telling her Maddox was here.

"Oh, okay," she smiled. "Don't do anything stupid." She gave me a stern look.

I laughed. "You have nothing to worry about mom."

"He's a teenage boy, therefore he's the one I'm worried about. I might like him, but I know what he's thinking about right now and it's not seeing your seashell collection. Don't show him your clam, Emma."

I stood there open mouthed.

"Oh, God. Ew. Mom!" I slapped a hand over my eyes, like my hand alone could block the visual in my head. "I cannot believe you said that!" I gagged. Like, seriously?! Who said that?!

She chuckled. "Okay, let me rephrase then… don't show him your vagina."

I'm pretty sure my mom just wanted to see me turn ten shades of red and stand there sputtering like an idiot.

"Please, mom! Stop!" Now I covered my ears. "Where's the bleach?" I asked. "I need to remove this nastiness from my mind."

She just kept laughing at me.

I finally walked out, leaving her to her hysterics.

Maddox tilted his head when I stepped inside the kitchen. "Interesting conversation?"

Oh, dear God! Please let him not have heard that exchange!

"No," my voice went high.

He raised a single brow, clearly not believing me.

I grabbed the vase of tulips and carried them back to my room, setting them on the dresser. They brightened up the space, and I found myself smiling at them. They were such a sweet gesture.

Maddox flopped on my bed and wiggled around. "Comfy," he grinned, crossing his hands behind his head.

I blushed. Even though Maddox had already seen my room I still felt uncomfortable having him in it. It suddenly felt so… girly.

The walls were painted yellow—not mustard yellow, but a light buttercup shade. I'd strung twinkling Christmas lights on the wall where my bed was, and they cast a golden glow on the room. A blue and teal quilt covered my bed and all the furniture was mismatched. I loved it, but I wondered what Maddox thought when he looked at it.

"Come lay down." He patted the empty space beside him.

I started forward, but then stopped.

"Hang on," I held up a finger, "I got you something."

Leaving Maddox lying on my bed I scurried to the living room and grabbed the bag from the flea market.

I sat down on the bed, pulling out the bubble wrapped metal drummer.

"Here," I handed it to him, "I hope you like it."

I suddenly felt very unsure if I should have gotten it or not.

He smiled at me, peeling away the tape and bubble wrap. He held the drummer and drums up, twisting it around. A slow, crooked smile lifted his lips. Turning to me, he said, "Em, this is the greatest gift anyone has ever given me. Seriously, this is amazing. I love it. Wow," he murmured, examining it from every angle.

"Really?" I asked, "you're not just saying that?"

"I love it," he repeated. "It's such a thoughtful gift." He continued to stare at it with a smile. "You didn't need to get me anything, you know?"

"I know," I replied, "but I wanted to."

He stared at me for a moment. His eyes were such an intense silvery gray color that I found myself squirming from his gaze.

"I-it reminded me of you and I had to get it," I stammered, needing to fill the silence.

His look never wavered and butterflies took up residence in my stomach.

He set the object aside and before I could blink he had me pinned to the bed. His muscular arms formed a barricade around me.

My breath rushed out of my lungs as he stared down at me. My heart thumped so loudly that I knew he had to hear it.

"Thank you."

"Thank you?" I repeated his words.

He nodded, a strand of brown hair falling over his forehead. "Yes, thank you for the extremely thoughtful gift."

"Oh, right," I stammered, "you're welcome."

His eyes darkened to the color of storm clouds. "I'm thinking I should kiss you. You know, as a proper thank you."

"You think so?" I gasped breathlessly.

He lowered, so his body was pressed against mine and his lips were only a breath away. "I know so."

He closed that last miniscule of distance, kissing me like a man that had been deprived of oxygen and I was his air—the only thing keeping him alive. His fingers tangled in my hair, pulling me impossibly closer and guiding me against him.

I wrapped my arms around his neck and moaned into his mouth.

It didn't seem possible that one person could create a hurricane of emotions inside you, but Maddox did that to me. He'd stirred up the calm waters my life had been and now everything was a chaotic storm. And I loved every minute of it.

He kissed me until my lips were red and chapped—branding me for the world to see that I was his.

He rolled over and curled my body against his chest.

"Goodnight, Emma." He whispered, kissing the skin where my neck met my shoulder.

I thought it would be impossible for me to go sleep after that kind of kiss, but I was exhausted. With Maddox's body heat wrapped around me like the coziest blanket in the world, I drifted off to sleep, having the sweetest dreams I'd ever had.

# CHAPTER SEVENTEEN

The rough clearing of a throat had me blinking my eyes open sleepily.

"Hi, mom," I yawned.

"Morning, Emmie… Maddox."

"Maddox?" I questioned.

She raised her brows and nodded her head.

I startled. I was still half asleep or I would've noticed sooner that a body was wrapped around me. He had me cocooned to his chest and his head was buried into the crook of my neck. His warm breath blew softly against my skin. He was sound asleep. At least we were both fully clothed so my mom couldn't accuse of us anything.

"Sorry," I mouthed. "We fell asleep."

"Obviously," she grumbled, putting on a motherly face. "I like him, I do," she said in a hushed whisper, "but I'm not okay with this."

I winced. I hated displeasing my mom. "I'm really sorry."

She nodded her head, as if my words somehow made it better. "I'll make breakfast. Wake him up."

I nodded, assuring her that I would.

With one last glance at us she left my room.

I tried to roll over, but Maddox's arm had me pinned to the bed. I tried to shove his arm off, but that didn't work. I finally pinched him and that got him moving.

"What the hell, Emma?" He cried, rolling onto his back and rubbing his eyes.

"My mom." It was only two words but his eyes widened in horror.

"Is she pissed?" He asked, scrubbing his hands through his already sleep mused hair.

I nodded.

"Fuck," he groaned, sitting up. "I'm really sorry. I was planning to leave once you fell asleep, but then I went to sleep too, and—"

"It's okay," I interrupted him. "We just can't let this happen again or she might kill me… and I'd really like to graduate high school."

He snickered. "Okay. No more sleepovers."

Something in his tone told me that there would, indeed, be more sleepovers.

Before I could give that much more thought I let out a squeak and rolled out of bed onto the floor.

"You okay?" Maddox asked.

"Yep," I cried, wanting to hide behind my hands. I'd suddenly realized that I'd just woken up in bed with Maddox and my hair was bound to be a mess and oh my God what if my breath smelled awful? I cupped my hands over my mouth and breathed, inhaling the scent a bit. "Ugh," I groaned. "That's nasty."

"What's nasty?" Maddox asked, striding around the bed and over to me.

"Nothing!" I cried, jumping to my feet. He probably thought I'd lost my mind. Maybe I had. I reached up, trying to tame my wild hair.

"I'm going to go brush my feet."

"Your feet?" Maddox repeated, biting his lip to stifle his laughter.

"I meant my teeth!" I ran past him and out of the room, straight into the bathroom. I slammed the door closed and leaned against it. I let out a pent up breath. Oh my God, that was mortifying. My feet? Seriously? Sometimes my brain and mouth did not communicate.

Even behind the closed door I could still hear him laughing. At least I amused him.

I shook my head and went to brush my teeth and hair, trying to make myself look halfway decent and not like the spawn of Satan… which was what I usually looked like when I just woke up.

When I padded back into my room I found it empty. I changed into a pair of shorts and loose tank top that showed off a bit of my stomach. It wasn't something I'd normally wear, but I was hoping to make Maddox forget about that embarrassing bit about my feet.

I found him sitting at the kitchen table, laughing with my mom. A plate sat waiting for me, along with a cup of tea.

"You look nice," Maddox grinned, surveying my body as I took a seat. "I can't say the same for myself." He winked, plucking at his wrinkled t-shirt.

I wanted to tell him that he always looked good, but I figured his ego didn't need any more inflation.

I took a bite of bacon and said, "Mmm, this is good, mom."

She smiled. "I figure the least I can do is make you a nice breakfast since I'm rarely around for dinner in the evenings… and now your time is… preoccupied."

She nodded her head at Maddox and he ducked his head to hide his smile.

When Maddox looked up he grinned at me.

"What?" I asked, lifting the cup of tea to my lips.

He nodded at it. "Tea Rex?"

I let out a soft laugh. "I had to have it."

"I can see why," he chuckled. "It suits you. It's quirky."

My brows rose. "Quirky? I'm not sure most girls would appreciate being called quirky."

He smiled crookedly, his silver eyes flashing. "But you're not like most girls. That's one of the things I like most about you."

"You like that I'm weird?" I suppressed a laugh. "That hardly seems like a winning attribute."

He shrugged, stabbing at his scrambled eggs. "I didn't say you were weird, Emma. I was just trying to say that you're different and I think that's a very good thing. You're not like other people."

We stared at each other, completely oblivious to the fact that my mom was still in the kitchen.

I swore the air began to crackle with electricity between us.

I'd only ever read about this kind of thing in the many books that lined my bedroom walls. Never, in a million years, had I believed it was real.

I broke eye contact first, unable to handle the intensity a moment longer.

We finished eating breakfast in relative silence.

I grabbed up our plates and proceeded to wash them in the kitchen sink. I heard the door to the garage close and knew my mom had gone into her studio. It had never bothered me how much she worked, I knew that for her it didn't feel like work. It was where her passion lay, just like me with music. Although, I doubted I'd ever pursue music as a career.

A moment later I felt Maddox step up behind me and my rambling thoughts cut off.

"Let me help." He grabbed a clean, but wet, plate from my hands and a towel to dry it with. He wiped it dry and set it aside, bracing his hands on the counter. He tilted his head towards me and I stopped what I was doing. "I want to show you something."

"Uh," I paused. "Okay?"

I didn't know why it came out sounding like a question.

He cracked a smile, his silvery eyes oddly serious.

I thought he was going to say more, but he took another clean plate from my hands and went about like nothing had happened.

Boys.

They were so damn confusing.

I really wondered what he could possibly want to show me. I thought it could be another 'adventure' but the serious look in his eyes had me doubting that. I felt like something important was about to happen, but then again I could've been reading too much into the situation.

We finished with the dishes and Maddox wanted to stop by his house to change before we went wherever it was that we were going.

I waited in the car, because frankly I didn't want to run into Mathias. I still hadn't recovered from his outburst over the girl named Remy.

In under ten minutes I saw Maddox emerge from the guesthouse. He'd changed into a different pair of jeans, a white shirt, with a button down jean shirt on top with the sleeves rolled up. When he turned around to shut the door I laughed at the fact that he had his drumsticks in his back pocket.

He hopped into the car, tossing the drumsticks in the cup holder, and backed out of the driveway, not uttering a word about our destination.

I decided to sit back and enjoy the ride. There was no point in stressing myself.

Twenty minutes later he pulled off the main road and onto a dirt road. I knew this road led to a pretty shitty neighborhood with run down houses—well, they were actually trailers—and scary people… mostly drug addicts.

"Why are we going here?" I asked, whipping my head back and forth.

Maddox winced, scratching at his stubbled jaw. He tapped his fingers against the steering wheel as he thought. "I've been thinking… since you had the breakdown in the bathroom." I winced, remembering how I'd cried on his shoulder like a complete baby while babbling about my asshat of a father. He glanced at me briefly before continuing, "And I realized I haven't been very forth coming about my life before Karen and Paul took us in as foster kids. I want to change that… so, I thought it best to start at the beginning."

I swallowed thickly. I didn't know what to say. This certainly wasn't what I had expected when he told me he wanted to show me something today.

"Maddox—" I started, but he held a hand up to quiet me.

"You don't need to say anything."

He pulled off the road onto a path that definitely wasn't a road and drove a short ways before stopping. Trees closed in around the vehicle, obscuring it and us from the sight of others.

He cut the engine and held the key in his hand. He didn't look at me, and I felt that he was probably giving himself a pep talk.

He took a few deep breaths and undid his seatbelt. He glanced at me with an indeterminable look on his face. "Are you ready?"

"Are you?" I countered. It seemed like the more important question.

He nodded his head, looking out the windshield. "Yeah, I am."

He climbed from the vehicle and I followed.

He slipped a pair of dark sunglasses on and looked over his shoulder where I stood by the car.

"Come on," he nodded.

"This way?" I pointed ahead. "I thought we were going that way?" I then pointed behind us to where the trailer park sat. "I thought you were just trying to hide your car. I'm no expert, but this looks like too nice of a car to have around here," I rambled.

He chuckled and came to my side. "No, we're not going *there*. Once I left I vowed never to go back."

"But we're here?" I was so confused. I wished he'd just get to the point.

"Even when things were really bad, I had one place to go—one place that didn't hold bad memories, only good ones. That's what I want to share with you today. My sanctuary." He reached for my hand and entwined our fingers together. "I'll tell you the ugly parts of my life too, the parts that are broken and ruined, but I want to show you the beauty first."

Without another word he guided me forward, pushing through the overgrown brush and errant tree limbs.

"It's not far," he told me.

He was right, within a minute we pushed through the last of the brush and a small creek appeared. I stopped and closed my eyes, listening to the sounds of the water flowing.

Opening my eyes, I smiled at him. "So, this is your happy place."

He sat on the ground, resting his arms on his drawn knees. "Yeah." He stared out ahead, his eyes shielded by the sunglasses.

To our left sat a large willow tree. A tire swing was tied to one of the limbs.

Maddox saw where my gaze had landed. "Ezra, Mathias, and I hung that up one year. I think we were ten." With a laugh, he added, "I thought I was such a dare devil climbing up there and tying it on." He shook his head and scrubbed his hands over his face, skewing his sunglasses. "We were so young," he said softly under his breath.

My brows furrowed. "You're still young."

His eyes narrowed as he righted the sunglasses. "Sometimes I feel so fucking old." He ran his fingers through his hair and it stuck up wildly. "Life was cruel to me early on, and while we lucked out—and things are great now—the past still haunts me."

I sat down beside him and wrapped my arms around his strong bicep. I then rested my head on his shoulder. He stared straight ahead at the creek. I knew he'd continue when he was ready.

"Sometimes I wonder if things were always so fucked up," he started, "if maybe there were some good times with my parents and I was too young to remember, but I tend to think not." His head drooped for a moment before he returned his gaze to the creek. "When we were really little, they used to yell and scream at us. Then once we got to be about five, both my mom and dad started hitting us."

I winced. *Five* was *'really little,'* but the way he said it made it sound as if he was so much older.

"My dad was an alcoholic like yours," he turned to glance down at me. "He was a mean drunk. He'd shove us into walls and scream in our faces. But I'd take that shit any day over my mom…" He trailed off, lost once more in memories of the past.

"My mom was just… *cruel*," he sneered, glaring at the ground. "She hit us more than my dad did. But… hitting wasn't her first weapon of choice. She liked words and," he looked to me once more, almost as if he was measuring whether or not I could handle what he was about to reveal, "she liked to choke us."

"Choke you?" I gasped. "*Why?*"

He shrugged. "I don't know… I think maybe she liked the thrill of it, of seeing the light fade in our eyes."

I wanted to throw up. What kind of mother could do that to her children?

"My dad died when we were seven. He crashed his car into a tree, because he was so drunk. She got worse after that. *A lot* worse," he added. "Paul and Karen lived in the trailer beside us—that's how we became friends with Ezra. They never knew how bad things were for us, or they would've intervened. Sometimes I wish I'd been strong enough to tell them what was happening, but I was terrified of my own mom—of what she might do to me." He swallowed thickly. "Mathias had it worse with her than I did. He was slow in school and had trouble reading, so that made her mad—even though she's to blame, it's not like she ever read to us or helped with homework. Anyway," he shook his head, "Mathias' teacher sent home a note from school one day when we were in sixth grade—something about how he was failing reading and she thought my mom should have him checked out for dyslexia. She was pissed when she read the note…" His teeth ground together and he removed his sunglasses to rub his eyes. "Even though I wasn't the one in trouble I ran away from her—scared she'd hurt me too. I hid underneath my bed and I heard Mathias fighting against her, trying to get away—we were both still really scrawny then," he laughed, but there was no humor in the sound, "I heard her drag him into the bathroom and the door slammed." His eyes pinched shut and his body trembled.

Even before he continued I was certain I knew where this was going.

"She tried to drown him in the bathtub like… like he was fucking animal or something." I expected him to be crying, but he wasn't. Instead anger simmered beneath the surface of his skin. His fists tightened like he wanted to swing out and punch something. "The most ironic part of it all is the fact that *she* was the animal. She was a drug addict and a whore—that's eventually what got her arrested and led to us being put in the foster care system. She was trying to trade sex for drugs from a cop that was working undercover. We were thirteen then, and even though we were rid of her," he stared straight ahead, his jaw set, "the damage had been done and it was irreversible."

He ripped at the grass, caking dirt beneath his fingernails. "Maybe it's because I didn't get it as bad as Mathias, or maybe I just coped differently, but for whatever reason I haven't stayed angry like him." He turned to glance at me. "My brother isn't an asshole for no reason, it's because she made him that way."

I winced, my heart breaking for Mathias and Maddox. No child should ever go through what they did.

"While we lived here," he waved a hand, "*this* became our solace. When things got rough we got out of the house and ran here. After all, the Collins' couldn't always let us into their home—and that was the first place my mom looked for us anyway. She never learned about this place. It was all ours."

A look stole over his face, one of peace and maybe even happiness.

"Nothing bad ever happened in this spot, and that made it special—no bad memories could haunt us here. We don't come here very often anymore, at least I don't, but it will always be special."

He trailed off, his eyes growing distant.

"You know, normally," he continued, "we would've ended up in a hellhole when we entered the system, but the Collins' stepped up to the plate. We basically lived at their place anyway—they'd moved out of the trailer park but were still close enough that we all rode the same bus, so we'd go there in the evenings. They saved us," he said with surety, "without them Mathias would be even more fucked up than he is, and me? I know I wouldn't be sitting here with you right now," he cracked a smile, "and I wouldn't feel so happy. I owe them everything. They loved us when no one else did—for years I struggled to find a way to repay them for their kindness, but I finally realized I already had, just by loving them back." He looked out at the creek, watching the way the sun shimmered on the surface. "They're the reason we got into music. They thought music might be a healthy outlet for our anger."

"Mathias plays too?" I had no idea that his twin had any kind of musical talent.

"Well," he chuckled, "he sings. He can play the piano too, and a little guitar, but he prefers singing."

"I would've never guessed," I said honestly.

"Mathias keeps to himself, don't take it personally."

"Why'd you choose the drums?" I asked curiously.

"I don't know," his lips turned down, "it just felt right."

We grew quiet—the only sounds around us were the creek, the rustling of leaves, and the caw of birds.

I let go of his arm and he stretched his legs out, coaxing me to lie down and put my head on his leg. He looked down at me, his face oddly serious. "You know," he started, reaching down to brush an errant blonde curl off my cheek, "I thought it would more difficult to tell you, but it was surprisingly easy." His fingers moved from my cheeks to outline my lips.

"Thank you for trusting me enough to tell me," I whispered.

His eyes zeroed in on my lips, following the path his fingers burned as he traced their contour. "You're too good for me."

"That isn't true," I grabbed his hand, wrapping my fingers around his and laying our joined hands on my chest. "I'm not too good for you. I'm average, Maddox. I'm just a girl and you're just a boy. But together," I reached up with my free hand, clasping his jaw so he was forced to look down at me, "we're more. Maybe not perfect, but we're something pretty extraordinary."

He grinned at that. "You could be a poet, Emma." He'd removed his sunglasses and they sat on the collar of his shirt, so I didn't miss his wink.

I laughed. "Maybe if you're nice to me I'll let you use it in a song."

"Or maybe you could write one with me?" He was still smiling, but his eyes shimmered with seriousness. "You told me you write."

"Me? Write a song with you?" I laughed. "Yeah, right. I can barely write a paper for English class." I *did* write songs though—at home, where no one would ever see them. I began to pale, recalling a long ago conversation where I'd told him I wrote songs. Jesus. Why couldn't I keep my mouth shut around him?

He bit down on his delectable bottom lip to stifle his laughter. "Writing a song is nothing like writing an essay. An essay comes from here," he tapped my forehead, "and a song," his voice lowered to a husky whisper and his darkened, "comes from here." He laid his hand on my chest, right over my heart. It started beating wildly at his touch, and with the way he grinned I knew he noticed.

"What are you doing to me?" The words tumbled out of my mouth, reminding me of a set of Jenga blocks falling to a table.

"Falling in love with you," was his quick reply.

I didn't know who made the first move, I guessed it didn't really matter, but suddenly I was in his lap with my legs wrapped around his waist as he kissed me passionately.

It was the kind of kiss that scorched your soul.

He nipped at my bottom lip and I wrapped my arms around his neck.

My chest pressed against his and I had the sudden urge to feel his bare skin against the palms of my hands. Almost as if he sensed what I wanted he stripped off both of the shirts he wore.

His bare skin scorched my palms.

"You're so beautiful," he whispered in between kisses. His hand found the nape of my neck, drawing me closer as his tongue brushed against the seam of my lips.

I opened for him, begging, wanting all he could give me.

My heart raced and my blood rushed through my veins.

I wanted him.

All of him.

Here.

Now.

I rocked my hips against him, needing to ease the ache I felt, and he grasped my thighs.

"Em," he whispered, "Emma, you have to stop."

He rolled over, pinning me to the ground and my hands above my head.

"Stop," he panted, his eyes so dark that there was only a thin ring of silver left. My lips ached from the loss of his. His tongue flicked out to wet his lips. "I want you, Em, God I want you so fucking bad. But not here, not like this."

I closed my eyes, realizing what I'd done.

"I'm sorry," I whispered.

"Don't be sorry," he shook his head. "Not for that, please."

My lower lip trembled and I was seconds away from tears—I felt like I'd basically thrown myself at him and been shot down. I knew realistically that wasn't what happened, and I'd gotten caught up in the moment, but it still hurt.

"Emma," he frowned, "don't cry. I'm trying to do the noble thing here, and your sad face is making it very difficult."

I managed a small laugh.

He smiled. "And can you honestly say you'd want our first time to be here?" He smoothed his fingers across my cheekbone.

"No," I replied. "I'm sorry," I repeated. "I don't know what's wrong with me."

He chuckled and ducked his head against my neck before rising to his feet. "There's nothing wrong with you, Em," he reached out a hand to help me up, "it's called hormones."

I still felt embarrassed and flustered as he grabbed his shirts, putting them back on.

He wrapped an arm around my shoulders and drew me against his body, kissing the top of my head. "Stop thinking about it, Em."

I let out a soft laugh. He could read me so well—*too* well sometimes.

Before he could guide me away, I asked, "What is this place, exactly?"

He looked out towards the water, his face darkening with… was that regret? "It's Willow Creek."

# CHAPTER EIGHTEEN

I followed Maddox back to his car—trying my best to forget about basically throwing myself at him. My cheeks were already heating just thinking about it, and I willed the redness to disappear. I needed something—anything—to talk about.

"So, you said Karen and Paul lived here too?" It was the first question that popped into my head.

He nodded, unlocking the car and we both climbed inside.

"How'd they get away?" I winced at my choice of words. It sounded so harsh and callous. "I'm sorry, I didn't mean it like that… I just meant that…" I rambled, unable to form a coherent sentence.

He reached over and squeezed my knee, leaving his hand there in the process. "It's okay. I know what you meant." He paused, appraising his next words. "Paul was able to get a promotion at work and they had to move to be closer—but they didn't move into the house they live in now, if that's what you're thinking." His hands tightened around the steering wheel.

He was obviously tense, and I worried that it came from telling me about his mom and dad—that maybe he'd told me before he was ready.

Maddox interrupted my thoughts with a statement of his own. "Your mom said your birthday is in a few weeks."

I winced. "What else did she tell you?"

He grinned at that—and even though his eyes were concealed behind the dark sunglasses I knew they were lit with laughter.

"She said you used to dress up and sing these little songs you made up."

My face reddened and I struggled to breathe. I could remember being five years old and dressing up in my sparkly red dress, black shoes, and getting into my mother's makeup—which wasn't much since she barely wore any—and singing a song about… cheese. Yes, cheese. Pretty much all the songs I made up related to my love of same random thing. Usually food. What could I say? I was always hungry.

"Hey, my songs were not *little*," I disagreed, "they were brilliant." The songs I wrote now were only for myself, though, and no one—not even Maddox—was ever going to see them.

"Do you still remember them?" He asked, an eyebrow rose in interest.

I squeaked. I felt like a cornered rabbit, and if we hadn't been in a moving vehicle I would've run away. "Maybe."

He laughed, trying to hide his smile behind his hand as he drove. "That's cute."

I wrinkled my nose with distaste. I wasn't sure I liked my boyfriend calling me cute. It seemed like a putdown, somehow—like something you'd call your little sister. Then again, I was probably being overly defensive due to my non-existent boyfriend experience. In the past I spent more time trying to push guys away than trying to figure them out.

"Mathias wants me to pick up some lunch to bring back with us, and then I was hoping I'd get to see you put those song writing skills to the test."

I blanched, shaking my head back and forth. "I'm hardly a skilled song writer," I defended. "Not like you," I added softly, remembering the day I played the song he wrote on the piano while he sang. The song had been beautiful—something I imagined someone much older than Maddox would've written. The songs I wrote paled in comparison.

"How would you know if you haven't let anyone hear them?" He countered.

Damn him. He had me there.

"What if I'm not good at it?" I asked in a small voice. I hated the thought of failing at something I loved so much.

He pulled into the parking lot of a local restaurant and turned off the car. He took his sunglasses off and leveled me with an indignant look. "How can any of us know if we're good at anything if we never at least try?"

I tried so hard not to smile, but I failed. "Okay, Yoda."

He chuckled. "I'm shocked you know who Yoda is if you didn't know Sonic the Hedgehog."

He was never going to let the hedgehog thing go.

I shrugged. "I watched them with my dad once." I didn't want Maddox to think I was going to burst into tears by talking about my dad again, so I was quick to add, "This is where Mathias wants us to get his lunch?" I pointed at the building.

Wait, lunch? Didn't we just eat breakfast?

My eyes widened when I looked at the time on my phone. It was after twelve—nearing one. Had we really killed that much time at the creek? Apparently so.

"Yep," Maddox nodded, hopping out of the car. He leaned his head through the open door. "Come on."

"Aren't you picking it up?" I asked, perfectly happy to stay behind in the car.

You know, to avoid people and all that jazz.

He shook his head. "*We're* eating here, while Mathias will eat alone and suffer in his self-imposed solitude."

My lips quirked at that, and I exited the car, following him into the building.

Before we entered the building he tugged on a beanie. Seriously, what was it with him and hats?

I followed him into the darkened building. It was relatively empty of a lunchtime crowd, although the bar did hold a few occupants. Maddox led me to a booth in the back and a waiter appeared quickly with menus.

"Have you ever been here before?" Maddox asked, twisting his bottom lip with his fingers as he perused the menu.

"No," I answered shortly.

He set the menu down, looking like I had offended him. "This place only has the best food ever. 'Tis a shame."

"I guess it's another first I'll experience with you," I said, and then immediately hid behind the menu because I started thinking about the naked kind of firsts. Seriously, my brain was all kinds of fucked up lately.

Maddox laughed at me, like a full belly laugh, which only served to leave me even more embarrassed.

He finally managed to compose himself and picked up the menu once more.

The waiter returned and we both ordered iced tea. I got a sandwich and Maddox ordered half the menu. I wished I was joking and I hoped that *some* of that food was going to be boxed up for Mathias.

Since my thoughts had already headed in that direction I thought now might be a good time to ask about the mysterious Remy.

"I've been wondering…"

"Yeah?" He prompted, his eyes skimming the restaurant like he was searching for something or someone.

"What's up with Remy?" I finally asked. "Who is she to Mathias? I mean, I assumed it was his girlfriend, or ex-girlfriend more likely, but then that night at dinner your dad said he knew you'd be the first to have a girlfriend." I knew I was rambling so I quickly shut my mouth. I hated to pry, but after Mathias went all Godzilla and threw a glass at us I thought I deserved to know—especially if I was about to willingly subject myself to his obnoxious presence.

The waiter sat down our drinks and Maddox nodded in thanks, waiting for him to walk off before he continued.

"Remy and Mathias…" He winced. "They dated briefly when they were sixteen."

"And that's it?" I asked. There had to be more to the story than he was letting on.

"Mathias is private—there are lots of things he doesn't even share with me—so

I honestly don't know that much. She never really came over to our house, but we'd all hang out. They were always all over each other, and they argued a lot. They've both got a temper and Remy didn't back down from his shit. She moved before our senior year of high school and they broke up. Mathias has been an even bigger asshole then usual since then, but I honestly don't know what transpired there. I have a feeling we may never know." He sat back and draped his arm across the top of the booth.

I frowned, suddenly gaining even more sympathy towards his moody and arrogant twin.

"Did he love her?" I didn't know why, but the question felt important to me.

He shrugged, taking a sip of his iced tea. "I guess in the only way Mathias Wade knows how to love—and that's to destroy." Maddox didn't seem bothered by his own harsh words about his brother. I think it bothered him that Mathias was so… broken… but he'd come to accept his twin as he was. Maddox straightened and I heard his boots stomp against the concrete floor. "Forget about my brother, let's talk about what we're going to do for your eighteenth birthday."

I squeezed my eyes shut. "No."

"No?" He chuckled. "I thought most girls loved talking about their birthdays and all the expensive shit they wanted."

"Not me," I shook my head. I used to love my birthday, until one year my father destroyed it in a drunken rage. It never felt the same after that—like it was tarnished somehow.

Maddox seemed to pick up on my feelings. He leaned forward, his hands crossing with interest. "Why?"

It was only one word, but it still made me squirm.

"Why do you think?" I countered with a question of my own, buying more time.

He quirked a single dark brow. "I'm going to go out on a limb here and guess your dad."

"Ding, ding, ding we have a winner."

His face wrinkled with disgust. "What did he do to ruin your birthday?"

I couldn't believe I was actually about to recount this story. I was eight years old and my mom had made me invite the entire third grade class, and not just Sadie. I'd been so embarrassed when my dad stumbled into the backyard drunk, muttering random nonsense under his breath. I was used to seeing him like this, but the other kids had no idea what was going on and had begun whispering amongst themselves.

"He showed up to my birthday party drunk," I mumbled. Closing my eyes I remembered the way the breeze had blown against my face—the orange balloons swaying. "Then proceeded to smash my cake and throw up in my lap."

Maddox snorted.

"It's not funny!" I cried.

"Sorry," he sobered, hiding his mouth behind his hand.

"I was traumatized," I defended. "Now whenever my birthday rolls around that's all I remember."

His eyes flashed with a silvery fire. "We're going to change that this year."

I shivered at the promising tone in his voice.

"What do you have in mind?" I asked, trying to pretend I wasn't all that interested in what he might come up with.

"I don't know yet," he rubbed his stubbled jaw in thought, "but I'll think of something."

I didn't doubt him.

"Here's your food asshole." Maddox tossed the bag of food at Mathias' chest.

Mathias fumbled to catch it. He'd been sitting on one of the barstools in the guesthouse's kitchen and hadn't been expecting us.

"Fuck, Maddox." Mathias managed to grab the bag before it fell to the floor. "I'm going to stick my cigarettes on your stupid hedgehog's fucking quills."

Maddox laughed, completely unaffected by his twin's words. "We both know you'd never waste your precious cigarettes to do that."

Maddox headed to the refrigerator, grabbing a bottle of blue Gatorade. While he spoke to his brother I headed to the side of the guesthouse that housed the instruments and simple couch.

Papers still sat scattered across the desk, and I wondered just how many songs he was working on. Skimming the papers, I guessed a lot.

I had a journal at home filled with songs—all written neatly and kept in some sort of order. *This* was a mess. Although, as I peered closer, I had to admit that he had ridiculously good handwriting. Couldn't he suck at something?

Another pair of drumsticks sat on the desk. I couldn't resist picking them up and tapping them against the top.

"Don't do that." A hand shot out, grabbing the sticks from my hands.

I pouted. "That wasn't nice." I wrestled them away from him and laughed in triumph, waving them in the air. "They're. Mine. Now." I accentuated each word by tapping the drumsticks against his chest.

He leveled me with a glare. "Don't do that."

"Do what, play with your sticks?" I grinned evilly.

"That sounded dirty." He fought a smile.

"You have a very dirty mind then," I told him, putting the drumsticks back on the desk.

I looked around, surprised Mathias hadn't interrupted us with a smartass comment, but he was gone.

Noticing my puzzled look Maddox said, "Mathias went to the main house to eat."

"Oh."

He grinned. "What? Are you suddenly afraid to be alone with me?"

"No," I scoffed.

"You should be."

His lips descended on mine, his hands on my hips. He lifted me onto the table, stepping between my legs.

He nipped lightly at my bottom lip and I'm pretty sure a moan escaped my throat. I really hoped he didn't hear it.

His fingers delved into my hair, musing it even more.

When I lost all ability to breathe he stepped back. He breathed heavily, looking down at me with a searing gaze.

"Afraid now?"

"Hardly," I panted.

He grinned at that. "Then I'll have to try harder." His eyes dipped to the swell of my breasts. Normally I would've covered my chest in mortification, but his kiss had killed a few of my brain cells and I couldn't move if I tried.

He dipped his head once more and I closed my eyes in anticipation, but his lips didn't touch mine. Instead he kissed my cheek, leaving me desperate for more. Jerkface.

"Think you can get off the table so we can write a song?" His hands landed on the table beside my thighs so he was now eyelevel with me.

He knew that there was no way I was peeling my body off this table. "You put me here."

He chuckled. "Oh, Emma." He helped me off the table and I stumbled against his side. "Go sit over there." He pointed and I saw that there were pillows, blankets, and beanbags sitting on the floor. They weren't normally there and I couldn't help wondering if he'd had this planned.

He carried over the papers where he'd already started songs, as well as blank sheets, and pencils. He sat them on the floor in front of me and went back, opening Sonic's cage.

I didn't even blink when he sat down with the hedgehog on his shoulder. At this point it was commonplace. I wouldn't have even been surprised if Sonic was wearing his knitted cape—he wasn't, though.

I stared at the spread out papers, grabbing a random one and starting to read.

Finished with that one I skimmed another.

I peeked at him, trying not to laugh at how adorable he looked with his hair ruffled and Sonic on his shoulder.

"These are really good, amazing actually," I waved the papers in my hands, "remind me again why you need my help?"

"Because I want it," he whispered.

I swallowed thickly, the look in his eyes was indescribable.

"I guess we better get started then," I smiled. I grabbed a piece of paper and one of the pencils. "Do you have anything specific in mind for this song?"

His eyes flashed a stormy gray. "Yeah, I want it to start with the piano and slowly build to the crescendo. As for lyrics… I hadn't gotten that far."

"It looks like we have our work cut out for us then," I laughed. My brows furrowing, I asked, "Do you mind me asking what you do with these songs?"

"I record them," he responded.

"Are you trying to get a record deal?" It was an honest question. Maddox never talked about his lack of a job or spoke of what he wanted to do in the future.

He looked away from me and mumbled, "Something like that."

I ignored him and tapped the pencil against the paper as I thought.

The words came to me easily and I scribbled them across the paper.

Maddox watched with rapt attention as I worked. I purposely sat with my shoulders angled in a way that he wouldn't be able to see the words on the paper.

Minutes passed before he couldn't take it anymore. "Can I see it?"

"No," I scolded, "not yet."

True, he'd asked for my help so we were supposed to be writing it together, but I wanted to get all my thoughts out on paper before he saw it.

By the time I finished an hour had gone by.

I looked over, laughing when I saw Maddox had dozed off. He lay in one of the beanbags with Sonic sleeping on his chest. They were quite the pair.

I almost hated to wake him—almost being the key word there.

I found a drumstick lying on the floor—seriously, he had them everywhere—and reached over to give his knee a tap. Okay, so I basically hit him with it, but whatever.

He sputtered awake, grabbing his knee. Sonic was knocked off his chest and into his lap with the motion.

"What was that for?" He groaned, rubbing the spot. "I think you gave me a bruise."

"Aw, poor baby." I pouted. "Here." I shoved the papers at him and scooted as far away as I could manage. No one—and I mean *no one*—had ever read one of my songs. I'd stopped singing them around the house about the time I stopped writing about cheese.

I honestly couldn't believe I'd let him talk me into this. He was such a charmer.

His mouth fell open the further he read and I resisted the urge to cringe. My songs were always so personal—like a diary entry—and it felt very much like I was baring my soul by letting him read one.

He picked up the pencil, crossing a few things out and adding his own lyrics.

Oh my God! He hated it! He totally hated it and he was trying to fix it.

I hid my face behind my fingers.

I couldn't stand the silence so I blurted, "It's okay if you hate it."

He was still quiet.

And then his hands were on mine, prying them away from my face.

His soft gray eyes met my blue ones. "Emma," he said my name slowly, "the song is amazing, truly. It… it blew my mind."

"But… but you were scribbling on it," I stuttered.

He grinned. "I'll admit to tweaking it a bit, but not much. Do you want to see what I changed?"

I nodded and he handed me the papers. He was right, he didn't change much, and what he did was for the better. It made it a stronger song.

"Normally I go through at least ten drafts before I get the lyrics right, and you just… did that in no time." He shook his head, running his fingers through his dark hair. "You're really kind of amazing."

I grinned. "Are you just now figuring that out?"

"No," he laughed, "I knew it the moment I saw you. It's why I talked to you in the first place."

His words warmed my body with a pleased flush.

"Now, the *really* hard part," he held out a hand to help me up. "Piano time."

Once again I found myself seated on the bench in front of the piano with him. The bench was so small that it left no room between us.

"I was thinking something like this…" He started to play, and I closed my eyes.

The notes drifted off and I opened my eyes in time to see him shrug. "Something like that. You're better at this than I am."

"Hardly," I snorted.

I'd heard enough to pick up on the sound he wanted, so I played while he wrote everything down.

Music was second nature to me—as easy as breathing.

I loved that it was the same way for Maddox. It allowed us to connect in a way many other people couldn't. It was a special bond we could share.

"I want you to start from the beginning," he said, standing up. "Just give me a minute."

He headed over to his drum set and pulled the drumsticks out of his back pocket. "Now you can start."

I laughed, shaking my head at his bossiness, but did as he asked.

I'd played a quarter of the way through the song when he started in on the drums. Just a rumble at first before it built—just like he said he wanted it to do.

We finished the song and he jumped up with the drumsticks clutched in his hands. He pointed the drumsticks at me, biting his lip excitedly. "*That*, Em, is what you call a hit song."

"You think so?" I asked, still doubtful about my lyrics.

"I know so," he chimed. He moved from behind his drum set and over to me. He bent down and pressed his forehead against mine. "You remember how you told me you didn't know what you wanted to do after high school?"

I nodded.

"I think you just figured it out."

"What?" I asked, confused.

"You're a song writer, Em. Plain and simple."

I gaped at him and then started laughing. "No, I'm definitely not."

"You are and I'm going to make you believe me when that song is a hit."

I snorted. "In case you're forgetting, we're two teenagers writing songs in your guesthouse. It's not going to be a hit."

"You'll see," he grinned.

And something told me I would.

# CHAPTER NINETEEN

Several days later I found myself hurrying to keep up with Maddox's long-legged stride in downtown Winchester. The sun was just beginning to set, bathing us in a red-hued glow.

"Where are we going?" I asked.

Maddox grabbed my hand and drug me down the street. Apparently I wasn't walking fast enough for him. As per usual he was dressed in jeans—with his drumsticks in the back pocket—a black t-shirt, and a beanie.

"If I told you that it would spoil the surprise." He glanced at me over his shoulder, his lips rising in a smile.

Damn these surprises.

I narrowed my eyes before he looked away. "Will this surprise also send me running down the street screaming?"

He chuckled. "I don't know… depends on what you're afraid of. You did tell me you'd jump out of a plane with me, and I don't think this is nearly as scary as that."

"I really don't like not knowing what *this* is," I growled. Something told me I wasn't going to like what he had planned.

"My lips are sealed."

"I'm going to unseal them," I grumbled.

He merely laughed at me.

He finally stopped and opened the door to a local coffee shop. I knew this place.

"Oh, hell to the no," I pried my hand from his. "I know what you're trying to do and it's not happening." I shook my head.

"Emma," he groaned—he rarely ever used my whole name so I knew he was serious—"People deserve to hear our song. I want to see their reactions."

I sputtered, "Absolutely not." I didn't consider myself a shy person, I just wasn't social, but putting myself on a stage singing in front of people seemed too much for even me.

"Em," he reached up to tenderly cup my cheek, the sweet look in his eyes nearly melting. "Please do this for me."

Oh God, he was giving me the puppy dog eyes. I almost expected his bottom lip to turn down.

He leaned in closer, brushing his nose along the line of my jaw. "Please," he begged again.

My eyes fluttered closed and I let out a small moan. "You're not playing fair."

"I never said I would."

"Fine, I'll do it." I gave in easily. I had to trust Maddox when he said the song was good—and really that's what scared me more than singing, the fact that this song came from my heart.

Maddox grinned triumphantly. "Thank you." He kissed me quickly, pulling away before things could get heated.

He stepped away from me to open the door to Griffin's—the local coffee shop/restaurant… it was kind of a weird place where mostly teenagers and college students hung out—and I instantly missed the heat of his body.

Upon stepping inside I was met with the heavenly sent of coffee and cake.

"Hey, Griffin," Maddox called to the burly owner, who manned the register.

He lifted his hand in a small wave. "You guys playing today?" He asked.

"No, just us." Maddox slung an arm around my shoulders.

Griffin chuckled. "I'm kinda relieved your brother isn't here. I had to break up a fight the last time he was."

Maddox sighed beside me. "Sorry about that."

Griffin shrugged. "It's in the past. Can I get you guys anything?"

Maddox looked to me.

"I'll have an iced coffee." I reached into my bag for my wallet.

"I'll have the same," Maddox told him, reaching for his own wallet in his back pocket.

I was determined to beat him. He was always treating me, now it was my turn. I bumped him with my hip, hard enough that he stumbled and dropped his wallet.

"Here," I handed Griffin a ten dollar bill.

The older man chuckled. "I like you."

"Jesus, Em," Maddox grumbled, wiping dust off his wallet, "I think you gave me another bruise."

I laughed. "Sorry, I had to."

Griffin handed me my change and went to make our drinks.

"I would've bought it," he grumbled, sliding his wallet back in his pocket.

"I know you would've," I assured him. "But I wanted to get this."

He mumbled something under his breath about me being so damn bossy sometimes. My lips lifted in a smile.

Griffin handed over our drinks and I followed Maddox to a table in the back corner that was partially hidden by a wall.

The coffee shop was fairly busy, but not as crowded as it was on open mic night. I'd come with Sadie once and the place had been *packed* with little room between bodies.

I began to fidget with nerves—first tugging on the ends of my hair, and then playing with the straw wrapper. I knew it was only a matter of time before Maddox dragged me onto the small stage and all the people here heard our song.

Maddox seemed equally as restless. He sat drumming his fingers against the top of the table. Then again, Maddox was always drumming or tapping on something.

"Can we get this over with?" I finally hissed.

He chuckled, his eyes crinkling at the corners. "We're singing a song, not going to the dentist. You don't just get it over with. You have to wait until it feels right."

"In that case, this doesn't feel right. I think we should leave."

I started to stand, but he grabbed my arm to keep me from running away. "Not so fast."

I sat back down. "What if people hate it?" I asked him, letting him see just how much that thought worried me.

He leaned forward with a contemplative look. "The way I see it, there are always going to be the ones that love you and the ones that hate you—let's face it, people love to tear others down, but as long as you're confident within yourself then nothing else matters."

"I was talking about the song, not myself," I countered.

He grinned, stifling a chuckle. "The same principle applies. If you're confident with the song, what others think shouldn't matter to you."

Why did he always have to be right? It was annoyingly unfair.

I squared my shoulders and jutted my chin out. "I believe in our song."

"I believe in *you*." He stood up and kissed my cheek before nodding towards the stage.

He didn't need to say anything. I knew this was it.

I followed him to the stage. There weren't any drums, but there was a guitar and a keyboard. Maddox picked up the guitar and sat on a stool, pointing at the keyboard for me.

Once I was on the stage, seated behind the keyboard, all my nerves disappeared.

I loved this song and I was proud of it. More than just the two of us deserved to hear it.

Maddox introduced us to the people hanging around the coffee shop.

"This is a little something we wrote together and I hope you guys will love it as much as we do."

He nodded at me and I knew that was my cue to start playing.

I took a deep breath, bracing my fingers above the keys.

And then I started to play.

You could tell the people were worried at first—since it started out so slow—but once we started singing and the song built towards the middle they got more into it.

It was an indescribable feeling watching people fall in love with our song.

When it ended I couldn't stop the goofy smile that lit my face.

I don't think I'd ever been happier in my entire life than I was right now.

I stood up from behind the keyboard, but before I could leave the stage Maddox had me in his arms, sealing my lips in a kiss that stole my breath. I clung to his shoulders, my cheeks heating with a blush as people gathered around the stage started to whistle and call at us.

When Maddox felt that he'd kissed me thoroughly he pulled away enough to put his forehead against mine.

I could see that he wanted to say something, it was there on the tip of his tongue, but he stopped himself.

He took my hand and we headed back to the table to grab our drinks before leaving.

I heard someone call after us as the door closed behind us, but Maddox didn't slow. In fact, he quickened his strides.

I basically had to jog to keep up with him as we headed to his car. Once safe inside he glanced over at me.

"After that adrenaline rush, I'm thinking we should do something else crazy. We're on a roll here."

I raised a brow. "Like what?" I had a feeling I already knew what he was going to say—and it was going to happen eventually anyway.

"I think it's time to go skydiving."

I buckled my seatbelt and smiled at him. "You know I'm in."

He grinned, his laughter filling the car. "You might be the only girl on the planet more scared to sing a song she wrote, than to jump out of a plane."

I shrugged. "There's no judgment with jumping out of a plane. You just do it. Singing a song you wrote… that's personal. Like someone reading your diary."

His eyes sparkled with that information. "You have a diary."

"*No*," I drew out the word.

Before pulling away from the curb he grabbed his phone. "Would you mind if the guys tagged along? I mentioned it to them awhile ago and they were pissed I was going without them."

"I don't mind at all," I assured him. Sometimes I spent so much time alone that it was all too easy to forget that he had friends, and I had Sadie. I'd been completely neglecting her this summer. If the situation was reversed and she'd ditched me the entire summer for a guy I'd be pretty mad. We'd hung out a few times, but not like we normally did. I was going to have to learn how to prioritize. I didn't need to spend all my time with Maddox.

"Great," Maddox grinned, either not noticing that I was lost in my thoughts or choosing not to comment on it.

I sat quietly while Maddox called Ezra to round up the guys. I heard him giving directions to the skydiving place.

I didn't feel nervous at all. Maybe there was something wrong with me. But I actually felt exhilarated at the thought of jumping out of a plane. It felt like I was literally going to spread my wings and fly.

I just hoped I didn't go splat.

Maddox, Mathias, Ezra, Hayes, and I all stood being instructed on what we could and could not do.

It was quite a lengthy explanation they went through.

Basically the gist was: Don't be a fucking idiot.

Easy enough.

We got strapped into the harnesses and my body buzzed with an excited energy.

This was hands down the most insane thing I'd ever done.

I knew a sensible person would be afraid—but all common sense had left me the moment I met Maddox. He had me throwing my rulebook out the window and living life to the fullest.

Once we were suited up they herded us onto the plane, going over a few more rules again. Since we were newbies we all ended up being strapped to an instructor.

I ended up paired with Tyler—an instructor that was only a few years older than us, and insanely good-looking in a California surfer type of way.

"Hi," he smiled, his blue eyes shining.

"Hi," I replied, glancing towards Maddox. He had his teeth barred and I swore he was growling.

"Down boy," Ezra told him, like he was a dog.

I couldn't help laughing and Maddox seemed to relax some when he realized he had my attention.

"What made you guys want to go skydiving?" Tyler asked. His question seemed to address all of us, but he stared at me. I squirmed, feeling uncomfortable. I mean, his question was innocent enough, but the way he was looking at me wasn't. His eyes perused my body lazily with a cocky smile curving his full lips. I imagined they didn't get very many girls willing to throw their body out of a plane, so he was probably intrigued by that.

"We just fucking wanted to," Mathias sneered, piping in before Maddox could say anything. "And while you're at it, maybe you could stop looking at my brother's girlfriend like you want to fucking lick her. M'kay?"

Maddox's lips quirked into a smile at his brother defending him. Ezra just laughed while Hayes shook his head. I stood shocked. I didn't think I'd ever heard Mathias use so many words at one time.

Tyler's head dropped and he took an uneasy step away from me.

The man that was supposed to be diving with Mathias switched places with Tyler. I guessed they wanted to avoid any unnecessary drama—and they might've been afraid of Mathias. His glare was icy and probably made small children cry.

Once the switch was made my new partner set about attaching us.

Maddox reached for my hand, giving mine a reassuring squeeze. I smiled at him, trying to show that I wasn't scared and he didn't need to worry.

Within minutes we reached the altitude we needed to jump.

This was it.

No turning back.

"Who wants to go first?" Tyler asked.

My hand shot in the air. No way was I letting the guys go first.

Maddox chuckled at my enthusiasm, ducking his head to hide his smile.

"Alright then," the guy strapped to me said. I didn't know his name.

The door slid open and I took a startled step back as the air swept into the plane. The guys laughed at me, but I ignored them.

"Ready when you are." The man told me.

I closed my eyes.

*One, two, three.*

And then I jumped.

# CHAPTER TWENTY

"That was amazing! Fantastical! Absolutely magical!" I exclaimed, twirling around in the grass.

"Someone make her shut up," Mathias groaned, puking his guts up.

"You're just jealous, because she didn't get sick and you did," Maddox countered. He came to stand by my side, his fingers grazing my hip. I stood on my tiptoes placing a light, chaste kiss on his cheek.

Mathias wiped his mouth with the back of his hand. "I can't fucking believe people do that for fun."

Maddox rolled his eyes. "Do you think you could try speaking without using a variation of the word 'fuck' in every sentence?"

Mathias laughed. "I don't fucking think so."

Maddox grumbled and turned to me. "He's ridiculous."

"He's your brother," I countered.

"And if we weren't identical I'd never know we were related," he retorted. Mathias overheard and gave him the finger.

"I fucking love you too, princess," Mathias sneered.

Maddox narrowed his eyes. "Now you're just saying it to spite me."

"Yes I fucking am," Mathias replied, trudging through the grass towards the building.

Maddox turned to me, his expression unreadable. "Be glad you're an only child," he grumbled. "Siblings suck."

I laughed, taking his hand in mine. "You love him."

He sighed, pinching the bridge of his nose with his free hand. "Yeah, I know. That makes it worse."

"Are you guys coming?!" Mathias called over his shoulder. Hayes and Ezra were specks in the distance.

"Yeah, yeah," Maddox waved him on.

"You know," I piped in, my voice low enough that Mathias wouldn't hear, "I'm really surprised he said what he did on the plane."

"Me too," Maddox agreed. "But Mathias is really protective of his family," he glanced down at me briefly, "and he considers you a part of our family."

My throat caught at that. "W-what?"

He grinned, drawing me close so he could press his lips to my forehead in a tender kiss. "You're not going anywhere, Emma."

I closed my eyes, reveling in his words. They were nice to hear. I was falling hard for Maddox and now I was starting to think maybe I wasn't the only one that felt that way.

Once in the parking lot we split up from the guys. The other three headed to Ezra's massive Yukon while Maddox and I made our way to his sports car. My poor little Volkswagen had barely been driven any this summer. I'd probably be lucky if it ran by the time school started.

"You know," Maddox started, buckling his seatbelt, "I've realized something."

"What?" I asked.

"We didn't need these adventures… yeah, they were fun, but we don't need them to have a good time. Being with you is enough."

My heart stuttered, skipping a beat in my chest. Since I was the least romantic person on the planet, I said, "Does this mean we don't have to go on that hike now?" If I recalled correctly the hike was the only thing we hadn't done.

He laughed heartily. "We don't have to do the hike."

"Thank God," I breathed a sigh of relief. "I was already dreading the blisters I was going to get from that."

He smiled at me—and that smile alone made my whole body flood with happiness. I'd never known that my feelings could be so in tune with someone else's, but with Maddox we were in sync.

I knew then that I was in love with him.

This wasn't the kind of love that was fleeting.

It was real and true.

It was a forever kind of love.

This realization didn't scare me—not the way it might have a few months ago. Instead, it made me smile. I'd managed to find the one person on the planet that was absolutely perfect for me.

"Where are we going now?" I asked, laying my head on his shoulder watching the world whip by us through the windshield.

"Does it matter?" He asked.

"No," I replied.

As long as I was with him I knew only good things could be headed my way.

"I've always wanted to come here," Maddox told me, parking the car along the side of the road.

We were high up on the edge of the mountain and I knew that straight down below us was the river.

Maddox slipped from the car, walking to the edge.

I did the same, sitting down so my legs dangled over the side.

Below us I could see people at the water's edge. It was flowing too fast for swimming or kayaking. It was beautiful though—the way the water lapped against the rocks and the greenery of the trees blanketing the area.

Maddox sat down beside me, looking up towards the sky before speaking. "Sometimes I forget just how beautiful it is here." He closed his eyes, letting out a deep breath. "For so long all I wanted to do was get away, and now I can't imagine living anywhere else."

I wrapped my hands around his arm and laid my head on his shoulder. "I know what you mean."

"Do you ever think you'll see him again?" He asked suddenly.

"Who?" I replied, confused.

"Your dad," he whispered.

I shrugged. "I doubt it. Yeah, it sucked that he left, but I'm better off with him gone. If he showed up tomorrow and apologized for everything he's done, then *maybe* I could forgive him and move on… but without an apology, he isn't worth my time. People should own up to their mistakes instead of brushing it under the rug. I *can't* forget about what he did, but I could forgive him if he asked me to—if he proved to me that he deserved it. But I don't think I'll hear from him ever again. I used to not be okay with that…" I trailed off. Refocusing, I added, "But now I am." I lifted my head to look at him. "Why do you ask?"

He shrugged.

"Maddox," I urged.

He glanced out at the water, a muscle in his jaw twitching. "I've been thinking about my mom lately… and wondering if I could ever stomach seeing her again… and I don't think I can. I know the past is the past, but I can't forgive her for everything she did to us. Especially to Mathias. Does that make me a shitty person?"

When he looked at me I could see the worry swimming in his silvery gaze. "Does that make me just like her?"

"No, not at all," I said quickly. "You went through a lot and someone like your mom—I'm sorry, but I don't think they change. Some people are just mean."

"You're right." He cupped my cheek, kissing the top of my head. He swallowed thickly, looking down at the water and kicking his feet against the ledge. "I never want to end up like her."

"You won't."

"How can you be so sure?" He asked, his eyes full of pain. I didn't like seeing him hurt like this.

"Because you're already nothing like her. You're a good, kind person."

He winced, like my words had stabbed him. "I'm a liar."

"No, you're not," I shook my head.

"I am." His jaw tightened and when he looked at me I swore there were tears in his eyes, but the moisture disappeared quickly. "But I can't regret my decisions. I won't."

"Maddox, what are you talking about?" I was completely lost. Where was this coming from?

He shook his head rapidly back and forth. He stood up, extending his hand for me. "Now's not the time."

"When will be the time?" I pestered. Something was really bothering him and I wanted to get to the bottom of it.

He looked away from my eyes and once again stared beyond at the breathtaking view.

"Never."

# CHAPTER TWENTY-ONE

"Happy Birthday to you," my mom sang, barging into my room before the sun was up, "Happy Birthday to you! Happy Birthday dear Emma! Happy Birthday to you!"

August twelfth. My birthday. I was shaking with excitement—*not*.

I threw a pillow over my face and groaned, "Thanks, mom."

My bed dipped when she sat on the end. She pried the pillow from my face. "I was thinking we could go to Marigold's for breakfast. Get some egg sandwiches."

"That sounds good, mom," I yawned. I'd come home late last night from Maddox's. We'd ended up having an all day Lord of the Rings movie marathon in the basement. Even Ezra, Mathias, and Hayes had joined us. I knew from some hints he dropped last night that he had something planned for my birthday, but I didn't know what. I only prayed it wasn't a party. I didn't do parties. Ever.

"Should we invite Sadie?" She asked.

I brightened at that. "Yeah, I'd like that."

"Alright, get out of bed, shower, and get ready." She tapped my foot before standing.

"Is that your way of telling me I stink?" I frowned.

"No," she laughed, "that's my way of telling you your hair looks like a rat's nest."

"Thanks, mom," I groaned, rolling out of bed. "Mornings suck," I grumbled, heading to the bathroom.

"Oh, Emma, don't be dramatic," she sighed, going to the kitchen—probably to make tea.

I showered, making sure to use half a bottle of conditioner on my hair to work out the knots and tangles.

I blow-dried my hair, trying to make it look halfway decent. Most days I just didn't care. But for my mom to comment on it, it had to be looking pretty bad.

I perused my closet for something to wear and ended up settling on my go to of shorts and a tank, but I opted to wear a loose one-shoulder sweater on top. It was cream colored and made my blue eyes appear even bluer.

I grabbed my phone off the night table and sent Sadie a quick text about breakfast. She was quick to reply that she'd go.

"Are you ready?" My mom asked, sitting at the table with her cup of tea.

"Yep," I nodded.

"Your hair looks better," she smiled. "You didn't happen to pull any furry creatures out of there, did you? Or maybe a hedgehog?"

I blushed, remembering the day I thought I'd lost Sonic. "No furry creatures here." I bent over, shaking my hair around.

She laughed at me, grabbing her keys off the kitchen counter. "Oh, Emmie," she sighed. "Are we supposed to pick Sadie up?" She asked, setting her mug in the sink.

I straightened. "Yeah."

She put her keys back down and said, "Oh, I want to give this to you first."

Before I could ask what it was she headed back to her room and returned with a carefully wrapped package.

I sat down on the floor—chairs were for the weak—and started ripping the paper off.

I lifted the lid of the box off and gasped. A pretty floral dress sat on the bottom, but it was the gold watch on top that had my mouth falling open.

"Mom," I choked. I knew, without even picking it up, that it was expensive. "It's so pretty. You didn't need to spend so much."

"I know," she smiled down at me, "but it's your eighteenth birthday and I wanted to do something special. I even had the back engraved."

I picked it up and flipped it over so I could read the tiny letters inscribed on the back.

**Emmie,**

**I believe in you. Always.**

**Love, Mom.**

I stood up, the watch clasped in my hand as the box fell to the side, and hugged my mom. "Thank you so much. I love it and I love you."

She hugged me back fiercely, like she never wanted to let go.

I'd never thought about it before, but it was probably scary for my mom knowing that this was my last year of high school.

It was scary for me too, in the sense that I had no idea what I wanted to do, and I wasn't sure if I was ready to leave my mom. It was terrifying thinking about going out on my own, but it would have to happen one day.

She let me go and I stepped back to snap the watch on my wrist. I was already thinking about wearing my new dress later for Maddox's mysterious plans. I carried the box with my dress back to my room and set it on the bed.

"I'll be in the car!" My mom called, and I scurried out of my room.

When we got to Sadie's house she already sat outside on the front porch steps, her eyes glued to her phone's screen. She looked up at the sound of the car and smiled. She stood, grabbing up a gift bag.

I already sat in the back and I reached over to push the door open so she could join me.

"Happy Birthday, bitch," she said, laughter twinkling in her voice as she handed me the bag and closed the door. I started to grab the tissue paper, but she stopped me. "You might want to wait." Her eyes flickered to my mom.

I paled. "What did you do?"

"Nothing bad," she assured me, reaching for the seatbelt.

"I don't believe you," I hissed, holding the bag out like it was grenade.

"Why do you have such little faith in me?" She sighed. "It's an awesome gift. I just want you to wait to open it."

"Okay," I said slowly, sitting the bag on the floor.

"How are things with lover boy?" Sadie asked.

"Great," I smiled.

She grinned evilly. "Then I got the perfect gift."

Screw waiting. I grabbed the bag, ripping away the tissue paper.

"What the hell?" I held the tiny lacy black bra and panty set in my hands. "No way." I shook my head, shoving it back into the bag. "You are the worst best friend in the history of best friends."

"Hey, just trying to help you out here." She raised her hands in defense. "That bra is a miracle worker. It makes your boobs look twice as big."

I crossed my arms over my chest. "I don't think I need any help in that department, thank you very much," I grumbled.

She laughed, grabbing her breasts. "Well I do."

"Then you can have it." I handed her the bag.

"Don't be absurd," she shoved it back in my hands. "You need some sexy lingerie. There you go."

I glared at the offending bag.

"There's also a gift card in there so you can go back and get more." She waggled her brows. "Because I know you'll want more."

"Stop it," I hissed, my whole face flaming. This would've been mortifying at any time, but having my mom driving the car made it a hundred times worse.

"And," she whispered, "condoms too."

"I need air!" I gasped, reaching to push the automatic button but apparently my mom had the child's lock on. "Air, please," I begged, trying to roll down the window with my bare hands. I wasn't opposed to jumping out of the moving vehicle to escape this conversation.

My mom obliged and as soon as the window was down I stuck my head out of it like I was a dog.

Sadie giggled. "Stop acting like you're five."

I wished I could, but I wasn't like her. I couldn't talk about sex as easily. It made me uncomfortable and squeamish.

"I was only kidding, Emma," she groaned, tugging on my shoulder to pull me back inside the vehicle. "You don't need to freak out. It was a joke."

When I managed to compose myself I slipped my head back into the vehicle and my mom rolled up the window. "I'm sorry," I mumbled, glancing at Sadie sheepishly.

"It's okay," she laughed it off, "but you've got to get over it eventually. You're not going to be a virgin forever."

I squirmed restlessly in my seat and whispered under my breath so my mom couldn't hear. "It's not the idea of sex that scares me, it's just talking about it. I feel like it should be a private thing."

"Oh. My. God." Sadie's mouth popped open. "You've already slept with him, haven't you? And you didn't tell me!"

My mom's eyes flicked up to look at me in the rearview mirror.

"No," I sputtered, "of course not." I scoffed at the idea that she'd suggest such a thing. Had I thought about it? Yes. I knew I was ready. I knew he was it for me.

She smiled slowly—like the cat that ate the canary. "But you want to, don't you? That's why you got so embarrassed."

"Shut up," I mumbled, looking away.

"Aw, my best friend is officially all grown up."

I whipped my head in her direction. "And your best friend is really beginning to question this friendship."

"Okay, shutting up now." She mimed zipping her lips and throwing away the key—but the effect was kind of lost when she smiled through the whole process.

"We're here," my mom announced.

I had never been so excited to get out of the car before.

I basically tumbled outside, catching myself before I could scrape my knees on the sidewalk. I straightened, pretending that hadn't happened—but Sadie's snicker let me know she saw.

"Don't say a thing," I growled.

"I wasn't going to." She hid a giggle behind her hand.

I hurried into Marigold's before I could make an even bigger fool of myself.

Two of the three tables were already taken, so Sadie and I snagged the last one, leaving my mom to place our order with Betty.

My mom joined us a few minutes later and crossed her fingers together, leveling me with *the look*. I was a second away from asking her what I did when she spoke. "Since you haven't let me throw a birthday party for you since you were in elementary school, I'm telling you right now that I *will* be throwing you a graduation party next summer. We have to at least celebrate that."

"Sure, mom," I agreed. I didn't need, nor want, a party but it was clear to me that she wanted one, so I'd suffer through.

"We should do a joint one," Sadie chimed in. "We could do something bigger and nicer than two separate parties."

"That's an excellent idea," my mom smiled. They launched into a conversation about all party related things, while I wanted to hide beneath the table to avoid a party that wouldn't be taking place for nearly a year. Actually, the thought of a graduation party didn't give me hives the way a birthday party would. What *really* scared me was the fact that I was going to be graduating and thrust into the real world. I wasn't ready. Not. At. All. Couldn't I stay a kid forever? That would be great.

In no time Betty was bringing drinks and our breakfast sandwiches to the table. "Happy Birthday, sweetie," she told me with a bright smile.

"Thanks." I smiled back.

My stomach rumbled at the sight of the food. I hadn't realized how hungry I was, but now I was starving.

I devoured my sandwich like I was never going to see food again, but I didn't really care.

"I'm stuffed," I declared, shoving my empty plate away from me.

As if conjured by my words Betty breezed over to our table again, this time with an elegant cake on a platter.

"Your favorite," she declared, "lavender cake with lemon icing."

Tears pricked my eyes at the kind gesture. "Thank you so much," I told her honestly. "And thank you." I turned to address my mom and Sadie. "I don't know what I'd do without the two of you."

"Don't make me cry!" Sadie pointed a finger at me, waving her free hand at her face as if the motion alone would dry the tears in her eyes.

I ignored her dramatics and turned to my mom. "Seriously, thank you for putting up with me for the last eighteen years. I know things haven't always been easy, but no matter what you've always been there for me, and I can't thank you enough for that."

My mom clambered out of her seat and wrapped her arms around me. "I love you so much, Emmie. You're the greatest thing to ever happen to me. Never forget that."

I hugged her back just as fiercely. I knew I was lucky to have a mom as amazing as mine.

When we broke apart I saw that Betty had returned with candles. "Shall we light them now?" She asked with a kind smile.

"Absolutely," I nodded.

She stuck eighteen candles into the top of the cake and lit them. The three of them began to sing and then it was time for me to make a wish and blow out the candles.

Only I didn't make a wish, because I had everything I could possibly ever want.

My phone rang and I hurried to answer it when I saw Maddox's name flashing on the screen. He still avoided texting me if he didn't have to. It was one of his quirks I'd grown to love.

"Hey," I answered the phone, sounding rather breathless.

"I'll pick you up at seven. Wear something nice."

I wrinkled my nose. "Are we going out?"

He chuckled. "I'm not answering *any* of your questions, but dress nice, and I'll be there at seven," he repeated.

"I have a car, you know." I put a hand on my hip, getting into a defensive stance even though he wasn't here.

"Yeah, and I'm pretty sure that thing needs to be driven to the nearest junkyard. It has rust all over it."

I gasped. "How dare you mock my car? Daisy has been a faithful companion."

He grew quiet and then his warm laugh sounded over the line. "You named your car Daisy?"

"Well you named your hedgehog Sonic," I countered, then wanted to smack myself in the forehead for such a silly comeback.

"And it's a damn good name—Mathias stop that! You're going to eat it all before we're done!"

"Uh… what's going on?" I asked.

"Nothing," he mumbled. "I've gotta go."

Before I could respond the line clicked dead. I stared down at the screen, shaking my head. What the hell just happened?

Since I still had a few hours before I needed to get ready I played the piano for a while and then read for a bit.

I decided to put a little bit more effort into my appearance than I normally did. My hair was already curly, but I did my best to tame the tendrils so I didn't look like Medusa. I even took the time to put on more makeup. When I finished I swore a different person stared back at me in the mirror.

I checked the time and saw that I had thirty minutes until Maddox was supposed to arrive—which meant he'd probably be here in fifteen.

I put on the new flower print dress my mom bought me. It was navy with large pink and orange flowers. The straps were thicker and thankfully it didn't dip low in the front. A thin brown belt cinched it in at the waist. I twirled in front of the mirror. The smile on my face was one I hadn't seen in a long time—and I knew I owed my newfound happiness to Maddox.

Turning away from my reflection I grabbed a cream colored cardigan, just in case I needed the extra warmth, and slipped on a pair of flats.

My phone rang and before I could say hello, Maddox said, "I'll be there in five."

I shook my head, and hung up, before heading outside to wait on the front porch.

I heard the low rumble of the car's engine before it appeared on the street.

I started towards the car, but he jumped out and held up a hand, "No."

Well then.

He ducked back inside the car and reappeared with a vase full of flowers.

"Those are beautiful," I gasped as he neared me. I grabbed my key and unlocked the door so he could set them inside. "Orchids, right?"

He nodded, grinning. "One for each day we've known each other."

My eyes widened in surprise and my mouth fell open slightly. "Maddox." His name was no more than a gasp on my lips. I was touched beyond words.

He headed straight back into my room with the flowers, sitting them on the nightstand. He appraised them for a moment and nodded in approval.

He whipped back around and his smile nearly blinded me. "Happy Birthday, Em." He said softly, taking my face in his large hands. Before I could respond he angled my head back, lowering his lips to mine in a soft kiss that still managed to flood my insides with butterflies. When he pulled away he placed a tender kiss on the end of my nose. A breathy sigh escaped my lips at the sweet gesture.

He reached down and clasped my hand in his. "I really hope I can make this birthday special for you." With his free hand he glided his fingers along my cheek.

"I want you to love your birthday again, instead of dreading it."

"You're one of a kind," I whispered. Most people wouldn't care the way Maddox did. His heart was so kind and pure, that at times I felt undeserving of his affections.

He shook his head, a small smile playing on his lips. "No, that's you, Em." He kissed my forehead and guided me out of my room and outside. He opened the passenger door for me and before I lowered into the car, he caught me by the arm and pulled me against his chest. "You look beautiful." His breath caressed the skin of my cheek and my body shook from the intensity of my feelings. I felt weak in the knees—and that was something I thought only existed in books and movies.

I swallowed thickly—trying to dam back the flood of emotions I felt—and looked him up and down the way he had me. I don't know how I'd missed it earlier, but he was dressed nicely in a pair of dark gray dress pants, with a crisp white button down shirt tucked into them, topped off with a black belt. He looked absolutely lickable. Yes, lickable.

When I didn't say anything, but continued to peruse his body with my eyes, he grinned wickedly. "Like what you see?" He leaned in, sweeping my hair over my shoulder so his lips could touch my ear. "Because I promise you'll love it even more when all my clothes are off."

I gasped and my arm whipped out to smack him in the shoulder. "Maddox," I scolded, but he simply laughed at me as I slipped inside the car.

I was pretty sure he only liked to say things like that to see what kind of reaction he could get out of me. Next time I was going to call his bluff and tell him to strip.

Oh God.

What if he wasn't bluffing and he actually started to take off his clothes?

I might die.

Of either embarrassment or the sight of his too perfect body.

My cheeks heated at the visual that began to play out in my head.

*Stop it!* I scolded myself, hoping the flush left my cheeks by the time Maddox jogged around the car and slipped in the driver's side. I did not need him asking questions, because when he did I usually ended up spilling the truth.

I buckled my seatbelt and didn't bother asking him where we were headed. It would've been a waste of my breath, because there was no way Maddox would tell me anything.

Since he told me to dress up I figured he was taking me to a fancy restaurant. Not really my scene, but it was the thought that counted.

However, I was surprised when he ended up driving to his house.

"Did you forget something?" I asked, my brows furrowing.

"Nope. This is our destination." He grinned, slipping out of the vehicle.

I scurried out and to his side—terrified that he'd thrown me a surprise party. I prayed to whichever god would listen that there was no party.

He wrapped an arm around my waist and guided my shaking body forward.

*Please, no party. Please. I'm begging you.*

My eyes had squished shut and when he swung the door open and I heard no shrieks of 'surprise!' I figured it was safe to open my eyes.

The guesthouse was surprisingly empty.

I stepped inside, half expecting someone to jump out at me.

Finally I turned to Maddox, my hands clasped together. "I'm so confused."

He smiled, crossed his arms over his broad chest and leaned against the wall. "Did you really think I'd throw you a party after you told me you didn't like that sort of thing?"

I shrugged. "Maybe."

He shook his head, his lips upturned slightly. He stepped forward slowly, like a lion stalking its prey. He took my cheeks between his hands and stared into my eyes. "That would not be the way to get you to love your birthday again. We're keeping things simple."

"Simple?" I repeated.

"Yes," he whispered, brushing his lips lightly against mine. It wasn't even a kiss, just a simple caress, but I still felt it all the way down to my toes.

He stepped back and I looked around, noting that the lights were dimmed and candles were scattered all over the place—already lit. It created a warm glow throughout the space.

"I gave the guys a heads up that we were almost here and they lit them. I don't want you to think I almost burned the house down," he chuckled.

"It's beautiful," I whispered in awe.

"This isn't even the best part." His voice lowered and his hand found my waist, pulling me against his body.

"I-It's not?" I stuttered.

He grinned, nuzzling my neck. "It's only beginning."

With those words he guided me into the small kitchen and motioned for me to sit on one of the stools.

"Birthday surprise number one… you get to watch me make you dinner." He smiled boyishly, backing towards the sink.

"And what will you be making Chef Wade?"

He washed his hands and swiveled to face me. "Your favorite."

"And what's my favorite?" I asked, raising a brow.

"Pizza." He answered with confidence.

I grinned. "I guess I've made no secret of that."

He grabbed a canister of dough from the refrigerator and before he could pop it, I asked, "Can I do it?"

"It's your birthday," he frowned, "you're supposed to sit there and watch me work."

I laughed. "But I want to help."

He grinned, his silver eyes flashing with my words. "Okay," he agreed, "only because it will be more fun."

I hopped up from the barstool and took the canister from his hands. "This is my favorite part," I told him, defending my actions.

He chuckled in response, opening a cabinet and grabbing a pizza stone. "Have at it, Em."

I smacked the canister against the counter and it popped open. I took out the dough, smoothing it onto the stone in a perfect circle.

Maddox grabbed the sauce and toppings from the refrigerator while I worked.

"This was a great idea." I smiled up at him, unable to hide my joy.

He dumped some sauce in the middle of the pizza and grabbed a spoon from a drawer to spread it around. Unable to control myself I stood on my tiptoes, kissing his stubbled jaw.

He smiled down at me. "What was that for?"

I shrugged. "It was because I wanted to."

He chuckled, lowering his head. "And maybe I want to do this." He pressed a light kiss to my lips. Even though it was only a quick touch of our lips it left my whole body tingling… and thinking about the fact that I'd put Sadie's gift to use. Yep. I was wearing the lingerie. But I was never telling her that. She'd be too satisfied with being right.

To distract myself from any possible naughty thoughts I grabbed the bag of cheese and began sprinkling it on the pizza.

I usually only ate cheese pizza, but we ended up adding green peppers, onion, pepperoni, and sausage, before sticking it in the oven.

Maddox set the timer and turned towards me. "How's your birthday so far?"

"Pretty perfect," I confessed.

His grin was infectious. "Good." He reached for his phone and pressed a button. Music began to play from a speaker and he grabbed me around the waist. "Dance with me," he whispered in my ear.

I nodded, lacing my fingers with his as we slow danced through the kitchen.

He lifted my arm spinning me around and into his chest. I let out a giggle, clinging to his neck. I was so full of happiness that I was ready to burst.

He began to sing the lyrics of the song softly under his breath.

He twirled me again, this time dipping me down and kissing my neck. I couldn't wipe the smile off my face, and I didn't want to.

When he stood up straight I tightened my arms around his neck, my fingers delving into the short strands of his hair.

"I love you." I stared into his eyes as I said the words, refusing to back down. Even if it was nerve-wracking laying my feelings out for him, I wasn't going to be ashamed.

His smile was blindingly bright. One hand stayed on the curve of my hip while his other found the nape of my neck. "Say it again." He pleaded with a look of awe on his face.

I leaned closer. "I love you." I swept my lips lightly over his as I said the words. "I love you." I brushed my lips against his jaw. "I love you." This time I stood on my tiptoes so my lips met his ear.

He lowered his head to the crook of my neck and my eyes fluttered closed. "I love you too," he breathed, then placed his lips lightly against the spot where my pulse raced. I shivered at the words. I hadn't expected them to sound that good rolling off his tongue.

For a moment we simply clung to each other, our words lingering in the air.

I loved him.

And he loved me.

I felt complete with that knowledge.

He brushed my hair away from my face, staring into my eyes. He opened his mouth, as if to speak, but silenced himself. With a low growl he dove for my lips. We crashed together, clinging to one another like we were the only thing holding each other up. He fisted the fabric of my dress in his hand, raising it dangerously high. One of my legs wrapped around his waist and before I could move any further he grasped my hips and lifted me onto the counter—all without breaking our kiss. With me sitting on the counter we were now at the same height. He stepped between my legs, grasping my thighs.

"I love you," he murmured against my lips.

I smiled at his words, loving the sound of them.

He placed light kisses along my jaw and down my neck. His lips headed even lower, towards my breasts, but then the timer went off and he jumped away from me like he'd been burned. He smiled sheepishly, running his fingers through his brown hair. He turned away from me to grab the pizza and while he wasn't looking I fanned my hands around my face. Holy Hell that had been hot—in both senses of the word.

He turned the oven off and grabbed the pizza, setting it on a rack above the counter.

After that kiss I'd lost my appetite.

All I wanted was Maddox.

And that was saying something, because I really did love pizza.

He left the pizza to cool and closed the space between us. His palms rested on the counter beside my hips. So close, but not close enough.

He leaned in, peering into my eyes. He tilted his head slightly to the side, his tongue flicking out to wet his lips.

"So, you love me?" He smiled happily.

I wrapped my arms around his neck. "Yes… do you need to hear me say it again?"

His eyes darkened with warmth. "I'll always want to hear you say it."

"Forever?" I asked hesitantly.

He cupped my cheek, smoothing his thumb over my skin. His eyes flicked from my lips to my eyes and he let out a small sigh. "For as long as you'll have me."

"Forever then," I reaffirmed, kissing him.

He broke the kiss before it could get too heated. "I want to give you your present… well one of them," he shrugged. "Wait here," he held up one finger.

He jogged up the stairs and returned a minute later with a package. It wasn't the best-wrapped package, but I wasn't going to diss his wrapping skills, because frankly it was better than anything I could do.

I ripped the paper off—I wasn't one of those people who removed it neatly. I always tore it off like I was an animal.

Beneath the paper was a plain brown box with colored duct tape holding the ends together. "Do you have a knife?" I asked him.

"Oh, yeah." He opened a drawer and handed me one.

I cut into the tape and opened the flaps.

Whatever was inside was wrapped in a thick brown paper. "You really don't want me to see this present do you?" I laughed.

He chuckled, ducking his head to hide his smile. "It came like that."

I lifted the item out and pulled away the paper, smiling at the object.

"I know it's silly," he started, "but it reminded me of us, and you like to drink tea, so…" He trailed off, looking slightly embarrassed. "If you hate it, just tell me, it won't hurt my feelings."

I clutched the mug to my chest. "Are you kidding me? This is my new favorite mug, it has officially beat out Tea-Rex."

He grinned. "Good."

I held the mug out, smiling at the design.

It had two hedgehogs on it, one stuck to the other, with the apt quote of: *I'm stuck on you.*

"It's perfect," I whispered. To some it might've seemed like a stupid gift, but for me he couldn't have gotten anything better.

"Do you want to see your second gift?" He asked, taking the box and paper so he could throw it in the trashcan.

I nodded eagerly.

He took my hand and I hopped off the counter. He led me over to the side of the guesthouse with all the instruments and Sonic's cage… only there were two cages now.

"What did you do?" I gasped.

"Your mom said it was okay…" He scratched the back of his head nervously.

"Did you seriously get me a hedgehog?" I asked, peering into the cage.

He shrugged. "I know I joked about it, but then your mom said you liked taking care of Sonic so I thought you might want one of your own."

"Where is it?" I asked, peering into the cage. I clapped my hands together excitedly. I might not have been able to keep a fish alive, but babysitting Sonic had proved that I could take care of a hedgehog—you know, except for losing him on my bed.

"Sleeping," he replied. He opened the cage and lifted up the little igloo thing, his body blocked the hedgehog from my sight. He gently nudged it awake and scooped it into his hand, slowly turning so I could finally see it.

"It's so tiny!" I squeaked, reaching out for the baby hedgehog.

He set it into my hand and it peered at me for a moment before falling back asleep.

"Is it a boy or a girl?" I asked.

"Boy, that way if you ever want to bring him over he can play with Sonic and we don't have to worry about any babies surprising us."

I laughed at that, gently stroking my finger along the small quills. It was the cutest thing I'd ever seen. "I'm taking your throwaway name and naming him Aquilla the Hun," I declared.

Maddox laughed. "Sonic and Aquilla… that ought to be interesting."

Since Aquilla clearly wanted to sleep I put him back in his cage and fixed the igloo in place. I wrapped my arms around Maddox in a tight hug. "Thank you so much. You've definitely made this the best birthday ever."

He grinned. "It's not over yet."

"It's not?" I gasped.

He shook his head. "Nope. There's more."

"You're spoiling me," I declared.

"Only because I want to. But before I show you the rest, I think we should eat."

I'd completely forgotten about the pizza, but now that he mentioned it I was starving.

He grabbed a pizza cutter and sliced it, placing pieces on two plates.

We sat side by side at the bar and he waited for me to take the first bite.

I let out a small moan. "Oh my God, this is delicious. We should make pizza every day."

He threw his head back, letting out a throaty laugh. "That good, huh?"

"Phenomenal."

He took his first bite and nodded his head in agreement. "You're right. This is delicious. Mom would be proud."

"We should take Karen a piece."

"Tomorrow," he agreed, "tonight is about you."

My body warmed at his words. We finished eating and set about cleaning up the kitchen together. While we cleaned we both sang along to the music he was playing—a few months ago I wouldn't have been able to sing along, but since he had given me his iPod I knew a lot of the songs now. At one point we started dancing again, so it took us longer to clean up than it normally would have, but I didn't care.

Once the kitchen was clean Maddox turned to me and wrapped his arms around my waist, pulling me against his chest. "Do you want your cake now?"

"You got me a cake too?" I asked, surprised.

He shook his head, grinning proudly. "No, I made you a cake." He paused, "Well, we all did. Mathias, Ezra, and Hayes helped too. So I can't promise it's the most delicious thing ever, but we tried."

Tears pricked my eyes. "That's the sweetest thing ever."

He chuckled, "You might not be saying that once you see it."

"Why?" My brows furrowed together with confusion.

"Well…" He started. "I'll show you."

He'd hidden the cake in a cabinet and brought it out to sit it on the counter. "It's yellow cake with chocolate icing—your mom said that was one of your favorites. We tried to make a layer cake, but it fell apart, and now it's kind of a blob."

"It's beautiful," I said.

"Beautiful?" He laughed. "Hardly. I also wrote Happy Birthday Emma on it, but you can't really tell now," he frowned.

"Maddox," I grasped his arm, "this is seriously so sweet. I don't care if the cake is a giant blob. It's the thought that counts."

"Are you sure?"

"I love it," I assured him. "Now stop frowning and let's eat some cake."

"Okay, okay," he chuckled. He stared at the mess of cake and mumbled, "I think we're going to need bowls, not plates."

"You're probably right," I agreed, lifting the glass top off.

He spooned some of the cake into a bowl and handed it to me, doing the same for himself.

"I can't believe the four of you made me a cake." I was still in a state of disbelief.

"It was fun," he shrugged. "Except Mathias kept eating the icing, so Hayes had to go buy more."

"Is that why you were yelling at him on the phone earlier when you called me?"

He chuckled. "Yeah. He wouldn't stay out of it. And then he kept telling us what to do… and laughed when the cake fell apart because we wouldn't listen to him."

"Does that mean Mathias was right?" I giggled, picturing the four guys arguing over the proper way to make a cake.

Maddox shrugged. "Probably. But I'm not telling him that."

Instead of sitting on one of the chairs I ended up cross-legged on the floor. Maddox joined me, stretching his legs out and resting his back against the cabinets.

"This is really good." I licked chocolate icing off my lip.

"Even if it's a lump and not a cake?" He asked with a raised eyebrow.

"That makes it better," I grinned.

We finished the cake and then he took my hand, guiding me to the stairs. "Your last present is up here… it's not really a present, it's…" He shrugged, looking sheepish. "You'll see."

I was very curious now.

At the top of the stairs there were two doors, one on the left and one on the right. He turned to the right one. He swung it open and motioned me into his bedroom.

I'd never seen his room before and my eyes flitted around curiously. The walls were painted a dark gray color. All his furniture was black with chrome accents. His bed was covered with a light gray comforter that was so fluffy I was pretty sure I could get lost in it.

But what took my breath away was in the corner.

He'd made a makeshift tent with twinkling lights strung around it. Blankets and pillows littered the floor and books lined the perimeter.

"You like to read so… I wanted you to have your own spot."

I threw my arms around his neck, kissing his cheek. "This is the best thing ever."

I released my chokehold on him and scurried over to the fort—I was calling it a fort anyway—and dropped to my knees on the pillows. One in particular caught my eye and I laughed. "Anatomy of a Hedgehog," I read on the pillow. Beneath the words was a picture of a hedgehog with lines jutting out. The line pointing to the hedgehog's bottom said, *'curlable posterior.'*

I lifted up the pillow, quirking a brow. "Really, Maddox?"

"There had to be a hedgehog," he declared. "Hedgehogs everywhere."

I put the pillow back and patted the empty space beside me for him to join. When he did I stretched out on my back, staring up at the top of the fort. Now that I was closer I could see that the each of the twinkling lights had a paper star attached to it.

I swallowed down the lump in my throat. "Thank you for the best birthday I could've ever asked for."

His eyes grew serious and he reached out to tuck a piece of hair behind my ear. "Does this mean you like your birthday now?"

"It means I love it," I whispered.

"More than you love me?" He joked, rolling onto his side and sitting up slightly so he looked down at me.

"Never."

He stared at me with an intensity that left me breathless. I'd never had anyone look at me like that before. Like I was everything.

He lowered his head, closing the space between us in tiny increments that drove me wild. When he was almost to my lips he stopped. I let out a small sound of protest. "I'm going to kiss you now," he growled low in his throat, "and I'm not going to stop until you forget your name."

I quirked my lips. "Promises, promises."

He chuckled and brushed his lips against my neck before gently nipping the spot with his teeth. "I always make good on my promises, Emma."

His lips sealed over mine and my back arched off the pillows. My hands sought his shoulders, needing something to hold onto, because I was pretty sure his kiss was about to make me fly away.

He pulled away enough to speak. "What's your name?"

"Emma," I rasped.

He grinned wickedly and kissed me again. Or maybe *devoured* was a more apt description. He nibbled lightly on my bottom lip and then his tongue smoothed over the spot, making me gasp. His hands delved into my hair, pulling slightly—enough that I felt a small sting, but not hard enough to hurt.

I was pretty confident in saying that every time we kissed it got better.

He pulled away again. "What's your name?"

My brows pulled together. "E-Emma?"

"Almost there," he growled.

This time his kiss set my whole body on fire. I felt heated all over and I clawed at him like a wild animal, trying to undo the buttons on his shirt. He broke away enough to rip the buttons off the shirt. Yeah, he *ripped* them. It was actually kind of hot.

He tossed the shirt over his shoulder, not caring that he'd just ruined what appeared to be a very expensive dress shirt.

When our lips collided together I stopped caring about the shirt too.

I ran my fingers along the dips of his abs, wondering how they'd feel pressed up against me with my dress gone.

He grasped my neck, tilting my head back. His hips pressed against mine. I let out a small gasp at the sensation, wrapping my legs around his waist.

His lips moved against mine slowly, leisurely, but with no less passion than he had exuded moments before. There was something infinitely better about this kiss—like we had all the time in the world.

He tore away from my lips, his chest rising and falling with every breath.

"What's your name?"

"I don't know," I panted, "and I don't care."

He grinned triumphantly, having won.

"Don't rub it in," I warned.

"Let me revel in my victory," he chuckled, all too pleased with himself.

I shook my head, my body aching to close the space between us. "Just shut up and kiss me."

Luckily he didn't argue with me.

After all, it was my birthday and he had to listen to everything I said. Right?

His fingers glided down my side, lighting me on fire. He wrapped his hand around my thigh, holding me more tightly against him. I gasped against his lips when he pressed into me.

He placed tender kisses to my neck and my body bowed off the pillows. "Maddox," I panted.

"What?" His voice was equally as breathless. "Tell me what you want," he murmured, tugging my bottom lip between his teeth and letting go.

I closed my eyes, swallowing thickly.

"Look at me," he growled, taking my chin between his fingers. "Tell me what you want."

The look of intense longing in his eyes made me shiver. I was sure the same look was reflected in my own eyes.

"You," I gasped, "I want you."

He lowered his head my chest, his ear over the spot where my heart beat madly.

"Are you sure?" He asked.

My heart sped up and he grinned.

"Positive." I assured him.

He lifted up slightly, staring down at me. I stared right back, refusing to look away.

Whatever he saw in my eyes must've been enough, because he nodded once and then he was kissing me again.

He lifted the dress from my body ever so slowly, like he was unwrapping a gift and wanted to savor every moment.

His eyes perused my body all over once it was gone—taking in the lacy bra and panty set I wore. Right now I was thanking God for Sadie.

"You're beautiful," he whispered, his eyes rising to meet mine, "and I love you."

I wrapped my arms around his neck and pulled him down so I could whisper in his ear, "Show me."

Our lips collided yet again and the rest of our clothes began to disappear.

Right there beneath the cover of the blanket fort and the glow of the starry lights he made love to me.

And it couldn't have been more perfect.

# CHAPTER TWENTY-TWO

My first thought upon waking was: *Man, Maddox's chest actually makes a really good pillow.*

I smiled, slowly blinking my eyes open. He was already awake, smoothing his fingers through my tangled hair.

"Morning," he grinned, kissing the end of my nose.

"Mmm," I hummed, reveling in the feel of his fingers skimming my bare back, "morning."

I cuddled closer to him, burrowing against his side. I never wanted to move from this spot or his arms. Seriously, I would've been content to stay right here forever as long as someone brought us food. Maybe we could sweet talk Mathias into being our butler—although he'd probably try to kill us in our sleep.

"How do you feel?" Maddox asked, taking my chin between his fingers and tilting my head up so I met his eyes.

I stretched my stiff muscles, taking inventory of how I felt. I didn't feel profoundly different like I'd had some sort of awakening. I still felt like me, just a little sore, and happy and in love.

"Amazing." It was the honest to God truth.

"Good," he rubbed his forehead against mine, his hair tickling me. "I was afraid I might've hurt you."

I shook my head rapidly. "No, no. Everything was perfect." *Because of you,* was what I left unsaid.

Maddox had been kind and gentle with me, his patience endless. Last night had been far more than I'd ever expected for my first time. It wasn't something I pictured often, but when I did it was usually dark and awkward and the worst thing ever. But with Maddox it had been so much more and I knew it was because we truly loved each other. That fact alone changed everything.

I splayed my hand on his chest, then began drawing random designs.

I knew that no matter how much I didn't want to leave our fort I was going to have to go home. If my mom was aware I hadn't come home last night I was surprised she hadn't already shown up here knocking down doors. I mean, she was more lenient than a lot of moms, but she was still a mom, so I knew she wouldn't be thrilled about me sleeping over at Maddox's. And she'd probably have a heart attack if she knew what we did. Yeah, parents were probably—okay, definitely— aware of what most teenagers were up to, but it didn't mean they wanted that information thrown in their face.

"I should probably go home," I whispered, almost afraid to voice the words out loud.

Maddox grasped my hand—the one I'd been using to doodle on his stomach— and entwined our fingers together.

"You're right—" I deflated at his words even though it should've been better that he was agreeing with me. "—But I'm making you breakfast before you go."

"Can we make it together?" I asked.

He chuckled, the sound rumbling through his chest, which my ear was currently pressed against. The steady *thump, thump, thump* of his heart was quickly becoming my favorite sound in the whole world. It was like a drum that beat only for me.

"We can do whatever you want." He sat up, the blanket pooling at his waist. His eyes flicked over my body unabashedly taking me in. A blush threatened to blanket my skin but I willed it away. His lips quirked into a half smile, and he leaned down. "I love you, Em." He pressed his lips ever so softly against mine. I was beginning to think I liked these kisses more than the soul scorching ones. There was something about the tender kisses that made me feel even more loved and cherished.

I grasped his hair between my fingers, holding him against me for a moment longer. "I love you too," I whispered against his lips.

His face split into a grin.

I wondered when, or if, we'd ever get tired of the impact of those words.

He stood, grabbing a pair of boxers and jeans from a drawer. He left the belt undone and chose to forgo a shirt—which left my eyes to feast upon his perfectly sculpted chest and arms… I really hoped I didn't get hit in the face with a door this time for looking. Although there were no doors near me so it would be more likely that the fort would collapse on top of my head.

That thought alone propelled me from beneath it and into the middle of his bedroom. I kept the blanket clutched to my body as I crawled around on my hands and knees in search of my clothes.

Maddox stood watching me with his arms crossed over his chest and an amused smile tugging up his lips. "What are you doing?"

"Looking for my clothes." Seriously, where were they? He'd basically ripped them off of me like a mad man so I knew they had to be on the floor somewhere.

Jesus, did he throw them so far that they ended up in another dimension?

"Uh… Em," he crouched down beside me and I ceased my frantic search, "they're right there." He pointed to his bed where they lay folded neatly.

"How'd they get there?" I asked.

"House elves," he replied with a chuckle. Sobering, he said, "I picked them up earlier."

"You were up?" I asked.

"I wanted to lock the door in case Mathias showed up," he shrugged. "He doesn't normally barge into my room but there's a first time for everything and I didn't want him to see you." His eyes darkened with possessiveness. "So I picked up your clothes while I was up." He shrugged.

"Well… thank you," I smiled. I reached for my clothes and saw that he was still watching. "Look away," I growled.

He grinned crookedly, tilting his head. "I've already seen everything there is to see, Em, so don't get embarrassed on me now. Besides, you watched me get dressed," he winked.

Damn him.

I grumbled under my breath and let the blanket drop. I knew I was being silly, but it felt different to be standing in front of him naked now than it did last night. Then we'd been in the heat of the moment, now we were just… us.

My heart thumped so hard that I was sure he could see it pulsing through my skin.

I dressed as quickly as I could, but never looked away from him.

When I was clothed he grabbed me by the waist and kissed me passionately, making my head spin. I forgot to breathe for a moment, so when he let me go I ended up gasping for breath like I'd just run a marathon.

He smirked, clearly pleased with his kissing abilities. He turned and unlocked the door. I followed him downstairs still in a daze. I'm pretty sure that kiss killed a few of my brain cells.

He turned on the lights and I blinked a few times from the sudden brightness.

"What would you like?" He asked, opening the refrigerator. "We have… eggs… and cereal… that's pretty much it breakfast wise."

"Let's make scrambled eggs." I reached around him to grab the carton. "Do you have any bread? We can make toast too."

"Uh… no," he frowned. "I'll go grab some. I'll be right back." He kissed my cheek quickly as he passed, almost as if the gesture was automatic.

While he did that I went to work on making the eggs.

"What the fuck are you doing?" A voice boomed.

I jumped, letting out a small scream. The bowl of eggs I was whisking nearly flew out of my hands but I managed to keep it from making a mess. I turned around to face Mathias.

"Making breakfast, obviously."

"Oh, fuck, Emma. I'm sorry." He squished his eyes shut, and appeared truly apologetic. "I thought you were someone else."

My brows wrinkled. "And who did you think I was?"

"I thought maybe I brought a girl home last night and she hadn't taken the hint to get the fuck out." He yawned, pulling out one of the barstools.

I stared at him, processing his words. "You *thought* you might've brought a girl home last night. Meaning, you don't even *remember?*"

"God, stop fucking yelling at me." He groaned, shoving the heel of his hands against his eyes.

"I'm not yelling," I glared. The unmistakable stench of alcohol wafted off of his breath, flooding me with memories of my dad.

He groaned, laying his head against the cool countertop. "I think I drank too much."

"You *think?*"

"Can you hand me a bottle of water?" He asked. "Please," he added, his eyes softening and his voice less gruff.

"Only because you asked without cussing," I sighed, opening the refrigerator door. I slid one of the bottles over the counter to him.

"Thanks." He gave me a grateful smile.

Maddox returned with the bread and Mathias winced when the door slammed closed.

"I'm surprised to see you up," Maddox said to his brother as he passed, "I thought you'd forgotten what it was like to wake up in the morning like a normal human being."

Mathias' gray eyes flashed with anger. "If I'm not a normal human being what the fuck am I?"

"An asshole," Maddox replied easily.

"Fuck you," Mathias sneered. "And here I thought if you finally got laid you might start being a joy to be around." He nodded his head in my direction.

Maddox's jaw tightened with anger and his fists clenched at his sides.

My cheeks began to redden and the bowl of whisked eggs did drop out of my hands from surprise this time. The gooey eggs splattered all over my legs and I cringed.

Maddox shook his head roughly back and forth. "Don't talk about her like she's nobody."

"Whatever," Mathias shrugged, standing up and grabbing his bottle of water.

He started towards the stare. "It was a fucking joke. Maybe you should lighten up some."

"Nobody is laughing." Maddox glowered, but Mathias never seemed fazed by his brother's anger.

"See you later," Mathias called, disappearing up the stairs and acting like he hadn't just majorly pissed off Maddox.

Maddox turned around to face me and I hastily bent down to grab the bowl. "I'm sorry. I didn't mean to drop it—"

He grabbed the bowl from my hands and tossed it in the sink. "I don't care about the bowl, I care about *you*. Are you okay?"

"Yeah," I shrugged, looking away from his eyes and to the floor.

"Talk to me, Em." He grabbed my chin forcing my eyes to his. "Tell me what's going on in that pretty little head of yours."

I didn't want to voice my fears, because I didn't want to even entertain the possibility that it could be true, but Mathias had already put doubts in my mind.

I squirmed uncomfortably, staring at the ceiling. I mumbled, "Did you just use me for sex?"

He let go of my chin like I'd burned him. "God, no. Em, I can't believe you'd even think that." He shoved his fingers through his hair, looking hurt.

I shrugged. "I didn't think that, not until—"

"My asshole of a brother opened his mouth." He let out a heavy breath. "I love him more than I can even possibly describe, but he always likes to cross the line. He's just bitter, because he doesn't have what we do." He wrapped his arms around me, hugging me to his chest.

I wrapped my arms around him, returning the gesture.

"I hope he finds it one day," I whispered, meaning it.

"Me too." He agreed. "But I'm afraid that day might never come."

Maddox took me home and stayed long enough to help me clear a spot for Aquilla's cage and get him set up in his new home—aka my bedroom. The hedgehog was so tiny and cute—even cuter than Sonic, but I might've been biased.

I lay across my bed now, staring at the ceiling with a giddy smile on my face. Last night felt like a dream, but my sore muscles argued that it was real.

It seemed so unbelievable.

This whole summer did.

I remembered zip lining with Maddox and asking him to kiss me afterwards—cementing our relationship.

I'd started the summer with no plans—and with two weeks until school started it was safe to say I'd had the best summer of my life.

Maddox and our adventures had been completely unexpected, but the greatest thing to ever happen to me.

Still unable to wipe the silly smile off my face I headed into the bathroom to shower. Since I planned on hanging around the house most of the day I dressed in a pair of gray cotton shorts and white t-shirt with a faded design of a butterfly on the front.

I padded into the kitchen to make some tea—planning to use my new cup from Maddox—and heard something clatter in the garage.

I opened the door and poked my head inside. "Mom?" I called. "Is everything okay?"

"Yeah," she responded, "just cut myself. Can you grab me a Band-Aid?"

"Of course."

I headed down the hall to the bathroom and grabbed a Hello Kitty Band-Aid—they were the only kind we had.

The doorbell rang and my mom called, "I'll get it," as I closed the medicine cabinet.

I walked into the kitchen to find Sadie standing beside my mom. "Hi," I smiled at my best friend. I opened the Band-Aid and my mom held her palm out for me to affix it to her cut. "That's probably not going to stay on long," I warned her.

"It'll be fine." She grumbled, heading back into her studio.

I'd have to keep an eye on the cut, though. Once, she'd needed five stitches, and had insisted she was fine. She ended up with an infection.

"We need to talk, *now*," Sadie hissed, grabbing my hand. She dragged me to my bedroom and slammed the door closed. I hadn't noticed it before, but she was livid. I couldn't understand where her sudden anger was coming from. What had I done? "Sit." She pointed to my bed and I suddenly felt like I was in for an intense interrogation.

She then shoved an *US Weekly* magazine into my hands.

With her hands on her hips she glared. "I'm so pissed right now that I can't even think straight. I can't believe you would keep something like this a secret from me. I thought we were best friends! And now I feel like you don't even care about me!" She started to yell, shaking with anger. "We're supposed to tell each other everything and you kept something this big a secret from me! That hurts, Emma. It really does." She frowned, tears clinging to her lashes. She was truly upset, but I had no idea what she was accusing me of and what the magazine had to do with this.

"I'm lost," I told her honestly.

She snorted, looking away. "Emma, you're dating *Maddox Wade*."

I narrowed my eyes. "How do you know his name?" I knew I'd never actually told her—having always evaded the topic. Yeah, that was shitty of me, and I'd willingly own up to it, but I still felt like she was making a bigger deal out of this than necessary. I didn't tell her his name? So what. She knew I was seeing someone and she'd been okay that I didn't want to talk about it. What was with her sudden change of heart?

She looked at me like I was stupid. "He's Maddox. Fucking. Wade."

"Yes," I replied. "That's his name. But I don't know what's so important about his name. I'm so confused right now." I was beginning to panic. What the hell was she getting at?

"Oh my God," she gasped, her hand flying her mouth. A single tear snaked down her cheek. "You don't know, do you?"

"Know what?" I hissed through my teeth, urging her to get to the point. "And why the hell did you shove this at me?" I waved the magazine through the air.

"Turn to page fourteen." She sat down and took it from my hands before I could even flip it open. Once she had it on the right page she handed it to me. "There," she pointed. "See."

I squinted at the grainy picture. "What the hell?" I gasped, my stomach rolling. The picture was grainy, like it was taken on a cellphone from quite a distance, but it was obviously me—if you knew me that is—and Maddox. My head was turned towards him and he looked down at me, both of us smiling. Drumsticks rested in his back pocket and I recognized our clothes from when we sang at Griffin's.

"Read it." Sadie pointed to the caption.

My eyes dropped away from the picture to read:

*Maddox Wade of the band Willow Creek has been spotted with an unidentified female companion that is believed to be his girlfriend. The two were seen together at a local coffee shop in Maddox's hometown. According to our source the duo even sang a brand new original song. Looks like love is in the air, which Willow Creek boy will be next?*

I threw the magazine down, clutching my stomach.

"I'm going to be sick." I slapped a hand over my mouth, running to the bathroom.

Panic snaked through my veins, suffocating me. This couldn't be real.

*Please don't let it be real.*

But it had to be.

The proof was in a freaking magazine.

"Emma!" Sadie cried, running after me. She grasped my hair as I heaved over the toilet. She rubbed her other hand soothingly against my back. "I thought you knew," she sobbed, "I'm so sorry. I thought you knew," she repeated.

I flushed the toilet and stood to brush my teeth. Tears coursed down my cheeks and I could do nothing to stop them. I was so full of rage that I was ready to explode.

I walked stiffly back into my bedroom and sat on the bed. I wrapped my arms around my chest, like I was trying to hold myself together. I couldn't even begin to process this.

"He didn't tell you?" She asked, even though it was unnecessary.

"No," I whispered. "I didn't know." I ripped at my hair and screamed, "God, I was so stupid! It was all right there in front of me and I couldn't see it!"

She handed me a tissue and I used it to dry my face.

"I feel so naïve," I sobbed.

"You can't blame yourself, Emma," she said softly, sitting down beside me. Her thin arms wrapped around my shoulders. "You don't listen to that kind of music, or read magazines. Hell, you barely watch TV and you don't even have a Facebook. You're kind of a mutant freak."

That got a small laugh out of me, but I quickly sobered.

"Seriously, I was so stupid. He plays the drums, has all that music equipment… Sadie," I shrieked, pulling out of her grasp as new tears poured down my cheeks, "he even took me to his special place and guess what it was called?"

"I don't know," she frowned.

"Willow Creek."

"Well, shit. You are kinda stupid," she joked.

"This is insane." I pushed my hair off my forehead and then began to flap my arms. "Jesus Christ, I'm hot."

"You are turning a bit red," she agreed.

Whenever I got angry it was like my temperature heated to two-hundred degrees.

"I can't believe it was right in front of me all this time and I didn't see it. Sadie, I was in the damn car with him and his friends when a song of theirs came on the radio. I made a comment about Willow Creek being from here and none of them even thought to tell me." My voice grew higher in pitch the madder I became. "I feel so used." My shoulders sagged in defeat. "What was I? His fucking plaything?"

Sadie winced. I hardly ever cussed or got this worked up over anything.

I mean, holy shit, my boyfriend was famous. This was insane. This kind of thing just didn't happen in real life. It was like I'd been transported to an alternate universe.

"I don't know," she whispered.

"He told me he loved *me*," my voice cracked. "Now it all feels like a lie."

Every look.

Every touch.

Every kiss.

All of it felt tainted now.

"We had sex," I hissed, "and now he's probably bragging about how he finally fucked me and screwed me over, because I'm the dumb naïve little girl that didn't know he was fucking famous," I shrieked, my hands fisted. My fingernails dug into the palms of my hands, leaving scratches.

"Emma," Sadie looked at me sadly, truly remorseful for dumping this kind of news on me, "what are you going to do?"

I took a deep, calming breath, and squared my shoulders. "What any sane person would do… I'm going to cut off his balls and feed them to his hedgehog."

She sat up, grinning evilly. "I'll help."

I grabbed my car keys off my dresser. "Then let's go."

# CHAPTER TWENTY-THREE

"Come on, start," I begged my car, turning the key. This time—the fifth try—the engine caught.

"Maybe we should take my car." Sadie pointed to the street as I backed out of the driveway.

"I'm not opposed to running him over and I don't think you'd approve of blood on your tires."

"You're right," she stared straight ahead. "I'm really sorry, Emma."

"You have nothing to apologize for. You're the only one to tell me the truth while he hid it from me, and so did Mathias, Ezra, and Hayes. I swear to God if they're there too I might punch them all." I flicked my gaze towards her. "Remind me to thank your brother for teaching me the proper way to punch someone."

She ignored that statement. "Hold up," she clutched the seatbelt, "you mean to tell me you've met *all* of them?"

"Yes," I growled, "those lying, worthless, pieces of shit."

"Is Ezra as hot as he looks in pictures?" She asked dreamily. "He has that gorgeous black wavy hair. God, I just want to run my fingers through it."

"Whoa, whoa, whoa," I shrilled, "whose side are you on?"

"Yours, of course. It was an innocent question," she frowned.

I shook my head, focusing my eyes on the road.

My anger was building by the second, but beneath that I was *hurt*. I loved Maddox and I trusted him too, and that's what pained me the most—the fact that I'd been so blinded by those two feelings that I hadn't been able to see the truth staring me right in the face. People were right when they said love made you a fool.

It felt like an hour had passed by the time we made it to his house, although I knew it had only been minutes.

"Stay here," I growled at Sadie.

"But what if you need backup?" She asked. "I have pepper spray."

I stopped with my hand on the door. "You have pepper spray?"

"My mom bought it. It's in a cheetah print canister." She held her keys up proudly, shaking them so that I saw the can.

I shook my head. "Just stay here for now." I grabbed the offending copy of *US Weekly*, ready to beat him over the head with it.

"Okay," she sat back.

I slammed my car door closed—instantly feeling bad for taking my anger out on an inanimate object.

I marched up to the guesthouse door and reached for the knob. It opened and music blasted me. All four guys were oblivious to me for the moment.

A scream tore out of my throat as I stormed forward. I saw a pair of drumsticks lying on the desk and grabbed one with my free hand, throwing it at Maddox with more force than I thought I had. It connected with his forehead, bouncing off and onto the floor.

The music stopped then as all the guys turned to look at Maddox who'd ceased drumming. He pressed a hand to his forehead, wincing in pain. He glanced up and spotted me, all the color draining from his face. "Emma, I can explain—"

"Explain, what?" I spread my arms wide. "That you lied to me? That you used me? Did you laugh at me behind my back? Did you even care about me at all?"

"Emma," he stood hastily, his stool clattering to the ground, "I love you. Stop this."

"Stop what? Stop telling the truth? You lied to me, Maddox!" I pointed at my chest, inhaling a heavy breath. Tears stung my eyes once more. "I have never felt so betrayed in all my life, not even the day my dad walked out on us and didn't even say goodbye."

He winced at my words, pain coating his features. "I never meant to hurt you."

"But you did hurt me!" I screamed. "Even if this was some stupid game to you, you still owed me the truth!" My chest heaved and I clutched the magazine so tightly that it started to crinkle. He stalked towards me and I shoved the magazine into his chest. He grasped it, not even looking at it. "*This* is not how I deserved to find out." My voice began to soften as the fight left me. "I'm a human being, I have feelings, and seeing the truth laid out to me in a magazine isn't fair." I choked on a breath.

"Guys, can you give us a minute?" Maddox asked.

The three guys shrugged and mumbled a few things, heading upstairs.

Once they were gone Maddox and I stood across from each other, neither of us saying a word.

"I never tried to play you," he finally said, his voice barely above a whisper.

"Then what do you call this?" I spread my arms wide. "This whole thing between us is a lie."

He winced like my words had stabbed him.

"God, Emma," he growled, hurt contorting his features, "it wasn't like that."

"Then tell me what it was like!" I poked a finger against my chest, leaning towards him.

His teeth clenched together, a muscle in his jaw ticking. "I wanted something for myself, okay? Because I'm a selfish fucking prick. The last year has been insane as our band has grown in popularity. *Everyone* wants something from us. And I was sick and tired of feeling used," he spat, tears shimmering in his eyes. "And then I met you and you didn't know who I was and… I felt like me again. I wasn't Maddox Wade the drummer from Willow Creek—I was just Maddox. I *craved* that."

"So, what? You only liked me because I didn't know who you were?" My own words began to slice me open.

"No!" He tore at his hair. "You're making this sound so much worse than it is!"

I flinched. "*I'm* making this worse than what it is?" I sputtered. "*You're* the one that hid your identity from me. I don't even know you!"

"Yes, you do," he took two steps forward, closing the distance between us. He reached up to clasp my cheeks in his hands. I flinched from his touch and he let his hands drop, his eyes haunted. "You know me better than anyone, Em." His voice was soft, pleading with me to believe him. "I've shared things with you that most people don't know about me. I know you don't believe it right now, but you are special to me, and I love you. That isn't a lie."

"Then why couldn't you tell me the truth? Did you think it would matter that much to me? Did you think I'd try to use you?"

"No!" He yelled, his hands flying through the air. "Jesus Christ, that's not what I thought at all! I tried to tell you so many times, I really did, I swear. But I never could. I just… the words would never come out right and…" He took a deep breath. "I was scared," he admitted. I started to reply but he cut me off. "I was scared to death that if you knew who I really was that my fame might push you away, and the last thing I want to do is live a life without you in it."

Tears coursed down my cheeks and I wiped them away as fast as they fell.

"Congratulations, Maddox," I sneered, wanting to hurt him as much as he had hurt me, "now you'll get to find out what your life is like without me."

With that I turned and started towards the door.

"Emma!" He yelled after me. "Please, stop!"

I did. My brain told me to move, but my heart said to stay.

I turned slowly and looked at him over my shoulder. He stood there, hurt shimmering in his eyes, and his fists clenched at his sides. His dark shirt molded to his tense muscles and he looked torn between staying where he was and coming after me.

Finally, he spoke. His voice was soft and cracking. "Loving you is my greatest adventure. Nothing else means anything without you."

"Then I guess you can live a life full of emptiness."

"Emma!" He roared again, starting towards me.

"Don't follow me!" I snapped, yelling at him. "You have no right to follow me! Just leave me alone! You've done enough damage! ... If you follow me I'll kidnap your hedgehog!" Yeah, that sounded like a good threat.

"*Emma*," his voice cracked. "Don't do this."

He fell to his knees and I closed my eyes as my heart ripped in two. I'd never experienced pain like this before and in that moment I swore it would never happen again.

"Too late."

I walked out the door and just before it closed I heard him cry my name again as the guys ran down the stairs.

I hurried to my car and raced away—just in case he did decide to follow.

Sadie stayed quiet, letting me cry.

Halfway home I couldn't see to drive through my tears. I pulled over and wrapped my arms around the steering wheel. My whole face was damp with tears. You would've thought I would have run out of them by now.

"Why does this hurt so bad?" I sobbed, my shoulders racking.

"Because you love him," Sadie whispered.

Her words made me cry harder.

I did love him. So much. And this wasn't fair. I'd deserved to know the truth and he hadn't given it to me. Maybe he was right, and it would've pushed me away, but he hadn't given me a chance. And now he'd betrayed my trust and that's what hurt the most. I gave it all to him and he only gave me half of who he was.

"Do you want me to drive?" Sadie asked softly.

I nodded. "And can we go to your house, just in case…"

She didn't need me to finish. "Of course."

"Thank you," I hugged her, my tears wetting her shirt, "you really are the greatest best friend in the whole world."

She laughed. "Are you just now figuring that out? I should be offended."

"No, I've always known." I assured her.

She let me go, giving me a serious look. "I know it doesn't feel like it right now, but you're going to be okay. Not today. And probably not tomorrow or even next week. But one day you're going to be okay."

"Thanks." I forced a smile but it quickly turned into a frown as more tears assaulted me.

I forced my stiff body from the car and switched places with her.

I laid my head against the window and closed my eyes, but darkness didn't greet me. Instead I saw Maddox falling to his knees calling my name, and my heart split even further.

I knew Sadie was wrong.

There was no getting over this.

Maddox had ruined me.

# CHAPTER TWENTY-FOUR

"Here," Sadie handed me a bowl of soup, "you have to eat something."

I shook my head, burrowing further under the covers of her bed. "I'm not hungry."

"You haven't eaten in two days. Please," she lifted the spoon, "you're worrying me." Her brow wrinkled and her lips turned down in a frown.

"I'll try," I conceded, only because I felt bad for worrying her. I sat up, the blankets pooling at my waist. She tried to feed me, but I glared. "I can do it myself."

"Okay." She handed me the bowl and spoon. "It's homemade chicken noodle soup."

I knew Sadie didn't make it, so that meant—"Did you tell your mom?"

She smiled sheepishly. "I kind of had too. She wanted to know why you were shut up in my room crying all the time."

"Have I really been that bad?" I asked, blowing on the hot soup.

She gave me a look like *are you kidding me?* "Yeah, it's been bad."

I winced. "I'm sorry."

The past two days had been hell. I missed Maddox more than I could describe. My heart ached for him. I'd never experienced a pain like this before—one that seemed to rip apart your insides leaving them raw.

My feelings were all over the place.

I loved him.

I hated him.

I missed him.

It was all so stupid and I was beyond angry.

I couldn't believe that he'd kept something like this a secret from me. If he really loved me like he said he did, he would've told me, right?

Sadie frowned, looking away. Her posture told me she was about to say something I wasn't going to like. She glanced back at me, her forehead wrinkled. "Can't you forgive him?"

I leveled her with a glare.

"He seems really hurt and sorry for keeping it a secret," she looked at me sadly. "Your mom said he's been stopping by several times a day to see you."

"And that's further proof as to why I should stay here," I frowned. "He *lied* to me, Sadie. About something big too. This wasn't like he told me he took the trash out and he didn't. This is… I mean, he's *famous*."

"So?" she shrugged. "He loves you."

I was tempted to throw the hot soup at her. "What happened to you? You were as mad as me," I hissed. "Besides, love doesn't fix everything."

"Well," she smiled sheepishly, "I talked to him. And Ezra too. They were at your house when I went to pick up your clothes. Not that you've changed." She wrinkled her nose and pointed at the dirty pajamas I was wearing.

"I'm *wallowing* and I'll wear what I want," I huffed. "This room is a no judgment zone."

"I think you're forgetting that this is my room, and therefore I can boss you around. Finish eating," she patted my leg, "then shower and change, please. I'm sick of seeing you so sad and maybe a shower will liven you up a bit."

I hated to tell her, but nothing was ever going to make me feel better.

"Yeah, sure." I agreed.

"I'll be back in fifteen minutes," she warned, eyeing me as she headed towards the door, "and if you're not in the shower I'll drag you there."

"I hear you," I grumbled. I paused, tilting my head. "I think maybe I should just go home."

She halted in the doorway. "Are you ready for that?"

I frowned. "He might show up, but it's not like I have to see him. I can't stay holed up in your room forever. I have to face this." My words sounded stronger than I felt.

She grasped the wooden doorframe, looking at me sadly. "I really think you should talk to him again."

"No," I hissed. The amount of venom in my tone surprised her.

She sighed, shaking her head. "Can you really blame him, though? For keeping it a secret? The guys deserves to have someone love him for who he is, not what he does. That's all he wanted, Emma."

"Stop it," I hissed. "I don't want to hear this." I needed my best friend to be on my side and she clearly wasn't.

"You don't want to hear it because you know I'm right."

I grabbed a pillow and threw it, but she was already gone and it thumped pathetically to the floor after colliding with the closed door.

I started to cry again—that's all I seemed to do the last few days—and tried to eat the soup. But it was useless. I didn't want to eat anything. I was miserable, and I knew the only way to move past this was to forgive him, but this betrayal cut deep and I wasn't sure I could look past it.

"I was beginning to think I didn't have a daughter anymore." My mom stepped into my room with a cup of tea for me—thankfully not in the cup Maddox bought for me.

"Ha, ha, ha," I droned. I took the tea from her and set it on the table and opened the cage to check on Aquilla. My mom had been tasked with taking care of him for the last few days. I felt bad about that, but I'd needed the time away.

"What exactly happened?" She sat on the end of my bed. "Maddox told me his side of the story and now I want to hear yours."

I sat down too once I was sure Aquilla was still alive, and she began to braid my hair like she used to do when I was little.

I hated that she'd spoken with Maddox. I wished he'd just stay away. When he lied to me he forfeited the right to care.

Even though this was the last thing I wanted to talk about, I started from the beginning, telling her everything—okay, not *everything*, but enough.

She listened, nodding her head and making a comment now and then.

When I was done she stood up and headed for the door.

"You're not going to tell me I should forgive him?" I asked, surprise coloring my tone.

"Emmie," she paused in the doorway, "do I think you should forgive him? Yes, I do, but that isn't my decision to make. You," she pointed at me, "have to make it. Whether you forgive him or not is entirely up to you," she shrugged, "and I'll support you either way."

"This sucks," I mumbled, grabbing a pillow and hugging it to my chest.

She let out a small laugh. "Love is never easy, Emmie. In fact, it can be impossible. But love is always worth fighting for—if it's the right kind of love."

I let out a shaky breath. "This feels like one impossibility I can't overcome."

"That's your choice," she shrugged. "You either love him enough to fight through your pain, or you let him go."

"I *trusted* him mom, and he *broke* that trust like it was nothing." My lower lip began to tremble.

She came further into my room and sat down again. She wrapped her arms around my shoulders and hugged me. "Sweetie, I think you forget that Maddox is just a boy. He's young and impulsive. He thought he was doing the right thing, for him and you. There was nothing malicious in his deception. Can you blame him?"

Sadie had asked me the exact same question.

"I don't *know*." My voice cracked. I was too upset to think clearly and all I wanted to do was hate him, but no one seemed to want to let me do that.

She nodded her head and let out a small sigh. "Just think about things."

I groaned and flopped back on my bed.

I wanted to kick and scream and cry, but I'd already done all those things and knew they did no good.

I loved him so much, and a huge part of me wanted to find him and run into his arms—to beg him to never let go. But I *couldn't*. Not now, and maybe not ever.

I honestly couldn't imagine my life without Maddox, but I was mature enough to know that life did go on, and it wasn't like this was the *end*.

And yet, it still felt that way.

I covered my face with my hands and groaned.

Why did everything have to be so messed up?

Why did my emotions have to be all over the place?

Why couldn't there be some clear answer in my mind?

Forgive him or move on?

It just wasn't that simple though.

Life rarely ever had a clear path set out for you, and this was one of those instances where the path seemed to have completely disappeared and I wasn't sure I would be able to find it.

# CHAPTER TWENTY-FIVE

Five days later and I still hadn't forgiven Maddox.

He'd shown up plenty of times trying to talk to me. The first few times I refused to even see him.

Another time I opened the door and yelled at him before slamming it in his face—sure that after that explosion he'd leave me alone.

He didn't.

Why?

Because he said he loved me—and that tore me apart more than anything else he could have said, because I loved him too, but I was hurting.

*"Please, Emma," he begged, his eyes pleading. "You have to believe me, I love you and I never meant to hurt you. This whole thing has spiraled out of control. Please, just listen to me."*

*"I don't want to listen," I growled.*

*He braced his hands against the front door, barring me from closing it. "I never intended to hurt you. I fell in love with you and it became impossible for me to tell you."*

*"Impossible?" I gasped. "Are you serious?"*

*He winced. "I didn't mean it like that. I just... I never wanted to hurt you."*

*"Stop saying that!" I screamed. "You did hurt me!"*

*He lowered his head and looked back up at me with pain filled eyes. "I'm so sorry, Em. I know you don't believe me, but I am. I'm so, so sorry I didn't tell you. I never meant to keep it a secret, but when I saw you didn't know who I was it just became so easy to pretend that other part of my life didn't exist."*

*Tears pooled in my eyes. I wanted him to shut up. I didn't want to hear this.*

*"Maddox," my voice cracked, "I need you to go away. Please. I can't think straight when you're around. Just give me a chance to breathe."*

*He took a step back and I closed the door.*

*"Please, Em," I heard him say through the door, "please forgive me."*

I needed *time* and he couldn't seem to understand that.

I needed a chance to think things through and let go of this anger. I kept reminding myself that Maddox wasn't my dad. Maddox didn't leave me. He lied. And lying was bad, but he hadn't abandoned me, and I knew in my heart he hadn't played me like I originally believed.

But I wasn't ready to run into his arms and act like nothing had ever happened.

This was *huge*.

Since finding out the truth I'd spent more time watching TV and on my computer than I ever had.

And what I'd learned was Willow Creek was blowing up.

Their EP had dropped at the start of the summer, three of the songs soaring into the Billboard Top 100 and one even going to number one. The level of excitement for their full-length album was insane.

The bottom line was: the Willow Creek boys were famous.

Which meant if I stayed with Maddox, I was going to be thrust into the spotlight.

Hell, I already had. I mean they had a photo of me in *US Weekly*. And eOnline had posted an article about Maddox and me—and my name had been included. How they found that out was beyond me, but I was thanking my lucky stars that no one had shown up outside my house to try and snap a picture.

The whole thing was a lot to process.

The doorbell rang—for the third time today—and I was tempted to chuck the mug in my hand at the door.

I ignored the doorbell, heading back to my room and closing the door. After speaking to him yesterday I had no desire to see him today. If he couldn't respect my wishes for space then I would tell him to leave me alone and that I didn't want anything to do with him anymore—that I couldn't forgive him.

My heart clenched at that thought.

The stupid organ still yearned for him.

It was annoying.

All I wanted was to be able to think clearly and rationally, but I couldn't do that when my heart wanted other things.

And maybe that was the problem, love wasn't rational, it just *was*.

"Emma!" My mom called.

Dammit, she got the door.

"I'm busy cleaning my room!" I called back. It was a pathetic lie, but all I could think of off the top of my head.

"Emma!" She called again. *"Come here!"*

Oh no. She used her stern voice. I was in trouble.

I grabbed Aquilla from his cage and cradled him in my hands. I figured if I was holding the baby hedgehog I'd be less likely to chuck something at Maddox's head.

I padded down the hall, my eyes on the hedgehog in my hands as I cooed at him.

When I stepped into the living room and looked up I promptly took two steps back, shocked to see Ezra, Mathias, and Hayes standing there.

"What are you guys doing here?" I asked, putting a hand on my hip and holding the hedgehog in the other. I felt like they were ganging up on me and I was probably about to endure an intense lecture. *Great.* It was really beginning to feel like no one was on my side. It was unfair. I wasn't the one that lied about who I was. I didn't betray anyone's trust. Maddox did. But everyone seemed to think I should let this go like nothing happened.

Couldn't they see that I was hurt? I felt like I'd had my insides ripped out. The boy I'd fallen in love with had been keeping a *huge* secret from me. He was no longer *Just Maddox.* He was also *Willow Creek Maddox.*

My boyfriend was freaking famous.

Or ex-boyfriend.

Ugh, whatever we were. I didn't even know anymore. It was all so confusing, not to mention exhausting.

"We wanted to talk," Mathias spoke. "Can we sit down?" He pointed at the couch. "Or will you pelt us with a fucking drumstick?"

"Language!" My mom warned as she left the room.

I sighed. "It was in the heat of the moment," I defended. I hadn't apologized to Maddox about that when I spoke with him. I'd wanted to, especially when I saw the bruise on his forehead, but I'd once again been too mad to be sensible.

Today, I didn't feel quite as angry. More sad. Defeated.

And frankly, I was really starting to miss him.

I just felt so conflicted.

It was like my emotions were one big ball of tangled yarn, and I couldn't unravel them. When I tried they just got more twisted.

"It was kind of funny," Hayes chucked, taking a seat. Even sitting the guy was a giant.

Mathias speared Hayes with a withering glare. "She could've given my brother a concussion. I don't find that funny."

Hayes' lips quirked into a smile, and even I had to smile. Mathias' fierce protectiveness for his twin was really quite adorable—even if I felt like throttling said twin.

Ezra sat down between the other two guys. He pushed his wavy black hair out of his eyes. "Why don't we just get to the point of why we're here? Okay?" He asked them.

"Sure, sure." Hayes agreed.

"He started it." Mathias pouted like he was five.

Ezra shook his head, sighing heavily.

Mathias turned to me, glaring. "We're here to talk about the fact that you broke my brother's fucking heart."

"Hey!" I cried, going on the defensive. "I'm not the one that lied!"

Aquilla curled into a ball in my hands, not pleased with my sudden outburst.

"Whoa, whoa, whoa." Ezra held his hands up in a placating manner. "We didn't come here to yell at you or try to make you feel bad," he glared at Mathias. "We just wanted you to hear our side."

"Yeah," Hayes agreed.

"Whatever," Mathias grumbled, crossing his arms over his chest and sitting back. He stared at the wall, his jaw clenched.

Ezra shook his head, his too long dark hair falling into his eyes once more. "We just wanted you to know that all of us wanted him to tell you."

"What?" I straightened. I hadn't been expecting that.

"We like you," Hayes piped in, "you're a nice girl and we didn't think it was fair for him to keep the truth from you."

"But," Ezra cut in, "we also understood where he was coming from."

"I think all of us can agree, that it would be nice to know that someone loves us for who we are. Not that we're rock stars or have a hefty bank account." Hayes shrugged. "So, we did see where he was coming from to an extent. But we also thought that he should've told you early on. You're not like other girls, that was obvious to all of us," Hayes waved his hand to encompass all three of them, "and we thought you might not be okay with this life. And if that was the case, he should've let you go."

Oh God. I was going to cry again. Imagining my summer without Maddox and all our adventures was heartbreaking. Even if I was hurt I would never take back any of those moments for anything.

"Honestly," Mathias sighed, his features softening, "I did get into it a few times with him after this. You shouldn't have found out the way you did. It would've been bad enough if he told you himself now, but seeing it in a magazine," Mathias winced, "I'd feel betrayed too." His eyes darkened and he growled, "But he's my brother and I know how upset he is and he misses you. I might not believe in love, but he does, and he loves *you*. Maddox doesn't let many people in. Remember that." He stood up, looking around the room momentarily. "I'll be in the car if you need me."

The front door closed behind him.

And then there were two.

I eyed the remaining guys across from me. "I don't know what I'm supposed to *do*." My voice cracked. It was doing that a lot lately thanks to all the waterworks.

Ezra shrugged. "All I have to say is, if you do take him back I think you can count on the fact that he'll never fuck this up again. He truly is devastated—he hates himself for not telling you himself sooner. He knows he was wrong, Emma. He's not trying to dismiss that fact."

Ezra stood up and I did too, clasping Aquilla to my chest. I was surprised when he opened his arms to hug me. He was a little shorter than Maddox and leaner.

"I'm really sorry," he whispered. He headed for the door.

And then there was one.

Hayes stood, grinning boyishly. He towered above me, his blond hair shorter on the sides and longer on top. "Come here," he opened his arms and I hugged him too.

When he pulled away he didn't head straight for the door. He paused looking at me carefully.

"We leave for L.A. in three days and I don't know when we'll get back. They didn't want to tell you, because they didn't want you to feel pressured, but I think you deserve to know."

I nodded, swallowing past the lump in my throat. "T-thanks for telling me."

"Always," he nodded. He stepped onto the front porch and caught the storm door before it could close. I stared at him, damming the tears back. "We're a family, Emma, and no matter what, you're always going to be a part of that. Okay?"

I nodded. "Bye," I whispered.

"I'll see you later, Emma."

He seemed sure of that, but I wasn't. I wasn't sure of anything anymore.

# CHAPTER TWENTY-SIX

I sat on the step of my front porch watching a plane fly overhead. I wondered, yet again, if Maddox was on that plane. Flying to L.A. to live his dreams, while I stayed behind and tormented myself with the decisions I had made.

After the guys showed up I expected Maddox to come by again.

He didn't.

Nor did he come the next day.

Or the next.

And today I knew he was leaving for L.A.

*I didn't go to him.* That thought broke my already splintered heart.

*I didn't go to him, because I'm a selfish grudge holder.*

*I just let him leave.*

I wanted to believe our love for each other was strong enough to weather any storm, but this was one of our own making. He'd lied. And I couldn't seem to forgive. But oh my God, I missed him more than I ever thought it was possible to miss someone. I felt like I was suffocating in his absence, like the air was slowly being sucked from my body.

I hadn't had this kind of reaction when my dad left.

The answer seemed obvious enough.

*Go to him.*

But he was gone now.

It was too late.

I'd let things go too far and now it was out of my control.

True, I could pick up my phone and call him, but after a whole week of *this* that didn't seem like enough.

Besides, there was a small voice in my head telling me he deserved more than me. A model. Or an actress. Not a girl who immersed herself in books and classical music. I was *nobody* and he deserved a *somebody*.

*But he wants you.* Another voice spoke up. I wanted to believe that voice so badly, but it was hard. We were so young, and Maddox was famous—I choked on the word—and therefore the odds were stacked highly against us.

*Some things are worth taking a chance.*

Was Maddox worth it?

Yes.

He definitely was.

Oh God.

A cry tore out of my throat and I ran into the house before one of the neighbors thought an animal was dying—because that's exactly what I sounded like.

"Emmie?" My mom called from the kitchen as I ran back to my bedroom. I heard her feet thumping against the floor as she hurried after me.

I collapsed onto my bed facedown, sobbing hysterically. "What have I done?" I mumbled, but it probably came out sounding like whathabidub because my mom responded with, "What was that?"

I rolled over and looked at her with my tear-streaked face. "What have I done?" I choked. "I threw away one of the best things to ever happen to me all because I was angry," I cried, my lower lip shaking, "I feel like dad."

"Oh honey," she took me into her arms, "you're nothing like your dad."

"I abandoned Maddox," I muttered.

She kissed the top of my head. "You didn't *abandon* him. You were upset and hurt, so you did the only thing you knew you cold do to protect yourself and that was to walk away. There's nothing wrong with that."

"I miss him so much, mom," I cried. "I've ruined everything and now he's gone."

"Shh," she hushed me, "that's not true."

I shook my head, wiping away my tears. "They left for L.A. today, and Hayes doesn't know when they're coming back. It's over."

My mom took me by the shoulders, forcing me to look at her. "Nothing is over until you give up. Are you giving up?"

"I don't want to," I answered honestly. "I want to fight for him."

My mom's whole face lit with a smile. "Now there's my Emmie. I've missed her."

"Mom," I groaned, looking away.

"Now we just have to figure out how to get you to L.A." She beamed. I was pretty sure she'd wanted to tell me I was an idiot for pushing him away, but she knew I had to come to this conclusion on my own. Yes, I was hurt that he'd lied to me. Yes, I knew it was going to be hard dating a rock star. But I also knew Maddox was worth it, and that was the only thing that kept me from freaking out.

"But flights are expensive," I mumbled.

She gave me a stern look. "Don't play dumb with me. We both know you want to do this in person and that boy deserves more than a phone call from you." She looked away, frowning. "I don't think I've ever seen someone look so heartbroken." I opened my mouth to tell her that I'd certainly been heartbroken, but she cut me off. "He looked even worse than you, so don't start with me."

"You like him," I laughed.

She smiled. "He's a nice boy and I can see he loves you. That's all I've ever wanted for you, Emma—to be happy and have someone love you the way you deserve to be loved. I never wanted to see you go down the same path as me." She patted my knee and stood up. "I'll see if I can book you a plane ticket."

"No, mom," I shook my head. I held up a hand when she started to retort. "No," I said in a firm tone, "I want to do this on my own. I can take care of it. This is my mess and I'm going to clean it up."

She smiled. "I'm so proud of you, Emma."

I snorted. "I don't think there's much to be proud of."

"That's because you don't see what I see."

She disappeared down the hall and I grabbed my phone. I'd never called this number before, but I knew he was my only hope.

"This is Mathias," he answered on the last ring.

"I need a favor," I whispered, like as if Maddox might here me over the phone.

I heard some shuffling and what sounded like a door closing. "I'm listening."

"I need a plane ticket to L.A. I'll pay you back, I swear."

Mathias didn't smile often, and even though I couldn't see him I was positive he was smiling then. "Text me all your information and I'll have the ticket sent within an hour. A driver will pick you up too."

"Thanks," I sighed in relief. I'd been terrified that I'd waited too long and Mathias wouldn't want to help me. "I'll need someone to pick me up when I get there too."

"I'll take care of it," he assured me. "Just make sure you get here."

"I can do that," I nodded.

"And Emma?"

"Yes?" I questioned hesitantly.

"If you break his heart again I won't be quite as nice."

"Understood."

"And since I'm not a one-sided bastard, if he hurts you again I'll punch him for you—no more projectiles on your part, m'kay?"

I laughed. "You've got a deal."

"See you soon." He hung up.

"See you soon." I whispered into the air, a grin transforming my face. I was going to get Maddox back.

*But what if he doesn't want you now?*

If he didn't, then I'd just have to live with my choices—even if it killed me.

"Holy shit," Sadie exclaimed, staring at the limo. The driver opened the door for me to slip inside, but Sadie cut me off and dove into the interior. "Emma! There are twinkling lights that look like stars on the ceiling! This is the coolest thing ever!"

I poked my head inside the door. "I called you to come over so I could say goodbye. Not so you could fawn over the limo." Mathias, unfortunately, hadn't been able to get me a plane ticket for yesterday, but I had a morning flight today.

"Right, sorry," she frowned, sliding over the seats and climbing out. "Are you going to be back before school starts?" She asked.

It was Saturday morning and school started on Tuesday.

"Of course," I replied.

She nodded and wrapped her thin arms around me in a tight hug. "Go get your man back." She slapped my ass as she walked away.

"Sadie!" I shrieked.

She simply laughed, backing away from the limo while giving me two thumbs up.

My mom stepped forward and I hugged her for as long as I could. I didn't want to let go—because this moment seemed symbolic. It was the first time I was ever really leaving my mom to go out on my own, and in a matter of months I would be graduating from high school and moving on with my life.

"Don't get into any trouble," she warned me. "I'm not bailing you out of jail."

I laughed under my breath. If only she knew.

"I'll see you in a few days," I told her.

"I'll miss you." Tears shimmered in her eyes and I wondered if she was thinking the same thing as me—that one day soon I'd be leaving home for good.

"I love you, mom," I smiled, slipping into the limo. "Don't miss me too much!" I yelled after Sadie who was hanging beside her car.

"Pssh, miss you? Never!" She cackled.

I nodded at the driver and he closed the door.

I sat back and closed my eyes.

I was about to get on a plane—and I'd never even flown before—to go across the country for a *guy*.

If someone told me that three months ago I never would've believed them.

Fate, it really was something else, wasn't it?

I stepped out of the airport doors, searching for Mathias'.

A hand rose in the air, and I glanced over, smiling when I recognized him. I moved through the crowd, my suitcase bumping behind me.

He leaned against a sleek black Cadillac Escalade, a navy blue baseball cap turned around backwards on his head. He was dressed casually in a pair of workout pants and shirt.

"Here let me take that." He reached out for my suitcase and put it in the trunk.

We climbed into the back of the Escalade. It was being driven by—

"Is he a body guard?"

"No, that's my boyfriend Hank," Mathias deadpanned.

The burly black man chuckled. "You wish, kid."

"I'm shocked he let you out of the car," I mumbled, looking out the window, taking in the palm trees and sunny skies.

"Hank and I have an understanding—he lets me do whatever the fuck I want—"

"Within reason," Hank piped in.

"And I pay his bills. He also keeps the grabby people away which is nice," Mathias shrugged. "Ezra had some girl try to cut off a piece of his hair. There are some psychos out there."

"Uh… that's… scary."

"Are you sure you can handle it?" His eyes glimmered with challenge.

I squared my shoulders, leveling him with a glare. "Of course I can." I knew it was going to be a huge adjustment—especially still being in high school—but there wasn't a doubt in my mind that didn't think Maddox was worth it.

Being without him had shown me just how powerful my love for him was. It wasn't going to go away, not ever, and I was going to fight for our happily ever after. I refused to think that I might live a life without him. I knew there would be ups and downs for us, and there was no telling what surprises the future may hold, but it would all be worth it.

"Where is he?" I asked, my eyes widening at the sight of the Pacific ocean.

"Photo shoot," Mathias replied. "That's where I'm supposed to be."

"Dressed like that?" I eyed his workout clothes.

"Hey, I showered," he pointed a finger at me, "besides, they'll have wardrobe for us."

My hands began to shake with nerves and I chewed on my bottom lip.

"Hey," Mathias said, placing his hand on mine. I turned to look at him and was surprised to see the compassion in his steady gaze. "It's going to be okay, trust me."

It might've seemed like an odd thing to trust brooding, anger-filled, snarky Mathias, but I did.

I nodded. "Okay."

While I believed him, that didn't take away my nerves. The last few times I saw Maddox I'd been less than friendly. I'd avoided him and snapped at him. And been a downright bitch.

If I were him I wouldn't forgive me so easily.

But I guess we were both in the wrong. Him for lying, and me for not listening to him.

I believed we could move past it, though.

He'd tried to reach out to me and I'd iced him out.

Now it was my turn to make this right.

"We're here," Hank said, the Escalade coming to stop.

I looked at the plain square gray building. It hardly seemed like the place for a photo shoot, but what did I know.

Mathias and I climbed out of the vehicle. He pulled a lanyard out of his pocket with some kind of ID badge on the end.

"Come on," he put a hand on my back, guiding me forward. Hank trailed behind us, the silent protector.

He led me through a winding hallway and down some steps.

He stopped outside another door. "You ready?"

"Absolutely." I rubbed my hands together.

He swung the door open and nodded his head for me to go in. I could hear the clicking of a camera and saw lights blinking. I really hoped I didn't get in trouble for this.

"Go," Mathias urged, waving me on.

I nodded and took two steps inside. He followed me and veered to the left. I started to follow, but he held up a hand to halt me. He pointed over his shoulder to where Ezra and Hayes sat on a couch. When they saw me they both perked up grinning from ear to ear. Ezra gave me a thumbs up and Hayes flashed an encouraging smile.

"That way," Mathias hissed, waving me in the other direction that was blocked off by a white sheet of some sort.

I turned my back on the guys and took one step forward and then two.

And then there he was.

He didn't see me at first, since he was listening to the photographer's instructions. I watched him for a moment at how effortless it all seemed for him as he posed with his drumsticks over his shoulder. He was looking away from me at the moment, but then he lifted his head and his mouth parted in shock.

"Emma?"

He said my name hesitantly, like he was afraid I was a ghost his mind had conjured and with the one word I might disappear forever.

"Hi." I waved weakly. I was frozen in my spot, my feet refusing to move forward.

The photographer looked over his shoulder and spotted me, his brows wrinkling in confusion.

"Can you give us a moment?" Maddox asked the man.

He mumbled something unintelligible, the tone coming across as harsh, and grabbed his camera bag as he headed out of the room.

"What are you doing here?" He asked, tucking his drumsticks in his back pocket.

"I-I came to see you," I whispered, terrified to close the space between us, because I feared his rejection.

"To see me?" He pointed at his chest. "Why? Because I got the impression that you never wanted to see me again." He looked away momentarily, trying to hide the sadness in his eyes from me.

I shook my head rapidly back and forth. "I was confused and hurt. I shouldn't have been the last to know, Maddox. *You* should've told me. Instead you made me feel like I was an insignificant part of your life and didn't deserve to know the truth."

"It was never like that," he winced in pain. "It wasn't my intention to keep the truth from you, it just happened. I liked spending time with someone that only wanted to be with me for me. The more time that went by the harder it became to find the words to tell you. I'm so sorry for that. But I don't, for one minute, regret it. I wouldn't take back every moment I got to spend with you for anything." He took a step forward. "And you're right, you shouldn't have been the last to know about me—not when the whole world already knows who I am," he grinned.

"Don't get cocky," I narrowed my eyes.

He chuckled, taking another step closer to me.

"But you know what, Emma?" Another step.

"What?" I asked, my eyes zeroing in on his hips.

Another step.

And another.

And then his sneakers were pressed right up against my boots. He reached up, smoothing his hand down my cheek. He leaned forward, his lips pressing against my ear. "You really aren't the *last to know*, because you're the only girl that knows the *real* me, and you're the only one I'll ever *love*." He pulled away, grasping one of my curls between his fingers. "Forgive me?" He pleaded, his eyes sincere.

Tears shimmered in my eyes. "You already were."

He grinned at my words. "Does that mean I get to kiss you now?"

"Since when do you ask?" I laughed.

He took my face between his hands. "Good point."

He closed his mouth over mine and wrapped me in his arms.

I heard the guys let out whoops and cheers, making me smile into Maddox's kiss.

"Welcome home, Em," he whispered, his fingers curling into my hair.

I grinned at his words, my whole body humming with happiness.

He was right.

I was home.

Right here in his arms.

"This is stupid," I groaned, "I don't even want to go." I complained, wincing when Sadie brushed through a knot in my hair.

"Shut up. It's prom. You're going. Even Maddox insisted upon it." She braided some strands of hair, pulling them back into a bun.

"I don't see why Maddox's opinion matters here, he's in L.A., so he shouldn't get to vote on whether or not I go. This isn't my thing," I insisted, eyeing the dress hanging on the back of my door. At least it wasn't that bad.

I'd picked it out on a shopping trip with Sadie and our moms. It had thin spaghetti straps, and dipped down into a V shape in the front—but luckily stopped before it became too revealing. The top was a light peach color fading into blue and purple in an ombre effect. It cinched in at the waist before flowing down. It wasn't a big ballroom dress or anything too flashy. It was simple and pretty.

"This is our senior prom, and I have forgone a date as a favor to *your* boyfriend, so that we can go as friends. So suck it up, princess." She stuck a flowered headband on my head.

"But everyone will stare at me," I mumbled, looking down at my lap.

This school year had been *awkward* to say the least. Everyone knew I was dating Maddox, so I'd gone from a nobody to the most popular girl in school in a matter of seconds. Everyone wanted to be my best friend in the hopes of getting close to the Willow Creek boys. It was annoying the lengths some people would go to, to try to get close to me. Luckily, I had Sadie, and she kept the crazies away with her cheetah print pepper spray. She made a good sidekick. Actually, she was probably the superhero while *I* was the sidekick, but I was okay with that.

She finished fiddling with my hair and stepped back. "Hair and makeup done." She clapped her hands together. "Now go put on your dress so I can see what the final product looks like."

"Yes, ma'am," I saluted her. I grabbed my dress off the back of my door.

She'd already changed into her dress—a pretty pale pink dress with silver detailing. With her tan skin and brown hair it was stunning.

I changed into my dress and turned to eye my reflection in the mirror.

"What do you think?" I turned to Sadie so she could see it from the front.

"If I were a lesbian I'd totally date you."

"Thank you," I rolled my eyes.

"Hey, that's a high compliment. There aren't many girls I'd switch teams for."

"Just stop talking," I told her, suppressing a laugh.

Sadie checked her phone. "We better get out of here."

"I thought we were supposed to be fashionably late?" I repeated her words from earlier.

"Emma," she eyed me, "we're already fashionably late. Prom started over an hour ago."

"Ohhh," I frowned. "I didn't know."

"Obviously," she laughed.

I followed her out into the living room where my mom and her parents waited. After snapping more than enough photos it was time for us to leave. We'd planned on just driving Sadie's car, but when we opened the door a limo sat parked on the street.

"Maddox," I smiled, sighing dreamily.

Sadie groaned. "I hate it when you get that dopey look on your face."

"You're just jealous that you're not in love."

"It's true," she shrugged. "One day. I hope."

"It'll happen," I assured her.

"Miss Burke," the driver called, opening the door.

Sadie and I hurried forward—well, as fast as we could go in heels.

A small part of me hoped that Maddox would be waiting for me in the limo, but of course it was empty. We'd facetimed earlier and it had been good to see him. I hated that he was so far away in L.A. I'd flown out at Christmas—my mom had been okay with it since Karen and Paul were there—and while I was in L.A. Maddox had dragged me to the recording studio so that we could record our duet. It was one of my fondest memories. And thanks to Maddox I no longer was scared of what the future held after graduation. I knew what I wanted to do, and that was to write songs. I didn't feel this impending fear when I tried to see my future. Instead, I felt peace.

The drive to the hotel where prom was being held was short, and my nerves started up once more. I *hated* being stared at, but I knew that's what I should expect. I already experienced it every school day in the halls.

"Show time." Sadie called, bounding up the steps of the hotel while I trudged along like a fifty-pound weight clung to my ankle.

We stepped into the ballroom, a really loud techno song playing in the background. Blue lights pulsed, giving the ballroom a club vibe.

I watched the way some of our classmates danced and wrinkled my nose in disgust. Um, ew.

"Come on, let's dance," Sadie dragged me onto the dance floor with our classmates. A few eyed me, but surprisingly most people seemed oblivious to my presence. I guessed their minds were otherwise occupied for the night. Thank God.

Between the dancing and the heat of the packed bodies it didn't take long for a fine sheen of sweat to coat my skin.

"I'm going to go get water," Sadie said, backing away from me. "You want some?" She asked, but was looking over my shoulder. I turned to see what she was looking at, but didn't see anything besides our classmates.

"Yeah, get me water," I told her, but when I looked back she was already gone, having abandoned me.

*Great.*

I started to dart off the dance floor, but was halted in my tracks when a familiar song began to play on the speakers.

A song that—as far as I knew—hadn't been released to the public yet.

I whirled around, trying to find the DJ—to demand to know how he got his hands on *my* song—and instead collided with a very solid chest.

"Whoa, Em. You're going to give yourself whiplash."

My heart skipped a beat and I closed my eyes, scared to believe it was really him.

"I'm here," he whispered, his fingers skimming along my neck and down my arm. "You can open your eyes now."

I did and was met with a silvery gaze. "H-how?" I stuttered. "I thought you were in L.A. this morning?"

"Did you really think I was going to let you go to prom without me as your date?" He asked, raising a dark brow. I noticed that instead of a tux he wore a crisp button down white shirt, a black bow tie, and black pants. I was sure that if I looked he'd even have his drumsticks in his back pocket.

"Well, yeah," I finally replied.

"Oh, Em." He grinned, shaking his head. "Why do you ever doubt me?"

I eyed him.

"Right," he chuckled.

"The song?" I asked, lifting a hand in the air as if I could touch the notes and our words.

He grinned. "The record label agreed to put it on our album as a bonus track."

"Are you serious?" I asked, my eyes threatening to bug out of my head.

"I wouldn't joke about that, Em."

I squealed and threw my arms around his shoulders, squeezing him tight.

"Careful." He wiggled away, reaching into his pocket. "You might squish Sonic."

My mouth fell open. "You brought your hedgehog to my prom?"

"Of course. Sonic deserves to go to prom too," he grinned, lifting the hedgehog onto his shoulder. "Look, I even knitted him a bow tie." He pointed to the item dangling around the hedgehog's body.

I dissolved into a fit of laughter.

Maddox simply grinned at my amusement. I think it was his goal to make me laugh as many times as he could in a day.

"Can I have this dance?" He asked, holding out his hand.

I looked from the hedgehog into his silvery eyes. "Yes, and each one after it."

His smile was blinding as he wrapped a hand around my waist and pulled me against his body. We swayed with the music—our music, and I smiled as I imagined all the adventures that were yet to come.

# THE END

# BONUS CONTENT

**Interviewer:** It's so nice to sit down with the both of you today. Your song *My Only* is climbing up the charts. Many people didn't know that you could sing Maddox. Is there anything else you're holding out on telling us? Any hidden skills?

**Maddox:** I'm a very skilled kisser. Like the best in the world.

**Emma:** Shut up.

**Maddox:** What? You don't agree? You've always seemed pretty impressed with my skills to me. I mean, it's not like I've ever made out with myself to know, but you always make these little noises—

**Emma:** I hate you.

**Maddox:** That's not what you told me last night. I'm pretty sure you told me you loved me and called me a God.

**Emma:** I'm leaving. You can finish the interview by yourself.

**Maddox:** Aw, don't go, Em.

**Interviewer:** <clears throat> Can you tell us how you got the idea for *My Only*?

**Maddox:** I think that's pretty obvious. She's the only one for me and I'm the only one for her. Case closed.

**Interviewer:** Are there any plans for a wedding in the future?

**Emma:** Uh… no. I'm only nineteen. There will not be a wedding anytime soon.

**Maddox:** Don't you want to marry me, Em?

**Emma:** Eventually.

**Maddox:** I can live with that.

**Interviewer:** Looks like we're out of time. Congratulations on the success of *My Only* and the whole debut album.

**Maddox:** Thanks man. <turns to Emma> I think I need to show you just how amazing my kisses are.

**Emma:** Oh God. You have that look that says I'm in trouble.

**Maddox:** <laughs> Oh you're definitely in trouble.

**Emma:** <screams and runs out of the room>

**Maddox:** You can run, Em! But I'm always going to catch you!

# MICALEA SMELTZER

- A WILLOW CREEK NOVEL -

"Music washes away from the soul the dust of everyday life."
—BERTHOLD AUERBACH

# CHAPTER ONE

I never thought I'd end up back here.

Back in the place where my whole life blew up into a million tiny pieces.

When we drove away with the moving truck in tow I thought I was saying goodbye to this part of my life forever.

I'd been wrong.

Anger simmered inside my veins—anger at the boy I'd loved and lost here. He'd discarded me like I was a piece of trash, just when I needed him most. I was nothing to him.

Back when we were sixteen he'd been nothing but a bad boy with a scowl on his face.

Now, Mathias Wade was the lead singer of Willow Creek—one of the most popular bands in the world.

I couldn't escape him.

Everywhere I looked his face was on a magazine, or one of their songs played on the radio.

At twenty-three years old I should've been over him.

I guess to an extent I was, but the pain and anger had never gone away.

Now I was back home, and according to the copy of *People* magazine clutched in my hand so was Mathias.

The pages of the magazine began to crinkle where I gripped it tightly.

I wanted to throw it down and stomp all over it—on *him*, just like he had done to me.

I wanted him to feel even a smidge of the pain I'd felt when he broke my heart into a million pieces.

I was convinced that once you fell in love with a Wade you could never stop loving them.

He should've been nothing more than the boy I loved as a teenager, but he wasn't.

He was everything.

And I was nothing to him.

"Ma'am?"

I startled at the sound of the cashier's voice.

"Do you want the magazine too?" She asked.

I'd basically mauled the poor magazine into oblivion so it would've been rude to put it back on the shelf. "Yeah." I handed it over. The way I figured it, I could burn it and chant some kind of spell that would turn him into a toad.

I swiped my credit card and she handed over the bag full of cat food, and the magazine.

I'd only gotten back into town last night and realized I didn't have cat food.

Percy was not pleased.

I made up for it by giving him too many treats.

He still wasn't happy with me, but at least I felt better.

I made the short drive home—still fuming over Mathias.

I couldn't believe that he was back in town. Although, I guess he never really left—according to the tabloids anyway. All the Willow Creek boys kept places in their hometown of Winchester, Virginia, even if they did spend a lot of time in L.A.

I pulled into the driveway, staring over at the plastic bag on the passenger seat.

I'd never finished reading the article, and now I was desperate to know everything it said.

I warred with myself, but finally I ripped the magazine from the bag and flipped through the pages.

Basically, the gist was that the guys were home for the holidays before their Coming Home Tour kicked off in the New Year.

I ran my finger over the picture of the four of them. I didn't know the blonde one, but I knew Maddox—Mathias' twin brother—and their best friend Ezra. While I'd mostly hung out with Mathias the other guys had been nice to me.

Even with the anger simmering in my veins I couldn't hate Mathias' success. I'd always wanted that for him. When we were young he'd never seen his own self-worth, but I'd always known he was remarkable. I hoped he saw that now too.

I still hated his fucking guts though.

I startled at a noise and realized I'd ripped apart the magazine.

*Oh well. There goes another one.*

Sadly, it wasn't the first time I'd torn apart a magazine because of Mathias.

I gathered up the torn shreds and put them in the plastic bag. I climbed out of the car, drawing my coat closer around me. After living in Arizona the last seven years I'd forgotten how cold it got here.

I stepped into the older home—inhaling the scent of freshly baked chocolate chip cookies.

"Grandma!" I called as I locked the door. "You're supposed to be in bed!"

"I wanted some cookies," she called back, "so I'm making some God damn cookies and no one can stop me."

It was safe to say I got my fiery personality from my grandma.

I stepped into the kitchen and set the grocery bag down on the granite countertop—my parents had paid for the whole house to be remodeled a few years ago.

I kissed my grandma's cheek. "Here, let me help." I took the bowl from her so I could mix it. "Go sit down and I'll finish this."

She glared and yanked the bowl from my hands with surprising strength for someone as small and frail.

"Grandma!" I admonished. "You're supposed to be resting. You had a heart attack."

"And yet I'm still here. It's going to take a whole lot more than a faulty heart to knock me down," she huffed.

"Like what?" I asked, hiding a smile.

She thought for a minute, turning her head to the side. Her white hair was fluffed around her head and her duster hung limply on her frail frame. "Hmm, that chick that's always sticking her tongue out on a wrecking ball. *That's* what will knock me down."

I busted out in laughter—not only at the visual that had formed in my head, but also at the fact that my nearly eighty-year-old grandma knew who Miley Cyrus was.

"Grandma, how do you even know that?" I asked, leaning a hip against the counter. Percy—my black cat—rubbed against my legs.

"I watch MTV. It's the most entertainment I get during the day," she frowned. Looking up at me she said, "I saw that young man you used to hang around on there one day. He was a bad influence on you."

I rolled my eyes. "I think we were an equally bad influence on each other."

She stared at me in disbelief and finally shrugged her thin shoulders. "You go finish unpacking your room while I do this."

"Grandma," I groaned, "if I do that then I'm already failing at taking care of you."

"And like I told your over protective father, *I'm fine.* I don't need a babysitter." She grabbed a spoon from the drawer and waved it around. "Besides, something is going to kill me eventually. I can't live forever."

"Aw, grandma, and here I thought you were invincible."

"The wrecking ball will get me one day," she winked. She began to spoon out the cookie dough onto a pan. "It's nice that you and your parents are worried, but I've been getting by fine on my own for years and I'll continue to do so." She glanced up at me. "You're young, Remy. You need to live your life, not take care of me. Go get a job, meet a guy, and have some fun."

I frowned.

"And give me some great grandbaby's before I die," I flinched at the mention of babies. "That's an order." She flicked the spoon at me and a glob of cookie dough landed on my shirt. I grabbed it and popped it into my mouth.

"You know my dad will kill me if I don't keep an eye on you." I warned her.

"Your dad is all the way in Arizona, what he doesn't know won't kill him."

I wasn't really into the idea of dating (or babies) but a job would be nice. I'd already been groaning about how boring it would be lazing around here day in and day out.

Back home I'd been working as a receptionist. I hated it. I wasn't a desk job kind of girl. I wanted to be moving.

I had a degree in marketing, but I'd never done anything with it—much to the irritation of my parent's. I'd only gone to college and studied that because I knew it was what they wanted and I'd been trying to please them. They'd never really understood me. They both had high paying jobs—my dad a doctor and my mom a lawyer—and then my big brother was an attorney. They never made me feel like I wasn't loved, but I knew they never really got me.

I was wild and spontaneous.

I was loud and obnoxious.

I was the girl that wasn't afraid to be crazy.

I'm sure my dad would bust a vein in his forehead if he knew some of the craziest things I'd done.

Like that one time I road tripped to California by myself and went diving with sharks.

Or the time I was riding in the back of a friend's truck and ripped my top off, letting my boobs fly free for the whole world to see.

Yeah… it was a good thing my dad didn't know these things. *He'd* be the one headed to the grave, and not grandma.

"Alright, I'll go finish unpacking and see if I can find any jobs online."

"I'll just be here, baking cookies, and not dying," she cackled.

I shook my head and clucked my tongue for Percy to follow me.

Grandma had long ago moved into the bedroom downstairs so she didn't have to use the stairs.

Fortunately for me this left the whole upstairs as my domain.

When I arrived yesterday afternoon she'd been quick to tell me I could do whatever I wanted with the whole space.

I was definitely considering painting my room a dark purple. Right now the walls were a pale green and everything was light and pretty in the room. My mother had clearly decorated it. While there was nothing wrong with her taste, it just wasn't me. I preferred darker colors.

Percy jumped up on the pale yellow quilt, his black fur already covering the thing. Percy shed on everything. I might find it more of an annoyance if I didn't usually dress in black.

I hadn't brought a lot with me from Arizona, just clothes, some towels, and necessities. Unfortunately, I didn't own much else, since I'd been living with my parents.

I was kind of a failure like that.

I frowned.

I hated feeling like a disappointment, but I did. When I was sixteen years old I lost all the trust my parents had in me, and I never really got it back. It didn't really bother me, in the sense that I still always did my own thing, but sometimes I wanted them to look at me the way they did Robert—my brother. I wanted them to be proud of me, but the fact of the matter was I never really did anything worthwhile.

All I did was fuck up.

Time and time again.

It was my specialty.

I sighed, yanking clothes out of my suitcase and dumping them on the floor. I wasn't a very organized person—but since grandma didn't come up here I didn't have to worry about anyone seeing my mess.

I leaned my head against the bed and heard a soft meow when Percy jumped down and climbed into my lap.

I scratched him under his chin and looked down at him. He opened one amber colored eye to peek up at me.

"Well, Perce, what kind of trouble do you think I can get into here?"

He closed his eyes and laid his head back down on my lap.

I answered for him.

*Lots.*

# CHAPTER TWO

I walked into the restaurant, heading straight for the bar with my red four-inch heels clicking against the concrete floors. I pretended to be oblivious to the stares of the men in the room, but I wasn't. I felt the way their eyes perused my body, admiring my curves. I didn't mind them looking. It was when they got touchy that I got pissed.

I strode right up to the bartender and leaned against the counter.

He turned to look at me, doing a double take. He couldn't have been more than two years older than me. He was good-looking with sandy brown hair, enough scruff to almost be considered a beard, and searing green eyes. Unfortunately for him I was only attracted to danger, and this guy seemed too normal for me.

"What can I help you with darlin'?"

Darlin'. Really?

I raised one pale blonde brow and leveled him with a glare. "I'm not your darlin' or hun or whatever else you might come up with."

He swallowed thickly and took a step back.

Yeah, that's right.

Be afraid.

Most people were.

Except for Mathias.

He embraced my prickly personality.

I closed my eyes momentarily dismissing all thoughts of the moody singer from my mind.

"Can I get you a drink?" He asked.

"No." I pouted my red lips. "But you can get me a job."

His eyes widened in surprise.

"You are hiring, correct? That's what the website said." I'd spent the afternoon browsing local online job ads and this was the only one that sounded mildly appealing.

I purposely leaned just a bit closer so he'd see a flash of my cleavage. Like all men his eyes dipped to my top. So fucking predictable.

"Yeah." He answered and his voice was surprisingly steady.

"So…?" I tapped my nails against the top of the bar. They were painted a shiny black and topped off with silver glitter.

"Hire her man, she's fucking gorgeous."

I leaned over to look at the man that had spoken from across the bar. He was probably in his forties, with a beer gut and balding, but I still sent a wink his way and with the way he sputtered you would've thought I kissed him.

"Well…" The bartender spoke. "I am the manager…"

"Great!" I chimed in before he could say anything else. "When do I start?"

"Tomorrow night too soon?" He asked.

"That would be perfect." I flashed him a flirtatious smile.

He seemed stunned for a moment, shaking his head. "I'm Tanner."

"Remy."

"Have you ever done bartending?" He asked.

I let out a twinkling laugh, drawing even more attention to myself. "Oh, Tanner, don't you think you should've asked me that before you hired me?"

He appeared sheepish.

"No, I haven't… well not officially." I flashed a smile and turned around. "See you tomorrow."

I heard one of the men at the bar say, "I'll be here every night you're working sweetheart!"

"No fucking nicknames!" I yelled and the men erupted into laughter.

Oh, this was going to be fun.

I dressed in a pair of black ripped skinny jeans, and a white V-neck tee that dipped low enough to show a bit of cleavage, but not enough to be obscene. I shrugged into a leather jacket and pulled on a pair of heeled black boots, fluffing my straight light blonde hair to give it some body. This wasn't exactly proper work attire, but it was a bar, and I had to dress a certain way to get bigger tips. Plus, these jeans made my ass look amazing, so bonus points for that.

"See you later, Perce." I scratched the cat behind his ears for a moment. He began to purr and leaned into my touch.

I'd found Percy on the side of the road. He'd been in a nasty shape from a fight with another cat. I'd taken him home and tended to his wounds, even though he clawed up both of my arms while I tried to help him. I wasn't normally a caring person, but I saw something in Percy that reminded me of myself. He was lost and hurt, and needed someone to love him. So I did and he never left.

I headed downstairs and said goodbye to my grandma, kissing her on the cheek.

Before we moved I'd always been close to my grandma. Our old house was in this very same neighborhood and when I was little I used to ride my bike over. We'd bake muffins and other treats together.

She'd ask me about school and boys, and let me gossip.

She never judged me the way my parent's did.

Well, not until…

I wasn't going to go there.

Not today.

Not ever.

I'd buried those memories for a reason.

I unlocked my car and slid inside.

I grasped the steering wheel in my hands so tightly that my knuckles turned white.

I leaned my head back and took a deep breath, in and out.

I wasn't going to start crying now.

Not about this.

I sat there, doing my breathing exercises, for as long as it took for the feelings to go away.

I'd started doing yoga a few years ago. I found that it helped soothe me. There was something so comforting about it.

I'd have to find a new studio to attend here. I didn't think I'd make it without my yoga.

Once I was composed I backed out of the driveway and headed to the bar.

I turned on some rock music and flailed about in my car.

I needed to prepare for my new job, and that meant getting myself pumped.

Most people turned to energy drinks, or drugs, for that.

Me? My drug was music.

That was another thing that Mathias and I had in common.

Fuck.

I was thinking about him again.

In Arizona I'd done a better job at pretending he didn't exist.

But here, where we grew up, it was impossible to escape his presence and the memories.

Oh, the memories.

I parked my car in the parking lot of the bar and leaned back; closing my eyes as I remembered the first time I ever met Mathias Wade.

*"You know those will kill you, right?"*

*I looked up to see the good-looking guy from my biology class standing in front of me. His messy dark brown hair fell into his eyes and he gave me that blinding smile that had most girls spreading their legs for him.*

*"Do I look like a care?" I puffed out some smoke right in his face.*

*He didn't cough or flinch away.*

*"Give me one." He said.*

*I raised a brow. "They'll kill you, you know?" I mimicked his voice.*

*He smiled slowly and straightened. "Something's going to kill me one day," he shrugged. Something dark flashed in his unique gray eyes. "I might as well do the killing. I'm already screwed."*

*I handed him a cigarette and lit the tip.*

*"Enjoy, because you're not getting anymore freebies from me."*

*His lips twitched with the threat of a smile before he settled with a brooding stare and leaned against the brick exterior wall of the school.*

*"How'd you find me out here?" I asked.*

*He pushed his hair out of his eyes. "I followed you," he admitted, not ashamed.*

*I stared at him. "Why?"*

*"Why do you think?" His eyes were serious and his mouth was a straight line. I found myself staring at his lips. They were slightly plump and pouty, but not in a girly way. They tempered the sharp cut of his jaw and I wondered if they were as soft as they looked.*

*I shook my head free of those thoughts, focusing on what he had said.*

*"I'm not sucking your dick," I sneered. "That's a vicious rumor Jake started because he's an*

*asshole.”*

*His eyes glinted dangerously and my stomach stirred with something I'd never felt before. Not lust, I'd felt that plenty. It was something else that made no sense.*

*"That's not what I wanted, but now that you mention it…" He reached for his zipper. "Ow!" He yelped when the tip of my cigarette burned the skin between his thumb and forefinger. "I was only joking. Fuck."*

*He waved his hand through the air.*

*"That's not something to joke about." I squared my shoulders. "And for the record, I'm not against blowjobs, I just don't want to be forced to give one."*

*He stared at me like I was the most mysterious creature he'd ever seen.*

*"I don't want to have sex with you… well I'd like to," he admitted sheepishly, "but that's not why I followed you out here."*

*"It's not?"*

*"No." He stared at me intensely. "I've been watching you, and I've realized that you're a lot like me."*

*"I am?" I looked at him like he was crazy.*

*He nodded and leaned close to me. "You're not like the other girls here who piss their pants if they see a fucking spider. You're wild. You don't care what people think of you. You're the bad girl they scoff at, but all secretly want to be."*

*"And you are?" I asked, lighting a new cigarette.*

*"I'm the fucked up bad boy everyone wants to save," his voice lowered, "but you wouldn't try to save me, would you, Remy? Because you're just like me."*

*My breath stuttered and he grinned at having made me react.*

*"I don't understand what you want." I stood tall and my voice never quavered.*

*"You."*

*He started to walk away, but promptly turned back around. He dug something out of his back pocket and I realized it was a pack of cigarettes. He handed me one of the slender white sticks and grinned. "No freebies, right?"*

*And then I jumped on his back and tackled him to the ground.*

*The rest is, as they say, history.*

I didn't know it then, but looking back I could see just how much Mathias changed the course of my life with only one meeting—and not for the better.

He'd screwed me up even more than I was—stirring up a fucking tornado in my life and leaving me behind to clean up the mess while he lived his life.

I hated him for that.

I hated him for leaving me.

I hated him for hurting me.

But most of all I hated him because I loved him.

And I didn't think I could ever stop.

# CHAPTER THREE

"You did good." Tanner commented, leaning against the bar with his arms crossed over his chest as I cleaned the glasses.

I arched a brow. "I think I did a little better than good. Have you seen my tips?"

"That's only because the guys that come in here are horny old men and if you shake your ass a bit they'll throw a hundred dollar bill at you."

I rolled my eyes. "Maybe you should shake your ass more then." I glanced up at him and smiled evilly. "You know, if you helped me with these we could get out of here sooner."

"I'm good." He sat on one of the barstools. "I like watching you work."

I rolled my eyes yet again. I did that a lot around Tanner. I grabbed a rag and threw it at him. "Help me, don't be a dick."

He chuckled and stepped behind the bar. "Okay, okay."

Tanner actually wasn't that bad to work with. He could be annoying, but that was only because he thought he was funny when he wasn't.

Working together we managed to finish in no time. Tanner locked up and we walked across the street to the parking lot.

"See you later, Red," he called, unlocking some small Dodge car.

I saluted him, making him chuckle.

Somewhere during the course of the evening he'd started calling me Red thanks to my signature red lipstick. Normally something like that would piss me off, but I found myself not caring. Maybe I was finally growing up—ha, not likely. I'd still sucker punch him if he tried to call me darlin' again.

I got in my car and sat there for a moment. It was well after three in the morning, so if I was smart I would head home and go to bed.

But I'd never been smart.

Instead, I found myself driving around town, reacquainting myself with my old haunts.

Somehow I ended up at my old high school.

Despite the chilly November air I slipped from the car and strode across the lot and around the building.

There.

Right fucking there, was where I met Mathias.

Where he forever changed the course of my life and fucked me up for anybody else.

My breath fogged the air as I stood there in the dark, staring at a damn brick wall like it held the answers to the universe.

Mathias and I had, had a… strange relationship.

We were friends.

We were lovers.

We were everything.

But in the end it wasn't enough.

We might've broken up and ended our relationship because of me moving—and because Mathias is an asshole—but I know in my heart we would've never worked anyway.

We were too much alike.

Both of us were like fire—loud, all-consuming, and willing to burn anything that got in our way.

I let out a sigh and crouched down, pulling up some of the dry brown grass.

Maybe there was something wrong with me, because even though I knew Mathias had been bad for me, I never wished I could take back everything that happened between us. The fact of the matter was I never felt more alive than I did when I was with him.

It was all so stupid.

I stood up again, kicking at the dirt.

It had been seven fucking years and I still couldn't seem to let go of the past.

I wondered if Mathias ever thought of me.

Probably not.

According to those celebrity news shows on TV he had a new plaything every day of the week.

I was nothing but a blip in his past. I didn't matter to him. I never had.

He told me he loved me once.

But if you love someone you don't destroy them.

# CHAPTER FOUR

"You look tired." My grandma commented, taking in the dark circles beneath my eyes.

"The night shift will do that to you." I took a sip of my too hot black coffee. "My body hasn't adjusted yet." I yawned.

It was well after ten in the morning, but I'd only gotten five hours of sleep.

"Let me make you some breakfast." She was already bustling about the kitchen, grabbing a pan.

"I'm supposed to be making *you* breakfast." I yawned again and laid my head on the table.

"I don't think you could lift a finger right now. Besides," I heard the refrigerator door open, "it does me good to take care of someone else."

I lifted my head up and propped it in my hand. "Why do I feel like I moved here to take care of you, but *you're* going to end up taking care of me?"

"Because I'm your grandma and I'm supposed to tend to you. I might be old, but I'm not completely useless." She rolled her eyes, scrambling some eggs. "I swear, your father thinks I just lay around and don't move or do anything." She waved a hand at me. "I'll have you know that I have a boyfriend."

I snorted. "A boyfriend?"

"Yes," she nodded rapidly. "I met him at the senior center during dance night—the way he moved his hips…" She licked her lips and made a noise in the back of her throat.

"Oh! Ew! Grandma!" I covered my eyes.

I might've seen and done a lot of crap in my life, but I did *not* need the visual of my grandma getting it on.

She snickered at me and said, "Oh, Remy."

She finished making the eggs and slid a plate in front of me along with some orange juice.

"Thanks," I smiled at her. "Now go lay down."

She glared at me, but I glared right back.

"Fine," she relinquished, "but only because Kathy Lee and Hoda are on the *Today Show* right now, and they crack me up." She started to waddle out of the room, but stopped. "How about you come back with me, we'll open a bottle of wine, and every time they laugh we'll drink."

I gaped at her. "We'd be drunk in no time."

"Exactly."

Only my grandma.

"You just had a heart attack. Let's lay off the alcohol for a while, okay?"

She sighed and mumbled, "Fun sucker," under her breath as she went back to her room.

I finished my breakfast and cleaned up before heading upstairs in the hopes of getting some more sleep.

Percy was curled up on my pillow and I scooted him over only for him to promptly move back to my pillow.

Cats.

I relinquished my pillow to him and lay down on the other side of the bed.

I'd been working at the bar for a full week now. I actually liked it. The people I worked with were nice and the patrons might've been rowdy, but they weren't rude. Yet.

I crooked my arm across my face—blocking out the sunlight that still streamed into the bedroom despite the closed blinds.

It didn't seem to matter how tired I was my brain didn't want to shut off.

I kept thinking about what a failure I was.

That at twenty-three years old all I had to show for my life was a degree I would never use, a job at a bar, and I was living with my grandma whom I was supposed to be taking care of, but really she was looking after me.

I was pathetic.

I covered my face with my hands and let out a small scream of pent up rage.

I had to get out of here.

I jumped out of bed and changed into yoga pants and a tank top. Since it was cold out I shrugged into a sweatshirt before putting on my tennis shoes.

Yoga would help calm and center me, then all would be well again.

I hoped.

I bound down the steps, said goodbye to my grandma, and headed to the nearby gym that had a yoga studio. I'd found it earlier in the week. Surely they'd have a class right now and I could join in.

I got there and hurried inside to escape the windy weather.

When I reached the room that housed the yoga studio it was closed.

"Fuck!" I screamed, kicking the door.

"Hey," a guy approached me slowly, "are you okay?"

"Do I look like I'm okay?" I glared, ready to kick him too if he pissed me off.

He held up his hands in a placating manner. "Sorry," he chuckled, flicking his head to the side so that his sweaty blond hair didn't hang in his eyes. "Is there something I can help you with? I own the gym."

I eyed him up and down. He seemed pretty young—definitely not in his thirties yet—with a lean athletic body.

"Yeah," I huffed, "I'd like to do some yoga." I tossed my thumb over my shoulder at the closed studio.

"Sorry," he shrugged. "I can't do that."

"But you're the owner!" I snapped.

He merely chuckled at my outburst. "I'm teaching a boxing class, why don't you check it out. You might find that it's more to your liking than yoga. That was one mean kick."

I frowned. I didn't want to do boxing, but I didn't see what choice I had. I needed to work off some of this pent up rage and at least boxing would allow me to hit something and pretend it was Mathias' face.

"Fine." I agreed reluctantly, lifting one of my shoulders in a half shrug.

"I'm Drew," he introduced himself.

"Remy," I replied.

His brows rose. "That's a unique name."

"So I'm told," I sighed.

I followed him through the building and into a room similar to the yoga studio. People were just beginning to arrive, standing in front of the punching bags. I was surprised to see that all the people were women.

"There's an empty one back there." Drew pointed and I detached myself from his side.

It was kind of surprising that I'd never tried boxing before. I guess maybe I'd been afraid it would only make my aggression worse, whereas yoga calmed me.

Drew came to my side with a wrap for my hands. He waited for me to hold my hands out so he could do it but I refused.

"I can do it myself." I wasn't helpless.

He raised a brow and leveled me with a look. "You haven't been taught the proper way. I'm doing it this time and next time you can do it on your own."

"Who said I'd be back here?" I challenged.

He smiled, ducking his head. "Trust me, you will be."

"You're very full of yourself."

He snorted. "I wasn't meaning you'd be back because of me, besides I'm married." He waved his left hand in front of my face. "I meant that boxing can be addicting. Sometimes it's nice to hit something."

"And kick something," I added, finally holding my hands out for him.

I watched what he did, careful to memorize the movements so I could replicate them the next time. *If* there was a next time.

He finished and flashed me a smile. "You're not going to kick me?"

"The day is young."

He chuckled and took a step back. "I like you."

"You might be the only one." I mumbled the words under my breath and he walked off, not having heard me.

He turned on some really loud rock music and I twisted my neck from side to side, smiling.

I listened to Drew's instructions on how we should position our feet and hips. Then he moved on to explaining what our fists should look like.

After that he basically let us have at it.

And I punched the shit out of that bag, wishing I could make it as broken as me.

An hour later I left the gym dripping with sweat, but feeling a hundred times better.

After the class I'd approached Drew and signed up to return to the classes.

Goodbye yoga and hello boxing.

I stopped off at Starbucks on my way back to the house, ordering an iced Caramel Macchiato.

I was waiting by the bar for them to make my drink when I heard a shriek of, "Remy Parker, is that really you?!"

I turned to look over my shoulder and my jaw dropped at the sight of one of my only high school friends.

"Lana?" I asked, my eyes zeroing in on her *very* round stomach.

"It is you!" She screamed again, drawing the attention of everyone in Starbucks. She threw her arms around me and I was reluctant to return the gesture. I couldn't remember Lana ever being this bubbly in high school. She'd been a lot like me, angry at the world. "You look so pretty!"

I took a step back. "You look… large."

She let out a giggle and rubbed her stomach. "It's twins!"

That explained it.

"So much has changed since I last saw you," she continued, forcibly pulling me over to a table.

"Yeah," I agreed. "I thought you hated kids."

"I hated everything when we were friends." She laughed, scooting the chair back to accommodate her stomach. She flipped her brown hair over her shoulder. In high school it had been dyed black with hot pink tips. "A lot changes in seven years."

"It sure does," I muttered, my eyes shifting around as I tried to formulate a plan of escape.

"So, how are you?" She asked.

"Good," I nodded.

"What are you doing back in town? I figured you were gone for good. You were always better than this place."

"My grandma needed someone to take care of her, so I volunteered for the job," I sighed, looking towards the bar and hoping my drink was ready.

"Oh, is she okay?" Lana frowned.

"It would take a lot to knock her down, trust me." I laughed. My drink order was called and I stood up. "That's mine," I pointed.

"Oh, okay," she smiled. "Would you want to meet up for lunch one day?"

I hesitated. I'd cut off contact with everyone I knew from here after I moved to Arizona. It had been easier that way. A clean break.

Looking at Lana now, she seemed like a stranger.

But I found myself saying, "Yeah, that would be fine."

Fuck, what had I just agreed to?

We exchanged phone numbers and I grabbed my drink, waving goodbye.

So far, moving back here wasn't going anything like I expected.

I thought it would be hard being back here—that the memories would overwhelm me.

And I guess in a way they were.

I was certainly thinking about Mathias more than I had in Arizona—and let's face it, I thought about him plenty there.

But it didn't *hurt* like I expected it to.

I didn't feel like my insides had been ripped apart and splayed open to be picked apart by vultures.

Maybe coming back here was actually a good thing and I'd finally be able to move on and let go.

Then again, maybe I was wrong.

# CHAPTER FIVE

"No more MTV!" I called over my shoulder as I left.

"I'm older, you can't boss me around young lady," my grandma yelled back.

I laughed at her response, shutting and locking the door behind me.

I was working another late night at the bar. The money was excellent, but I wasn't sure if I liked how many hours Tanner had me working. I was quickly becoming exhausted. I wasn't a night owl like I used to be. I kept hoping my body would adjust, but so far it hadn't.

I parked my car, grabbed my purse, and scurried inside and away from the cold.

"Hey, Tanner!" I called, heading to the back.

I tucked my purse away, reapplied a coat of red lipstick, and put on my game face.

When I worked I put on a show.

I strode back out into the bar, swaying my hips and smiling as I felt the men's eyes zero in on my ass.

*You can look, but you can't touch.*

"Evening, Red." Tanner nodded when I slid behind the bar. "Todd needs a refill." He nodded to the end of the bar where one of the regulars sat.

I might've only been here a week, but I'd already memorized what most of these guys ordered.

I grabbed a Bud Light, popped the cap off, and handed it over to Todd with a wink.

I swore the poor guy blushed.

Bless his heart.

I quickly picked up where Tanner needed help.

When the bar and restaurant area were packed it became insane trying to keep up with all the orders.

Not to toot my own horn, but I honestly didn't know what Tanner did before I came along.

Hours passed and I never got a break—and someone spilled their beer and it splashed on my shirt, so that kinda sucked. The good news was I was wearing a black shirt, the bad new was that despite that I still looked like I was competing in a wet t-shirt contest. At least I got bigger tips.

The bar began to empty out as closing time approached.

I was ready to collapse with exhaustion. Tonight had been one of the times where there never seemed to be a moment to catch your breath.

I wiped down the bar and got the lone guy there another drink.

I had my back turned when I heard another stool pull out behind me. "I'll have the usual."

Ice.

My body was a frozen block of ice.

Seriously, give me a tap and I'd go crumbling to the floor.

There was no fucking way.

It couldn't be possible.

I had to be imagining that voice.

"Hello? Did you hear me? I said I'd have the usual. If you don't know what that is, maybe you should find a new job."

Nope, I definitely didn't imagine it.

I turned around, facing a ghost.

I watched all the color drain from his face and he reared back, nearly falling off the stool.

"Remy?" His voice was nothing more than a whisper, but it still managed to affect me.

"The usual?" I asked. "Let me guess, that?" I pointed at the most expensive bottle of scotch the bar had—something that no one else had ordered at this point.

He nodded woodenly, still stunned.

I grinned evilly and reached for the bottle.

I took the cap off and acted like I was reaching for a glass, but instead I lunged forward and tilted the bottle, dumping all of the contents on top of his head.

I let the bottle drop to the ground where it shattered at my feet.

I didn't care if I got fired.

I'd wanted to do that—or something like it—for a long time.

The lone man at the bar looked like a deer caught in headlights. He probably thought he was next. He pulled his wallet from his back pocket, slapped some bills down, and grabbed his coat before hauling ass out of there.

Mathias looked at me with a sneer on his lips and anger in the depths of his eyes. The amber colored liquid stained his crisp button down white shirt and dripped from his hair onto his face.

He barred his teeth, a growl rumbling in his chest. He slammed his palms against the top of the bar. "You always did know how to piss me off. Would you like a fucking medal?"

I smiled, batting my eyes innocently. "What did I do?"

"Why are you back here?" He seethed, leaning forward. His look was menacing, and most people probably would have been shied away from him, but I'd never been scared of Mathias. Then again, I wasn't very smart, so maybe I *should've* been afraid. "You shouldn't be here."

I widened my eyes. "Really? It's a free country. I'm pretty sure there's no rule against me being here. Although with all the money you have now you can probably pay to have someone kick me out of the state."

His eyes flashed with danger. He opened his mouth to speak, but was cut off by Tanner.

"Did I hear something break?" Tanner asked, returning from the bathrooms. "Oh." He frowned when he took in the drenched Mathias. He turned to me and said simply, "You're fired."

"What?" I gasped. I mean, I'd been expecting it, but still.

"You can't pour drinks on customers," he flailed his arms. "Especially not that one." He pointed a finger at Mathias.

I rolled my eyes. "Whatever," I sighed.

I wasn't going to argue with him. I knew it had been a dumb move, but I didn't regret it. I marched around the bar, leaving behind the broken glass, and pushed open the door to the backroom.

Since I was fired I wasn't going to stay there a second longer and be subjected to Mathias' presence. I wasn't a masochist.

I let out a startled scream when a heavy body grabbed me from behind and pushed me against the wall.

Mathias pinned my hands above my head and pressed his hips into mine so that there was no way I could move. I couldn't see much of him like this, but I could take in the broadness of his shoulders and the way the wet shirt stuck to his sculpted chest. Mathias had always had a nice body, but now? Oh my God, the guy was built, and feeling him pressed up against me like this was doing all kinds of crazy things to me.

Fuck.

I bit down on my tongue until I tasted blood—the pain burning away my treacherous thoughts.

"What are you doing here?" He asked through gritted teeth.

"I'm not here for you, if that's what you're getting at. You always were such a pretentious asshole. I don't know why I ever liked you."

His anger seemed to disappear momentarily and he leaned in close. He glided his nose along my neck, like he was inhaling my scent, and my pulse jumped.

"You loved me Remy."

I jerked in his grasp. "The love of a sixteen year old doesn't count," I spat.

He grinned. "Jumpy?"

"Let me go." I bucked against him, trying to twist away.

"No." His eyes darkened again as his anger returned.

He pressed into me further so that our chests were pressed together.

"How'd you get back here?" I asked.

"I know, Tanner," he shrugged. "You're not fired by the way." He grinned like he was so fucking wonderful.

"I don't need help from you." I wiggled again, testing his grip to see if I could slip away or knee him in the groin.

He clucked his tongue. "You always were so unwilling to take help from anybody."

"Don't act like you know me." I was seething, a cobra coiled and ready to strike.

His voice lowered and rumbled against my body. "I know you very well, Remy."

"Sex doesn't count."

He chuckled, his breath fanning against my neck. "Oh, Remy. We both know it was so much more than that."

"Let me go." I bucked against him again.

"That's not allowed." He growled.

"What are you going to do?" I taunted. "Tie me up?"

"I'm considering it." His gray eyes were serious.

"What do you want with me?" I asked, my voice sounded breathless—not with want or desire, but with pain and suffering.

He leaned close and his delectable lips touched my ear. "I want you to stop haunting my fucking dreams."

And then he let me go and walked away, like nothing ever happened.

Just like the last time.

I lay in bed, with Percy hogging my pillow, convinced the whole thing had been a hallucination.

There was no way that had happened, right?

I mean, I didn't really pour a bottle of scotch on his head and then have him pin me to a wall?

The tender spots on my wrists where he'd held me disagreed with my thoughts.

When I saw the article saying that Willow Creek was back in town for the holidays I'd known there was the *possibility* of bumping into Mathias. I just never expected it to be like that.

So… explosive.

But that was our way.

It always had been.

People had never understood our relationship.

We spent most of our time arguing and the rest fucking each other's brains out.

It was how we functioned.

Despite all that, we still knew each other better than anyone else did. Within each other we found someone we could confide all our deepest, darkest secrets in.

After that first day where he approached me for a cigarette our strange friendship bloomed, and then blossomed into something more.

Were we ever boyfriend and girlfriend?

I suppose we were together in the only way two fucked up sixteen year olds knew how to be together.

He'd been my everything.

And I'd been his… I don't know.

Sometimes I wondered if I ever really mattered to him.

I rolled onto my back, squishing my eyes closed and wishing for sleep, but it was futile.

I'd always been a strong girl who didn't take any shit.

But Mathias was my weakness.

With him I turned into someone I didn't recognize.

And it was all because I'd given him my heart and never gotten it back.

It was time to turn the tables.

I was going to make him fall in love with me, and when he didn't see it coming I'd break his heart just like he'd done mine.

I smiled up at the darkened ceiling.

Let the games begin.

# CHAPTER SIX

"I need your help with something." I leaned against the bar, giving Tanner the most sincere look I could muster. I really hoped it didn't look like I was constipated. That would be tragic.

He eyed me, tucking the rag he'd been using to wipe down the bar into his back pocket. "My help, Red? Why would you need my help?" He scratched at his beard.

"You're friends with Mathias, right?"

He straightened. "I'm not getting you his autograph, if that's what you're asking for."

I snorted. "You do recall the fact that I poured a five-hundred dollar bottle of scotch on his head, right? Do you *really* think I would've done that if I wanted his autograph?"

"Good point." He shrugged his wide lumberjack shoulders. "We're not really friends. More like acquaintances. He likes it here because no one bothers him and I always keep his drink of choice on hand."

"Whatever." I sighed, not interested in the details of his relationship with Mathias. "I just wanted to know if you knew some way I could contact him to apologize?"

Step One of my plan was to ambush him— preferably wearing a slinky dress and killer heels. I knew Mathias' tastes and there was no way he'd be able to resist that. Once I had his attention I'd seduce him, drag him almost to the edge, and then leave him hanging and begging for more.

I hadn't really thought of a Step Two yet.

I figured it would come to me when the time was right.

"Sorry," Tanner turned his back on me, drying off the clean glasses, "it's not like I have his phone number or anything."

Dammit.

This was not going according to plan.

*Think, Remy. Think!*

I came up with nothing.

"He lives in the penthouse of that fancy shmancy hotel around the corner. That historical one or whatever."

I perked up with interest. I couldn't believe Tanner was actually giving me some details after the stunt I pulled. Maybe he was high or something. It honestly wouldn't surprise me.

"The George Washington Hotel?" I asked.

"Yeah," he glanced at me over his shoulder and nodded. "That one."

If I was a hugger I would've hugged Tanner in that moment.

It might take a few tries, but if I started hanging around the hotel—which was coincidently on the same block as the bar—I was bound to run into him.

I resisted the urge to rub my hands together like some evil mastermind and cackle insanely.

"But I didn't tell you this!" Tanner leveled me with a glare. He seemed to have come to the sudden realization that he probably shouldn't have extended this kind of information to me.

Too late now buddy-boy.

"No, you didn't." I agreed.

I hopped up on the counter and pointed at the glass Tanner was currently trying to dry. "You missed a spot."

He looked up at me and glared. "Get off the bar, Red. And if you think you can do better, maybe you should take over."

I climbed down and took the glass and cloth from him.

"I will." I bumped his hip with mine.

He had me working an earlier shift today and the bar was relatively dead. Even the waitresses didn't have many tables to tend to. I decided then, that even though it was exhausting, I'd rather work late. Not only did I earn a hell of a lot in tips, but it was a lot more fun.

Right now I was bored, and cleaning this glass was the most fun I'd had in an hour.

Pathetic, I know.

Once I'd dried all the glasses and put them away Tanner found me and told me to head on home since it was so dead.

On my way to my car my phone buzzed in my back pocket. An unfamiliar number flashed on the screen.

"Hello?" I answered hesitantly.

"Remy!"

"Oh hi, Lana." For a moment I'd thought it might be Mathias. How stupid of me.

"I'm free and was wondering if you might want to meet for dinner? How about Toulouse?"

"Where is that?" I asked with a small laugh. "It's been so long since I've lived here."

"It's the new French restaurant at the George Washington hotel."

I stopped in my tracks in the middle of the road, causing cars to honk at me. I hurried to the other side, internally doing a cha-cha at the perfectness of the situation.

"Sounds good. What time are you thinking? I just got off from work and smell like a bar."

"Is two hours from now too soon?"

I slid in my car and cranked the engine, looking at the time that flashed on the dashboard. "That'll be perfect."

"See you then!" She chimed cheerily, completely oblivious that she'd just given me the perfect excuse to run into Mathias.

But first, I had to buy a new dress.

And shoes.

Yes, definitely shoes.

I curled my blonde hair, running my fingers through it to make it more loose and natural looking. I sprayed it with enough hairspray that it was probably a miracle I didn't pass out. But my naturally straight hair had never held a curl for long and I needed these to last.

Not that I was planning to stay the night if I ran into Mathias.

I needed to leave him wanting more and not show all my cards up front.

Once my hair was finished I moved on to makeup.

I used smoky grays around my icy blue eyes, layering on the mascara to make them pop even more. I coated my lips with my favorite red lipstick and stepped back to appraise my appearance.

Perfect.

I padded down the hall and into my room, so I could slip on the new black dress I got.

The dress fit me like it was tailored specifically to my body. It had random triangular cutouts that showed bits and pieces of my skin.

I slipped on a pair of red heels and grabbed a clutch.

"See you later, Perce."

I gave the cat a quick belly rub before going downstairs to say goodbye to my grandma. She was in bed watching recorded episodes of *Arrow* and drooling over Stephen Amell's abs. My grandma was one of a kind.

"I'm going out," I told her, poking my head in the doorway.

She shushed me for interrupting her show.

That woman.

"There's a pause button," I commented with a grin.

She grabbed a pillow to throw at me, so I hurried away.

I'd made dinner for her earlier when I got home, even though she insisted she could do it herself. The woman was so God damn stubborn.

But then so was I.

My heart raced as I drove to the restaurant to meet Lana. The possibility of running into Mathias again had my body humming.

I was a bit afraid that the humming had nothing to do with my plan for revenge and everything to do with the way he affected me.

I turned up the music, hoping it would help center me and give me the strength I needed to do what I had to do. I could not forget the mission.

I parked my car across the street and deposited some change in the meter.

I wrapped my knee length black coat tighter around my body and ran across the street to the hotel—well, ran as fast as I could in the heels I was wearing.

I stepped into the warmth of the hotel and let it wash over me for a moment.

The hotel was surprisingly fancy—but I should've expected as much with a rock star supposedly living in the penthouse suite. It's not like he would live in a dump.

The floors were a shiny marble and the walls were painted a buttery gold color accented with dark wood tones.

It was beautiful and looked like something you'd see in New York City—or so I assumed, since I'd never actually been there.

In front of me sat a round table with the largest vase of flowers I'd ever seen. I stepped closer, reaching out to touch one of the delicate petals and gasped when I realized it was real.

The bar was to my left, and I knew that would most likely be the best place to search for Mathias, but I was supposed to be meeting Lana at the restaurant. Which sat to my right. So close, and yet so far away.

I started over to the restaurant and immediately spotted Lana sitting at a table waving at me like she was trying to land a plane.

I was going to need Vodka if I was going to make it through this dinner without gagging.

I couldn't believe this was the girl I'd been friends with in high school.

Back then she'd been just like me and even had her eyebrow and tongue pierced. Now she was like a fucking Stepford wife. It was scary.

I pulled out a chair and sat down. "Thanks for calling me." I smiled, smoothing my hands down my dress.

"I wasn't sure you'd be able to join me." She admitted with a shrug, taking a dainty sip of her glass of ice water. Jesus Christ. Had she been to some kind of etiquette class? She held her glass like she was the Queen and sat perfectly straight.

"Normally I wouldn't be able to. I usually work at night." I picked up my own glass of water that had already been filled before I arrived.

Lana set her glass back down and I got an eyeful of a very large engagement ring on her finger. The thing was massive and looked like it needed a crane to lift it. Her wedding band was just as flashy, with diamonds going all the way around. She was only twenty-three like me and that seemed so young to be married with a baby on the way. *Babies*, I corrected myself.

"So, who's the guy?" I asked, nodding at her hand and glancing down at the menu.

"Uh… you remember Clayton Jamison?"

My head shot up. "That asshole football player who's the Mayor's son?"

She nodded.

"You married *him*?" I scoffed, feeling like I was choking on something sour. "*Why?*"

"People change, Remy." She huffed, fiddling with the cloth napkin already placed in her lap.

"I guess they do," I agreed, taking a sip of water to have something to do.

I didn't feel like I had changed at all from the girl I was in high school. I guess I knew more now, and was therefore a little wiser, but I was still a bitch. I didn't care what people thought of me. I was always going to do my own thing.

A waiter appeared to take our order and I told him to bring me whatever their specialty was. I didn't really care what I ate at this point.

"This place is nice," I commented, trying to steer the conversation in a different direction.

"It's one of Clayton's favorite's," she smiled.

I arched a brow. "And what's Lana's favorite?"

She frowned, mulling over my words. "I'm not sure."

"Are you happy?" I asked her suddenly.

Her nose crinkled. "Yeah?" She framed it as a question. "I mean, not all the time, but usually."

"Good," I nodded, sitting back. "That's nice to hear."

I might've thought it was weird that Lana grew up to marry one of the biggest jerks we went to school with, but if she was genuinely happy then I was happy too. She deserved the fairytale ending.

Bitches like me?

We didn't get the fairytale or the romance.

We got the raw and the real, and then we got dumped on in the end.

It was the way of the world.

We spent the rest of the dinner catching up and trying to get to know each other again. It was weird and definitely awkward at times, but while talking to Lana I discovered how starved I'd been for a friend.

A real friend.

Someone you talked to.

And not someone that constantly got you into trouble.

I walked with Lana to her car—frankly I was afraid if I left her alone her water might break and she'd end up being one of those people you heard about on the news that had their kid in the back of a car.

I watched her taillights disappear around the corner and I headed back into the hotel and to the bar.

It was nearing ten and the place wasn't packed like where I worked.

It was mostly lone businessmen sitting around nursing a drink.

I sat down on one of the barstools and ordered an ice water.

I needed to keep my head right now, not end up drunk.

Time trickled by slowly and Mathias made no appearance.

Maybe he didn't drink as often as he used to—where he drank himself into oblivion every night so he didn't have to relive the horrors of his past.

Or maybe tonight he was drinking alone in his penthouse.

Or he could even be at the bar I worked at.

My throat closed up at the fourth possibility—the one that said he might be on a date.

I wasn't supposed to *care* about him.

He broke my heart and didn't bat an eye.

This was about revenge, not about being in his arms again.

The stool beside me slid back and my body sparked with hope, but when I looked the man sitting down next to me wasn't Mathias.

Of course not.

The man eyed me, unashamed in his perusal of my body.

I wasn't vain, but I knew men admired my body and I used it to my advantage.

"Here on business?" I asked.

"You could say that," he replied, his dark eyes flickering over the tops of my breasts. He turned away briefly to signal the bartender. Once he had the man's attention he placed his order and turned to me once more. "I'm Gavin."

"Remy," I replied, taking a sip of my water.

His eyes zeroed in on the way my lips wrapped around the straw, and I was sure he was picturing my lips around something else.

"Why are you alone here, Remy?"

I shrugged, counting the bottles behind the bar. Gavin was boring me and he was also distracting me from my mission. "Because I want to be."

His hand landed on my knee, snaking up my thigh and I stiffened.

"How much?" He asked me.

I reared back. "Excuse me?" He couldn't be asking me what I thought he was.

"How much?" He repeated. "For the night."

Before I could respond—and my response probably would've been to slap him—a heavy hand descended on Gavin's shoulder.

"I suggest you leave," the new arrival growled lowly.

Gavin glanced up and smiled cockily. "Sorry, I didn't know she was already taken for the night."

"She's not a fucking prostitute."

I closed my eyes. I didn't know what to make of Mathias showing up and defending me. This was not how I'd planned this.

"I couldn't tell the difference," Gavin spoke.

Mathias growled unintelligibly and cocked his arm back, ramming his fist into Gavin's face.

Gavin fell out of the chair and onto the ground.

Mathias dove after him, punching him again.

When Mathias got like this I knew to get the hell out of dodge.

I grabbed my clutch and hurried away—the bartender already rushing to break up the fight.

My heels clacked against the marble floors as I hurried for the bathrooms to compose myself.

The door swung closed behind me and I grasped the nearest porcelain sink in my hands, trying to slow my breathing.

I couldn't believe that had happened.

Shockingly, the most unbelievable part of the situation had been Mathias coming to my defense.

My hands shook like I was coming down from an adrenaline rush.

I hadn't been scared of the man, though. I'd handled plenty of guys like him before.

No, this reaction was only caused by one person.

He stirred up my insides, shaking me around until I couldn't make sense of anything—and he hadn't even said a single word to me.

The door opened and I grabbed my clutch to leave, not wanting another woman to be a witness to my breakdown. Or whatever this was.

But it wasn't a woman.

Mathias stood in front of me, his pressed white button down shirt now wrinkled. The suspenders he wore were slightly crooked and I itched to straighten them.

Instead, I said, "You've really changed, Mathias. What is this? Nerd chic?" I waved a hand at his clothes that probably cost more than I made in a month.

"Shut up." He sneered, crowding into my space.

"Make. Me."

With a growl he grasped my hips and pushed me into the wall. His hands moved down to my thighs, lifting my legs so I was forced to wrap them around his waist.

His lips descended on mine before I could take a breath, and then he seemed to become my air.

His touch sparked an electric current in my body.

His hips pressed into mine and I moaned into his mouth, pulling at his hair.

When his lips tore from mine for a moment, I panted, "I could've handled that guy myself."

He didn't reply, he just kissed me again.

Our hands seemed to be everywhere at once.

I wanted to weep at how good his hands and lips felt on me. No one had ever compared to Mathias and what he could do to me. A spark like the flow of an electrical current seemed to flow through my veins anytime he touched me. Hell, sometimes I felt it with a single glance from him.

Suddenly my plan to seduce him seemed so stupid, because here he was seducing me. Or at least it felt that way.

I was in over my head when it came to this guy.

I always had been.

Yet here I was, once again, unable to let him go.

He was like my drug—an intoxicating high but the crash left me defeated, alone, and searching frantically for the next hit.

He ripped his body away from me and I dropped to the ground, barely catching myself.

Without a backwards glance he was out the door.

I would've thought I imagined the whole thing if it wasn't for the swinging door.

Instead of standing there I stormed after him and jumped on his back, much the way I had the first day we ever talked.

This time he didn't fall to the ground.

It was like he expected me to jump on him.

I wrapped my arms around his neck and my legs around his waist, holding on for dear life.

"You don't get to do *that* and just *leave*." I hissed the words in his ear. "You're always walking away from me, but not anymore."

"Get the fuck off me," he growled, swatting at my limbs like I was pesky fly.

"No!" I shouted not caring who heard me.

"Remy—"

I dropped from his body, the fight leaving me—for now at least—and he swiveled around to face me.

"I really don't know why I ever liked you," I spat. "You kiss me like I'm everything to you—after all the shit you said to me—and then you just walk off! You're so fucking confusing!"

"I didn't like him touching you." Darkness flashed in his gaze.

"So, what? You had to kiss me to get rid of his hands being on me? That makes a whole lot of sense." I laughed manically.

Tonight was not going at all how I had planned. I had no idea how to rein this in and put my plan in motion. I wasn't sure my plan even mattered, because the way that kiss made me feel proved to me that I wasn't over him. I thought I'd stopped loving him—that all I felt for him was this searing hate and anger—but I'd been wrong. I wasn't sure I could do this without getting hurt again. If I was smart I'd shut my mouth, walk out of here, and be done with this.

He looked away, not giving me an answer.

Once upon a time we might've known everything about the other person, but right now I felt like we were strangers. I guess we were. We had seven years of mistakes and experiences to change us from the people we knew.

"I'm going back to the bar, finding Gavin, and seeing if he wants to have a little fun."

I started to saunter away but his hand snapped out to grasp my wrist.

"You'll do no such thing." He pulled me against his chest. "I will fucking handcuff you to me if that's what I have to do to keep you from spending the night with that guy."

"Let me go." I tried to pull away. "You have no say over what I do."

His eyes flashed with silver fire. "No say?"

I nodded.

He leaned in close, rubbing his lips against my ear before he whispered, "I fucking *own* you."

I ripped away from him and rushed out of the hotel as fast as I could manage with my heels.

I heard his heavy footsteps behind me.

He wasn't running, but he was keeping a quick pace.

I reached my car and I wasn't surprised when he stepped up behind me, pinning me to the door.

His chin rested on my shoulder, his stubble tickling my bare skin—because I'd been stupid and left my coat in the bar.

"Why can't things be like they used to be?"

His question surprised me, and I opened my mouth to say, *because you destroyed it*, but stopped myself.

This.

Right here.

This was the moment I'd been waiting for in order to put my plan into motion.

It was the perfect opening and I jumped on it.

"It can be," I whispered.

His body pressed more firmly into me. "I hated you for leaving," he admitted, his voice sounding pained in my ear. "But seeing you again…"

"I know what you mean," I panted.

My body seemed to be humming at the way he was pressed up against me.

"I want you." His lips ghosted against my cheek and then he turned me around so we were face to face. "Come inside."

"Yes."

# CHAPTER SEVEN

"Mathias!" I screamed—and not from ecstasy might I add. "If you do not unlock this right now I swear to God I will *kill* you when I finally get my hands on you."

He stood at the end of his massive bed, grinning with his hands shoved into the pockets of his dark colored pants. His dress shirt was gone, leaving him in only a thin sleeveless t-shirt with the suspenders dangling below his waist.

My dress was gone as well, leaving me in my lacey bra and underwear.

"Unlock it now!" I yelled, shaking my wrist that was handcuffed to the elaborate wrought iron bed.

"No."

"Mathias!"

"I had to make sure you didn't try to go find that guy." He said simply, like that explained everything.

"I'm with *you*, not him!" I roared, trying to shake free of the handcuffs. I was going to end up rubbing my wrist raw, but I didn't care. I also didn't want to think about who else he might've handcuffed to his bed.

He shrugged. "I know you, Remy." He leaned forward, bracing his hands on the end of the bed. The movement did incredible things for his chest muscles. "And I know you like to play games."

"This isn't a game." I groaned, my arm starting to hurt the more I pulled at the handcuffs. I guess it *was* kind of a game to me, but not in the sense that I would've fucked that other guy just to mess with Mathias. I wasn't *that* crazy.

He clucked his tongue like he didn't believe me. "Get some sleep."

He started for the door of his bedroom.

"Where are you going?" I practically shrieked in panic. Was he seriously going to leave me alone handcuffed to his bed?

"Out."

The door closed behind him, and I started screaming, cursing his name and threatening him in every way I knew how.

But the door never opened again and eventually I fell asleep.

I woke up when someone touched my arm. I jerked away, barring my teeth like I was about to hiss.

"Don't be so damn skittish." Mathias growled, holding me still so he could undo the handcuffs.

My shoulder and arm were numb from being in that position all night, but that didn't stop me from launching myself at him like a crazy person—a scream tearing out of my throat.

I tried to scratch at him, but it was useless. He was so much bigger and stronger than me.

He slammed me down onto the bed, wrapping his hands around my wrists, and pushed his whole body into mine. He was so heavy I felt like I couldn't breathe.

"Let me go, you stick twisted bastard."

He smiled slowly. "I like it when you call me names."

"Ugh! You are impossible!" I bucked my hips against his, trying to throw him off, but it was futile.

"Why are you here?"

"In your bed?" I sneered. "Because you tricked me and then fucking handcuffed me!"

He rolled his gray eyes. "I know why you're in my bed, I didn't forget. I want to know why you're *here*, back in town."

"How is that any of your business?"

He glared down at me, pressing me harder into the bed so my back rubbed against the smooth sheets. "Anything to do with you is my fucking business."

"Oh, really?" I snorted. "I'm pretty sure you gave up any right to know anything about me when you walked away from me."

He winced, no doubt remembering the day he cut me open with words and left me alone in a parking lot feeling like I was bleeding out.

"That was a long time ago," he sneered. "We were both kids then, let's act like fucking adults."

"Says the man that handcuffed me to his bed all night for no good reason!"

His lips threatened to turn up into a smile but he schooled his features. "Just tell me why you're here, Remy. Why did you come back?" There was an almost reverent look on his face.

Now it was my turn to cut him. "I didn't come back for you if that's what you're thinking."

His face fell slightly, but then his gaze heated and I knew I was in trouble.

"You mean," he lowered his head, pressing his lips to my neck where my pulse jumped, "you haven't thought about me at all over the years?" He pressed another kiss to the spot behind my ear. "Not about how we used to talk for hours about anything and everything? Not how my lips felt on yours?" He ghosted his lips over mine in a teasing touch. "Not how I felt inside you?" His voice dropped to a husky whisper and his eyes had deepened with lust.

"Stop." My voice came out weak sounding.

"Tell me," he growled, "tell me you haven't thought about me, about *us*, at all, and I'll stop."

I swallowed thickly. I couldn't say anything.

"Just say the words, Remy, and I'll let you go. I'll let you walk out of here and that'll be the end." His dark brown hair brushed against my forehead.

He grasped my chin, forcing me to look at him. "Say it!" He roared. "Tell me you don't want me the way I want you! Fucking say it!"

My chest heaved, and if I'd been a weaker woman I would've started crying. "I *can't*."

With my admission his lips crashed into mine. We collided angrily, clawing at each other like wild animals.

He kissed me until my toes curled, and my skin felt like it was on fire, but then pulled away roughly before things went too far.

He backed away from the bed like my touch had electrocuted him.

I sat up slowly, trying to catch my breath and calm my racing heart.

"You can't kiss me like that and then not do anything about it." I glared, looking around the room for my dress. When I found it I grabbed it up and slipped into it.

He sat down on a high-backed chair in the corner, resting his elbows on his knees and his head in his hands. "You confuse me like nobody else can."

"Back at ya." I nodded, heading for the door to his bedroom.

"Don't leave," he called.

"Why shouldn't I?" I stopped, not looking over my shoulder at him. Instead I stared straight ahead with my shoulders squared. "It's what we do best, right?"

"What the actual fuck?" I whispered to myself, pacing my bedroom. Percy cracked one amber eye open to watch me from where he snoozed peacefully on my pillow.

I kept replaying everything that transpired last night and this morning and I was no less confused each time I analyzed it. Mathias was so hot and cold. One minute he was all over me and the next he acted like my touch was going to poison him.

He wanted me, that much was clear, but he was fighting it.

*Why?*

*He* was the one that broke up with *me*.

*He* was the one that hurt *me*.

This should've been easy—but it wasn't.

I needed to continue with my plan. I knew that for sure. He was clearly still attracted to me—despite the fact that he was always photographed with a brunette on his arm—so I needed to turn up the seduction a notch and work on my acting skills. I couldn't let him realize this was a game. It had to look real.

And that's where it would get difficult, because in the hands of Mathias Wade what was left of my heart just might be obliterated all together.

Then I'd be left with nothing.

# CHAPTER EIGHT

I finished my workout and sweat dripped off my body.

I grabbed a clean towel as I headed towards the locker room and used it to dry myself off some.

A hand clamped down on my shoulder and I turned to find Drew, the boxing instructor and gym owner, standing behind me.

Once he had my attention he released me and took a step back. "I just wanted to tell you that you're doing an excellent job."

"Oh, thanks." I spared him a smile.

"It's better than yoga, right?" He joked.

"Only a smidge." I held my thumb and forefinger up with a tiny bit of space between them.

He chuckled. "And yet, I don't think I've seen you attend a yoga class since you started boxing."

"Touché."

"Anyway, that was it," he smiled. "I'll see you soon."

"See you," I replied as he walked away.

When I started towards the locker rooms I stopped in my tracks.

Mathias.

Oh, fuck.

I hadn't seen him in over a week. I hadn't sought him out and he hadn't come by the bar.

I was unprepared for this encounter, so I darted around a pillar out of his sight and into the locker room. I showered and changed into clean clothes. I had to head straight into work from here so I took extra time in front of the mirror applying my makeup.

When I left the locker room I looked left and right and didn't see any sign of Mathias—thank God.

With Mathias' celebrity status he probably had his own fucking room to workout in.

Sometimes it still surprised me that he was actually famous. To me, he would always be Mathias. I didn't look at him and see dollar signs. Instead I saw a guy that was lonely and begging for someone to understand him.

There was so much more to him than what he showed to the world. All everyone else saw was a brooding lead singer going through more booze and women than should be allowed. But I saw past that. I saw the pain he was trying to hide. He might've been a bad boy through and through, but I believed wholeheartedly that there was *good* in him. He just chose to hide those bits and pieces from the world so they couldn't be held against him.

I shook my head free of my thoughts. I needed to focus and get to work, not think about Mathias.

The drive was short and inside the bar was dead but the restaurant area was packed. Before I could get behind the bar Tanner threw an apron and notepad at me. I caught both easily. "We need you out there today."

Waitressing would be harder for me than manning the bar since the customers were more diverse. But since the bar was dead this would give me more tips.

I tied the apron around my waist and grabbed the notepad. A pen was already clipped to the end.

I spoke with the other waitress, Amy, and she told me which tables to take—flashing me a relieved smile in the process.

Hours passed and we finally began to slow down. I was getting tired though. Being a waitress was hard, carrying the heavy trays and running here and there. I wanted nothing more than to go home and take a long hot bubble bath.

When Tanner said I was free to go I couldn't get out of there fast enough. I grabbed my bag and twisted my hair up on top of my head in a messy bun. My neck was damp with sweat from all the running around I'd been doing.

I grabbed my purse and headed out, waving goodbye to Tanner and the other waitress that had come in.

I hurried outside and immediately encountered a wall of smoke.

I coughed, waving it away.

I hadn't smoked since I was sixteen and now the smell made me ill.

The guy sitting on the steps with a cigarette dangling between his lips looked up at me, his gray eyes stopping me cold.

He dropped the cigarette on the ground, snuffing it with the toe of his shoe, and stood up blocking my way before I could even process the fact that he was sitting there.

"What are you doing here?" I asked when it became obvious that he wasn't going to move.

"Waiting for you." He shrugged, running his fingers through his hair in a nervous gesture.

"Why?"

"I think that's pretty obvious," he looked at me like I was stupid. "I wanted to see you."

"I'm tired," I stood up straight, "and I'm going home to take a long hot bath. I don't have time to get into it with you again." He got under my skin so bad that I couldn't even think about trying to implement my plan.

I went to brush past him, but he grabbed my wrist and said something that very rarely passed through his lips. "Please?"

"What do you want?" I stopped, looking at him sadly.

He rubbed at his now clean-shaven jaw. "Dinner. That's what I want." He nodded, like he was agreeing with his words. "Come back to my place and we'll have dinner."

"Okay," I agreed, "dinner would be nice." And maybe it would give me enough time to get my shit together and actually go in for the kill.

I *had* to make him fall in love with me again.

I *had* to break his heart.

And I *had* to stop getting so mad and flustered around him, so that I could actually do it.

I'm sure that sounded twisted, especially since I'd loved him once, but after the hell I went through he deserved to hurt too. Right?

"Good, come on." He placed a hand on my waist, guiding me forward.

"I have my own car, you know." I looked up at him through my lashes.

"I know," he replied. "But we're going in mine."

He led me to a brand new shiny red Corvette. When I knew him, he didn't even own a car, he had a skateboard.

I slid into the car and he got behind the wheel. "Why did you drive here if your penthouse is around the block?" I asked.

He chuckled huskily. "Because I didn't come here from the penthouse."

"Oh, right." I mumbled, looking out the tinted windows. From the outside the windows were so dark that no one could see in. I'm sure Mathias enjoyed the privacy. It had to be hard having practically the whole world watch your every move. When the band was in L.A. the paparazzi relished in following their every move. Right now, Mathias and Maddox seemed to draw the most attention—Maddox, because the paparazzi expected him to propose to his girlfriend Emma any day, and Mathias because he was always getting into trouble. I'd lost count of all the articles I'd read where Mathias had been kicked out of a bar or restaurant for being drunk and causing a problem. Not to mention, the paparazzi loved how he went through women. Mathias was gorgeous, and despite the fact that he was a very obvious player, women flocked to him. Even me. After all, I was here wasn't I?

But this was different.

This wasn't him batting his eyes at me and making me lose all sense.

This was *me* going after *him*.

Right?

Fuck. My brain was all kinds of rattled where Mathias was involved.

This was never going to work.

But I had to try.

Even if I broke myself in the end, it would be worth it if he experienced even the tiniest bit of heartbreak I'd felt.

Mathias was quiet when he parked the car in the underground garage attached to the hotel.

He climbed out of the car and I knew I was expected to follow.

We stepped into an elevator and he inserted a key, pushing the PH button.

"It must be nice," I said, leaning against the wall of the elevator, "being here and not having to deal with the paparazzi."

He shrugged. "Yeah, that's nice, but that doesn't stop random people from stopping me on the street for pictures or taking one from afar and trying to sell it online." He ruffled his hair and his brows furrowed, wrinkling his forehead. "But this place… it's home. It always has been and it always will be."

The elevator dinged and opened into the penthouse. He grabbed the key and pocketed it, pressing his arm against the door so it wouldn't close and I could exit first.

"You hate it… don't you?" I asked hesitantly. I wasn't sure if my question might piss him off, because with Mathias the stupidest things could make him explode. But I also knew I was one of the few people to know everything about him—at least, I used to. Like I knew that he was dyslexic. It was something that had always bothered him and made him feel like he was worthless and stupid. But that was the farthest thing from the truth.

"Hate what?" He asked, striding past me and into the open concept kitchen.

I followed, looking around the space. The last time I'd been here I'd been otherwise occupied thanks to Mathias' heated kisses—but then the fucker had to go and trick me and handcuff me to his bed. Jerk.

The kitchen boasted white cabinets and white marble countertops. The floors were a gray hardwood looking tile that extended through the whole living area, but turned into a plush carpet in the bedrooms.

"The fame." I shrugged.

He braced his hands on the countertop, tilting his head to study me as if weighing his options. Finally, he nodded. "I do hate it. I mean, this is what we always dreamed of, but now… sometimes I wonder if getting to live our dream is worth all the other things we've had to give up." He looked down at the countertop, his knuckles turning white. "I love the music. I love feeling it. But having people judge me for being human? It fucking sucks. We all mess up and make mistakes, but when you live in the spotlight people act like you're supposed to be a fucking saint," he shook his head, "and that's not fair."

I couldn't believe he'd said all that and been so honest.

I jumped up on the counter and he moved to stand in front of me, bracing his hands beside my hips. I kicked my legs against the cabinets like a little kid as he stared down at me intensely. I wasn't sure what he was looking for in my eyes, but he must have found it, because he cupped my cheek and leaned in.

"This feels like when we were younger," he whispered. "Like no time at all has passed."

I closed my eyes, feeling his breath fan across my lips.

God, I'd missed him.

It didn't seem possible to miss someone I'd grown to hate, but I did.

I was pretty sure that when someone like Mathias came into your life they were impossible to forget.

He was like the sun, burning so bright that even once he was gone I was still blinded.

"Did you ever miss me?" I asked. "Even once?" I held my breath, waiting for him to explode—because that was Mathias. He could be nice one minute and an asshole the next. I wouldn't put it past him to kick me out for my question.

Instead he surprised me by leaning in impossibly closer and nuzzling my neck. "Always."

I opened my mouth to say something back, or maybe to kiss him, but a high-pitched whimpering cut me off.

"What was that?" I asked, jumping against him and grasping his shoulders like his body alone would protect me from whatever the beast was.

He chuckled, unhooking my arms. "Stay here. I'll show you."

He sauntered off to a back part of the penthouse suite. I watched him go, my eyes glued to his ass. His dark gray pants hugged it perfectly and his navy sweater pulled taut against his wide shoulders.

He returned a moment later with the cutest gray and white pit-bull puppy in his arms.

I jumped off the counter, my mouth hanging open. "Mathias Wade has a puppy? You realize you have to feed it right? And give it love and affection?"

He rolled his eyes at me. "No, Remy. I thought she lived off of the air."

"She?" I asked, raising a brow.

"She," he repeated. "Her name is Shiloh. I… I rescued her." He shrugged. "I stopped by the shelter and she just looked at me and…" He looked away from the puppy, glowering at me now. "I had to have her."

"Do you go to the shelter often?" I asked reluctantly, fearing his wrath.

He shrugged, putting the puppy on the ground. She promptly made her way over to me, sniffed my feet, and must have deemed me okay, because she licked my toes.

"Hey," his eyes narrowed, "I'm not a heartless bastard you know? I went in to donate some money and they were showing me around the place and…" He trailed off.

"And?" I prompted, bending down to pet the puppy. I swore Shiloh smiled at me.

"And she chose me," he mumbled, looking away.

"She chose you." I repeated, fighting a laugh.

"Well it sounds stupid and improbable when you say it that way." He crossed his arms over his chest and leaned against the wall.

"She's very sweet." I gathered her into my arms and she licked my face. "And for the record, my cat is going to be livid when he smells her on me."

"You have a cat?" He asked, looking adorably confused.

"Yes," I nodded. "Percy chose me, the way you say Shiloh chose you… okay, that's probably a lie," I laughed. "I found him in a really bad shape and took care of him, tending to his wounds, that kind of thing. He scratched the shit out of me, but then he never left and became mine."

Mathias nodded, looking distracted. "I better take her out." He mumbled, taking the puppy from my arms. He grabbed a leash and fastened it onto her collar. I bit down on my bottom lip to keep from laughing at the sight of Mathias walking a dog with a hot pink leash.

While he was gone I snooped around—because why wouldn't I?

I didn't find anything of merit though. The place was pretty empty and there was nothing personal around. Not even a picture of his friends and twin brother.

I didn't understand how he could possibly like this starkness.

It made the otherwise lovely penthouse seem cold and depressing.

I vacantly wondered if his home was as empty as his heart.

When Mathias returned he was like a whole new person, he smiled when he entered, Shiloh right on his heels. "I'm going to order room service. Why don't you go take that hot bath you talked about wanting?"

My eyes widened. "Are you serious?"

"Of course." He stepped closer to me but left an appropriate amount of space between us. If Mathias Wade had a theme song it would be 'Hot n Cold' by Katy Perry. Mathias would hate the cheesiness of that, but it was true. I guess I was the same way with him, though. We were quite a pair. It was like neither of us could ever decide what we wanted.

"I don't have any clean clothes to change into," I argued.

He laughed but there was no humor in the tone. "Remy, with my money I'm pretty sure I can get you some clean clothes delivered."

I bristled at that. "You don't need to flaunt your wealth in my face," I spat. "I'm not some model or actress you need to impress. I'm *me*. I'm the girl that knew you when you were nobody."

"It's not flaunting when it's the truth," he countered easily.

I narrowed my eyes on him. "What do you want with me?" I finally asked.

His eyes flooded with confusion. "I don't know," he answered. At least he was honest. His fists clenched at his sides. "You infuriate me like nobody else," he continued. "But you also make me feel better than anyone else. You've always been able to get under my skin. And I've *never* stopped thinking about you, Remy. Every day I wondered about you. But I was never man enough to find you." I closed my eyes at his words, biting my tongue so I didn't tell him he wasn't man enough even now to apologize for what he did. "You scared me when we were teenagers. What I felt for you scared the shit out of me, because it shouldn't have been possible. I thought then that the feeling would go away once you were gone, but it only got worse. I *ached* for you." I don't know when he moved, but suddenly he was right in front of me. "I still do." There was a pain in his eyes I'd never seen before. "When you left I was a scared teenage boy that had no idea what he was doing. I pushed you away, because I thought that was easier. I felt like you were abandoning me. But it was all me. I was the one that abandoned *us*." Years of pain and torment echoed in his words.

Was it possible that Mathias was as torn up about what went down between us as I was?

"I still don't know what I want with you." He leaned his forehead against mine, his Adam's apple bobbing. "I don't know if I'm even *right* for you, but God dammit I want you so fucking bad right now. I want you in my arms, in my bed. I want a chance to make this right between us." His voice lowered and his lips brushed against my jaw. "Give me a second chance. Please tell me it's not too late for us."

I wasn't used to this Mathias—a pleading one.

"But-but," I stuttered, "you seemed so angry that I was back in town."

"I was," he admitted, one of his hands cupping the side of my neck. I was sure he could feel how fast my heart was racing. "I thought you were here to destroy me all over again. But then I decided I didn't give a fuck, because I only feel like I'm alive when I'm with you."

I leaned forward, pressing my face into his chest. I didn't want him to see my face right now and all the emotions raging across it. I needed a moment to think.

*This* was exactly what I had wanted to happen. *This* was my in to destroy his heart the way he had mine, but suddenly that didn't feel right. I felt dirty and ashamed to have wanted to hurt him, but I couldn't get my feet to move—to walk away and end this.

"What do you want to happen between us?" I lifted my head and peered into his eyes.

"I want you to be mine," he growled lowly, "and only mine."

"Does that mean you'll be mine and only mine?" I twisted his words around. My heart clenched painfully as I recalled all the photos I'd seen of him with different women. Mathias got around, that much was obvious.

"I've only ever been yours." He ghosted his lips against my neck. "I might not be a hearts and flowers kind of guy, but it's the fucking truth."

"The-the women?" I panted as his lips explored further and my eyes fluttered closed.

He pulled away, glaring down at me. "Are you telling me you haven't been with anybody since me?" His look said *not likely*.

"I've been with other guys." Of course I had. It had been seven fucking years, and I thought I'd never see him again.

"And I've been with other women." He shrugged. "But right now, here we are, just the two of us." His voice lowered to a husky murmur. "Tell me that you want me as much as I want you."

"I do." I gasped the words, a small cry accompanying them. I wanted Mathias more than I wanted my next breath. We were made for each other. They might say opposites attract and never to fight fire with fire, but neither of those things applied to us. We defied the laws of the universe.

"Just like old times?" He asked. "You and me against the world?"

I nodded, afraid that if I opened my mouth the truth would spill out and I'd tell him he was playing into my plan exactly as I wanted.

"Just like old times."

# CHAPTER NINE

I sat in the bathtub with bubbles up to my chin.

Mathias was somewhere in the penthouse ordering our dinner.

His open vulnerability had me worried.

I was playing games, and Mathias… what if he really did want me?

That should've been a good thing for my 'love him and leave him' plan, but suddenly I felt sick to my stomach and I wasn't sure I could go through this. It felt wrong.

I drew my knees up to my chest, water sloshing over the sides.

Mathias had always been able to wrap me around his finger better than everybody else. He was so fucking charming and I fell for it every time. He could just as easily be playing games with me.

*But what if he's being honest? What if he really does want you?* A little voice in my head spoke up.

*It doesn't matter.* I lied to myself.

I'd barely been around the guy and he already had my thoughts all kinds of messed up.

It was like a storm was roaring through my mind, kicking up dust and overturning everything in its path to the point that I was lost and confused.

I climbed out of the bathtub, wrapping a towel around my body.

I stared at my reflection in the mirror. "You can do this, Remy." I whispered. "Revenge, remember?" I nodded to myself. "You have to destroy him like he did you. He ruined your life and he's not good for you. Do *not* let him into your heart again. Do *not* let him trick you into thinking he's changed. He doesn't care about you. He didn't care about you then and he definitely doesn't care about you now."

I probably looked like a crazy person standing there talking to myself, but let's face it, I lost my mind a long time ago.

I closed my eyes, remembering my last conversation with Mathias before I left for Arizona.

*The stifling humidity of the summer heat made my clothes stick to my body. I was tempted to take my tank top off and leave myself in my bra and jeans, but I was still on school property and I wouldn't put it past one of the teachers to report me even though it was the last day of school—and after school hours.*

*Mathias' hand was clasped in mine as we walked together.*

*My heart beat irregularly in my chest.*

*I had to tell him that I was leaving.*

*I'd been putting this talk off—and another—for weeks.*

*But time had caught up to me and now I was left with no choice but to break the news.*

*"Mathias?" I spoke, stopping in my tracks.*

*He stopped too and looked at me questioningly. "What is it? You're not sick are you? You've been looking a little pale."*

*"I'm fine, but there's something I have to tell you…"*

*He stopped and crossed his arms over his chest like he knew whatever was going to come out of my mouth was going to be bad.*

*"What's going on, Remy?" He asked. "Is this some sort of intervention? I didn't drink that much at that party, I swear."*

*"No, it's not about that," I mumbled.*

*I shook my head, tears clinging to my lashes. I never cried, so Mathias knew this was bad.*

*"Rem?" He prompted.*

*"We're moving." I choked on the words like they were something physical lodged in my throat. "We leave in a week."*

*"Moving? Where?" He asked, his dark brows furrowing into a straight line.*

*"Arizona." I squeaked.*

*"Arizona?!" He roared. "Next week?! That might as well be all the way across the world!" He threw his arms in the air.*

*"Mathias," I said his name calmly, "we can do the long distance thing."*

*He shook his head roughly back and forth, his shaggy brown hair falling into his eyes. He pushed it back and slapped his baseball cap on backwards.*

*"No. No. No." He seemed to be in a state of disbelief. "You can't fucking leave me."*

*I closed my eyes. He'd once told me he had abandonment issues. His dad had driven his car into a tree on a drunken binge and his mom was in jail. Even though his foster parents were great people, I knew he feared they'd grow tired of him and kick him out.*

*"I'm not leaving you by choice," I reached for him and he flinched away from my touch. "This is my dad's job, I have to go."*

*A look of hatred settled over his face. "Just go then."*

*"Mathias—"*

*"GO!" He yelled right in my face. "I always knew you would! I knew you were too good for me and that's why I fucked Josie!"*

*"What?" I gasped, taking a step back and clenched my heart like I'd been shot. Josie? Josie Miller? That girl that was always batting her eyes at him in our biology class? How? What? When? Why? We spent so much time together, I didn't see how…*

*"You heard me," he seethed. "I fucked her, because you'll never be enough for me."*

*Tears coursed down my cheeks at his cruel words. "You cheated on me?"*

*I'd fallen in love with Mathias in a way I didn't know you could at sixteen years old. I'd given him parts of myself I never shared with anyone. He knew everything about me, and right now he was destroying me.*

*He nodded, his teeth clenched together. "Did you really think I'd settle for you?"*

*I flinched. Those words were like a slap to my face. "I don't know what I thought." My voice came out as no more than a whisper. I was normally a strong girl, but right now all my strength had left me. I felt like a piece of me was dying.*

*"She wasn't the only one. There've been more."*

*He continued to drill holes in my heart.*

*"How many?" I asked, gasping for air.*

*"More than you want to know," he spat.*

*"I hate you!" I shouted, a sob cutting through my throat.*

*"Good, because I hate you too!" He yelled back.*

*"You're nothing but a lying, cheating, filthy bastard and I'm sorry for thinking there was more to you than that." And then my hand reared back and connected with his cheek. My hand left behind a red imprint on his cheek.*

*He nodded once, like he was agreeing that he deserved that, and then he turned and walked away.*

*He left me standing there crying in the school parking lot as my entire world blew up in my face.*

*When his body was nothing but a speck in the distance, I whispered, "You're going to be a dad."*

*And then I fell to the ground in the fetal position and cried until a teacher found me.*

# CHAPTER TEN

I ate dinner with Mathias last night and then had him drive me back to my car with the excuse that I had to check on my grandma. It was the truth too. I'd been gone all day. I was really sucking at the whole Babysit Grandma thing. I should be fired.

The sunlight streamed in through the kitchen windows as I made breakfast. I felt like shit today, and I knew it had everything to do with remembering that day in the parking lot. I purposely tried not to think about it, because every time I did it filled me with the same feelings of loss and emptiness.

Grandma came out of her bedroom, hobbling with her cane. I set the plates of poached eggs down on the table and hurried to her side to help her to the table.

"Are you okay?" I asked her.

She waved away my concern with an age-spotted hand and said, "It's this damn arthritis getting to me. Nasty stuff makes me ache like I've been run over by a car."

"You've been run over by a car?" I joked.

She narrowed her eyes. "You know what I mean."

I laughed at her and got each of us a glass of orange juice before sitting down.

"Do you have to work today?" She asked me.

"Not today." I took a bite of my breakfast.

"Good, you can drive me to bingo. Normally Charlene picks me up and takes me," she said, referring to one of her elderly friends, "but she drives like this is the Indy 500. The last time I swore my false teeth were going to come flying out."

I laughed, choking on a bite of egg. She reached over and beat my back with a surprising amount of strength. I coughed up the lodged eggs and spit it into a napkin.

"Can you try not to make me laugh when I have food or drink in my mouth?" I asked, reaching for my glass of orange juice.

"What's funny about my dentures falling out? That's a tragedy, Remy."

I shook my head. "It was funny, trust me. Anyway," I continued, "I can definitely take you to bingo."

"You better stay in the car when you drop me off, though. If you come inside the old farts might try to flirt with you, and the women there get jealous easily."

"Grandma," I laughed. "I think I'm a little young for those men."

She eyed me. "They don't know that. Men are men, and they think anything with two legs and a pussy is fair game."

"Grandma!" I exclaimed, stifling a laugh. "Stop it!"

"It's the truth." She nodded her head, finishing off her breakfast. "You stay here with me for very long and I'll teach you everything I've learned over the years, like the fact that men think their penis is a gift to womankind. It's not."

At this point I was laughing so hard at her that tears were streaming down my face and I could barely breathe.

She soon joined in with my giggles.

Living here with my grandma actually wasn't that bad. I mean, I did get free comedic entertainment with breakfast.

Once I had composed myself I cleaned our plates and glasses before guiding my grandma into the living room and getting her situated on the couch with the TV on.

"You know," I said to her as I plopped in the rocking chair, "if there's ever any place you want to go to I'd be happy to take you."

She turned to look at me. "Do I look like I want to go anywhere?"

"Well, you did say you wanted to go to bingo," I laughed. Sobering, I added, "I hate you being cooped up in this house all the time. If it was warm outside I'd try to get you out for a short walk. I could always take you to the mall," I suggested.

"No," she growled. "No malls. Annoying teenagers frequent that place. The last time I was there I had to hit one with my cane to get him out of my way."

"Grandma!" I felt like I was shouting that a lot, but she kept surprising me.

"What?" She looked at me innocently. "He kept standing in my way and wouldn't move, not even when I asked politely. A little tap to his knee and he was out of my way."

"If you keep this up I'm going to pee my pants," I warned her.

"I honestly don't see what's so funny," she huffed, "it wasn't a joke."

I shook my head and stood up, stretching my arms above my head. "I'm going to head to the gym for a while. I won't be gone long."

"Can you pick up Chinese for lunch?" She asked, perking up. "I haven't had that in forever."

"Of course," I replied. "Let me get you a notepad to write down what you want."

I left her with the pen and paper and went upstairs to change.

Percy was sitting on top of the dresser. His tail swished lazily back and forth as he watched me.

I grabbed my gym bag and headed downstairs. She handed me the piece of paper as I passed her on the way to the kitchen. I grabbed a water bottle from the refrigerator and put it in my bag.

I stopped and kissed her wrinkled cheek. "Bye," I called over my shoulder.

She mumbled something under her breath that I didn't catch as I locked the door.

There wasn't a boxing class today, so I planned to run a few miles on the treadmill in order to feel like I had accomplished something.

I was halfway through my run, and damp with sweat, when a dark form strolled over beside me.

When I looked over and saw that it was Mathias my feet stumbled and I would've face-planted if it weren't for his quick reflexes. He reached out and grabbed me around the waist and yanked me off the treadmill into his arms. I stumbled against his hold, feeling slightly dizzy.

"Are you okay?" He asked, reaching up with his free hand to turn off the treadmill.

I nodded weakly, struggling for air. My legs seemed wobbly and I was glad he hadn't let me go yet.

"What are you doing here?" I panted, my chest rising and falling with each breath.

"Exercising." He gave me a 'duh' look.

"Obviously," I huffed, "I meant here scaring me half to death."

He chuckled. "That was an accident. I saw you and I couldn't resist coming over."

"Uh huh," I nodded, finally letting him go since my limbs no longer felt like Jell-O. "Next time give me a warning."

"Are you finished?" He asked, nodding his head at the treadmill.

"I am now," I grumbled, crossing my arms over my chest. The movement pushed my boobs up and his eyes zeroed in. He quickly looked away though, clenching his jaw. It wasn't like Mathias to be this way. In the past he'd never tried to hide his ogling.

"Go to lunch with me."

I was startled by his words. I hadn't been expecting that. His gray eyes narrowed on me, as if daring me to say no. "I can't," I replied. He opened his mouth to argue with me, but I cut him off by holding my hand up. "I promised my grandma I'd bring Chinese home for lunch. I'm taking care of her, remember?"

He leaned against the side of treadmill. "No, I think you conveniently forgot that bit of information."

"Oh, right," I mumbled. Squaring my shoulders I jutted out my chin defiantly. "Well, that's why I'm here. To take care of her."

His eyes flashed a dark gray and he glowered at me. "Does that mean you're leaving again? You're just here to check on her and then you'll be gone?" He turned away, shaking his head, and mumbled something under his breath. It sounded a lot like, "I knew you'd never stay."

Mathias being, well, *Mathias*, he started to leave.

I grabbed his arm and he turned around sharply to glare at me. He shook my hand off and spat, "Forget it, Remy. Forget everything I said last night. I don't want to see you." He stalked off once more, towards the exit.

"Hey!" I yelled after him and he stopped. He didn't turn around though. "What the fuck is your problem?" I seethed. "I'm not going anywhere. I don't know what the future holds for me, but I like it here."

He continued to stand there, not looking at me.

"You know what, you're a fucking coward. That's all you are." I let out an exasperated sigh and stormed away to the locker room. I didn't care if I looked like a five year old. Mathias was so damn confusing. He was giving me whiplash. One minute he was coming on to me and the next he was pushing me away. At this point I was starting to not give a fuck about trying to break his heart, because he was exhausting me so damn much.

I opened my locker to grab my things—I'd shower at home—and a hand slammed into the metal door closing it.

I whipped around and came face to face with Mathias.

"Stop doing that!" I yelled.

His body caged me in against the lockers. The room was empty except for the two of us. In the corner a leaky faucet dripped, the quiet splashing the only other sound save for our breaths.

"Stop doing what?" He tilted his head, leaning so close that his nose touched mine.

"You know what," I snapped, spitting the words through my teeth. "One minute you're nice to me and the next you push me away. It's unfair!"

He shook his head, his face darkened with shadows. "You don't know what you do to me, do you?" He asked.

I shook my head, my breasts brushing his chest every time I took a breath.

"You've done nothing but haunt me since you left. No one and nothing compares to you," he nuzzled his face against my neck and I arched against him. "One taste of you and I was fucking ruined." I squished my eyes closed and winced in pain. Hadn't I said basically the same thing about him? "What I feel for you scares me," he breathed, his lips brushing over mine. I whimpered at the feel of them. "When we were teenagers I thought for sure it would go away, that I'd grow sick and tired of you, but I was wrong," he growled lowly, "I only ever wanted you more."

I couldn't seem to stop myself from saying, "But Josie?"

He shook his head, his hair brushing against my forehead. "I don't want to talk about that."

"You never want to talk about anything!" I roared, struggling against him.

"That's how I am." His eyes seared into me, his nostrils flaring with anger. "It's in the past. Let it go."

I squished my eyes closed, anger boiling my blood. Anger was good though. That's what I wanted to feel for him. It made it all the easier to play the game.

"Fine," I panted. "We'll forget the past," I agreed. "It'll be like it never existed."

"I want this to be a second chance for us," he whispered, brushing his lips over my cheek. My anger began to dissipate and lust filled its place with one simple touch. Mathias was the only guy that had ever been able to make me go weak in the knees, and I hated him for it. "But I keep fucking it up." He bit my earlobe, tugging it gently between his teeth. "And I'm sure I won't be able to stop, because that's what I always do… ruin everything." His lips grazed my chin. "But I'm not strong enough to walk away from you. You're my fucking addiction. Always have been. Always will be."

He grasped my chin and tilted my head back, capturing my lips with his. He tugged on my bottom lip with his teeth and let it go with an audible pop. My blood heated with want and desire. I grasped his hair, pulling sharply and a hiss escaped between his teeth.

"You want it rough?" He growled, his eyes flashing with heat.

"Don't I always?" I panted, my eyes flaring with desire. Just because I was playing a game, didn't mean I couldn't reap the benefits. I needed him to ease the ache inside me.

He chuckled huskily in approval, grasping my thighs and lifting me up so my legs were wrapped around his lean waist. The cold metal lockers dug into my back, but I didn't mind.

I took his face in my hands, angling my mouth over his. I normally wouldn't be able to kiss him like this, but since he was holding me it put me higher up than him.

While I kissed him he tore away from the lockers and moved through the room. I didn't care where he was going as long as he didn't stop touching me.

One of his hands left my body as he tore open one of the shower curtains and carried us inside the stall. He closed the curtain and reached over to turn on the water, dousing the both of us and drenching our clothes.

I didn't care and neither did he.

He tore off my wet tank top and palmed my breasts that heaved against the confines of my sports bra.

"It's been too fucking long since I've had you like this," he growled, kissing my neck.

"Since when did you become such a talker," I groaned, bucking my hips against his as the shower streamed down us. "Just shut up and fuck me."

He chuckled in a way that let me know I was in trouble.

Oh, how I loved being in trouble.

The shower beat down on us, scalding our skin—or maybe that heat was from our touch.

He ripped my sports bra off and then his mouth was on me and I let out a long moan—not caring if someone walked in and heard us.

I tugged at his white t-shirt and he pulled away just long enough to discard it.

One by one our clothes landed in a wet heap on the tiled floor of the shower.

Our hands and lips seemed to be everywhere at once. I couldn't get enough of him. For seven fucking years I'd been missing this. It didn't seem possible that I had survived that long without this… this… whatever this was.

With a groan he pinned my hands above my head and a look of anguish stole over his face.

"Condom," he ground out, "I forgot a fucking condom."

"Don't need one." I nearly cried the words. I needed him inside me and he was taking too damn long.

"Are you sure?"

"Mathias!"

He laughed, taking my lips between his and thrusting into me instead of responding with words.

I clenched around him, nearly weeping with joy at how fucking good he felt inside me.

My head fell back, soft pants passing through my lips as he fucked me just the way I liked.

It seemed he'd never forgotten my body and the way it responded to him. He still knew the exact right things to do to get to me.

His tongue swirled over one of my swollen nipples and I cried out from the sensation, clenching around him.

"You feel so fucking good," he growled, biting down on my shoulder and I knew a mark would be left behind.

He rolled his hips against mine and I let out a small scream. "Do that again." I pleaded. He did. "Oh God."

"No, my name's Mathias." He smiled. The arrogant bastard.

"Harder, please." I begged.

Normally he would go against my requests because he liked to drive me fucking insane, but this time he obliged.

He let go of my hands, holding my hips, and I grasped his wet shoulders.

I flicked a wet piece of hair out of my eyes, fighting to gain control of my breaths.

"Fuck, right there," I urged. "Oh, God." I fell over the edge with a small cry that he covered with his mouth and I panted his name against his lips.

He growled low in his throat and rested his head in the crook of my neck as he found his release.

He stayed there for a moment, letting his breath even out. The water was turning cold but neither of us moved to turn it off.

Finally he raised his head and kissed me deeply before murmuring, "Fuck I missed this."

"Me too," I agreed, clinging to his shoulders as he lowered my legs to the ground. When I was sure I wouldn't fall I released my hold on him.

He shut off the water and poked his head out of the shower so he could look around.

"No one's in here." He reported. "Wait here, I'll grab us some towels."

I did as he asked, shivering slightly from the cold water that still clung to my body. He returned only seconds later with a fluffy white towel for me—one already tied around his lean waist. I wiped myself off and then wrapped it around me.

"I might have a change of clothes here," I told him, eyeing the pile of soaking wet clothes, "but I'm guessing you don't." I laughed. "I mean, this is the women's locker room," I joked, winking at him.

He leaned against the tiled wall and my eyes zeroed in on a water droplet that dripped from his chin onto his collarbone, slid down his abs, and disappeared beneath the towel.

He shrugged, not caring. "What's the worst that can happen? Someone snaps a picture and sells it to a magazine? They've printed plenty of shit about me, so I really don't give a fuck at this point."

"Aren't you supposed to care about your public image?" I asked. It was pretty obvious that he didn't when you bothered to look at most of the headlines sporting his name or image. He was always being photographed in some compromising position—the last one I'd seen had been when he attacked a paparazzi for tailgating him. I couldn't say I blamed him for getting pissed about that. I would too.

"Does it look like I care?" He raised a single dark brow. "I'm sure you've seen the headlines."

"I have," I confirmed, "I've also seen all the women."

He smiled at that. Not even the slightest bit embarrassed. "I like women," he replied. His eyes darkening he added, "But I don't like any of them the way I do you."

"Good to know," I huffed. "I also noticed most of them were brunettes."

He chuckled, shaking his head, a playful smile on his face. "You noticed that, huh?"

I nodded. "I've got news for you, Mathias. I'm not a brunette." I grabbed a piece of my wet hair and waved it in his face. "Never have been."

"I know." He closed the space between us. He placed his hands on either side of my head and leaned in so he could whisper in my ear. "But there's only ever been one blonde I wanted. No one else compared to her."

I closed my eyes, breathing in his words.

And when I opened them he was gone.

# CHAPTER ELEVEN

Mathias was waiting for me in the parking lot when I stepped outside the gym. He was leaning against the back of his red Corvette, smoking a cigarette. He'd changed into a pair of nice jeans and… was that a cardigan? Normally I would make some dig about him turning preppy, but he looked too hot in it for me to complain.

"I can't believe you still smoke," I sighed.

"You don't?" He asked, a brow rising in interest. "You used to smoke more than me."

That was true. "I quit." I stopped smoking after I found out I was pregnant and never picked up the habit again.

"Shame." He let out a puff of smoke and we both watched it circle the air. He reached up, ruffling his now dry hair. Looking at him standing there so calm and composed you would have never guessed that not too long ago he had me pinned to a wall in a shower fucking me senseless.

"So, I was thinking," he started, putting the cigarette out, "you and I should go get lunch and then you can take your grandma whatever it was she wanted."

I looked down at my watch. "I have an hour."

"Good," he nodded, not smiling, "now get in."

I stared at the pile of pasta in front of me. "How is one person supposed to eat all this?"

Mathias lifted a single brow and looked at me like I was crazy. "It's family portions, or whatever. That means you have to share with me." He smiled like the cat that ate the canary.

"I forgot you can never get enough to eat," I laughed.

"It's my superpower."

"A bottomless stomach?" I asked.

He nodded, dipping a piece of bread in olive oil. "Yes, that and my ability to get you to scream my name."

I rolled my eyes. "I can make you scream my name too. Or have you forgotten?" I winked, kicking his shin lightly with my foot beneath the table.

He grinned and when he smiled it transformed his whole face. Normally he looked so angry at the world, but when he smiled… it was magical. "I haven't forgotten anything about you." He let out a sudden laugh and leaned forward, lowering his voice. "Do you remember Mr. Johnson?"

"That really mean history teacher?" I asked, racking my brain.

He nodded. "We glued all his stuff to his desk after he gave you an F on that one paper."

"Oh yeah." I laughed with fondness at the memory.

"I ran into him the other day in town," Mathias snickered, "and he asked me for my fucking autograph."

"Oh God." I laughed, hiding my face behind my hands. "What did you do?"

"I pretended to give him an autograph, but instead I drew a penis and said SUCK THIS."

"Mathias!" I giggled. "What are you? Twelve?"

He chuckled. "Well that's what I used to put instead of my name on all those stupid worksheets he gave us, so I thought it was fitting."

"And that'll probably end up in the news next week," I told him. I could see the headline now: *Mathias Wade gives former teacher penis drawing.*

"Probably," he agreed. "I fucking hate the media," he speared a piece of pasta, "but I'm learning to ignore it. It's easier that way. I went out of my way to purposely piss them off and look like an asshole."

"Why?" I asked, confused.

"It's what I do," he answered simply. "They don't know me, but they think they do, so I just give them what they want. It's easier than letting them see the truth." He stared down at his plate of food, his brows furrowed together.

"Why are you so intent on making people hate you?" I asked, even though I already knew what the answer was.

Mathias always pushed people away. If they didn't care about him, then they couldn't get close enough for *him* to care, and ultimately end up hurt. I'd been one of his only exceptions—and I didn't think I'd ever know what it was that drew him to me in the first place—and look how we ended up? We crashed and fucking burned down the entire forest.

"You know why," he grumbled.

"I wish," I took a deep breath, twisting the wrapper from my straw around my finger, "that you would let people see the real you."

"That is the real me, Remy," he growled, glaring at me. "I'm harsh and a jerk. I'm the alcoholic womanizer everybody loves to hate. I hurt people because it makes me feel good. I like to make other people as miserable as I am, so that maybe, for one fucking second, I won't be alone in my suffering."

I remained steady, looking right at him. "I know you think that's all you are, but you're wrong. You can't lie to me."

He grabbed his glass of wine and took a sip—that sip turning into him downing the entire thing. "I am what I am."

I sighed. This was going nowhere.

Finally I changed the subject. "You've never really explained to me what we are?" I questioned.

He glowered at me and spat, "I think I've been pretty fucking clear."

"Nope," I shook my head, "with you there are a lot of gray areas."

He rolled his eyes. "You're mine and I'm yours. End of fucking discussion."

"Yes," I started, "but are we like a couple? Or fuck buddies? I'd like to know upfront before I see a photo of you in some magazine with some other woman and it catches me off guard."

"We're Mathias and Remy—that's all that matters. The rest will fall into place."

Ha! If only he knew.

"Ah, yes. I'm sure it will just be that easy." I laughed, taking a sip of wine.

He glared at me, anger simmering off of him. "Why is it so fucking hard for you to believe me?"

"Because," I sat back, the picture of ease, "I've seen photos of all the women you go through, and I doubt I'll be enough for you." I laughed. "And on top of that, I've only been in town all of three seconds and you've been nothing but hot and cold. It's so hard to read you."

"Just because I don't profess my fucking feelings by shouting them from the rooftop, doesn't mean I don't have them," he snapped, his irritation with me leaking into his words. "It's not like I'm sitting here telling you I love you, we both know how that ended up the last time. I'm just…" He looked away for a moment. "I don't really know what the fuck I'm asking for." He shrugged. "I told you I wanted this to be a second chance for us," he whispered, "and I meant that, but I…"

"But you're not going to promise me forever," I supplied.

"Yeah, I guess that's what I'm saying." He sat back in the booth, glaring at his food like it had offended him somehow.

I smiled slowly and lifted my glass of wine. "Lucky for you, that's fine with me."

His eyes closed and he looked almost pained.

Shouldn't he have been relieved that I was agreeing with him?

Instead he seemed tortured. It made no sense.

Mathias wiped his hands on a napkin and set it on the table. "I'm not very hungry anymore."

I looked down at my food and realized I'd only been pushing it around. "Me either."

He motioned for the waiter and asked for the check and boxes.

After paying we headed out to his car and he drove me back to the gym so I could get mine.

He parked beside it and I glanced at him.

He stared moodily out the window, not looking at me.

I had no idea what he was pissed about, but with Mathias it was always something.

I wore a challenging smile and undid my seatbelt. Instead of getting out of the car like he expected I climbed onto his lap. Up until this point Mathias had been playing into the game better than me, and he didn't even know it.

He looked at me, startled.

I took his face in my hands, kissing him deeply with every ounce of passion I had left in my body.

The goal was to leave him aching and begging for more.

He let out a low, pleased growl, and his fingers tangled into my hair, tugging lightly.

When we were both panting for air, I pulled away and slid off his lap.

I was out of his car before he knew what happened.

I sauntered over to my car, swaying my hips more than necessary.

When I heard his car door open I smiled with satisfaction and looked at him over my shoulder.

"Come by tonight?" He asked, rubbing his fingers over his lips.

I let out a soft laugh and shrugged. "Maybe."

He narrowed his eyes on me as I got in my car.

God, I loved playing with him—and it was only just beginning.

# CHAPTER TWELVE

"You didn't come over."

I looked up from the glass I was drying to see Mathias standing in front of the bar with his hands flat on the shiny wood top.

"Was I supposed to?" I asked, raising a brow.

"Um, I'm pretty sure I asked you to come by last night." He slid onto one of the barstools.

"I'm sure you were heartbroken by my absence." I put a hand over my chest.

"I was hoping for a repeat of the shower." His eyes raked over my body, and it felt like he was undressing me. Some of the other guys sitting around the bar perked up with interest and started watching the two of us. Apparently we were more entertaining than whatever football game was playing.

"I was busy." I gave him a look that said, what-was-I-supposed-to-do, and shrugged my shoulders while lifting my hands innocently in the air.

"Busy?" He repeated, making a face like the word tasted sour on his tongue. "What could possibly be more important than me?"

I rolled my eyes at his arrogance. "Bingo." I said in an even voice.

"Bingo?" He snorted.

"You betcha," I nodded, grabbing another beer for Melvin and sitting it on the bar before he could ask. "I won a hundred bucks. Most fun I've had in a while."

He narrowed his eyes until they were nothing but thin slits. "You're such a fucking liar."

I propped my elbows on the bar in front of him and leaned forward. "Should I come over tonight?"

He nodded eagerly, his eyes dipping to the swell of my breasts as his tongue slid out to moisten his lips. "And I'm going to sit here until your shift ends to make sure you don't flake again."

"I didn't flake," I leveled him with a glare, "I was playing bingo, remember?"

"Uh-huh," he nodded, scratching his slightly stubbled jaw. "Now get me my scotch."

Now it was my turn to narrow my eyes. "Are you really going to wait here until my shift ends?"

He nodded, looking up at the TV screen.

"I'm here until midnight." I warned him.

"And I'll be right fucking here," he said, never taking his eyes off the screen. "Put in an order of cheese fries while you're at it."

"Scotch and cheese fries," I mumbled, "that sounds delightful."

He still didn't look at me, but I saw his lips twitch and knew he was fighting a smile.

I put the order in first and then poured his drink. I set it on the bar and his eyes flickered to me. "You know," he said, his voice serious, "I like that when I'm here no one tries to take my fucking picture."

One of the guys sitting at the bar—a regular named Jason—piped in with, "That's because we don't like you pretty boy and your music sucks."

Mathias grinned. "See? This place is wonderful."

I shook my head. "I think you forget that it's also a restaurant." I pointed over his shoulder to a table of giggling high school girls who were pointing at him—a few tearing apart their purses, probably in search for something for him to sign.

"Fuck," he groaned, not even turning around.

"Be nice," I warned, "their money makes your life nice and cozy."

"It was never about the money," he told me, "just the music."

"Then prove it," I challenged. "Go say hi to them."

"Fine, I will." He finished off his scotch and stood up. He sauntered towards the girls, but suddenly turned and changed course.

My mouth fell open when I saw him stop at a different table—this one occupied by a mom, dad, and their daughter—who couldn't have been more than thirteen and her head was bald from chemo treatments, concealed behind a bandana. The girl looked up at him with an awed expression as he spoke, waving his hands through the air. He must've asked to join them because suddenly the little girl was sliding over and he sat down beside her.

"Remy!" He called to me where I stood open mouthed behind the bar. "You can bring my cheese fries to this table and whatever they ordered make sure it gets put on my tab."

I nodded woodenly, watching in surprise as he interacted with the parents and daughter. The little girl seemed enamored with him and I was shocked that he'd managed to bury his usual asshole attitude for a moment.

Mathias stayed at their table until they had desert and then moved back to the bar—but not before giving the girl a hug and posing for pictures.

My icy heart might've melted a teeny tiny bit. A miniscule amount really.

I wiped down the bar and said, "That was quite a show you put on."

He snorted. "It wasn't a show. I'm not quite the asshole the world believes."

I crossed my arms over my chest. "Why wouldn't you want the world to see that part of you?" I nodded my chin at the family walking out the door.

"Because," he replied, "it's the only good part of myself I have left, and if the media found out that I'm actually a softy when it comes to kids then they'd twist that somehow and taint it." He stared at me, his forehead wrinkling as he thought. "No matter how much I might wish it so, moments like that don't make me a good person. I'm still a piece of shit."

Mathias used to say that about himself all the time when we were teenagers. Nothing I said to the contrary could prove him wrong, and it seemed with the media's scrutiny his self-hatred had only become worse. That should probably please me since I was hell bent on seeing him suffer, but it didn't. I felt bad for him. He shouldn't have hated himself the way he did.

"I hate that you think that," I whispered, almost hoping he didn't hear the words.

"Why?" He asked, truly curious.

I shrugged, busying myself by rearranging some glasses. "Because you're not a bad person. You're good, Mathias, you've just… you've made some bad choices." I flinched, thinking about the pain I felt when he told me he'd cheated on me. Despite how much I worked to *not* be like every other girl, once I got with Mathias that's exactly what I became. I went from the girl who wanted to rule the world, to the one that dreamed of marriage and a happy life for our baby. But all of that was ripped away from me, because of the choices we made.

"Bad choices?" He laughed. "I've fucked up at every turn."

I opened my mouth to reply, but was cut off by Tanner scolding me to get back to work.

"Later," I warned Mathias.

The minute we walked into his penthouse suite I started in again. "For someone that thinks they've fucked everything up, you've done mighty good for yourself." I twirled around, my arms lifted in the air.

He stood with his hands in his pockets watching me. "Trust me, I've fucked up everything that matters." He glowered at a wall. "Luck is what got me all of this." He waved his hand to the fancy furnishings.

I shook my head in disagreement. "Talent is different than luck."

"So what? I can *sing*, yeah that's such an amazing talent." He sat down on the couch while I stood by one of the windows, looking down at the empty street below us.

"But it is," I replied.

"You call it a talent," he mumbled, leaning his head back to look up at the ceiling, "I call it a curse."

"Why are you such a pessimist?" I marched toward him, sitting on the coffee table in front of him.

"It's not pessimism, it's realism. I don't deserve this," he waved his arms around. "Not any of it."

"*Why?*" I pestered.

He scrubbed his hands over his face. "I don't want to talk about this."

"You always used to say that," I sighed, "but you know what?" He looked at me, not saying a word, so I continued, "You would tell me anyway."

"Things are different now. I might want you just as much now as I did then, but it doesn't change the fact that we're strangers now."

"Do you really believe that?" I asked.

He looked away and I knew I had my answer.

"You trusted me then, why can't you trust me now?" I asked. Even if I had ulterior motives for being with him, I would *never* betray his trust in the sense that I'd run to the media and sell a story.

"I don't know." He growled.

"Think about all the things you told me then, and I've never told another soul."

He closed his eyes, and I wondered if he was reliving one of the countless memories we shared. I knew I was.

*Tap. Tap. Tap.*

*I slid out of the warmth of my bed and over to the window. I pushed the curtains aside and found Mathias looking at me through the window, perched on the roof outside. I opened the window, and muttered, "What the hell are you doing here?"*

*"I needed to see you," he said, reaching for my hand.*

*I slipped outside and sat beside him on the roof.*

*Now that I was closer to him and the light from the moon was shining on his face I could see the bruise covering his cheek. "What happened?" I asked, reaching out to tenderly stroke the side of his face. He relaxed into my touch and let out a content sounding sigh.*

"I got into a fight with some older guys. They outnumbered me."

"Over what?" I gasped.

"I started it," he whispered, drawing up his knees and draping his arms overtop, "I wanted to fight them."

"Why?" I couldn't understand.

"I wanted to feel something," he admitted.

"Why can't you feel something without punching someone?" I spat. It wasn't the first time I'd seen bruises on him, he'd just never told me where he'd gotten them from before.

"I'm fucked up," he whispered.

I shook my head. "Only because you let yourself be. Maybe you should try being a man and stop looking for trouble."

Mathias sought out pain like it was a drug, the way I way I found things to get my adrenaline pumping.

"What if those guys beat you unconscious and left you for dead?" I asked him. "Have you even thought about that?"

His jaw clenched together. "It's what I deserve."

"No, it's not." I shook my head.

He nodded. "It is. You don't understand…"

"Then explain it to me!" I raised my voice and quickly put a hand over my mouth, afraid I might wake up my mom and dad. Or worse, my brother.

"You can't tell anyone," he warned, glaring at me.

"Who am I going to tell? Lana? She's barely my friend," I snorted. "You know you're like my best friend, and that's only because you're so fucking stubborn that you won't leave me alone."

"It's only because you're hot." He cracked a smile.

I rolled my eyes. "I'm still not sleeping with you. So nice try."

He chuckled, but quickly sobered. "My real mom's in jail," he whispered. I knew he was a foster kid—everybody did—but no one knew anything about his real parents. "For prostitution. Awesome, huh?" He laughed humorlessly, ducking his head. "And my dad's dead, but he wasn't a fucking saint either. He was nothing but an alcoholic with anger issues."

"So?" I asked, missing the point.

"With parents as fucked up as that it's only inevitable that I follow in their path." He sighed, looking up at the stars.

I put a hand on his shoulder and he tilted his head down to look at me. "We might be made up of our parent's DNA but it doesn't mean that we're them. We make our own choices and become our own people. There's not some predetermined future for us at birth. We have the choice to be anyone we want to be."

His jaw ticked. "It doesn't feel that way." He winced as if he was in pain. "…I can still hear her yelling in my head about how I was worthless, and stupid, and nothing but a fuck up…"

"Your mom said that about you? Your mom that's in jail?"

*He nodded.*

*"Um…" I started, "I think those things apply to her. She's the one that's in jail for making bad choices."*

*"But I'm her kid. Cut from the same cloth."*

*"But not the same person," I countered.*

*"She was right though… I am stupid," he mumbled.*

*"No, you're not. Hating school is different than being dumb."*

*He shook his head. "I can't read."*

*"What?" I asked.*

*"I. Can't. Read." He said each word slowly. "I'm dyslexic. Anytime I look at a piece of paper all the words get all jumbled and I can't read it."*

*"So what?" I asked. "There are plenty of people with dyslexia. I'm sure there's some kind of exercises for your mind or something."*

*"You have an answer for everything," he chuckled, glaring out at the night.*

*"Maybe you should shut up and accept my help," I snapped, "instead of being so fucking stubborn."*

*He glanced at me, smiling slowly. "I love it when your sass comes out."*

*"You're so weird," I rolled my eyes.*

*"I'm surprised you're not looking at me like I'm a piece of trash," he said suddenly, startling me with the turn of conversation. "I told you the kind of parents I had, and here you are living in this nice house with your doctor dad and lawyer mom."*

*"So? Having successful parents doesn't make me better than you. We're all just people in this world," I leaned back, resting my elbows on the roof, "and that's it."*

That was the first night Mathias ever appeared on the roof outside my window. But it soon became a nightly routine where we'd sit outside for hours, talking about anything and everything. Sometimes we discussed something that happened at school, and other times our conversations got deeper as he opened up more about his childhood. He told me some horrible things, but none of it made me love him any less, and love him I did.

"Why didn't you ever tell anybody?" He asked, looking at me with a perplexed expression. "There were so many things you could've told on me. You could've ruined my career if you wanted to."

"I didn't want to," I shrugged. "Things between us might've ended on a sour note, but I loved you once and how could I possibly hurt someone I used to love?" My voice cracked, and I frowned. Wasn't that what I was trying to do now? Arguably, breaking his heart wasn't the same as destroying his career, but it was still bad, wasn't it?

I drew my knees up to my chest and hugged my arms around them.

Mathias stared at me for a moment before shaking his head. "You were always too good for me."

I shook my head, smiling sadly. "You're wrong."

He chuckled, leaning forward and prying my arms from around my knees and yanked me onto his lap. I straddled him, wrapping my arms around his waist.

"Okay," he smoothed a hand down my back, resting it at my waist, "then you're the less fucked up one."

*Wrong again.*

Mathias had no idea how messed up I was and I hoped he never found out. Better to break his heart on purpose than to shatter it with the truth.

# CHAPTER THIRTEEN

He held me in his arms for a few minutes and then placed me on the couch in a manner that was far too gentle for the Mathias I was used to.

"Do you remember all the movies we used to watch?" He asked suddenly, reaching for the remote.

"You mean when we'd watch those old kid's movies and recite all the lines?" My nose crinkled as I thought.

He nodded. "Yeah. Let's do that." He reached for the remote and brought up Netflix. Our weekly movie night had been one of the few things we did together that was actually relatively normal. Most everything else we did involved some kind of trouble—a lot of it illegal.

He typed something in and I turned to look at him, stifling a laugh.

"Little Rascals?"

"Wasn't that always your favorite?" His pouty lips turned down in a frown.

"It is," I nodded, "I can't believe you remembered."

He looked at me strangely. "I remember everything about you, but that doesn't change the fact that I don't feel like I know you now." He got up abruptly and headed to the kitchen, opening and closing drawers. A moment later I heard the telltale pinging of popcorn popping.

The movie began to play, but I was too busy looking behind me waiting for him to return.

He strolled back into the room, shoving a handful of popcorn into his mouth. He sat down right beside me, so that his thigh touched mine, and put the bowl in his lap. "It has extra butter and that powdered cheese you always liked."

I shook my head at his thoughtfulness. He was hurting me with his kindness and he didn't even know it. I reached over and grabbed a handful of popcorn, popping one into my mouth.

Looking around the spacious penthouse, I ignored the movie and asked, "Why did you decide to live here? In a hotel?"

He chuckled. "The penthouse might be attached to the hotel, but it's still my place. I mean, look around," he waved a hand, "does it *look* like a hotel to you?"

"No," I agreed, taking in the sparse white decorations that hardly matched the rest of the hotel, "but isn't it a part of it?"

"It's attached to the hotel, obviously, but the top floor was originally divided up into two apartments for sale. I bought both so I could turn it into one large apartment. So, it's not a fucking hotel room, m'kay?"

I rolled my eyes. "You didn't need to get nasty. It was just a question."

"I have a home in L.A. and I guess I wanted something different while I'm here. I mean, I could've stayed at my mom and dad's place, but that felt weird. Besides, Maddox and his girlfriend have taken over the fucking guesthouse, so I didn't really want to stay there anymore. This place is all mine," he waved a hand to encompass the space. "Plus, I can still order room service, and have access to the indoor swimming pool. I wouldn't have had that in a house."

"Yeah, but you could've built a huge mansion to be whatever you wanted it to be," I argued.

He shrugged. "I don't want a mansion, besides…" He trailed off, letting out a sigh. "I didn't want a house, because being in a big space like that makes me realize how alone I am and then that makes me feel fucking depressed. That's why I hate my house in L.A. It's not even that big, but when I'm there it's… it's so quiet. I don't like it. At least here," he shrugged, "I can look out the windows and see the town and I can walk down the street to a restaurant or bar if I want to. I'm not isolated, and I don't have to worry about being bombarded by paparazzi."

"And now you have Shiloh," I added.

As if she heard her name the little puppy began to whine.

Mathias chuckled and stood up, pausing the movie. "I better walk her, do you want to come?"

"Sure," I agreed, surprised he asked.

I followed him back to a laundry room and he let her out of her crate. "I have to keep her in here when I'm gone," he glanced up at me, "she chewed through five pairs of my shoes and then started in on a belt."

"At least the suspenders weren't harmed," I joked.

"You love my suspenders." He grinned, holding Shiloh in his arms and standing up to leash her.

"I do," I agreed, because it was true. He definitely made those suspenders look hot.

I followed him to the elevator and out onto the street. The hotel didn't have a grassy area so poor Shiloh was forced to do her business on the sidewalk. Once she was done we headed back inside and sat down on the couch with Shiloh. She sat in Mathias' lap and kissed his chin, then tried to steal the popcorn every time he took a bite.

I finally took pity on her and gave her a piece.

Mathias narrowed his eyes at me. "Did you just give my dog popcorn?"

"I did," I smiled innocently. "I felt bad for her."

"She's not supposed to eat people food," he glared, now holding the bowl in the air so Shiloh couldn't get into it.

"Aw, come on," I pouted, "I hardly think one piece of popcorn is going to hurt her."

His eyes darkened for a moment as he stared at me and then before I knew what was happening, the bowl clattered to the ground, popcorn going everywhere with Shiloh running after it. But Mathias paid no attention to that. Instead, he pounced on top of me, pinning me to the couch.

His lips devoured me, biting and nibbling and staking his claim.

My heart beat madly behind my ribs as my fingers wound around his neck.

His touch scorched my skin, burning me from the outside in.

He cupped my face in his large hands, angling my head back and sweeping his tongue against my parted lips. I gasped against him, tugging sharply at the short strands of hair at the back of his neck. He bit down on my plump bottom lip in retaliation.

I knew my lips would be bruised later from the force of his kisses, but I didn't care.

His hips dug into mine, pushing me further into the plush cushion of the couch.

He grasped my neck, kissing over my breasts and heading lower.

"God I fucking want you again," he growled, slowly lifting my shirt up my stomach. "I always want you. The ache never goes away."

I breathed deeply, trying to steady my racing heart, but it wasn't working and I feared it might beat right out of my chest.

"I knew something was missing from my life, I just didn't think…" He paused, glancing up at me, his breath tickling my exposed stomach.

"You didn't think, what?" I prompted, needing to hear what he had to say.

"I didn't think it was you." He whispered the words, almost as if he didn't want to give voice to them.

He moved up my body and was about to press his lips to mine when we heard a high-pitched whining sound.

"Oh shit." He jumped away from me and off the couch.

Shiloh had eaten most of the popcorn on the floor.

Mathias looked at me with panic in his eyes. "I think I just killed my dog."

Shiloh laid on her side and let out a burp.

"She looks fine to me." I bent down, looking at her closer.

"I need to get her to the vet." Panic edged his voice. "This can't be good. I mean, she ate a shit ton of popcorn."

"She's probably only going to have a really bad stomach ache."

Mathias ignored me, instead running around the penthouse looking for his phone.

He called someone and paced back and forth. I ignored his portion of the conversation and kept an eye on Shiloh, just in case something bad did happen.

He hung up the phone and crouched down beside the puppy, lifting her into his arms, cradling her like a baby.

"The vet's coming over," he mumbled, rubbing the top of Shiloh's head.

"At one in the morning?" I gasped.

He glanced at me, his eyes flashing a silvery hue. "Yes. Sometimes having money comes in handy."

"Of course," I sighed, sitting back and feeling like I was in his way. I stood up and looked around for my purse and jacket. I'd tossed them onto the floor on the way in, but they weren't by the entry. I finally found them sitting on a side table. Mathias must've picked them up. He'd always thrived on order while I needed chaos.

I shrugged into my coat and pushed the button for the elevator.

It pinged and I heard a rustling behind me.

I looked over my shoulder and found Mathias standing up with Shiloh in his arms. The look in his eyes reminded me of a lost little boy. He seemed hurt, confused, and desperation clung to his shoulders.

"Please, don't go," he begged.

A lump formed in my throat and I tried to swallow past it. "I thought you wanted me to go." The elevator doors opened behind me, but I made no move to step inside.

"I never said that."

"But you made me feel that way," I countered, crossing my arms over my chest. "You can't have it both ways—if you want me to stay you need to make me feel like I'm wanted, not like I'm a fucking inconvenience."

He sighed, glancing down at Shiloh in his arms. "I'm sorry for being an asshole, but that's me, Remy, and you know it. You've always known it. I can't be any other way."

I wanted to argue with him on the matter—because he'd certainly been sweet with the little girl at the restaurant tonight, and then again with his concern for the puppy. I wished he could see how thoughtful and caring he was, instead of only seeing the bad. Every person had good and bad traits, but Mathias thought he was bad through and through. He was so incredibly mistaken on that matter. He had more good in him than most.

When I stayed quiet, anger flashed in his gaze. "Fine, go. Leave. I don't give a fuck."

He stormed out of the living room and down a hallway. A moment later a door slammed.

I closed my eyes, warring internally. Did I go after him? Or leave? Neither seemed to be the right option, but I figured if I left he might never want to see me again and I *needed* him to want me around. So I set my purse down on the table again, and marched down the hall.

I pounded my fist against the closed door that led to his bedroom.

"I swear to God Mathias Wade if you don't let me in there right now I will throw something at this fucking door and break in. And once I do that, you'll be the one handcuffed to the fucking bed."

The door swung open and he waved me inside. "Oh look, you stayed," he sneered, "there's a first time for everything."

I winced, but turned away so that he didn't see the pain etched on my face.

"Maybe if you weren't always pushing me away, I wouldn't be leaving."

He growled something under his breath and sat down on the bed, laying Shiloh down beside him. He looked at her worriedly, his forehead wrinkling.

"She's going to be fine," I assured him, climbing on his massive bad and sitting so that the puppy was between us.

"She's so little," he whispered, rubbing her stomach as she slept, "this could be really bad."

"Well, the good news it's not chocolate. I read somewhere that, that's really deadly for dogs." I hoped the tidbit of information would make him feel better.

He jumped up from the bed and raced out the bedroom door.

I hurried after him, nearly tripping over my own feet in my haste to keep up. "What are you doing?" I hissed, finding him rummaging through every drawer and cabinet in the kitchen.

"Making sure I don't have any chocolate." He looked at me like *I* was the crazy one.

I rolled my eyes. "You can have chocolate in the house. Just don't give her any."

"But what if she finds it," he hissed, dropping to his knees to search one of the bottom drawers.

"She doesn't have thumbs. The chances of her opening a drawer or cabinet are impossible."

"What if she nudges it open with her nose?" He asked, making a huge mess as he tossed stuff out of a drawer. He found a Snickers bar in there and held it up triumphantly before throwing it away.

"I highly doubt that would happen." I pinched the bridge of my nose.

"But it *could* happen," he argued.

I sighed, crossing my arms over my chest. "I'm going back to check on Shiloh. I'll leave you to your raid."

He ignored me, continuing to tear apart his poor kitchen. All that stuff was going to be a pain in the ass to put away. Good thing I didn't live here.

Shiloh perked up a little when I entered the room, cracking her eyes open. I was sure she was fine, but Mathias' concern for her was adorable, although a bit annoying. He tended to go overboard with all things.

I made myself comfortable on his bed, grabbing the remote off the side table and turning the TV on. I lay down, flipping through channels, and Shiloh moved to lay curled up next me.

I stifled a yawn, my eyes growing heavy.

I was about to drift off to sleep when Mathias strolled into the room with a man trailing behind him.

The man introduced himself to me and then immediately checked on Shiloh.

He looked her over carefully and then turned to Mathias.

"She's fine," he declared. "She might have a stomach ache and nausea depending on how much she ate, but it's nothing to worry about."

Mathias let out a deep sigh of relief. "I'm happy to hear that. I was really worried."

"I know." The vet smiled. "But she's okay."

Mathias nodded and pulled out his wallet to pay the man. He led him out of the suite and returned, taking off his shirt and undoing the belt on his pants.

I sat up and moved to get off the bed, because clearly it was time to go home, but he stopped me.

"Stay the night, please. We don't have to do anything. Just sleep."

I stared at him like I didn't know him.

"I don't have any pajamas." It was the only excuse I had to leave. I *wanted* to stay. I *wanted* him to hold me in his arms. And that scared me like nothing else could, because wanting led to caring, and caring led to heartbreak.

He strolled to his dresser and opened the top drawer. He rummaged around and pulled out an old Willow Creek tour t-shirt. He tossed it at me and I caught it easily. "You can wear that. There are extra toothbrushes under the sink." He nodded his head towards the bathroom.

"Thanks," I mumbled.

I had no excuse now.

I padded into the bathroom and closed the door behind me. I changed and brushed my teeth. Normally I would've left my clothes lying on the floor, but I knew Mathias hated that, and besides I'd need to put them on again in the morning and I didn't want them wrinkled.

Mathias was already in bed when I opened the door and even though the lights were now dimmed I could still feel his stormy gaze lingering on my body, particularly my legs.

I slipped into bed, Shiloh snoozing between us.

He reached up and turned the last light off, plunging us into complete darkness.

Neither of us said a word. The only sounds in the room were our breaths and Shiloh's light snores.

Back when we were young, our late night roof chats often led to him staying the night in my bed and sneaking out before my parent's woke up. I'd always felt comfortable then and safe in his arms.

But right now safe was the last thing I felt.

I knew I was in danger of falling in love with him all over again—because love is the one thing that can over power hate.

I was becoming tangled in the web of my own making, and I was afraid I might suffocate.

# CHAPTER FOURTEEN

I woke up with Mathias' body wrapped around mine, and his breath tickling the skin of my neck. Our legs were intertwined and he had my body hugged to his chest. I kind of felt like a human teddy bear.

I tried to pry his arm from around my torso but it wasn't working. He was too heavy.

"Mathias," I groaned, wiggling against him.

He tightened his hold and let out a soft growl. "You're not going anywhere."

"You're squishing me," I groaned, thrashing my body and trying to throw him off.

I squeaked when he moved lightning fast and pinned me to the bed, hovering on top of me.

"You're always so damn feisty." He blinked sleepy eyes at me and kissed my neck.

"I thought you liked that." I muttered, still fighting against him.

"Only when it's you." He cracked a small smile and rolled off of me. He grabbed a pair of black-framed glasses off of the night table and slipped them on, ruffling his brown hair further by running his fingers through it.

"Nice glasses Clark Kent."

He narrowed his eyes on me and glowered.

"What?" I shrugged. "It was a compliment. You can totally pull off the look." I left out the part where he could pull off anything… or nothing at all.

I slipped out of the bed and started towards the bathroom when I heard him hiss between his teeth. "Are you naked under my shirt?"

I looked back at him, quirking a brow. "Maybe," I said coyly.

"Fuck," he cursed.

Before I could make it to the bathroom he grabbed me around the waist and tugged me back into his bed. He lifted the shirt off, his eyes roaming over my body.

"I can't believe you slept in my bed all night practically naked. That's like torture." He pouted and I wanted to reach up and pull on his perfect bottom lip.

I shrugged. "You didn't know."

"I know now." His eyes skimmed over me again, and he bit his lip, looking pained.

"You can touch me, you know." I whispered conspiratorially.

"I'm enjoying the view." His eyes lifted to meet mine. So many different emotions flickered in eyes so fast that I couldn't even begin to decipher them.

His hand lightly grazed my sides and my blood roared in my veins with the simple touch. Goosebumps broke out over my skin and I closed my eyes as his lips met mine.

His kiss ignited a fire inside of me and I grasped onto his shoulders, wrapping my legs around his waist. Only his boxer-briefs separated us, and I wanted them gone.

"Mathias," I breathed his name against his lips, "please."

Oh God. I was *begging*. This was bad. He'd barely even touched me and I already wanted his cock inside me.

He pressed light kisses down my neck, between my breasts, and over my stomach. He grabbed my legs and parted them. He rained kisses on my right thigh and I squirmed against his hold.

"Mathias." Again with the begging.

"Hmmm?" He hummed. "Do you want something?"

"Please."

"Please?" He questioned. "That doesn't tell me what you want." He looked at me with an evil smirk. I wanted to slap it right off his arrogant face for toying with me.

"You know what I want." I fisted the sheets tightly in my hands as he moved closer to the spot where I needed him most. He just hovered there, not moving and not touching. "Dammit Mathias!"

"I want to hear you say it." He took my chin between his fingers and angled my face to look at him. "Say it, Remy. Say it and you'll get exactly what you want."

"I want you to fuck me."

He grinned triumphantly. "Now that wasn't so hard was it?"

"You're hard."

He let out a bellowing laugh and pressed against me. I was tempted to rip his damn boxers off. "So it would seem."

"Would you please just shut up already?" I begged, grasping his hair and pulling his mouth to mine.

He resisted and my lips ached with the need to touch his. I think I let out a whimper.

Suddenly he pulled away and stood up, smirking at me as I lay naked on his bed. "You know what, I changed my mind."

"Wh-what?" I stuttered. No. He couldn't do this.

"Yeah," he shrugged, feigning that he was unaffected. "I think I'm just going to go make some breakfast." He grabbed a pair of sweatpants and pulled them on.

I stared at his bulge with narrowed eyes. "You realize that in punishing me you're also punishing yourself, right?"

He grinned, crossing his arms over his chest and I stared up at the ceiling so that I wouldn't drool over his abs. "I know," he said in a silky voice, "but it's the anticipation that always makes it so damn sweet with you."

With that he walked out of the room, closing the door behind him.

I couldn't believe this. I'd freaking begged him like a crazy person, giving in and telling him what he wanted to hear, and the asshole was still leaving me hanging.

I threw a pillow at the door and yelled, "You bastard!"

His only answer was to laugh at me.

I took a shower, hoping that would help get rid of my aching desire.

No.

It made it worse.

Why?

Because I had to use his damn soap to wash with and now I could smell him all around me, it was the worst kind of torture imaginable. If he wanted me aching with want and desire he'd succeeded, but I wasn't going to ask him to fuck me. Nope. *He* was playing games, and I wasn't going to lose. I was going to make him so mad with desire that *he* lost his mind. He thought he held all the cards in his hands, but he was wrong.

I stepped into his bedroom with a towel wrapped around me and found him shrugging into a plain t-shirt. He wore khaki colored pants and sneakers. It was the most dressed down I'd seen him. He reminded me more of the Mathias I knew in high school when he was dressed like this.

"I got you some clothes."

"What?" I looked at him, confusion written plainly on my face.

"Clothes." He pointed to a shopping bag sitting on the floor.

"You left?" I didn't know why this tidbit of information was so important to me.

"No," he looked at me strangely, "I had someone pick it up and deliver it."

"Are you being sarcastic or serious?" I questioned, wrinkling my nose. "Because with you I can never really tell."

"Serious." He replied, grabbing a leather jacket. "I have to go meet up with the guys. Get dressed and we'll go."

"Wait… you want me to go with you?" I pointed at myself.

He rolled his eyes. "That's what I said."

And then he marched out of the bedroom, Shiloh at his heels.

I shook my head, baffled at his behavior.

I picked up the bag and dumped out the contents, finding a new pair of jeans, a red blouse—that was practically see-through—a black leather jacket, a pair of heels, and even lingerie.

I changed into the new clothes and found him in the kitchen, sliding a homemade waffle across the counter when I entered.

"You're a man of many talents," I said as I picked up the plate.

He merely pursed his lips in response and continued on with the task at hand. I sat down at the counter, glancing around. The penthouse was clearly decorated to his specifications, but it still seemed so cold. There were no personal photos or mementos. It was barren. I kind of wanted to go buy him some art for the walls and some colorful throw pillows. The white, black, and gray color scheme was so boring.

Mathias sat down beside me with a cup of coffee. He raised a brow when he noticed I wasn't eating. "Is something wrong?" He asked.

"No," I stuttered, "not at all."

He looked at me doubtfully.

"How long have you lived here?" I finally asked.

A wrinkle marred his forehead before he straightened out his features. "Almost two years. That seems like an odd question to ask."

I shrugged, getting up to pour my own cup of coffee. "It's just… I mean, this place is nice, don't get me wrong…"

"But?" He prompted, raising a brow. "There's always a but, so get to the point Remy."

"It's so boring," I frowned. "There's no color, or pictures. Not even personal photos." I sat down once more, watching him carefully.

He frowned, looking around. "I guess I never noticed. I like it."

"You like this?" I asked, sounding incredulous.

"I don't like clutter," he muttered.

I rolled my eyes. "Clutter is different."

He shrugged. God I hated it when he did that and looked at me like I was crazy.

"Would you like me to give you my credit card so you can go to Pier-Fucking-One and make the place all feminine and prissy?" He waved a hand wildly through the air.

I sucked my lips together, trying to contain my laughter. "I'm shocked you even know what Pier One is."

His lips quirked into a small smile. "Only because it's beside Petsmart and Target." He finished his waffle and stood to clean the plate. "Hurry up and finish eating," he growled when he saw that I'd barely made a dent in my plate of food, "or I'm leaving your ass here handcuffed to my fucking bed again."

"You wouldn't dare." I gave him a challenging look.

He leaned forward, resting his elbows on the counter and quirking his head to the side. "Want to try me?"

I scarfed down the waffle in record time and shoved the plate at him. "Happy?" I asked around a mouthful.

"Very." He suppressed a chuckle, washing the plate while I finished my coffee.

I put the empty cup in the sink and he huffed at me. "What am I, your fucking maid?"

I grinned evilly. "I'd love to see you in an apron."

"Only in your dreams." He rinsed out the cup.

I hopped up on the counter beside him, clucking my tongue. "Sorry, my dreams are a little more creative than that."

"Oh, really?" He chuckled, opening the dishwasher drawer. "I'd love to hear this."

"Hmm," I started, tapping my chin with my finger as I thought, "let's see, if I was dreaming about you, you'd probably be naked." He glanced at me, his lips twisting together as he fought a smile.

"Continue," he prompted, looking at me instead of focusing on the dishes.

"And then I'd get on my knees…"

"Remy," he growled.

"And wrap my mouth around you…"

"Fuck." His eyes widened.

"And then, just when you were about to come I'd stop, and then you'd slide inside me. I'd already be wet and aching for you and—"

One of the coffee mugs slipped from his hands and crashed to the floor.

"Shit," he cursed, bending down to pick up the pieces and throwing them in the nearby trashcan.

I hopped off the counter and smirked. "I'll let you figure out the rest." I winked and he cursed again.

"You're mean."

"I'm not the one that stopped this morning." I crossed my arms over my chest.

He winced. "I'm beginning to really regret that idea."

"Too late to change your mind now," I clapped a hand on his shoulder as he stood, "we've got to go."

He stood in front of me, crowding my space until my back was pressed into the counter. "I should take you back to my room right now, tie you up, and show you what happens when you play with me."

"Sounds kinky." I grinned, sliding away from him and heading to the elevator. I glanced at him over my shoulder and gave him a coy smile. "Coming?"

"Oh we will be," he nodded, sauntering forward like a lion stalking his prey, "later."

# CHAPTER FIFTEEN

"Nice house," I commented, when we pulled into the driveway of the large cape cod style home.

"Maddox, Ezra, and I bought it for our parents." He shrugged like it was no big deal. "It was the first big purchase we made once we signed our record deal."

Something in my heart warmed a bit.

"That was nice of you guys."

He glanced at me, seeming oblivious to his kindness. "Maddox and I owe Karen and Paul everything. They took us in instead of letting us get placed with some random family." Mathias had told me a long time ago how Karen and Paul had been their neighbors growing up, and the twins had become best friends with their son—Ezra, of course—so when Maddox and Mathias were put into foster care they stepped up to the plate and took in both boys. "They loved us when no one else did," he whispered, looking down and putting the car in park. He removed the key and sat back.

I wanted to tell Mathias that he was wrong—that I had loved him too.

But something told me that if I opened my mouth and uttered those words, they'd be nothing but a lie, because I *still* loved him. Against logic, against everything, I did and I think I always would. The kind of love we shared didn't go away easily—even when we crashed and burned, a lingering spark still burned. That's why, after seven years, I never stopped thinking about him. It was more than the fact that he hurt me, it was because he owned me. Mind, body, and soul. I was his. I didn't want to be, but I was.

When I didn't reply, he muttered, "Come on," and slipped out of the sports car.

He led me into the house—it was decorated with rich dark hardwood floors, pale gray walls, and comfortable looking furniture—and down a hall where he opened a door that revealed a set of steps.

He nodded his head for me to go first, so I did.

At the bottom of the steps we were met with an open living area set up for movie watching.

But that wasn't our destination.

He moved in front of me and I knew I was meant to follow.

Down another hall he opened a door and we stepped inside a fully functioning recording studio.

"Hey, Mattie Boy!" Ezra chimed from where he leaned back on a brown leather sofa. Even if I hadn't seen his picture in any magazines, I'd still recognize him. Although, he'd done a lot of growing up since we were sixteen. He was still thin and not as muscular as Mathias, but he had filled out more. His cheekbones were sharp, but softened by the heavy scruff on his cheeks. His black curls fell over his forehead and when he smiled a dimple pierced his cheek. "Nice of you to join us."

Mathias grunted in reply and sat down in a vacant chair.

The guys hadn't noticed me yet.

I spotted Maddox in the recording part, banging away at his drums. A girl around my age stood watching him with rapt attention. I recognized her from the magazines as his girlfriend Emma.

Ezra looked my way then and noticed me standing by the door, half in the room and half out.

"Remy?" He gasped my name, shaking his head and then rubbing his eyes like he couldn't believe what he was seeing.

I waved.

"It really is you." He stood up, moving towards me. I didn't know what to do when he wrapped his arms around me in a hug. I wasn't expecting that kind of reception at all. "I can't believe this."

"Remy?" Emma spoke. "Like, Remy *Remy?*"

My eyes widened in surprise. Had Mathias talked about me?

The girl spoke into some sort of mic and Maddox ceased drumming, looking up. His mouth fell open when he saw me.

He rushed out of the recording part and walked up to me.

"Remy?"

"That's my na—*ow!*" I rubbed my arm where he pinched me. "That was rude."

"Just making sure you're real."

"Shut up and leave her alone." Mathias growled, finally butting into the conversation. He grabbed me around my waist and pulled me onto his lap.

They all continued to stand there staring at me.

"I got the drinks!" A new voice joined us, the person it belonged to appearing in the doorway a moment later with a bunch of water bottles in his arm. "Why are y'all just standing there? I thought we were supposed to be working?"

Then the guy's eyes settled on me as he finally noticed that everyone was staring in my direction.

I recognized the tall blond guy as Hayes, the guitar player. He hadn't gone to school with us, so he definitely didn't know who I was.

"Uh… hello?" His eyes shifted around. I kind of felt bad for him. He was clearly out of the loop. "Who are you?"

"Remy." Everyone echoed.

"Nice to meet you, Remy," he muttered, setting the bottles of water down. "I'm Hayes."

"Oh, and I'm Emma." Maddox's girlfriend smiled apologetically. "I'm sorry I didn't introduce myself sooner, but I was taken off guard."

"I'm surprised you know who I am."

Emma's face wrinkled and she looked up at Maddox and then at Mathias. There was definitely a story there.

Mathias was still holding me, so I leaned my head back on his shoulder to look at him. "Talk about me often, darling?" I kept my tone light and playful, but I was really curious to know how Emma knew about me.

"No." He growled the single word, but his fingers curled possessively against my waist.

I raised a single brow, waiting for him to elaborate.

He huffed and glared at his twin brother. "If we're not going to work, I'm going to fucking leave."

Maddox crossed his arms over his chest. "And I've told you a thousand times that you don't need to use the word 'fuck' in every sentence."

"Sorry, but I fucking like it."

Maddox tossed his hands in the air, grabbed a water bottle, and headed back into the recording part. Emma glanced at me for a moment and left the room. Hayes and Ezra sat on the couch, and silence descended on us.

I'd often found silence to be more deafening than a roomful of people talking. There was something so heavy and oppressive about silence. It amplified everything and made you notice things you normally wouldn't. Like the way Mathias' forehead was wrinkled and his gray eyes were shadowed with thought.

I pulled my body from his hold and walked out of the room.

I thought he might follow me, but he didn't.

I found Emma sitting on the large couch in front of the massive TV in the basement. She was curled up with a book in her lap. I guessed the whole situation had made her feel awkward and she'd decided to retreat.

"Hi," I smiled, sitting down beside her.

She closed her book and glanced at me, looking sheepish. "Hi. I'm sorry we all kind of pounced on you. We were just shocked."

"I noticed." I let out a small laugh. "But I'm wondering how *you* know me?"

Emma winced. "By accident."

"That doesn't tell me much. Did… did Mathias tell you about me?" I closed my eyes and looked away so she couldn't see my face. I wanted so badly for her to tell me that he had, and that pissed me off. I wasn't allowed to want things like that.

"No," she shook her head. "Once… he… uh… walked in on Maddox and I making out and he made some smartass comment… I'm sure you know how he is. Then Maddox mentioned you and…" She trailed off, biting her lip and looking unsure with whether or not she should continue.

"And?" I prompted, needing to hear what she had to say.

"He threw a glass at us."

"He threw a glass at you?" I repeated. "*Why?*"

"Because he's Mathias," she shrugged, like it was no big deal. "A little while after that I asked Maddox about you and he said you guys had been together in high school and that Mathias—" She stopped herself and looked up.

That's when I glanced behind me and saw that Mathias had joined us. He glared at the two of us and cleared his throat. "I think that's enough story time."

Emma gave me an apologetic look and said, "Excuse me," as she passed me.

"Care to join us?" Mathias asked, pointing over his shoulder back where the recording room lay.

"Yeah, sure," I mumbled.

I stood up and awkwardly followed him back to the room. I felt like a teenager again who'd just been caught doing something really bad. Only I hadn't done anything wrong.

Maddox and Emma were now sitting on the couch, along with Ezra. Hayes had moved to sit in front of the control panel and fiddled with some of the buttons there.

Mathias pointed a finger roughly at the chair, telling me to sit down.

Without saying a word he stepped into the recording space and the door closed behind him. I could still see him through the glass partition, but I couldn't tell if he was mad or irritated.

He stuck some earmuff looking things on his head and grabbed the microphone, sitting down on a stool.

"Are you guys recording new stuff?" I addressed all of them.

Maddox nodded. "Yeah, we're hoping to have a new album out by this time next year, but it might get pushed longer than that since we're going on tour from January until June."

I swallowed thickly, passed the lump in my throat. I'd forgotten about that—

that in less than two months they'd be gone.

I glanced at Mathias through the glass, wondering why I suddenly felt so empty at the thought of him leaving me.

This was only supposed to be revenge.

But it was quickly becoming so much more.

My eyes never left him as he began to sing.

He looked so peaceful and content as he sang. He closed his eyes, feeling the words and the power of the song. He was so raw and real in this moment, and it was a beautiful thing to see.

I found myself leaving the chair and moving to stand in front of the glass.

I wanted to get closer to him. I wanted to sink inside him and feel everything that he felt.

I reached out, my fingers touching the glass the way I wished I could touch his voice.

He finished the song and his eyes opened. "How was that?"

*Perfect.*

"I think we're good, but do it one more time," Hayes told him.

His eyes met with mine briefly, giving me a small—almost shy—smile, before he started singing again.

I sat down once more in the chair and drew my legs up to my chest, wrapping my arms around them.

I felt Maddox's eyes on me, watching me carefully. I knew from the thin set of his lips that he wanted to say something but wasn't sure he should.

I looked in his direction. "Say it. I'm a big girl."

"What are you two doing?"

That hadn't been what I expected him to say.

"I don't know," I answered honestly. I knew what my motives were, but Mathias' were a complete mystery to me. He was always photographed with different women all the time, so I doubted I was special to him. On some of the nights I left him, I wouldn't have been surprised if he didn't go find someone else to keep his bed warm.

*I wasn't special.*

*I wasn't special.*

*I. Wasn't. Special.*

I repeated the mantra over and over again in my head, wondering why I wished the opposite to be true. I wasn't supposed to want a relationship. Not with anyone, but definitely not him. Not the guy that broke me in every way imaginable.

Maddox stood up slowly, shaking his head and his face twisted with indecision. He finally relaxed and let out a sigh. He looked at me dead on and said, "He still loves you, you know? I think you're the only girl he's ever loved, and the only one he will."

He nodded his head in goodbye and left the room, while I was left holding the ticking time bomb he'd planted in my hands.

This should have been good news for me.

After all, that had been my plan all along—to get him to fall in love with me.

Suddenly I hated my plan.

I hated myself.

I didn't want this bomb.

I didn't want it to blow up.

I didn't want to hurt him the way I had.

I didn't want him to feel the pain I'd experienced—because I might know all of Mathias' secrets, but he didn't know *mine*.

# CHAPTER SIXTEEN

"Why are you so quiet?" Mathias asked, parking his car in the garage attached to the hotel.

I shrugged. Apparently it was okay for *him* to be silent, but not me. I was consumed by my thoughts and the confusion I felt. Revenge had been my only goal and now… now I didn't know anything. I felt dirty and wrong and like the shittiest person on the planet. What kind of twisted person wants to hurt someone like that? Hadn't we both been through enough already? Why was I letting my demons rule my life?

"Remy," he growled my name. "Talk to me."

I shook my head back and forth.

It was amazing how quickly things could change. This morning I was begging him to fuck me and now I wanted to be as far away from him as possible. I needed to sort out my feelings and emotions.

Maddox claimed Mathias still loved me.

But how could you cheat on someone you loved?

None of it made any sense.

God, this was making my brain hurt.

I climbed out of the car and started walking away. I had no idea where I was headed, but I didn't care as long as it was away from him.

Mathias clouded my thoughts. He confused me, and made me want things I wasn't allowed to have. He made me *like* him again. All I'd felt for seven years was hate, and then the last few weeks… that hate had gradually been leaching out of my body. Once Maddox said what he did, I knew I couldn't go through with this. I couldn't become someone so sick and twisted that they were willing to hurt someone else for revenge.

I wrapped my arms around my body and walked as fast as my feet could carry me in my heels.

"Remy!" He shouted my name, but I didn't stop. I didn't look. I didn't give him anything.

This time *I* was the one walking away from him.

"REMY!"

His voice was closer this time, and I could hear his feet slapping against the concrete.

I took my heels off and started to run, but not soon enough.

His hand closed around my arm and he yanked me against his chest.

"Why are you running away from me? What did I *do*?" Hurt leached into his words. He smoothed a thumb over my cheek. "You're crying."

I was. My cheeks were covered in wetness and I couldn't seem to stop it. I think I was finally crying for everything that had happened.

"Let me go." I wiggled in his grasp trying to get away.

"*No.* I let you walk away once before, but I won't do it again." He touched his forehead to mine.

"Stop it," I begged, pressing my forehead against his chest. My tears soaked his shirt, but he didn't push me away.

"Why are you crying?" He asked, awkwardly rubbing my back. Mathias didn't do comfort. "I don't think I've ever seen you cry." He whispered the last part.

I wanted to tell him that I might seem tough, but I wasn't. It was all an act. A mask I put on along with my red lipstick. It wasn't the real me. The real me was weak. The real me couldn't own up to the truth. The real me was just a scared little girl sitting alone in a hospital bed holding her stillborn daughter in her arms. I closed my eyes, clinging to him as the memory flooded me.

*"What's happening?" I pleaded with them. "Where are you taking her? Is she okay? Why isn't she crying? Please, let me hold her!"*

*They told me nothing.*

*"Shh," my mom wiped a piece of sweaty hair off my forehead. Tears streamed down her cheeks.*

*"Mom?" My voice cracked on the single word. "Why won't they let me hold her?"*

*"I'm so sorry, honey." She held my hand, like she thought the simple gesture alone would hold me together.*

*"Let me see my daughter!" I screamed. I wanted to hold her, and kiss her, and tell her how beautiful she was. I wanted to see if she looked like Mathias or me. Even if I hated him now, I still wanted her to look like him. I hoped she had his dark hair and lips.*

*The doctor and nurses huddled around her small body, pressing her and poking her.*

*"Please," I begged, tears clinging to my lashes. "Please let me see her. Please. Please. Please."*

*"Remy," my mom said my name quietly, "she's gone."*

*"NO!" I shouted the word. "No, she's not! She's okay! She's okay! Just let me hold her and you'll see!"*

*"No, honey." She shook her head, tears clinging to her lashes.*

*My lower lip began to tremble with the threat of tears. "She's* fine.*"*

*If I kept saying it, it had to be true, right?*

*"I'm sorry," she said again.*

*"Stop saying that!" I screamed at her. I shouldn't have been yelling at her right now. She was the only one that supported me when I wanted to keep my baby. My dad had been adamantly against it, and even my brother had sided with him. I guessed they were getting their wish now. I wasn't getting my baby.*

*The doctor carried my daughter over to me, a forlorn look on his face. "I'm sorry, there was nothing we could do. These things… they just happen sometimes and we don't know why."*

*He placed my stillborn daughter in my arms and they cleared out of the room, leaving my mom and me alone with her.*

*A gut-wrenching sob raked my body and I curled her tiny body into my neck. I never wanted to let her go. I wanted her to know that her mommy loved her. Her skin was still warm, but she was pale. Too pale. I cradled her in my arms. She didn't have Mathias' hair. She had mine. But she did get his lips and that made me smile through my tears. I'd thought I knew heartbreak before, but I was wrong. This* was *heartbreak. This* was *having my whole world ripped from my hands. It wasn't fair.*

*"Life never is," my mom whispered, and that was when I realized I'd said the last part out loud.*

*I wanted to know why this happened to me.*

*Why my daughter?*

*Why anybody's child?*

*This was the cruelest form of punishment that ever existed.*

*Her eyes were closed and I could almost pretend that she was sleeping.* Almost.

*I kissed her forehead. "Mommy loves you, Hope," I whispered.*

*"Hope?" My mom repeated.*

*"Hope," I said again.*

*She was my hope and now she was gone.*

"Remy? Remy? Remy?"

My body was shaking.

Why was my body shaking?

"Why are you shaking me?" I asked.

He ceased the movements and stared down at me with confusion. "You just… zoned out. What's wrong with you?"

I closed my eyes, reaching up to wipe away the wetness on my cheeks.

I couldn't tell him.

Not because he didn't deserve to know, but because I wanted to spare him the *pain*.

That was comical really, since I'd spent the last few weeks planning to break his heart.

It was funny how quickly your thoughts and opinions of a person could change.

"I have to go." I tore out of his hold and this time he let me walk away.

I should've been happy about that, but I wasn't.

# CHAPTER SEVENTEEN

"You really should stop moping around the house." My grandma spoke up from the kitchen table.

I glanced at her, adding more sugar to my cup of coffee. "I'm not moping."

"You are." She declared, spreading out the newspaper on the table. "Want to tell me *why?*"

It had been a week since I left Mathias standing in the parking garage. He hadn't reached out to me, but I hadn't expected him to. It was better like this anyway. I didn't have to pretend anymore, and he could go back to his old ways. It was how it had been for the last seven years and it should stay that way.

Stupidly, I did miss him. He was my fucking kryptonite.

After that day in the garage, when I had to relive losing Hope, if I hadn't had my grandma to take care of I would've been on a plane out of here.

It was too much.

I tried not to think of Hope.

I tried to pretend she didn't exist.

But that was wrong of me. She was my daughter and her brief existence should've been celebrated.

It was too hard though. The pain of losing her would never go away, I knew that now.

And I guess, when I came up with my game plan to seduce Mathias, I thought it would help if something crushed him the way I had been. I'd been a bitch and wanted someone else to lose something too.

And by doing that, I had let Hope down.

I think I let myself down too.

I didn't know who I was anymore since I lost her, and that scared me.

I needed to rediscover myself.

"Hey," she snapped her fingers, "I'm not getting any younger here. In fact, with every second I'm getting closer to death. So come here and tell your dear old grandma what's wrong, after all, chances are I'll take your secrets to my grave." She winked.

I laughed, for the first time in what felt like a while.

I pulled out a chair and sat down at the table. "It's Mathias," I started.

"That boy?" She glared. "The one that got you pregnant and left you all alone?"

I sighed. "He didn't know, grandma."

She rolled her eyes. "Well what is it about him that's been bothering you?"

"Everything," I muttered, doodling on the table with the edge of my fingernail. "I… I was seeing him again. And… I wanted to hurt him the way he hurt me…" I frowned, lifting the cup of coffee to my lips. "Isn't that awful?" I looked up at her. "I mean, what kind of sick twisted person does that?"

She stared at me, her expression sad. "You've been through a lot, Remy. You've handled it like a champ. But even the best of us crumble eventually."

I didn't feel like I'd ever handled anything at all. I'd closed myself off and pretended to be okay. Pretending was not reality. I'd done crazy, stupid things all because I was trying to feel *something*.

The only thing that made me feel anything—good or bad—was Mathias.

I felt like a part of my soul was tethered to him.

Maybe that was the real reason I came up with the game—as an excuse to get close to him.

I wanted to laugh at that stupid thought. I'd never been the girl to believe in fate and destiny and other mystical things.

"I don't know what I want anymore," I whispered, burying my head in my hands. "I still like him even though I shouldn't… even though I know he's bad for me. But I *can't* stop these feelings and that scares me. I don't think I can be with him again, because what if he hurts me?"

She looked at me seriously. "What if he doesn't?"

"You're not helping," I snapped, "you're only confusing me more."

"It's a legitimate question." She shrugged her thin shoulders.

"I don't think he wants me like that… he doesn't see a future for us." I nodded my head, agreeing with my own words.

"How do you know that?" She asked.

"Because he's Mathias," I answered simply. "He doesn't do commitment."

*But he did with you.* My conscience spoke up.

*Until he cheated on you.* I reminded myself.

She tapped her fingers against the table. "I think you're holding on too tightly to the past. It's done. It's over with. You can't change it. But you can change your future, because it's not set in stone. You're both adults now. Act like it."

She got up from the table then and waddled back to her room, leaving me alone to ponder her words.

"Percy, life sucks." I mumbled to the cat that currently hogged my pillow. Always with the damn pillow. Couldn't he find a new spot?

Of course in typical cat fashion he ignored me. He didn't even crack one of his eyes open.

I didn't know what to make of my grandma's advice. It seemed too simple to let go of the past and move on.

The doorbell rang and I groaned. I didn't want to deal with anyone today.

"I've got it!" I yelled, just in case my grandma decided to get out of bed and go to the door.

I bound down the steps, ready to tell whoever was standing there to go to hell, but when I opened the door all the words died on my tongue.

"Mathias?"

He stood in front of me looking impeccably put together like always. His brown hair was swept away from his piercing gray eyes and he was dressed in a pair of jeans, a nice shirt, and jacket.

"Can I come in?" He asked, clearing his throat and pointing to the interior of the home.

"Uh… yeah. Sure." I was shocked and couldn't wrap my brain around the fact that he was here.

He took a seat on one of the couches in the living room and I took a few tentative steps toward him.

"I wanted to see you," he said the words slowly, "but I wanted to give you time to cool off."

"I'm fine," I grumbled.

"What happened that day?" He asked. "You just… you freaked out on me, Remy, and… you actually scared me."

I couldn't believe Mathias was admitting something like that to me. He might've shared things about his past with me, but he'd *always* guarded his feelings.

"Talk to me," he demanded when I stayed quiet. His features contorted with anger and I knew he was seconds away from blowing up.

"I don't know what to say," I admitted.

"Why does it always have to be a fucking rollercoaster with us?" He asked, staring up at the ceiling like it held all the answers in the world.

"Because that's how we are," I shrugged, sitting down in the chair across from him. "We're a hurricane raging."

He stared at me through hooded eyes. "Are you saying we're a catastrophe?"

"I guess so," I shrugged.

"You don't think there's more for us? You don't think there's a reason why we ran into each other again?"

"No," I said adamantly. If I believed there was a reason for us meeting again, then I would be forced to believe that there was a reason for Hope's death, and I'd never accept that.

"Who are *you?*" He asked. "Because this," he waved a hand at me, "this isn't the Remy I know. The Remy I know doesn't sit back so quiet and meek. The Remy I know shouts her feelings for the world to hear."

"Stop it."

"Come on, Remy, let it out." He stood up, stalking towards me. "Tell me what your problem is."

"My problem is you!" I yelled, shooting up into a standing position. If he wanted a reaction from me, I'd make sure he got one.

"Me?" He seemed confused.

"Yes, you!" I threw my hands in the air. "You're just… ugh! You're *you* and you confuse and frustrate me like nobody else can."

"I feel the same way about you." He said the words calmly, evenly.

"I don't know what you want from me," I whispered, "from this." I waved a hand between the two of us. "From us. Together."

Even though I had been playing a game, *real* feelings had developed again, because it was fucking impossible for me not to love Mathias Wade. He was planted into my DNA. He was my air. My life. Even though I didn't want him to be, he was. He always had been and he always would be. From the first moment he spoke to me, it was over then. For both of us. We were never going to be the same, because I was perfect for him and he was perfect for me. We were two pieces of a puzzle that fit together just right. That kind of love… it didn't go away. No, it only grew, even in the absence of each other it continued to blossom and grow into something stronger. Even my hate hadn't been strong enough to snuff it out. I'd been too blinded by revenge to see that.

He glowered down at me. "I think I've been pretty fucking clear, Remy."

"Nothing is ever clear with you!" I poked a finger against his chest. "You're so damn confusing and hard to read!"

"Me?!" He looked shocked. "What about *you?*"

"What about me?" I countered.

He groaned, shoving his fingers through his hair. "God, we are so fucked up. We can't even have a normal conversation." His jaw clenched and he shook his head back and forth. He scrubbed his hands over his face and let out a groan. "Why can't things ever be easy with us?"

"Because things that are easy aren't worth fighting for," I whispered.

One of his hands fell to my waist, his fingers tightening around one of the belt loops so I couldn't get away, and the other cupped my cheek. "Are you saying that *we're* worth fighting for?"

I swallowed thickly. "I don't know." And that was an honest answer. I loved Mathias when I was sixteen years old, but I wasn't sure if what I felt now was love, or a desire to hold on to the past. I also couldn't overlook the fuckedupness of the fact that a week ago I'd been set on destroying him. We were a disaster. Pure and simple.

He stared at me for a moment, his face void of any emotion. "If I walked out this door right now, and you never saw me again, how would you feel?"

I didn't even have to say anything, the flicker of pain that twisted my face spoke volumes.

"Tell me you want me, Remy." His fingers ghosted over my lips and my eyes closed.

"No."

"Tell me," he growled.

I shook my head. "I can't."

"Why?" His fingers skimmed down my neck and over my collarbone.

"You'll only hurt me." My eyes opened and I looked at him, letting him see the pain in my eyes that I always kept carefully hidden.

He pulled his bottom lip between his teeth and let it go. "I won't. Things are different now. Let me prove it to you."

My body unconsciously curled into his until I was tucked against him. I laid my cheek against his chest, my emotions raging.

"I'm not a kid anymore, Remy." The sound of his voice rumbled against my ear. "I won't fuck this up again. I swear. I know I'm not a good guy. I know I've done horrible things. But the only time I've ever felt halfway decent was when you were mine, and I was yours."

My heart stuttered in my chest and then began to beat more rapidly.

I took a step back and squared my shoulders. Jutting out my chin, I said, "Okay, but if you screw this up I'll hurt you. I don't know how yet, but I promise it'll be extremely painful."

He chuckled, reaching up to scratch his jaw. "I wouldn't expect anything less from you."

"Good." I nodded, wondering if I'd done the right thing—or if I'd just willingly handed over the last piece of my shattered heart for him to obliterate. I guessed the good news was if he completely destroyed my heart I really could be the heartless bitch I pretended to be.

"And now," he closed in on me once more, "I'm going to kiss you."

"Don't be so arrogant," I rolled my eyes, "maybe I don't want you to kiss me."

He chuckled, rubbing his thumb against my bottom lip. "I *know* you do."

"Oh, really?" I quirked a brow.

"Mhmm," he nodded, his eyes falling to my lips. His were only a breath away from mine when he let out a yelp and jumped away from me.

He swatted at something on his leg and I began to laugh manically. Percy was wrapped around his leg, trying to claw his way up his body.

"Jesus Fucking Christ, this thing is a demon!"

I probably should've helped him, but I was too busy wiping the tears of laughter from my eyes. "That's what you get for trying to kiss me."

"Remy," he groaned, his eyes pleading with me, "I think I'm bleeding."

"Alright, alright, you big baby," I chuckled, bending down to pry Percy off.

Percy did not release him easily. "Good kitty." I petted him on top of his head when I finally had him cradled in my arms.

"Your cat hates me."

"He does," I agreed, "I think he wants to be the only man in my life."

Mathias frowned, glaring at Percy. "He looks like he wants to eat me."

"Aw, he'd never eat you. He has better taste than that." I made a kissy face at the cat.

Mathias narrowed his eyes. "He's plotting to kill me. I can see it in his eyes."

"He truly is my soul-cat then," I joked.

He gave me a challenging look and I knew I was in trouble.

Feeling like a kid again I let out a squeal and ran for the stairs, running up them as fast as I could with Percy in my arms.

I dove into my room and tried to close the door, but Mathias caught it in his hand and pushed his way through.

Percy meowed and jumped out of my arms, running from the room.

"Oh, you're in trouble now." He stalked towards me.

The backs of my knees hit the bed and I fell down. He was quick to lower his body on top of mine, caging me in with his arms.

"Looks like you've got me right where you want me," I grinned.

He chuckled, kissing my neck. "Yeah, but you're not naked so that's kind of a bummer."

Then he covered my lips with his, kissing me deeply and reminding me how much I'd missed him this week—how much I'd *always* missed him. The thing about the heart is, once it's given itself completely to someone it's theirs forever, no matter the circumstances.

Once my lips were bruised with the imprint of his he pulled away. He lay on his back, staring at the ceiling, and I did the same. I was reminded of a time where things were simple and we were just Mathias and Remy. Now he was famous and I was keeping secrets. That right there was a lethal combination.

"I did come here for another reason," he said, reaching for my hand. He wound our fingers together and my whole body hummed with the touch.

"And what would that be?" I asked.

"I wanted to see if you and your grandma wanted to come to my parent's place for Thanksgiving tomorrow." He cleared his throat. "I mean, you don't *have* to, but I'd like you to be there. Never mind. You probably already have plans. Forget I said anything." He rambled in a very un-Mathias-like fashion.

I was shocked he was extending an invitation. When we… dated… before he *never* introduced me to his foster parents. Only his brother and Ezra knew about our relationship—and my parent's of course, who were never quiet about their disapproval of him.

"You didn't even give me a chance to respond." I laughed.

"Then do you want to go or not?"

"We would love to," I assured him. Sitting up I looked down at him. "But who am I going as? Your friend? Your fuck buddy? I want to be clear on how you're introducing me to your parent's. I don't want any surprises."

He glowered at me. "You're mine."

"Like I'm a toy to you?" I pushed, wanting to hear him say it.

"No, you're mine like you're my fucking girlfriend."

"So… I'm just your girlfriend that you only fuck?" Now I was messing with him.

I let out a small scream when he grasped my wrists and rolled me back onto the bed. He glared down at me. "You're my girlfriend. Although, that seems like too insignificant of a word for what you are to me."

"Are you okay with this?" I asked. "With us?" I didn't want to get my hopes up that there could be more for us, if this was only something casual and temporary for him. When I was young I never sat around and dreamed about a wedding, babies, and happily ever after's, but once I met Mathias I wanted all of that. He'd taken it away from me once, and I didn't think I could handle it if he did it again.

His tongue snaked out to moisten his lips. "Let's get one thing straight, Remy, and this is going to be the *last* time I say it. I want this. I want you. I want the good and the bad and whatever the hell else you throw at me. You're the only girl I've ever wanted and I refuse to let you get away from me again."

I wanted to tell him that he didn't let me get away, he *pushed* me away, but I kept my mouth shut. Some fights weren't worth it.

"I don't know what the future might hold for us," he continued, his hair brushing against my forehead, "so for now we take this one day at a time."

I nodded my head in agreement. "Okay."

"And if you ever freak out on me again, you have to *talk* to me." His lips brushed against my ear when he spoke. "Don't run away from me."

I closed my eyes, frowning. "You don't talk to me when you have one of your… moments." I didn't know what else to call the times where he snapped.

He took my chin in his hand and forced me to look at him. "You know my darkest secrets, Rem. Don't ever say I don't talk to you."

"You don't talk to me *now*."

He sighed, rolling away from me, and pulled roughly at his hair. "We really are going to have to get to know each other all over again, aren't we?"

I shrugged.

He held out his hand to me, smiling boyishly. I liked this smile, and it wasn't one he wore often. "Mathias Wade. It's nice to meet you."

I shook my head, laughing under my breath. Taking his hand I said, "Remy Parker."

"Remy, how about we don't fuck this up this time?" He raised a brow, smiling crookedly.

*But that's what we do.*

"Sounds like a plan."

# CHAPTER EIGHTEEN

"Grandma," I groaned, "could you try not looking like you want to kill him?" I asked her, watching Mathias get out of a black SUV and head for the front door.

"No. He's bad. He hurt you," she snapped, "and if he doesn't keep his manner's in check I'll take him out at the knees." She waved her cane around for emphasis.

"I'm considering hiding that from you," I told her, crossing my arms over my chest.

"Oh, Remy, we both know you wouldn't take an old lady's cane from her." She smiled. "That would be far too cruel for even you."

"But you're not a lady," I laughed, heading to the door when I heard a knock. "Ow!" I turned back around hastily. "Did you poke me in the butt with that thing?"

She nodded, trying to hide a grin.

"You're bad," I narrowed my eyes. "I'm going to have a bruise from that."

"Well then, that young man can kiss your ass and make it better. Lord knows you should make him grovel," she muttered under her breath.

"Shh," I hissed.

I'd already swung the door open and Mathias stood there grinning. "What is this about your ass?"

"You both suck," I glared, stomping out the door and to the waiting SUV.

I then realized that I'd left my poor grandma alone to make her way to the car by herself, so I quickly did an about face to go back and get her.

Only Mathias was helping her.

Oh. My. God.

I think hell froze over.

Mathias Wade was helping a little old lady—but not just any little old lady, nope, he was helping my grandma… who hated him… and she wasn't even trying to hit him with her cane.

I grabbed my phone from my pocket and snapped a picture.

"What are you doing, missy?" My grandma asked, holding onto his arm as she climbed down the porch steps. "You know I hate having my picture taken."

"This is for blackmail," I joked, tucking my phone back into my pocket.

Mathias glared at me for that one and I simply laughed. I headed over to my grandma to take her from Mathias, but she swatted my arm with a loud smack. She might look little and frail, but that hurt.

"He's got me," she scolded, "and he's a lot better to look at than you."

"I thought you hated him," I snickered.

She glanced up at Mathias who shrugged in response, clearly not bothered by my statement.

"I might not like him, but that doesn't change his looks."

I snorted and Mathias' lips twitched with the threat of a smile. I wanted to tell him that it was okay to smile—that he didn't have to hide those things, but I left the words unsaid.

"Have you been working out?" My grandma asked him, reaching up to grasp his bicep through the material of his shirt.

"Grandma!" I scolded.

"It's like a rock." She rapped a fist against his arm.

Mathias looked at me, biting his bottom lip to hide his laughter. "Let's get her in the car before she gropes you some more," I shook my head, "she has wandering hands."

"Yeah, better stop her before she gets to the best part." He winked at me.

Grandma made a tsking sound and picked up her pace.

Mathias helped her into the back of the car and then opened the front passenger door for me. I looked at him like he'd grown three heads.

"What?" He asked innocently. "I can be nice."

I smirked and leaned forward so I could whisper in his ear. "Don't be."

There was nothing wrong with tender moment with Mathias, but I preferred him to be himself, which was raw, and smart-mouthed, and rough, and… I could go on forever.

Neither of us was perfect, and that's why we complimented each other so well.

He shook his head and stepped away. "Get in the fucking car, Remy." He paused, tilting his head. "Was that better?"

"Much," I nodded.

I climbed into the car and glanced back at my grandma. She sat watching me with a small smile on her lips. Something told me I was going to be listening to an epic speech later tonight.

"Nice suspenders," I commented, as I watched Mathias help my grandma out of the car—because she refused my help. I think she was testing him, to see if she could make him mad. So far it wasn't working.

He chuckled, shaking his head. "You love my suspenders."

"You can definitely pull them off," I assured him. He was dressed nicely in a pair of gray slacks, a white button down shirt, black tie, belt, and the suspenders. I was glad I'd worn a black dress and heels. "Although, I don't know where your obsession with them came from."

He closed the car door and started guiding my grandma forward. "They had me wear them during a photo shoot once, and I liked them," he shrugged.

When he brought up things like photo shoots it reminded me that he wasn't just Mathias anymore. Instead he was a world famous rock star.

I followed him up the front porch steps and he reached for the doorknob. He glanced at my grandma and then at me. "Be prepared for my mom to ask you five-hundred questions."

"Does she know I'm coming?" I asked, my eyes widening as I glanced at the door.

He nodded. "Did you really think I'd ask you to come and not tell my parents beforehand?"

"Well… yeah." I kept forgetting that things were different now, for the both of us, and we didn't have to hide our relationship.

He shook his head, laughing in a self-deprecating manner. "You have such little faith in me."

I frowned.

"I told them I was bringing my girlfriend, and they tried to ask me about you then, but I shut them up, so… they're chomping at the bit. Especially my mom."

"Great." I squared my shoulders.

I'd never met Mathias' foster parents since he'd always been secretive about our relationship. After him, I never dated again. Just a one night stand here and there, which meant I'd lived twenty-three years of my life without ever having to do the meet the parent's routine.

And to make it worse, it was Thanksgiving.

I needed a shot.

Something strong.

Where was the fucking tequila?

Oh dear God, he hadn't even opened the door yet and I already wished I was drunk. I hoped this wasn't an omen as to how the evening would go.

"Are you ready?" He asked me, and I realized he'd been giving me a moment to gather myself.

"Yeah." I smoothed my fingers through my straight hair and squared my shoulders as I plastered on my game face.

"Show time," he muttered, and pushed the door open.

Almost immediately I heard a high-pitched shriek and a woman say, "You must be Remy!"

I shot Mathias a scared look and he shrugged, letting me know I was on my own. Fucking Traitor.

His mom pulled me inside and enveloped me in a bone-crushing hug.

I was pretty sure my lungs were about to collapse.

"Can't. Breathe."

"Mom, let her go." Mathias groaned, passing by us as he toted my grandma along.

"I can't believe you brought a girl home." She pulled back, but kept her hands on my arms so that I couldn't go anywhere. "And she's real."

"Very real," I nodded.

"And pretty," she continued.

"Mom," Mathias pleaded, sounding very much like the teenage boy I remembered. "You're embarrassing me."

His mom grinned. "That's what mom's are for."

"Shit," he cursed, "this is only the beginning isn't it?" He waved a hand at his mom and me.

She nodded and he muttered something under his breath. Pushing a strand of hair from his eyes, he asked, "Should we get seated in the dining room or do you want to eat later?"

"Now," she nodded, "everybody else is seated."

Mathias tightened his hold on my grandma and the two left the foyer, leaving me completely alone with his mom.

I was going to kill him for this.

"I'm Karen," she smiled brightly. "You have no idea how nice it is to meet you."

"I'm Remy, but I guess you already knew that." I forced a smile, but I was afraid I looked like I was choking on something.

"Mathias has never even mentioned a girl around us, so when he said he was bringing his girlfriend to dinner I almost peed my pants with excitement." She danced on the balls of her feet.

"Uh…" I was at a loss for words.

Sobering, she grasped my hands. "My husband, Paul, and I have always worried about him more than the other boys. He's had a hard life, and we've been afraid he'd never find someone he trusted enough to let in."

I glanced down the hallway where Mathias had disappeared, her words having sparked a curiosity in me. I'd never once bothered to question what it was about me that made me different. When we were teenagers I figured we were drawn together because of our likeness, but he'd sought me out first and things escalated from there. So, what on earth did the enigmatic Mathias Wade see in *me?*

"I know he's not the nicest nor the easiest person to be around," she continued, turning my attention back to her, "but there's a goodness in him. He has a heart that's much kinder than he realizes."

"I know," I whispered. And I did know that, which only served to make me feel even guiltier for my previous intentions.

"I guess we should join them." She smiled politely and motioned for me to follow her.

When we reached an archway that led into the dining room Mathias was about ready to jump out of his seat. "Thank God." I heard him mutter.

There was an empty seat between Mathias and my grandma and he stood up hastily to pull out the chair for me. "Thanks." I shot a smile in his direction.

Maddox and Emma were seated across from us, along with another woman that I assumed was Emma's mother. They looked enough alike that they had to be related. Down on the other end sat Ezra, who seemed highly amused. I glanced down the other way and saw Karen take her seat beside her husband who sat at the head of the table.

He said a few words over the food and then stood to carve the turkey.

Underneath the table Mathias' hand landed on my knee, snaking slowly up my thigh and underneath my dress.

I jerked, nearly spilling the glass of water beside my plate.

Mathias let out a low chuckle and his hand came back to rest on my knee. He gave it a soft squeeze and then left his hand there.

My body heated at his touch, desire curling low in my belly.

Jesus Christ, the man could make me want him while sitting at a table with his fucking parents. He was dangerous to be around.

I piled food onto my plate, but I'd lost my appetite. …Unless wanting to lick Mathias counted as having an appetite, because in that case I was *starving.*

I nibbled at my food, pushing most of it around my plate. Everybody else chatted and I kept quiet until the attention was turned to me.

"What do you do Remy?" Karen asked.

I gulped down the rest of my wine—I was on my second glass, but unfortunately it would take a lot more than that to get me drunk.

"I'm working at a bar." I cringed once the words were out of my mouth. It sounded pretty bad. I was working at a bar, while her son was a famous rock star. She was definitely going to think I was using him. Fuck. I hastened to add, "I have a degree in marketing, but when I moved back here I needed to get a job and they hired me on the spot at the bar, so…" I trailed off and my grandma made a snickering sound beside me. She knew I was trying to impress them.

Mathias gave my knee a slight squeeze, as if he was telling me it was okay. He knew I didn't get nervous, like ever, so this was new for me. But this was also his *parent's* and dammit, I wanted them to like me. I wanted their approval. I wanted them to accept me the way my parent's never had with Mathias—and my poor father would bust a vein in his forehead if he knew where I was right now.

With his free hand he reached for the bottle of wine and poured me another glass.

"That's nice." His mother smiled.

I wanted to crawl under the table and hide, but since that wasn't in my nature I squared my shoulders and smiled instead. "Thanks."

"So you've lived here before?" Paul, Mathias' father, asked.

I nodded. "Yeah. Mathias and I…" I paused, not sure how to continue. Finally I settled on the safest thing to say. "We knew each other in high school."

"Oh," Karen's eyes widened in surprise. "He didn't tell us that."

I glanced at Mathias. "Of course he didn't."

He shrugged, tapping his fingers against the table. "I didn't think it was important."

"It's not," I snapped. It had been obvious that he hadn't told his parents about our past connection, and I'd been fine with that, but when he said it wasn't important that grated on my nerves. It made me feel like *I* wasn't important to him, which then made me wonder what the fuck I was doing here.

His hold on my knee tightened and I glared at him. He gave me a look that told me I needed to chill out. I resisted the urge to stab the heel of my shoe into his foot.

"They dated in high school." Maddox piped in.

"Oh fuck." Mathias dropped his head in his hands and for the first time through the whole meal my body was free of his touch.

"What?" Karen gasped, looking around at all of us.

I grabbed my glass of wine and chugged that sucker.

Paul looked like he was going to fall out of his chair.

This had officially turned into the most awkward Thanksgiving/Meet-The-

Parent's dinner, ever. Seriously, I think we deserved an award for this.

"I didn't know you ever dated anyone." Karen fiddled with the napkin in her lap, a frown marring her pretty face. "I feel like we don't know you at all." Tears pooled in her eyes. "Why is it, that even after all this time, you feel like you can't talk to us?"

"Fuck, fuck, fuck," Mathias cursed, shaking his head, "here we go again." He threw his hands up and said, "Please, for the love of God can we *not* turn this into a fucking therapy session where we all sit around and talk about How-To-Fix-Mathias. Frankly, I'm not in the fucking mood for it."

"Mathias," his mom scolded, "don't be like that."

"Then stop making me feel guilty." He leaned around me to glare at her. "And stop trying to fucking fix me."

Holy shit, I felt like I was sitting between a tennis match and any minute I was going to get pelted in the head with a ball.

Karen sighed. "Mathias, that's not what I'm trying to do. All we've ever wanted to do is help you, because we love you. You're blowing everything out of proportion."

"Like always," Maddox muttered from across the table.

Mathias sent a withering glare in the direction of his twin.

"Help me? You think you can help me?" He shook his head, letting out a breath. "There is no helping someone like me."

With that he stood up from the table and I half expected him to throw his plate or do something stupid, but instead he stalked out of the room, leaving us in silence.

We all stared around at one another, wondering what to do.

Grandma was the first to speak.

"Can we have desert now?"

We all laughed and she smiled at having succeeded in ridding the room of tension.

"Yes, I think it's time for desert." Karen pushed back her chair and left the room.

I stood too, and muttered, "I'll be right back."

Before I could leave the dining room, Maddox spoke. "He'll be in the guesthouse."

I stopped and looked at him over my shoulder. "Thanks."

I passed Karen in the kitchen and she smiled knowingly. "Are you looking for Mathias?"

I nodded.

"Come on." She ceased cutting the pumpkin pie and led me through the house and to a set of French doors. They opened into the backyard where a large pool sat—currently covered for the winter months. She pointed to the guesthouse, even though it was easy to see, and whispered, "Good luck."

I strode across the yard and paused in front of the door, taking a deep breath before pushing it open.

Immediately the light twinkling sounds of the piano floated through the air.

I paid no attention to my surroundings, instead striding up to Mathias and wrapping my arms around his wide shoulders. He instantly relaxed into my touch, but kept playing the piano. I didn't recognize the song, it was something soft and haunting sounding.

When he finished he sat still as a stone. He didn't even seem to be breathing. I didn't move either, and continued to stand with my arms wrapped around his neck. Eventually he turned and looked up at me. I swore tears shimmered in his gray eyes.

"What's wrong with me, Rem? Why do I do this? Why do I push everybody away?" He looked pained, and I hated that he hurt so much, and I hated even more that I had wanted to add to that pain. Mathias already hurt enough as it was. Now, I wanted nothing more than to make it all go away.

"I don't know," I whispered, rubbing his shoulders. "I guess maybe you're scared to let people in."

He took a shuddering breath. "I don't want to be like this. I don't want to be this guy, but I am." His hands quaked and he clenched them into fists, his knuckles turning white.

"Your family loves you, regardless," I told him. "You have to stop pushing them away."

"How could anyone ever love me?" He asked, his eyes desperate for an answer.

"I loved you." My voice cracked and he wrapped an arm around my waist, pulling me down onto his lap.

He burrowed his head into my neck and I startled when his wet tears stung my skin. He pulled away slightly and grasped my cheeks, staring at me with an intensity that left me breathless. "Do you think you can ever love me again?"

"I don't know," I lied.

He nodded his head and swallowed thickly, like he expected that answer.

He smoothed his fingers through my hair and cupped the back of my neck. "I'm going to do whatever it takes to change that answer to yes, because," he whispered in my ear, "I never stopped loving *you*."

I closed my eyes, soaking in his words—basking in them. I wasn't sure I believed him, but I wanted it to be true. I wanted to believe his feelings for me never dimmed, the way mine hadn't for him. Even when I hated him with every fiber of my being I still loved him—because it was so much easier to hate someone you loved. And I loved him now, God did I ever. I'd believed I was over him, that my feelings had left, but if the last few weeks had proven anything it was that I was always going to love Mathias Wade, whether we were together or apart.

Despite our undeniable love and connection I still had a hard time believing we could make it. I *hoped*, but it seemed impossible.

He wrapped his arms around me and held me for a moment. It was a sweet gesture, and one I wasn't used to from him. I liked this side of him, but I still preferred the rougher, rawer Mathias. However, I knew right now he just wanted to hold me, so I offered him as much comfort as I could.

The door to the guesthouse opened, but Mathias didn't move. I glanced over and saw Maddox standing in the doorway. "Your grandma is ready to go home."

I nodded. "Give us a minute."

"Sure thing." He gave me a small smile and closed the door.

Mathias had burrowed his head against my neck, but now he looked at me, tucking a piece of hair behind my ear. "Do you think we'll ever not be a fucked up mess?"

I smiled, letting out a small laugh. "I like our mess. Except…"

"Except what?" He prompted, his fingers skimming over my collarbone like they had a mind of their own.

"Except when you said you cheated on me. That was one mess I hated."

He swallowed thickly. "When you said you were leaving…" He looked away, his face contorting in pain. When he looked back at me his gray eyes were light and pleading with me. "It hurt so bad. *Nothing*, none of the shit I went through compared to the pain of knowing you were leaving, and you know how bad it was for me with my mom… you know what she did to me…" He closed his eyes and I knew he was thinking of his real mom, and all the evil things she'd done to him— like trying to drown him in a bathtub. Not to mention all the times he told me that she choked him, or hit him, or belittled him with harsh words. I hated that he'd had to go through that as a little kid and never got a normal childhood. By the time Maddox and he were put into foster care they were already older, and the damage had been done. "None of it was as bad as the thought of losing you. I didn't see how two fucked up kids like us could ever make it work, so I lied to you. I broke you the way you broke me."

A weight lifted off of my shoulders and I gasped.

"Say it," I pleaded, "I need to hear you say it."

He grasped my face in one hand, holding me tight enough that I couldn't move. Staring into my eyes he said, "I never cheated on you. When I was with you, I was only ever with you. You're the only girl I can say that to."

I closed my eyes, letting the truth of his words wash over me, and it felt so, so good.

"You're not lying now, are you?" I asked, hoping he couldn't hear the quiver in my voice.

He shook his head. "I was angry at you for a long time for leaving me, and since I'm such a selfish asshole the only thing that comforted me was knowing that you might be hurting as much as me… just for a different reason."

His reasoning for hurting me was twisted and sick, but that was Mathias.

His version of love was all kinds of fucked up thanks to his parents. He got the worst of it over his twin brother, and even today he still bore the scars of his past.

I clung to him, breathing harshly.

Despite the fact that he was telling me now that he had lied about Josie and the other girls it didn't erase the years of hurt I'd had to cope with. It didn't change what happened to our baby. His words had no magical powers to erase the past, but maybe they could help mend what was left of my heart. I hoped so anyway.

"You know I had no choice in leaving," I glowered, "how could you be so cruel?" I hit my fist against his chest, but he grabbed my hands to stop me before I could do anymore damage.

"Because that's what I do," his eyes were serious, "I destroy the things I love."

I swallowed thickly, damming back tears. I wouldn't cry. I refused.

"I'm so, so sorry for lying to you—for hurting you. I was… I wasn't in a good place, and I can acknowledge that what I did was wrong." He leaned his forehead against mine and his breath fanned across my lips. "I want to get better, for you, for me, for our future."

"For our future?" I whispered, my voice sounding awed.

He nodded, running his fingers reverently along my jaw.

"Do you really see a future for us?" I asked, grasping his hair between my fingers. It didn't matter how many times he told me, I still had a hard time believing he wanted more from me. "After all the shit we've been through, and put each other through, do you really think we can make it work?"

He nodded, placing his hand on my wrist and pulling my hand away from his hair to entwine our hands together. "Yeah, I think we can." He swallowed thickly, his face darkening with shadows. "If our years apart have taught me anything it's that my feelings for you are never going to go away. It doesn't matter how much I drink, or who I fuck, I only want you."

I winced at his words, hating the thought of him being with so many other women, but it wasn't like I'd been a saint either.

I knew that in order for us to truly work we'd have to put the past behind us and start anew. Which meant I needed to be honest. I could be honest about wanting to hurt him, but I couldn't tell him about the baby. Not now, maybe not ever. That was one hurt I wanted to spare him.

"Since we're being honest and all…" I started, glancing away and biting my lip.

He grabbed my chin and forced me to look at him. His eyes were steely. "What did you do, Remy?"

I squared my shoulders and jutted out my chin defiantly, refusing to cower. "After the first time I saw you at the bar I decided I wanted to hurt you the way you hurt me. I wanted to make you fall in love with me again, and break your heart like you did mine." I stroked my fingers against his slightly stubbled cheek. "It didn't take me long to realize that I couldn't do that to you." I took a shuddering breath.

He chuckled, shaking his head. "We're a fucked up pair, aren't we? Always trying to hurt each other." A small smile played on his lips and he cupped my cheek. "We really need to work on that."

I laughed, glad that he wasn't pissed. "Yeah we do. No more lying and no more games?"

He smiled crookedly. "That might be impossible for us." He smoothed his fingers through my hair and then the tips of his fingers grazed my collarbone. "But I think we can do it."

I hoped so. I really did.

Mathias helped my grandma out of the car and inside. I took over from there and guided her to her bedroom. She lay down and reached for the remote.

"I'm ready for some trashy reality television," she declared.

"Of course you are," I sighed, reaching for her shoes. She swatted at my hand and I glared at her. "That hurt."

"Don't be a baby," she admonished me. She continued to push my hands away. "I can do this myself."

I rolled my eyes and stepped away from her. "Remind me again why I'm living here with you?"

"The free food?" She suggested.

I laughed, shaking my head as I walked to the door.

"Remy?" She stopped me.

I turned back to look at her, raising a brow as I waited for her to continue.

"He's not so bad." She shrugged her slender shoulders.

I laughed, smiling at her. "Are you going soft, grandma?"

She scoffed. "Hell no. If he hurts you again I won't hesitate to end him."

"Grandma!"

"I'm dead serious. If you see me in the backyard with a shovel don't come out. I don't want you to become an accessory in a murder charge."

I stared at her, fighting the urge to laugh. "I think you've been watching too much CSI."

"Oh no, I don't like that show. I watch Criminal Minds. That Morgan…" She licked her lips. "The things I'd like to let that man do to me."

"Oh my God," I gasped, this time unable to hide my laughter. "You're a piece of work."

She smiled widely. "That's why you love me." Sobering she said, "Go on. I'm sure he's still waiting for you and I doubt you want to spend your evening here with me. I'm *fine*." She waved her hand, shooing me on.

"Are you sure?" I asked, hesitant to leave her.

"I'm fine," she assured me yet again, "I was fine before you lived with me and I'm fine now."

"Okay, but if you need me call me." I pointed a finger at her warningly.

"Just go." Her attention was already focused on the TV.

I headed back down the hall and into the living room. Mathias still stood there waiting, his back turned to me as he appraised the photos on the wall. I noticed his eyes lingered on my high school graduation photo.

He heard me approach and turned, his hands shoved into the pockets of his pants. "Do you ever wonder what would have happened if you hadn't moved away?" His eyes were far away, remembering a time when things were simpler even though they'd seemed impossibly complicated.

My breath left me in a small gasp. "Every day," I admitted. For a long time that had been a question I'd obsessed over, especially when it came to Hope. If we hadn't left might I still have had my daughter? It was a question that was impossible to answer. "But the reality is, if we hadn't left I'm sure we would've ended eventually."

His eyes narrowed as he glared at me. "Why do you say that?"

"We were just kids." I shrugged. "Do you really think we would've lasted?"

His mouth twisted into a grimace. "Probably not."

"Exactly," I nodded, stepping closer to him. "At least now we have a chance to make it work. We're older and… I was going to say wiser, but I don't think either of us is very wise," I laughed.

He chuckled softly. "Definitely not." He brushed his fingers over my cheek and leaned in.

I closed my eyes in anticipation of his lips, but they never touched mine. Instead he nuzzled his head into my neck and his breath tickled my skin when he said, "Stay the night with me."

"Why?" I asked, keeping my voice steady.

"Because I want you to." This time his lips barely brushed mine. Tease.

One of his hands wound around my waist and he drew our bodies together. My hands moved to his chest, and I could feel the steady beat of his heart. I swallowed past the lump in my throat as I stared into his eyes. He made me crazy in the best way possible.

"I'll pack a bag," I whispered, leaning up to press my lips to his.

He pulled away before I could make contact and I glowered at him. He was trying to kill me. I was sure of it.

"Excellent. I'll wait here."

"You don't want to come upstairs?" I nodded my head at the stairs, surprise coloring my words.

He shook his head. "Nope. Your demon cat might attack me again."

"I'll hurry then." I swayed my hips as I headed for the stairs. I was on the third when I stopped and looked at him. "And Mathias?"

"Yes?" He prompted, a slight smirk lifting his lips as he tilted his head to the side.

"I swear to God if you don't fuck me tonight I will kill you in your sleep," I warned playfully.

He snorted, covering it with a cough. "Rem, I'm not much good to you if I'm dead," he winked.

Shaking my head I climbed the rest of the stairs and packed a small bag of clothes and checked on Percy, making sure to give him fresh food and water.

No more than five minutes later I was hurrying back down the steps, but with Mathias' glare you would've thought I'd taken an hour.

He took the bag from me and slung it over his wide shoulder as he reached for the door. I turned on the front porch light before following him out and locking the door.

Neither of us said much on the drive to the hotel, but sexual tension was thick in the air. He gripped the steering wheel so tight that his knuckles turned white, while I kept my eyes trained out the window—afraid that if I looked at him I might end up attacking him with my lips.

When Mathias parked the SUV in the parking garage beside his Corvette I nearly sighed in relief.

We stepped onto the elevator, keeping a careful distance between the two of us. My fingers itched to touch him so I clasped them together, refusing to be the first to give into temptation.

When the elevator opened he finally reached for me, taking my hand and pulling me into his arms.

Immediately I found my back pinned against the wall of the penthouse suite with my arms held above my head as his lips ravished mine.

340

It felt like it had been forever since he touched me this way, when in reality it had only been a week. I didn't know how I ever made it seven years without this… without *him*.

My legs wrapped around his waist and his hips pressed into mine. Our collective pants filled the air. I wiggled my fingers, itching to reach out and touch him, but for now my hands were held immobile above my head.

His tongue brushed against my lips and they parted with a gasp.

A low groan resounded in his throat and he bit lightly on my bottom lip, pulling it between his teeth and letting it go. His eyes were lust filled when they met mine.

A shaky breath left me, startled by the way he was looking at me—like I was his everything.

He ducked his head, kissing my neck and down over the tops of my breasts. Suddenly my dress felt too tight and restricting.

He finally let go of my hands and I wound my arms around his neck. He grasped my thighs, carrying me through the space.

He didn't put me down until we were in his bedroom.

He turned me around, sweeping my hair over my shoulder. He pressed a kiss to my neck and I relaxed against him as he eased the zipper down on my dress.

My dress started to fall and I pushed it off the rest of the way.

It fell into a pool of black fabric and I stepped out of it, kicking it and my heels away.

His eyes appraised me approvingly and my heart thundered in my chest.

I didn't get shy, but Mathias made me feel the closest thing to it.

He stalked forward, his moves lithe like a panther. He took my face between his large hands and slanted his lips over mine. I worked my fingers over the knot in his tie and removed it before starting in on the buttons of his shirt. I pushed the fabric over his shoulders along with the suspenders.

His chuckle vibrated against my lips. "Slow down, Rem."

"We have time for slow later." I stood on my tiptoes to whisper in his ear.

His chest rumbled with a low growl. "You'll be the end of me."

"Back at ya." I kissed him, slowly at first and then with more passion.

His fingers dug into my hips and I soon found myself flat on his bed.

His large body pressed into mine, making me feel incredibly small and protected in his embrace.

He pressed small kisses down my torso, reaching behind me to unsnap my bra.

My back arched off the bed as he tugged away the lacy fabric.

"Please," I begged.

He kissed me again, rolling his hips into mine. I gasped, my hands reaching for his pants.

"Remy," he warned with a low growl.

I took his face between my hands, rubbing my thumb over his lips. "I can't wait. Please, for the love of my sanity, don't draw this out."

He reached for my panties and tugged them down and I nearly did a victory dance—but it would've been in vain, because the bastard didn't listen to me.

His fingers pressed into me and a small scream escaped my throat as I fisted the sheets between my fingers.

"You like that?" He grinned.

I nodded, at a loss for words.

"See, slow is good."

"Shut up." My fingers tangled in his dark hair, drawing him to me for a kiss. I gasped against his lips when I felt my orgasm begin to build. "Oh, fuck. Right there. Keep doing that."

His fingers moved in and out of me, and he watched me with a look of awe on his face as I fell apart.

"You're so fucking beautiful," he whispered, sucking on my bottom lip.

I undid the button his pants, pushing them down.

He stepped back and removed the rest of his clothes, before grabbing a condom and rolling it on. He hovered over me, kissing me as he pushed inside me.

I let out a gasp, arching my neck and back as he pumped into me hard at first.

When I wrapped my legs around his waist he moved his hips slowly, drawing out every moment and savoring it.

We didn't normally do sweet, but this was exactly what this was and I kind of liked it. A lot.

He grasped my thigh, drawing one of my legs higher and I gasped at the sensation.

I panted, grasping his hair roughly between my fingers.

He growled, biting down on my lip in retaliation.

His hips continued to move in a tantalizingly slow rhythm.

He grasped the sheets roughly in his hands beside my head and his jaw was clenched tightly together. He was holding back and that was the last thing I wanted.

I grasped his chin in my hand, breathing, "Let go."

A look of pain flickered over his face and I knew he didn't want to. "Please," I begged, "let me see you."

"Fuck," he growled, and all restraint left him.

His hands and mouth were everywhere—nipping, biting, gripping.

The air was filled with our groans and pants.

I could feel myself building to another orgasm and I wrapped my arms around his neck, holding on for support.

He pushed deeper into me and a small scream left me.

The look on his face was full of satisfaction. God, he was beautiful and he didn't even know it. He looked at me with such honest trust and openness that I had a strange desire to cry. For some reason I was reminded of our first time together, and how closed off he'd been. He wasn't that way now, not at all. For once I could see all his emotions plainly on his face and I reveled in it.

I touched his cheek reverently; a part of me believing this might be a dream.

It didn't seem real that after all this time he was actually mine. I thought the book had been closed on our story a long time ago, but I'd been wrong. It had only been the beginning.

My back arched once more and he peppered kissed over my breasts as I came.

Sweat coated our skin as we moved together, always in sync.

His eyes closed and his teeth snapped together. I knew he was close. He buried his head against my neck, his breaths fanning across my shoulders.

"Oh, fuck." He growled softly and I felt him twitch inside me.

He held his weight above me as we both fought to catch our breaths.

His chest rose and fell sharply. He looked at me like I was a mirage beneath him and if he looked away I might disappear.

I reached up, pushing his hair away from his eyes before grasping his face in my hands. "It's okay. I'm here."

The fear didn't leave his eyes as he rolled off of me and disposed of the condom. He climbed back onto the bed, and lying on his side he pulled me against his chest. His arms wrapped protectively around me and my eyes closed, a soft sigh escaping my parted lips.

Minutes passed and sleep threatened to overtake me. I was beginning to think he'd drifted off to sleep when he spoke.

"Don't go," he whispered, pressing a kiss to the back of my shoulder. "Don't leave me."

"I won't," I assured him.

I couldn't. Not even if I wanted to.

# CHAPTER NINETEEN

"She liked to hit me a lot," Mathias spoke, laying in my bed and staring up at the ceiling. "Maddox didn't get it as bad as I did… and I guess in a way I'm thankful for that. I could take the pain and the emotional toll, but he's got too much of a kind heart. It would've hurt him deeper than it has me."

I lay beside him, not touching. I wanted to reach out and wrap my hand around his, but I knew he wouldn't have wanted that, so I forced myself to keep still.

I wanted to argue with him and tell him that he was wrong, that he'd clearly been hurt by the abuse, but I knew that wasn't what he wanted to hear.

"Did you ever fight back?" I asked.

I heard the sheets ruffle as he shook his head. "No."

"Why?"

He was quiet for a moment and I worried I had pissed him off. That happened a lot—and he'd usually jump out of my bed and pull on his clothes, climbing out the window without a second glance at me.

But he didn't do that tonight.

Instead he seemed to be weighing his words carefully.

"I thought I deserved it," he finally whispered, his voice cracking. "I believed her when she said all those things about me."

I rolled over onto my side. This time I was unable to stop myself from touching him. I reached out, tracing my finger along his collarbone. He stiffened at first, but then relaxed into my touch. I laid my palm on his chest, right overtop of his racing heart. His hand came up to clasp mine. I thought he might push my hand away, but he held it there like he was afraid of me letting go.

"Nobody deserves to be treated like that. Definitely not you."

He stared into my eyes, a range of emotions warring on his face. "Haven't you met me? I'm not exactly the nicest fucking person to be around," he growled.

"No, not all the time," I agreed, ducking my head to avoid his intense stare. "But I see past *that, and I know it's only a front. You're actually a pretty nice guy, Mathias."*

*The breath was knocked out of me when he rolled over suddenly, pinning me to the bed.*

*"I'm not a nice guy and you'd do well to remember that, sweetheart." He said the words with a sneer.*

*I wigged one of my arms free and reached up to cup his cheek. "You can try and scare me, but it won't work. I'm not afraid of you."*

*"You should be," he whispered.*

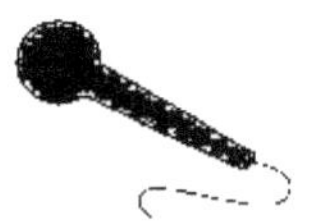

I woke up with my head resting on Mathias' bare chest as his fingers brushed softly through my hair. I wiggled closer to his warmth, blinking the sleep from my eyes.

"Hey," he murmured, his fingers stroking lower over my arm.

"Morning." I tilted my head back to look at him.

He gave me a small, adorable smile. "I was going to get up and make breakfast, but then I decided I'd rather lay here and wait for my girls to get up."

"Your girls?" I asked, putting a hand over my mouth to stifle a yawn.

He nodded his head to the bottom of the bed and that was when I saw Shiloh snoozing peacefully near his feet on her back with her paws in the air. She was honestly the cutest puppy ever.

He brushed his lips tenderly against my forehead and my eyes closed, a soft sigh escaping my lips at the sweet gesture.

"Now that you're up I'll take Shiloh out and make something."

"But I don't want to move," I whined, tightening my hold around his torso.

He chuckled, brushing my messy blonde hair away from my eyes. "Breakfast in bed then?"

I nodded. "That would be perfect. What time is it anyway?"

He glanced at the nightstand. "A little after eight."

"I have to go into work tonight." For the first time since I'd taken the job at the bar, it made me mad that I had to work. I wanted to stay in with Mathias.

He chuckled, playing with a strand of my hair. "At least I'll have you all to myself for most of the day." His voice lowered and he leaned down so his lips brushed my ear with his words. "And I'd really like to try out those handcuffs again, but for fun this time."

I tried to hide my smile. "Later."

He grinned, sliding out of bed and away from my hold.

The cold air hit my body and I immediately wrapped the sheets around myself like a burrito.

Mathias laughed at me, pulling on a pair of low hanging sweatpants.

"Comfy?" He asked, his hands propped on his hips.

"Very," I nodded. "I'm not coming out of here, ever."

He climbed onto the bed and made like he was going to pry the covers off of me, but I rolled away, only tangling myself in them further.

"Nope," I warned him, "I'm not coming out, now go make me breakfast."

He chuckled and grabbed Shiloh, heading for the bedroom door. "You're so damn bossy."

"Says the bossiest man on the planet." I stuck my tongue out at him.

"Yeah, and you're even bossier than me." He stopped in the doorway.

"Just so you know, if I had use of my hands at this moment I'd throw a pillow at you."

He threw his head back and laughed. "Remy, Remy, Remy," he chanted my name, "you're in trouble for that one."

Before I could retort he closed the door and I was left alone.

I truly didn't feel like moving out of the bed, but I decided a shower would be nice.

I untangled myself from the sheets and grabbed my bag that sat by the bottom of the bed. I couldn't remember him bringing it in with us last night, since we'd been otherwise occupied. I figured he must've grabbed it when he got Shiloh.

I closed the bathroom door behind me and turned towards the walk-in shower.

"Holy shit," I muttered, taking in all the controls. The thing was like a spaceship. I opened the glass door and reached inside to turn the nobs. After a few minutes of messing with it, I finally got it set to my liking.

I took as quick of a shower as I could manage and changed into a pair of jeans and plain white t-shirt.

When I opened the bathroom door Mathias was stepping into the bedroom with a tray full of food. A girl could get spoiled to this.

"You showered?" He asked, setting the tray down on the bed.

"Obviously," I replied, gathering my damp hair up and securing it in a bun.

"Why?" He asked, arching a brow. "I'm only going to get you sweaty again." His voice lowered with promise.

"Then I guess I'll have to shower again." I shrugged, smiling playfully.

As much as I loved the aggressive side of Mathias, I was growing to love this side even more. I liked being able to laugh, and smile, and joke with him. It was a welcome difference.

We sat on the bed together, Shiloh between us.

He handed me a plate filled with scrambled eggs, toast, and bacon. "I can't eat all this," I told him, pinching a piece of bacon between my fingers.

"Hey, I made you a nice hot meal so you'll eat it and be happy about it."

I laughed, shaking my head. It was really good though, so I did end up eating it all.

"I think you should cook for me from now on." I put the plate down on the tray.

"Is that so?" He asked, raising a cup of coffee to his lips to hide his growing smile.

I nodded, rubbing my stomach. "You're a much better cook than me. Besides, I hate cooking."

"I think next time I'm going to make you help." His gray eyes flashed with amusement.

"If your kitchen burns down don't blame me." I shrugged.

"You're not going to burn the kitchen down." He rolled his eyes, standing and grabbing the tray. "I'll be right back."

He headed out of the room and my eyes zeroed in on a tattoo between his shoulder blades. I hadn't noticed it before, but then again my mind was usually otherwise occupied when I was around him. Shiloh jumped off the bed and trotted behind him like she was attached to his shadow.

I grabbed my phone from my bag and checked to see if I had any messages.

There was a text from my mom asking how I was.

Another was from my dad checking in on grandma.

There wasn't a message from anyone else, because honestly I didn't have anybody. Any friends I'd made in Arizona hadn't been true friends and we drifted apart. I'd known when I moved here that I would never talk to them again. I didn't have any desire to, and I think a part of me was kind of relieved to say goodbye.

I quickly typed back a response to each of my parents and by the time I was done Mathias was sauntering into the room in all his shirtless glory.

He sat down on the bed and bent over to pick Shiloh up.

Up this close there was no missing his tattoo. It was an intricate compass and beautifully designed.

I reached out to touch it, my fingers grazing his skin. He stiffened at my touch and I quickly withdrew my hand.

"When did you get this?" I asked.

"A while ago," he shrugged.

"Why a compass?" I asked curiously.

"Why so many damn questions?" He snapped.

"Don't get pissy about it," I muttered, "it was a simple question."

He sighed and mumbled, "Sorry."

I was taken aback by his quick and seemingly sincere apology.

With a sigh he ran his fingers through his hair and the brown ends stuck up wildly. It made him look younger and more vulnerable. He looked at me, his gaze steady. "I got it because I wanted something to remind me that no matter how rough the waters might be, I can always find my way back home. It's like my beacon of hope."

I closed my eyes, thinking briefly of my own *Hope* and how I lost her.

"That's a really beautiful reason," I finally replied.

He laughed. "Beautiful? Now you're making my tattoo sound girly."

I pushed his shoulder. "That's not what I meant and you know it."

His lips quirked with a small smile.

"Do you have any other tattoos?" I asked.

"One more," he answered. "But since you've been up close and personal with my body I'm shocked you haven't found it yet."

"Usually when we're naked you're kind of aggressive. It doesn't leave me a lot of time to… explore."

He snorted and I was glad that I could amuse him. "Well, we're not naked now so why don't you try to find it?" He smirked.

"Challenge accepted." I grinned gleefully.

I scooted over, closing the space between us and swung one of my legs over his lap so that I was straddling him.

Kissing his neck I murmured, "There's not one here." Moving lower I kissed his chest, right overtop of where his heart beat. "Not here either."

"Remy," he warned with a low growl, grasping my hips in his hands.

I grabbed his left arm, kissing his bicep and down his arm. "Nope, not there either."

He shifted restlessly and I smiled in satisfaction when I felt him harden beneath me.

I grabbed his other arm and kissed my way down, stopping when I reached his wrist. The tattoo was small, so small that I had to squint to make out the letters. When I read it a gasp escaped between my parted lips.

My head shot up, my eyes connecting with his.

"M-my name. You have my name tattooed on your body. Like permanently."

He huffed, rolling his eyes. "Yeah, that's kind of the point of a tattoo."

I held his wrist still and looked down at the tiny letters again.

R E M Y

"Why?" I asked, baffled. "After how things ended why would you have wanted this?"

I was lost and confused, and honestly very rattled—and it took a lot to unnerve me.

He shrugged, looking away.

"Mathias," I snapped, tightening my hold on his wrist, "tell me." In a softer tone I added, "Please?"

A muscle in his jaw twitched and he slowly returned his gaze to mine.

"Because I always knew you were the only girl I'd ever love." He smoothed his fingers over my cheek. "I wanted to immortalize that. I'm not ashamed of what I feel for you and I'm not going to hide it like a pussy. I made the mistake of pushing you away and thinking that our love wasn't strong enough to last, because I was an insecure kid with abandonment issues. It didn't take me long to realize my feelings were never going to go away and that I'd been a fucking idiot. A love like ours… it doesn't fade in absence, instead it keeps growing. It's all-consuming." He grabbed a piece of my hair, wrapping it around his finger. He leaned forward, pressing his forehead to mine. "It's a rare kind of love, and one that should be celebrated and embraced, so that's what I did, because trying to pretend it didn't exist was fucking impossible."

I closed my eyes, a wave of emotions threatening to drown me.

I took a deep breath and looked up at him. "How come you never tried to find me?" I traced my finger over his chest and down his stomach. "You could have found me if you wanted to," I said with surety.

He swallowed thickly, reaching up to rub his stubbled jaw. "Because I had convinced myself you would have moved on. I couldn't bear the thought of finding you, only to see you happy with some other guy—even though that's exactly what you deserved to have. So, me being the asshole that I am, drank and slept around." He sighed heavily. "I've done nothing but fuck up at every turn for the last twenty-three years of my life and I refuse to do it anymore, especially now that I have you back. I want to be worthy of you."

I wrapped my arms around his neck and laid my head on his chest. His arms wound around my body, hugging me to him.

"You're already worthy," I whispered.

A shaky sigh left him and when I tilted my head back to look at his face he seemed relieved.

He looked down at me, playing with my hair. "I know I can be harsh and an asshole most of the time and I'm not the most romantic guy, but I can promise you that I'll love you every day for as long as my heart beats. I want you to know that *this* is what I want." He lowered his mouth to my ear and whispered, "You. Here.

In my bed. With me. Always.”

I took a shuddering breath, soaking in his words.

Before I had a chance to respond I found myself roughly tossed onto the other side of the bed, and then he was on top of me, pinning me against the bed with his arms.

“Enough serious talk,” his lips turned up into a smirk, “I’m going to fuck you now.”

I smiled when his lips touched mine. The man could be deep one minute, and then an animal the next. I think that’s why I loved him so much.

# CHAPTER TWENTY

I propped my elbows on the bar and leveled Mathias with a glare.

"So, what are you going to do? Sit here the whole time I work like a bodyguard?" I raised a brow, waiting for his reply.

He lifted his glass of water to his lips, not saying a word.

"Mathias," I snapped. "This is my job. I don't need you to babysit me."

His eyes darkened and he set the glass down. "I've seen the way the men in here look at you. You're fucking insane if you think I'm not going to sit here and look out for you."

"I can protect myself," I sneered, hands on my hips. If there was one sure way to piss me off it was to treat me like some Barbie Princess.

"I'm not leaving." He leveled me with a glare, taking another drink of water, "but if you keep bitching at me I might need something stronger than this." A small smile lifted the corners of his lips so I knew he was joking.

"Whatever. Just don't cause any trouble," I warned, walking away to busy myself with actually working.

"When do I ever?" He chuckled.

I rolled my eyes, sighing at his response. "Hey Jeff, you're here early. It's only five," I remarked, noticing one of the regulars sidling up to the bar. "Are you lost?" I laughed.

"I've got a date," he grinned, pointing over his shoulder.

I peered around him and noticed a pretty brunette around his age sitting at a booth. "She's pretty," I smiled, "so what are you doing over here talking to me?"

"Uh…" He started and I noticed a sheen of sweat on his forehead. "I'm kind of nervous. I don't know what to say to her." He frowned. "I haven't been on a date in years, not since my wife left me. I'm too old for this."

"Aw, Jeff, you're not old."

"Fifty is old, Red."

I couldn't help smiling at the nickname—the one Tanner had given me, and all the regulars picked up on. I *hated* nicknames, but this one I liked. It wasn't condescending.

"No it's not." I shook my head. "Go back over there and talk to her. About anything… except the weather… or your dick. Don't do that."

He chuckled. "Thanks, Red."

"Anytime." I gave him a reassuring smile before he walked away.

I grabbed a rag and began wiping down the counter.

"Who was that?" I heard from behind me.

I stopped wiping and turned to glare at Mathias. "I'm working."

"You were talking and that wasn't working. Who was he?" His face was contorted in a grimace.

"Are you jealous?"

"No," he drew out the word, "that guy just seemed extra friendly."

I tucked the rag in the back pocket of my jeans and crossed my arms over my chest as I stared him down. "Jeff is a regular, and he's also practically as old as my dad. So, really not my type." Stepping forward I smiled coyly. "Besides, I already have a guy."

"You do?" He chuckled. "Tell me about him."

"Well," I started, clucking my tongue, "he can be kind of an asshole. But he's immeasurably sweet when he wants to be. He also has a huge heart, but he doesn't let many people in. He's smarter than he thinks he is and he's fiercely protective— so much so that apparently he has to come stand guard over me at work."

He chuckled, ducking his head. "He sounds like an incredible guy."

"He is," I agreed seriously. "I wish he could see that."

His fists clenched where they rested on the bar top and he looked away.

"Remy?" A new voice broke into my thoughts and I turned away from Mathias.

"Lana?" I questioned. "Are you sure you should be in a bar in your… state?" I asked, staring at her large stomach. Jesus, she looked like she was ready to give birth any second.

She laughed. "I'm not here to drink, obviously." She rubbed her stomach. "I remembered you mentioned you worked here, and I wanted to invite you to my baby shower." She held out an envelope for me. "I didn't have your address and I thought if I called you might forget about it. It's next Friday."

I held the envelope like it was a bomb that was going to explode in my hand. "Uh…" I didn't know what to say. Baby showers were not my thing. In fact, anything involving a baby wasn't my thing. It only served to remind me of what I didn't have.

"Please say you'll be there," she begged.

"I-I—" I stuttered, unable to form a coherent sentence.

"She'll be there," Mathias interrupted, "I'll make sure of it."

Lana's attention swiveled from me to Mathias and her eyes narrowed. "Mathias Wade? Wow. I haven't seen you since… well, since high school. Um… how are things? Like with the band? I just… oh my God, you're famous now and it's just… can I have your autograph?"

I snorted and Mathias glared at me for my rudeness—I don't know why he cared, since he normally acted like an asshat.

"It's good to see you, Lana," he said in an even tone.

"I… I can't believe someone we went to school with is famous…" She gasped, looking back at me. "And I mean, you *dated* him, like… whoa."

I rolled my eyes and reached into my pocket for the rag so I could return to cleaning.

"Lana, please pick up your jaw from the floor before you leave," I remarked.

Her eyes widened and her cheeks flamed with redness as she realized what a fool she was making of herself.

"I'm sorry," she blabbered, "please forget I said anything… wait," she looked from me to Mathias, waving a finger, "are you guys like… together again?"

"Yes.'"

"No."

I glared at Mathias.

"No," he repeated. "We're not together."

"Oh," Lana frowned, "my bad." She seemed to realize she'd stirred up something bad because she slowly backed away. "I'll see you at my baby shower, Remy!" She called, running out of the building.

I threw the rag down on the floor and stormed off towards the backroom. I didn't give a fuck if Tanner fired me again. Right then, if I didn't get away from Mathias, I might launch myself across the bar top and strangle him. I didn't want a murder on my hands, so I figured it was best to remove myself from the situation.

I was beyond livid that after everything he'd said he was now saying we weren't together. He was giving me fucking whiplash.

I sat down at the small table in the backroom and rested my head on the table. The cool surface helped to soothe me, but nothing could completely take away the anger raging inside me.

"Remy," Mathias growled my name as he stormed into the backroom, "don't fucking run away from me."

I turned my head away from him and mumbled to the wall, "I wasn't running away. I was removing myself from the situation."

"What are we, five? Let's talk about this like adults."

I snapped towards him and he backed a step away when he saw the anger on my face. "Adults? You want to talk about this like adults? Okay, how about you don't tell me we're together and then tell Lana we're not." I pushed at his shoulders and beat my fists against his solid chest.

He grabbed my hands and cradled them between his, holding on tight enough that I couldn't pull them away.

"Shh," he crooned, trying to calm me.

"Let me go!" I wiggled against his hold.

"No," he growled, wrapping his arms around my body and holding my back against his chest. I kicked him in the shin and he grunted, but didn't let go. "Rem, listen to me," he said in that silky voice that normally had me melting, but right now I was too mad for it to affect me. "Listen," he pleaded, tightening his hold against my struggles. His lips brushed my ear and I jerked away. "Remy," his voice rose with anger, "I only said that because she went all fan-girl and I didn't want her to go blabbing about it to someone else, who would tell someone else, who would then contact the media, and so on and so forth."

I stopped struggling, becoming dead weight in his arms. "So, what if she had?" I countered. "If we're together for real why would you give a fuck if the media found out?"

I felt his forehead press against my back. "I don't know," he mumbled. "I just… I hate the media. I hate what they do and say and how they misconstrue things. I don't want them to drag you into that. I was only trying to protect you."

"I can protect myself." I spat the words through clenched teeth.

"What's wrong with letting me take care of you? You don't have to do everything, you know."

"Let me go," I pleaded, trying to pry his hands off of me.

"Not until you listen to me."

"I am listening," I mumbled.

"No, you're not. You're fighting me. Please," he begged and I felt his teeth nip lightly at my shoulder, "believe me. I wasn't trying to hurt you, I was doing what I thought was best."

"So what? I'll always be your dirty little secret? Your whore on the side while some model is draped on your arm?" I panted, trying to catch my breath.

His hold loosened, but only enough so that he could turn me around to face him. He kept a tight hold on my wrists so that I couldn't get away.

"Don't you *ever* say that about yourself ever again." His eyes held a dangerous silvery glint.

"Why not? That's how I feel." I swallowed thickly, my mask slipping as my vulnerability shown. "That's how *you* made me feel."

He closed his eyes and his Adam's apple bobbed. "God, I'm sorry, Remy. I didn't mean it like that at all. My wanting to keep you away from the media has nothing to do with wanting to hide this. I promise you that."

"You know they'll find out eventually," I whispered, the fight leaving my body, "so why does it matter so much?"

His eyes popped open and his chest heaved with a heavy breath. "Because they ruin everything and I refuse to let them ruin this, the one good thing I have left."

I shuddered, folding into his arms and letting him hold me. "Okay," I said, resting my head on his chest, "I'm sorry for overreacting."

He laughed, his whole body shaking. "We wouldn't be Mathias and Remy if we didn't overreact."

"I guess you're right about that." I joined in with his laughter.

He took my chin between his thumb and index finger and lifted my head so I was forced to meet his gaze. "And you're going to her baby shower. Even if I have to kidnap you and throw you in the trunk of my car."

"Why?" I frowned. "I don't want to go." I pouted like a small child, panic rising inside me at the thought of being surrounded by all the baby things. I could handle being around pregnant women—and maybe that was because I hadn't had my pregnancy stolen from me—but babies and baby things sent me into a tailspin.

"Because you need friends."

"I have friends… I have you… and my grandma… and I kind of have Tanner," I rambled, "and we can't forget Percy."

"I don't count." He chuckled.

"Why not?"

"Because," his voice lowered with a sensual tone, "we have sex, therefore we're not friends."

"I'd say we are friends," I countered. "Look at all the conversations we have. I know more about you than most people."

"You're not winning this argument, Remy," he glared. "And who the fuck is Percy?"

"My cat," I reminded him.

His face crinkled with disgust. "Fucking demon cat," he muttered under his breath.

"That's not his name. It's Percy. P. E. R. C. Y."

"Such a smartass," he mumbled and I fought a smile. "But don't think I haven't forgotten what you're trying to do. You're going to the party, Remy. Lana was your friend and she wants you there."

"Why do you even care?"

He frowned, my question having taken him off guard. "I don't know," he answered honestly, his brows furrowing together. "I guess I don't want your life to become consumed by mine."

"Wow, egotistical much?" I joked, biting my lip to contain my laughter. "Besides, *you're* the one sitting at the bar while I work."

He shook his head. "Fuck, I can never win with you."

"Nope." I grinned triumphantly.

"Hey, Red," Tanner poked his head into the backroom, "you have a job to do. Get out here."

"Fuck off, Tanner." I gave him the finger.

He shook his head and walked away. He was used to my antics by now.

I stepped away from Mathias and straightened my clothes. "I'm not going," I declared as I walked away—sure that I'd had the last word.

"Yes, you are," he sing-songed, and I knew he wasn't going to let this go.

Wonderful.

He sat down at the bar once more and feeling devilish I grabbed one of the kid's menus and crayons. I set them in front of him and he looked at me with a perplexed expression. "What the fuck is this for?" He waved a hand at the kid's stuff.

I smiled, but there was nothing nice about it. "If you're going to act like a child, I'll treat you like one."

"Now who's acting like a child." He waved a hand at me. "I don't see what the big fucking deal is. It's a baby shower. It's not like you're going to get pregnant by breathing the same air as her."

I sighed, closing my eyes. I took a deep breath and tried to center myself. I needed to let this go and give in. I couldn't tell him the truth behind why I didn't want to go. It was time to put my big girl panties on. "Fine, whatever, I'll go. This is stupid." I shrugged, turning away from him and getting back to work. Tanner really was going to fire me if I didn't get my shit together, and unfortunately I wouldn't even be able to blame him.

"And now you're mad at me." I heard him mumble behind me. I didn't bother responding. He'd already distracted me enough.

"You okay, darlin'?" One of the men at the bar asked.

"Yeah," I muttered, not even bothering to see who had spoken to me.

I hurried around taking new orders and refilling old ones—as well as tending to a few tabletops because one of the waitresses called in sick.

All the while Mathias sat at the bar—coloring that damn kids menu I'd put in front of him as a joke. His water was gone though, replaced by a glass full of scotch. I didn't know how he drank that stuff. It was lethal.

I shook my head as I passed him, heading over to one of the tables to take an order.

A good hour passed before I had a chance to catch a breath.

"Why don't you just quit?" Mathias asked while I fixed him another drink.

I raised a single brow, looking at him like he'd lost his mind. "Number one, I like working and number two I need the money. Most people aren't like you." I reminded him.

"I know," he took the glass from me, his eyes dark and serious, "but I would take care of you."

My mouth fell open and I stared at him, at a loss for words. There was no way I possibly heard him right.

"What?" I voiced.

"You heard me," he repeated, slowly raising the glass to his lips.

"You would take care of me?" I parroted his words back to him. I shook my head, laughing under my breath.

"I don't know why you're laughing. I'm serious." His brow wrinkled with frustration.

"I can't even get into this with you right now." I shook my head again, still mystified by what he said.

"Why not?" He asked. "I mean, I think I've made it pretty clear that I want you by my side for the rest of my life, therefore me wanting to take care of you shouldn't come as a shock."

My throat tightened up and I couldn't breathe. "Mathias, we've only been together for like… a month," I said, frazzled by his declaration. "You can't say stuff like that."

His teeth snapped together, a muscle in his jaw ticking. "So what? The fucking year we spent together means nothing to you?"

"I don't know," I cried, throwing my hands up in frustration. "It's just a lot for me to process when you say things like that. I've taken care of myself for so long that I can't just become some trophy wife for you to have to prance around on your arm."

"You think that's what I fucking want?" He glared, his hand tightening around the glass. "That's not what I want at all. I love you for *you*. I'm not trying to change you, I'm just saying that… well, that I would take care of you. Isn't that what most girls want? To be taken care of? Fuck," he muttered, clutching his forehead, "you make my brain hurt."

I would have laughed at him if he didn't look so despaired.

"I'm sorry," I apologized, "I shouldn't have freaked out, but I'm happy here. I like doing something."

He nodded. "Yeah, I understand. I shouldn't have said it," he mumbled, raising the glass to his lips once more.

I reached out, placing my hand over his—suddenly feeling horrible for my behavior. He was only trying to be nice and I twisted that. "Don't feel bad," I pleaded with him, "what you said was a nice thing to say, but I'm not that girl. You should know I'm far too independent to sit back and do nothing," I winked.

He sighed heavily and looked up at the ceiling briefly—like maybe it held the answer to everything—and then his eyes lowered to mine. "We really fucking suck at this whole relationship thing."

I laughed, taking a step back. "That's because we're far from normal," I cracked a smile, "and I wouldn't have it any other way."

He smiled at that too, and reached into his pocket for his pack of cigarettes. He took one and stuck it between his lips.

"No smoking in here," I warned, pointing a finger at him like he was an unruly child.

A single brow arched as he raised the lighter to the tip. It caught and he sucked in the smoke before slowly blowing it out. Smiling crookedly he said, "I'm Mathias Fucking Wade and I can do whatever the fuck I want."

I turned my head away so he couldn't see me smile at his words.

For the rest of my shift I pretended he wasn't there, and when it ended we walked together back to his penthouse, where we both showered and collapsed in bed exhausted but happy.

# CHAPTER TWENTY-ONE

"I can't believe you're making me do this," I muttered, walking up and down the baby aisle in Target with Mathias. If I wasn't so mad it would be kind of funny to see him standing between all the baby stuff and looking like a fish out of water.

"She's your friend and you need to go," he stated, picking up a box. "What the fuck is this?" He asked, his brow wrinkling as he inspected the box.

I peered over his shoulder and laughed. "It's a breast pump for mother's that breast feed."

His eyes widened and he quickly returned the box. He ventured further down the aisle and picked up a blue stuffed elephant. "How about this?"

"Well, it's blue, and I don't know if the twins are boys so no. Let's keep this gender neutral."

He groaned, muttering under his breath about me being unreasonable.

"Don't complain," I lightly punched his shoulder as I passed him, "this was your idea."

"Ugh, whatever." He pinched the bridge of his nose. We headed down another aisle and he grabbed two gray blankets. "How about these?"

I reached out, rubbing the soft knitted fabric between my fingers as a lump formed in my throat. I'd had a similar blanket for Hope, one I had planned to bring her home from the hospital in.

"No, not that one."

"It's a fucking blanket, how does it not work?" He snapped, replacing the blankets.

"I don't think she'll like it." I saw a pale yellow blanket with a bee design on it and grabbed two. "This one is cute."

"Great, then let's buy it and get out of here." He tossed a thumb over his shoulder.

"Allergic to baby stuff?" I joked, but was truly curious to know what he thought of kids.

He wrinkled his nose and looked around. "No, it's just weird. I mean, who knew babies needed all this stuff. They're so small."

I draped the blankets over my arm, heading towards the gift-wrapping aisle. He fell into step beside me, shortening his strides to match mine.

"So, would you want kids one day?" I ventured to ask. I didn't know why the question suddenly felt so important, but I needed to know. The doctors had assured me that what happened with Hope was random and that I wasn't defective—like I'd kept shouting in the hospital. They promised me that one day, when I was ready, I could have a baby. I knew it was silly, since we hadn't been back together long, but I couldn't stop myself from imagining a future that included more than the two of us.

He glanced at me, his eyes widening in surprise. "Uh…" He paused, scratching at the back of his head nervously. "Yeah, I guess so."

"You guess so?" I repeated, waiting for him to elaborate.

He frowned, his brows drawing together. "I *like* kids, but the thought of having a kid of my own is really fucking scary… what if… what if I'm a fucked up parent like mine were?"

I exhaled a breath I didn't know I was holding. Smiling, I grasped his forearm. "You would be an amazing dad." I meant those words wholeheartedly. I *knew* without a shadow of doubt that Mathias would be the best dad imaginable.

If things had been different and Hope had lived, I knew that once Mathias found out about her he would've been there for her in a heartbeat. He wouldn't have abandoned her the way he did me.

"You think?" He asked, his expression softening.

"I know."

He grinned and his smile made my stomach fill with a million butterflies. His smile was so rare, but one of the most beautiful things I had ever seen. Every time he graced me with its presence was a moment I cherished.

Sobering, he said, "What are we looking for now?"

Once more his steely mask fell into place.

"I was going to grab a gift bag and a card."

"Oh, right," he mumbled. "I'm going to go grab a coffee. I'll be at the front."

Without waiting for me to say anything he turned, shoving his hands into his pockets and walked away.

I turned down the gift bag aisle and grabbed one with zoo animals that was large enough for the two blankets. Stopping off at the cards I grabbed the first baby one I saw and headed to the checkout.

Lana's baby shower was starting soon, so I needed to hurry.

Mathias had insisted on driving me to Target for the gift, and then to the party, because he was convinced I was going to flake. Let's be honest, I probably would have.

I put the items on the conveyer belt and the cashier rang them up and put them in the plastic bag. He held the plastic bag out to me and I stared at him quizzically. "I haven't paid yet." I tried to hand him the cash in my hand but he dodged it.

"Mr. Wade has taken care of it."

"Mr—Oh fuck him. I can't fucking believe him. This is ridiculous. I can pay for my own damn stuff. Who the fuck does he think he is? *Mr. Wade.*" I mimed the cashier's tone, and snatched the bag from him. I probably should've felt bad for being so rude in front of the cashier, but I couldn't find it within myself to care.

I marched over to Starbucks and glared at Mathias who stood by the counter holding two cups of coffee, a smug smile on his lips.

"Seriously, Mathias?" I snapped. "I could've bought it."

He shrugged. "Too late."

"That's why you wanted to get coffee," I muttered, taking the cup he offered me, "so you could give the cashier money."

"You bet." He lifted the cup to his mouth.

"Did you also tell him to call you Mr. Wade?" I asked. I tried to sound angry, but I was really trying not to laugh.

He nodded. "Yep. It has a nice ring to it, doesn't it?"

I shook my head, trying to hide my smile at his antics.

"You know what else has a nice ring to it?"

"What?" I asked as we headed outside to his car.

"Remy Wade."

I spit out the coffee in my mouth all over the ground. I'm pretty sure a dribble got on my shirt too.

He stopped and looked at me, appearing slightly mad by my reaction. "Does the thought of marrying me make you gag?"

I wiped my mouth with the back of my hand. Shaking my head I said, "No, I was just surprised that you of all people would ever think about marriage." I might've had hopes for a future with him, but a huge part of me still doubted that he'd ever want that with me… or anyone.

His dark brows furrowed together. "Why is that so shocking?" He seemed truly confused.

I waved a hand at him, scoffing, "Because you're you."

"Oh come on, Remy, you can give me a better reason than that."

I sighed heavily and let it spill out. "It's just that you've never been Mister Commitment. Since you guys got famous you're *always* photographed with a different woman. You don't date so why would you ever want to get married?"

He took a step back and looked away, but not before I saw the hurt on his face. "I was committed to you," he said softly. "I *am* committed to you," he added with more force. "Is it so impossible to believe that I might see a future for us? I mean, I know I'm not the kind of guy who wears his heart on his sleeve," he waved his arms dramatically through the air. "I don't do romantic bullshit and I'm not going to give you some epic poem declaring my undying love, but I do—love you, I mean. I love you in the only way I know how and I'm sorry if it's not good enough and I'm sorry if it's flawed, but at least it's real."

The last thing I had ever expected was for Mathias to make a declaration like that.

I stood there, staring at him with an open mouth. I had no idea what to do or say. He'd officially stunned me into silence—which was kind of a miracle.

Finally I said the only thing that made any sort of sense to me.

"I love you *too*," I whispered, my voice cracking.

He lovingly stroked the side of my face with a sweep of his fingers before lowering his lips to mine.

Despite the cold temperature I suddenly felt like I was on fire.

His tongue swept against mine, drawing a moan from me. My fingers grasped at the soft material of his leather jacket as I angled myself against his body, wanting to get impossibly closer.

We startled apart a moment later when a car honked.

Mathias let out a low throaty laugh and stepped back.

He took the bag from my hands and wrapped an arm around my waist, pulling me along to his car since apparently I'd become immobile.

"Come on, Rem," he grinned, "there's a party for you to attend."

"Don't fucking remind me."

He laughed, opening the passenger door for me. "You sound like you're headed to the slaughter house."

"Might as well be," I muttered.

"It won't be that bad," he assured, handing me the bag.

The passenger door closed and he walked around the front with a lethal cat like grace. Everything he did was always done with such precision… at least when he wasn't pissed off about something. When he got mad he turned into a raging bull that took out everything in its path.

Once he was in the car I handed him the invitation with Lana's address and then I set about fixing the card and the blankets in the bag.

I had hoped the drive would take an hour, but it didn't take any more than ten minutes to reach her house.

This was going to be like walking into my own personal hell.

Mathias parked on the street and turned the car off.

I looked at him quizzically.

"I'll walk you to the door," he said in answer.

I knew that he was making sure I didn't make a mad dash for it and hop over the fence.

Mathias met me at the side of the vehicle, laughing at the expression on my face. "You could try not to look so miserable."

I forced a smile and he grimaced.

"Never mind, smiling is worse."

"Thanks a lot," I mumbled. "You know, since you're my boyfriend you should really be nicer to me."

He shrugged, trying to hide a smile as he put a guiding hand at my waist—not so subtly pushing me up the fancy brick walkway.

"If I was nicer to you, you might start thinking there was something wrong with me."

"That's true," I agreed as we stopped in front of the door. It was painted a deep shade of red with a heavy knocker.

I took a deep breath, holding the air inside my lungs. Surely if I passed out Mathias would take mercy upon me and this whole debacle could be avoided.

The front door opened and with it the air rushed out of my lungs. Fuck. There went that plan.

"Remy! Mathias! Get in here you two!" Lana exclaimed in an overly bubbly manner as she wrapped her arms around my neck. I awkwardly hugged her back, silently counting how many minutes I needed to stay before I could leave without seeming like a party pooper.

Letting me go she hugged Mathias. His eyes just about bugged out of his head and he mouthed, "Help me."

I shook my head, smirking at him.

"Come on, come on." Lana grabbed each of our hands, pulling us inside. For being so pregnant she possessed an awful amount of energy.

"Oh, I was leaving," Mathias muttered, tossing his thumb over his shoulder. "I just gave her a ride."

"Oh, don't be silly," she giggled, closing the door and locking it. "All the husbands stayed."

Mathias paled and his eyes shifted to me and back to Lana. "But we're not married."

"Yeah, but you're friends, right?" She asked, clapping her hands together. My God she could give a cheerleading squad a run for their money with all this pep.

She was never this happy when we were in high school. Had love seriously turned her into this creepily happy robot drone?

Mathias mumbled under his breath and pinched the bridge of his nose. "Whatever, I'll stay."

"Yay!" Lana did a little dance and I really hoped a baby didn't come flying out. "Follow me! The party is in the living room."

Mathias glanced at me, then at Lana's retreating form, and then back at the locked door. "Did you see how fast she locked that door? I feel like we just walked into the house of a serial killer and we're not getting out alive. If we make a mad dash for it, do you think she'll notice."

I smiled sweetly and started after Lana. "You're the one that was so insistent on me attending this baby shower, so we're staying."

"Fuck me." He cursed, tapping his fingers against his jeans. I knew he was itching to grab a cigarette but was trying to resist the urge.

I was a few steps in front of him now, so I stopped and smiled coyly. "Oh, I will later."

He grinned at my words and then seemed to remember where we were and mumbled, "This better be the fastest fucking baby shower ever."

"I think we should make a game out of this."

"What kind of game?" He whispered skeptically.

"Every time you complain I get to be on top for a minute."

"No fucking way," he shook his head. "I'm in charge. Always."

"Are you sure?" I asked, running my fingers along his chest. I hadn't even realized we'd stopped following Lana. "I think it could be fun."

He scrubbed his hands over his face and muttered, "Alright, but this better be worth it."

"It'll be the best sex of your life," I promised.

"Remy! Mathias!"

"Oh, shit," I muttered, hurrying after the sound of the voice. We stepped into an open living room with high-vaulted ceilings and beige walls. A large tan sectional took up most of the space, positioned in front of a gas fireplace with a TV over it. A few extra fold-up chairs were scattered throughout the room for the party, as well as a table for the cake and gifts.

I put my gift with the others and then Mathias and I took a seat.

He rubbed his hands against his jeans and glanced around like he was looking for the nearest exit.

This was going to be epic.

One of Lana's friends stood up, clapping her hands together to get everyone's attention. "First up we're going to play a game called Applesauce Never Tasted So

Good. This'll be done in teams of two so we'll divide off as couples. I'll be handing out a trash bag for each of you to wear as a bib and the applesauce. Whoever eats their applesauce the fastest is the winner."

Mathias looked at me with a horrified expression. "This is barbaric."

"One," I coughed.

"Huh?" He looked at me, his brows furrowing together in a dark line.

"One. Minute."

"Fuck."

"Two."

"Shit."

"Three," I laughed.

He put a hand over his mouth.

The woman finished passing out the stuff and I felt bad that I didn't know her name. Hell, I didn't any of the people here. I figured Lana knew most of them through Clayton, her husband.

"You go first," I told Mathias, setting the bag and applesauce I'd been handed on the floor.

He glared at me, wringing the plastic trash bag between his hands.

"Come on, be a team player," I coaxed.

"This is fucking ridiculous," he spat, tying the bag around his neck.

"Four," I grinned.

He narrowed his eyes at me. "You're really enjoying my pain right now, aren't you?"

"Oh, I am." Plus, his utter contempt for the baby shower was distracting me from thinking about Hope.

"Oh, I forgot the blindfolds!" The woman that handed out the previous items jumped up from her seat with ties clutched in her hands.

"This keeps getting worse and worse." He rolled his eyes.

"Five."

"Hey!" He glared at me, snapping his fingers. "I wasn't complaining, I was merely stating a fact."

"Fine, four then." I shook my head, positioning my chair in front of him.

I took the tie from the woman and shielded Mathias' eyes, securing it in a knot.

"You know, this would have possibilities if you were the one blindfolded," he whispered under his breath.

I rolled my eyes even though he couldn't see me. "You wish," I muttered.

I sat back down and took the lid off the applesauce and grabbed the baby spoon.

"Is everybody ready?" She asked, holding up her phone to start a timer.

"Yes," everyone replied, except for Mathias and me that is.

"Annnnd Go."

I shoveled a spoonful of applesauce into his mouth and he turned away, covering his mouth with his hand. "Jesus Christ, Remy. I think you cracked one of my teeth."

"Don't be a baby," I laughed, attacking him with another spoonful.

He made a face much like a disgruntled small child would. "What the fuck is this? It tastes terrible."

"It's applesauce, remember?" I gathered another spoonful and prepared to attack him.

"It tastes fucking awf—"

I nailed him with the spoon and then he reached out, trying to push me away, which resulted in me losing my balance and falling out of my chair—which somehow made him fall over as well. Our legs ended up tangled together and we were covered in spilled applesauce.

"That didn't end well." I frowned, holding a piece of blonde hair that was sticky.

"This was a fucking terrible idea. Remind me never to force you to do something ever again." He chuckled, pulling the blindfold off. There was applesauce smeared across his cheek and I reached out, wiping it away with a swipe of my finger.

"We're kind of a mess." I bit my lip to stifle my laughter as I pointed to our clothes.

"Does this mean we can leave?" He asked, his eyes brightening.

"Ahem." Someone cleared their throat and I looked up to see the woman that was in charge of the game towering above us. "Do you think you two could compose yourselves long enough for us to finish the game?"

"Uh…?" I looked from her to Mathias. He held a hand over his mouth, trying to hide his laughter but his shaking shoulders gave him away.

She began to tap her foot.

"Yeah," I finally said, feeling like I was a child getting scolded by a parent.

Mathias and I both picked ourselves up off the floor and sat down—choosing to sit out the rest of this game.

I glanced at my phone, frowning when I saw that not even ten minutes had passed. This was going to end up being the longest day of my life.

The game finally ended and a winner was declared.

What did they win?

The satisfaction of being covered in applesauce.

I guess in that case we were all winners.

Mathias turned to me, his mouth parted as if he'd had some sudden realization.

"Do you think they'll make us play pin the tail on the donkey?" He reached up trying to wipe applesauce from his hair, but his efforts were futile since it was already drying.

I snorted at his ridiculous question. "No, it's a baby shower not a kid's birthday party."

His eyes widened in horror. "They're not going to make us pin a tail on a baby are they? Because that's just wrong."

I stared at him for a moment, biting my lip to contain my laughter. Eventually I couldn't hold it in any longer and it burst forth, causing all the eyes in the room to draw our way, but I didn't care.

Mathias glared at me—daring me to keep laughing at him, but I couldn't help it.

Once I had control of myself, I held up a hand and said, "You may continue now."

And so they did, moving on to another ridiculous game—one where they'd melted chocolate onto diapers and you had to smell it and guess what chocolate bar it was. I thought it was disgusting. Mathias apparently did too, because after the second diaper he refused to play anymore.

After a few more ridiculous games we were finally rewarded with cake.

Mmm, cake.

That made this suckfest so much better.

The woman in charge of the games cut up the cake and dished out the plates.

Several of the attendees chose this time to approach Mathias, fawning over him and asking him for pictures. He took it in stride, even though I knew he hated the attention. It was a part of his job and he couldn't be too rude.

"Is this almost over?" Mathias hissed in my ear.

"I really hope so. I want to wash this applesauce out of my hair and I'm really looking forward to my sixteen minutes on top," I grinned triumphantly.

"We'll see about that, m'kay?"

I lifted a bite of cake to my lips, licking off the icing. "I'm not afraid to use your handcuffs against you." I warned him.

"Good luck finding them." He grinned.

I flicked icing at his face and it landed in a yellow blop on his cheek. He narrowed his eyes until they were nothing but thin slits and wiped the icing off. Holding out his finger to me he demanded, "Lick."

I did, not even caring that we were engaging in foreplay in front of a group of strangers.

His eyes darkened until they were nearly black.

"Now I just want to drag you out of here and fuck you in my car," he hissed under his breath.

"Presents first." I nodded my head towards the table of gifts.

He mumbled under his breath about not having the patience to wait.

"Seventeen," I sing-songed.

"Stop it," he growled. "I'm in pain over here and now you're mocking me. Don't kick me while I'm down."

I snickered, eyeing his jeans. "Looks like you're up to me."

"Shut up, Remy," he growled, wiggling uncomfortably in his seat.

Personally, I wanted to leave as badly—if not more than he did—but now that I was here I didn't want to be even ruder by walking out early.

We finished eating the cake and I took Mathias' plate, dropping both of ours in the waiting trash bag.

Everybody else had finished as well, which meant Lana and Clayton were about to start opening presents.

"Thank God," Mathias muttered when the first gift was handed to Lana, "it's about time."

*It's almost over.* I told myself.

Wrong.

They took their time, opening each gift slowly and carefully, then thanking the person who gifted it to them at least ten times.

I was pretty sure today was designed to be my own personal hell.

Not only was this boring as fuck, but all of the baby items were a huge reminder of the fact that I didn't have my baby.

My chest felt raw and cut open as I remembered coming home from the hospital with empty arms, only to see Hope's crib still set up in my bedroom. When I'd cried out my mom had come running to me and then scolded my dad and brother for not doing away with it.

For a long time after that I was a shell of who I used to be. But gradually I went back to my wild ways. It wasn't the same though. It was like I was living someone else's life—acting the way I thought I was supposed to. I think a part of me had hoped that if I acted like I was fine eventually I would be. But I'd learned that the pain of losing Hope would never go away. It was something I would have to carry with me for the rest of my life and it was *okay* to *not* be *okay* all the time.

I closed my eyes, momentarily blocking out Lana and Clayton's smiling faces. I needed to regroup.

I'd been able to block out the memories while we'd been playing those ridiculous games and Mathias had been making me laugh, but now there were no distractions. It was all right there in front of me. Baby this and baby that. It was like being stabbed repeatedly in the chest while someone twisted the knife around.

"Are you okay?" Mathias asked, grasping my knee.

I nodded my head. "Mhmm."

He looked at me doubtfully, his brows drawn together. "You look like you're feeling sick."

"I'm fine. Honestly," I assured him—trying not to flinch when Lana held up a two tiny pink onesies.

"Rem—" He started, concern radiating off of him.

Sometimes it really sucked that Mathias was the only person that could read me so well. Most people probably didn't notice the stiffness in my posture or the way my lips tightened to hide my frown—but he did.

"I'm just getting antsy," I mumbled.

He looked at me doubtfully and shrugged before turning away. I knew he didn't believe me, but was letting it go. For now at least.

The next gift they opened was the one from Mathias and me.

"Aw, these blankets are lovely!" Lana chimed.

Lovely? Who in the their right mind used the word lovely?

"Thank you so much," she continued. "The girls will love them."

"Great," I forced a smile, "you're welcome."

Mathias glanced at me again, having noticed the slight waver in my voice. I had to get it together.

He didn't say anything this time. Instead he reached for my hand, entwining our fingers together. Mathias rarely ever held my hand and I let myself take a brief amount of comfort in his touch.

Once the last gift had been opened I stood hastily. I was leaving whether anybody else did or not.

I strode over to Lana—giving her a brief hug.

"We have to get together and have lunch soon." She grasped my hand, refusing to let go.

"Uh… yeah, sure." I agreed, in the hopes of getting away faster. "I really have to go."

"Oh, right, of course." She shook her head and let go of my hand. "See you soon. Bye, Mathias!" She called over my shoulder to Mathias who I was sure was leaning broodily against the wall and giving off a Stay-The-Fuck-Away-From-Me vibe.

When I turned around I saw Mathias saluting her with two fingers.

Before anyone could stop us we hurried to the front door and out to his car.

Finally in the safety of the Corvette I breathed a sigh of relief.

Mathias started the car and pulled away from the curb. I felt the heavy weight of his eyes every few seconds as he glanced in my direction.

"Rem, are you okay?" He asked again. Before I could respond, he continued,

"You got kind of weird in there."

"I'm fine, honestly," I mumbled, looking out the window.

Mathias tapped the breaks and pulled off the side of the road. "What the fuck is going on with you? You were fine earlier and now you're…" He clenched his teeth and shoved a hand through his hair so that the dark brown strands stuck up wildly. "I don't know what you are, but something's wrong, and I know it. Talk to me."

I couldn't talk to him. Not about this. Not about Hope.

He stared at me and I was stuck, unable to look away no matter how hard I tried. Those strange gray eyes of his were pleading with me, begging me to open up.

My throat constricted as I remembered the boy who used to sneak in my bedroom window—who shared his darkest moments and deepest secrets with me, and now here we were back together again years later and I couldn't confide in him the way he had me. The difference was Mathias' secrets had never been something that might break me, but the one I was keeping from him would shatter him into a million pieces.

I couldn't hurt him like that.

I had to carry around the gut-wrenching loss of Hope *every single day*, but he didn't have to. If I never told him, he wouldn't have to experience the heartbreak of mourning a child.

"Rem," he pleaded, reaching up to cup my cheek. His palm was warm and rough. "What's going on?"

I swallowed past the lump in my throat and tried to clear my face of any emotion. "It's nothing."

"You're lying." The words came out in a harsh bite, a stark contrast to the way he lovingly stroked my cheek. "You keep getting weird on me, like that day in the garage. What is it, Remy? Do you owe someone money? Are you tangled up in something illegal? What the fuck is it? Tell me so I can help you."

I continued to stare at him, unable to form a coherent sentence.

He stroked his thumb in slow rhythmic circles against my cheek; like the small gesture alone could coax the words I refused to say from between my lips.

"I have a lot going on," I whispered after a minute. "It's all starting to catch up to me." That wasn't a complete lie. "I feel like I need a break—not from you, but from life," I hastened to add. "I wish for a moment I wouldn't have to deal with all of this and I could just… breathe."

He continued to stare at me, his eyes seeming to calculate something. His tongue flicked out to moisten his lips and I couldn't help the way my body responded by tightening all over.

"Come to L.A. with me."

I shook my head, my brows drawing together. I couldn't have possibly heard him right. My ears must've been broken. "What?" I croaked, my voice seeming to have left me.

"Come to L.A. with me," he repeated. "Next week. We have to take care of a few things before our tour so I have to go back for a few days, but let's make a trip out of it. We can get away, just you and me."

My mouth opened and closed as I tried to form words. "What about my grandma?" Was my intelligent response.

He chuckled, tangling his fingers in my hair. "I can have someone check on her."

"L.A.?" I repeated.

"That's what I said."

"I… I don't know," I frowned.

"You're the one that said you needed a break. Here's your break."

"What about the paparazzi?" I asked him. "They might photograph us together and then—"

He shut me up with his lips. Grinning like a mischievous little boy, he tucked a piece of hair behind my ear and said, "I'm done caring about them and the media. This is my life and they can fuck off." He took a shaky breath. "I know I told you a while ago that I couldn't promise you forever, but I was wrong to say that. I can't live my life without you," he whispered, his fingers gliding down my neck and lower where I was sure he felt how fast my heart was beating. "Those seven years without you were some of the worst of my life, and that's saying a lot considering all the shit I went through with my real parent's but it's the truth."

"Mathias—"

"Shh," he whispered, resting his forehead against mine. "Please say you'll go."

I contemplated for only a few seconds before saying, "Yes."

He kissed me again, this time his lips lingering longer against mine. He grasped my hand and pulled back onto the road.

I closed my eyes, knowing that right here beside him was where I had always belonged—and I only hoped that nothing would take us away from each other again.

# CHAPTER TWENTY-TWO

I let out a small squeak when the shower door opened. I had my towel thrown over the top of the glass and it was fogged up, so I hadn't noticed Mathias coming into the bathroom.

"I fucking hate applesauce now," he muttered.

"I have to agree." I leaned under the spray of water, trying to get the gunk out of my hair.

"Here," he batted my hands away, "let me do it."

I stood still, Goosebumps dimpling my skin as he worked his fingers gently through my hair. I closed my eyes, leaning my head back further.

I was glad to be away from the baby shower—and even happier at the thought of escaping to L.A. in a week with Mathias. I knew we had plenty of privacy here, but it would be nice to get away for a bit—to a place where the memories weren't quite as stifling.

"That feels good," I murmured as his fingers rubbed against my head.

He chuckled warmly and my eyes opened at the sound. He reached over and grabbed the bottle of shampoo, lathering it in his hands and then rubbing it into my hair.

A part of me still couldn't believe that I was here with him. I'd spent so many years hating him for abandoning me and the lies he'd told me, but despite all that I knew there was no place I'd rather be.

He rinsed the soap from my hair, kissing my shoulder before moving onto the conditioner.

It was nice to let him take care of me for a change. We were both always so stubborn, never wanting to let the other have more control that moments like this were rare for us.

"It's all gone now."

His voice startled me and I opened my eyes to find him grabbing the shower gel.

"But I think you're still dirty."

Oh, God.

He had a dangerous glint in his eye—one that had my throat constricting but my pulse racing at the same time.

"Is that so?" I asked, fighting a smile.

He nodded, stalking towards me until my back was pressed against the shower wall and the water cascaded down on top of us.

He lowered his head, the wet strands of his dark hair brushing against my forehead. His eyes flashed and his tongue flicked out to catch a drop of water on his lips.

"Are you afraid, Remy?"

My heart thundered in my chest, threatening to beat right out of the protection of my ribcage.

"Of you?" I asked, my voice barely above a whisper as my body arched towards him in anticipation. "Never."

He grinned at that, and then slammed his lips against mine in a bruising kiss. His hands braced against the shower wall beside my head, trapping me against him. When his chest brushed against my sensitized skin I cried out softly.

Heat soared through my body at his touch.

He bit my bottom lip and I whimpered as his lips moved down to my breasts.

All of my thoughts left me as his lips danced over my skin. The only thing that existed was him, the touch of his fingers, and the smooth feel of his lips.

I leaned my head back, letting the water pour down on my face as his hands ventured lower.

A small breathy gasp escaped me and his chest rumbled with a chuckle.

One finger slipped inside me and I moaned. "Mathias, please," I begged, even though I didn't know what I was begging for.

His body pressed into me—so close that I wasn't sure where I ended and he began. "I love hearing my name roll off of your lips," he murmured, taking my bottom lip between his fingers and letting it go.

"Is that so?" I asked, fighting to stay upright from the dizzying array of sensations rolling through my body.

He nodded, nuzzling my neck as his finger moved slowly in and out of me. The stubble on his cheeks scratched my skin, adding to the sensations.

It was all too easy for me to get lost in him and with a sudden clarity I realized what he was up to.

With a great deal of effort I pushed him away. Immediately I was overcome with a sense of loss.

"What?" He looked at me, confused.

"I know what you're trying to do." I glared daggers at him, trying not to let him see how much my body ached for his touch.

He ducked his head, trying to hide his smile. "You figured that out, huh?"

"I did," I nodded, moving around him so that I could reach the door of the shower. I needed to get away from him before I gave in and told him to take me here and now. I looked at him over my shoulder and forced a smirk. "I'm getting my seventeen minutes."

He narrowed his eyes.

"Have fun getting the gunk out of your hair and thanks for washing me," I sing-songed, winking at him before stepping out of the shower and grabbing the towel to wrap around my body.

I heard him let out a low growl and then mutter, "This isn't over yet."

"You're right," I agreed, poking my head back inside the shower. "It's just getting started."

With that, I turned and left him to finish showering.

I brushed my teeth and then my tangled hair before padding into his spacious bedroom.

I heard the shower cut off and my heart began to race ten times faster.

It didn't matter how many times I was with Mathias—it always got better and I always wanted more.

I lay down on his bed, the fluffy white towel still wrapped around my body.

He appeared in the doorway of the bathroom a moment later. He'd forgone a towel and water still clung to his body.

"That wasn't nice, Remy," he glowered.

"Being nice is overrated."

He stalked towards me, his hands landed on my knees before skating up my thighs and beneath the towel. With one flick of his hand the towel fell from my body.

"Are you ready to finish what you started?" I asked, tracing my fingers over his full lips before trailing them down his neck and over his pecks before venturing even lower to his abs.

"Oh, I'm more than happy to finish it," he growled, claiming my hands and pinning them above my head.

"Nuh-huh, I don't think so." I broke his hold and pushed him down on top of the bed, straddling his hips. "A deal is a deal."

His lips twisted into a frown.

"You know," I smiled, rolling my hips against his and eliciting a groan from his throat, "I thought guys liked it when the girl was on top."

"I don't care what other guys might like. *I* like to be in control." His eyes darkened to a stormy gray.

I lowered until my chest was pressed against his and my lips grazed his ear. "Well, right now *I'm* in control."

He grasped my hips, his hold almost bruising.

Air hissed between his teeth and he growled, "And it'll be the last time."

My hair brushed against his chest as I sat up. "We'll see about that."

He started to say something else, but I cut off his response by kissing him. My tongue brushed against his and his fingers tangled in my hair, holding me to him.

I broke away from his lips and kissed down his neck and over his pecks, before circling my tongue around his nipple and blowing softly.

He hissed, his hips bucking. "Fuck, Remy," he groaned.

I smiled against his skin, and moved even lower as I kissed his abs.

His erection pressed against me and I rolled off of him so I could take his cock in my hand.

I circled my thumb around the tip and he closed his eyes as a low groan rumbled in his throat.

I smiled in satisfaction before lowering and wrapping my mouth around him.

"Fuuuuuck." He pulled my hair back and when my eyes rolled in his direction he muttered, "Wanna watch."

I kept my eyes on his as I moved my mouth up and down. His stare was heated, sending tingles of anticipation all throughout my body.

"Stop." He pleaded after a few minutes. "Need to be inside you." He panted, gasping for breath.

I sat back, smirking at him. "So bossy."

"Damn right. You didn't think I'd give up *all* control, did you?" He looked at me like I was crazy. He opened the drawer beside the bed and grabbed a condom.

"Let me." I took the packet from his hand and tore it open, rolling the condom on.

"Fuck. You're really trying to kill me." His eyes were hooded with lust.

"Aw, Mathias, if I wanted to kill you that's what the knives in the kitchen are for."

He growled and grabbed my thigh, pulling me on top of him. "Now is not the time to tease me." His voice was low with warning.

I wanted to tell him that anytime was always the time to tease him, but in that moment he took matters into his own hands and slammed into me.

"Oh God." I wrapped my arms around his shoulders.

He chuckled, giving me a self-satisfied smirk. Jerk.

"You aren't allowed to do that," I hissed.

"Too late."

"I don't think so." I pushed my palms against his chest so that he lay on his back. I rolled my hips against his, going slow and enjoying the way his fingers tightened against my thighs as he fought his need for control. I leaned down, whispering in his ear, "Don't think, just feel."

He closed his eyes and when they opened they were surprisingly calmer.

I leaned down and kissed him, long and slow.

He cupped my breasts, rubbing his thumbs against my nipples.

"Mmm," I hummed against his lips. His teeth lightly nipped my bottom lip before pulling it between his teeth.

I sat up, my palms flat on his chest as I worked my hips.

"At least the view is nice," he panted, his eyes glued to my breasts.

I wanted to laugh, but all I could do was focus on the different sensations rolling through me. I slowed down, wanting to enjoy every single second of this.

"Rem," he growled, fighting his desire to slam into me.

"No," I hissed, trailing a finger down his chest. He shivered beneath me. "So close," I breathed, rubbing my breasts before one of my hands skated down my stomach and below. His eyes followed the trail of my hand to where it disappeared between us.

His teeth clamped together and he mumbled a curse.

My pants grew louder until I was crying out in ecstasy. I collapsed against his solid chest and he wrapped his arms around me, holding me against him as our hearts raced in sync. He was still, but his body was taut as he fought his natural reaction. I guess he finally decided he didn't care what I wanted, because suddenly I was flat on my back as he braced his hands beside my head.

"Time's up." His voice was a husky growl as he began to move.

It felt so good that I couldn't find my voice to complain about him taking away my time on top.

He pushed into me with hard, deep thrusts that made me cry out with pleasure.

"You're mine, Rem," he hissed, biting the sensitive skin where my neck met my shoulder. "Don't ever forget that."

With every thrust he growled, "Mine. Mine. Mine."

And when he collapsed on top of me after finding his own release, I whispered in his ear, "Yours."

We were still lying in the bed curled around each other when my phone rang.

"Ugh," I groaned, not moving to grab it.

"Shouldn't you get that?" He asked, drawing lazy circles on my arm.

"No," I groaned, closing my eyes and snuggling closer to him. It was nowhere near time to go to sleep, but I didn't want to move from this bed until tomorrow morning.

It stopped ringing, only to start up again a few seconds later.

"I think you need to get that." He released his hold on me and climbed out of bed, heading over to his closet. "It might be your grandma."

Shit. He was right. I was really sucking at this whole responsible adult thing.

I rolled out of bed and grabbed my phone out of my purse that lay haphazardly on the floor.

"Hello?" I answered, padding across the room to the dresser. I opened the top drawer, grabbing the first clothes I could find. Yes, I was keeping clothes at Mathias' place. It was weird, but with as much time as I'd been spending here it had become necessary.

"Charlene can't take me to bingo."

"Grandma?" I asked, putting the phone on speaker so I could get dressed.

"Yes, who else would it be?" She snapped.

Mathias snickered from the bathroom.

"Anyway," she continued, clucking her tongue at my stupidity, "I need you to drive me."

"Alright I'll be there in a few minutes." I shimmied into a pair of jeans.

"Good. Hurry. Bingo is important and I can't be late."

I sighed. "On my way."

I ended the call and finished getting dressed. Mathias emerged from the bathroom dressed in a pair of jeans, a black sweatshirt, with a baseball cap perched backwards on his head. It was strange to see him dressed so casually, but I kind of liked it. Although, those suspenders had certainly grown on me—but I'd never tell him that. He'd be too pleased with that information.

"So, we're going to bingo?" He asked, grabbing his wallet.

My eyes widened. "I was just going to take her and wait in the car."

He shook his head. "Where's the fun in that? Let's go too. Your grandma is hilarious."

"You like my grandma?" I tried to hide my smile.

"Of course. She's pretty cool for a grandma. I mean, she did read me the riot act the other day about how a gentleman should treat a lady."

"Oh God." I shook my head.

He fought a smile as he spoke. "To which I replied that I wasn't a gentleman and she smiled at me and said, 'Good.' I'm telling you that woman must've been something else in her day," he chuckled. "Now I know where you get it from."

I covered my face with my hands, my shoulders shaking with silent laughter.

It was kind of hysterical how my grandma used to hate Mathias. Granted, she never met him when we were teenagers so her opinion had only been based on the bashing from my father, no doubt. And Mathias could come across as an arrogant jerk, but when he showed his true colors he was impossible to resist.

"I'll walk Shiloh while you finish getting ready." He leaned down and kissed my cheek. My skin warmed with the simple touch.

I hurried into the bathroom and tried to do something with my hair. It was a gigantic mess since it had been wet and then we ended up rolling around in the sheets. After a few minutes I deemed it a lost cause and pulled it back into a messy bun. I applied a minimal amount of makeup, topping it off with my red lipstick.

I slipped my feet into a pair of black-wedged boots as Mathias strode back into the bedroom. "Ready?" He asked.

"Yeah," I said, just as my phone rang again. I grabbed it out of my pocket and looked at the screen. "Crazy old lady," I muttered as I answered. "Yeah, grandma?"

"Where are you? It's been ten minutes and I need to be there in—"

I stood from the bed, following Mathias through the penthouse and into the elevator. I tried not to pay attention to how the sweatshirt pulled taut across his wide shoulders and how his jeans hugged his ass. Oh, fuck. I wanted to beg him to take me back to his room—or better yet, beg him to fuck me against the wall. Oh, yeah. That had possibilities.

Realizing that my grandma was still on the phone, I said, "We're getting in the car right now."

"Lies!" She cried.

I automatically looked around like the batty lady would be standing behind me, glaring, and pointing an accusing finger. But of course she wasn't actually there.

"I would never lie to you, grandma," I assured her, even as I was lying to her. Granddaughter of the year right here.

She snorted and said, "Just get your ass here."

And then the line clicked off. I glared down at my phone and then looked at Mathias. "She hung up on me. How rude."

We stepped into the elevator and Mathias pushed the button to take us to the garage.

"She's sassy. I like it."

"Ew," I frowned, glaring at him, "it's like you have a crush on my grandma or something."

Mathias threw this head back and laughed. Like a real, genuine, body shaking laugh. I couldn't help the smile that lifted my lips at seeing him let loose. He was normally wound so tight that even when he laughed you could tell he was holding back.

"She is pretty cute." He finally replied with a shrug.

I shook my head, crossing my arms over my chest. "This conversation got weird really fast."

"You're the one that started it." He grinned.

I couldn't argue with that.

The elevator doors opened and Mathias pushed a button on his key, the brake lights on his SUV lighting up.

"How many cars do you have?"

He glanced down at me as he strode past. "Just the Range Rover, Corvette, and my motorcycle." He pointed to a sleek sporty looking bike.

"Jesus." I whistled in appreciation. "That's nice."

He smiled, his eyes lighting up like a little boy. "I have one just like it in L.A. We can take it out while we're there."

Me, Mathias, and a motorcycle… oh yeah, that sounded like a good time.

"We have to," I told him, still staring at the shiny red motorcycle. It had been forever since I'd driven one, and if it hadn't been December with snow on the ground I might have begged him to let me drive it.

"Rem," he warned, "we've got to go."

"Oh, right. Grandma," I muttered, hurrying over to the SUV and away from the motorcycle.

I slipped into the sleek SUV and he started the engine. It was so quiet you could barely tell it was running.

He pulled out of the parking garage and we were immediately greeted with a red light.

And then another.

And then my phone started ringing again.

"I swear to God we're on our way," I said into the phone.

My grandma huffed over the line. "I'm about to walk there. I'm sure I'd beat you."

"Don't you dare," I warned, terrified that she might actually do it.

"I'll be waiting outside," she said.

"It's too cold," I protested.

"Then you better hurry."

She hung up on me… again.

"I'm pretty sure she's determined to worry me to death." I pinched the bridge of my nose and glanced over to see a smile curling his lips.

"She's probably just lonely since I've been monopolizing your time."

"Oh, please," I laughed, "she doesn't want me there. The other day I tried to talk to her for a while and she told she didn't have time to listen to me ramble because Pretty Little Liars was coming on."

He shook his head, turning into the neighborhood.

When we reached the house I saw the crazy old lady waiting at the end of the driveway.

"She's going to get hypothermia," I muttered to myself, "and die, and it'll be all my fault and I'll never forgive myself."

Mathias put the car in park and undid his seatbelt, stepping out of the car before I could even blink.

My grandma smiled at him as he helped her into the car.

She sat down in the back and Mathias closed the door.

"At least one of you has some decency," she huffed, but when I glanced back at her she was smiling.

"Ha, ha," I rolled my eyes. "You didn't give me much of a heads up."

"Well, neither did Charlene—you know she normally picks me up," she rambled, clutching her purse in her slender age-spotted hands, "and she just didn't show. It was incredibly rude. Bingo night is my second favorite night of the week."

"What's the first?" I asked in wonder.

She gasped, like there was something seriously wrong with me for not knowing. "Vampire Diaries night, of course. Damon is delicious."

I snorted, turning it into a cough as Mathias got back in the car. My outburst didn't go unnoticed by him though.

"What did I miss?" He asked, clicking his seatbelt in place.

"Grandma has a crush on a vampire," I laughed, covering my mouth with my hand to stifle the sound. Oh God, this woman, she was seriously a hoot.

"What the fuck?" He looked at me and then back at my grandma. She must've glared at him because he paled and retracted his previous statement. "Sorry, I meant what the hell—HECK, what the *heck*."

Mathias trying not to curse was quite possibly the funniest thing I'd ever seen. His forehead was wrinkled with deep concentration and his fingers tapped restlessly against the steering wheel—although that nervous tick probably had more to do with him craving a cigarette.

After a minute of complete silence Mathias finally spoke. "Ladies, you do know I have absolutely no fuc—freaking—idea where I'm going, right?"

"Good catch," I laughed, reaching over and giving his knee a light squeeze. "You know where the old fire hall is?" I asked.

He nodded.

"That's where we're going."

"Easy enough," he muttered.

Five minutes later we pulled into the parking lot and my grandma was ready to jump out of the SUV.

"Whoa, slow down. Let me help you," I warned her.

"Oh please, you've helped me enough by making me late. I doubt I'll be able to get a seat near the front now."

I opened her door and held my hand out to help her. She reluctantly took it.

Mathias joined us and walked on the other side of her.

"Honestly, you two act like I'm going to fall over dead any second. I can certainly walk in here on my own."

"Grandma, there's snow on the ground. It's slippery, therefore we're helping you."

She muttered something about me being a pain in her ass, to which Mathias shot me look as if to say *why is it okay for her to cuss and not me?* Sorry bud, Grandma made the rules and the rest of us had to follow them—unfortunately she was usually exempt from her own rules.

We headed into the room that was blocked off for bingo and it was surprisingly full.

My grandma glared at me and mumbled, "You see, all the good seats are gone. Now I'm stuck sitting in the back."

"Why is this my fault?" I muttered, following her to a table.

"What are you doing?" She glanced at us, where we hovered behind her.

"Staying for bingo," I replied, pulling out a chair and urging her to sit—but not before removing her heavy winter coat.

"I don't need a babysitter," she pouted like a surly teenager. "Oh, hi Howard." She waved at the lone man sitting at the table.

"I'll get our boards," Mathias said, heading over to the side of the room.

"He does know he has to pay for them right?" Grandma asked, fixing her hair, which had been ruffled by the wind. "That's how they get their money for the prizes, you know."

"He knows," I assured her, taking my seat beside her.

Mathias returned a moment later with three boards. They hadn't started calling out numbers yet, so at least she couldn't bitch about missing that part.

"Y'all don't need to stay," she huffed. "I highly doubt you want to play bingo with a bunch of old farts."

Mathias snickered, covering his face with his hands.

"Stop your whining," I smiled at her, "we're here to spend time with you."

"Maybe I don't want to spend time with you," she huffed, squaring her shoulders and glaring daggers at us.

"So sassy." Mathias chuckled under his breath.

"We already paid for our boards," I told her, "so we're staying."

She sighed, exasperated. "You could always give them to me."

"Nuh-uh, not happening." I shook my head.

Before she could argue the matter further a man stepped up on a small podium, welcoming everybody, and got right down to business of calling out numbers.

I couldn't stop my smile when I glanced over at Mathias and saw his lips pursed in concentration as he stared at his board, the little chips resting in his open palm.

Apparently bingo was serious business.

I tried my best to pay attention, but my mind began to wander.

I was truly excited at the idea of escaping to L.A. with Mathias. I knew the whole band was going, and he'd have work things to do, but it would still be nice to get away for a while.

Glancing towards my grandma, I frowned. I felt bad for leaving her on her own for a few days or a week—but the fact of the matter was, she'd made it pretty clear that she didn't need me around. It was my dad that had decided she needed supervision. While I was gone I'd definitely call her as often as I could—which would probably be only once a day, because on days where I stayed with Mathias she got mad if I called her more than that. She really was a stubborn lady, but I loved her for it. I hoped I could be just as badass as her when I reached that age.

Another letter and number was called and I scanned my page, groaning when there was no match. My grandma already had a few of the tokens on her board and Mathias had more than her.

Mine was blank.

That's what I got for not paying attention.

I forced myself to focus on the game and only had two chips down on the board when Mathias jerked beside me, shooting up into a standing position. "Bingo! What did I win?!"

I laughed at his adorable exuberance. I loved that these moments were becoming more commonplace with him. It was like he was finally letting his guard down.

The man on the stage came over to verify the board and then informed Mathias that he'd won fifty dollars.

"I don't need your money," Mathias scoffed—not rudely, "I should be giving you money."

"Uh…" The man looked at Mathias, studying his face. His eyes suddenly lit with recognition. "You're in that band, uh…" He snapped his fingers together. "Willow Creek! That's the one, right?"

"Yeah," he nodded. "I'm Mathias." He held out his hand.

"Wow, I can't believe you're here! Playing bingo of all things. Wow. Just wow." The man stammered, shaking his head as if he was in shock.

Mathias stood awkwardly with his hands shoved into the pockets of his pants. It seemed that when Mathias attended an event he put on his game face and acted a part—at least that was what I'd deduced from seeing photos in magazines—but in situations like this, where there were no cameras or roles to play, he became almost shy under the scrutiny.

Finally the man seemed to recover and said, "Since you don't want the money we can give you a shirt."

"Yeah, that's fine," Mathias shrugged.

Appearing almost sheepish the man asked, "Would you mind signing some?"

"Uh…" Mathias glanced at me and then around the room where all eyes were on him. "Sure. I can do that."

"Excellent," the man said. "I'll be right back."

Mathias sat back down beside me, his shoulders hunching as he glanced down at the table—like he thought if he didn't look at anyone then they couldn't look at him.

"Hey, it's okay." I reached over and squeezed his knee, trying to give him a reassuring smile.

He ignored me.

"You should sing us a song." I looked up, finding that the words belonged to the man sitting with us whom my grandma had called Howard.

"Yeah," someone else piped in, "we need some more fun around here. The most exciting thing to happen here was when Marvin peed his pants and that was more messy than exciting."

"Hey!" Yelled someone else—my guess being the man named Marvin.

Mathias finally looked at me. He didn't appear mad by the sudden recognition, but apologetic—like he was worried the attention bothered *me*.

"Yeah, I can do that," he said, standing. He removed the baseball cap he wore and set it on the table before shoving his hands in the pockets of his jeans and heading up to the podium area. Ignoring the microphone, he stood in the center of the small stage and asked, "What would you guys like to hear?"

Everyone shuffled their seats to see him better, a few people shouting out songs.

"That's a good one," Mathias smiled—a real smile—pointing to an older lady near the front. She blushed at the attention and ducked her head, her white hair fluttering around her face. It was pretty adorable.

"What's happening?"

At the sound of the voice I turned to find the man that had went in search of the shirts standing beside me.

"They wanted him to sing," I shrugged, smiling straight ahead at the man I loved even though he wasn't looking at me, "so he's going to sing."

"Oh," the man nodded, smiling slowly, "excellent. I'll leave these here then." He dropped a few black t-shirts with the fire hall logo on them onto the table.

"Do you have a stool?" Mathias asked suddenly.

The man beside me took off like a rocket, grabbing a stool from a closet and giving it to Mathias.

Mathias grabbed the microphone and took a seat on the stool.

He began to sing, and like every time I heard him sing a sweet feeling of calm washed over me. His voice was soft and husky with a raspy edge to it. He closed his eyes, feeling the song.

The people slowly began to clap along, but I was too enamored with watching Mathias to join in.

I'd seen clips of him performing on stage—and he always commanded the large space—but here, he was toned down and just letting himself love the music and the moment.

As the song came to a close he lifted his head, his eyes meeting mine. An invisible cord seemed to tie us together, and nothing—not time, or hate, or *anything*—could break it.

# CHAPTER TWENTY-THREE

"You look really hot doing that," I commented, watching Mathias use the pull-up bar in the gym. He was shirtless and sweat glistened on his muscles while the loose shorts he wore hung low on his hips. I would not deny the fact that there were about a hundred naughty things running through my mind right now. Oh, the things I wanted to do to him.

"Stop. Looking. At. Me. Like. That." He huffed out between breaths.

"Like what?" I asked, watching the way the muscles in his arms flexed.

"Like. You. Want. To. Lick. Me."

"Oh," I nodded, wetting my suddenly parched lips, "I want to do much more than lick you. Trust me."

"Fuck," he groaned, dropping down. "I'm not coming to the gym with you anymore." He sucked in a lungful of air—and I was positive his sudden lack of oxygen had more to do with me than the pull-ups. "You're far too much of a distraction."

I grinned. "So are you."

He shook his head, grabbing a pair of boxing gloves. He nodded his head at a pair of pink ones. "For you."

I wrinkled my nose with distaste. "I might be a girl, but that doesn't mean I want everything under the sun in pink. Give me yours."

"Hell no," he said, the black gloves already fixed onto his hands.

I glared at the offending pair of pink boxing gloves. They were just so glaringly bright and attention grabbing. Why couldn't they be red? Red, I liked.

"Fine," I shrugged, taking a step back, "I'll just watch."

He turned around to glare at me. "I can't concentrate when you watch me."

"Too bad." I hopped up on a stack of mats, swinging my legs back and forth.

He turned back around, his shoulders visibly tense as he stepped up to the punching bag.

He slowly glanced over his shoulder and his eyes connected with mine. I gave him a winning smile. "Stop watching me," he growled lowly, a challenge in his eyes.

"Make me."

He stalked over towards me, his hands slamming down against the mats, one on either side of my legs. He leaned in until the tip of his nose touched mine and his full lips brushed my lips when he spoke. "Keep this up, Rem, and I will flip you over right here, right now, and fuck you so hard that everyone in this building will think my name is a prayer."

I licked my lips, nodding in appreciation. "I like the sound of that."

He ducked his head and his soft hair tickled my collarbone. His whole body visibly shuddered and when his gaze rose to mine his eyes were dark with lust. My insides stirred with delight at that look—the dangerous, promising glint shimmering in those stormy gray eyes.

His lips crashed against mine. I whimpered when his teeth sunk down on my bottom lip, pulling it into his mouth and letting it go with an audible pop.

I wound my legs around his waist and my arms around his neck, holding him close to me. If he wanted to get away he was going to have to physically pry me from his body.

A small sound escaped me before he swallowed it with another slam of his lips. His fingers wound into my hair at the base of my skull, tugging at the strands causing a gasp to emit from my throat.

God, he was fucking dangerous. I wondered if he had any idea the amount of power he yielded over me.

He pulled away roughly, taking two hefty steps back. Both of our chests rose and fell heavily with each labored breath. He looked absolutely delicious—yes, *delicious*—standing there with his lips roughened from our kisses and his hair tousled from my fingers.

With a cocky smile, he said, "I hope that'll hold you over for now."

I was tempted to launch my body at him and tackle him to the ground for that comment. I didn't though, because Drew, the owner of the gym, chose that moment to walk into the room.

"Behave." He smiled at me as he passed. To Mathias he said, "Are you ready for your lesson?"

Mathias nodded, putting the boxing gloves back on. I hadn't even realized he'd thrown them on the ground before attacking me with his lips.

Oh, his lips… I was positive that Mathias had the best lips on any man ever, and he definitely knew how to use them. And his tongue. And his—

"Remy!"

His sudden snarl jolted me from my thoughts as fast as being doused with ice-cold water.

"What?" I asked innocently.

"You know what." He stood in front of me with Drew hovering near the center of the room.

"I don't know."

"You were definitely undressing me with your eyes, and it's beyond distracting." His voice lowered and he growled lowly, "Be good and I promise to reward you later."

"Now you make me sound like a dog getting tossed a bone." I narrowed my eyes.

He chuckled, reaching out to skim the backs of his fingers across my cheeks. "Rem, you're going to get much more than a bone."

"Fine," I sighed, crossing my legs—trying to alleviate the pressure between them. "I'll sit here and be good."

He looked at me doubtfully, but backed away before jogging over to where Drew stood.

This was going to be fun to watch.

Drew gave Mathias some instructions and then they started throwing punches.

If I was a normal girlfriend I'd cheer for Mathias, but I definitely was as far as it got from normal. So, naturally, I cheered for Drew, which only served to piss off Mathias. He kept snarling—at Drew, or me, I wasn't sure, but I really enjoyed watching him get rowed.

Thirty minutes later the guys finished and I hopped off of the mats.

"Good job," I smiled at Mathias, kissing his cheek.

"Oh, so now you're nice to me." He rolled his eyes, trying not to smile.

I shrugged, following him out of the private room. "Normally I'd root for the underdog, but I wanted to piss you off so…" I left my sentence unsaid.

He stopped walking and grabbed my arm so that I was forced to stop too. "Whoa," he shook his head, "I'm no underdog."

I shrugged out of his hold. "I think Drew has a lot more experience than you, therefore you are the underdog." A playful smile quirked my lips and I crossed my arms over my chest.

His eyes narrowed and I let out a small squeal of surprise when he grabbed me and I suddenly found my back pushed up against the wall. He pressed his whole body against mine so that there was no room for me to wiggle away. My palms pressed flat against his sweat-dampened chest, waiting for what came next.

He lowered his head, brushing his lips against my ear and then grazing them along my chin. He repeated the same movements, going back up. His lips paused at my ear and he growled, "Baby, I'm no underdog." His hips ground into mine and I gasped.

Apparently, going to the gym was excellent foreplay. I didn't understand why people avoided it like it was the second coming of the plague.

"Mmm," I hummed as my eyes closed. I completely forgot about what he was saying.

He chuckled lowly and cold air blasted my suddenly heated skin when he stepped away.

Fuck.

He was so talented at starting something and then never finishing it.

Mathias Wade was the king of the tease.

"I'm going to shower," he called over his shoulder, heading over to the men's locker room.

I frowned at his retreating figure and tried to pretend that the deep-seated ache currently residing in my body was going to go away soon—ha, yeah right.

With a shake of my head I turned to the women's locker rooms. I needed to get to the bar for my shift, and then I'd be spending the evening packing before we left for L.A. in the morning.

I couldn't remember the last time I'd ever been this excited for anything. It was nice to finally have something to look forward to.

"Just make yourself comfortable," I said sarcastically as Mathias sprawled out over my bed. He looked huge on the small bed. My queen-sized bed in no way compared to the massive one he owned.

"Is that sarcasm," he fake-gasped, wiggling around on my bed and adjusting the pillows. Percy hissed at him and Mathias—being such a nice guy—gave my cat the finger. I didn't bother to point out to him that the gesture was probably lost on Percy. "Demon cat," he muttered, glaring at my cat.

"Hey," I scolded, opening my closet door, "I don't say mean things about Shiloh, so don't say mean things about my cat."

"Shiloh is an angel," he rolled his eyes, crossing his arms behind his head, "therefore there is nothing mean you can say. Your cat is evil."

I rolled my eyes. "He's protective."

"Of you? Hardly," Mathias snorted. "He's more protective of this fucking pillow." He patted the one his head currently rested on.

"That's because you stole it from him," I reasoned, dragging my suitcase out of the closet. I stood with my hands on my hips, appraising my clothes and trying to decide what I wanted to take.

"We have plenty of room on the jet, take whatever you want," Mathias said, like he could read my thoughts.

I glanced at him over my shoulders. "You have your own jet?" I gaped.

He shrugged, reaching over to grab the picture frame I kept beside my bed. It was a photo of my family at Christmas years ago. We were all wearing these hideous sweaters and my brother and I were bickering in the photo, but it was one of my favorites. With his eyes perusing the photo he finally said, "It's the record company's but we have exclusive use."

"That's pretty cool," I said in awe. I knew Mathias and his band were famous, there was no denying that when the proof was everywhere, but having known him growing up I couldn't think of him any other way than as himself. I didn't see a famous rock star. I just saw the boy I'd always loved. Something told me though, that this trip to L.A., was about to show me exactly what Mathias' fame status meant for him and now for us.

"Yeah it's nice," he shrugged, setting the picture frame back on the end table. "It means I can bring Shiloh."

I perked up at that. "Does that mean I get to bring Percy?"

He glared at my cat, who sat on the end of the bed glaring right back. "The demon cat is staying."

"Nuh-uh," I shook my head, placing my hands on my hips, "if Shiloh is coming than Perce is too."

He pinched the bridge of his nose and muttered, "Fine, but keep that demon far, far away from me."

"Did you hear that, Perce? You're going to L.A.!"

Percy flicked his tail and turned his glowing orange eyes in my direction. He didn't seem to care that he was getting to go across the country. Cats could be so ungrateful.

I packed my stuff while Mathias meandered around my small room. "This room doesn't really seem much like you," he commented, taking in the muted palate.

I was sure he was comparing it to my room I'd had as a teenager. The walls had been green with furniture in every color imaginable—because just to spite my mom I'd gone to yard sales every day all summer one year, buying the crappiest furniture I could find and then painting it a bright hue. I'd spent years balking my parents, especially my mom, but when I went through everything I did with Hope she was the one person that was there to pick me back up. I'd never thanked her though, and I guess that made me a crappy person, and an even crappier daughter.

"It's not really my style," I agreed, shrugging my shoulders as I zipped up my suitcase. "My grandma said I could redecorate and I had planned to, but then we started spending so much time together and I've been at your place most nights so it just felt sort of pointless."

He nodded, sitting down on the end of my bed. "Are you ready to go?" He asked.

"Our flight doesn't leave until morning." I glanced up at him, confusion wrinkling my brow.

"Yeah," he chuckled, "aren't you staying at my place, though? The car is picking us up at five in the morning."

"I thought I should stay with my grandma tonight." I frowned, standing up and brushing lint off my jeans.

"You're at my place most nights. What makes tonight different?"

"I feel bad," I admitted with a small shrug. "I'm supposed to be here looking out for her and now I'm off gallivanting around with you."

His lips twitched. "Did you just use the word gallivanting in a sentence?"

"I did."

He shook his head and reached out to pet Percy, but then realizing what he'd been about to do he quickly retracted his hand. Percy hissed at him and jumped off the bed while I tried not to laugh.

"I've got someone checking on her." He assured me. "She'll be fine. She knows how to call you and I even gave her my phone number."

"You gave my grandma your number?" I laughed. "You have met my grandma, right? She'll probably give it out to all her bingo friends."

"Nah," he waved a hand in dismissal, "she wouldn't do that. She says I'm too hot to share."

I snorted, covering my face with my hands. "The fact that my grandma has a crush on you is hysterical. She used to hate you, you know," I admitted, lowering my hands.

He shrugged his wide shoulders, completely unaffected. "Most people hate me before they love me."

I frowned at that, but his words were true. It was all too easy to hate Mathias. He came across as an asshole smart-mouth most of the time, but if you stuck around long enough and got to know him it was impossible not to love him.

I was glad I'd stuck around.

He stood, stretching his arms above his head. His white t-shirt rode up, exposing those delicious indents that disappeared beneath his jeans.

"You're staring, Remy." I could hear the smile in his words.

I raised my eyes to his. "You're my boyfriend, therefore I'm allowed to stare."

He suppressed a smile. "Good point." He reached for my suitcase and picked it up with ease—despite the fact that I was pretty sure it weighed a hundred pounds since I'd packed every single pair of shoes I owned. And clothes. Yeah, there were clothes in there somewhere. "Don't forget your demon cat."

I rolled my eyes. Percy was not a demon. I glanced at the cat and his glare was withering. Okay, so maybe he could be kind of demonic.

"Come on, Perce," I picked him up, tucking him under my arm.

When I reached the bottom of the stairs Mathias was already opening the front door to put my suitcase in the car.

"I'll be right there," I told him. "I have to say goodbye first."

I headed back to my grandma's room and found her absorbed in another show—this one they seemed to be dressed in period costumes.

"I'm heading out," I sat down on the end of the bed, "our flight leaves in the morning so I'm staying over there."

"Shh, it's just getting to the good part! I think Mary and Francis are about to kiss for the first time!"

"Huh?" I glanced from her to the television.

"Reign," she said, throwing up a hand to halt anything I might say, "this is my new addiction. God I love Netflix. If Netflix were a man I would so do him. Netflix brings me nothing but pleasure."

"Oh God, grandma!" I shrieked. "Keep your sexual comments to yourself!"

"I'm old, not dead. My lady bits still function you know."

If I hadn't been holding Percy I would've slapped my hands over my ears.

"*You* need your own show." I shook my head. "They can call it, *Grandma's Gone Wild.*"

She rolled her eyes at me and finally paused the TV once the blond guy swooped in for a kiss. "Alright, give me a hug and get out of here. You're irritating me."

She held her thin arms out for a hug and I dove into her embrace. "I love you, you know that, right?"

She nodded against my shoulder. "Of course you do," she patted my back, "I'm impossible not to love."

I laughed, kissing the top of her head before pulling away. "You've got that right."

"Have fun, sweetie," she sobered. "I'll be fine, honestly."

"I know," I smiled.

I hated to leave her—not just because I was responsible for her, but because I loved her. However, she was the toughest person I knew and if she'd made it all these years by herself I knew one week wouldn't kill her.

"I'll see you soon." I stood up, switching Percy to my other arm. "Call if you need anything."

She waved her hand in dismissal and her show resumed once more.

I knew then that she was done talking.

Outside Mathias was waiting in his car. As he drove away from my grandma's home I couldn't help feeling like the next time I saw this place everything would be different. I only hoped things would be different in a good way, but something deep in my gut suggested otherwise.

# CHAPTER TWENTY-FOUR

Warm lips pressed against the soft skin of my neck. I began to wiggle around and soon a laugh vibrated against me.

"Time to get up, Rem." Fingers tickled down my bareback.

"Don't want to," I mumbled, wrapping my arms tighter around the pillow.

"The car's waiting for us." Those same lips pressed against my ear. "We have to go."

I made some noise that was completely unintelligible.

"You never were a morning person," the voice mumbled.

Cold water prickled my skin and I groaned in protest.

"That's only a taste of what you'll get if you don't wake up."

I sat straight up. "I'm up. I'm up." I repeated, as if he didn't hear me the first time.

Mathias lounged in bed beside me, already dressed in a pair of tan colored pants, a white button down shirt, and a navy cardigan. He even wore his Clark Kent glasses. Normally I'd poke fun at him, just because I could, but I was too tired and he did look pretty hot so I couldn't complain.

"Do I at least have time to shower?" I pouted.

"No," he smacked my butt and stood. "We need to go. Like now."

After some more grumbling I managed to drag my sleepy self out of bed. I had planned to wear a sweatshirt and jeans, but then I began to panic, realizing we might be photographed together.

I decided to keep the jeans but chose a black peplum top with lace sleeves and my knee length red coat.

I brushed my straight hair and applied a minimum amount of makeup—and of course my red lipstick.

No woman could conquer the world until she'd put on her red lipstick.

"Remy!" Mathias yelled through the penthouse.

"I'm ready!" I yelled back.

My stuff was already waiting by the elevator since we left it there last night, so I had nothing else to grab. Except Percy—who had taken up residence on Mathias' pillow.

I slipped on a pair of heels and grabbed Percy.

Mathias was pacing in the kitchen. "God, woman," he groaned, "could you be any slower?"

"I guess you should have woken me up sooner," I reasoned, lifting my shoulders.

He mumbled under his breath and went to get Shiloh, returning a moment later with her on a leash.

Together we managed to get the animals and the suitcases into the elevator, but instead of taking it to the parking garage we stopped in the lobby and headed out front where an SUV was waiting for us. A big, burly driver in a black suit stood waiting.

"Is that your body guard?" I asked.

Mathias nodded. "Yeah. That's Hank. Hank, this is Remy. Remy, Hank."

We each said awkward hellos as he opened the car door for us, before putting our bags in the trunk.

When we slipped inside the vehicle I was surprised to find Maddox and Emma sitting in the back. I mean, I knew from what Mathias said that the whole band would be going to L.A. but I just figured we'd be meeting up with them there. Silly me.

"Hi," I smiled at Maddox. Emma was currently passed out asleep with her head on his shoulder. On his other shoulder sat... "Is that a hedgehog?"

He smiled crookedly. "Yep. Sonic," he pointed to his shoulder, "Aquilla," he then pointed to his lap. Two hedgehogs. Wow.

"Uh…" I didn't know quite what to make of the spiky creatures. Percy finally seemed to notice them and hissed before scratching at me and jumping on the floor of the SUV. He glared up at me with disdain.

"I told you we should've left the demon," Mathias muttered, having witnessed the whole situation.

I rolled my eyes and relaxed into the seat.

"Ezra and Hayes are already on the plane." Maddox spoke from behind me.

"Of course they are," Mathias griped.

The trunk closed and Hank slid into the driver's seat, pulling away from the hotel.

The sudden jolting of the car caused Emma to momentarily wake up. I heard her mutter something before promptly falling back asleep cuddled against Maddox with her wild blonde hair hiding her face. I couldn't help watching as Maddox smiled lovingly down at her and kissed the top of her head. I quickly turned around before he could catch me watching them. Mathias didn't miss it though. He reached over, taking my hand in his. It wasn't much, but it was a simple gesture to show me that he cared. A smile touched my lips as I looked at our hands. It was cute that Mathias thought he should show more affection—and even though I'd been admiring the sweetness of Maddox and Emma's relationship, I didn't need that. All I'd ever wanted and needed was Mathias, just the way he was.

I relaxed into the plush leather seat, settling in for the long drive to the airport. I was surprised though when Hank didn't get on the interstate.

"Where are we going?" I asked stupidly.

"To the airport." Mathias answered immediately with his usual sass.

I rolled my eyes. "I know that, but shouldn't we be going in that direction?" I pointed the opposite way.

He shook his head, glancing down at our joined hands like he wasn't quite sure what to make of them. "We're going to the airport here."

I racked my brain, trying to recall an airport here. "You mean that really small one?"

He nodded. "Yeah. It's easier for us to fly in and out of there. The private plane isn't that large and we can avoid getting mobbed by a crowd. Unfortunately," he winced, "we'll have to land at LAX so brace yourself. It's going to get crazy."

"Yeah." Maddox piped in from behind us.

"Great." I glanced out the window. I wasn't ready for this, but I had to be.

We arrived at the airport no more than ten minutes later. It was nice not having to go through security and then wait for the plane to be ready to board. Hank literally drove right up to the plane and we got out of the car, climbed up the steps, and took our seats.

Hayes nodded as we got on the plane. Ezra was already asleep in his chair with his headphones on.

Poor Emma was still half-asleep and Maddox had to practically carry her to a seat.

"She really hates getting up early." He told me when he caught me staring.

"I'm with her," I agreed.

I took my seat and clicked the seatbelt into place. Percy sat in my lap and Shiloh snoozed peacefully on Mathias'.

"Go back to sleep," he urged.

I shook my head. "I don't think I can."

"Of course you can. I'll sing to you."

I looked up at him wide-eyed. "You're going to sing to me?"

"Sure," he shrugged, stretching his legs out. That was a major bonus of a private plane—lots of leg-room. Not to mention the seat was super plush and the interior was shiny and clean. I wouldn't feel the need to bathe in Germ-X like I normally did after traveling.

"Uh…" I didn't know what to make of that.

"Just get comfortable," he huffed.

"Alright, alright," I mumbled, trying to hide my smile.

I wiggled my butt around in the seat, trying not to jostle Percy too much, and then laid my head on his shoulder.

I was surprised when he laid his head on top of mine.

A smile of contentment lifted my lips and I scooted as close to him as I could get.

Closing my eyes, I waited for him to start singing.

When he did I immediately felt a flush of warmth in my body and tingles in my toes. I would never grow tired of hearing him sing at any time, but there was something I enjoyed infinitely more about having him sing only to *me*. I didn't recognize the song, but if it was one of Willow Creek's that wasn't surprising. I'd never let myself indulge in their music. It was too painful to hear Mathias' voice. But now I never wanted him to stop singing to me. I wanted to wrap myself up in the softness of his voice and stay there forever. His voice had a slight husky rasp to it that I loved. It made it rougher and more unique than everything else you heard on the radio. It was just as raw and beautiful as the man it belonged to. He'd hate it if he knew I thought everything about him was beautiful, but it was the only word to describe him. He was beautiful inside and out.

I closed my eyes, letting his warmth and voice envelope me.

Soon I found my eyes growing heavy and I was lulled into a deep sleep as his voice carried me into my dreams.

We landed at LAX and it was time to depart the plane. Mathias grabbed a black baseball cap and stuck it on his head, pulling the brim low before covering his eyes with a pair of dark sunglasses.

"You want one?" He asked, pointing to a stash of baseball caps and beanies kept in a basket on the plane.

"Uh…" I paused, debating. "Yeah." He handed me a red cap and I smiled.

"Thanks."

I put it on and adjusted it so I wore it the way he did—hiding half of my face. The media didn't need to know who I was. I might've fought with him on that fact before, but that was only because I thought he was ashamed of me or something. In all honestly, I'd rather keep my anonymity for as long as possible.

"Show time," he muttered.

Taking my hand he led me off the plane and through the gate. We were the last to depart—the other band members having ditched us.

"Hank will bring our stuff and Shiloh and Percy to my place later. I thought it was best that they avoid this," he said to me, just before chaos erupted and I learned what *this* was.

High-pitched shrieks echoed around the airport as a group of teenage girls spotted Mathias.

"Fuck," he groaned.

He grudgingly posed for pictures and signed autographs before Hank and another large beefy guy showed up.

They ushered us out of the crowd and through the airport.

Outside I saw photographers lined up, their cameras flashing as they tried to snap photos through the glass.

Mathias wrapped an arm around me, holding me tight against his side, while Hank and beefy guy number two flanked us.

When we stepped outside the clicking of cameras and shouts from the photographers were nearly overwhelming.

"Mathias! Over here!"

"Mathias!"

"Who's the woman?"

"Mathias, are you dating now?"

"Is it serious?"

"Who is she?"

"Who are you?"

Oh, look, a question finally directed at me.

We reached the vehicle and Hank opened the back door. Mathias pushed at me, trying to get me to go in first, but a photographer chose that moment to practically shove a camera in my face and scare the crap out of me. The flash went off, momentarily blinding me and I covered my eyes.

A new arm came around me, and I started to scream when I realized the arm was so large it had to either belong to Hank or beefy guy number two.

I was lifted into the SUV and I immediately scurried to the other seat so Mathias could get in.

He sat down, letting out a hefty sigh as the door closed—helping to drown out some of the noise. Beefy guy number two got in the driver's seat and Hank took the passenger's.

"How do you live with that?" I asked Mathias.

He shrugged, removing the baseball cap and ruffling his hair with a quick swipe of his fingers. "I don't like it, but it's part of the job."

"That was insane."

He nodded in agreement. "It was worse than I expected." His jaw clenched and he turned his gaze on me, his gray eyes so icy that I found myself shivering. "Does it scare you? Because if it does you should just leave now. This is one part of my life I can't change."

I gaped at him. My mouth opening and closing as I tried to form words.

"Do I like it? No. But it's not going to scare me away from you," I spoke fiercely. "I choose to be with you, because I love you, and nothing, not even this, can change that." I couldn't help muttering, "Don't be such a damn drama queen." I crossed my arms over my chest and glared out the window. I was slightly hurt that he thought that something as simple as a photographer snapping my picture would send me running. Sure, I didn't like it, but I expected it. I wished he'd have more faith in me.

"Rem," he started, and then grunted in annoyance before turning to look out the opposite window. In many ways we were far too much alike, one of those ways being our stubbornness. It always seemed to get us in trouble.

I noticed Hank reach up and turn the radio on to drown out the awkward silence. In that moment I was incredibly thankful for Hank… and you know, also when he saved me from some crazy photographers.

Despite the fact that it was cold back home, it still looked like it was summer here.

That was one thing I missed about Arizona, even though when I left to take care of my grandma I'd known I'd never go back there.

I hadn't planned to stay in Virginia either, but sometimes life had other plans for you. I turned to look at Mathias, taking in his steely posture and sharp jaw. I hadn't expected to find him again, once I did I'd wanted nothing but revenge, and now all I wanted was for us to finally get our happily ever after. We'd both been through hell and back—together and apart—and I felt we deserved to be happy, but dread slid like a thick serpent through my veins, because people like us didn't get a happy ending. In a movie we'd be the bad guys that everyone loved to hate, and secretly rooted for their demise. We didn't get to skip off into the sunset. No, we ended up alone and miserable—left questioning every decision we'd ever made and how it led to this… to nothing.

I didn't want to end up with nothing.

I wanted to end up with Mathias, but I *knew* that in order for that to happen I'd have to tell him about Hope and I… I just couldn't. Not only did I want to spare him the hurt, but I wanted to avoid the pain telling him would cause me.

Selfish? Yeah, I'd agree with that. I was a selfish person. So were most people, even though they didn't want to admit it.

But if being selfish meant that he'd never have to experience the hurt of losing our daughter then I would be selfish for the rest of my life and take my secret to the grave.

The car came to a stop in front of a set of wrought iron gates and I was jolted out of my less than happy thoughts.

The gate swung open and we drove through a slightly overgrown tree line before they parted to show a large white, rectangular home with a balcony wrapping around the second level. The entire home was covered with wall-to-wall windows.

"This is home when I'm here." He shrugged, finally speaking.

"It's gorgeous." There was no denying that fact.

"Let me show you around," he said as the car came to a stop.

Hank opened the door for us and said they'd return soon with our luggage and the animals. I really hoped Percy and Shiloh were okay.

Mathias guided me to the heavy wood front door with a hand at my waist. He dug a pair of keys out of his pocket and slid it into the lock.

A gasp escaped my parted lips.

While the penthouse at the hotel was muted colors and decorated sparsely this house was the complete opposite. Despite the fact that all the outside walls had windows the house was relatively warm looking, with rich woods and brown hues decorating the space. It was definitely masculine, but I loved it. Due to the style of the home I expected it to be decorated like the penthouse, but I was pleased I'd been wrong.

He led me into the family room where a tan suede sectional was positioned in front of a fireplace with a flat screen TV mounted above.

Decorative burnt orange pillows and a throw blanket decorated the couch.

"I hired an interior designer," he admitted with a sheepish shrug. "There was no way I could do this on my own, let alone ever have the time. I think you're right, I should do something else with the penthouse. When I moved in there…" He turned away from me, his jaw clenched tight. "I guess I wanted it to reflect me—to be just as empty as I was on the inside. I'm not so empty anymore." His gray eyes flooded with love and I swallowed thickly.

I couldn't stop myself from wrapping my arms around him. He was slow to do the same, but eventually he did. I rested my ear against his chest and closed my eyes as I memorized the steady *thump, thump, thump* that was the beat of his heart.

He rested his head on top of mine and we stood there silently as minutes passed, neither of us willing to let go.

"I love you," I finally whispered. "I know I never say it, but I do. I love you so much that it scares me." My voice cracked and I clung tightly to his shirt.

"I love you too." He pulled away just enough to press a tender kiss to my forehead. I sighed softly and my eyes closed at the sweet feel of his lips.

I knew I needed to release him so I did just that, instantly missing the warmth his body provided.

Reaching for my hand he flashed me a small half-smile. "Let me show you the rest of my place."

The floor plan was open so I could practically see the whole downstairs from where we stood, but I wasn't going to complain.

He led me from the family room into the dining room. It was decorated with a dark wood table and beige fabric covered chairs. I doubted the room had ever been used.

From there he guided me into the kitchen. Like the rest of the house the walls were a light golden hue with espresso colored cabinets and gold-flecked granite countertops. It was gorgeous and I couldn't help picturing the two of us cooking in here together—you know, after I learned how to cook. I was turning into a sap, so sue me.

I was too busy looking around the kitchen in awe to notice him approach. He grasped my hip, turning me around to face him, and pressed me against the edge of the center island.

His eyes were dark with lust and he lowered his forehead to mine.

"I think we need christen every room."

I tossed my head back, laughing. "Oh, do you now?"

He nodded, skimming his lips along my jaw before nipping my chin lightly with his teeth. "Definitely. I want a different memory for every room."

"Mmm," I hummed as his lips captured mine.

His tongue slid against mine, eliciting a moan from my throat.

"I. Thought. You. Were. Going. To. Give. Me. A. Tour." I panted in-between kisses.

"Fuck the tour."

I was okay with that.

His hand skimmed up my thigh, cupping my butt, and then he lifted me onto the countertop. My legs parted and he stepped into the space between, never breaking his lips from mine. He reached up, cupping my face in his large hands and holding me prisoner.

In the small space between us I began to undo the buttons of his cardigan, pushing it off his wide shoulders. Next went his white button down shirt. Then he removed my coat and shirt.

Bra.

Jeans.

Panties.

Gone.

Gone.

Gone.

I lay down with my back pressed flat against the countertop. The cold surface made me shiver and my nipples tightened in response.

"Fuck, you're beautiful." He growled lowly as his eyes raked over my body.

I bit my lip, watching as he rolled on the condom.

Once it was in place he grabbed my hips and pulled me over.

He slammed inside me and I let out a small cry.

"I didn't hurt you, did I?" He asked, suddenly stilling.

"Please, for the love of God," I reached forward, my fingers grazing his abs, "don't fucking stop."

A small smile touched his lips and he began to move.

I let out a small moan, clenching around him.

He palmed my breast, rolling his thumb over my swollen nipple while his other hand roamed lower. When his fingers found my clit I gasped, my back arching off the countertop.

"Oh God," I whimpered.

He lowered his head, sucking on my other nipple.

I was a goner.

He continued to pump into me at a vicious pace and I found myself coming a second time with him.

He collapsed with his chest on top of mine, our sweaty skin sticking together. I wrapped my legs around his waist as we both tried to even our breaths.

He was the first to recover. He pulled out of me and removed the condom, tying it off before tossing it in the trashcan.

I was too tired to move, but luckily I didn't have to. He reached for me and pulled me off the counter and into his arms.

"Next room," he growled.

I nodded, more than happy to indulge his fantasy.

After having sex in every room downstairs we finally were too tried to continue. We got redressed and collapsed on the couch in the family room. He turned the TV on and I laid down with my head resting on his thigh. I paid no attention to the TV as my eyelids grew heavy.

Just as I was about to doze off asleep there was a knock at the door.

Mathias groaned and tapped my shoulder so I'd sit up.

"That'll be Hank with our stuff."

"Percy!" I cried with sudden renewed energy.

I tumbled off the couch and hurried after Mathias, reaching him just as he swung the door open.

Shiloh immediately bound inside, tearing her leash out of Hank's hand.

Poor Hank let out a curse and that's when I noticed Percy clawing at the large bear of a man.

"I'm so sorry!" I cried, rushing forward to grab Percy from his hands.

"It didn't hurt," Hank shrugged, but the claw marks on his arms and neck told a different story.

Percy wasn't too pleased with me either and scratched at me so I'd put him down. As soon as I did he promptly ran into the dining room and hid under the table.

"Demon cat," Mathias muttered.

For once I agreed with him.

He took the bags from Hank and they said their goodbyes.

"I'm hungry," Mathias announced.

"Okay," I said slowly. "Do you want to go out, or—"

"Let's make frozen pizza."

I nodded my head in approval. "So fancy. I like it."

He chuckled, shaking his head as he started in the direction of the kitchen. "You're lucky I like your sarcasm."

I padded after him, rolling my eyes despite the fact that he couldn't see me. "And you're lucky I tolerate you."

"Good point," he shrugged.

In the kitchen he opened the freezer and pulled out a box of pizza with practically every topping on it. I had no idea where anything was located so I hopped up on the counter while he fixed everything. Besides, watching him was way more fun than helping.

Shiloh joined us shortly, sniffing every surface.

For kicks I almost reminded Mathias to get rid of any chocolate, but I decided that would be too mean even for me considering the panic attack he'd nearly had the last time.

He finally slid the pizza into the oven and set the timer.

He turned to me, placing his hands on the counter beside my legs. "So," he started, lowering his head so he could peer into my eyes, "do you like it here?"

I let out a small laugh. "I haven't seen much, you know, besides your cock. But it was pretty nice. I quite like it actually."

He ducked his head to hide a smile. Raising his eyes to mine he brushed his thumb against my bottom lip. "You and your dirty mouth."

My eyes dropped to his lips. "That wasn't even dirty."

He tucked his head into the crook of my neck and I felt him smile.

I expected him to say or do something else but after a pause he took a step back and held out his hand for me.

"Come with me."

I tucked my hand into his and hopped off the counter.

He led me to a wall of windows and I gasped. I'd been too preoccupied by the opulent inside to notice the beauty that lay beyond the windows.

The house was nestled high on a hill over looking a barren, private beach. Directly outside the windows sat a large swimming pool with shimmering blue water. Lounge chairs were set up by the pool, and off to a corner was an area sectioned off with rocks and chairs surrounding a fire pit.

He slid open a door—that I'd actually believed was a window since it blended in so effortlessly—and guided me outside.

The air was warm with a slight breeze.

I released his hand and started removing my clothes.

"What are you doing?" He asked, watching my movements.

"What does it look like I'm doing?" I raised a brow as my fingers found the button on my jeans. I left my bra and panties on just to mess with him.

He shook his head, looking at me like I'd lost my mind as all my clothes fell in a heap on the grass.

I dove into the water and found that it was actually warm. I guessed he kept it heated.

I rose to the surface, pushing my wet hair away from my face.

"Aren't you coming?" I asked, treading water.

He shook his head yet again, as if he couldn't believe he was about to do this. He stripped down to his boxer-briefs and dove into the water. He surfaced in front of me and shook his head, sending water droplets flying all over the place.

"You're crazy, you know that, right?"

I smiled, wrapping my arms around his strong shoulders. "I know," I agreed, watching a droplet of water cascade down his cheek and over his lips. "But life is pretty boring without the crazy moments."

He chuckled. "You've got that right."

Before he could say anything else I leaned in and kissed him, stealing away that drop of water.

He swallowed thickly, his eyes growing serious. The strands of his wet hair brushed against my forehead as he spoke. "To think, we almost missed out on this. On us." He brushed his fingers lightly over my cheek. "I never thought I was the kind of person who had good luck or got second chances, but here I am, defeating the odds—living my dream, and getting my girl back."

*My girl.*

I didn't know what to say to that. I was so overcome by his words that for once in my life I was actually speechless. "I guess some things are meant to be," I whispered when I realized he was still waiting for a reply.

His tongue slid out to wet his lips and his forehead wrinkled with thought.

I didn't know what he was going to say, and nothing could've prepared me for the words that left his mouth.

"Marry me."

I choked on a gasp. "What?"

"Marry me," he repeated, dead serious. "Not right this second, but soon. Like this week. We're playing a show in Vegas while we're on the west coast. While we're there let's get married."

"Are you insane?" If he wasn't holding onto me I was pretty sure his words would've sent me sinking straight to the bottom of the pool.

"On the contrary, I think this is the most sane I've ever been." He cracked a smile. "Now, please, don't make me ask again."

"I-I—" I stuttered, shaking my head back and forth as every reason why I should say no flitted through my mind. Unfortunately, one word outweighed every negative thought I had. "Yes." Tears pricked my eyes. I never thought I'd be one of those girls that cried when she got engaged—in fact, I'd rarely even imagined this moment. "Yes," I said again, loving the sound of that word. "Yes. Yes. Yes."

His lips smothered mine in a bruising kiss as I continued to whisper, "Yes," over and over again. Now that I'd said it, it was my new favorite word and I never, ever wanted to stop saying it.

# CHAPTER TWENTY-FIVE

After Mathias' surprise proposal we'd gotten out of the pool and dried off. The pizza had finished baking, and although it was a little burnt, I still declared that it was the best thing I'd ever eaten.

Now, Mathias guided me up the staircase with a twinkle in his eyes.

My heart thumped steadily in my chest. Each beat seemed to say, *He wants to marry you.* I was still in shock. The last thing I had ever expected was for Mathias to ask me to marry him. Even if someone had asked me where I thought we'd be in five years I definitely wouldn't have answered with married. I never thought it was something he'd want, and I'd always been okay with that. Now, though, as his warm hand enveloped mine, I couldn't help smiling with glee at the thought of calling him my husband. I had to admit, I really liked the sound of that.

He paused in front of a door, glancing back at me with an almost shy smile.

Pushing the door open he stepped back and let me step inside the room first.

I let out a small gasp and spun around, trying to take in all the details.

The bed took up most of the space. It had four posts that soared high and was a deep rich brown. The wall behind the bed was covered in what looked like wood flooring. It sounded strange but it actually worked. Two of the other walls were painted a deep burnt orange color, while the last wall was a solid window over looking the pool and the beach below. The bed was covered in a thick brown comforter with orange pillows. Surprisingly this room had carpet. It was thick and plush and for some reason I had the urge to kick my shoes off and dig my toes into it, so I did just that.

Mathias chuckled as he stood watching me. He leaned casually against the wall with his hands in his pockets. He hadn't bothered to put his shirt or cardigan back on so his chest was left bare. I never knew a body could be a work of art, but his was. With soft skin and hard planes of muscle, he was nothing less than magnificent—and mine.

"Like what you see?" He grinned, while his own eyes scoured my body.

I licked my lips and nodded. I glanced at his bed and back at him, frowning.

He noticed the downturn of my lips and strode forward, taking my face between his hands. "What is it?" He asked, his eyes scanning my face for any explanation of my sudden sadness. "What's wrong?"

"It's stupid," I winced, refusing to speak the words aloud.

"Tell me," he coaxed, his eyes pleading.

"I…" I gaped at him open-mouthed like a fish. "It's just that… Fuck." I cursed, wishing he'd release me so I could escape the intrusiveness of his gaze.

"Remy," he warned, "tell me what's wrong so I can fix it."

I swallowed past the lump in my throat. I felt silly and oh-so girly in this moment. "It's so dumb," I frowned, biting my lower lip in the hopes that I could stop the tumble of words, "but I *hate* the thought of you fucking me in this bed where you've brought countless other women." I'd never had that worry at his penthouse because he was never photographed with women at home—then again, the paparazzi didn't seem to want to bother hanging around our small town. But I *had* seen countless photos in magazines of him with different women in L.A. and the thought of him bringing them back here, to this bed, literally made me sick to my stomach.

He stroked his fingers lightly over the curve of my cheek, his eyes darkening. "One, I've never brought any woman back here. This is my home and I don't want it tainted with meaningless hookups. Two," his voice lowered and his lips pressed against my neck, right over the spot where my pulse raced wildly, "I'm not going to fuck you in this bed."

"You're not?" My voice came out sounding surprisingly strong despite how weak I suddenly felt.

I felt him shake his head and I shivered as his hair tickled my neck. He pulled back, looking into my eyes. His Adam's apple bobbed and his eyes flicked down to my lips and then back up. "No," his voice was barely above a whisper, "I'm going to make love to you."

That was the last thing I'd ever expected him to say.

My heart raced in anticipation at the promising glint in his eyes.

"No one's ever made love to me before," I whispered, my chest heaving with each breath as I struggled to get enough air.

He pushed forward and I was forced to take a step back, and then another, until the backs of my knees hit the bed and I was forced to lie down.

"I've never done it," he admitted, his fingers skimming down my neck, all the way to the bottom of my shirt. His fingers wrapped around the end of it and he slowly tugged it upward, stopping when he reached the bottom of my bra. My skin felt heated all over and when he kissed my stomach I was sure his lips would be burned. He lifted his head, his eyes connecting with mine yet again—and my body clenched all over from the intensity of his gaze. "But something tells me I'm going to enjoy this."

My heart beat so fast that it sounded like thunder in my ears—a steady roar promising more.

He sprinkled kisses all over my stomach and small little sounds escaped my throat.

I was used to hard and fast with us, and this was anything but that.

His fingers dipped beneath the edge of my jeans, teasing me as he went no further and made no move to remove them. I covered my mouth with my hand to resist the urge to beg him for more.

He kissed his way up my stomach, this time lifting my shirt off and gently removing it. My blonde hair tumbled forward and he pushed it away, his eyes feasting upon my breasts, which were barely contained in a lacy black bra.

"I never thought I'd get you *back*." His voice cracked. "I believed I was nothing but a sick bastard that didn't deserve you. I was wrong though. I do deserve you. I deserve happiness and you bring me that." His lips skimmed down my neck and over my breasts. "I'm done punishing myself for things that were out of my control." His eyes met mine and it was like he was peering straight down into my soul. "My parent's might've been bad people, but I realize now that it doesn't mean I am just because their blood runs through my veins. Loving you has shown me that."

I closed my eyes, soaking in his words and the beauty of them. "You were never a bad person," I whispered after a moment.

He looked at me doubtfully, his chest shaking with a silent chuckle.

"Misunderstood, yes," I continued, "but you've never been a bad person. Beneath all your… assholishness," I said for lack of a better word, "you have a heart of gold." I placed my hand over his heart, feeling it thump steadily in time with mine.

"If I had a heart of gold I wouldn't have lied to you when you left," he growled. "I wouldn't have done half the shit that I have."

I swallowed thickly, remembering back to that day and everything that happened after. "Even good people make mistakes."

He shook his head, but instead of arguing with me he simply said, "I'm done talking now."

In an achingly slow manner he removed the last of my clothes and proceeded to kiss every inch of my body.

My whole body tensed with the desire to connect with his.

Grazing my fingers down his bare chest until I reached his pants, I said, "I think you're wearing too many clothes."

"Slow, Rem," he growled, nipping my earlobe.

"This is slow," I argued.

He merely chuckled, sweeping his lips over my breasts.

He would be the death of me, but at least I'd die happy.

While he kissed my neck his fingers slipped inside me. I gasped at the same time he groaned.

"Christ, your pussy is always so wet for me."

I wanted to come back with some witty response, but my brain had shut down for the moment. Words fled my mind and all I could focus on was the touch of his fingers and the feel of his weight resting on top of my body.

His fingers rubbed against me, working me into an orgasm. As I came, panting his name, his eyes never left mine and his contained a gleam of satisfaction.

"I like it when you say my name like that," he growled, undoing the button of his pants.

Sweat dotted my skin and I struggled to catch my breath. "Like what?"

"Like I'm everything to you."

Before I had time to process his words he'd stepped out of his pants and he gave his cock a light stroke before slipping on a condom and covering my body with his.

Pushing my hair from my eyes he whispered, "I love you," before slowly sinking inside me.

My breath caught on a gasp as my whole body shook with his intrusion.

I wrapped my legs around his waist, my fingernails digging into his back as he rolled his hips against mine in a leisurely pace.

He rested his forehead against mine, peering into my eyes as he made love to me—and he was right, this was definitely making love, not fucking, and I loved it. I never knew sex could be like this. So powerful. It was like we were connecting not only physically, but spiritually as well. It was a beautiful thing and I never wanted it to end, and I realized it didn't have too, because I was going to be his wife.

Tears pricked my eyes and one slid down my cheek.

His eyes followed the trail of the tear. "Why are you crying?" He asked, still pushing into me at that deliciously slow pace.

"I don't know," I whispered, taking his chin between my thumb and forefinger. The light stubble on his chin scratched my fingers, but I didn't mind the roughness.

He wiped away the wetness with a swipe of his large thumb.

"I don't want you to be sad," he frowned.

"I'm not," I shook my head, "I'm so undeniably *happy*."

Confusion marred his brow, but he let it drop. His pace picked up slightly, but was still slower than our normal frantic coupling.

He sucked at the skin on my neck, no doubt leaving behind a mark, before trailing his lips over the valley between my breasts.

I could feel another orgasm approaching and my whole body clenched.

"Fuck," he groaned, kissing me.

I gasped beneath him when my orgasm hit and cried out his name. My nails dug sharply into his back and he hissed. I shook all over and sweat dampened my skin. I'd never had an orgasm that powerful before.

He wasn't far behind me, growling lowly as he found his own release.

We stayed connected and he was careful to hold his weight so that he didn't hurt me. When he caught his breath he slipped out of me and disposed of the condom. Returning to the bed he lay down beside me, pulling me against his side.

"Fucking hell," he muttered, staring up at the ceiling while I still struggled to get enough air into my lungs, "if I had known it would be that good I would've made love to you a long time ago."

Despite my lack of oxygen I still managed to laugh. "Well, there's always next time."

"Hell yeah."

And then he proceeded to show me over and over again why making love was better than fucking.

The early morning sun filtered in through the open windows, bathing our bodies in a golden glow. I trailed my fingers lightly over his chest, watching the way his muscles clenched and danced at my touch. Neither of us had gotten much sleep, maybe two hours at the most, having spent the entire night wrapped in each other's arms.

"Why do you want to marry me?" I asked. My breath tickled his chest and his nipple tightened at the sensation.

"Why would you ask that?" He sounded mad.

I tilted my head back to peer up at him. His dark brows were pulled together and his forehead was wrinkled with irritation. "I was just wondering. I mean… I never thought you'd want that."

"I didn't," he admitted on a sigh, "but with you I want it all."

My heart skipped a beat at that. "*Why?*"

"Because I love you." He answered simply, his fingers resuming their slow rake through my hair before stopping at my neck. He began to massage the stiff muscle and I nearly moaned. His fingers stilled once more and his whole body went rigid against me. "Have you changed your mind?" The fist on his free hand clenched. "Do you not want to marry me?"

I sat up, my blonde hair forming a silky sheet around us. "That's not what I was getting at, at all." I reached forward, stroking my fingers along his cheek. He sighed happily at my touch and began to relax. "I want this, I want *you*, more than anything. It's just hard for me to see why you would want me. You talk about how you're a bad person, but what about me?"

I was pretty sure it was a safe bet that my sins were far worse than his. After all, I was hiding a massive secret from him. Yeah, I was trying to protect him, but that didn't make the fact that I was keeping a secret from him okay.

He sat up too, clasping my hands in his like he was afraid I might run away and he needed to keep a tight hold on me. "What's going on Remy?"

"Nothing," I lied, hoping he couldn't see the tears shimmering in my eyes. "I just wanted to know why."

"Fuck," he growled, looking away. A muscle in his jaw ticked. Looking back at me he said, "I want to marry you, because you're my best friend. I want to marry you, because I love waking up beside you. I want to marry you, because I love seeing you strut around in my shirts. I want to marry you, because I love having you in my house, in my space and I love knowing you've been there and that you're coming back. I want to marry you, because without you my life feels incomplete." He paused, taking a deep breath. "But most importantly, I want to marry you because I love you—I have since I was sixteen years old—and I'll never stop."

Happy tears pricked my eyes for the second time in a matter of hours. Clearly I was turning into a sap.

I wrapped my arms around his neck and kissed him long and deep. "I love you too," I said on a breath.

He smiled against my lips. "So, you're really going to marry me?"

I nodded and was rewarded with one of his rare blindingly bright smiles that made my insides dance and sing.

He kissed me quickly, his lips a bruising pressure against mine.

His fingers curled against the nape of my neck and his smile never wavered.

"Did you really think I had changed my mind?" I asked.

He shrugged, laying back down and pulling me with him so I was once again lying in the same position with my head cradled on his chest. "You looked so upset…" He trailed off. "So, yeah, I guess I did think that."

"I'm sorry, I didn't mean to scare you like that. But I wondered why, because I know I'm not always the nicest person."

He laughed, his whole body shaking with it, which in turn made mine shake.

"And neither am I. That, my dear Remy," he kissed my forehead, "is why we work."

I closed my eyes, breathing in his scent.

"Get some sleep," he whispered, brushing his lips against the top of my head, "I have to film a commercial in a few hours."

"A commercial?" I questioned.

"Yep," he grabbed the edge of the sheet and brought it over our bodies, "for Pepsi."

"You're so cool," I yawned, "and you're going to be my husband."

"Just go to sleep, Rem," he growled.

I didn't think I'd be able to fall asleep, but like on the plane he began to sing softly and in a matter of minutes I slept peacefully.

# CHAPTER TWENTY-SIX

We stepped into the garage and I followed Mathias over to a sleek cobalt blue Honda motorcycle. It looked fast, and that fact made me excited.

"Are we taking this?" I asked, practically dancing on the balls of my feet.

He looked at me like he didn't even recognize me, which was understandable since I rarely got excited over anything.

"Yeah," he nodded, heading over to a row of silver lockers that lined the back of the garage. He also owned a sleek silver car that looked like nothing I'd ever seen before. Something told me I didn't want to know how much it cost.

Opening one of the locker doors he grabbed two helmets. I was already wearing a black leather jacket while he wore a brown one.

"So…" I reached out, taking the offered helmet, "are you going to let me drive it?"

"Fuck no." He pushed a button to open one of the garage doors before slipping the helmet on his head.

He tossed his leg over the side of the bike and a moment later the engine roared to life.

I had to admit he looked mighty sexy straddling the sleek motorcycle. Downright lickable.

"Hurry up, Rem," he growled over the motor. "We're going to be late."

"Oh, right," I muttered to myself, getting into place behind him. My hands lightly grasped his sides and when he knew that I was comfortable we shot out of the garage. The bike was crazy fast and my hair whipped around me as the air stung my skin even through my layers of clothes.

I was enjoying every moment of it though.

The L.A. traffic was insane and we got stuck in traffic before arriving at a building that looked like a rundown warehouse. I spotted several cars in the parking lot and figured the rest of the band was already here.

We dismounted from the bike and removed our helmets. I pulled my hair back into a ponytail to help tame the strands.

Taking my hand Mathias led me through a backdoor and down several hallways.

The space opened up and a whole set was in front of us along with cameras. Off to the side sat a rack of clothes and a makeup team.

"They're going to put makeup on you?" I tried, and failed, to suppress a laugh.

"Yes," he growled.

Maddox approached us from off to the side. He was dressed simply in a pair of loose jeans and a white t-shirt that molded to his chest. His drumsticks rested in his back pocket. "Emma's over there," he nodded his head in the direction of another doorway. "Free food," he whispered conspiratorially, "and lots of Diet Pepsi. It's like heaven."

Mathias released my hand. "Go on." He nodded as well. "I have to go get ready anyway."

I watched as he strutted over to the wardrobe like he owned the damn place. He oozed effortless confidence.

Maddox cleared his throat, forcing my attention back to him. "So," he started, "how are things?"

"Uh… Good?" I didn't know why it came out sounding like a question. He'd caught me off guard though and I had no idea how to respond. I had no knowledge of how much Mathias shared with his twin, and I definitely didn't know if he wanted to tell his brother we were planning to get married or if he wanted to keep it between us for now.

Maddox nodded, looking over at where Mathias argued with the stylist about the wardrobe. "That's good." He stuck his hands in his pockets as his silver eyes swiveled back in my direction. "I can tell he's happy."

I nodded too, feeling extremely awkward. I didn't know Maddox very well. When we were teenagers we only hung out a few times, and it wasn't like we'd ever been friends.

"Are you happy too?" He asked, reaching up to sweep his dark hair away from his eyes.

A small smile touched my lips as I watched Mathias. "Yeah, I am. The happiest I've ever been."

Maddox grinned. "It's crazy how after so many years apart you guys still connected. What you have is special. Anyone can see that."

I nodded, smiling at Maddox. "Yeah, it is."

Just then Mathias voice raised and we looked over to see him yelling at the poor stylist. It looked like a vein was about to burst in his forehead and his face had turned red.

"I better go calm him down," Maddox groaned. "Emma's in there," he repeated, "she'd love to see you so feel free to say hi."

I nodded as he took off to calm down his twin and I went in search of Emma.

I found her just where he'd promised. This room was sectioned off with a long table covered in various food items, and a couch and chair set. Emma sat in the chair and Ezra and Hayes occupied the couch.

When Emma saw me she instantly brightened, waving me over. "Grab a muffin!" She cried, pointing to the table overflowing with food. "They're delicious. This is my third." She held a half-eaten blueberry muffin aloft.

I grabbed a muffin, my mouth already watering. Mathias had let me sleep in, which meant once he did wake me up there'd been no time for breakfast, so I was starved now.

"It's so nice to not be the only girl around here anymore," Emma said when I dropped into the chair beside her.

Hayes turned his attention in our direction and mock-glared at her. "You know you love us."

She sighed, smiling. "Yeah, I suppose I do. You guys are like the annoying over protective brothers I never had."

Hayes chuckled, leveling his eyes on me. "Joshua Hayes," he stuck his hand out for me to shake, "better known as Hayes or The-Greatest-Member-Of-The-Band." His smile made his eyes crinkle at the corners. "I'm sorry I didn't properly introduce myself to you the first time we met. I was in quite a bit of shock that Mathias brought a girl to the studio. He's never done that, but these guys filled me in," he waved his hand around, "and now I understand. So, anyway," he rambled, "I wanted to apologize. I hope I didn't come across as rude, I was just shocked."

I cracked a smile, peeling the wrapper off the bottom of the muffin. "If I'd been in your position I would've been just as shocked and confused, so I understand."

"So, you guys were like high school sweethearts I hear?" He pried.

I coughed on the bite of muffin I'd taken, the small crumbs tickling the back of my throat. I grabbed a water bottle, and after a moment managed to compose myself. "We were hardly high school sweethearts."

His lips turned down. "But you dated?"

I shrugged. "I suppose." It was nearly impossible to define what our relationship had been. "I mean, we were *together*, but… it was complicated."

Hayes scratched the top of his head, his blond brows pulled together. "God, this is making my brain hurt."

I laughed, setting my half-eaten muffin aside. "We were together in high school, and we're together now. The rest is…" I shrugged, letting my sentence drop.

Hayes shook his head and glanced at Ezra with a wry smile. "What the fuck is wrong with the world that Mathias would get a girl before us?" Grinning at me, he said, "I honestly thought the fucker was going to be alone and miserable his whole life. He's not exactly the easiest person to deal with."

"Neither am I," I countered.

Hayes sat back, tapping his fingers along the armrest of the couch. "Mhmm, I can tell," he smirked. "I think I can see why you two work so well."

"We need you two out here." A woman called, poking her head through the doorway.

Ezra sighed and stood up, stretching his arms above his head before heading out of the room. He hadn't spoken at all since I'd entered the room and from the dark circles beneath his eyes and the pale hue to his skin, I thought the guy might be sick—and yet here he was, showing up to work.

Standing, Hayes smiled down at me. I had to crane my head back to see his face. The dude was a giant. "I'm looking forward to getting to know you, Remy."

I smiled in return and he ducked out of the room. Seriously, he literally *ducked* so his head wouldn't hit the doorway.

I grabbed my muffin up once more, hoping this time I might actually get it eaten.

"I know they can be weird sometimes, and rather nosy, but they're all great guys. We're a family. You included."

I laughed, wiping the crumbs off my jeans. "What an unconventional family."

"I suppose so," she smiled, her shoulders shaking with soft laughter, "but a loving one." Sobering, she turned towards me, tucking her legs behind her on the chair. "When Maddox told me about you and Mathias I always hoped that maybe you guys would find your way back to each other."

"Like fate?" I asked, quirking a brow.

"Yeah, or like soul mates or something."

My lips twitched with the threat of laughter. "I don't believe those things exist."

"How can you say that?" She asked, seeming confused by my easy dismissal of her notion. "You don't think it's possible that there's some cosmic force out there and that nothing, not time nor distance could've prevented you two from ending up together?" Before I could respond she let out a soft curse and covered her mouth. "Shit, I sound like my mom."

I laughed at her, shaking my head. Despite the fact that I didn't really know Emma I still felt comfortable around her. She had one of those easy-going personalities that instantly made you fall in love with her. She was adorably irresistible.

She joined in with my laughter. "This is what I get for being raised by a hippy."

I grinned at that. "Your mom sounds awesome."

"Oh, she is," Emma agreed, "but she's a little out there. I love her for it though."

"What does your mom think of you dating a rock star?" I asked. If my mom knew I was dating Mathias again she'd probably pass out and my dad would grab a gun. I didn't even want to guess at what their reaction to marriage would be.

Emma smiled, wiggling around in the leather chair. "My mom loves Maddox. I think she might love him more than she loves me," she giggled. "He's quite the charmer."

"It's good that your mom likes him."

"Definitely," she nodded. "I really lucked out." She glanced wistfully at the doorway like Maddox might appear any second. "He was my first boyfriend, my first everything. I also know he'll be my last and I wouldn't have it any other way. I know some people think it's crazy to only ever be with one person and that you're living in a fairytale to think it'll ever last, but I know it will with us."

"I think that's pretty beautiful," I said, and meant it.

She smiled bashfully, her cheeks coloring. "I'm lucky."

"So is he."

She tucked her hair behind her ear and pointed to the doorway. "I guess we should go watch them in action."

I nodded in agreement, throwing away the muffin wrapper and empty bottle of water.

The guys all stood on the stage set up. Well, except for Maddox—he sat behind his drum kit.

Mathias had changed into a pair of gray pants, a button down white shirt tucked into them, with a black belt and tie. His hair was styled away from his face, making his unique gray eyes stand out.

Music pumped out from a pair of speakers and the guys went through the motions of actually performing.

Emma stood beside me, watching them with love in her eyes. To me, she said, "Maddox is obsessed with Diet Pepsi so he was thrilled when Pepsi wanted them to do a commercial. I think this is honestly the highlight of his career," she laughed, shaking her head.

"It's crazy isn't it?" I nodded towards the guys on the stage.

She glanced at me, raising her brow in question.

"I knew them—except for Hayes—way before they were a band. I mean, they still played and Mathias sang some, but it was just something they did. I never imagined it would become who they are. I knew they jokingly talked about trying to make something happen with it, but I guess… I never imagined it would actually happen."

In high school I'd been to a few of their gigs, mostly performances in small venues around our hometown, and I never believed then that it would turn into something more—that they would actually make something out of it. I felt bad for that—for not believing in them more.

Emma shrugged. "Some dreams do come true."

My gaze rose to Mathias and I took a deep breath as his eyes connected with mine and a slow smile graced his lips as he continued to mouth the words to the song. "Yeah," I agreed, "some do."

After the commercial ended we all decided to grab a bite of lunch together before heading over to the recording studio.

The recording studio was located in a plain looking building on the outskirts of L.A. I was sure it had been purposefully designed to look non-descript.

We were the first to arrive and I climbed off the motorcycle, removing the helmet and trying to tame my hair. Mathias stood and took off his helmet as well. He grabbed mine and secured both to the bike.

I startled when he took my face between his hands and placed a soft, chaste kiss on my lips.

"What was that for?" I asked, sounding breathless despite the simple kiss.

He shrugged. "It was because I can."

I let out soft laugh. I should've expected that answer, it was so very Mathias.

Before the others showed up I hastened to ask, "Are you going to tell them? That we're getting married?"

He took my hand, leading me towards the entrance of the studio. I glanced down at our hands. I still wasn't quite used to his new displays of affection, but I was enjoying them.

"I haven't decided yet," he replied, holding the door open for me. I slipped into the darkened space and then followed him down a plain hallway. He opened another door that opened into a private recording studio.

"I don't care," I whispered to his turned back and he glanced at me over his shoulder. "Either way, I'll be happy, but I do think you should say something to your brother. I think he'd be hurt if we excluded him."

Mathias winced and nodded his head. I figured he was agreeing with me, but he still didn't confirm whether or not he'd tell them so I decided to let it drop.

A few minutes later a man entered the studio. He was tall and slender, older— probably in his fifties—with a shiny baldhead.

"This is Julian, our manager." Mathias introduced me with a groan. He was clearly irritated by the man's sudden appearance.

"Hi." I took his outstretched hand. "I'm Remy."

He smiled, his grip firm. His dark eyes shifted from me to Mathias. "Can I talk to you for a moment? Alone," he added, as if his tone hadn't already suggested that I wasn't welcome for this conversation.

Mathias gave me an apologetic look before ducking out of the room behind Julian.

I sighed heavily, taking a seat on the plush leather couch.

A moment later the muffled sound of raised voices could be heard through the door. They sounded like they were arguing and I felt like it might be about me.

A minute later Mathias strode back into the room, slamming the door closed behind him. His hair was mused like he'd been tugging on it.

"Is everything okay?" I asked.

He dropped down onto the seat beside me. "Yeah."

"No, it's not. I can tell." My hand rested on his thigh as I leaned towards him. He slowly turned to look at me and I could see the frustration in his eyes. "What's going on?"

"Just Julian being an ass," he grumbled, his jaw tight with tension. "He needs to mind his own fucking business."

"Was it about me?" I whispered the words, afraid of his answer.

He didn't need to speak though. His eyes said it all.

I let out a disgusted laugh. "Why?"

He shrugged, picking at an invisible piece of lint on his pants. "Julian hates me. I never bring the right kind of attention to the band and I guess he assumes that the same will be true of you."

I narrowed my eyes. "But you never even told him that we were together."

He chuckled, scratching at his lightly stubbled jaw. "Julian is very… perceptive. It's why he's good at his job."

"I'm sorry," I mumbled.

He looked at me quizzically. "Why are you apologizing?"

"I don't know. I just don't want you to be on the outs with your manager because of me."

He snorted. "I'm always on the outs with Julian. He hates me and I hate him, but I can't deny what he's done for the band."

Before the conversation could go any further the rest of the band joined us along with a few other people.

In no time they were taking turns in the booth.

"Why are you recording a new song?" I asked curiously. "I thought you guys were focused on the tour."

Hayes answered me, but his eyes were trained on the sound booth where Mathias was currently singing. "We're always working on new music. There's never any down time for us."

I processed his answer and sat back against the plush couch. I was beginning to see that all the time I'd been spending with Mathias was rare. More often than not the guys were busy doing something music related. That would be hard to adjust to, but watching Mathias sing and seeing how much he truly did love it, I knew I'd put up with anything for him.

That's what love did to you.

It made you willing to sacrifice your happiness for someone else's.

# CHAPTER TWENTY-SEVEN

I stood by the wall of windows in the family room. My arms were crossed over my chest as I watched the sunset. It was a beautiful kaleidoscope of reds, oranges, pinks, and even purple. It was made even more stunning by the way it reflected off of the ocean.

I felt Mathias walk up behind me. His warmth and solid body was a steady presence.

I leaned against him and his hand settled on my waist.

"I got you something," he whispered, his lips ghosting along the shell of my ear.

"You did?" I asked, turning in his arms so that the view was now behind me.

He nodded, reaching into the pocket of his black pants. He pulled out a navy colored jewelry box. Cracking a smile he said, "Don't expect me to get down on my knee. I'm not romantic enough for that."

I tossed my head back, my hair swishing around my shoulders as I laughed. "And yet you bought a ring."

"Arguably, you don't know it's a ring yet, but that is, in fact, the case." He opened the lid, showing me the stunning ring inside.

I stared at the ring with a look of awe. The center was some sort of amber colored jewel, square cut, with small diamonds surrounding it. It was unique and different—beyond anything I could've imagined for myself.

"I didn't think you'd get me a ring." I don't know why those were the first words out of my mouth.

He chuckled, shaking his head and smiled wryly. "I'll admit, I got it for entirely selfish reasons."

"Mhmm, I see." I clucked my tongue.

He took the ring out of the box and reached for my hand. I gave it to him willingly and he slid the ring over my finger. It was a perfect fit. "You're mine, Parker," he smiled triumphantly, "and now everybody else will know too."

I wrapped my arms around his neck and leaned up to kiss him. "Such a caveman," I murmured against his lips, "and for the record, I'm not yours yet, Wade."

He lifted my hand, kissing my fingers just below the ring. "You've always been mine." His eyes were filled with desire and I felt my belly dip with excitement. Cupping my cheeks between his large hands he lowered his head. His voice was nothing more than a soft growl. "Don't deny it."

A sound that could only be described as half-moan, half-sob bubbled out of my throat. I swayed against him, clutching the fabric of his cotton t-shirt between my fingers.

His fingers slid down to my chin and he grasped it between his fingers. I saw a million different thoughts and emotions flicker through his eyes. To anyone else, his eyes were nothing but liquid steel. However, with me, he was never able to mask them so easily.

I waited with baited breath for what he would say.

"Tomorrow."

"Huh?" My brows rose with confusion at his single word.

"Tomorrow. We're leaving for Vegas in the morning, and by this time tomorrow night you'll be my wife."

Before I had a chance to respond he lowered his mouth to mine, stealing all my thoughts, my breath, and maybe even a piece of my soul.

The airport in Vegas had been just as insane as L.A. if not more so, probably brought on by the fact that Willow Creek was playing a show there tonight.

The craziness had followed us all the way to the hotel, where security had to form a barricade for us to reach the door. Emma and I dashed inside while the guys signed autographs and took pictures.

Now, the group of us poured into an elevator, heading up to the penthouse suite of The Mirage. I was wondering how it would work with the group of us sharing a suite, but when the doors opened revealing the massive space I knew it wouldn't be a problem.

"We get the biggest room." Mathias grabbed my arm, rushing around to find it.

Nobody bothered to object and I figured none of them really cared.

When Mathias finally found the room he deemed the biggest he pulled me inside and closed the door.

The room was decorated in muted grays and whites with a bed low to the floor.

I figured his urgency was due to a desire to get naked, but I was wrong.

He paced the length of the room, steepling his fingers beneath his chin.

"Mathias—" I started and he stopped in front of me. He looked worried, little wrinkles turning down the corners of his mouth.

"I don't know how to tell Maddox."

"Oh," I mumbled, sitting down on the bed. "Uh… I guess that is a problem."

Still frowning, he added, "He might try to talk us out of it."

I shrugged, unaffected. "So? When have we ever listened to anybody else? This is what we want."

"Right," he nodded, resuming his pacing. "It's just… He's my brother. My *twin*. No matter how much I might act like I don't care, I *do*."

"Sit down," I told him, patting the space beside me on the bed. After a few more paces he did. "Stop worrying. We'll go out there and tell him together."

"He's going to be pissed," he warned. "Especially over the fact that mom and dad aren't here."

"We can wait," I whispered, that thought filling me with sadness. "If that's what you want."

"No, absolutely not." He shook his head roughly, rubbing his hands on his jeans. He reached up and removed the baseball cap he wore, spinning it around in his hands before putting it back on, but backwards this time. "This is what I want. I want you to be my wife and I think I might die if I have to wait."

I rolled my eyes, bumping my shoulder against his in jest. "Don't be so dramatic."

He wrinkled his nose and grumbled, "I'm not being dramatic."

I wanted to argue that matter further, but before I could speak he was standing up and heading for the door with a purposeful stride. I guessed he'd made up his mind that it was now or never.

I hurried after him and we found Maddox, Emma, Ezra, and Hayes all hanging out in the living room part of the suite watching TV.

Mathias stood directly in front of the TV, diverting their attention.

"I have something I need to talk to you about." He looked right at Maddox when he spoke. "All of you," he added, his gaze landing on each one of them.

I stepped forward and wrapped my arms around in his, leaning against him.

"What's going on?" Maddox turned the TV off and gave us his full attention.

Mathias wrapped his arm around my waist and cleared his throat. Taking a deep breath the words tumbled out. "A few days ago I asked Remy to marry me and she said yes."

Everybody looked shocked. Seriously, all of their mouths fell open and they looked at us like we were some exotic species they'd never seen before.

Maddox recovered first. "Uh… Wow." He shook his head. "Congratulations guys, that's awesome." He stood, as if to come towards us.

"That's not all." Mathias held up a hand.

"You're having a baby too?!" Emma shrieked so loud that my ears began to ring.

At the word baby I flinched and felt Mathias stiffen against me. "Uh… no. No babies."

"Oh." Emma frowned, looking devastated.

"We're getting married."

Maddox's lips twitched and then he began to laugh. "That's typically what an engagement means." He glanced towards Emma with a wistful look, as if he was imagining what it would be like to be married to her.

"No," Mathias shook his head, "what I mean is, we're getting married today."

He held his head high, his shoulders squared as he braced himself for whatever his twin might say. Mathias didn't care what many people thought of him, but his brother's opinion was one that mattered.

Maddox looked shocked, as did the others—even more shocked than when Mathias said we were engaged.

"But mom and dad aren't here," Maddox argued. "You know mom will be devastated if she misses this."

"I'm doing this for me, not mom and dad."

"Dammit Mathias!" Maddox roared, standing up with his fists clasped at his sides. Emma looked flabbergasted at his sudden outburst and I got the impression that Maddox didn't get mad about much. "Sometimes you have to think about other people besides yourself!"

Mathias grasped my hand and positioned his body slightly in front of me, like he was protecting me. "I don't expect you to understand our decision, but this is what we're doing. We're getting married today whether you like it or not."

Maddox glared at his twin, anger rolling off of him in waves. "You are the most stubborn, arrogant, asshole I've ever met."

Mathias shrugged. "You're not telling me anything I don't know." Despite his carefree attitude I could tell his brother's words had upset him.

"I can't believe you." Maddox's jaw was clenched so tight I was surprised we couldn't hear the grinding of his teeth. Glancing at his watch, he muttered, "Call mom. Before you do this. Call her. And I really hope to God that she makes you feel guilty as fuck."

I watched Mathias' lips twitch. "You never say fuck."

"Yeah well, I'm really fucking pissed off and I guess you're rubbing off on me."

Mathias shook his head. "I'll call her," he promised, turning to leave the room with a tight hold on my hand. Glancing back at his brother, he added, "I don't expect you, or any of you," he added to the rest of the group, "to come but I…" He cleared his throat. "I'd really like for you to be there."

With a nod he ducked out of the room, dragging me along behind him.

Once we were safely in the bedroom he collapsed on the bed. He reached into his back pocket, his fingers fumbling as he pulled out a pack of cigarettes and a lighter.

"I don't think you're allowed to do that in here," I warned.

He glared at me, the cigarette dangling between his pursed lips. "I'm Mathias Fucking Wade and—"

"'I can do whatever the fuck I want,'" I mimed his tone.

He cracked a smile before lighting the cigarette and taking a drag. Blowing out the smoke he watched it circle up to the ceiling before disappearing. "Well, that went about as well as I thought it would."

"Maddox is right, you know," I whispered, fearing his wrath—and sure enough his eyes were cold as ice when they landed on mine. "Your parents should be here. Hell, so should my grandma and my parents… although my dad would probably try to kill you," I mused, shrugging apologetically.

"Are you saying we should wait?" His words were laced with anger.

"No," I shook my head. "I'm just as ready as you are. All I'm saying is, I get where Maddox is coming from and our family is going to be pissed at us."

Mathias shrugged, propping his head up on a pile of fluffy pillows. "Most people are always mad at me for something. I'm used to it."

"Yeah, but your mom and dad also love you."

He turned his head towards me and rolled his eyes. "I've been nothing but a pain in their ass."

"So? You're a pain in mine too, but I still love you."

He stared at me for a moment. "I also fuck you. There's a difference."

I snorted. "Are you saying I love you for the sex?"

"Well, no," he frowned. "I don't really know what I'm saying."

"Obviously," I muttered.

Putting out the cigarette in a decorative vase on the side table he then crossed his arms behind his head. "What time is it?" He asked.

"Ten," I replied.

"Would you be opposed to getting married tomorrow evening instead of tonight?"

"Uh…" My brows furrowed. "What are you thinking?"

"Postponing would give me enough time to get my mom and dad on a plane—your grandma too."

I smiled at that, nodding eagerly. I would be fine with it only being the two of us standing in a chapel somewhere, but it felt *right* having our family there. It made it more real.

"What about your mom and dad?" He asked.

I frowned, thinking of them and my brother. I shook my head, hoping he didn't notice how much my next words bothered me. "They wouldn't understand."

"Rem." His voice deepened as he reached for me. He pulled me down onto the bed beside him. I tossed one of my legs over his and he wrapped his arms around me. My hand rested on his chest as I curled against him. His heat warmed me, instantly filling my body with calmness. "I'm sorry."

"Don't be," I whispered. "I love you and that's all that matters."

He kissed the top of my head and my eyes closed as a happy sigh escaped my parted lips. "I'm one lucky bastard."

I poked his side, grinning. "And don't you ever forget it."

"Never." He pressed closer to me, lowering his lips to mine. The kiss was slow and deep, making my toes curl. Kissing my forehead he pulled away and sat up, grabbing his phone. "I have some phone calls to make."

I nodded, my heart beginning to race with anticipation. Be it today, or tomorrow, the thought of marrying him filled me with the kind of excitement I so very rarely felt. I knew that if this was any other person I wouldn't feel this way.

This was once in a lifetime—and I got it twice, because I got a second chance.

"You can stop glaring at me like you want to kill me." Mathias snapped at his twin when we joined the others at the hotel restaurant for dinner.

After making all the arrangements for his mom, dad, and my grandma to fly out to Vegas we'd emerged from the bedroom to find that everyone else had left. I knew that pissed Mathias off, but he managed to keep his anger tamped down. I saw now that it might still be unleashed.

"We're getting married *tomorrow*," he emphasized the word, "and mom and dad will be here *tonight*."

"They're coming?" Maddox asked, brightening with this news.

Mathias nodded and looked at me before speaking. "We agreed that it would be best to have them here."

"Good." Maddox plucked at the collar of his shirt like it was suddenly too tight.

Mathias sighed, grabbing my hand beneath the table. I knew he wouldn't say it, but he was relieved to have Maddox back on his side.

A waiter appeared to take our orders and I picked the first thing I saw on the menu. I wasn't very hungry. I was nervous to see them perform tonight. I knew it would be a vastly different experience seeing them on a concert stage versus hanging around in the recording studio. But I was actually the most nervous for the questions I might be asked.

On our way to the restaurant I saw someone reading a magazine.

My face was on the cover, with the caption *Who is she?*

I'd known going into this that my life was going to change, but imagining it and seeing it were two different things.

"Are you okay?" Mathias whispered in my ear, picking up on my distress.

"Yeah," I nodded. I didn't want to worry him with my silly fears. I was strong and I'd get through this. Nothing knocked me down for long, not even my own self-doubt.

He looked at me doubtfully, but since the others were around he didn't press the issue.

Emma waved her hand, trying to catch my attention. I raised my chin in her direction to let her know I was listening.

"Since y'all are postponing until tomorrow this means we can get you a wedding dress."

I blanched. "Uh… I was just going to wear jeans."

Emma looked like she'd been shot she was so shocked. Her eyes threatened to bug out of her head. "Jeans? You can't wear jeans to your wedding! I mean, I'm all for non-traditional but there has to be some sort of dress."

I hung my head. Shit.

I glanced at Mathias. "Are you wearing a tux?"

"Yes," he replied.

"Of course," I sighed. I shouldn't have expected any less since he was always dressed impeccably.

"We might be getting married in Vegas," he tapped his chin, "but this won't be a typical Vegas wedding. We're definitely not getting married by an Elvis impersonator."

"Does that mean we're going to the drive-thru chapel?"

He snorted. "I love that you sound excited by that idea, but no. I have something else in mind."

"What is this 'something else' you have in mind?" I coaxed, rubbing my hand up his thigh.

He grabbed my roaming hand and put it back in my lap. I pouted—not even caring if someone noticed my downturned lip.

"This might be a last minute wedding, but it's still going to be a wedding," he promised.

"You're making my brain hurt," I grumbled.

Everybody else was watching the volley of our conversation with rapt attention.

"Just don't worry about it. I have it taken care of."

Of course he did—and I wasn't surprised he wasn't going to tell me more than that. Typical Mathias. I was secretly glad that I didn't have to be a part of whatever he was planning. He was better at that kind of stuff than me. All I wanted to do was show up—and I guess now wear a dress.

Talk of our wedding ceased and the guys lapsed into conversation about the concert and what songs they were performing.

Mathias chatted easily with them, even throwing in a smile or two. Based on the reactions from the other three guys it was easy to guess that this was a new development. I knew Mathias was usually extremely quiet around others—and when he did open his mouth it was usually to say something rude.

Emma asked me questions about which kind of dress I thought I'd like. I tried to answer as best as I could, but when I proved useless she finally smiled and said, "We'll go to a store and take a look around. You can try on a few and we can even Facetime my best friend. She's a stylist and has her own store now, so she might be able to help us. She's better at this kind of thing than I am."

After we finished our dinner we were ushered out of the restaurant by a group of body guards, through the lobby, and out into a waiting limo.

"A limo?" I asked Mathias, arching a brow as I climbed inside. Lights flashed around us and the roar of the crowd was deafening—and I knew it was only going to get worse once we arrived at the venue.

"It was the only thing large enough so that we didn't have to take separate vehicles."

He was right about that, but I still found the massive machine to be obnoxious.

"What's this concert for?" I asked him.

We sat at the end of the limo in front of the divider that separated us from the driver. Hayes sat to our left, Ezra to our right, and Emma and Maddox occupied the seats in front of us. There was still enough room for a few more people.

"It's a benefit concert so there are a few more artists here. We're all playing two songs," he replied, adjusting his bow tie. I *really* liked that bow tie. I hoped he wore it tomorrow too.

"So what's the cause this is for?" I was prepared for him to snap and tell me I was asking too many questions, but he didn't.

"Kids with cancer."

I snorted. Why did they pick Vegas for this? Also, I couldn't help thinking of the little girl at the restaurant who he'd been so kind too. So many kids had to suffer and it was heartbreaking.

As if answering my unspoken question, he said, "I think they chose Vegas because so many people are here on break for Christmas and New Year's. Drunk people like to spend money."

I snorted at his serious tone. Sobering, I said, "I can't believe it's almost Christmas. Wasn't it just Thanksgiving?"

He chuckled, leaning over to graze his fingers along my collarbone, and eliciting a shiver from me. "Feels that way, but we've been a little too wrapped up in each other."

I guessed that did explain it.

The limo came to a stop and a moment later the door opened.

Before we even got out of the car the flashes and clicks of cameras was nearly overwhelming—not to mention the screaming.

Mathias held tightly to my hand like he was afraid I might get sucked into the crowd and lost forever.

People screamed the guys' names, thrusting out scraps of paper and boobs for them to sign. Ezra and Maddox stopped to sign a few autographs, Mathias ignored everyone like they didn't even exist, and Hayes dove after the boobs with a grin on his face like he'd just one the lottery. Maybe he had. The Boob Lottery.

We were ushered through a backdoor and then into a large waiting area. Willow Creek was written on a piece of paper and taped to the door.

"Who are the other artists?" I asked anyone that would answer me.

Hayes began naming different bands, ticking each one off on his finger. There were four other bands besides Willow Creek performing and each one was a big name.

There was still an hour before they went out so everybody settled into the room. Maddox sat in the corner knitting—yes, knitting—Hayes tuned his guitar, Ezra napped on the couch, and Mathias was busy fixing his hair.

I joined Emma in the corner where she sat on the floor.

"I can't believe I'm getting married," I admitted to her. "I never thought I would."

Her smile was kind. "There are a lot of things we all think we'll never do, and then life throws you a curveball and you see that the things you didn't want are exactly what you need." Clearing her throat, she added, "As long as you're happy that's all that matters."

"I am happy," I nodded, rubbing my suddenly sweaty palms on my ripped jeans. "So," I turned to her, "what was your curveball?"

She sighed dreamily and smiled at Maddox. "Him."

I liked her answer.

Because mine was the same.

Just a different guy.

It wasn't long until a man walked by the door and said, "Thirty minutes." Then, "Fifteen."

When it was five minutes until Willow Creek went on stage they were ushered out of the room. Maddox stopped to give Emma a kiss and I was surprised when Mathias did the same with me.

His hand was a steady weight against my waist. He lowered his voice to a whisper. "It makes me happy to know that you're going to be standing out there watching me."

With those words he pulled away and hurried after the guys.

Emma and I lagged behind talking while the guys got wired up or whatever it was they were doing.

I gave Mathias a smile and thumbs up before he stepped out on the stage. It was an awkward gesture, but he grinned and tipped his head in my direction, so at least he seemed to appreciate it.

Emma and I stood off to the side of the stage, against the wall so that we weren't in the way of the people working.

I watched Mathias walk up to the microphone and the others took their places as well.

He spoke to the crowd for a moment, working them into a frenzy.

Mathias might not have been the best people pleaser, but when it came to the band he knew how to put his game face on and make people fall in love with him.

The crowd chanted, "Willow Creek!" over and over again to the point that when he started to sing I doubted they even heard him.

Where Emma and I stood the view of the stage was rather awkward, but I wasn't going to complain. We were incredibly close to the stage, but positioned to the left and a little behind them.

"They're breathtaking, aren't they?" She asked, swaying to the music. The purple hue of the stage lights made her face glow with an ethereal light.

"That they are." I agreed wholeheartedly.

In the blink of an eye their set came to a close and they drifted off the stage.

Their clothes and hair were damp with sweat, but they all smiled victoriously like they'd just run a marathon and come in first place.

Mathias brushed his hair away from his eyes with a sweep of his long fingers. "So, what did you think?" He asked, looking down at me.

"You were amazing. So you think you can sing to me all of the time?" I joked.

"Our life can be one big cheesy musical."

He tossed his head back and his laughter echoed around us. It didn't escape my notice how his brother, Emma, Hayes, and Ezra looked at him like he was a stranger when they saw him laugh. Slinging his arm over my shoulder he guided me back to the room we'd been in before. "How about I stick to singing you to sleep?"

"He sings her to sleep?" I heard Ezra whisper under his breath behind us. I snorted and hastily tried to turn the noise into a cough.

"Yes, I do," Mathias chimed, having heard his band mate.

"Who the fuck are you?" Ezra asked, shaking his head so that his black curls bounced.

"The new and improved Mathias," he joked, releasing me from his hold.

They had some clean clothes stashed in a duffel bag so each of the guys took the time to change.

There was nothing left for us to do there so we headed outside and into the waiting limo. There was still a crowd but it had thinned out a lot.

"I think we should go dress shopping," Emma announced.

I looked at her like she was crazy. "It's after midnight."

Now it was her turn to look at me like I was the crazy person. "This is Vegas. It only comes to life at night."

Across from me Maddox frowned and when I looked at Mathias he had the same look on his face. They both spoke at the same time, saying the same thing. "I don't want you out at night by yourselves."

Emma and I looked at each other, both breaking out into laughter.

"Stop laughing," Mathias groaned.

Maddox shook his head, rubbing his chin to hide his smile.

"Ezra will go with us." Emma pointed to the bass player currently sprawled out on three seats.

"Me?" He pointed at his t-shirt clad chest. "Why me?"

"Because I know you're just going to go back to the hotel and do nothing," she reasoned.

"What about Hayes?" He swung his arm in the direction of the giant guitar player. The guy had to be well over six-foot-four, but he was thin and lean.

"I'm sure Hayes wants to go out."

"Mhmm," Ezra hummed in agreement, "therefore he can go out with you. I'm tired."

"And awfully cranky," she added on. "What's wrong with you?"

"Nothing," he grumbled, looking away.

She clearly didn't believe him, but let it go. "I think Hayes' idea of going out is to a club, not wedding dress shopping."

"You've got that right." Hayes finally piped in.

"Maddox and I can go with you," Mathias added.

"No!" Emma cried, leaning forward like she was ready to lunge at him. "You're the groom, therefore you can't see the dress beforehand. Besides, you two can have some twin bonding time or whatever."

Mathias rolled his eyes and huffed a sigh. "I don't see what difference it makes. I'm going to see the dress at some point, and then I'm going to rip it off of her later."

"We don't need the details." Maddox held up a warning hand, but was fighting a smile.

Mathias shrugged. "Don't be such a fucking priss. Everybody knows what happens after the wedding and it isn't playing Scrabble."

I laughed, burying my face into the curve of his shoulder to muffle the sound.

"Fine, fine, fine." Ezra sat up, his messy black hair sticking up wildly around his head. "I'll go with them so you two don't have to worry and you," he pointed at Hayes, "can go have fun."

"Thanks, Ez." Maddox reached forward, clapping Ezra on the shoulder.

Ezra finally cracked a smile, his dark brown eyes lightening. "Yeah, well, you guys are right. They shouldn't be out on the streets alone. Not here."

The limo came to a stop at the hotel and after a quick kiss Mathias ducked out along with Hayes and Maddox.

Emma spoke to the driver, telling him where we wanted to go. A moment later we pulled away from the hotel.

Ezra stretched out once more on the seat, crooking his arm over his eyes. "I could be sleeping right now. Instead, I'm going to look at wedding dresses. Remind me, how did I get talked into this?"

"Because you love me." Emma laughed, kicking his knee with her foot.

He grumbled, but smiled in her direction. Yeah, yeah. I guess I do."

"I'm extremely lovable," she agreed.

The two bickered back and forth for a while like siblings.

It didn't take us long to arrive at the dress shop. I could tell from the outside alone that this place was going to be crazy expensive. Before I could tell Emma we needed to find another store she held out a shiny black credit card.

"Mathias gave me his card. Don't worry about it."

I still didn't breathe a sigh of relief. It seemed unfair for Mathias to be spending a ridiculous amount of money on a dress I'd wear once. Not to mention the expensive ring he'd already put on my finger, and there was no telling what he had planned for tomorrow.

"Don't worry about it," Emma repeated as Ezra headed for the door of the building. "Seriously. He just wants you to be happy and…" She blushed. "He also said the dress was for him too—he told me to make sure you got something sexy so that all he can think about is… uh… all the ways he… uh…" Her cheeks went from pink to red. "…wants to fuck you… His words. Not mine."

I laughed at poor Emma, following behind her and Ezra.

Emma pulled out her phone and glanced at me over her shoulder. "Do you mind if I Facetime Sadie?"

"Sadie?" I asked, confused.

"Yeah, my best friend. The stylist."

"Oh, yeah. Sounds good." I shook my head, noticing the way Ezra's whole body tensed at the mention of Sadie's name.

"What's wrong with him?" I asked, pointing to where Ezra stood broodingly against the wall with his arms crossed over his lean chest.

She followed my gaze and frowned. "He's not normally so forlorn," she shrugged, "but…" She paused, as if she wasn't sure how much she should say. Finally she sighed and seemed to decide to tell me the whole thing. "He became really good friends with Sadie after Maddox and I started dating—I guess you could almost say they're best friends. They bonded over their interests and then Maddox and I kind of ditched them a lot, which forced them together. Anyway," she took a deep breath before pushing forward, "Sadie's been dating this one guy, Braden, and he's kind of an asshole. I don't like him and Ezra definitely hates him. He's just a jerk and he doesn't treat her very well, but he asked her to marry him over Thanksgiving and she said yes. Ezra thinks she's absolutely stupid, and said as much, so she's not speaking to him right now. I think she's being dumb too, but Sadie always does what Sadie wants." She shrugged, trying to act like she didn't care, but I could tell she did.

"Well, that sucks," I said, for lack of anything else to say.

She nodded, and her eyes looked haunted. The guy must've been a real tool. I really hoped her friend got away from him before she ended up married with a kid.

"Enough of that." She waved her phone around. "Sadie will want to help."

"Isn't it like four in the morning there?" I asked before she could call her friend.

"Crap," she put her phone away, "you're right. Sadie will be pissed if I wake her up. I guess you're stuck with only my help. I'm really not good at this kind of stuff, but I can pass my opinion."

"Sounds good," I agreed.

A woman approached to help us and proceeded to ask me a million questions about what kind of dress I wanted. She very quickly learned I had no idea.

The only word I could give her was, "Sexy." It was what Mathias wanted and me too. I didn't want the typical wedding dress. I wanted something daring.

She nodded and said, "I think I know just the dress."

She dashed off through a door, mumbling that she'd be back in a minute.

"We need a dress for you too," I told Emma.

"Me?" She pointed at herself, looking shocked.

"Yeah, you," I laughed. "You're going to be my bridesmaid."

"Me?" She repeated. "Are you sure?"

"Absolutely."

I didn't know Emma well, but I really liked her. And now that Mathias and I were tying the knot Emma and I would be spending a lot of time together. I felt that given enough time we could become really good friends. Maybe even best friends. I'd never had a best friend before. Yeah, Lana and I had been friends in high school, but I'd never confided in her the way best friends did. I wasn't a very trusting person, but there was something about Emma that made me feel instantly at ease. I knew I could tell her something personal and she wouldn't go blabbing to anyone, not even Maddox.

"Wow," she smiled. "I'm honored."

"You can pick whatever you like," I told her, waving my hand to encompass the store. "It's not like I have anything in mind."

"But it's your wedding."

I shook my head, smiling. "That might be true, but I don't care about the details. All I care about is the fact that the man I love will be waiting for me at the end of the aisle."

Her smile lit her whole face. "That is the important part. A lot of people seem to lose sight of that."

I nodded in agreement.

The sales lady returned a few minutes later with three dresses in garment bags tossed over her arm.

"Dressing rooms are back here," she nodded, "follow me."

Ezra grunted, looking extremely uncomfortable. "I'll stay here."

Emma followed me back to the dressing area and took a seat while the woman ushered me into one of the closed off rooms.

I undressed and she helped me into the first gown. I glanced at it in the mirror, my eyes widening.

"Do you like it?" She asked.

"I love it," I breathed. I ran my fingers along the lacey fabric, admiring my reflection in the mirror.

The dress was stunning. But it was also daring and sexy, just like I had asked for. The top was done in an intricate lacey design with a nude colored background. It had short-sleeves, but somehow it didn't look stuffy and added to the sexiness of the dress. It dipped down low in the chest area, showing off my cleavage, but not enough to be trashy.

It was then accented with a thick gold belt.

The bottom of the dress was a loose tulle-like fabric with a high slit on the side. In the back there was a short train.

I also liked that it was cream colored instead of stark white.

I spun around, looking at the dress from all angles.

I could tell the saleslady was pleased that I loved it.

"Would you like to show your friend?" She asked.

I nodded, unable to form words at the moment.

She opened the door and I stepped out so that Emma could see.

She gasped, her hands flying up to cover her mouth. "Oh my God," she gasped. "Please tell me you love it. It's… Wow."

I stood up on the podium, looking in the mirrors once more. "I think I'm in love."

Emma squealed, clapping her hands together.

I turned towards her and frowned. "Do you think it's wrong to fall in love with the first one?"

"Sometimes the first one is the right one."

Her words hit me hard as I realized how true they were.

Mathias was the first guy I ever loved, and he'd be the last.

The same was true for her and Maddox.

Any worries I had about choosing the first dress I tried on evaporated.

"I'll take it." I told the saleslady.

"Excellent."

She took me back into the room and helped me out of the dress.

"We'll have this dry cleaned and sent to your hotel by tomorrow afternoon. Just leave us with your information."

I nodded. "I'd also like to get a bridesmaid dress for my friend.

"Of course," she smiled. "What do you have in mind?"

"Something gold or champagne colored."

I hadn't had anything in mind for Emma's dress before, but since my dress had the gold belt I thought it would be nice to have her dress in that color tone.

"I'll be back with a few options."

She took my dress and slipped out of the room while I finished putting my clothes back on.

"She's going to grab some dresses for you." I told Emma when I emerged from the room.

"This is so exciting! I can't believe Mathias is going to be the first to get married."

I laughed. "Yeah, I'm pretty sure everyone thought that would be you and Maddox."

She smiled, giving a slight shrug. "He would've married me years ago if I let him, but I wanted to wait. We met so young and I wanted us to have fun being a couple before we put such a heavy label on our relationship."

"That's wise," I agreed.

"I think I'm ready now, though," she added.

"Have you told him that?" I asked, sitting down beside her.

Her nose crinkled. "No."

The saleslady breezed up to us with a selection of dresses. I immediately vetoed a few, but one in particular caught my eye. "This one," I said.

It was an elegant gold sequined dress that shimmered when the light hit it. It was in a similar style as my gown, with slightly longer sleeves and no slit. I thought it would be gorgeous on Emma, with her fair complexion, freckles, and wild blonde hair.

"That one is my favorite too," Emma whispered.

This time it was her turn to be ushered into one of the closed off dressing rooms. I sat waiting patiently.

When she stepped out of the room I gasped.

"You like it?" She asked, spinning in a circle.

"It's perfect!" I couldn't hide my smile or the excitement I felt.

This was really happening.

And while I wouldn't have minded it just being Mathias and I, it was even better knowing the ones we'd love would be there.

I knew it wouldn't be a lavish wedding, and that was fine by me, because it was still going to be perfect for us.

After paying for the dresses, and leaving the information for the hotel so they could deliver, we headed out.

"That was surprisingly fast." Ezra commented, as we walked down the street to where the limo was parked waiting for us. "I thought we'd be there for a few hours."

"I'm not like most girls," I quipped.

He chuckled, flashing me a genuine smile. Bumping my shoulder playfully, he said, "I know. You couldn't be like most girls in order to deal with all of Mathias' bullshit."

I laughed in agreement.

"I want you to know that all of us think you're really good for him," Ezra confessed, his voice dropping low. "I don't think any of us have ever seen him so happy. So… uh… well, thanks."

We slipped into the limo and I stared at Ezra, not knowing what to say.

He stretched out on the seat and closed his eyes, saving me from having to reply. "I'm going to sleep," he announced.

"We'll be back at the hotel in like ten minutes," Emma cried.

Ezra yawned. "And that's ten minutes of sleep I can have. Now shush."

Emma shook her head and mouthed, "Boys," to me.

I was with Ezra though. I suddenly felt absolutely exhausted and all I wanted to do was go to bed.

When we arrived at the hotel the three of us made our way clumsily to the elevator. It seemed the need to sleep had finally caught up to Emma as well.

I swore Ezra fell back to sleep standing in the elevator, but when the door slid open he promptly strode off towards his room.

"Goodnight," Emma chimed, waving at me before walking in the direction of the room she shared with Maddox.

I stopped off in the kitchen and grabbed a bottle of water.

The bedroom was dark when I opened the door, but the sheets rustled and a light soon flicked on.

"Hey," Mathias greeted me, his voice thick with sleep. "You're back. Did you find a dress?"

"I did," I smiled, leaning over to kiss him. He groaned low in his throat at the feel of my lips and cupped the nape of neck, deepening the kiss. "You're going to love it." I told him when he finally released me.

He looked me up and down, his eyes darkening to the color of storm clouds. "Not as much as I love what's underneath."

"Pig," I scolded, taking my shirt off and throwing it at him.

He deflected it easily, his eyes roaming my body hungrily as I changed into my pajamas.

"Don't get any ideas, Wade," I warned, peeking at him over my shoulder. "I'm exhausted."

He pouted like a five year old, and instead of it making him look silly he was made even more irresistible. Damn him.

I padded into the bathroom to brush my teeth and returned to bed.

He lifted the sheet up and I slipped in beside him. I was instantly cradled against his large body.

"I missed you." He whispered the words so low it was like he didn't want me to hear them. "It's the craziest thing, even when I know you're coming back and won't be gone long, I still miss you. While you're gone there's this ache in my chest that won't go away." Kissing the top of my head, he murmured, "I ached like that for seven whole years, Remy. Seven. It was like my own personal hell."

Tears pricked my eyes at his confession. "It was hell for me too."

In those seven years my hatred had tried to overshadow my love for him. I'd still missed him though, against all logic. I'd ached and pined for him. I'd tried so hard to extinguish the flame that burned bright inside me for him, but I never could—and if I had succeeded we wouldn't be here right now. Nothing would've been able to stop me from my plan to hurt him. But love is a funny thing, once it's given you can't take it back. It's forever, no matter what happens. You might move on, but at the end of the day you can't change the fact that you loved someone and they'll always own a piece of your heart. Mathias owned all of my pieces.

"Let's never hurt each other again." His voice was a soft sigh in the dark. "Deal?"

"Deal."

Craziness ensued from the moment I woke up. Mathias and the guys bowed out, citing that they were working to get everything set up for the wedding.

That left Emma and me alone.

"I hope you don't want help with your hair or makeup," she told me over breakfast, "because I suck at that."

I assured her I could manage. I didn't bother telling her that Mathias had already offered to hire a hair and makeup artist, but I refused. I didn't want today to turn into a circus.

Time passed in a blur and before I could blink it was evening and time to finish getting ready.

Emma had already helped me into my dress and I now stood freshening my makeup.

She poked her head into the doorway of the bathroom.

"Maddox just texted me and said to meet them in the ballroom. There will be bodyguards waiting for us when we get off the elevator."

I frowned. "Is it crazy down there or something?"

She sighed. "Someone from the hotel tipped off the media that there was going to be a high profile wedding here tonight, so they've swarmed the hotel like the vultures they are. Apparently they're camped out in the lobby." She rolled her eyes and glanced down at her phone. Looking back up at me, she said, "You'd think they'd have something better to do than stalk famous people."

I added a pale pink gloss to my lips and another swipe of mascara. My makeup was understated, but I didn't want an overly dramatic look. My hair was simple too. I'd curled the normally straight strands into loose waves.

"You look gorgeous," Emma smiled, leaning against the doorjamb.

"Thank you."

"Are you ready?" She asked, checking her phone again.

I took a deep breath and smiled at my reflection. "Yes."

I was nervous, but also incredibly excited.

I followed her out of the suite and into the elevator.

My heart thumped so loud that I heard every beat ringing clearly in my ears like it was counting down the seconds until Mathias became my husband.

I never thought I would be the kind of person to get emotional over this sort of thing but I was seconds away from bursting into tears—happy ones and some sad ones too, because Hope wasn't here to see this.

Emma and I were silent on the ride down in the elevator. I think she knew that I didn't want to talk.

As soon as the elevator doors opened the two hulking bodyguards turned and spotted us. They managed to block us with their large bodies as paparazzi scrambled to take a photo and hotel management yelled at them to get off the property.

We were quickly ushered out of the space and down a hallway.

Tall wooden double doors came into view and my heart raced impossibly faster.

I knew that Mathias was behind that door.

Waiting for me.

This was it.

A woman I'd never seen before handed Emma and me a bouquet of flowers.

"Ready?" The woman asked.

Emma looked to me for confirmation.

"Yes." The word was barely a breath.

The doors swung open and Emma stepped forward, gliding down the aisle.

Then the music changed and that was my cue.

I took a step and halted, taking in the magnificent room.

The ballroom had been sectioned of with thick sheets of gold hued fabric, creating a more intimate space.

The only guests seated were Hayes, Ezra, Karen, Paul, and my grandma.

I knew to most people that was hardly an appropriate amount of guests to have at a wedding, but for us it was just right.

The lights were dimmed and the aisle was covered in white rose petals. For someone that claimed to be so unromantic Mathias was actually quite good at it.

At that moment my eyes landed on him and everything else—the room, the music, and even the people—ceased to exist.

It was only the two us tethered together by a connection so intense that even if we lived a hundred years we'd never understand it.

I felt weightless as my feet carried me up to the altar where he stood waiting for me.

I knew people always talked about the bride taking away the breath of the groom, but right now I'd say we were equally breathless.

His broad shoulders were accentuated by the cut of the black tuxedo. It was adorned with a bow tie—which made me smile—and I was pretty sure he was probably hiding some suspenders under there. He was right, while I might make fun of him, I really did love those suspenders.

Emma took the bouquet of flowers from me and Mathias clasped our hands together.

Somehow over the pounding of my heart I managed to hear the words the minister—or whoever he was—spoke. We took our turns saying our vows and when he slipped the simple silver band on my finger I knew I'd never felt more complete than I did right now.

My whole life, the good and the bad, had all been leading to this one single moment.

I knew, in Mathias, I had found my home.

Emma handed me my ring for Mathias and I shook my head, beaming at him.

He truly had thought of everything.

He didn't think he was a Prince, or a knight in shining armor, or anything worthy of a title or praise.

But he was all those things and more to me.

I slid the ring onto his finger, staring at the thick band that symbolized our love and commitment to each other.

I was filled with such joy that I thought I might burst. I never knew it was possible to be this inexplicably happy.

Something was said about kissing the bride and then Mathias took my face between his hands, lowering his lips to mine. I clutched at his arms to keep myself upright. I really thought I might pass out.

His lips glided against mine and I moaned into his mouth.

With a chuckle he broke the kiss, placing one last tender kiss to the end of my nose.

He leaned his forehead against mine, his hands still cupping my face tenderly.

"Hello, wife."

"Hello, husband," I replied breathlessly.

His tongue flicked out to moisten his lips and he kissed me softly once more.

He took a step back and his hand slid down to hold my mine.

Facing our family and friends we were introduced as, "Mr. and Mrs. Wade."

I smiled, happiness fluttering through my body. Normally I'd argue that it was archaic for the woman to have to take the man's name, but I didn't care.

I was proud to be a Wade now and even prouder to be his.

# CHAPTER TWENTY-EIGHT

Since there were so few of us Mathias arranged for all of us to have a nice dinner versus a reception.

"I can't believe you were really going to do this without me here." Grandma glared at me from across the table.

"I'm sorry," I shrugged, leaning against Mathias. Since the moment we'd said 'I do' we had yet to cease touching one another in some way. "You're here, that's what matters."

"And I have him to thank for that." She pointed her fork at Mathias.

Mathias smiled at her. In fact, he hadn't stopped smiling since his eyes landed on me when I stepped into the ballroom. I couldn't recall a time I had ever seen him this happy.

"Yes, ma'am." He tipped his head in her direction.

"See, he's a good boy, and you're just a disgrace."

I sighed. My grandma was always going to love to poke fun at me.

"Not that we're not thrilled," Paul, Mathias' foster dad, spoke up, "but what made you guys decide to do this?"

I looked at Mathias and he looked at me.

Shrugging, Mathias said, "It was going to happen one day. Why wait?"

Paul nodded, absorbing Mathias' words.

After chatting for at least an hour everybody stood to head off to their rooms.

Mathias grasped my wrist, brushing my hair away from my ear so that he could whisper, "I got us our own room."

"Why?" I asked. "We have plenty of space in the penthouse."

He shook his head and his breath fanned across my cheek, making me shiver. "I plan on hearing you scream my name all night long and nobody but me is going to hear that."

I shivered again. I nodded, having momentarily lost my voice.

Before we could head off in the direction of our own room my grandma cleared her throat. "Can I talk to you?" She asked me.

I glanced at Mathias and he waved his hand in her direction and walked off to give us some space.

"What's wrong?" I asked.

She stared at Mathias over my shoulder and then back at me. "Does he know?"

My heart stopped beating in my chest.

It was one thing knowing in my heart that it was wrong to keep Hope a secret, it was another hearing the complete disapproval in my grandma's voice. She looked at me with angry, accusing eyes.

"He has a right to know, Remy."

I didn't know how my grandma could possibly know that I'd never told Mathias about Hope. But then again, she always did seem to have some kind of freaky telepathy.

I swallowed past the lump now lodged deep in my throat. "I know." My voice cracked. "Fuck, I know," I groaned. I buried my face in my hands, trying to force back the sting in my eyes.

"That baby was his too." She reached up and pulled my hands from my face, her grip surprisingly strong despite her frail frame. Her eyes were now filled with sadness. "I know it killed you, pretty girl, but this is the kind of secret that can destroy a relationship and now…" She trailed off.

"A marriage," I supplied for her.

She nodded, patting my cheek. "Tell him. Keeping this a secret will tear you apart. You're a strong woman Remy, but there are some things not even the strongest person can bear to live with. He can handle it. I have faith in the both of you."

I took a deep breath and nodded. "I will. I just… I need some more time." I bent down and wrapped my arms around her. She hugged me back fiercely—like she was trying to infuse her strength into me so that I would be strong enough to do this.

"I love you," she whispered, kissing my cheek. "And I'm so proud of the person you've become."

"Thank you." I hastily wiped away a tear. "I love you too."

She headed off in the direction of the elevators and I turned to Mathias. He'd long ago removed his jacket and was left in a crisp white shirt and, no surprise, suspenders.

"What was that about?" He asked, meeting me halfway.

"She just wanted to give me some marriage advice," I lied.

He chuckled, not picking up on the note of falsity in my tone. "I'm sure that was some epic advice."

"Yeah, it was great," I mumbled, following him to the elevators.

I needed to get my emotions under control before he noticed something was wrong with me. The last thing I wanted to do was ruin tonight for us.

"Care to share?" He asked as the elevator doors slid open. We stepped inside and he pushed the correct floor number, spinning the room keycard between his fingers.

"Oh, um, she'd probably kill me if I told you. It's a secret."

He stared at me, his eyes flitting over my features. His lips turned down into a frown. "Are you okay?"

"Yeah," I assured him quickly. "I'm a little emotional, but okay." That sounded believable, right?

He reached out, brushing his fingers lightly down my cheek. His touch sent little sparks zinging through my body and I closed my eyes, inhaling a ragged breath. I hoped that my body never stopped reacting to him like that.

I absorbed the feeling of his fingers on my face and leaned into his body, my palms flat on his chest.

I feared that when I told him about Hope he'd hate me. That it would truly be the end of us and I would never be touched, held, or loved by him again. I'd lived without him once and it had been the worst kind of torture imaginable. I wasn't sure I could go through that again.

But I also knew that this secret would strangle me from the inside out if I kept it much longer.

*Soon*, I chanted in my head. *I'll tell him soon.*

The elevator doors slid open and he took my hand, leading me down the hallway. He looked at me over his shoulder, a small smile curving his full lips.

He quickly opened the door to the room and yanked me inside. As soon as the door was shut he pushed me against it, his lips coming down to cover my own. A little hum worked its way out of his throat and I gasped when his fingers dug into my thighs, lifting me up. My legs wound around his waist and my fingers grasped at the short strands of his brown hair, holding him to me.

His tongue slid past the seam of my lips and I moaned, my hips rolling against his.

He carried me away from the door and a moment later I found myself sprawled on the bed.

He gazed down at me with dark eyes, licking his lips.

"God, that fucking dress couldn't have been more perfect."

"You like it?" The words came out as a gasp as I struggled to get enough air into my lungs.

"I fucking love it."

He pulled at his bow tie and it dropped to the floor, then the suspenders, and his shirt.

"What? I don't get the whole striptease?" I pouted as he stalked towards me.

He chuckled huskily and leaned down, kissing the spot on my neck where my pulse fluttered like a frightened bird. "I want this to last as long as possible, and if my pants come off now it'll be over before it even starts, and that would be embarrassing." He rose up and winked at me.

I took his face between my hands, the light stubble scratching the palms of my hands. I ran my finger along his bottom lip and his eyes closed as he sighed.

"Fuck," he groaned, his eyes liquid fire when they opened. "This doesn't feel real."

"I know what you mean," I whispered.

He swallowed thickly and kissed me, his hands roaming down my body. One hand landed on my bare thigh and snaked up through the open slit in the dress.

"I've never seen anything more beautiful than you in this dress, standing in front of me, saying 'I do.'" He whispered against my lips before kissing his way down my neck and over the exposed curves of my breasts.

"I t-thought you said you w-weren't romantic," I panted, trying to catch my breath.

His chuckle vibrated against my chest. "I'm not, but I'm working on it. I find that you make me want to do and say things I would normally find repulsive."

"Uh… thanks?"

He stared down at me with a contemplative expression. "It's a good thing, Rem."

"Just shut up." I grabbed his hair between my fingers and hooked a leg around his waist, pushing so that he fell with his back on the bed and I was on top.

Oh, yes.

I covered his mouth with mine, kissing him so deeply that the texture of his lips would be imprinted on mine for days.

My hands snaked down his hard chest and over his abs.

When my lips and tongue followed the journey of my hands he groaned. "Oh, fuck."

I reached for the button on his pants and he grabbed my hand.

"No," he growled, his eyes darkened with desire.

"Yes," I countered, but before I could move any further I found myself flat on my back once more. "That's not fair," I pouted.

"Do I look like I care?" He growled.

He flipped me again, this time so he could undo the zipper on the back of my dress. He slid the dress off and hissed between his teeth when he realized I was only wearing panties and no bra.

"Thank God I didn't know you were wearing practically nothing under this dress or I would've pulled you into a closet and fucked you until you passed out."

"Why don't you just fuck me now?" I asked, rising up on my knees with my hands on the bed. I glanced back at where he stood and gave him a coy smile.

He pursed his lips, running his fingers languidly down my bare back. "Oh, I will, trust me. But first I'm going to make love to you the way a man should his wife."

Oh fuck me. Sweet words from Mathias were better than his dirty talk.

He placed soft kisses down my back and Goosebumps broke out across my skin.

He flipped me over onto my back again, much more gentle with me this time.

He cupped my breasts in his warm hands and my body ached with the desire for more.

He rubbed his thumbs over my nipples before his lips replaced them.

His hands skimmed down my sides, hooking into my underwear and tossing them into a far corner of the room.

Kissing his way down my stomach his lips found my core and my back arched at the feel of his tongue. My fingers wound into his hair and I wasn't sure if my objective was to hold him to me or push him away.

Sweat dampened my skin and little sounds kept escaping between my parted lips.

I gripped the bed covers in my fists so tightly that I was surprised they didn't rip in half.

When I came I screamed his name so loud that I put a hand over my mouth to muffle the sounds.

He rose up, giving me a self-satisfied smile.

I tried to catch my breath, but something told me it was gone for good.

He undid the button on his pants and ever so slowly slid the zipper down.

My eyes followed his movements and my tongue flitted out to wet my lips.

His pants dropped to the floor and my whole body tightened with anticipation of what was to come.

He grabbed a condom and put it on and I nearly cried out with impatience at having to wait a second longer.

I thought he might truly be trying to kill me.

He lowered on top of me, carefully holding his weight above me as he gazed down at me. I pulled him closer to me so that his chest was pressed against mine. I didn't want there to be one inch of my skin not covered by his.

One of my hands rested on his chest, over his steadily beating heart, while the other cupped his neck and I played with the short strands of his hair.

"I love you," I whispered as he pushed inside me.

"I love you more," he breathed.

With every thrust and every breath we continued to whisper *'I love you'*, as if neither one of us wanted to stop hearing the words.

We came together and he held me in his arms before taking me again even slower and sweeter than the first time.

Eventually we passed out from exhaustion, our limbs and hearts tangled together.

Forever intertwined.

"Morning, wife." Mathias smiled, stepping into the bathroom and wrapping his arms around me from behind.

"Husband," I replied, rolling the foreign word around on my tongue.

It seemed strange that we were both so at ease with those words, but I guess when you marry the right person for you they don't seem so scary.

His hands rose and he tugged at the top of the towel I had wrapped around my body from my shower.

"Again?" I asked, looking at him behind me in the mirror and raising a brow. We'd had sex so many times since stepping into our hotel room last night that I had lost count. My body was tired, but when the towel fell from around my body and he cupped my breasts in his hands I couldn't stop the moan that passed through my lips.

His voice was a husky growl in my ear. "I haven't *fucked* my wife yet."

"Ohhh." The word came out as one long moan.

"Bend over," he commanded.

Fuck. Yes.

I did as he asked, my tender breasts pressing against the cool granite countertop. My hands planted on the counter and my feet stayed firmly on the ground.

His fingers skimmed over my ass and his eyes connected with mine in the mirror. "I want you to keep your eyes on the mirror and watch everything I do to you."

My fingers flexed at his words and I spread my legs wider.

I watched with baited breath as he grabbed a condom from his pocket and then dropped his low-slung basketball shorts.

Despite the stiffness in my muscles I still yearned for the feeling of his body connecting with mine.

He thrust inside of me and I cried out. My fingers flexed, reaching for something to hold onto but there was nothing.

"Look at me," he growled, and his hand connected sharply with my ass. He then smoothed his hand over the spot that stung.

I opened my eyes, I hadn't even realized that I closed them, and kept my focus on his in the reflection of the mirror.

I didn't think I'd ever seen anything more erotic than watching him fuck me.

He held my hips in a bruising grip and the veins in his arms stood out against his skin.

He lowered his torso and skimmed his lips over my back.

"Please," I begged.

He reached between us, his fingers rubbing against my clit. Between the sensation of him pounding into me, his roving fingers, and watching him in the mirror, I was a goner within minutes.

He wasn't far behind.

"Remy." He growled my name over and over again. His sweat-dampened body stuck to mine as we sunk to floor, clinging to each other. My legs rested on either side of his and my arms wound around his neck.

I didn't see how I'd find the strength to move.

Mathias rested his head against my neck, his heavy breath tickling the skin of my chest.

He cupped my cheek and lifted my lips to his, kissing me long and deep. When our mouths parted, he whispered, "We have to go."

"Now?" I asked, not caring that there was a slight whining tone to my voice.

"Now," he repeated.

"I don't think I can move," I warned him. "Possibly for the next five years."

He ran his fingers through my slightly damp hair. I was sure it was a wild mess after what we did.

"I can carry you."

"Uh-huh," I muttered.

"Don't doubt me, baby." He growled lowly.

"Never," I said sarcastically.

He pinched my side and I yelped.

"Jerk," I snapped.

"But I'm *your* jerk," he grinned, kissing the end of my nose.

"That's right." I laid my head against his chest and my eyes began to drift closed. We'd been up most of the night, with only a few hours of sleep in-between our love making, so I had no idea how he expected me to get ready to head back to L.A.

I let out a small squeal when my equilibrium shifted and I opened my eyes to see that he was standing up with me cradled in his arms.

"Put me down." I smacked his chest.

"You said you needed to be carried." His gray eyes were lit with laughter.

"I was joking."

"Well, I was serious when I said I'd carry you."

"Are you going to dress me too?" I asked when he sat me down on the bed.

He grabbed a pair of jeans from his suitcase—he'd had all our stuff transferred to this room yesterday without me knowing.

Stepping into the jeans he pulled them up and secured the button and zipper. The knowledge that he was boxer-less beneath those jeans was going to kill me today.

"Stop staring at me," he said, but smiled cockily so I knew he liked the attention.

With a groan I stood from the bed and got dressed. I pulled my messy hair back into a bun and within minutes we were packed and ready to head down to the lobby.

Two bodyguards waited outside our hotel room door.

That was something that would take me a while to get used to.

They grabbed our luggage and flanked us on each side as we headed into the elevators.

"Are you ready?" Mathias asked me, taking my hand and squeezing it tight.

He didn't wear a baseball cap this time, and he didn't offer one to me.

There was no hiding anymore.

I nodded and he pushed the button for the lobby.

With each floor we descended my heart lurched a little.

Everything was about to change.

Despite the fact that it took us no more than three hours to finally reach the front door of Mathias' L.A. home I felt absolutely exhausted.

I dove for the couch, landing flat on my stomach and wrapped my arms around a throw pillow. Shiloh and Percy trotted over and I laughed when they both jumped up on the couch, snuggled together.

"Look who made friends," I called to Mathias, as he strode through the house turning on lights and staring angrily at his phone. "What's wrong?" I asked, not liking the wrinkle marring his brow.

"Fucking Julian," he cursed.

"What happened?" I asked, sitting up.

I pulled my hair out of the bun and let the blonde strands flow around my shoulders.

"It's all over the internet that I married a mystery girl," he rolled his eyes at the title, "and apparently it's creating a shit-ton of trouble for him, but I don't really give a fuck."

"Mathias—" I frowned.

"Don't," he hushed me, pinching the bridge of his nose. He let out a loud groan and sunk down onto the couch with his head in his hands. Leaning back, he growled, "Julian's on his way over, and I really don't want to have to deal with his bullshit."

"What's wrong with us getting married?" I whispered, reaching over to pet Percy since I needed the comfort at the moment. The cat glared at me first, but then gave in to my touch. I figured he was pissed that we'd gone off and left him with a stranger to pet sit.

Mathias glanced at me sadly. "My reputation."

"Oh," was all I said.

He nodded. "The media is assuming the wedding was a drunken mistake and they've already confirmed that you're the same woman I showed up at LAX with, so now… now they're digging around trying to find your name and any information on you that they can."

"Oh," I said again. It seemed to be the only word my brain could produce at the moment.

"Fuck, I'm so sorry, Rem."

"Why are you apologizing?" I finally seemed to snap out of my haze. I stood and made my way over to him on the opposite side of the couch. I sat down beside him and wrapped my arms around him, laying my head on his shoulder.

"You shouldn't have to deal with this kind of shit."

"Mathias," I said his name sternly, "I knew that things would be this way. You can't change the fact that you're famous and people want to know every detail of your life, which includes me if we're together."

He sighed heavily and his fingers stroked my knee. "I love that I get to live my dream, but I really fucking hate the baggage that comes with it. Having the whole world want to know all about you makes it hard to keep something to yourself. Something to hold onto that's real."

"I'm real," I whispered.

He swallowed thickly and looked into my eyes. "You're right."

He kissed me slow and sweet, sucking on my bottom lip like it was his favorite candy.

We jumped when there was a loud banging at the front door, accompanied by the ringing of the doorbell.

"Julian," he muttered. "That was fast. He must've been in the area already."

He untangled from my hold and went to get the door.

"You might want to go upstairs," he warned.

I steeled my shoulders as he reached for the doorknob. "I'm not going anywhere."

It was going to take a lot more than a psychotic manager to scare me.

Julian burst inside as soon as the door opened. His face was red and a vein in his forehead bulged.

He was speaking so fast and so loudly that I couldn't understand a thing he said at first.

"What the fuck were you thinking?!" He roared, pacing the floor. "Did you have another one of your drunken binges and think it would be a great idea to marry some redneck hick from your hometown?!"

"Hey!" Mathias yelled back, shoving a finger into Julian's chest. "Don't you ever fucking talk about her like that!"

"Do you have any idea what kind of PR nightmare you've pulled with your little stunt?!" Julian gesticulated his arms around the room in a wild manner.

"Stunt?" Mathias pointed at his chest. "This is my life! And *that*," he pointed at me, "is my future! So get that through you're thick fucking skull or you're fired!"

"You can't fire me!" Julian spat. "We have a contract!"

"You can fucking sue me, because if you don't learn to accept that Remy is my *wife* then I refuse to work with you!"

Julian stood in front of Mathias, breathing deeply as his nostrils flared like a bull's.

"What the hell am I supposed to say to the press about this?" Julian asked, his tone much calmer than before, but from the clenching in his jaw I knew he was trying hard to hold back.

"How about the truth?" Mathias spread his arms wide. "That I reconnected with my high school sweetheart recently and we decided to get married." He shrugged. "It's that simple."

Julian shook his head. "Do you really expect people to believe that of *you*? The bad boy of the band? Suddenly you're some romantic guy falling back in love with some girl from your past."

"It's the fucking truth," Mathias spat.

Julian shook his head. "And no one will believe it."

"Then you figure something out, that's why you're our manager."

Julian stood for a moment longer, shaking his head like he was debating with himself on whether or not to say anything more.

After a minute he spoke. "I want you two to pack your shit and get back to Virginia while I deal with this. Just stay out of the spotlight for a few weeks, okay?"

"Sure thing." Mathias saluted Julian mockingly.

With a shake of his head Julian headed for the door.

It slammed behind him—Mathias' doing, not his.

"So…" I started, smiling sheepishly. "Now what?"

Mathias ran his fingers through his hair and then crossed his arms over his chest. "We do what he said. We go home."

Home. I liked the sound of that.

# CHAPTER TWENTY-NINE

Time seemed to pass in the blink of an eye.

Christmas came and went without much pomp and circumstance. Mathias and I exchanged gifts and set up a tree in his penthouse. We spent the day watching movies before having dinner at his parent's house—grandma tagged along, of course.

My parent's hadn't been happy when they found out about us getting married. I had expected that, and frankly that's why I hadn't bothered to tell them. They saw it on TV and I couldn't even feel bad about it since my dad acted like a raging dickwad when he called. My mom took it much better—after telling me how disappointed she was that I was doing this to myself *again*, she finally sighed and said it was my life and she'd support my decisions even if she didn't like them. My brother never called. Shocker. We were just one big happy family. Not.

I still hadn't told Mathias about Hope yet. Each time I opened my mouth ready to tell him, it was like my throat closed up and I couldn't form a single word.

I knew I had to, and soon, but it seemed impossible.

"Where is this party again?" I asked, adding another layer of red lipstick to my lips. My dress was also the same shade of red, falling all the way to the floor. The top was a sweetheart neckline with sleeves that swept down to my elbows. It was backless as well. When Mathias first saw it on me his eyes had flashed with lust.

"It's at the Wentworth's mansion," Mathias said, stepping into the bathroom and glancing at his reflection in the mirror so that he could straighten his bow tie. "They have a fancy New Year's Eve party every year and they asked us to play. We said yes since Hayes is Lily's nephew." I shook my head and at my noticeable confusion, he added, "I'll introduce you to everybody and explain the dynamics, don't worry."

"I still don't see why we're leaving so early. It's barely five o' clock." I fluffed my curled hair one last time and padded into the bedroom to slip on my heels.

"There's someone I want you to meet." He said vaguely.

"And you're not going to tell me who this someone is?" I placed a hand on my cocked hip, staring him down.

"Nope." He smiled boyishly and grabbed a black bag so I couldn't see what was in it. "But he's important to me, so I want you to meet him."

I sighed, grabbing my black sparkly clutch. "Okay."

If he wanted it to be a surprise I'd keep my mouth shut… for now.

Instead of hiring a driver for the evening Mathias chose to drive his Range Rover. I was glad for that. I didn't really like having a driver. It was so foreign to me.

The sky was already growing dark, and since it was a cloudy night you could barely see the crescent shaped moon.

Mathias drove a few towns over, turning into a neighborhood. The homes were small, and mostly rundown with paint peeling off of the siding and broken shutters.

He pulled into a gravel driveway of a home that appeared to be in better shape than most.

I didn't recognize the house, or even the neighborhood, so I honestly had no idea who he could be bringing me to meet.

He unbuckled his seatbelt and his sigh echoed through the car. "This is it."

"I deduced that."

His lips twitched. "Don't get sassy with me."

He slipped out of the car, grabbing the black bag from the backseat.

I followed him to the front door and after he knocked we waited for a moment.

The door opened to reveal a frazzled looking woman that appeared to be in her early thirties. Her brown hair was frizzing out of its ponytail and her clothes hung loosely on her thin frame. She smiled pleasantly at Mathias and opened the door wider.

"Collin will be happy to see you. He's been asking when you're coming to see him for weeks."

As if summoned by her words a little boy of about six came running towards us, his brown hair blowing with the speed.

He jumped into Mathias' arms, and Mathias caught him easily.

"Mattie you're here! You're finally here!" The little boy wrapped his arms around Mathias' wide shoulders.

"I told you I'd be back to visit soon." Mathias hugged him back just as fiercely.

I stood mystified, watching them. I couldn't figure out who the little boy was and how Mathias knew him.

"I know I'm late," Mathias set the boy down, "but I brought you some Christmas presents."

"Presents?" The little boy beamed. "Gimme!" He reached up and Mathias handed him the bag that had fallen on the floor.

Once the bag was in his grasp Collin took off running once more.

"Who is this?" The woman asked, eyeing me warily.

Mathias grasped my waist, pulling me firmly against his side. "This is Remy, my wife."

"Oh, right," the woman shook her head. "I remember seeing that on TV. I'm sorry. I tend to tune that stuff out."

"Might as well," Mathias muttered, "all they do is tell lies."

I gave his hand a squeeze and he looked down at me. "I'm so confused," I frowned. "Who is Collin?"

"My Little Brother," he replied.

I opened my mouth to retort that Maddox was his brother and he didn't have any others, but he beat me to it.

"I'm his Big Brother—you know, the Big Brothers Big Sisters club."

"Oh," I drew out the word. "Now I get it."

"This is Laura, Collin's mom," Mathias introduced me to the woman.

"Hi," she gave a small wave. "I'll be back there if you need me," she pointed towards a bedroom. "I know Collin doesn't want me around right now." She rolled her eyes, but laughed and you could tell she was happy Mathias was there.

"So… explain this to me?" I asked in a hushed voice.

"I decided to get into the program because I wanted to help children in a small way. You know I didn't grow up with the best parent's and get the support I needed, so I wanted to be that mentor I never had." He shrugged like it was no big deal, but it *was*. He had the biggest heart, bigger than anybody else I knew. "I got paired with Collin, and it's really been perfect. His dad walked out a few years ago and he barely remembers him, so I'm proud that I can help fill that role with him." Mathias' chest swelled with pride as he spoke. "He has dyslexia like me too, and so I'm working with him on things to help him learn to read that *I've* learned over the years. I don't ever want someone to tell him he's stupid, just because he has a learning disability. It might take him longer, but he *will* learn how to read."

"Mathias…" I started, and then didn't know what else to say. He was the most remarkable man that I had ever met.

"You don't need to say anything," he whispered, caressing my cheek.

"Mattie!" We heard yelled from the other room. "Get in here so I can open my presents!"

Mathias chuckled. "That's our cue."

I followed him into the small living room that also doubled as a dining room. The carpet was new and the furniture looked new as well.

Collin sat beside the tree that glowed with colored lights and was covered in more tinsel and ornaments than it looked like it could hold.

He'd dumped out the contents of the bag, revealing four wrapped presents.

"Come on, open them, bud." Mathias coaxed, sitting down on the floor beside Collin.

I took a seat on the couch.

"Who is she?" Collin asked, reaching for a present—the largest one.

Mathias chuckled and ruffled the boy's hair. "My wife."

"Wife?" Collin wrinkled his nose. "Does that mean you're going to have babies? That's what mommy says husbands and wifes do."

"Wives," Mathias corrected automatically. "And yes, one day we'll have babies."

"Will I be their big brother?" Collin asked with wide eyes.

"Of course," Mathias grinned.

"Good," Collin beamed, and then began to tear into his presents.

The first one turned out to be a remote controlled car. The second a remote controlled airplane. The third a remote controlled train set. Clearly the kid had an obsession and Mathias knew it. Collin gushed over the presents, throwing them at Mathias with cries for him to get them out of their boxes.

"Sure thing," Mathias said, standing up and heading over to the small kitchen to grab a knife. "You've got one more present."

"Oh, right." Collin clapped and grabbed the present. "What is this?" He asked, holding up the box that contained an iPad.

Mathias sat down beside him once more, and began cutting at the tape on the box for the plane. "It's an iPad, so you can Facetime me and we can see each other even when I'm gone."

And my heart just melted.

That's right, Remy Parker's—correction, *Wade's*—heart just melted into a pile of goo at the cuteness.

"So I can see you anytime?" Collin asked, joy lighting his little face.

Mathias grinned and nodded. "Pretty much. Unless I'm working."

"Cool!" Collin cried, diving into Mathias arms—thank God Mathias had set the knife on the floor on his other side.

He held the little boy tight, like he never wanted to let go.

"I love you," Collin said into Mathias' neck.

"I love you too, bud."

Tears pricked my eyes.

I wished he could see himself right now. If he could he wouldn't think he was a monster. He would see himself for the beautifully broken, tormented, but kind soul that he is.

Collin let go of him and Mathias finished unboxing the gifts. Soon the plane buzzed around our heads, crashing into walls. Collin's giggles became infectious.

Watching Mathias with Collin was bittersweet, because I couldn't help thinking of Hope who would've been the same age had she not been stillborn

Mathias let go of Collin and the little boy grabbed the control for his plane once more. While the plane zipped around, Mathias picked up the control for the car, racing it around the coffee table.

"My plane is going to beat your car!" Collin cried, racing his plane around the table above the car.

"No way," Mathias chuckled. "I'm going to win."

"No, me!" Collin's tongue stuck out between his teeth as he concentrated on making a turn. "I won! Did you see, Mattie? I won!"

Mathias grabbed the little boy, tickling his stomach. "Yeah, yeah. I saw."

"Stop tickling me!" The boy wiggled, tears of laughter tracking his cheeks.

Mathias let him go and Collin ran off. A moment later Christmas music began to play.

Bursting back into the room with energy that never seemed to wane Collin cried, "Let's dance! You too!" He grabbed my hand, yanking on my arm. I stood up and he pointed to Mathias. "With Mattie."

Mathias smiled boyishly and held out his hand to me. "You heard the kid. Dance with me."

I smiled and placed my hand in his. He pulled me against him and murmured, "Closer," when I kept a respectable amount of distance between us.

I shook my head, prepared to tell him no when I saw that Collin had disappeared once more.

One of his hands rested on the small of my waist while the other held my hand firmly.

He sang the words of the song softly under his breath, swaying us back and forth.

Soon the giggles of Collin returned and I looked over Mathias' shoulder to see the little boy plugging in a set of Christmas lights.

Before I could ask him what he was doing he grabbed the string of lights and started running around us.

Soon our legs were tangled together with the lights and I grasped Mathias' shoulders to stay up right.

"Whoa, careful, Collin." Mathias warned.

"Mommy! Come help me!" The little boy called, jumping up so he could try to get the lights higher.

Laura appeared in the doorway and shook her head when she saw what her son was up to. "Collin, take those off of them. Now."

"It's okay," Mathias told her, "let him finish."

She sighed, looking weary. "Are you sure?"

"Of course," Mathias replied, and I figured he'd do pretty much anything to make sure Collin was happy.

Laura helped Collin finish wrapping us in lights and then he demanded that we pose for a picture.

"Grab my phone." Mathias nodded to where he'd left it on the coffee table.

Collin picked it up and handed it to Laura. Cupping his hands around his mouth, he whispered, "I don't know how to work it. Will you do it for me?"

She laughed at her son and ruffled his hair. "Sure."

"Smile you two. One, two, three."

The flash on the phone went off.

"Another!" Collin clapped his hands.

This time Mathias leaned in and kissed me, which made Collin cry, "Ew, gross!"

"Alright, one more," Mathias said. "You better get in this one, bud, since this was your idea."

Collin bounced over to us eagerly and stood in front of us with his arms crossed over his chest. Based on Laura's laugh I assumed he made a funny face.

"Okay, you have to undo us now," Mathias said.

"Does this mean you have to leave?" Collin frowned.

Mathias nodded and the little boy's head hung limply. "How long will you be gone?"

"A while," Mathias' Adam's apple bobbed. Laura began to undo the lights from our bodies. "I'm going on tour with my band. You might see me on TV. And remember, I got you the iPad so we can Facetime. We're still going to see each other."

"You promise?" Collin asked, wrapping his arms around his small body. "You're not going to leave forever like my daddy are you?"

The lights fell on the floor and Mathias stepped over them, bending down in front of Collin. "I would never leave you forever."

"You didn't promise," Collin pouted, tears falling from his eyes.

"I promise, bud."

"Okay," Collin's voice cracked, and he reached his small arms up to wrap them around Mathias' neck.

When I looked over at Laura I saw that she had tears in her eyes just like I did.

I could tell it was breaking both of their hearts to say goodbye.

The tour didn't start up until mid-January, but I knew Mathias would be busy working on other things and probably wouldn't have a chance to see Collin again before we departed.

Mathias finally let go and kissed Collin on his forehead.

Holding out his fist Collin bumped his smaller one against it. "See you later, right?" Mathias asked.

Collin nodded, reaching up to wipe away his tears.

"I love you," Mathias told him. "And whenever you miss me, just place your hand over your heart like this," Mathias held his fist against his chest, "and know that I'm missing you too."

Collin nodded and mimed the gesture, hugging Mathias one last time.

We hurried outside then and into the car. As we drove away I turned to look at him. "You give me a new reason to love you every day."

He took my hand, entwining our fingers together and lifted our joined hands to his lips so that he could kiss mine. "I guess that means you'll never fall out of love with me then." His eyes were serious.

"Never," I vowed.

He nodded, his eyes on the road.

Tomorrow, I told myself.

Tomorrow I would tell him about Hope. No excuses.

Even if *he* might fall out of love with *me*.

"Whoa," I gasped as I stepped out of the car. "They *live* here?"

Mathias closed the car door, locked it, and took my hand. A cigarette dangled precariously between his lips.

"Yep," he nodded.

"How do they not get lost?" I hissed as we walked up to the large front doors. I kept looking around with my mouth hanging open. It was completely dark now, but the whole front of the house was lit brightly with strategically placed spotlights.

Mathias shrugged in answer to my question and reached up to grab the cigarette. He blew out a string of smoke and dropped the finished cigarette on the ground, crushing the lit tip with the edge of his shoe.

He reached out and opened the front door.

We stepped inside a massive foyer and people stood around mingling.

My head swiveled around, trying to take in every elegant detail of the home.

"This way," he tugged on my hand, leading me away, "we need to go to the ballroom."

"They have a ballroom?!" I shrieked. "In their house?"

Mathias merely chuckled at me, but I couldn't believe that someone had a ballroom in their house—although, it was a mansion, not a house, so I guessed they could have whatever they wanted.

We followed the sounds of music and chatter, soon stepping into a room that was the size of the whole house I grew up in.

I spotted Emma and Maddox speaking with Hayes and a few other people. Ezra was there too, with his back turned to us.

We joined them and I immediately complimented Emma on her dress. It was a beautiful floor length gown in a deep blue color with a beaded top. It made her blue eyes seem even bluer and her hair was pinned back elegantly.

"Thank you," she smiled, "yours is amazing too."

Squeezing my hand to get my attention, Mathias began to introduce everybody. "This is Trace Wentworth and his wife Olivia," he pointed to a couple. The man was tall with the greenest eyes I'd ever seen and an easy smile. His brown hair flopped over his forehead into his eyes. Olivia looked like a small little pixie next to him. She was dressed in a pretty pale pink dress, her dark hair curled down her back, and she held a baby boy in her arms. He couldn't be more than a few months old, with dark hair like his parents. He was dressed in a tiny suit, with a small pair of converse on his feet.

He began to fuss and Trace reached for the baby. "Dean wants his daddy."

Olivia sighed good-naturedly and smiled at her husband as she handed over the baby. "He really needs to go to bed."

"I can do that," Trace smiled lovingly at his wife and lowered to kiss her cheek. "It was nice to meet you," he turned his attention to me. To the rest of the group, he said, "I'll be back soon."

Mathias took the interruption in stride and moved on to the next person. "This is Trenton Wentworth."

This guy was just as tall as Trace, with the same facial features and build, but blue eyes instead of green.

"I'm the rude one's brother," Trent winked playfully, eliciting a growl from Mathias.

I gave his hand a small squeeze and he quieted.

"This is…" Mathias paused and frowned. "I don't know who the fuck you are."

The girl rolled her eyes and her plump lips pulled down in a pout. Flipping her fiery red hair over her shoulder, she said, "Just because you're famous doesn't mean you're allowed to be rude. I'm Avery, Olivia's best friend—also know as the life of the party and all around greatest person alive. This is my boyfriend Luca." She pointed to the big bear of a man beside her. He grunted in response and looked like he'd rather be anywhere but here. Poor guy.

"Avery," Mathias repeated, trying to repress a laugh.

"And don't you forget it." She rolled her eyes.

Moving on to the last person standing there, he said, "This is Lily Wentworth, Hayes' aunt."

Hayes stood beside the woman with his arm thrown over her shoulder, smiling widely. "I'm her favorite nephew," he boasted.

"You're my *only* nephew," she countered, shaking her head. I could tell she was fighting not to laugh.

"Same difference," Hayes chimed. "So, anyway, in case that got really confusing for you, Lily is my aunt and this is her house. Trace and Trent are my cousins."

I laughed. "Thanks for the repeat, but I think I got it."

He tipped his head in my direction with a smile.

"Well, that's everyone you need to know," Mathias said, releasing my hand and placing his at the small of my back instead.

"Not everyone," Emma interrupted, her eyes near the entrance of the ballroom.

A moment later we heard a high-pitched shriek and Emma was nearly tackled to the ground. If Maddox hadn't grabbed Emma around the waist, both girls would've went falling to the floor.

After the girls recovered, both laughing, Emma turned to me. "This is Sadie, my best friend that I was telling you about."

"Hi," Sadie smiled, stepping forward to hug me. I was surprised by the gesture, but quickly returned it. She was gorgeous, with sun-kissed skin like she'd just been to the beach, and brown hair curling halfway down her back. Her brown eyes were sweet, but twinkled with mischief. "You must be Remy."

I nodded.

"Emma's been telling me a lot about you. I'm starting to get jealous. I think she's replacing me," the girl jested.

A loud clearing of a throat had all of us turning in the direction of the man standing behind Sadie. He was tall and wide, like a football player, with short blond hair. There was something about him I instantly didn't like.

"Oh, right," Sadie's face turned red, "this is my fiancé Braden."

Even after being introduced the guy said nothing, just glared at all of us.

"Excuse me," Ezra muttered, breaking through the group. He strode up to Braden and clapped him on the shoulder. Ezra was a little bit taller, but definitely not wider, than the guy and used that to his advantage by looking down on him. "I think we should have a little chat."

"Stop it," Sadie hissed under her breath.

Ezra glanced at her and shook his head. His look said she was stupid to think he was going to drop whatever this was.

"I don't have anything to say to you." Braden finally spoke, his voice booming around us and drawing the attention of those near us. He crossed his arms over his massive chest, his feet planted firmly apart.

"Really? That's great, because I have some things to say to you, so you can stand there and listen."

Braden rolled his eyes. "Is this because I told her she couldn't hang out with you? As her fiancé it's my right to decide who she's *friends* with," he sneered the word, "and I don't want her to be friend's with any man. Especially one I'm pretty sure she's fucked."

Sadie gasped, her whole body flushing with embarrassment.

Ezra clenched his teeth, his hands fisted at his side. "What the fuck did you just say?"

Braden didn't back down. "Are you deaf? I said I'm pretty sure you fucked my girl, so as long as I'm in the picture, you won't be."

Ezra cocked his fist back and punched Braden in the face. Braden then threw a fist into Ezra's side.

As the guy's scuffled we all looked on in horror.

No one seemed to know what to do.

Maddox and Mathias were the first to move. Each one grabbed a different guy and tried to get them off of each other. Neither Ezra nor Braden was willing to back down from the fight which made things even more difficult for the twins.

Tears streaked down Sadie's cheeks and I felt so sorry for her. I could see the confliction on her face.

The guys finally broke apart and Lily came scuttling forward. "I'm sorry, but you two need to leave." She pointed to Sadie and Braden.

Sadie nodded, like she had expected as much.

Braden threw a fit about how he hadn't done anything, blah, blah, blah. But Sadie simply grabbed him by the arm and quietly towed him from the room.

You could feel the shame rolling off of her shoulders, and I wondered how she'd ever gotten involved in a guy like that.

"I hate him," Emma spoke up, glaring at Braden's back until he disappeared.

"Me too," Ezra said, clutching his side. There was a small cut on his upper lip that trickled blood.

Emma sighed when she saw him. "We have to respect her decision. It's her life."

"Well, she's making the worst mistake of her life," he seethed, reaching up to wipe away the blood from his lip.

"I know that, and you know that, but she doesn't. The more we balk her on this, the closer it will drive her too him," Emma reasoned.

Ezra tugged at his hair and let out a growl.

Emma stepped forward and grabbed his hand, forcing him to look at her.

"I know you love her—" Ezra opened his mouth to argue with her, but she held up a hand and he shut up. "—like a friend and want what's best for her, but she's stubborn. Nothing you do or say is going to make her change her mind about him. You have to let his go."

Ezra closed his eyes and his whole body shook with a breath. "I'll try, but she deserves better."

"I know," Emma agreed.

Taking a step away Ezra mumbled, "I'm going to the bathroom. I'll be back in time for our set."

Emma frowned at his retreating form.

"Dinner is going to be served in a few minutes if you'd like to take a seat." Lily swept her hands in the direction of the tables scattered around the space.

Mathias steered me towards one and Hayes, Trenton, Maddox, and Emma joined us. Olivia, her friend, and her friend's boyfriend sat at the table beside us since there was no longer enough room at ours.

Ezra didn't return for dinner, and his absence weighed heavily upon all of us. When Maddox and Emma excused themselves from the table and left the room I knew they were going to look for him.

The tables were soon cleared of dirty plates and it was time for Willow Creek to perform on the stage setup in the corner of the ballroom.

Maddox, Emma, and Ezra returned just in time. The guys immediately climbed on stage. Maddox pulled his drumsticks out of his back pocket and sat down behind his kit, banging out a beat.

Mathias took his place in front of the microphone and winked when he caught me looking at him.

Emma stood beside me, swaying to the music as they played. Despite the fact that she'd probably seen them perform hundreds of time she still looked on with awe.

Mathias' eyes connected with mine as he sang, and to me it felt like we were the only two people present. He had this way about him that made me forget anything else even existed.

The first song ended and they moved into another one, this one a little more fast-paced.

Emma grabbed my hands and cried, "You have to dance, Remy!"

At first I was hesitant—mostly because this dress was tight and the last thing I wanted was for it to split up the sides—but Emma was impossible to resist. Soon the two of us were laughing and dancing, not caring if we looked like complete and utter goofballs.

The guys played a few songs and then there was some more entertainment before we were all ushered outside.

"What's going on?" I asked Mathias.

"You'll see," he smiled, shrugging out of his tux jacket and draping it over my shoulders so that I wouldn't be cold.

Somewhere, someone began to countdown to midnight and we all joined in.

"Ten, nine, eight, seven, six, five, four, three, two, one!"

Mathias leaned down and kissed me, murmuring, "Happy New Year," against my lips.

Fireworks went off all around us and now I knew why we'd all been dragged out into the cold air.

"Happy New Year." I mimed him as a heavy weight settled on my chest.

Off to our right a gasp had us turning to look.

"Oh my God," I smiled, lifting a hand to my mouth.

Maddox kneeled on one knee in front of Emma. From where we stood we couldn't hear anything that Maddox was saying, but tears shimmered in Emma's eyes. She nodded her head yes and he slipped the ring onto her finger. She dove into his arms and he spun her around, their lips pressed firmly together.

Even though I feared that my life might be falling apart, I was still happy for them. I eventually looked away, wanting to give them any amount of privacy that I could offer.

I turned my face towards the sky, watching it explode in a fiery cascade of silver and gold.

Mathias' fingers tapped against my waist and I rested my head on his shoulder.

Each bang of the fireworks sounded like a bullet lodging itself into the beating heart of our relationship. Nothing would be the same once I told him, and I only hoped we could make it through this. I believed our love was strong enough to overcome anything, especially as hard as we fought to get to where we were now, but this might be one sin that not even that love could overcome. That thought left me bereft and empty inside.

# CHAPTER THIRTY

I woke up the next morning with what felt like a fifty-pound weight on my chest. I knew today was the day. I couldn't keep this a secret any longer. I still had no clear idea on how to tell him. This wasn't exactly easy news to break to someone, and knowing Mathias he would snap at me and not let me finish explaining.

I slipped out of the bed and went over different scenarios in my head, wondering how would be the best way to tell him.

My heart clenched with fear.

I didn't want to do this.

But I had no choice.

I thought I might throw up.

Nope. No. I was good.

I could do this.

I padded out of the bedroom, heading towards the kitchen for coffee.

"Remy."

I stopped in my tracks at the icy tone. He didn't shout my name, but the single word was lined with steel.

I closed my eyes.

He knew.

I didn't know how he knew—unless I'd been talking to myself out loud and didn't realize it—but somehow he did.

I rounded the corner and came face to face with him.

I thought I'd seen Mathias angry before, but nothing, and I mean *nothing* compared to his anger now.

He was pale, his skin a ghostly white. A vein in his forehead pulsed and his hands were scrunched into fists.

"What the fuck is this?" His voice was still that deadly calm before the storm.

"What?" I was surprised by how strong the single word sounded. On the inside I was freaking out.

He grabbed my arm and pulled. I nearly tripped over my feet.

"Ow, Mathias, you're hurting me," I cried, prying my arm from his hold.

He didn't say he was sorry, but his eyes appeared to be slightly apologetic.

"Tell me they're lying." He pointed at the TV and I looked to see some celebrity gossip show on TV. There was a picture of the two of us, and they were talking about how it was so romantic that we'd gotten back together all these years later after the death of our daughter. They were saying some other things too, but all I could focus on was the daughter part.

I sunk to my knees, tears rolling down my cheeks.

That was answer enough for him.

"Fuck!" He screamed, grabbing the coffee table and turning it over with a crash that I was sure was heard through the whole hotel.

I tried to get oxygen into my lungs, but it was like I had forgotten how to breathe.

I knew it was going to be bad telling him, but this was the worst way possible for him to find out.

*You should've told him a long time ago*, my conscience piped in. I told her to take a fucking hike. There was nothing I could do now to change my decisions. All I could do was explain my side and hope he saw that I'd meant well.

He paced around the room, cursing and throwing things when he felt like it.

"Mathias, please—" I started.

He stopped with his hands on his hips and glared at me like I was the most disgusting thing he'd ever laid his eyes on. I felt so small beneath that gaze.

"Explain!" He shouted. "Fucking explain this to me!"

"I don't know where to *start*." My voice cracked.

"How about at the fucking beginning? You…" He stopped, his breath coming out in ragged pants. "You were pregnant?"

I nodded, tears stinging my cheeks. "Yes. When I left. I was going t-to tell you that d-day in the parking lot and then…" I trailed off, he knew what happened, what *he* said to me, so there was no point in continuing.

"And then you never fucking thought to give me a call and say, 'Oh, hey, Mathias, I thought I should let you know I'm pregnant and the baby is yours.'"

"I was a kid!" I yelled, rising to my feet. "I was a kid and so were you! I was a kid that was madly in love with you and you *broke* my fucking heart! You crushed me! Excuse me for thinking you wouldn't want anything to do with me or our daughter!" My chest rose and fell with rapid breaths.

"I had a right to know!"

"I would've told you eventually had she…" A sob raked my body and I bit down on my fist to stifle the sound. "…Had she lived." I finally managed to get the words out.

"What the fuck happened?!" He asked. "I want to know everything! I deserve to know!" He thrust a finger against his chest and I swore there were tears in his own eyes.

I wrapped my arms around myself, sniffling as I fought more tears. "I don't *know*." My voice cracked yet again. I could see that he was about to argue with that statement, so I quickly continued. "Everything was fine. I did everything right, Mathias! You have to believe me! I stopped smoking, I ate healthy, I did everything the doctors told me to do, but then she stopped moving as much and… and they induced labor, but it was too late." My lip trembled with my tears. "She was already gone."

I buried my face in my hands, crying harder than I had let myself cry since the day the doctors took her from my arms.

Mathias stared at me, his mouth moving back and forth, but no words came out. He seemed at a loss as to what to say.

"After that… it didn't seem important to tell you. She was gone, and even though I thought I hated you, I still loved you. And because of that love, I wanted to spare you the pain I had to live with." More tears flowed down my cheeks. I was drowning in them. "Every single day since then I've had to live with the fact that I'll never see her grow up. I'll never get to hear her call me mommy. Or take her to her first day of school. I'll never get to teach her how to ride her bike. I'll never get to brush her hair, or tuck her into bed at night. I'll never get to tell her I love her, and that kills me a little inside every day. Can you blame me for wanting to spare you that torment?" I wiped at my face, struggling to breathe.

"You still had no right to take that choice away from me!" He yelled, a muscle in his jaw twitching.

"I know. I can see that now, and I'm sorry. But *please* understand where I was coming from. I was going to tell you, today actually, but I… I didn't get the chance." That was taken away from me like so many other things.

"Fuck," he cursed, pulling at his hair, "I want to believe this is a fucking nightmare." His voice was suddenly soft and defeated sounding.

"It feels like it sometimes," I whispered.

"What was her name?" He asked, startling me.

"Hope," I whispered. "Hope Wade. I didn't give her a middle name."

His shoulders hunched forward, as if by having a name she suddenly became even more real to him.

With a growl he picked up his phone and slammed it into a wall. A dent was left behind and the phone shattered.

"It's not fair!" He screamed, losing all control.

He destroyed everything in sight—shattering lamps, ripping the couch cushions off. The whole room soon looked like a disaster zone.

I stood there, unable to move.

I didn't know what to do or say to calm him, and something told me there was *nothing* I could do.

When he finally stopped raging he returned to his icy calm. He pointed a finger at me and hissed, "I hate you and I will *never* forgive you for this."

I nodded, and my tears began to flow at a faster rate.

I had expected his words, but they still hurt.

Numbness spread through my limbs and I sunk to the floor, my back against the wall.

He glared at me for a long moment, before shaking his head and storming away.

I heard the sound of the elevator doors opening and then he was gone.

I knew that this very well might be the last time I ever saw him.

I couldn't blame him for hating me.

This really was my fault.

My decisions led to this moment.

And I would have to live with that regret for the rest of my life.

When I finally pried my body off the floor I tried to clean up the space, but I soon felt far too tried to deal with anything.

Sluggishly I made my way back to our bedroom and immediately fell asleep.

I was pretty sure I could sleep for a thousand years.

Anything to avoid having to deal with the mess my life had become.

I stared at the plate of food I had warmed, but I wasn't hungry.

Mathias hadn't come home yesterday, and today was a new day with still no sign of him.

I was supposed to work at the bar today.

I called in and quit.

I figured Mathias was done with me—he was probably getting divorce papers drawn up already—and I would be moving back to Arizona. There was no way I could stay here after this and I had no place else to go. My parent's would say, 'I told you so,' but I honestly couldn't fault them for that. They had every right to rub it in my face that I'd screwed up yet again.

I threw the food away and cleaned the plate, before sitting down with my laptop and playing the video once more. The one brief news clip that ruined my life.

Over and over again, I watched it.

So much for staying out of the spotlight. I was sure Julian was about to have a heart attack trying to deal with this.

It was clear that the so-called journalists had been digging into my past, trying to find out anything they could about Mathias' mystery girl. I guess they were trying to find a reason for why Mathias would choose me to settle down with. I knew it wouldn't have taken much sleuthing for anyone to find Hope's death certificate. Coupled with all the hospital visits and timing, it was easy to put two and two together.

He shouldn't have found out like that, though, and it was nothing but my own fault for not having the guts to tell him.

There wasn't much I feared, but losing him was number one.

That didn't matter now, because regardless, I had lost him.

I wished he could see where I'd been coming from, though. My intention had *never* been to hurt him. It had been the complete opposite.

The elevator dinged and hope soared in my chest.

Disappointment quickly replaced it when Emma stepped out of the elevator and not Mathias.

She winced when she looked around and saw the mess.

Her eyes landed on me and she frowned. I was sure I looked scary. I hadn't showered yesterday or this morning. I hadn't even bothered to brush my hair or change my clothes. I didn't have the energy to do anything.

"Hey," she smiled.

I closed the laptop and set it beside me on the couch.

"Are you here to kick me out?" I asked.

I expected Mathias to show up for that part, but maybe he was still so angry that he couldn't bear to look at me, even to tell me to get the fuck out of his place.

"No," she shook her head, her brows furrowing together as she navigated the mess and sat down beside me. "Why would I do that?"

I turned red-rimmed eyes in her direction. "Because I'm sure Mathias doesn't want me here anymore."

She shrugged.

"Have you seen him?" I asked, swallowing past the lump in my throat.

She nodded. "He showed up at the guesthouse. We'd already seen the news and Maddox didn't think Mathias knew about the baby. Maddox said Mathias might not be the most open person, but that he'd never keep that a secret from him." She sighed, tapping her fingers along the back of the couch.

"Do you think I'm a horrible person for not telling him?" I knew she'd be honest with me.

"No, I don't think you're horrible. Do I think it was wrong? Yes. But I can also understand why you did it. You were young and you lost your baby. You probably thought you'd never see him again, so what difference would it have even made? But when you reconnected with him now… you should've been honest."

"I didn't want him to have to grieve every day for the rest of his life like I do. I didn't want him to ask himself the endless amount of questions that I ask myself. I wanted him to be able to live his life without asking *what if.*" I reached up, swiping away a tear. You would've thought I would have run out of tears by now, but somehow they kept flowing.

"I think he knows that, but he's still…"

"Mad?" I supplied for her and she nodded.

"You should've told him, Remy, instead of letting it get this far. It wasn't fair to him to find out like this. I know, because I've been in a similar position." She reached forward, grabbing my hand and holding it in comfort.

"You have?" I asked.

"When I met Maddox, Willow Creek was already gaining popularity, but I had no idea who they were. I'm kind of aloof like that," she rolled her eyes and laughed, "anyway, he never told me that he was in the band, and I found out by accident when Sadie saw a picture of Maddox and me in a magazine." She shook her head, letting out another small laugh. "I was so mad at him for not telling me—for not trusting me. I was so angry that I found out who he was in a magazine. *He* should've told *me* just like *you* should've told *Mathias.* When you're in the spotlight like they are… there are no secrets. Everything comes out eventually." She frowned.

"I don't know what to do," I whispered. "He probably wants nothing to do with me. He has every right to hate me." I bit down on my bottom lip to stop the trembling and turned the bands around and around on my ring finger. "But I can't imagine my life without him."

"Then don't," she said, placing her hand on my knee. "Don't give up on him. Fight for him the way Maddox fought for me. Love isn't easy. In fact, it's downright painful sometimes. But when you find the right person for you, those bad moments are worth it."

"I can't expect him to forgive me for this." I shook my head.

"You have to make him understand," she argued.

"How?" I pleaded.

"Be honest."

"I've already told him why and I don't think he cared." I picked at a loose thread on one of the throw pillows, needing to do something to keep my hands busy.

"Then tell him again. He was angry before, but after he's cooled off he might be more willing to listen to you."

I didn't believe her. "He's never going to get over this."

"He will." She assured me. "He's just in shock right now. In the span of a few minutes he learned not only that he had a daughter, but that she was gone too."

I wiped away my tears and reached to grab a tissue to blow my nose.

I nodded, processing her words. "I want to make this work."

"You're a fighter, Remy," she gave my hand a squeeze, "so just keep on fighting for a little longer."

"I think I can do that."

"Good." She reached out and hugged me. "You two will work it out. I know it."

Her words made me feel better, even if I didn't quite believe them.

# CHAPTER THIRTY-ONE

*Just keep fighting.* Emma's voice echoed in my mind.

I didn't know how much longer I could.

I stepped into the bar and took a seat. "Give me something strong. I want to be so drunk that you have to drag me out of here covered in my own vomit."

Tanner stared at me with disbelief. "You quit."

"Yes, I quit my job. That does not mean I quit drinking… I mean, I never really drink, but right now I need to get shit-faced."

Yep, getting shit-faced sounded like the best idea ever right now.

After tucking me into bed with a cup of tea Emma had left me alone. I'd tried to go to sleep, but it was fucking useless.

So here I was.

At the bar.

Three o' fucking clock in the afternoon.

But it's always five o' clock somewhere, right? Isn't that how the saying went?

"What's going on, Red?" Tanner braced his hands on the bar in front of me. His lips were turned down in true concern. "Is this about what they're saying on TV about a baby?"

"You would be right." I snapped my fingers.

He narrowed his eyes. "Are you already drunk?"

"Possibly," I admitted.

"Shit." He scrubbed his hands over his face. "Okay, okay," he muttered, "so why are you so upset about this?"

"He didn't know," I mumbled.

Tanner's eyes widened. "Well, fuck." He reached for a bottle beneath the bar, grabbed two shot glasses, and poured the drinks. He shoved one in front of me and held the other.

"Are you supposed to drink on the job?" I raised a brow.

He lifted it to his lips. "I'm the manager," was his response.

I took mine and he refilled both.

"I can understand your desire to get drunk now," he admitted.

I glanced down at the second shot with a frown.

Getting drunk wasn't solving anything.

Instead it was making me feel worse.

"I miss him," I whined. "He hates me now and I can't even blame him." I hiccupped, and covered my mouth. "Excuse me."

Tanner stared at me for a moment. "That was a big secret, Red."

"I know," I agreed, laying my head on the counter. "This is so bad."

My tears began to dampen the bar and Tanner poked my shoulder.

I sat back up and glared at him. "That wasn't nice."

"You're getting your germs all over my clean bar. Now take your shot." He thrust the shot in my direction.

I downed it, wincing at the aftertaste.

"Listen, I like you, Red," he started, "but that's some bad shit not telling a guy about his kid and then…" He trailed off, having heard about her death on the news. I fucking hated that the details surrounding Hope were out there for the world to hear and know.

"I know, I know." I agreed with him, burying my face in my hands. "I fucked up so bad. That's what I do. It's what *we* do," I mumbled, lumping Mathias into my equation, "we fuck up everything."

I laid my head back down on the counter. Tanner scolded me again, to which I gave him the finger. Some guy at the bar laughed so I gave him the finger too.

Tanner sighed heavily. "This doesn't seem like you, Red. Sitting here sniveling."

"I'm *wallowing* not sniveling. There's a fucking difference. Get it right, doucheknozzle." I sat back up, waving my arms wildly through the air.

He snorted. "Wow, you're highly entertaining when you're drunk."

"I'm not drunk I'm…" I paused. "Okay, yeah, I'm totally drunk."

Tanner shook his head, crossing his arms over his chest. "I'd like to think we're friends…" He waited for me to nod in agreement, before continuing. "So, I'm going to be straightforward with you."

"Oh, great." I rolled my eyes. "You better give me another shot for this."

He did, forgoing one for himself.

His elbows rested on the bar and he leaned towards me. "This is some bad shit you've got yourself into."

"Yeah, I know. I didn't come here to hear you tell me that. Trust me, I've been telling myself that plenty."

He glared at me to shut up and I mimed zipping my lips and tossing away the key.

"But as your friend, I'm here to tell you it's not irreparable."

I snorted.

"I'm serious," he continued. "I've known Mathias for a few years now since he started coming in here, and let me tell you, there's been a huge change in him during the time he's been with you. Trust me, that guy isn't going to walk away from this—and by this, I mean you."

My lips flattened into a thin line. "You think?" I asked, daring to let myself feel a smidgen of hope.

He nodded. "I'd be shocked if I was wrong. Wanna bet on it?"

I shook my head. "I'm too drunk to bet. You'd take advantage of me."

His body trembled with laughter. "God, I love you, Red. Best thing that ever happened to this bar was you walking in here and demanding a job."

"I am pretty fucking awesome," I agreed.

He chuckled, grabbing the glasses off the counter and dropping them into the sink. "Why don't you go rest up in the back?" He suggested. "You look like you're dead on your feet. I'll get you home after my shift ends."

I stood up, ready to disagree with him, but my legs began to shake and I knew there was no way I was walking out of here and all the way down the street back to the hotel.

"Okay," I agreed.

When I didn't move and he noticed the shakiness in my legs he sighed and came around the bar. He put a hand around my waist and guided me to the backroom and onto the couch.

"Stay." He pointed at me like I was a disobedient dog.

"Yes, dad," I sassed.

He shook his head and left me alone.

I might not have been able to sleep earlier, but with all of the alcohol in my system I soon passed out.

"Fuck, Red," Tanner groaned, "I think you just clawed the shit out of my arm. Trim your nails or something."

I flopped onto the couch, and out of his arms, feeling like I was going to throw up.

I told Tanner such and he promptly said, "Oh, hell no, Red. Hold it in."

Yeah, that so wasn't happening.

I jumped up from the couch and nearly tripped over something that was broken. It was anybody's guess as to what the object was since most things in the suite were broken now.

"Fuck," Tanner said.

He grabbed for me, trying to help me.

"Tanner, no—" I tried to warn him, but it was useless. He was in the way and my vomit wasn't staying down a second longer.

His shirt got splattered and he made a face of pure disgust.

"Ew," his nose wrinkled, "you owe me a new shirt for this and like fifty bucks, because I don't get paid to deal with drunk people. I just supply them with the liquor."

"Sorry." I put a hand over my mouth. I did feel bad. I hadn't meant to get sick all over the guy, or show up at the bar for an impromptu therapy session.

"It's okay," he grumbled, removing his shirt.

I lay down on the couch once more and Tanner went to the kitchen to dispose of his shirt in the trashcan.

"Is there someone I can call to come sit with you?" He asked, his footsteps coming closer. Suddenly he peered at me over the top of the couch.

"No," I answered with a sad lilt to my voice, "I don't have anybody."

That was the sad truth.

I was all alone in the world.

Shit. There came the tears again.

"Fuck, Red," he frowned, "I didn't mean to make you cry."

"S'okay," I muttered, "it keeps happening."

He swallowed thickly and stepped around the couch, taking a seat near my feet. Percy hissed and Tanner reared back, not having realized the cat was on the couch. Percy was sneaky like that.

"What're you doing?" I mumbled, hoping my words weren't slurred together.

"You said you didn't have anybody to sit with you, so this is me babysitting you so that you don't choke and die on your own vomit. I don't want your death on my hands," he rambled, trying to hide a smile, "mostly because I'm afraid your husband might kill me."

"He's not my husband anymore," I muttered, staring up at the ceiling.

"Says who?" He countered.

"Trust me," I turned my head in his direction, "he doesn't want to be. Not after this."

"You don't know that, Red. Give him a chance."

It grew quiet between us, but after a while I couldn't stop myself from saying, "I think we're out of chances."

"There's *always* a chance."

I wanted to believe him.

Oh, God, how I wanted to.

# CHAPTER THIRTY-TWO

It had been a week since Mathias walked out. A week since I'd seen his face or heard his voice. A week of nothingness. And in another week he would be gone on tour.

He didn't even come back for Shiloh and the poor thing kept moping around as pathetically as me.

Emma kept me updated by sending random texts here and there on how he was doing.

It didn't matter though.

Because *he* wasn't the one telling me.

All I wanted was some sign of communication from him.

But I got nothing.

Nothing but the fear that he really might be planning to divorce me.

The pain of that thought nearly ripped my heart out of my chest.

I had no idea how to fix this.

And maybe that was the point—that there was no way to fix it.

I just had to live with it.

But I didn't want to have to live with this.

I *wanted* to get my happy ending.

I used to think that girls like me didn't deserve a happy ending, but I was wrong. I deserved to be happy just as much as the next person, and despite my choices I deserved to have Mathias in my life. If he still wanted me, that is.

I just didn't know how to make him understand.

I finally made myself shower and get dressed.

Tanner called to check on me. He'd done that three times a day, every day, since I got drunk and he had to drag my sorry ass home. I had to admit, he was a pretty nice guy.

"How are you feeling, Red?" He asked.

I grabbed a water bottle from the refrigerator, the phone cradled between my ear and shoulder.

"Not drunk," I replied.

He chuckled. "That's a good thing."

"We'll have to agree to disagree," I muttered, lifting the water to my lips and taking a sip.

"Seriously, though, how are you feeling today?" He pestered.

I leaned a hip against the counter. "The same as yesterday and the day before that and—"

"So, basically like shit," he interrupted.

"Yep," I mumbled. "At least I showered."

"Thatta girl."

"Shut up."

"Hey, don't be mean to your best friend."

"You're *not* my best friend."

"You threw up on me," he countered, "that's practically a blood bond."

I rolled my eyes. "Whatever. I think I'm going to go see my grandma."

"That sounds like a good idea," he agreed. "Talk to you later."

"M'kay," I said, and frowned. Jesus, I sounded like Mathias. "Bye."

I set my phone on the counter and buried my head in my hands. I had made such a fucking mess of things. I'd spent most of the week crying, gorging myself on ice cream, and avoiding alcohol because that turned into such a mess the first time.

But enough was enough. I had to get out of here and return to the real world. Life went on whether or not I was present for it.

I headed over to my grandma's like I told Tanner I was going to. My grandma was the only person I had here and I hoped she could make me feel better. Then again, she'd probably be too busy watching some trashy reality TV show to talk to me.

Since I didn't have my car I took Mathias' Range Rover. I figured he was already so mad at me that using his car wouldn't matter much.

I parked in the driveway and clenched the steering wheel in my hands, banging my head against the headrest.

*Why?*

*Why me?*

*Why did my life always have to get crapped on?*

*Why couldn't I be allowed to be happy?*

My eyes burned with the threat of tears, but they'd dried up a few days ago so none spilled over.

With a sigh I turned off the car and walked up to the front door.

I still had my key, but suddenly I felt like I didn't belong here.

Like I didn't belong anywhere.

Fuck, this had been a bad idea.

I doubted she wanted to see me.

She'd probably take one look at me and say, "Remy, you really fucked things up this time."

She wouldn't be lying. I had.

I knocked loudly on the door so she would hear me.

I stood with my hands clasped together, praying that she didn't turn me away.

A few moments later I heard her grumbling on the other side.

When the door opened she glared up at me. "Oh, it's you."

I flinched at that. I deserved it, but her tone still stung.

"Can I come in?" I asked hesitantly.

"If you must," she huffed.

The door closed and I followed her into the kitchen, sitting across from her at the table.

She proceeded to glare at me.

Neither one of us would speak.

I began to wonder why I even came here, but I made no move to leave.

Minutes passed and finally she was the first to break the silence. "He came over here you know."

I perked up at this information. "He did?"

She nodded. "I saw on the TV that they were talking about the baby, but I hoped you told him beforehand."

"I was going to tell him that day," I whispered, tracing the edge of my fingernail around a ring on the table.

"You should've told him a while ago, Remy."

"Fuck," I buried my face into my hands. "I know. Okay." I let my hands drop. "I know I fucked up."

"Yes you did," she nodded. Sobering, she added, "But everybody makes mistakes."

"Not mistakes this big," I countered, hanging my head in shame.

"A mistake is a mistake. Some *are* bigger than others," she agreed, "but any mistake can be forgiven," she spoke wisely.

"I don't know how to ask him to forgive me."

"You just *do*." She took my hand. Hers looked so small against mine, but right now she was the stronger of the two of us. "Life is full of hardships. You act as if what you did was unforgivable, but Remy, you didn't do anything wrong."

"But I did!" I cried. "I didn't tell him about Hope! How can he ever trust me again?!"

"Shhh," she patted my cheek, "calm yourself."

I took a few hiccupping breaths and seemed to gain control of myself once more.

"I'm not saying what you did wasn't bad, all I'm saying is it wasn't *wrong*. You did the right thing for you and him at the time. You lost your daughter and honey," tears shimmered in her eyes, "from the things your parent's told me… it sounds like we lost you too for a while." I watched as she began to cry. "You were so young and you made the only decision you knew how to make. No one can blame you for protecting yourself."

"*I* blame *me*." My voice cracked.

She shook her head. "There's no point. Instead, you need to tell yourself how strong you are. You should be proud of the person you are today. I know your daughter would be proud of you."

"Don't say that," I begged, my eyes stinging with tears. They began to cascade down my cheeks and dripped onto my shirt. I guessed they hadn't dried up after all.

"It's the truth, honey."

I began to sob, because she was wrong. So, so wrong. There was no way my daughter would be proud of me, of the things I'd done, and the way I had hurt Mathias. I was a shameful excuse for a human being.

"Do I think you should've told him back then?" She started in again. "Yes, yes I do. But I've also never been in the position where I lost a child, and thank God for that, so there's no telling what I might've done in your shoes. We all make decisions in life, and we have to own them."

I wiped my face on the sleeve of my shirt, not even caring that I was smearing mascara all over it.

"Why are you being so nice to me?" I whispered. "You seemed awfully pissed off when I showed up."

She shrugged. "I wanted to be mad at you, but frankly I can't. Not because I'm your grandma, but because you look miserable. Seriously, you look awful," she reiterated.

I began to laugh—the first time in a week—and it felt so good.

I hugged my grandma, kissing the top of her head. She might've been batshit crazy, but I loved her to death.

"Thank you."

"For what?" She asked, returning the hug.

"For making me feel better."

"Yeah, yeah," she patted my back and let go, "but if you don't work things out with him then I'm disowning you."

I snorted. "You used to hate him based off everything mom and dad told you about him. What made you change your mind with him? And be honest. Don't give me one of your bullshit answers." I warned her with a smile.

"I saw the way he looked at you."

My brows pulled together.

"He loves you, Remy," she said, "a strong, fierce kind of love—one that's rare and doesn't go away."

I nodded at her words and took a deep breath. "Thanks for the talk. I'm going to head out."

"Okay," she nodded. "I love you, but you seriously need to do something about all of that." She waved a hand at me.

It was then that I noticed my jeans were dirty, my shirt was on inside out, and my shoes didn't even match.

And here I thought I'd been doing so well this morning.

Leaving my grandma's I headed to the gym—thankful that not only did I have gym clothes stashed in my locker, but regular clothes as well. You know, since I dressed like a bum this morning.

Once there I took out my aggression on the punching bag.

I kicked and hit it until my arms were sore. Every single piece of sadness, anger, and resentment that had been bottling up inside me for the last six years poured out of me as I hit it.

When I was finished I showered and changed into fresh clothes.

I was torn between heading to Maddox and Emma's—where I was sure Mathias was still holed up—and going back to his place.

I finally settled for the former.

This girl that kept sitting around moping, and crying, wasn't me. I wasn't weak. I was loud mouthed and I fought for what I wanted. I didn't sit back and wait for somebody else to take action first.

I took charge.

I was the hero of my own fucking story.

I beat on the door of the guesthouse with the side of my fist. I didn't care if I had to stand there all day knocking. I wasn't leaving until I saw Mathias and had a chance to talk to him. I wasn't wallowing anymore. I was taking charge and doing what I wanted.

The door finally swung open and I nearly fell inside, but I quickly righted myself, squaring my shoulders.

Emma stood in front of me. She didn't look too happy.

"He's not here."

"What?" I gasped, and suddenly it felt like the ground had disappeared from beneath my feet.

"He left a few hours ago and I don't think he's coming back."

Air rushed in and out of my lungs as I processed her words.

"Did he say where he was going?" I pleaded with her.

She shook her head. "No, he's just gone."

Gone.

*Just gone.*

This was what I deserved, but it didn't make it hurt any less.

"I… uh… better go then."

I turned away hastily and hurried back to the car.

I kept my head held high.

I would not break.

I drove slowly back to the penthouse, silently inventorying everything of mine at his house that I would need to pack. Sadly, it was mostly clothes and Percy. Not that I would pack Percy in a box, that would be cruel even if cats did love boxes.

I pulled into the parking garage and slammed on the brakes when I saw the Corvette parked in its usual spot.

For the first time since he said my name so icily a week ago, my heart began to beat at a steady pace.

He was here.

He was really here.

I parked the car and all but ran to the elevator.

As it soared to the top floor I willed it to go faster.

When the doors opened I called out, "Mathias!"

I rushed forward and heard the sound of his footsteps approaching.

The air was sucked out of my lungs when he appeared.

We stood, staring at each other, separated by our own pain and suffering.

I couldn't move or speak for a moment. My eyes roamed over his body, as if I was looking for some significant change that had happened in the last week. He did look rather tired, with purple rings beneath his eyes.

"I'm sorry," he spoke. "I'm sorry I told you I hated you. I don't. I fucking hate myself." He scrubbed his hands over his face. I took a tentative step forward. "I've had a lot of time to think and I'm sorry for my reaction, but most of all I'm sorry for lying to you that day in the parking lot so long ago. It's my fault. I set this whole thing in motion," he rambled, barely able to catch a breath.

"No—"

"I pushed you away! I hurt you and I abandoned you when you needed me most!"

I took another step forward, and then another, until he was so close I could reach up and touch him if I wanted to.

I tilted my head back and looked up at him. "It was no one's fault. Trust me, I know. I wanted to blame myself for a long time. I even blamed you. I blamed everybody, to be honest. But I was wrong to do that. These things… they just happen."

"Why did it have to happen to *us?*" He countered, his eyes two dark storm clouds.

"Because," I placed my hands over his chest, comforted by the familiar beating of his heart, "we're stronger than most people."

"I don't feel very strong right now." His voice lowered to a soft whisper. "All I can think about is this tiny baby that needed her daddy and I wasn't fucking there. I wasn't there, because I pushed you away. I broke you and I broke her. I broke us all. I keep feeling like if I had been there this wouldn't have happened." Tears filled his eyes, one spilling over and rolling down his cheek. I wiped it away and his breath caught in his throat.

Shaking my head, I said, "You're wrong. There was nothing you or I, or anyone, could've done to prevent this."

He swallowed thickly and stared down at me, fighting his emotions. "I was with Collin yesterday and…" He closed his eyes. "Every time I looked at him I kept thinking about the fact that if she were alive she would be his age. And then I thought about all the things you said you'd never get to do with her, which made think of all the things I wouldn't get to do with her and fuck I *want* those things." He wet his lips, pulling in a lungful of air. "I know we were just kids ourselves and would've had no business raising a child, but it's unfair that we didn't even get a chance." This time it was his turn to wipe a tear away from my cheek. "I don't even know who she *looked* like." His voice cracked and more tears filled his eyes.

I closed my eyes, steeling myself. Recalling those final moments with Hope was always painful. "She had blonde hair, so light it almost looked white." A wistful smile touched my lips. "And she had your lips. She was so tiny and perfect. I kept looking at her, trying to find something wrong with her. Some outwardly proof as to why this happened to her. But she was honestly perfect. The most beautiful thing I had ever seen."

Mathias scrubbed his hands over his face. "I can't believe you had to go through that by yourself."

"Now do you see why I didn't want to tell you? I *love* you and I never wanted you to have to hurt like this."

He took my face between his large hands and we breathed the same air for a moment. "Remy, this was always our hurt. It was never your burden to bear alone."

I let out a small cry and clung to his shirt, burying my face in his chest. I wanted to hold on to him forever. I didn't want to ever have a fight like this again or to have to watch him walk out and leave me.

"Shh," he murmured, stroking his fingers lightly through my hair. "I'm so sorry. For everything."

"Me too," I whispered.

He reached down and grabbed my chin, forcing me to look at him. "I forgive you."

At those three words I breathed a sigh of relief and a weight lifted off of my shoulders.

He stroked his fingers down my back.

"I was so mad, but I realized I was more mad at myself than you. I was being stupid to walk out. This is just another part of our story, right?"

"One of the worst parts." I laughed, releasing him from my hold.

"It's not too late for us, is it?"

I wiped away the last of my tears and shook my head. "It's never too late."

"Thank God for that," he growled, taking my face between his hands and lowering his mouth to mine.

Mathias and I had been through a lot at a young age, and we'd always have our ups and downs, but no matter what we would always work it out, because our love was forever.

He pulled away and smiled down at me. "No more secrets?" He asked.

"No more secrets," I vowed.

"Good." He pressed his forehead to mine.

Wrapping my arms around him, I said, "I'm so happy you came back."

"Me too," he murmured, holding on to me too.

"I expected you to divorce me," I admitted.

He chuckled. "I'd be lying if I didn't say there was a moment of weakness where I considered it. But in the end, the thought of my life without you in it was far too painful. I've changed a lot, Remy. I'm not that same guy I used to be. I'm working on thinking things through and not being so impulsive. My impulsivity tends to ruin things," he frowned, stroking my cheek. "Think of me as the new and improved Mature Mathias."

I laughed. "I still liked the old Mathias."

"How about a happy medium?" He suggested, guiding me over to the couch.

He collapsed onto the cushions, pulling me down with him. I landed with a thud on his hard chest and he grunted from the impact.

"Sorry," I mumbled.

He put a pillow behind his head and soon Shiloh and Percy joined us on the couch. He wrapped his arms around me and we lay there together, breathing in each other's presence and reveling in what we could've lost again if one or both of us chose to be stupid.

Mathias was right. He had changed, but so had I.

Both of us for the better.

We were both stronger, happier people now.

He smiled and laughed more. He listened to his heart instead of running away.

And me?

I didn't hide behind the persona of my red lipstick anymore.

I was just Remy and he was just Mathias.

Things might not have been perfect, but I knew they never would be with us.

All that mattered was that we had each other.

"It's this way." I held tightly to Mathias' hand, guiding him around the grassy area.

His hand was slightly sweaty in mine and I knew he was nervous.

I was too.

I'd been shocked when he told me he wanted to visit Hope's grave after the tour ended, but I didn't object.

I might've gotten my closure with her death, but he never did.

The sun shined down us, bathing us in a warm golden glow. I was excited for the summer, especially since the tour was finally over and we'd have a chance to relax.

"It's this one." I stopped in front of the small grave with her name, birth and death date. It broke my heart that the dates were the same. It still seemed unfair, but I'd long ago stopped questioning it. Sometimes things happen in our life that are out of our control, and you either let it make you or break you.

Mathias' hand slipped from mine and he let out a ragged breath, dropping to his knees in front of the stone. He ran the tips of his fingers over the indented letters that formed her name.

A dark gray splotch landed on the headstone and I looked up, expecting to see that the sky had darkened and it was starting to rain, but no, that wasn't the case.

Mathias was crying.

The kind of cry that made his whole body shake from the force.

I reached out, placing my hand on his shoulder.

I didn't say anything. I gave him his moment.

"It never really seemed real before," he whispered.

He slowly raised his head and his tear-rimmed eyes met mine. I stroked my fingers over his cheek and then his lips.

"I wish it wasn't," I murmured.

He stared down at her grave once more and I startled when he began to sing a lullaby.

Now I was the one crying.

Damn him.

I hurriedly wiped the tears away before he could see.

When he finished singing the song, he whispered, "Daddy loves you."

He rose to his feet, drying his face with the back of his hand. "How did two fuck-ups like us get lucky enough to have a second chance?" His hands fell onto my rounded stomach. We hadn't been trying to get pregnant, and we'd both been shocked over the news, but also incredibly happy.

"I don't know. I guess maybe it was fate." I smiled at him as he lovingly stroked my stomach.

"Or maybe," he kissed my forehead, then my cheeks, and finally my lips before murmuring, "it was Hope."

# THE END

# BONUS CONTENT

**INTERVIEWER:** Thanks for sitting down with us today. Every celebrity news station has been vying for this interview and we're honored you chose us. You don't normally do interviews, correct Mathias?

**MATHIAS:** No, I fucking don't. And I'm only doing this one because my manager made me. He's a real prick.

**INTERVIEWER:** <clears throat> Alright, then… <shuffles notes> Everybody has been looking forward to hearing from you both about your sudden decision to get married and now the news that you're having a baby. Congratulations, by the way.

**REMY:** Well—

**MATHIAS:** I wouldn't call it sudden. Not when you've been in love with the person for seven years. <rolls eyes> This is why I fucking hate interviews. None of you do any fucking research.

**INTERVIEWER:** Uh… moving on then… are you enjoying being married? Remy, how are you adjusting to life in the spotlight?

**MATHIAS:** Being married is just like dating. Except the sex gets better. Don't ask me how. But it does.

**REMY:** I guess I'm adjusting fine. <shrugs> It's just a part of his life, and mine now. So I roll with it. I also wear lots of hats now.

**INTERVIEWER:** <chuckles> How was life on the road with the *Coming Home Tour*?

**REMY:** That was hard. I missed being home and relaxing on the couch, watching movies. Whatever.

**INTERVIEWER:** Now that the tour is over what are your plans?

**MATHIAS:** Baby proofing the fucking house.

**REMY:** <laughs> And working on Mathias not cussing so much.

**MATHIAS:** Good fucking luck. <mumbles> I need a cigarette.

**INTERVIEWER:** Do you know if the baby is a boy or girl?

**MATHIAS:** We do and it's none of your fucking business.

**INTERVIEWER:** You lost your first child together when you were only teenagers, does that leave you with any fears this time around?

**REMY:** <looks at Mathias> Yeah, of course. I mean, there's *always* the possibility that something could go wrong. We see the doctor regularly and he assures us that everything looks as good as it can.

**INTERVIEWER:** Mathias, I heard that you actually didn't know about your first child, is that true?

**MATHIAS:** <glares> I'm not answering that.

**INTERVIEWER:** <shrugs> It seems that if it were true, that would be something difficult to work through? Yet, you both seem incredibly happy and you're having another baby together.

**MATHIAS:** Look, people make mistakes. I've made a hell of a lot them myself. We've made a lot of mistakes together. <reaches for Remy's hand> And we'll continue to make mistakes, because we're far from fucking perfect. But when you love someone as much as we love each other, and you've fought as hard as we have to get to where we are, you don't fucking let go of that. <kisses Remy>

**INTERVIEWER:** Well, I think that's all the questions we have time for today. Thank you for joining us.

**REMY:** Thanks for having us.

**MATHIAS:** Thank God this nightmare is over. See you never, asshole.
Twitter: @msmeltzer9793 (https://twitter.com/msmeltzer9793)
Instagram: micaleasmeltzer (http://instagram.com/micaleasmeltzer)
Pinterest: http://www.pinterest.com/micaleasmeltzer/

# IN YOUR HEART

## MICALEA SMELTZER

- A WILLOW CREEK NOVEL -

"Music exists to speak the words we can't express."
—Unknown

# CHAPTER ONE

I WAS GETTING married in two weeks.

I was getting married in two weeks and I was standing here watching my so-called fiancé stick his dick in a woman that wasn't me.

An inhuman shriek crawled out of my throat and I grabbed the first thing I could get my hands on which happened to be one of Braden's baseball caps—granted, it wouldn't do much damage, but at least it was something—and threw it at his bare back. He was already turning to look at me over his shoulder, his hips still thrusting against the skank beneath him, when the cap hit him.

"What the hell?" He glared at me.

At *me*, like I was the one doing something wrong.

"Excuse me?" I stormed forward. My whole body shook with barely contained rage.

Before I could reach them he stood up, wrapping the bed covers around his waist and leaving the woman in *our* bed lying there completely naked.

That was Braden for you, ever the gentlemen.

He held his hands up in a placating gesture. "Let's talk about this, Sadie."

"Yeah, let's *talk!*" I screamed, waving a hand in the direction of the woman lying on *my* sheets. "Let's talk about the fact that apparently you slipped and fell and your penis ended up in someone else's vagina! Thank God she was there to break your fall!" I yelled sarcastically.

"It's not what—"

I slapped him across the cheek. My hand left behind a red imprint on his skin. His teeth snapped together and he glared down at me.

"Don't you fucking *dare* tell me it's not what it looks like," I shouted, my hands shaking at my sides.

The woman in our bed was still lying there. Why, I didn't know. Maybe she thought I'd be kind enough to leave and let them finish.

As. Fucking. If.

"Sadie—"

He grabbed my arm and I screamed so loud that I was sure everyone in the apartment complex heard me. "Take your fucking hand off of me!!"

Braden, surprisingly, let me go. He took a step back and I swore his skin had paled a shade.

That's right asshole, be afraid. Be very afraid.

I poked a finger into his chest—a chest I had once found to be a magnificent piece of masculine perfection.

"I can't fucking believe you! After *everything* you've put me through you go and do this! Seriously?! What the fuck did I ever see in you?!" The words poured out of my mouth. I was beyond hurt and pissed off. This was the man I'd planned on spending the rest of my life with, the man I'd given up so many important things for, and here *he* was fucking another woman only weeks before our wedding.

It was comical really, the irony of it all, since he'd been convinced I was sleeping with my friend Ezra. I thought of all the ridiculous accusations Braden had lobbed my way, and I couldn't help wondering if his own indiscretions led to his insecurity.

Hell, Braden had practically forced me to end my friendship with Ezra.

Why? Why had I been so blinded? When did I become this weak, sniveling excuse for a person that I let an asshole like him walk all over me? And *why* did it take me seeing him fucking someone else, to finally snap back into reality and realize what a complete asshole he was?

Fuck.

It was like I'd been brainwashed.

I tore at my hair, my breaths coming out in little gasps.

Anger at myself, at him, and at the bitch in my bed simmered dangerously in my veins. It wouldn't take much for me to snap and lose my ever-loving mind.

"Sadie, let's talk about this—"

"Should I get dressed?" The woman in our bed spoke up.

"Yes!" I screamed.

Her eyes widened and she slipped from the bed, looking around for her clothes.

With another scream I started for the kitchen.

"Where are you going?" Braden asked, trailing behind me.

He kept stopping to untangle his feet from the too-long sheet wrapped around his waist.

I wished he would trip and die.

"Sadie," he started in again.

I opened one of the various drawers in the kitchen and pulled out a knife, waving it around like a crazy person.

He paled further.

"Sadie, put down the knife."

"No!" I screamed. "I think I should cut your dick off so you can fuck yourself with it! Would that suffice?!"

Braden's mouth fell slightly open.

He was afraid.

Good.

The asshole should be afraid for his life.

Or the life of his penis, which was really the most important thing to him.

"I'm calling 911!" I heard the woman shout from my bedroom.

"Go ahead, bitch!"

"Sadie, be reasonable," Braden started.

I thrust the knife in his direction, flailing my arms about like I'd seen jousters do on TV. "Reasonable?! You want me to be reasonable?!"

"I'm a man, I have needs—"

"Oh for fuck's sake!" I threw my hands up in the air. "Your *needs?* That's seriously the excuse you're using? Wow, you're dumber than I thought." Laughing manically, I cried, "Who am I kidding? *I'm* the dumb one for being with you."

When I met Braden he'd been…perfect. I knew that sounded cliché, but it was true. He was everything I'd always wanted and more. He treated me nicely and was always a gentleman. Once things got serious he started changing. I chalked it up to the fact that he'd recently started a new job. When things got worse after our engagement I found every excuse possible to explain his behavior. I'd been so naïve.

Everybody had tried to warn me that something wasn't right.

But I'd been blinded by…love?

No, that wasn't the right answer.

I think I'd been more blinded by my own need not to be *wrong.*

It was like I felt by giving up on my relationship with Braden it was admitting defeat—admitting that everyone else had been right about him.

*Look where that got you?* My conscience piped in.

"Sadie." He took a few steps forward.

"Stay away from me!" I jabbed the knife in his direction. I wasn't *really* going to hurt him, but oh how I wanted to.

"Sadie, put the fucking knife down and let's talk about this," he pleaded.

I wiped the back of my hand over my tear stained face.

Why the fuck was I crying over this loser? He didn't deserve a single tear from me.

"Talk about what?" I spread my arms wide. "The fact that I've wasted the last two years of my life with you? Or the fact that if I hadn't caught you in the act I would be your *wife* in two weeks." I shook my head, laughing under my breath. I began to slow clap. "Thanks for saving me the nightmare of divorce court, asshole."

"We can work this out—"

"Work this out!" I shrieked, charging forward. "Are you fucking crazy? I am *done* with you!"

To further prove my point I pried off my engagement ring, throwing it at his head. He tried to catch it, dropping the sheet from around his waist in the process.

"You disgust me," I spat through clenched teeth.

He hurried to grab the sheet to cover himself once more, as if I might charge forward and make good on my previous threat.

He opened his mouth to speak, but I stopped him.

"I swear to God, if you say my name *one more fucking time* I will cut off your tongue too!"

"Don't worry, babe," the slut from my bed strolled down the hall, dressed only in skimpy lingerie, "I called the police and I recorded everything she said on my phone."

I gulped, suddenly not feeling so bold.

The evil glint in her eye told me I was in trouble.

She leveled me with a smirk. "I'm a lawyer," she said the words slowly like I was too dumb to process them, "and this," she waved her phone around, "is enough to get you arrested."

Oh, fuck.

I steeled my shoulders, refusing to let the bitch know her words had gotten to me.

Braden glanced from her to me, not saying a word.

Two years together and the asshole couldn't even come to my defense and tell the bitch that I hadn't really meant anything by it. Heat of the moment and all that jazz.

Nope, he just stood there blinking like it was the only thing he was capable of doing.

My teeth gnashed together and I dropped the knife on the floor. I wanted to launch myself at the bitch with my claws out, but she'd already won.

Although, that was laughable, because apparently the prize was Braden and I could see now that he was hardly worth bragging rights.

She could have him.

And I would laugh when he cheated on her.

Because he would.

Men like him didn't change.

I turned to Braden, my shoulders slumping with exhaustion. I'd been so wound up and now the air had left my sails. I was just…done. I wasn't going to waste another breath yelling at him. Nothing I said would penetrate its way through his thick skull the way he penetrated his mistress. He definitely wasn't worth it either. I'd been crazy to ever think he was the guy for me.

Sirens sounded outside the apartment building.

"I'll go let them in." The tramp smiled.

"Shouldn't you go put some clothes on," I snapped.

She looked down. "Oh, right."

She disappeared back into the bedroom while Braden and I stood staring at each other. When she returned she was wearing *my* ripped shorts and *my* lavender tank top.

The calm defeat I'd felt a moment before instantly disappeared.

How dare she wear *my* clothes.

I screamed again, charging forward, and grabbed the bitch's hair before Braden could stop me.

That's when the cops knocked on the door.

From there, things escalated.

I scratched her.

She hit me.

I hit back.

She pulled my hair.

I bit her.

And then I got arrested.

Today was not my day.

# CHAPTER TWO

I SAT ON the cold metal bench inside the holding cell, contemplating my life choices.

I wondered what shitty decision led me to this moment.

Was it when I attacked the bitch?

Or grabbed the knife?

Or when I first started dating Braden?

I was betting on the latter.

From the first moment I met him he screwed with my life and I let him, because I'd been dumb. There was no other explanation. I'd been so desperate to love someone that I'd tricked myself into thinking he was better than he was.

I kept going over and over in my head different things he'd said and done, and wondered why I'd always swept his behavior under the rug.

When did I become this girl that turned a blind eye?

I'd always spoken my mind, but with Braden I let him speak for me.

I put my head in my hands, letting out a small groan.

I wasn't going to be that girl anymore. I was going to get my fire back and conquer the world.

Well, as soon as I got out of this jail cell.

Footsteps sounded on the concrete floors and I stood up, praying that they were coming to let me out.

A moment later a figure appeared.

He was tall and thin. He kept his head ducked down and his unruly black hair hid his face.

Slowly, he lifted his head to face me. His dark eyes were hidden behind a pair of round glasses and his cheeks and chin were covered in scruff like he hadn't shaved in a week or more.

My breath caught on an embarrassing gasp.

It'd been six months since I'd seen him and he still took my breath away—not that I would ever tell him that.

Once upon a time I'd had a crush on Ezra Collins, but soon his friendship became too important to me to ever cross that line.

He tilted his head to the side, shoving his hands into the pockets of his jeans.

"I thought I'd never hear from you again." His eyes bore into me, hurt lacing his words. Chuckling, he added, "Let me tell you, I was quite surprised to answer the phone and hear your voice. Jail? Really, Sadie? What is it with you and Emma getting arrested?"

I lifted a finger. "That wasn't her fault." I reminded him. "This…" My lower lip began to tremble with the threat of tears. "This is all me."

And that was the sad truth.

"What exactly happened?" He asked.

I stepped forward, wrapping my hands around the metal bars. "Do you think you can get me out of here first and then we can chat?"

"Oh, right." He shook his head, pushing his too long hair out of his eyes. He cracked a small half smile. "They didn't want to let me back here, but I had to see this for myself."

I sighed, sitting back down on the bench with my hands splayed on my legs. "I'm glad you find this amusing, Ezra."

He shook his head, his eyes growing serious once more. "I'm sorry."

I flinched. I'd told him when I called that I caught Braden cheating on me.

"Why?" I found myself asking. "You hated him."

"But I love you." He paled, lifting his hands in surrender. "Not like that," he added. "You're my best friend, Sadie. I might've hated the asshole, but I still wanted you to be happy. This was the last thing I wanted to happen to you."

"But you knew it would," I whispered, looking away from him and staring at the cinderblock cell wall instead, "you warned me and I didn't fucking listen."

"You were in love." He defended my actions.

I turned back towards him. "Was I?" I retorted. "Because I don't know anymore."

My shoulders sagged with my words. I didn't think there had ever been a time in my life when I felt this defeated.

He frowned, his mouth twisting as he struggled with something to say. Finally he muttered, "I better go take care of this."

"Yeah, that would be great," I sighed. "I mean, this bench is nice and all, but I don't really want to sleep here."

He shook his head and walked back down the hall.

I felt bad that after six months with no communication this was what I called him for, but I knew I could count on him to bail me out.

My parent's would have too, but frankly I wasn't ready to tell them all the gory details.

Plus, my dad might kill Braden when I told him.

I knew Ezra would keep his cool, even if he probably did dream about maiming my ex-fiancé.

In fact, the last time I saw Ezra he punched Braden in the face.

Now, I wished I could go back and give Ezra a round of applause for that one.

It took a while, but eventually they released me.

Neither of us spoke as we walked out of the building. Ezra guided me through the parking lot and to his shiny black Cadillac Escalade.

As soon as we were both seated in the car I broke down in tears.

He didn't say anything, which I was thankful for.

He reached for my hand, holding mine in his and offering the smallest amount of comfort that he could.

After a few minutes I wiped my face free of tears and he started the car.

He pulled away from the police station and I watched the trees and traffic go by.

"I don't have anywhere to go," I realized.

I'd moved into Braden's place when we got engaged. At the time I'd still been living with my parents but they'd since downsized. I wouldn't have wanted to impose on them anyway.

I couldn't stay with Emma either—my best friend since we were in diapers. She and her fiancé, Maddox—the drummer for Willow Creek, the band Ezra played in—still lived in the guesthouse behind his foster parent's house. Maddox's foster parents also happened to be Ezra's real parents. They'd taken in Maddox and his twin brother Mathias when they were put into the system as teenagers. Maddox and Ezra were close, like brothers, while Mathias had always remained distant. That seemed to be changing though, according to things Emma had told me. Apparently, since Mathias rekindled with his high school love, Remy, and subsequently married her, he'd stopped distancing himself from his brother and band mates. They were also having a baby. Mathias Wade as a dad…I definitely hadn't seen that one coming.

"You'll stay with me." Ezra said simply, his eyes on the road ahead.

I shook my head. "No." My voice was firm. "I can't impose myself on you like that. I *won't*," I reiterated.

He glanced at me and then his eyes went back to the road. "You're not *imposing*. You're my friend and I'm doing you a favor."

"I don't want any favors," I ground out between my teeth, "this was enough." I added, referring to him bailing me out of jail.

"Yeah, care to explain the details to me? Seriously, what the fuck did you do to get arrested?"

I swallowed thickly and looked out the window once more. I could see my reflection in the glass. My lips were turned down in a frown and my light brown hair hung limply.

"I grabbed a knife and told him I was going to cut off his dick and then I threatened to cut off his tongue too. The bitch he was cheating on me with happened to be a lawyer. She recorded the whole thing and it was enough for them to arrest me." I shrugged, playing it off. "Can you believe that?"

I glanced at him. A muscle in his jaw twitched and I knew he was irritated. Not at me, but at the situation.

"It's like the world is conspiring against me," I muttered, picking at the tear in my ripped jeans. "No, not conspiring…it's laughing at me. At how completely fucking stupid I am." I shook my head back and forth, swallowing past the lump in my throat. Tears stung my eyes once more. "I hate myself so much right now."

"Don't," Ezra snapped, his tone harsh as he spared me a glance, "don't fucking say that."

"But I do."

"Everybody makes mistakes, Sadie," he interjected, turning down a street and heading out of town.

"I was going to *marry* him." My voice cracked. "I was going to marry an asshole that treated me like shit, who cheated on me, and who just isn't a very nice fucking person, and *why?*"

His Adam's apple bobbed as he swallowed. His lips pursed as his tongue rolled around, searching for the right words. "I don't know," he answered.

"Yeah?" I laughed, but there was no humor in the tone. "Me either." I buried my head in my hands and let out a small scream. "Why didn't I listen to you? Why didn't I listen to any of you? *Everybody* warned me against him."

"You're stubborn," he responded, his voice flat.

"Yeah," I agreed, "and look where that got me. I'm now fiancé-less and homeless. I'm such a role model."

His lips twisted. "Now's not the time for your sarcasm."

"Are you mad at me?" I asked, hating that I sounded hurt. But I was. Hurt, that is. He had every right to be mad at me though. I mean, what kind of crappy friend calls a person up because they're in jail and then doesn't even have a place to stay?

"Yes, I am mad at you," he replied, "but not for the reason you think."

He always did know me so well, like he could read my mind. We'd only become friends when our best friends fell in love four years ago. They were so enamored with each other that we both ended up being left out. We started hanging out and bonded, soon becoming best friends ourselves. The last six months without Ezra in my life had sucked, to put it bluntly, but Braden was my fiancé so I thought I was doing the right thing by cutting Ezra out of my life since that's what Braden wanted. Little did I know that was simply another way he was manipulating me.

"So, why exactly are you mad at me?" I asked.

"Because," he took a deep breath, trying to calm himself, "you're acting like this is your fault. You're not the one that cheated, Sadie."

"But I'm the one that stayed with an asshole for no good reason. I mean," I pushed my hair away from my face, "I don't feel like I ever really loved him…if I did I would feel more hurt, right?" I asked him. "Because that's not what I feel, instead—"

"Your ego is bruised," he supplied, turning down another road. Farmland stretched as far as I could see as he drove to his house.

"Exactly," I agreed, nodding.

"I think you *wanted* to believe he was the one for you," he glanced at me for a moment, his dark eyes serious, "but he wasn't."

"Maybe I'm meant to be alone for the rest of my life," I mused, "with like fifty cats."

He chuckled, shaking his head. "You're twenty-one. You have plenty of time to find the guy for you."

"I think I'm just going to become a nun." I nodded, affirming my words.

He snorted and I glared at him. "I think it's a bit late for that."

I crossed my arms over my chest, the seatbelt digging into my collarbone. "I'm glad you find amusement in my suffering."

"Don't be like that." He chuckled. "Think about all that you've accomplished. You own your own store, Sadie. That's a big deal. Be proud of yourself. Focus on that and not trying to find a guy to settle down with."

"I wanted so desperately to be in love," I confessed. "Real, soul deep, shaking in the knees, forever, kind of love."

"You'll have that one day," he assured me.

I sighed heavily. "But not now."

He shook his head and took my hand once more, giving it a reassuring squeeze before letting go. "This is a good thing. You're going to be a stronger person because of this."

"I hope so," I agreed.

I knew I was better off without Braden, and I hated that it had taken *this* to get me to see that. But it still hurt. I'd spent two years of my life with him, and there had been good memories with him. I stayed with him for stupid reasons, and I was mad at myself for that. I'd given up so much for an ideal I'd conjured up in my mind of what my life was supposed to be like. I would not let this break me. Nope.

Oh God, was I crying again?

I tentatively reached up and there were more tears.

Shit. So much for not letting this break me.

Ezra turned onto the driveway leading up to his house. Although, calling it a house was a stretch. His home was small, more like a cottage. I'd been there plenty of times before…well, *before*. It was cute and nestled between shady trees with a lake in the back. There were also no other houses close, which I knew was a big draw for Ezra. Seclusion from nosy people and the media was highly coveted among the Willow Creek boys.

He parked the SUV in the detached garage he'd had built to match the house. Both were covered in dark blue siding with white shutters beside the windows. I'm sure most people expected a rock star like Ezra to live in a mansion, but that'd never been what he wanted. I admired him, and the other guys too, for not letting fame go to their heads. Not that they didn't love their shiny toys, like their various cars.

He turned the vehicle off and sighed into the silence.

"How about I make some dinner? Fettuccine?"

I flinched. Fettuccine Alfredo was my favorite meal. Ezra knew that, but that was something Braden could never remember.

"I'm not very hungry," I muttered, reaching for the door handle.

Before I could slip out of the vehicle he grabbed my arm, halting me. "Don't let him win." His eyes bored into me, burning me with their seriousness.

"I'm not," I argued.

"That's exactly what you're doing," he snapped. "He's not worth it."

I sighed, scrubbing a hand over my face. "Ezra," I huffed, "this *just* happened. I think I'm allowed a day to wallow over the complete shit-fest that is my life."

His lips quirked into a small smile and he ducked his head. Releasing my arm, he sobered. "Yeah, you're right. I'm sorry."

"I'm sorry too," I whispered, a frown turning down my lips. He gave me a quizzical look so I quickly explained. "I'm sorry for throwing away our friendship like it meant nothing to me. I was wrong to do that."

"You felt like you had to." He sighed heavily. Shaking his head, his black curls tumbled forward to hide his gaze. "I'd be lying if I said that didn't hurt, especially since Braden is such a prick," his teeth ground together, "but it was your life and I couldn't force myself to be a part of it. So, I let you go."

"And yet, you didn't let me spend the night in jail. It's what I deserved."

He stared at me for a moment. The intensity in his dark eyes rooted me to the spot. "I'll always have your back."

I lowered my head, feeling forlorn. Ezra was much too kind to me.

"You should hate me," I breathed, my words hanging heavily in the air.

He grasped my chin, forcing me to look at him. His eyes seared into me as he spoke. "Friendship doesn't work like that. I could never hate you for making the decision that you did."

"Even if it was the wrong one?"

His fingers momentarily tightened against my chin and anger pulsed in his brown eyes. "For you, it was the right decision at the time. Life is a series of choices that we make, some of them are good, and some of them are not, but everything always works out in the end. Things will be better now, you'll see."

He released his hold on me and I looked away with a sigh. "Better," I repeated. "I hope so."

"I know so." He reiterated with a smile. "Everything happens for a reason, Sadie. Sometimes we don't understand why, but eventually we look back and can see that everything worked out."

"I think it already has," I whispered.

He nodded at my words, processing them. "Come on," he reached for the car door handle, "let's eat. I'm starving."

This time at the mention of food my stomach came to life.

I climbed out of the large SUV and followed the gravel pathway over to the front porch steps.

He pulled out his house key and swung the door open.

"After you." He waved a hand.

I stepped inside the cottage and immediately felt an overwhelming sense of comfort. The home was decorated with the coastal colors of navy and white. The floors were a dark hardwood that shined as if they'd just been cleaned. The family room sat to my left with a white couch and chair, with blue and gray throw pillows.

Across from the family room sat the kitchen. It had white cabinets with concrete countertops. The appliances were shiny stainless steel. It was a work of art, and almost looked untouched, but I knew that Ezra wasn't that kind of guy. He actually enjoyed cooking. His mom had made sure that he, Maddox, and Mathias, all knew how to cook and not just microwave frozen pizza rolls like most guys.

Beside the kitchen was a small table with four chairs, but the area wasn't large enough to be considered a dining room.

The downstairs also had a small powder room and the laundry room—the laundry room being an addition Ezra had insisted on since the home didn't have one when he moved in.

Upstairs there were two bedrooms and a shared bathroom.

Straight ahead lay a pair of French double doors that led out to a large deck overlooking the lake. I knew if I went out there he would have several rocking chairs lined up, a grill, and a fire pit. The view of the lake, and the deck, had been one of the things Ezra loved the most about this place.

He'd dragged me to various homes during his house hunt. That seemed like a lifetime ago even though it hadn't been more than three years.

"You act as if you've never seen the place before." He chuckled, noticing my lingering stare.

I lifted my shoulders in a shrug and gave him a small smile. "I missed this place."

He beamed at my words. "Yeah?"

I nodded. "This has always been one of my favorite places."

I always felt at peace here. I didn't know why. Maybe it was the fact that the home was so cozy and welcoming, or maybe it was the breathtaking view of the lake. Or maybe it was simply because this was where my best friend lived, and being near him filled me with a sense of security.

"You can stay here as long as you need," he said, moving into the kitchen. He began to rifle through cabinets, setting out pots.

I wrapped my arms around my body, as if I could hold myself together. "Thanks," I forced a smile. I hated intruding on Ezra's space, but I was truly thankful for his kindness. Especially after the last six months with no contact. Without him…I didn't know where I would stay. I couldn't afford my own place right now.

He flicked a piece of dark hair out of his eyes. "Want to help?" He asked me.

I nodded, stepping around to the other side of the counter beside him. He quickly gave me instructions and I went to work.

We laughed and joked as we cooked, slipping into our once familiar roles as best friends. God, I'd missed this. Ezra might not have been my friend for as long as Emma—who I had known since we were babies—but our bond was just as strong. Sometimes I even felt like it was stronger.

We fixed the table and sat down across from each other to eat.

"So," I started, picking up my fork, "how was the tour?"

Willow Creek had been on a tour across the United States since January. They'd only been home a few weeks.

"Good," Ezra nodded. "Tiring, but fun. It was nice to get back out there and play on stage, but I'm also ready to get back in the studio."

"So, you guys are already working on the next album?" I swirled the noodles around and then took a bite. "Oh my God," I moaned, "that's delicious."

Ezra smiled at my words. "I'm glad you like it."

"It's certainly better than a restaurant."

He'd made the sauce from one of his mom's recipes and it was as good as I remembered.

"To answer your question," he reached for a wine bottle, filling each of our glasses, "yes we're already working on it."

"Do you guys ever sleep?"

He choked on a laugh. "No, not very much."

"You all have lots of dedication," I told him.

He tipped his glass in my direction. "So do you."

Me?" I snorted. "No."

He clasped his fingers together, studying me like I was some fascinating specimen. "I don't know how you can dismiss your accomplishments so easily."

"They don't feel like accomplishments when I'm currently homeless."

He set his glass down, crossing his fingers together. "You're too hard on yourself. Why?"

It was a simple question, one I should've been able to answer, but I couldn't.

"I think," he continued when I didn't speak, "that you need to focus more on your accomplishments and less on your failures." He slowly raised the glass to his lips.

I sighed, taking another bite of fettuccine to stall for time. "I'll get right on that."

He shook his head, fighting a smile. I expected him to call me on my sarcasm like he usually did, but he didn't.

"You know," he said, "when I met you, you were…" He paused, his lips twisting as he searched for the right words. "So vibrant," he settled on, "and from the moment you got with Braden I've had to watch him strip your identity from you. You went from this carefree girl to this…shell. It's like you're a stranger."

"I was a teenager then. I grew up," I defended, his words stinging me.

He shook his head, looking at me pityingly. "No, it's more than that."

I knew he was right, but that didn't make it hurt any less to have him point it out to me. Reluctantly I mumbled, "Yeah, I know. You're right."

"We're going to change that," he stated. He tilted his head to the side, daring me to contradict him.

"How?" I asked, not even bothering to hide the challenging tone in my voice.

He tapped his lips. "I don't know yet, but I'm going to figure it out."

I believed him.

In fact, I always believed in Ezra, because he'd never let me down.

We grew quiet as we finished our dinner. I offered to wash the dishes, but he refused my help and I reluctantly settled on the couch.

Ezra joined me a little bit later, turning on the TV and settling into the chair.

The silence between us should've been awkward since we hadn't seen each other in so long, but it wasn't. In fact, it was like no time at all had passed.

I let out a heavy sigh, suddenly feeling exhausted. It wasn't even eight o' clock yet and I felt like I could pass out asleep any second.

At my sigh Ezra cast his dark eyes in my direction. "Tired?" He asked, the corners of his mouth wrinkling with concern.

I nodded. "Yeah, I think I'm going to go to bed." I stood up, as if to do that and my face crumbled with the realization that I had no clothes, no toothbrush, nothing. "I don't have any of my stuff," I sniffled.

"Sadie," Ezra's eyes darkened with worry, "we can get your stuff tomorrow. We'll make do for tonight."

"Right." I nodded, rubbing a hand over my face. I couldn't believe I didn't have *anything*. Not even my purse. I'd been so distracted by my anger, and then getting arrested that I hadn't even thought about all my shit at Braden's place. I really hoped that tramp didn't do anything with my stuff.

"Sadie," his eyes narrowed on me as he repeated my name, "are you sure you're okay?"

I wrapped my arms around myself, my eyes shifting to the stairway. "No," my lips began to tremble, "I'm not."

I *wanted* to be okay. I knew I was better off without that asshole and should've dumped him a long time ago, but it still hurt. I might not have been *in* love with him like I thought I was, but I had loved him in some way or I wouldn't have been with him.

Ezra didn't say anything. He simply stood up and wrapped his arms around me. I didn't return the embrace at first, but slowly I wrapped my arms around his lean chest. I inhaled his familiar woodsy scent as my tears stained his white t-shirt.

"This is the beginning of new and better things," he vowed.

I nodded against his chest.

Taking a step back I dried my tears with the back of my hand, silently vowing that they'd be the last tears I cried over Braden. He wasn't worth my sorrow.

Ezra stared down at me, his eyes raking over my face as he looked for any signs of another imminent breakdown.

"I'm okay," I assured him. "I just needed to cry again."

"And that's fine," he reached out, wiping away a tear I had missed, "tears aren't a sign of weakness, but of strength of the heart. They show you care and caring is never a bad thing."

"Even when it gets you hurt?" I questioned, leaning my head back to look up at him. At six-foot Ezra was much taller than me.

"Even then." He nodded at his words like he was agreeing with them. He turned for the stairs. "Come on, I'll let you borrow a shirt to sleep in. I have some extra toothbrushes too."

I followed him upstairs and stood awkwardly in the doorway of his bedroom.

He opened his dresser drawer, rifling through it and procuring a plain black t-shirt. His heavy boots clapped against the creaking hardwood floors. "Here," he held the shirt out for me.

"Thanks." I mustered a genuine smile for him as I followed him down the short hallway into the bathroom. He grabbed an unopened blue toothbrush from beneath the sink and gave me that as well.

"If you want to shower you can use my soap. I don't care."

I nodded. "A shower would be nice."

He cleared his throat and stepped out of the bathroom. "You know where the guestroom is, and I'll be downstairs for a while if you need me."

I nodded, sliding the door closed. "Thanks for everything, Ezra."

"Anytime." He nodded his head once and then bound down the steps.

I closed the bathroom door completely and laid the shirt on the shiny marble countertop. I turned on the shower, letting the water grow warm before stripping out of my clothes.

I stepped beneath the spray and the heat began to work out the tension in my coiled muscles. An audible sigh of relief passed through my lips.

I didn't bother washing my hair—not wanting to deal with the tangled nightmare it would become if I didn't use conditioner—but I used Ezra's soap to wash my body. It smelled like mahogany with hints of oranges, nothing like the coconut-scented body wash I usually used.

I turned the shower off and grabbed a clean towel, drying off my body. I returned the towel to the rack and shrugged into the t-shirt. It fell to the center of my thighs and was incredibly soft. I knew that even though it was a plain t-shirt it probably cost more than my car payment.

I had a ponytail holder on my wrist and I used it to pull my hair back while I scrubbed my face clear of makeup.

I gathered up my clothes and opened the bathroom door, promptly bumping into Ezra as he topped the stairs.

"Sorry," he grabbed my arms, righting me from my stumble, "I wanted to check on you."

"I'm fine," I assured him, edging towards the bedroom.

He stared at me for a moment, dissecting my words and trying to find the truth in them.

"Yeah, okay," he finally mumbled, starting back down the stairs. "Good night," he called.

"Night," I said back, but it was merely a whisper and I doubt he even heard it.

I stepped into the guestroom and closed the door behind me.

The room was small, but cozy. The walls were painted a pale yellow with white furniture and soft gray bedding. I'd helped Ezra decorate it. In fact, he'd asked for my opinion on lots of things when he'd been renovating the cottage. He'd fussed that he was a guy and had no idea what matched and what didn't. I'd loved helping him.

I sat down on the edge of the bed, running my fingers over the silky fabric of the bedspread. I'd missed out on a lot these past six months. Not just with Ezra, but with Emma as well. She'd gone on tour with the band and we'd hardly been able to talk. I'd become so out of the loop, and I couldn't help wondering if that was something Braden wanted. He'd always hated it when I spent any time with someone that wasn't him.

With a groan I stood up, pulling back the bed covers and climbing beneath.

I reached for the remote, turning on the small TV and keeping the volume low for background noise in the hopes that it would help muffle my racing thoughts.

I turned on my side, facing the window that overlooked the lake. It was completely dark, no moon in sight, but out this far in the country I could still see the twinkle of stars.

I closed my eyes, wishing upon a star—wishing for happiness and most importantly wishing that I would find my true love.

# CHAPTER THREE

I WOKE UP, struggling to understand my surroundings. The room wasn't familiar and there was nobody lying beside me.

It all came rushing back to me and I lowered my head in my hands.

In my dreams I'd been able to believe it wasn't real, simply a figment of my imagination, but with the sunlight streaming into the room that wasn't mine I couldn't deny the truth.

My life felt seemingly over.

Melodramatic? Yes.

But also the truth.

The life I'd had was no more. From this point forward things were going to be different. My future was now heading down a new path.

One for the better.

But I knew I would stumble and fall before this path felt like the right one.

I eased out of the bed, the TV in the room now off. I hadn't turned it off so Ezra must've checked on me before he went to bed.

I opened the bedroom door and stepped out into the hall.

It was early, around seven, but Ezra was already up.

The bathroom mirror was still slightly fogged so I knew he'd already taken a shower and from the sounds of cabinets banging downstairs he was making breakfast.

I brushed my teeth and hair, braiding it on the side so it rested against my collarbone. I had no makeup with me and my skin looked pale with purple rings beneath my eyes. I hoped I didn't scare Ezra.

I dressed in my clothes from yesterday, silently squirming at the fact that they were dirty, but I knew I'd get my stuff today.

I padded down the stairs and rounded the corner, smiling at Ezra.

"Morning," I said, feigning cheer.

Ezra glanced over his shoulder where he stood at the stove making scrambled eggs. He was already dressed for the day in a pair of jeans and a heather gray t-shirt. His black hair was still damp from the shower, one curl sticking to his forehead.

"Hey. I'm almost done with this."

"You didn't need to make me breakfast." I walked over to the refrigerator and grabbed the bottle of orange juice and then the glasses from the cabinet by the sink.

Ezra shrugged, sliding the eggs onto the plates and topping both with a sprinkle of cheddar cheese just the way I liked. Toast popped up from the toaster and he added it to the plate.

"It was no big deal."

"Don't dismiss your kindness so easily," I told him, setting our glasses down on the table. He'd already put out paper napkins and utensils.

He glanced at me out of the corner of his eye as he sat the plates down. "It's breakfast, Sadie," he chuckled, "it's not a kitten."

"Does that mean you got me a kitten?" I joked.

His lips quirked into a smile. "No kitten. Sorry."

"Darn," I tsked, reaching for the fork.

Ezra sat down and began to eat, keeping a careful eye on me like he was waiting for any signs of an imminent breakdown.

"I'm okay," I assured him, piercing a piece of egg, "I'm not going to crack."

"It would be the normal thing," he argued.

I stared across the table at him. "I'm not normal."

"No, you're not," he agreed, "but it's okay to break."

I leaned forward, lowering my voice like I was letting him in on a secret. "I might bend, but I will not break. Not because of this at least."

His dark eyes seared into me and he nodded once.

He returned to his food and I sat back once more.

"I thought we would eat and then go get your things."

I glanced at the old-fashioned cuckoo clock—a quirky gift I'd bought him as a joke. "Braden won't be up until at least ten."

He gave me a disgusted look and spat, "Do I look like I give a fuck?"

I fought a smile at his use of the word *fuck*. Ezra wasn't one to curse a lot. That was usually left to Mathias—the lead singer of the band.

I shrugged. "I just want you to be prepared to deal with his wrath."

His brown eyes narrowed on me like laser beams. "*He* should be the one prepared to deal with *me*."

"Are you going to punch him again?" I asked, recalling their last encounter.

"I'm not planning on it," he violently speared an egg like he wished it was

Braden he was stabbing, "the last thing I want to do is stoop to his level again, but I might be unable to control myself."

"Well, if you do punch him make sure you punch the right side of his face."

Ezra's brow wrinkled with confusion and he flicked a stray curl from his eyes. "Why the right side?"

"Because he thinks it's his good side."

Ezra snorted and shook his head. "The guy has no good side. He's ugly through and through."

I nodded in agreement, glaring down at my food.

"Sadie," his voice was soft, "there's nothing wrong with you for not realizing how bad he was."

"I know," I replied softly.

The look he gave me clearly said he didn't think that I did know.

He finished eating and I gathered our plates to clean them.

As I ran water in the sink I felt him standing near my back but I refused to acknowledge his presence.

Eventually he spoke. "You don't have to do the dishes you know."

"I want to help," I shrugged, rinsing a plate, "I don't expect to stay here scot-free. I'll help out."

"You know I'd never ask that of you."

I spared him a glance. "And I don't want to be a charity case."

He sighed heavily, his chest expanding as he let out a breath. "I have a maid, so don't start trying to clean the floor with a toothbrush or something," he muttered, rubbing the back of his head awkwardly.

I fought a smile. "I'll stay away from the toothbrushes then."

"I mean it," he warned, pointing a finger at me, "you don't need to do anything."

I turned the water off and opened the dishwasher so I could place the dirty plates and cups on the rack.

"Ezra," I started, "this makes me feel better."

He looked like he wanted to argue with me, but he surprised me by saying, "Alright. Fine. Whatever."

I nodded my head in thanks.

I closed the dishwasher and he grabbed his keys off the kitchen island. "Are you ready to go then?"

"Yeah," I said, even though *ready* was the last thing I felt. I didn't want to face Braden. I never wanted to see him again.

I also knew that today I would have to call my parents and Emma, break the news to them that my engagement was no more and the wedding was off. I would also have to call and cancel everything to do with the wedding. I didn't want to deal with any of those things, but I couldn't ignore my responsibilities.

I followed Ezra outside, the front porch steps creaking as we stepped down. I liked that he hadn't fixed the creaky floors in the cottage. It was things like that, that gave a place character and charm.

Above us the summer sun already shined brightly, promising a day of scorching temperatures. The Virginia summers could be brutal, the humidity alone was enough to kill you, not to mention the bugs. I would never survive living somewhere further south.

Ezra opened the garage door and I tried to ignore the way he watched me—still waiting for another breakdown.

I kept my shoulders back and my chin held high.

I was fine.

I was fine.

*I was fine.*

Maybe if I repeated it enough I would start to believe it.

Not likely, but it was worth a shot.

While I was having my internal debate Ezra unlocked the SUV.

"Are you coming?" He asked, opening the driver's door and looking back at where I stood.

"Yeah." I shook my head free of my thoughts and joined him.

We were silent on the drive over to Braden's apartment. The radio provided background noise, but it wasn't loud enough to drown out my racing thoughts as I imagined all of the different ways this meeting with Braden could go.

None of them were good.

On the way, Ezra stopped by the office supplies store and picked up some boxes. I hadn't even thought of that.

When we arrived at the apartment Braden's truck was nowhere to be seen in the parking lot. I said a silent thanks to whatever god or deity had been on my side today.

Ezra glanced over at me. "This is it."

It was, in more ways than one.

I nodded, reaching for the handle and stepping out of the vehicle.

I trudged slowly up the steps and stopped in front of the door, letting out a string of colorful curses.

"What is it?" Ezra asked, fighting a smile as I kicked the door.

"I don't have my key." I groaned, slamming the heel of my hand against the door like I could force it open.

Ezra lightly pushed my shoulder, forcing me to step away from the door.

"I've got this." He flashed me a crooked smile.

I stood back with my arms crossed over my chest, trying to peer over his shoulder to see what he was doing, but he was careful to shield me.

The door swung open and I stared at him open mouthed. "Did you just break into my apartment?"

He suppressed a laugh. "For starters, it's not your apartment. Secondly, it was already unlocked." He winked.

"No, it wasn't," I defended.

His lips twitched. "Are you sure about that?"

I sighed. "Fine, if the cops show up again I'll stick with the story that it was already unlocked."

"That's all I ask." Pausing, he tilted his head to the side and muttered, "They better not show up."

I shrugged and moved past him to step inside the apartment.

Twenty-four hours ago this place had been home, and now I wanted nothing more than to destroy it. I had to put a lid on my temper. It was going to get me in trouble again.

"Do you have tape?" Ezra asked, laying the flat boxes down on the small kitchen table. "I can start putting these together while you gather your stuff."

"Yeah." I padded into the kitchen and rifled through the junk drawer, producing a roll of packing tape. "Here you go." I held it out to him and he took it with a small smile. He knew this was hard for me, but he also didn't know what to say to make it better.

I left Ezra to assemble the boxes and headed back to the bedroom.

I glared at the bed, remembering what I'd walked in on yesterday. I'd left my store early hoping to surprise Braden and maybe have a nice dinner since it was Friday night. Braden had obviously had other plans.

With a violent yank I began to pull the sheets off the bed.

I would never use them. Not now anyway. But I bought them and I refused to let him have them on principle.

Tears clogged my eyes as I tossed the sheets out into the hallway. Ezra would pack them up for me.

First I grabbed my stuff from the dresser, careful to keep everything folded so I wouldn't have to do it again later.

I strode over to the closet, yanking the doors open so that they clattered harshly against the walls.

"Is everything okay in there?" Ezra called, the concern evident in his voice.

"Just dandy," I said sarcastically.

I heard his chuckle echo through the small apartment.

I took everything off on the hangers and laid them on the bed.

Soon nothing was left in the closet except for Braden's clothes and one lone garment bag.

I grasped the bag, rubbing my fingers against the material that hid my wedding dress.

Stupidly, I reached for the zipper, exposing the white princess dress.

My lower lip began to tremble as I pulled it out of the bag and clutched it to my chest.

I sunk to the floor with the white fabric billowing around me.

Tears fell from my chin onto the dress.

I was crying for so many things.

For my life that imploded in my face.

For the love I'd thought I had that was nothing more than a farce.

For hurting Ezra and pushing him away.

For pushing *everyone* away.

"Sad—oh shit," Ezra cursed, stopping in the doorway of the bedroom. He set the boxes down hastily and hurried to my side. He crouched down beside me, pulling me against his chest. I tried to push away, ashamed of my tears, but he wouldn't let me. "Shh," he cooed.

I finally stopped fighting and relinquished myself to his embrace.

He smoothed his long fingers through my hair and then kissed the top of my head.

I clung to his shoulders, trying to even my breaths and stop sniveling.

He rested his chin on top of my head and he leaned his back against the open closet door.

I fisted the tulle fabric of my dress in my hand.

"I want to burn it." I confessed to him.

He rocked me back and forth, not saying anything for a moment. "Then we'll burn it," he declared.

"Thank you."

I pressed a palm flat against his chest and pushed away.

I dried my eyes with the back of my hands.

Before he could say anything else, I said, "Let's get this stuff packed and get out of here. I don't want to see this place ever again."

Ezra nodded and stood, holding out a hand to haul me up.

I flashed him a grateful smile.

He had all the boxes assembled and we hurried to get all my stuff in them.

I left Ezra in the bedroom to finish, while I tucked an empty box under my arm and headed into the bathroom. I flicked the light on, ignoring my reflection in the mirror. All my makeup and hair things were thrown haphazardly in the drawer, but a hot pink straightener lay on the counter—a straightener that wasn't mine.

Anger overrode me and I picked it up, throwing it at the mirror. The mirror cracked and began to shatter, the pieces raining down.

"Sadie!"

Ezra came running into the bathroom and his mouth fell open at the mess.

I acted like nothing had happened. I started grabbing my things and dropping them into the box. "I hate him," I muttered under my breath, "I hate him so damn much."

Ezra lingered in the doorway. "I know."

"You don't have to watch over me," I assured him.

He still stayed. After a pause he pulled away from the wall. "I'll start loading the other boxes in the car."

He walked away, the sound of his heavy boots muffled by the carpet, and then I heard the front door close.

Once the drawer was empty I grabbed my shampoo, conditioner, and body wash from the shower.

In the kitchen I grabbed the tape and secured the flaps of the box. It felt symbolic somehow. Like I was taping up the wound Braden had left on my life.

I'd begun stacking the boxes by the door when Ezra ran inside. He rested his back against the closed door and his chest rose and fell as he gasped for breath.

What the hell did he do? Run up all three flights of stairs?

"Braden," he panted, waving a hand to point out the door, "is here. He saw me."

My eyes widened.

"Shit," I cursed.

Not only did I never want to see him again, but I also didn't want to deal with his bullish behavior. He'd be intolerable since he saw Ezra.

I squared my shoulders. "We haven't done anything wrong."

"We haven't," Ezra agreed. "But I wanted to beat him here to tell you so you were prepared."

At that moment the door began to move behind Ezra's back and he stepped away so it could swing open.

Braden's large frame took up the whole doorway as he stared angrily at me.

I kept my chin held high, refusing to cower in his presence.

Ezra stood beside me, his hand grazing my waist like he was trying to remind me that I wasn't alone.

Braden's eyes flicked down to where Ezra's hand sat, and let out a growl as he stomped forward. He raised his arms, as if he was going to physically push us away.

"I can't fucking believe this," he spat, glaring at me like I was a disgusting piece of scum stuck to the bottom of his shoe, "not even a day later and you're with him. I always knew you two were fucking."

Ezra growled, ready to barrel forward but I put a hand on his shoulder to halt him. He looked down at me and I shook my head.

This wasn't his fight.

It was mine.

"If I've told you once, I've told you a thousand times, Ezra is my *friend*. F. R. I. E. N. D. The definition being, a person attached to another by feelings of affection. Not attached by a penis and vagina, which is apparently *your* definition." I crossed my arms over my chest, glaring at him. "Don't try and put your transgressions on my shoulders. I've been nothing but faithful to you. Now that I know you're nothing but a cheat I completely understand your insecurity."

He stared at me, baffled. His face began to turn red. "Insecure? I'm not insecure."

"Of course you're not." I patted his chest in a placating manner.

He grabbed my wrist and something in me snapped. My right arm shot out, my closed fist connecting with his jaw.

"Oh motherfucker!" I cried, clutching my fist. "That hurts!" I fanned my hand around like that alone would remove the sting of pain.

Braden started towards me, whether to offer assistance or not I didn't know, because Ezra stopped him from approaching me with a withering glare. "I've got her," he spat at my ex-fiancé. "I think you've done enough, don't you?"

He turned me into his arms and inspected my fist. The skin around my knuckles was red and throbbed painfully. "He has a hard head." I defended my pathetic punch.

Ezra twisted my hand around looking at it closely. "You can wiggle your fingers?" He asked.

I did.

"It's not broken and I don't think it's sprained either, so that's good news." Lowering his voice, he whispered, "He's going to have one heck of a bruise on his face to try to explain."

"Really?" I brightened.

The pain in my hand would be worth it to know that my asshole ex was walking around with a black eye.

He nodded and I heard the freezer open. When I looked over my shoulder I saw that Braden was getting a bag of ice for his face. I hoped his face hurt as bad as my hand. He deserved worse than that, but I'd settle for this.

Ezra let my hand drop and took a step back. "I think we should go now."

I nodded. I was done here. There was nothing else I needed, or wanted, to say to Braden.

When I turned around fully I saw that Braden leaned against the kitchen counter, holding the ice to his cheek. He seemed resigned and I was glad that I wouldn't have to argue with him about it anymore.

Ezra grabbed two of the last three boxes and waited by the door.

I grabbed my keys off the counter where they'd been left yesterday and took off the key to Braden's apartment.

I swallowed thickly as I looked down at the key, remembering how happy I'd been when he'd asked me to move in. Now, my happiness seemed so silly.

I held the key out to him. "Here," I waved it at him.

He took it with his free hand, his fingers grazing my hand. His touch had once filled my body with a pleasant warmth and now I felt nothing.

We stared awkwardly at each other for a moment, neither of us knowing what to do or say.

Finally I shrugged and said, "Well, goodbye."

He nodded once and I knew I'd been dismissed.

Ezra stepped outside and I grabbed the last box.

The door had almost closed behind me when Braden cleared his throat and grabbed it, holding it open so he could peer outside at me.

He stared down at me from his looming height and his lips twisted. "I'm sorry," he finally said, and I reeled back in surprise at his apology.

He eased the door closed before I could react.

I turned to Ezra, gaping like a fish. He looked just as surprised as me.

"That was interesting," he muttered before starting down the stairs.

I nodded my head in agreement even though he couldn't see me.

I followed him over to his car and we put the last of the boxes into the trunk.

"Thank you," I told him yet again. Something told me I was never going to run out of reasons to thank Ezra.

He tipped his head in acknowledgement of my words.

"I'll meet you back at the house," I said, tossing a thumb over my shoulder to point at my white Jeep Wrangler.

"Oh, wait." He caught my arm to stop me from leaving. He shoved his hand into the pocket of his jeans and rummaged around. His tongue stuck out adorably from the corner of his mouth. "Ah, there it is." He held a key up.

I outstretched my palm and he placed it onto my hand.

"What's this?" I asked, closing the fist of my uninjured hand around it.

"The key to my house." He shrugged, shoving his fingers through his unkempt curls. "If you're staying with me then you need to have a key."

"Yeah, I guess so." I frowned, squinting up at him. "I really don't want to be in your way."

"You're not," he assured me, "don't worry about it."

That was easier said than done.

He leaned against his vehicle. "I have to make a couple of stops before I go home."

"I need to go by the store," I mused.

Arden was manning my store today, so it was really unnecessary for me to swing by, but I always liked to check on things. My store was my baby in many ways and I wanted to keep things running smoothly.

"I'll see you later then." He flashed me a smile before turning to get into his SUV.

I waved goodbye, even though he couldn't see me, and crossed the lot to my car.

When I started the car the radio was loud enough to give me a headache. That's normally how I loved to listen to it, but right now I craved silence so I turned it off.

I backed out of the parking space and ended up behind Ezra at the exit.

He turned right while I turned left.

My store was about fifteen minutes from the apartment; so it didn't take me long to get there.

It was located on the walking mall with an antique store to its left and a pizza shop on the right.

I didn't know what had possessed me to decide to open a clothing store. One day I just woke up and it felt right. So, after getting my degree I went for it. People thought I was crazy, but it worked.

*Sew in Style* was my baby, a complete labor of love.

It had been scary going out on a limb and starting a business at my age, but I'd done it. It also helped that my best friend was a rock star and had been willing to loan me the money to start up. Ezra had already been paid back months ago, and he never brought up his helping hand in my business. In his eyes I had done this on my own.

I parked on the side of the building and grabbed my purse as I headed in the back.

I set my bag on a working table and stepped out into the store.

Arden was one of my two employees, and she stood by a rack speaking with a woman about a green and white polka dotted dress. Arden spoke softly, her long red hair curling down her back. She was pretty, with fair skin and a smattering of freckles across her face. The day she'd walked in here asking about a job had been my saving grace. Even though the store wasn't hers, I knew she loved it as much as I did. She'd been working here for the last year and over that time we'd become friends.

When she saw me she lifted her hand in a small wave before returning her attention to the customer.

I busied myself straightening a few racks of clothing.

The woman decided to buy the dress and Arden rang up her purchase. Once the woman left Arden turned to me with her hands on her hips.

"What are you doing here?" She asked. "Shouldn't you be working on last minute details for your wedding."

I flinched and held up my left hand, wiggling my fingers. "I'm not getting married."

Her mouth fell open. She scurried forward and grabbed my hand like she thought the ring was going to magically reappear.

"What happened?" She took a step back, trying to look remorseful even though I knew she wasn't. She, like everyone else, hadn't hid her distaste of Braden. She'd said once that he reminded her too much of her ex-husband. She'd gotten married young, just out of high school, and then got pregnant only for her husband to bail. She'd remained strong through it all, and I admired her for that.

I turned around and began to refold some shirts on one of the tables near the front of the store.

"He cheated." I said the words fast, like ripping off a Band-Aid.

Arden followed me, her lips downturned in sympathy. "Are you okay?"

I smoothed the wrinkles out of the shirt and stood up straight. "Yeah," I held my head high, "I am."

My pride had taken a major bruising, but I really was okay with all of this. It had been eye opening.

"Well, that's good," she said, although her tone suggested she was doubtful of my sincerity.

"This is a new beginning," I stated.

She leaned her hip against the table. "We'll have to get dinner soon if I can manage to get a sitter for Mia. I think we both need some girl time."

"That would be nice," I agreed, moving through the store.

There wasn't anything else for me to fix. Arden was always on top of things.

"I guess I'll head out."

"I have everything covered," she assured me.

"Thanks." I flashed her a grateful smile.

She reached her arms out and hugged me briefly. "The best is yet to come," she whispered in my ear.

I closed my eyes, hanging onto those words and praying that she was right.

# CHAPTER FOUR

IT FELT WEIRD being in Ezra's house by myself. I knew he would want me to make myself at home, but it *wasn't* my home.

I'd been here for hours and he still hadn't come back. It was late afternoon now and I'd spent the whole day making phone calls to cancel everything associated with the wedding, as well as to let my family know. My dad and brother had both offered to castrate Braden for me. I turned down their offers, as tempting as they might be. When I told my mom, she said, "Oh thank God." I would've been more hurt by her words if I hadn't come to see what an asshole he was. Emma hadn't said much when I told her. I got the impression that she was afraid, "I told you so," might pass through her lips while she was trying to be supportive.

I heard the roar of a car and rolled off the couch, hurrying to the front window.

Ezra's large SUV zoomed down the drive with Maddox's sleek sports car behind him. I saw Emma sitting in the passenger's seat and a smile spread across my face. She hadn't said anything about coming over when I talked to her earlier and I hadn't wanted to ask and sound whiny, but I really needed her right now.

I waited for them to park before opening the door and rushing outside.

Emma had barely gotten out of the car before I crashed into her arms, squeezing her tight. I'd seen her only a week ago when we got together to catch up after her being gone on tour with the guys, but it felt like so much longer.

She hugged me back just as fiercely.

"Why are you guys here?" I asked, flicking my head in the direction of Maddox and giving him a small wave.

He smiled and waved back. His brown hair fell messily over his forehead and stubble dotted his jaw. He crossed his arms and laid them on the roof of his car. "This one," he pointed at Ezra who was walking towards us, "said something about a party."

"A party?" My brows rose in interest.

"Yeah," Ezra nodded. "I'm calling it the Thank-God-That-Asshole-Is-Out-Of-Your-Life party."

Laughter burst free of my lungs and I couldn't seem to stop. "That's quite a long name for a party."

He shrugged. "It seemed appropriate."

"I hope you got alcohol."

At my words he walked over and opened the trunk of his SUV, revealing two twelve packs of beer stacked beside my belongings.

I put a hand to my forehead and pretended to swoon. "You're a life saver."

"I also got cake." He smiled proudly. "And fireworks, because what party is complete without blowing some shit up."

"Yeeeaaah!" Maddox clapped his hands together. "Beer and fire, I like this party." He held out his fist for Ezra and Ezra bumped his against it.

Boys.

Emma shook her head, a small smile turning up her lips. She eyed the boxes in Ezra's car. "Do you want me to help you unpack?"

I had told Emma on the phone that I would be staying with Ezra for the foreseeable future.

"That would be great." It would make the time go faster and we could talk.

We each grabbed a box and Ezra told me that he and Maddox would bring in the rest. I flashed both guys a grateful smile.

Emma followed me up the porch steps and into the cottage. Since Maddox and Ezra were best friends she'd been here plenty of times before.

I trudged up the steps and pushed open the door to the guestroom with a shove of my shoulder.

I set the box in my hands down on the bed and Emma did the same.

The guys were right behind us with more boxes.

Ezra lingered in the doorway, looking back at Maddox and then Emma before his eyes landed on me. "I…uh…" He scratched the back of his head, a nervous habit. "I cleared out a drawer in the bathroom for you to put your things."

"That's nice of you, but you didn't need to do that. The last thing I want to do is disrupt things for you." I felt like I kept telling him that over and over again, but I sincerely meant it. It was never my intention to swoop in and unsettle things.

"You're not disrupting anything." He assured me.

Emma watched our exchange with a careful eye.

"Well, thanks for the drawer then. If you're sure?" I questioned further.

"I am." He nodded.

He ducked out of the room then with Maddox behind him.

Emma's lips twisted as she fought a smile.

"What?" I asked, knowing exactly where this was heading but refusing to be the one to initiate the conversation.

"What's going on with you guys?" She asked, trying to hide her growing smile.

I fiddled with my keys, looking for the chain with the small pocketknife. My dad insisted I always have one with me, and he'd also stuck a can of pepper spray in my car. He took the over protective parent role very seriously.

Once I found the knife, I used it to slice open the tape on one of the boxes.

Shrugging, I began to lay the stuff on the bed. "We're friends. We have been for years. Nothing has changed."

She eyed me for a moment and then let out a sigh. She opened another box and started unpacking that stuff.

"You haven't talked to him since New Year's," she whispered, "that hurt him." She glanced at me out of the corner of her eye, waiting for my reaction.

I set a stack of jeans on the bed before turning to the dresser and opening a drawer.

"I did what I had to do." I swallowed past the lump in my throat, waiting for her to ridicule me for my stupid decisions.

"I know," she replied, shocking me. "There's something I've been wondering, though," she started.

I raised a brow for her to continue when she trailed off.

"Why did you call him when you got arrested and not me? I can see why you wouldn't want your parent's to know, but you and I have been best friends for longer than you and Ezra."

I hadn't told my parent's about getting arrested, but I had let Emma in on that detail.

I began to place the jeans in the drawer, weighing my answer. "I guess I was afraid you'd judge me." I shifted my eyes nervously in her direction.

She reeled back, shocked by my admission. "How could you think that?"

I put the last pair of jeans away and closed the drawer.

I waved a hand at her and said, "Look at you, Emma! You have the perfect relationship with the perfect guy. You're *happy*. You didn't get with some fuck up like I did." I opened another box, my back now turned to her.

"You think my relationship is perfect?" She snorted. "I assure you, it's not. We have our ups and downs like everybody else."

"Yeah," I agreed, grabbing the stack of clothes from the box. These were on hangers so I walked over to the closet to hang them up. "But you guys are…ugh…. You're *perfect* for each other. Braden and I were not. You warned me that he was the wrong guy, so I guess I was afraid you'd say 'I told you so.'"

"You know I would never do that," she defended, "and Ezra could just as easily have said that to you. My God, he's the one that punched Braden, not me."

I finished hanging up the clothes and faced her with a frown on my face. "I didn't want to be a bother to you, okay? You're always wrapped up in Maddox and now you're planning your own wedding," I pointed to her hand where a unique purplish pink diamond glittered, "so I didn't want to be an inconvenience. I knew I could count on Ezra."

"But you can count on me too." Her voice was no more than a whisper and hurt swam in her blue eyes. Her mouth fell open and she let out a small gasp. "Are you lying to me? Is something going on between you guys and that's why you and Braden broke up?"

I snorted. We were back to square one. "No," I emphasized the word. "We're only friends and Braden is a lying, filthy, cheating scumbag." My fists tightened at my sides.

"Did you start the name calling without us?" Maddox joked as he and Ezra arrived with more boxes. "I'm hurt." He set the boxes on the floor and then swooped down to give Emma a kiss on her cheek.

Ezra smiled as he watched the gesture. We were both so used to Maddox and Emma's constant displays of affection that we were no longer grossed out.

"Do you have enough room for everything?" Ezra looked concerned as his eyes flitted about the area. He seemed to be taking stock of the furniture to see if there was enough space for all of my belongings.

"It's fine," I assured him, my hand briefly landing on his arm. I let go hastily when Emma's eyes fell to where I touched him. She was reading into nothing. "You don't need to worry about me," I told him, pretending Emma wasn't listening to and analyzing every word that left my lips, "you letting me stay here is enough."

It was kind that Ezra was going out of his way to try to make me feel comfortable but it was completely unnecessary. I couldn't help but feel safe in his presence. Was it my ideal scenario to be crashing here for a while? Definitely not. But I was okay.

He nodded and flashed a small smile. "I'll try to stop worrying then."

Expecting Ezra not to worry would be like anticipating the sky turning green. It was never going to happen.

Ezra was usually a laid-back guy, but when he cared about someone or something it worried him endlessly.

Ezra turned to leave once more but Maddox appeared in the doorway. I hadn't even realized he left.

"These are the last two," he declared, setting the new boxes on the floor beside the others.

"We'll be out back while you finish unpacking." Ezra nodded at Emma and then me.

The guys left, their shoes smacking against the wood stairs.

I went to work opening the new boxes and noticed that the one containing my wedding dress and the sheets were suspiciously absent.

Emma eyed me with a speculative look as she set about removing items from boxes. "So…you don't have any feelings for him?"

I sighed. This wasn't a new question.

"I love Ezra as a friend. Nothing more." I muttered the words as I stuffed my bras and panties into the top dresser drawer. I could refold them later.

Emma made a noise that sounded like a grunt of disagreement. "You guys have been skirting around your chemistry for years. It's only a matter of time…"

"A matter of time until what?" I asked.

"Until you fuck each other's brains out."

I laughed, the kind of laugh that came deep from your belly. Before Emma met Maddox she blushed as red as a tomato at any mention of sex. That girl was long gone.

"That's not going to happen," I declared once I'd sobered.

She quirked a brow and eyed me with indignation. "We'll see."

We finished unpacking all of my stuff and I changed into a pair of jeans and a lightweight sweater. While the summer days were scorching hot, the evenings could be downright chilly where you wanted to snuggle beneath a blanket.

Emma and I found the guys out back seated around the fire pit. A fire roared and the makings for s'mores lay on a side table.

Emma scurried over to the chair beside Maddox, but he snagged her around the waist before she could sit down, and she fell onto his lap with a giggle.

I took the chair beside Ezra, wanting to distance myself from their sickeningly sweet displays of affection. Their relationship was one for the storybooks—one I didn't think I'd ever find for myself.

Was I jealous?

I didn't think so. I was happy that Emma had found something so special, but I was also smart enough to know that it was rare and the chances of me finding it were slim to none.

"Did you get everything unpacked?" Ezra asked, stealing me from my thoughts.

"Yes," I answered, staring at the roaring fire as it soared higher. I leaned back in the Adirondack chair, making myself comfortable.

"Good," he replied.

I felt like there was a slight awkwardness between us at moments, and I guessed that was perfectly understandable since I'd ignored him for the last six months and then come barreling back into his life with a mountain of baggage.

"Oh, here," he said suddenly, reaching down. He removed the top on a longneck bottle of beer and held it out to me.

"Thanks," I smiled, taking it.

Maybe to someone else it would seem surreal to be sitting around drinking beer with the bassist and drummer for one of the most popular bands in the world, but for me it felt right. Initially, when I first met the guys I'd been starstruck. I'd been a fan of their music before I knew Emma was dating Maddox, so it was bound to happen. But you didn't have to be around them long before you realized they were like everybody else.

"It's been a long day," he commented, leaning back in the chair and stretching out his legs.

"It's been a long *two* days," I corrected.

He chuckled and the shadows of the flames danced over his handsome face.

Across from us Maddox nuzzled Emma's neck and she let out another giggle before kissing him on the lips. He grasped her hair in his fingers and murmured, "I love you."

I let out a sigh.

Ezra's head swiveled in my direction. "You'll have that one day," he declared.

"I hope so," I replied, "I really hope so."

He lifted his bottle of beer to his lips and drained what was left. He stood up, placing the empty bottle on the nearby table.

"I think it's time for us to get to the real reason for this gathering."

Emma and Maddox immediately broke apart, giving him their full attention.

My brows rose in interest and I set my beer on the ground beside my chair.

"I'll be right back." He looked at me when he said the words, warning me to stay in my seat.

I raised my hands in surrender and sat back.

He disappeared inside and I looked at Maddox across the fire. "What is he up to?" I asked, giving Maddox my best glare—daring him not to tell me the truth.

He chuckled. "You'll know soon enough."

He was right.

Ezra breezed out onto the deck with two boxes and down the steps over to where we sat around the fire.

When I saw the boxes I knew immediately what he was up to. He set them both in front of me and smiled down at me.

"You said you wanted to burn it," he kicked the box where my wedding dress overflowed from the open flaps, "and I thought you might want to burn this too." I looked at the other box and my suspicions were confirmed when I saw the sheets from the bed I had shared with Braden.

"You're the best," I told Ezra, meaning those words more than he could possibly understand.

He grinned a mega-watt smile at my words. "Ready?"

"Do you even need to ask?"

He chuckled and stepped back, giving me access to the fire.

Emma and Maddox both watched with a smile.

I grabbed the sheets first.

With a cry I launched them into the fire.

The flames licked the fabric, slowly burning away the floral material to a black crisp.

Emma let out a whoop and waved her hands in the air. Maddox said something to her that sounded a lot like, "You're so adorable."

"How do you feel?" Ezra asked, standing beside me. His arm brushed mine and my body hummed with familiarity.

"Unstoppable." I answered with the first word that came to mind.

He smiled down at me, his hands shoved into the pockets of his jeans.

The four of us watched the fire eat away the sheets until they were barely recognizable.

I headed for the dress, struggling to get the massive thing into my arms.

Ezra grasped my elbow and I stopped what I was doing.

"Are you sure?" He asked, his eyes flicking from me to the dress.

I took a deep breath. "Yeah, I am. If I get married I won't be doing it in this dress."

"When," he said.

"Excuse me?" I questioned, confused by his seemingly random response.

He smiled crookedly. "*When* you get married."

"Right," I sighed. That possibility seemed so far in the future now that I couldn't even picture it happening.

Without a second of thought I launched the dress into the fire. Smoke licked the sky as the dress went from white to black.

How symbolic.

Ezra's arm fell around my shoulders and I leaned against his body for support. His lips pressed against my forehead in a quick kiss and then the warmth of his lips was gone, replaced by his fingers as he wiped tears away from my cheeks.

"I'm okay." I assured him before he could ask. "I really am."

These tears weren't of sadness. They were cathartic, clearing away all the negativity that had been clinging to my shoulders the last few years.

I felt it all drift away like a seed carried away by the wind.

I knew in that moment that I would be okay. Everything happened for a reason, and I needed this speed bump to teach me a lesson.

"Can we have s'mores now?" Emma asked, interrupting my thoughts.

Ezra's arm dropped away from my shoulders and he grabbed the bags of stuff, passing them half.

I sat down once more and he set the items between us. I grabbed a marshmallow, sticking it on the skewer. I held it over the fire until it was a soft golden color. When I pulled it away from the fire Ezra already had a graham cracker with a block of Hershey's chocolate on it waiting for me. He was always looking out for me, no matter the situation.

I bit into my s'more and the gooey marshmallow clung to my lips.

Ezra noticed and began to laugh.

"Don't laugh at me." I leveled him with a glare.

He shook his head. "You're cute."

I rolled my eyes, wiping the sticky residue off my lips. He was still laughing at me, so with narrowed eyes I reached out and wiped the goo on his arm.

He glanced down at his arm and his mouth parted slightly with disbelief.

"I can't believe you just did that," he muttered.

I grinned, bouncing in my seat like an excited child.

"You're going to pay for that," he warned.

I prepared to spring from my chair and run away, but he was faster.

His finger had dipped into the melted chocolate of his own s'more and he reached out, swiping his finger down my nose.

A gasp emitted from my lips. "Ezra!" I shrieked.

"Payback's a bitch." He grinned.

I shook my head. "You're just mean."

He chuckled, the sound warm and husky. "We both know that isn't true."

"Right now it is." I stuck my tongue out at him.

He smiled at me, flicking a piece of hair away from his eyes.

Before I could retaliate Maddox called, "What about the fireworks?"

"Oh, right." Ezra shoved the last of his s'more into his mouth and hurried over to where he'd left the boxes of fireworks. Maddox joined him and while they got everything set up I made myself another s'more.

Emma stood from her chair and made her way over to Ezra's now vacant one. Her wild blonde hair blew around her shoulders from the evening breeze. She plopped into the chair, crossing her legs.

"Do you feel better now?" She asked.

I nodded, my eyes flitting to the fire where the remains of my wedding dress and those blasted sheets were barely distinguishable. "Much."

"I'm sorry you have to go through this, but I'm also happy that he's out of your life."

My lips lifted with a smile. "You're not the only one."

She opened her mouth to reply, but was cut off by a loud boom. We both turned to look at the same time as a small firework fizzled.

Maddox stood with his hands on his hips beside Ezra, both guys looking at the disappearing firework with a *what-the-fuck* expression.

"Well, that was anticlimactic," Maddox muttered. "Should we try another?"

Emma and I both laughed as we watched the guys fiddle with another firework. It went off, burning out quickly like the last.

"Where did you get these?" Maddox asked, picking up one of the boxes and inspecting it from all angles.

Ezra shrugged. "It was a booth beside the gas station."

Maddox huffed and threw the box on the ground. "That explains everything. The next time you decide to buy anything explosive call me, or Hayes. But not Mathias, he's not to be trusted with fire."

Emma and I both laughed again. It didn't seem possible that I should feel this *happy* only a day after finding my fiancé in bed with another woman, but I did, and it was all thanks to the fact that I had the greatest friends in the whole world.

"So these are a bust?" Ezra pointed to the unopened fireworks.

Maddox nodded. "Sorry, bud." He clapped Ezra roughly on the shoulder. "Those sparkers are doable, but rather boring."

Ezra grunted and rolled his eyes, but picked up that box and opened it. He extended it in Maddox's direction and he removed two of the sticks, one for himself and Emma. He ventured over to us and handed one to her.

Ezra grabbed two as well and gave me one. He held out a lighter and lit the tip of mine, then Emma's, before lighting his own and Maddox's.

I stood up from my chair and he eyed me, wondering what I was doing.

I waggled my brows and grinned. "Catch me."

I took off running, swirling the sparkler through the air.

Ezra's feet pounded behind me, urging me to run faster.

"Sadie!" He cried suddenly. "The lake!"

Oh, shit. I'd completely forgotten about the lake and it was dark enough that it completely blended in with the grass.

Before I could slow down my feet landed in the water, sinking into the mud.

I went down into the water, getting my whole body wet. The poor sparkler got lost in the water, extinguished by the wetness before it could meet its own fiery demise.

I came up gasping for air as his arm snaked around my waist.

Ezra pulled me against his now wet body and muttered, "You're honestly the craziest person I've ever met."

I laughed, clinging to his shoulders. "I'm not crazy, I'm *alive*."

He shook his head, hauling me out of the water like he was afraid if he didn't I wouldn't get out on my own.

"Why'd you come in after me?" I asked, shivering when the cool night air touched my wet body.

He set me on the ground and tucked a piece of hair behind my ear that clung to my forehead.

"Because that's what friends do," he replied with a small shrug of his shoulders, "you jump, I jump. Always."

My lips quirked into a smile. "I didn't jump, though. I face-planted into the water."

He laughed, hooking his thumbs into the back of his wet t-shirt and pulling it off. His lean chest was exposed with a smattering of dark hair trailing beneath his belly button. I tried not to notice how my heart pitter-pattered.

"Same difference," he claimed, shaking his head so that water droplets flew from his hair.

"What are you guys doing?" Maddox called. It sounded like he had his hands cupped around his mouth.

Ezra scrubbed a hand over his heavily stubbled jaw. "I think the party is over."

I shivered, my teeth chattering together. That water wasn't exactly the warmest. "I think so too," I agreed.

He tucked his t-shirt into the back pocket of his jeans and started back to the house.

It was easier to see going this way since the fire was in front of us.

When we approached, Emma rushed forward. "Are you okay? We heard a splash."

"Just peachy," I replied, wringing out my wet hair.

I shivered again and she said, "You need to get inside and take a hot shower. You're going to get sick."

"Yeah," Ezra agreed, "go ahead. I've got to clean up down here first."

"Are you sure?" It was his house and I felt bad for going first. He had to be as cold as I was.

He nodded. "Positive."

I didn't fight him on it, because I was freezing and a hot shower sounded like the best idea ever right now.

"Thanks for all of this," I waved my hand around, "and thank you guys for being here." I looked at Emma and Maddox then.

Maddox dipped his chin in acknowledgement.

Emma smiled sweetly. "There's nowhere else we'd rather be." She paused, biting her lip. "I'd hug you goodbye, but you're soaking."

I laughed. "We can save the hug for later."

She nodded and watched me head up the porch steps. I hadn't missed the flash of worry and speculation in her eyes. I knew she thought there was something more between Ezra and me, but she couldn't be more wrong. We were friends and that's all we ever would be.

# CHAPTER FIVE

"GET UP." Ezra demanded, turning on the ceiling light in the guestroom.

I sat up in bed, the blankets pooling at my waist. "What the hell?" I blinked sleep from my eyes and looked at him dazedly.

"Get up," he repeated.

"What are you *wearing?*" My eyes widened at the sight of him. He had on a pair of khaki shorts, a white sleeveless shirt, and…was that a fisherman's hat on his head? One of those with the little dangly things? Oh my God, it was!

"We're going fishing," he stated, which explained the hat, "so get your ass out of bed, get changed, and meet me downstairs. You have ten minutes."

He slipped out of my room and closed the door.

I would've thought the whole thing was a strange dream if it wasn't for the fact that the light still blinded me.

I glanced at the clock on the bed and gasped. "It's six o' clock!" I screamed. "I'm going back to bed." I lay back down and tossed the blankets over my head.

The door creaked open and his shoes slapped against the hardwood.

The covers were yanked unceremoniously from my body.

I gasped, trying to grab the sheets from his hands.

"No," he demanded. "We're going fishing."

"It's six o' clock," I repeated, a whining tone to my voice, "on a *Sunday*. The day of *rest*." I made a grab for the covers once more, but he yanked them completely off the bed and threw them on the floor. "Ezra!" I yelled.

He ignored my outburst and headed out the door once more. "You're down to eight minutes now. Tick, tock."

I hated him.

No, I didn't.

But seriously?! Six o' clock on a Sunday?

He better have at least made breakfast or I might turn into a raging beast.

I forced my tired body out of bed and changed into a pair of jean shorts, a tank top, and sneakers. I grabbed my sunglasses from my purse and stuck them on top of my head.

When I reached the stairs Ezra was starting up them. "Coming to get me?" I asked, a brow rising in interest.

He grinned and nodded. "Yep. I thought you were flaking."

"Did you think I might try to make a break for it and climb out the window?"

He shook his head as I joined him downstairs. "I wouldn't put anything past you," he confessed. "I made biscuits and gravy if you want any."

"Is there anything you can't cook?" I asked him, heading over to the coffee maker.

Oh sweet sustenance.

He chuckled, rubbing his stubbled jaw. "Not really."

"You're going to make some girl very happy one day," I told him, standing on my tiptoes to grab a coffee cup from the top cabinet.

He grunted in response to my comment and came up behind me to grab one of the mugs for me so I didn't topple them over.

"Thanks." I took the cup from his hands and filled it with the steaming black liquid before I added a heart attack inducing amount of sugar. "What ever happened to you and that actress?"

A few months before I stopped speaking to Ezra he'd gone on a few dates with an up and coming actress. She'd been gorgeous and exactly the kind of girl you'd expect a rock star to date.

I'd asked him before why things ended and he never wanted to tell me.

Today, he shrugged and leaned his backside against the kitchen counter with his arms crossed over his chest. "She was too vain. I want someone with a little more substance. Someone who's…" He paused, staring off as he searched for the right word. "Real," he finally settled on. "I want someone I can picture myself growing old with and who doesn't throw a temper tantrum at the sight of a wrinkle."

I nearly choked on my coffee. "She did that?"

He nodded reaching up to further secure the hat on his head.

"Is that why you haven't dated since then?" I asked.

He shrugged. "No, I just haven't found anyone worth my time."

I fixed myself a plate of biscuits and gravy, taking a seat on one of the barstools.

Ezra pulled out the one beside me and sat down as well.

"So," I started, shoveling a fork full of food into my mouth, "why do you want to go fishing?"

"The better question is why *wouldn't* I want to go fishing." He smiled boyishly, fiddling with the edge of the hat. He propped his elbows on the countertop and tilted his head in my direction. "I thought it would be fun. We haven't hung out in a long time."

I raised a brow, fighting a smile. "Admit it, you only want to see me scream and run away from a worm."

He tossed his head back and his laughter echoed around the kitchen. "You caught me." He reached into his back pocket. "Here," he extended a baseball cap in my direction, "you'll need this."

I took it and removed my sunglasses from the top of my head so that I could put it on. Pouting my lips I turned to him. "How do I look?"

"Beautiful." He answered without a second of thought. He promptly cleared his throat and looked away. He jumped up from his seat like he'd been burned. "I'll be outside."

He hurried away and I watched him leave, wondering what I'd done.

I didn't dwell on it for long.

I finished my breakfast and cup of coffee, washing both the plate and mug before joining him outside.

I saw him standing on the small dock that led into the lake. His hands were on his hips and he had his head turned towards the sky. When he heard me approach he turned and smiled. The sun glowed behind him, making him look otherworldly.

I stopped in front of him, fixing my sunglasses onto my face.

"I wasn't joking about the worms. I will scream like a five year old girl if you make me touch one."

His lips twitched as he fought not to laugh. "Fine," he agreed, "I'll do your dirty work."

I grinned. "Does this mean if I decide to kill Braden you'll help me hide his body?"

This time he couldn't contain his laughter. "That's what best friends are for, right?" He reached for a fishing pole. Glancing at me over his shoulder, he whispered, "I'll even be your alibi."

"How kind of you."

Sobering, I sat down on the edge of the dock, kicking my legs back and forth over the open air. The dark lake water glimmered with the reflection of the sun and nearby trees. Above us birds chirped happily.

I closed my eyes, letting the sun warm my face. A small smile lifted my lips.

It might've been too early to be up on a weekend, but this was actually nice.

Ezra handed me a fishing pole and sat down beside me with his own.

He instructed me on what to do and soon the hook, or whatever it was called, was bobbing on the surface of the water.

We sat in silence for a while, enjoying the peaceful setting.

I was the first to break the quiet minutes later.

"I'm sorry I missed your birthday." My throat closed up. I'd spent his last few birthdays with him, well not just *me*, but all of us—Emma, Maddox, Mathias, and Hayes. "I wanted to call you," I confessed, looking straight ahead at the water.

He swallowed audibly. "Why didn't you?"

"I was afraid if I did I wouldn't be able to stop at a phone call. I've missed you."

I'd missed him more than I'd been willing to admit to even myself. The last few years we'd been so impossibly close—and anybody that said that guys and girls couldn't be friends were liars, because in a way I was closer to Ezra than I was Emma. Girls were always quick to judge, even I was guilty of that, but guys were different.

"I can't believe I'm twenty-four," he whispered.

"You say that like it's a bad thing."

He shrugged. "I feel like I haven't accomplished much."

I snorted. "You have a Grammy, Ezra," I said, referring to their recent win, "I'd say that's pretty accomplished."

He turned to me, his dark eyes shielded by the flap of the hat he wore. "I don't mean with my career, I just mean with my life in general. I've traveled to all these places and had so many amazing opportunities, but I feel like I haven't ever really *lived*."

I mulled over his words, seeing how that would be true. The last few years of his life had become so consumed with music, performing, and traveling, that he hadn't really had a chance to be his own person. He wasn't just Ezra Collins. He was Ezra the bassist for Willow Creek.

I rested my head on his shoulder. "We need to change that."

He chuckled. "How?"

"I don't know," I answered truthfully. "I guess by finding what makes you happy."

"Music *does* make me happy," he replied. "It's more that…it feels like something is missing from my life."

I lifted my head. "We'll have to keep searching until we find what that is."

He smiled over at me. "Even if it takes a long time?"

"You know me," I bumped his shoulder with mine, "stubborn to a fault. I won't give up until we find it."

He shook his head, a small smile playing on his lips. "That's one of the things I like most about you."

I frowned, ducking my head. "Even when it made me stay with a guy that wasn't worth my time?"

His thumb and forefinger grasped my chin, lifting my head so I was forced to look at him. "I don't believe it was stubbornness that made you stay with him."

"What was it then?" I asked, truly curious.

He stared down at me for a moment, his lips twisting. "You're one of the kindest people I know. You love with all your heart and you're extremely passionate. You choose to see the good in people even when you shouldn't. I think that's why you stayed with him." He nodded at his own words, squinting against the sun.

I swallowed thickly, my chest feeling tight. "You're too nice to me."

He shook his head. "I'm being honest."

Suddenly I felt a tug on the line and let out a small cry. "I think I caught something!"

"Reel it in," Ezra commanded, gesturing with his hand.

"Oh, right."

I began to do as he said, fighting against the pressure on the fishing line. He gave me a few pieces of advice, but mostly left me alone.

With a groan I pulled and the fish came out of the water, dangling from the end of the line.

I glared at the tiny thing. It couldn't have been bigger than five inches.

I turned to Ezra, my mouth turned down in a grimace. "Well, that was anticlimactic."

He looked from the fish to me and we both burst into laughter.

All the seriousness from our previous conversation drifted away.

"Hold it steady," he commanded. He'd already reeled his empty line in and set his fishing pole on the dock.

I tightened my hold on the pole and he got the wiggling fish free. He clasped it between his hands. "Do you want to put it back in?"

"I'm not touching that thing!" I cried, scuttling backwards like he might toss it in my lap any second.

He shook his head, laughing under his breath at my antics. He bent forward, lowering his hands into the water. He let go and the little fish swam away.

He grabbed the pole from my hands and fixed more bait onto the end before handing it back to me.

I settled myself beside him once more and we both cast our lines.

"This is pretty nice," I admitted.

He chuckled. "Does this mean you won't kill me for waking you up early?"

I smiled, adjusting the brim of the baseball cap I wore. "The day is young."

"How's your hand?" He asked me suddenly, steering the conversation in a different direction.

"A little sore," I admitted, "but it's worth it."

He smiled and little wrinkles creased the corners of his eyes. "I'll never get the image of you punching him out of my head. It was awesome."

"Even better than when you punched him?" I questioned with a laugh.

He nodded his head eagerly. "Way better. The look on his face was priceless. He didn't see that coming."

"Why did he cheat on me?" I asked, looking up at Ezra. "You're a guy, so tell me, what's so repulsive about me that he had to seek it elsewhere?"

Ezra reared back, surprised by my random question. "There's nothing *repulsive* about you." He mimicked my tone. "Some guys can't be satisfied with anybody because they're not happy with who they are."

"I feel like I must have done something wrong."

He looked at me like I was crazy. "Sadie, the only thing you did wrong was loving someone that wasn't good enough for you."

I took a deep breath and let it out slowly. "I feel like I should feel more hurt, devastated even, but really I'm just confused." Panic snaked its way through my veins and I looked at him with widened eyes. "I didn't love him the way I should have. What if I don't know how to love someone in that way?"

"You do," he assured me, looking out at the shimmering water, "but you haven't found him yet."

I looked up at the sky and the birds flying above us. "I feel like I don't know who I am anymore. I spent two years with a guy that stripped me of my identity. I feel like all I have of myself is my store and the rest I'm left questioning. I tried so hard to please him, to make him happy, and in the end I made myself miserable. I was so desperate for it to work out that I overlooked how toxic our relationship was. How stupid is that?"

"You're human," he replied. "We have this inane desire to belong to something that is greater than we are on our own. That desire is so strong that we can fool ourselves into believing things that aren't true."

"So, I'm not crazy?" I cracked a smile.

"Definitely not crazy."

His smile was comforting and I reminded myself for the hundredth time that everything would be okay.

I rested my head on his shoulder and then his head rested on top of mine.

A smile touched my lips.

I'd missed this—having someone that understood me completely, even when I didn't know myself.

# CHAPTER SIX

I LOCKED THE door leading into my shop, switched the sign to CLOSED, and shut the blinds.

I was exhausted, and certain that this had been the longest week of my life. It had seemed unending as I dealt with phone calls from family and endless Facebook notifications from people wanting to know why Braden and I broke up so soon before our wedding. The gestures would have been nice, if I hadn't believed that most of them were only asking because they were nosy and didn't really care that I'd been hurt. I told them all that we decided mutually that we weren't meant to be. It seemed unfair to let the scumbag off the hook so easily, but I didn't need everybody knowing all of my business and talking behind my back.

I straightened the clothes and shoes, making sure everything was in order for the next business day.

I closed out the register and turned off the lights.

I headed into my office and sat down in the chair behind my desk, letting out a hefty sigh. I glanced at all of the papers on my desk, the numbers and information blurring together. I'd planned to stay a little while longer, but I was beginning to think that wasn't the smartest idea. I'd probably end up messing something up and having to start my paperwork over again tomorrow.

I decided to leave it until tomorrow and stood, grabbing my purse.

I reached for my car keys and flicked off the light on my desk.

I'd only taken one step when I heard someone knock on the front door of the store.

Oh, shit.

I froze where I stood, holding my breath.

The knock sounded again.

I had no idea who could possibly be at the door and I certainly wasn't going to check.

My phone buzzed in my purse and I thanked God that I always kept it on vibrate. If the person outside was a murderer I didn't want to alert them to my location.

I checked the screen and read a text from Ezra.

**EZRA: I'm outside.**

I breathed a sigh of relief and put a hand over my racing heart, silently scolding myself for my silly thoughts.

I hurried to the front door and opened it.

He stood there in a pair of jeans and a black t-shirt. His dark curly hair tumbled over his forehead, shielding his eyes.

"You scared me," I scolded him.

"Sorry." He appeared sheepish. "Are you done?" He asked, flicking his finger towards the darkened store. "I thought we could get dinner and celebrate."

"What are we celebrating?" I asked.

"The fact that it's been a week." He shrugged, toeing the ground with his booted foot.

"A week since I've been dumped?" I raised a brow.

"Well, it sounds insensitive when you say it like that," he grumped, brushing his long fingers through his shaggy hair. "You've been strong through all of this and I think you deserve to celebrate that." He leaned against the side of the building and lowered his head as he looked at me. "Don't you?"

I tapped my lip. "Are you buying?"

He snorted. "Of course."

"Then yes, I do deserve to celebrate, and I plan on getting shit-faced." I pumped my fist in the air.

He shook his head and tried to hide a smile. "Are you ready to go?" He asked.

"Yeah," I nodded. "I just need to lock the back door first. Are we going in your car?"

"I thought we could walk." He pointed across the street to where one of my favorite local restaurants sat.

"Wait here." I held up a finger, telling him I'd only be a second.

I quickly locked the back door and the door to my office before rejoining him outside. I stopped, locking that one as well.

Ezra shoved his hands into the pockets of his jeans as we crossed the street onto the back patio of the local pub. You seated yourself, and we managed to snag a seat on the upper deck.

Within a minute a waitress hurried over with menus and silverware.

"What can I get you guys to drink?"

"Alcohol," I answered. "You can surprise me."

She looked at me like I was crazy. "I'll have the bartender make you our special…

it's kind of strong."

"Perfect," I grinned.

"For you?" She turned her attention to Ezra and her mouth fell open. "Oh my God!" She jumped up and down—I kid you not. "You're Ezra, from Willow Creek! Oh my God, I can't believe this! I mean, I knew you guys lived here, but I never thought I'd meet one of you. Wow! This is amazing! Can I get a picture and an autograph?"

Ezra flashed me an apologetic smile before smiling full watt at the waitress. "Absolutely. Anything for a fan."

I sighed and looked around at the attention her scream had drawn our way. In no time we would be swarmed.

She pulled her cellphone out of her apron and he posed for a picture. She then gave him a pen and he signed a piece of paper on her notepad.

"Thank you so much!" She gushed. "I'll be right back with your drinks."

"You didn't get mine!" Ezra called after her.

She quickly did an about-face, her face flushed with embarrassment. "I'm so sorry about that. What can I get you?"

"Water," he replied, "and an order of nachos. They're her favorite." He pointed at me.

She glanced at me and I could tell she'd already forgotten my existence.

"I'm sorry," Ezra mouthed as a group of girls rushed our table.

I shrugged. I was used to this happening when we went out in public. Usually it happened in L.A. and not here, but it was the same thing. Besides, a bunch of squealing teenage girls were nothing I couldn't handle.

Ezra posed for picture after picture and signed autographs. Our waitress had to fight her way through the mob to give us our drinks and nachos. Then I had to yell over the screaming girls to give her my order, and Ezra's too, since he was currently occupied and couldn't order for himself.

Before the waitress left I grabbed her arm. "Would you mind getting management to break this up?" I asked.

The girls had already gotten what they came for, so I wasn't being rude, but they had overstayed their welcome.

"I'll send the manager over," she assured me.

I took a sip of whatever concoction she'd brought me. Whoa. She hadn't been lying. It was strong.

I sipped some more and the burn gradually disappeared.

The guy that was obviously the manager showed up and escorted the girls away.

"Your ticket is on me. I'm so sorry for this inconvenience," he apologized.

Ezra shrugged, sitting down once more. "It's not a big deal. I'm used to it." He smoothed his fingers through his ruffled hair—one of the girls had mused it. I hated that so many people treated the guys like they weren't even human.

"Still," the manager said, "I'd like to take care of it."

"Of course." Ezra smiled and nodded. He hated getting special treatment so I wouldn't be surprised if he ended up leaving a wad of cash on the table before we left.

The manager smiled in goodbye and I was finally alone with Ezra.

"Is anybody else joining us?" I asked. It wasn't unusual for the other guys to join us, and Emma of course, and I guess Mathias' wife now—but I'd only ever met her once and the meeting had been brief since that happened to be the time Ezra punched Braden. Braden had spent half the night bitching about that and had continued to grumble for a good month afterwards. He was such a diva.

Ezra shook his head. "Just us. Something wrong with that?" He asked, bringing the glass of water to his lips.

"Of course not."

Ezra and I went out just the two of us plenty of times in the past, not so much when I started dating Braden. He was too jealous.

"I ordered that burger you like," I told him, finishing my drink.

"Thanks," he smiled. "Was it good?" He nodded at my now empty glass.

"Fan-freaking-tastic, but it will take more than that to get me drunk."

"Why do you want to get drunk?" He asked. "You'll only regret it in the morning when you feel sick."

"Because, for the last few years I've been nothing but responsible. Tonight," I lifted my empty glass, signaling the waitress, "I want to be a normal twenty-one year old." I answered with complete honesty. "And I know you won't try to take advantage of me in my inebriated state," I added.

He laughed, hiding his smile behind his hand.

"Also," I continued as the waitress set down a new drink, "we live together. Therefore, you can haul my drunken ass home and not have to make an extra stop. It's very considerate of me, I know. No need to praise me," I joked.

"I'm happy to see you're finally regaining your sense of humor. I was beginning to worry I was stuck with this melancholy version of you for a friend and that was really beginning to suck." He winked.

I thought winking was the most ridiculous gesture ever, but Ezra made it downright sexy.

Wait…did I just call my best friend sexy?

What did they put into this magic potion to make me think such things? I proceeded to glare at my drink.

Eh, whatever.

I picked it up and drank half, wiping my mouth on the back of my hand.

So lady like.

I grabbed my fork and put some of the nachos on the plate the waitress had brought. Ezra was already devouring his own pile.

"These are so good," I moaned, stuffing one into my mouth. This wasn't a date so I could be as messy as I wanted.

He nodded his head in agreement, wiping his hands on his napkin.

"When was the last time you ate?" He asked me, noticing how I was devouring the chips.

My nose scrunched as I thought. "Uh…breakfast. I had a cereal bar for a snack."

He glared at me. "You've only eaten once today?"

"I had a cereal bar!" I defended, gesticulating wildly with my free hand.

He shook his head as his teeth ground together. "Sadie, you can't skip meals like that."

I frowned. "I know, but I forget."

"How do you forget to eat?" His hands landed roughly on the table as he leaned forward.

I shrugged, picking up another nacho chip and eating it. "I get busy and forget how much time has passed."

He wasn't pleased by my explanation and his nostrils flared.

"I'll set a reminder in my phone," I mumbled to appease him.

He still looked doubtful.

"Look, at least I'm eating now." I pointed at my plate of nachos. Lifting my drink in the air, I added, "And drinking. Oh, alcohol, how I love thee." I downed the rest of the drink. When a frown still marred his face, I said, "Eat, drink, and be merry. Your sourpuss vibe is killing my buzz and I need this right now."

He laughed, the tension easing from his shoulders.

"Okay, I'll let it go…for now." He eyed me for a moment, letting me know that this conversation was far from over.

We'd unintentionally been leaning towards each other and jerked apart when the waitress appeared with our meals.

She set the burger in front of Ezra and a small pizza in front of me.

"Would you like another drink?" She asked me.

"Yep," I nodded eagerly. "Go ahead and bring two."

"Sadie." Ezra warned with a low growl.

"Don't listen to him," I whispered conspiratorially, "someone pissed in his cheerios this morning."

She glanced at Ezra, back to me, and then to him once more.

"Just bring her the drinks," he grumbled. "Don't make me regret this." He warned me.

"However would I do that?"

"Wow, the stars look so pretty from here."

Ezra kicked the car door closed with his booted foot. "That's because I'm carrying you."

"Look at all of them. They're so sparkly. Can I have one?" I reached my hand up and tried to grab one. I frowned. "I can't reach it. Can you get it for me?"

"You're never drinking ever again," he groaned, adjusting his hold on my body as he climbed the porch steps. "Wrap your arms around my neck," he demanded. "I have to put you down so I can get the door open."

I did as he asked and my shaky feet touched the ground. I wobbled and he wrapped an arm around my torso, holding me against his chest so that I didn't fall.

The door swung open and cold air hit my face.

"Oh, that feels good." I smiled, leaning forward and trying to get closer to the deliciously cool air.

Ezra chuckled. "Come on, up you go."

My legs were whisked out from under me once more and I tightened my hold around his neck.

"Are you carrying me across the threshold?" I asked, laughter filling the words.

"No," he groaned, "I'm carrying my drunk best friend home. And could you loosen your arms? You're choking me."

"Oh, sorry," I giggled. I leaned my head back and looked up at the ceiling as he started up the steps. "Everything looks so different like this. Oh, ew, you need to clean up there." I pointed to a cobweb.

He sighed as we reached the top of the stairs and he turned down the hallway to the guestroom.

My fingers tangled in the silky strands of his black hair as he pushed the bedroom door open with a nudge of his shoulder. "Your hair is so soft," I gasped. "Like a puppy." He snorted. "I want a puppy," I told him, my words slurring. "Can you be my puppy?" I rubbed his head as he laid me down on the bed. "I'd name my puppy Oliver. Isn't that a good name for a puppy? I think it is."

He chuckled, untangling my fingers from his hair. "Sadie, you might be the most hilarious drunk person I've ever met."

"Aw, thanks." I reached for his hair again—seriously, it was the softest thing I'd ever felt—and he grabbed my hands and held them in both of his.

"Sadie, stop," he warned.

"I want to pet the puppy!" I pouted.

"My hair is not a puppy."

"Well it sure feels like one. Could've fooled me," I huffed.

He sighed heavily and released my hands. He grabbed my shoes and began removing them.

"Are you trying to get me naked?"

"No," he glared at me, "I'm trying to get your shoe off."

"I'd be fine if you wanted to get me naked."

"Sadie," he warned.

"I haven't had sex in…" I tried to count, but my brain was too muffled to form a coherent thought. "A long time. That should've been another tip that Braden was cheating. I'm so stupid." I smacked my forehead.

He grabbed my hand. "Don't hit yourself." His voice softened.

He finished removing my shoes and they dropped to the floor with a crash.

"What's so wrong with me?" I asked him. "Am I so repulsive?"

"Sadie, repulsive is the last thing that you are. Braden is just…well, there are no words for what Braden is."

"I used to have a crush on you," I admitted. "Shit," I slapped my hand across my mouth, "I wasn't ever supposed to tell you that. I'm never drinking again."

He chuckled and shook his head. "Yeah, you won't be drinking again if I have anything to say about it. So," he grinned, "you had a crush on me?"

"Well, yeah," I shrugged. "You're hot. Who wouldn't?"

He laughed and grabbed the blankets, trying to tuck me beneath the covers. My stomach rolled and I grabbed his wrist.

"I'm going to be sick," I warned.

"Shit," he cursed. In a lightning fast move he grabbed the small trashcan and held it over for me. He held my hair back with his free hand as my body heaved.

I panted heavily, sweat breaking out across my skin. "Yep, I'm *never* drinking again," I vowed.

He set the trashcan aside and looked me over. "Are you okay?"

"I think so." I replied, my eyes growing heavy.

"Don't go to sleep yet," he warned. "I'll be right back."

He eased out of my room and flicked the light on in the hallway. I heard him fumbling in the bathroom and the sink running.

A minute later his shadow darkened the doorway and he strolled forward with two cloths in his hand. He crouched down beside me, his dark eyes full of worry.

Ever so gently he cleaned my mouth and then laid the clean cloth across my forehead.

"I'm not done yet." He warned with a pointed look.

"I'll try not to fall asleep, but no promises."

He left me again and the stairs creaked as he went back downstairs.

I rolled onto my side, forcing my heavy lids to stay open.

Sleep. I needed sleep, and maybe some duct tape for my mouth before any more truths slipped past my lips.

When Ezra returned he had a glass of water and two pills.

"Here, take this." He thrust the pills out to me.

I took them and the water. I set the glass on the table and he glared at me.

"What?"

"You need to drink all of the water."

"Ezra." His name sounded like a whine.

He crossed his arms over his lean chest and stared down at me. God, he was fucking relentless.

With a groan I picked up the glass once more and downed it.

"Happy?" I asked him, thrusting the empty glass into his outstretched hand.

"Immensely."

He turned to leave and I grabbed his wrist. His steps halted and he looked down at me, his eyes shielded by his shaggy hair.

"Stay with me," I begged. "I don't want to be alone."

Indecision warred on his face.

"Please?" My hand wrapped around his, tugging with as much force as I could muster, which admittedly wasn't much in my current state.

"Why can I never say no to you?" He mumbled, looking up at the ceiling as if it held all the answers in the world.

"Because I'm irresistible?" I supplied.

He chuckled, his shoulders shaking. "Yeah. That must be it."

He tugged his hand from my hold and started to leave. I let out a small sound of protest and he glanced back at me.

"I have to turn the hall light off." He pointed.

"Oh."

He did just that and darkness blanketed the space. I blinked my eyes, trying to get them to adjust to the now darkened room.

He left my bedroom door open and kicked off his boots before removing his shirt. Sadly, his jeans stayed on. I might've pouted. I really hoped it was too dark for him to see that.

He padded over to the other side of the bed and climbed in behind me, pulling the covers up and over us both.

I rolled over onto my other side to face him. He lay on his back and turned his head to look at me.

"Go to sleep," he warned, his voice a low gravel.

"I don't want to sleep," I sulked.

"You need to."

"You're such a buzz kill." I proceeded to poke his face.

He pushed my hand away. "And you're drunk."

"Really? I hadn't noticed."

He shook his head and put his hand over his mouth to hide his laugh. I sat up a bit, propping my body weight on my elbow.

"How come you've never made a move on me?" I asked, the words tumbling out of my mouth. "Why don't you like me as more than a friend? I admitted to having a crush on you, but you've always been indifferent."

He reached up and grasped my cheek. I startled at the gesture and my small gasp echoed through the room.

"I'm far from indifferent," he growled lowly. "Trust me, there have been plenty of times where I wanted to make a move, as you put it, but I never did because your friendship is far more important to me than a quick fuck."

I reached out with my other hand, laying it flat on his chest over his heart. "So, that's all you thought we'd be if we moved past the friend stage? A quick fuck?"

I didn't know why I felt so hurt by his words.

He put his hand over mine and swallowed thickly. "We were both young and the chances of us making it as a couple seemed slim to me. I wasn't going to throw our friendship away to test the waters, so to speak. And then you started dating Braden. But if you really must know, I am insanely attracted to you." His voice lowered to a husky whisper.

My breath came out in small little pants. I wanted desperately to lean down and kiss him, but something told me that he didn't want that, and also I'd yet to brush my teeth after vomiting so that was a kiss no one wanted.

"You are?" I asked stupidly, blinking my eyes rapidly like he was a mirage that might disappear at any second.

"I don't lie."

I continued to stare down at him, not sure what to do with this information.

Ezra made the decision for me. He pushed me down lightly and pulled me against his chest.

"Sleep, pretty girl," he commanded.

I didn't know how he could possibly expect me to sleep after he told me he was attracted to me. The man was lucky I hadn't thrown my panties across the room and mauled him with my vagina.

His fingertips brushed lightly against my neck as he pushed away my hair. My skin prickled with Goosebumps when his lips replaced his fingers in the barest of touches. My eyes fluttered closed and a happy sigh fell from my lips. Ezra was never so bold, and I wondered if he was only being this way because he believed I'd be too drunk to remember in the morning.

I would remember though. There was no way I could forget this.

# CHAPTER SEVEN

DAYLIGHT SPILLED ACROSS my body and I groaned as it penetrated my closed eyelids.

"It's time to get up." A hand smacked my foot. "It's noon already."

"Go away," I groaned, burying my face in my pillow.

"No."

"You're killing my buzz."

"Your buzz wore off hours ago, now you're just hung over. Get up, we have to go."

"I'm not going anywhere." I hugged the pillow tighter to my body and slowly peeled open my eyes. I was supposed to do paperwork at the store today since I put it off last night, but there was no way I was doing that now. "Gah!" I quickly covered my eyes with a hand. "Turn the fucking ceiling light off," I spat.

"No," he said again. I really hated that word. "Get out of bed and then *maybe* I will."

"You're evil."

"Get out of bed, Sadie. Seriously, we have to go in…" He looked down at the shiny watch on his wrist. "Thirty minutes."

"Where are we going?" I whined, still not making a move to get out of bed.

"Mathias called, he and Remy are moving into their new house today and he needs me to help."

I reached out and poked his chest. "You said he needs *your* help, not mine."

He captured my hand in his. "And *I* want you to come. Everyone will be there. Come on."

I pried my hand away from his hold. "Fine, but I'm going to need more Advil."

"I can get that," he chuckled. "Anything else?"

"My sunglasses."

He grabbed them off the dresser and handed them to me. I slipped them on and sighed in relief. "Much better."

"Shower and get dressed."

"Do I stink?" I asked, lifting my arm to smell.

He laughed and paused in the doorway. "You smell like a bar."

"Lovely," I sighed.

His boots slapped against the steps as he went downstairs, leaving me alone.

It took more effort than it should have to shower and get dressed. I chose to forgo drying my hair and instead tied it back in a messy bun. Even though I felt like shit I took the time to apply my makeup. Nobody wanted to see me looking like this. It was scary. And Mathias was the kind of guy to make a rude remark. I didn't think he honestly meant to be so rude to people, he was just crass and didn't think before he spoke.

I met Ezra downstairs and he already had a glass of water waiting with Advil. I'd tell him he was a saint, but he did wake me up so he was still on my shit-list for the moment.

I took the pills and emptied the glass of water. I poured some more water into the glass while Ezra fiddled with the toaster. After a minute two browned pieces of toast popped up.

He buttered them both, sticking one in his mouth, and put the other on a plate before handing it to me.

I waved it away. My stomach was too queasy to eat.

"Come on." He set it in front of me, chewing on his. I swore the thing was gone in three bites. "It's just toast. It'll help."

"You know what else will help?" I asked, pushing my sunglasses further up my nose. "If I poke you in the eyeball with a fork."

"I don't think rendering me eyeless would be helpful in this situation." He washed his hands in the sink with his back turned to me. I was tempted to pelt the buttered toast at his back, but I refrained.

He turned back around, crossing his arms over his chest. "Eat, Sadie. You're holding up progress."

I rolled my eyes and stuck the toast in my mouth, making a very dramatic show of taking a bite. Crumbs dotted the corner of my mouth and I wiped them away.

"Happy?" I asked.

"For now."

He smacked his hand on the counter. "Eat in the car. Mathias has already texted me ten times in the last five minutes."

I followed Ezra out to the garage and paused. "When can I get my car?"

"Later," he answered vaguely.

"You're testing my patience," I muttered under my breath.

He merely chuckled at me.

I was glad that he was still acting like himself though, after the truths we shared last nights.

And those truths…well, they had me thinking.

Thinking things I should not be thinking, that is.

Like me, and Ezra, naked and rolling beneath the sheets.

Yep, my thoughts should *so* not be going there. Especially after I had *just* ended my engagement to the Douche Lord.

Damn you treacherous thoughts!

Maybe I was still drunk…yeah, that explained it.

We didn't talk on the way to Mathias' house. Frankly, my head couldn't take it. How he expected me to act like a civilized human being today was beyond me.

Ezra turned into the neighborhood, one I recognized since it was where his parent's house was.

"Mathias bought a house in your parent's neighborhood?" I asked, not bothering to hide the shock from my voice.

He nodded. "Yeah, a few streets over. He and Remy liked the fact that the houses were a nice size, but not too large, with decent sized lots. You know how Mathias is, he didn't want to be too close to neighbors."

I laughed at that. Mathias Wade might've been the lead singer of Willow Creek, but he was not a people person.

Ezra turned into a driveway, and I gaped at the pretty home. It wasn't what I was expecting. The driveway wound up a hill, where the house sat overlooking the street.

The two-story home was covered in light gray siding with white trim. It had a gorgeous wraparound porch with a swing. There was a glass double front door and the windows were large, giving it an airy appearance. The grass was so lush and green that it reminded me of a golf course, and pretty flowers were planted across the front.

A moving truck was parked on the driveway and guys unloaded furniture and boxes.

"Why do they need our help again?"

He sighed. "It's Remy and Mathias."

I didn't know much about Remy, but I did know Mathias, so that was enough of an answer for me.

Maddox's sports car was parked in the grass and a large pickup truck that I knew belonged to Hayes took up another space.

Ezra put his car in park, blocking the exit of the driveway.

Before I could ask him why he was doing that and not parking in the grass like the other guys, he said, "Mathias is going to shit a brick when he sees that those two idiots parked in the grass. Just wait."

I managed a small laugh and then winced when my head pounded. I rubbed my temples, trying to get the throbbing to go away. I really shouldn't have drunk so much. Lesson learned.

Ezra slipped out of the vehicle and I was forced to follow him.

Immediately we stepped into drama.

"I'm going to kill him!" Remy shouted—I recognized her immediately with her platinum blonde hair and signature red lipstick. "I swear to God I'm going to smother him with a fucking pillow." She stomped down the porch steps, Emma hurrying behind her. "Oh," Remy paused suddenly, her hand falling to her small baby bump, "sorry baby, mommy said a bad word. Please forgive me, but your dad is being a pain in my ass. Butt. I meant butt." She frowned at Emma, not noticing our presence yet. "Between Mathias and me our baby's first word is going to be 'fuck'. This kid is doomed."

"Hopefully 'mom' will be a close second in the word department." Emma shrugged.

"Eh," Remy shrugged, "second will probably be 'asshole' because that's what I keep shouting at Mathias. He is driving me nuts."

"Ahem," Ezra cleared his throat as we approached them.

Remy glanced away from Emma and sighed in relief. "Oh, thank God you're here. Maybe between you and Maddox you can talk some sense into my husband. He's trying to bubble wrap the fucking walls." She winced and mumbled, "Crap, I did it again." Taking a deep breath, she continued, "Anyway, he's going way overboard with this whole baby-proofing thing and it's just…a nightmare." She rolled her eyes. "And he's getting in the way of the movers, so they're getting mad."

Ezra saluted her. "I'm on it. We'll tag team him."

I watched him leave, disappearing into the house. I was left alone with Remy and Emma—and the moving guys that were wrestling with a massive dining room table.

"I'm sorry you had to walk into all of this drama," Remy sighed, her hand rubbing absentmindedly against her stomach. "Mathias has been… extremely overprotective since we found out that I was pregnant." She glanced at Emma and then me. "Do you know the other day he got mad at me for picking up my *cat*. He thinks if I pick up anything that weighs more than five pounds that the baby is going to fall out of my vagina. I've got news for him, the process of childbirth, sadly, isn't that simple."

Emma laughed and patted Remy's shoulder in a familiar gesture. "He loves you."

"He's smothering me with his love. Seriously, I'm suffocating. And he will too if he doesn't stop."

I snorted and then burst into laughter, Remy and Emma joining in too.

"Ow," I groaned when my head pounded with renewed vigor.

Note to self: Stop laughing while hung over.

"Are you okay?" Emma asked.

"Yeah," I nodded, closing my eyes behind my sunglasses as I tried to get the blinking white lights to go away, "just a little too much to drink last night."

"Why'd you have too much to drink?"

"Because I wanted to," I replied. "Anyway," I rubbed my hands together, "what can I do to help?"

"Whoa, whoa, whoa." Emma shook her head. "Who did you go out with?"

"How do you know I went out? I could've gotten shit-faced at Ezra's place and passed out in my vomit on the kitchen floor."

"Did you?" She asked doubtfully.

"Well, no." I admitted.

"Then answer my previous question."

"Ezra took me out." I squirmed, wanting to run back and hide in the safety of the SUV.

"And let you get drunk? Did you have sex?"

"No!" I screamed a little too loudly, causing the moving guys to turn and look at us. "Why are you so convinced that there's something going on with us? I *just* broke up with Braden."

Emma stared at me with a calculated look as if she was measuring the weight of her words. "I see the way you look at him." She said the words slowly, gauging my reaction to them. I gave her nothing and remained stone faced. "The way you've *always* looked at him," she reiterated. "I'm not sure if you even realize it."

"I realize that you're absolutely insane. He's my *friend*. Nothing more." I pushed the sunglasses further up my nose, hoping my cheeks hadn't reddened with the lie. Only minutes ago I'd been picturing him naked, and now I was having to steadfastly defend the fact that were only friends. It was the truth though. Ezra didn't want to take things further. He'd said as much last night.

"Who are you trying to fool?" She raised a single brow. "Me or yourself?"

"Nobody," I replied easily.

"Mhmm," she mumbled in disbelief.

"Haven't you ever heard of friends with benefits?" Remy asked, interjecting herself into the conversation.

I choked on a laugh. "Of course, but me and Ezra? No way."

"Crazier things have happened." Remy shrugged. "I mean, I married that asshole." She pointed at Mathias who stormed down the porch steps and proceeded to yell at the movers. From what I could gather they'd scratched a piece of furniture.

Behind him a large dog and cat bound out the door, down the steps, running through the yard. It didn't look like the dog was chasing the cat, but more like they were playing.

"Mathias!" Remy yelled, heading over to her husband. "You let Shiloh and Percy out again. They're going to get hit by a car."

Mathias turned his attention from the movers to Remy, his hands resting on his hips. "Your cat is a fucking demon, Rem. You have to let it out once a day so its toxicity doesn't pollute the house. It's in the *Taking Care of a Demonic Creature Handbook*. You should read it. It's also how I've learned to deal with you." He grinned.

"You are so lucky that I love you more than I hate you." She laughed, fighting a smile.

"Back at ya." He smiled lovingly at her and grasped her waist, pulling her in for a kiss.

I quickly looked away when it became heated.

"No surprise why they have a baby on the way, right?" Emma laughed at the expression on my face.

"None at all." I shook my head.

"We'll leave them to it," she said, starting towards the moving truck.

I followed, happy to have something to do. She ventured onto the truck and grabbed a box labeled KITCHEN and handed it to me before grabbing another for herself.

Mathias and Remy were still making out in the front yard while their pets played. Maybe Mathias would be so distracted he wouldn't notice the vehicles parked in the grass.

Emma knew the layout of the house already, so I trailed behind her to the back where the kitchen sat overlooking the backyard. There was a large pool and since the lot was so high up you could practically see the whole town from here. It was spectacular.

Emma sat her box down on the island in the middle of the open kitchen, and I did the same.

"This house is gorgeous," I murmured, looking around in awe.

The floors were a dark, luxurious hardwood. The walls were all painted a neutral cream color that brightened up the space. The cabinets in the kitchen were also cream colored with a gold-brown granite countertop. The kitchen even had a built in bench with a table. Across from the kitchen was the family room that was currently in disarray. To our left was an archway where I figured the dining room was meant to be.

"Yeah, it's amazing." Emma grabbed a knife off the counter and cut into the tape. She handed me the knife before opening the flaps on the box.

I opened my box and discovered it was full of plates.

"Just pick a cabinet and start putting stuff away. They don't care where it goes, and Remy wasn't kidding about Mathias freaking out over her lifting things. He'd bust a vein in his forehead if she was in here trying to organize those." She nodded her head at the plates I now grasped in my hands.

"It seems like they'd want some say," I started.

She gave me a look. "I've been here since seven, so trust me when I say it doesn't matter."

I looked at her in disbelief. "Since seven? But you hate mornings."

"I know," she groaned. "Maddox bribed me."

"With what?" I asked, mystified.

She cracked a smile. "Sexual favors."

I laughed, shaking my head. The naïve little Emma I once knew was no more.

I carried the plates over to the counter by the sink and opened one of the upper cabinets. I carefully stacked the plates on a shelf—terrified I'd chip them. The last thing I wanted to do was break something that wasn't mine. Except Braden's nose. I'd enjoy breaking that.

Once those were put away I went to work on organizing the utensils in a drawer. Remy joined us, sitting on the floor to put away dishtowels. The guys argued by the staircase about how to install a baby gate.

"I don't know why he insists on putting that up now," Remy muttered, folding a towel. "We still have four months until the baby comes, and he won't walk for a while."

"*He?*" Emma shrieked, dropping the cup she was holding. Luckily it was plastic and didn't break.

Remy's smile was blinding. "Yeah, it's a boy. We just found out this week."

"I'm so excited." Emma bounced on the balls of her feet. "There's going to be a Willow Creek baby!"

I looked at her like she was crazy.

She frowned when she saw my expression. "Sorry," she mumbled, "I'm just a little excitable these days. I think being cooped up on tour was really bothering me. So," she turned back to Remy, "names? Spill."

Remy bit her lip and peered around the edge of the counter where the guys stood.

"We already have a name picked out, but Mathias doesn't want us to tell anyone the gender or name, in case it gets back to the media. He said this was a moment in his life he refused to share with the world until he had to." She shrugged.

"You're really not going to tell me?" Emma put her hands up in a begging motion. "Please, please, oh please tell me."

Remy sighed. "Give me one of those." She snapped her fingers and pointed to the knives I was currently organizing.

"Uh, why?" I asked, holding the knives against my chest like she might maul me for them at any second.

"Because I'm pregnant and I said so," she huffed. I reluctantly handed her one. "If I'm going to tell you guys, and go against my husband's wishes that *no one* know, then you're going to have to swear a blood oath."

Emma held her hand out.

"Are you crazy?" I asked Remy.

"No," she drew out the word, "I'm a Mama Bear protecting my cub, work with me here."

I grumbled, but held my hand out.

She nicked the meaty part of my hand, Emma's, and her own. She joined our hands together and peeked around the corner at the guys one last time.

"You both have to swear on your lives that you'll tell *no one* the name of the baby or the gender. And by no one, I mean these words better not even be muttered to your reflection in the mirror. Got it?"

"Got it." I said.

"You have to swear." Remy huffed in exasperation.

"I *swear.*" I had to resist the urge not to roll my eyes at her melodramatics.

"I swear," Emma piped in, vibrating with excitement.

Remy smiled, satisfied with our vow. "There are paper towels over there if your hand is still bleeding."

I looked at mine and saw that it had already dried since the cut was so small. Emma made no move either.

"Come on," Emma pleaded, "the suspense is killing me."

Remy laughed and rubbed her stomach. "His name is Liam Maxwell Wade."

"Awwww," Emma clapped her hands together, "I love it! It's such a strong name."

"We think so too." Remy beamed.

"It's adorable," I piped in, because I felt like I needed to say something.

"Thanks." Remy smiled in my direction. "Now get back to work," she shooed us, "Mathias will get suspicious."

Emma reluctantly returned to organizing the pots and pans while I finished with the utensils.

Several hours later all of us were tired and starving, so we took a break and ordered pizza.

We sat around on the floor of the family room, using paper towels as our plates. Emma and Maddox talked quietly together. Remy and Mathias were absorbed in their own little world as Mathias sang lovingly to her stomach in-between bites of pizza.

That left Ezra, Hayes, and me as the odd ones out.

Good times.

I sat sandwiched between the guys, eating my pizza in small dainty bites compared to the way they gobbled it.

Ezra stretched out his long legs and picked a piece of pepperoni off his pizza. He handed it to me and I gobbled it up greedily. I loved pepperoni.

"Thanks." I bumped his shoulder with mine.

"So, how have you been?" Hayes asked. "I haven't seen you since…" He scrunched up his nose, thinking. "New Year's? Whoa, has it really been that long?" He muttered the last part in disbelief.

I turned to the band's guitar player.

Josh Hayes was a good-looking guy, with angular cheekbones and sandy dirty blond hair that he kept swept away from his face. He was put together in a way that looked effortless, but you knew it actually took him quite some time to achieve it.

"Yeah, that long." I took a sip of orange soda.

He shook his head in disbelief. "What have you been up to?"

"Catching my fiancé fucking someone else."

Hayes shook his head. "Uh, yeah, Ezra told me." He awkwardly scratched the back of his head and glanced over at Ezra, as if he was worried he wasn't supposed to admit to knowing this bit of information.

"I'm pretty sure the whole town knows," I mumbled, spinning the white soda bottle cap between my fingers.

"I'm sure it's not the whole town." He cracked a grin. "I bet those old ladies that Maddox knits with don't know."

"Hey!" Maddox glared, pointing a finger at Hayes. "Those ladies are my friends, don't diss them."

Hayes raised his hands in surrender, laughing under his breath.

"They're sweet old ladies," Maddox continued, "who not only teach me how to knit *all the things*, but they also bake me pie. Do you have pie, Hayes? I think not!"

We all busted out laughing, even Maddox.

I wiped tears away from eyes and said, "If you had a super power you'd be The Knitter."

"And I'd knit my little minion creatures." He grinned.

"Oh God," Hayes laughed, "do you realize if our fans heard half the shit we talk about they'd realize what a bunch of nerds we are."

"Speak for yourselves." Mathias glared, huffing under his breath.

"Dude," Hayes waved a hand in Mathias' direction, "you wear fucking suspenders and look at those glasses you have on. You're a nerd too."

Mathias frowned and whispered something in Remy's ear. She said something back and he kissed her, a smile tugging up his lips. In all the time I'd known the guys I'd never, not once, used the word *happy* to describe Mathias, but he definitely was now.

"So," Hayes turned his attention back to me, "now that you're single we should go out." He grinned, waggling his brows.

Ezra stiffened beside me, but said nothing.

"Uh…" I started. I had no idea what to say.

"Come on," he said, when I took too long to speak, "I don't bite and I hear I'm a lot of fun."

I laughed at that. "I don't know."

"Give a guy a chance, Sadie," he pleaded, grinning at me, "don't bruise my ego. It's a gentle, easily hurt, thing. It's just dinner."

"Fine," I agreed. I wasn't ready to date, but I figured one night out with Hayes could be fun. He was a nice guy.

Ezra stood up and threw away his pizza crust, mumbling that he was going to the bathroom.

"Did I piss him off?" Hayes asked. "If y'all have something going on I don't mean to butt in."

"No, nothing's going on," I said quickly.

Hayes seemed appeased by my words and smiled broadly. "Good. I'll call you."

Across from where we sat Emma's gaze seared me to the spot. She was mad.

I turned to look at her and mouthed, "What?"

She didn't respond and instead continued to glare.

Ezra returned to the room, not making eye contact with anyone. "I have a few things I need to do." Finally his gaze dropped to me. I couldn't read anything in his brown eyes. They were flat. Emotionless. "I'll drop you off at your car."

"Uh…yeah, okay." I stood up, putting the slice of pizza back in the box that I hadn't finished yet.

Hayes stood up too, looking between Ezra and me. "I can take you to your car," he said.

I knew he was only trying to be helpful, but I really wanted to kick him in the shin right now.

Ezra smiled weakly. "Great, Hayes can take you then." He clapped his hands together and somehow it felt like a gesture that he was washing his hands of me.

Before I could respond Ezra turned sharply on his heel and stalked out of the house.

I was left there wondering what I had done to piss him off.

"I'm really sorry," Hayes apologized yet again, "I didn't mean to make things awkward for you. You said there was nothing going on with you guys, and he said he had somewhere he had to go. I was trying to be helpful," he rambled.

"I know," I assured him. "I don't know what's going on with Ezra."

While Ezra might've been one of my closest friends, there were still times where I felt like I didn't know him at all. Today, being one of those days. Sometimes he retreated into himself and there was no prying his thoughts past his lips.

Hayes parked his truck beside my car and turned the volume down on the radio. "So," he started, "it's still okay if I call you?"

"Yeah, that's fine." I laughed lightly, reaching for the door.

"You don't feel weird about it, right? I mean, I know you just broke up with Braden, so I don't want you to feel pressured."

His sincerity was endearing.

"Just dinner?" I confirmed.

"Only dinner," he nodded, "and then we go from there."

"I'm okay with that." I gave him a small smile.

He nodded. "I'll see you soon."

"Bye."

I slipped out of the vehicle and into my store. I was feeling better and determined to put a dent into finishing up my paperwork and doing inventory.

Hours passed and when I finally left it was after six in the evening.

Once again, the whole day had managed to go by without me realizing it.

Ezra wasn't at his house when I got there.

He wasn't there when I made dinner either.

He still wasn't home when I went to bed.

And I couldn't help feeling that his absence was my fault.

# CHAPTER EIGHT

I SAT AT the kitchen island, eating a bowl of cereal, and flipping through a magazine when Ezra walked into his house.

I glanced over at him, noting that he was wearing different clothes.

I quickly looked back at the magazine, refusing to let him know that I'd been waiting anxiously for him to return. I'd worried something bad had happened to him, but after three unanswered texts I'd stopped bugging him—knowing that if he'd been hurt Maddox and Emma wouldn't have kept me out of the loop.

"Did you have a good night?" I asked.

He stepped into the kitchen, dropping his keys and wallet on the countertop. "Not in the way you're implying."

"I wasn't implying anything." I shoveled a mouthful of Cheerios into my mouth.

He propped his elbows on the counter and stared down at me with those intense dark eyes. "Yes, you were."

I shrugged. "You were gone all night. What you did isn't any of my business."

And it wasn't.

I didn't care either.

That was a lie. I did care, even though I shouldn't.

My feelings seemed to be swirling in a whirlpool and I couldn't make sense of them. I'd always *liked* Ezra and there'd been attraction mixed into that, but I'd never planned to act on it. This jealousy I felt at the possibility that he spent the night with a woman was ridiculous. I'd not only just ended my engagement, but I'd also agreed to go on a date with Hayes, so I shouldn't have been thinking of Ezra in that way at all.

I was also wondering if I'd agreed to go on a date with Hayes too soon after breaking up with Braden. But when was the right time to move on? Did I have to live my life on some invisible timeline that was respectable to what people found appropriate? I didn't want to spend the next six months, or year, sniveling over the end of my engagement to a man I now realized never even owned my heart. I *wanted* to move on and live my life the way I chose.

"Sadie, did you hear me?"

"Huh? What?" I snapped my head up, my gaze colliding with his.

"I stayed at my parent's house." He turned and grabbed a mug before pouring himself a cup of coffee. He leaned against the counter once more, arching his brow as he waited for a response from me.

"Did you not come home because of me?" I asked, swirling my spoon through the milk. Suddenly, I wasn't very hungry anymore. "This is your house, Ezra, and I don't want to keep you from it."

He pinched the bridge of his nose. "That had nothing to do with you and everything to do with me," he sighed.

"Is this because I told Hayes I'd go out with him?" I asked, lowering my head and staring down at the cereal like it was the most interesting thing I'd ever seen.

"Yes. No. I don't know." He mumbled, running a hand nervously through his hair. "Things are complicated." His jaw snapped together and he glared at the nearby window.

"How so?" I prompted.

"You're my best fucking friend." He slammed his palms down on the countertop. "It can't be more than that. I told you I wouldn't lose you, and I meant that." He dumped out his coffee in the sink and muttered, "I'm going to shower," before heading upstairs.

I sat dumbfounded, not knowing what to do or say.

So, I did nothing.

Several days passed, and Ezra kept his distance from me.

Boys could be so incredibly frustrating, and they thought girls were complicated creatures.

Hayes called and texted me some, but we'd yet to go on an actual date. Although, we'd made plans to go out for dinner next Friday, so it was still happening.

Now, it was the Fourth of July and everybody was headed to a party at the Wentworth's. The Wentworth's were a wealthy family in town, and Hayes happened to be related to them.

I rode with Ezra, but the entire car ride was filled with awkward silence.

I didn't know how to fix this, mostly because I didn't know what I'd done wrong in the first place.

He'd made it clear that he didn't want a relationship with me beyond friendship, and frankly I didn't feel that I was ready for more with anyone. I already regretted saying yes to a date with Hayes, but I hated to let him down now. Besides, one date wouldn't hurt anything.

We arrived at the mansion and I took a deep breath. Things had changed a lot since the last time I was here. Then, I'd been engaged and blissfully ignorant.

Ezra got out of his car and I was forced to follow, more awkward silence descending upon us.

Normally, it was a comfortable silence between us, now it felt like he was building an invisible wall between us to block me out.

I followed him to the backyard. Although, calling it a *yard* seemed an injustice. The space was expansive with a beautiful pool and the greenest grass I'd ever seen. There were several cabanas set up so that you could escape the boiling hot July sun and servers walked around with trays of food and drinks.

A gust of wind blew by and my skirt billowed around my legs.

"Hey, you guys are here!" Hayes waved from a nearby cabana. He stood up and grabbed two beers from a cooler before jogging over to join us. He only wore a pair of navy board shorts slung low on his lean hips. His chest and arms were sculpted and on the start of one arm was a half-sleeve tattoo. Dark sunglasses covered his eyes, but nothing could hide his blinding smile. I felt bad that his smile did nothing to me, but it wasn't…I refused to finish the thought.

Hayes held out a beer to Ezra and then me, the caps already popped.

"Thanks," I said, taking it. It wasn't my favorite beer, but it was the thought that counted, right? Although, the way Ezra glared at the drink in my hand I knew he believed differently.

"I'm okay," Ezra replied, waving away the beer, "maybe later."

Hayes shrugged, unfazed by Ezra's dismissal.

"I'm going to see Maddox." Ezra pointed and strode off, leaving me alone with his band's guitar player.

I forced a smile for Hayes and tried to give him my attention, but my gaze kept drifting in the direction of Ezra.

"How have you been?" He asked, lifting his beer to his lips.

"Uh…good," I replied, shielding my eyes from the sun. "Busy with the store."

"'Course," he nodded. "Fuck," he rubbed his forehead, "it's blazing hot out here. I'm getting back in the pool. You want to?" He tossed a thumb over his shoulder at the crystal blue water.

"Sure." I shrugged, not knowing what else to say.

I'd worn my bikini underneath my skirt and tank top so I followed Hayes to the cabana he'd commandeered and stripped them off. My bikini top was bright orange, flowing down in a triangle cut. The bottoms were orange and blue zig zags that tied at the sides.

Hayes' cousin, Trace, occupied one of the lounge chairs with his baby son sitting in his lap. The baby—who was probably old enough to walk now—was dressed in a pair of pale blue plaid swim trunks with oversized red sunglasses perched on his tiny nose. The baby blew bubbles, spit dripping down his lips and onto his chubby stomach. Trace chuckled and kissed the baby's cheek before looking up at me.

"Sadie, right?" He asked.

"Yeah," I nodded.

I hadn't seen Trace Wentworth since the disaster last New Year's. He had been absent from the ballroom when Ezra and Braden got into a fight, but he'd caught Braden and me in a hallway on his way back from putting his son to bed. Braden had been shouting at me, making everything out to be my fault, and I'd stood there, mute, as I took his verbal assault. Trace interrupted, cutting Braden down with quick, sharp words. Braden didn't yell at me again that night—he still bitched though.

"How have you been?" He asked. "Where's…?" He paused, waiting for me to fill in the blanks.

"Sleeping with someone else," I replied, not batting an eye. I didn't even care anymore.

Trace winced. "Sorry?"

"You said that like a question." My lips quirked into a half smile as I folded my skirt and top to tuck into my bag.

"Well," he paused, seeming to search for the right words, "he didn't seem very nice, which wouldn't be much of a loss in my book." He shrugged.

The baby made a noise and Trace started playing peek-a-boo with him.

"Yeah, I'm glad it's over." It was the first time I'd said the words aloud and I felt a stirring in my gut at the truth in them. I was better off without Braden. Bigger and better things were headed my way, and when the time was right I would fall in love again, for real this time.

Trace rubbed his finger against his son's lips so that the baby made a whirring noise. Turning to look at me, he said, "I'm happy to hear that."

"Are you ready?" Hayes asked. He'd slipped off somewhere and I hadn't even noticed he was gone.

"Yeah."

I put the untouched beer back in the cooler and followed him to the pool. I'd put on sunscreen before I left the house, so I wasn't worried about getting burnt.

It was a humid day and sweat already clung to my neck as I stepped into the cool water. It felt amazing against my heated skin.

Hayes chose to forgo the steps leading into the pool, and instead padded over to the diving board. Before he stepped up on it he rubbed his hands together and blew into them. He pointed in my direction and grinned. "Cheer for me!"

"I've got my Pom Poms at the ready." I shook my fists in a mock cheer.

He chuckled and stepped up onto the board. It wobbled with his weight.

He bounced several times before soaring into the air, doing a somersault, and diving into the water.

When he surfaced he swished his wet hair away from his eyes while I cheered. That had been impressive. I'd been expecting a belly flop.

He swam over to me and a dimple pierced his cheek when he smiled. "Some party, huh?" He asked, looking around.

"They go all out," I commented, taking in all of the decorations and guests. I didn't know how they knew so many people. "Are your parent's here?" I asked.

I knew Hayes was related to the Wentworth's, Trace being his cousin, but I'd never actually met his parents.

"Nah," he said, pushing his wet hair away from his blue eyes.

"You're kind of a lone wolf, aren't you?"

He chuckled. "I am, but they're on vacation in Hawaii. I sent them there for their anniversary."

"That was sweet of you," I commented, swimming over to the side of the pool and resting my arms on the concrete side. I kicked my legs out behind me as Hayes joined me, mimicking my position.

"I figure I owe them." He smiled. "They put up with all of my teenage angst and paid for my guitar lessons."

"I guess those definitely paid off."

"They did." He smiled, squinting against the sunlight. He stretched his palms out on the concrete and I noted the callouses on his hands. Ezra had similar ones. They came from all of the hours of playing the string instruments.

I'd asked Ezra if they hurt once and he said it looked worse than it felt.

"How was your tour?" I asked.

"Fun," he grinned.

I chose not to comment. I'd heard stories of what Hayes did on tour and most of them involved him getting naked with groupies.

"I wish I could've gone to a show." I'd been planning to attend their concert in D.C. at the Verizon Center, and maybe two others in Virginia, during their Coming Home tour, but after the blow up at New Year's I'd decided it was best not to go. I'd seen them in concert plenty of times, though, and the excited rush I felt never diminished.

"There's always next time." Hayes winked, his arm bumping into mine as he drew closer to me.

"Yeah—" I started to say, but the word quickly turned into a scream when someone cannonballed into the pool right behind me, drenching my upper body which had remained dry up until this point. I turned, ready to go off on the ignorant asshole, when Ezra surfaced beside me. "Ezra?" I asked. "What the hell are you doing?"

He shook his head, sending water droplets flying. "I was hot, so I'm cooling off."

I was tempted to shove him under water. I glared at him, my tongue working behind my closed mouth as I tried to form words. "You're ridiculous," I finally settled on. With an apologetic smile thrown in Hayes' direction, I said, "Excuse me."

I swam to the steps and climbed out of the pool. I rang out my hair, heading for the side of the house. I needed a moment to collect myself before I hit my best friend. His odd behavior the past few days, coupled with his obvious attempt to disrupt my conversation with Hayes, was more than enough to piss me off. And let's face it, with all the shit thrown my way lately I was already a little testy.

I'd barely rounded the house when a warm hand caught my elbow. Tiny little pinpricks zinged down my spine and I knew before I turned around who would be standing there.

"Let me go." I jerked my arm from his grasp and he did.

I glared at Ezra, letting him see the anger simmering in my eyes.

His bronzed chest glimmered in the sunlight from the reflection of the water droplets and his flowered board shorts hung dangerously low on his hips, enhancing the V shaped muscle that disappeared beneath along with the trail of dark hair.

"What do you think you're doing?" I snapped at him, my tone venomous as I crossed my arms over my chest. "Because from where I'm standing you're acting like a five year old."

He looked away from me, a muscle in his jaw ticking. He turned back, lowering his face into his hands. He let out a small groan. "I don't know what the fuck I'm doing," he admitted.

"You cannot tell me that you want nothing more than friendship from me and then get into a pissing contest. This isn't high school. This is my *life*." I stared him down, daring him to dispute me. "I've been through a lot in the last few years, especially the last few weeks, and I don't need to be worried about my best friend hating me for trying to rebuild my life."

"I know," he hung his head in shame, "I'm sorry."

"I'll call my brother tomorrow and see if I can crash on his couch. I'll be out of your way," I vowed. I felt like living with him was only serving to bother him more. The close quarters were wearing thin for both of us because they only served to intensify the attraction between us.

"No," he said adamantly, shaking his head, "that's not necessary. I'll get my shit together. I promise."

I stared at him, calculating the sincerity in his words. Finally, I nodded. "Okay, I believe you." Anytime Ezra had made me a promise in the past he'd always kept it.

He swallowed thickly and took a deep breath. His lips lifted in a slow smile of relief. "Let's pretend the last few days didn't happen."

"I can do that." I smiled and his shoulders relaxed.

He rubbed his hands together and pointed over his shoulder. "I guess we should get back over there."

I nodded and followed him. We'd no more than rounded the house until we bumped into Hayes. He gave us each a sheepish smile and rubbed the back of his head.

"I thought I should come check on you in case you guys were trying to claw each other's eyes out or something." He shrugged, letting his hand drop.

I lifted my hands and wiggled my fingers. "No claws. See?" I joked, hoping to ease the tension.

It seemed to help as both of the guys relaxed.

"I'm going to go see Emma." I nodded towards the cabanas. Before either of them could reply I ran off. I hoped if I left them alone for a bit that it would help ease the awkwardness between them that was my fault.

I found Emma and Maddox in one of the various cabanas along with Remy and Mathias.

Remy and Mathias shared one of the lounge chairs with her sitting in front of him. Mathias rubbed her shoulders and she relaxed against him.

Maddox and Emma occupied two of the other chairs, quietly talking together. They looked up when I entered and I grabbed one of the regular chairs and pulled it over to Emma's side.

Her blonde curly hair was piled on top of her head in a messy bun and she was wearing a cute pale blue floral bikini set. The top came down farther on her midriff, reminding me of a corset.

"We saw what happened." She said immediately, refusing to let me skirt over the events of a few minutes ago.

I sighed, propping my feet up on her lounger. She made no move to push them away.

I sat back, weighing my words. "You know Hayes asked me on a date," I started, "and Ezra has been weird since then. This was the culmination of that. I think everything's settled now, though." I shrugged.

"Settled?" She repeated and Maddox leaned forward to peer at me around her.

He lifted his black Ray Bans to the top of his head. "I've never seen Ezra act like this before and I've known him since we were little."

Emma turned to look at him and then back at me. "We've noticed things…"

"Oh my God," I groaned dramatically, "here we go again. Ezra and I don't like each other like that. Stop trying to make something out of nothing. It's annoying."

"I think you guys would make a cute couple." Remy piped in behind me and I heard Mathias chuckle.

I ignored those two, remaining focused on Emma and Maddox.

Emma looked at me pityingly. "You don't really believe that, do you?"

I glared out at the pool and away from my friend. When I looked back at her I let out a sigh. "It is what it is."

I jumped when Mathias yelled behind me, "Collin, stop that!"

I looked over to see a kid of about six or seven running after people, squirting them with a water gun. I'd never met him before and I was confused as to why Mathias would be calling him out.

I swiveled around in my chair to look at the brooding lead singer. His lips were pursed in a snarl as he pointed a finger in warning at the boy.

"Who's Collin?" I asked.

Mathias hands fell to Remy's exposed baby bump. She was dressed in a white bikini with a crocheted black tank top that covered her top half. A floppy hat was perched on her head and when she turned to look at me it smacked Mathias in the face. He laughed and reached up to remove it, smoothing down her ruffled blonde hair with a stroke of his fingers. I never thought I'd see the day where Mathias was a loving and doting husband. It was weird, but a good weird.

"He's my little brother," Mathias replied, returning to massaging Remy's shoulders. "I signed up with the Big Brothers Big Sisters program a while back and they assigned Collin as my Little Brother," he explained. "His mom had to work today, so I offered to watch him so that she didn't have to pay a babysitter."

"That's…nice of you." I mumbled, shocked that those words had left my lips.

He smiled, ducking his head. "I can be nice when I want to be."

Remy reached back, rubbing his thigh. "Go get in the pool with him. He's restless."

Mathias sighed. "But what if—"

"If I need something I can get it myself." Before he could protest she leaned back with her head on his shoulder and covered his mouth with her hand. "Or ask Emma to get it for me."

"Fine," he agreed, albeit reluctantly.

He slipped out from behind her and ran after the little boy that was currently using his squirt gun to water the grass since he'd been scolded.

I turned back to Maddox and Emma and adjusted my chair so that I was sitting more angled and not blocking Remy.

"How are the wedding plans?" I asked them.

Emma hadn't peeped one word about her upcoming wedding since my engagement fell apart. I knew she thought it would make me sad hearing about her dream wedding when mine wasn't happening, but I was truly okay with everything. I wished everyone would stop treating me like glass. I wasn't going to break.

Emma was slow to smile. "Good."

"Good? That's all I get? You're getting married in September, I know you have more details than that."

She frowned, her nose crinkling. "Are you sure you want to hear about this?"

"Yes!" I threw my hands up, sighing in exasperation. "I'm your best friend, so yes, I want to know about your wedding and I want to help if you want me to! I'm *okay*," I emphasized the word, "so stop treating me like I'm not."

She looked at Maddox and back at me. "Okay," she replied. "I'll stop." A smile broke out across her face as she launched into details on the wedding. I listened and inserted comments here and there, getting excited. She deserved this and so did Maddox. I was honestly kind of surprised they'd waited this long to get married. I knew it was Emma's doings though. Maddox would've married her as soon as she graduated high school. I had no doubts on that.

Halfway through our wedding talk Maddox left, joining his twin, Hayes, and Ezra in the pool.

Remy ditched us too, saying that she was starving.

Emma finished gushing about her wedding plans, her cheeks flushed a pleasant pink color.

"So," she started, reaching over to grab a drink off the table, "you're really okay?"

"Not one-hundred percent," I answered honestly, "but I'm getting better." I draped my arms over my bent knees. "I realize now that my life was headed in the wrong direction. Braden and I would've ended up divorced within a year, I'm sure of it." I sighed, looking off in the distance. "It sucks feeling like I'm back at the starting line while all of you are moving on to the next step. Everything happens for a reason, right?"

She nodded, setting her now empty glass aside. "It does." She stood up, stretching her arms above her head. "I'm getting in the pool, before I die and all they can find of my body is a puddle of sweat."

I laughed at her and pushed up from the chair. "Good idea."

Sweat clung to my arms and the back of my neck. I'd lived here my whole life and I still wasn't used to the summer humidity.

We joined the guys in the pool. They played with Collin, all of them now the proud owners of squirt guns. When Emma and I stepped into the pool all of them turned their water guns on us and squirted us in the face. Even in their twenties they all still acted like a bunch of little boys.

Emma yelped holding her hands up in defense. "Maddox! I'm going to kill you!"

"Hey!" Trace yelled and I turned to see that he and his wife were in the pool now, their son sitting in a tiny float. "Don't get my kid wet."

"Sorry," the guys chimed, lowering the guns.

"Where's Remy?" Mathias asked, his voice sounding panicked as he swam for the stairs.

"Stop getting your panties in a bunch," Remy's voice boomed as she neared us, "I'm fine. I wanted something to eat." She held a plate piled high with food in her hand. She stuffed a grape in her mouth. "You worry too much."

Mathias sighed, his shoulders sagging in relief. "You can't scare me like that." He swam over the edge of the pool and I noticed he'd gotten a new tattoo. I'd missed it before since Remy was sitting in front of him. Above his heart was one word: *Hope.*

I swallowed thickly, knowing the significance behind the tattoo.

"Aw, poor you. Would you like me to put a tracking monitor on my ankle so you know where I am all the time? I can be your prisoner. Maybe," her voice lowered, "if you don't irritate me too much, I'll even let you use your handcuffs on me."

Maddox cleared his throat and muttered, "Well, this got awkward really fast."

Remy gasped and the plate tumbled out of her hands, falling to the ground. I knew her reaction had nothing to do with what Maddox said.

In a lightning fast move Mathias leapt out of the pool and over to his wife. "What's wrong?" He asked, fear sticking to his words. He looked her over, searching for what had caused her distress.

She grasped his wrist and brought his hand to her stomach. "The baby. I felt it." Her mouth parted in wonder and tears pooled in her eyes. "It's kicking. Do you feel it?" She asked, looking up at Mathias with wide, love-filled eyes.

He held his hand to her stomach and gasped when he felt it too. "Wow," he murmured, looking at her lovingly. "That's amazing."

"I never thought I'd see the day," Maddox whispered.

When I turned to look at him he was smiling at Mathias and Remy with a look of awe. I think we'd all worried that Mathias would remain angry and brooding for the rest of his life—and he still was those things occasionally—but you couldn't deny the fact that for once he was actually *happy.* Seeing someone that had once been so miserable find a light in their life was a truly beautiful thing.

"What are you guys looking at?"

We all turned around to see a pretty redhead standing on the other side of the pool, her hand clasped tightly in the hold of the guy beside her. The guy was wearing a fedora—yes, a fedora—with his sandy colored hair peeking out of the bottom. They were both dressed in swimsuits, but the girl had a bag slung over her shoulder like she'd only just arrived at the party.

"Avery!" Olivia, Trace's wife, chimed. "I was afraid you weren't going to make it."

The woman named Avery straightened her pale blue bikini top that had white stars. I noticed that her bottoms had red and white stripes. It was the perfect bikini for the holiday. "Yeah, we spent more time at Luca's parent's house than we meant to." She shrugged. "Where should I put my stuff?"

"Our cabana's fine." Olivia pointed.

"Thanks." Avery set off in that direction and the guy, I assumed he was Luca, followed her like a puppy.

The next interruption came in the form of Trace's younger brother, Trent. He let out a war cry and bound towards the pool, executing a perfect cannonball, and drenching all of us in the process. It was a good thing we were already wet.

Trent surfaced, grinning.

Dean began to cry, not pleased that his face got wet. Trace pulled Dean out of his float and into his arms as he glared at his little brother. "Look what you did. Now my kid's going to be terrified of the water."

"Oh, shut up," Trent kicked his feet swimming away, "a little water won't hurt him."

Trace continued to glare at his brother, but chose not to argue, and instead bounced the baby in the hopes of cheering him up.

Ezra swam over to me, his curls plastered to his forehead. He cracked a small smile and treaded water. "Enjoying the party."

I smiled back. "It's nice to be with my friends."

"I'm still your favorite, right?" He joked, winking.

I mock gasped. "I don't pick favorites."

He chuckled and lowered his lips, blowing bubbles in the water before speaking. "But if you did I would be number one?"

"Maybe." I splashed him.

He splashed me back and soon it was an all out war.

"You guys are children!" Maddox called, he and Emma now at the other end of the pool to avoid our splash fight.

"Coming from you that means nothing!" Ezra laughed, shoving a wall of water at me.

I didn't turn away in time and some of it went up my nose. I coughed and sputtered.

Ezra immediately ceased his attack. "Are you okay?" He asked.

I nodded. "Yeah, I'm fine."

Before I knew what was happening he had my back pinned against the pool wall with his arms on either side of me. He stared down at me, his dark eyes intense. I watched as a droplet of water fell from one of his curls and onto his nose, before rolling down his lips.

My heart thudded in my chest at his proximity and my muscles locked up. When he got this close I never knew what to do. My body had *always* reacted to Ezra, I just denied what I felt. I tried to pretend it didn't exist, because it was easier that way. He was right, we couldn't ruin our friendship even if I did daydream about the way his lips would feel against mine. Even when I was with Braden I'd still felt this intense connection to Ezra. I guessed maybe Braden had been right to be so jealous.

"So, we're good?" He asked.

"Huh?" My brows knit in confusion. I'd been too busy staring at his lips to process his words.

"Are we good?" He repeated. "After our talk earlier…we're still good, right?"

"Oh," I shook my head, "yeah."

His smile was blinding, shedding light on all the darkest parts of myself. Ezra, in many ways, was the best parts of me. There was something about him that was so pure and good that you couldn't help but be affected by that if you were around him for long. I swore he had one of the kindest and pure souls that ever existed. There weren't many people like him and I was lucky enough to call him my best friend.

"I want you to know that I really am sorry for acting like such an asshole the past few days. It was wrong of me." He took a deep breath. "I'm going to be a better friend to you." He reached up, tucking a piece of hair behind my ear.

My eyes closed and the skin on my cheek tingled where his fingers had brushed against it.

I swallowed past the lump in my throat. I hated that I was so affected by him— that I *wanted* him in a way that he refused to want me. I knew it was still too soon to want a relationship—and I didn't—but I hated that he refused to even entertain the idea of an *us* one day. My feelings were obviously stronger for him than his were for me. I'd been denying my feelings for so long, trying desperately to ignore them, but from the moment Ezra dove in the lake after me during my Thank-God-That-Asshole-Is-Out-Of-Your-Life party they'd become impossible to ignore. At least the night I got drunk he admitted to being attracted to me. If it weren't for that I'd still be convinced that my feelings were entirely one-sided.

"You already are the best friend I could ask for. You've gone above and beyond best friend duties," I joked, finally answering him.

"I'd do anything for my friends. You're my family." He waved his arms, encompassing his band mates and their girls.

The Willow Creek boys really were like family, and by extension the people they brought into their inner circle became family too.

I knew I'd become a better person by knowing them, especially by befriending Ezra. He'd become my anchor when I was lost and confused. I knew without him I would've never had the courage to pursue my dream and own a store. He believed in me when most people didn't—but as a teenager I'd given people a reason not to have faith in me. I'd spent more time chasing boys than figuring out what I wanted in life. And then once I had things figured out, I'd met Braden. He'd completely fooled me. I'd believed I'd finally found the right guy for me, but I'd never been more wrong. I didn't regret my time with Braden though. The way I saw it, being with him taught me a valuable life lesson—to appreciate the good in my life, and to stop striving for an unrealistic ideal.

Ezra snapped his fingers in front of my face. "Sadie?"

"Sorry, I zoned out," I laughed. I squared my shoulders, the water sloshing around my body as I swam away from the edge of the pool, putting more distance between us.

I hated the way my heart came to life when I was near him. The stupid, treacherous, organ didn't seem to know that he was off limits.

Ezra swam away, back to the guys.

Emma and I got out of the pool to grab some food. We ended up back in the cabana and I took over the lounger Maddox had vacated.

Emma put on her sunglasses, smiling out at the scene that played before us.

Chatter, music, and laughter filled the air and children ran around with sparklers, their happiness contagious.

Off in the distance a group of guys, Trace and Trent included, began to set off fireworks.

I smiled at the sight, then at Emma, and the guys as they got out of the pool.

Hayes ran over to us, his hair slicked back off of his forehead. He held his hand out for me. "Come on, you can't see the fireworks from over here."

I wanted to argue that it was still daylight, so even up close you'd barely be able to see them, but I let him lead me away.

We joined the group I'd watched earlier and they set off another round of fireworks.

"Wait until you see the ones they have for tonight." Hayes whispered in my ear. "They're epic."

I believed him. The Wentworth's were loaded, so they could pay to have the best.

"This is nice, huh?" He asked as a firework crackled, sparks flying low to the ground.

"Yeah," I replied, but I couldn't keep my eyes from drifting behind us to Ezra.

I'd tried many times to get over my ridiculous crush on my best friend, but it was impossible.

Even when I thought I'd moved on with Braden, a flame in my heart still burned for Ezra—reaching and hoping that maybe he felt it too.

He lifted his head, as if he felt my gaze on him, and his eyes collided with mine.

I quickly looked away, focusing back on what Hayes was saying, but that one look from Ezra had revealed so much and it only served to make the ache inside me grow stronger.

# CHAPTER NINE

"MOM, I'M FINE," I assured her for the thousandth time since I'd answered my phone. I had her on speaker while I folded my clothes and put them away.

"But Sadie," she started in again, "you were supposed to get married today. I know it has to be bothering you. You're my daughter, I can sense these things."

I sighed. "Things are hitting me harder today," I confessed, "but in all honestly, I dodged a bullet. I wouldn't have been happy with Braden in the long run. You know that. You never were his biggest supporter."

"That's because he treated you like you were beneath him. You need a man who wants to stand at your side, not one that acts like you're a child."

My mom. So, wise. Too bad I tended to ignore her advice.

"I know," I agreed, putting away the last of my laundry.

"Why don't you come over today, sweetie?" She asked. "We could bake cookies like we used to."

"I just don't feel like it." I grabbed my phone off of the bed and switched it off of speaker before holding it to my ear. "I have some things I need to do today," lie, "and I really am fine. You don't need to worry so much. I'm a big girl."

Her sigh echoed over the speaker. "Sadie, you'll always be my baby to me. The sooner you realize that, the better."

"Okay, okay." I tucked the phone between my ear and shoulder as I reached for the water bottle on my nightstand and took a sip. "I have to go now, mom."

"Alright, but if you change your mind and want to come over I'll be home all day."

"Okay," I said again. "I love you."

"Love you too."

I hung up the phone and grabbed my tennis shoes, sitting on the edge of the bed as I tied them on. I hoped going on a run would help clear my head. I hadn't lied when I told my mom I was okay, but it was still a hard pill to swallow.

Downstairs I found Ezra lying on the couch, reading a book.

He laid the book on his chest when he heard me and crossed his arms behind his head. "Where are you going?" He asked.

"For a run," I replied, heading to the refrigerator for a fresh bottle of water.

He sat up, dropping the book on the coffee table. "Mind if I join you?"

I paused with the water bottle halfway to my lips. "I don't mind…but I don't think I've ever seen you run."

He laughed. "I might not be the most fit of the guys, but I *can* run." He stood up, heading for the steps.

I didn't bother to tell him that I thought his body was perfect, even though the words were on the tip of my tongue. The last thing I wanted to do was make things weird between us again. We were finally getting on normal footing again. Although, with my upcoming date with Hayes I feared things might be headed for another nosedive.

While Ezra changed I stepped out on the front porch, inhaling the morning air.

Here, on the lake, there was something magical about the mornings. Everything sparkled with dew and the animals weren't afraid of us. From where I stood I could see a deer grazing in the woods and a squirrel scuttled along the porch railing.

Smiling to myself, I sat down on the top step and stretched my legs.

Behind me I heard the screen door creak open. I peered over my shoulder at Ezra and oh my Lord I think he was trying to kill me.

"What are you wearing?!" I squeaked, hating the appalling way my voice spiked.

His dark brows furrowed together and he looked down. "Uh…shorts?"

"Where's your shirt?" I huffed, staring at his bare chest and those low slung basketball shorts that were like the worst kind of delicious torture on the planet. It seemed wrong to be checking out my best friend on the day I should've been married, but let's face it, a lot had changed in the last two weeks and I no longer gave a crap about Braden. He could move on with his bitchy lawyer and I could do whatever I wanted with my life—including drooling over Ezra.

"I'm not wearing one…obviously."

I let out an exasperated breath and jumped to my feet.

"Besides," he continued, "where's *your* shirt?"

Now it was my turn to look down. I wore a pair of running shorts and a jog bra.

"Forget I said anything," I huffed, glancing away in embarrassment and cursing myself yet again for my ridiculous feelings towards him. I wished there was some magic potion I could drink to make them go away, because now that I'd realized how strong my attraction to him was I couldn't tamp it down like I had in the past. It didn't help that he was one of my best friends, and therefore a truly decent person. He was the whole package and I hadn't lied when I told him he'd make someone very happy one day. But I knew if he had his way—which he always did—I wouldn't be that person.

His lips quirked as he fought a smile clearly amused at my dismissal of the conversation.

I started down the porch steps and looked back at him. "Are you coming?"

"Always, sweetheart." He joked, tossing in a wink for good measure.

I rolled my eyes and started to run, setting the pace. He fell into step beside me.

Since the road leading to his house was dirt and cut a windy path through the woods it was the perfect place to run.

Even though it was early in the morning it was no time until sweat clung to my body and my breath came out in small pants.

Ezra kept up with me, unfazed by my fast pace.

The sun filtered between the branches of the trees and I watched the way the shadows from the leaves danced over the dirt path.

That was the thing I loved most about running, how it allowed me to empty my mind completely and focus on the beautiful things in front of me that I normally overlooked.

We came to the end of the driveway and turned right, heading down the dirt road that led to another house several miles away. Ezra had once told me it belonged to an old guy that owned a farm and all of the surrounding land. He'd actually owned the cottage Ezra bought, but decided to sell it when it began to fall apart and he didn't have the funds to fix it.

"How are you holding up?" I asked him between breaths.

"I'm fine."

I picked up my speed, enjoying the burn in my arms and legs.

After two miles I turned around. Ezra managed to stay by my side the whole time, even though he looked like he was about to keel over dead.

When his house was in sight I veered off of the path and into the grass. I sat down and brought my knees up to my chest.

Ezra followed, his body wet with sweat. He collapsed beside me onto his back with his knees bent. His chest rose and fell with each lungful of air he pulled in.

"You're insane." He panted a few minutes later. "Completely and utterly insane."

"Then why did you come with me?" I asked, my breath under control now.

He turned his head to look at me, pushing the damp black curls away from his dark eyes. "I know what today is." His voice was barely a whisper. "I wasn't going to let you go off by yourself."

I cracked a smile. "Were you afraid I might hang myself from a tree?" I stuck my foot out and lightly kicked his leg in jest.

"No," he shook his head, "but I still didn't think you should be alone."

"Well, thanks." I smiled, truly grateful.

"Let's do something today."

"Like what?" I plucked a piece of grass from the ground and wrapped it around my finger.

He shrugged. "How about we watch a movie and just hang out? We haven't had a chance to do that in a while."

"No, we haven't," I agreed. Smiling, I nodded. "Yeah, that sounds good."

He grinned and stood up, extending a hand to me. "We better shower first."

I took his hand and couldn't stop myself from saying, "Together?"

He reared back in shock.

"I was kidding, Ezra." I bumped his shoulder with mine and started walking. I turned around backwards to face him. "First one to the house gets the shower!"

I took off running and when I reached the porch I turned around to see that he was still walking leisurely down the driveway. He lifted his hand to wave when he saw me looking.

"You lose!" I called to him.

"Really, because I feel like a winner from where I'm standing! You have a nice ass!" He yelled back.

My mouth fell open in shock and I turned abruptly to head inside without comment, but his laughter followed me.

We both showered and after a quick snack we sat down on the couch with a bowl of popcorn. Ezra had already picked out the movie and the previews began to play. Most people skipped through this part, but we never did.

"What did you pick out?" I asked, curling my legs beneath me. My damp hair tickled my shoulders and I reached for the cream colored blanket that sat on the back of the couch and wrapped it around me.

"*Benchwarmers*." He reached for the popcorn and shoved a handful in his mouth.

"A classic," I responded, wiggling around until I got comfortable.

He stretched his long legs out on the coffee table and chuckled under his breath. "Only you would consider this a classic."

I smiled. "And what would you consider a classic?" I countered, popping a piece of popcorn into my mouth.

He pursed his lips in thought. "*The Godfather*."

I shook my head. "Okay, so maybe *Benchwarmers* isn't a classic."

He chuckled, crossing his arms over his chest. "You gave in easily. That's rare."

I shrugged, grabbing another piece of popcorn. "I'm tired." And I was, for so many different reasons.

"Come here," he coaxed, moving the popcorn bowl to the coffee table.

"What?" I asked stupidly.

He put a pillow on his lap and motioned for me to lie down. After a reluctant sigh, I did. I felt weird about it, which was stupid, because I'd done this often with him in the past. But with the way my 'crush' had intensified since he let me live with him, it suddenly felt different. You know, typically when you live with someone it's hard in the beginning working around each other's quirks—Braden and I had fought a lot when I first moved in—but Ezra and I flowed naturally together.

"Comfortable?" He asked, fixing the blanket so that it covered my shoulder.

"Yeah, thanks." I said when he grabbed the remote and pressed play.

I tried to relax and watch the movie, but it was impossible.

Ezra was everywhere, invading my senses and making my brain fuzzy.

When his hand settled on my arm I nearly jumped out of my skin.

I knew he meant nothing by the touch, but I couldn't stop myself from wishing it was more.

So much more.

Crushing on my best friend really freaking sucked.

# CHAPTER TEN

MY HEART POUNDED in my chest as I swiped pale pink lip-gloss over my lips. Hayes would be showing up any minute to pick me up and I felt sick to my stomach. I didn't know why I'd agreed to do this. I felt like I was cheating, even though that thought was beyond silly considering I was no longer with Braden and I certainly wasn't with Ezra either. But that knowledge didn't stop me from feeling dirty. It was all so stupid and ridiculous.

I took a deep breath and closed my eyes.

I had to get a grip.

Hayes was a nice guy and it was one date.

This wouldn't change anything.

I nodded my head in affirmation at my own thoughts and put the gloss away.

I sprayed on some perfume and turned out the bathroom light before heading downstairs. I grabbed my purse from the counter, checking my phone for any messages. There was one from Hayes saying he'd be here in ten minutes that was sent five minutes ago.

"You look nice."

"Ah!" I let out a scream and whipped around. "Jesus, Ezra, you scared the crap out of me. I thought you were still out."

"I got back early." He leaned against the back of the couch with his arms crossed over his chest. "Seriously, you look nice."

"Oh, thanks." I mumbled, still scattered. I'd dressed in a long white skirt with a loose over the shoulder beige sweater on top. I was going for nice, but casual.

Ezra shoved his hands into the pockets of his khaki cargo shorts. "So…Hayes?"

"Yeah." I nodded, tucking a piece of wavy hair behind my ear. "You're okay with that right?"

He'd been fine since the Fourth of July party, but the way he stood now with squared shoulders and a tense jaw only reiterated my feelings that I was doing something wrong.

"Of course," he scoffed. "Why would I have a problem with it?"

I shrugged. "I don't know."

My hand tightened around my phone, willing Hayes to get here faster so that I could end this awkward conversation.

"What are you going to do today?" I asked him.

He shrugged, scrubbing a hand over the heavy stubble on his cheeks. "I need to mow, so I guess I'll do that."

It always amazed me that Ezra liked to do things such as mowing his own grass. I mean, he was a rock star. He could easily pay people to mow his yard—which was far bigger than most—but he wanted to do these things himself.

"Maybe we can watch a movie later?" I suggested, wanting to get rid of the mountain that seemed to be growing between us.

"I'm not in the mood."

"Oh." I sighed, glancing towards the door. My phone buzzed in my hand and a second later the sound of a car horn could be heard outside. "I guess I better go." I pointed at the door stupidly.

He nodded, forcing a smile. It was so incredibly fake that I nearly called him out on it. "Have fun," he said, the tone lacking any enthusiasm.

"Thanks," I mumbled, for lack of anything else to say.

I headed to the door and before it closed behind me Ezra caught it. I turned back to look at him, raising a brow. "What?" I asked.

He stared down at me and then up at Hayes who was climbing out of his truck. When his eyes fixed on me all he said was, "Be careful," and the door closed in my face.

I was tempted to barge back inside and yell at him—to tell him he was being a jackass *again*—but Hayes was waiting on me so I plastered on a smile and headed over to his truck.

He stood waiting by the passenger door. "Hey, you look beautiful," he greeted me, lowering from his towering height to kiss my cheek.

I smiled up at him. "Thank you."

He opened the truck door and held onto my hand as I climbed inside. His hand was warm and calloused like Ezra's from all his hours of playing guitar.

He jogged around the front of the truck and climbed inside. The music was blaring and he reached over to turn it down.

"Where are we headed?" I asked. I'd been surprised when Hayes wanted to pick me up at one in the afternoon, but I rolled with it.

"I thought we could go to the park and have a picnic." He nodded to the backseat of the truck and I turned around to see an old-fashioned looking picnic basket.

"That'll be fun." I grinned, truly meaning it. "But won't you get mobbed?" I asked.

"Aha." He reached down between the seat and kept his eyes on the narrow driveway as dirt billowed around us. "That's what this is for." He held up a baseball cap and sunglasses. I looked at him in disbelief. "It helps, believe me." He added.

"I'll take your word for it," I laughed.

He grinned, his eyes crinkling at the corners.

I began to relax once he pulled out onto the main road. "Why a truck?" I asked.

"Huh?" He glanced in my direction.

I shrugged. "Maddox and Mathias drive sports cars, Ezra has an Escalade, and you drive a truck. Granted, this is a fancy truck, but it's a truck," I remarked.

He laughed, shaking his head. "I'm a country boy, Sadie, and country boys drive dirty, mud covered trucks." He took on an exaggerated southern drawl.

"Did you grow up around here?" I knew a lot about the other guys in the band, but Hayes had always been a mystery to me. He didn't open up easily.

He nodded. "Yeah."

"How'd you get to know the other guys?" I knew it sounded like I was prying, but this was one story I'd never been told.

He glanced at me briefly before his eyes returned to the road.

"We went to school together. I was two years ahead of them, and I'd always played guitar so when they started their band and needed a guitar player they reached out to me. They're cool and we all clicked. It was easy to become friends with them and then everything else sort of fell into place," he shrugged.

"Do you like living the rock star life?" I knew his answer—Hayes was the band member that most took advantage of his celebrity status.

"Absolutely," he answered with an easy going grin. Sobering, he added, "But I like being home and living a normal life too. I guess I like having the best of both worlds."

"I can understand that."

"So…" He started, glancing in my direction with an awkward smile. "How's Ezra with this?" He waved a finger between us. "Is he cool now?"

I shrugged. "Fine, I guess." Based on his odd behavior this afternoon *fine* was the last thing he appeared to be, but I didn't want to tell Hayes that. "Let's not talk about him." I didn't want my thoughts to become entirely absorbed in Ezra.

"Okay, that's off the subject table then." He smiled over at me, tapping his fingers against the steering wheel in time with the beat of the song playing softly on the radio. "What do you want to talk about?"

I thought for a moment. "If you weren't in Willow Creek, what would you be doing?"

He didn't hesitate to answer. "Working in construction. My dad owns a company. It was my plan to work for him while I was in high school, get a degree in business management, and take over the company one day…but plans," he pursed his lips in thought, "they have a funny way of changing."

He pulled into the parking lot of the park and turned the vehicle off. He put the red baseball cap on, making sure the brim covered half of his face and added the sunglasses.

"How do I look?" He asked me, striking a playful pose.

"Like a rock star in disguise." I laughed.

He smiled crookedly. "Come on, it totally works."

"Yeah, it kind of does," I agreed.

The baseball cap kept most of his sandy hair hidden from view and the dark sunglasses obscured his blue eyes. But if someone were observant he'd still be easy to spot.

"Are you just saying that to make me feel better?" He frowned.

"No." I shook my head.

He rubbed his hands together before reaching for the door handle. "Picnic time! I'm starving!"

I rolled my eyes as I got out of the car and met him on the other side of the truck. "You guys are always hungry."

He laughed and nodded his head in agreement, reaching inside to grab a blanket and the basket. Once he had both secured in his hands we started in the direction of the grassy area. There were picnic tables, but Hayes chose a spot beneath a large tree that was shaded by the sun.

He set the basket down and shook out the blanket. We sat down and he opened the basket. He handed me a sandwich and smiled sheepishly. "I asked Emma what your favorite was. I hope that's okay."

My mouth fell open as I unfolded the saran wrap. "You *made* this?"

He shrugged like it was no big deal. "It's only a sandwich."

"Which you made…with your hands…by yourself?"

He snorted. "Is it really that surprising to you?"

"Yes," I answered without hesitation.

He ducked his head. "You don't know me at all."

"You've never given me the chance to know you," I countered, "over the years you've kept yourself pretty separate from the rest of us."

He sighed, pulling out a bag of chips and bottles of water from the basket before closing it. "Yeah, I guess I have…I feel like I've always struggled to fit in with the band."

"Why is that?" My brows furrowed in confusion. Hayes was a confident guy that wasn't afraid to speak his mind, so I was surprised that he'd feel that way.

He unwrapped his sandwich and took a bite. Once he'd swallowed he finally answered me. "Don't get me wrong, I consider all three of those guys as my friends…but they've known each other since they were kids. They're like brothers while I'm the outsider."

I couldn't stop myself from laughing. "I have to admit, Maddox and Ezra have one hell of a bromance going on."

Hayes laughed to. "You've got that right." He shrugged and took a sip of water. "I guess Mathias is a bit of an outsider too, but he's been changing since he married Remy and now he's having a fucking kid." He shook his head and his whole body shuddered with a sigh. "It's too weird to think about him being a dad."

"Yeah, I have to agree with that."

Mathias was the last guy in the band I ever pictured settling down so early, but people change.

I bit into my sandwich, surprised by how good it tasted. "Hey, this is delicious." I told him.

He chuckled. "It's just a sandwich."

"It's a yummy one," I countered.

"So, I did okay?" He asked, motioning to our set up and lunch.

"You did great." I smiled at him. I was actually having a really nice time with him, which surprised me completely.

"How are things with your store?" He popped a chip into his mouth.

"Good," I answered vaguely.

He raised a brow. "That's all I get."

"There's not much to tell." I shrugged. "It's just a store."

"It's what you love, though, right?"

"Yeah."

He cracked a small, half smile. "That's good to hear. Too many people these days are miserable."

"Are *you* miserable?" I asked.

I expected an immediate answer, but he surprised me by pausing and mulling over my question.

"Not miserable, per se," his lips pursed, "but sometimes I feel like something is missing from my life."

"Is that why you asked me on a date?" I questioned. "You've always…uh… gotten around." I frowned, hating to sound so blunt, but it couldn't be avoided.

He chuckled. His laugh was deep and husky sounding. "Yeah, yeah, I know." He hung his head, hiding a smile. "I love women and I'm not ashamed of that. But I guess…the meaningless hookups have gotten a little old. Is it stupid that I see Maddox and Mathias with their girls and I want that?"

"Not stupid at all." I finished my sandwich and wiped my hands on a napkin that he'd so thoughtfully packed. "But why ask me? You've never acted interested in me before. Even when I was single," I added.

He shrugged. "You're different, Sadie. You're not like the girls that throw themselves at us when we're on the road. Besides, I might not know you well, but I do know you'd never be with me because of my money and status."

He leaned towards me and I held my breath as the distance between us lessened. My heart thundered in my chest—not because I was excited by the thought of Hayes kissing me, but because I couldn't decide whether I wanted him to or not.

His fingers tangled in my hair and his breath fanned over my lips, waiting.

I closed my eyes, my thoughts and feelings a raging inferno inside me.

I was promised to no one, but my heart didn't know that.

"I'm sorry," I mumbled, turning my head away.

His hand fell and he sighed, not in disgust but resigned. I felt bad, because Hayes truly was a nice guy and I believed him when he said he wanted more than a meaningless hookup, but I couldn't see myself with him.

"Is it Ezra?" He asked. He didn't sound angry.

I winced and reluctantly raised my head to look at him. "I know it's stupid, he doesn't even like me like that," I winced, hating the fact that I sounded like I was in elementary school, "but yeah…I can't feel this way towards him and kiss you. It's wrong and I won't use you like that."

"I can respect that." He sat back, putting distance between us. He surprised me by holding out a hand to me. "Friends?"

"No," I put my hand in his, "family."

He grinned—the smile lighting up his whole face. "The Willow Creek family."

"Exactly."

"Thanks for…uh, giving me a shot, I guess." Hayes said with a laugh when he parked his truck in Ezra's driveway.

I laughed too. "Hayes, you're going to find the girl for you someday, it's just not me."

He nodded. "I know."

He leaned over and kissed my cheek before I slipped out of the truck.

He waited in the driveway until I had the door unlocked and then he turned the truck around to leave.

I stepped inside and locked the door behind me.

A small squeal left my lips when I turned around to find Ezra standing behind me.

"You have got to stop sneaking up on me like that." I put a hand over my racing heart and moved to drop my purse and keys on the kitchen counter.

"Sadie?" He swallowed thickly.

"What?" I looked at him curiously. He didn't look right, slightly sweaty and pale. His fists opened and closed at his sides.

I was about to ask him if he was sick when he threw his hands in the air in defeat, cried, "Fuck it," and stormed towards me.

I stood frozen, completely transfixed as he closed the space between us in three powerful strides.

He cupped the back of my neck and my back hit the wall beside the refrigerator as he towered above me. Before I could blink his lips were on mine.

Let's face it, I'd fantasized about kissing Ezra. He was hot, and I had an unrequited crush so it was bound to happen.

In those fantasies he'd always been sweet and tender.

But I would never use those two words to describe this kiss.

His lips were rough and demanding.

There was something feral about the way he moved—how he *consumed* me.

He growled low in his throat and my own moan captured the sound.

Holy shit, I was kissing Ezra.

Actually, he was kissing me and I was just along for the ride, but oh what a fun ride it was.

My hands began to wander up his chest and he grabbed my hands, pinning them above my head.

His hips dug into mine, and—*holy hell.*

A breathy sigh escaped me and his tongue pressed beyond my parted lips.

My knees began to quake.

I had never been kissed like this before.

No, that was a lie.

A kiss had never *felt* like this before.

Our lips moved together like they were singing the same song.

My fingers twitched in his grasp, desperate to touch him, but his hold only tightened.

I had never expected Ezra to be this rough, and aggressive, and *hot.* He was always so nice and gentle, but apparently there was a side to him I'd never experienced before and I was all for getting to know this part of him…intimately, and by the bulge pressing between my thighs he was up for that too. No pun intended.

"Finally." He breathed the word against my lips before pulling my bottom lip between his teeth and letting it go.

I moaned and my hips jerked forward.

A chuckle rumbled in his throat and then he deepened the kiss.

My brain grew fuzzy from the lack of oxygen, but the last thing I wanted to do was stop kissing him.

With one last slow stroke of his tongue he retreated and he let go of my hands. They fell onto his shoulder and my chest pressed against his with each breath I took.

He reached up, caressing his fingers lightly against my cheek. "I've wanted to do that for so long. You have no idea."

My eyes closed and I chanted in my head, *this has to be a dream.*

But when I opened my eyes Ezra still stood there and my lips were swollen from his kisses.

"Why now?" I couldn't stop myself from asking.

"Because," his teeth ground together, "seeing you with Hayes…" He looked away, fighting to gain control of his temper. "It was even worse than seeing you with Braden. At least I had a legitimate reason to hate him, but Hayes? I couldn't hate that guy if I tried, and that made it a thousand times worse."

"What do we do now?" I asked.

"It was only a kiss." He started to pull away, but I tightened my hold around his neck.

"No, don't you *dare* say that," I spat.

"Sadie—"

"Please, stop." I laid my head against his chest. "Please, don't take it back."

"I wasn't going to." I felt his fingers smooth through my hair.

"Why won't you let this—let *us* happen?"

His Adam's apple bobbed and he peered down at me. "You're my best friend," he reminded me yet again, "what if things didn't work out between us? I can't lose you."

"And I'm not worth the risk," I snapped, the words laced with venom as I reared back. I shook my head at him and stormed away, up the steps, and slammed my bedroom door like a surly teenager.

Rejected, yet again.

# CHAPTER ELEVEN

IT HAD BEEN a week since our kiss.

Seven whole days.

And in those seven days I hadn't spoken one word to him.

He'd talked plenty though. He liked to tell me my behavior was 'childish' and I guess the silent treatment was childish, but I was afraid if I opened my mouth to talk to him I might scream.

I was so incredibly frustrated, and hurt, and…horny.

Yeah, that last one *really* sucked.

I'd avoided Ezra's place as much as I could—usually hanging out with Maddox and Emma. But they were annoying to be around after a while. I honestly didn't know how they were still so lovey dovey after being together for four years. Or was it five? I'd lost count. But they were still all over each other and I could only handle Maddox sticking his tongue down her throat so many times.

Now, I was sequestered in my bedroom while Ezra made dinner.

He always made enough for me too—and then I would make a point of not eating it. Even if it meant I OD'd on sour patch kids or something else equally sugar filled that I kept hidden in my room.

Tonight was different, though.

I had an idea, one I hoped he'd go for.

Although, after my silent treatment he was probably apt to kick me out and not listen to what I had to say.

I paced restlessly around the small bedroom that had become mine the past month.

This idea of mine…it was crazy.

Stupid, even.

The chances of Ezra agreeing were slim.

The chance of him laughing in my face, however, was a high percentage.

I blamed Remy for this idea.

Yep, it was all her fault.

She'd planted the seed in my brain and now I couldn't get this festering thought out of my head and I had to act on it.

I had to do something.

Because tiptoeing around this was impossible.

I pressed my ear against my bedroom door, listening intently like a nosy teenager eavesdropping on a conversation. I waited until I heard the kitchen chair scrape against the hardwood floors before darting down the stairs.

I had to do this fast before I lost the courage.

Ezra looked up when he heard me, the burger he'd grilled halfway to his mouth and another sitting on a plate in front of him waiting for me.

Before he could say anything the words tumbled out of my mouth.

"I have a proposition for you."

His brows quirked and he set the burger down without taking a bite. He motioned to the empty chair in front of him and I quickly sat.

He folded his fingers together and stared at me with that intense dark gaze that always sent me reeling.

"You haven't spoken one word to me in a week, and the first thing you say to me is that you have a proposition for me…I'm really looking forward to hearing this." He tipped the chair back so that the front two legs came off the ground.

While I tried to gather myself he continued to stare at me, his fingers stroking the heavy stubble on his face.

I laid my palms flat on the cool surface of the table and took a deep breath.

*You've got this, Sadie!* I tried to pep talk myself, but it wasn't working.

"I want you to fuck me." Shit. That hadn't been how I was planning to lead into this. I quickly added, "Just sex. That's it. Not a relationship. You don't want to lose our friendship, and I don't either, but we have a mutual attraction and I don't think we should fight it. I'm proposing that while I live here—which I promise to be out in the next two months or so—we should have sex."

The chair clamored back to the floor and his mouth hung open.

"Don't look at me like that," I squirmed, "I'm not crazy. This is a rational idea. We're adults. We can have sex without it complicating things."

"So…" He started, shaking his head like he couldn't believe what I'd said. "You want us to be friends…with benefits." His lips twitched with laughter.

I squared my shoulders and lifted my chin defiantly. "That's exactly what I'm saying."

"You're serious?" He sobered, his expression back to shock.

"Very serious."

He looked at me carefully, like he was searching for any sign that I might be lying.

"Sadie—"

"Don't say no yet," I pleaded, "and don't say yes either. Just…just think about it. *Please?*"

He breathed in shakily. "Okay."

I was surprised he agreed to that so readily. I expected him to slam me with a firm no and tell me there was no way he would ever sleep with me.

I wanted so much more from him than sex, but I knew he would never cross that particular line with me.

But sex, he might.

Sex did not a relationship make.

Four days passed and neither one of us peeped a word about my proposal. I was too embarrassed to bring it up, and I guessed he'd been counting on that.

I turned on the TV switching it to Hallmark and sat down to watch whatever sappy movie they were playing. I needed a good cry and a bowl of cookie dough ice cream—which reminded me Ezra had mentioned picking some up at the grocery store. Well, actually his groceries were delivered so he could avoid getting mobbed at the store, but logistics.

I didn't bother with a bowl. I grabbed the gallon carton of ice cream, a spoon, and made my way to the couch. Despite the fact that it was eighty degrees or more outside I was dressed in sweatpants, a sweatshirt, and had a blanket wrapped around me like a burrito.

I needed comfort in my time of sorrow and warmth brought me that.

Although, I was positive Ezra's warm body wrapped around mine would bring me *a lot* of comfort.

Fuck.

I had to stop thinking about him like that.

It was never going to happen and it only made me depressed thinking about it.

Especially, after that kiss.

Oh, sweet Lord, *that kiss*.

It had been everything dreams were made of.

It was downright magical.

I'd felt it all the way down to the tips of my toes.

And even now, almost two weeks later, my lips still tingled from the bruising pressure of his possessive mouth.

I shoveled a mouthful of ice cream between my lips and focused my eyes on the TV screen.

No more thoughts about Ezra.

Which should be easy, since he wasn't home. So it wasn't like he was sitting around tempting me or anything.

But I was always tempted when it came to him.

My God I wanted to lick him all over like I was currently going after this ice cream.

I had problems.

I put the ice cream away. It was making things worse.

I burrowed into the couch once more and this time I did manage to get sucked into the movie. It also made me cry, so bonus points for that.

It ended and another one came on. I lay down with my head on a pillow and tried to keep my eyes open.

As a teenager I'd been wild.

As an adult, this was as exciting as my Saturday's got.

I was pathetic.

I needed more excitement in my life than sitting around watching Hallmark movies.

I startled from my thoughts when the front door opened.

"Hey," Ezra said in greeting, his back to me as he closed the door.

"Hi." I squeaked. Yes, *squeaked* like a mouse.

He set the case he kept his bass in beside the door. The guys were already working on their new album as much as they could, but things were slow since their personal lives kept complicating things.

"What are you watching?" He came around from behind the couch and lifted my legs before sitting down and placing them in his lap.

"I have no idea," I answered honestly.

He tapped his fingers against my leg and focused on the TV.

"Are you seriously going to watch a girly movie with me?" I glanced away from the TV at him, raising a brow.

His gaze swiveled in my direction. "Sure, why not?" He shrugged. "I don't have anything else to do."

"Okaaaay, then." I drew out the word, looking at him like he'd grown another head.

"Hey, I can watch a chick movie and not shrivel up and die." He defended, scrunching up his face to appear mad.

I tried to hide my smile but it was impossible.

"Are you laughing at me?"

"I would never laugh at you," I scoffed.

"You definitely are."

Before I could respond he pounced on me. Giggles burst forth from me when he tickled my stomach.

"Stop! Stop!" I pleaded between bouts of laughter.

"You have to promise never to laugh at me ever again." He grinned, moving to my side where I was even more ticklish.

"I promise!" I cried. "Please stop tickling me!"

Miraculously his assault ceased. We were both panting and out of breath, although I had no idea why he was so breathless.

His hands moved down from my sides, over my hips, and stopped at my thighs.

My throat closed up as his thumb rubbed slow circles against my thigh.

His chocolate colored eyes darkened even more.

My heart sped up and I struggled to find my voice. "What are you doing?" I finally asked.

His tongue flicked out to moisten his lips and his eyes remained steady on mine.

"Accepting your proposition."

My body clenched all over and I ceased breathing. "What?" Surely I didn't hear him right.

"I'm accepting your proposition," he repeated.

Sweet baby Jesus. Was this real life? I had to be dreaming, right?

I pinched myself.

Yes, it was real life.

Ezra chuckled, the sound of it vibrating through my body. "Did you just *pinch* yourself?"

I nodded my head. I had no words. Every single word in the English dictionary had fled my mind.

He chuckled again, hovering above me. "You don't believe me, do you?"

I shook my head.

"I guess I'll have to show, not tell."

Before I could inhale my next breath his lips were on mine and he became my oxygen. My fingers tangled in the silky soft strands of his hair and I let out a small moan as his hips ground against mine.

"Are you sure?" I asked between kisses.

"Abso-fucking-lutely."

He gathered me in his arms so that he was sitting on the couch and I was straddling him.

He cupped the back of my neck, holding me to him as he kissed me thoroughly.

A rush of emotions flooded my veins.

Excitement.

Lust.

*Fear.*

His hands moved lower, to the hem of my sweatshirt and he pulled it over my head, revealing my thin tank top. He cupped my breasts and let out a satisfied growl when he discovered I wasn't wearing a bra.

He kissed his way down my neck and then back up.

I leaned forward to kiss him when he stood up with me gathered in his arms. My legs automatically wound around his waist and I held on tight to his neck.

"Where are we going?" I panted the words.

"To my bed. Did you really think I was going to have sex with you on the couch?"

"We're having sex *now?*" The words came out as a screech.

He topped the stairs and stepped into his bedroom. "Only if you want to."

He set me down on his bed and took a step back, waiting for me to make up my mind.

I kept running through silly thoughts in my head. Like, did I brush my teeth? What about my hair? Oh my God, did I *shave?*

Finally I said, fuck it, and dismissed every last one of them from my mind.

I stood up and grabbed his t-shirt, pulling it over his head. He continued to stand there, not touching me. He tilted his head to the side, waiting.

I knew he wouldn't do anything until I gave him permission.

My palms pressed against his chest and slid down, stopping at the belt that held his jeans on his narrow hips.

"I'm not walking away," I breathed, "this is what I want."

"We're really going to do this?" He asked, his Adam's apple bobbing. "Once we cross this line we can't go back." He stared down at me from his looming height, as if he was hoping he could intimidate me into chickening out.

"Just shut up and kiss me."

Surprisingly, he listened.

He lowered his mouth to mine, sealing our lips together in a soul-stealing kiss.

He backed me up until the backs of my knees bumped into his mattress.

I lowered onto the bed and he followed, his body blanketing mine.

My heart beat in an out of control rhythm as his hands snaked under my tank top and he touched my bare skin.

A shiver raked my body and he smiled against my lips.

"Lift your arms," he commanded.

I did as he asked and he pulled the tank top off, throwing it into the corner of his room.

I resisted the urge to hide my body.

I'd never been shy or self conscious before, but I suddenly felt that way.

He pulled back, his eyes skimming over my body hungrily. I shivered and Goosebumps dotted my skin.

His lips pressed lightly against my neck and he murmured, "You're so beautiful."

I closed my eyes, letting his words sink in. I grasped onto them, believing them because of the depth of his conviction when he spoke them.

My breath came out in a short gasp when his lips trailed between the space between my breasts and down lower. His fingers found the waistband of my sweatpants and he yanked them off forcefully like he couldn't wait to get to what was underneath.

He grinned when he saw my underwear. "Iron Man? Really?"

"Every girl wants Tony Stark a.k.a. Robert Downey Jr. in her pants."

He snorted. "Well, *I'm* the one getting into your pants so…"

"Robert was here first." I snapped the band of my underwear.

He growled and with a sharp pull he removed them as well.

I pouted. "You better not have ripped those. They're my favorite pair."

"I'll buy you new ones," he promised, covering my body with the heat of his as he kissed me all over.

My fingers tangled in his unruly mane of hair when his mouth found my center. "Oh God," I panted in a long moan.

Lights sparkled behind my closed lids as his tongue swirled around and around. It had been far too long since I'd had sex and my body was overly sensitive to every stroke of his tongue and fingers. I felt like a rocket, ready to go off at any second once the right button was pushed.

"Ezra." I panted his name like a prayer.

I felt him smile against me and his fingers crooked inside me.

"Oh God," I moaned as my orgasm hit me. My whole body shook and he held tightly to my thighs so I couldn't get away.

He kissed his way back up my body and took my lips between his own. My heart pounded in my chest like a caged bird fighting to get free.

With shaky hands I framed his face.

"I want you inside me," I begged. I'd been waiting for this moment for what felt like years, and now that it was here I didn't want to wait a second longer.

"Eager, are we?" He chuckled, kissing the sensitive skin behind my ear.

"Very."

He kissed me again, long and deep, imbedding himself on my heart and soul. I would never be the same after this, but I couldn't stop it. I didn't want to. I needed this—I needed *him*—more than I needed my next breath.

Once my lips were tender from his kisses he pulled away from me and stood up.

I swallowed thickly and watched as he walked the two short steps over to his bedside table and grabbed a condom.

The rush of my blood roared through my ears as it raced towards my heart.

He stood in front of me, his eyes capturing mine as he reached down and undid his belt oh-so slowly. Next, his fingers went to the button and then the sound of the zipper going down on his jeans filled the silence between us.

He reached out, grazing his fingers against my bare thigh and I shivered.

Raising a brow he stepped forward and bent down so his lips brushed my ear when he spoke. "This will change everything."

"This changes nothing."

Neither one of us believed my words, but both of us were too needy to back out now.

He crawled back until he towered above me once more.

I held my breath in anticipation of what was to come.

He kicked off his jeans and removed his boxer-briefs, leaving himself bare to my viewing pleasure. I licked my lips and he chuckled.

"Like what you see, sweetheart?"

I sat up and my hands landed on his chest. His skin was heated and his heart beat as fast as mine. At least I wasn't the only one affected and we'd barely even started.

My eyes flicked down taking in the impressive length of his cock.

Gazing back up at him I said, "I like it…a lot…but don't call me sweetheart ever again."

He grinned and stuck the foil condom wrapper between his teeth, ripping it open. "Whatever you say…sweetheart." He winked.

My heart stuttered and then stopped before picking up speed once more.

"Lay down." He commanded in a soft voice.

I wasn't one to take orders, but I listened to him.

Once I was lying down he grabbed my thighs and pulled me to the edge of the bed. He'd already put the condom on, but he didn't push into me. Instead, he stared down at me and several emotions flashed in his dark eyes. I was terrified that he was going to back out and leave me naked and wanton on his bed, but he didn't.

He grabbed the base of his cock and guided it inside me.

My body tensed all over at the delicious pleasure coursing through my body.

With one hard thrust he was all the way inside me. We both gasped and then I swore he said, "It's better than I fucking imagined."

"What did you say?" I wanted to hear him repeat them so that I'd know I wasn't crazy.

"Nothing." His teeth gnashed together and a vein pulsed in his forehead.

His hands tightened around my thighs.

"Uh…Ezra?"

"Yes?" He ground out between his teeth, his head ducked so that his dark curly hair concealed his eyes.

"This is the part where you should be moving your hips. Just saying."

He let out a breathless chuckle and raised his head to look at me. "Sadie, if I move I'll blow my load like a fourteen year old kid. Bear with me for a minute."

"Well, we can't have that." I took a deep breath and let my body relax.

He shuddered and slowly pulled back before sinking back inside me.

My eyes closed and a long moan left my parted lips. My hands landed on his shoulders and when I opened my eyes he was staring at me with a look of awe, his mouth slightly parted.

"Kiss me," I pleaded. Not only was I desperate for the feel of his lips on mine and his stubble rubbing my face, but I needed him to stop looking at me like that, because that look…it showed me more than he was willing to give and I refused to get my hopes up.

He brushed his lips against mine in the lightest, most fleeting of kisses and I groaned out loud. My fingers fisted around his silky hair, holding him to me as I arched my neck to kiss him more fully. A growl vibrated in his chest and his teeth nipped my bottom lip. His hands roamed over my hips, down my sides, before he palmed my breasts. I moaned when he rubbed his thumbs over my nipples.

"Fuck," he growled, his lips sucking against my neck. "This is everything."

My hips lifted to meet his and I saw stars behind my eyes.

I'd never known sex could be like this, and if I had I think maybe I wouldn't have given up my virginity at such a young age. He was right when he said this was everything.

His hands left my breasts and he grabbed my hips, lifting them off the bed. He hit something deeper inside me and I let out a small cry.

He paused, his face tightening with the effort it took to hold back. "Are you okay?" Sweat clung to his skin and the pupils of his eyes were dilated.

"Yes," I panted, "don't stop. Please, for the love of God don't stop."

With a deep exhale he let himself go and we both became lost in the feeling of each other.

He was wild and unrestrained as he fucked me. It was a beautiful sight to see and to know that *I* made him come undone like that.

I felt myself building to another orgasm and I gasped when it hit, my back arching. Ezra watched me with a look of awe and delight. A moment later he reached his own peak. He growled lowly, a curse passing between his lips, and his fingers dug harshly into my thighs. I wouldn't be surprised if it bruised.

He collapsed against me, his head buried in the crook of my neck. Our bodies stuck together from our perspiration and he was careful to brace his weight on his arms so he didn't crush me.

After a long moment he sat up slightly and kissed me deeply.

He took my chin between his fingers and forced me to look at him. My chest rose and fell harshly with each gasping breath I took.

His tongue flicked out over his lips and he breathed, "I think this is the best idea you've ever had."

I smiled and said, "Yeah."

Even though I already knew this was the *worst* idea I'd ever had, because I was dangerously close to falling in love with my best friend and I'd only end up with my heart broken.

# CHAPTER TWELVE

I SAT ON the dock, dangling my bare feet out over the water. The sun warmed my exposed skin and I reached up to adjust my sunglasses.

"You're unusually quiet today." Emma commented from beside me.

I guessed I was. I kept replaying what had happened yesterday with Ezra, then again in the shower, and then yet again this morning. We were both insatiable.

I shrugged. "I have a lot on my mind."

"Want to share?" She asked, adding another layer of sunscreen to her nose, momentarily hiding her freckles beneath the white lotion like substance.

"Not really."

"Everything's okay, though, right?" Her voice was full of concern.

"Yeah, of course." I forced a smile.

"You know…" She started and then trailed off like she wasn't sure she should continue.

"Come on, spit it out." I bumped her shoulder with mine.

She winced—not in pain, but at whatever she had to say. "It's just that…I thought after you broke up with Braden you'd return to the normal, bubbly Sadie you used to be, but you're still…"

"I'm still what?" I didn't snap at her, even though a part of me wanted to.

"Withdrawn." She settled on.

I guessed that was an accurate description of what I'd gradually become over the last two years.

"I'm working on it," I mumbled, adjusting the straps of my bikini top.

"Is there anything I can do?" She asked, her toes skimming the surface of the lake.

"Nah," I shrugged, "I have to find my way back to myself on my own."

"Hey, Em!"

We both turned to look behind us, and saw Maddox barreling straight for us.

"What is he doing?" She mumbled.

He wasn't slowing down and reached us in a matter of seconds. Somehow, without stopping, he grabbed Emma around her torso and jumped into the water with her in his arms. Water splashed everywhere, and I ended up drenched.

They surfaced a few feet in front of me and Emma smacked her fists against his muscular chest. "You asshole! That was mean!"

"Aw," he reached for her, pulling her body against his and she immediately melted into his embrace, "you know I love you."

"I think you just like dragging me into bodies of water," she mumbled, but she was smiling. She kissed him quickly and swam away.

"What are they up to?"

I jumped at the sound of Ezra's voice. I tilted my head back and—oh Lord. I swallowed thickly at the sight of him in a pair of white low hanging swim trunks and a blue baseball cap sitting backwards on his head. Pieces of his black curls curled around the edges of the baseball cap, refusing to be tamed.

"Oh, you know, the usual, being the sickeningly cute couple that they are." I hoped he didn't notice the pitch in my voice but based on the quirk of his lips he definitely saw how I was eyeing him. I felt like I was dehydrated and stranded in the middle of the desert, while Ezra was the cool glass of water just out of my reach.

While we might be having sex now, our friends didn't know that and they had to remain blind to our deal. They wouldn't understand.

Unfortunately, that meant around them we had to keep our hands to ourselves.

When Ezra said Maddox and Emma were coming over I hadn't expected that to be a problem, but even though they hadn't even been here an hour I was ready for them to leave so I could have him all to myself.

"Oh, here." Ezra mumbled and handed me a bottle of beer. I hadn't even noticed he was holding two, one for me and one for himself, since I was too busy checking him out. "You only get one, though." He joked.

"Ha, ha, ha." I rolled my eyes. "I'm an awesome drunk and you know it."

He sat down beside me and brought the beer to his lips. "You're definitely entertaining, that's for sure."

"Darling!" Maddox called in a joking voice to Ezra. "Are you going to sit there all day or join us?"

"I'm fine right here." Ezra chuckled. "*Darling.*"

"You guys are so weird." I snorted, shaking my head.

Ezra shrugged. "We're practically like brothers, after a while you find you don't care what the fuck you say to each other. Besides, if you can't joke around life gets pretty boring."

"That's true."

I set my beer aside, not bothering to take a drink. The last thing I needed was a buzz right now.

"Come on! Get in! It's hot!" Emma called, floating on her back. Maddox splashed her and she retaliated with an even bigger splash.

"They're not going to leave us alone until we get in," I told Ezra.

He sighed. "You're right."

He emptied his beer and stood up, tossing his baseball cap onto the dock. He reached a hand down to me and I took it, letting him haul me up. I stumbled into his chest and he steadied me before we both toppled over.

He chuckled lowly and smoothed my hair away from my face. "Are you okay?"

I swallowed thickly. "Mhmm, yeah. Great." I definitely was not affected at all. Nope. Not even a little bit.

"We have an audience," he whispered in my ear.

I jerked away from him like I'd been electrocuted.

When I looked out at the lake Maddox wasn't paying attention to us, but Emma was. Her eyes were narrowed and I could tell she'd be asking me about this later. Fantastic.

Ezra reached for my hand again and we stepped up to the edge of the dock. I wanted to pull away since I knew Emma was watching, but I didn't.

"Ready?"

"Yeah."

Together we jumped into the water. The temperature of it was cool, but it felt like heaven against my heated skin.

We came up and Maddox hollered. "Perfect score!"

"That wasn't even a dive!" Ezra yelled back as he swam towards his friend.

Emma was already headed my way and I wished I could sink beneath the surface of the water and disappear.

When she reached me she pushed the wet strands of her blonde hair away from her eyes. "Are you still going to tell me nothing is going on with you guys?" She arched a brow.

"I think you need your eyesight checked," I quipped, "because you're seeing things."

"I'm not blind or stupid." She glared at me, the skin beneath her freckles turning red—and not from a sunburn. "You used to tell me everything, even things I didn't want to know, and now you tell me *nothing*. I feel like I don't know you anymore." She frowned, her shoulders sagging even as she moved her arms to stay afloat.

The truth was, Emma and I had been growing apart for a while. That was why Ezra and I had grown so close the last few years. Our best friends ditched us for each other, so we ended up becoming friends. While Ezra had maintained his close relationship with Maddox I hadn't done the same with Emma. It wasn't all her fault though. She'd been wrapped up in Maddox and I'd been wrapped up in Braden.

"We used to do everything together," she continued. "I miss our sleepovers and pigging out on way too much pizza while watching those stupid shows you seem to love."

I laughed and began to smile. "Yeah, that was always fun."

"Maybe we should do that again?" She suggested, her voice meek sounding.

"We're grown ups now, Emma."

"So?" She countered. "Maybe the mistake in growing up is thinking that everything you used to do was childish."

"You really want to have a sleepover?"

She nodded eagerly. I hated to let her down, because lately I'd been letting everyone down, including myself.

"Let's do it then. You provide the pizza, I'll pick the *stupid shows*." I mimed her tone with a laugh.

"Deal." She smiled back.

"We'll have to do it at your place, though," I told her, "I wouldn't feel right taking over Ezra's place with girly stuff."

"Sounds good. Tonight?"

"Sure," I said, even though I cringed

I sent up a silent prayer that at this sleepover she'd let the topic of Ezra go, but I knew that wasn't likely. Emma was too perceptive. Besides, she'd already brought it up too many times for me to believe she'd suddenly stop asking me about it.

She swam away from me, over to Maddox, no doubt to tell him about our plan for a sleepover.

Ezra swam over to me, his dark hair plastered to his forehead. "Is everything okay?" He asked. "It looked like you were having an intense conversation."

"Everything is fine," I assured him, "but we're going to have a sleepover tonight. Emma wants us to…reconnect," I said, for lack of a better word.

"Reconnect, huh?" He arched a brow.

I shrugged. "We haven't hung out much in a long time."

"Ezra!" Maddox called, drawing his attention away from me and over to his friend. "The girls are having a sleepover tonight, which means we are too! Are you ready for me, buddy?" Maddox raised his fists in the air. "I'm going to whoop your ass on Call of Duty."

"You wish." Ezra rolled his eyes.

They began bickering back and forth about different video games and Emma swam back to me.

"We've lost them to nerd land," she declared, but she smiled when she said it. She glanced over at Maddox and love shone in her eyes.

I wondered if I'd ever looked at Braden like that—like he was my whole world. I doubted it.

I swam away from Emma and onto the shore. I grabbed my towel and shook it out before lying down on top. Emma joined me, doing the same with her towel. The guys continued to goof around in the lake. No surprise there.

It grew quiet between us when Emma picked up a book to read, but a little while later she voiced, "Are you happy?"

I glanced over at her, puzzled by the random question.

"I'm just wondering," she defended, "after everything that's happened the last month if you're happy now."

I looked away from her and out at the shimmering water of the lake. "No," I answered honestly. "I mean, I'm not miserable, but I'm not exactly happy either." How could I be when I felt like a shell of the person I used to be?

Emma rolled over onto her stomach and propped her body up on her elbows. "What can I do to help?"

I gave her a small smile. "No one can help me with this. This is all on me. Don't worry," I assured her, "I'll find my way back to my happy place one day."

"Good." She reached over and gave my arm a playful squeeze. "I miss the peppy Sadie."

I laughed. "Admit it, you totally want to choke me when I get hyper."

She grinned. "Okay, so I have had some fantasies of knocking you out when you get a little crazy, but I miss that you're not like that anymore. Maybe the sleepover will be step one into resurrecting you," she winked.

"Yeah, maybe so," I agreed.

I really hoped so.

"I can't believe you're abandoning me so soon after our…arrangement."

I turned around sharply at the sound of Ezra's voice.

"That's it, you need to wear your boots all the time so that I can hear you, because otherwise you sneak up on me all stealth-like. Stop trying to be a ninja, Ezra." I scolded him, taking a deep breath to calm myself.

He chuckled, leaning against the doorway. His hair was still damp from his shower and the woodsy scent of his soap filled the air. He'd changed into a white wifebeater and a pair of basketball shorts. I hated how he made such a simple ensemble look so amazing. It was completely unfair.

He strode into the room and sat on the edge of my bed. Or—er—I guess technically it was his bed, since this was his house, and—why the hell was I obsessing over this? The answer was simple, because I was trying to ignore the searing force of his dark gaze.

"Going away for a while?" He arched a brow.

"I'm a *girl*," I defended, zipping my overnight bag closed, "we need a lot of stuff."

Sobering, he bowed his head and his shoulders tightened with tension. When he looked up at me there was worry in his eyes. "You're not leaving tonight because of me, right? Because of what we did?"

I expelled the breath I'd been holding. "No, definitely not," I shook my head. "I…I don't regret what we did." My hands shook at the memories.

He cleared his throat. "Good."

He looked so awkward sitting there that I had to feel sorry for him.

"I promise I'm not running away. And," I grew bold and sat down in his lap, his hands landed on my hips and the tips of his fingers dug into me, "I'm really looking forward to doing it again."

Before he could reply I kissed him.

His body instantly relaxed at the feel of my lips and a low growl rumbled in his throat. His hands fisted the fabric of my t-shirt, like he was tempted to tear it off of me but knew he shouldn't.

The kiss quickly grew heated and desire blossomed low in my belly.

I felt him harden beneath me and within seconds he'd maneuvered us so that I was lying flat on the bed with him above me.

I wrapped my legs around his waist, our lips never breaking.

He began to ease my shirt up while I reached for the band of his shorts and that was when the doorbell rang.

Ezra tore his lips away from mine and rested his head in the crook of my neck while he tried to regain his breath. "Fucking hell. I'm going to kill Maddox. He has the worst timing ever."

Maddox and Emma had left a little over an hour ago so that they could shower and Maddox could grab a change of clothes since he was staying the night here. Emma was supposed to ride back with him and pick me up.

"Hello!" We heard called downstairs. "Honey, I'm hoooome!"

Ezra cursed and pulled away from me, muttering under his breath. "And why the fuck did I *ever* think giving him a key to my house was a good idea?"

I laughed, biting my lip. "Uh, Ezra…you might want to hide that?" I pointed to his hard-on tenting his shorts.

He cursed again and headed for the bathroom.

"Are you seriously going to jerk-off?" I hissed under my breath.

He started to close the bathroom door, but poked his head out so he could see me sitting on my bed. "I don't have much of a choice, do I?" He slammed the door closed and I dissolved into a fit of laughter.

"Is everything okay?" Maddox called and I heard him start up the steps.

"Yeah," I yelled back, grabbing my bag. I met Maddox at the bottom of the stairs and he took my bag from me.

"What the hell do you have in here?" He groaned against the weight.

"It's not that heavy." I smacked his side, heading for the door.

He mumbled, "Yeah, it is."

I shook my head and stepped outside. I was surprised to see Emma had brought her car, but I guessed that made sense because she hated driving Maddox's since it was a stick shift. She didn't like the SUV very much either, but that was only because she thought spending a lot of money on a vehicle was ridiculous. It was a nice car though, a pretty white Porsche Cayenne. I'd been happy when Maddox got it for her. The old Volkswagen beetle she'd been driving had definitely seen better days.

Maddox put my bag in the backseat and leaned in through the open driver's window to kiss Emma goodbye.

"I love you," he told her, grinning widely.

"I love you too." She kissed him quickly one last time as I climbed into the car.

Maddox jogged up the porch steps and disappeared inside.

"Ready for girl time?" Emma asked.

"Definitely."

"I like that color." Emma pointed to my pale blue toenails as we left the nail salon.

"Me too," I agreed.

When we left Ezra's house we ended up stopping off to get a manicure and pedicure. I'd been shocked when Emma pulled into the parking lot, because I knew this wasn't really her thing. I had to give her credit; she really was trying to cheer me up.

We walked over to the nearby pizza place to grab our order that Emma had called in a few minutes ago.

Once we had that we got back in her car and she drove us to her house. Well, it wasn't really a house since she and Maddox still lived in the guesthouse behind his parent's house. It was funny, since they could afford to live elsewhere, but they loved the guesthouse. I knew they were planning to move soon though since they were getting married in a few months.

"Have you guys found a house you like, yet?" I questioned, getting out of the car and grabbing the pizza boxes.

Emma wrinkled her nose as she fiddled with her keys, looking for the right one.

"No," she sighed, opening the door and waving me inside. "Maddox wants to buy a piece of land and build a house, but that seems like a major headache to me. I'd rather get something older and remodel. Who knows what we'll do," she shrugged, tossing her keys on the kitchen counter.

The guesthouse was actually pretty large. It was two-stories, with two bedrooms upstairs along with a bathroom. Downstairs was the kitchen and living room. The living room used to be where the guys had band practice, but they'd long ago moved most of their instruments into the recording studio they'd installed in their parent's home. The piano still remained though.

I took a seat on the couch and Emma turned the TV on before handing me the remote. The TV was huge—which I knew was Maddox's doing. Emma rarely watched TV. She preferred her books and music.

I put the TV on one of the entertainment channels and set the boxes of pizza on the coffee table.

Emma lifted the lids and grabbed a slice. "I love pizza," she moaned, taking a bite. "Pizza is life."

I laughed, grabbing a piece for myself. "Do you love pizza more than Maddox?"

She pretended to ponder my words. "It's a tie." She tucked her legs underneath her and turned towards me. "This is nice. I can't remember the last time we did something like this."

"I think we were still in high school," I mumbled around a bite of pizza. After we graduated Emma jetted off to L.A. with Maddox, and started writing songs for the band. I stayed behind and went to college. It'd been weird being without her at first, since we'd been friends since we were kids. Luckily, Ezra spent most of his time in Virginia so I'd still had him.

"Yeah," Emma nodded her head in agreement, "it probably was."

"Have you found a wedding dress?" I asked her. She was still struggling to discuss her wedding plans with me, but I really didn't care. My relationship with Braden might've fallen apart, but I wasn't angry with everyone else for being happy.

She bit her lip and set her pizza crust in the box. "I've been meaning to talk to you about that…I know it's short notice, but I was kind of hoping that maybe you'd make my dress." She held her breath while she waited for my answer.

Tears stung my eyes. "You want *me* to design your wedding dress?"

Let's face it, Maddox was loaded and Emma made plenty of money on her own writing songs, so she could definitely afford to have one of the top celebrity designers to make her dress, but she wanted me.

"Of course," she gasped. "Your designs are amazing! And I know you focus mostly on styling, but you're an amazing designer as well, Sadie."

I tackle hugged her and she laughed, wrapping her thin arms around me.

"I take it this means you'll do it?"

We sat back up and I brushed my tears away. "Absolutely. Let's brain storm tonight."

She smiled widely. "Thank you."

"No, thank you," I told her. "So, have you picked a venue yet?"

She nodded. "Yeah, we're going to get married here. We want to keep the wedding small, just our family and friends, so there's enough space for that."

"That'll be nice."

"I want to keep things simple," she grabbed another piece of pizza, "you know me. I'm low maintenance."

"It'll be beautiful." I knew whatever she had planned would be.

"I can't believe I'm getting married." Her face flushed with a pink hue. "I was never like you," she continued, "I didn't dream of falling in love and getting married, and yet here I am."

"Things change," I commented.

"They do," she agreed.

I ate another slice of pizza and drew my knees up to my chest. "What kind of dress do you think you want?" I asked, already brainstorming in my head.

"Simple," she said, and then laughed. "Can you tell that's my thing?" Sighing, she tapped a finger against her lips. "I want it to be lightweight. It's still going to be blazing hot in September, so I don't want it to be heavy. Maybe something with a thin strap," she suggested, "my boobs are too big to go strapless, I'd be afraid they might pop out."

I laughed at her, making a mental note of the things she'd said. "I'll get to work on some designs. We don't have much time."

She clapped her hands together, vibrating with giddiness. When we were younger Emma was always quiet and guarded, once she met Maddox she really came out of her shell. It was nice to see her so vibrant and living life, instead of hiding behind the pages of a book.

"You know," she sobered, draping her arm along the back of the couch, "for a while I was scared to get married. I know Maddox has wanted us to get married for a while, but I thought it might change things—put more pressure on our relationship," she shrugged. With a wistful smile she added, "But it hasn't. In fact, I think I've fallen more in love with him through this whole process and I can't wait to have him be my husband."

I smiled, reaching for her hand and giving it a squeeze. "I'm glad. You deserve all the happiness in the world." And that was the truth. Emma had been through a lot at a young age and having a drunken asshole for a father had made her untrusting of guys. But Maddox had barreled into her life, breaking down all the walls she'd built around herself.

She tilted her head, a small smile gracing her lips. "So do you."

I sighed. I should've known she'd find a way to circle back to my happiness, or lack thereof, eventually.

"I'll find my happiness again," I muttered, picking at a loose thread on the couch. "Things are just…rough right now."

The breakup with Braden had taken a lot out of me. Even though I knew in my heart I'd never really loved him, I'd still spent two years with the guy, and there'd been fondness there. Throw on top of that the stress of running my store, and then skirting around my feelings for Ezra, and I was exhausted. Maybe things would get better in the Ezra department now that we had our agreement, but it was doubtful. I just hoped it didn't make things worse.

"You know what you need?" She grinned, leaning towards me. "A vacation!"

I snorted. "I don't have time for a vacation. I can't leave the store."

She shook her head rapidly. "You had a two-week honeymoon planned, Sadie. I think you can take a week off and go on a vacation."

"By myself?" I hissed.

"No," she shook her head, "we'll all go. The guys, Remy, me and you."

"I don't know about this…" I trailed off. A vacation sounded nice, but…

"Please, oh please." She held her hands beneath her chin and pouted her bottom lip. "We can get a beach house somewhere. I'll plan the whole thing…okay, that's a lie, I can't plan very well so I'll get Maddox to do it, but you won't be bothered with any of it. I promise."

"Do you think the others will agree?"

She pointed to her face and pouted again. "No one can say no to this face."

I smiled, feeling myself grow a little excited. "Let's do it!"

"Yay!" She stood up and started dancing around. Pulling her phone out of the pocket of her shorts she pressed a button and music flooded the small space.

Laughing, I stood up too and joined her crazy dancing.

Our laughter filled the air as we tripped over our own feet.

I'd been reluctant to agree to this sleepover, but it was proving to be exactly what I had needed.

# CHAPTER THIRTEEN

HIS LIPS MOLDED to my neck and my fingers tangled in his silky soft hair.

It was safe to say I had an obsession with Ezra's hair.

Actually, I had an obsession with the man himself. It was completely unfair how amazing he was. Inside and out.

His fingers skimmed down the sides of my bare torso and my body arched at the sensation.

His touch electrified me.

His hips rocked against mine and my nails raked his back.

I was so close.

He sat up suddenly, pulling me with him so that we never separated. I let out a long moan at the new sensation. I rolled my hips and he cursed.

He grasped the nape of my neck and pulled my lips to his, kissing me deeply. Our lips parted and I panted from the lack of oxygen.

I closed my eyes, tightening my hold on his shoulders. "I'm coming," I warned.

"Fuck, I'm close too," he breathed, his lips skimming mine when he spoke.

Our chests pressed together, adding even more friction.

I moved faster and his own thrusts sped up.

I tipped over the edge, and my cry filled the room. With a groan he came too and we fell back onto the bed in a tangle of limbs.

My chest rose sharply as I struggled to get enough air.

I didn't think it was possible, but it got better every single time.

I didn't know how I was ever going to give this up, but I knew eventually our arrangement would have to come to an end.

He wrapped an arm around my waist and pulled me against his body, tenderly kissing the crook of my neck.

My eyes closed as a happy sigh escaped me. The gesture had been so sweet, something a real boyfriend would do, but I had to remind myself that we weren't really a couple.

All too soon he pulled away and rolled out of bed. He put on his boxers and stuck his hands on his narrow hips.

"We better get ready."

I glanced at the clock on his nightstand. He was right. It was a little past noon, but the guys were playing at a local festival later this afternoon. Even though the guys were a big deal now they still made an effort to perform local gigs. I thought it was nice that they still appreciated their roots.

I sat up and began gathering my clothes strewn about his room. With them clutched in my arms I mumbled that I was going to take a shower.

He nodded, already distracted by something on his phone.

After my shower I dried and curled my hair. Instead of putting on a pair of shorts I opted to wear a dress. It was new and I hadn't had a chance to wear it yet. I wasn't dressing up for Ezra, though. Nope, definitely not.

I slipped the dress on and admired my reflection in the mirror above the dresser in my bedroom.

It was white and hugged my body. It had an open design in the middle that exposed parts of my stomach and the design continued at the bottom of the dress. The back was low cut, and my tattoo was on full display. It was a dream catcher that started between my shoulder blades with the feathers extending down my back. I got it a while ago, straight out of high school. Ezra had been with me when I got it, since I didn't want to go alone. I'd gotten it, because at the time my dreams had seemed so far out of reach and I wanted something to remind me that I could go after them and, well *catch* them.

Satisfied with the dress I put on a pair of strappy gold flats and added a flowered headband to my hair.

"You look beautiful," Ezra commented, appearing in the doorway.

"Thanks," I smiled at him.

He was dressed simply in a pair of khaki shorts and a white t-shirt.

"I thought we'd head on over now," he looked at the large watch on his wrist, "and have some time to do a few things before the show."

My brows rose. That sounded suspiciously date-like to me, but I wasn't going to say anything.

"Sounds good." I swiped some more gloss onto my lips before following him outside.

"Security is meeting us at the festival. Just to be safe," he told me, slipping inside the Escalade.

I didn't like going places where their security tagged along, but it was better than being swarmed. Most fans were pretty chill, but there were still the crazy ones. Someone gave Mathias a lock of hair one time. The look of disgust on his face would've been comical if it hadn't been downright gross. She literally ripped it out of her head and thrust it at him. She'd also said something about them being destined to be together and that she'd already picked out the names of their children. She then proceeded to rub her stomach and told him that little Leopold would be arriving in the fall. Mathias hauled ass out of the meet and greet room after that.

They were actually doing a meet and greet today after they performed. Hopefully no more scenarios like that one played out.

Ezra and I were quiet the whole drive over. He parked in a section off to the side where the people working at the event parked their cars. I immediately spotted two hulking security guards. Each of the guys had two of their own security personnel. Ezra's were named Jon and Kenny. They were massive—all of their bodyguards were—and built like linebackers.

Ezra hopped out of the car and the bodyguard's met us at the parking lot exit. They flanked us on each side as we headed into the festival.

It was already packed, and as we walked the whispers and stares started up. Soon it would be all over the festival that Ezra was here walking around.

The guards kept people from approaching, but it didn't stop them from taking pictures as we passed.

"I thought we could go see the circus." Ezra glanced down at me to see if I was in agreement. He was completely oblivious to the crowd growing around us. He was so used to it at this point that he didn't even bat an eye. "It's supposed to be one of those aerial acts. Not clowns," he winked.

"You're never going to let me live that down, are you?" One time I confessed that I was terrified of clowns and Ezra thought it was the funniest fear ever. But those things were scary. Yes, things, because I did not believe clowns were people. They were far too horrifying to be human.

"Definitely not." He smiled at me boyishly, a slight skip in his step.

He seemed to know where he was going so I followed him, while the bodyguards kept the crowd at bay.

He approached a red and white striped tent and ushered me inside. One of the guards stayed by the entrance while the other followed us.

The place was packed with people waiting for the start of the show.

Ezra continued forward and I grabbed his elbow, hissing, "I think they're sold out."

"Just trust me."

He turned to the first row and sure enough there were three empty seats. "After you." He waved his hand dramatically.

I shook my head and took the end seat. "You had this planned," I accused.

He smiled and sat down beside me with his bodyguard on his other side. "Maybe," he whispered in my ear.

A girl, no more than thirteen, sat beside the guard. She leaned forward, peering around his massive body and let out a small shriek of excitement before skirting back and hiding her red face behind her hands.

Ezra chuckled and leaned forward. "Hi, I'm Ezra." He held out a hand to the girl who was still hiding behind her hands. Her friends sat beside her, both of their mouths hanging open in shock.

The one beside the girl bumped her with her elbow and said, "He's talking to you!"

The girl lowered her hands. "I'm Sarah." When she noticed that he was holding out his hand she stuck hers in it.

He gave it a quick shake before letting go.

Sarah looked like she'd just won the lottery. "You're my favorite," she exclaimed suddenly, finally finding her voice. "I know most people overlook the bass player, but yeah, I love you."

Ezra chuckled, flashing a smile. "I'm happy to not be overlooked."

"We're going to the concert later." The girl that elbowed Sarah piped in.

Ezra grinned, pushing strands of his dark hair away from his eyes. "Cool. Hey, Jon make sure these ladies get passes into the meet and greet." He pointed to Sarah and her two friends.

The one that had been quiet up until now let out a shriek that had everybody in the nearby vicinity covering their ears. "You mean I get to meet Maddox?!" She gasped, fanning her suddenly flushed face. "Oh my God, I love him so much. He's beautiful and when he plays the drums…" Her whole body shook with excitement. "He's amazing."

It was then that I noticed her shirt.

SAVE A DRUM. BANG A DRUMMER.

Oh shit. We were in for it.

I gave Ezra a look and he merely chuckled.

Maddox had no idea what was headed his way.

The lights began to dim and then everything began to glow with a purple and blue hue. Ezra sat back and the girls grew quiet, only the occasional whisper and giggle, as the show began.

Music began to play, something slow and haunting.

Dancers came out with some sort of white glow stick clasped in their hands. As they danced the lights began to blur, creating an otherworldly effect.

The music began to quicken and then stopped all together.

The tent went black.

I blinked my eyes, trying to see anything.

My heart picked up speed at the total darkness, and I was tempted to reach for

Ezra's hand, but we were in public and I was afraid someone might snap a photo of us on their phone and the rumors it would cause weren't worth it.

Before my panic could escalate the lights came back on, pointed at the peak of the tent.

I gasped in awe when I saw that heavy looking lengths of fabric now dangled from the top. A female had the fabric wrapped around her arm and spun through the air. On the other fabric piece a man spun in the opposite direction.

Their faces were tortured and full of longing as they reached out for each other, always failing to reach the other one.

The music sped up again, as did their movements. They began to blur and then she let go of the fabric. He caught her easily and their bodies tangled together as he held them up with only one hand.

The lights changed to a pink hue and their expressions became filled with lust.

They were absolutely incredible.

I'd never seen anything else like it.

"This is amazing," I breathed.

When I glanced over at Ezra he was looking at me and not the show.

"You're missing it," I hissed, pointing in the direction of the aerialists.

He shook his head, his dark brows drawn together. "I'm not missing anything."

My heart stuttered and skipped a beat and I looked away from him hastily.

But still, his eyes lingered upon my face.

When the show ended we headed back out into the festival once more. The crowds had doubled in size and I worried the two guards might not be enough.

I stuck close to Ezra's side, trying to ignore the stares.

I should've been used to them by now since I was friend's with him, but I was convinced the prying eyes and nosy looks from strangers was something you just didn't get accustomed to.

"Let's go get some cotton candy." He slung an arm over my shoulder, steering me over to a cart.

The guy working it quickly handed over a cone of cotton candy. He didn't appear starstruck by Ezra, but I could tell the growing crowd was freaking the guy out. They were turning into vultures.

Ezra handed me the cotton candy and turned us away from the cart.

I dug my heels into the ground. "Aren't you getting one?"

He shook his head and grinned. "Nope. I thought we could share." He then leaned over and took a bite of the cotton candy, shoving the strands that stuck to his lips into his mouth.

He was definitely trying to kill me.

Or my ovaries.

What he did shouldn't have been so hot, but it was, and based on the swooning going on around us I wasn't the only one affected.

I continued to watch as he reached out and pried away a small handful of the blue fluffy sugar goodness. He then proceeded to stuff it in my mouth.

"What the hell, Ezra?" I chewed and swallowed.

He grinned, rocking back on his heels. "You were drooling. I was trying to clean up."

"I was not drooling," I defended, squaring my shoulders. "I was merely… appreciating the view."

"Mhmm," he smiled, biting his lip. He glanced away and pointed, "Let's go over there."

"To the games?" I questioned. "You know those things are rigged, right? They only want your money."

"I think I can afford to lose a few bucks." He winked.

"True," I agreed.

He stopped in front of a booth, one where you had to throw baseballs at different targets.

"What do I get if I win?" Ezra asked the guy manning the booth.

"A goldfish," the guy replied, pointing to where several goldfish swam in mason jars.

"Sweet," Ezra rubbed his hands together, "Sadie, why don't you think of a name for our future pet."

I raised a brow, taking another bite of cotton candy. "*Our* pet? Do you really think I could manage to keep that thing alive for more than a day?" I pointed at one of the happily swimming fish. "I can't even remember to feed myself."

He laughed, ducking his head. "Fine, I'll take care of it."

He laid some money on the counter and the guy handed over several baseballs. "You get three tries on each target and you have to knock down all three targets to win."

"Easy enough." He smiled, rolling his shoulders.

He blew out a breath and I laughed. "You're really taking this seriously, aren't you?"

"I always take my balls seriously."

I rolled my eyes and poked him in the ribs.

"Hey, you gave me the perfect opening. I had to take it."

I shook my head, smiling even though he was ridiculous. I'd missed our banter though. It felt like it had been missing the last month, but with everything that had been going on and the months we went without speaking to each other it was reasonable for us to be a little wary around one another.

But now we were back to the old Sadie and Ezra.

Only we were sleeping together.

But that wouldn't change our relationship.

Nope.

Definitely not.

I forced myself to pay attention to the silly game. He'd already knocked down one of the targets and had moved on to the second. That one fell too and he stepped over to line up with the third target. He missed, and then missed again. When he raised the final ball I couldn't stop myself from lightly kicking the back of his knee. It wasn't hard enough to hurt him, but it messed up his aim.

"Sadie," he groaned, but then began to laugh. "You really don't want me to bring that goldfish home, do you?"

I shrugged innocently. "I just thought you should work harder for Toby. You know, show him that you really want him."

"Toby?" He raised a brow.

I feigned a gasp. "You said I could pick a name."

"And you said you didn't want a pet."

"Well, I mean, I do already have a puppy." I reached up, ruffling his hair.

He laughed and ducked away.

Around us strangers took photos and videos on their phones. I did my best to ignore them.

"You want the fish or not?" He asked, already pulling his wallet out of his back pocket.

I shrugged again, fighting a smile. "Only if you think your balls have what it takes."

"You're baiting me and it's working." He chuckled, smacking a twenty-dollar bill on the booth counter.

"That's what I'm here for."

The guy handed him his change and some more baseballs.

"You've got this, Ez." I gave him a thumb's up while making a silly face.

He batted me away and mumbled, "You're distracting me."

"Come on, you've gotta show Toby that you're serious about this life-changing adoption. Work for it."

"Shhhh," he covered my mouth with his hand, "I can't concentrate with you babbling."

I licked his hand.

He lowered his head and muttered, "I should've known you'd do that."

"I'll be on my best behavior now." I raised my hands and took a step back. I bumped into the solid steel wall of Kenny and stumbled. The large ogre of a man grabbed my elbow and immediately steadied me. Thank God for that, the last thing I wanted to do was fall and show the world my Britney. Granted, I was wearing underwear, but accidents happen.

Ezra successfully knocked down all the targets this time since I didn't distract him. He gladly accepted his new pet goldfish with a boyish grin. As we left the booth a crowd of people rushed it, all of them now wanting to win one of Toby's brothers or sisters.

It was getting close to the start time for their set so we didn't have time to do anything else.

Jon and Kenny ushered us both into the talent tent.

"Dude," we heard almost immediately, "why the hell are you carrying a goldfish?" Hayes strode forward, holding a bag of chips.

"I won him," Ezra said, setting the jar down on a table.

Hayes merely shook his head. "How are you?" He asked, nodding at me.

"Uh, good." I smiled awkwardly. Hayes was a nice guy and I felt bad about how things had gone on our date, but the way he acted he didn't seem to have any hard feelings.

"Has Ezzie-poo taken you on a date yet?" He grinned, looking between the two of us with a knowing smile.

"No," I said adamantly.

Ezra changed the subject by asking where his bass was. Hayes told him and he hurried off, leaving me alone with his band mate.

"So," Hayes started, chewing on a mouthful of chips, "you two haven't banged each other's brains out yet?"

I rolled my eyes and took a seat on one of the plastic chairs dotting the tent.

"Why does everyone think there's something going on with us?"

"Um…" Hayes looked at me like I was crazy. "Number one, we're not blind. Two, the sexual chemistry stemming off the two of you is about to smother all of us. Just do it already so things can go back to normal." He leaned his hip against a table covered in food, waiting for my reply.

I simply laughed. "You're crazy."

"Maybe," he agreed, and tipped a finger in my direction, "but I'm not stupid."

"Touché."

Behind me the tent opened again and Mathias walked in. Immediately Hayes groaned, waving his hand dramatically at the lead singer.

*"Duuuude,"* he drew out the word, "you cannot wear a fucking nerdigan on stage. Plus, it's like ninety degrees. Aren't you dying?"

"What did you call my cardigan?" Mathias stopped in his tracks, glaring at Hayes.

"A nerdigan. It's the proper name for it. Seriously, take it off. You look ridiculous."

Mathias smirked. "If you wanted me naked all you had to do was ask." His hands went to the belt on his jeans.

Hayes sputtered. "No dude, just the fucking nerdigan."

Mathias shook his head and took it off. Hayes smiled in glee. "I'm only taking this off because it's fucking hot out there and I don't want to pass out on stage. So stop gloating."

"I'm not gloating." Hayes defended.

"You're smiling," Mathias' glare was icy, "it's the same thing."

"Where's Remy?" I asked.

Mathias turned his attention to me. His lips turned down into a deeper frown. "She doesn't like dealing with the crowds now that she's pregnant. It makes her nervous."

"Her or you?" I countered.

His lips twitched. "Mostly me."

"That's what I thought." I smiled. Mathias was crazily overprotective of Remy, but even pregnant the chick was a definite bad ass.

At that moment a woman working for the festival entered the tent, wheeling a cart with audio equipment to wire the guys.

Maddox and Emma entered right behind her.

"I need you guys back here." The woman pointed to the back of the tent.

"See you soon." Maddox leaned down and kissed Emma quickly.

He waved at me and then playfully shoved his twin before the three disappeared behind a curtain.

"Have you been here a while?" Emma asked, plopping down in one of the other plastic chairs. She wore a black crop top and pale yellow skirt that came up higher in the front and was long in the back and sides. Her favorite floppy black hat sat on her head with her wild blonde hair curling beneath it. I was slightly envious of her effortless, almost hippy, style. I knew Emma spent hardly any time picking out her clothes, and yet she still managed to look gorgeous. Although, she'd argue the fact that she looked like she'd just rolled out of bed.

"Uh, yeah. I guess." I replied. "Why?"

"You look a little sun burnt."

I turned my head to look at my shoulders and discovered that they were slightly red in color. "I forgot to wear sunscreen."

"Yours?" She nodded at the fish swimming lazily in the jar.

"Ezra's. He won it in one of those stupid games." I waved my hand to encompass the festival.

"Have you been having fun?" She asked, straightening her skirt and crossing her legs.

"Yeah," I nodded. "We saw the aerial circus act and it was amazing."

"Oh!" Emma clapped her hands together and leaned forward. "So, Maddox found a great place for us to stay in the Florida Keys. Do you think you can be ready to leave in a week?"

I nodded. "I can make it happen."

"Perfect!" She did a little dance. "This is going to be so much fun!"

I smiled in agreement. I hadn't been on board with this in the beginning, but the more I thought about it the more excited I became. I knew being around everyone for a week would make it hard for Ezra and I to get any alone time, and that sucked, but I needed this.

Maddox returned, smacking his drumsticks against his legs and jumping up and down. "Are you guys ready to rock? Because I'm ready to rock."

I glanced at Emma. "Did he drink too many Diet Pepsi's again?"

She smiled and shrugged sheepishly. "Maybe."

"Dude, chillax." Hayes appeared next, his bright blue guitar slung across his body. "You're like a fucking monkey on crack. What's with the jumping?"

"We haven't performed in a while and I'm really excited," Maddox replied gleefully, still drumming his drumsticks against his leg.

Hayes' face crinkled in thought. "We just finished a six month tour a month ago."

"I know but it feels like forever." Maddox went back to jumping.

"He's going to give me a headache," Hayes pinched the bridge of his nose, "I never thought I'd say this, but someone get that guy his knitting bag."

"It's in the car," Emma said, digging through her clutch for car keys.

"Hey, you." Hayes grabbed one of the festival workers that was milling around the tent. "Go get Maddox his knitting supplies before he blacks out from excitement. He needs to calm the fuck down."

The worker's eyes widened. "Uh…"

"I'll get it," Emma stood, heading for the tent flap. "You," she pointed at Maddox, "try not to break anything."

Maddox grinned, now tapping his drumsticks on the concession table. "No promises."

Emma sighed and left.

Mathias returned, fiddling with his earpiece.

He strode over to his twin and snatched the drumsticks.

"Hey!" Maddox made a grab for his stolen drumsticks, but Mathias was faster and turned away. "Give those back!" Maddox demanded, jabbing at his brother.

"Ladies and gentlemen, I present to you the Wade Brothers: forever twelve years old." Ezra entered the room, carrying his bass.

The twins continued to scuffle, completely oblivious to Ezra.

"You want some water?" Ezra asked me, striding over to the small refrigerator in the corner.

"I would love some, darling," Maddox called, still trying to get his drumsticks back from Mathias.

"I wasn't talking to you," Ezra chuckled.

Maddox gasped, forgetting his drumsticks. "Lovebug, have you moved on? I thought what we had was real. I'm devastated."

Ezra rolled his eyes and grabbed a bottle of water, tossing it to Maddox.

"You guys have the weirdest bromance ever." Hayes shook his head.

"Aw," Maddox reached up to put his arm around Hayes' shoulders, "Ez and I are open to making this twosome and threesome." He winked.

Hayes shrugged out of Maddox's hold and his lips twitched with suppressed laughter. "Yeah, I don't want in on this particular threesome."

"Such a shame," Maddox shook his head, "Ezra and I are a lot of fun."

"I'll live." Hayes chuckled, leaning his hip against the concession table. He grabbed a handful of chips and started munching.

"Here," Emma grouched, shoving the tent flap open, "now chill out." She held out a blue duffel bag to Maddox.

"Ooh," Hayes smiled, "sounds like someone's in trouble. Will he be sleeping on the couch tonight?" He turned to Emma.

She smiled, laughing under her breath. "Possibly."

"If I knit you a sweater will I redeem myself?" Maddox asked, his eyes round and his lower lip jutting out.

"It's ninety degrees outside. Do I look like I want you to knit me a sweater?" She tried to sound serious, but laughter soon infused her tone.

"You look like you want to be wrapped in my arms."

She snorted and then laughed out right. "That's quite possibly the cheesiest thing you've ever said to me."

"Come on," Maddox held his arms out, his t-shirt stretching to fit across his broad chest, "let's hug it out. Hugs make the world a better place."

Hayes gagged. "I'm choking on the sweetness. I need to breathe normal air." He set his guitar aside and headed for the back part of the tent. Bright sunlight streamed in for a moment when he exited and then the tent was plunged into its shaded state once more.

Ezra appeared in front of me and handed me a bottle of water before sitting down in the chair. "There's never a dull moment around here," he commented.

I nodded in agreement. I sipped at my water as Maddox and Emma pulled up another set of chairs.

Mathias paced in the corner, talking on his phone. From the sounds of it he was checking in on Remy.

Maddox sat the duffel bag on the ground and began rummaging through it. Small items fell out and I eyed them before reaching out and picking one up.

It was a tiny sweater and I had no idea why he would make something so small. I fit it onto my hand and eyed him. "What did you make this for?"

He looked at me like *I* was the crazy one. "For Sonic of course. He gets cold."

"Your hedgehog?"

"Do you know any other Sonic's?"

"I guess not." I tossed the small sweater back into his duffel bag.

He began knitting and I couldn't make out what it was. "What is that?" I asked, my brows wrinkling in confusion.

He held it up. "It's baby socks. For my future niece *or* nephew, since my asshole brother won't tell me what his kid is." He raised his voice and glared at his twin. Emma tried not to smile since we both knew the gender of Mathias and Remy's child.

Mathias ended his call and stuffed the phone in his back pocket. "It's a fucking boy!" He lifted his arms at his sides. "Happy now?"

"Immensely." Maddox grinned, sitting the yellow yarn away and pulling out baby blue. "Now I can make my *nephew* a proper sock and blanket set."

Mathias closed my eyes. "How on Earth are we twins?"

"Well, you see," Maddox started, "a sperm met an egg, and said, 'Oh hello, Imma fertilize you.' So then the fertilized egg split in utero—"

"M'kay, I got it." Mathias held up a hand for Maddox to shut up.

"Does my nephew have a name?" Maddox returned to the previous conversation.

Mathias scrubbed a hand over his lightly stubbled jaw. "It's Liam."

"So…are you going to tell mom she's having a grandson named Liam, because you know she's pissed you guys haven't revealed the gender."

"I might as well now." Mathias tossed his hands in the air. "Can't keep a fucking secret in this family. Everybody has to know everything." He grumbled under his breath.

"You guys are going on in five." A guy appeared at the front of the tent, holding up five fingers and wiggling them around. "Are you going to be ready?"

"Absolutely." Maddox said, packing up his knitting supplies. "Although, we're currently missing our guitar player. He's probably getting a blowjob behind the tent. Would you mind fetching him for us? I've seen his dick one too many times."

"Maddox!" Emma hissed, smacking his arm.

He chuckled and kissed her. She made a big show of wiping her mouth off with the back of her hand.

The festival worker looked at Maddox in horror.

"He's messing with you," Ezra put the poor guy out of his misery, "don't worry, I'll get Hayes."

"Uh…okay…thanks." The guy ducked away.

"You know that guy is probably going to blab what you said and it'll end up on TMZ by tomorrow." Ezra eyed Maddox.

Maddox dismissed his words with a wave of his hand. "The media has said worse things about all of us before. This is nothing. Besides, Hayes has a sense of humor so he'll think it's funny. Unlike some people." His gaze swiveled to his twin brother.

"Two minutes!" Someone called.

Hayes reappeared at this call and the guys headed to the back of the tent and out into the open air.

Emma and I went in the opposite direction to join the spectators.

The crowd was huge, but that was really no surprise.

The stage was fairly large with a screen behind it, flashing the Willow Creek logo.

Maddox's drum kit already sat on the stage and I had to laugh. He'd had it custom painted with Sonic the Hedgehog—the video game hedgehog, not his pet.

Maddox was the first to bound onto the stage, so full of energy. He sat down behind his kit and began to tap out a beat as the other guys climbed the steps to the stage.

The girls had screamed at Maddox's appearance, but now that the rest of the band had joined him the screams became deafening.

"Oh my God, Oh my God, Oh my God," a girl beside me fanned her face, "I think I'm going to pass out."

If she did I wouldn't catch her.

Okay, that was mean of me, so I probably would help her out if she actually passed out but hopefully she could keep it together.

Emma snickered beside me.

Mathias grabbed the microphone, putting on his game face. He spoke charmingly to the crowd for a moment, hyping them up while Maddox continued to play a light beat in the background.

Mathias nodded to Hayes, giving him the cue.

Hayes began to play and the sound of his guitar blasted through us.

Mathias started to sing and Ezra joined in with the bass.

I loved watching Ezra play. He was always so in the zone, completely absorbed in the feel of the song. His foot tapped against the stage and he leaned into his bass, almost like he wished he could slip inside and become one with it. He bit his bottom lip and his eyes closed momentarily.

He was so beautiful.

And maybe that was a weird thing to think about a guy, but it was true. When he was up on stage, living his dream, and loving his music, he truly was beautiful.

Beside me Emma sang along to the song, really getting into it. She even busted out a few dance moves. Before Maddox she didn't even listen to this kind of music. I loved that she'd managed to come out of her shell.

I joined her, singing and dancing to the song.

It was humid and in no time sweat drenched my body, but I didn't care. I was having too much fun.

When I glanced back up at the stage my eyes connected with Ezra's. Somehow he'd spotted me, even from this distance. He flashed me a smile before ducking his head and focusing on playing.

Mathias grasped the microphone, belting out the song like his very soul demanded he sing the words.

Hayes jumped around on the stage like he was possessed. I didn't know how he managed to jump like that and play guitar at the same time.

Maddox's drumsticks clashed against the cymbals and his shirt stuck to his chest with sweat. His messy brown hair was just as damp.

When the guys were on stage they truly *performed*, they didn't just stand there. They made you feel and live the music with them.

When their set ended fireworks went off. I turned to Emma with surprise in my eyes.

"What did you expect?" She laughed. "It's Willow Creek. This town pulls out the big guns for them."

"Obviously."

We ducked out of the crowd and headed back into the tent.

The guys joined us a few minutes later. All of them were sweaty, their faces flushed from the heat. Hayes grabbed a bottle of water, drinking at it greedily. The other guys grabbed waters as well.

Maddox stripped off his shirt, giving everyone an eyeful of his abs. One of the women working in the tent sighed happily and Emma glared at her.

"Put your shirt back on before you get mauled." She demanded.

Maddox grinned, wiping a dribble of water off his chin. "Aw, babe, are you jealous?" He glanced in the direction of the woman who was trying to busy herself by restocking the refrigerator, but kept stealing glances at the half-naked drummer.

"Of course not." Emma scoffed, crossing her arms over her chest.

"I think it's hot when you get jealous," he told her, striding over. "But the shirt is staying off for now. I'm too hot." He fanned himself. "This heat is ridiculous. Are you sure you want us to vacation at a beach? Because right about now, escaping to some place cold sounds like a mighty fine idea, don't you want to see my epic snowboarding skills?"

"Don't go changing plans now," she warned him, "you'll confuse everyone."

"When are we supposed to leave for this *vacation*?" Mathias asked, sinking down into a chair. He said the word vacation like it left a sour taste in his mouth. I figured after being on tour for so long he didn't want to travel, but Emma was adamant that she wanted all of us to go, and I knew all of the guys would do anything to make her happy.

"Next Friday, and we'll be gone for a week," Emma replied.

"When does the meet and greet start?" Hayes interrupted, running his fingers through his damp hair.

"Thirty minutes," Maddox said, looking at the watch on his wrist.

"Good. I'm starving, so that gives me a chance to stuff my face."

"Didn't you eat before you guys went on stage?" I asked.

He shrugged, grabbing a plate and piling food on it. "I'm already hungry."

"Hayes is always hungry." Mathias rolled his eyes. "He's a bottomless fucking pit."

"When you have a kid are you still going to use the word *fuck* in every sentence?" Maddox glared at his brother.

"Hey, I'm working on it," Mathias growled, "it's pretty fucking hard to stop using a word you've said all of your life."

Maddox sighed. "My nephew is going to have a potty mouth." He tossed his hands up, like he was already resigned to this fact. "He's going to end up calling me Uncle Fucking Maddox."

"Sounds good to me." Mathias grinned. Actually *grinned*—like his lips lifted and he showed his teeth and everything.

Maddox laughed and so did Mathias. They looked more like twins to me in that moment than they ever had. Despite being identical, it was always easy to tell them apart. Maddox had an easy smile, while Mathias' face was usually pinched with irritation.

Ezra came over to stand beside me, his fingers purposefully grazing my arm.

A small gasp escaped between my lips and I forced myself to remain still. I didn't want him to know how much his touch affected me. But based on the way

623

his lips danced, he was *very* aware of what he was doing to me.

With the remaining free time we all ate the food provided and the guys attempted to regale their appearances so they didn't look so sweaty and dirty. I didn't think the fans would mind, though.

For the meet and greet more chairs were brought in and the guys sat down. I noticed they did that a lot and I figured it was to seem more approachable. When you had four giant rock stars staring down at you it could be intimidating.

"Are you excited for your little friends to joins us?" I joked, looking at Ezra.

He shrugged. "You betcha."

"Friends?" Maddox leaned around his twin to look at Ezra. "Honey, are you cheating on me? I thought our friendship was real."

Ezra laughed. "Yeah, sorry dude, you just don't do it for me."

"I feel like everything I've known to be true is now a lie." Maddox gasped, putting a hand over his heart. "What a cruel, cruel world we live in."

Ezra shook his head. "It's just a few fans that were at the circus and I told them they could come." He grinned suddenly, no doubt remembering the girl with a clear crush on Maddox. "I think you're really going to like them."

"Hey," Emma interrupted, snapping her fingers, "what are you up to?" She narrowed her eyes on Ezra.

"Nothing." He raised his hands innocently.

"We're going to start letting them in." One of the festival workers, who I had learned was named Hannah, stood by the tent entrance.

"Bring it on," Maddox clapped his hands together, "I'm ready for battle."

At his words Hannah opened the tent flap and she started letting people in.

The guys graciously doled out hugs and posed for pictures and signed whatever was tossed their way. I knew they had to be exhausted from their set, but they all kept smiles on their faces. Even Mathias.

I spotted the girls from the circus and the one with the drummer shirt looked like she was ready to pass out.

When she saw Maddox she lost all control and ran right at him.

Maddox was quick and caught her in a hug before they could fall to the ground.

He placed her down gently, but was obviously rattled.

"Hi," she peered up at him with wide eyes, "I'm Taylor and I'm your biggest fan ever. Like *ever*. Wow, I can't believe I'm meeting you. You're even hotter in person." She reached out to touch his jaw and he flinched away as she stared at him in awe. "Your jawline is more structured than my life."

Maddox's lips pressed together and the other guys dissolved into laughter.

The other girls—and reluctant parent's—gathered for the meet and greet watched the exchange.

"Uh…thanks?" Maddox said. I'd never seen him so unsure before. Normally you could count on Maddox to have some sort of witty comeback.

"I'm sorry," the girl put a hand to her forehead, "you probably think I'm so weird."

Maddox grinned, his charm slipping into place. "Weird is beautiful."

She giggled, her cheeks flaming red.

Beside me Emma laughed, shaking her head. We'd moved to the back corner to be out of the way. "I'm so afraid that poor girl is going to pee her pants."

"It's a possibility," I agreed.

Another hour passed while the guys conversed with the meet and greet attendees and I lost count of how many pictures they continued to pose for.

Finally everyone was cleared out of the room and we were free to go.

It was getting late now, and darkness had settled into the summer sky.

Mathias grabbed his cardigan and hauled ass out of there before any of us could tell him goodbye. I knew he was probably worried about Remy. Those two were almost as bad as Maddox and Emma.

Maddox and Emma headed out next, leaving Ezra and I alone with Hayes.

Hayes paused by the tent entrance and looked back at us. "I'm hanging out here for a while longer, y'all wanna come?"

Ezra was quick to shake his head. "No, I have to get Toby home."

"Toby?" Hayes asked, his forehead wrinkling in confusion.

"The goldfish." Ezra pointed at the lazily swimming fish.

"Oh, right." Hayes raised two fingers in a salute. "I'll see you later then."

Ezra lifted his chin in goodbye and waved.

Once he was gone Ezra admitted that he was tired.

"Me too," I agreed, and I hadn't even been the one performing.

We gathered up our stuff, including Toby, and met his bodyguards outside the tent so they could escort us back to his car.

The festival was still raging and seemed even more crowded than it had been earlier.

Luckily, most people seemed too drunk to recognize Ezra so we made it to his car without incident.

I held Toby's jar tightly in my hands, afraid that the car ride might jostle him too much. It would totally suck if Ezra and I ended up killing the goldfish before we even made it home.

Ezra backed out and started the drive home. Since he lived in the middle of nowhere it took us a while to get back to his place.

I dropped my bag on the floor as soon as we got in and set Toby on the counter.

"We need to get him a little fish tank," I told Ezra as I headed for the stairs.

"I'll take care of it," he assured me, grabbing a bag of chips and a drink before following me

I took a quick shower and changed into my pajamas.

I was starting into my room when Ezra called my name.

I padded down the short hallway and stood in the doorway. "Yeah?" I asked, as his eyes raked over my body. My pajamas consisted of a pair of shorts and a tank top. The shirt was pulled taut against my breasts and I was sure he was getting quite the show.

"Sleep in here tonight." He patted the empty space beside him. He was shirtless and the glare from the TV screen made his chest glow.

"What did you say?" I wet my lips. I couldn't possibly have heard him right.

He turned back the blankets on the other side and patted the empty space again. "Sleep in here," he repeated, "we don't have to do anything, but I…" He paused, clearing his throat. "Please?" He settled on.

I began to sway, suddenly feeling lightheaded, and I realized I'd been holding my breath.

"Okay," I squeaked like a mouse. I'd never been so unsure of myself before. I'd always been a confident girl, comfortable in my own skin, but Ezra shook up my insides to the point that I didn't recognize them.

I tiptoed into his bedroom and slipped beneath the smooth, silky sheets.

Ezra turned off his bedside light, but left the TV on.

He burrowed under the covers and I jolted when his arms wrapped around me.

He pulled me against his body and tucked one of my legs between his.

My heart raced a million miles an hour.

This…this was so much more than just sex.

This was something real couples did. He held me tightly, like he didn't want to let go.

He pressed a tender kiss to the back of my neck and then lower between my shoulder blades over my tattoo.

"Goodnight, Sadie," he whispered in the darkness.

"'Night."

*This was nothing.*

*It meant nothing.*

*We were nothing.*

*Nothing.*

*Nothing.*

*Nothing.*

So why did it feel like everything?

# CHAPTER FOURTEEN

MY PENCIL DRAGGED lazily across the blank white page. I could see the dress perfectly in my head, now I just had to get it down on paper.

I'd drawn a few possible designs for Emma's dress already, but I vetoed them without even showing her. They were all lacking something. I wanted this dress to be one hundred percent Emma, and the idea I had now I knew was perfect.

The dress slowly appeared before my eyes and I began to flesh it out, adding the smaller details.

Downstairs something fell over and Ezra yelled, "I'm okay. Don't come down yet!"

"Alright!" I called back.

He'd banished me upstairs and told me he had a surprise for me. I was definitely curious to know what he was up to, but luckily I'd been distracted by my design. Without a distraction I would've forced myself past his barricade—yes, he made a barricade—just to see what he was up to.

I finished my drawing and I smiled at it. I *knew* Emma would love it and I couldn't wait to see her face when I showed her. I was already planning out the fabrics I would need to buy and how much time it would take to make the dress. It wasn't too complicated of a design, but I knew to account for the fact that I might run into a problem.

"I'm ready!" Ezra called. "You can come down now!"

I set my sketchpad aside and scurried down the stairs, nearly falling in my haste.

He'd cleared away the barricade and when I reached the bottom of the steps I saw that he'd moved the furniture out of the way and covered the floor with a large white sheet.

On top of the sheet was a Twister mat—yeah, like the game—and on top of each colored circle was a splattering of a matching paint color.

"What is this?" I asked.

"Twister…with a twist." He chuckled, standing with his arms crossed over his chest as he admired his handy work.

"Why?" I stood beside him, staring at the mat on the ground in wonder.

He glanced down at me. "We leave for Florida tomorrow and I know it'll be nearly impossible for us to get any time alone, so I thought we would do something fun today."

"So…you want us to roll around in paint?"

His laughter vibrated through his chest and he shoved his unruly black hair out of his eyes. "Getting you dirty has a certain appeal."

"At least you're honest. But I'm not sure how I feel about ruining my clothes."

"Such a girl," he muttered, then cracked a smile, "it's a good thing I think of everything."

He grabbed a pair of brand new white shorts and a white t-shirt. I noticed then that he was dressed in white jeans and a white shirt. By the end of this both would be covered in a kaleidoscope of colors.

I took the clothes from him and stripped down right there. I didn't think there was any reason to be modest at this point. I folded what I'd been wearing before and set it on the steps.

"You wanna go first?" He asked me, a challenge gleaming in his eyes.

"Sure." I agreed, stepping over onto the sheet beside the mat.

He picked up the board and spun. "Right hand green."

I crouched down and put my hand on one of the circles, right smack in the middle of the paint. It squished between my fingers and felt cold and gross, but I kept my face straight so that he wouldn't make fun of me.

"Your turn," I declared, waving my hand for the board so that I could spin for him. He held it out to me and I flicked the spinner. "Left foot yellow."

He stuck his foot out and immediately spun for me. "Right foot red."

"I'm not that flexible!" I groaned, stretching out to reach a red circle all the way on the opposite side of the mat while still keeping my hand on the green circle.

"I'd beg to differ," he whispered under his breath.

I rolled my eyes and spun for him. "Left foot blue." He moved his foot. "Ugh," I groaned, "that's so not fair! My muscles are screaming and you only had to move your freaking foot!"

"Don't hate the player, babe," he grinned, lifting his shoulders in a small shrug.

"I'll show you a player," I grumbled.

"Don't be like that." He continued to grin, definitely unconcerned with my current pissed off state. He spun and called out, "Left hand blue."

"Motherfucker," I cursed, trying to position myself. I ended up bumping into Ezra and my hands landed on his butt to steady myself, leaving behind streaks of paint.

He stumbled from the impact of my weight and then tripped over me.

We fell together in a tangle of limbs, paint getting all over our clothes and hair.

"Well, that didn't go according to plan." I muttered, laying flat across his chest.

"Really? Because getting you in my arms was my end game." He winked.

I glared down at him as his hands tightened around my waist. I reached out, smearing my hand in a glob of paint. Before he realized what I was up to I pressed my hand to his cheek, the red paint getting all over his face and into the scruff on his cheeks.

His eyes narrowed on me. "Oh, you're in trouble now."

I squealed when he grabbed my wrists and twisted to pin me beneath him. Paint squished beneath me, coating my hair and clothes.

"Ezra!" I screamed.

I smeared my hand in paint again and wiped it in his hair.

He laughed and grabbed my breasts, leaving behind handprints on my boobs.

We continued to roll around in the paint, smiling and laughing, as we tried to get the other person dirtier than we were.

I fell onto my stomach and he landed on top of me, carefully holding his weight slightly above me so that he didn't squish me.

I tapped my hand against the mat. "I'm out, I'm out."

He laughed and rolled off of me, lying flat on his back. I raised my head slightly to look at him and laughed when I saw he was entirely covered in paint. I'm sure I looked much the same.

"We're a mess." I giggled, sitting up.

He grabbed my waist and towed me towards him. I slid easily on the slick surface. "Come here," he growled lowly, and I swung my legs so that I was straddling him. He sat up, wrapping his arms around me. Slowly, one hand slid up the bare skin of my arm and then he grasped my chin. "I'm going to kiss you now," he breathed, his dark eyes flicking down to my lips.

Not one to wait, my fingers delved into his hair and I pulled him closer, angling my mouth over his. He exhaled a deep moan and I swallowed it with a kiss.

I rolled my hips against his and his fingers tightened around my waist.

"Fuck," he growled, "I need you." His fingers skimmed underneath my top and he pulled it over my head, tossing it so that it landed on the sheet. He lay down, and my lips never parted from his. He sucked my bottom lip between his and I let out a mewling sound.

"You kill me," he breathed in-between kisses, "you absolutely shatter me."

I clasped his face in my hands and stared down into his warm eyes. There were so many things I wanted to say—to confess—but I refused to give life to the words. I'd been hurt enough, and I had to protect my heart at all costs, especially from someone who didn't want it.

Instead of saying anything I kissed him again.

His tongue swept past my lips and I breathed him in.

He was everywhere—his taste, his scent, his touch, it was all too much.

It didn't matter how many times he touched me, it always lit me on fire from the inside out. It was like my body was programed to come to life when he touched me.

He turned, pining me onto my back and his lips left mine to kiss a trail down my neck, between my breasts, and over my stomach.

My back arched above the mat and I fisted my fingers in his hair, tugging slightly and he growled in response.

Before I could take my next breath he ripped my shorts off—seriously, *ripped* them because he tugged them off so harshly. I couldn't complain about him ruining them since he'd bought them and they were already covered in paint. Plus, seeing him do that was pretty hot. My underwear and bra went next and both were removed with just as much vigor.

I palmed my breasts as he removed his clothes. His eyes darkened with lust as he watched me. I didn't have much going on in the boob area, but the way he looked at me made me feel good.

He undid the button on his paint covered white pants and started to tug them down, but cursed.

"What's wrong?" I asked, my voice sounding breathless.

"I don't have a condom," he hung his head, smiling sheepishly he added, "this wasn't about sex." He gestured to the twister mat and paint. "I really did want us to do something fun."

"Well, now it *is* about sex." My voice was full of want and desire. "Just forget the condom. I'm on birth control and I'm clean. I got tested after…well, after." He knew what I was talking about.

His whole body shook when he inhaled a breath. "Are you sure? I'm clean too."

"I trust you."

I trusted him completely—with my life, but not my heart.

He nodded once and removed his pants and boxer briefs.

My eyes immediately dropped to his erection. I couldn't help myself. I reached out, wrapping my hand around him and rubbing up and down. Air hissed between his teeth and he let out a curse.

"I need to be inside you," he murmured, grabbing my hands and pinning them above my head. He captured my lips with his and thrust inside.

I gasped at the intrusion and then my body began to relax. Pleasure zinged through my veins. I'd never known how potent and special sex could be until Ezra. I had thought I'd known, but I'd been oh-so wrong. Everything from my past paled in comparison, and I feared that anything after would never live up to this. But from the first time I let him touch me it had been a risk I was willing to take.

His hips rolled deliciously slow against mine and a breathy sigh escaped me.

He stared into my eyes, the feelings and moment far too intimate for two people that were only supposed to be friends with benefits.

I stared right back, unflinchingly.

I don't know what he saw in my eyes, but his darkened with heightened passion and he pulled his bottom lip between his teeth.

Letting go of my hands he skimmed his down my sides and then back up to palm my breasts.

My naked body was covered in paint, as was his, but I didn't care.

He lowered his head, sucking my bottom lip into his mouth. I moaned and his tongue swirled against mine.

My body began to shake as I soared to that place high among the sky.

When I fell his lips silenced my small cry.

I wrapped my fingers around his neck, holding him to me. I kissed him back with every ounce of desire that my small body possessed.

His thrusts quickened and he rested his forehead against mine, still looking into my eyes.

I knew I should look away, that watching him like this would only make me fall harder for him, but I couldn't let this moment leave. I wanted—no, *needed*—to see if any part of him cared for me the way I did him. Even if it was only a fleeting look, I would treasure it forever, because for that single suspended moment in time we would be one.

He groaned, his body shaking as he found his release.

I held his face in my hands, refusing to let him look away.

And then I saw it—that look, so full of love and longing.

I held onto it, tucking the moment into my heart where I could treasure it forever.

I knew I had to let him go, but I raised my head and kissed him again.

His lips were a brand against mine. His fingers fisted in my hair and he kissed me with fervor, like he needed me to survive.

He broke the kiss first and pressed a single, tender kiss to my forehead before pulling out and rolling onto his back.

We both lay there, covered in paint, unmoving except for the heavy rise and fall of our chests as we struggled to get enough air into our lungs.

So much hung unsaid in the air between us.

And it would remain that way.

# CHAPTER FIFTEEN

"WOOO! WE'RE IN MIAMI, BITCHES!" Maddox yelled, grabbing up Emma and tossing her over his shoulder. He ran straight for the blue-green colored ocean water. She beat at his back, laughing wildly at his antics.

"We're not even in Miami!" Hayes hollered after him, shaking his head. "Fucking psycho."

"Do you think we could, um maybe keep the cussing to a minimum?" Arden asked, covering her daughter's ears.

I'd ended up closing down my shop for the week and after talking to the guys, Emma, and Remy to see if it was okay, I invited Arden and her daughter Mia to go on vacation with us. I knew it had been forever since she'd had a break—being a single mom was hard—and I felt bad that I'd blown her off a few times when she asked to get lunch or something.

"Oh, right. Sorry." Hayes smiled sheepishly at her. "That might be difficult between the two of us." He tossed a thumb in Mathias' direction.

Mathias rolled his eyes and finished unloading the suitcases from the trunk of one of the SUVs we'd rented for our stay.

I glanced up at the gigantic mansion we were staying in.

It had four stories—the bottom story was a massive garage, but the other three still remained a mystery. The siding was a pale blue and it had windows everywhere. It was just starting to get dark, but the house glowed from within making it obvious someone had been there earlier to get it ready for our stay.

On the outside palm trees and an endless amount of sand surrounded it.

I breathed in the crisp, salty air.

This was exactly what I had needed.

Glancing over at Ezra as he finished unloading the car we'd rode in I couldn't help thinking about how difficult this week would be for us.

While Maddox and Emma played in the water—meaning he dropped her in the ocean on purpose and she retaliated by dunking him—the rest of us carried our bags into the house.

"Oh my God," Arden gasped.

My gasp echoed hers.

The house was stunning.

Actually, that was an understatement.

Magnificent was a more accurate description.

The walls and furniture were all white with pops of turquoise and hot pink in the form of pillows and vases. It was so simple, but beautiful.

But the view? That was to die for.

I dropped my purse by the set of stairs and walked straight ahead to gaze out the windows. The ocean glimmered in the last of the setting sun and below on the beach Emma ran away from Maddox. He caught her around the waist and spun her around. It was a picture perfect moment.

Ezra stepped up beside me, his arm brushing mine. Body heat radiated off of him and I found myself leaning closer to him. I itched to be wrapped in his arms, but I fought off that urge.

On my other side Arden stood with three-year-old Mia on her hip. "Wow," she gasped, "it's so beautiful it doesn't seem real."

I nodded in agreement.

"Thanks for inviting me." She glanced at me with a smile. "All of you." She glanced at the guys and Remy.

"Of course," Hayes huffed, setting down a heavy bag by the stairs. His face was red and he looked like he was starting to sweat. "What was in that bag?" He addressed me. "Fess up fashion Queen. It's yours right?"

"Not mine." I shook my head.

Beside me Arden's cheeks flamed red, making her freckles appear even more vividly. "Uh…it's mine," she admitted. Hayes began to laugh. "In my defense," she held up a hand, halting whatever he was about to say, "that's my only bag and it has all of mine and Mia's stuff."

Hayes' eyes sparkled with barely contained laughter. "I guess I can forgive you for that."

She smiled at him, tucking a piece of bright red hair behind her ear.

I eyed the two carefully, trying to hide my smile. I turned away and back out at the beautiful view.

"I'm starving," Mathias declared, heading over to the kitchen. He swung open the stainless steel refrigerator doors and cursed. "Motherfucker."

"Language!" Arden admonished, covering Mia's ears once more.

"Oh, right. Sorry."

Holy shit, Mathias Wade apologized. Somebody, put that down in the record books.

"The fu—idiot only has the refrigerator stocked with Diet Pepsi."

Ezra snorted. "Why am I not surprised?"

"I'm going to run to the store to get some food and I'll just pick up pizza for tonight or something." Mathias swiped the car keys off a side table.

"I'll go with you." Remy piped up.

He shook his head and kissed her tenderly. "No, stay here and rest for a bit."

She didn't put up a fight, which led me to believe she did need to rest. Remy wasn't one to listen to what she was told.

Mathias left just as Hayes returned with the last bag.

And by bag I meant cage.

Maddox and Emma brought their pet hedgehogs.

I wished I was joking.

Maddox and Emma ran up the beach and onto the deck steps.

Ezra unlocked the door to let them inside.

"You guys are soaking wet," I said unnecessarily.

"It's his fault." Emma poked Maddox in the side.

"Mathias went to get food since *someone* only stocked us with Diet Pepsi." Hayes muttered, strolling over with his arms crossed over his chest.

Maddox grinned crookedly and tossed an arm over Emma's shoulder. "What else does a man need in life, besides the love of a good woman and Diet Pepsi?"

"A hedgehog," Ezra chuckled.

"How could I forget?" Maddox mock winced.

Hayes sighed, but I knew he was secretly amused. "Why don't we figure out the sleeping arrangement?" He suggested. "That way we can put all this shi—crap—away." He pointed to the mountain of suitcases by the stairs and flashed Arden an apologetic smile.

"Sounds good." Emma clapped her hands together.

We each grabbed a bag and started up the stairs. The same color scheme was carried throughout the large home.

On the second level—or I guess technically it was the third—there were five bedrooms, all with their own bathrooms. There was even a little nook with a chaise lounge and a bookshelf.

Everyone picked a room and that left me. "I guess I'll take a room upstairs," I mumbled, heading for the second set of steps.

"Uh," Ezra interjected, "I will too. I don't want you to be alone."

Emma stopped outside a bedroom door with a hand on her hip and a calculating look in her eyes. "Or Sadie could take the extra room down here and *you* could go upstairs."

"But then *I'm* alone," he countered, "what if I get scared at night? Are you going to come hold my hand, Emma?"

Her lips pressed together as she held in laughter. "Does that mean Sadie is going to hold your hand?" She folded her arms over her chest. She was so on to us. She had been from the start.

"Of course." He grinned, trying to play everything off as a joke.

Emma finally shrugged. "Whatever."

The two of us headed up to the second level. There were only three bedrooms up here—and two bathrooms, one room had it's own and the other was Jack and Jill style. The nook up here was larger and had a baby grand piano and art easel. This place was so incredibly peaceful that I knew I wouldn't have any trouble unwinding.

The three bedrooms were similar in size, so I picked one based on the view of the beach and the fact that it had a balcony. Ezra chose the room across from me and set his bags inside before joining me in my bedroom.

I opened the French doors and stepped out onto the balcony. I leaned against the railing and he stepped up beside me with his hands shoved into the pockets of his khaki shorts.

"You realize I'll be sleeping in here, right?" He winked.

I cracked a smile. After the night where he asked me to sleep with him without sex we'd continued the tradition.

"I expected so."

"I've grown so used to the privacy we have at my house that being here with everyone is going to test the limits of my sanity." He grabbed onto the railing, the last of the blazing sun haloing his body. I itched to lean forward and kiss him, but he wasn't mine and I couldn't risk someone catching us.

"I know what you mean," I agreed.

Ever so slightly he brushed his pinky against mine, and then rested it overtop.

I closed my eyes, treasuring the brief touch.

"Hey, what are you guys doing?"

Maddox.

Ezra's finger fell away from mine and he whipped around with a smile on his face. "Admiring the view," he replied.

Maddox stepped outside with us and I noticed he'd changed his clothes to something dry, but his hair was still wet.

"Isn't this place great?" He grinned. "I couldn't believe I found it on such short notice."

I had to admit I was surprised too. Plus, it was nice that the houses on either side were off in the distance. I doubted we'd have to worry about any crazy fans in this neighborhood, homes this big could only be owned by celebrities and CEOs.

"Anyway," Maddox clapped his hand on Ezra's shoulder, "I just came to tell you guys that Mathias is back already and I thought you might be hungry."

"Sure," Ezra nodded, "we'll be right down."

"Cool." Maddox began to back away, watching us carefully. He was just as suspicious as Emma.

When he disappeared Ezra reached up and gently stroked my cheek.

I sighed happily and leaned into his touch. He placed a feather light kiss on my forehead and held his lips there when he murmured, "How can I do this for a week? How can I pretend I'm not spending every second thinking about the way your body hums when I touch you and you sigh when I kiss you?"

A week? How was I going to pretend to not be thinking about those things for the rest of my life? Our agreement was going to come to an end in a matter of months, maybe even less, and then…and then I didn't know.

I grasped his shirt in my hands and leaned forward, inhaling the scent that was uniquely Ezra.

I answered truthfully. "I don't know either."

# CHAPTER SIXTEEN

"UP! UP! UP! GET UP!" Maddox drummed his fist against the door to my room.

"Go away!" I yelled back, tossing a pillow over my head. If I had to deal with Maddox's chipper personality at the crack of dawn every morning I might murder him, which would suck for Emma since she loved him and all. But, seriously.

The door to my room swung open and I sent up a silent prayer that Ezra had snuck over to his room early in the morning.

I tossed the pillow off of my head and rose up on my elbows to look at Maddox. I was sure my hair was a wild untamable mess, but for once in my life I didn't care.

"I made breakfast." He grinned, clearly pleased with this news, like he'd done me some kind of favor.

"It's too early," I groaned.

"It's eight o' clock," he tossed his hands up in exasperation, "that's not early. You're as bad as Emma. Now come on and get ready. We're all going snorkeling."

"Snorkeling?" I sat up completely, this bit of news making me a little excited despite the early time.

He nodded. "Yep…or you could stay here and sleep. Your choice." He shrugged nonchalantly.

I pointed a finger at him in warning. "Don't you dare leave without me."

"Wouldn't dream of it, Westbrook." He flashed his winning smile and closed the door.

I immediately tossed the covers off and ran over to my suitcase.

I pulled out all of my bikinis and dropped them on the floor, rifling through them. I ended up picking a solid black one. The top made my breasts appear larger than they actually were and had several overlapping straps in the back. The bottoms exposed more of my ass than I was used to, but let's face it, I was planning on driving Ezra crazy.

I put on a pair of old ripped jean shorts and a see-through blousy white top over my bikini.

I brushed my hair and it hung in soft natural waves just past my shoulders.

I didn't bother applying makeup, just a bit of gloss.

Before I left my room I grabbed my sunglasses and stuck them on top of my head.

Ezra's bedroom door was open, but I didn't see him inside so I figured he'd already joined the others downstairs.

Everyone was seated at the dining room table and a smorgasbord of breakfast food was sitting on the table. An empty seat was left between Arden and Ezra.

Ezra looked up when I entered the room, his dark eyes raking over my body. They flared with hunger and he sucked his bottom lip between his teeth. His eyes rose to meet mine and he winked.

I sat down and Arden smiled. "Morning."

"Morning." I reached for a biscuit and put it on the plate that was already waiting for me.

"They all made breakfast," she hissed like it was some kind of secret, "the guys."

"We have many talents." Hayes quipped, having heard her. "Did you know Mathias can rap?"

Mathias rolled his eyes. "I can do a lot of wicked things with my tongue."

Emma snorted and Remy nudged his arm with her elbow in a silent gesture to tell him to shut up. She also threw in a glare for good measure.

"Sweetie, do you want another biscuit?" Hayes asked.

At his words we all turned to look at him and saw that he was talking to three-year-old Mia. Her hair was a vibrant red like her mother's and she looked up at Hayes with wide blue eyes.

She nodded her head and he grabbed one for her.

Arden watched the two in awe.

"She doesn't normally like strangers," she whispered.

"Everybody likes me," Hayes scoffed, flashing a wide smile, "I'm irresistible."

"I'm beginning to think so," she agreed.

Beneath the table Ezra's handed landed on my thigh and he gave it a soft squeeze. I closed my eyes and my lips parted on a breath. He quickly let go before anyone could notice and my body instantly ached for his touch.

Once breakfast was done we all cleaned up and then piled in the SUVs to head over to a different beach.

There, we met with a guy that went over instructions and what to do in case of an emergency—mainly if a shark happened to swim by. It wasn't likely to happen, but they still had to warn us.

I bounced with excitement, eager to dip my toes into the blue-green water and see the creatures that lived inside.

"I'm going to stay behind with Mia," Arden said, holding her daughter's hand and moving back a few steps.

Hayes paused what he was doing and frowned. "Come on, Arden, you don't want to miss out on this. I'll stay with her."

"No, no," she waved him away when he started forward, "I don't want to be a bother. We're fine here."

He shook his head adamantly. "Go," he said firmly. "Mia loves me," he grinned, bending down to the little girl's level. "We'll go hunt for seashells while you snorkel."

Arden seemed to be contemplating his words. "Are you sure?"

"Absolutely." He reached a hand out to Mia. She put her much smaller one on top and her pale pink nail polish sparkled in the sunlight. A little yellow hat was perched on her head to block the sun from her eyes and she was dressed in a cute bathing suit with little ruffles on her butt. She was such a cute kid.

"Okay." Arden agreed, watching as Hayes swept Mia up into his arms. He tickled her stomach and she giggled happily. I'd never seen this side of Hayes before and it made me smile. He really was maturing and I was beginning to think what he told me on our date about settling down wasn't a lie.

Arden had brought a beach bag with her and she rifled through it. She pulled out a small bucket and handed it to Hayes.

"For the seashells." She smiled at him, tucking a piece of hair behind her ear. "Thanks for doing this."

"It's not a problem. Mia and I will have lots of fun. Won't we?" He addressed the little girl. She nodded eagerly.

Arden stepped away slowly, still a little reluctant to leave her daughter behind.

I put the goggles on that covered my eyes and nose and turned to Ezra. "How do I look?" My voice sounded thick and funny since it had a nosepiece.

"Adorable." He grinned and kissed me quickly.

I froze and so did he. We both turned to see if anyone saw.

Luckily everyone was busy putting their own masks on and didn't notice.

We both let out an audible sigh of relief.

That had been a close one.

My heart still pounded in my chest and I eyed them all warily in case one of them was pretending not to have seen.

"Relax," Ezra whispered, his lips near my ear.

I didn't know how he expected me to do that with him standing so close.

We followed the others to the water's edge and I giggled when it tickled my toes. It was warm and the sand squished between my toes, which were painted a pretty pale purple.

I walked out into the water until it hit my hips. I fixed the mouthpiece between my lips and then dove slightly into the water, making sure to leave the snorkel sticking out so I could breathe.

Beside me Ezra did the same. Arden was close by with the others a little farther out.

Beneath me tiny bright colored fish swam around. They were gorgeous and seemed unafraid of us. One tickled my arm as it swam by.

I swam farther and saw a crab scuttling over a small rock.

The coral was gorgeous and in a rainbow of colors.

I'd never seen anything so beautiful before and I was flooded with inspiration for designs.

Seeing all of this beauty made me realize I'd been missing out on so much that life has to offer. I'd been stuck in my hometown for so long that I forgot that magic was all around us.

A piece of aqua colored coral—or maybe it was some kind of weird grass—swayed from the ocean current.

A finger tapped against my elbow and I jolted.

I turned to look and saw Arden. Her red hair billowed around her like a flame. She pointed to my right and I glanced that way.

It was a turtle and it swam right up to us, completely unafraid of us like the other fish had been. I itched to reach out and touch its shell, but the man we met with on the beach warned us to not touch any of the animals. After all, they were wild and this was their home.

I don't know how long we swam around, but eventually we all emerged from the water with wrinkly fingers and toes.

Instead of returning to the beach house and hanging out there, we set up on this beach.

Hayes met us with Mia—the bucket now full of seashells. Mia was grinning from ear to ear and clinging onto him. I'd say the little girl had a crush.

Arden went over to join him, smacking a loud kiss on Mia's cheek. Mia giggled merrily and reached for her mom.

I headed over to my bag and pulled out my towel, using it to dry my body before sitting down.

I grabbed my tanning oil and started rubbing it on my body.

Arden put her towel down beside mine and sat with Mia between her legs. Mia immediately toddled off of the towel and into the sand. She picked up a handful of sand and threw it at her mom's legs. Arden merely shook off the sand.

"It's unfair that you can get a nice pretty tan and I'm going to end up looking like a lobster and I'll probably gain a hundred more freckles." She nodded at my already natural olive-toned skin. She tugged her hair back into a ponytail and then began slathering herself in sunscreen before grabbing Mia and putting some on her too.

"Hey, I might get a tan but I'd kill for your hair."

"I guess we all want what we can't have," she quipped.

Hayes strolled over to us and squatted down so that he was at our level. "I thought Ms. Mia might want to dip her toes in the ocean, if that's okay?" He addressed Arden.

"Sure, if she wants to."

Hayes turned to Mia. "Want to be a mermaid?"

The little girl nodded her head enthusiastically and I wondered if she actually knew what he said. I wasn't around kids enough to know what they understood at what age.

Hayes picked up Mia and lifted her onto his shoulders. She grabbed the longer strands of hair on top of his head and tugged. "Horsie!" She cried.

Hayes winced and loosened her fingers. "Don't do that."

"Sowwy." She frowned.

Before she could get too upset he took off running, holding on tight to her, and her giggles trailed behind her.

Beside me Arden shook her head. "It's the craziest thing. Normally Mia hates strangers, so I don't know what it is about him that she likes so much."

"He's a nice guy," I supplied.

"I suppose so." She shadowed her eyes with a hand to her forehead as she watched Hayes and Mia in the ocean. He was holding her now, barely dipping her toes into the water. She giggled and her legs flailed wildly.

Mathias and Remy sat in chairs off behind us beneath an umbrella, far enough away that they had some privacy from the rest of us.

Emma and Maddox were talking to the man we'd seen earlier about something, while Ezra was walking down the beach.

I itched to join him, but I knew Emma would see and draw conclusions.

I hated keeping our arrangement a secret from her, but I had to. No one could know. It was already messy enough with only Ezra and I involved. But if the others found out, I knew they'd root for us to end up a couple, and when we didn't I feared that would lead them all to feel like they had to pick sides. If they didn't know, they couldn't form an opinion and pass judgment.

I watched Ezra pause and stoop down to pick something up out of the sand. He turned it over in his hand before tucking it into his palm. He squeezed it tight and continued on.

"I'm going to take a nap."

Arden glanced at me and arched a brow. "Didn't you go to bed early?"

"Uh…yeah. But the beach sun makes me really sleepy," I lied. I couldn't tell her the truth—that Ezra had kept me up most of the night. The possibility of getting caught had heightened every sensation in my body, and the effort to quiet my cries of pleasure had been exhausting.

"Okay," she said doubtfully. "I'm just going to read for a little bit since Mia's occupied. I never get to read anymore."

I nodded and laid back. My sunglasses shielded my eyes from the sun and the warmth from the rays felt like a blanket.

I really was sleepy and in no time I drifted off.

Cold water prickled the skin of my stomach and I jolted into a seated position.

"What the hell?!" I exclaimed and looked up to find Hayes standing over me with a squirt gun. Where he found that I had no idea.

He smiled boyishly. "I didn't think you'd want to miss this."

"Miss what?"

He pointed to the sky.

"What the hell?" I repeated, blinking my eyes. "Is that—?"

"Yep," he answered, grinning at the sight before us with his hands on his narrow hips.

"They're insane!" I stood up, leaning my head back so I could see better.

Maddox and Emma were parasailing. To say they were adrenaline junkies was an understatement. They were always looking for another crazy adventure.

Ezra stood a few feet away with his phone held aloft, videoing our crazy best friends.

"One day they're going to get themselves killed," I groaned.

Zip lining, skydiving, and now parasailing. What was next? Cliff-jumping?

"Probably," Hayes answered.

"Did I say that out loud?"

He chuckled and nodded.

"Oops." I glanced away and noticed that Arden and Mia were gone. "Where did Arden go?"

"Mia was sleepy so she headed back to the car. We're leaving after these two finish." He pointed up at the sky.

"I'm posting this on YouTube," Ezra chuckled, "the whole world needs to see these fools."

"Wouldn't your manager have a heart attack if he knew Maddox was up here?"

"Hells yeah," Hayes laughed. "He'll probably shit his pants. Julian is such a fucking fun-sucker." He paused, his lips pursed in thought. "Maybe if he got laid he'd be happier." He snapped his fingers together with a sudden though. "Ez, we should hire a hooker for him."

I reached out and smacked the back of his head.

"Ow," he rubbed the spot and mockingly glared at me, "that hurt."

"Aw, poor baby." I pouted. "I think you'll live."

Hayes smiled and his eyes dipped to my breasts.

I rolled my eyes and pointed to my face. "Eyes up here Hayes."

"Sorry," he cleared his throat, "I just can't help myself. They're just right in my face."

"Dude," Ezra glared, anger flashing in his eyes as he completely forgot about the video he was currently taking, "do you *want* me to punch you in the face?"

"Oh, so are you two—?" He trailed off, waving a finger between Ezra and me.

"No," Ezra said adamantly, tucking his phone into the pocket of his board shorts, "but have some respect."

Hayes made a sound in the back of his throat that made it obvious he didn't believe Ezra. "Whatever. I'm going back to the cars. You guys can wait for them."

Ezra let out a heavy sigh and crossed his hands behind his head. He wouldn't look at me and that began to worry me. I stayed where I was, refusing to be the first one to break the silence.

"What have we done?" He asked, staring out at the sparkling ocean.

"What do you mean?"

He lowered his hands and plopped in the sand, draping his arms over his knees. "I knew this was a bad fucking idea, but I wanted you too much to say no," he continued, "but this fucking sucks, Sadie. Anytime another guy even glances in your direction I want to punch him in the face." He slowly raised his head and his dark gaze connected with mine. "I'm not allowed to have those feelings. You're not mine."

*You're not mine.* Those words stung like a slap to my face.

"This is just sex. It's not real."

*It's not real.* Another slap.

It was tearing me apart that he didn't return my feelings, but I was still all too willing to take what he would give me for however long. The pain was worth knowing what it felt like to be held in his arms.

"Right?"

His voice startled me from my thoughts. I sat down beside him, crossing my legs in the sand. I picked up a handful of sand and watched it sift through my open fingers.

"Right," I echoed, immediately hating that word. How could a word that by its very definition meant *correct* feel so undeniably *wrong?*

He reached over and took my hand in his, holding it until he was forced to let go.

I wished so desperately that we could have more than stolen moments, but wishing gets you nowhere, because wishes don't exist.

As our friends joined us once more we headed out to lunch and then back to the beach house. Both of us forced our conversation out of our minds.

We had to.

At least I did, because letting myself believe for one single second that I'd heard a note of longing in his voice when he asked me if he was right, would lead me to feel nothing but anguish later on because it would give me *hope*, and hope was suffocating.

We laid around on the beach for a while before the guys got the brilliant idea to play beach volleyball. They were forcing all of us to play too, except for Remy. Mathias glared at his brother and friends, daring them to go against his wishes and let her play.

Remy was fine with sitting out though, which I knew made Mathias feel relieved.

There was already a net set up on the beach, between our house and the next one, which was currently vacant, but we didn't have a ball. All three guys—minus Mathias who chose to stay behind with Remy—headed to the store.

While they were gone the rest of us ventured into the house to cool off. My skin felt heated to the touch, but I wasn't burned, unlike poor Arden who was starting to look a little red. She hadn't been exaggerating about the whole lobster thing.

I poured myself a glass of ice water and took a seat at one of the kitchen stools.

Emma ventured in and fixed a glass of water too. Her blonde hair was piled on top of her head in a messy bun and she wore a sheer ivory cover-up over her bikini. It had fringe on the hem, which made it very Emma-like.

She sat down beside me and I smiled. "So…do you want to see what I've sketched for your dress?" The wedding was fast approaching so I had to start the actual process of making her dress soon, so I hoped she loved what I'd come up with.

"Ooh! Yes!" Her blue eyes glimmered with excitement. "I wanna see!"

"Wait here." I instructed her before running upstairs to grab my sketchpad.

I returned with it clutched in my hands and I bounced with excitement. I was nervous too, though. There was the very real possibility that she might hate what

I'd come up with.

"Lemme see!" She held out her hands in a grabbing motion.

I suddenly felt very unsure of my design. I reluctantly handed it over. I wanted to close my eyes so that I didn't have to see her reaction if she hated it, but I manned up and held my chin high. It was her dress and if she didn't like it, that was her right, but my designs were my babies.

Her mouth fell open and a small gasp emitted from her lips. "Sadie," her voice was full of awe, "this is amazing."

"Really?" A huge weight lifted off of my shoulders.

"I know I didn't give you much to go on, but this? This is perfect. It's more than I could've dreamed of." She reached out and tentatively ran her fingers over the sketch.

I'd opted to go simple for the dress, but kept within Emma's personal bohemian style. I wanted her to be comfortable in it and feel like herself. The shoulders were bare, but a lace draping went around the top of the dress adding more support and ending above her elbows. The dress was fitted against the stomach and then billowed out slightly around the hips, before ending in a short train with more lace detailing.

"I'll get your measurements when we get home and then we can look at fabric together so that you get something you like."

"Thank you." She set the sketchpad aside and reached out to hug me.

I hugged her back fiercely. She might be driving me nuts with her meddling, but she was still my best friend. We'd grown up together, shared each other's good moments and the bad ones too, and I knew I was lucky to have her on my side.

The front door opened and Emma thrust the sketchpad into my hands. "Hide this before Maddox sees," she hissed.

I hurried for the stairs and had only climbed three when I felt eyes glued to my ass.

"Where do you think you're going?" His voice poured over me like sticky honey, rooting me to the spot.

I casually looked over my shoulder, taking in his tousled black curls and searing brown-eyed gaze. He could be so intense sometimes.

"To my room," I answered, finally finding my voice.

He opened his mouth to say something, but Maddox strolled by then and asked him a question.

The spell was broken.

I ran up the rest of the stairs, and the next set as well.

I was out of breath from the climb, but my racing heart? That was all Ezra.

I quickly put my sketchpad away before joining everybody outside for volleyball.

"I think we should do guys versus girls." Hayes declared. The other guys nodded in agreement.

"That's not fair," I argued, "There are four of you and three of us since Remy's sitting out."

"I'll sit out." Mathias volunteered. His eyes already strayed to Remy where she sat a few yards away on a beach towel with her hands resting on her round stomach.

The other guys nodded at his declaration. They probably didn't want the liability of having him on their team anyway, since he'd be distracted checking on Remy every five seconds. Hopefully he'd relax once she had the baby, but somehow I doubted it.

"So, now are we good with guys versus girls?" Hayes asked me, grinning widely.

"I don't know," I shrugged, "depends on if you're ready to lose or not."

"Ooh," Hayes mock-winced, "the trash talking has begun already. Me likey."

"Shut up." Emma glowered, and stole the ball from his hands.

"Somebody woke up on the wrong side of the bed." Hayes whispered conspiratorially. "Maddox, you better do a better job of making sure your woman wakes up happy. You know, maybe a little oral in the morning."

Emma gasped and threw the ball at his head. It bounced off and Ezra caught it.

Hayes rubbed the side of his head, and mumbled something, before joining the other two guys on one side of the net.

"We better beat them." I told Emma and Arden.

"Oh, it's on," Emma agreed, still glaring at Hayes.

"I'm not very good at sports," Arden admitted, glancing over in worry at Mia.

Mia was sitting with Remy and Mathias. Remy had the little girl sitting in front of her and was braiding her hair.

I quickly went over the rules of beach volleyball with her, but she still didn't look very enthusiastic about playing.

Hopefully Emma and I would be able to pull off a win just the two of us.

We lined up with me on the front left, Arden to the right, and Emma behind in the middle.

Ezra tossed me the ball. "Y'all can serve first."

"Aw, look at you guys trying to be all gentlemanly." I laughed and threw the ball to Emma. "You're still gonna lose," I warned.

"We'll see." He grinned.

Emma served and the ball went over the net. Maddox hit it back over in Arden's direction. She screamed and started to run away, but I managed to bump it back over the net.

"Get your head in the game!" I yelled at her. Yeah, I was competitive. So what?

"Did you just quote High School Musical to me?" She laughed.

The ball came sailing back over the net and Emma ran forward to hit it back over.

"Oh my God," I groaned, "just play."

Arden joined in after that, but it was up to Emma and me to make sure we didn't lose. Poor Arden would never make it in sports. It was a good thing she worked in retail.

We ended up tied and my body pulsed with adrenaline. We were so close. We had this. I knew we did.

Hayes served it and it headed in Emma's direction, but was low to the ground. She dove into the sand and bumped it up. Arden hit it and it went a little higher, but not enough to go over the net. I ran over and spiked it over the net.

It landed in the sand before Maddox could get to it.

"Did we win?" Arden screamed in excitement. "We won, right?"

"Yeah, we won," I grinned, sticking my tongue out at the guys. Childish? Yes, but when you were friends you were allowed to do those silly things without it seeming rude.

Emma dusted sand off her body and I did the same.

"I think I have sand between my boobs," she groaned.

Maddox strolled over and kissed her cheek. "I'd be happy to help you clean them."

"Of course you would." She snorted. "I really do need a shower, though."

"Good, me too. We can shower together. You know, save the planet and conserve water. I'm very environmentally conscience like that."

"Mhmm," she hummed in agreement, "and it has nothing at all to do with getting me naked."

"None at all."

She shook her head, fighting a smile.

We all headed inside to shower and relax for a while. We were all tired from being outside all day.

I grabbed a quick snack before heading upstairs to my room to shower.

The bathroom attached to my room was just as dazzling as the rest of the house. Metallic glass tiles covered the walls and the floor was some kind of white tile that resembled wood. The shower was glass and there was a large Jacuzzi tub. I'd have to put that to use at least once before we left.

I turned the water on and let it get nice and warm before peeling off my bikini and stepping inside.

I felt my stiff muscles instantly uncoil and relax at the feel of the warm water.

I began to sing—don't judge me, everybody did it—and didn't notice when the door to the bathroom opened.

When the shower door jerked open I let out a scream. Ezra stepped inside, his hand falling on my mouth to stifle the sound. "Shh," he warned, his dark brows drawn together, "you don't want anyone to hear you."

The noise coming out of my throat cut off and he dropped his hand.

"What are you doing in here?" I hissed, glaring at him. I refused to let my eyes stray over his body and his hard cock jutting proudly from his body. Nope, I wasn't looking. Not. At. All.

He grinned. "You've been prancing around in that tiny excuse for a bikini teasing me all fucking day. Do you have any idea how difficult this has been to hide?" He pointed to his cock.

I swallowed thickly, pulling my bottom lip between my teeth.

"It's been the best and worst kind of torture imaginable." His voice dropped to a husky whisper. He stalked forward, like a panther cornering its prey. My back hit the tiled shower wall and water poured down around me. He placed his hands on either side of my head and leaned in close. "And now," he continued, "if I don't get to touch you, I think I might die."

"Dramatic much?" I quipped, trying to hide how much my body was reacting to him.

"Just the truth, baby."

*Baby*. I'd never liked pet names. I found them degrading and annoying, but hearing that word roll of Ezra's tongue gave it a whole new meaning.

He continued to hover there, the water pouring down around us, like he was waiting for something.

Finally, he spoke again. "I won't touch you until you give me permission."

I stood on my tiptoes, holding onto the wall for added support. My lips grazed his ear and I whispered, "Touch me. All of me."

Those words seemed to spark a fire inside him, one that burned for me and me alone.

He grasped my hips and lifted me up. I wrapped my legs around his waist and he pressed me into the wall.

He kissed me deeply, like he was trying to memorize the contours of my lips with his.

My fingers delved into his wet hair, tugging him impossibly closer. Our chests were pressed together fully and all he had to do was pull back and move his hips slightly and he'd be inside me.

Our pants filled the steaming air and I moaned into his mouth.

His hands palmed my ass and he lifted me up slightly, breaking our endless kiss.

"Hold onto my shoulders," he commanded.

I did as he asked and the moment I did he thrust inside me. We both let out embarrassingly loud moans. He'd fucked me senseless the night before, and yet somehow it felt like it'd been forever since we were joined like this.

He rested his forehead against mine, not moving his hips as we both struggled to compose ourselves.

When he looked into my eyes I hoped he couldn't see the fear there—the fear that I would never find this with anyone else.

His head moved from my forehead to the crook of my neck and his lips pressed gently against the spot where my pulse raced. Ever so slowly he pulled back slightly and then pushed inside me. He did it again and I thought I might cry. I wanted hard and fast, I didn't want this. This was too much like making love and things like this weren't allowed in our arrangement. Okay, so maybe it hadn't been defined that way, but in my mind it wasn't allowed. This felt too real.

"Harder," I begged, clinging to his wet shoulders.

"No," he growled lowly. He nipped my chin and then took my bottom lip between his teeth before letting it go.

"Please," I panted, trying a different tactic.

"No."

I really hated that word.

I tried to take matters into my own hands and began to circle my hips faster.

He grabbed my hips and held hard enough that I couldn't move them. "I said *no.*"

"Ezra," I begged.

"Stop thinking," he whispered, his lips a breath away from mine, "just feel."

God, I wanted to. I wanted to let myself go and revel in the way it felt to be held and loved so gently by him, but I was scared. So, undeniably, terrified that I'd end up ripping my heart out of my chest and handing it to him in the process.

"Feel, Sadie," he said again, kissing me sweetly. "Feel how good we are together."

Didn't he know that was the problem? We felt too good together. Not just when we had sex, but at all times. He was my perfect other half.

A tear fell down my cheek, getting lost in the shower water.

I didn't know how I would ever find the strength to let this go.

I didn't want to.

But I had to.

I closed my eyes as his lips ghosted down my neck.

He clasped my hands in his and held them above my head. I gasped when he hit something deeper inside of me. "Ezra." I panted his name over an over again. "Ezra. Ezra. Ezra."

I was desperate to touch him, but he held my hands prisoner.

He angled his mouth over mine, and his tongue brushed into my mouth.

I was consumed.

Devoured.

Obliterated.

I did not exist.

Somehow I managed to let go of my thoughts and soon I was hurdling over the edge as an orgasm hit me.

I clung to him desperately, my legs shaking, and he let go of my hands to grasp my thighs.

He pushed into me a little harder, but still at an unhurried pace.

In a matter of minutes I was close to another orgasm.

I cried out, and he tried to silence me with a kiss.

"Fuck," he growled against my throat, nibbling the tender skin there. "Oh, fuck you feel so good. I'm gonna come."

When his orgasm hit he growled low in his throat and burrowed his head against my neck. His wet hair tickled me, but I was too tired to try to move away.

Still inside me, he murmured, "That was fucking amazing."

I nodded.

He gently lowered me to the ground and he slipped free of my body.

Before I knew what he was doing he had my shampoo bottle in his hand, and poured some into his open palm.

"Turn around," he commanded.

I did as he asked.

He lathered the shampoo into his hands and worked it into my hair. He rinsed it out and did the same with the conditioner.

When my hair was clean he reached for the body wash. He worked it into his hands and rubbed my shoulders and my arms, before cupping my breasts.

I leaned against him, absorbing his touch.

His hands roamed over my stomach and my body clenched with desire once more, hoping his hand would venture lower, but he didn't. Instead he rinsed me off and used my shampoo to wash his own hair. I really hoped no one noticed that we both smelled like strawberries.

He turned the shower off and we stepped out. I wrapped the waiting towel around my body and grabbed another one from underneath the sink for him.

When I stood back up he was *right there.* I let out a startled squeak and jerked backwards, knocking into the large decorative vase that had some kind of wooden sticks in it. It fell to the floor and shattered with a loud clamor.

I looked at Ezra with panic in my eyes. "Oh, shit."

He grabbed the towel from me and used it to rub his hair before tying it around his narrow waist. "No one probably heard." He swept his thumb over my bottom lip, like it pained him to not touch me.

I glanced down at the shattered vase. "Yeah, you're probably right."

"I'm always right." He chuckled.

He took my face between his large hands and kissed me long and deep, before stepping back. "I never want this to end."

He said the words so quietly that I didn't believe I heard him right, and was convinced they were merely a figment of my imagination.

He headed out of the bathroom without a backwards glance and I stood there, hating myself for letting my feelings get the best of me.

"What are you doing in Sadie's room in only a towel?"

Ice drenched my veins. Oh, we were so fucked and not in the good way. I *knew* someone had to have heard the vase break and of course it would be Emma. I had the worst luck on the planet.

"There was a spider in the shower. She screamed and I came running over to see what was wrong."

"And you got wet in this shower?"

I peeked around the edge of the bathroom doorway, but I couldn't see Emma. All I could see was Ezra standing there, wet, in nothing but a towel. Normally this would be a wonderful sight to see, but not right now.

"Well, the shower was running so yes I got wet. But I came from my bathroom, where I'd been taking a shower, which is why I'm in a towel."

Man, Ezra could lie pretty well under pressure. It was kind of scary.

"Mhmm, I'm sure that's what happened," she said doubtfully. "Is everything okay though? We heard something crash, so that's why I came up here."

"Uh, a vase might've been broken in the process of trying to kill the spider. It was huge. Mammoth sized. And fast. I'm lucky I escaped with my life intact."

"Yeah, well, I'm happy to see you're alive. Try not to hurt yourselves too much *killing spiders.*" She said the words like they were code for something. Maybe they were.

I heard her steps retreat away and a second later Ezra closed the door and turned to look at me. Panic shimmered in his dark eyes.

"We are so screwed."

# CHAPTER SEVENTEEN

IT WAS OUR third night at the beach house and Ezra and I hadn't had any more close calls. But that was only because we were doing our best to ignore each other.

"Where are we going again?" I asked Emma.

"I can't remember the name," she said, pulling on a pair of flowered wide leg pants. She was also wearing a white crop top. "But it has karaoke."

"Karaoke, great," I mumbled.

"Hey, it'll be fun," she said, swiping a clear gloss over her lips.

I leaned closer to the bathroom mirror, blending my eye shadow. I was going for a sultry smoky eye. I'd curled my hair and braided a few pieces before pulling it back into a bun. The dress I chose was hot pink with a dipping neckline and a short skirt. It made my already golden skin appear even darker.

Remy was already dressed in a simple long black dress, accented with a necklace. Her blonde hair was styled straight and she wore her signature red lipstick.

Arden hadn't joined us. She wasn't going out, instead she was staying home with Mia. I felt bad ditching her, but she had insisted that the rest of us not stay behind because of her.

Since my dress and eye makeup was bolder I opted to wear a nude colored lipstick with a pale pink gloss on top.

When my makeup was done I grabbed my strappy pale pink heels and put them on. Not to sound egotistical, but I knew those heels made my butt look amazing and my legs impossibly long. Even if Ezra and I were trying to avoid each other right now, so that we didn't get caught, it didn't mean I couldn't try my best to drive him mad.

We headed downstairs to meet the guys. They were all hanging around the TV, but looked up when we approached.

Ezra looked at me like a starving man seeing food for the first time, and I'd be lying if I didn't say it made me feel good.

I knew the others were speaking, but I couldn't hear a word they said.

For the moment, all that existed was Ezra and I.

His hands rubbed against his jeans and he bit his bottom lip. I wanted desperately for him to take me in his arms and kiss me, but that was impossible.

"You look beautiful," he said.

They were innocent words. Words he'd spoken to me many times in the past through our friendship. But somehow, right now, they felt different. The others didn't notice though, so maybe the difference was merely a figment of my imagination. Something I conjured up in an effort to make his feelings as strong as mine. I had to keep reminding myself that while I wanted more with him, he didn't want the same. Friends. We had to remain friends.

The others moved around us, heading to the door, and I snapped back to reality.

I hastily turned away from him, breaking the spell he'd cast over me. For the moment at least.

"Is Hayes not coming with us?" I asked, noticing that he'd disappeared.

Emma turned to give me a puzzled look. "Did you not hear him when he said he wanted to stay with Arden so she wasn't here alone?"

"Uh, must've missed it," I muttered.

"Are you okay?" She asked, genuine concern coloring her tone.

"Yeah, yeah," I rushed to assure her, "I think the sun is just getting to me." I laughed it off and then my body went ramrod straight when I felt the commanding presence of Ezra behind me. My whole body reacted to his proximity. It was entirely unfair. My only saving grace was that I was starting to believe that he wasn't as immune to me as he seemed.

"Should we go?" Ezra prompted.

"Oh, yeah." Emma seemed to realize that Maddox, Mathias, and Remy were already outside waiting.

We all managed to pile into one SUV, so that the other was left in case Hayes and Arden needed it. When we got home, or if I got a chance to catch her alone, I'd have to ask Arden what was going on with the two of them.

Great, now I was going to act like Emma.

Scratch that, I wasn't asking Arden anything.

I would not be the annoying, nosy friend like Emma. God, I loved the girl, but she was getting on my last nerve. She kept bringing up 'killing spiders' in small talk and then eyeing Ezra and me for a reaction. She'd yet to get one. We were masters of disguise. Okay, so not really, but neither one of us wanted to deal with the drama-fest of our friends finding out we had a friends-with-benefits relationship. They'd be mad, tell us we were stupid, and that we should stop immediately. While stopping would probably be the best thing to do the thought of it scared me more than anything else ever had and filled me with a pain far worse and than the crippling betrayal I'd felt when I caught Braden cheating on me. God, that seemed like a lifetime ago.

"We're here," Ezra said, bumping my elbow and jarring me from my thoughts.

I looked up to see that we were outside a shack looking building. It had bamboo sides and what looked like a straw roof. A neon sign decorated the front. It was pretty non-descript and I wondered how anyone ever found this place since there were no other establishments nearby.

We filed out of the vehicle and into the building.

It was pretty busy, which shocked me. I figured it would be empty.

A hostess greeted us and led us to a table, setting the menus down.

We were seated near the stage, where karaoke was well underway. The poor girl up there now was butchering a Mariah Carey song. I was pretty sure my ears started to bleed.

"Ow." Ezra winced.

At least I wasn't the only one that thought the girl was horrible.

When she finally finished the song I sent up a prayer that she wouldn't sing again.

She didn't.

I eyed the menu and ended up ordering a cheeseburger and salad. It seemed safe enough, and I could trick myself into thinking I was being healthy.

"So, are you guys going to sing?" I asked, eyeing Maddox and Mathias. Mathias was the lead singer of the band, but Maddox could sing too. Ezra, however, sounded like a dying cow when he sang. I knew this because I dared him to sing one time.

"Nah," Mathias shook his head, draping his arm over the back of Remy's chair, "I don't want the attention."

Remy automatically leaned into his body and smiled up at him. "And what makes you think anybody would be paying any attention to you?"

He cracked a half-smile. "Have you seen my face? And this voice? It's the sound of an angel. The combination is an attention grabber and a panty dropper."

She rolled her eyes at him and reached down like she was going to feel beneath her dress. "Really? Because my panties are still on."

He brushed his lips against her chin and growled, "Not for long." He kissed her then, and not an innocent kiss either. It was the kind that made you feel dirty for looking too long.

"Dude, stop," Maddox groaned, covering his eyes. "I'm too young to see this."

Mathias punched Maddox in the arm, all without breaking his kiss with Remy. That took some major skill.

Finally he pulled away and Remy was left breathless. Somehow her lipstick was still perfectly in place and none lingered on Mathias' lips.

Now that Remy was available to talk, I said, "So, ladies, does that mean we're going to sing?"

"Absolutely," Emma chimed.

Remy grimaced. "And this is when I wish I could drink. I hate the thought of doing this stone cold sober, but for you guys I will. The Willow Creek ladies have to stick together." She held out her fist for a bump. Emma and I quickly obliged.

I liked that. The Willow Creek ladies. But I couldn't help feeling like I wasn't really a part of that term. After all, Remy was married to Mathias and Emma would soon be married to Maddox. I was nothing but the friend, the outsider. I existed on the fringes, but not a part of the actual family. I knew if I voiced that aloud everybody at the table would tell me I was crazy, even Mathias, but it was how I felt.

Our food came and we all chatted while we ate.

We continued to talk after the food had been cleared away. It was nice for all of us to hang out and it reminded me of what things had been like before I started dating Braden. Remy hadn't been a part of our group then, and Mathias had kept to himself, but we all clicked.

"Alright, ladies," Mathias slid his chair back and crossed his hands behind his head, "it's now or never. Quit stalling."

Remy glared at him. "We're not stalling, we were having a conversation."

He reached over and rubbed her shoulder. "It's getting late. We need to head back soon. The baby—"

"Okay, okay," she agreed, and her face crinkled with worry, "you're right. One song and then we're out of here. Sound good?" She turned her attention to Emma and me.

"Yep." Emma stood quickly, nearly knocking her chair over. Luckily Maddox caught it before it fell. "Oops." A blush stained her cheeks.

"Have fun," Maddox told us, sliding Emma's now vacant chair into the table.

We went over and put our names on the list and picked a song. We were next, which didn't give us long for the nerves to set in. I knew I didn't have the best voice in the world, but I wasn't horrible. Emma was amazing though. Her vocals were featured on several of Willow Creek's songs and she even had a duet with Maddox.

The guy on stage finished his song and we were handed microphones.

"Ready?" Emma asked.

"Of course," I answered.

Remy took a deep breath, her face slipping into a mask of confidence. "I got this."

We all laughed and then stepped up on stage.

Maddox, Mathias, and Ezra began to clap for us before the song even began and Maddox threw in a loud whistle for extra effect.

The music began to play and the lyrics to Fifth Harmony's *Worth It* appeared on the screen.

Emma started singing the first part. Maddox hollered and pumped his fist in the air.

I came in next, feeling bold and daring I started to move my hips to the song. I shimmied and tried to be as sexy as possible.

If Ezra's darkened gaze, and the way he carefully covered his lap with closed palms, was any indication then I was doing a pretty good job.

Remy took the next part and she wasn't bad at all. Although, it wasn't that difficult to sound better than the girl who butchered Mariah Carey.

We took turns singing verses and even the other two joined in with the sexy dancing. I was shocked when Emma started swaying her hips, and running her hands through her hair sexily, but the fact of the matter was loving Maddox had made her more comfortable in her own skin.

The song ended and the room erupted into cheers—mostly from the guys, but whatever, it still counted.

We bowed and my hair brushed the stage floor.

We hopped off the stage and joined the guys. They'd already paid the bill so we headed outside to the car.

As we were about to exit the building I was jerked roughly into a darkened hallway by Ezra.

Before I could make a sound his lips crashed down on mine.

He pulled away within seconds, but I was still left breathless.

He grabbed my hand and put it over the hard-on straining against the zipper of his jeans. "Do you feel that?" He asked unnecessarily, but I nodded anyway. "That's what you do to me. I'm hard for you all the fucking time and it's killing me." He pressed his forehead against mine. "*You're* killing me…but I can't walk away. I don't want to."

With one last tender kiss to my forehead he tore away and I was left alone, but the ghost of his lips and words still lingered.

# CHAPTER EIGHTEEN

I BLINKED MY EYES.

One time.

Two.

The sight before me was still there.

"What the hell are you guys doing?" I asked.

Maddox looked up at me from where he sat on the floor beside Emma. "We're having a hedgehog race."

"I need some coffee," I mumbled, striding into the kitchen. Surely once I had coffee all of this would make more sense.

When I returned to the living room they were still on the floor with dividers set up and each one held their pet hedgehog.

"We need to set some rules," Maddox declared, lifting the hedgehog up to perch on his shoulder.

Emma sighed. "What kind of rules is a hedgehog going to understand?"

"Shh," he scolded her, reaching up to cover Sonic's ears, "he'll hear you."

Emma shook her head. "I say we just let them go and whichever one gets to the end first is the winner. Stop trying to make things complicated."

I sat down on the couch, drawing my legs underneath me and sipped at my coffee as I watched them bicker.

"Fine." Maddox relented, and scooped Sonic off his shoulder.

"What's going on?" Ezra asked as he yawned. His hair stuck up wildly around his head, making him adorably rumpled, and to torture me even more he was shirtless and wearing only a pair of loose gym shorts that left my ovaries panting. Yes, panting.

"They're having a hedgehog race," I answered.

He shook his head. "I need coffee."

I raised the cup to my lips to hide my smile. I'd said the same thing.

Ezra returned and sat down beside me. The couch dipped with his added weight and I drifted towards him.

"How'd you sleep?" He asked, making small talk.

"Awful," I supplied.

"And why was that?"

I shrugged, pretending not to know. "I got cold."

He smiled. "Hmm, we'll have to get you some extra blankets."

"Yes, hopefully that will suffice."

Below us, Maddox began to count. "One, two, three."

They let the hedgehogs go.

Aquilla, Emma's hedgehog, laid down and refused to move.

Sonic veered off to his right, knocking down the makeshift divider they'd made from cardboard.

"I don't think they like this game," Emma whispered conspiratorially.

"Sonic is clearly the winner, though." Maddox argued.

"He didn't do it right!" She countered.

"At least he moved," Maddox reasoned.

She shook her head. "Fine, whatever, Sonic wins."

"Thanks for seeing things my way." Maddox grinned and leaned over to kiss her cheek.

She tried to feign that she was mad, but it didn't last for long. Soon she was leaning into his touch and giggled when he kissed her neck.

I wanted that so bad, that sweet carefree kind of love, but the problem was I wanted it with someone that didn't want me forever. I was nothing but a temporary pleasure and I hated that I'd reduced myself to that, but when you wanted something as bad as I wanted Ezra you'd do things you never thought you were willing to do. Maybe, I'd hoped that he would change his mind once we were together that way, but despite the things he said we were still nothing but a dirty little lie. Hiding from our friends, and even ourselves.

"Are you okay?" Ezra asked, his fingers lightly grazing my thigh before jerking away as if he'd forgotten we were in the presence of our friends.

"Yeah, why wouldn't I be?"

More lies.

Lies.

Lies.

Lies.

So many little lies, that I didn't even know what the truth was anymore.

He looked at me like he didn't believe me, but I stood up and left for the kitchen before he could say anything else.

I started pulling out the cartons of eggs, cheese, and spinach, to make omelets for everyone.

I heard footsteps entering the kitchen and my body tensed. "I said I was okay!" I snapped.

"Whoa! What did I do?"

I jerked. That wasn't Ezra.

I turned around quickly, nearly rolling my ankle in the process, and found Hayes entering the kitchen.

"I thought you were someone else," I confessed.

"Obviously," he muttered, musing his sandy colored hair. He passed me and opened the refrigerator so that he could grab the orange juice. "I'm assuming you thought I was Ezra." He said the words slowly, like he was dropping a bomb and waiting to see what I would do when it blew up.

His tanned, muscled, back was to me as he poured the juice

I still hadn't spoken when he turned around and eyed me over the rim of the glass. "You gonna answer me?"

"I wasn't planning on it."

"No answer, is an answer." He smiled gleefully and took a sip of the orange juice. "What did he do?"

I narrowed my eyes. I didn't want to have this conversation with anybody, but definitely not with Hayes. He'd been so sweet to me and I'd thrown away any possibility with him because I was so hung up on my best friend.

"Ah," Hayes snapped his fingers together, a dimple appearing in his cheek when he smiled, "it's what he *didn't* do, isn't it?"

"He's just being a guy," I finally replied, "besides, friend's fight."

Although, this wasn't really a fight since I was mad at myself, and my stupid, illogical, feelings.

"Uh-huh," Hayes nodded, "*friends*. Sure."

"I don't know what you're implying." I played stupid as I got back to work making breakfast. Maybe if I ignored him long enough he'd go away.

He didn't.

Instead, he made himself comfortable by leaning against the counter right in my personal space. If he was trying to intimidate me into spilling the beans it wasn't going to happen. I grew up with a brother, sister, and two nosy parents whom I all loved dearly, but it taught me to keep my mouth shut on things better left unsaid.

"So, Arden," he started, and I breathed a sigh of relief over the subject change, "what's her story?"

"Why do you want to know?" I asked. I wasn't just going to hand out free information. The boy had to work for it.

He shrugged his lean shoulders and tried to appear nonchalant. "She seems cool."

"Are you interested?" I continued to pester him. Yeah, I knew I was doing to him exactly what I hadn't wanted him to do to me, but he brought this subject up so he should've known it was coming.

"Maybe." He set his glass down and propped his elbows on the counter. "Obviously there's not a guy in the picture…" He trailed off, wanting me to fill in the blanks.

"Her husband left her shortly after she got pregnant." He opened his mouth to speak, but I silenced him with a glare. "That's all I know. She's my friend, but I haven't wanted to pry. I can tell it's a sore subject for her. I don't think he was a very nice guy."

His lips pursed in contemplation and he grew quiet.

Minutes passed and finally I stopped what I was doing and looked up at him. "She's a nice girl and she has a kid. Don't try to pursue something with her if you're not serious about it."

Hayes cracked a smile and leaned forward. "Yeah, I know. I wouldn't fuck her and bail. I'm done with being like that. Empty, meaningless, sex isn't worth it to me anymore. I want someone to share my life with, not just my bed. And Arden…I really, really like her."

I couldn't believe how honest and open Hayes was being with me. I was used to the fun, joking Hayes, not one that carried on such serious conversations. I liked that I was getting to see a different side of him.

"Don't hurt her," I warned him. "She's a good person and she doesn't deserve to have her heart broken."

"Hey," he held up his hands in surrender, "don't give me the third degree before I even fuck it up. Have some faith, Westbrook."

I shook my head at him and turned towards the stove.

A tingling sensation came over me and I knew instantly that Ezra had entered the room. Whenever he was near my body tingled. I should've known Hayes wasn't him.

"Hey," he said softly.

"I'm going down to the beach." Hayes announced suddenly. "Just yell for me when the grub's ready."

He hightailed it out of the kitchen like his ass was on fire. For all I knew maybe he did feel the simmering heat of the flame that burned between Ezra and I.

I didn't bother to turn around and acknowledge Ezra. I continued on making breakfast, like his presence didn't affect me at all.

He said nothing as I finished making one of the omelets. I grabbed a stack of plates and slid the omelet out of the skillet onto the top one. I picked up the plate and handed it to him.

"Hungry?" I asked.

I wasn't mad at him. On the contrary, I was mad at myself for expecting more. I was pathetic.

He grabbed the plate and opened a drawer to grab a fork. He speared a bite and I watched as he raised it to his mouth and chewed, waiting for his reaction.

"Not bad," he cracked a smile, "in fact, it's pretty damn good."

I smiled despite my dour feelings. I set about making the rest and I was sliding the third onto a plate when he spoke again.

"Would you be opposed to going somewhere with me today?"

I arched a brow and set the skillet aside. "Just the two of us?" I wondered.

He nodded, striding over to the sink to wash his plate. "Yeah, just you and me."

"What do you want to do?" I questioned, crossing my arms over my chest as my suspicions rose.

He shrugged casually and stared at me from across the kitchen island. "I can't tell you."

I let out a sigh. Despite not knowing what he had planned, I refused to say no. "When do I need to be ready?"

"After you eat breakfast," he mused. "And wear something stretchy."

"Stretchy?" I repeated. What the hell did he have planned? "We better not be biking. That shit makes my vagina hurt, and don't get me started on guys. Seriously, where does your junk go? It's one of the many mysteries of the world."

He snorted. "Sadie, you're one of a kind. And no, we're not going biking. Think outside the box a bit more." He winked and then strode out of the kitchen, leaving me alone to wonder what he was up to.

No matter how much I racked my brain I couldn't come up with one single idea.

"Ezra," I whined, looking out the window as he continued to drive farther and farther away, "where are you taking me? If you wanted to kill me and feed my body to the sharks we could've done that back at the house."

He stopped singing along to the radio and chuckled. "Come on, you have to have more faith in me than that."

"My faith in you sailed away approximately five minutes ago. We've been in the car for an hour. I'm going stir crazy."

"Be patient."

"Why does my gut tell me I'm not going to like whatever it is you're up to?"

He grinned and shook his head like I was oh-so-cute. I wondered if he'd still think it was cute when my panic caused me to jump out of a moving vehicle.

Ten minutes later we turned into a parking lot in front of a plain building. I swung my head around wildly, looking for a sign or any sort of clue to the origins of the building.

"High Flyers," I read. "Please tell me you're not making me jump out of a plane. I know you did that with Maddox and Emma, but I'm not as brave as Emma," I admitted.

"No planes." He assured me and got out of the vehicle.

I hastily followed after him. "Then what is this place?"

"You'll see."

I was tempted to run back to the safety of the car, but something told me he'd only chase after me and drag me back.

He opened the glass door to the building and waved me in ahead of him.

We were standing in some sort of lobby. The floors were a beige tile and the walls were a pale yellow.

I rubbed my hands together nervously as he strode over to the counter and spoke with the lady sitting behind it.

She answered him and I saw her point to a doorway.

"This way." Ezra nodded his head.

I followed him and when I saw what was behind the door I thought I might throw up. "No, no, no, *no* fucking way am I doing this."

I darted for the door and he caught me around my waist, dragging me into his body.

"I'm going to die," I said dramatically. "I will fall to my death."

"You'll be fine," he chuckled, "there's a net."

"So, you're implying that I will fall?"

"Well, you have to get down somehow."

"I can't do this." My stomach rolled, looking up at the sight before me once more.

We were in a training facility of some sort and above us were these *things* hanging from the ceiling. People held onto the bars and jumped from one to the next. One man hung upside down on one, holding a woman's hands in his and spun her around. In another corner of the gym long pieces of fabric hung from the ceiling with a woman spinning from one, exactly like we'd seen at the circus.

"Ezra," I started, throwing in a dramatic gulp for good measure, "this was awesome when we saw it at the circus, but there's no way in hell you are ever getting me up there."

"Come on," his hand landed on my butt and he gave it a small squeeze, "it'll be fun. It's something we'll remember forever."

I wanted to argue with him that I would remember every single moment we shared together for the rest of my life, but I knew he'd just find another argument for getting me up there.

"If I die you better tell my parents that I love them…and tell my brother that I was the one that broke his BB gun when we were little. He was really mad about that and I blamed the dog."

Ezra snorted. "Anything else?"

"Not at the moment, but something might come to me before I plummet to my death."

He shook his head, trying to hold in his laughter and failing miserably. "If you're falling to your death then I hardly think you can impart any last words."

I shrugged, rearing my head back to watch as the man swung back and forth gaining momentum before throwing the woman into the air. She easily caught onto one of the metal bar things.

"Then I guess the world will never know my last words of wisdom. 'Tis a shame. Maybe we should leave before the world has to deal with the burden of such a loss?"

He crossed his arms over his chest. "Or maybe you shouldn't be such a scaredy cat."

"Scaredy cat?" I wrinkled my nose. "What are we? Five?"

He chuckled. "You're the one acting like a baby."

"Ooh," I mock winced, "that hurts, Ezra."

"Just calling it like I see it." He smiled innocently.

"You must be Ezra and Sadie." A voice sounded behind us.

I turned around hastily and had to rear my head back to see the face of the man standing there. He was so tall that he made Hayes seem short. He had to be at least six-foot-seven.

"That's us." Ezra reached out to shake his hand.

The man held his hand out to me next. I placed mine inside his open palm and watched it nearly disappear in his gigantic grasp.

"I'm Oscar. I'll be your instructor today."

I glanced over my shoulder once more and gulped.

"Don't be scared," Oscar said, drawing my attention back to him, "it's not as scary as it looks."

"I don't believe you," I muttered.

He chuckled, amused by my words. "You'll change your mind once you get up there."

"Why?" I asked, curiously.

He shrugged and a look of contemplation stole over his face. "Because," he replied, "when you're up there…it feels a lot like freedom."

I sighed and lifted my hands in the air. "Alright then, let's do this."

"Are you sure?" Ezra questioned. He might've been pushing me to do this, but he'd never make me do anything I absolutely didn't want to do.

"Yeah," I nodded, steeling my shoulders, "let's go make some memories."

Oscar went through countless instructions and made us do several exercises on the ground before letting us go up high. We weren't made to wear harnesses since there was a giant net beneath the bars to catch us. I would've felt better wearing a harness, but I didn't say anything. I'd already made enough of an embarrassment out of myself.

We climbed the ladder on opposite sides. Oscar chose to come with me. I think he was afraid I'd chicken out. But I'd committed to this. Besides, seeing how happy Ezra was and the effort he'd gone through to make this happen was pretty sweet.

I'd learned that Oscar, and all the professionals here, were a part of a circus in Orlando. This was their training center and they were on a break right now, preparing for a brand new show opening in a few weeks.

I watched as Ezra pulled one of the bars towards him. When he grabbed the bar he hung from it upside down, swaying in the air. I let out a scream like I was the one swaying like a pendulum.

"Your turn," Oscar spoke.

I shook my head. "I can't do that."

"You don't need to do it upside down. Just grab it like we practiced down below."

My feet tapped restlessly against the platform. "I can't do this," I whimpered.

"Come on, Sadie," Ezra pleaded. "For me."

I closed my eyes.

*For him.*

I reached out and jumped, grabbing onto the bar. I screamed as I swung back and forth, my feet dangling below me. I had no idea how far the fall was, and I hadn't wanted to ask. Instead I kept reminding myself that there was a net that would catch my fall.

My arms began to burn. "I'm going fall," I cried.

Ezra swung towards me. "Jump to me."

"No! Are you crazy?!" I shrieked, trying to hold myself up. Running clearly wasn't doing anything for my upper body strength. I was going to have to work on that.

Ezra's face was turning bright red from hanging upside down. "Do you trust me?"

I squished my eyes closed. "That's a stupid question."

"Sadie," he growled, "do you trust me?"

"Yes!"

"Then fucking jump. I've got you. I've always had you."

My throat closed up and I swung back gaining momentum.

I waited until I was in the right position and I let go, hurtling my body towards him.

I reached for his hands and he caught mine, somehow managing to hold onto me.

"See," he said, "I'll always catch you when you fall."

"Except when you drop me onto the net," I mumbled, my legs swaying.

He laughed, but it sounded more like a cough since he was upside down. "But it'll be a gentler fall."

I guess I couldn't argue with that.

"Ready?" He asked.

"Ready," I answered.

He let me go.

He was right. It was a gentle fall.

But when we inevitably ended I knew the fall would be anything but gentle. It was going to be fucking brutal and I wondered if either of us would come out unscathed.

# CHAPTER NINETEEN

EZRA AND I spent the whole day together after leaving the training facility. We did random silly things, like racing go-carts and hanging out at this little diner. We laughed and joked, and for the moment at least it felt like we were the old Sadie and Ezra. We had no pressure from our friends, or ourselves.

When we returned to the house it was already getting late and the sun was setting.

"I thought you guys were never going to get back," Emma cried impatiently.

"Did you miss us that much?" I laughed, setting my bag down and kicking off my flip-flops.

Ezra walked past me, his arm grazing mine in the process and headed into the kitchen.

"We're going out," Emma declared.

"We are?" I raised a brow. "I didn't know."

"Well neither of you would answer your phones," she huffed, tapping her foot impatiently. "There's a club Hayes wants to go to. Mathias and Remy are staying behind and watching Mia, so Arden's going too."

"What does that have to do with me?" I questioned, dropping into one of the chairs in the living room. Mathias sat on the couch and raised his chin slightly in greeting.

Emma followed and perched her butt on the coffee table in front of me. "Maddox and I are going too, and so are you and Ezra."

I raised a brow. "Maybe I don't want to go."

She shook her head. "You know, you were always the one pushing me to do things out of my comfort zone. *You* were the crazy one in this friendship that had all this experience and now you act like an old lady."

I snorted, fighting a smile. "I am old."

"I'm sorry," she said, grabbing my hand, "I'm really not trying to be bossy, and I'm sorry I keep coming across that way. I don't know what's wrong with me lately…" She paused, taking a breath. "But we only have one more day here and I wanted us to spend tonight and tomorrow together. Once we get home things will get crazy with the wedding and it'll be hard for us to have any girl time."

I frowned. I could see where she was coming from. We'd also both been far too bitchy to each other lately and I knew it was my fault. If I would just confess everything that was going on to her I knew this tension would disappear, but I just wasn't ready to talk about it. I knew she wouldn't approve of our arrangement. She wanted to see us together as a real couple, not as fuck buddies.

"I'm in…but you better let me do your hair and makeup."

She winced. "Just don't make me look like a hooker."

"And when have I ever done that?"

"Middle school. Lauren Hanagen's thirteenth birthday."

I laughed. "I think I've learned a few things since then. Have no fear, you're in good hands."

"So what are we doing?" Ezra asked, walking into the room with a bag of chips in his hands.

I glanced over at him and said, "We're going clubbing."

"That sounds like a disaster." He mumbled around a mouthful of chips.

Emma threw her arms in the air. "Y'all act like this is a death sentence."

"I'm sure it'll be fun as long as no one gets a roofied drink."

Emma threw a pillow at him and Ezra tried to duck away, but it still collided with his shoulder before falling to the ground.

Backing into the kitchen he held his phone up and waved it around. "It's getting late, so you ladies might want to get ready. I know it typically takes you five hours."

This time I was the one to throw a pillow at him and his laughter carried from the kitchen all the way into the living room, and I couldn't help but smile.

I finished styling Emma's hair in a loose fishtail braid and moved on to Arden.

I'd already done my own hair and makeup. I chose to straighten my hair since I'd been leaving it wavy so much and left it down. For my makeup I'd gone in a more dramatic direction—red lips and smoky gray eyes.

"I'm not sure I should go." Arden frowned, biting at her nails. "What if Mia needs me?"

I smacked her hand away. "Mia is already asleep. She's not even going to know that you're gone. And if for whatever reason she would wake up Mathias and Remy will be here. Plus, we all have cellphones if we need to get ahold of each other. It'll be fine."

I wanted Arden to go out and have fun, even if it was only for one night. Being a single mom didn't afford her much time to do things for herself. She deserved this.

"You're right, you're right," she chanted, like she was trying to convince herself.

I went to work curling her long red hair and then fluffed it out with my fingers.

"Thanks for letting me borrow this." She pointed to her clothes.

Arden hadn't packed any "party" clothes as she called them, so I'd lent her some to go out. Since I didn't have a spare dress, she was wearing a pair of black skinny jeans, and a gold-sequined strapless peplum top. It looked amazing next to her vivid red hair. We wore the same shoe size so I also lent her a pair of black pumps. She wobbled a bit in them, but I doubted Hayes would leave her side tonight so I wasn't worried about her falling over.

"Ladies," I said, giving them each a once over and then myself in the mirror, "I think we're ready."

Downstairs the guys were waiting for us. They were all dressed casually in jeans and t-shirts. No surprise there.

"You look beautiful," Maddox told Emma, his eyes moving from her head down to her toes and back up again. Even after being together this long his words still made her cheeks tinge pink.

She was dressed in a sparkly flapper style dress in colors that reminded me of a mermaid.

Maddox nuzzled her neck and kissed her cheek before they headed to the door. Arden and Hayes were right behind them, which left Ezra and I alone for the moment.

I hadn't looked at him when I entered the room, but now I lifted my eyes to his.

The look in his eyes could be described in one word. Hunger.

He was starved for me, and I reveled in that fact.

I loved knowing that my very presence had an affect on him. That it killed him that right now he could only look and not touch.

"That dress," he growled lowly, his eyes scanning my body slowly like he was savoring every inch.

"You like?" I did a little spin, showing it off. The dress was short and tight, but had three-quarter sleeves and covered me fully in the front. The back, however, was open to just above my butt and crisscrossed at my shoulders. The fabric was purple and shimmery, so it appeared to sparkle any time the light caught it.

"Fuck." He groaned, looking pained, and scrubbed his hands down his face.

I couldn't hide my grin. I loved being desired by him and pushing him past his breaking point. I wanted him to lose control.

I turned and headed for the door, purposely putting a little more sway in my hips than usual.

I heard him let out a string of curses behind me and I smiled like the cat that ate the canary.

I could feel things changing between us and I was scared as to where it was headed, but for tonight all I wanted was to feel his hands on my skin.

Music poured out of the speakers so loud that I wanted to cover my ears, but then I'd just look like an idiot. I couldn't believe that as a teenager I'd liked this sort of thing. While my teen years technically hadn't been that long ago, it felt like a lifetime. I'd changed and matured so much in the last few years. Okay…matured, not so much.

 Inside the club was far nicer than the ones I'd snuck into when I was in high school.

The ceiling had these unique triangle dropdowns that glowed with different colors and the floor was shiny and clean—not covered in a layer of sticky grossness like most were.

The bar was lined with every drink imaginable and backlit in varying colors like the triangle tiles on the ceiling.

"Boys," I patted Ezra on the shoulder, "why don't you go grab a table and some drinks."

Ezra eyed me, his hands shoved into the pockets of his jeans. "And what are you ladies going to do?"

I grabbed Emma and Arden's hands. "Dance of course."

Before either of them could protest, like I knew they would, I dragged them onto the dance floor.

It was a fast paced song that immediately had my heart racing.

"I can't dance," Emma whined.

"I *shouldn't* dance," Arden interjected. "At least not like this. I'm a mom." She glared at the people around us with disdain in her amber colored eyes.

"First off, you can dance." I pointed a finger at Emma. "Secondly," I narrowed my eyes on Arden, "just because you're a mom doesn't mean you lose all sex appeal. Own it, girl."

When neither of them moved I started to dance. I reached out and grabbed Emma's hips, getting her to sway in time to the music. Once she had it I set my sights on Arden, but I was pleasantly surprised to see that she was already loosening up. She was clearly still nervous, and rather awkward, but I knew in a matter of minutes she'd let the rest of her reservations go.

Since both girls seemed to be fine on their own now I closed my eyes and let myself enjoy the moment.

All that existed was me, the music, and how it made me feel.

I swayed my hips, lifting my hair off of my shoulders when my skin began to dampen with sweat. There were a lot of people packed in here and the air was stifling, but it was all a part of the experience.

Three songs later I finally opened my eyes and saw that Emma and Arden had disappeared.

I searched the crowded dance floor for them and came up empty.

Feeling irritated I started towards the tables.

I finally found them sitting at a large booth with the guys.

I stuck my hands on my hips and gave them both the most withering glare I could muster. "You bitches ditched me."

Emma giggled. "We were thirsty." She pointed to her drink.

I shook my head. "What are you even drinking?" I asked, sliding into the booth beside Arden.

Emma lifted her brightly colored drink. "I have no idea, but it's delicious. We got you one too." She pointed at a drink in the center of the table.

I took it and cringed. It was too sweet for me, but it packed quite the punch. For someone like Emma, who didn't drink much, she'd be wasted in thirty minutes… maybe less.

"Are you drinking?" I asked Arden.

She shook her head. "No."

I couldn't blame her. She had a kid and dealing with a hangover and a three-year-old in the morning would be killer.

"Hey, hey, hey," Hayes chanted, lifting his drink in the air. "We should toast."

"To what?" Ezra asked.

Hayes' lips twisted in thought. "To the Willow Creek family and all the adventures that are headed our way."

"Hell yeah I'll toast to that." Maddox lifted his drink—which I'd bet was diet Pepsi, since he was tonight's DD, and tapped it against Hayes', before we all followed suit.

I downed my drink, and upon seeing the empty cup Ezra signaled someone over to our table.

Without me even getting a chance to open my mouth, Ezra ordered me a new drink—something completely different than the one I'd had. I'd bet money Emma had ordered the first drink for me, and of course Ezra had noticed that I detested it. But hey, it was doing its job of getting me buzzed, so it was still a winner in my book.

"Thanks," I mouthed to him, where he sat across from me.

He waved his hand in dismissal.

Emma finished her drink and bumped Ezra to move so that she and Maddox could slide out of the booth.

"Outta my way!" She cried. "I want to dance with my man!"

Maddox snorted, fighting a grin. "I think someone's buzzed already."

"Absolutely not." She pouted, standing with her hands on her hips.

Maddox leaned down and took her lips between his, kissing her long and deep. She melted into his touch and then they disappeared onto the dance floor.

Beside me Arden let out a dreamy sigh. "Is it just me or are they the cutest couple ever?"

"They are," I agreed.

"I've seen cuter," Hayes piped in.

Arden and I swung our gaze in his direction. "Like who?" I questioned, as a fresh drink was set down for me.

"One time I saw these two puppies that were clearly in love. Their little tongues kept hanging out and their tails were wagging. It was the epitome of cuteness." He grinned easily, stretching his arm out along the back of the booth.

"Aww, that sounds precious," Arden cried, clasping her hands together.

At the same time, I said, "You're so full of shit."

Arden narrowed her eyes on me. "That was an adorable story."

"And you're drunk."

She wrinkled her nose in confusion. "I'm not even drinking."

"Exactly."

I finished my drink and stood. "See you losers later. I'm going to get my dance on."

Before anyone could protest I stepped back and allowed my body to be carried away by the crowd.

The room was pulsing with energy and you couldn't help but respond to it.

I let the music flow through my veins as I swung my hips to the beat of the song. My arms swayed above my head and I truly let myself go for the first time on this trip.

I closed my eyes and the glowing lights glittered behind my eyelids.

One song blended into many and my body grew damp with sweat as my heart beat like a drum.

A smile touched my lips when I felt arms wind around me from behind.

I'd recognize the feel of that body anywhere.

"Do you have any idea how long I've been watching you?" He growled lowly in my ear, his teeth grazing my lobe. "You're so fucking sexy it was killing me that

I could only look and not touch. It was like having my favorite candy dangled in front of me and saying one bite would kill me."

"And yet," I panted, leaning my back against his front as I opened my eyes, "you're here touching me."

"I decided it was worth the risk."

"They might see us," I warned.

I waited for him to say he didn't care, that he wanted me and it didn't matter anymore—that this arrangement was futile and he wanted me forever, as his future and not just his temporary pleasure.

But he didn't say that.

Instead he whispered, "Then we'll just have to make sure they don't see us."

I squished my eyes closed once more, silently reminding myself that I was being silly. He was sticking to our agreement and I couldn't fault him for that. But my heart was breaking a little more every day and the sex—as amazing as it was—wasn't enough to keep me whole. I couldn't keep doing this to myself, and I vowed in that moment that once we got home I'd find my own place. This needed to end before I broke completely, but for now I would let myself enjoy the feel of his body wrapped around mine for just a little bit longer. Selfish? Maybe so. But if I was going to be forced to go the rest of my life without him then I wanted to make the most of every second we had left.

"Sadie." He prompted when I'd been silent too long.

"Just dance with me."

He obliged.

I never knew Ezra was such a good dancer, but the way he moved his body against mine should've been a crime. It was one of the most erotic things I'd ever experienced, and he wasn't even being sexual about it. Not at all, actually. He felt the music and it pulsed through him and into me. It was like the beat of the song made us one.

His hands roamed down my hips to my thighs, and back up again. His fingers edged underneath the bottom of my dress and I hissed between my teeth as my core clenched. But he didn't move his hands up any further. He kept them right where they were, every once in a while his fingers would lightly stroke my skin and I would clench again.

I wound my arms behind me and around his neck. He burrowed his head against mine, nipping at the spot where my neck met my shoulders, and then smoothed the spot with a slow flick of his tongue before pressing his lips to the spot.

I let out a long moan.

Jesus Christ, the way the man could affect me was entirely unfair. He knew how to stroke and play all the right strings on my body.

"Sadie." The way he breathed my name made me shiver.

"Please," I begged. I didn't even know what I was begging him for.

To say my name again.

To touch me.

To love me.

I felt his fingers flex against my thighs, the pressure increasing as he pulled me more fully against him.

I rolled my hips and smiled in satisfaction when he hissed between his teeth.

"Fuck, Sadie."

"Yes," I purred, "fuck Sadie, please."

I didn't care that we were in the middle of a dance floor surrounded by people. I needed him to touch me in all the ways I needed to be felt.

"We can't." He breathed, sounding like those two words pained him.

"Ezra," I panted his name and I felt him growl in approval at the sound, "I need you. Here. The bathroom. The wall. The fucking car. I don't care. Take me, I'm yours."

His fingers tightened against my skin even more and I wouldn't be surprised if I found bruises in the morning, but I didn't mind. I wanted him to brand me physically the way he was already branded on my heart and soul.

I turned around so that we were now facing each other and let him see the desperate want in my eyes.

"Sadie, you've been drinking…" He trailed off.

My palms landed on his hard chest and slid up around his neck, where I curled my fingers into the silky strands of his hair. Despite our conversation we both kept moving to the beat of the song.

"You know two drinks will hardly get me drunk," I argued.

"Fucking hell." He muttered, and kissed me right there on the dance floor.

For the moment, at least, he didn't seem concerned about getting caught.

He nipped my bottom lip and I moaned into his mouth.

He tasted like cool lemonade on a warm summer's day.

"Touch me," I begged, "I need you to touch me."

I needed to get my fill of him before I was forced to say goodbye, but something told me I'd never feel satisfied.

His hands roamed up my sides, the pads of his thumbs grazing the undersides of my breasts concealed by my dress.

"More," I pleaded.

"Fuck being good," he growled, taking my hand and pulling me through the crowd. He barreled past people, making sure they didn't ram into me.

I didn't look around to see if our friends saw. My head was too clouded with lust to care.

He found a hallway and dragged me down it.

I had no idea where we were going, but Ezra seemed to be navigating the space with no problem.

He reached out and pushed a door open and we stepped into a back alley. It was littered with trash and there was a dumpster nearby.

He led me away from the mess and before I could blink he had my back pinned to the brick wall and his lips devoured mine. His kiss was nothing like the one inside. This was rough, and tinged with desperation, like he too felt that time was running out for us and wanted to make the most of it.

I started pulling at his shirt, but he grabbed my hands and pinned them above my head.

"No." He glared at me.

"But—" I protested.

"No," he said again, "I want you. God, believe me I do," he ground his hips into mine so that I could feel how much, "but not here. This, right now, is about your pleasure. Not mine."

I opened my mouth to argue that his pleasure was mine, but he silenced me with a breath-stealing kiss.

He broke the kiss when my brain grew foggy from lack of oxygen and his lips trailed down my neck and over my collarbone before he sunk to his knees in front of me.

He glanced up at me and his dark eyes were hooded with lust.

"Do you trust me?" He asked.

"I think I proved that today," I panted.

He let out a husky chuckle. "That you did."

His hands skimmed up my calves and thighs, disappearing beneath the dress. He grabbed the sides of my underwear and pulled it down roughly until it stopped at my ankles.

"Step out of them," he commanded.

I did as he asked and watched as he stuffed my underwear into his pocket.

He looked up at me again and licked his lips in anticipation. "Hold on."

"Huh?"

I let out a small squeal of fright when he grabbed my legs and placed them on his shoulders. He pushed the bottom of my dress out of his way and looked at me one more time. "Ride my face like you mean it, sweetheart."

And then his mouth was on me and I lost all trace of coherent thought.

Pleasure hummed in my veins and my limbs grew weak. He seemed to sense this and grabbed my ass to hold me steady.

"Ezra." I panted his name over and over again in the darkened alleyway.

I leaned my head back against the wall, looking at all the stars that shimmered above us. They were the only witness to the sublime pleasure Ezra was giving me. The stars saw everything. Oh, the secrets they could tell.

I felt my body begin to tighten and my legs shook. "I'm going to come," I warned, my back arching against the wall. "Oh God," I moaned. "Ezra!" I cried out his name loud enough that people nearby probably heard.

His tongue swiped against me one last time and he lowered my legs to the ground. He kept ahold of me as he stood, and brushed the dirt and gravel off of his pants with his free hand.

"Fuck you taste amazing," he growled, turning me on all over again. He swiped his thumb over his bottom lip and sucked it into his mouth. Damn him. My body was coiled tight with the need to sink myself down onto him, but I knew he wouldn't allow that.

I leaned up and kissed him, the taste of me lingering on his lips. "I think that's the hottest thing anyone has ever done to me."

"Go down on you in an alley?" He questioned, raising one dark brow.

"When you put it that way it sounds gross, but it was…incredible." I grabbed onto his shirt, my body leaning heavily against his. He wrapped an arm around me and started leading me towards the door we'd come through.

"I'm glad you thought so…it was equally as pleasurable for me."

"But you didn't get off," I whispered, like it was some sort of secret.

He grinned down at me. "Giving pleasure can be as good as receiving, and that," he nodded behind us at the alley, "was fucking amazing."

I bit my lip, wishing desperately that we were anywhere but here right now so that I could make love to him the way I wanted.

Whoa, *no*.

Not make love.

We didn't do that.

We fucked.

Because we were friends with benefits.

And that was it.

Ezra held my hand through the darkened hallway, but once we reached the main room he let go.

We found the table and all our friends, who looked grumpy and irritable.

"Where have you been?" Emma asked, her eyes were filled with worry, but her words were laced with anger. "We've been looking for you guys for forever."

"We were dancing," Ezra replied. I didn't know how he appeared so at ease after what we did. My body was still shaking with after shocks.

"We checked the dance floor five times," she argued.

"Must have missed us." Ezra shrugged indifferently. "Are you guys ready to go?"

"Dude, what the fuck is on your jeans?" Maddox sputtered, eyeing all the dirt and gravel still stuck to Ezra's jeans.

Ezra looked down and shrugged again. "Huh? That's curious."

"Curious," Emma shook her head, "y'all think we're so dumb." She muttered something to herself and then glared at us both. "Why don't you both do us all a favor and admit you're madly in love and fucking like rabbits behind our backs? Okay?"

Before either of us could protest she was out of the booth and hurrying towards the exit.

Maddox smiled apologetically and hurried after her.

Ezra let out a hefty sigh and mused his hair. "Well, I guess that's our cue to leave."

Hayes and Arden slid from the booth and we all headed towards the exit.

The ride home was completely silent and I knew Emma was beyond irritated. I hated having my best friend mad at me, especially when I knew it was my fault because I wasn't being honest with her. But I couldn't tell her, not yet at least. She'd get her hopes up that things would work out with Ezra and I, and we'd ride off into the sunset on the back of a white horse.

Or worse…

She'd tell me I was crazy and that I'd ruined everything. That by doing this I was not only going to break my own heart, but lose Ezra in the process.

Not just as a lover.

But as my best friend too.

# CHAPTER TWENTY

"I DIDN'T EVEN drink that much and I've already thrown up three times this morning." Emma groaned beside me, a book propped on her knees. For now at least, she seemed to have forgotten her irritation with me. "I think this is my first official hangover, though. Does that make me an adult now?" She laughed.

I rolled over onto my stomach so that the sun could tan my back. "You barely had enough to drink to have a real hangover, so no you have not been inducted into adulthood. Secondly, if you're so hung over how are you reading?"

She sighed, turning the page. "It doesn't make me as nauseous as looking at the ocean does." She lowered her book and eyed the ocean, as if testing herself. She gagged and mumbled, "No," before returning to her book.

I pillowed my head on my arms and closed my eyes. It was our last day at the beach. Tomorrow morning we were flying home, and I knew everything was going to change once we got there. So to say I felt a little melancholy at the thought of leaving was the understatement of the century. I was downright sick and it had nothing to do with the two drinks I had last night.

"Hey, I brought you some water," Maddox said, sinking down into the sand beside Emma.

"I love you." She took the bottle of water from him and gulped it greedily.

"Here's one for you too."

I lifted my head to see that he was leaning around Emma and offering me a bottle.

"Oh, thanks." I took it. The cool water soothed my dry throat.

Instead of lying back down I stayed sitting, watching Hayes and Ezra fight over a soccer ball down on the beach.

I couldn't help smiling at the way they bickered over the ball, pushing each other out of the way—but all the while laughing.

I stood up and slipped my flip-flops on.

"Where are you going?" Emma asked.

"To play."

I grinned and ran towards the guys. They didn't see me coming and I jumped on Ezra's back. He grunted from the surprise attack, but quickly held the back of my knees so I didn't fall.

I knew Emma would probably try to make something out of this, but I'd been doing things like this with Ezra long before we started having sex, because he was one of my best friends. I'd lost sight of that fact the last few weeks. I knew when our arrangement came to an end it might also destroy our friendship, so selfishly—even if it was only for right now—I wanted to forget all about the sex and remember why it was that we were friends to begin with.

"How do you expect me to play with you hanging off my back?" He jested, glancing over his shoulder with a half smile.

"I don't. I wanted Hayes to beat you."

Hayes grinned and pointed a finger at me, while kicking the ball back and forth. "That's my girl!"

Ezra let out a growl and I poked him in the ribs so he would stop.

"Actually," I dropped off Ezra's back, "I wanted to join you."

"Sure," Hayes nodded. "As long as you're okay with losing."

I grinned widely. "I never lose."

Before he could blink I stole the ball from him and started running up the beach, kicking the ball as I went.

"Get her!" I heard Hayes bellow, which only made me laugh harder.

I made it a few more feet when an arm collided with my middle and I was jerked against a chest.

I kicked my legs wildly as Hayes dragged me into the ocean.

"Let me go!" I laughed, fighting against his hold.

On the beach Ezra laughed hysterically.

"Nope. Cheaters have to get punished."

I had a three second warning before he plunged me into the water. Luckily none got up my nose, but he was going to pay for that.

Hayes was a hell of a lot taller than me, but I grabbed onto his arm and pulled, dragging him deeper into the water.

"Westbrook, you're like a fucking piranha." He laughed, letting me drag him. I say letting, because we all knew he was strong enough to escape my hold.

"I do have sharp teeth." I flashed him a menacing smile. Well, as menacing as I could muster.

"I'm terrified." He pretended to shake.

I let him go and started to swim back to shore. "By the way," I called to him, "I'm not a piranha, I'm a siren, and you've just been led to your death." I began to cackle as evilly as I could, but I knew it sounded pathetic. I didn't care though, because this was the most fun I'd had in a long time.

Hayes swam towards me, sweeping the longer strands of his sandy hair away from his eyes.

"Apparently your siren buddies didn't like me too much. I was too handsome to kill." He joked as we stepped onto the beach once more.

Ezra stood with his arms crossed over his bare chest. His skin had grown tan while we were here and with his dark curly hair and eyes he reminded me of a Greek god of some sort.

"Does this mean I won?" He smiled crookedly, one foot resting on top of the soccer ball.

"Only losers have to ask if they've won." I winked at him as I adjusted my bikini top. When I looked up his eyes were zeroed in on my boobs. If Hayes noticed he said nothing.

Clearing his throat, Ezra said, "I think I'm going to go make a sandwich. Are you guys hungry?"

I nodded.

"Starving." Hayes rubbed his stomach.

"Cool, I'll go…uh…yeah…sandwiches." He was still staring at my chest and apparently my boobs had magical mind jumbling powers.

"I'll help." I clapped my hand on his shoulder and the gesture seemed to snap him out of his thoughts.

Hayes headed on down the beach to where Arden and Mia were building a sandcastle with Mathias and Remy's help. Maddox and Emma were where I left them. Emma was laughing at something he said, and with as crazy as Maddox could be there was no telling what came out of his mouth.

I walked up to them, and Ezra paused behind me.

"Hey, we're going to make sandwiches for everybody. Do you guys want some?"

"Yeah," Maddox nodded, "and bring some diet Pepsi." He waved an empty bottle around.

"You got it," I nodded. I looked at Emma and arched a brow. "Do you want something to eat?"

She turned a bit green at the mention of food. "No. I'm good. Just more water, please."

I nodded. I hoped she wasn't getting sick. I honestly didn't think she'd drunk enough last night to feel so ill, but then again she rarely drank so maybe it just hit her hard.

Ezra and I walked up the deck steps and into the back of the house.

The air-conditioned space felt like heaven. I hadn't realized I'd gotten so warm outside.

I followed Ezra into the kitchen and he got out the meat and cheese from the refrigerator while I grabbed plates. We worked in silence as we made the sandwiches, but it wasn't an awkward silence. The air was charged with the energy between us and I think we were both afraid that if we spoke sparks might ignite.

It was getting harder every second to pretend there was nothing between us. At least for me. It was impossible to know what was going through his mind sometimes. Ezra could be extremely difficult to read since he internalized things. He was the person that stood in the background, carefully reading and interpreting a situation, instead of jumping right in. He liked to know all the facts and predict all the outcomes before moving forward. And maybe that's why he refused to give into what I knew already—that we were perfect for each other—because he was scared, since he couldn't see where it would lead.

He was afraid of losing me forever.

I was afraid of never getting to experience what it truly meant to be *us*.

The rest of the day passed in a blur and as night fell we all gathered outside.

I was dressed in shorts and a lightweight sweater, with a blanket wrapped around me.

The fire pit was lit and we all sat around, roasting marshmallows, and telling silly stories. Mia was asleep, so luckily we didn't have to worry about filtering ourselves.

When my marshmallow was toasted to perfection I layered it between a graham cracker and a piece of chocolate. I took a bite and moaned. S'mores were one of my favorite things ever.

Ezra chuckled beside me and reached out, brushing his thumb against my bottom lip. "You've got some marshmallow stuck."

He swept it away and started to put his thumb in his mouth, but instead wiped it on his jeans when he realized what he was doing.

Across from us on the opposite side of the fire pit Emma cleared her throat and stood up so that we could all see her better.

Eyeing the two of us, she said, "I think we should all play a game of truth or dare."

My body stiffened. Something told me this wasn't going to bode well for me.

"I don't know…" I mumbled.

"It'll be fun," she protested. "Besides, it's our last night here and we might never be able to go on a trip with all of us ever again. Things are changing." She looked around at all of us with a sad look. "We're growing up and starting our own lives." Her gaze settled on Mathias and Remy before moving on to Maddox.

She did have a point there.

"Okay, fine," I agreed.

"Yay!" She clapped her hands together and sat back down, this time propped on her knees.

My stomach coiled with tension.

"Can I go first?" Hayes raised his hand like we were in elementary school.

"Sure," Emma shrugged.

"Cool." He grinned, rubbing his hands together. "Who shall be my first victim?" He looked around at everyone before his eyes settled on me. "I dare you to kiss…" He paused and I expected him to say Ezra, but instead he surprised me. "Arden."

"Me?" She squeaked, pointing a finger at her own chest. "Why me?"

"A little girl-on-girl action never hurt anybody." He grinned widely.

I laughed and shook my head. "Aren't I supposed to get to pick truth *or* dare?"

His smile grew even more. "Not the way I play. There's dare or dare."

"Ooh, that makes it even better," Emma chimed in.

"So…"Hayes sat back, "get to it."

I shook my head and stood up, walking over to where Arden sat.

"Just a quick peck, right?" She questioned.

I shook my head. "Where's the fun in that?"

Her eyes widened and before she could freak out even more I took her face tenderly between my hands and sealed my lips over hers. It wasn't a quick peck like she wanted. Instead I kissed her like I would any guy. I was never one to back down from a challenge. I swiped my tongue past her parted lips and she gasped. She surprised me when she kissed me back and behind us I heard Hayes mutter, "Fuck, that's hot." I threw in a little hair pulling to make it even hotter.

When I turned around I smiled smugly at him. "Was that good enough for you?"

"Yes." His voice sounded like that of a prepubescent teen boy. I noticed he conveniently covered his crotch with one of the outdoor throw pillows.

I sat back down beside Ezra and glanced at Arden. "You taste good," I told her. Hayes made some kind of noise of distress.

Her cheeks reddened. "It's strawberry lip gloss."

"Does this mean I get to dare you now?" I eyed Hayes.

"Uh…sure…I guess." He seemed extremely uncomfortable now.

I tapped my lips, trying to think of something good. "I dare you to shave your legs."

"What?" He gasped. "Come on!" He extended one leg out and pretended to pet it. "Do you have any idea how many years it took me to get a nice fur coat?"

I snorted and everyone else laughed. "Well, I mean I could've asked you to make out with Mathias…so…"

"I'll shave my fucking legs," he grumbled. "Give me the stuff."

I hurried inside and grabbed a razor, shaving gel, and a bucket of water.

I set the bucket of water down in front of him and held the other items out to him.

"Both legs too," I eyed him, "don't get skimpy on me."

He dunked one leg in the water and then slathered it in shaving gel. "Oh, fuck, now not only am I going to be hairless but I'm going to smell like a girl too. I think I would've rather kissed Mathias."

Mathias glared at him, his dark brows knitted together. "Try it and I'll bite your tongue off."

"Sounds kinky," Hayes jested. Taking a deep breath he made the first swipe over his leg. Seeing the bare patch of skin he let out a small fake cry. "I'm so sorry," he muttered to his leg, cracking all of us up.

Once he finished he let out a roar and flexed his arms. "Who's my next victim?" His eyes landed on Maddox. "I dare you to do a handstand for one minute."

Maddox snorted. "That's easy."

"We'll see if you still think that in twenty seconds," Hayes challenged.

Maddox shook his head and stood up. "Start a timer."

I grabbed my phone and set it. "Are you ready?" I asked him.

He nodded.

My finger hovered over the start button. "Go!"

Maddox got into the handstand position and at fifteen seconds cried out, "How much longer?"

"Ha!" Hayes clapped his hands together. "Told you!"

Suffice to say, Maddox only made it until thirty seconds and he wasn't very happy about this fact.

The dares began to escalate. I knew it was only a matter of time before it circled back to me.

Emma eyed me smiling like the cat that ate the canary. "I dare you to give Ezra a lap dance."

I closed my eyes. It wasn't the worst thing she could've come up with, but it was bad enough. I wanted to protest, but I knew that would only highlight the fact that something was indeed going on. In the past I wouldn't have hesitated, because we were friends and it didn't mean anything. It was just a game.

I stood and Ezra grabbed my arm. "Sadie," he started, and when I looked into his eyes I saw what he wanted to say—that I didn't need to do this.

But I did.

I gave Emma a look and said, "Challenge accepted."

I was slightly pissed off, because I knew this dare had an ulterior motive for her.

"If I'm going to do this right, I need some music."

A moment later Mathias' phone lit up and music pumped around us.

Tipping my head at Emma, I began to dance.

Ezra cleared his throat behind me and when I turned to face him I saw that he was looking away.

That only served to spurn me on.

Our friends might've surrounded us but I was still going to make sure he enjoyed this.

I grabbed his chin and forced him to look at me, still swaying my hips to the beat of the song. "Don't think."

He swallowed thickly and his eyes dilated.

I turned back around and lowered my body, rolling my hips against his groin. His hands that had been lying flat on his knees curled into fists. I smiled in satisfaction.

I moved against him as sensually as I could and my hands skimmed underneath my shirt, exposing my stomach.

"Sadie," he growled, grabbing my hips and pulling me more fully against his growing erection.

I removed his hands and turned around to scold him. "Nuh-uh," I wagged a finger in front of his face, "you can look, but you can't touch."

He swallowed thickly and pulled his bottom lip between his teeth.

I laid my hands on his thighs and bent forward so my chest was right in his line of sight—thank God for push up bras—and then moved my hands up his legs, over his stomach, and settled on his chest. His heart thundered madly beneath my palm, like it was racing to escape the confines of his chest. I leaned in and skimmed my lips down his neck and he gasped.

"I thought you said no touching."

"I said *you* couldn't touch. I never said anything about me."

He looked tortured.

I turned back around and practically sat in his lap. I lifted my arms behind me and wrapped them around his neck. All the while I kept moving my body along to the fast pace of the song. I could feel how turned on he was and it made it all worth it. Hell, even I was getting turned on. Bless the poor souls watching us.

The chemistry between us burned brighter than the hottest star.

"That's enough." Emma said and the music cut off.

I moved my hips for a few more seconds before standing and moving back to my chair. I crossed my legs, trying to relieve some of the ache in my center, but unfortunately it wasn't going anywhere.

"Satisfied?" I asked Emma, tilting my head to the side.

She stood with her hands on her hips. "I'll be satisfied when you two finally admit that you're more than friends. I know you think it's not obvious, but it most definitely is," she fumed.

I shrugged innocently. "It was just a lap dance."

She groaned and sat down, muttering, "You're driving me nuts."

Something about her words made me snap. I stood up this time and leered across the burning fire at her. I probably looked menacing but I didn't care.

"Forget a fucking dare," I seethed, spitting the words between my teeth, "I want the truth…why are you so obsessed with my love life? The last time I checked it was none of your business!" The last words were pretty much a lie, yeah my love life wasn't her business but in the past I'd never kept those things a secret from her.

Her face crumbled and I instantly felt like a piece of shit. "I just want you to be *happy*," she cried. Legit *cried*. I made my best friend cry and I felt ashamed of the tear that rolled down her cheek. "That's all I've ever wanted for you. To be happy. Is that such a bad thing?" She sniffled. She wiped at her face and groaned. "I don't know why I'm crying. I'm sorry." She dashed into the house, running away from me as fast as she could.

Upon her exit I was met with silence.

"I'm sorry," I whispered, even though she wasn't there to hear it.

Ezra stood and wrapped an arm around me. He was always there to comfort me when I made a mess of things. I loved him for that.

Maddox stood too and cleared his throat. "She's been really emotional lately…I think it's the wedding. I'm going to go check on her. 'Night."

Without a backwards glance he was gone and I felt even worse.

"I feel awful," I whispered. "I didn't mean to yell at her."

"It's okay." Ezra kissed my forehead.

The others sat watching us. "No, it's not." I pushed myself away from him. I glanced at all of them before my eyes landed on Ezra.

I kept pushing away the people I cared about the most, and what for?

Fear.

I pushed Ezra away, because I was scared of what Braden thought.

Look at how that turned out.

And now I was pushing Emma away because I was scared of what she'd think if she found out the truth.

Fear was a crippling emotion and I hated it. I hated what it was doing to me. I was becoming a monster. I kept hurting the people I cared about the most and that wasn't okay.

"Sadie," Ezra pleaded, reaching for me.

I startled at the worry in his eyes and realized that now I was crying.

I wiped my tears away on the back of my hands and held my chin high. "I'm going to bed."

No one protested when I left.

I couldn't blame them. I wouldn't have stopped me either.

I headed upstairs to my room and took a quick shower. I put on my pajamas and set out my clothes for tomorrow—packing up everything else.

I climbed into bed and willed myself to go to sleep, but not even the soothing lull of the ocean could put me to sleep tonight.

I heard my bedroom door creak open and my body stiffened when a sliver of light poured across the bed before disappearing.

"Go away." I said the words with as much venom as I could muster.

The bed dipped and his warm body slid in behind me. His strong arms wrapped around me and I was too weak to fight him.

"No," he growled angrily in response to what I'd said, "you can yell, and cry, and try to push me away, but I'm not going anywhere. I'm here for you, always. You're my best friend, Sadie, and when your heart hurts so does mine."

I rolled over so that I was facing him and curled my body into his. My fingers fisted his shirt and I burrowed my head into the crook of his neck.

"You're too good to me." I cried into his chest.

He smoothed his fingers through my hair. "No I'm not." He brushed his lips against my forehead. "A good friend wouldn't have used you the way I have."

"You didn't take anything I wasn't willing to give."

"Exactly. That makes me even more of an asshole."

"Do you think we can just forget both of our assholish ways for tonight?"

He chuckled, his laughter rumbling against my ear. "We can do that."

A minute passed. "And Ezra?"

"Yeah?"

"Please, don't let go of me," I begged, my hold on his shirt tightening.

"Never, sweetheart."

I woke up a little after five in the morning.

Ezra was still wrapped around me, his dark hair tousled over his forehead, and his lips parted with sleep.

I sat up, my hair sweeping over my shoulder. I smiled at the sight of him sleeping so peacefully in my bed.

I couldn't seem to stop myself as I reached out and traced my finger over the contours of his mouth. He was entirely too perfect.

I was too restless to stay in bed so I slipped out of his arms and padded out of the room.

The house was silent and I knew it would be hours before the others began stirring since our flight didn't leave until eleven—and since we'd flown in on the record company's private jet that was reserved for Willow Creek's use, we didn't have to worry about being at the airport crazy early to get through security.

I opened the refrigerator and blinked rapidly at the sudden brightness. Once my eyes had adjusted I reached inside and grabbed a bottle of water.

I sat down at the kitchen table and looked out the window at the darkened ocean as I sipped at my water.

I tried my best to silence my mind and it must've worked, because I didn't notice when Ezra came into the room.

"Are you okay?"

I jumped at the sound of his voice and looked over my shoulder to see him standing there adorably rumpled in his pajamas with his round Harry Potter looking glasses perched on his nose.

"Yeah," I nodded, "I'm fine."

"Do you mind if I sit?" He motioned to the chair.

"I don't care."

I expected him to sit in one of the empty chairs, but instead he picked me up and took mine, before depositing me in his lap.

I settled against his chest as my body automatically curled into his. We felt so right together.

"You know more about me than anybody." I whispered into the darkened kitchen and tilted my head back so I could see his reaction.

His dark brows furrowed together and he gave me a peculiar look. "I'm your best friend. I'm supposed to know."

"Yeah…but don't you think it's more than that? Like maybe…" I trailed off, brushing my fingers against this collarbone.

"Maybe what?" He asked, his eyes drifting away from me as he looked out the window. It seemed like he didn't really want to hear what I'd been going to say.

"Never mind," I sighed.

While I felt that my connection with Ezra was deeper than friendship, he clearly didn't feel the same way. I'd thrown away our friendship once, and I refused to do it again by trying to pursue a feeling he didn't even return, although I was afraid I was going to end up losing our friendship anyway. It would be too hard being close to him and not being able to have him. I used to pride myself on being a strong girl, but even the strongest people eventually reach their breaking point. This was mine.

I sighed and leaned my head on his chest, wrapping my arms around his neck.

"I love you," he whispered, kissing the side of my forehead, "you know that, right?"

"Yeah." And I did know it. I also knew he didn't love me in the way I wanted him to.

"Good." He took my chin and tilted my head up so that he could kiss me.

"Ohhh shit."

I jumped away from Ezra, falling onto the floor and bruising my butt in the process.

Hayes stood in the kitchen with a hand slapped over his eyes.

"I saw nothing. I know nothing. I am nothing."

I snorted.

"I am a mist. I do not exist," he chanted, backing out of the kitchen with his eyes still covered. His hand fell suddenly and he grinned. "Oh, hey, look at me rhyming. Maybe I could be a rapper."

"Don't quit your day job," Ezra laughed.

"Yeah, you're right." He grumbled and started to leave.

"Didn't you come down here for something?" Ezra asked him and reached down to help me up.

"Oh, right. I wanted water." Hayes grabbed his water and started his chant all over again. "I saw nothing. I know nothing. I am nothing. I am a mist. I do not exist."

We could hear him still continuing on with his mantra through the living room and up the steps.

Ezra and I both dissolved into a fit of laughter.

"Thank God it was Hayes," he chortled, "and not someone else."

I nodded my head in agreement. That could've easily been a disaster.

"Are you ready to go back to bed?" He asked.

"I think so."

He took my hand and led me up the stairs.

We cuddled into my bed once more and Ezra fell right to sleep. When he'd been asleep for a while, and I knew there was no chance of him hearing, I whispered into the darkness, "I'm in love with you."

# CHAPTER TWENTY-ONE

WE'D BEEN HOME from the beach for two weeks and in that time frame I'd been slowly distancing myself from Ezra. I knew he noticed the change, but he didn't say anything. I could tell from the way his brows seemed to be permanently furrowed together that he was worried about me. I was fine though. Really, I was.

"So, what do you think?" The guy showing me the apartment asked.

This was the fifth one I'd seen in a week, and I felt I'd finally found the one. It was small, the kitchen, living room, and bedroom were all a part of one space. The bathroom was the only thing that was closed off. But I loved the charm. It had brick walls, an open ceiling, and touches that harkened to the era in which the building was built.

"I'll take it."

"I'll get the paperwork drawn up." He strolled from the room, leaving me alone in the open space. There was no furniture so I'd have to go shopping, but that was okay with me.

I crossed my arms over my chest and strolled over to one of the long windows that overlooked the street below. The apartment was only blocks from my store and if the weather was nice I could walk there. This was going to be good for me. I needed to distance myself from Ezra and the things that could not be.

I tapped my finger against the window and watched outside as a bird swooped down, landing on the edge of the window. It stared at me intently and tilted its head at me before flying away once more.

Behind me the door opened and the landlord stepped back inside. "I'd really like to get a renter in here as soon as possible, so there's no contingency on the move in date. The place is ready for you when you want to move in…as you can see my last renter hauled ass out of here as fast as possible," he griped. "I do require you to pay the first three months up front to lock in the place. Is that okay?"

"It's not a problem." I set my purse down on the counter and listened as he went over the paperwork. It was pretty basic and when he was done I signed my name on the bottom and handed him a check.

Once he had his money he seemed to be in a better mood. He led me outside and told me to have a good day. I waved goodbye and slid into my car, heading over to my store.

I was meeting Emma in thirty minutes for her second dress fitting. As soon as we got back from the beach I'd went to work on making it since time was not on our side. Plus, it was a valid excuse to avoid Ezra. We hadn't had sex since we got back from the beach. I hadn't slept in his bed either, even though he'd asked. A part of me wanted to jump his bones every second of the day while I still had the chance, but it hurt too much. That's why I was moving out. I couldn't shove my feelings to the side anymore and he didn't have any for me, so I wasn't going to fight this.

I pulled into the parking lot behind my store and headed inside.

Arden was working today and she greeted me with a cheery smile. "Hey, I ordered you a sandwich when I got my lunch. I figured you probably forgot to eat. It's on your desk."

"You're a life saver," I told her honestly. I didn't know what I'd do without her.

I headed into my office and set my bag down before tearing into the sandwich. I hadn't realized how hungry I was until she mentioned food.

By the time I finished and washed my hands Emma was breezing into the store. She greeted Arden before heading towards me. I motioned her into my office and closed the door.

"I feel like crap." She declared, sitting down in the chair across from my desk. "I swear I've been fighting a bug for weeks."

"You need to go to the doctor," I scolded her, grabbing her dress from where I'd stashed it.

She waved away my concern. "I don't have time."

I put my hands on my hips. "Emma Rayne you do so have time to go to the doctor."

She rolled her eyes and kicked off her combat boots. "You sound like my mother…only she'd be shoving some kind of herbal tea at me."

"That's because your momma is a smart lady. Now strip down."

She laughed. "Just try not to poke me with seven hundred pins this time."

I glared at her with my hands on my hips. "Then don't wiggle so much."

Once she was down to her bra and panties I went to work helping her into the dress. It'd been a week since she last tried it on and now it looked like a real dress. She couldn't see herself yet and I hoped she loved the dress as much as I did. It fit her perfectly and the design was so her. To say I was pleased with my handiwork was the understatement of the century. It still needed some tweaks, but it was pretty close to perfect.

I covered Emma's eyes and led her over to the floor length mirror.

"One, two, three." I counted and dropped my hands.

Her gasp of delight was exactly what I wanted to hear. "Sadie," tears welled in her eyes, "this…this…is amazing." She twirled around, examining it from every angle. "I love it. I really do."

I grinned. "I'm glad."

I was stunned when she tackle hugged me.

"Whoa," I held her, trying to keep us upright.

"Thank you so much," she cried against my shoulder, "I know I've been such a bitch to you lately, and I'm sorry. Please forgive me."

I rubbed her back. "There's nothing to forgive."

"I don't know what I'd do without you." She stepped back, wiping her face.

"I think you'd be just fine." I laughed and pointed towards the stool. "Stand up there. I need to fix a few things."

She did as I asked and I grabbed my pins and tape measure.

I turned on some music while I worked and we talked for a bit as I marked things and scribbled notes down.

"Sadie," she said suddenly.

"Yeah?" I didn't look up from my notebook.

"I don't feel so good."

I looked up just in time to see her start swaying. "Emma!"

She fainted and fell off the stool. By some miracle I managed to catch her in my arms but I sagged under her dead weight.

"Arden!" I yelled. "Arden! Hurry, please!"

The door to my office crashed open and when she saw me holding Emma her hands flew up to her mouth. "Oh my God! Is she okay?"

"I don't know!" I cried, my body shaking with worry. "Help me lay her down and then call 911."

Arden nodded and rushed forward, helping me lay Emma down on the floor before dashing away for her phone. I grabbed a bundle of fabric from another project I was working on and bunched it under her head. I felt panicked and I kept trying to run through a checklist of things to do when someone fainted, but my mind was empty.

I sat down on the floor beside her and smoothed her hair away from her forehead.

"Emma," a tear coursed down my cheek, "wake up. Please."

"An ambulance is on the way." Arden burst back into the room and knelt on Emma's other side. "I thought this might help." She laid a dampened paper towel over Emma's forehead.

"Do you think she'll be okay?" I asked Arden.

Before she could answer Emma's eyes started to open. When she went to sit up

I forced her back down with a hand to her shoulder.

"Just relax. The ambulance is coming."

"Ambulance?" She asked, blinking her eyes wider. She seemed confused.

I nodded. "You fainted."

"I've never fainted before." Her voice was nothing but a whisper.

"I know. That's why the ambulance is coming. I think you need to be looked over."

She nodded slightly, surprisingly not fighting me on this. Her eyes closed once more, but she wasn't asleep. Her hand felt around blindly and I reached out to hold hers.

The ambulance arrived and everything from there happened in a blur.

I followed the ambulance in my car since the assholes wouldn't let me ride in it and then had to park a mile away.

By the time I made it into the hospital and found her room she'd already had blood drawn and was lying in a bed looking incredibly weak. How had I not noticed how thin and pale she'd become? Or the purple rings beneath her eyes? Had I become so absorbed in what was going on in my personal life that I'd stopped paying attention to the things around me?

"Can you…" Her voice was barely above a whisper and she pointed to a cup of water on a tray beside her bed. Some idiot had put it far enough away that she couldn't reach it.

I grabbed it and held it for her while she took a few slow sips.

When she spoke this time her voice sounded a tiny bit stronger. "Can you call Maddox?"

"Oh! Of course!"

In all the madness I'd forgotten to call him.

"I'll be right back," I told her.

I stepped outside of her hospital room and searched my purse for my phone. The stupid thing was buried all the way at the bottom. I pulled it out and rang Maddox's number.

I never called him and when he answered he seemed to sense that something was wrong. "Sadie?" He questioned, confused as to why I'd be calling him. "Is everything okay?"

I swallowed thickly. "No, it's not." I pressed the heel of my free hand against my forehead.

"What's wrong?" His voice grew high with fear. "Is it Emma? Is she okay? Are you okay?"

"It's Emma. We're at the hospital—"

The line went dead.

I really hoped he didn't get himself killed trying to get here.

Before I could step back into Emma's room my phone was lighting up. Only the caller wasn't Maddox.

"Sadie," Ezra's voice was panicked when I answered, "are you okay?"

"I'm fine," I assured him. "Emma was at my store and we were doing a fitting for her dress and she passed out. She hasn't been feeling well so I made her go to the hospital…although, she didn't protest, so I think she realized it was past time to see a doctor."

"We'll be there in twenty minutes. I've got to go catch Maddox before he leaves. I don't think he should be driving right now."

"That's probably a good idea."

"Bye." He hung up the phone, but not before I heard him yell, "Get out of the fucking car, Maddox!"

I stuck my phone into my pocket and stepped back into Emma's room.

She slowly rolled her head towards me. "You look like shit." I tried to laugh, but it was forced.

"I feel like shit." She tried to push herself up so that she was sitting, but it wasn't working. I rushed over to help her, trying to get her more comfortable. I hated seeing someone I loved so miserable. I hoped it was nothing bad. "I should've gone to the doctor a while ago," she mumbled, "but I've been so focused on the wedding that I just assumed it was stress."

"This," I pointed at her, "is way more than stress."

"Yeah, I can see that now." She nodded at the stark hospital room. "God I hate hospitals. They smile like death and bleach."

I pulled up one of the chairs closer to her bed and sat down. "Do you want some more water?"

She nodded and was able to drink a little more this time. "Did you get Maddox?"

"Oh, yeah." I nodded. "He's on his way…or actually I think Ezra was about to forcibly remove him from his car so that he could drive him. He was afraid Maddox might crash his car or something."

Emma laughed, but it wasn't her normal one. Instead it was more rough and tired sounding. "Maddox freaks out if I get a splinter. I can't imagine his reaction to this kind of phone call."

"He loves you." I defended his actions.

"I know." She smiled. It was a small one, but still managed to glimmer in her eyes.

I sat back and we grew quiet. I knew Emma was tired and I hoped maybe she could drift off to sleep for a little while, but a doctor ended up coming into the room.

"Ms. Burke," the doctor said, stopping at the end of the bed. "We have your results back from the blood test." The doctor was pretty, maybe in her early forties, with black hair and unique blue eyes that popped against her dark skin.

"That was fast," Emma commented.

The doctor nodded. "I had your tests fast-tracked."

That wasn't a surprise to me. Everyone in this town—unless they lived under a rock—knew who Emma was because of her association with Maddox and the whole band. All of them were practically royalty in this town.

The doctor's eyes shifted to me. "Would you mind stepping outside for a moment?"

Emma's eyes widened in fear and she grabbed onto my arm with a surprising amount of strength. "No, I want her to stay. Please. She's my best friend and I don't want to be alone."

"If it's okay with you…" The doctor paused, waiting for Emma to confirm.

"It is." Emma nodded, resolute.

I sat back down once more, hoping this was nothing bad. I wasn't sure I would be the best person to console Emma if the doctor had bad news.

*Please let everything be okay,* I silently chanted.

"Well," the doctor started, "the good news is nothing is majorly wrong with you."

"Majorly?" She repeated. "So something is wrong?"

"Not wrong per se," the doctor hedged.

Emma paled even further and I feared she might pass out again.

"I'm hoping this will be good news." The doctor glanced down at the chart. "According to your blood work you're about seven weeks pregnant."

Oh.

My.

God.

"What?" Emma shook her head and her eyes bugged out. "Can you repeat that? I don't think I heard you right."

The doctor smiled. "You're seven weeks pregnant."

Emma's hand went to her stomach. "I'm having a baby?" Tears filled her eyes and I really hoped they were tears of happiness.

"Yes," the doctor nodded. "We'll do a sonogram soon. We're just waiting on the technician."

"Wow." Emma wiped at her tears. "This is insane." She looked up at me with wonder and awe in her eyes. "I'm going to be a mom, Sadie. How crazy is that?"

"Pretty crazy. But you're going to be an amazing mom." I knew between her and Maddox this baby would be the luckiest kid on the planet.

"I need a tissue," she said, reaching out and failing to find one.

The doctor grabbed one for her and handed it over. "It seems that it's a combination of things that led to your extreme fatigue, the baby being one of those causes. You need to eat more balanced meals and drink a lot of water. I'll be back soon and we'll go over a few things," she said, before leaving.

Emma nodded as she left and continued to dab at her eyes. "I can't believe I'm getting married *and* having a baby."

"Life is changing," I agreed.

My phone buzzed and I stood up. "I'll be just outside the door."

"Is it Maddox?" She asked.

I shook my head. "Ezra."

"Oh. Okay."

I stepped into the hallway and closed the door behind me.

Before the phone could stop ringing I answered. "Hello?"

"Hey, I wanted to let you know I just let Maddox out at the front and I'm parking the car. I thought you should be warned though because he's on a rampage."

"Noted," I said, just as I heard a commotion around the corner. "I have to go."

I hurried in the direction of all the sound and stopped when I saw a cart had fallen over on the floor and Maddox was pushing people out of his way.

"Move! Get out of my way!" He yelled as he shoved people. "My woman needs me!"

I couldn't help but snort at that last part. Emma would throw one of his drumsticks at him if she heard him refer to her as his "woman".

Maddox saw me and ran forward. "Sadie!" He cried. "Where is she?"

"This way." I led him down the hall and pointed to her room.

He didn't pause as he threw the door open and hurried inside. "Emma." His whole body sagged as he collapsed beside her bed, taking her hand in his. His body shook and I realized he was crying. She consoled him, saying something softly under her breath, and running her fingers through his hair. I took a step back, feeling like I was invading on an intimate moment between the two. After all, Maddox was about to find out that he was going to be a dad.

I eased the door closed and slid down against the wall until my butt hit the floor.

I heard the telltale sound of boots slapping against the linoleum floors and looked up to find Ezra hurrying down the hall. Mathias and Hayes were right behind him.

"You all came," I whispered in surprise.

"Of course we did," Hayes replied. "We were worried."

"Is everything okay?" Ezra asked.

"Yeah," I nodded. "It's fine." I wasn't going to tell them about the baby. That was Maddox and Emma's good news to share.

Suddenly I felt incredibly tired. I rose shakily to my feet and Ezra grabbed my arm to steady me.

"I'm *fine*." I jerked out of his hold.

I hated being so angry in a moment like this, but Maddox and Emma's happiness was my pain. She was getting her happily ever after and riding off into the sunset with her Prince Charming, while mine refused to see that I stood right in front of him open and willing to love him. I couldn't do it anymore. I couldn't keep this up.

I started off down the hallway and Ezra hurried after me. "Sadie, where are you going?"

He grabbed my shoulder and I skirted away from his touch like I'd been burned. I whipped around in anger. "I can't keep doing this!" I cried, not caring who heard me. I was done. I wouldn't put myself through this anymore. I couldn't make him love me anymore than I could will the ocean to turn pink. Some things just weren't going to happen ever. I could see now that we were one of those things. "I can't keep tiptoeing around my feelings like they don't exist! I can't fuck you and pretend that it doesn't mean more to me than some quick satisfaction! I love you! I. Love. You. And I thought maybe you loved me too, but it's pretty obvious to me that I was wrong." I wiped at my tear-streaked face. Mathias and Hayes stood a few feet away watching our exchange in shock. "I can see that you're never going to let me into your heart." I stabbed a finger at his chest and he flinched, but I knew it wasn't from the pressure. "I'm leaving," I said the words steadily. "I found a place of my own. So I'll be out of your place today."

Moving out today would be inconvenient, but it had to be done. I'd suck it up and crash at my parent's house for a few days while I bought furniture and had it delivered to my apartment.

Ezra stood shell-shocked. His mouth opened and closed as he searched for words. "You don't need to do this."

I flinched. He wasn't stopping me. He wasn't saying he loved me.

"Yeah," I nodded, "I have to." I waved a hand at him. "You saying that is exactly why I have to leave. My feelings for you…they're far more than what you feel for me and I can't allow myself to get hurt any more than I already have. I know our deal wasn't your idea. I take full responsibility; so don't feel bad, please. I'm a big girl and I knew what I was doing, but I stupidly thought it would help me get over my ridiculous crush on you. I thought if we had sex then you wouldn't live up to my fantasy, or it would get dull after a while…but it didn't. It got better and you… well, I think I fell in love with you long before we slept together. If I'm honest with myself I think maybe I loved you even before I met Braden, but I knew you'd never go for someone like me. And I was right." I took a deep breath. "But I can't turn my feelings off, so I'm leaving."

"Sadie—" He reached for me.

I took three steps away from him. "No," I said firmly. "Don't touch me. Don't try to stop me. Don't say anything. I don't need you to feel sorry for me."

He swallowed thickly and he looked like he was in pain. "I never meant to hurt you."

"I know." I nodded. "You're a good guy, Ezra. Really, you are. This isn't your fault."

I turned to go and he whispered, "I don't want you to go."

I closed my eyes and paused for one short second. "I have to."

I walked away as fast as my legs would carry me and behind me I heard the guys berating Ezra. I even heard Maddox step out of the room and say, "Dude, if you love her make her yours."

But he didn't love me, because if he did he would've never let me walk away.

# CHAPTER TWENTY-TWO

I WAS NUMB.

That was the only excuse I could come up with as to why I wasn't currently bawling my eyes out. Especially considering all the tears I shed over Braden and I hadn't loved him the way I loved Ezra.

God, my life was a fucking mess.

I stuffed all of my clothes and toiletries into my suitcase. It didn't take long until there wasn't a single trace of me left in his house. Selfishly, I hoped a small part of him would miss me. It was stupid, but I wanted him to hurt in some way. Although, his hurt would never compare to the pain I felt when walking out of the hospital and leaving behind my mangled heart crushed in his hands.

I hurried down the steps, my heavy suitcase clomping behind me.

I paused in the kitchen and removed his key from my key ring. I tossed it haphazardly on the counter and it clanked against the goldfish bowl. Toby swam into his lime green castle to hide away from the sound.

"Sorry Toby," I muttered.

A part of me wanted to take the fish with me, but I didn't know the rules when it came to fish-parent custody and I didn't want him to use that as an excuse to come after me.

Although, I guessed if he was going to come after me he would've followed me here, which he hadn't.

"Fuck you, Ezra Collins," I muttered angrily to myself as I threw open the door, "fuck you and everything you make me feel."

Outside I shoved my suitcase into my car.

When I drove away I didn't look back.

I pulled into the driveway of my parent's home and knocked on the door. I had a key, but I didn't want to intrude.

My mom opened the door after only a few seconds.

"Sadie, is everything okay?" She was surprised to see me.

"No." I began to wilt as she pushed open the screen door and pulled me inside. "Everything is a big puddle of suck. Why are boys so stupid?"

"Aw, Sadie." She wrapped her arms around me and hugged me fiercely. "Boys never grow up. That's their problem."

"Is it okay if I stay here for a few days?"

She held me back by my shoulders and nodded. "You can stay here as long as you need to, sweetie. You know that." She took my hand and led me into the kitchen. "Your dad's out back starting the grill, but I made brownies this afternoon. Do you want some?"

I perked up slightly. "Do you have whipped cream?"

"Of course," she said, heading to the refrigerator.

She fixed me a piece of brownie on a plate with whipped cream and chocolate syrup. It was delicious, but it did nothing to fill the gaping hole in my heart.

The back door slid open and my dad stepped inside. "Hey, Princess." He greeted me with a kiss on the top of my head.

My dad was a tall, large, bear of a man. Some people found him scary and intimidating, but he was really a big softy. Especially when it came to my little sister and me.

He pulled out a chair and sat down beside me. "Have you been crying?" His eyes zeroed in on my face. I was sure my mascara was smudged and my eyes were probably red. When I didn't answer he huffed, "Okay, who do I need to punch in the face? If it's that prick you were going to marry I might just run him over with my car."

I laughed. Leave it to my dad to make me laugh even when I felt like curling in a ball to die.

"No, it's not him."

"Richard," my mom said lightly, "why don't you take the burgers out and put them on the grill."

"But—" He protested.

"Now, please."

"Fine." He grumbled. He stood and pointed a finger at me. "She might be dismissing me, but I *will* find out who hurt my baby girl."

He grabbed the plate from her and headed out the back door once more, grumbling the whole way.

"Why don't we go to the living room?" She suggested. "We'll be more comfortable in there."

"Sure…and do you think I could have another brownie?"

She laughed and took the plate from me. "You might as well eat them now. Once your dad starts in on them they'll be gone in minutes."

She fixed me another brownie and I followed her into the living room. The couch was a large black leather sectional that they'd had since my siblings and I were kids. There was still a long streak on the back of it from a silver sharpie.

I sat down and the cushions molded around me.

"Now, tell me what happened." My mom sat down beside me and patted my knee gently.

While devouring my brownie I told her everything. I told her how Ezra had always been there for me, and how great he'd been when I needed a place to say. I even told her about our deal. I explained how I'd always felt around him and how in the past two months I'd discovered that I was in love with him, but that he didn't feel the same way about me.

"Honey," she looked at me sadly, "how would you know he doesn't love you. Did you ever really give him a chance?"

I wiped a streak of whipped cream off of my lip. "He had plenty of chances."

"Well…" She paused. "He's a guy, Sadie. You know how boys are with their feelings."

"I told him I loved him and he just stood there." I looked down at the now empty plate.

"Maybe he was shocked," she defended.

"Hey," I pointed my fork at her, "whose side are you on here?"

She smiled. "Yours. Always. You know that. But I've also seen Ezra enough to know that he's the quiet, guarded type. You're…" She paused, searching for the right words. "You're like a tornado. You blaze through town with this wild energy, not caring what kind of disruption you cause." I pouted and she laughed. "That's not a bad thing, Sadie. I'm just saying he's different. He's the quiet moody poet in the corner while you're the one spinning through the room making a spectacle of yourself. All I'm trying to tell you is not everyone deals with things the same way."

I leaned my head back on the couch. "It doesn't matter."

"Doesn't it?"

I shook my head. "I just want to move past this."

She grew quiet and stared at me for a moment. "I think you should talk to him."

I grunted in response. "I don't think so. I did plenty of talking today."

"It sounds to me like you didn't really give him a chance to respond."

"No, I didn't," I agreed. "But I couldn't stand there in the middle of a hospital and let his friends hear him shoot me down. I know he would've told me that he only ever wanted to be friends and that he was sorry he couldn't return my feelings."

"But how do you know he would've said that?" She argued.

"I just know." I grumbled. "Look," I stood up, "I don't want to talk about this anymore."

"Okay." She sat calmly with her hands in her laps. "The conversation is forgotten then."

"Good," I nodded. Wringing my hands together, I smiled sheepishly. "Are you sure it's okay if I stay here? I found a place of my own, but I need to get furniture and everything."

"You know you don't need to ask."

"Thanks, mom." I lowered and kissed her cheek.

"Are you still hungry after all of those brownies?" She asked, standing up and heading towards the back door. "I'm sure your dad's finished with the burgers by now."

"Nah," I shook my head. "Maybe later. I think I'm going to get my stuff and lay down for a bit."

"Okay." She hugged me, the kind of hug that made me feel like I was going to suffocate, but secretly loved. "Everything's going to be okay." She took my face in her hands. "You'll see."

"I hope so," I replied. My mom had never been wrong before, but there was a first time for everything.

I was sitting at the table eating breakfast when the doorbell rang.

"I'll get it!" My dad called from his den.

My body had completely frozen over.

Could it be?

"Emma!" I heard my dad boom and my shoulders sagged. It wasn't him. Of course it wasn't, but I'd dared to hope.

Footsteps sounded towards the kitchen and then Emma and my dad appeared in the doorway.

"You look a lot better." And she did. Her skin was back to its normal color and there was some pink in her cheeks. She didn't look as tired either.

"I feel better." She pulled out a chair and sat down.

My dad quietly left the room.

"So..." She tapped her fingers restlessly against the tabletop. "I was right about you and Ezra?"

I rolled my eyes. "I'm sure he told you everything."

"He didn't say too much," she shrugged, "but it was impossible not to hear you yelling in the hallway."

"Oh, right." I winced.

She gave me a sympathetic look.

"I really made a fool of myself, didn't I?"

She shook her head. "I don't think so. I think it's about time you stood up for your feelings instead of burying them."

I stared up at the ceiling, my bowl of cereal forgotten. "I tried so hard not to fall in love with him," I whispered.

"We can't control who we love. We just do."

"It just sucks when the person you love doesn't love you back."

Her lips pressed into a thin line, but she said nothing.

"Anyway," I stood up, emptying my uneaten cereal into the sink, "I'm going shopping today for my place. Do you want to come with me? I could always use your opinion."

When I turned back around Emma was smiling. "I'd love to help. And maybe while we're shopping you could tell me all about what's been going on this summer that you tried so hard to hide." She stood and bumped her shoulder against mine.

"We were pretty obvious, huh?"

"You think?" She laughed. "I've always been rooting for you guys though. I just…I guess I always thought *you'd* be the stubborn one about a relationship, not him. It's always been clear to me how he feels about you."

"What do you mean?" I asked, padding down the hall to the tiny guestroom. It had a futon instead of a bed, and my back was aching today from how uncomfortable it had been.

"He loves you. I think he's scared, though."

"He doesn't love me," I protested, shaking my head as I searched through my suitcase for something to wear.

Emma sighed and sat down on the edge of the bed. When I looked over my shoulder at her she seemed torn about something.

"What is it?" I asked.

"Nothing," she responded quickly, too quickly.

I arched a brow.

"It's nothing," she repeated.

"Whatever." I wasn't in the mood to argue with her. We'd done far too much of that the last few months. It was time to put everything in the past.

I dressed in a pair of shorts and a loose top. I pulled my hair back into a ponytail and grabbed my purse.

"I'm ready."

We drove around to the various furniture stores in town and I was able to find everything I needed.

From there we headed to Target so I could get things for the kitchen and bathroom. I had nothing of my own to take to my place, so it was fun to be able to pick out new things. It gave me something to smile about when it felt like my life had gone to shit around me.

All while we shopped I explained to Emma about my arrangement with Ezra, and why I hadn't wanted to tell her. She seemed to see where I was coming from and gave me much needed support.

"I feel like such an idiot," I confessed to her, when we sat down at a little café to get a bite to eat.

She stayed mysteriously quiet, perusing the menu like it was the most fascinating thing she'd ever seen.

"Come on, Emma. You have to have some sort of opinion on my idiocy."

She shook her head and finally lowered the menu. "I think you're both idiots."

"What?" I laughed.

"He's a dumb boy that was too stupid to realize his feelings until it was too late, and you're stupid to have walked away without giving him a chance to explain where he was coming from." She sat back and crossed her arms over her chest, leveling me with a glare.

"What do you mean about that first part?" I asked hesitantly.

She waved away my words. "I said I wouldn't say anything. And Ezra's my friend too, so my lips are sealed." She mimed zipping her lips. "You need to talk to him though."

I shook my head and picked up my glass of water the waiter had left. "I'm not ready. I need some space to clear my head."

She narrowed her eyes. "Y'all better not mess up my wedding. You do remember that he's supposed to escort you down the aisle?"

"Unfortunately, I hadn't forgotten that tidbit of information."

"No fighting at my wedding. I mean it," she warned. "I'll kick you both. Don't doubt me."

I managed to laugh. "I'll be on my best behavior."

Ezra might get the silent treatment, but I'd never do anything to jeopardize Emma's special day.

"Promise me you'll talk to him."

"I promise," I whispered, but we both knew those words were a lie.

# CHAPTER TWENTY-THREE

WE NEED TO TALK.

The four words glared up at me from the screen of my phone.

Please Sadie.

Don't ignore me.

I stuffed my phone in my back pocket. I didn't have time for this. I didn't need him to tell me to my face how he was sorry for everything, and that he'd never meant for any of this to happen, that everything was supposed to be simple until I had to go and ruin it.

I set the shopping bags down on the kitchen counter in my new place. All the furniture had been delivered and Emma had come by to help me unpack. Not that there was really anything to unpack. I think she just didn't want me to be alone.

I rifled through the bags until I found the one with the plates. Once I located it I sat it on the dining room table and took a seat to start peeling off the price stickers.

"This place is nice," Emma commented, looking out one of the tall windows.

"Thanks. I really like it."

She took a seat and grabbed half of the plates.

My phone buzzed in my pocket and her brows rose in interest. "Is that him?"

"Possibly."

She slapped her palms against the table. "I'm getting married in a *week*. Fix this," she hissed.

I rolled my eyes. "I promise that my love life will not interfere with your wedding."

She groaned. "Forget messing up my wedding, think of this as a gift instead. You two working out your problems would be the best wedding gift you could give me."

I eyed her. "Better than your dress?"

"Yep, that would be even better than my dress."

"I don't even know what to say to him." I dropped my head in my hands, the plates lying forgotten on the table.

"Then don't say anything to him. Let him do all the talking."

I nearly rolled my eyes out of my head. "Ezra? Talking?"

"It's true that he's a man of few words, but when he does have something to say it's usually important and you should listen."

"When did you become my therapist?" I jested.

She tucked a piece of unruly blonde hair behind her ear. "When you started being so blind."

I grumbled under my breath. I wasn't blind. I saw what was right in front of me and it was blatantly obvious that he didn't love me. Or, he did, but not in the way I wanted him to.

I finished peeling off the stickers and set the plates in the sink to wash them later.

"Can you do these?" I asked Emma, handing her the bag with the cups.

"Sure."

"Oh, and here's this." I grabbed a spare key off the counter. "I wanted you to have this just in case."

She smiled and tucked the key into her pocket.

While she was helping me with the cups I made my bed since it'd been lying bare.

The place was starting to look better. Even still, I missed Ezra's cozy little cottage on the lake. It felt like home. This still didn't feel quite right, and I was reminded of a quote I'd once seen that said it's the people that make the place, not the things.

After another hour of unpacking shopping bags and putting things away, Emma and I walked the two blocks over to my store for her final fitting.

Remy and Arden were already waiting, because they needed to try on their bridesmaid dresses.

I put Emma in her dress and stood back to admire my handiwork. I might have to add custom wedding dresses as something I offered in my store. It had been hard, but worth it.

Emma spun around, admiring her reflection. "This dress is so beautiful, Sadie. I can't thank you enough." She hugged me fiercely. Into my ear she whispered, "You're going to get your happily ever after too. You'll see."

I wanted to believe her, I really did, but at some point you have to grow up and stop believing in fairytales.

She patted my cheek in a gesture similar to something my mother would do.

"Chin up, buttercup."

I giggled and she smiled at having had her intended effect.

I helped her out of her dress and put it away in its garment bag.

"Alright ladies, you next." I motioned Arden and Remy over.

Originally Hayes wasn't going to escort anyone down the aisle since Emma didn't have another bridesmaid in mind, but after our vacation she'd asked Arden to be in the wedding. Arden had been surprised at first, but quickly agreed. Arden fit into our group seamlessly.

"Don't forget you have to try on your dress too!" Emma warned.

"I burned my dress." I said it as straight-faced as I could.

Her mouth fell open. "Sadie! You better not have!"

I began to laugh and she eased. "You know I would never do that."

"You scared me there for a second. I think my heart stopped." She put a hand to her chest.

"You're feeling okay, right?" I asked, suddenly worried as I pulled the dresses out of the closet in my office.

"Yeah, I'm fine. I've been a lot better since I was in the hospital."

"I'm so excited that our kids will be the same age," Remy beamed, taking the dress from my hands.

"Me too," Emma agreed. "I hope they'll be really close."

"Best friends," Remy agreed.

It was a happy moment, but my heart sagged. I'd once dreamed of having that same conversation with Emma. Only we'd been older and both married. Now she was moving on and starting a whole new chapter of her life without me.

I handed Arden her dress and grabbed mine. We didn't bother with modesty as we all stripped down and slipped into our dresses.

Emma clapped her hands giddily. "You all look beautiful!"

"I feel fat," Remy grumbled, putting a hand over her swollen stomach.

"How far along are you now?" I asked her.

She fanned herself with a spare piece of paper. "Almost eight months."

"You're getting close then," I commented.

"Not close enough," she sighed. "I'm ready to get this baby out. He's killing my back."

"If you're trying to scare me," Emma gulped, "it's working."

Remy laughed. "It's not that bad…sometimes."

Emma took a deep breath. "No more baby talk. I have enough anxiety at the moment."

I looked over Remy and Arden's dresses and everything seemed fine. I hadn't made these, but I had done the tailoring.

I stood so the three of us were lined up in front of Emma. "Do they get the bride's approval?"

She clapped her hands giddily. "They're perfect!" Standing, she threw her arms around us in a group hug. "Guys! I'm getting married in three days! This is it!"

"I still think you should have a bachelorette party," Remy said, grinning widely. "We could go to the bar where I used to work. I'm sure I could bribe Tanner into doing a striptease." She cackled.

Emma wrinkled her nose. "I never wanted a party, and definitely not any stripping."

"You suck." Remy stuck out her tongue and then reached for the zipper on the back of the dress. When her arms didn't reach Arden slid it down for her.

"Maddox and I wanted to keep everything low key." Emma reminded us. "You know us. We don't like to cause a fuss."

"That's okay," I piped in, trying to be positive, "when I get married I'll have the strippers."

Emma rolled her eyes. "Then I'm not coming."

"More strippers for me then." I laughed heartily. I hadn't laughed this much, or this genuinely, since everything blew up with Ezra.

"Amen to that."

I glanced over at Arden in surprise. "What?" She batted her eyes innocently. "Just because I have a kid doesn't mean I'm dead."

We all laughed at that and I couldn't wipe the smile off of my face if I wanted to. Everybody needed girl time now and then.

# CHAPTER TWENTY-FOUR

CHAOS.

That was the only way to describe the mess surrounding me.

For a "small" wedding there sure were a lot of people running around.

I sat in a chair, trying not to wiggle so much as the makeup artist expertly applied my makeup. Across the room someone was doing Emma's hair. Beyond this room people ran through the Wade's house trying to get everything set up in time. The wedding was being held in the backyard, but they were decorating the interior for the event as well.

"I'm so nervous," Emma confessed, her fingers dancing along the arm of the chair. "What if they tell me to say 'I do' and I say 'I don't' by accident?"

I wanted to laugh, but the makeup artist was applying false lashes and I really didn't want to incur her wrath.

"That's not going to happen, Emmie." Her mom breezed into the room already dressed with her hair and makeup done.

"Looking good." I told her mom.

"Thanks, Sadie." She smiled in my direction.

"I'm sweating so bad right now," Emma continued, "I'm going to look like a hot mess, literally, when I walk down the aisle. Oh my God, what was I thinking telling that boy I'd marry him?" She rattled. "We would've been fine without all of this." She waved her hands wildly and the hair stylist scolded her.

Emma's mom pulled out a chair across from her. "Honey," she took Emma's hand, "he loves you and you love him. Stop worrying so much about everything else and focus on that fact, okay?"

Emma nodded. "I think I can do that."

"Alright," she stood, "I'm going to go find Karen and see what I can help with." She turned towards me. "Keep her calm."

"I can do that," I assured her.

The woman doing my makeup finished and went on to Remy.

I'd already done my own hair and the other girl's in a simple fishtail braid.

I slipped into my dress and went to sit beside Emma. Her hair was being styled back in a simple bun with a few strands framing her face.

"Have you talked to Ezra yet?"

I glared at her. "Today is your wedding, Ezra and I should be the last thing on your mind."

"I'm worried about you guys," she confessed with a frown.

"Don't be. Seriously, don't waste your time worrying about us."

"I'll try," she mumbled, but I doubted she'd be able to let it go.

"Think about that cute little baby you're going to have soon." I pointed to her still flat stomach. "And just so you know, I'm going to spoil that kid silly."

She laughed and began to relax. "Yeah, this will be one spoiled baby." She stroked her fingers over her stomach. "You know, this wasn't expected, and I would've liked to have waited a few more years, but…I'm really excited."

"You should be," I assured her. "You and Maddox will be the best parent's ever. And hey," I grinned, "think of all the cute baby clothes Maddox can knit."

She snorted. "He was already going crazy making things for baby Liam," she pointed towards Remy, "he's going to be even worse now."

"I guess this means you guys will be moving out of the guesthouse?" I raised a brow.

She wrinkled her nose and groaned. "Don't remind me. Normally Maddox and I are on the same page, but not when it comes to what kind of house we want. It seems like neither of us will get our way now. With the baby coming, we don't have time to build a house or remodel."

"I'm sure you guys will figure it out."

"Thirty minutes ladies," Karen, Maddox's foster mom, poked her head through the doorway.

"I'm going to be sick." Emma paled.

"You can do this," I assured her.

She took a deep breath. "I feel like my heart is going to beat right out of my chest."

"That's normal." I assured her.

The woman finished her hair, accenting it with a few small white flowers pinned into her hair.

Before Emma could freak out too much I managed to get her in her dress and then gave her a pep talk before it was show time.

We lined up at the French doors in the kitchen that led out into the backyard. All of the windows were lined with lavender tulle and string lights, thick enough that we couldn't see out and no one could see in.

I was acutely aware of Ezra standing in the corner. Even though I told myself not to look every few seconds my eyes flicked in his direction anyway. He was always looking at me too.

He looked amazing in the black tuxedo with his hair tamed away from his forehead. He'd shaved, so he wasn't as scruffy as normal, but there was still a little bit of stubble dotting his cheeks and chin.

Somebody yelled for us to get lined up and he started towards me.

I swallowed past the lump in my throat, hating how my heart sped up the closer he got to me. We were to walk out last since I was Emma's Maid of Honor and he was Maddox's Best Man. You would've thought Mathias might have been pissed that his twin didn't choose him as his Best Man, but he didn't care. He was still too busy flying high about his epic love with Remy to care about anything else.

Ezra crooked his elbow and I slid my hand inside the space.

Someone handed me my bouquet and went over a few more instructions, but I couldn't hear a word they said, because Ezra chose that moment to lower his head and brush his lips against my ear. "We need to talk. You can't avoid me forever."

"I'm not avoiding you." I was surprised by how evenly I was able to say the words.

He made a noise in the back of his throat. "Bullshit. You need to give me a chance to explain. After the ceremony, please talk to me."

"No," I said firmly, "there's nothing to say. Besides, I won't ruin Maddox and Emma's wedding by arguing with you."

"Dammit, Sadie," he growled, anger lacing his words. I'd never heard him sound so pissed and hurt in all the time I'd known him. Ezra was always even-tempered. "You *will* talk to me."

I shook my head as the French doors opened.

Hayes and Arden walked out first, and then Mathias and Remy, leaving Ezra and I to take our places.

He straightened then and we both plastered on fake smiles.

I counted the steps in my head, trying not to think about how tense Ezra's arm felt against my hand or the words he'd spoken.

As soon as I could let go of him, I did, and took my place beside the altar.

The backyard had been transformed into a magical wonderland. Small fairy lights glimmered everywhere and fake walls decorated in green foliage and flowers hid the guesthouse and surrounding homes. The pool was decorated with glowing orbs that floated on the water. I knew when the sun went down it would be even more beautiful.

I giggled when I saw what came out behind us.

Sonic, Maddox's hedgehog, scampered down the aisle in a bow tie with the rings tied around his body.

"Come here." Maddox crouched down when Sonic veered off the path. At the sound of his voice Sonic righted himself and scurried into Maddox's empty hands.

Maddox untied the rings and handed them to Ezra to hold.

He sat the hedgehog on his shoulder and then turned towards the doors.

I felt, rather than heard, Maddox's intake of breath when he saw Emma. It was like with that one single inhale he stole all of the air around us.

I glanced over at him and saw tears shimmering in his eyes, but he was trying to play it cool. Ezra clapped him on his shoulder and said something under his breath.

It must've done the trick, because Maddox let go, letting the tears flow freely.

Since Emma's dad wasn't in the picture her mom was the one that walked her down the aisle.

She placed Emma's hand in Maddox's and kissed each of their cheeks. "I love you," she whispered to the two of them before taking her seat.

Emma handed me her bouquet and flashed a smile as she turned to face Maddox.

The preacher began to speak and I tried to focus on what he was saying, but it was impossible when I could feel the weight of Ezra's eyes on me.

I heard the preacher say it was time to kiss the bride, and Maddox grabbed Emma's face between his hands and gave her a very dramatic kiss before the two of them headed back down the aisle.

"Take these." I shoved the two bouquets I held at Remy and took off away from the ceremony.

I hurried behind the fake walls and ran over to the guesthouse where I grabbed the spare key from underneath the mat and let myself inside.

I knew I couldn't run away from my problems forever, but tonight I had to. I was afraid if I spoke to Ezra I'd either scream at him or throw myself at him. Neither of which was an appropriate option at the moment.

I sat down on the couch and put my head in my hands, trying to compose myself.

I hadn't seen him since that day I walked away in the hospital and I stupidly thought that the time apart would have desensitized me to his affect. Wrong. So, very wrong. If anything it had made things worse.

The door to the guesthouse opened and I immediately jumped into a standing position, turning around sharply. I was braced for a fight, but it wasn't Ezra.

Instead Arden stared back at me with wide eyes. "Are you okay?" She asked, stepping forward hesitantly like I was a wounded animal that might snap and bite her hand off. "You ran away so fast...I was worried."

"I'm fine."

She raised her brows, urging me to be honest.

"Okay, I'm not fine," my shoulders sagged, "but I don't want to talk about it."

"Fair enough." She gave me a sympathetic smile. "I know you really want to hide in here, but they need you for pictures."

I closed my eyes and my teeth snapped together.

"Come on," Arden urged, stepping around the couch to take my hand, "it won't be that bad."

"You have no idea."

If this wedding hadn't been planned for months in advance, I'd be convinced Emma was doing everything she could to torture me.

While we were taking an endless amount of photos the wedding organizers were busy setting up tables and chairs in the backyard.

I found my name written elegantly on a piece of parchment and looked beside my plate to see Ezra's name written down.

Fuck my life.

I sat down just as Ezra appeared. He'd ditched his tux jacket and if anything he looked even more lickable. The sleeves of his white dress shirt were rolled up to his elbows and his slick black tie lay flat.

I quickly turned my head away when he saw me looking.

The chair to my left slid out and he sat down.

"You keep running from me," he drawled, "and yet we keep ending up together. Think there's something to that?" He propped his elbows on the table and tipped his head in my direction, a dark curl tumbled forward across his forehead refusing to be tamed.

"Yes," I agreed and he smirked, "the world hates me."

His smile fell. He leaned forward, his eyes flicking all across my body before he ever so slightly drew his bottom lip in between his teeth. Fuck me. He wasn't playing fair.

His lashes lowered, fanning across his cheekbones, and his breath tickled the skin of my neck. "I'll leave you alone…tonight. But soon I'm going to talk and you *will* listen."

I swallowed thickly, hoping he couldn't see the way my pulse fluttered in my throat.

"Is that a threat?"

His lips quirked up into a crooked smile and he leaned impossibly closer. "No, sweetheart, that's a promise."

I suddenly felt light-headed. Even when he sat back, out of my personal space, I still couldn't seem to get enough oxygen into my lungs.

Our food was served to us, but I merely picked at mine. My appetite was completely gone. I wished I could bow out, but since I was the Maid of Honor I was stuck here.

The tables were cleared away to make room for a stage and room to dance.

Emma and Maddox had their customary dance together before Hayes and Maddox took the stage.

"Emma," Maddox spoke into the microphone, "you haven't heard this song yet and I've been hiding it for a while. This is for you. Only you."

She smiled up at him from the edge of the stage.

He sat down on a stool beside Hayes. He tipped his head in Hayes' direction and the soft sounds of the acoustic guitar filled the air.

With a small smile Maddox began to sing. His voice was similar to Mathias', but softer.

Emma swayed to the song, looking up at her new husband with love shining in her eyes.

I was so happy for her, but that happiness didn't fill the ache in my heart.

"Dance with me."

I turned and looked up at Ezra. I said nothing as I quickly looked away.

He moved to stand in front of me and held out his hand. Other couples were already filling the dance floor.

I saw Hayes dragging a giggling Arden out onto the dance floor.

"Take my hand, Sadie." His eyes pleaded with me. "If you don't you'll regret it."

I wanted to be mean and tell him that I already regretted everything between us and that I could handle one more, but the words would be a lie, and I was done with all of the lying. It was exhausting.

He crooked his fingers, beckoning me to trust him for the moment and to put my hand in his.

Exhaling a deep breath, I somehow found the courage to give him my hand.

He smiled triumphantly and pulled me onto the dance floor.

I couldn't help the blush that colored my cheeks when I thought about what happened the last time we danced together.

He held my one hand and his other settled on my waist, above the curve of my butt, and I stiffened. "Relax," he coaxed. "I'm not going to hurt you."

"You already have." I whispered the words so softly that I thought he might not hear them, but he did.

He pressed a kiss to my forehead and I closed my eyes. "I'm going to make this up to you," he vowed, "you'll see."

I wasn't going to hold my breath.

# CHAPTER TWENTY-FIVE

I CLOSED THE door to my shop and locked it behind me.

The night sky glittered above me with a thousand shining stars and a brief smile touched my lips. It had been three days since the wedding, and I was feeling surprisingly good. It was one of the first days where I'd actually felt like my normal self.

I adjusted my purse strap on my shoulder and walked in the direction of my apartment. The weather had been perfect today, so I'd wanted to walk. Walking helped me to clear my head. It was helping me to gain a new perspective, and maybe the next time I saw Ezra I wouldn't feel quite so angry. After all, none of this was his fault.

I crooked my head back, enjoying the evening breeze tickling the bare skin of my neck. Fall was in the air and I couldn't wait to wear fuzzy pajamas, and drink pumpkin spice lattes every chance I got.

My building came into view, the old brick glowing with a golden hue from the old fashioned streetlights.

My strides quickened and I hurried up the steps, passing one of my neighbors. "Hey, Frankie." I waved at him before grabbing my key and unlocking the door to my place.

I stepped inside and immediately knew something wasn't right.

The floor lamp beside the couch was turned on and I knew it had been off when I left.

I turned slowly, circling the room with my eyes, and stopped when I reached my bed.

My breath was sucked out of me and my whole body shook at the sight of the boy perched on the end of my bed.

"What are you doing here?" I gasped, my purse and keys falling from my hands onto the floor. "*How* are you here?"

He shoved his dark unruly hair away from his eyes and stood with a gentle grace as he untangled his long legs.

He held up a key. "Maddox and Emma let me borrow this."

"They're on their honeymoon," I said stupidly.

"I know." He took a step forward, his boots crunching something. "I've been planning this for a little while."

"Planning what?"

"This?" He spread his arms to encompass the space.

I finally allowed my eyes to leave his face and I looked around me in awe. Everywhere I looked pieces of paper littered the floor.

I bent down, picking up the piece of paper nearest my shoe.

I gasped, my hand flying up to cover my mouth. "Ezra." It was only one word, but I knew he could hear the surprise and overwhelming love behind the word.

On the piece of paper was a drawing of the first time we met. He'd sketched every little detail, and while he wasn't the best artist it was flawless in my eyes.

I clutched the piece of paper to my heart, hugging it against me, wishing that I could squeeze it tight enough to melt inside of me.

A tear brushed against my cheek and I reached up to wipe it away. In the process, my eyes met his.

"You wouldn't let me explain." His voice was soft, hesitant, almost scared. "So I thought I could show you."

"Show me what?" My voice was thick with the threat of tears.

"That I've loved you from the beginning." He pointed to the drawing I held so protectively against me. "There's not been one single moment that I've known you where I haven't loved you. And somewhere along the way, that love became something bigger, something so undeniable that the force of it scared me more than anything else ever has." He took a measured step towards me. "Somewhere along the way I fell in love with you. I think I fell in love with you a long time ago and I was too fucking stupid to admit it, because the thought of loving you and *losing* you was too painful to contemplate. I would rather have you as a friend than not at all." Another step. "But I realized something when you walked away from me in the hospital. No matter what, I was still going to lose you, because being your friend isn't enough anymore, Sadie. I know now that falling in love with you isn't wrong. It's the best thing I've ever done. And I'm so, so sorry that it took me so long to see that." He took yet another step towards me and now no more than three feet separated us. "I've made a mess of things. Please, tell me it's not too late to fix this. I love you. I'm *in* love with you. And I will spend the rest of my life making this up to you if that's what it takes. Forgive me, please."

His Adam's apple bobbed and he suddenly seemed unsure. He clasped his hands in front of his body and rocked back on his heels, waiting for my response.

"How long?" I questioned.

"How long what?"

"How long have you been planning this?" I waved my hand around to encompass all the drawings. There had to be at least a hundred of them, if not more. Some appeared to be larger and more detailed while some were smaller. From where I stood I could see one with Toby drawn on it in his goldfish bowl.

"Since the moment you walked away from me and I realized how in love I am with you. I would've told you then, but you were gone so fast, and I also knew that it was going to take a lot more than pretty words to make you believe me." He shrugged, his hair tumbling forward across his forehead. I itched to run my fingers through its softness, but so much still needed to be said.

"You hurt me." I whispered the words, handing them to him like they were a grenade. "I told you that I was in love with you and you just *stood* there."

"I know," he said sadly, nodding his head, "and I'm sorry for that. I'm sorry for a lot of things. But even if you tell me to walk out that door right now," he pointed behind me, "and tell me you never want to see me again, I'll never apologize for every moment I spent with you." He motioned to the drawings around us. "Not just this summer, but every single time I smiled or laughed with you. I'll cherish all of it forever." He closed his hand into a fist and placed it over his heart.

"I don't want you to walk out that door," I confessed, wiping away more tears.

Damn that boy for making me cry.

A slow smile crept onto his face. "You don't?"

I shook my head. "I want you to stay." I pointed to my heart and I hoped he got my meaning.

"In your heart?"

I nodded. "I couldn't get you out of there if I wanted to. You're too much of a part of me."

He crept closer to me and touched his heart. "You're in mine too, sweetheart. You're in me so deep that I don't know what to do when you're gone. I feel like half of a person."

I took a deep breath and finally I made that final step, the one that closed the distance between us. I leaned my head back to look up at him.

"So what does this mean for us?"

He tilted his head to the side. "I hope it means that you're my girlfriend…" He paused. "Although, I really hate that word, because I feel like it diminishes how much you mean to me."

I reached up and wrapped my arms around his neck and we both sighed at the contact. "No more hiding?" I questioned. "This is real?"

"It was always real, sweetheart." He cupped my cheek. "We were only trying to pretend that it wasn't."

A question glimmered in his eyes and he must have found the answer in mine, because he lowered his head, slanting his lips over mine.

I moaned into his mouth, my body relaxing at the contact. I stood on my tiptoes and my fingers tangled in the curls of his hair as I tried to get closer.

His hands pressed into my waist, moving lower, and I startled when he grabbed my legs to lift me up.

He carried me over to my bed and laid me down. Paper crinkled beneath my back and I pulled away enough to breathe, "Don't mess up the drawings. I want to look at all of them later."

"Later?" He chuckled, brushing his lips so lightly against mine it couldn't even be called a kiss. "How about now?"

I leaned up, finding his ear. "I was kind of hoping my boyfriend would fuck me first."

He framed my face with his hands and shook his head. Before I had a chance to be upset he said, "I'm not going to fuck you, Sadie. Not right now, at least." His voice lowered to a husky whisper and his lips ghosted against my neck over the spot where my pulse raced. "I'm going to make love to you the way I've always wanted to."

I shivered at his words. "I like the sound of that."

He grinned and kissed me again, deeply, with a hunger that could never be filled. I kissed him back just as urgently and with no less passion. As hot as all our other encounters had been we'd both been holding back on the emotion part, and now it was here in full force and couldn't be denied anymore.

He slanted my head back with one hand and his tongue pressed against mine. I gasped into his mouth and the sound was drowned out by his groan. His other hand slid down the side of my waist and over my thigh. He grabbed my knee, lifting my leg so that he could fit himself more firmly against my center. His hips ground into mine and I gasped again, my hands sliding down his chest until I found the bottom of his shirt.

I tore it off of him and he chuckled at my enthusiasm. His shirt fell to the floor somewhere and I relished in the feel of his smooth, tanned skin beneath the palms of my hands.

"I love you." The words came out as a breathless gasp and I reveled in the feel of being able to say them with no restraints.

"Fuck, I love you too." He ran his thumb over my bottom lip. "So much. Don't ever doubt that."

With all the drawings of our best moments lying around us, there was only one answer. "I won't." I couldn't doubt his love for me anymore, not when he'd gone to this much trouble to literally illustrate how much I meant to him.

He kissed me again. The kind of kiss that stole your breath and maybe your soul too.

He took his time peeling off of my clothes, like he was unwrapping the most precious gift he'd ever received.

He kissed every inch of my skin that he uncovered and my heart raced impossibly faster. Surely, eventually, it would stop beating all together. At least I would die happy and knowing what it felt like to have Ezra love me.

His lips skimmed between my breasts, over my stomach, and stopped when he reached my underwear. His hands slid up my thighs and hooked into the sides. All the while his eyes stayed on mine. He pulled them down and tossed them behind him and he finally let his eyes drop to feast on my bare skin.

"You're so beautiful." The words were a whispered rasp that covered my body in Goosebumps. He said the words with such conviction that I could never doubt them. Even as his eyes fluttered over my body I didn't feel a desire to cover myself. I wanted him to see me, all of me, and the love I had to give.

He sucked his bottom lip between his teeth and his eyes finally met mine once more. "I love you," he said, ducking his head to kiss the space where my neck met my shoulder. "I love you." A kiss to my collarbone. "I love you." He kissed my chest, over my heart. "I love everything about you."

"Everything?" I questioned with a giggle when he kissed my side, his stubble brushing against a ticklish spot.

"Everything," he repeated.

He removed the rest of his clothes and grabbed my hips, easing inside of me. We both sighed in relief at the feeling.

My hands roamed down his back, grabbing his ass. "Harder," I pleaded desperately.

He grabbed my hands, entwining our fingers together. We fit together seamlessly, another reminder of why we were so perfect for each other.

"I never want you to walk away from me ever again," he confessed.

"Then don't give me a reason." I breathed against his lips.

"I won't," he vowed.

With the amount of love and truth swimming in his gaze I had to believe him.

His thrusts sped up and my fingernails dug into his back.

My body tightened all over and I gasped, "I'm close."

"Me too." His hold on my hips tightened and his forehead creased.

We came together, both confessing our love for the entire world to hear.

When he fell asleep I crept out of the bed, wrapping my robe around me, as I padded around the apartment, collecting every single drawing. I sat down on the bed once more, beside his sleeping body. He was lying on his stomach, with his arms hugging the pillow. His dark hair was wild and unruly and perfectly him.

I giggled at the first drawing.

Paint twister. That had been fun.

Next was a drawing of the two of us getting milkshakes at this cute little diner in town. I remember the day well. It was before we really knew each other that well, and my crush had been raging in full force that day. I'd spent a good two hours picking out my outfit, only to spill milkshake on myself. I'd been upset at first, but then Ezra took his glass, spilled his own milkshake on his jeans, and shrugged, saying, "Now we match." Laughing, I'd scolded him for wasting a perfectly good milkshake. He told me it was worth it to see me laugh and ordered two more.

I set that drawing aside as well and looked down at the next one. I couldn't figure out what it was at first, but then realized it was a picture of me sleeping peacefully in his bed. Scrawled in the corner he'd written, *You belong here.*

I laughed at that, but my laugh didn't sound right. It was more like a choked sob and I realized I'd started crying again. But these were happy tears and I was thankful for them. Just like I was thankful for the drawings and the boy sleeping in my bed.

I thought I'd never have this.

This soul-stirring, intense, all-consuming, once in a lifetime kind of love.

But I got it.

With my best friend.

And you didn't get any luckier than that.

"I CAN'T BELIEVE I let you talk me into this," I mumbled, carrying the second to last box inside the house. Ezra was behind me, carrying the final box—the one that marked the fact that this was my home now too, not just his. I was here to stay. "You know my lease wasn't up yet."

He set the final box down on the floor along with the others.

He cracked a smile and leaned his hip against the kitchen counter. "This is your home. This is where you belong."

"With you?" I smiled widely.

"Yes." He framed my face, kissing me deeply. "And Toby of course." He nodded towards the fishbowl. "Toby has really missed you. He cries every night. I have to rock him to sleep."

I busted out in laughter. "Oh I'm sure, seeing as how rocking a fish would kill him."

He mock winced. "Yeah, that's why that's Toby 2.0."

I gasped. "What? You killed our baby!"

He laughed so hard that he was bent over at the stomach. "You should've seen your face!" Straightening, he sobered. "That's the original Toby, I assure you."

"It better be," I muttered, fighting a smile.

I stepped forward, wrapping my arms around him. His lips brushed against the top of my head.

"So, what do you say Westbrook, are you ready to try out this love thing with me forever?"

"I don't know," I hedged, clucking my tongue, "forever is an awfully long time."

"I'm good company, I promise." He grinned down at me. The kind of smile that made him seem boyish and young.

"Hmm, sounds tempting."

"Do I need to do more convincing?" He asked, his fingers gliding beneath my sweater.

"*A lot more.*" I whispered breathily in his ear. "Preferably naked."

"I can do that." A mischievous glint sparkled in his eyes.

I squealed when he grabbed me, tossing me over his shoulder as he ran up the steps.

Instead of stripping me naked and making love to me for the rest of the day and night we ended up jumping on the bed like two little kids.

Because that was us.

Our relationship was intense, passionate, and full of fun.

And I wouldn't have it any other way.

# BONUS CONTENT

Interviewer: Good afternoon, Ezra. Sadie. Thanks for sitting down with us.

Ezra: Thanks for having us.

Interviewer: Of course I have to ask you if Willow Creek is working on any new music? Can we expect a new release any time soon?

Ezra: I'm not really allowed to say, but we're working on it.

Interviewer: Good, good. So it's recently come out that you two are indeed a couple now. <points at both Ezra and Sadie> I don't think I'm speaking too broadly when I say everyone was expecting this. You've been photographed together numerous times and there's been several headlines hinting at a possible relationship, but nothing concrete. So, is this relatively new, or have you been able to hide your romantic relationship well?

Ezra: <glances at Sadie> Our romantic relationship is new, yes, but we've been best friends for a while now. But yes, I think everyone seemed to sense there was a connection between us…I just didn't want to see it. I didn't want to ruin a good thing. You know?

Interviewer: Mhmm. Sadie, do you have anything to say? You're awfully quiet.

Sadie: I read magazines. I know how you guys twist things, so no I'm not talking to you.

Ezra: <chuckles and leans in to kiss her> I love you so much.

Interviewer: <straightens clothes> I'm sorry you feel that way. Ezra, seeing as you two have known each other for a while, can we expect an engagement any time soon? Especially considering two of your band mates are now married?

Ezra: <glances at Sadie with a smile> I love this girl with my whole heart, and yes I'm going to marry her someday, but I don't know when. Besides, that kind of thing is private and none of the media's business.

Interviewer: Ah, yes. We all know how you and your band members feel about your privacy.

Ezra: <laughs> We might be famous, but we still deserve to keep certain parts of ourselves private.

Interviewer: Yes, well, I suppose…

Ezra: Do you have any more questions?

Interviewer: <looks for notes> Uh…

Ezra: <reaches for Sadie's hand> Bye. <they run down the hall laughing>

Interviewer: <watches them leave and pushes glasses up nose> And that's why Maddox is my favorite. At least he'll actually talk and not ditch an interview. <grumbles and packs up stuff> I better not get fired for this.

# TAKE A CHANCE

## MICALEA SMELTZER

- A WILLOW CREEK NOVEL -

A painter paints pictures on a
canvas.
But musicians paint their pictures on
Silence.
—Leopold Stokowski

# CHAPTER ONE

"GO," I URGED my boss, Sadie, out the door. "I can handle this place and your guy is waiting for you." I pointed to where her boyfriend Ezra lingered outside the store with two coffees in his hands. Beyond him, several people snapped photos of him on their cellphones. That might've been weird if it weren't for the fact that he was a member of the band Willow Creek.

"Are you sure?" Sadie asked, worrying her lip between her teeth.

"Positive." I nodded my head, resolute. "You need to finish packing so you can move back in with your man." I bumped her hip with mine. I was lucky that my "boss" had become one of my best friends.

She swished her brown hair over one shoulder and rolled up the sleeves of her shirt. "I can't believe I let him talk me into moving back in with him. My contract on my apartment isn't even up. But I swear that boy could sweet talk me into an orgasm." She shook her head, smiling at him through the glass door.

I snorted and moved behind the counter. "I'm fine here," I told her, "the store closes in an hour and I've closed it by myself plenty of times."

She straightened her shoulders and nodded. "You're right. I'm sorry for being such a worrier."

"This store is your life, so I get it."

She grabbed me into a hug and said a quick goodbye before running outside to join Ezra. I watched as she kissed his cheek and took one of the coffees. He saw me watching and waved before they got into his SUV.

Since the end of the day was nearing not many people strolled inside. So I busied myself with straightening racks and refolding clothes. That way I might be able to go straight to the babysitter's house and pick up my daughter. I hated that I couldn't be a stay at home mom like I'd always dreamed of, but at least I was making things work.

Outside a continued commotion had me turning to look. My face fell into a glare and I stormed forward and out the door.

"Hey! What do you think you're doing?" I yelled at the guy who had been skateboarding by the store—several times might I add—and was now attempting to slide against the metal bench outside the door.

The guy's back was to me as he slid off the bench, his skateboard landing on the concrete sidewalk with a clank.

He kicked the skateboard up and held it in his hand and turned around to face me.

The air was stolen out of my lungs when my eyes connected with his baby blues.

I hadn't recognized him from behind with a baseball cap worn backwards obscuring his hair.

But there was no mistaking those eyes, or those angled cheekbones, and definitely not the wry half-smile he wore so well.

"Hayes." His name fell from my lips as a gasp. I'd been doing my best to avoid him the last two months. I'd ignored his texts, phone calls, and I'd even been avoiding gatherings Sadie invited me to because I was afraid I might run into him. I hadn't wanted to see him after the passionate night we shared at his band mate's wedding. It shouldn't have happened, and I figured Hayes, being a known player, would be content to let that night be added to his countless list of others. I'd been wrong. The guy was relentless. Now he was here, right in front of me, and I couldn't run away.

"Arden." A smirk lifted his lips when he said my name. The way it rolled off his tongue sent a shiver down my spine.

"What are you doing here?"

He turned his head slightly to the side and removed his hat, scratching at his head before replacing it. He held up a hand, ticking a list off on his fingers. "Well, you've ignored my phone calls, my texts, and even my handwritten letter. Do you have any idea how long I slaved over those heartfelt words?"

My brows furrowed together. "It said: 'Stop ignoring me'. How is that heartfelt?"

He snapped his fingers together. "Ha! So you did read it!" Straightening, he towered above me and I felt slightly intimidated beneath his looming height. "So now I have stooped to showing up at your job in the hopes of having an actual conversation face to face." He nodded towards the store. "You're closing soon, right?"

"Uh…"

"Perfect." He strode past me and into the store.

I sighed heavily, my shoulders sagging.

I'd managed to avoid Hayes for two months and now my time was up.

I followed after him and looked at the time on the clock hanging above the register. One minute until closing. It figured.

I turned back around and locked the door, flipping the sign to CLOSED, and shutting the blinds.

It was all done in an effort to distract myself from Hayes' potent presence.

*The feel of his lips on my naked skin.*

*The searing warmth of his gaze.*

*The smooth glide of his fingers.*

I was tempted to open the door and go running, but I was wearing heels, and something told me Hayes wasn't going to let me get away so easily anymore.

I forced myself to face him and saw that he was standing by the counter with his hip leaned casually against it, and his strong arms were crossed over his chest.

My heart pulsed in my throat as his eyes swam all over my body, lingering on my breasts, lips, and finally connecting with my stare.

Silence stretched endlessly between us. I licked my suddenly dry lips and his eyes narrowed on my mouth. The sexual tension roaring between us was unlike anything else I'd ever experienced. Even in our better days my ex-husband—Todd—and I had never had this kind of chemistry.

Tapping his lips, he finally spoke. "I never expected you to be one to fuck and duck."

"Excuse me?"

"You know…fuck and duck. Where you fuck and then duck away like a coward." He didn't say the words with anger, just a resigned irritation.

I flinched, wringing my hands together. "I don't know what to say."

He grinned, leaning more fully against the counter and crossing his feet. "I know, how about you say, 'I'm sorry, Hayes. Let's go on a date.'"

I coughed on my own saliva, gasping for air. "You want to go on a date with me?"

He nodded. "Yes, I believe that's what I said."

"But…but…but you're *you*." I floundered, my whole body shaking from shock. "You're Joshua Hayes, Willow Creek guitar player, and also a major player when it comes to women. I read magazines, Joshua."

"Ooh, bringing out the first name." He grinned, rubbing his hands together. "Yes, I am both of those things…or was, because I'm not much of a player anymore. I'm a changed man."

I snorted in disbelief and rolled my eyes.

He started forward and in three long strides he'd closed the distance between us. He grasped my chin, sending a jolt through my body, and lifted my head so I was forced to look at him.

"Don't roll those pretty whiskey colored eyes at me or I'll have to spank you."

Why did my whole body have to clench with desire at his words? And from the glimmer in his eyes he noticed.

He gently stroked his fingers against my cheek and a soft sigh passed through my parted lips.

"You like it when I touch you." His thumb brushed my bottom lip and his eyes darkened.

I was frozen. Every word I'd ever learned flew from my mind and I was left with nothing but the ability to pull air into my lungs and notice the way my skin prickled where he touched me.

I'd tried so hard to pretend for the last two months that there was nothing between us, nothing more than a one-night stand at least. But all of my pretending had been in vain because there was no denying the electricity that pulsed between us. It was magnetic, sucking all of the energy from the room into our orbit.

Air rushed back into my lungs when his hand fell away and he took step back, distancing himself.

Immediately I ached for his touch and I silently scolded myself for being so weak.

I pulled in a lungful of air and tried to gather my scattered thoughts.

"Why are you here?" That seemed like a safe enough question.

"I'm pretty sure I already answered that when I said we should go on a date." He crossed his arms over his lean chest, the material of his shirt pulling taut over his muscles. Muscles I'd spent a night running my tongue over. I really needed to stop thinking about that night if I was going to keep a clear head.

I shook my head. "I meant, why are you here after all of this time? Why not give up? I read magazines and I watch TV so I know you have no shortage on admirers and I know that you also use them to your *full* advantage."

His lips twitched with laughter. "You sound jealous."

I snorted. "Hardly."

He bit his lip to hide a grin and fuck me if it wasn't the hottest lip bite I'd ever seen. Jeez, my lady parts were going nuts in his presence. It's not like I could really blame them. Not only was Hayes gorgeous, but he was the first man I'd been with since my husband left me. A toddler didn't give me much time to date.

"We'll have to agree to disagree on the state of your jealousy." He smirked, looking me up and down like something in my posture gave me away.

Deciding to move things along I brushed past him and strode into the back. "You're making me late and I have to pick up my daughter."

He trailed behind me, his sneakers squeaking on the concrete floors. "How is Mia?" His voice sounded soft, almost hesitant. I turned to look at him and saw that his shoulders were slumped and he was toeing the ground.

Hayes had bonded with my daughter when we went on a vacation together—not the two of us alone, of course, but when he and his band mates went on vacation with their girls. Sadie invited me and Hayes had immediately hit it off with Mia. My daughter didn't like most people, so it had surprised me that she took so readily to Hayes. I believed it had something to do with his carefree attitude and easy going smile. It was hard not to like the guy. But that's exactly what I'd spent the last two months trying to accomplish.

"She's good," I finally answered. "She'll be four soon. December fourteenth."

"Would it be okay if I got her a present?" He asked.

"Uh…" I was surprised he'd even offer. He wasn't her father, and he wasn't anything to me. "If you want to."

"I do," he replied quickly. "Anyway, about that date…"

"Oh, right." I rolled my eyes and he clucked his tongue, reaching out to capture my hand in his.

"What did I tell you about rolling those eyes at me?"

I swallowed thickly, my throat dry.

Before I could respond he let go of my hand and trailed his fingers down my cheek. "Like I was saying, tomorrow is *my* birthday and I want *you* to be my date."

"But I have Mia." My protests were weak as my eyes fluttered closed and I found my back pressed into the wall. I felt his nose glide against my neck and his lips briefly touched the spot where my pulse jumped erratically. When I opened my eyes he'd taken a step back and my body felt cold without his touch. His blue eyes sparkled with the knowledge of what he was doing to me.

"Bring her. Something tells me she might like what we have planned."

"She's three," I stated. "Do you really want a three-year-old at your birthday party?"

"Absolutely," he nodded, "she'll fit right in with Maddox."

I laughed at the mention of his band's erratic drummer. Sobering, I shrugged, "Why do you want us at your party?"

"Because," his voice lowered to a husky whisper, "I like you. A lot. You're beautiful, and funny, and nice, and you have a wonderful daughter who thinks I'm fucking awesome, and if she thinks I'm awesome then so should you." He chuckled, the sound of his laughter filling my body with warmth.

"So, I should base all my judgments on what my daughter thinks?"

"Absolutely," he nodded, "she's smart like her mom."

Now it was my turn to nod. I snapped my fingers together. "I see what you did there. You're good."

He grinned. "Does this mean you'll come?"

He looked so earnest when he asked the question and I felt bad for how I'd avoided him. "Fine, I'll be there, but it's not a date."

He clapped his hands together and did some kind of happy dance. There was a lot of hip thrusting involved.

"*This* might not be a date," he started, staring down at me with determination swimming in his eyes, "but I *will* get you to go on a real date with me. I'm going to prove to you that there's more to me than you think."

"And how are you going to do that?" My brows rose in interest.

His lips lifted in a smirk. "One day at a time."

# CHAPTER TWO

WHEN I INPUT the address Hayes gave me into the navigation system the last place I thought I'd end up at was a Chuck-E-Cheeses. I'd predicted a restaurant, maybe a house, not a kid's birthday place. I guess, this being Hayes, I should've expected something this wacky.

I parked my car and helped Mia out. I fixed her braid and made sure her dress was lying flat.

"Do I look pwetty like you, momma?" She asked.

I nodded, smoothing down a stray piece of red hair behind her ear. "Even prettier."

She giggled with glee. "Where's my pwesent for Hayes?"

"Right here, baby girl." I led her to the trunk of my car and handed her the bag.

I'd stopped by Target before coming here, refusing to show up empty handed, and Mia had insisted on getting something for Hayes as well. Granted, I didn't really think he needed a cheese grater shaped like an alligator, but I figured he'd appreciate the gesture nonetheless.

I handed Mia her gift bag—which I'd taken the time to put together in the Target parking lot—and grabbed the other bag. I closed the trunk and locked the car before taking her hand and heading inside the building.

The place was practically empty and it seemed oddly eerie without the sounds of children's laughter.

Someone was waiting near the front and smiled as we approached. "Are you Arden and Mia?" She asked.

I nodded. "Yeah…"

"Excellent, the birthday boy is waiting for you."

"Oh, I bet he is," I mumbled under my breath.

She stamped each of our hands, which I found hysterical. This was Chuck-E-Cheese, not a club.

I followed the sound of voices to the back of the building where I found Hayes surrounded by his Willow Creek band mates, their girls, two people I assumed were his parents, and a couple with a little boy whom I didn't recognize.

"Arden! You're here!" Hayes tossed his hands in the air and that's when I noticed that he was wearing a crown on his head. My God this was getting better by the second.

"Yeah, we're here, woo!" I threw in a fist bump, trying to act like I was excited to be in a Chuck-E-Cheese. It actually wasn't that bad with no kids around, but still…

"Take a seat," he pointed to some empty chairs, "the pizza will be out in a minute and then we're going to play."

I fixed Mia into a chair and sat down. It didn't escape my notice that he'd kept two seats in front of him empty for us.

"I brought you dis." Mia slid the bag across the table. "Momma says it's your birfday."

Hayes nodded, smiling widely at my daughter. "It is. Do you know how old I am?"

She shook her head and leaned shyly against my arm.

"More than all these fingers that fit on my hands." He held up both of his hands, wiggling his fingers.

I looked down and saw Mia's eyes widen in awe. "More dan dat?"

Hayes nodded. "Yeah, I'm twenty-seven today. I'm officially an old man. Unfortunately I still can't grow a beard to save myself." He rubbed his smooth cheeks. "Unlike the bearded wonder over there." He pointed at Ezra.

Ezra laughed, and ducked his head so that his black curls hid his face.

"Huh?" Mia looked at him with confusion.

"It's okay, most people don't understand half of the things that come out of my mouth. Oh! Look! Pizza!"

It was safe to say Hayes was like a two-year-old on a sugar high—hyper and easily distracted by food and shiny things.

Several large pizzas were set at different intervals on the table and paper plates were passed around. They also brought out huge pitchers of different sodas and water so that we could serve ourselves.

I grabbed a piece of pizza for Mia, making sure it was cooled before she started eating it. Once she was happily occupied I grabbed a slice for myself.

A squawk to my left had me jerking in my seat.

At the end of the table Remy sat rocking a tiny baby boy. Remy was the wife of Mathias—the lead singer of Willow Creek. Sadie had mentioned to me about a month ago that Remy had given birth, but since I'd been avoiding everyone I'd promptly dismissed the bit of information from my mind.

"Sorry everyone." Remy winced when the baby let out an ear-splitting scream.

Hayes spoke around a mouthful of pizza. "It's okay. Babies cry."

She bounced the baby, cooing to him softly. Mathias reached over, rubbing the fine strands of brown hair on the baby's head.

"Let me sing to him." Mathias pleaded, holding his arms out for the baby.

Remy handed the baby over and Mathias cradled his son carefully. The baby was so small that he nearly disappeared in Mathias' arms.

The moment Mathias began to sing the baby stopped crying.

"Every time." Remy smiled widely at her husband and he leaned over to kiss her.

"Is the pizza okay?"

At the sound of Hayes' voice I turned towards him. "Yeah, it's fine. Why?"

He shrugged, chewing on what looked to be his third slice. "You've taken two bites."

"Oh, right…sorry."

"It's okay." He smiled at me. "Do *you* like your pizza?" He ducked his head, addressing Mia.

She nodded eagerly. "It's good."

I finished off my piece of pizza and wiped my hands. "Who are they?" I asked, nodding towards the couple at the end of the table that I didn't recognize.

"That's my cousin Trace," he pointed at the guy wearing a plaid shirt, "his wife Olivia," his finger moved to the pretty brown-haired woman, "and their son Dean." The little boy couldn't have been much more than a year old. "And this," he slung an arm over the shoulder of the woman beside him, "is my dear mother and the old fart beside her is the man I call dad. You should thank them, they created me."

"Joshua." His mother scolded, brushing his arm off.

Beside her Hayes' dad cackled with laughter. Something told me that he was responsible for Hayes' sense of humor.

Hayes shrugged in a what-are-you-going-to-do gesture and picked up another slice of pizza. He was so thin that I didn't know where he could possibly fit all of that food.

"So, Ms. Mia," he eyed my daughter, "once we eat this not-so-nutritious pizza will you do me the honor of joining me in the plastic ball pit? I need someone to score me on my belly flopping skills."

Mia nodded eagerly. "I can do dat."

"That's my girl." He held his hand out for her to give him a high-five.

My heart clenched at his words though. *My girl.* Something her father should've been saying to her. Instead, the asshole had skipped out on her whole life. He'd never even asked for her picture. It broke my heart that Hayes—someone that was practically a stranger to her—cared for her more than her own father.

Hayes seemed to notice a sudden shift in me, because he tilted his head towards me. "Are you okay?"

"Mhmm," I nodded, "yeah."

Little wrinkles marred the corners of his mouth when he frowned. "Arden," he started.

I shook my head. "It's not important."

He looked doubtful, but thankfully let it drop.

Mia finished her pizza and I cleaned her up.

Everybody chatted with one another, but I sat quietly. I'd gotten to know the whole band pretty well, which consisted of Maddox and Mathias, who were twins, Ezra, and Hayes of course. I'd also grown close with Emma, Maddox's wife. Upon noticing me she leaned forward and said hi.

"Hey," I replied, "how have you been?"

"Great." She replied cheerily, her hand falling to her tiny baby bump.

"How far along are you now?" I asked, keeping an eye on Mia so that she didn't run off.

"Almost seventeen weeks." Maddox answered for her.

I wasn't surprised that he knew. He was so wrapped up in his love for Emma that I sometimes wondered how he managed to play the drums. At least his love for her gave him lots of material for songs since he was the songwriter for the band.

Maddox reached over and rubbed her stomach. "We'll be finding out the gender of baby W.C. very soon."

"W.C.?" I questioned, confusion wrinkling my brow.

"W.C.," he repeated. "Willow Creek."

"Ah," I nodded. "That makes sense."

"Enough of this chatter," Hayes declared, tossing his napkin on the table, "the birthday boy declares it's time to play!"

With that, he pushed away from the table and came running around to grab Mia. She giggled as he swooped her up into his arms.

"To the balls!" He began to run away.

I shook my head and called after him through my laughter. "Please don't corrupt my child!"

He paused in his running and Mia held tight to his shoulders. He mock gasped. "I'm appalled that you'd think such a thing of me. I'm an excellent role model for children." Before I could respond he was gone and a moment later we heard Mia let out a laugh as she was tossed into the ball pit.

Across from me Hayes' father shook with unrestrained laughter. "Excellent role model?" He cackled. "Now that's hilarious. This is the guy that once tricked the neighbor's kid into eating rat poop because he told him it was raisins."

His father's statement had my stomach lurching in fear and I took off in the direction of the sound of laughter.

Hayes had been excellent with Mia when we went to the beach together, but that had been a while ago.

When I rounded the corner I saw the two of them sitting in the middle of the brightly colored balls. They were laughing and smiling while tossing them at each other.

There was no reason for my worry and I couldn't help but smile at the delight that lit my daughter's face.

"You know," Sadie sidled up beside me, crossing her arms over her chest as she watched Hayes and Mia, "I warned Hayes not to hurt you." Turning to look at me, she narrowed her eyes to thin slits. "I never thought I'd need to warn *you* not to hurt *him.*"

I backed a few steps away so that there was no possibility of Hayes overhearing our conversation.

"I don't have time for a relationship, I have a daughter."

Sadie rolled her eyes at me and made a noise in the back of her throat. "You're a mom, he knows that, we all know that, now stop hiding behind that as an excuse not to date."

"Date?" My eyes widened. "Wow, that escalated quickly."

Sadie sighed, her arms falling to her sides. "All I'm saying is he *likes* you, a lot. And for Hayes…well, that must mean you're pretty damn special to him. I'm not asking you to fall in love with the guy, but look at him." She pointed to where he was tossing Mia up in the air so she could fall into the ball pit and her delighted giggles filled the air. "He's a good guy. Let him prove it to you that you're more than a one-night stand."

I gasped, my eyes threatening to pop out of my head. "He told you about that?" I hissed, my heart speeding up.

"Well, *something* was going on with you guys and I knew there was no way you'd tell me, so yes, after some persuading, he told me that you slept together."

"I'm going to kill him," I mumbled.

"Hey, don't blame him." She scolded me. "I really had to pry it out of him."

I hung my head. "I…I don't know what to do. I feel like my life is such a complicated mess. Guys want easy, and I'm anything but."

She grabbed my arm and wrapped her hand around my wrist, giving it a squeeze before letting go. "Don't give up on him before you even start something."

I sighed, glancing at Hayes and unable to hide my smile as I watched him and Mia climbing through the indoor jungle gym. I knew Sadie had a point, but Todd had cut me so deeply with everything that he had done that I was afraid to open up my heart and lay it bare to him.

"Just think about what I said." She hugged me and then went back to the table.

Olivia and Trace were up with Dean, letting him toddle around, and I noticed Mathias and Remy were watching a child playing on one of the arcade machines. I hadn't noticed the kid earlier, but I'd been too taken with the baby.

"Alright, it's time to play!" Maddox jumped up from the table while Emma shook her head at him, fighting a smile.

Maddox started running towards me and I thought he was going to mow me right down, but he ended up skirting around me and cannonballing into the ball pit. Multi-colored balls exploded, raining everywhere as some escaped over the netting.

Emma busted out laughing. "Please tell me someone got that on video."

"I've got you covered," Ezra chimed, holding up his phone with Sadie curled in his lap.

"Momma! Momma!" I looked up at the sound of Mia's voice and found that she and Hayes were above me, in one of the higher compartments of the jungle gym—or whatever you called it.

Mia tapped her chubby fingers against the plastic bubble.

"Hey baby girl." I blew her a kiss.

Hayes tapped the plastic and said, "Where's my kiss?"

I resisted the urge to smile. "You're going to have to work harder than that to get a kiss from me."

His eyes gleamed behind the plastic. "I like a challenge."

I shook my head as he and Mia disappeared into a bright yellow tunnel.

Since I knew in my gut that Mia was safe with Hayes I went back to the table and sat down.

"So…" I started, all eyes turning towards me. "Why did Hayes want to have his birthday here?"

"It's Hayes." His parents and friends answered in unison. I couldn't help but giggle at that.

"We're pretty sure Hayes is actually a ten year old stuck in a twenty-seven-year-olds body," Ezra cackled, ripping a paper napkin to shreds.

"Aw, give him more credit than that. He's sweet." Sadie elbowed Ezra in the gut.

Ezra nipped playfully at her ear. "He took you on a date before I did, therefore I'm not giving him any credit ever." He growled.

Sadie giggled and whispered something in his ear, which made Ezra kiss the end of her nose.

I felt a pang in my gut. Todd had been like that once upon a time, before the pressure of married life got to him and then his fists replaced his lips.

"What's up with you?" Emma asked, bumping my shoulder lightly with hers. "I don't think I've seen you since the wedding."

"Yeah, that's because she's avoiding us." Sadie piped in and I glared at her.

"Avoiding us? Why?" Emma's mouth turned down in a frown.

"Yeah, Arden, tell us why." Sadie smirked. I narrowed my eyes even more. I knew she'd hated it when Emma butted into her love life, but I guess now that she was blissfully in love she'd forgotten all about that and was now determined to subject me to that torture.

"Tell you what?"

I jumped at the sound of Hayes' voice and nearly fell out of my seat.

"Whoa, steady there sailor." He grabbed ahold of my chair to keep it from tipping over.

Instead of taking the seat across from me where he'd sat previously he took Mia's and placed her in his lap.

"Momma, dat was fun." Mia pointed over my shoulder at a slide.

"It was baby girl?" I asked, pasting on a bright and happy smile. "Did Hayes go with you?"

She nodded. "We said, 'Weeeeeee!'"

I ran my finger over her pink cheek. "Do you want momma to go down with you this time?"

"No, no," she shook her head. "Hayes again."

Hayes grinned, bouncing her on his lap. "Of course, princess. But first we must eat cake."

"Cake!" Mia exclaimed. "Wis it chocolate?"

"It's marble, do you know what that is?" He asked her.

She shook her head and he explained.

"You mean it's bof?" She questioned him with wide eyes.

"It sure is."

"Momma, dat's my new favorite."

I laughed. "I'm not surprised. But maybe you should try it first before you tell me it's your favorite."

She nodded her head eagerly. I knew that child well enough to know that it didn't really matter what kind of cake it was, she was really more interested in the icing. What could I say? She was my kid, and like mother like daughter.

The others ventured back to the table and I nudged Hayes.

"Who's that kid?" I pointed at the young boy with Mathias and Remy.

Hayes leaned around me to see who I was pointing to. "Oh, that's Collin. He's Mathias' little brother from the Big Brother Big Sisters program."

"Oh," I nodded, "that was nice of them to bring him."

"Mhmm," Hayes hummed, "Collin is a cool kid."

"Oooh! Momma! Look!" Mia pointed and I raised my head to see what caught her attention.

A large cake shaped like a guitar was being carried out and once it was set on the table the candles were lit.

As a group we began to sing, and Hayes ducked his head in embarrassment, his dimple piercing his cheek with his smile.

"Make a wish," I told him.

He stared at me for a moment, the weight of so many things unsaid swirling in his blue depths.

He looked away, breaking the spell.

His cheeks hollowed as he blew out the candles and smoke wafted through the air.

We all clapped and Hayes chuckled, kissing Mia's cheek.

"Princess Mia gets the first piece."

"But it's your birthday." I reminded him as someone came out with paper plates, utensils, and a cake cutter.

"Ah, that might be true, but Ms. Mia is the real star. Isn't that right?" He tickled her stomach and she giggled.

"You really do like her, don't you? It's not an act?"

His brows drew together and for once his face fell into serious lines. "Yeah, I do. Did you think I was faking it or something so you'd like me?"

"I..." I gaped at him open-mouthed like a fish.

"Seriously, Arden?" He sounded slightly irritated. With a deep sigh he relaxed his features and closed his eyes. He seemed to be counting silently in his head. Opening his eyes he looked directly at me. "I can see where your thoughts might go in that direction, but I'm anything but a faker. What you see with me is what you get. Remember that."

I swallowed thickly, past the large lump currently lodged in my throat.

Unbidden, my thoughts went back to the passionate night we spent in each other's arms.

*"Do you feel that?" He placed my hand on his chest, over his steadily beating heart.*

*I nodded. "I feel it."*

*"I don't think I've ever felt more alive than I do right now. Here, with you."*

My eyes connected with his and it seemed like he knew where my thoughts had strayed. The night we spent together had been one of the best of my whole life, but I was scared. Terrified, really, because what I felt for him was so potent that I knew if given the chance it could grow into something monumental. If I gave him my heart I feared I'd never get it back. And what if things ended? What kind of state would that put me in?

"Life is nothing without risks." He spoke, like he had a looking glass straight into my thoughts.

My pulse jumped and I continued to stare at him. I knew that beyond us plates were being passed around and our friends were chattering, but despite that it still felt like it was only the three of us—Hayes, Mia, and me—existing in our own orbit.

"One date. That's all I ask for. If after that one date I haven't proven to you that I'm worth it I'll leave you alone and you'll never hear from me again."

Why did those words fill me with such hollowness? The thought of existing in a world where I never spoke to Hayes was painful to contemplate. The last two months had been sucky enough and *he* had been talking to me.

"Deal." I finally managed to find my voice.

Joshua Hayes was impossible for me to resist. The rock star bad boy should've been the last guy to strike my fancy, but there was something about him that drew me in unlike any other guy ever had.

"Seriously?" Hayes flashed his mega-watt smile, all traces of seriousness leaking out of his eyes and posture. "That was easier than I thought it would be."

"What can I say?" I shrugged, reaching for a fork. "You're kind of annoying so I wanted to shut you up," I jested.

He grinned at my words, adjusting his hold on Mia.

I loved how we were able to go from serious to joking to flirting in a matter of seconds.

Grabbing up his fork he speared a large piece of cake and shoved it into my mouth.

Crumbs got all over my clothes. "Hayes!" I scolded, trying to keep the food in my mouth.

He laughed merrily and even Mia joined in, clapping her hands. "Now I shut you up."

"Oh, it's on." I reached across the table and grabbed a huge chunk of cake, throwing it at his head and messing up his perfect hair before he could even blink an eye.

"Now you've done it!" He laughed.

An all out attack was launched and soon everybody was participating. Cake went everywhere, icing smearing across my face and into my hair, but all the while I laughed and couldn't get rid of my grin. This was the most fun I'd had in a long time.

Mia grabbed a handful of cake and smeared it on my skirt. "I gots you, momma!"

"Yes you did baby girl," I told her, smearing my hand in icing.

Unable to resist myself I lunged towards Hayes and pressed my hand into his butt, leaving behind my handprint in blue icing.

"I knew you liked my ass." His blue eyes glimmered and he grasped my wrists, holding tight enough that I couldn't get away but not hard enough to bruise.

I laughed, trying to squirm away and in the process our legs tangled together sending both of us falling to the floor.

He waggled his brows, a grin splitting his face. "And now I have you underneath me, right where I want you."

My eyes flicked to his lips and my heart tripled in speed. "You're bad."

"On the contrary I think I'm very, *very* good." His voice lowered to a husky whisper. He let go of one of my wrists and tenderly stroked the backs of his fingers against my cheek. "Honestly, I should be applauded for the amount of restraint I'm exhibiting right now."

"And why is that?" The question came out as a breathless whisper.

"Because," he lowered his lips until they grazed the shell of my ear. "You have no fucking idea how bad I want to kiss you right now."

His fingers smoothed through my hair, further smearing the icing lodged there, and his eyes roamed all over my face before settling on my mouth.

His tongue flicked out and his Adam's apple bobbed. "Those lips were made to kiss mine."

Before I could form a coherent response he rolled off of my body and into a standing position. He held out a hand and helped me up, purposely holding me close to his body for a moment before letting go. That one moment was enough to further shake my already jumbled insides. He smelled downright lickable…which was plausible considering he was covered in cake and icing.

While we were on the floor the food fight must have ceased because no one was throwing anything anymore and the employees were looking on with disgust at the mess.

Hayes clapped his hands together, drawing attention to himself. "Considering we're all a mess I think it would be best if we moved on to the present opening before these lovely people over here kill us." He pointed at the employees and then hissed behind his hand, "They have murder in their eyes."

Maddox snorted and Mathias shook his head. Mathias had a dollop of icing on the end of his nose and Remy promptly leaned over to lick it off, eliciting a chuckle from his throat.

Hayes' parents were covered in cake too, and I wasn't even surprised they'd partaken in the madness.

Hayes sat down and I followed suit, scooping up Mia and sitting her in my lap.

Hayes reached for a present and Mia smacked her chubby palm against his muscular arm. "Mine first." She pointed at the purple gift bag—I'd tried to talk her into a manlier birthday bag, but purple was her favorite color so she thought Hayes would like it too.

"Which one?" He asked her.

"Dat one." She pointed again, wiggling her finger around.

He grabbed the one she indicated and held it up. When she nodded her head enthusiastically he set it in front of him and started pulling out the tissue paper.

His lips quirked with the threat of laughter as he held up the alligator shaped cheese grater.

"This is a wonderful gift Ms. Mia. Thank you. I'm going to use this every day for all of my cheese shredding needs."

She clapped her hands together and wiggled out of my hold, reaching for Hayes. He took her and his eyes widened in surprise when she kissed his cheek. Blushing, she bashfully hid her face in the crook of his neck. Hayes smiled widely and smoothed his hand against her back.

I couldn't help smiling at him with my daughter. It was a beautiful thing that she had taken so quickly to Hayes. But if I let him into my life and then things didn't work out I feared what it might do to her. Her dad had already abandoned her before birth, so what kind of psychological effect would it have on her if I let a man into my life again only for him to leave too?

Hayes grabbed another gift, and I forced my thoughts away.

When he got to my gift I bit my lip nervously. It wasn't much, but what did you get a guy that had everything?

He pulled it out of the gift bag, flipping through the pages.

I'd ended up getting him one of my favorite books and while in the parking lot I'd sat and made notations throughout it, pointing out my favorite quotes, and my thoughts while reading.

"Thanks Arden," he glanced at me, "this is really special."

I worried my bottom lip between my teeth. "It's just a book."

"No," he shook his head, reaching up to rub his forehead and further smearing the icing there, "it's more than that." The way his voice dropped it seemed like he was leaving something unsaid, but I was afraid to say anything in front of everybody.

"I'm glad you like it." The words were clogged with barely contained emotion— an emotion I couldn't even begin to decipher.

I didn't know what this boy was doing to me, and at this moment he wasn't even trying to woo me with sweet words or the caress of his fingers. I didn't know how I'd managed to avoid him for so long, because from where I was sitting there was no denying that there was something between us. Something infinitely more than a one night stand. It was a connection that if we followed it, it might lead us down the road of the greatest adventure of our life. But all roads had bumps, and I was afraid ours might be filled with craters.

His blue eyes sought mine and the way his softened with understanding it was like he was saying that he knew why I'd stayed away, but determination still glimmered in his eyes and I knew nothing I did or said was going to get me out of the date I promised him.

When he looked away the spell was broken and I hastily stood, grabbing Mia from his arms. "Well, we should be getting out of here."

Before anyone could blink I hurried out of the building and to my car.

I was finished buckling Mia into her car seat when the sound of sneakers hitting pavement assaulted my ears.

I closed the car door and turned around to face Hayes.

His normally perfectly coifed hair was now a mess, but it only served to make him look even more handsome, and to remind me of what he looked with it mused from my fingers.

He stopped in front of me, so close that his sneakers nearly touched the tips of my shoes.

"You ran away so quick that I couldn't even say goodbye."

I shrugged, feigning that I was completely unaffected by his presence. I was such a liar. "I remembered I had to get home and check something."

"Check something?" He repeated, fighting laughter. "What exactly was it that you had to check?"

"Uh…"

He pressed his arms on either side of the car behind me, effectively caging me in. "Don't try to lie to me, Arden, it's unbecoming of you."

My skin pricked with awareness at his close proximity.

He lowered his head, skimming his nose along the bare expanse of my neck.

"What are you doing to me?" I asked breathlessly.

"Seducing you," he replied with a soft chuckle. "Resist all you want, Little Bird, but I'm not giving up on you."

"Little Bird?" I don't know why those were the words that I latched onto.

"Yes, Little Bird," he repeated, his lips barely touching my neck, "because whenever I touch you your heart speeds up so fast that it reminds me of the beating of a baby bird's wings."

I pressed my hands to the flat expanse of his chest, in the plans of pushing him away, but somehow my treacherous fingers ended up wrapping around the fabric and holding him to me so that he couldn't get away.

He rested his forehead against mine, staring into my eyes and straight down into my soul that yearned so desperately for his. It begged me to give in and see where things might go, but one date was all I was giving him—giving *us*. I couldn't risk more. I'd never been a gambler, but I'd once put all my money on a sure bet and he ended up hurting me in more ways than one person should be hurt. And

Hayes? He was a wild card for sure. He would shake me up and spit me out, but the question was would he still be there to catch me when I fell? He was a player, plain and simple, and I didn't know if I could trust that I was different.

But my God I didn't think I could stay away any longer either.

One day with him—hell, not even a *whole* day—and he'd already crumbled every single wall I'd built around myself the last two months.

It was more than his charm and good looks.

It was just *him*.

"It's my birthday," his breath skirted over my cheek, "therefore I think I should get a kiss."

Oh God.

I knew I should push him away, I really did, but instead I only held on tighter.

It was like I was under a spell. Those blue eyes of his had hypnotized me, that was my story and I was sticking to it.

"One kiss?" I asked breathlessly, not having forgotten that my daughter sat in the car where my back was pressed.

"Only one," he tilted my head back, "but I *fully* plan on making it count."

He slanted his mouth over mine stealing the words on the tip of my tongue and swallowing them. I let out a soft moan and his own drowned out the sound. He cupped my face between his hands holding me as his willing prisoner.

My mind shut down and my body took over.

I stood onto my tiptoes, grasping at the longer strands of his hair, and licked my tongue between his parted lips.

He let out a soft groan, nibbling my bottom lip before stroking his tongue over the same spots where he'd just peppered small bites.

His hands slid from my face, down to my waist, where he grasped my hips.

My body arched completely into his and his tall frame shadowed over me.

With one last sweep of his tongue he pulled away and brushed his lips against my ear.

"Dream about me tonight."

When I opened my eyes he was gone, but the imprint of his lips still lingered on mine.

# CHAPTER THREE

*DREAM ABOUT ME tonight.*

Those four words kept replaying in my mind as I drove home. I would never tell him, but I'd been dreaming about him almost every night. Actually, it was more like a memory than a dream as my brain looped every detail of the night I spent wrapped in his arms. Even in sleep my brain was trying to tell me how good it was with Hayes—how what he made me feel shouldn't be denied.

My thoughts and feelings were a complicated and twisted mess.

I'd spent enough time with Hayes, before I started avoiding him, to develop real feelings. But it was difficult to decipher exactly what those feelings were. Was it simply lust? Or was it more?

The way my chest clenched and my body hummed with electricity I knew it was more than lust.

Sweat dampened my skin.

I was so screwed.

This was bad, really bad.

I pulled into the driveway of my modest two-bedroom house. It was small, with only one bathroom and a kitchen you could barely turn around in, but it was home and I loved it.

I pulled a sleepy Mia from the car and carried her inside and straight to the bathroom. I started a tub of warm water and stripped off her icing covered dress.

I lifted her into the bathtub and the bubbles foamed around her.

She giggled, grabbing some and making a fake beard around her chin.

"Look at me, momma! I haz a beard!"

"Yes you do silly girl." I tweaked her nose.

"Read me a stowy," she pleaded with wide blue eyes.

I narrowed mine on her. "What do we say?"

"Pwease and tank you?"

"That's right." I smiled down at her.

I was so thankful to have my daughter. Despite the shit I was put through by my ex I couldn't regret Mia. She was the bright light in my otherwise dull life. "Which story do you want?"

"Um…" She put a finger to her lips. "Ariel!"

"Ah, *The Little Mermaid*. I should've known."

I grabbed the large storybook and sat down on the tiled floor.

"I wanna be a mermaid when I grows up," Mia chimed, kicking the water.

"Don't do that baby," I scolded lightly. "You'll get the book wet."

"Sowwy." She ceased her kicking and sat still, waiting for me to start reading.

I flipped to the right page and began to read. Mia sat, listening with rapt attention despite the fact that she'd heard this story a million times.

When I finished the story I set the book aside and washed her hair.

Once she was clean I dressed her in pajamas, even though it would still be a while before she went to bed, and put a movie on for her in the living room.

I showered as quickly as I could, hating to leave Mia unsupervised for even a second, but it was necessary to remove the hardened icing from my hair and skin.

Once I was clean I put my hair up in a messy bun and dressed in a pair of sweatpants and an old t-shirt.

Mia was still right where I left her and I sat down on the couch beside her. Immediately, without tearing her eyes away from the screen, she crawled into my lap.

I grabbed the fluffy blanket off the back of the couch and fixed it around us both.

Mia snuggled even closer to me and I brushed my lips against the top of her head. "I love you baby girl."

"I know, momma."

I couldn't help but grin at her response. It warmed my heart to know that my daughter knew I loved her. I never wanted her to ever doubt that. She was my world. She had been since the moment I knew she was growing inside me, and it would remain that way until I took my last breath.

I eased the door closed to Mia's room and backed down the hallway.

I turned the lights off in the living room and grabbed a bottle of water from the refrigerator.

I'd started in the direction of my bedroom when I heard a soft knock on the front door.

I froze mid-step. No one knocked on my door.

I set the bottle of water down and tiptoed into the living room and stood by the window beside the front door in the small foyer. I edged back the curtain, barely risking a peep out the window.

When I recognized the tall figure all of the worry seeped out of my body.

I threw the door open and hissed, "You scared me!"

"Sorry." He raised one hand in surrender, a box clasped in the other. "Can I come in?" He swept two fingers to the side, indicating the living room.

"Uh…"

"Excellent. You're so kind." He breezed right past me, through the living room, and into the kitchen.

Stunned, I closed the door and followed after him.

He'd set the box on the kitchen table and proceeded to poke at my coffee maker.

"What are you doing?" I stepped up behind him, trying to peer over his shoulder but since he was a giant my efforts were futile.

"Trying to make coffee, obviously." He said in a sassy tone.

"Don't break my coffee maker." I shoved at his heavy body, but didn't succeed in moving him even an inch. "Move. Let me do it."

He sighed and stepped aside.

"Why exactly am I making coffee?" I asked as I reached for the filters in the cabinet above.

"I brought cake."

"Cake?" I glanced over at him. "*Why?*"

"Because you ended up wearing it, not eating it. I thought you and Mia might like some."

I leaned back, scrutinizing the box on the table. "That looks like a new cake." While the coffee began to perk I walked over to the table and picked up the box. Yeah, it was definitely a new cake and not the remnants of his original birthday cake. "Why does it say *Happy 50th Birthday Barbara?*"

Hayes bent over me to look at the cake. "Shit, I must've grabbed the wrong one. I was going to get one with the Teenage Mutant Ninja Turtles on it but then I got distracted."

"By what?"

"Well, someone recognized me and then there was a lot of screaming, some tears, and some declarations of desires to birth my children. So when that happened I grabbed the first cake I could get my hands on and ran out of there…I also forgot to pay. Fuck. I should probably call the store."

"What store was this?" Curiosity was taking over.

"Walmart."

I snorted. "You mean to tell me that *you*, Joshua Hayes, willingly went into

Walmart to buy a cake?"

He paused, scrutinizing my face. "I also had to buy toilet paper. Forgot that, though."

I snorted, covering my face with my hands. "I can't take anything you say seriously."

"Hey, I can be serious," he defended, the warmth of his body leaving mine as he began opening cabinets in search of coffee mugs, "but life would be pretty miserable without laughter. Aha!" He cried, finally finding the mugs. He grabbed one and began to laugh. "Mickey Mouse? Really, Arden?"

"Mia saw it and insisted I buy it. She's a bit Disney obsessed. Hopefully I'll be able to take her to Disney World sometime. Although, she might pass out from excitement."

He chuckled and set the mug down, pouring the steaming hot liquid inside. "Where is she anyway? With her dad?" He looked around.

I swallowed thickly. I didn't know how much Hayes might know from Sadie about my ex, but I figured it couldn't be a lot since even she didn't know the whole story.

"He's not in the picture."

Hayes stared at me for a moment, seeming to read so much in the hollowness of my eyes. "I'm sorry."

"I'm not." I shrugged.

He shook his head. "I'm not sorry for the reason you're thinking."

"Then what are you sorry for?" I asked, confusion coating my words.

He stepped towards me and my small gasp echoed through the kitchen as he smoothed his calloused fingers against my cheek. "I'm sorry that he hurt you, but I'm not sorry that he's out of your life. Because if he wasn't gone I wouldn't be standing right here with you, where I'm meant to be."

"Hayes—" I started.

"No," he said firmly, clasping my face between his large hands, "don't try to deny it. I see it in your eyes. You know we belong together just as much as I do. You've been skirting around this for *months*. Remember this summer? At the beach house and all the time we spent together? Not once did I try to make a move even though I wanted to. I know you want to believe that this is just sex for me, but it's not. That night with you…" He closed his eyes briefly, swallowing thickly. "It was fucking amazing, but one night will never be enough with you. Hell, I'm not even sure the rest of my life would give me enough time to get my fill of you."

"This is…it's too sudden."

He dragged a breath into his lungs and nodded his head as he stepped away.

"You're right. I'm sorry. I'm getting ahead of myself." He smiled wryly. "My mom always did tell me I liked to push things too far, too fast, and that the most important things in life take time." He nodded at his own words. "You owe me one date and I'll stick to my word that after that date the ball's in your court. But Arden?"

"Yeah?"

"I don't promise to fight fair."

Before I could blink he shoved one of the coffee mugs in my hand.

"Enough serious talk. It's time for us to gorge ourselves on poor Barbara's cake. I should really send an apology letter."

"What is it with you and letters?" I mumbled, grabbing two forks and not even bothering with plates.

"It's a lost art form. People are too impersonal these days," he mused, taking the fork I offered him.

I sat down and removed the lid. We both took a bite of cake and sat in silence.

Finally, I spoke. "You know…you're kind of a strange guy, but I mean that in the best way possible. You're nothing like I thought you'd be."

He grinned, his adorable dimple making an appearance on his cheek. "I'm full of surprises, Arden. Appearances can be deceiving. Never forget that."

Little did he know, but I had already been schooled in that thanks to my asshole ex.

We continued to sit, even after we'd finished with the cake and our coffee had long since grown cold.

It was like both of us were content to sit there and simply enjoy being in the presence of the other person.

As much as I might fight my overwhelming feelings for the cocky rock star I couldn't deny that in his presence I felt that I'd finally found where I belonged.

# CHAPTER FOUR

AGREEING TO GO to lunch with Sadie during my break had been a bad idea.

Possibly the worst decision I'd ever made in my entire life.

Okay, so maybe I was being a bit—or a lot—melodramatic, but the girl was getting on my last nerve. I wished I had Mia here as a buffer, but since I was working today she was at her baby sitter's house.

"So, you and Hayes?" She waggled her brows. "What's going on there? It seemed like there was a little somethin', somethin' going on at his party."

I rolled my eyes. "What you sensed was merely my irritation at being in the same room with him."

She picked up her glass of water, glaring at me across the rim. "Arden, everybody could see your lady boner from a mile away."

I choked on the bite of food in my mouth.

While I was hacking away and trying not to die Sadie sat there calmly.

I gulped greedily at my water and once I had myself composed I glared at my so-called friend. "Lady boner? Really?"

"Hey," her hands rose innocently, "I call it like I see it. Lady. Boner."

I narrowed my eyes further. "You know how mad you got when Emma kept asking you endless questions about you and Ezra?" I waited for her to nod. "Well that's exactly what you're doing to me. It's annoying. Quit it."

Her face fell. "You're right. I'm so sorry. I'll stop, I swear…but for the record, I'm totally one hundred percent rooting for you guys to be a couple."

I took a deep breath, trying to steady myself. "I agreed to go on a date with him," I admitted.

Sadie lit up, clapping her hands together in glee.

"But I only agreed to *one* date." I held up one finger, wiggling it around to drive home my point. "No more."

"Oh there will be more!" She did a little dance in her seat. "You'll see."

"I don't know what he sees in me anyway," I mumbled. "Didn't he go on a date with you this past summer? I mean, I'm nothing like you."

"It was *one* time." She stared me down as she ripped her straw wrapper into tiny pieces. "And yeah, we don't have chemistry—and let's face it I was madly in love with Ezra even then and I was too blind to see it—but that one date was enough to tell me that he's a genuinely nice guy." Worrying her bottom lip between her teeth, she admitted, "He told me that he was ready to settle down, and to be honest I didn't quite believe him at first, but I can tell now that he wasn't lying. He hasn't been going out and partying, or bringing around random play things."

"Really?" My brows rose in interest.

She nodded. "I know you think that he might grow bored with you, or that it would only be about sex, but need I remind you that you already slept with him and the boy's still pursuing you relentlessly. Cut the guy some slack."

"My life is complicated," I mumbled.

Sadie snorted and shook her head like I was beyond silly. "*Everyone's* life is complicated in different ways. That's a pathetic excuse and you know it."

My face crumbling, I admitted, "I'm scared. What if I let him in and he leaves? What if he hurts me? I've been through so much already and…I honestly don't know if I'm strong enough to go through it again."

Sadie softened, her shoulders slumping. "Oh, Arden." She reached for my hand that rested on the table. "I know things were rough with your ex, but you can't base every guy off of him." I hastily looked away from the pity in her eyes. The last thing I ever wanted was for someone to feel sorry for me. "You can't lock your heart away forever, that's only letting the bastard win."

I sighed and my eyes dropped to my plate of food. "You're right," I agreed.

And she was, but it felt like it would be impossible for me to let go of four years of hatred and fear. I had to try though, because like she said, I couldn't let Todd win.

Braving the throngs of the grocery store with a tired three-year-old was not my idea of a good time. But I hadn't had time to stop off before picking her up and we were out of a few things.

"Momma, I wanna go home," she whined, crocodile tears streaking her cheeks.

"I know baby girl." I pulled in a lungful of air, trying to stay calm.

I loved being a mom, don't get me wrong, but it was moments like these that tested the limits of my sanity.

Wiping away her tears I stopped on the cereal aisle. "If you're a good girl I'll get you those popsicles you like."

Instantly, the tears stopped.

Yes, I'd stooped to bribery, but what parent didn't?

"Really?" She asked, her bottom lip jutting out.

I nodded. "But you *have* to stop whining, okay?"

"O'tay," she said around some final sniffles.

I grabbed the cereal I needed and then consulted my list before heading to another aisle.

"Coffee, peanut butter, and macaroni." I read the words softly to myself and steered the cart down the pasta aisle.

I grabbed the family pack of Kraft mac n' cheese and dropped it into the shopping cart.

"Momma," Mia hissed, grabbing my shirt.

"What?" I looked down at her, confused by her odd behavior.

With her other hand she waved me forward.

I lowered and her small hands grabbed my face, holding me close so that she could whisper in my ear. "Dat man keeps watching us."

"What man?" I whispered back.

She pointed over my shoulder.

I pulled back a bit and kissed the top of her head. If someone was watching us the last thing I wanted to do was clue them into that I knew. Although, Mia pointing probably gave it away.

I turned slightly and peeked behind me but the aisle was empty.

"He left," she announced softly.

I smoothed my fingers through her hair. "Tell me if you see him again."

She nodded.

I grabbed the last of the items I needed, including Mia's popsicles, and headed to the check out.

I was still on edge from Mia's words, the little hairs on the back of my neck standing up straight. I wanted to pretend it was nothing, but Mia wasn't the kind of child to make something like that up. If she said someone was watching us then they were.

I stepped into line and began unloading my groceries onto the conveyer belt.

"Fancy running into you here."

"Ah!" I jumped and turned around, clasping a hand over my heart. "You scared me!" I scolded.

"Sorry." Hayes smiled sheepishly and gave a small shrug.

"Why are you here?" I asked as I pushed the cart forward.

"Well…this is a grocery store. I needed food…you know, in order to keep living and all. As well as toilet paper." He proudly held up the plastic wrapped rolls. "I remember, mentioning that to you last night. Oh, and we can't forget that I had to reimburse poor Barbara for her delicious cake."

"I forgot about Barbara," I muttered.

He shook his head, his lips turned down in a frown. "How could you possibly forget Barbara? She gifted us with the most delicious cake to ever pass through our lips…although, calling it a gift is kind of a stretch since I stole it. Does it count as stealing if you didn't intend to steal it?"

Uh…"

"Never mind," he waved his hand in dismissal, "and in case you were wondering, I got Barbara a gift card to make up for eating her cake."

"How generous of you," I commented as the checker began to scan my items.

"I like to think of myself as a very giving guy." Hayes mused. "Especially when it comes to the pleasure of a certain red head." He stared at me with hooded eyes and my body heated all over.

"You don't play fair," I accused.

"I told you I wasn't going to."

"Ma'am?" The checker called to get my attention.

I looked and saw all my stuff bagged and waiting.

"Oh, sorry." I jumped into action, swiping my credit card and loading the bags into the cart.

The cashier handed me my receipt and I started to push the cart towards the doors, wanting to get out of there as fast as I could.

"Hey, Arden?"

I was forced to turn around at the sound of Hayes' voice.

"Yeah." I paused, waiting for him to speak.

"I'll see you later."

"Oh, right…of course."

Still scattered, thanks to his sudden appearance, I hurried to the doors.

I loaded the groceries into the car and buckled Mia into her car seat.

As I was backing out, it finally occurred to me to ask her if Hayes had been the man she saw.

"No, momma," she giggled, "I know Hayes."

"So, Hayes wasn't the one watching us?" I confirmed.

"No, swilly."

I swallowed past the lump in my throat as fear slid like a slimy serpent through my veins.

I prayed silently that it was nothing, but my gut told me otherwise.

# CHAPTER FIVE

IT'D BEEN A week since I'd heard from, or seen, Hayes. Stupidly, I thought maybe he'd given up on me. I should've known better.

I looked down at the text message flashing on my phone.

**You. Me. Date. Tomorrow. No excuses…or I'll spank u.**

A second later my phone chimed with yet another text.

**On 2nd thought, pls give me a bullshit excuse so that I can spank you.**

I laughed.

**I like your ass.**

**You're so weird.** I sent back.

**Weird in a charming way, right?**

I didn't reply and a few minutes passed.

**Did I scare you away?**

**I did, didn't I?**

**Shit. I know my enthusiasm can be a bit much. I'll try 2 dial it back.**

**Stop sweating.** I sent him.

**Phew. Ur mean. I'll pick u up at 7.**

**I don't have a baby sitter and I doubt I can get one this last minute.**

**Already got u covered. Sadie and Ezra volunteered.** Even though it was only a text message I knew he was grinning widely, pleased that he'd thought of everything.

**Ur good.** I replied.

**I like to think so.**

**How should I dress?** I asked him.

A minute passed before he replied.

**Comfortably.**

**I like the sound of this date already.** I replied with a smile on my face.

**U should. It's going 2 b the most awesomest first date in the history of**

**dates. Brace ur self.**

I shook my head, smiling like a giddy schoolgirl.

**Bracing.**

I did something I never did.

I stood in front of my closet and carefully planned out what I was going to wear.

Normally, I'd grab the first thing my eyes landed on, yank it off the hanger, and pull it onto my body as quickly as I could. Then I would usually tie my hair back into a ponytail, or if it looked halfway decent leave it down. Having a three-year-old daughter didn't allot me much time to pamper myself. Hell, peeing without an interruption was a luxury.

Mia bounced excitedly on my bed. When I explained to her that I was going on a date with Hayes I think she'd been more excited than me. Not that she really knew what a date was at her age; she'd asked me if this meant Hayes was taking me to the playground.

Since Hayes told me to dress comfortably I avoided my dresses.

I grabbed a pair of jeans off the shelf and shook them loose. They were one of my nicer pairs and I knew my ass looked amazing in them, and since Hayes had already admitted to liking my butt I figured I might as well torture him a bit. I liked watching him squirm.

I perused my shirts, settling on a gray loose tee. Since it was chilly out I topped it off with a jean jacket in a lighter shade of fabric than my pants.

I changed in the bathroom and opened the door to find Mia waiting.

"What do you think?" I asked her. "Do you approve?"

She cocked her hip to the side and looked me up and down. "Hmm…"

"What is it?" I asked, looking down to make sure there wasn't a stain or hole in my clothes.

"You sood wear a dress if you wants him to kiss you."

I squished my lips shut, trying not to laugh.

"I won't be kissing him, baby girl."

She scoffed, her tiny pink lips parting in an O. "Then I twill kiss him for you."

This time I couldn't contain my laughter and full on snorted.

"What's so funny?" She put her hands on her hips, glaring at me.

"You are, cutie." I ran my fingers through her red curls.

She turned her head to the side. "I was swerious."

I chuckled. "I know."

She looked me up and down one more time. "You sood change." With a swish of her hips she turned and strutted out of my bedroom.

"That child," I muttered to myself, "I fear the teenage years."

I turned around and stepped back into the bathroom to put on some makeup, careful to keep it light and simple. I curled my hair and let it cascade down my back.

Satisfied with my appearance I checked the time and saw that Sadie and Ezra should be arriving any minute…and so should Hayes.

My hands began to prickle with nerves and I silently scolded myself for being so silly.

This was *Hayes.*

I knew him.

This wasn't some stranger I had to pretend to be polite to.

I was comfortable with Hayes…but suddenly I felt anything *but* comfortable and he wasn't even here yet.

I slipped into a pair of converse sneakers and grabbed my purse just as there was a knock on the door.

My heart rate spiked and I held my breath as I swung the door open.

I instantly deflated when I saw that it was Sadie and Ezra.

I waved them inside and closed the door.

"That's what you're wearing?" Sadie wrinkled her nose with distaste.

Sadie, being the fashionita that she was, I'd expected such a reaction.

"Hayes told me to dress comfortably," I defended with a frown.

"You need to dress to impress."

Ezra chuckled, shaking his head. He wrapped an arm around her waist and tugged her against his side. "She looks nice, sweetheart. Leave her alone."

Sadie huffed in exasperation, but let it go.

"You remember Sadie and Ezra, right?" I asked Mia.

She sat with her back turned to us, her eyes glued to the TV screen where *Frozen* was playing.

"Mia," I prompted, and she finally turned around. "Say hi to Sadie and Ezra. They're watching you tonight."

"Hi," Mia mumbled, her attention quickly returning to the TV screen.

I sighed and shook my head.

"She goes to bed in an hour. I always read her a bedtime story. But only one. She'll try to sweet talk you into more so she can stay up late. I know she's cute when she bats those eyes, but stay strong." I joked.

"We've got it." Ezra nodded.

"Oh, and she likes a sippy cup of water when she goes to bed. I set it on the counter for you. If she asks for a snack she can have some gold fish crackers, but *no* sweets. Seriously, she'll get a sugar high and never go to sleep."

"We'll be fine." Sadie assured me.

I nodded, taking a deep breath. I trusted them both and Mia knew them so it should be fine.

A knock sounded on the door and Sadie gave me a knowing look. "There he is."

I stood still, completely frozen. My palms began to sweat and I tried to inconspicuously wipe them on my jeans but Ezra saw and let out a small chuckle.

"Are you going to get the door or should I?" Sadie prompted with a raised brow.

"Oh, right…me. I've got it."

I strode over to the door and after another deep breath I opened it.

Hayes stood there looking as handsome as ever. His hair was still damp from the shower and brushed over to one side. Like me, he was dressed casually in a pair of slim legged dark jeans and a long sleeve gray shirt. Even still, he made the simple ensemble look like he'd plucked it straight off a model on the runway.

His hands were clasped behind his back and when he brought one hand forward he held a bouquet of white daisies beneath my nose.

"For you." He grinned proudly.

Behind me, Sadie swooned. "Awww, how sweet!"

I glared at her over my shoulder and then quickly gave Hayes my undivided attention. Smiling at him, I said, "They're beautiful."

"Are dose for me?" Mia asked, *Frozen* completely forgotten for the moment.

"No, Ms. Mia," Hayes shook his head, "these are for your mommy, but these," he drew his other hand forward and proudly held out a bouquet of hot pink daisies, "are for you."

She clapped her hands together excitedly and ran forward to take them from him.

"Day're bootiful." She grinned up at him and he bent down to be at her height so that he could hand them over.

"I'm happy you like them." He smiled at her like she was the cutest thing he'd ever seen, and something inside my chest stirred.

He stood back up and smiled at me, his dimple flashing.

"I'll go put these in some water and then we can head out. Mia, can I have yours?" I asked her, holding my hand out.

"Can I puts dem in my room?" She asked, not wanting to let go of the flowers.

"Absolutely."

"O'tay."

She handed the flowers over and I fixed each bouquet in a vase before heading back to the door. Hayes dropped his hand to my waist and waved at Sadie and Ezra with the other. "We won't be out late."

"Oh," Sadie grinned, "take all the time you need."

"Sadie," I hissed, pink staining my cheeks.

She laughed. "I feel like a parent sending my kid out for prom. Quick, Ezra, get your phone and take a picture."

"No! No pictures!" I cried, embarrassment deepening the color in my cheeks.

It was too late though, Ezra was already snapping away while Sadie clapped her hands and danced on the balls of her feet.

"You kids have fun." She winked, all but pushing us out the door.

When the door closed behind us I turned to Hayes with wide eyes.

"She is so bossy," I grumbled.

Hayes merely chuckled and reached for my hand. He guided me to his truck and then helped me climb into the massive thing. His hand landed on my butt and he gave me a small push.

Once I was seated I turned to glare at him. "You did that on purpose."

His eyes sparkled with laughter. "Maybe."

I huffed and reached for the seatbelt as he closed the door.

He hopped into the truck and the engine roared to life a moment later.

He turned the volume down on the radio and glanced at me. "You know," he smiled sheepishly, "I haven't put this much effort into impressing a girl in…well, a long time."

I laughed. "Is that a good thing or a bad thing?"

"Good, definitely good." He nodded. "It means I care enough about you to try." He winked.

I guessed he had a point there.

Taking a deep breath, he said, "I know you have your reservations about me. Hell, the magazines don't tend to paint me in the best light…and I have done some shitty things in my life. But I'm different now. This isn't a game to me. Okay?" He gave me an earnest look before his eyes fell back to the road.

I nodded. "I know," I whispered.

And even though it was hard to acknowledge I *did* know that. The Hayes I'd gotten to know this past summer was amazing, and kind, and…maybe a little—or a lot—naughty at times.

"Where are we headed?" I asked, glancing out the window at the darkened sky.

"My house."

"Your house?" I echoed.

"Mhmm," he nodded, tugging his delectable bottom lip between his teeth before letting it go. "Is that okay?"

"Yeah, of course. I'm just surprised, that's all."

He shrugged, adjusting his hold on the steering wheel. "I'm not going to lie, I thought about taking you to a fancy restaurant, or whisking you away to D.C. or Baltimore for the evening, and about a million other things. But in the end I decided that none of those things were *you*. I knew I could do something special just by sharing myself with you." Smirking, he added, "And by 'myself' I do mean my person and not my cock."

"Oh my God," I muttered, fighting a laugh as I leaned my head back against the seat.

"And I'll be making dinner of course."

"*You're* making dinner?" I couldn't keep the surprise from my tone.

Smiling crookedly, he said, "I might be a rock star, Little Bird, but I'm not completely incompetent."

"What are some of your other talents?" I joked.

He tapped his lips as he pondered the question. "Hmm, well I think you're well acquainted with them." He winked.

"Hayes!" I lightly smacked his arm, my whole body blushing an unattractive shade of red. I was sure it matched my hair and my poor freckles probably stood out even more.

"Hey," he raised his hands in defense before grabbing the steering wheel once more, "I don't know what you're thinking in that pretty little head of yours, but I was referring to my wicked awesome skateboarding tricks. Granted, I'm a little rusty, but I'm getting back into it. The teenagers at the skate park can be real dicks though." He turned to me with a sad face. "I wiped out and tore up my elbow and the fuckers laughed."

Now *I* was laughing at him.

"You're just as mean as them. You should be saying, 'Oh, Hayes, let me kiss your war wound and make it all better.'" He mimed in a high-pitched voice.

I snorted. "Not happening."

"I had a feeling you'd say that." He sighed.

He turned off the main road and the truck wound around the mountain, going higher and higher. We passed a few homes—ones so large I could fit my whole house into it three times.

When we could go no higher he turned into a driveway.

I gasped in awe. The home was huge, but not as large as some of the others we'd passed. Even still, it didn't lack grandeur.

It was done all in brick with a three-car garage jutting out the front. Above the front door was a large window and through it I could see a lit chandelier.

I'd never stopped to wonder what kind of home Hayes lived in, but if I had thought about it this was the last thing I would've expected.

"What do you think?" Hayes asked, seeming a bit embarrassed. "I know it's quite large for one person, but I fell in love with this land and I wanted to build my dream house here."

"It's beautiful," I answered honestly, "but not what I was expecting."

"What were you expecting?" He asked, truly curious.

I shrugged, still staring at the home in awe. "I guess I expected something more modern. Like a sleek condo or something."

He chuckled. "Yeah, that's not really my style." He parked the truck and turned off the engine. "Are you ready to check out the inside?"

"No, I was planning to climb a tree first."

He threw his head back and laughed. "I should've expected that kind of response."

"Yes, you should've." I scolded him lightly with a smile touching my lips.

I undid my seatbelt and he grabbed my hand to halt me from getting out.

"Let me help you. I wouldn't want you to break an ankle getting out of this thing." He winked playfully and jumped from the truck.

No way in hell was I waiting for him so I quickly opened the door and hopped out, landing on my feet.

Hayes stopped in front of me, shaking his head. "Why can't you listen to anything I say?"

"Aw," I patted his chest mockingly, "now where's the fun in that?"

Huffing a breath he closed the door and locked his truck.

He led me to the front door and grabbed his keys, digging around for the right one.

"I normally go in through the garage," he explained. "Aha!" He chimed, holding up a key. "Found it."

He slid it into the lock and swung the door open.

My eyes were met with dark hardwood floors, toffee colored walls, a sweeping staircase, and arches leading back into what appeared to be a family room. To my right sat a home office that was decorated pretty sparsely with a wooden desk, heavy chair, and a sleek laptop. On my left was a little nook with filled bookshelves and several comfy looking leather chairs.

"This way."

Hayes took my hand, leading me deeper into his home.

"This is the kitchen." He pointed unnecessarily to the room.

It had tall cherry wood cabinets, golden colored granite countertops, and appliances any chef would drool over.

"Dining room." He motioned to the room across from the kitchen.

A large table sat beneath a glimmering chandelier. I'd never seen such a big dining table before and I figured he must have had it custom made to accommodate all off his friend's and family.

"And the family room."

"This might be my favorite room," I breathed, craning my neck back to take in the massive cathedral like ceilings.

The wall across from me was covered in windows, while the one to my left boasted a massive fireplace surrounded by intricate woodwork. The other walls were painted a darker shade from the one in the entryway and it made the large room seem cozy. In front of the fireplace was a tan suede sectional positioned on top of a fluffy beige rug.

"It's my second favorite," he grinned, "my bedroom is number one of course." His perpetual smirk stained his lips. "My bed is *super* comfy. Would you like to test it out?"

I tried to hide my smile but failed miserably.

"Ah, there it is." He poked my cheek. "Your smile is beautiful, but you hide it."

I lowered my head, my hair falling over my shoulders.

I startled when his warm fingers touched my chin, lifting my eyes to his.

His face was shadowed with seriousness as he stared at me.

"Don't hide yourself from me." His voice was nothing more than a husky whisper. "I want to see it all. Your smiles. Your frowns. Your worries. Your pleasure. Everything that makes you *you*. Give it to me."

I pulled in a lungful of air, overcome by his beautiful words. "I'm scared," I admitted. Those two words took every ounce of courage I possessed in my body. Admitting you were afraid was one of the most difficult things to own up to as a human being. We were programmed to always say that we were *fine* or *good*—that showing fear is a sign of weakness. But it's not. It's one of the bravest things you can do to surrender that fear from yourself and place it into the open palms of someone else.

"Don't be," he breathed, closing his eyes and leaning forward to press his lips to the top of my forehead. "I've got you."

His hands skimmed up my arms before coming to a rest against my cheeks.

His stare was unwavering and I couldn't look away from him if I wanted to.

"Take a chance on me, Arden. I know it might not seem like it, but I'm a sure bet."

I pulled in a shaky breath. "Don't break me." I whispered into the heated air between us. "I know I might not seem fragile, but I am."

He smoothed his thumbs against the round curves of my cheeks. "I'll take care of you," he vowed, "I could never hurt you."

I grasped his shirt between my hands. "I trusted a man once, I loved him with all of my heart, and he hurt me in ways you can't even begin to imagine. But getting to know you these past few months…" I paused, laughing under my breath. "You've managed to breach every barrier I built around my heart without even trying."

Hayes' whole body had gone rigid at the mention of my ex. "What did he do to you?" He pleaded with me to open up, to spill every dark secret that tormented my brain. "Tell me." His fingers tangled in the silky hair at the base of my skull, tilting my head back so my gaze was locked on his.

"Not yet," I shook my head adamantly, "I promise I'll tell you, but please, *not tonight*."

I didn't want this night to be tainted with memories of Todd.

This was the night I was willingly handing over my heart to Hayes and I wouldn't let Todd take this moment from me. I'd been letting him rule my decisions for far too long, it was the only reason I'd been able to resist Hayes for four months— because even before I slept with him that boy had been weaseling his way into my heart from the moment I met him.

"Okay," Hayes relinquished to my pleas. "Not tonight, but soon?"

I nodded.

"I can live with that…although I might hunt down the fucker and kill him with my bare hands." His words were a growl and a muscle in his jaw jumped.

I reached up, taking the side of his face into one of my hands. His body instantly relaxed at my touch and I smiled at the fact that I affected him as much as he affected me.

"He's not worth it," I told him, "trust me."

"He must've been a fucking idiot to treat you horribly and abandon his daughter."

"You have no idea," I sighed.

Breaking away from his hold the tension from my body slowly leaked away.

"No more mentions of him tonight." I gave Hayes the best stern expression I could muster. It probably wasn't all that scary considering it never fazed Mia.

"Who?" Hayes winked.

I smiled. "So…are you going to feed me on this date or let me starve?"

"Baby, I'm a feast for your eyes, isn't that enough?" He jested.

Laughter burst free of my mouth and I doubled over clutching my stomach. "That's the cheesiest thing I've ever heard." I wiped tears from my eyes.

He shrugged, his grin firmly in place. "I thought it was pretty decent considering I saw it on a Popsicle stick."

I laughed harder.

Only Hayes could go from super serious one second to giving me an idiotic pickup line the next.

He held out his hand, waiting for me to place mine on top.

When I did he guided me out of the family room and into the kitchen.

He pulled out one of the barstools for me and urged me to sit down.

He strolled over to the refrigerator and began pulling out various dishes. He set them on the counter and then grabbed two wine glasses.

"Do you want any?" He asked, uncorking a bottle and pouring one glass, but hesitating over the other.

I gave a small nod and he filled it up halfway.

I took the glass while he turned on the grill built into the countertop.

"What are we having?" I asked, trying to peer at the plates he was slowly uncovering.

"Steak, baked potatoes, roasted vegetables, and dessert of course." He grinned boyishly as he arranged the plates.

"You've put a lot of thought into this," I commented.

He ceased what he was doing and looked up. "Of course I have."

He seemed offended that I would think anything else.

"It's nice," I assured him, "better than nice actually."

Like Hayes had said, he could've taken me to a fancy restaurant—and that's what I'd expected—but this was a thousand times better. I didn't need to be impressed, I just needed him in his true form.

I finally picked up my glass of wine and took a tentative sip. I was a picky drinker, but the delicious liquid that splashed against my tongue before sliding down my throat was absolutely incredible.

"Wow, that's good," I commented, taking another sip.

Hayes chuckled, laying two thick steaks on top of the grill. "I have it shipped in from this little vineyard I stumbled upon in Napa Valley."

"You went to a vineyard?" My eyes widened in surprise.

I had a hard time seeing Hayes, with his perfect hair, fancy sneakers, and straight-legged pants, traipsing through a vineyard.

"Hey," he put a hand to his chest, "I'm cultured. Just because I'm a rock star doesn't mean I'm all about the party life…okay, I will admit that I used to be, but the last six months or so…it hasn't been appealing." He shrugged. "But yes, I went to a vineyard."

"You're full of surprises," I shook my head, mystified, "what else do you have up your sleeve?"

"I like to hike."

"Hiking? Really?" I mused.

He grinned and rubbed his jaw. "I know I might look more like a Renaissance sculpture, or so I've been told," he shrugged, "but I'm all for getting down and dirty now and then." He winked before turning his back to me and opening the oven door to check on the baked potatoes he'd left cooking while he picked me up. Turning back around he placed his hands on his narrow hips. "Now you have to tell me something about yourself that I'd never guess."

"Hmm," I mused, trying to think of something. I was really a rather boring person. "I'm a beast at ping pong."

He chuckled, leaning forward to rest his elbows on the counter. "Really?"

I nodded. "My brother had a table when we were younger and I got really good at it because I wanted to beat him."

"You have a brother?" His brows rose in interest.

I nodded. "He lives in North Carolina now with his wife and kids. We don't see him much anymore." I frowned, shrugging my shoulders.

"Any other siblings?" He asked.

"No," I took another sip of wine, "you?"

"Two sisters." A wistful smile touched his lips. "One older and one younger. Jessica, my older sister, lives in Manhattan now. She's married with a son. She's a lawyer. And Jaclyn, my younger sister, is currently living in Washington state." Frowning, he mumbled, "I'm pretty sure she sells pot for a living."

I snorted, unable to help myself. "Seriously?"

He nodded. "She's always been a bit of a…"

"Free spirit?" I suggested.

He pointed at me. "I was going to say oddball, but let's go with that one. It sounds nicer. She's cool though. I miss her. I miss both of them actually…fuck, I never thought I'd say that when I was growing up. Let's just say, growing up the middle child with two sisters wasn't always fun."

"Aw, did they turn you into their doll?" I cackled mercilessly.

He frowned. "How'd you know? They were very into blue eye shadow, hot pink lipstick, and bows. Oh, God, the *bows*." He buried his face in his hands, stifling his laugh.

"I bet you made a very pretty girl," I joked.

He looked up and his eyes had darkened to a stormy navy blue. He stalked around the counter and slid the barstool out so that he stood between my legs. Looking down at me from his looming height, he growled, "I'm all man, Little Bird. And don't you forget it."

He lowered his head, suckling my neck before going higher and tugging my earlobe between his teeth.

An unwanted moan slipped free from my lips and he hummed in response.

This man was a deadly potent force to my senses.

His thumb brushed my bottom lip and I ached for his kiss.

I'd agreed to this date, believing I was strong enough to make it a one-time thing, but I had no strength when it came to Hayes.

Before I could beg him to kiss me, and maybe even to take me right there on his kitchen counter, he pulled away and resumed his position beside the grill.

I was panting, my whole body aching for his touch, and he stood there smirking at me. He knew exactly what he did to me. Damn him.

I moved my chair back into place and picked up the wine glass.

"Tell me something else about yourself."

Despite the fact that I'd known Hayes for months we still didn't really *know* each other.

"When I was six I set a trap to catch the tooth fairy…my dad was pissed when he tripped over my booby trap. My childhood was also ruined in that moment because then I began to think everything my parent's had ever told me was a lie. I cried for like…" He tapped his chin in thought. "Three days. My dad finally gave me a hundred dollars to shut me up. Not that I really had much concept of how much money that was, I just knew I could buy some Hot Wheels."

I laughed. "I hope Mia never tries anything like that. I want her to believe in that stuff as long as possible. When you're a child magic and possibilities seem endless. All too soon you grow up and that innocence disappears in the blink of an eye," I mused, a frown down turning my lips.

Hayes checked the steaks and returned to his propped position against the counter. "It's your turn again, tell me something else."

"My favorite color is pink…cliché, I know," I laughed.

"Come on, you've gotta give me more than that."

"That was something!" I defended.

He shook his head. "A color doesn't tell me much about you personally."

"I'm not a very good cook," I admitted.

He chuckled. "Oh, I doubt that."

"I burned water one time. *Wat-er.*" I drew out the word. "I'm lucky Mia is pretty easy to cook for. And I do make a pretty awesome grilled cheese." I grinned. "*But it's definitely not that.*" I pointed at the steaks.

"Well, aren't you lucky to have me now." He gave me a half-grin. "These should be done now." He muttered to himself before checking the steaks. "Yeah, they're ready."

He removed the steaks and grilled the vegetables before pulling the baked potatoes from the oven.

I offered to get the plates, but he insisted on doing everything on his own.

He refilled my glass of wine—his still untouched, and guided me into the dining room. He set the plates down at seats across from each other and then pulled out a chair for me. I hadn't expected Hayes to be such a gentlemen, but I was discovering that he was full of surprises.

He turned on the chandelier that sparkled above the table and then dimmed it so that it wasn't so blindingly bright.

"One second," he said, running from the room.

When he returned he had two candles clasped in his hands.

He lit them and sat down, all the while I watched him in awe.

"You've thought of everything, haven't you?"

He shrugged sheepishly. "I tried. I'm sure I've forgotten something, though."

"You're amazing." I whispered the words. I wouldn't normally have said such a thing, but I thought he deserved to know.

"I'm just me." He reasoned.

"Hmm, you're being humble, I'm shocked." I laughed as I cut into my steak. I took a bite and let out a moan. "Oh my God, that's fantastic."

He grinned, lifting his glass of wine to his lips. "I'm glad you approve."

"Can you cook for me all the time?" I asked, taking a bite of my baked potato.

He chuckled, cutting into his own steak. "While I *can* cook, I must admit this is a rare occurrence." He winked. "The lure of ordering take-out is far too potent for me to resist."

"Ah," I nodded, "I should've known."

"But hey, if I had a beautiful woman to cook for every evening I might change my mind."

"When can you move in?" I joked.

He let out a laugh, the kind that came from deep within your gut. "Would I get to sleep in your bed?" A smirk lifted his lips.

I pretended to ponder his words. "Possibly, although I hear dogs like sleeping on the floor."

He let out another laugh, this one even more booming than the last. "Fuck, I like you. You're a spitfire, you know that, right?"

"So I've been told." I shrugged.

We continued to chat as we ate and soon my plate was empty.

"I'm stuffed," I declared, rubbing my stomach. "I don't think I can move."

"That's okay. I'll let *you* sleep in *my* bed," he jested, sliding his chair away from the table.

He began to gather the dirty plates and I said, "How very accommodating of you."

He shrugged, trying to hide a smile. "I like to think so."

I managed to push myself away from the table and followed him into the kitchen where he stopped at the sink and ran hot water for the dirty dishes to soak.

"Come on." He took my hand, leading me back into the family room.

He turned on a few lights, but kept the room relatively dim. With a push of a button the fireplace roared to life and I gasped in awe.

We sat down in front of the fireplace on the fluffy rug and he reached for a blanket, wrapping it around our shoulders.

Everything about tonight had been simple, but so overwhelmingly perfect.

I found myself scooting closer to him and laying my head on his shoulder.

He smoothed his fingers through my hair and his lips touched my forehead.

"Wanna know something?" He murmured, the sound of his voice vibrating against the sensitive skin of my neck.

"What?" I prompted, reaching up to cup his jaw.

He turned his head to press a tender kiss to my palm.

He swallowed thickly, his Adam's apple bobbing with fear.

"I'm terrified that tomorrow, I'm going to wake up and you're going to have changed your mind…that you don't want me as much as I want you."

I stared into his eyes, seeing the fear shimmering in the twin blue pools. "I might be stubborn, and prideful, and a bunch of other things, but I'm not stupid. I tried ignoring what I feel for you," I sucked in a breath, "but look where I am now. I'm here, with you. Hell, I even swore to myself that this date would change nothing, but I was wrong. What I feel for you transcends logic. I'm done denying myself what I want."

"And what *exactly* is it that you want?"

"You," I breathed, "only you."

He closed his eyes, his whole body shuddering with my words.

"You have no fucking idea how badly I've wanted to hear you say that."

Before I could respond, his lips stole my next breath and I dissolved into his arms.

I hadn't been lying when I told him I wanted this. I did. So badly. I'd resisted for so long because of silly fears, but everything he shared with me tonight—his kind words, and the little tidbits that made him *him*—was enough to crack my resolve for good.

I just hoped I didn't end up getting burned.

# CHAPTER SIX

BLISS.

It was the only word to describe how I felt.

Well, maybe that and giddy.

I felt like I was in school again, enjoying the high of a new relationship.

I knew it had only been a week and that it wouldn't *always* feel like this, but I was determined to enjoy it while it lasted.

"So, things are going good?" Sadie asked me from where she stood at the register while I refolded a stack of shirts.

"Yeah," I smiled at her over my shoulder, "we haven't seen much of each other this week since the guys are busy in the studio, but he calls me every night when he gets home."

"That's so sweet." Sadie swooned—I'm not kidding, she put a hand to the back of her forehead and did a little dip.

"Yeah, I just hope it works out," I mumbled.

She frowned. "You don't sound so certain that it will."

I finished with the shirts and turned around to face her. "I fell for a guy once before and he turned out to be the complete opposite of who I thought he was."

"Well," she grinned, "the good news is, you thought Hayes was a bad boy through and through, so if he's the opposite of that then it means he's perfect."

Leave it to Sadie to come up with that reasoning.

"Your brain must be a strange place," I commented, heading into the back of the store for a box of new clothes that had arrived earlier.

"You guys are good together," she called to me, "and I'll be saying I told you so on your wedding day."

I shook my head. "Not likely."

I was saved from her response by the sound of the chime above the door dinging and signaling a customer.

"Hayes is here!"

Or not exactly saved.

Not that I wasn't happy he'd stopped by, but I knew Sadie would give me hell for this later.

I emerged from the back with a smile on my face.

Hayes stood by the counter with his skateboard clutched in his hands. He was dressed casually in a pair of jeans and a t-shirt with a logo I didn't recognize. A beanie hid his normally perfectly styled hair.

"I brought you ladies lunch." He proudly held up a bag from Chick-fil-A.

"Aw, how nice of you." Sadie nudged my shoulder as if to say, *see he's a nice guy.*

I already knew that, though, and I also knew it was wrong of me to expect him to change like my ex had. Most people weren't like Todd. But when you'd been treated as horribly as I had by someone it became harder to trust. I was making the effort to work on that, because I really did like Hayes, and I didn't want the ghost of my past relationship to hurt a good thing.

"I would've gotten you drinks too," he explained, setting the bag down on the counter, "but I couldn't really carry drinks, a bag of food, and skateboard."

"This is more than enough." I reached for the bag, suddenly ravenous.

"Also…" He paused, shrugging his shoulders like he was afraid to say what he needed to say. "I wanted to see if Arden could possibly have next Thursday through Sunday off?" He addressed Sadie.

"Uh, don't you think you should ask me if I *want* to be off first?"

"Shh, woman, I have to find out if this is even a possibility before I make plans with you." He threw up a hand, silencing me. I would've been mad if it wasn't for the fact that he said it jokingly and his smile was large.

"Yeah, she can be off…*if* the reason you want her off is for what I think it is."

"What is going on?" I asked, groaning in irritation. "I feel like the odd man out here."

Hayes turned to me, his smile even more beaming than before if that were possible. "The guys and I are making an appearance on *The Today Show*. They want to interview us and have us play one of our songs." Shrugging, he said, "We all decided to head down Thursday and make a weekend out of it."

"You're going too?" I asked Sadie.

She nodded, sweeping her brown hair to the side of her shoulder. "Yeah, of course. Do you really think I'm going to let a bunch of fan girls fawn all over my man and try to touch his hair? That hair is mine."

Hayes and I both laughed.

"I'm pretty sure the hair that resides on Ezra's head belongs to him." Hayes informed her.

She crossed her arms over her chest. "He belongs to me, therefore so does his hair. I've seen your groupies try to pet him before. Only I'm allowed to do that."

Hayes snorted. "Okay, then."

"Shouldn't you be getting back to the studio, *Joshua*?" She sneered.

He chuckled, rubbing a hand over his smooth jaw. "Why does everyone start calling me by my first name when they get pissy?"

"Because, you don't like your first name and I want you to be as pissy as I am." She joked, reaching for the bag of food and pulling out a container of waffle fries. "Thanks for this, though."

"You're welcome." He cracked a grin, the dimple I adored making its appearance.

"So what do you say Little Bird? You, me, Ms. Mia, and NYC next weekend?" His eyes pleaded with me to say yes, but I was worried. Not about me, but Mia. The trip we went on to the beach with the Willow Creek gang had been the only time she'd ever been away from home and slept in a bed that wasn't hers. But even then we'd been staying in a *house* not a hotel.

"I don't know," I hedged, "Mia might not be too happy about it."

"I can handle a cranky three-year old—not that I think she'll be bad—but I do deal with Mathias on an almost daily basis, and he's worse than most children."

Sadie snickered. "He can be bad. But he's getting better."

"Eh," Hayes shrugged, "a bit. He's at his best when he's around Remy and the baby. When he's on his own he starts to get a bit grumpy and he bitches about," he lifted his fingers into quotation marks, "'Missing out on important milestones in Liam's life.'" He lowered his hands. "The kid's only like a month old, all he does is shit, eat, shit again, and throw up on himself. What exactly is there to miss?"

"You'd be surprised," I replied.

"I guess I'll understand one day." He winked at me and my stomach dipped with…excitement? Fear? Nervousness? With a wave he started towards the door. "Don't back out on me, Little Bird." He stopped and pointed a finger warningly at me. "It's going to be a blast and Mia will love it, you'll see."

He disappeared, hopping onto his skateboard and zooming down the sidewalk.

"Little Bird?" Sadie eyed me with one brow raised in questioning. "He gave you a nickname?"

"Yeah," I admitted reluctantly, reaching for the bag of food.

"You've been holding out on details with me, haven't you?" She looked me up and down, scoffing under her breath. "And here I thought we were friends." She laughed.

I stuck a fry in my mouth and said, "I don't kiss and tell."

"Hmm," she hummed, "whatever. Keep the details for yourself. It's not like my panties are dry and I need the stimulation. I've got a smokin' hot bass player waiting for me at home, and let me tell you, that boy might look all cute and innocent…but you get him into bed and BAM! it's a whole other guy. He's quite rough in bed and I love it." She waggled her brows and reached down to open a box that contained a chicken sandwich.

"I didn't need to know all that," I told her, holding up a hand in an effort to halt anything else she might say.

"I know, but I can't help but brag." She joked with a smile. "Especially since *you* don't want to share."

"I think some things should be kept private." I reasoned. "Besides, we only slept together the one time."

Her jaw came unhinged and she grabbed my arm, forcing me to look at her. "You mean you didn't have sex the other night? I sent you a text and told you to make sure he got it in." She began to thrust her hips. "You need some lovin'."

I rolled my eyes at her crudeness. "That night was…special without that."

"Aw," she clasped her hands. "I bet it was sweet, but I wouldn't know since you won't tell me anything." She jutted out her bottom lip.

"That doesn't work on me when Mia does it and it won't work on me now, either."

"Fun sucker." She pouted. She picked up the sandwich once more and smiled. "Just kidding. I can't be mad when I have Chick-fil-A. I'm pretty sure the inside of Chick-fil-A is what heaven looks like."

I tossed a napkin at her head. "You're insane."

She grabbed the napkin from where it landed on her boobs and set it on the counter. "Where's the fun in being sane? Because apparently you're implying that *you're* sane, and you're not having sex, so I want no parts in sanity."

"You're worse than a guy," I muttered, munching on a waffle fry.

She wiggled her hips again. "Only with Ezra. I could ride that boy all day and all night." She winked.

"Gross." I wrinkled my nose.

"Prude," she countered, bumping my hip with hers. "Now shut up and eat this delicious food your man brought us. He's a keeper, I'm tellin' you."

I shook my head, fighting a smile. "I hope so."

She stared at me for a long moment. "I *know* so."

# CHAPTER SEVEN

I HAD NO idea what to pack for New York Freaking City.

I was a small town girl. I'd been born and raised in Virginia and my traveling had been kept to a minimum. Sure, I'd been to the beach plenty, and D.C. since it was so close, but I knew that didn't compare to New York City. It was a whole different ball game out there.

Irritated with my lack of presentable clothes I decided to pack Mia's stuff first. You'd think since we were only going to be gone a few days that I wouldn't need to pack much. Wrong. A three-year-old could get into more messes than you'd believe. Not that Mia wasn't well behaved, but accidents did happen.

I pulled out Mia's carry-on size hot pink suitcase and sat down on the floor in front of her dresser.

It wasn't long until she found me, a half eaten popsicle dripping onto her hand as she struggled to finish eating it.

"Aw, Mia," I groaned, standing up. "You're going to be all sticky."

"I taste yummy, momma." She proceeded to lick her hand.

I took a deep breath and guided her into the kitchen where I lifted her onto the counter and cleaned off one hand while she finished the Popsicle with the other.

Once she was completely clean I put her down.

"I'm going to pack your stuff. You want to help?" I ruffled her hair as I smiled down at her.

Being a parent was hard, especially doing it on your own, but at the end of the day this little girl was the reason I lived and breathed.

She nodded her head eagerly. "Can I twake my dresses? I wants to be pwetty."

"You're always pretty." I told her as I padded down the hall with her right on my heels.

"Duh, but dresses make me pwettier."

I laughed. "Okay, baby girl."

We sat down on the floor together and went through the clothes in her dresser. Even though she insisted she only wanted to wear dresses I still packed her a few pairs of pants to be on the safe side. It was already getting chilly here, and I knew it would be even colder up north.

Once she was all packed I had to face the reality of my closet once more.

It was Wednesday afternoon and we were flying out tonight. I felt so unprepared even though I'd had a week to plan. It was safe to say I'd procrastinated my time away.

Mia hopped up onto my bed with her favorite purple stuffed bunny clasped in her chubby hands. She burrowed into the pillows on my bed and I chuckled.

"Are you going to take a nap?" I asked her.

"No, swilly," she scoffed. "I'm a big gurl. Naps are for babies."

I shook my head, laughing under my breath as I scanned my closet.

I ended up packing mostly jeans and sweaters. I did pack two dresses though, to be on the safe side. I didn't want to get caught like I did at the beach when I didn't have anything dressier to wear.

I set the packed suitcases by the front door and then packed a small bag with hair and makeup supplies.

By the time I was done I knew Hayes would be here any minute.

I scurried around the house in an effort to double check that I'd packed everything I might need. I hated to over pack, but with a child you had to make sure you had certain things. Like medicine and Band-Aids…and I forgot both of those things.

I ran back into the bathroom and grabbed the children's Motrin and the small first aid kit.

I put both in my purse and stood with my hands on my hips. I took a deep breath as I ran through a mental checklist. This time I was sure that I had everything I could possibly need.

It was crazy to think I'd gone on a vacation with everybody only a few months ago, but this time Hayes and I were a couple. It seemed too weird to use the word *boyfriend*. I hadn't called someone that since high school. After Todd left I had no desire to date and having a baby left little time for a relationship. Besides, most men could barely handle the baggage of a woman, let alone one with a child. But Hayes was different. From the moment I met him he'd been enamored with Mia. In fact, if you wanted my complete honesty I think he liked her before he did me. While shy, she could charm the best of them with a bat of her lashes.

"Mia, what are you doing?" I called when I noticed her bouncing on the couch as she looked out the window.

"Waitin' for Hayes."

She never ceased to amuse me.

Turning to look at me over her slender shoulder, she asked, "Is he going to be my new daddy?"

My whole body clamped up. I'd known these kinds of questions were inevitable from a child her age, but I'd hoped to avoid them a little while longer. I mean, Hayes and I hadn't even been on an official second date yet. It was way too soon to be talking about anything permanent, but explaining that to Mia would be nearly impossible.

"No," I replied as I sat down beside her. I gathered her into my arms and kissed the top of her head, inhaling the scent of her shampoo.

She pouted, tears sparkling in her large blue eyes. "But udder kids have daddies. Day pick dem up at school."

My heart broke at her words. Three days a week Mia went to a preschool in the mornings before being picked up by her baby sitter. I hated that she had to sit and watch other kids interact with their dads while she was left to wonder why she didn't have one.

"I'm so sorry, baby girl." My throat suddenly clogged with emotion and I struggled to get enough air. "One day you're going to have a daddy."

She gave me a sad little look and snuggled into my body. "At weast I have da best momma in the world."

I smiled at her words. "I'm glad you think so." I kissed her forehead, hoping that even with the simple gesture she could feel how much I loved her.

A car horn sounded outside, breaking the moment.

I stood with Mia gathered into my arms and went to the door.

Hayes was already getting out of his truck and I nodded towards my car. "Can you grab her car seat for me?"

"Sure thing." He jogged over to my car and had the seat out within seconds.

He installed it in his truck like he'd done it a million times before and I walked down the porch steps with Mia still in my arms.

Hayes tugged on the seatbelt strap to make sure there wasn't any give and grinned in satisfaction at his handy work.

"Hey, Ms. Mia," he held out his arms, "are you going to let me put you in your seat?"

She nodded and leaned from my arms towards him. He grabbed her and buckled her into the seat, placing a kiss on her cheek and melting my heart in the process.

I turned to head back inside but Hayes reached for my arm to halt me while he closed the truck door with the other.

"You get on in," he nodded at the truck, "I'll get your stuff and lock up."

"Are you sure? They're heavy," I joked.

He gasped like he was offended. "Have you seen these guns?" He proudly flexed his arms. "I think I can handle your bags."

I shook my head, unable to hide my smile. "The bags are by the door and my keys are on the kitchen counter."

"You got it." With a salute he jogged away and up the porch steps.

I climbed into the massive truck and turned around to check on Mia.

"Are you strapped in good there, baby girl?"

She nodded. "Yep." She tugged on the straps.

I smiled at her. "We're going on an adventure. Are you excited?"

Her tiny pink lips pursed together. "...Will I get a new Barbie?"

I grinned. "Only if you're good."

"I'll be da best."

"I know you will."

I turned back around and saw Hayes had both of the suitcases sitting on the porch while he locked the door. He kept staring at the knob and studying the doorframe.

Before I could hop out of the truck he grabbed up the suitcases and started forward.

He put them in the back on the opposite side of Mia and when he climbed in the driver's seat his brow was wrinkled with worry.

"What's wrong?" I asked, placing my hand on his forearm. The muscle was taut beneath my fingers.

"It looked like your door had been tampered with," he whispered, backing out of the driveway. "I'm going to call someone to change your lock while we're gone."

"What?" I gasped, my heart stopping and then speeding up in fear. "Do you really think it's necessary?"

His worried blue eyes connected with mine. "Yeah, I do. If someone's messing around..." He pulled in a lungful of air. "I'd never forgive myself if I did nothing and you or Mia ended up hurt."

"You're right," I agreed, glancing back at Mia. "I can't let anything happen to her."

Suddenly, my eyes widened with clarity.

What if the person messing around my house was the man Mia saw at the store? Could someone be stalking me? But why? It wasn't like I had much. It was all strange, but I was going to have to be more alert. Not only for my safety, but for Mia's.

The last few hours had proven to be some of the craziest of my life.

I could now check off riding in a private jet and a limo off of my bucket list.

Back at home it was all too easy to forget that the guys in Willow Creek were *famous*. They had perks most people only dreamed about, but it was their reality. I didn't know how they'd managed to remain humble through it all.

The limo pulled up in front of a fancy hotel and everyone moved to get out. When I started to slide towards the open door Hayes grabbed my arm to halt me.

Mia was passed out asleep on his lap and there was a wet spot on his shirt from her drool but he hadn't, not once, complained.

"We're not staying here," he stated, releasing my arm.

"We're not?" I frowned as the driver closed the door. Through the window I could see the others heading inside the hotel while someone pushed their bags in on carts.

"No," he shook his head, "Trace, my cousin…you remember him, right?" I nodded so he continued. "They own an apartment here. I thought it would seem more like home to Mia instead of staying here."

How did he think of these things? I'd never met anyone so kind and thoughtful before.

The driver pulled away from the hotel and I settled back into the seat.

Despite my exhaustion I still took time to look out the windows and appreciate the view. I'd never seen the city before and while beautiful with its soaring skyscrapers and bright colors I felt entirely out of my element and I hadn't even set foot out of the car. One of the things that boggled my mind the most was the fact that it was so late—or early, depending on your perspective—and the city was still teeming with life. Did no one ever sleep?

Minutes later the limo stopped in front of a large building that screamed rich people. Money dripped from the stone encasing the building and the marble steps leading up to the entrance. Beyond it I could see a lobby of sorts with heavy leather chairs and couches with a gleaming chandelier hanging above.

The door swung open and I slid out, my mouth parted in awe.

Hayes glided out behind me with a grace no man that tall should possess. Mia was still cradled in his arms sleeping peacefully.

"I'll bring your bags up for you." The driver said.

"Thanks." Hayes flashed him a smile as he adjusted his hold on Mia. "This way, Arden." His hand landed against the small of my back and he guided me forward and into the building.

We headed straight for the elevator. Hayes fumbled in his pocket for a key and inserted it into a slot before pressing a button for the penthouse.

It seemed to take forever for the elevator to finally reach the top floor, but when it did it was well worth the wait.

"Oh, wow." I gasped, stepping forward.

The foyer was covered in marble floors with a round wooden table that had a large flower arrangement perched on top. I reached out, taking a petal between my fingers to see if it was real. It was.

Hayes stood quietly behind me, letting me explore.

I stepped through an archway and gasped at the view. There was a whole wall of windows that showcased the city. It felt like we were a part of everything happening below us.

"This place is beautiful," I commented, turning around to take in the rest of the space.

I was surprised to find that the penthouse wasn't cold and barren looking. Instead it had a lived-in feel to it. There was a large sectional covered in thick pillows and a leather ottoman sat in the middle. Above a fireplace was a flat screen TV.

"Yeah it is," Hayes agreed. "I've only been here once before a few years ago so I forgot how nice it is."

"Where do you normally stay when you're in the city?" I asked, skimming my hand along the soft fabric of the couch.

He shrugged and glanced down at Mia in his arms. "Usually at the hotel with the guys, or at my friend's."

"Who's your friend?" Curiosity colored my tone.

He smiled wryly. "Not a girl if that's what you're implying. Have you ever heard of the band Fallen Invasion?"

I scoffed. "Of course. I don't live under a rock."

He chuckled. "Asher Robinson, the lead singer, let's me crash at his place sometimes."

"Wow," I breathed, "you know famous people."

He laughed softly. "Baby, I *am* famous people."

"Oh, right." I glanced down. "I keep forgetting that."

"I like that you forget that." He said the words softly and with so much meaning that I felt the words down in the very depths of my heart. He paused as he started past me and leaned down to graze his lips against the top of my head. "Come on, bed time."

I followed him down the hall to a guestroom where he pulled back the covers and gently placed Mia on top. She snuggled into the bed as he covered her body.

We tiptoed out of the room and he started to close the door, but left a small crack so that her room wouldn't be completely black.

I smiled at the small gesture that he probably hadn't even realized he'd done.

Hayes stood against the opposite wall from me and crossed his arms over his chest.

"There are plenty of rooms in this place so feel free to take one of those or you can share with Mia."

My brows furrowed in confusion. "I won't be sleeping with you?"

His eyes widened in surprise and his Adam's apple bobbed. "I'm okay with that if you are."

I nodded. "I am, but I'm exhausted so don't get any ideas…yet." I winked.

He groaned and reached out to grab me around the waist. He pulled my back against his chest and hugged me tight. "You really know how to play with a man, you know that, right?"

I smiled and leaned into his touch. I'd long ago forgotten how good it felt to be held by someone you cared about.

"Only you."

He chuckled against my neck and then his lips pressed tenderly against the spot where my pulse raced. "I like the sound of that."

# CHAPTER EIGHT

NEVER IN A million years did I think I'd be waking up in a king size bed, in a penthouse located in Manhattan, with the arms of Josh Hayes wrapped around me. But man, I could definitely get used to this.

I snuggled closer to his warm, bare chest, and pressed my lips to the crook of his neck.

He made a tiny little sound in the back of his throat but still didn't wake up.

He looked so peaceful in his sleep. The normally sharp edges of his cheekbones were softened and his lips were pouted to perfection. He oozed sex appeal without even trying and my long dormant hormones were ready to wake up and say hello. He was irresistible.

I reached up and traced my finger along his top lip. When I started on the bottom his eyes popped open and he playfully nipped at my roaming finger. I let out a squeal and he rolled over to pin me to the bed.

I pouted up at him as he caged me in with his arms.

"That's not fair," I protested.

He grinned. "What's not fair pretty girl?"

"You scared me and now you've trapped me."

He chuckled, leaning down to brush his lips over mine in a barely there kiss. "Trapped? Nah, you're not trapped. You could get away if you wanted to." His eyes darkened and his eyes fell to my lips. "But you don't want to."

This time his kiss was anything but brief.

He slid his lips over mine, gently coaxing my mouth open with his tongue.

I let out a soft moan and my hands delved into his hair. My legs wound around his waist and I urged him closer. I could feel him growing hard between my legs and I reveled in the power I had over him.

With one hand he grabbed my neck, tilting my head back as he deepened the kiss.

He tugged my bottom lip between his teeth and bit down, hard enough to sting but not enough to actually hurt, then he smoothed his tongue against the spot like he was wiping away the pain, although there was none.

My heart felt like it was going to jump right out of my chest and into his.

"Hayes." I breathed his name and he moaned like the sound of his name on my lips was the sexiest thing he'd ever heard.

He broke the kiss and looked down at me. He smoothed his fingers over my collarbone as he tried to steady his uneven breaths. "You have no idea what you do to me." His blue eyes shimmered with delight. "You have absolutely no fucking idea what you make me feel. Hell, sometimes I don't even understand what I'm feeling."

I cupped his jaw as I stared into his eyes. "I think I know."

I rose up, closing the short distance between us, and kissed him once more. Gaining leverage I pushed against his chest so that he was now the one lying and I hovered above him. His hands roamed down my sides, settling on my ass as his mouth explored mine.

I rolled my hips against his, itching to reach down and remove the barrier of clothing that separated us. I'd wanted to take things slow, but with Hayes it was impossible. What I felt for him couldn't be explained and I was sick of trying to define it by my own insecurities and preconceived notions. For once in my life I wanted to let myself go and enjoy the ride, wherever it might take me.

"Momma!"

And apparently I needed to get off this ride for the moment.

I pulled away from Hayes and flashed him an apologetic look. "I'm so sorry."

"Don't apologize." He rubbed his hands up and down my arms. "Go. It's okay." He smiled reassuringly. "Don't worry about me. I'll just be over here taking a cold shower and jacking myself off." His dimple flashed with a grin.

I buried my head in the space where his neck met his shoulder to stifle my laughter.

"Go." He urged, giving my ass a squeeze. "She needs you."

He kissed my forehead and I scurried out of the bed and to the door.

I found Mia in the hallway, rubbing her eyes.

"Hey, baby girl." I dropped to my knees and grabbed her hands. "Are you okay?"

She shook her head. "I woked up and I wasn't in my room so I gots scared."

"Aw, I'm so sorry. I should've been there, sweetie." I smoothed my finger over her plump cheek.

"S'okay."

"How about we go make some breakfast?" I asked her.

"We're going out for breakfast!" Hayes called from the bedroom.

"Never mind," I sighed. "Why don't we put on one of those beautiful dresses you picked out?" I tweaked her nose.

She nodded. "Will you make my hair pwetty?"

"Of course, but it's already pretty," I assured her.

I stood and lifted her in my arms.

I set her down on the bed she'd slept in and went in search of our bags. They'd been left in the foyer so I grabbed Mia's and rolled it into her room. I unzipped it and let her pick the dress she wanted to wear. The top was a light purple and it fanned out in the bottom with a tutu type material. I'd packed her a pair of tights to wear under it so that she wouldn't get too cold.

"Do I look pwetty, Momma?" She spun in a circle, her giggles filling the room.

"Beautiful."

I looked up at the sound of Hayes' voice and found him standing in the doorway, still shirtless, with a pair of jeans hanging loosely on his hips. He held a cup of coffee in his hand, the steam billowing in the air around him. He was oblivious to my scrutiny, though. His eyes were glued to Mia who was dancing around the room in her dress with a pair of black converse on her feet. My girl was equal parts princess and tomboy.

"Hey, Ms. Mia?" He called and she stopped twirling, looking up at him with interest.

"Yeah."

"Why don't we go do something and let your mommy get ready?"

She frowned, pursing her lips in thought. "But my hair?"

"I can do your hair." He shrugged.

"Really?" I asked at the same time Mia squealed in delight.

Hayes nodded. "How hard can it be?"

He had no idea.

"Okay. Well here's her brush, and hair ties." I pointed to the items on the bedside table. As I passed him I patted his bare chest. "Good luck."

He snorted like he wasn't going to need any.

Poor Mia. Who knew what kind of mess Hayes would make with her hair. I'd have to have my camera ready so that I could have photographic evidence of this.

Back in the bedroom I'd shared with Hayes I saw that he'd carried our bags in here and set them in the corner. I rifled through mine, procuring one of my nicer pairs of jeans, a white billowy top, and my favorite Aztec print cardigan.

I took a quick shower and styled my hair back in a ponytail.

By the time I finished my makeup I was starving and hoped that wherever Hayes wanted to go for breakfast was nearby.

In the living room of the penthouse I found Hayes and Mia sitting on the couch watching cartoons.

My mouth dropped open when I spotted Mia. She had two, perfectly braided, pig-tails tied with purple ribbons.

Hayes got a look at my face and laughed heartily at my shock.

"You really didn't think I could do it, did you?" He tried to hide his grin behind his hand.

"Nope."

"Two sisters, remember?" He winked.

"Remind me to thank them." I laughed, still amazed that he'd done her hair so beautifully. Even the middle part was perfect and not skewed.

He hopped up from the couch. "I'll be ready in five minutes."

"Good, because I'm starving."

"Me too." His eyes narrowed, raking down my body. "But not for food."

My whole body tingled with those words as my imagination ran wild. The promises that sparkled in his eyes were enough to excite any girl.

While he was getting ready I sat with Mia while she watched Doc McStuffins.

Hayes emerged from the bedroom a few minutes later with a white t-shirt on and a light denim shirt overtop. As he walked he fiddled with the sleeves of the denim shirt, rolling them up to his elbows. On his head he wore a dark gray beanie that hid his hair.

He shrugged into a black coat and then clapped his hands together. "Are my ladies ready to go eat?"

"I am! I am!" Mia jumped up and down on the couch, waving her hands in the air.

"Don't jump on the couch, Mia," I scolded lightly.

She stopped jumping and hopped off the couch. She ran over to Hayes, nearly falling over her own two feet in the process.

She batted her eyes up at him and asked in her sweetest voice, "Will you carry me?"

"Of course, sweetheart." He bent down and scooped her up.

I followed them to the elevator and when we exited the building Hayes turned to his right.

"It's only a few blocks away."

I looked down at my boots, silently grateful I'd worn them and not heels.

When Hayes stopped in front of the restaurant I was surprised to find that it was a little hole in the wall of a place. He opened the door and ushered me inside first.

There was only room for three booths and two tables. All of which were occupied. But there were two stools open at the counter.

"I can hold her on my lap," he assured me.

We seated ourselves on the stools and menus already sat on the counter ready. Before I could pick mine up, Hayes said, "The egg sandwiches here are amazing, and you can't go wrong with the pancakes."

"I'll have the egg sandwich then." I smiled over at him, amazed at how perfectly at ease I felt here with him. "What do you want baby girl?"

Mia scrunched her nose and pursed her lips. "Pancakes!" She finally declared with an exuberant flick of her arms.

"Whoa, there," Hayes warned her, moving out of her way, "you almost hit my nose."

"Sowwy." Mia appeared sheepish.

"It's okay." Hayes was quick to assure her. "I know you didn't mean it."

A frazzled waitress popped up behind the counter in front of us. Blowing a piece of stringy brown hair from her eyes, she asked, "What can I get you to drink?"

"Orange juice and coffee," I replied. "She'll have milk." I pointed at Mia.

"Orange juice for me as well." Hayes told her.

"Are you ready to order?" She eyed the menus we weren't looking at.

Hayes nodded and gave her his order.

"I'll have the same, and she wants a pancake."

"It shouldn't be too long." She grabbed the menus off the counter and stowed them away.

"How did you ever find this place?" I asked, looking around our dingy surroundings. "I'm sure there are a lot nicer places around here."

"I'm sure there are," he agreed, bouncing Mia up and down on his knee while she giggled, "but I like this place."

"So, what's on the agenda for today?" I tapped my fingers restlessly against the countertop. I hated not knowing what Hayes had planned for our stay, but at the same time it was freeing not to have to be the one in control all the time.

"After breakfast I thought we could take Ms. Mia to Toys-R-Us." He tickled her stomach and her laugher bounced around us. "What do you say to that?" He asked her.

She nodded her head eagerly. "I say yes!"

"You've gone and done it now," I warned him, trying to fight a smile.

"I think I can handle it." He winked.

The waitress set down our drinks and disappeared.

I sipped at my orange juice, completely astounded that I was in New York Freaking City with none other than Joshua Hayes—guitarist for Willow Creek. It sounded like the opening of a movie. Normal girl gets sucked into the whirlwind life of a rock star. Only this wasn't a movie.

It was one hundred percent real.

Weighed down with shopping bags—all full of stuff for Mia, since that girl could bat her eyes and sweet talk Hayes into anything, because the man had no willpower—we made our way towards Central Park.

"I'm going to have someone come get our bags and take them back to the penthouse," he told me as he struggled to hold on to all of them.

"Yeah, that's probably a good idea…wait, you can have someone get these from us?" I tightened my hand around Mia's when a group of rowdy teenagers passed us. I glared at them as they passed. Shouldn't they have been in school anyway?

Hayes chuckled, fumbling to get his phone out of his pocket. "Yeah, there are people who do that. At least when you're me." He winked, his grin tugging up his lips in a crooked smile.

I rolled my eyes and laughed under my breath. "Of course, how could I forget. You're *Joshua Hayes.*"

"Keep saying my name like that, baby, and I'll have to spank you later." His eyes twinkled with his threat.

"Momma," Mia tugged on my hand, "spanking is for bad girls. Are you bad?"

"Yeah, Arden, are you *bad?*" Hayes couldn't hide his grin. He was clearly enjoying putting me in an awkward position.

"Everybody is bad sometimes," I answered Mia as diplomatically as I could, "but we should all always strive to be our best."

Mia nodded and I took a deep breath, pleased that my answer had sufficed.

Luckily Hayes said nothing else and made his phone call.

He hung up and pointed across the street at a coffee shop. "We'll wait there for Greg to meet us."

"Sounds good. Come on, baby girl, this way." I guided Mia towards the crosswalk where we waited for our turn.

The coffee shop was packed with people waiting in line, but Hayes was large enough that he was able to push through the crowd and locate an empty table in the back.

"You want anything?" Hayes asked, tossing his thumb over his shoulder.

I helped Mia into a chair and pursed my lips in thought. "Anything mocha is fine."

"Coming right up."

With a clap of his hands he went to join the line.

A few people eyed him in recognition and one girl asked for an autograph. Others stood a few feet away, taking his photo like they were afraid to approach. I felt bad for the guys sometimes. It had to suck feeling like a zoo animal stuck behind a glass partition while people leered at you.

When Hayes sat down at our table with drinks and a cake pop for Mia the interest in him was renewed when people realized he was with me. I'm sure they were wondering who on earth I was.

Another girl approached our table, jutting out her chest and smiling down at him seductively.

"Hey, you're Hayes, right?"

"I am, and you are…?" He smiled up at her, but not in a flirtatious way, just friendly. If it *had* been flirtatious I might've kicked him.

"Melanie." She twirled her hair around her finger like she actually thought that was sexy or something.

"What can I do for you Melanie?"

She shrugged and bent forward so that her large chest was practically shoved in his face.

"A few of my friends and I are going to a club tonight. It just opened a few weeks ago. We thought you might want to join us and we could show you a good time." She threw in a little hair flip and lowered her voice. "We're very…adventurous." She nodded in the direction of two other bimbos taking residence at a nearby table.

"I'm sorry but I'll be unable to join you. I'm here with my girlfriend, and you see that little doll there?" He motioned to Mia. "I'll be tucking her into bed tonight and reading her a story. But I hope you ladies have a wonderful time at the club."

Melanie's mouth popped open and her gaze slid to Mia. "I didn't know you had a kid," she sneered.

"Well, now you know." He grinned at her retreating back.

"Hayes…" I started.

"I deal with people like that all the time. It's no big deal and comes with the territory," he said warningly, like he thought I was about to snap his head off.

"I know, it's okay…but…"

"Yeah?" He prompted with a raised brow, lifting the white plastic coffee lid to his mouth.

"You made it seem like Mia was your child. Why would you do that?" My voice grew soft and tentative. I really didn't know what to make of his gesture.

"We're dating, right?" He tilted his chin down, giving me the full force of his icy blue gaze.

"Y-yes." My voice shook with a sudden case of nerves.

"Therefore I feel that Mia is very much mine. Yeah, maybe she's not my biological child, but as long as we're together she's my kid. And I'll take care of her just as much as I will you. I promise you that."

Tears swam in my eyes.

"Shit, Arden, I didn't mean to make you cry."

"It's okay," I assured him, wiping away a stray tear, "they're happy tears. You're too sweet. You know that?"

He smiled widely. "I do now that you told me."

I leaned over and kissed his cheek. My lips lingered against his cheek a little longer than necessary, but I hated to break the contact.

"Ahem."

I sat back at the sound of a man clearing his throat.

The man stood in front of our table, towering above us. He was huge, and so tall that if Hayes was standing I think even he would look short. He looked young though, definitely not in his thirties yet, with a mop of curly blonde hair that reached his shoulders.

"I'm your bodyguard, not an errand boy. And seeing as how I'm your bodyguard I should be *guarding* you while you're in the city. You were supposed to call me this morning before you left, but nooooo, you had to go on out by yourself. At least you weren't mobbed, but if you think I'm leaving your side now you're sorely mistaken."

Hayes glanced from the man to me and said simply. "In case none of his gibberish made sense, that's Greg, my bodyguard, not my errand boy."

I laughed.

"Don't laugh," Greg growled, but not in irritation, "you'll only encourage the idiot."

"Hey, I might be an idiot, but I'm alive."

"Not good enough," Greg declared. He reached for a pile of bags on the floor. "Hurry up, let's go."

Hayes picked up his coffee and stood. "He's so bossy."

"Only because I'm stuck babysitting you." Greg muttered under his breath.

To me, Hayes said, "He loves me."

"You wish." Greg smiled. They seemed to have an easy banter, born of people who had to spend a lot of time together.

Hayes reached down to Mia. "Wanna ride on my shoulders?"

"Yes!" She clapped her hands together and let out a little giggle-scream when he lifted her up.

He headed for the door with Greg trailing behind. Somehow Greg had managed to grab all of our bags so I had to do nothing but follow.

Outside, Greg opened the trunk to a Chevrolet Suburban and began piling things inside.

We walked the few blocks over to the park with Greg keeping a close eye on us.

A few people stopped Hayes for pictures. Even so, he refused to lift Mia off of his shoulders. I smiled up at her. Her happiness was infectious.

We finally managed to make it into the park and snagged a patch of grass in the sun. The November air was chilly and I was thankful for the blanket of warmth the sun provided.

Hayes set Mia down and she ran in circles around us, at one point falling to her knees and promptly jumping up before either of us could make a move to check on her.

Hayes sat down in the grass, stretching out his long legs, and patting the space beside him.

I curled my legs beneath me and sat down, leaning my body slightly against his. He reached for my shoulder, pulling me more fully against him so that I all but fell into his lap.

"Hey, Greg," Hayes called to his bodyguard.

"Yes?" A single brow rose on Greg's forehead.

"Why don't you go fetch Ms. Mia some bubbles or something?" He pointed to Mia who was now dancing around us.

Greg scoffed, crossing his arms over his massive chest. "I'm your *bodyguard*. Not a Golden Retriever."

Hayes chuckled. "You look the same to me."

Greg sighed in disgust. "How did I get stuck with you?"

Hayes grinned, completely unfazed. "*Stuck?* I'd argue that it was luck that landed you with me. I'm a delight."

Greg chuckled. "More like a pain in my ass. I'll call Casey to bring some kid stuff, okay?"

"Who's Casey?" I asked, confusion rippling through me.

"My other bodyguard," Hayes supplied. "Unlike this one," he pointed at Greg, "Casey will actually leave me alone."

"That's because Casey is lazy and would rather watch *The Real Housewives* than deal with hunting down your sorry ass."

"Language," I warned.

"Oh, sorry." Greg smiled sheepishly, glancing at Mia.

Hayes' phone began to buzz in his pocket and he pulled it out, frowning at the name on the screen.

Before I could ask who it was, he said, "Sadie's calling me. That's odd. Hello?" He held the phone to his ear. "Ah, I see." He smirked. "Yeah, that's fine. We're in Central Park…mhmm, okay. We'll wait here."

He hung up the phone, grinning like the cat that ate the canary.

"What's going on?" I asked.

"The girls are kidnapping you."

"Oh, dear God," I groaned. "What do they have planned?"

"Shopping."

Well, that wasn't too bad…except for the fact that I could barely afford to buy a water here.

"The guys and I will watch Mia."

"You will?" I lifted a brow.

"Hey, we've kept ourselves alive for twenty-plus years, therefore I think we're more than capable of handling a three-year-old for a few hours. Besides, Mathias is a dad now, and Maddox is going to have a kid soon, so I think it's about time we all learned, right?"

I laughed, shaking my head. "Knock yourselves out. Just don't give her a lot of sugar or we'll all regret it."

"So, that's a no on the twelve cupcakes I was planning to feed her, then?"

"A definite no."

"Well, there goes that plan." He snapped his fingers together.

"So, what do you think you guys are going to do while we shop?"

He shrugged and smiled as he watched Mia. "Probably just head to the hotel and hang out there. We'll get mobbed if we try to go somewhere and Mathias is so worried about something happening to Liam that I know he won't want to risk it."

I nodded.

"Oh, and I made reservations for us to get dinner."

"And by us, you mean…? I prompted.

"The two of us. I've already arranged it with Maddox and Emma to watch Mia…if you're okay with it, of course."

"I trust them, but I wish you would've asked me first."

He chuckled, rubbing his jaw. "You would've protested too much if I'd done that." He was right. "I knew you'd agree easier if I already had a game plan in place." Right again.

I twisted my lips as I fought a smile. It blew my mind that he knew me so well. Hayes was the kind of guy that seemed aloof, but in actuality he paid close attention to everything around him.

Before I could sprinkle him with a compliment that would only serve to inflate his ego, we heard Maddox calling our names.

"That's our cue to leave."

He stood and extended a hand to help me up before scooping Mia into his arms.

He ran towards Maddox with Mia's giggles trailing behind him.

Two SUVs were parked illegally and people were getting fussy, but I tried my best to pay them no mind.

"You're in that car, Arden." He pointed to the first SUV.

Sadie rolled down the back passenger window and hung out of the opening. "Get in loser, we're going shopping."

"Did you just quote *Mean Girls*?" I asked her.

"Duh, it's only one of the greatest movies ever."

I shook my head and started to get in the car, but Hayes grabbed my arm to halt me.

"I'll see you later." He lowered his head, placing a quick chaste kiss on my lips.

"Bye." I said breathlessly and climbed into the car.

"Oh, and Sadie," Hayes strode up to the vehicle and leaned inside, "take care of my girl."

I watched, open-mouthed, as he handed her a shiny black credit card.

"Hayes!" I yelled after him but he was already getting in the other SUV and we were pulling into traffic.

There were two bodyguards accompanying us, and I figured the guys had insisted on it.

I sat beside Remy in the back and I turned to smile at her. "Hi, how are you?"

"Good." She smiled. "Tired," she added with a laugh, "but good. Having a newborn is exhausting—add in Mathias, and I'm about to lose my mind."

I laughed and patted her arm. "It'll get better."

"Oh, I'm sure the baby will…Mathias, not so much." Despite her words, she smiled widely and happiness shimmered in her pale blue eyes. Her light blonde hair was pulled back into a sleek ponytail and her makeup was minimum. It was a change since Remy was usually dolled up. "So, you and Hayes?" She wiggled her brows and bumped my shoulder. "It's about time that boy settled down."

A blush stained my cheeks. "Yeah, me and Hayes." There was no skirting around it anymore. Hayes and I were…well, a couple. God, that was weird to think about. I hadn't been someone's girlfriend in ten years.

"Where are we going first?" I asked Sadie, because I had no doubts that she was the ring leader of my kidnapping.

She peered back at me with a smirk. "First up, the hair salon."

"The hair salon?" I asked incredulously. "*Why?*"

"We have to get you ready for your date tonight," she huffed.

And now I was officially terrified.

"Don't look so scared," she laughed, "it'll be fun. You'll see."

Yeah, we would see.

# CHAPTER NINE

I'M PRETTY SURE my body was sparkling.

If it wasn't, then it should have been.

Not only had my hair been cut and styled to perfection, but I'd also had my body buffed, cleansed, and shined. I kind of felt like a car getting a major detailing. I couldn't say I hated it, though. There had never been a time when I was pampered like this, and I was going to allow myself to enjoy it.

A makeup artist expertly applied my makeup while someone else painted my nails in a pale pink.

The other girls sat chatting off to the side.

"And done." The makeup artist—named Kara, took a step back and let me finally see my reflection in the mirror.

My hair had been trimmed, and my normal waves had been styled straight and sleek. The makeup was impeccable, but not over dramatic.

"Thank you," I told Kara. "I'd give you a hug, but…" I nodded at the woman doing my nails.

Kara laughed. "I'm glad you like it. Enjoy your evening."

She packed up her supplies and went to help someone else.

Within a few minutes my nails were done, which I was grateful for since my butt had long since gone numb.

"How do you feel?" Sadie asked.

"Amazing," I replied honestly. "And that facial was everything dreams are made of."

Sadie's laughter rang through the room. "We have to get you out more."

"Well, it's kind of hard to do these things when I have a kid," I mumbled.

"I know." Sadie reached out and gave my arm a squeeze. "Even so, that doesn't mean you should neglect your needs. Everyone needs 'me' time now and then."

I eyed her, suppressing a laugh. "Tell me that again when you have children."

She snorted. "Me? A child? I can't even imagine."

"You don't want kids?" I asked, completely surprised.

"No, I do," she rushed to assure me, "it's just…with everything that's happened in my life in the past few months kids are the last thing on my mind."

"Can't say I blame you," I shrugged. "Although, between those two," I pointed to Remy and Emma, "you're going to end up getting baby fever."

Sadie busted into laughter. "Yeah, probably. But Ezra better put a ring on this," she began to dance, waving around her left hand, "before he even *thinks* about putting a baby in me." She settled and clapped her hands together, sobering. "Phase One is complete. Now we move on to Phase Two."

"What's Phase Two?" I was a bit afraid to know. I mean, this part hadn't been bad, but who knew what Sadie had up her sleeve.

"Shopping, of course."

"I should've known."

"Ladies!" She called to Emma and Remy and they immediately snapped to attention. "It's time to go *shopping.*"

There was something about the way she said the word *shopping* that had me worried.

I was drug from the building and into the SUV waiting outside.

Sadie rattled off an address to the guy driving and I settled into my seat, knowing that with this traffic it could take us an hour to go five blocks.

When we finally stopped outside a store my mouth dropped open.

"Have you lost your mind?" I shrieked at Sadie, pointing out the window at the displays of sexy lingerie. "I can't wear that! That covers *nothing!*"

"Stop being dramatic." She shook her head at me and slipped from the vehicle. I stayed seated. "So help me God, Arden, I will climb in that vehicle and drag your ass out here if I have to."

I took a deep, steadying breath. I knew she'd make good on her threat if I didn't get moving.

I climbed out of the car, Remy and Emma already waiting on the street with Sadie.

The bodyguards stayed in the car and I was thankful that they weren't about to witness my complete embarrassment.

"Come on," Sadie grabbed my hand, hauling me forward, "it won't be as bad as you think."

It was worse.

Once we entered the store the garments only became skimpier and more lavish.

The thin, barely-there, lingerie oozed money. I was sure a pair of underwear cost more than I made in a month.

The marble floors shined beneath my feet and above us a huge chandelier shimmered, casting rainbows throughout the large space.

"Can I help you?" A saleswoman strode up to us, all business.

"Yes," Sadie stepped forward, dragging me with her, "our friend Arden here has a hot date tonight, and we need her to look sexy. Not only for her man, but for herself."

"I'm sure we'll be able to find something. I'll set up a room for you. Are you ladies shopping as well?" She looked from Sadie to Emma and Remy.

"Possibly." Remy reached out, running her fingers along the black lace of a bra that left little to the imagination. "Maybe when I'm not breastfeeding," she added as an afterthought, her hand falling away as she sighed.

The four of us followed the sales lady back to an elegant changing room. There was a large space with lounge chairs set up between the dressing room and we took a seat while we waited for her to come back.

My hands shook with nerves and I buried them between my knees in the hopes of stilling them.

The woman returned what felt like an eternity later with several different items in varying colors.

She hung up the items in one of the rooms and motioned for me to enter.

I stepped inside, closing and locking the door behind me.

"Don't freak out!" Sadie called.

"Too late," I mumbled.

I grabbed the first item, a lacey pale pink bra and pantie set.

I shoved my fear down and removed my clothes so that I could slip into the lingerie. I had to admit, it fit well, but that didn't change the fact that it was see-through. Not even kidding. You could see my nipples.

Oh dear God.

I'd never worn anything this revealing, and definitely not since my pregnancy.

My body had changed after I had Mia.

My curves were fuller and there were still the faint lines of stretch marks on my stomach.

I wasn't ashamed, but it was hard not to be embarrassed at the thought of prancing around in something like this.

"Arden!" Sadie pounded on the door. "Let us see."

"Uh…"

"Oh my God, you're not embarrassed are you? Come on, we're all girls here! If it makes you feel better I'll strip down to my skivvies. I happen to be wearing Thor today."

Before she could ramble anymore I opened the door, resisting the urge to hide my body with my arms.

Remy let out a wolf whistle. "Look at you hot mama!"

I hid my face in my hands.

Sadie pinched my side. "Why are you embarrassed? You're hot!"

"It's just weird," I admitted, "I feel so exposed."

"That's kind of the point." She eyed me. "Anyway, this isn't the one. You need something sexier."

"Sexier?" My voice spiked in pitch. "Isn't this sexy?!"

"Yeah," she shrugged, "it's just a little too sweet."

"You can see my nipples."

"I noticed that." She laughed. "But it's not good enough. You need something so hot that the moment he sees you in it he comes in his pants."

"Um…"

"Just trust me." She pushed me back into the dressing room.

I tried on another set, this time in black. It covered more skin, but was still sexy. I felt more comfortable in it but as soon as she saw it Sadie vetoed it.

"Let me see what you have in there."

Before I could respond she strode past me and into the room.

"No, no, maybe, yes!" She cried triumphantly. "*This one!*"

She shoved the silky garment into my hands. "It's white," I said unnecessarily.

"Guys dig the whole innocent virgin look. Just trust me on this. And that garter belt…oh yeah, he's gonna lose his mind."

"Who said I'd be having sex tonight?" I countered.

She grinned and patted my head. "You're so cute."

She slipped out the door and closed it behind her.

"Put it on!" She yelled through the door.

I sighed and changed into the one she'd chosen.

I looked at myself in the mirror and let out a surprised gasp.

I had to admit, Sadie had been right.

The white popped against my creamy skin and made my red hair seem even redder. I wasn't sure about *virginal*, but it was definitely sexy. Very sexy, actually.

The bra was lace and completely see-through with a matching set of panties. A lace corset type thing was wrapped around my middle with the ends of the garter belt dangling from it.

"Let me see!" Sadie pounded on the door, always impatient.

I opened the door and admitted, "You were right."

"Ah!" Sadie clapped her hands together and began to do a victory dance. "Nailed it! *That* is perfect! Hayes is going to lose his mind. You can tell him to thank me later." She winked.

I blushed, trying not to think about the purpose behind what I was wearing.

Yes, I'd slept with Hayes already.

But that had been months ago and we'd both had a few drinks. It had been entirely spontaneous.

I wasn't sure lingerie was going to give me the courage to initiate anything as much as I might sort of want to.

Besides, Mia…

"Maddox and I will watch her all night if you're okay with that," Emma spoke up, almost as if she'd read my mind. "We better get used to taking care of a kid." She rubbed her round stomach.

"Have you found out the gender yet?" I asked her, slipping back inside the dressing room to change into my clothes.

"Oh! That's right, you don't know yet!" I heard her clap her hands. "I'll tell you when you come out."

A few minutes later I opened the door and Emma burst out with, "It's a girl!"

"Aw!" I ran over to hug her. "I'm so excited for you!"

"Thank you." She glowed. "It has made it even more real knowing the baby is a girl. Maddox is absolutely giddy—and gloating. He was convinced it was a girl. I didn't want to guess."

"Do you have a name picked out?" I asked her, handing over my chosen garment to the saleslady.

"Willow Elise."

"Willow?" I asked, surprised.

Emma nodded. "Willow Creek has a deep meaning for Maddox, beyond the band, so Willow was the only thing that made sense."

"Well, it's a beautiful name."

We gathered our things and followed the saleslady to a cash register.

She rang up the items and Sadie handed over Hayes' card.

Suddenly, my eyes landed on the total. "Wait, what?!" I screeched, causing everyone near us to turn and look at my outburst. "Almost two-thousand dollars for *lingerie?!*"

"This isn't just any lingerie," Sadie countered, "it's La Perla."

"And I'm going to pass out." I fanned my face.

"Oh calm down." She waved a hand in my direction. "Hayes can certainly afford it."

"That's not the point." I tried to take a deep breath.

I'd only ever spent that much money on the down payment for my car. I would never dream of spending that kind of money on underwear. And only *one* pair at that.

Holy shit.

I needed a drink.

The saleslady handed me the bag and I wrapped stiff fingers around it.

"You need to wipe that deer in headlights look off your face." Sadie told me as we headed for the exit.

"It's just so much money," I mumbled.

"Remember," she stopped me with a gentle hand on my wrist, "this is just as much for him as it is for you."

"I know, but I still don't think that justifies—"

She put a hand over my mouth. "Zip it. I don't want to hear it." Letting her hand fall she turned to Remy and Emma. "All that's left is a dress and some killer heels. There's a store just around the corner that I think might have something so let's just walk."

"Sounds good." Emma chimed as we stepped outside. She signaled to the bodyguards and they got out of the car to join us.

I followed behind the three girls, trying to stop obsessing over the cost of the fancy lingerie.

Sadie noticed me lingering and shook her head. "Arden, I swear to God if you're still thinking about the cost I might smack you upside the head."

"Sorry," I mumbled. "Do you think I could return them?"

"You're not returning them." She rolled her eyes and grabbed my hand to pull me along. "You're going to wear them."

"Okay."

Wiggling her brows, she added, "And you'll be thanking me tomorrow."

"I hope you're right."

She scoffed. "I'm always right. Oh! Here it is!"

She yanked me into a small boutique that was easily missed the way it was nestled between two larger stores.

The store was decorated in all black and white with pops of hot pink. Round black leather ottomans took up much of the floor space with racks of clothing lining the walls.

"You. Sit." Sadie pushed me onto one of the ottomans. "Remy and I will find something for you."

The two bodyguards took up residence beside the entrance and I felt bad for them that they were being subjected to this. It couldn't have been very fun.

I startled when Emma joined me on the ottoman and flashed me a smile.

"Seriously, don't worry about any of this." Emma pointed to the bag I held and then the store around us. "Hayes told us to spoil you at any cost and he'd be pissed if we spared any expense." She assured me. "I get it though. Maddox and I are married now and I still have a hard time letting him spoil me. I didn't come from much," she shrugged, "and I don't *need* much. So when he does something outlandish for me sometimes it makes me feel guilty, but I shouldn't feel that way because it makes him happy."

"Yeah, you're right," I agreed, pulling in a lungful of air. "I'll try not to feel so guilty about it."

"What do you think of this dress?" Remy held up a tight, very revealing, black dress.

"Uh…"

Sadie snatched it from her hands. "No that's too revealing. We need something a little classier. Like this…" She produced an emerald green dress.

"I like that one." I admitted.

"Go try it on." She strode over to me and shoved the dress in my arms. "Changing rooms are back there." She pointed. "We'll look for shoes and jewelry while you put it on."

She turned her back and I knew I had been dismissed.

I walked into one of the empty changing rooms and drew the curtain closed.

I slid the dress up my body, the silky fabric hugging my curves. The neck dipped down only a bit, giving a small glimpse of cleavage but not enough to be obscene. The bottom of the dress ended just below my knees with a bit of it coming up higher in the front. Even I had to admit I felt good in it.

I opened the curtain and stepped out to find the girls waiting for me.

"You're a bombshell!" Sadie squealed. "You have got to stop hiding your body!"

I ducked my head, hoping to hide the blush staining my cheeks.

"Here, put these on." Sadie handed me a pair of gold pumps. I slipped them on and admired my reflection in the mirror.

"Damn, I'm good," Sadie laughed, "Hayes might come in his pants before he even gets to the good stuff."

I paled and an older woman coming out of a dressing room scoffed, sticking her nose up into the air as she passed us.

"Sadie," I groaned, burying my face in my hands.

"What?" She batted her eyes innocently. "It's not my fault some people are prudes." Pushing me back into the dressing room, she said, "It's obvious this dress is perfect. So get changed and we'll head over to the hotel so we can make sure the guys haven't burned down the building or anything."

"They better not have done anything stupid." Remy groaned through the curtain.

I heard Emma snort. "This is Maddox, Mathias, Ezra, and Hayes, with two kids, so they're definitely up to no good."

I changed quickly and after buying the dress, shoes, and a few pieces of jewelry Sadie insisted I needed, we headed down the block to the waiting SUV.

Forty minutes later we were let off outside the hotel.

Emma studied her phone as we went inside. "Maddox hasn't responded to my text. That's weird."

"Whose room are they in?" I asked.

"We're all staying in the penthouse suite," Emma mumbled, still staring down at her phone.

We stepped into the elevator and headed to the top floor.

Remy produced a plastic keycard from her purse and waved it against the door.

"Oh. My. God." She stopped in her tracks, staring at whatever was in front of her.

"What is it?" I asked, panic rising in my chest.

The three of us stepped behind her, peering around her shoulders.

"Oh my God," we all echoed.

Hayes, Maddox, and Ezra sat around a table wearing dresses and makeup, with tiaras on their heads.

"Are you wearing my heels?!" Remy shrieked, storming towards Maddox.

Mathias chuckled from where he laid on the couch, bare-chested with his son sleeping on top. "I told you she'd rip you a good one."

"Is that my dress too?! Why were you in my stuff? Jesus Christ! That's my lipstick." Remy pointed at Maddox's mouth.

"We were playing dress up." Maddox said, stating the obvious. He reached up to grab his hedgehog, Sonic, from his shoulder and held him in his hands.

"What Ms. Mia wants, Ms. Mia gets," Hayes added.

I snorted. "She has you wrapped around her finger real tight. Nice crown." I nodded at his head.

"Am I a beautiful princess?" He batted his eyes.

"You're something else, that's for sure."

"There are bows in your hair." Sadie laughed, standing beside Ezra. Shoving her hand into her pocket she said, "I have to get a picture of this." She promptly began snapping photos of all of the guys.

Emma stepped up beside Maddox, placing her hand on his shoulder. "Are you going to play dress up with our daughter?"

He put his hand on her round stomach and grinned up at her. "Absolutely. Whatever my little girl wants me to do, that's what I'll do."

Emma bent down and pressed a kiss to his stubbly cheek. "I love you," she murmured.

I turned away before those two could get any more sickeningly cute.

I bent down beside the chair Mia occupied, a full tea set—a real one—sitting in front of her along with little sandwiches.

"Are you having a tea party?" I asked her.

She nodded. "Try it."

She held out one of the finger sandwiches to me. I took a bite and she set it on the plate.

"Very good." I told her, kissing the top of her head. "So you had fun."

She nodded again and let out a giggle. "Lots!"

I turned my attention to Hayes and smiled at him. My stomach fluttered, full of a million feelings, when I looked at him. I was falling, falling hard and fast, and I was helpless to stop it.

"You make a pretty girl." I told him with a wink.

He chuckled, staring right back at me unashamed. "It's the hair, isn't it?"

"Actually, I'm really digging that shade of lipstick on you."

"I pitcked it!" Mia raised her hand triumphantly in the air.

"And that blue eye shadow really makes your eyes pop," I continued.

"Really?" He smirked.

"Oh yeah, you should wear it more often."

I let out a small scream when he reached out and grabbed me. He pulled me onto his lap and I wrapped my arms around his shoulder.

Smoothing his fingers down my cheek, he said, "*You* look beautiful. Did you have fun?"

"I did. Thank you, but you didn't have to do that."

"I know." He held my chin so I couldn't look away. "It's just like I didn't have to do this." He motioned to the dress and makeup he wore. "But I *wanted* to. I enjoy making you and Mia happy. So let me."

In a rare moment of affection in front of our friends I nuzzled my head into the crook of his neck. I felt his lips press tenderly against the side of my forehead and I relaxed into his hold.

"I better go shower and get ready." He spoke after a minute of silence between us. Our friends had continued to buzz around us while we shared our moment.

I stood up from his lap and he disappeared into one of the bedrooms.

"You." Sadie grabbed my hand forcefully, yanking me towards her. "It's time to finish getting you ready."

I took a deep breath and smiled over at Mia. "Do you want to help mommy get ready?"

She let out another giggle and climbed off the chair.

I let Sadie drag me into the room she was sharing with Ezra. She shoved me into the bathroom along with the shopping bags.

"Change." She demanded, stepping out of the bathroom and closing the door. Through the door, she said, "Then we'll touch up your makeup and go over a few things."

"What kinds of things?" I opened the door a smidge so she'd hear me.

"Things," was her only response.

I gulped in fear.

Something told me I didn't want to know what kind of *things* she needed to discuss.

Regardless, I closed the door and changed into the lingerie and dress, fixing the garter belt onto the pair of stockings she'd somehow slipped into the bag.

I stared at my reflection in the mirror, my red hair brushing against my arms, and my amber eyes shining with happiness. My cheeks were stained with a flush and if I was honest, I was glowing.

And it was all because of Hayes.

# CHAPTER TEN

I FELT LIKE I was getting ready for prom.

Not only was I wearing a dress and all dolled up, but Sadie kept tearing up like an overemotional mother. She also gave me the sex talk—and by sex talk, I mean she listed off all of the creative positions she thought I should test out with Hayes. She'd then proceeded to try to tuck several condoms into my bra. I'd thrown them away when she wasn't looking.

Sadie ran the brush through my hair one last time.

She'd debated about styling it in a sleek bun or ponytail, but ended up deciding to leave it down.

Her reasoning?

"That way when he fucks you good he can fist your hair in his hands."

I told her if she had sex on her brain that bad she needed to go find Ezra.

She'd smirked and told me she'd ride him hard later.

The girl was insane.

But I loved her.

She was so much more than my boss. She was a genuine friend, and while she could be a bit crazy, she was one of the nicest people I knew.

There was a knock on the bedroom door and Sadie yelled, "Come in!"

Ezra poked his head inside, his hand slapped over his eyes. "Is it safe?"

"Yes, it's safe you dumb ass. That's why I said you could come in."

Ezra chuckled, lowering his hand. "We've been waiting forever. I think Hayes is about one minute from storming in here and throwing you over his shoulder." He spoke to me.

"Perfection takes time." Sadie told him, her hands on her hips.

Ignoring his girlfriend, Ezra asked me, "Are you ready?"

Sadie huffed and crossed her arms over her chest. "She's ready when I say she's ready."

Ezra let out a full belly laugh. "Man, power sure does go to your head." He stepped into the room and bent down to kiss her quickly. She turned her head so that his kiss landed on her cheek and he only laughed harder. "God, I love you." Sobering, he said, "So, *boss*, is she ready?"

Sadie looked me up and down once more and nodded. "My work here is done."

"Are you ready?" Ezra asked me, pushing his unruly curly black hair from his eyes. "Or is this one getting overzealous?" He tossed a thumb in Sadie's direction.

She retaliated against his comment by poking his side.

"Yeah, I'm good."

I followed them out of the bedroom and into the living room of the suite.

I caught sight of Mia sitting on Maddox's lap, watching Beauty and the Beast on TV. I smiled at the sight, pleased that Mia was being so well-behaved. It gave me hope that she'd be okay tonight. I was still unsure about being without her for the night. I'd never spent the night without her, so I'd have to see how things went.

Suddenly, the air in the room grew heavy and heated and I knew that Hayes had emerged from wherever he'd been.

I looked up and my breath caught in my throat.

You always heard guys say that their girl took their breath away, but Hayes had certainly stolen mine.

He towered above everyone in the room. His presence was commanding without him even trying, but his goofy smile softened the effect.

He was dressed nicer than I'd ever seen him—outside of Maddox and Emma's wedding—with a pair of slim fitted black pants hanging perfectly on his narrow hips. A white dress shirt was tucked into the pants with the sleeves rolled up to the elbows, leaving the bottom of the tattoo on his arm visible. A buttoned gray vest completed the ensemble.

My eyes lifted higher, to his clean-shaven face, the solid black gauges in his ears, and his blond hair styled to the side. He smiled crookedly, taking me in as unabashedly as I was him.

"That dress…" He made a noise in the back of his throat. "That dress is giving me all kinds of fantasies."

I laughed, refusing to shy away from his words like I normally would. "Thank Sadie."

"Thank you." He nodded at Sadie, but kept his eyes on me.

Sadie snorted. "Oh, don't thank me yet. You haven't even gotten to the best part."

Hayes gulped, his hands trembling at his sides. "It gets better?"

"You have no idea," she told him.

He scrubbed a hand over his face. "We better go before I decide against dinner." He closed the distance between us and took my hand, lowering his head to whisper in my ear. "You're stunning. The most gorgeous creature I've ever laid my eyes on."

"You're not too bad yourself," I jested.

"Go on, get out of here. Have some fun! Use those condoms!" Sadie pointed a finger at me, grinning from ear to ear.

"Sadie!" I hissed, nodding towards Mia.

"Oh! Oops!" She slapped a hand over her mouth. "My bad."

Mathias laughed loudly and strode over, clapping a hand on Hayes' shoulder. "He cleans up well, doesn't he?" He smirked at me. "Look at Joshie all grown up." He pinched Hayes' cheek.

"Dude, stop." Hayes pushed him away.

"Just saying you should thank me is all." Mathias held up his hands innocently. "I mean, that's my shirt and vest."

Hayes grumbled under his breath. "You also tried to make me wear one of your dorky nerdigans at first. That's not happening. Ever."

Mathias chuckled, backing away and pulling Remy into his arms. "Hey, those nerdigans, as you like to call them, get me laid, so who's the real winner here?" Mathias chuckled, kissing Remy's neck.

Hayes rolled his eyes and his hand settled at my waist. "And that's why you should never ask Mathias for help."

"You asked him for help?" My brows rose high on my forehead.

Hayes shrugged. "I don't normally dress up, but that one," he pointed at Mathias, "always acts like he's on a fucking runway or something."

"Language!" I warned him.

"Oh, right. My bad." He frowned. "I've really been trying to be better about that." He gave me a puppy-dog face.

"You have," I agreed, "and I thank you for it."

Disentangling myself from his arms I went over to Mia and she glanced away from the movie.

"Mommy's going to leave for a little while. Are you okay?" I asked, smoothing her hair away from her eyes.

"Of course," she said, like I was so silly to be worried about her.

"Love you baby girl." I hugged and kissed her, never wanting to let go. I wished she could stay this little forever. I didn't know what I'd do with myself when she grew up and went to school, started dating, and left me.

I stepped away and was surprised when Hayes went over to her.

He dropped to his knees in front of her so that he was at her eyelevel where she sat on Maddox's lap.

"I'm taking your mommy to dinner. Is that okay with you?"

She nodded and leaned in, whispering something in his ear.

His whole body stiffened and I swore his eyes pooled with tears but they disappeared too fast for me to be sure.

"Maybe one day Ms. Mia." He told her, his voice cracking.

He kissed her cheek and she wrapped her arms around his neck.

I smiled at the sight of them together. It made me so happy that Mia liked Hayes and that he liked her too.

He met me by the door, grinning from ear to ear.

"Ready?" He asked.

I nodded, trying to ignore the stares of our friends as they watched us leave.

Hayes guided me down the hall and to the elevator. We were both silent. I searched for something to say and kept coming up empty, but it was especially hard to think with my pulse pounding like a drum in my ear.

In the lobby we were met by a bodyguard I didn't recognize.

Hayes sent the guard a speculative look. "I thought you guys were waiting in the car?"

"Greg is, but he sent me in here since the media has descended onto the hotel like fucking vultures. It's madness out there."

Hayes sighed, seeming irritated by this new development. "Do you think we can lose them before we get to the restaurant?"

The guard frowned, crossing his massive arms over his chest. "Not likely. This is Manhattan after all."

"Right." Hayes muttered, pinching the bridge of his nose.

He wrapped his arm around me, pulling me more fully against his side.

"Just stay calm," he told me, "there will be a lot of yelling and camera's flashing."

"I'm okay." I assured him.

But when we stepped out I was definitely not okay.

The experiences I'd encountered today in no way compared to this. It was mad.

Hayes was right, there was a lot of yelling.

"Hayes, over here! Hayes who's the woman?! When is the new album coming out? Hayes! Hayes! Hayes!"

"Don't let go of me." I pleaded with him, tightening my grip around the vest he wore.

Greg had been waiting in the driver's seat of the car but he came barreling out, pushing back the paparazzi since the other guard wasn't having much luck.

Somehow we managed to make it into the car but even once the door closed behind us the flashes and questions were endless.

"Are you okay?" Hayes asked, looking me over.

"Yeah. Just frazzled." I reached up to smooth my hair down.

Suddenly his hand shot out to grab my arm. He stared at the skin near my elbow, his brows narrowed in concentration.

"What is it?" I asked.

He reached up, turning on the light in the car as Greg pulled us away from the hotel.

"When did this happen?"

I looked down at my arm where his eyes were pinned.

"Uh…" I started. "I think one of them hit me with their camera. It all happened so fast," I rambled.

He glared at the red mark on my arm for another moment before letting go.

He sat back against the leather seat, a muscle in his jaw ticking. "Fucking paparazzi," he muttered, more to himself than me. He glared out the window for a moment and I watched as he closed his eyes, taking several deep breaths to calm down. Turning to me with sorrow filled eyes, he asked, "Does it hurt?"

"Only a little."

Now that my adrenaline was fading the spot on my elbow throbbed in time with my heartbeat. It wasn't *that* bad though. Sure, it would bruise, but I'd suffered worse.

Hayes frowned at my words.

"It's not a big deal to me," I assured him.

Fire ignited in his eyes. "It is to me! They *hurt* you, Arden! What if they'd hurt Mia? It's not okay!" He bellowed and I was shocked by his raised tone.

I'd never heard Hayes mad before and I couldn't help but recoil into my seat, drawing my legs up as if to protect myself from him. It was a reaction I couldn't control. Flashbacks of Todd, of his hate-filled words and heavy fists filled my mind.

Horror settled onto Hayes' face and his mouth fell open in shock. "Arden," he said my name softly, just a faint whisper. "Fuck," he pulled at his hair. "Do you think I'm going to hurt you?"

I didn't respond.

I couldn't.

It was like my limbs were locked and my voice was gone.

"Arden," he pleaded, his eyes filled with regret, "I would *never* hurt you."

*He isn't Todd.*

*He isn't Todd.*

*He* isn't *Todd.*

I chanted over and over again in my head, but it did nothing to erase my fear.

"Arden, I would never hurt you." Hayes pleaded with me, trying to reach me through the dark place I had retreated to in my head. "What did he *do* to you?"

It was only then that I realized I was sobbing. I was sure the makeup that had been expertly applied to my face was now running in rivers down my chin.

I knew Hayes said something to Greg then, but I couldn't hear him over the memories assaulting my mind.

*Todd in my face.*

*His spit on my shirt.*

*His fist slamming into my stomach. My face. Everywhere.*

Suddenly the car jerked to a stop and I fell from the seat, having forgotten to buckle my seatbelt.

"Stay put." Greg turned around to glare at Hayes. "Let us push them back."

Hayes nodded, looking down at me with shock and pity in his eyes.

I didn't want him, or anyone, to pity me, but I knew I must be a pretty sad sight lying on the floor of the car.

"Will you let me touch you?" He asked, reaching his hand out to me.

He was giving me the power.

I could find the strength to reach out and take his hand or I could refuse and essentially let Todd win.

That's all I'd been doing for years.

Letting him *win.*

I'd avoided men like wildfire, terrified that they'd treat me the same way he did.

Until Hayes.

For some reason, just like Mia, I'd trusted him from the moment I'd met him, and right now I needed to let go of my fears. They were crippling me. I didn't want to lose out on things in life because I was *scared.*

Slowly I raised my hand, my fingers trembling, and sat my hand onto his open palm.

He swallowed thickly and let out a sigh of relief as his hand closed around mine.

"That's my girl," he murmured, helping me up and out of the car.

As soon as we were out of the vehicle the flashes of a hundred cameras blinded me and Hayes had to carry me inside the building.

When the little black dots from the flashes stopped swimming in front of my eyes I was surprised to see that we were at the building where his family's penthouse was located.

"W-why are we here?" I stuttered as he guided me to the elevator.

"I didn't think you were in much shape to go to a restaurant, Little Bird."

In the elevator I leaned against the wall and he let me go, seeming to know that I needed the distance.

"Are you mad at me?" I asked and instantly regretted my words at his look of horror.

"Mad at you? Are you fucking crazy? Mad is the last thing I am." He shook his head. "I'm…I don't know what I am. Hurt, I guess. Hurt that you'd think I'd harm you, but more so that someone treated you so badly that that's immediately where your thoughts went." He scrubbed his hands over his face. "Fuck, Arden. The last thing I'd ever do is raise a hand against you."

The elevator doors slid open and he waved his hand for me to exit first.

My feet only carried me as far as the couch before I collapsed. I was completely exhausted from the last fifteen or so minutes. It felt like so much longer. I guessed maybe it was. Todd's torment hadn't ended when he left me. I carried the physical and mental scars of what he did to me every single day of my life.

Hayes crouched down beside me, staring at me for a moment. I'd never seen someone look so tormented and worried before. I hated that I'd freaked out, therefore putting that look in his eyes, but my reaction had been uncontrollable.

He reached out tentatively and stroked his fingers against my forehead and then into my hair.

"Tell me, Arden." He pleaded with me. "Tell me everything. I need to know."

My throat closed up and I shook my head. "I can't." Tears stung my eyes.

He pulled his lip between his teeth, seeming torn between begging me for answers and letting it go.

"Please, baby, you have to. I need to understand so that I never, *never*," he reiterated, "make you feel that way again."

I squished my eyes closed, a single tear escaping and sliding down my cheek.

I felt his finger touch my skin hesitantly and the tear disappeared.

"I never want you to cry because of me. Not unless it's happy tears."

I sat up then and wrapped my arms around his shoulder, burying my head into the crook of his neck. My tears dampened his shirt but he never pulled away. Instead he held me tighter. It was like he was trying to remind me silently that he wasn't going to let me go.

My whole body shook and his hold on me tightened. Not in a constricting way, but like he was trying to hold me together.

"Why do you want to know this?" My voice was muffled against his neck.

He didn't say anything and I thought maybe he hadn't heard me, but then he spoke and each word was said carefully. "Because, I want to know everything about you. No one's life is all rainbows and sunshine. There's going to be good and bad. And fuck it, Arden, I want all your good moments and the bad ones too. I want to help you bear the burden of your past so that you don't have to do it alone."

This man.

This crazy, perfect, silly man was too good to me.

"Why are you so perfect?" I asked him.

He disentangled himself from my arms and took my face between his large hands. "I'm not perfect. *Nobody* is perfect. Get that notion out of your head now. I'm going to mess up and make mistakes, like back in the car," his fingers flexed and the muscle in his jaw jumped, "but I will always do my best to fix them."

I inhaled a shaky breath and confessed, "I don't want you to think differently of me. That I'm weak."

"Fuck," he growled, "you're the strongest woman I know. I could never think you were weak."

He sat down on the couch beside me and pulled me onto his lap so that I was straddling him.

Holding my chin captive, he said, "Bravery comes from the most dire of situations and I think we both know you've proven how brave you are."

My tears only fell harder at his beautiful words.

I knew I needed to tell him about Todd, about how horrible he'd been, but opening myself up like that was going to be difficult. Maybe even the hardest thing I'd ever done. I'd kept so many of the awful things he'd done to me a secret. Heck, even my parent's didn't know all the details. No one did. I'd buried everything deep down inside me, suppressing it so that I could make it through each and every day without suffocating.

"Todd had always been quick to anger…you know, the kind of person who would be grinning from ear to ear one second and spitting mad the next. But he never, not once had laid a hand against me. It was usually other guys that pissed him off. They'd say something stupid or look at me for too long and it would set him off."

I inhaled a shaky breath, my hands quaking against his shoulders.

"When he asked me to marry him I was so, naively, thrilled." I laughed self-deprecatingly. "Things were good…for a while. Then they started changing. Slowly at first. He'd yell at me, a lot. But the yelling I could handle. The hateful things he'd call me…I could take it. And then one day he came home from work early and his dinner wasn't ready—I mean, it's not like the bastard called to let me know he'd be early or anything" I chuckled, staring off into the distance—into a past that still seemed so much a part of my present and future. "That was the first time he hit me." I whispered the words, hating to give voice to them. But Hayes was right. He needed to know. He *deserved* to know what he was dealing with. I was damaged goods after all.

I grasped the collar of his pressed white shirt between my fingers, rubbing my fingers around and around on the fabric, like I could harvest strength from it to carry on with what I needed to say.

"That time it was just a slap on my cheek. It hurt, but the mark faded quickly. It was like it gave him a rush, though, some sick twisted sense of satisfaction for having physical power over me and from there it just escalated." I pressed my lips together tightly, trying to hold in the sob that was so desperate to break free.

"Let it out, Arden." He caressed my cheek with the most gentle of touches. "If you need to cry, or scream, throw something, whatever it is, do it."

"Just hold me."

He smoothed his fingers through my hair. "I think I can do that."

I sobbed against his chest. The kind of sobs that shook your whole body and left you feeling exhausted, but it was past time that I let these emotions out.

It was hard to let my guard down and allow Hayes to see me like this, but I knew it was necessary for the both of us.

Minutes, or maybe it was hours, later I dried my tears on the back of my hands and opened my mouth to finish my tragic tale.

"The abuse lasted for years," I confessed. "Someone on the outside might view me as weak for not having the guts to leave, but I was terrified. Completely scared out of my mind. The threats…I believed he'd make good on them if I left him. He was so violent there was no reason to doubt him. And then…" I squished my eyes closed. "And then I got pregnant. I kept it a secret for as long as I could. He didn't want children and I was afraid of what he might do." I bit down on my lip hard enough to taste blood. "But eventually I couldn't hide it anymore and he found out. One day I came home from work and the house was eerily quiet. There was a stillness in it and it seemed…empty. When I searched the house I found that all of his belongings were gone. He just…left. No explanation. He was gone and I…I was so *relieved*. I think a part of me thought he might kill me one day and I feared what he'd do to our baby more than that."

Shrugging, I ran my fingers down his solid muscular chest, playing with the buttons on his shirt and vest to keep my hands busy.

"The divorce papers came a few weeks later and that was that. I never heard from him again."

"Fuck Arden." His hands roamed up and down my sides. "I'm so incredibly sorry that you had to go through that."

"I'm not," I sighed. "Without Todd I wouldn't have Mia and I wouldn't trade her for the world. She's worth everything I went through and more."

He took my face between his hands, staring straight through me. "You are the most remarkable woman I've ever met and I'm so damn lucky to be with you."

"Are you sure about that?" I asked, stroking my fingers along his jaw. "I'm kind of a mess."

He chuckled and his hands settled at my waist. "Lucky for you I like cleaning."

"Is that another cheesy popsicle joke?" I cracked a smile, and while small it was genuine.

"Nah, baby, that's all me. And if you're going to remain my girlfriend you better get used to all the ridiculous things I say, because I'm not changing." He grinned crookedly.

"That's okay," I leaned forward and lay my head against his chest, "I like you just the way you are."

"Back at ya." His lips pressed tenderly against my forehead.

With my skin still tingling from his kiss, and his strong arms wrapped around me, I wondered idly if he was falling for me the same way I was him.

Teasing my hand against the part of his chest that was exposed above the top button of his shirt, I asked, "I'm sorry for ruining tonight. I know you probably went through a lot of trouble and—"

He cut off my next words by pressing his hand against my mouth.

"You didn't ruin tonight, Little Bird. If anything you've made it one of my best because you *trusted* me enough to let me into your darkest places." He grazed his fingers down my cheek. "I regret that my actions led us to this moment, but I don't regret knowing."

Quiet settled around us and I knew he wouldn't be the one to break it. Something told me that from this moment on he was putting the power in *my* hands. I'd never had that with Todd.

"Kiss me."

His body stiffened. "Arden—"

"Kiss me," I said again, this time the words were stronger and I stared into his eyes, letting him know I was serious. There was no fear.

Only desire.

He cupped my chin, his eyes remaining on mine as he brought our lips closer and closer.

I gasped at the feel of his lips so near to mine.

His eyes held a question though. He was waiting, once more, for permission.

"Kiss me," I said again.

Without hesitation he did.

His lips glided over mine.

Teasing.

Biting.

Searching.

My body melded into his and I couldn't get close enough. I wanted to sink inside him and let everything that was so beautifully him wash over me and mend the parts of me that Todd had left broken.

My hips rocked against his and he let out a husky moan that only spurned me on more.

Nibbling my bottom lip, he breathed my name and I never knew so much meaning could be reflected in so few syllables.

My fingers delved into his hair, tugging on the perfectly styled strands and turning them into a wild and chaotic mess.

I wanted to unravel him in the same way he'd done me from the moment I met him.

He was breaking apart everything I'd thought I knew about life and love and completely redefining the definition—showing me the beauty that had been destroyed by Todd.

"I want to touch you so bad." He confessed, tilting my head back so he could rain kisses down my neck.

"Then touch me."

He hesitated, ghosting his fingers down my back before settling his hands at my waist.

"You're testing my limits." He said through clenched teeth.

"Hey," I leaned my forehead against his, holding his chin between my fingers, "I said it was okay. I…I know I freaked out earlier, but I'm good now. In fact, I haven't felt this good in a long time. Telling you has lifted a weight off my chest and now all I want is for you to—"

Instead of silencing me with his hand this time it was his delectable lips.

I let out a small sound of surprise when he stood with me in his arms.

I wrapped my legs around his waist as he carried me through the space and back into the bedroom.

He laid me down on the bed and his lips finally parted from mine.

"If this gets to be too much, just tell me and I'll stop."

I grabbed the vest he wore and yanked him towards me. "You act like we've never done this before. Trust me, I won't be stopping you."

His hand settled over mine, but he didn't pry my hand off his vest. He let out a low, dangerous chuckle. "If you think that time will in any way compare to this one you're mistaken."

Something about the naughty glint in his eyes made my whole body tighten in anticipation. My nipples pebbled and he seemed to sense this as his eyes dipped to the front of my dress.

He wet his lips and growled, "I'm thoroughly going to enjoy devouring you."

I shivered at his words.

His hands shook as they roamed down my legs to my feet where he removed the heels.

I knew, despite his words, that he was holding back—that he was afraid I wasn't ready for this.

"Don't hold back," I pleaded with him, reaching up to cup his jaw. "I want this just as much as you. Please, give me everything. Give me *you*."

He lowered his head and whispered against my lips, "You already have me."

I closed my eyes, relishing in those words.

His hands slid under my dress and stilled when he felt the cool metal of the garter belt connecting to the stockings.

"Is that what I think it is?" His eyes were wide with wonder.

"I guess you'll have to wait and see."

"Wait?" He scoffed and pulled the dress up and off my body in one hard jerk. It fell to the floor somewhere in the room and he grinned down at me. "I don't *wait*, Little Bird." His Adam's apple bobbed as he stared down at me. "Holy Fuck, you are the most beautiful woman I've ever seen." His tongue slid out, wetting his lips as he stared at my chest, completely exposed with the see-through material.

Goosebumps pimpled my skin at his words and intense stare.

"You make me feel beautiful," I confessed. "The way you look at me...I love it."

He kissed his way down my neck, over my chest, and to the small bit of my stomach exposed above the corset.

"God, look at you," he growled lowly, "you're like a fucking dessert."

He stood up, staring down at me. "As much as I love this, it's gotta go. I need you naked. Now." His voice was urgent.

I stretched my arms above my head and the movement made my breasts push out even further. He groaned, palming himself through his pants.

"I want to take my time with you. I want to make this good. But fuck, I don't know if I can."

"Stop thinking," I told him, stretching my neck to reach his lips.

He kissed me deeply, so passionately that I thought my body would ignite from the inside out.

Idly, I acknowledged the fact that I'd never felt this way before with another man. Hayes made me feel happy, and crazy, and like I could do anything, but he also made me feel comfortable and despite my earlier reaction I knew he'd never hurt me in that way.

But my heart?

Piece by piece it was becoming his, and if things ended I knew it would be destroyed.

Falling for him was a risk, but it was one I was willing to take.

His touch sent scorching flames up my spine as his hands slowly curved around my torso. His fingers inched under the edge of my bra but he didn't remove it.

His mouth closed over one of my breasts, sucking on the skin through the lacey fabric and the sensation of the rough material and his soft tongue was jarring.

I hooked a leg around his waist, pulling him against me and I felt his hardness settle between my legs.

"Oh God." I moaned, shaking all-over. I wondered if maybe he could make me come this way. The way my body pulsed and hummed, I was thinking yes. My hands clutched at his hair and he let out a groan when I tugged on it. Moving my hands to his shoulders, I begged, "Please. Oh, please. Touch me."

"Tell me want you want." He lifted above me, his eyes twin blue pools of desire. "Tell me and it's yours."

My throat bobbed. I didn't know if I could say it. The only man I'd ever been with before Hayes was Todd and things between us had hardly been adventurous or passion-filled so I felt a bit shy when it came to sex.

Hayes grasped my chin, his thumb brushing against my bottom lip. His eyes were sincere when he spoke. "Don't be nervous with me. Say what you want. I'm not judging you. I'm here to please you."

He kissed me then, slow and drawn out, and he didn't pull back until my toes tingled and I was completely relaxed.

He knew exactly what to do to calm me down.

"Ready to tell me?" He asked, his breath warm against my neck as he pulled my earlobe between his teeth.

"I-I want you t-to…"

"To what?"

"Touchmypussy." I said the words really fast, like by somehow slurring them together I wouldn't actually be saying them.

He let out a warm chuckle and pressed a kiss to my neck.

"So," he began, "you want me to touch your pussy…with my fingers or with my tongue? Be more specific to get what you want, Little Bird."

"B-both." I stuttered, hoping I could gain control of myself in the next ten seconds.

"Say it like you mean it, Arden." His eyes were bright in the darkened bedroom.

My breasts pushed against the confines of my bra as I took a deep breath. "Both," I said again, this time with more strength. "I want your fingers, and your mouth, and then I want your cock."

He grinned triumphantly. "That's my girl."

I glowed under his praise.

His fingers looped into the sides of my underwear and he slid them down as slowly as he possibly could until they landed on the floor. As he removed them his lips glided along the insides of my thighs and calf muscles. My body felt strung tight, waiting with rapt attention for what was to come.

"God, you're so fucking beautiful. How did I get so lucky?" He murmured, kissing his way up my legs. His eyes flicked up to mine and let out a small groan.

"Seeing you like this, spread apart for me and dripping wet, with your eyes hooded with lust…fuck, it's the best thing ever and I haven't even really touched you yet."

"Please," I begged.

His hands slid up my back and the clasp on the bra popped.

"That had to go first." His eyes grew dark as he pulled the fabric down, freeing my breasts. He pulled the fabric completely off, dropping it onto the floor along with everything else.

"Your shirt too," I reached out and began undoing the buttons on the vest, "I need to feel your skin."

The last button slid free and the vest was gone. The sight of him in the button down white shirt shouldn't have been such a turn on, but it was. He was a gorgeous man, inside and out, and he was here with me—a fact that might always baffle me. He could have his pick of women and he wanted to be here with broken, damaged, single-mother, *me*.

He deftly unbuttoned his shirt and his muscular chest was exposed for my viewing pleasure. My eyes fell to the hard lines of his stomach, dipping down into the black pants that hung low on his narrow hips.

"I'm going to make you feel good, Arden. So fucking good that this whole city will know my name."

"I'm pretty sure they already do."

His lips quirked. "Now's not the time for jokes, woman, not when I'm about to lick your pussy."

I shivered and he grinned in response.

He lowered his massive body over mine, shielding me like a blanket.

I gasped when I felt his fingers press into me and his mouth close around my sensitive flesh.

I gripped the sheets in a tight fist. In no time I was cursing, panting, sweating, and begging for him to make me come.

His fingers hooked inside me and I bowed off the bed, my fingers locking into his hair and holding him against me.

"Faster," I pleaded, "Harder. Oh God. Like that. Keep doing that."

My legs shook and my hand fell limp from his hair.

Black and white dots pulsed beneath my closed lids. I sucked in a lungful of air but it wasn't nearly enough. I was sure all the oxygen had been sucked from the room with my cries.

His lips glided up my stomach, leaving behind a wet trail of kisses.

His mouth settled on my lips, his tongue swiping against mine as he coaxed me back to life.

"You're gorgeous all the time, but when you come…you're a fucking goddess."

"I need more," I begged wantonly.

He chuckled, his hand wrapping around my neck. He tilted my head back and nipped at my jaw. "So eager. I like it."

"You're wearing too many clothes." I plucked impatiently at his belt. The need to feel him was all consuming. Even when things had been good with Todd I'd never desired him like this—where each breath was an effort and I thought I might pass out if I didn't feel his skin sliding against mine.

He stood and I sat up, making the process of undoing his belt and pulling it through the loops so much easier.

With my fingers shaking against the button on his pants I looked up at him through hooded eyes.

I knew there was something I had to say before we continued.

"I don't want you to think I want this because of what I told you earlier—like by being with you that will somehow erase my memories or something. I want this, right now, here with you, because of *you* and no other reason." I stared at him, allowing him to let my words to sink in.

His eyes softened and he reached down, lovingly stroking my face.

"I didn't know I needed to hear that, but I did. Thank you."

He lowered from his looming height and cupped my cheeks between his hands. His lips settled over mine in a slow, leisurely pace that somehow only served to make me crave him even more.

He stood up again and his fingers stroked against my cheek.

"Have at it, Little Bird. Take what you want. I'm yours."

I closed my eyes, my heart thundering in my ears as I lowered his zipper.

This was so different from the first time we'd been together. We'd both been tipsy then, definitely not drunk, but the alcohol had made me more comfortable. Now, I didn't have the alcohol in my system to dull my senses. Everything was heightened.

I stroked my fingers against the hard ridge of his length pressing against his pants and he shivered.

Ever so slowly I began to pull his pants and boxer-briefs down like I was opening the best present I'd ever been given.

I looked up, watching as he tilted his head back and his eyes fell closed.

I ran my thumb over the tip of his cock and around the barbell piercing going through the top and bottom.

"I never even knew something like this existed before that night." I confessed into the darkened room.

He leaned over, turning on one of the bedside lights and bathing the room in a warm golden glow.

"I needed to see you," he whispered, reaching down to tangle his fingers in my hair. Eyeing my hand wrapped around his length, he said, "Does it scare you?"

"The piercing?" I waited for him to nod. "No, not at all," I admitted, rolling my thumb around the tip and eliciting a soft moan from his throat. "I like it."

He grinned at that but his smile soon disappeared when I dropped to my knees and wrapped my mouth around him.

"Oh holy fuck." He cursed, fisting my hair in his hands and holding it away from my face.

I swirled my tongue around his tip, getting used to the foreign feeling of the piercing.

In the past, oral sex had never been something I'd enjoyed giving—and Todd certainly didn't reciprocate—but with Hayes, I loved it. I loved watching him lose all control. I loved the soft pants that passed through his lips and the way he mumbled curse words under his breath and bit at his lip. Mostly, I loved the way he looked at me. Like I was the most amazing creature he'd ever seen.

I held the base of his cock in my hand, rubbing up and down as I took him as far into my mouth as I could.

I wanted to watch him come undone—to completely unravel from my touch.

But he wasn't having it.

Just when I knew he was close he pushed me away and lifted me onto the bed.

He grabbed a condom, putting it on as quickly as possible, and then he was on top of me, in me, all around me.

Everything was Hayes.

I knew nothing but the feel of his fingers, the glide of his skin against mine, and his mouth pressed to my ear whispering sweet words.

My hands roamed down his back, grabbing his ass and tightening my legs around him.

"Harder," I begged.

He kissed my collarbone and over my breasts before grabbing me by the waist and lifting my hips off the bed. He thrust against me, sweat dampening his brow, and his chest heaving with each labored breath.

"Like this?"

"Oh God," I moaned, grabbing at the sheets, "just like that. Don't stop."

He ducked his head down and kissed me long and deep.

"Fuck, you feel so good. Never been like this before," he said brokenly.

His words were my undoing and I fell apart around him. My legs shook uncontrollably and I let out a cry that could've been his name, but with my blood roaring in my ears I had no idea what I'd said.

"I love watching you come," he confessed, biting my earlobe.

He pulled out of my body and before I could protest he'd flipped me over onto all fours and slid back inside me.

"You're so wet. So fucking wet for me." He murmured, placing small kisses down my spine.

A sharp sting on my ass had me turning my head to look at him and the fucker was grinning like the cat that ate the canary.

"You spanked me." The words were breathless and barely audible.

"Hell yeah. This ass—" He spanked me again. "—is very spank-able."

"I like it," I confessed.

His grin widened. "I knew you were a naughty girl. You're so fucking perfect for me it doesn't seem real."

He spanked me again and I let out a long moan, my hair falling forward to conceal my face.

Immediately he reached out, pushing my hair over my shoulder so that he could see every expression that settled on my face.

"You're mine, Arden," he growled, pulsing inside me. "Not because I own you, but because you own *me*."

He sped up, angling my hips so he hit deeper inside me and the piercing rubbed against something that had me falling apart again in a matter of seconds.

He was right behind me.

His body fell over mine with one arm wrapped around my stomach and his chest pressed into my back while he used his other hand to hold himself above the mattress.

"You've fucking ruined me."

I couldn't seem to find enough air to produce words, but I wanted to tell him that it was the other way around.

He'd ruined me.

Completely.

And I'd never be the same.

# CHAPTER ELEVEN

LAST NIGHT HAD been amazing—as cliché as that sounded, but it was true.

After making love for a second time, and with his arms wrapped around me, he'd said, "Let's go get our girl."

Despite the late hour we'd dressed and driven over to the hotel to pick up Mia. She'd been asleep and Hayes had scooped her up into his arms. She'd woken up, but once she saw that it was us, and knew we were bringing her home with us she fell back to sleep.

It took my breath away the way he loved my daughter as much as I did. He didn't begrudge the fact that I was a mother. Instead, he embraced it, and treated her as if she were his own.

Now, we stood in back of the studio, watching the guys give their interview with the show hosts.

Maddox and Hayes stole the show, but there was no surprise there.

Mathias looked like he didn't want to be there, and Ezra, being the shyest, kept quiet unless addressed directly.

Maddox gestured wildly with his hands, telling some outrageous story about one of his and Emma's many adventures.

"Momma, I'm firtsy."

"Come on, we'll find some water." I reached for her hand.

I headed back towards the room we'd been waiting in before the guys were called out. There had been a fruit basket and bottles of water sitting on a side table.

I stepped into the room with Mia glued to my side and grabbed a bottle. Unscrewing the lid I handed it over to her.

She sipped at it greedily and smiled up at me beautifully. "I wuv you, momma. You're the best momma in the whole world."

My heart warmed. "I'm glad you think so baby girl."

With the water bottle and an apple in hand we headed back out to join the girls.

The guys had already started their set and Mia squealed excitedly, darting away and in front of the cameras before I could blink. I started forward to grab her and pull her away but I caught Hayes shaking his head.

The show hosts laughed as Mia began to dance around, shaking her butt, and giving it her all.

Even I had to laugh.

Hayes went over to her, leaning down as he played his guitar. Mia jumped up and down before dancing around him. Hayes tossed his head back, his body shaking with laughter. He grinned from ear to ear, appearing to have the time of his life.

The song came to an end and the show went to commercial. Hayes removed his guitar and set it down before picking up Mia and tickling her stomach.

"We didn't know you had a daughter." One of the show hosts said. "She's adorable."

Hayes shrugged, his smile making his dimple appear. "I didn't, but now I do." He caught my eye and winked.

Beside me Sadie sighed dreamily. "Is anyone else swooning? Because I'm definitely swooning."

Emma laughed, wrapping her arms around Maddox as he approached. "I think everyone is swooning."

It was then that I turned to see several other women staring with lust-filled eyes at my boyfriend. I wasn't jealous, and frankly I couldn't blame them. The sight of a hot rock star with a child in his arms would send any woman's ovaries into overdrive.

"Over me?" Maddox asked in response to what Emma said. "Of course they are, Em. I'm irresistible."

She poked him in the ribs. "We were talking about Hayes."

"Hayes?" He scoffed, wrinkling his nose. "Everyone knows I'm the swoon-worthiest. There's no competition."

"Swoon-worthiest? I'm surprised you even know that word." Emma laughed, leaning her head on his shoulder.

"Yeah, Maddox, enlighten us on how you know this." Mathias said, taking his son from Remy. He immediately melted into a pile of goo as he gazed down at Liam, peppering kisses onto the downy brown hair that covered his head.

Ezra snorted and covered his face. "This oughta be good."

Maddox shrugged, stroking his fingers absentmindedly against Emma's hip. "You left your computer open on some blog and they had a list of the most swoon-worthiest book boyfriends." He paused, seeming to contemplate something. "What the hell *is* a book boyfriend?"

"Don't worry. You'd never be one." Emma smirked at him and reached up to pat his head.

He tried to glare at her but instead laughter reflected in his eyes. "Come on, Em, we all know I'd be number one."

"You keep telling yourself that." She patted his stomach.

He lowered his head, grazing his lips against her ear. "Maybe later I'll show you my most swoon-worthiest qualities."

He pinched her butt and she squealed jumping away. "I hate you!" She laughed.

"Yeah, tell that to my child growing inside you. It looks like you hate me a lot." He grinned crookedly and crossed his arms over his chest.

"You're on a roll today." She shook her head.

"What did I miss?" Hayes asked, suddenly appearing at my side.

"Nothing." Emma insisted.

Hayes looked around at us doubtfully. "Something tells me I don't want to know." He adjusted his hold on Mia. "We should probably get going."

Maddox looked down at his watch. "Yeah, you're right."

Hayes had told me this morning that we were all going out for lunch together and then he had a surprise planned for Mia. A surprise he wouldn't even tell me. I hoped it didn't involve sugar.

We were ushered out of the building by the band's security team and immediately I was thankful for their presence when the hundreds of fans gathered outside all began to scream.

Signs were held up, names were called, cameras flashed, and requests for autographs sounded around us.

The guys stopped and posed for as many pictures as they could and signed everything that was shoved in their face.

All the while their security detail worked to keep the women from grabbing any of them, or us.

When we finally reached the SUVs I would've sworn it had taken us twenty minutes to get to them even though they were only about thirty feet from the exit.

I climbed into the back of one of the SUVs and Hayes was right behind me, lifting Mia into the car so I could grab her and put her in her car seat. He joined me in the back, slightly out of breath from the chaos. Mathias and Remy joined us with Liam and the others scurried into the other car.

"It's getting worse all the time," Remy commented, buckling Liam into his baby seat. I leaned forward and noticed her hands shaking. "It scares me with the baby. I don't want someone to hurt him by accident."

"I know," Mathias said, kissing the side of her forehead. "I'll call for more security detail."

"What about when we're home and there is no security?" Her voice rose in pitch. "What then?"

Mathias grunted and glared out the window. "I don't fucking know, Rem. We can't bubble wrap the kid for his whole life. I can't change who I am and I can't change that this kind of thing follows us everywhere." She opened her mouth to say something and he held up his hand to silence her. "I don't like it anymore than you do. But it is what it is. This is why I don't ask you to come to many of these things, but the reality is we can't avoid it all."

"I know," she finally sighed, "I'm sorry for getting upset. It's just hard and I'm still new at this whole mom thing."

Mathias softened and reached over to cup her cheek. "I'm sorry too. And for what it's worth, I think you're the best fucking mom there ever was."

She laughed and leaned over to kiss him.

Mathias and Remy were…explosive, to say the least, but no one could deny that they were madly in love with each other. I was sure there was no one else on the planet that could handle either of them. They were meant to be.

We pulled up to the back of the restaurant in order to avoid the crowd that had followed the cars and from there we were led into a private dining room. There were no windows and silence surrounded us. Quiet was rare in this city and I took a moment to let it sink in.

Hayes pulled out a chair for me and then requested a booster seat for Mia. I didn't know how he managed to remember such simple things, but I was thankful for it.

Menus already sat on the table waiting for us and I scanned the items, looking for something that would be okay for Mia. Everything my eyes landed on was far too fancy for a three-year-old. She'd look at the food in disgust and ask me for chicken nuggets.

Hayes leaned over to whisper in my ear. "I asked Casey to run and pick her up something from McDonalds. I hope that's okay. I didn't think she'd like any of this."

I gaped at him and he grinned, reaching over to push my chin up.

"It's like you read my mind sometimes. It's scary."

He chuckled. "I'm perceptive, but definitely not a mind reader."

"Can I sit on your wap?"

I looked down at Mia and found that she was staring with wide eyes at Hayes.

"Sure thing, Ms. Mia." He slid his chair out and she scurried off of hers and climbed into his lap.

The waiter returned with a booster seat and fixed it in the now empty seat, but I doubted Mia would be returning. Her favorite spot was apparently in Hayes' lap.

The waiter took everyone's drink order and disappeared from the room.

I picked up the menu once more, trying to find something I could eat that didn't cost the same amount as a kidney on the black market. I knew Hayes wouldn't let me pay for my own meal, but regardless these prices were ridiculous, and the menu items were outlandish. I wanted something normal to eat, not something that sounded like it'd been made up.

By the time the waiter had returned I'd decided on a cheeseburger—although, according to the menu it was far superior than a regular cheeseburger and had a list of fancy cheeses and toppings, but I figured it was safe enough.

Hayes got the same thing while everyone else seemed to either order steak or seafood.

A few minutes after the waiter left us again Casey appeared with a happy meal box.

"Is that for me?" Maddox grinned. "Case, you shouldn't have." He chuckled, tipping his chair onto the back two legs.

"I didn't." Casey huffed, clearly not pleased at being made errand-boy, and placed the box in front of Hayes before exiting the room.

"He's always so chipper," Hayes jested, "remind me to give him a raise for being such a joy to be around."

He reached for the box and set out the apples and chicken nuggets.

"Toy!" Mia chimed happily when he grabbed the plastic wrapped toy. He opened it and handed her the cheap plastic Barbie necklace, but the way she lit up you would've thought he'd given her a diamond.

That was the beauty with kids, normal every day things seemed so grand and monumental.

"I'm really bummed I don't have any chicken nuggets or a toy. It's not fair." Maddox mock pouted.

Mia picked one up and held it out between her chubby fingers. "I twill share wit you."

Maddox grinned widely. "That's sweet of you princess, but I won't eat your food."

She shrugged her shoulders. "Tat's otay. Moar for me."

We all burst into uncontrollable laughter at her comment.

"Wat's so funny?" She asked innocently, blinking her wide doll-like eyes.

"You, cutie," Hayes kissed her cheek, "you're so adorable."

My heart.

It was melting.

And I was helpless to stop it.

Hayes and I stood on the street with Mia, surrounded by four bodyguards, as the rest of his band members and their girls drove away in the SUVs.

Hayes crouched down so he was closer to Mia's eyelevel.

"Want a piggyback ride?"

She nodded her head eagerly and he turned around and crouched down so she could hop onto his back.

He seemed to know what direction to head so I fell into step beside him while the bodyguards flanked us, keeping the growing crowd at bay.

The fans were far more eager today than they had been yesterday and I was sure the band's TV appearance today might've had a hand in that.

Hayes was completely unaffected by all the attention, and for some reason Mia was too which I was grateful for. When she was two she'd gone through a nasty spell of crying and yelling about anything that upset her. Thank God she'd finally grown out of that stage before I pulled out all of my hair.

A few blocks later my eyes landed on a building and my steps faltered.

"No." I gasped the word.

"Yes," Hayes said, somehow managing to hear me over the chaos surrounding us.

"No," I repeated.

"Don't look scared. It's only dolls."

I let out a laugh. "Aren't *I* supposed to say that to *you?*" I asked, staring up at the *American Girl* logo on the building.

He shrugged, stepping up to the crosswalk. "It's just a bunch of dolls and little girls. What's there to be afraid of?"

*A mob of horny mothers*, but I didn't say that out loud.

We reached the store and stepped inside.

Pink.

Pink and red *everywhere*.

Mia squealed in delight and Hayes let her down, quickly grabbing her hand before she could run off and be lost in the throngs of people.

Since Christmas was only a month away they'd already put up a tree—a pink one covered in so many decorations you could barely see a branch.

Mia spotted it and tugged on Hayes' hand to get his attention. "Twee!" She cried. "I wants to see the twee!"

"Of course, Ms. Mia. Shall we take a picture with the tree?"

She beamed up at him and nodded eagerly.

"Greg, take a picture of the three of us." Hayes commanded, pulling his phone out of his pocket and tossing it at his burly bodyguard.

Somehow Greg managed to catch it despite the ginormous bear paws he had for hands.

"Arden," Hayes called, waving me over to stand beside him in front of the tree.

When I stood beside them Mia beamed up at me. "I wuv you, momma."

I smiled down at her. "Love you too baby girl."

I lifted my head and found Hayes staring at me, and what I saw in his eyes said so much more than any words could express.

The flash on the camera phone went off.

"Smile!" Greg called to get our attention this time.

I reluctantly turned away from Hayes and gave the camera the cheesiest smile I could—but while cheesy, it was one hundred percent genuine.

It always was with Hayes.

# CHAPTER TWELVE

HAYES PULLED HIS truck into my driveway and my shoulders sagged in sadness at the fact that our mini-vacation was over.

It was dark out and in the backseat Mia was passed out asleep, drool dripping from her chin onto her pajama shirt.

"The new key should be around here somewhere." Hayes muttered more to himself than me as he got out of the truck and began searching.

I climbed out of the truck—which meant I basically fell onto my driveway. Why his truck needed to be so high I'd never know or understand.

Hayes had procured the new key from somewhere and the door to my house now stood open.

I went to get Mia out of the car but Hayes jogged over and gently pushed me out of the way. "I've got her."

Since it would be easier for him to grab her I let him.

"Don't even think about grabbing your bags either." He warned when he noticed me moving to the other side of the truck.

"You're so bossy." I stuck my tongue out at him in jest.

He pulled a sleeping Mia higher into his arms and started for the house. "I want to take care of my girls."

I followed behind him and directed him to Mia's room. She was still sound asleep as he laid her in her bed and I turned on her butterfly nightlight so she wasn't in the dark.

"She looks so peaceful and happy." Hayes whispered, pushing a piece of red hair away from her face.

"She's probably dreaming about floating on cotton candy clouds again."

He chuckled and quickly put a hand over his mouth to stifle the sound. We both eased from her bedroom and I closed her door halfway.

"Cotton candy clouds?" He asked now that we were safely outside her room.

I shrugged. "That's what she told me one time. Apparently they were delicious… but then she ate a hole into the cloud she was floating on, and she fell in her dream, which means she woke up and ended up in my bed," I rambled.

Hayes snorted. "She's so fucking adorable."

"No cussing in my house." I jested, poking his side.

He mock-winced and said, "Sorry."

We strolled out into the living room and he told me to wait there while he carried Mia's and my stuff inside.

When the last of the bags sat on the floor we stood across from each other, me leaning against the wall and him with his hands shoved awkwardly into the pockets of his jeans. He stared at me with this unfiltered innocence that I'd never seen before.

He swallowed thickly, his lips parting as if he wanted to speak but then thought better of it.

"Say it," I pleaded.

"I don't want to leave," he confessed. He shook his head, laughing under his breath. "It's crazy, really, what you've done to me. Before you I thought the way I was living my life was great. I *thought* I was happy, but that couldn't be further from the truth. I haven't been in a committed relationship…ever—because two months in high school doesn't count. Then I met you and suddenly I couldn't stop thinking about you, or wanting to be around you. I wanted to see you smile and hear you laugh and for the first time in my life it wasn't about *sex*. Although, I have to admit with you it's better than it's ever been before. But what I'm trying to say," he rambled, his hands waving through the air, "is that you're all I want and what I feel for you is never going to go away. And maybe it's too soon to say I love you, but I know I do. I love you. I love you so damn much that it scares me more than anything else ever has." He spoke passionately, the fierceness in his eyes rooting me to the spot. "It scares me more than when we signed our record deal or the first time I was on stage in front of thousands of people. But just like those things, it doesn't scare me enough that I want to walk away, it only makes me want to fight that much harder. I love you," he said it again, like he never wanted to stop saying it, "and I love your daughter too. She's the most brilliant little girl I've ever met."

I stood staring at him, at a loss for words. I hadn't been expecting that. Not at all. And my brain couldn't seem to function to form even a single sentence.

Hayes swayed awkwardly where he stood. "Uh…this is kinda the part where I thought you would say something. Either tell me you loved me too, or that I'm a major weirdo and to get out of your house, so…"

"Shut up." I closed the distance between us and jumped into his arms.

He caught me easily and I wrapped my legs around his waist, taking his face between my hands as I lowered my mouth to his. I kissed him slowly at first, but the fire that always seemed to burn between us sparked into a raging inferno.

I found my back pressed into the wall as he angled his mouth over mine completely devouring me. His unique scent—a mix of the woodsy soap he used and something else that was inherently Hayes—swam around me. His large body completely covered mine and in his arms I felt safe and protected. That was a miracle considering everything Todd had done to me. When he first left I'd believed I'd never feel comfortable in the presence of another man, but that was before Hayes came along and completely shattered my world in the best way possible.

His lips left mine but he still held me in his arms. His breath fanned across my lips as he fought for air. I was equally as breathless and with each inhale of breath my breasts brushed against his chest.

Somehow, I managed to find the words to whisper, "I love you too."

He closed his eyes as several different emotions rippled across his face. "Say it again," he pleaded, placing a tender kiss to my chin, "please say it again."

"I love you."

He let out a low growl that made my entire body clench with desire. "I never knew it would feel so good to love and be loved." He admitted, sadness glimmering in his eyes. Brightening, he cracked a small smile, "But I'm really fucking glad I waited for you."

I grinned too as he lowered my legs to the ground. I grabbed ahold of the sides of his open plaid shirt and held on so he couldn't move away. "I am too." I leaned my head against his chest, my ear pressed against the spot where his heart thumped loudly. His arms wound around my body and he simply held me, resting his head on top of mine. It was such a sweet, simple gesture but it filled my whole body with a fluttery happiness I hadn't felt in so long.

"Stay here tonight," I begged. "I don't want you to leave."

Confessing that I wanted him to stay was a vulnerable moment for me. I'd been on my own so long now, refusing to accept help or comfort from anyone, but Hayes was different. He didn't make me feel like a charity case, instead he made me feel…well, *loved*.

"Are you sure?" He asked, holding my face between his large hands so I was forced to look at him.

"Yes. I-I mean I know this can't be an every day thing, but for tonight…please stay."

He grinned—my favorite smile of his, the one that made him look like a goofy little boy.

"I'd do anything for you, you know that, right?" He asked and waited for me to nod. "Then trust me when I say that staying the night with you is hardly a burden."

I stood on my tiptoes to kiss him. "I love you," I whispered again.

"I love you too, Little Bird."

Taking his hand I locked up the house and led him back to my room.

"Nice room." He commented, taking in his surroundings.

I laughed, turning the bed back. "It's pretty boring," I admitted. "The room was already painted this color when I moved in," I motioned to the lavender walls, "so I decorated the room around it. And it seems a stretch to even call it decorating. One vase doesn't really count." I shrugged and headed over to my dresser to grab a pair of pajama bottoms and a tank top. "I'll be right back." I pointed in the general direction of the hall bathroom. "Make yourself at home."

Before he could respond I hurried down the hall and into the bathroom. I closed the door, leaning my back against it as I struggled to gain control of my breaths.

I didn't know why I was freaking out so much. I'd just told the guy I *loved* him, and yet the sight of him standing in my bedroom was making me nervous. Maybe it was because he was so tall and imposing and seeing him in my super girly bedroom had been strange. Or maybe it was because he'd looked so *right* there.

"Get it together, Arden." I whispered to myself with a shake of my head.

I turned on the shower and stripped myself of my travel clothes. I'd showered this morning, but after the flight and drive I knew my stiff and tired muscles needed it. I squirted my body wash into the palm of my hand and lathered my body until I smelled like peaches.

When I returned to my room I had to put a hand over my mouth to suppress a laugh.

Hayes was sprawled on the bed, his arms and legs spread wide like a starfish, with his mouth hanging open. He snored lightly, completely sacked out.

I climbed into bed beside him, lifting one of his heavy arms and moving it over to his side so I'd have more room. He mumbled something in his sleep and I giggled as I turned out the light.

I drew my legs up and rolled closer to him.

As if he sensed me even in his sleep he turned on his side and wrapped an arm around me.

I burrowed my head against his neck and closed my eyes, falling asleep instantly.

I awoke with a start.

There was too much light in my room. Normally when I woke up it was still dark out, but not this morning.

Nope.

The sun filtered in through the open blinds, bathing the whole room in a golden shimmer.

Hayes wasn't in bed and I wondered if he'd left at some point in the night—the thought making me sadder than it should have.

My eyes finally landed on the alarm clock on the bedside table and I blanched when I saw it was nearly nine in the morning.

I normally woke up on my own around six so I would have some free time before Mia, invariably, woke up at seven on the dot.

In a panic I shoved the blankets off my body and ran out of my bedroom.

The amount of trouble a three-year-old could get into without supervision was endless. Already I was imagining Sharpie scrawled across the walls.

Instead I was met with her light musical giggles coming from the kitchen.

I rounded the corner and stopped in my tracks.

The kitchen was a disaster, but I couldn't bring myself to care, because Mia sat on the counter helping Hayes make breakfast.

From the looks of it he was making pancakes.

They hadn't noticed me yet and I took a moment to watch them together.

"Do you know who the most beautiful girl in all the land is?" Hayes asked her while he dumped ingredients in a bowl.

"Who? Who?" Mia asked eagerly. I noticed her hair was neatly braided down her back. Since Mia couldn't braid, and her hair had been loose last night, I knew Hayes had taken the time to do it.

"You." He tapped her nose, leaving behind a streak of flour.

"Me?" She beamed, pointing at herself. "What about momma?"

Hayes grinned, stirring whatever he'd put in the bowl. "She's the prettiest *woman* in all the land."

Mia nodded with a grin lifting her lips, clearly pleased with his answer.

She tilted her head, inspecting his exposed arm. "Why dids you draws on yosef?"

Hayes chuckled, scooping some of the mixture onto the hot griddle. "I didn't draw on myself. They're tattoos."

"Wat are tat-tat-tatoooos?" She squished her nose, clearly confused by the new word.

"I guess you could say they're permanent drawings." He shrugged and his thin t-shirt pulled taut across his chest and shoulders.

He looked up then and spotted me in the doorway. "Morning." He tipped his head in my direction, a grin splitting his face.

"Morning," I whispered, leaning against the archway, content to continue watching him and Mia.

"We're matking pantakes, momma!" Mia chimed, clapping her hands together in her excitement. "Ooh! Ooh!" She exclaimed suddenly. "Will you matke me Mickey Mouse ones?" She addressed Hayes, looking up at him like he was some sort of God.

"Sure thing, sweetheart." He flipped the pancakes and a few minutes later removed that batch. "Wanna watch me make it?" He asked her.

She nodded and he picked her up, settling her onto his hip. With his free hand he poured the batter into the shape of Mickey Mouse and Mia squealed in delight. It obviously didn't take much to make her happy.

While Hayes finished making the pancakes I finally got my feet working and grabbed the plates from the cabinet. I set them on the table along with forks, napkins, syrup, and drinks.

Hayes turned the griddle off and carried Mia and the plate piled with pancakes over to the table.

We all sat down together at the table, digging into our food, and I marveled at how normal it felt to sit around a table together and eat breakfast.

Yeah, we'd eaten meals together in New York, but for some reason I thought it'd be different here in my house.

And…I guess it was, but not in the way I expected.

It felt like—

"Are we a famalee?" Mia asked, looking from Hayes to me.

I smiled at her and my gaze rose to Hayes to find him smiling too. It had happened so fast, but Mia was right. The three of us were a family. An unconventional one, that was for sure, but what family was perfect?

Hayes had busted into my life this past summer, festering beneath my skin where I couldn't rid myself of him, and now I didn't want to.

"Yeah baby girl." I kissed her sticky cheek. "We're a family."

# CHAPTER THIRTEEN

I WAS A lovesick fool.

You know the person constantly walking around with a goofy smile and acting like they're high? Yeah, that was totally me and I wasn't ashamed of it. I was going to embrace this giddy feeling for as long as it lasted.

I danced around the store, straightening items of clothing and singing along to the radio.

Nothing could possibly dampen my mood.

The door leading into the store opened, the bell chiming with the new arrival.

"Welcome to *Sew in Style*." I chimed happily as I turned around, beaming at the customer.

When my eyes connected with the man's my smile bled away, as did my happy mood that only moments before I'd believed was impenetrable.

I felt like all the air had been sucked from the room and I was slowly beginning to suffocate.

I hadn't seen him in over four years and yet he still looked the same.

His light brown hair was trimmed short and his dark blue eyes were as lifeless as I remembered. He wore a beard now, which made him appear older than what he was. He was tall—not as tall as Hayes—with wide shoulders that had once made me feel so protected but ended up only making me feel caged. His lips tugged into a smile but there was nothing nice about it. He looked like a robot. Fake and emotionless.

"Todd." I whispered his name, hating to give life to it and show any sort of fear.

"Arden." He sauntered forward, smirking at me as he tucked his sunglasses into the collar of his shirt. "Long time no see."

I stood straight, squaring my shoulders. I refused to cower in his presence. He'd hurt me once but I wouldn't let him hurt me again.

"Yes, well, that's typically what happens when one up and leaves their pregnant wife."

He rubbed his jaw, trying to appear unaffected. "You always did have a mouth on you."

"And you never did like that, did you?"

He stepped closer and I clasped my hands together in the hope that he wouldn't notice how badly they shook.

He picked up a bracelet; twisting it around in the light like it was the most fascinating thing he'd ever seen. "A woman should listen to her husband."

"And I guess you also believe it's okay for a husband to *hit* his wife." I stepped behind the counter, using it as a barrier between us.

He grinned, noticing the gesture.

"Yes, I do believe that's okay, especially when his wife is a nagging, defying bitch." He replaced the bracelet and stared at me, waiting for me to make some kind of response. It was a great effort not to roll my eyes.

"Why are you here?" I finally asked, lifting my arms in resignation. He was obviously here for a reason and I'd rather he get to the point instead of dragging it out with his stupidity.

"To see my daughter."

I snorted. "Don't be absurd."

His thick brows furrowed together. "She's my daughter. I have as much right as you to see her."

I crossed my arms over my chest and lifted my chin. "I'm pretty sure you gave up that right when you abandoned her before birth. Not that I'm complaining," I hastened to add, "the best thing you ever did for me was leave."

He snarled, his nostrils flaring. "You're a real bitch."

I laughed, shaking my head. "Coming from you that means nothing."

His eyes narrowed to thin slits and he snarled. Once upon a time that look on his face would've sent me running. Not anymore. I wasn't his prisoner and I wouldn't allow him to think he intimidated me—even if on the inside I was scared to death.

"You never knew when you should shut your mouth."

"Get out," I pointed over his shoulder at the door, "you have no right to come to my *job* and try to berate me."

He shook his head, his lips lifting in a sneer. "Make me."

"You're such a child." I huffed under my breath.

He stepped up to the counter, laying his hands flat on the surface.

"I will see *my* daughter." He growled. "And if you don't watch your fucking mouth you'll never see her again." He began to back away. "It was good seeing you."

I scowled at him, my lips twisted as I held back the words I wanted to scream at him. I wanted to yell and tell him he'd never see or get close enough to lay his hands on her, but I knew he wanted a rise from me and I refused to give it to him. He could go fuck himself.

"Goodbye, Todd." My voice was cold and detached.

He braced his body against the door and chuckled under his breath. "I'll see you later."

Ice slithered down my veins as he exited the store and disappeared around the corner.

The adrenaline that had been surging through my veins only moments before suddenly disappeared and I was left feeling cold and shaky. I couldn't believe that had just happened. I blinked my eyes and pinched my arm, wanting to believe it was a bad dream, but it was most definitely real.

Todd was back.

"Momma," Mia called from the backseat, "turn up da song. I wike dis one."

I did as she asked, wishing the music could drown out my racing thoughts. Somewhere in the back of my mind I registered that it was a Willow Creek song playing on the radio, but I couldn't even take a moment to enjoy it because all I could think about was Todd.

It all made sense now.

The guy Mia saw staring at her in the grocery store.

Hayes saying it looked like someone had messed with my front door.

If Todd had gone that far before even speaking to me it scared me to consider what he might be capable of.

My eyes flickered to Mia smiling happily in the backseat and kicking her feet. Keeping her safe would always be my number one priority and there was no way in hell I was going to let Todd anywhere near her.

My knuckles turned white where I gripped the steering wheel and I pulled in a lungful of air, trying to calm myself. I was supposed to meet Hayes for dinner after he finished band practice—or whatever it was that the guys were up to. We wouldn't be going out for dinner, instead we'd be having dinner with Ezra's mom and dad—who were also Maddox and Mathias' foster parents. I'd met Karen and Paul a few months ago at Maddox and Emma's wedding. Karen had been kind and welcoming to me, despite the fact that she'd never met me before that day. Hayes was close with them though, they were almost like second parents, and he'd wanted me to get to know them better.

I turned into the neighborhood, glancing in awe at the large homes. They weren't monstrous by any means, but they were certainly bigger than what I lived in, though smaller than Hayes' home.

I pulled into the driveway of the beautiful white cape cod style home and smiled at Mia in the rearview mirror. "Ready, baby girl?"

She nodded, curly hair bouncing.

I helped her out of her car seat and then held her hand as we climbed the steps of the front porch.

"Do you want to ring the bell?" I asked her.

She nodded eagerly, beaming with a gaped toothed smile. I lifted her onto my hip and leaned forward so she could push the button. I quickly grabbed her hand and held it in mine before she could get too excited and push the bell ten more times.

Within seconds the door swung open, revealing Karen. Her smile was blinding—like she was absolutely thrilled to see us—and she stepped back, waving us inside.

I inhaled the homey scent of a roast baking and suppressed the urge to moan. I'd been too busy stressing over Todd to eat lunch and now I was starving.

"Hello, Arden." She chimed. "It's so nice to see you. And *you*," she turned her smile to Mia, "must be Ms. Mia. Hayes has told us all about you."

"He did?" She asked shyly, burying her face in the crook of my neck and peeking at Karen through the thick strands of my hair.

"He has," Karen assured her, unfazed by her shyness. "I'm baking some cookies for dessert. Would you like to help me?"

She waited patiently, letting Mia ponder her words. Finally, a full minute later, Mia nodded and I set her down.

"You're welcome to help too, Arden," Karen lifted her gaze to me as she held her hand out to Mia, "but I figured you'd want to join everyone in the basement. The girls are here too."

"Uh," I hedged, unsure with whether or not I felt comfortable leaving Mia with a virtual stranger.

Karen smiled thoughtfully. "I've been in your position before. It's hard to let go of our little ones. Especially when they're not little for long."

I let out a breath I didn't know I was holding. "It's been the two of us for so long that it's hard for me to let someone else help."

She nodded, staying quiet and letting me work through my inner turmoil.

"Mia, will you be okay with Mrs. Collins for a little while?"

If Mia wasn't comfortable with me leaving, I wouldn't—and frankly, after Todd showed up at the store it was a little unnerving to have her out of my sight for even a second.

Mia looked up at Karen with wide blue eyes, seeming to assess her in that quiet knowing way kids had about them, and then nodded at me.

"If you need me," I told Karen, "just let me know."

"We'll be fine." Karen assured me, leading Mia down the hall towards the kitchen. "They're down there." She pointed at a door and smiled at me over her shoulder before she disappeared.

Once they were in the kitchen I heard Mia ask her what kind of cookies they were making. I smiled to myself, pleased that she was getting better about speaking to people.

Before I could talk myself out of it I reached for the basement door and headed downstairs.

I could hear the twinkling sounds of the girls laughing and some of the tension began to leak from my body.

I rounded the corner and saw the three of them sitting in a nicely decorated living room space—complete with a massive flat screen TV and sectional.

"Hey!" Emma grinned when she saw me and waved me over to the couch. "You're here for dinner?" She asked eagerly.

I nodded, tucking a stray piece of hair behind my ear as I took a seat. "Yeah. Hayes invited me…that's okay, right?" I was suddenly nervous as I eyed the three girls.

"Of course! I just can't believe he didn't tell us you were coming over. He was probably hoping he could manage to keep you all to himself." Emma winked.

"What are the guys doing?" I wiggled around, trying to get comfortable, and ended up with my legs crossed beneath me. "All Hayes told me was that they were in the studio, but I don't really know what that means."

Emma hastened to explain. "They have a studio here in the basement so they don't have to stay in L.A. all the time, so right now they're putting the final touches on their album so it'll be ready to release in a few months."

"Ah, I see." I turned my gaze to Remy where she bounced a fussy Liam. I couldn't believe how big he was getting already, but that was the thing with kids, you blinked and suddenly they weren't babies anymore. "Can I hold him?" I asked, a little uncertain. I remembered when Mia was born how I was terrified to let a stranger hold her. Heck, I even freaked out over letting my mom and dad hold her and they were my parents.

"Sure," Remy held him out to me, "but be warned, he can scream like a banshee. He's already moody like his dad."

The baby squirmed in my arms, clearly not happy to leave his mom. I stroked his plump cheek and cooed softly to help calm him. He gazed up at me with wide blue eyes, his dark brown hair making them appear even bluer.

His lower lip trembled with the threat of tears and I began to rock him. He quickly settled and I smiled down at him.

"Sometimes I miss Mia being this little. I mean, it was hard taking care of a baby by myself, but when they're this small…every little thing they do is so special."

It was quiet around me and I looked up to see that the guys had appeared and Hayes was staring at me with such intensity I was surprised I didn't combust on the spot.

"How's the recording going?" I asked as I rubbed my fingers along the soft downy hair coating Liam's head.

Hayes took a seat beside me, between Emma and I—well technically it was Maddox now, since he'd taken Emma's spot and deposited her in his lap.

"Good. I think we're all excited to release something new."

"Does this mean you'll be going on tour soon?" I inquired, staring at the baby so he wouldn't know how curious I was about his answer.

"Nah," I felt him shrug, "it'll be a few more months before the new album is out—these things take time, and then it'll probably be another six or so months after that before we're ready for a tour, maybe longer since everyone keeps popping out babies." He glanced towards Sadie and Ezra.

Sadie held up her hands in defense. "Don't look at me. He's not getting any babies out of me until he puts a ring on it."

Ezra laughed under his breath and leaned over to whisper something in her ear. Sadie batted at his shoulder and pushed him away, but couldn't feign being mad for long as she leaned over to kiss him quickly.

Hayes reached for one of Liam's sock covered feet and gave it a little tug. "He's so small."

"Do you want to hold him?" I asked.

His eyes widened and he frowned, unsure. "What if I break him?"

I laughed and Liam blinked his wide blue eyes up at me, clearly not happy with being disturbed. "You don't worry about breaking Mia."

Hayes wiggled uncomfortably where he sat. "Yeah, but Mia is like a tiny *person*. And she can talk. Babies just spit on themselves and poop their pants. It's scary."

Mathias and Remy laughed at his discomfort. "He's yet to hold Liam," Remy informed me.

"Oh, you're definitely holding him then. Lift your arms like mine."

"He's going to fall through," Hayes muttered, "I have long arms."

"That's why you *cradle* him." I bit my lip to contain another bout of laughter at his expense.

Hayes looked like a deer caught in headlights. "I don't want to drop him."

"You're not going to drop him." I held Liam out and placed him in Hayes' waiting arms.

Hayes' eyes widened with panic.

"It's okay," I assured him, "he's not as breakable as he looks. Just be sure to support his neck."

Hayes gazed nervously down at the squirming baby. "Uh…"

"He's a baby," I giggled, "he's going to move."

"I'm afraid he's going to roll out of my arms."

Mathias cackled merrily somewhere to my left. "I never thought *you'd* be the one of us most afraid of a baby."

"Dude, shut up," Hayes groaned, staring at the baby so intensely it was like he was willing him not to move, "go iron one of your nerdigans like a dutiful little housewife."

Mathias laughed even harder. "That's the best comeback you have?" He shook his head. "You're losing your touch."

"I also have your spawn in my hands and don't want to kill him, so my brain is kind of focusing on that right now…and for the record, if I had use of one of my hands I'd be giving you the finger right now."

Mathias chuckled and rubbed his jaw.

"It's not so bad, is it?" I asked Hayes, reaching over so the baby wrapped his tiny fingers around one of mine.

"Yeah, not so bad," he mimicked. His lips were turned down in a frown and he still looked scared to death, but his arms had relaxed some.

I leaned my head on his shoulder and hummed softly under my breath. It was an old lullaby I used to sing to Mia every night. I didn't have the best signing voice, but it had always calmed her down.

Liam, instantly, focused his eyes on me. His small pink lips pouted as he regarded me with curious eyes.

I began to sing the words, oblivious to the others surrounding us.

When the last note hung in the air I looked up to find Hayes staring at me, his mouth parted in awe.

"I didn't know you could sing."

I ducked my head, my whole body heating with embarrassment. "I can't."

"Uh, you definitely can." He assured me.

I laughed, trying to hide my discomfort at all the attention that was suddenly directed my way.

"You're in a *band*, a world famous band at that—so I know you're lying." I poked him in the ribs.

He brushed off the gesture. "You're cute when you're embarrassed."

His words only served to make me blush even more. I was sure my freckles looked startling on my nearly red skin.

"Hey!"

We all turned towards the stairs at the sound of Karen's voice, and my heart lurched as panic slid through my veins. I stood, my motherly instincts kicking in as I feared Mia had been hurt or was having a meltdown.

"What is it, mom?" Ezra asked. He sat lazily on the couch, with his foot resting on his leg and his arm swung across the back of the couch behind Sadie.

"I wanted to let you guys know dinner was ready."

I suddenly felt silly for my gut reaction to jump to attention, but I couldn't help it.

"We'll be up in a minute," Mathias called. He stood and crossed over to Hayes. "Give me my kid," Mathias held out his hands, "before you drop him and split his skull open."

"Don't scare him," I scolded Mathias.

He turned amused gray eyes in my direction as he lifted his son to his shoulder. "I like you," he said, completely catching me off guard.

"Uh…" Before I could form a coherent thought he had started up the stairs.

Everyone else filed up the stairs, leaving Hayes and I alone for a brief stolen moment.

I wrung my hands together, suddenly nervous about being alone with Hayes. I hadn't decided whether or not I was going to tell him about Todd's surprise visit to the store. We'd only been an official couple for a few weeks, and before that I was used to taking care of everything on my own.

"I thought they'd never leave." He chuckled, reaching down to take my chin between his thumb and forefinger. "I've been thinking about your lips all day." His eyes flicked down to my mouth.

At his words my mind instantly emptied and my fingers wrapped around the soft cotton of his shirt. "Then kiss me."

He made this half-growl, half-hum sound in the back of his throat that made me feel lightheaded. Since he was so tall, and I was on the shorter side, he had to lean way down to kiss me. I didn't mind though. I liked having his larger body envelope my smaller one. I felt so safe wrapped in his arms.

Even though I could've stood here kissing him all day I reluctantly took a step back, letting my hands fall from his shirt.

He was slightly out of breath when he asked, "What's wrong, Arden?"

I looked down at the ground, tugging my bottom lip between my teeth.

"Arden," he prompted again, the tips of his shoes coming into my line of sight when he stepped forward. "You can tell me anything…you know that, right?"

I took a deep, steadying breath. I knew that if I didn't tell Hayes about Todd it would make me feel like shit and eat away at my insides. This was too big of an issue for me to try to hide it and it definitely wasn't something I could fix on my own.

I straightened my shoulders and I looked up, meeting his curious gaze.

"I saw Todd today."

"Todd?" His brows furrowed in confusion. Suddenly, his eyes widened and his lips parted with a gasp. "*Todd*, as in your ex *Todd*?"

"Yep, that one." I sighed, feeling sick to my stomach. I perched my bottom on an armrest of the couch, unable to hold my body up any longer after my admission.

He ran his fingers through his hair, musing the once perfectly styled strands. "Fuck. What did he want?"

"To see Mia." My stomach rolled with the words. I desperately wanted to go back to only a minute ago where his lips had been on mine and life had felt good.

"Double fuck." He groaned, raking his hands down his face. "This isn't good."

"I know." I rubbed my hands nervously on my jeans. "I don't know what to do. I mean, he's her *father*, it's not like I can keep her away from him forever."

"Oh yes you can," Hayes thundered. "He gave up any right to her when he left you pregnant and alone."

"I feel that way too, but he's her *dad*," I groaned, anger surging through my body. "I told him he couldn't see her, but I don't know how much longer I can keep him away. When Todd wants something…" I let my thought hang in the air.

Hayes looked at me with horror. "Your door…before we left for New York, do you think that was him?"

I sighed. "Probably. Who else would it be?" I lifted one shoulder in a shrug.

"You're staying with me," Hayes nodded to himself, "yep, that's the solution. You'll both stay with me."

I rolled my eyes, laughing under my breath. "I can't uproot my whole life, and my daughter's, and saunter into yours like everything is fine. It's not fine."

"It's not fine if you're there in your house, which he tried to break into, either!" He spread his arms wide. "This isn't about being *fine*," he spat the word, "it's about being *safe*."

I dragged air through my lungs and yet I still felt like I wasn't breathing. After a moment of silence, my voice finally punctured the air. "I'll think about it, okay?"

Hayes frowned, clearly not pleased with this compromise. His shoulders sagged. "That sounds fair." Pointing a finger at me like I was an unruly child, he added, "But if he shows up again you call me immediately and you're coming to my house."

"Hopefully there won't be a next time. Maybe he just wanted to rattle me and now he's gone." As soon as the words left my mouth I knew how wrong they were. When Todd wanted something he'd go through hell until he got it, and right now he had his sights set on our daughter. He definitely wouldn't be leaving, even if I wished it were true.

Hayes looked at me skeptically, not believing my words anymore than I did.

"Are you guys coming?" Maddox yelled down the stairs. "And I mean coming upstairs, not coming in the sense of the sexual relations kind of coming…because in that case, that's gross, we sit on that couch and there are children in this house now!"

Hayes snorted and shook his head. "We're coming!" He called and Maddox mock-gasped. "Upstairs," he added while laughing hysterically. "Get your head out of the gutter, Wade."

I heard Maddox chuckle before the door to the basement closed.

Hayes smirked at me. "I guess we better join them before Maddox has them convinced we're doing the other kind of 'coming.' " He winked, lifting his hands and flicking his fingers in quotation marks.

I shook my head at his antics and stood up.

Before I could move towards the stairs he grabbed me around my waist and pulled me into his arms. Laying his head on top of mine, he whispered, "Everything is going to be okay, Arden. You'll see."

I wanted to believe him, I really did, but I couldn't.

When we topped the stairs the sounds of voices drifted from the dining room and Hayes dropped his hand to the small of my waist, guiding me forward.

Everyone was already seated and looked up when we stepped inside.

"Hi," I mumbled awkwardly, making a beeline for the empty chair beside Mia.

Hayes was right behind me and held the chair out and slid it back in before taking the seat on the opposite side.

"Look at you being all gentlemanly," Maddox chortled. "Who are you and what have you done with the real Hayes?"

Hayes ducked his head, laughing under his breath. "He grew up," he shrugged

"Took him long enough." Mathias grumbled, reaching for a roll.

His mother swatted his hand and glared at him like he was an unruly child. "Be nice," she hissed, "and we're saying grace before we eat. Stop acting like a savage."

Mathias muttered something under his breath, but sat back and bowed his head.

Paul, Karen's husband, spoke for all of us.

Once he finished speaking we all chimed in with a collective, "Amen."

"Now you can eat." Karen eyed Mathias. "But mind your manners."

"Yes, ma'am," Mathias mumbled, reaching for a roll once more.

Before I fixed my own plate I tended to Mia, making sure she got a bit of the roast, potatoes, and carrots. I cut it all up into small, easy to manage pieces for her.

"This looks delicious," I told Karen, shoveling food onto my plate. Beside me, Hayes was already halfway through his first plateful. "Thanks for having us."

"Anytime, sweetheart." She smiled kindly at me.

I took a bite of roast and tamped down the moan that wanted to bubble out of my throat. The food was even better than it looked. Nothing beat having a home cooked meal—one that you didn't have to slave over. I was convinced everything tasted better when someone else made it.

Idle conversation was made as we ate, but for the most part it was relatively quiet. Karen spent a good time cooing over Liam, and it was obvious she was smitten with her first grandson.

When we'd finished eating I offered to help clean up, but Karen waved me away. "That's what my sons are for," she said with a wink.

Poor Mia was nearly asleep from a food coma so I guessed it wasn't such a bad thing that Karen dismissed me.

"I'm going to head out," I told Hayes, sliding my chair back and picking up Mia. She wrapped her arms around my neck and legs around my waist. "I think it's safe to say this one is ready for bed." I bounced her in my arms slightly. She was already asleep, and within seconds I felt her drool dampen the sleeve of my shirt. When they were babies you got spit up on, when they reached this age it was drool instead…and the occasional booger.

"I'll walk you out." Hayes wiped his hands on a napkin and stood from his chair.

"Not fair! We have to clean up and he gets to go suck face!" Maddox bellowed as he gathered up a stack of plates.

"You're my son." Karen swatted his side with a towel. "You can suck face later."

"But—"

I didn't hear whatever he was about to say as Hayes and I left the room.

We were both silent as we stepped outside. It was already completely dark, and since the night sky was cloudy you couldn't see any stars or even a sliver of the moon.

Hayes held the door open and I bent to put Mia in her car seat. She roused a bit, but was already asleep again by the time I closed the door.

I turned around to face Hayes, drawing my cardigan tight around my body.

"I'm worried," he admitted. "I don't like him being back here."

I sighed and my breath fogged the air. "Me either, but what can I do?" I shrugged nonchalantly. I desperately wanted to brush off the fact that Todd was back, but realistically I couldn't. It would be stupid not to think him being back didn't pose a threat to Mia or myself. Todd was…unstable to say the least.

Hayes cupped my cheek in one of his large hands, smoothing his thumb over the top of it. "Just…be careful, okay? And if you get scared or…fuck, if *anything* happens, call me and I'll be there."

I nodded. "I will."

He leaned his forehead against mine. "I love you, Arden, and the thought of him trying to weasel his way back into your life scares me so fucking much."

"Why?" I questioned. "I would never go back to him."

"I know that, Little Bird. That's not what I meant. I'm afraid of him hurting you again, or Mia, and…" His eyes squished closed and he looked anguished. "If he lays a hand on either of you I can't be held accountable for my actions," he warned.

"He's not going to bother us."

Hayes looked at me doubtfully. "We can hope." He whispered, his breath feathering against my forehead. "On a lighter note…Thanksgiving is next week. What are your plans?"

My brows furrowed in confusion at his sudden change in topic. "I'll probably go to my parent's."

He reached down and entwined our hands together. Staring at our joined hands, he said, "What if you came to mine?"

"You want me to come to your parent's house for Thanksgiving?" I didn't believe I could've possibly heard him right.

"Yes, I know you've already met them, but not as my girlfriend. And," he hedged, seeming nervous, "my sisters are flying in and I want you to meet them, and for them to meet you."

My heart lurched and then sped up. "I'm not sure…" It had been so long since I'd met anyone's family—and he was right, I had met his parent's but not as his girlfriend and that made it feel like I was meeting them for the first time.

He ducked down so his baby blue eyes met mine. "Don't make me beg." He jutted out his bottom lip. "Please? There's no way you can resist this face."

I laughed despite my nerves. "I'll go," I agreed.

"Yes!" He clapped his hands together and did a little victory dance.

"Don't make me regret this," I warned him, unable to keep a smile off my face.

"You won't, trust me." He took my face between his hands and lowered his mouth to mine. He kissed me leisurely like we had all the time in the world.

When he pulled away we were both slightly breathless. He caressed my bottom lip with his thumb, his eyes a dark navy blue now. "I love your lips," he murmured. "They're so soft and plump. Kissable."

"Mmm," I mumbled, unable to form a word when he was looking at me like he was now. Unconsciously my tongue slid out to wet my lips, as if called forth by his attention.

"You're killing me," he growled, kissing me again.

His tongue slid past my lips, stroking against mine and eliciting a moan deep from within my throat. My heart thumped madly behind my rib cage and I was sure he could feel it with how closely our chests were pressed together. I hadn't noticed, but somehow while we were kissing he'd grabbed my waist and my body had automatically bowed into his.

When he broke the kiss, I whispered, "I love you," so our lips brushed with my words.

He growled low in his throat and kissed my forehead gently before murmuring,

"I'll never get tired of hearing you say that to me."

"I really need to go now," I whispered, disentangling myself from his arms.

"I know." He took a step back, like he was afraid if he didn't distance himself he might maul me with his mouth again.

"Bye," I told him, slipping into my car.

"Goodnight, Arden," he murmured as I closed the door, his words slipping over me like warm honey. I'd never known *goodnight* could sound so sexual, but the way he said it made me think of how desperately I wanted to spend the night with my naked body wrapped around his.

"Night," I mouthed through the door, turning the car on.

I backed out of the driveway and he stood, watching my car until we were out of sight.

# CHAPTER FOURTEEN

I STARED AT the pile of brand new clothes on my bed. I'd already tried on countless new dresses and nothing seemed appropriate for spending the day with Hayes and his family.

Just thinking about it nearly had me running to the toilet to throw up.

I didn't know why I was so nervous.

I'd met his parents already and he assured me that his sisters would love me, but that did nothing to calm my nerves.

I picked up a simple black dress and put it on, quickly vetoing it.

Hayes was going to be here in less than an hour and I hadn't even done anything to my hair. At least Mia was ready…although, that fact could prove to be a disaster if she tried to get into anything.

I picked up the last dress I had to wear, vowing that this would be the one.

The fabric felt silky as it rubbed against my skin. It was on the shorter side, ending above my knees, and a soft cream color. I closed my eyes before I looked in the mirror, saying a little prayer.

When I opened my eyes I was pleasantly surprised by what I saw in the mirror. The dress was simple but pretty. I looked dressed up, but not like I was trying too hard.

Satisfied, I stuffed the rest of the dresses back into the bag and stuck it in my closet.

"Momma! Momma!" Mia chanted, running into my bedroom and face planting into my legs.

I laughed and reached out to steady her. "Hey, silly girl, are you okay?"

"Yeah," she pushed her hair out of her face, looking up at me sweetly, "I haz a qwuestion."

"And what's your question?" I asked, moving into the bathroom.

She bounced behind me and stood by the counter while I tried to make my hair presentable.

"My bwirthday is soon…and I want a kitten."

"A kitten?" I laughed.

She nodded her head eagerly, her red curls swinging around her shoulders. "Day're so fluffy and cute."

"And who would take care of the kitten?" I smiled down at her, amused by the random ideas she always came up with.

"You would swilly."

"Ah, I see." I nodded, fluffing my hair and leaving it hanging down my shoulders in soft waves. "I'll think about it, how does that sound?"

"Sounds wike a deal." She nodded adamantly and flounced out of the bathroom.

I applied my makeup, opting for light and natural—like usual—and added some pink lipstick and gloss for a pop of color.

I grabbed a pair of heels from my closet and dangled them from the end of my finger as I padded through the house.

Mia was sitting in the living room, playing with her new baby doll Hayes bought her while we were in New York City. It was her new favorite toy and she could barely stand to go five minutes without it in her sight.

I set my shoes by my purse and grabbed my phone.

There was a text from Hayes telling me he was running a little late since he had to stop for gas.

"Mia, do you want to leave your hair down or put braids in it?"

Her lips pursed as she pondered my question. "Can Hayes do it?"

"Um…" I paused, shrugging. "If he's willing to do it when he gets here."

Mia returned to playing with her doll and muttered, "Den ask him."

I chuckled. "I'll ask him when he gets here, baby girl."

Ten minutes later a shadow fell across the front of the house as Hayes pulled his massive truck into the driveway.

Mia gasped and ran to the door, looking out through the glass. "Hayes is here, Hayes is here!" She chanted, jumping up and down.

You know, if I was going to fall in love with someone it was only appropriate that Mia loved him too. In fact, I think the fact that she loved him so much was one of the reasons I fell so hard and so fast.

Hayes jumped out of his truck and stole the breath from my lungs.

He was dressed nicely, in a pair of dark jeans, a button down shirt worn open over a shirt with the sleeves rolled up, and a pair of black boots. His hair was perfectly styled like always. The sun hit his hair making the normally sandy, almost brown, strands look even lighter. He wore a pair of stylish sunglasses that I was sure cost more than I made in a week.

He looked up and saw Mia and I standing in the doorway and a smile split his face. My stomach was assaulted with butterflies from that one smile.

I pushed the door open and he stepped inside, immediately bending down to pick up Mia and plant a loud kiss on her cheek. "Hi, Ms. Mia," he greeted her, removing his sunglasses and tucking them in the collar of his shirt.

"Hi." She wrapped her arms around his neck. "Will you bwraid my hair?"

Hayes chuckled and set her down. "I might be able to do that."

His eyes swam to me and he looked me up and down. His Adam's apple bobbed and he finally met my eyes. "You look stunning. You're always beautiful, but that dress…your legs…" He stepped impossibly closer and bent to whisper in my ear. "All I'm going to be able to think about tonight is burying my face between your legs and licking—"

"Hayes," I groaned, pushing him away as a blush blossomed over my cheeks, down my neck, and into my chest.

He shrugged, smiling innocently. "Sorry, Little Bird. I got a bit carried away with my thoughts." He winked.

I closed the front door as Mia took Hayes' hand and led him to her room.

I followed, watching as she handed him her brush and ponytail holders.

She sat on the floor and he sat behind her, spreading out his long legs. He ran the brush through her hair, separating it into two even sections.

"What have you and your mommy been up to?" He asked her, beginning to braid her hair.

"Um," she tapped her chin thoughtfully, "we whatchted a movie last night?"

"Which one?" He secured the first braid before moving on to the next one.

"Tangled!" She cried gleefully.

Hayes chuckled at her exuberance. "Was it good?"

She nodded her head eagerly.

"Hold still," he warned gently, finishing the second braid.

"Sowwy." She frowned.

"It's okay," he assured her. With a pat on her shoulder he said, "All done."

She jumped up and tackle hugged him.

He rocked back, bracing an arm against the floor to keep from falling over. "Whoa," he chuckled.

"Tank you." She told him before letting go and running off, probably in search of her doll.

Hayes grinned, jumping to his feet. "She's so adorable."

"I tend to agree." I laughed where I stood in the doorway.

He sauntered towards me in that lethal way he had and I found myself stuck in the doorway, my back pressed into the wood molding as he blocked me, pressing in so there was no room for me to escape—not that I wanted to.

"I haven't had a chance to kiss you properly," he breathed, his eyes flicking down to my lips. My heart thumped madly, it always did when he was near. "The problem is," his fingers ghosted against my chin, "once I start kissing you I never want to stop." His lips replaced his fingers and they glided up my jaw to my ear. "It feels like it's been ages since I touched you…*really* touched you. I'm desperate to hear the sound of you falling apart in my arms."

My eyes closed and my shaking hands landed on his forearms, holding on so that I didn't fall over. "I want that too." I admitted, tugging my bottom lip between my teeth and wishing it was his teeth instead—nipping and biting all over my body.

I felt the barest touch of his lips to mine. "Soon." He promised.

Cold air whooshed around me and I looked up to see that he was gone.

I took a moment to calm my racing heart before finding him and Mia waiting in the living room.

"Ready?" He asked.

"I just need to put my shoes on." I grabbed the heels and slipped them on while Hayes put Mia's car seat in his truck.

When I stepped outside he was already buckling Mia in.

He turned and saw me, freezing in his tracks. "Jesus Christ…those shoes… between them and this short dress I'm going to spend all day walking around with a hard-on in front of my parents and sisters and that's pretty fucking embarrassing."

I laughed and rose—still having to perch on my tiptoes even in my heels—and kissed him lightly. "You'll live." I patted his chest.

"I might die," he argued. "From blood loss," he added, "since all the blood in my body will be going straight to my dick."

I couldn't help myself and busted out laughing as I strolled around to the other side of his truck.

He followed, helping to boost me into the truck. "Don't laugh at my pain, it hurts my feelings."

I only laughed harder as he closed the door. My laughter was a welcome relief after all the stressing I'd done the past few days in preparation of today.

It was the first Thanksgiving I hadn't spent with my parents in a long time. My mom had been understanding when I called to tell her, but insisted that she and my dad got to meet Hayes soon. I hadn't said anything to Hayes about that yet, and I figured now was as good a time as any.

I waited for him to back out of the driveway before dropping the grenade.

"So…" I started.

He glanced at me. "Yes?" He prompted.

"When I called to tell my mom that Mia and I were having Thanksgiving with my boyfriend's," I thrilled at the word, "family, she was kind of shocked since I hadn't told her about you yet. But she was happy too, since she's been telling me to get out and date for a while." My hands wrung together. "Anyway, she and my dad want to meet you soon."

Hayes grinned his signature goofy smile. "Look at us being all official and meeting the 'rents."

I busted out into laughter once more. Of course Hayes wasn't going to freak out over this. I was pretty sure nothing ever fazed him. He went with the flow of things.

"So, you're okay with meeting them?" I questioned.

"'Course," he shrugged, "granted, I've never actually met a girl's parent's before…" He frowned. "That makes me a pretty pathetic twenty-seven year old, doesn't it?"

I shrugged, glancing out the window at the trees and houses whipping by. "You got famous at a young age, therefore I think you acted like most guys in your situation would. Not everyone is Maddox and Emma who meets the person they're supposed to be with for the rest of their life at such a young age."

"True," he shrugged, concentrating on the road ahead. "I envy him though, for finding that special person so young…then again, I think if I had found you when I was nineteen I probably would've screwed up everything." He chuckled, shaking his head. "I was a bit…wild."

"A bit?" I laughed. "I read magazines."

"Okay, so maybe I was a right piece of work. Regardless, it's made me who I am today and brought me to this point here with you and Mia and I'm happy…" He paused, mulling over his words. "I feel like I'm happier than I've ever been, and I would say I've always been a fairly happy person. It's just that I feel…" He glanced at me and whispered, "Complete."

I was unable to stop the smile that spread across my face. It felt good to hear him say that—almost better than when he told me he loved me. I didn't want to be a burden to him and hearing that he felt like I completed him made me feel all warm and fuzzy inside.

Hayes reached over then and took my hand, entwining his fingers with mine.

I smiled at him and then at Mia sitting happily in the back seat.

My life had been a series of shit storms thrown my way and it made me wary to trust when something good happened, but I wasn't holding back anymore.

Screw Todd.

Screw my own insecurities.

Screw it all.

"We're here," Hayes declared, pulling into the driveway of a modest two-story brick front home in Middletown.

The home was simple, but pretty. Even though it was November the lawn was well kept—not a leaf in sight, and I was sure in the spring and summer the bed out front bloomed with a kaleidoscope of colors.

"It's beautiful…is this where you grew up?" I asked, wanting to know a little more about his past.

He nodded. "I've tried to move them to a newer place, but they're both stubborn to a fault. My dad says he bought this house to die in and that's what he's going to do." He shook his head. "Silly man," he muttered, cutting the engine.

"Are your sisters here already?" I asked.

"Yeah," he replied. "They got in yesterday."

I took a deep breath before climbing out of the vehicle. I caught the movement of a curtain in a front room and stiffened, knowing that someone was watching us.

By the time I made it around the side of the vehicle Hayes was already holding Mia in his arms. She laid her head on his chest, content to be held.

"Show time," Hayes grinned, reaching for my hand.

We followed the brick walkway up to the front door.

"Breathe," he whispered to me a moment before the door swung open.

His mom greeted us with a huge smile. "My favorite son!"

"I'm your only son," Hayes chortled, stepping inside the home.

"Same thing." His mom shrugged. To me she said, "Josh didn't introduce us properly the first time we met. I'm Darla."

"Arden," I replied. "Thank you for having me."

"Of course, dear." She reached out, opening her arms for a hug.

While I hugged his mom Hayes eyed me, seeming to silently say, *See, I told you they would love you.*

She let me go and smiled warmly. "James is in the family room fiddling with that new TV you got him. Can you help him?" She asked Hayes. "The poor thing doesn't know how to work anything that was made after the year two-thousand."

Hayes laughed and set Mia on her feet where she quickly scurried to my side and grabbed ahold of my leg.

"Sure thing, mom." He kissed her cheek before striding down the hall.

I silently cursed him for leaving me alone with his mom. I wasn't good at this kind of thing. Having him near acted as a buffer, but alone I had no idea what to say.

"And this is your little girl?" Darla asked me, looking down at where Mia hid her face against my leg.

"This is Mia." I rubbed the top of her head in a soothing gesture.

"She's beautiful."

"Can you say thank you, Mia? She's talking about you." I smoothed my finger down her cheek, but she didn't budge. Looking up at Darla, I shrugged, "She's shy."

"That's okay. Why don't you join Josh in the family room? That's where everyone else is. I'm almost done in the kitchen and then we'll be ready to eat."

"Uh…okay." I squirmed uncomfortably. "I don't know where the family room is though."

"I'll take you."

She led me down the hallway and I tried not to gawk at the walls which were covered in family photos as well as photos of Hayes from magazines. It was like taking a step back in time. The further we walked, the older the pictures became. I stopped at one of Hayes as a toddler wearing a pair of cowboy boots, naked except for his diaper, and covered in mud.

"He was a cute thing, wasn't he?" His mother mused beside me.

"He's still pretty cute," I laughed.

"This is when we brought him home from the hospital." She pointed to another picture of a younger version of herself holding a baby wrapped in a blue blanket. She stood in front of this house, with her husband by her side, and her oldest daughter clinging to her leg much the way Mia was to me right now.

She smiled wistfully at the photo. "It seems like this was just yesterday." With a shake of her head she turned down the hall and an archway appeared. "Mind the stairs," she pointed to the three stairs descending into the family room, "if I don't tell people they don't seem to realize they're there."

I smiled at her as she passed and I stepped down into the room.

I saw Hayes fiddling with the large TV. He'd pulled it out and was redoing the wires while his dad stood with his hands on his hips, surveying what his son was up to.

As much as I wanted to keep staring at Hayes, I couldn't. The weight of other eyes in the room was too much to bear.

His sisters sat on the couch side by side appraising me like I was some organism shoved under a microscope. I felt exposed beneath their cutting glares and I had the sudden urge to run from the room.

Adrenaline surged through my veins as I felt my fight or flight senses kick in.

Somehow, I managed to stand my ground.

"Hi, I'm Arden." I said it as pleasantly as I could. Unfortunately, my voice shook, giving away my fear. "And this is my daughter Mia."

Mia scooted behind me, hiding even more.

The sister closest to me stood, extending her hand. She smiled, but it wasn't a friendly smile and did nothing to end my fears. "I'm Jessica."

I took her hand and she shook it roughly.

I remembered Hayes saying Jessica was his older sister. She had the same sandy colored hair as his, but her eyes were brown. Her face was thin with angular cheekbones. She looked so much like Hayes that there was no mistaking them as siblings.

"I'm Jaclyn." His other sister stood. Instead of shaking my hand, she actually hugged me but it was rather awkward and ended quickly.

Jaclyn had a softer face than her sister, making her look infinitely kinder. Her hair was dyed in a rainbow of colors. There was something relaxed and subdued about her. Like she didn't have a care in the world. I was beginning to understand why Hayes said he thought she sold pot.

A door from the outside opened and a little boy ran inside with a man behind him. The boy was maybe a year or two older than Mia and when he saw her he immediately ran behind me to greet her.

"Hi," he said cheerily, "I'm Ian. Wanna play?" He held up the bouncy ball in his hands.

Before Mia could respond, Jessica spat, "Ian!" Snapping her fingers she motioned him over to her side.

Frowning, the little boy hurried to his mother. She placed her hands on his shoulders like she was afraid he might escape and try to make friends with Mia again.

"This is my son Ian." Jessica squared her shoulders, sticking her chin in the air haughtily. I knew you shouldn't judge some you'd only just met, but I really didn't like her. "And this is my husband Grant." She nodded at the man.

I didn't even bother to acknowledge her husband. I was afraid if I spoke to him she might put him in the corner like an unruly child.

"I'm going to see if your mom needs help in the kitchen," I mumbled. I took Mia's hand and hurried out of the room.

"Arden!" I heard Hayes call after me, but I didn't stop. I wasn't going back in that room to speak to his judgmental sister. "What did you say to her?" He growled at his sister.

She responded, but I was already out of earshot.

Tears stung my eyes, but I dammed them back. I wasn't going to let his rude sister make me feel inferior. I knew me being here meant a lot to Hayes and I didn't want to make a scene.

I followed the homey scent of a home cooked meal and found the kitchen nestled in the back of the house.

"Is there anything I can help you with?" I asked, the sound of my voice echoing around the kitchen.

Darla jumped, raising a hand to her racing heart. "You scared me," she said unnecessarily.

"I'm so sorry," I apologized quickly.

"It's okay." She waved away my words. "Help," she mumbled to herself. "Ooh! Could you ice that cake for me?" She pointed to where a three-tiered chocolate cake waited with a bowl of chocolate icing.

"I sure can." I sighed in relief, pleased to have a task to complete and not feel like a useless pile of crap.

I helped Mia onto a stool and Darla handed me a knife.

I scooped some icing onto the cake and began to swirl the knife, spreading the icing around.

Hayes breezed into the kitchen. "Ooh! Cake!" He crowed, swiping his finger into the icing I'd already layered onto the cake.

"Hayes!" I scolded, laughing at him.

I bumped him with my hip and he chuckled, bending his head to kiss me quickly and smearing icing on my lips in the process. "Love you," he murmured, and I thrilled at how easily he said it—and in front of his mother no less.

Once he'd grabbed a screwdriver from a utility drawer he was gone again.

I became lost in my own little world as I frosted the cake, but my solace was short-lived when Jessica entered the kitchen.

She strolled right up to where I stood in front of the cake and leaned her hip against the counter. She held a glass of deep red wine and slowly raised the glass to her mouth, taking a delicate sip so as not to ruin her lipstick.

"So…you're a single mom, obviously."

My spine stiffened, but I wasn't going to let her words get to me. "Obviously." I said the word flatly, refusing to let her hear how upset I was.

"Did you get knocked up in high school and the baby daddy didn't stick around long enough for the paternity test to come back?" She sneered, looking me up and down. "Cute dress…did you get that at K-Mart?"

"Jessica!" Her mom yelled, looking horror stricken.

"It was just a question, mom." She batted her eyes innocently.

"What's your problem with me?" I asked softly, continuing to ice the cake and refusing to look at her.

"Problem? I don't have a problem." She put a hand to her chest and looked at me like she was shocked I would ask such a thing.

I suppressed the urge to roll my eyes. I'd only met her five minutes ago and she'd made it pretty obvious she didn't like me. But the last thing I was going to do was stand here and pick a fight with Hayes' sister.

She must've grown bored with me, because eventually she drifted away. Probably back out to the family room.

"I'm so sorry." Darla hurried to my side. She appeared appalled at her daughter's behavior. "I don't know why Jessica would say such horrible things to you…well, I do know," she frowned, "Jess is…very over protective when it comes to Josh.

He's her little brother, and as the oldest she think she has to look out for him and Jaclyn. Hayes has never, and I mean *never* brought a girl home before and I think it's throwing her." With a sigh, Darla shrugged. "She forgets he's almost thirty and not a baby anymore."

"It's okay," I mumbled.

She placed her hand on my arm, squeezing softly and giving me a sad look. "No, it's not." Stepping away, she seemed to gather herself. "Would you mind helping me set the table? It's almost done, I only need to carry the food out."

"I'd love to help," I assured her. I rinsed the knife off in the sink and then let her dictate which dishes she'd like me to carry to the table.

Hayes rounded the corner and caught sight of me carrying a bowl of mac n' cheese and another of mashed potatoes.

"Whoa, babe, let me get that." He skidded to a top and took the dishes from my hands.

I halted, shock widening my eyes.

"What?" He asked innocently. "Is something on my face?"

"You…you called me babe," I stuttered.

He chuckled. "How about that? I didn't even realize it." He bent and kissed the corner of my mouth. "Want me to say it again?" He grinned. Before I could respond he lowered his head and murmured, "Babe," into the crook of my neck.

I shivered and he pulled away with a laugh, disappearing into the dining room before I could collect my wits.

In no time the whole table was set and we sat down for our meal. Hayes, Jaclyn, Mia, and I were on one side, with Jessica, Grant, and Ian on the other. Darla and James sat at the heads of the table.

Food was passed around and I piled it onto my plate, even though I doubted I'd be able to eat much. I was still too worked up from my encounters with Jessica— and as luck would have it, she was seated across from me where she could glare at me. I really wanted to ask her who pissed in her Cheerios, but I doubted that would score me any points.

Conversation circled the table, but for the most part I kept quiet unless addressed specifically. I wanted to avoid the wrath of Jessica as much as I could.

"You were in Manhattan recently?" She questioned Hayes, her fork poised inches from her mouth with a piece of macaroni dangling from the end of one of the spears.

"Yeah, why?" Hayes asked, shoveling food into his mouth so fast I didn't know how he didn't choke.

"I just find it odd that you were in Manhattan, where I live, and you didn't bother to try to see me. It's not like I get out here often to visit, and when I do you're usually on tour or screwing anything with two legs and a decent ass."

"Jessica!" Darla slammed her hands on the table. "Stop this nonsense."

Hayes bristled beside me, glaring at his older sister. "Maybe this is why I didn't want to see you? Did you ever think of that? Huh?" He waved his hand at her husband. "Ever since you met Mr. Goody-Goody over there you've been nothing but a pretentious snob living in your nice Manhattan apartment, with your perfect robot husband and robot kid."

"Oh my God, you two! Stop it!" Darla pointed at her children. "If you act like five-year-olds I'll treat you as such and put you both in time out. I mean it!" She warned.

Across the table James and Jaclyn laughed manically at the scene playing out before them. If I were them I'd laugh too, but since I was part of the reason they were fighting I wanted to sink under the table and hide until it was time to leave.

"What do you know about this girl?" She pointed at me. "Tell me, Joshua?! Because I've got news for you, she's just some gold-digging whore looking to get your money! Wake up, Josh!"

Hayes was eerily silent beside me. "So, what? I'm so unlovable that a woman would only want me for my money? Is that what you're saying?"

"She has a kid! Don't you see that she's using you? You're her golden ticket to give that brat a better life."

That was it. I'd had it.

I pushed away from the table so roughly that Jessica's wine glass fell onto her lap, staining her blue dress. She said something else, no doubt rude, but it was like I was in a tunnel and couldn't hear anything she said.

Without saying a word I grabbed Mia's hand and walked out of the room.

I didn't have a car, so I couldn't leave, but I wasn't going to sit there and let his sister belittle my daughter and me. It wasn't right.

Somehow I found myself in the family room and I pushed the door open onto the outside. Mia followed, quiet at my side.

Before I closed the door I heard more shouting coming from the dining room.

A tear fell down my cheek.

I hated that my presence was ruining the Thanksgiving dinner Hayes should've been enjoying with his entire family. I'd known I shouldn't come, but I'd let his charm talk me into it.

Once the door was closed I turned around to find Mia running through the yard with her arms spread out at her sides. She was clearly happy to be out of there too. Even though she was young I knew she understood enough to know that we'd been insulted.

A tire swing hung from a branch of one of the large trees in the massive backyard. We'd had one similar in my yard growing up. I made my way over to it and swung my legs through the hole and wrapped my arms around the top of it, holding on as I spun around.

Today had turned into a huge clusterfuck of epic proportions and I was exhausted.

"Momma! Wook at me!" Mia called, spinning around and around the yard.

"You're going to get dizzy," I warned her.

"I won't!" She said as she stopped, swaying slightly. She let out a small giggle and grinned her adorable toothy grin.

His sister could think and assume what she wanted, but that little girl was the single most important thing in my life. And yes, I did want her to have a good life, but that wasn't why I was with Hayes.

The fact that she thought I only liked him for his money was insulting and revolting.

"Momma," Mia called, running over to me on the tire swing, "can we go home now?"

"In a bit," I assured her. I wasn't going to rush Hayes. If he worked things out with his family and wanted to stay, that was fine. I wasn't going to force him to cut his day short, but I also wasn't going to be in any room his sister frequented.

I wasn't sure how long we were outside, but eventually Hayes emerged from the family room with hunched shoulders, looking forlorn.

Mia ran up to him and said something and he nodded before she took off again. He made his way towards me with his head ducked so I couldn't see his eyes. My stomach dipped in fear that maybe his sister's words had had some effect on him and he was going to tell me this wasn't going to work.

He stopped in front of me and finally his head rose as he looked at me.

"Arden," he cleared his throat, "I was afraid you'd left when I couldn't find you in the house," he rambled. "I'm so sorry. I can't believe she said those things. It's unforgivable and—" He rubbed his hands over his smooth cheeks. "I never expected her to act like that."

"It's not your fault," I mumbled, holding onto the tire swing rope.

He grabbed ahold of the tire to keep me from spinning away. "In a way it is. I asked you to come here. I thought today was going to be great, and I was wrong."

I twisted my lips. "She hurt my feelings," I admitted, "and I know I should be an adult and not let silly things like that get to me, but she was so mean, and for her to think I'm only with you for your money…" I let my sentence drop and shrugged. "You know I love you for *you*, right?"

He chuckled, sweeping his fingers against my cool cheek. "I know, Little Bird."

He let go of the tire, and I began to swing around, letting out a laugh. I caught his grin at my laughter and my heart skipped a beat. After Todd I'd never believed I'd find someone I trusted and loved so completely and then Hayes came barreling into my life.

He stopped the swing once more and pulled it close, lowering his head to kiss me. "Let's go," he whispered.

"Are you sure?" I asked. "I don't want you to leave because of me."

He grinned. "S'okay. Mom's packing up some food for us and I figured I'd sweet talk my way into your house and you, me, and Mia could have our first Thanksgiving as a family instead." My heart sped up in excitement at his words. "Because I plan on there being many more." He kissed me again.

"You're kinda sorta amazing, you know that, right?"

"I do," he grinned cheekily, "but I like hearing you say it." He winked. "Come on, let's get out of here."

He helped me out of the swing and Mia came running over to us. He scooped her up and spun her around like she weighed nothing. Her laughter filled the air and I couldn't contain my smile. I was so happy that Mia finally had a man in her life, one that was good and kind, that she could look up to.

I saw his mom standing on the other side of the glass sliding door and when she noticed us approaching she slid it open.

"I'm so incredibly sorry," she told me immediately, "I hope you come back to see James and me. We would both love to get to know you better."

"I'd like that," I said, even though I was afraid that I'd only be able to think of Jessica's cutting words every time I saw this place.

"I fixed a bag of food for y'all and set it by the door." She patted my cheek gently in a motherly gesture.

"Thank you. I'm sorry I ruined your dinner."

She dismissed my words with a wave of her hand. "It's not ruined, dear. I got to see my kids, and you, and your adorable little girl. But most importantly I got to see how foolish my son is when it comes to you and it's good to finally see him settle down."

"Maybe we could have dinner at Hayes' place soon?" I suggested.

"That sounds like a great idea." She hugged me.

Hayes was waiting for me and together we headed towards the front entry.

His dad and Jaclyn came out of the kitchen and said their goodbyes.

I didn't see Jessica, her husband, or her son, and I wondered if they'd left or if she was avoiding us. I guessed it didn't really matter. I had a feeling nothing I did or said would ever make her like me, and that was fine. The only person's approval I needed was Hayes'.

"I'm really sorry this happened." Hayes apologized again as he lifted Mia into the truck.

"Stop apologizing," I told him, "it's over and done with and now all I want is to go home and spend some time with you. Okay?"

He nodded as he closed the truck door, but his eyes were still haunted.

His sister's words had hurt, but I knew it wasn't his fault. She had her own issues, clearly, and I wasn't going to blame him for that.

Standing on my tiptoes I wrapped my arms around his neck. "Maybe you could stay the night." I said coyly.

His hands ghosted down my sides, settling on my hips, and a slow smile appeared on his lips.

"Mmm," he hummed, "I like the sound of that."

"Good." I kissed him quickly and hurried around to the other side of the truck.

On the drive home, Mia chatted endlessly—telling Hayes all about her favorite Disney movies, which princess was her favorite, and which prince she was going to marry.

When she got to the prince part, Hayes replied with, "You won't be getting married for a very long time if I have anything to say about it."

Mia mused quietly. "Even when I'm tirty?"

"Never." Hayes chuckled.

Mia crossed her arms over her chest and pouted in the backseat. "Dat's not fwair."

"Sorry, Ms. Mia." He shrugged, turning onto my street.

"You don't sound sowwy."

Hayes pulled into the driveway and put the truck in park.

He ignored her, staring intently at the front of my house. "What the hell?" He whispered to himself, reaching for the handle and climbing out of the truck.

Mia gasped. "Momma, Hayes said a bad word."

"I know, baby, that wasn't nice of him." I undid my seatbelt and leaned forward, trying to see what he was looking at, but my efforts were futile. "Mia, mommy will be right back."

I hurried out of the vehicle and over to where Hayes stood in front of the window beside the front door.

I opened my mouth to ask him what he was looking at, but the words quickly turned into a gasp when I saw. The window was completely broken in—the screen that was normally in front of it was lying on the grass completely useless.

"Get back in the car with Mia and lock the doors," Hayes warned.

My eyes widened in horror. "Do you think he's still in there?"

"I don't know, but I'm going to find out." He declared, standing with his hands on his hips like he was poised to take on the world.

"You can't go in there!" I cried. "What if he has a gun?"

"I'll be fine." He assured me.

"You're not invincible," I reminded him, "and I'd never forgive myself if you were hurt because of me."

"Don't worry about me," he turned away from the broken window to look down at me, "go be with her. She shouldn't be by herself." He nodded towards the car. I knew he was right, so I headed back to the truck without protest. "Oh, and Arden?"

"Yeah?" I paused, hesitating on my next step.

"You're staying at my house for the foreseeable future. Don't even try to argue with me. *This*," he pointed over his shoulder at the shattered remnants of the window, "is not okay."

"I know," I replied. "I won't argue."

He nodded once and waited for me to get in the truck and lock the doors before he opened the front door. Since it was unlocked—and hadn't been when we left—I let out a sigh of relief, believing that if Todd had broken in then he must've already left. And who was I kidding using the word *if?* Of course it was Todd. It couldn't be anyone else.

Even though I believed he was already gone my heart thundered like a vicious storm in my veins while I waited for Hayes to emerge.

I busied myself by calling the police and reporting the break in. Someone was to be dispatched within thirty minutes.

I hugged my knees to my chest, waiting for him to emerge from the house. Each minute that ticked by on the dashboard clock was a minute too long.

I was just about to bust inside when he finally stepped outside with two large suitcases in tow.

He wheeled them down the driveway and hefted them into the truck beside Mia.

"I wasn't sure what all you'd both need, so I grabbed pretty much everything."

"The police are on their way," I informed him as he climbed into the driver's seat, "so we should wait."

"Okay." He agreed, pinching the bridge of his nose.

"Did it look like anything had been taken?" My voice sounded small when I asked the question.

"Some pictures were missing," he shrugged, "looks like that was it."

"I don't understand why he's doing this now?" I whispered, more to myself than him.

Hayes sighed heavily, turning to look at me with sorrow filled eyes. "Do you want my honest opinion?"

"Always." I didn't hesitate to reply.

"I think he's probably always been hanging around, back in the shadows watching you, and then I showed up." He frowned, his brows crinkling together. "And now he feels like his territory is threatened."

"Territory?" I scoffed. "I'm no one's *territory*."

"I know that," he rushed to assure me, "but I think someone as twisted as he is probably thinks you both belong to him."

"Ugh," I groaned, burying my face in my hands, "this is all so messed up."

"I know and I'm sorry." He reached over, massaging the back of my neck. "We're going to fix this."

My body relaxed at his use of the word *we're* as opposed to *I*. He wasn't trying to be all macho and saying that he'd get everything under control. No, he was saying that *we*, he and I, would do it together as a couple.

I think I fell in love with him a little more in that moment.

The police arrived a few minutes later and we each gave a statement before they searched the house. I was required to go along this time and list off anything I noticed was missing.

By the time they finished and we were allowed to leave, I was completely exhausted.

Hayes took my hand as he drove, slowly stroking his thumb over my fingers.

"We've got this," he whispered at one point, "you and I…we're going to get through this."

"I know," I whispered.

I was just afraid of how far it would go before Todd was stopped.

# CHAPTER FIFTEEN

"WHOA," MIA GASPED, "do you wiv in a cwastle?"

Hayes chuckled as the automatic door on his garage went up and he parked inside.

"If you think it's a castle, then it's a castle."

Exhausted, I climbed from the vehicle.

This whole day had been one major suck-fest.

All I wanted to do was give Mia a bath and put her to bed so that I could relax. I needed a moment to breathe and decompress and that was hard to do with a three-year-old.

Hayes opened the door leading from the garage into the house, and a giggling Mia immediately ran inside.

I hurried after her; afraid she'd make a mess or ruin something without meaning to.

"Dis pwace is huuuuge." She cried, spinning around with her head craned back to take in the expansive space. "Can we wiv here, momma?"

I chose not to answer her.

"Come here, baby girl." I walked over and picked her up, waiting for Hayes to come in with our bags. "Do you want something to eat?" I asked her.

"I'm not hwungy." She rubbed her face against my arm.

"Bath time, then?" I asked her, tucking an escaped curl behind her ear.

She nodded and rubbed sleepily at her eyes.

"Where's a bathroom I can use for her?" I asked Hayes as he set the suitcases down by the stairs.

"I'll show you." He grabbed one of the bags and started up the steps.

I followed him down a long hallway and he pushed open a door, revealing a beautiful guestroom done in a muted gray color with pops of green.

He set the suitcase down on a striped chair and opened another door that revealed a bathroom done entirely in black and white.

"Thank you." I set Mia on the floor and reached over to start running the water.

"I'll be downstairs if you need me." He scratched the back of his head awkwardly before disappearing.

I opened the suitcase he'd brought up and grabbed a pair of pajamas for Mia as well as a bottle of shampoo and her toothbrush and toothpaste. No wonder he'd been in the house so long. He wasn't kidding when he said he packed everything.

I pulled out Mia's braids and undressed her before lifting her over into the claw foot bathtub. I hadn't expected such a character filled bathroom from a house so modern and I was pleasantly surprised by the touch it gave.

Bubbles tickled Mia's chin and she laughed, blowing at them and giggling further when they made funny shapes.

I washed her hair and scrubbed her body before letting the water swirl down the drain.

I found a fluffy black towel under the sink and I used it to dry her body before helping her into her pajamas.

Once she was in her pajamas she scurried away from me and into the bedroom where she somehow managed to climb onto the high bed.

"I'm tired, momma." She rubbed at her eyes.

"Me too." I yawned. "But I have to brush your hair first before you go to sleep."

"O'tay." She sighed, giving me room to sit behind her and comb out the long strands of her vivid red hair.

Once I was finished she pleaded, "Will you lay wif me?"

"Of course, baby girl."

I pulled the covers back and climbed into the massive bed beside her. She rolled towards me, looking at me with her wide blue eyes.

"Momma, why are we hwere? Are we having a sweepover?"

"Something like that." I pushed a piece of hair off her forehead and glided my fingers down her smooth plump cheek. She was so unbelievably perfect in every way, and despite all the crap I went through with Todd—and was going through now, thanks to him—I wouldn't take any of it back if it meant not having her.

"Go to sleep baby girl." I coaxed gently.

"Will you swing me a swong?"

I stifled a laugh. "Of course."

I began to sing to her softly, an old country song that I'd loved years ago, and within minutes she was asleep.

I slipped out of her bed and tiptoed from the room.

I eased the door closed, terrified of waking her, and jumped when I turned to find Hayes standing in the hallway.

"Is it wrong that I got hard listening to you sing?" He asked, brushing my hair over my shoulder so that it cascaded down my back.

"I think everything makes you hard," I joked.

"When it comes to you," he lowered his head, "that's a pretty accurate statement." He nodded towards the stairs. "Come on, I warmed the food and poured you a glass of wine. I know you're probably about to tell me you're not hungry, but you need to eat."

I wrinkled my nose. He knew me too well. But he was right, I did need to eat something whether or not I thought I wanted it.

I followed him downstairs to the kitchen where he already had two plates waiting on the counter in front of the barstools.

I took a seat and inhaled the scent of the food. My stomach came to a sudden, roaring life and Hayes chuckled when he heard it growl.

"See?" He grinned, wiggling his brows. "I told you that you were hungry. I know everything." He bumped his shoulder with mine before pulling out the other chair and taking a seat.

"Yeah, yeah." I leaned over and kissed his cheek before digging into my food in a very un-lady like manner. "This is really good," I said, spearing a piece of turkey and swirling it in gravy. "I hate that we weren't able to eat with your family."

"Things happen." Hayes ripped apart a roll, shoving the pieces into his mouth one right after the other. "And what Jessica said was inexcusable."

"She's still your sister, though," I said sadly.

He frowned. "She's been blowing up my phone, but I don't feel like talking to her."

I was quiet for a moment, mulling over what I wanted to say. Finally, I settled on, "I wouldn't be mad if you wanted to talk to her. You don't have to pick sides. You know I would never make you do that."

"I know," he assured me, "but I really don't want to hear anything she has to say right now." He sighed heavily and scrubbed his hands over his face. "She can blame her actions on being overprotective but she didn't even *try* to get to know you, she immediately started in with that shit and it's ridiculous. I've *never* brought a girl home to meet my family, so that alone should've assured her that you were different."

"I just don't want you to not speak to her because of this," I whispered, staring down at my plate of food. "I won't get in the way of you and your family."

"Hey," he grabbed my chin, forcing me to look at him, "*you* and Mia are my family now too. Family is so much more than blood. It's like me and the guys… we're not related but we're still family. Some connections and bonds *are* more important than blood."

My eyes flitted down and I let out a soft sigh. "How is it that you always know the right thing to say to me?"

"I'm magical."

I picked up the glass of red wine he'd poured and took a small sip. "Mmm," I licked my lips, "that's good."

When I glanced over at him I saw that he was staring at my lips and his eyes had dilated.

"Fuck," he groaned, "I'm so desperate to touch you that I can't even think straight. I want to spread you out on this counter and eat *you* for dessert."

I shivered at his words. I wanted to tell him to do it—the idea of him taking me on the counter already had my panties soaked—but with a three-year-old in the house who could wake up at any moment we needed a room with a lock.

"I want you to touch me," I whispered, my wine and food lying forgotten. When Hayes looked at me like he was now, like I was the center of his universe and he was high on my presence, I couldn't think about anything else.

He growled low in his throat and my whole body clenched at the possibility of what was to come.

Before I could blink he was off the stool and he'd grabbed the back of my neck, angling his lips over mine. He stole the air from my lungs and every coherent thought from my mind with one sweep of his velvety tongue against mine. He kissed me thoroughly, leaving my body heavy and aching for his touch.

"Please, don't stop," I begged when his lips parted from mine, "I need to feel you inside me."

His hands dug into my hips and he lifted me from the stool. My legs wound around his waist as he carried me from the kitchen and up the stairs. He never broke the kiss, and by the time we reached his room I was gasping from the lack of oxygen.

He pushed the door closed behind us and I heard the lock click.

I was too busy kissing him to even bother looking around his room.

He set me down and dropped to his knees, skimming his hands up my calves and thighs, stopping when he felt my panties.

"Fuck," he cursed, air hissing between his teeth, "you're soaked."

"Touch me, please." I begged. I didn't care if I sounded desperate, because I *was*. I needed him to touch me more than I needed my next breath. It felt like it had been forever since the night in New York and I knew I'd need *hours* to reacquaint myself with my favorite parts of his body.

He lifted my dress, ever so slowly revealing the skin of my thighs. He kissed a path along the skin that was slowly revealed. His lips swirled up over my stomach and then he stood, sweeping the dress over my head and leaving me standing there in a matching bra and panty set—I could thank Sadie for those. After New York she'd shown up at my house with five bags full of new clothes and lingerie. She called herself the Sex Fairy Godmother and told me I was welcome before departing as fast as she'd arrived.

"You're so fucking beautiful." He murmured, cupping my breasts in his hands before lowering his head to kiss the swells. My back bowed and I moaned.

"Please," I gasped into the room, "I need more."

His hand skimmed up my back and a second later the clasp on my bra came undone. The silky straps fell down my arms and he yanked the bra off completely, tossing it into some far corner of his bedroom.

"That lingerie is sexy as fuck, but I prefer you like this…all creamy skin." He ducked his head again, this time taking a nipple into his mouth. My fingers tangled into his hair and I cried out, my legs buckling beneath me from the overload of sensations assaulting my body.

He grabbed ahold of me and lifted me onto his bed.

The smooth, cool feel of his bed sheets pressed into my back and my nipples tightened beneath his intense stare.

"I could look at you in my bed all day."

"It's more fun up here," I whispered breathlessly.

He chuckled huskily. "Mmm, it sure is." He stood between my spread legs and grasped the sides of my panties, sliding them all the way down.

It was strange to have a man staring at me so intimately when I'd gone without sex for so long, but I didn't feel shy beneath Hayes' stare. If anything, I felt powerful. There was a satisfaction in seeing the desire shimmer in his normally playful eyes.

"From the moment I met you, I've been yours," he confessed. "I didn't realize it then, but somehow you etched your way inside me and there was no ridding myself of you. Not that I wanted to." His fingers glided down my sides and in between my legs, stopping before he reached the place I needed him to touch me the most. "I never knew it would be like this," he admitted, bending to glide his lips between my breasts.

"What?" I gasped, my brain beginning to turn to mush as his tongue swirled around my belly button.

He glanced up at me, his blue eyes glowing in the darkened room. "I didn't know falling in love would be this easy. Everything with you is." He placed small kisses over my stomach. "I think I always thought that if I fell in love, I'd feel tied down, but it's the complete opposite. Instead, I feel free…like I've finally found my real purpose in life."

His words warmed my body and tears of happiness stung my eyes.

"I love you," I whispered, cupping his jaw.

He growled low in his throat and his large hands skimmed over my ribs before settling on my breasts. "I'll never get tired of hearing you say that."

"Then I'll never stop." I panted into the room as his mouth closed around my breast. My fingers tangled in his hair and my other hand pulled impatiently at his clothes.

He shrugged out of his shirt and pulled the other over his head. I sighed in relief at being able to touch his warm, bare skin.

His hips ground against mine and I gasped at the feel of his jeans rubbing against my sensitive flesh.

"Hayes," I moaned. "I need you."

"Shh," he pressed a finger to my lips, looking at me through hooded eyes. "In time."

I nearly sobbed. The desire to feel him moving inside me was all consuming.

He kissed me deeply then, silencing my cry of irritation. My cry quickly turned into a gasp when I felt two of his fingers press into me.

"Oh God," I moaned into his mouth, "like that. Please don't stop."

My hips moved against his hand and I grabbed onto his arm. My eyes met his and he was watching me with a look of fierce concentration.

He pressed his thumb against my clit and my back bowed off of the bed. Sweat dotted my body and all my thoughts were focused on him and what he was making me feel.

My body vibrated with barely contained energy and I came apart with a loud cry that he silenced with a kiss.

He waited for me to come down off my high before he pulled his fingers from my body. I watched in fascination as he lifted his fingers to his mouth, sucking away my wetness. His eyes darkened as he stared at me and then he climbed off the bed, despite my protests.

My indignation was short lived when he kicked off his boots and removed the last of his clothes. He started towards the bed, but I stood and placed my hands on his shoulders.

"Not yet," I pleaded, "I want to taste you first."

"Fuck yes." His eyes were hungry.

I dropped to my knees and took the base of his cock in my hand, stroking up slowly before closing my mouth around the head and rolling my tongue against his piercing. He gathered my hair in his hands, holding it away from my face.

I swirled my tongue around him, relishing in the unique taste of him and the small sounds of pleasure that he made.

"Your mouth is fucking amazing." He groaned as his head fell back. "Feels so good."

I took him as far as I could into my mouth before pulling back slowly. I did it again, and again, moving a little faster each time.

"Fuck, Arden." He growled into the room. "Stop, stop," he pleaded breathlessly, "I need to be inside you."

I pulled back, looking up at him with lust filled eyes and he growled in approval.

I turned climbing onto the bed. I spread my legs and began to stroke my fingers over my center.

"Hurry," I pleaded, "I need you."

"Fuck yes you do," he agreed, his eyes zeroed in on where my fingers stroked.

He grabbed a condom from the drawer and I reached out for the package. "Let me," I pleaded.

He gladly handed over the packed and I ripped it open. I sat up and he moved to the end of the bed, standing between my legs.

I rolled the condom down his length, careful not to tear it on the piercing, and once it was on he wrapped his hands around my thighs and pulled me even closer to him. He slid into me easily and I moaned at the feel of him. My arms stretched above my head and my fingers twined into the bed covers.

After everything I'd been through today it felt good to let go and seek pleasure in his arms.

"You feel so fucking good," he murmured, pulling my bottom lip between his teeth.

I reached out, running my fingers up his smooth, muscled chest and down his back.

I dug my nails lightly into his skin and he hissed.

"That's it," he growled, sucking on my neck, "mark me."

He kissed his way over my breasts and down my stomach before pulling out and climbing onto the bed.

"Is this okay?" He asked, grabbing me and lifting me onto him. His cock teased my entrance but he didn't push inside.

"It's perfect," I assured him, sinking down. "Oh God," I moaned. He felt deeper this way, filling me even more.

I rocked my hips slowly and he grabbed my breasts, licking a trail across each one.

He sat up, holding me so we were chest to chest, and our eyes met.

I'd never experienced a moment so intimately perfect as this one. I wrapped my arms around his neck and kissed him. Hoping, that without words, he'd know how much he meant to me—because while you could say I love you all you wanted, it was another thing to *show* someone you loved them and allow them to *feel* the depths of your emotions.

I began to roll my hips faster and my breath panted through my lips, caught by his kisses.

"I'm going to come," I warned him.

"I'm right there with you," he whispered.

Holding my hips steady he moved faster beneath me and stars blossomed behind my eyes. My nails dug into his back and I fell apart with a sharp cry. He groaned with his release and his breath fanned over my ear.

Instead of pulling out of me, he kept holding me with his forehead pressed against my chest.

He raised his head, pushing my sweaty hair away from my face.

"I'll never get tired of this." His voice was thick. "Of *you*."

I couldn't find the words so I only nodded my head in agreement. Being with Hayes…it didn't matter what we did, I always loved it. But sex with him was mind-blowing. I'd never known it could be like this and how having a true connection could make it even better.

He lifted me off of him, groaning from the loss of contact, and removed the condom. He tied it off and tossed it into a nearby trashcan.

Rolling over, his eyes slid over my body and then his fingers followed the same trail.

"I want you again already."

"Mmm," I hummed, "I'd like that."

"You're not too sore?" He asked, concern coloring his tone.

I reached out, rubbing my fingers over his strong jaw. "No."

"Thank God." He rolled on top of me and kissed me deeply. "And this time," he ducked his head, ghosting his lips against my ear, "it's going to be slow. The exact definition of what making love should be."

My body tightened at the promise in his voice as he reached over and grabbed another condom from the drawer.

He put it on and rocked his hips leisurely against mine before sliding in completely.

He held still once he was all the way inside and gathered his breath.

And then he did as he promised and made love to me again and again and again until we both passed out from exhaustion.

# CHAPTER SIXTEEN

I WOKE UP with Hayes between my legs and I decided then and there that I never wanted to wake up any other way ever again.

I didn't know how after last night he'd possibly have the energy for another round, but the man was insatiable.

My muscles were sore, but in the best way possible, and I couldn't wipe the grin off my face if I tried.

"I'm going to go make breakfast." Hayes said as he stepped out of the bathroom, drying his hair with a towel.

He'd asked me to join him in the shower, but I'd been too tired and ended up falling back to sleep. Besides, I knew if I'd taken him up on the offer *showering* would have been the last thing we were doing.

"Mmm," I hummed in response.

He chuckled. "Any special requests?"

"Mmm."

"Can you form any coherent words this morning?"

"No." I smiled at him.

He grabbed a pair of sweatpants from a drawer and let the towel around his waist drop to the floor before slipping them on. He remained shirtless and I took the opportunity to let my eyes feast on his sculpted chest and the intricate tattoo adorning the top of his left arm. It was beautiful with bright swirls of colors creating the image of an octopus, mermaid, a turtle, and fish on the blue ocean back drop.

"Like what you see?" He grinned at having caught me gawking at me.

I nodded, wrapping my arm around the pillow. It smelled like him and I was once again reminded at how crazy it was that I was here with him. I'd thought if I gave him a chance I'd be just another girl that the playful rock star took for a ride, but I'd been wrong. I was glad that he'd been so persistent and hadn't given up on me when I kept pushing him away. Most guys would have. Not Hayes, though. He was one of a kind, and for some reason he loved me.

"I *love* what I see." I finally replied.

His smile widened and he took me in where I lay in the middle of his bed, wrapped in his sheets.

"And I love what I see." Tossing the wet towels into a hamper, he said, "I was going to make egg sandwiches, does Mia eat those?"

I nodded. "She's not super picky like most kids. What time is it?" I asked, glancing around for a clock.

"A little after six," he replied.

I yawned. "I feel like I didn't sleep at all."

"Well, that's because you kind of didn't." He winked.

I sat up, holding the sheet to cover my chest. "I'm going to shower really quick before Mia gets up."

"If she gets up early I'll tend to her," he assured me. "Don't feel rushed."

I rubbed at my sleepy eyes. "You're too good to me."

"Only because I love you." With a small, almost shy smile he disappeared from the room.

I knew this whole thing was probably as strange and exhilarating for him as it was for me. But while I'd been in love before—because I had loved Todd before things went to shit—Hayes never had been.

I saw my suitcase sitting on the bench in front of the bed and I scurried out of the bed and grabbed some clean clothes and my shower things Hayes had so thoughtfully packed.

Now that it was morning, and Hayes wasn't around to distract me, I could finally admire his bedroom.

It was done in mostly gold and brown, with dark wood furniture. The walls were painted in two colors of gold, forming horizontal stripes around the large room.

His furniture was massive, but the room was so large that it actually made the furniture seem normal-sized. To my right was the bathroom, and even from here I could tell it was ginormous, and to my left was a sitting area complete with a couch, two chairs, and a TV over a fireplace. In the sitting area there was a counter with a sink, mini-fridge, and a coffee maker. You would never have to leave this room if you didn't want to.

Clutching my clothes I stepped into his bathroom.

The gold and brown glass tiles glimmered from the chandelier hanging from the ceiling. The counter boasted two sinks and was so long that if two people were getting ready there would be no chance of them bumping into each other.

A large soaker tub sat in front of a window overlooking the backyard—where I could see a covered pool, pergola, and a small pool house.

I always knew there were people who lived in spectacular homes like this one, I just never expected to meet one, let alone *date* one.

I turned away from the bathtub and stared open-mouthed at the shower.

Although, calling it a shower hardly seemed to do it justice.

You could probably fit ten people in this 'shower'. There were several sprayers in the walls and a showerhead hanging from the top. I thought I'd remembered hearing this kind called a *rain* shower.

The shower was closed off from the rest of the bathroom by an open piece of glass.

I set my clean clothes on the counter and stripped down, fiddling with all the showerheads until I got it right.

I stood underneath the water and let it uncoil my stiff and sore muscles.

Once I was showered I dressed and brushed my hair and teeth. Since my hair was still damp I pulled it back in a messy bun so that the strands didn't drip and make my shirt wet.

When I left his room I went to check on Mia and found that she was just waking up. She was slightly disoriented with waking up in a strange place, so I was happy I was there to calm her down.

After some coaxing I managed to get her out of bed and dressed before we headed downstairs.

In the kitchen Hayes was finishing up and slid the third egg sandwich onto a plate.

"There's my girls!" He crowed. "Did you sleep good, Ms. Mia?" He asked her, tweaking her nose before lifting her into his arms.

She nodded. "I felt wike a princess. Dat bed was huuuuge." She held her arms out as wide as she could.

He tickled her stomach and picked up a plate. "Wanna carry those into the dining room for me?"

"Of course." I gathered the other plates and followed him.

Mia was telling him all about her dream—it involved a unicorn and a prince—when I went back to the kitchen to grab glasses and a bottle of orange juice.

By the time I returned Mia still hadn't finished her talc, but Hayes listened with rapt attention, hanging on to every word she said like it was the most important thing he'd ever heard.

I loved that he didn't ignore her and try to brush her aside. Most guys dismissed kids, even their own.

Mia sat at the head of the table, which left Hayes and I across from each other.

I poured each of us a glass of orange juice and slid his across the table. He smiled at me before fixing his attention on Mia once more—she'd now launched into a story about preschool.

I marveled at how *right* it felt to be sitting here the three of us.

In a short time, we truly had become our own little family, and that thought brought tears to my eyes.

"Arden?" Hayes prompted, his brows wrinkling together in concern. "Are you okay?"

I nodded. "Yeah," I rushed to assure him, dotting my wet eyes with a napkin. "Everything is perfect."

And for now it was.

# CHAPTER SEVENTEEN

"WHY THE HELL did you not tell me you were staying with Hayes?" Sadie asked the moment I entered through the back of the store.

I sighed and set my purse down on a small chair and removed my coat.

She stood, blocking the entrance into the main store and crossed her arms over her chest, tapping her foot impatiently.

I'd had the last four days off for a short Thanksgiving break and all of that time had been spent at Hayes' house watching movies—although, we did go into the city one day to get out, and Mia had loved strolling the streets of D.C. But in that time, I hadn't bothered to inform my friend that I was staying with Hayes. I knew she'd be excited, but also curious as to *why* I was staying with him. She knew I was a sheltered person and that there would have to be a reason for me to be there.

"Who told you?" I hung my coat up on the rack.

"Emma—Hayes told the guys, so naturally Maddox told her, because those two tell each other everything. I'm pretty sure if he farts he sends her a text to let her know."

I snorted.

"It's true," Sadie demanded, "anyway, why didn't you tell me?"

"It didn't seem important," I shrugged innocently.

"Not important?!" Her voice spiked with impatience. "Of course it's important. And I know you, Arden, so tell me what happened. Why are you staying with him? Did a pipe burst or something?"

I was a terrible liar, but she gave me the perfect opening. "Hot water heater burst, and they can't fix it until the end of the week."

Maybe it was silly, but I felt like by telling her about Todd showing up I was only giving him more power to hurt me. I wanted to pretend his threat didn't exist, and the less people that knew he was back the easier it would be.

"Aw, that's awful," she frowned, "but at least Hayes is taking care of you."

"Mhmm," I nodded.

She narrowed her eyes on me. "What are you not telling me?"

"Nothing," I breezed past her, into the main store.

She followed, and unfortunately the store was empty so I couldn't use a customer as a buffer.

"You are such a liar, Arden."

I busied myself by straightening the display on the checkout counter.

"I'm no such thing," I said, refusing to meet her eyes.

She rolled her tongue around her mouth and waved a finger at me. "I'm going to find out what's really going on. You can't keep any secrets from me." Straightening, she grabbed her purse from where she'd stashed it behind the counter. "Luckily for you, I have a dentist appointment, so I can't bug the shit out of you at the moment."

"Bye, Sadie." I laughed at my crazy friend.

"I was a detective in another life," she said, easing towards the back, "so don't dismiss my sleuthing skills. I'm watching you." She pointed at her eyes and then me. Letting the façade drop, she added with a smile, "And we need a girl day sometime. With Emma and Remy too."

"Sure thing," I saluted her, "now go before you're late for your appointment."

"See ya!" She called over her shoulder.

She hadn't been gone more than two minutes when my phone vibrated in my pocket. I didn't receive many phone calls so I immediately grabbed it, afraid that something had happened to Mia with the sitter.

The caller ID flashed MOM though.

"Hey," I answered, "I'm at work, can I call you back?"

"This'll only take a minute…okay, more like five. But it's important." Her rapid sentences and overall distressed tone of voice immediately had me on edge.

"What is it?" I asked, watching the front of the store for any possible customers so I could hang up quickly if I needed to.

"Todd showed up."

"At *your* house?" I leaned against the wall for support.

"*Yes*," she replied, her tone as shocked as mine, "he started asking all of these questions and—"

"Whoa, whoa," I halted her, "what kind of questions?"

"Mostly about you, and Mia, of course. He wanted to know if Mia was in school," I scoffed at this, the idiot didn't even realize she wasn't old enough to be in school, "and he asked for some pictures."

"Please tell me you didn't tell him anything."

"Of course not." She seemed appalled that I'd think such a thing.

I pinched the bridge of my nose, feeling a headache coming on.

Clearly, trying to pretend the Todd problem was going to go away was not working in my favor.

"Has he talked to you?" She questioned.

"Yes," I admitted reluctantly. "It wasn't a very pleasant conversation."

"I didn't think it would be…Arden," she started, "this has me worried."

"I know," I sighed, fighting the urge to breakdown, "it's worrying me too."

My parents, at the time, hadn't known how bad I'd had it with Todd. Around them he'd always been a perfect gentleman, kind, and carrying. I recalled my dad once telling him that he couldn't have picked a better man for me to marry. But once Todd disappeared I had to explain everything to them so they'd understand. My mom had cried for a weak straight and my father swore if he ever saw Todd again he'd kill him with his bare hands, chop up his body, and feed it to the bears.

"Just…be safe, sweetie. Okay?"

"I will." I assured her.

"Your father and I still want to meet Hayes," she said. "Could you come over for dinner Friday evening?"

"Friday…" I mulled over my schedule. "I'm free. I just have to talk to Hayes."

"Excellent!" She chimed. "Well, that was all. I'll talk to you soon. Love you!"

"Love you too," I said, but she'd already hung up.

Hayes picked me up from work since my car was still at home.

"How was your day?" He asked, leaning over to kiss me.

"Todd showed up at my parent's house," I admitted.

He cursed, tightening his hands around the steering wheel as he pulled away from the store and headed in the direction of Mia's sitter's house.

"That guy…" He hissed. "He's asking for it."

"I don't know what to do," I whispered. "I'm scared."

It was the first time I'd said those two words out loud, but they were true.

The fear that had cloaked me like a blanket while I was married to him had disappeared once he was gone, but now it was back and even heavier, like a weight around my ankle dragging me down.

Hayes reached for my hand and kissed the tops of my fingers as he drove. "Everything will be fine. I'll never let that asshole touch you."

Tears pricked my eyes. "Isn't this too much for you? I mean, we've only been dating a month and now my ex is back and wants Mia…or at least that's what he's saying. Who knows what he really wants." I laughed, but there was no humor in the sound. "You didn't sign up this. I'm nothing but a burden."

He glared over at me. "You're right. I didn't sign up for this."

I gasped and started to pull my hand away, but he only tightened his hold.

"You know what I did do? I met this crazy, beautiful girl this past summer, with an equally amazing daughter, and she wound her way into my heart where I fell irrevocably in love with her. I didn't ask to fall in love with you, but I *did*, and I don't fucking regret it. And correct me if I'm wrong, but when you love someone you're supposed to fight your battles *together*. That's what I'm doing Arden. I'm fighting *with* you." He pulled off the road and stared into my eyes, trying to sear each and every word into the recesses of my mind. His fingers delved into the hair and the base of my neck and he pulled me forward, pressing his forehead to mine. "You will never, not *ever* be a burden to me. And yes, this is still a new relationship for the both of us but when something's right it just *is*. Let it be and stop questioning every little thing. I'm here and I love you and I'm not going anywhere." He pressed his lips against my forehead tenderly. "I've waited a long time to give my heart to someone, and at times I never thought I would, but it's yours Arden, and I never want it back."

My lower lip trembled with the threat of tears.

"Aw, fuck, Arden. I didn't mean to make you cry. I'm sorry."

"No, no," I waved away his concern, "I don't even know why I'm crying…it's just…that's the most beautiful thing I've ever heard." Shaking my head I wiped at the silly tears streaking my face. "How did I get so lucky?"

He grinned, brushing a piece of hair away from my forehead. "Nah, I'm the lucky one. Before you I didn't know what I was missing, and now that I know how much better my life is with you in it I can't go back. I *won't* go back." Clearing his throat, he added, "From now on we fight our battles together. Got it?"

I let out a small laugh as he pulled back onto the road. "You know, for someone that's never been in a relationship before you're awfully good at this."

He flashed me a cheeky smile and winked. "I'm good at everything."

I rolled my eyes, laughing fully at his comment. I loved Hayes at all times, but I especially loved him when he was being his silly, cocky self.

A few minutes went by as he drove to the sitter's house and finally I broke the quiet by asking, "So, my mom wanted to know if we could have dinner with them Friday night?"

His lips twisted together in thought. "Yeah, that should work…your dad's not going to whip out a massive gun collection and show me a bunch of mounted animal heads before telling me my head will be mounted next if I hurt you, is he?"

I snorted. "That was a very specific scenario."

"Just answer the question, Arden." He chuckled, rubbing his hand over his jaw in a nervous gesture.

"I know they'll love you once they get to know you, but…" I hedged, taking a deep breath. "Expect them to be slightly wary in the beginning. After what happened with Todd…they're going to be protective since you're the first guy I've been with since then. Okay?"

Hayes nodded. "I can handle wary."

I grinned up at him. "I expected you to tell me you could handle anything."

"That too." He winked as he pulled into the sitter's driveway.

I hopped out and went inside to grab Mia. When she saw Hayes standing by his truck she took off running straight into his waiting arms. He lifted her up and spun her around, her giggles filling the air, and when she was sufficiently dizzy he buckled her into her car seat.

Instead of heading straight back to Hayes' house we stopped by mine first so I could grab my car.

"I'll just be a second," I told Hayes. "I have to go inside and grab my keys."

"I'll wait," he said. *Just in case*, was what he left unsaid.

I hurried inside, surprised at how in only a few days this place didn't seem like home anymore.

I shivered as I headed into the kitchen, feeling extremely creeped out, and terrified Todd might jump out of some random hiding place.

I tiptoed over to the counter, like I was the one breaking and entering, and searched for my keys.

My eyes halted though on a piece of paper

One I *knew* hadn't been there when the police had searched the house.

Which meant Todd had been back.

And could still be here.

Blood roared through my veins and my heart beat so fast that it was the only thing I could hear.

I reached out with tentative fingers, the hair on my body standing on end once the piece of notebook paper was in my hands.

I lifted it to eyelevel, trying to make out his chicken scratch.

In horror, I read the four words written on the torn piece of paper.

*I'll get what's mine.*

Those words bounced and ricocheted inside my head.

*I'll get what's mine.*

*I'll get what's mine.*

*I'll get what's* **mine.**

Mia.

# CHAPTER EIGHTEEN

I DIDN'T TELL Hayes about the note.

I knew I should have, but I couldn't. I was too horrified to repeat it.

I spent the whole week walking around like a complete mope, barely uttering more than the necessary response to anything he said. Even Mia could tell something was wrong with me and was constantly asking me if I was sick or had a fever. I was sick, but not in the way she thought.

I stood now, in Hayes' closet, getting ready for dinner with my parents. Since my parents weren't fussy people I decided to wear a pair of jeans and a black and white striped long-sleeved shirt.

Hayes strode into the closet wearing nothing but a pair of low-slung dark jeans with the belt hanging undone.

He was trying to kill me.

I itched to reach out and run my fingers over the curves of his abs, but I wouldn't. It felt wrong to touch him when I was keeping the note a secret from him.

Hayes eyed me, lifting his lips slightly in challenge. He knew *exactly* what he was doing to me. The jerk was trying to break me.

"You look beautiful," he said, his muscled back to me as he flicked through the shirts hanging in his closet, "you'd look even better naked on your back, all sweaty and freshly fucked, with my come on your stomach."

I squeaked like a small mouse and he chuckled.

Glancing over at me, he narrowed his eyes, "Something's going on with you, Arden, and you'll eventually spill the beans."

I ran from the closet and he cackled behind me.

Jerk.

I hurried downstairs before he could tempt me further and joined Mia in the family room where she was watching *The Little Mermaid*—her obsession.

Hayes came down the steps a few minutes later, the sound of his sneakers slapping against the steps alerting me of his presence.

He strolled into the family room looking ridiculously too good-looking to only be wearing a simple pair of jeans and a t-shirt. Or maybe I was so horny that anything he wore would make him appear devilishly handsome and extremely fuckable.

Jeez, my head was too far-gone in the gutter to be having dinner with my parents.

Hayes glanced down at his watch. "We better go. We're going to be late if we don't."

"Right," I sighed. "Come on, Mia." I reached for her hand. "You can finish your movie when we get home."

She pouted, crossing her arms over her chest and refusing to grab ahold of my hand. "I don't wanna go. I wanna watch my movie."

"I know, sweetie, but Grandma and Grandpa are waiting for us. We need to go."

"Ugh." She groaned, kicking her legs.

Normally I was lucky with Mia, and she didn't give me too much sass, but then there were moments like this when it came out in full force.

Hayes paused the movie and turned the TV off which sent her screaming with crocodile tears streaming down her face.

I was already wound so tight that I couldn't handle a meltdown. "Mia!" I yelled. "Stop this! This behavior is unacceptable!"

She only cried harder and I pressed my face into my hands, letting out a frustrated groan.

I took a few deep breaths, trying to calm myself.

Straightening, I said in a soft tone, "Mia, we have to go. The movie will be waiting for you when we get back."

Still pouting, she stomped out of the room and towards the garage door.

I pinched the bridge of my nose and closed my eyes.

I opened them when I felt the brush of Hayes' fingers against the exposed skin of my stomach where my shirt had ridden up.

His eyes were filled with concern and his lips turned down into a frown. "Talk to me," he pleaded. "Please."

I took a step back and his hand dropped from my side. I shook my head and started for the garage.

He sighed behind me, and mumbled, "You are infuriating."

I swallowed thickly, knowing that my silence was hurting him.

The drive to my parent's house was filled with awkward silence, only broken by the occasional direction I lobbed his way.

Hayes glared out the windshield, a muscle in his jaw ticking.

I knew he probably wanted to snap at me, but he also didn't want to scare me, which led to him sitting broodingly in the driver's seat.

By the time we reached my parent's house I was tempted to tell him to turn the car around and go home—that neither of us were in any shape to spend the evening with my parents.

Hayes pulled into the driveway of the modest, one story ranch style home, and killed the engine.

He sat with his fists clenched in his lap, but made no move to get out of the vehicle.

I cracked.

"I'm sorry," I cried, "I know I'm being a horrible person right now and you don't understand and I'm so sorry." I pressed the heels of my hands into my eyes, probably streaking my mascara in the process, but not really caring. "Please," I begged, "I have my reasons and I just…I don't want to talk about it."

He glared at me with steely blue eyes. "You *need* to talk about it with me. Remember, you don't have to fight alone anymore, Arden. I'm here and I'm not going anywhere." His face softened and he reached over to trail his finger over the curve of my cheek.

My eyes closed and I breathed in a shaky breath.

"Stop trying to take on the world alone," he whispered, "a battle fought alone is a battle lost."

I swallowed thickly, the note burning a hole in my purse.

I should've told him from the moment I saw it, but I'd stupidly kept it to myself. Apparently, when it came to Todd, I became a big ball of dumb. I'd been so hurt by him in the past, and my silence had been my protection, but also my downfall, and now I was letting history repeat itself.

Before I could grab the note, the front door opened and my mom came running out.

"Later." I told Hayes, my stomach twisting with the thought.

He nodded once.

I scurried out of the truck and greeted my mom with a hug.

She held me tight, squeezing until I felt like I couldn't breathe.

"I've missed you." She patted my cheek. "You don't visit enough."

"I know. I've missed you too."

My parents lived almost an hour away from me, which made visiting difficult with my schedule.

"Let me see this man of yours and my grandbaby." She winked.

I laughed and turned to see Hayes walking over to join us with Mia in his arms.

"Hello," he extended his hand to my mom. "I'm Joshua, but I go by Hayes."

At only five-foot-two my mom had to crane her head back to look at him.

"My God, you're tall." She said.

He chuckled. "Yes, ma'am, I am."

"Oh!" She seemed to then realize what she said. "Forgive me for forgetting my manners. I'm Stella." She paused. "I'd hug you, but you currently have your hands full."

Hayes grinned, his dimple making an appearance—I was happy to see it, since it'd been missing all week.

"Yes, quite full," he agreed.

"It's cold out here," she clapped her hands together, "come on, come on." She turned, heading back towards the house and waving for us to follow. "Dinner is ready and waiting…if your father hasn't eaten all of it, that is." She cackled merrily.

"I like your mom," Hayes whispered. "She's funny."

"She's something else," I agreed.

We entered the quaint dining room and my dad stood from the table to great us.

"Josh," Hayes held out his hand, "but you can call me Hayes."

Since I only called Hayes…well, *Hayes*, it was always weird to hear his first name. It didn't seem to suit him the way Hayes did.

"Nice to meet you." My dad shook his hand. "I'm Henry. Here," my dad pointed to one of the chairs beside him, "why don't you sit there, so uh, we can get to know each other."

"Dad." I glared venomously at him.

"I'll be nice." He rushed to assure me.

I gave Hayes an apologetic look, but he merely chuckled and took the seat.

My mom took the one across from him and I sat beside him with Mia to my left.

"This smells delicious, mom." I commented, inhaling the scent of homemade lasagna.

"I know it's your favorite." She smiled, cutting into it and heaping a serving large enough for three men onto my plate. "You're too thin. Eat up."

My mother, always the worrier.

She was right though, I was too thin at the moment. All the stress I'd been under with the Todd situation had led to me skipping meals and losing sleep.

She cut a piece even larger and put it on Hayes' plate.

"Thank you." He smiled at her and I breathed easy, glad his irritation from earlier had disappeared for the moment. Not that I could blame him for being irritated with me.

"Thanks for having us, mom." I said as I cut up the small piece she'd put on Mia's plate.

"We've really been looking forward to meeting you." She glanced up at Hayes and brushed her red hair from her eyes. It was beginning to gray slightly and she had crow's feet beside her eyes, but I still thought my mom was beautiful inside and out.

"Likewise." Hayes smiled, reaching for the basket of garlic bread. He grabbed a piece and put it on my plate before taking one for himself.

"So…you're in a band?" My dad asked, raising a brow in disbelief.

Hayes chuckled and ducked his head to hide his crooked smile. "Well, yes, but it's not like how you're making it sound."

"You don't play in a garage and live in your parent's basement, then?" My dad asked.

"Daddy!" I scolded, my face reddening in embarrassment.

My dad chuckled. "It's just a question sweetheart. Simmer down."

"No, I don't live in my parent's basement." Hayes was doubled over in laughter.

"What's the name of your band?" My mom asked.

When I'd told her about Hayes on the phone I'd mentioned he was in a band, but didn't tell her it was Willow Creek. In this area *everyone* knew of them since they were local. So while my mom didn't recognize *his* name, she'd definitely know the band.

"Willow Creek."

Like I expected both of my parents' eyes widened and my mom looked close to passing out.

She coughed, choking on a piece of lasagna noodle.

"Mom?" I asked worriedly. "Are you okay?"

She gulped greedily at her glass of water. "Fine, fine." She waved away my concern. "I just wasn't expecting that."

"Wow," my dad gasped, "you're in a *real* band."

Hayes chuckled, unaffected by their surprise. "Yes, sir."

"Does this mean Arden and Mia will be going on tours with you?" He flicked his fingers in my direction.

"Dad," I scolded yet again, "don't."

Hayes shrugged. "I don't know. It'll be a while before we go on tour again, but I'd love for Arden and Mia to come if that's what they'd like to do."

"And if they don't go does that mean you'll be banging groupies every night and bringing back every STD imaginable to my daughter?"

"Dad!" I groaned, burying my face in my hands.

Hayes took it all in stride. "No, sir. I love your daughter and there definitely won't be any groupies in my future."

My dad harrumphed. "You better not be lying to me."

"I wouldn't dream of it sir."

My dad seemed to be contemplating something and finally said, "I like you." Hayes grinned at this. My dad leveled him with a glare and his smile disappeared. "But if you hurt her I'll break your bones. I didn't get the chance with the first one and I won't miss my opportunity this time should the need arise."

Hayes pressed his lips together, trying to look scared, but I knew in actuality he was trying his hardest not to laugh.

"I won't hurt her," Hayes vowed.

My dad chuckled. "We'll see."

Before Hayes could take another bite of lasagna my mom launched into a barrage of questions. "What's it like being famous? Is it fun traveling the world? What's the craziest thing you've ever done on the road?"

Hayes answered each question and didn't seem at all perturbed by it.

We'd finished our meal and I was helping my mom gather the plates—Hayes and my dad having retired to the living room where my dad was probably drilling him on his knowledge of all things football—when she said, "I can't believe you're dating someone so famous."

My mom was officially star-struck.

But having lived in rural Virginia her whole life it wasn't like she'd met that many famous people—exactly zero until now—so I chose to let her enjoy the moment.

"He doesn't feel famous to me." I shrugged, carrying the plates into the adjoining kitchen. The counters were the same old gray corian they'd always been with white cabinets that had chipping paint. The whole house needed a sprucing up, but it still felt like home. "He's just Hayes."

"He's *very* handsome." She grinned, bumping her hip with mine.

I blushed and set the plates in the sink before running water and adding a bit of soap. "He's okay I guess."

"You *guess*?" She laughed, poking my side. "I see the way you look at him and how he looks at you…it's nice to see you happy, Arden." She reached out, wrapping her arms around my shoulders in an awkward side hug. "I've missed seeing that light in your eyes." She paused, seeming to search for the right words. "Not that I don't think you've been happy with only you and Mia, but something's been missing for a while and I think you've finally found it. I like him. A lot."

Until that moment I hadn't realized how much I needed my mother's approval.

"You do?" My voice sounded meek.

She nodded, nudging me out of her way so she could rinse the dishes off. She handed me a towel to dry the plates.

"I really do," she said, "and you don't realize it, but when he looks at you… you light up Arden. I've never seen you like that before. I'm really happy for you."

"Thanks mom." I set the dry dish down and hugged her.

She kissed the top of my head and handed me the next plate. "Have you heard anymore from Todd?" She asked, lowering her voice and shifting her eyes towards the entrance to the kitchen. "I didn't tell your dad he showed up," she admitted with a shrug. "I was kind of afraid if I told him he might end up in jail for attempted murder."

She probably wasn't joking.

My dad was beyond angry with Todd—not that I wasn't too, but I think it really hurt my dad to feel like he hadn't been protecting me when he should have. But it was my own fault for never telling anyone about the abuse. For people that had never been abused it was easy to think someone was dumb or naïve for keeping their mouth shut, but they didn't realize how manipulative an abuser was and how the victim felt *terrified* for their *life*.

"I haven't heard from him anymore," I lied. There was no point in telling her about the break in, or note, because there was nothing she could do, and I didn't want her to worry herself to death.

"That's good." She nodded, handing me the last dish. "He's an odd one."

I snorted and began putting the dry dishes away. "Odd doesn't even begin to cover it."

She laughed. "Yeah, I guess that's true…you know," she mused, propping a hand on her hip, "he was always nice enough, I suppose, but there was this underlying… darkness in his eyes. I should've known something was up." She frowned, the lines in her face deepening.

I reached out and hugged her, placing a kiss on her cheek. "You couldn't have known mom."

"Still…" She mumbled and tears shimmered in her eyes.

"No," I took her by the shoulders, "don't blame yourself for any of that, okay? Just be thankful that he's out of my life now."

She nodded, sucking in a lungful of air to calm herself. "Well, if he shows up again you let me know."

"I will, mom." I hugged her again, even tighter than before. "I love you."

"I love you too."

"We better head back," I told her. "It's getting close to Mia's bedtime."

"Of course." She pulled her hair back and secured it with a clip that had been pinned to her sweater.

I found Hayes and my dad in the family room and Mia was curled up in Hayes' lap with her head rested on his chest, fast asleep. Her mouth was wide open and her drool had left a wet spot on his gray t-shirt, but he didn't seem to mind. He was lying back on the couch with his arms crossed behind his head while my dad sat in his favorite weathered recliner. The recliner looked like it needed to be tossed in the nearest dumpster—it was ripped in places with stuffing coming out, and dirty, but he refused to get rid of it.

"We need to head home," I told Hayes, leaning against the archway that led into the living room.

Hayes lowered one of his arms and looked at his watch. "Yep, you're right."

He held onto Mia and came into a sitting position before standing. Mia blinked her eyes open briefly before promptly falling back asleep.

Seeing her so content in Hayes' arms made me smile.

"It was really nice meeting you both." Hayes nodded at my dad and then my mom. "Next time we'll have dinner at my house."

"That sounds lovely." My mom chimed, completely swooning over my boyfriend.

"Bye, dad." I bent over to hug my dad, knowing that there was no way in hell he was getting out of his recliner.

"Bye." He kissed my cheek and hugged me tight. "Visit your old man more often. I'm not getting any younger."

"Sure thing." I laughed. "Love you."

"Love you too, buttercup."

I hugged my mom goodbye and hurried outside.

Hayes had already put Mia in her car seat and started the car. The vents blew out warm air, which I was thankful for since even in the short time it took me to get from the house to the truck my cheeks and hands had grown cold.

Hayes had turned on the radio and some old rock song played softly out of the speakers.

"That wasn't too bad," Hayes chuckled, backing out of the driveway.

"It could've definitely been worse," I agreed. "And by the end there my dad seemed to really like you."

"It's impossible not to like me," Hayes chortled, "I'm a fucking awesome human being."

I glared at him. "No cussing." I pointed over my shoulder to the backseat where Mia was.

"Sorry," he smiled sheepishly, "but she *is* asleep."

"No excuses," I grinned, poking his side.

I was glad that, for the moment at least, we were back to ourselves. I knew my melancholy attitude the past week was driving Hayes insane. At one point I'd heard him mutter to himself, "Fucking PMS always ruining everything."

I wished my problem was as simple as PMS, but nothing with Todd was ever simple, and I knew that I had to share the note with Hayes tonight. The only person I was protecting by keeping it a secret was Todd and he was the last person who needed to be safe in this scenario.

"What are you thinking about over there?" He questioned, glancing over at me briefly before his eyes drifted back to the road ahead. "You have a wrinkle between your brows that tells me you're thinking really hard about something. Care to share?"

My plan had been to wait until we got home to tell him, but what was the point in that?

"I figure it's about time I explain why I've been so weird the last week," I shrugged.

Suddenly, he paled and seemed to choke on his own saliva. "You're not pregnant are you?"

"What?" I gasped, suppressing a laugh. "No! Of course not."

"Oh, thank God," he breathed a sigh of relief. He glanced over at me, even more horrified than he had been a moment ago. "Not that a baby would be a bad thing…I mean, I want kids…someday, not now. I think we already have our hands full." He tossed his thumb over his shoulder and I smiled at his use of the word *we*, like Mia was his. "Alright," he adjusted in the seat, "tell me what's going on."

"That day you took me by my house to get my car?" I prompted.

"Yeeeeaaah?" He drew out the word, waving a hand impatiently for me to get to the point.

"There was a note on the counter. A note that hadn't been there."

His teeth snapped together with a loud clank. "You have got to be kidding me," he muttered, shaking his head roughly. "What did it say?"

" 'I'll get what's mine.' " Bile rose up in my throat from having to say the words out loud.

"Todd?"

"It was his handwriting," I sighed.

I glanced behind me at my sleeping daughter in the backseat. She was so beautiful, and perfect, and sweet, and a million other things, and I'd never forgive myself if Todd used her to hurt me.

"We need to tell the police," he said, his hands flexing around the steering wheel.

"What are they going to do?" I laughed humorlessly. "He hasn't done anything physical and we have no solid *proof* that he's the one that broke into my house. The fingerprints they found came back without a match, which I figured would be the case."

"I'm flying Casey and Greg in." Hayes said forcefully, like he was daring me to contradict him, which of course I did.

"And what are they going to do? They're *your* bodyguards, not mine."

"They do what I tell them," he countered. "I'm their boss, and if I tell them not to let you and Mia out of their sight that's what they're going to do."

I shook my head and glanced out the window where small flakes of snow swirled around and around in the night sky.

"I hate this," I muttered to myself, "I hate this whole situation and I hate him for doing this to me. For making me feel scared—and not even scared for myself this time." I turned back to look at Mia before staring at Hayes' profile. "I'm *terrified* of what he might do to her. I know that he wouldn't think twice about hurting her just to get back at me, and look at her Hayes!" My voice rose with fear. "She's so small and innocent. She might not be a baby anymore, but to me she is, and I never want her to have the kind of memories I do from what he did to me. I don't want her to live in fear that every man or boy she meets is going to raise a hand against her."

"And that's exactly why Casey and Greg are getting their asses on the first plane I can get them on." He nodded his head adamantly.

I scrubbed at my face, suddenly completely, and overwhelmingly, exhausted. "This should be a happy time for us," I sighed, tears stinging my eyes, "we should be basking in our new relationship glow, and I should be excited about Mia's birthday and Christmas coming up, but instead I have *this* to deal with." I clenched my teeth together. "I'm so angry that he's once again ruining my life. I was so naïve to think he was gone for good." I shook my head, glaring out the window once more.

Hayes reached for my hand and squeezed it tightly, reassuring me without words that he was here and we could get through this.

I was glad one of us had faith that everything would be okay, because right now I was just done.

By the time we arrived back at his place I was ready to fall over asleep, but I had to get Mia in her pajamas and into bed.

Hayes carried her inside and up to her room.

While I was changing her, because she was too tired to dress on her own, he went downstairs to fix her a glass of water since she'd been waking up the past few nights thirsty.

I lifted her into the bed and tucked the blankets around her. "Snug as a bug in a rug." I bent and kissed her forehead as Hayes strolled into the room, placing her cup of water on the nightstand.

"Goodnight, Ms. Mia." He said, kissing her forehead in the same spot I had.

She blinked sleepily up at us and yawned. "Night, night, Momma. Daddy."

Beside me Hayes froze.

I was pretty sure he stopped breathing all together.

Mia yawned once more before her eyes closed and I knew she'd fallen back to sleep.

Hayes turned to me slowly, his eyes wide with wonder. His lips were parted with a silent gasp.

"Wow." He murmured. "That was…wow." He rubbed at his jaw, stifling a small grin, and I swore tears swam in his eyes. "I didn't know it would feel like that to hear someone call me daddy," he admitted as we backed out of her room, and I eased the door partly closed.

"And what does it feel like?" I stretched onto my tiptoes and wrapped my arms around his neck.

"It's hard to describe," he admitted, kissing the end of my nose, "but I liken it to that rush I got when I jumped out of a plane one time—like I'm invincible and can take on the world. Like I am someone."

"You are someone," I whispered in his ear.

He bent to kiss me softly, his lips lingering against mine. "And now I know it."

# CHAPTER NINETEEN

"SO, I'VE BEEN thinking…" Hayes started, trailing his fingers down my bare hip.

"About what?" I snuggled closer to his warmth.

"I know you mentioned wanting to take Mia to Disney sometime and with her birthday and Christmas coming up, I thought maybe we could take her now. I would pay for the trip of course."

I sat up and my hair swept forward over my chest. My mouth parted with shock.

"That's expensive, Hayes. You can't do that."

"But I *want* to." He sat up too and reached out to cup my cheek. "I want to do something special for her."

My lips turned down into a frown. "I don't know," I hedged.

"Please," he coaxed, nibbling on my chin.

"Hayes," I groaned, pushing at his shoulders.

"Please." He said again, this time kissing me on the lips. "Please." His lips grazed the shell of my ear. "Don't you want to make a little girl's dreams come true?"

"Of course I do."

"Please, Arden. I want to do this, so let me."

"Ugh," I groaned as his lips trailed down my neck, "fine," I relinquished. Pouting, I added, "You don't fight fair."

"Where's the fun in that?" He winked, climbing from the bed and pulling on his boxers. He padded into the bathroom and turned around. He reached up and grabbed ahold of the frame above the doorway and the muscles in his arms flexed. "Oh, Greg and Casey are flying in this afternoon, so don't complain when they watch your every move." He warned, staring at me with narrowed eyes.

I sighed. I wasn't thrilled at the thought of being tailed by Hayes' bodyguards, but I knew at this point their protection was necessary.

"Oh and one other thing…" He tapped his fingers against the top of the doorframe. "I know it's last minute but the guys and all the girls are going to the

Winter Festival in town tomorrow evening and they asked if we'd want to go."

I wrinkled my nose with distaste. "I'm not really in the mood for socializing."

Hayes snapped his fingers together. "And *that* is why I said yes."

I flopped back on the bed and tossed an arm over my face. "Won't you get mobbed?"

"People are pretty chill around here. I mean, yeah, I'm sure people will ask for pictures, but it's never gotten too crazy."

"This feels like a very bad idea." I lowered my arm and turned to look at him.

He ran his fingers through his messy hair before standing with his hands poised on his slender hips. "We need to get out and have fun. All this shit lately with Todd has been taking a toll on both of us, heck even Mia. She certainly hasn't been her normal bubbly self."

"Ugh, you're right." I finally agreed.

He grinned and his whole smile transformed his face, somehow making him look younger and softer. "I'm always right."

"I hate you." I stuck my tongue out at him.

"Love you too, babe," he said as he closed the door, "Love. You. Too."

"Are you sure you want to do this?" My voice shook with nerves as Hayes scanned his laptop for flights to Orlando.

"Absolutely. Stop asking me that." He found what he was looking for and bought the tickets on the spot.

He'd already booked the hotel and bought the Disney park passes.

Once Hayes made a decision he didn't mess around. That thought made me smile because he'd done the same way with me when he knew he wanted more.

"She's going to be so excited." Hayes smiled widely. "I can't wait to see the look on her face when we tell her."

We were going to be leaving next week, so we'd be at Disney for Mia's birthday on the fourteenth, but home in time for Christmas because we knew there was no way either of our parents would forgive us if we weren't home for the holidays.

"She's going to scream—in a good way." I laughed.

Hayes grabbed me around the waist and pulled me into his lap. He nuzzled his head against my neck and I squealed, kicking my legs, when I felt his wet tongue swipe against my skin.

"Please, for the love of my sanity, don't forget I'm in here." Greg fake-gagged and held up a hand to block his eyes.

"Don't be a baby." Hayes chuckled.

Greg lowered his hand and Hayes seized the opportunity to basically shove his tongue down my throat to piss off his bodyguard.

"I liked you better when you were single." Greg grumbled, hiding his eyes once more.

"That's a lie and you know it." Hayes smoothed down my hair where he'd mused it. "You love me at all times. I'm irresistible to both males and females."

"You're a cocky asshole."

"Hey!" Hayes scolded with a raised finger. "If I'm not allowed to cuss in my own house then neither are you."

Greg huffed a breath. "I don't get paid enough for this."

"Ignore him," Hayes told me, sweeping his lips against mine in a gesture so light it couldn't even be called a kiss, "he's just jealous that he's single."

"Yeah, yeah, yeah." Greg grumbled.

Kissing Hayes on the cheek, I disentangled myself from his arms. "I better go relieve Casey of babysitting duties. Besides, we need to get ready to meet everyone at the festival."

"You're right," Hayes agreed, shutting his laptop. He stood and stretched his arms above his head. "I'm going to go shower."

I found Mia in the family room where I'd left her with Casey. Casey was being a good sport and watching *Pocahontas* with her.

"Momma!" Mia cried excitedly when she saw me and began to tell me everything I'd missed in the movie while I was gone.

"That's great, baby girl." I ruffled her hair and bent to kiss her forehead. "Do you want to go out in the outfit you have on, or wear a dress?"

"Dress!" She cried enthusiastically. I wasn't one bit surprised.

I took her hand and led her upstairs to the room she'd claimed as hers. In the short time we'd been here the room had exploded with stuffed animals and dolls everywhere. It was safe to say that Hayes liked to spoil Mia.

Mia hopped up on the chair in the corner while I pulled two dresses from the closet.

"Which one?" I held each up for her inspection.

She tapped her lip with her index finger like she was thinking long and hard about this decision. "Da blue one!"

I put the other dress away and grabbed a pair of black tights and her shiny black shoes. I helped her into the tights and she giggled when she kept tripping over her own two feet.

"Silly girl," I tweaked her nose, "hold still."

With another giggle she finally stayed still long enough for me to finish putting her tights on and pull the dress over the top of her head. It fell to the tops of her knobby knees and had long sleeves with black polka dots.

I led her into the bathroom and lifted her onto the counter so I could brush her teeth and then her hair before braiding it in two pig-tails—her signature style.

She turned to look at herself in the mirror and smiled as she stroked the ends of her hair. "I'm bootiful."

I laughed and kissed her forehead before helping her down. "Yes, you are." I agreed.

Once her feet touched the floor she went running out of the room and I heard her shoes clap against the stairs.

"Cwasey!" She called and I shook my head.

Poor Casey. She wouldn't leave the guy alone.

I headed down the hall to Hayes' room so that I could change. I didn't think my leggings and thin t-shirt would be acceptable with the suddenly frigid weather.

Hayes stepped out of the bathroom as I was closing the bedroom door and I stopped in my tracks, letting my eyes roam over him from head to toe.

He looked completely fuckable—he always did—but suddenly, I was overcome with the fact that he was mine.

He was my guy.

The one I woke up thinking about and fell asleep looking at.

The one that stirred butterflies in my stomach every time he smiled in my direction.

"You're looking at me funny," he frowned, "did I miss a spot?" He rubbed at his freshly shaven face.

I stepped closer to him and stretched onto my toes to wrap my arms around his neck. "Nothing's wrong," I assured him, kissing his chin, "I was just thinking about how good it is to love you."

His blue eyes sparkled with excitement. He wrapped an arm around my waist and lowered his head to kiss me. His tongue pressed against my lips and my mouth parted with a gasp.

Once I was breathless he pulled away with a pleased smirk.

With a chuckle, he pinched my butt and let me go. "You know," he said as he started towards the bedroom door, "I used to make fun of the guys for being such saps when it came to their girls and now look at me. I'm the worst one of the four of us."

"That's okay," I smiled widely, "love looks good on you."

He grinned at that. "It looks good on you too, Little Bird."

He'd been edging to the door, but now he strode towards me with a purpose.

Before I could blink he'd grabbed me by the waist and pressed my back into the wall beside the bathroom. His lips claimed mine in a bruising, take control, kiss that drew a long moan from my throat. I wrapped my arms around his neck and my body arched into his. I loved when he was like this, wild and unrestrained.

"We're supposed to leave in thirty minutes." He growled as his hands slid under my shirt, pushing it up and over my head.

"I guess we'll have to be fast then."

"Fuck yes." He nipped my bottom lip and I moaned at the stinging pulse that was left behind.

Within seconds my bra landed on the floor and he'd slid my leggings off as well.

I fumbled with his belt while he grabbed a condom from his wallet.

"This is going to be fast and hard." He warned when I freed him from his pants.

"Shut up." I grabbed the short strands of hair on the back of his head and pulled his lips down to mine.

His chuckle vibrated through my body and his fingers dug roughly into the skin of my thighs. He lifted me and positioned me above his already hard cock.

"Hayes," I pleaded, completely breathless, when he continued to hold me there teasing me with the barest brush of his tip.

"Say it," he begged, his blue eyes shimmering with longing.

I started to ask him what he wanted me to say, but with a sudden clarity I seemed to *know*.

"I love you."

A rumble shook his chest. "Best fucking thing I've ever heard."

He thrust into me and I cried out, the sound quickly dropping into a moan.

"And that's the second best thing I've ever heard."

His fingers dug into my thighs as he held me, fucking me so hard I swore stars swam before my eyes.

I moaned his name brokenly.

*Hayes.*

*Oh my—*

*More*

*Harder*

*Fuck*

*Please*

*I'm gonna—*

I came around him, my body pulsing and shaking. I didn't know if I'd ever had such an intense orgasm before. If he hadn't been holding me so tight I would've surely fallen to the floor in a puddle.

His pace never slowed and he burrowed his head against my neck. His hair brushed against my sensitive skin and I shivered, rocking my hips to meet his thrusts.

I felt his hold tighten on my legs to the point of bruising and with a growl he found his own release.

We'd been fast and frantic, but it'd been just as perfect as every other time we were together.

Hayes didn't let go of me immediately. Instead, he waited, letting both of us catch our breath. When he knew I had the strength to hold myself upright he set me down, pressing a tender kiss to my lips.

I slipped into the bathroom for a quick shower while he redressed.

Hayes was gone from the bedroom when I emerged from the shower.

I strolled into the closet and slipped into a pair of dark jeans, a thick gray cowl neck sweater and a pair of chestnut colored boots.

My hair hung down my back in thick red waves. My eyes were lined with a smoky gray shadow and my lips were a deep cherry red.

For the first time in a long time I felt good about myself and I knew it was because I was so happy.

"Arden! Are you ready?" Hayes called up the steps.

"Just a minute!" I yelled back, looking around for my purse. Once I located it I grabbed it and hurried down the stairs.

Hayes was waiting in the foyer with Mia in his arms and his bodyguards at his sides.

"I'm ready," I declared, slightly out of breath and nearly tripping down the last step.

Hayes chuckled and reached out with his free hand to steady me. "I didn't mean for you to try and kill yourself."

"Sorry." I ducked my head in embarrassment.

Glancing over his shoulder at his bodyguards, Hayes said, "Are you boys ready to roll?"

Greg snorted. "Only if you promise to never refer to us as boys ever again."

Heading towards the garage, Hayes questioned, "What would you prefer then? *Ladies?*"

Greg shook his head. "Such a smart ass," he muttered under his breath.

"Language!" Hayes yelled after him and I laughed.

Since there wasn't enough room for all of us in Hayes' truck, Greg and Casey ended up following us in a black SUV.

Hayes and I were relatively silent on the drive to the festival, but Mia made up for our silence by chatting endlessly about her birthday and Christmas and how excited she was.

By the time we made it to the downtown area it was packed and I had no idea how we were ever going to find a place to park.

Hayes ended up turning down a random side street and parking in an alleyway.

He undid his seatbelt and pulled his phone from his pocket to check his text messages.

"Maddox says they're waiting by the entrance so we'll meet them there."

I climbed out of the truck and met Hayes on the other side where he'd already grabbed Mia. She held his hand, looking up at him like he was the greatest thing she'd ever laid her eyes on.

"I had no idea we actually had a Winter Festival here," I admitted with a shrug. "I really need to get out more."

Hayes' laughter echoed off the nearby buildings and his guards trailed behind us as we headed for the festival entrance.

"This is actually the first year they've had it. If you ask me, I think it's being done in an effort to drum up some business for the local shops."

"Makes sense." I shrugged, drawing my coat closer to my body and watching the trail of my breath disintegrate in the air.

A light dusting of snow covered the ground and more flakes stirred around us. I watched as a flake landed on Mia's nose and her giggle filled the air.

Hayes grinned down at her and I couldn't get over the love I saw in his eyes for my daughter.

We came out of the alley and stepped into the crowd, moving towards a large arch covered in some sort of evergreen with white lights wrapped around it with a red bow in the top center.

Greg and Casey pressed closer into us so that we didn't become separated from them.

"This is really crowded," I told Hayes, nerves seeping into my bones.

"It'll be fine," he assured me.

We finally made it to the entrance and I spotted everyone waiting for us.

Sadie saw me at the same time and waved us over.

"Hey!" She greeted, wrapping her arms around me in a tight hug. She narrowed her eyes at the guards over my shoulder. "Why are Dumb and Dumber here?"

I winced. Sadie still didn't know that Todd was back in town.

"It's a long story," I hedged.

She narrowed her eyes on me and tapped her foot impatiently. "Don't feed me that line," she warned.

I groaned and shook my head. "My ex is back and creeping around, so…" I lifted my shoulders in a small shrug, trying to brush it off.

Sadie's mouth popped open and she gasped as we stepped beyond the entrance, following the rest of the crowd.

"Why didn't you tell me?" She questioned.

I sighed heavily. "I think I stupidly thought if I didn't talk about it then it wasn't real."

"So, you've spoken to him?"

I nibbled on my bottom lip. "Yes," I mumbled, "he showed up at the store one day."

"The store? As in *my* store?" She pointed at her chest.

"Yep, that one." I looked away and towards the guys ahead of us. Hayes still held Mia's hand, and beside him Maddox spoke to Emma, while Mathias and Remy were a few feet ahead pushing Liam in a stroller. Ezra hung back a bit, waiting for Sadie to rejoin him.

"That asshole." She hissed. "If I'd been there I would've kicked him in the balls."

Despite how gloomy this conversation made me feel I managed to laugh at that. "I don't doubt you."

"If he knows where you work then does he know where you live too?" Her voice grew soft, almost scared sounding.

I winced. "Yes," I admitted, the word feeling like shrapnel clawing at my throat.

"Oh wow." She blew out a breath and it fogged the air. "Now I understand the need to have Dumb and Dumber here. This is not good."

"You're telling me." I pinched the bridge of my nose, feeling a headache coming on.

"Do you know what he wants?" She asked, her brown eyes full of worry.

"To mess up my life even more?" I suggested with another sigh.

Sadie winced. "I'm so sorry, Arden."

"It is what is," I mumbled.

"Well, I'm here for you," she said. "Anything you need, don't hesitate to ask."

"You're a good friend."

She smiled. "I love you and I don't want to see you hurt. So be careful, okay?"

"I will." I promised her before she ran off to join Ezra.

I hurried forward and grabbed Mia's free hand. She looked up at the feel of my hand and smiled when she realized it was me.

"We're heading over to the ice rink." Hayes informed me.

"Ooh." I squeezed Mia's hand. "Are you going to ice skate?"

She nodded her head eagerly. "I hwope I don't fwall."

"Well," I smiled at her, "if you do fall, you know what you do?"

She shook her head.

"You stand back up, dust yourself off, and try again."

She smiled her toothy grin. "Will you do it wif me?"

"Of course."

"You too?" She turned to look up at Hayes.

"Will you hold my hand?" He asked her.

She squished her nose in thought. "Maybe."

His chest shook with laugher.

The ice rink was set up in the center of the promenade and seemed to be the hottest—and possibly only attraction. The festival didn't seem to be much of a festival. There was a band playing live music and the stores seemed to be having special sales, but that was about it besides the skating rink.

We paid for skates and then had to join a long line to wait our turn.

"You're not skating." Maddox told Emma as he reached up to tug his gray beanie further down his ears.

"I am too."

"No, you're not," he argued. "You're pregnant."

"I'm pregnant?" She gasped in wonder. "Thanks for enlightening me, Maddox. I had no idea."

"Em," he groaned, "you might fall and hurt the baby or yourself."

"For the record, I wasn't going to actually skate, but now I want to do it just to spite you." She crossed her arms over her chest.

Maddox growled and mumbled something under his breath. "You're making me exhausted."

She narrowed her eyes on him. "Exhausted? You want to talk about exhausted? You're not the one carrying a massive child inside you! I swear she must weigh ten pounds and she's nowhere near ready to come out of here yet."

Maddox's lips pinched together and he appeared to be trying not to laugh at her.

Suddenly, an ear-splitting scream pierced the air.

"OHMYGOD! It's Willow Creek!"

"I told you that you were going to be mobbed," I mumbled to Hayes, moments before a group of about ten teenage girls came barreling towards us with cellphones held out.

Hayes chuckled. "All part of the job, baby."

The guys posed for photos for the girls, but by that point their exclamation had caused more people to find us and the small group was quickly turning into the mob that I'd feared.

Casey and Greg pushed forward, trying to clear a space around the guys before they were completely swallowed by the ever-growing crowd.

Hayes looked back at me with an apologetic smile as an overzealous fan pulled on his jacket.

"Sorry," he mouthed.

"It's okay." I mouthed back as my body was jostled by even more people trying to get to the guys.

Mia's hand slipped from mine and I grasped at air, trying to get ahold of her again. When my hand didn't immediately connect with hers I looked down and panic squeezed my chest like a vice.

The space where Mia had been standing only moments before was now empty.

"Mia!" I screamed, fear spiking my voice.

Bile rose up my throat as I twisted around frantically searching for her.

"Mia! Mia! Where are you?!"

My cries were drowned out by the crowd of people.

I clutched at my chest, gasping for air. "Mia!" I yelled, pushing through the throngs of people. "MIA!"

There were plenty of times in my life where I'd thought I'd known true fear, but all of those moments paled in comparison to this one.

The overwhelming terror that my child was *gone* sent sharp pains shooting through my whole body. My vision began to swim with black dots and I realized I'd stopped breathing.

"Mia!" I spun around and around, searching for her red hair in a sea of dark coats.

Over the top of the crowd my eyes connected with Hayes' and his skin turned an ashen color when he saw the panic overwhelming me.

He pushed people out of his way, not caring if he came across as rude.

The other guys saw that he was trying to get to me and immediately started helping him clear a path.

It felt like an hour when in reality it was only seconds until Hayes was in front of me, taking my face in his hands.

"What is it?" He asked, searching my face for signs of an answer.

"M-Mia! She's gone!" I twisted out of his hold, searching the area for her once more.

"Gone?" He echoed, his eyes widening in horror.

"I was holding her hand," I panted, out of breath from my panic, "and then I felt her hand slip from mine and when I looked down she was just gone. Oh my God," I grabbed Hayes' shirt between my fists, "she's gone. She's *gone*, Hayes!"

My breath came out in short, sharp pants and tears stung my chilled cheeks.

"Hey, *hey*." He grabbed my face once more, forcing me to look at him. "We're going to find her."

"How can you be so calm?" I pushed away from him. "She's missing!"

"I'm far from calm," his blue eyes flashed, "but one of us has to think straight right now."

A sob raked my chest. "Hayes," I said his name brokenly, "she's gone." I buried my face in my hands, streaking my mascara everywhere.

By now all of our friends had formed a ring around us and knew what was going on.

"We have to call the police," Hayes said, trying to be the voice of reason since I couldn't seem to gather my thoughts.

I was pretty sure I was having an out of body experience, because surely this wasn't actually happening.

It had to be a dream.

Or a figment of my imagination.

Mia couldn't just be *gone*.

But she was.

I let out a broken sob.

"Come here." Hayes coaxed, trying to hug me to his chest.

"No," I pushed against him. "Don't touch me!"

His face fell. "Arden—"

"This is your fault!" I screamed at him. I didn't want to be mad at myself so I directed all of my anger and blame onto him. "I didn't even want to come here and you made me!"

"Arden, please—" He reached for me, but I backed away.

"No," I said firmly, holding my hands up in a barricade to keep him away.

Sadie wrapped an arm around my shoulders and guided me away from the crowd.

She found a spot for me to sit on a stonewall and pulled her phone from her purse.

I knew she was calling the police and reporting Mia as missing, but I didn't hear the words.

I *couldn't*.

Because I didn't want to face reality.

# CHAPTER TWENTY

WHILE WE'D WAITED for the police to arrive we'd all scoured the area for Mia, checking every shop and every street she might've been hiding in.

But Hayes and I both knew that Mia wasn't hiding.

Deep down in my gut, call it mother's intuition if you want, I knew that Todd had taken her.

The asshole had probably been watching us—even at Hayes' house—for weeks, waiting for the perfect opportunity to strike and he'd finally found it.

The police asked me an endless amount of questions, ones that were simple but I was too flustered to answer, so Hayes jumped in.

*What color is her hair?*

*What color are her eyes?*

*Approximate height and weight?*

*What was she wearing?*

*Did you notice anyone acting suspicious?*

I broke down with that last question, my sobs thundering the air. I should've done *something*. Maybe gotten a restraining order against Todd. I'd never thought he'd try something like this, though. Try to get custody? Yeah, that seemed like Todd. But kidnapping? That seemed low even for him.

"Ma'am?" The officer prompted when I stopped sobbing. "Did you see someone?"

"No." I wiped at my face, streaking mascara all over my arm. "But I think it might've been her dad."

"Her dad?" The officer prompted.

I nodded. "He left before her birth and he's been in town the past few weeks. Someone broke into my house and I think it was him. We filed a police report. You'll see." I waved at his notebook like it held all the answers in the world. "He's crazy," I babbled, "he wouldn't think twice about taking her."

The officer looked at me like I was the crazy one and resumed speaking to Hayes.

"Please," I begged him, "stop standing here talking to us. You need to be out there looking for her. She's just a little girl. She's probably scared to death and crying and she needs me. Please." I struggled to pull enough air into my lungs and grew dizzy.

"Whoa, steady." Hayes grabbed my shoulders, keeping me from swaying. "You're not going to be able to help Mia if you pass out. You need to calm down."

"I can't calm down!" I yelled, pissed off that he'd suggest such a thing. "My *daughter* is out there," I waved my hand around to encompass the area, "probably with a man that hates her and wouldn't think twice about hurting her."

"Ma'am do you know what kind of car he drives? That might help us locate him."

"No," I shook my head, more tears rolling down my cheeks. Before this moment I didn't know it was possible to cry so much. "I haven't seen him in one and I doubt he has the same one he had years ago…that was a silver Honda Civic."

"We'll look into it." The officer assured me with an apologetic smile. "Why don't you go home and get some rest? We'll continue the search."

"*Go home?*" I repeated. "*Get some rest?* Are you crazy? My little girl is out there scared to death and you think I can just go home and sit around and *wait?* No way in hell! I'm going to be looking for her too!"

"Arden." Hayes said my name in a low warning tone and guided me away.

"He's crazy," I hissed. "CRAZY!" I yelled louder so the officer was sure to hear me.

Hayes guided me over to our group of friends.

"Nothing?" Sadie asked, her face etched with worry. Ezra had his arms wrapped around her body like he was trying to keep her warm.

Hayes shook his head. "They don't think she's at the festival anymore. Whoever took her is probably long gone."

"*Whoever?*" I spat. "We know who it was. The asshole!" My whole body shook with my barely contained rage. "I swear to God if I *ever* see him again I'll gouge out his eyes with my fingernails."

"Whoa," Mathias' eyes widened, "remind me not to piss that one off."

"Bite me." I snapped my teeth together.

Apparently no one was immune to my anger at the moment.

Hayes rubbed his hand up and down my back in an effort to calm me. I had to give him credit, despite yelling at him earlier he hadn't abandoned me. He knew that I didn't actually blame him. It was the anger and fear talking.

"We're going to get her back. I promise." He pressed his lips to my forehead.

I closed my eyes and let myself absorb the small bit of comfort. "I hope so."

But I knew that if Todd was capable of hurting me the way he had, there was no telling what he might do to our daughter to get back at me.

Mia had been missing for three days.

Three whole days of no sleep, and little food or water for me since I couldn't seem to stomach anything, and I was afraid that if I closed my eyes for even one second there might be some new piece of information.

Every day, for hours, Hayes and I drove around and around looking for *anything* that might be a clue as to where Mia was.

But the more time that passed the more I feared she wasn't even in the state anymore.

The police had issued an Amber Alert—blasting Mia's face everywhere, and Todd's as a possible suspect.

My mom had proved helpful, when she found out that Mia was missing she came forward to say that Todd had been driving a small, dark green or black truck when he showed up at her house.

But there still wasn't a lead.

And I began to fear that Todd *wasn't* the one that took her.

If that was the case there was no telling where my baby girl might be.

"Arden…" Hayes stepped hesitantly into the guestroom.

At first I'd wanted to return to my house, like I'd stupidly believed Mia might come strolling up the front walk, but Hayes hadn't let me. He thought it would be better for me to continue to stay with him.

I think he knew I wasn't going to let *him* stay with *me* and he was afraid I might do something dumb…like hang myself with the shower curtain.

"Go away." I mumbled the words as I wrapped my arms around the pillow Mia had slept on only a few nights earlier.

"You need to eat something. Please."

His normally happy and smiling face was gone, instead replaced with a frown and worry lines.

"I can't eat."

"I know you don't think you can, but you *have* to." He strolled forward, a steaming mug of some kind of soup clasped in his hands. "You won't be able to help look for Mia if you're passed out from exhaustion and lack of food."

I clutched the pillow tighter. I knew he was right, but I was afraid I wouldn't be able to even swallow.

"Arden, *please.*" His eyes shimmered with worry.

I forced my weakened body into a seated position and held my hands out for the mug. He gladly handed it over, his shoulders sagging in relief that I'd finally accepted some sort of nourishment.

He sat by my feet, staring straight ahead at the wall and not me.

I lifted the spoon to my lips and sucked down the vegetable soup. I assumed it was homemade, and probably tasted delicious, but my taste buds didn't seem to be working.

"I'm doing everything I can to find her." Hayes whispered, finally turning to look at me with forlorn eyes.

"I know you are." I forced myself to swallow another spoonful. "I just worry that it's not enough."

He winced, and I knew it'd been the wrong thing to say, but I was only being honest. I was afraid that nothing *anyone* did was going to be enough.

If Todd had taken her, that was *bad*.

But if it was someone else? Well, that was even worse and I didn't even want to consider that possibility at all.

With that last thought I couldn't stomach any more soup and thrust the mug back into his hands.

"I'm done. I'm sorry."

"I'm sorry too," he whispered. "So fucking sorry. You were right when you said this was my fault. We shouldn't have gone to the festival."

I shook my head. "No," I said adamantly, "I was wrong to say that to you. You didn't know that was going to happen. None of us can see the future. And Todd would've found a way to take her eventually." I shrugged, ridding my mind of the possibility that it could've been someone else. "We could've been at the grocery store and he might have snagged her." I sighed, drawing the blankets closer around my suddenly freezing body.

"I hate this." He buried his head in his hands and let out a loud groan. "I've never felt so helpless in my entire life."

"Me either," I admitted, sinking back into the pillows. "And I thought I knew what it was like to be afraid. Todd made me fear for *my* life. But from where I'm standing now, it's an even worse kind of torture to fear for someone else's."

Hayes took a deep breath. "Can you *please* try to get some sleep? We'll head out in an hour to drive around some more."

"I'll try," I conceded.

He stood and started to leave.

"Hayes," I called.

He stopped and turned to look at me over his shoulder. "Yeah?" He raised a single brow.

"Stay with me?" I patted the empty space in the bed beside me.

For the past three days I'd done nothing but push him away and keep him at arm's length. I couldn't bear to be around anyone right now. But I knew Hayes loved my daughter and was worried sick too. I wasn't being fair to him.

"Are you sure?" His mouth turned down in a frown and he started forward hesitantly.

I nodded. "I don't want to be alone right now."

He seemed torn, but finally he placed the mug down on the dresser and lay down on the bed.

He kept as much space between us as he could, trying to be respectful.

I rolled over onto my side and scooted closer to him.

"Arden," he warned.

"I just want you to hold me. *Please?*" I begged brokenly.

His body was stiff at first, but slowly he began to relax and wrapped his arms around me. I wiggled around, trying to get comfortable. I laid my head on his chest, taking comfort in the steady *bud-m, bud-m, bud-m,* beating of his heart.

"I love you," he whispered.

"I love you too. I'm sorry I've been such a bitch." I smoothed my fingers down the soft cotton of his shirt.

"You've had every reason to be a bitch," he chuckled, "I don't blame you. I haven't been very tolerable to my friends."

"You've been patient with me," I whispered.

"You're the only one." He smoothed his fingers through my hair. "I've been yelling at everyone else."

"I'm so scared," I admitted, clutching onto his shirt like it was my lifeline. "I've never felt so helpless before and I hate it. My little girl is out there without me, probably terrified out of her mind and nothing I do is helping."

"I know what you mean…she's not even my daughter, but fuck…I love her like she is. And you're right, I feel so helpless. It's not a good feeling."

"Why does he keep ruining my life?" I whispered.

I felt Hayes shrug. "No idea. My guess is he wants you to feel as miserable as he does."

"Probably," I agreed.

"Now, *please*, be quiet and try to get some sleep."

"Don't leave me," I begged him, holding onto his shirt even tighter. I was terrified that if I managed to get some sleep I'd wake up and not realize what had happened, and then have all the emotions come flooding back to drown me.

"I wouldn't dream of it, Little Bird."

Hayes let me sleep for four hours before he woke me up so we could continue our own search.

We'd dropped Casey and Greg off on a side street to sweep the town on foot, while we drove around. They both felt partly responsible for what happened to Mia, since they were supposed to be keeping an eye on her and me, but had been distracted by the mob forming around the boys. I'd blamed them at first—I'd tried to blame anyone I could, wanting to find someone I could lash out and hold responsible for this situation.

Today, I didn't feel anger anymore. All I felt was fear and worry.

It was afternoon time, but the sky was overcast, painting the area in a dreary gray color that seemed to echo my mood.

Inside Hayes' truck we were both silent, scanning the streets as he drove by at a snail's pace.

I knew our efforts were most likely futile, the chances of her still being in town were slim, but I had to do something. I couldn't do what the police said and stay at home and wait for an update from them.

"Anything?" I asked Hayes.

"No."

This was always his response.

"Anything?" He asked me.

"No."

That way always my response.

I was growing wearier with every passing second that there was no news, no shred of evidence.

Hayes continued to drive, circling around the downtown area again and again.

On our fifth time around, something caught my eye. "Stop!" I yelled, throwing my hands out. "Stop!"

He slammed on the brakes and I jumped out of the truck. "Mia!" I yelled, running down the street and around the corner after the little girl I'd seen. "Mia!"

I spotted the little girl up ahead, wearing a bright red coat, with her red hair hanging in waves down her back.

"Mia!"

She didn't turn around. Her hand was clasped in someone's, but I couldn't bring myself to notice who it was. All of my focus was trained on my daughter.

Footsteps pounded behind me and I knew Hayes had joined me.

"Mia!" I called again as I neared her.

I reached out and grabbed her shoulder to turn her around.

"Hey!" The woman with her yelled.

And that's when I looked down and saw that the little girl wasn't my daughter. She had the same red hair, but her eyes were a warm brown and she was definitely older, probably six or seven.

"Sorry." I removed my hands from her quickly, like I'd been burned. "I'm sorry," I repeated. "I thought…"

"Arden." Hayes caught up to me and grabbed my hand, pulling my body into his like he was trying to shield me from the fact that this girl was not my daughter.

The mother of the girl seemed to finally notice us and her mouth widened in horror. "Oh! You're the one with the missing daughter."

I winced like I'd been slapped.

The police had me do an interview, pleading for the safe return of my daughter, and it had been blasted everywhere so there was no surprise that she recognized me.

"Yeah," I admitted, taking a step back.

"I'm so sorry. That's horrible. I hope you find her." She smiled sympathetically.

"Mhmm, yeah, thanks." I mumbled, and turned sharply, hurrying back to the parked truck.

"Arden!" Hayes called after me. "Arden!"

He grabbed my arm, effectively halting my hurried steps.

Tears streaked my cheeks. I felt like my face was constantly damp with tears right now.

"Are you okay?" He peered down at me, trying to see into my eyes.

"No, I'm not." I wrapped my arms around my body in a futile effort to hold myself together. "This is tearing me apart," I choked.

He took my face between his hands and lowered to press his forehead to mine.

"I know and I'm so sorry."

"What if I never see her again," I sobbed, holding onto his body for support.

"Hey, hey," he cooed, "don't think like that. She's *fine.*"

"I want to believe that, but it's been three days with *nothing*. Not one shred of evidence or a tip on their whereabouts. Todd is a conniving son of a bitch, and I know him well enough that if he took her then he had a plan and I don't know what that plan might be."

Hayes held me for a moment, rocking back and forth in an effort to comfort me. "We're going to find her. The police have been working tirelessly to find her. It's just a matter of time."

Drying my eyes I stepped away from him. "Let's go. I want to keep looking."

He nodded once and followed me back to the truck.

We picked up Greg and Casey and drove around for hours and hours, but just like the previous days there was no sign of Mia or Todd.

It was scary how easily someone could disappear and cease to exist.

# CHAPTER TWENTY-ONE

"We have a lead."

With those four words I fell out of the chair I occupied in the kitchen.

Hayes quickly helped me up and back into the chair.

"A lead?" I repeated. "What kind of lead?"

"Someone spotted what we believe to be Todd's vehicle outside an abandoned warehouse in the New York area. Officers in that area are heading over to investigate now."

For the first time in the five days since Mia went missing I was able to breathe.

I pulled in a lungful of air, letting it soothe my aching soul.

"Remember, this is only a lead," Officer Myers reminded me, "it could be nothing."

"But for now it's something." I said, my body relaxing with relief at finally having some sort of information. "She might be there." I looked from the officers around the room to Hayes. "Right?"

"Possibly," Officer Myers replied.

"How long until we know more?" I pleaded.

He shrugged. "Within the hour, I'd say."

I smiled and my face felt stiff and awkward from the motion since I hadn't smiled in days.

"I'm going to call my mom and let her know." I told Hayes as I jumped up from the chair. I kissed his cheek as I passed.

Out in the hallway I pulled my phone from my pocket and called my mom. She answered on the first ring.

"Do you know anything?" Were the first words out of her mouth.

"Someone reported a truck that could be Todd's outside an abandoned warehouse."

Her sigh of relief echoed across the line. "Oh I hope this is it. I hope they find her."

"Me too." I leaned my head against the wall. "It's the first lead we've had, so I hope it's not too good to be true."

"Think positive, sweetie. Do you want your dad and I to head up there to be with you?"

I shook my head, which was silly since she couldn't even see me. "No," I tucked a stray piece of hair behind my ear, "it's too far for you guys to come here. I'm fine. I have Hayes and the officers are here right now."

"Okay. Well, we'll come if you want us. Just call."

"I know. I love you, mom."

"Love you, sweetie."

I hung up the phone and tucked it against my chest, saying a silent prayer that they finally found my daughter.

Hayes and I sat on the couch in the family room while we waited for news.

Well, he sat.

I paced.

Up and down the room I walked, over and over again.

I couldn't sit still if my life depended on it.

"Arden," he warned lowly, "you're wearing a hole in the rug. Sit down, please."

"I can't!" I wrung my hands together and continued my pacing.

Hayes sighed, resting his elbows on his knees and his head in his hands.

"I hate waiting," I muttered, walking by him.

"At least we know *something*," he replied. "It's better than the whole lot of nothing we've been hearing the past few days."

"That's true," I agreed, but didn't cease my endless pacing.

"Arden." He snagged my arm the next time I passed him and pulled me down on the couch beside him. "You're giving me heartburn just watching you."

"I don't know how that would happen, but whatever." I crossed my arms over my chest, but one of my legs bounced restlessly.

In front of us the news played. They were talking about Mia's abduction and pleading with the public for help—they hadn't been given the updated information on the lead yet.

"I hope she's okay," I whispered, leaning my head on his shoulder.

"She *is* okay," he vowed, resting his head on top of mine, "we just have to find her. That's all."

"He hit me, Hayes. He *abused* me over and over again. What's to say he won't do the same to Mia?"

He let out a weary sigh. "There is no guarantee, but I have to believe that even he isn't so fucked up that he'd hurt a child. *His* child."

Beyond the room I heard a flurry of activity and the officers voices rose.

I ran from the room and into the kitchen where they'd taken residence.

"What is it? What do you know?" I clasped my hands together and bounced on the balls of my feet.

Officer Myers stepped forward and he was *grinning*.

"You found her!" I exclaimed. He had to be smiling because they found her, right? "Please tell me you found her!"

He nodded his head eagerly. "We found her. She was in the abandoned warehouse and the truck that was spotted belonged to Todd James."

"So, she's okay? She's not hurt? When do I get to see her?" I rattled off question after question.

"She appears to be fine, maybe a few scrapes and bruises, but nothing serious. A medical team will be looking her over to be sure, though. Once they know she's indeed okay, and stable enough to travel, she'll be brought back."

"Oh, thank you! Thank you! Thank you!" I basically tackled the poor officer in my haste to hug him.

Officer Myers lifted his arms and awkwardly patted my back in his pathetic attempt to show affection.

Pulling away from him I stepped back into Hayes' embrace. He held me tight, burying his face into the skin of my neck and that was when I felt his wet tears.

He'd had to be the strong one through all of this, and now was his moment to break.

I held him tight. "I love you," I whispered. "Thank you for being you. Thank you for putting up with me. Thank you for everything."

"That's what love is," he murmured against my neck, "it's loving someone through every storm. You don't ever need to thank me for that."

"Yes, I do." I assured him, pressing a wet kiss to his cheek.

I turned to Officer Myers and Hayes wrapped his arms around me, his front to my back, not wanting to let me go.

"Is it possible for us to meet them halfway and get her ourselves?" I questioned—throwing in some puppy dog eyes for good measure.

Officer Myers winced, his lips twisted with displeasure. "Well, you see…there's a bit of a problem."

My blood ran cold. "What kind of problem? You said she was okay? What could possibly be wrong?"

Office Myers looked behind him at another officer. When that officer nodded he turned back to us.

"We found *Mia*."

"Yes, I got that." I grinned. "You found her and she's okay."

"But that's it," he said, his dark brows furrowed with worry. "We only found *her*. Todd was not in the warehouse."

"Oh my God." My eyes widened in horror. "So you mean he's still out there? He could do this again?"

Officer Myers nodded sadly. "I'm afraid so. We'll be releasing a statement soon about Mia being found, and we'll blast Todd's face everywhere. We *will* find him."

"So what does that have to do with us not being allowed to get her?"

Officer Myers nodded to himself. "This has been a high profile case due to your…uh…*status*." He glanced at Hayes. "We just want to make sure we do this right and keep her safe so she'll be in police custody the whole way here. It's the safest option with Todd still on the loose."

"I understand." I was disappointed, but I didn't want to do anything to jeopardize Mia.

I couldn't believe she was safe and okay and that she was coming home.

"I need to call my mom and our friends, to let them know."

"Of course," Officer Myers nodded, taking a step back. "We'll be here until she arrives and if there are any updates regarding Todd I'll let you know."

"Thank you," I said again.

I backed out of the room and called my mom while Hayes called his.

When his mom found out that Mia was missing she'd been beyond hysterical that this was happening. Hayes told me she was the one that had made the soup he'd gotten me to eat. She'd driven all the way here to deliver the soup herself, and had wanted to see me, but Hayes had talked her out of seeing me since I hadn't been in the best frame of mind. Thank God for that, since I might've thrown something at her. Not that I'd thrown things at people or anything. Okay, only once, and it was at Casey.

My mom answered on the first ring, just like the last time. I was pretty sure her phone was permanently glued to her hand at this point.

"Anything?" She said in greeting.

"They found her." A sob bubbled out of my throat. I was so *relieved* and now my emotions were all over the place.

"Oh thank God!" She cried and her own sobs filled the line.

"I feel like I can finally breathe," I admitted.

"Oh, I'm sure sweetie. I can't believe this happened, but at least she's been found and safe."

"I know. But Todd wasn't with her, which means he's still out there and could try something like this again."

She clucked her tongue. "That isn't good."

"No, it's not," I sighed, "but Mia's okay and that's all that matters."

"When will she be home?"

"Hopefully tonight." I pushed my hair away from my face. "I don't know if I could stand it if they made me wait until tomorrow."

"Once she's there and everything is settled your dad and I want to come see her."

"Sounds good. Thanks for all your help, mom."

"Of course. I love you."

"Love you too."

I hung up and called Sadie to let her know everything and she promptly burst into tears of relief. We were all an emotional bunch right now—but I was thankful to have friends that cared so deeply.

By the time Hayes and I finished making our rounds of phone calls I felt more exhausted than I had in days. Now that I knew that Mia was safe my adrenaline had faded.

We found ourselves back on the couch, and I lay down on my side with my head in his lap.

"It's over," Hayes said, stroking his fingers through my hair before settling his hand on my neck.

"Is it?" I questioned, worry still plaguing me.

"It has to be," he whispered.

The sky was dark, completely black with not even the hint of stars or the moon, when the cop car containing Mia pulled into Hayes' driveway.

I'd been on the front steps for the last fifteen minutes, waiting anxiously for her arrival, despite Hayes' demand that it was too cold for me to sit outside. He'd joined me anyway, and wrapped a big fluffy blanket around my shoulders to help keep me warm.

When I saw the car turn into the driveway I took off running. I didn't think I'd ever run that fast in my entire life.

The car stopped and I pulled the door open.

Almost immediately Mia dove into my arms, her tears dampening my shirt.

"Oh, baby girl," I sobbed holding her tight and inhaling her scent in an effort to convince myself of the fact that she was really here, "I'm never letting you go," I vowed.

"Momma," she sobbed, "I twas so scared."

"I know, baby, I'm so sorry." I squeezed her tight and then peppered her face with kisses. There was a small scratch on her nose, but other than that she appeared to be fine. "I love you so much." I held her tight again.

I felt the warmth of Hayes' hand on my shoulder and I turned to look up at him, surprised to see that he was fighting back tears.

"Come here," I told him.

Without hesitation he squatted down beside me and wrapped his arms around Mia and me.

"I was so worried about you, Mia," he choked. "I missed you."

I watched in quiet fascination as tears streaked his face.

"I'm so happy to have my family back," he whispered, kissing my forehead and then Mia's.

Mia pulled from my arms and dove into his, squeezing him as tight as she had me. "I mwissed you too. I wuv you." She sniffled, choking on her own tears.

"I love you too." He closed his eyes and wrapped his arms around her, laying his head on hers.

He stood, picking up Mia in the process. She wrapped her arms around his neck and held on tight as we trekked back to the house.

The officers were standing outside waiting for us, unable to hide their own smiles.

"Thank you," I said again for the millionth time, and proceeded to hug each and every one of them.

I'd admit, I hadn't been the nicest to them—when you were worried out of your mind about your child you weren't nice to *anyone*—but they'd done their job and brought my daughter back to me. I knew some parents weren't as lucky as I was.

This could've been a whole lot worse.

Hayes set Mia down inside the foyer and thanked the officers like I had.

"We're going to continue searching for Todd, this isn't over yet," Officer Myers warned us forlornly. "The officers discovered some evidence in the warehouse that he was planning to hold her for ransom." He glanced at Hayes when he said this. "Just be careful, alright?"

"We will," I promised, reaching out and holding Mia's hand.

I wouldn't be letting Mia out of my sight until she was like…thirty, and maybe not even then. I was going to be taking 'over-protective' to a whole new level.

"We'll pack up our stuff and head out. If you see anything suspicious call me." Officer Myers handed me a card with his information and headed back into the kitchen with the other officers following him.

"I'm going to go give her a bath and put her to bed," I told Hayes as I absentmindedly stroked my fingers down Mia's cheek, "can you stay and see them out?"

"Yeah, of course." He nodded.

I picked Mia up and carried her upstairs—despite the fact that she was now too big for me to do this—I just needed to hold her close.

I set her down in the bathroom and began to run warm water, adding in a dash of bubbles.

"Momma missed you so much, baby girl." I took her face in my hands before helping her undress.

She had a few more scrapes aside from the one on her nose, and a couple of bruises too. I felt relieved, because I knew it could've been a lot worse.

"I mwissed you too." She sniffled, wiping at her nose.

"Let's get you cleaned up and into bed."

I lifted her into the bathtub since it was too high for her to climb in by herself.

She splashed in the bubbles for a minute, before she said, "Momma?"

"Yes, baby girl?" I rested my arms on the top of the bathtub.

"Will you sweep in my bed tonight?" She wouldn't look at me when she asked the question, like she was embarrassed.

"Of course, honey."

I'd always do anything for her, and if she wanted me to sleep in her bed tonight then I would. But I was beyond worried about what kind of effect this would have on her. Could children develop PTSD? I'd have to Google that later, although knowing Google that would only scare me further.

I figured I'd need to have Mia see a therapist. That seemed a bit drastic at her age, but she'd been *kidnapped* by her own father and he'd planned to hold her for ransom, so in my book that seemed like something a therapist would need to help with. I didn't want to do nothing and have this affect her for the rest of her life.

Mia grew quiet, so I quickly washed her hair and body before helping her out and wrapping her up in the fluffiest towel I could find.

"You're a brave, strong girl," I told her as I put her pajamas on her.

"I am?"

I nodded emphatically. "The strongest."

That got her to smile and I felt the vice around my heart start to lessen a bit.

Neither one of us was going to be okay tonight, or tomorrow, or even the next day, but eventually all would be well again.

Mia fell asleep as soon as her head touched the pillow.

I propped my head in my hands and lay watching her sleep. I was afraid if I closed my eyes I'd wake up and find that this was all a dream and she was still missing. I wasn't sure my heart could take that. It'd been beaten enough.

Eventually the door creaked open and between the slice of light from the hallway I could see Hayes' silhouette.

I waved him forward and he tiptoed into the room so that he didn't wake Mia.

Leaning over the bed, he whispered, "They're gone."

I nodded in response and patted the empty space beside me in the large bed. "She wants me to sleep in here tonight. Will you stay too?"

His eyes shimmered with relief. "I don't want to be without either of you," he confessed, slipping into bed behind me and leaned around me to look at Mia. He smoothed his large fingers over her small cheek. "I didn't know it was humanly possible to experience what I've felt the past few days."

"I didn't either," I concurred, burrowing under the covers.

Hayes lay back and wrapped his arms around me. "Go to sleep, Little Bird. It's over now. Rest." His lips brushed against my ear as he spoke, sending a shiver down my spine.

"I don't know if I can."

"Try," another brush of his lips, "she needs you to be strong for her and you can't do that if you're dead on your feet."

I peered around him at the clock on the nightstand and saw that it was nearing one in the morning.

"I'll try."

His hand slid up my back, settling on my neck and he massaged the tense muscle. My eyes grew heavy and I yawned.

When he started humming I was a goner, and sleep claimed me peacefully.

I sat bolt upright from a dead sleep.

The clock flashed that it was nearing five o' clock in the morning, so I'd only been asleep for a few hours.

Beside me, Mia slept peacefully and Hayes was completely knocked out with his arm crossed over his face.

My heart raced inside my chest and I rubbed my hand over it, like somehow that gesture would slow it.

And that's when I heard it.

Footsteps downstairs.

Casey and Greg were staying in the guesthouse over the garage, and it was complete with a kitchen and everything, so there was no logical reason as to why one of them would be in the house.

My throat closed and I shook with fear.

Something told me that this was bad.

Very bad.

Bad with a capital B.

I shook Hayes awake.

He startled awake, slinging his arms around. "Huh? What is it?"

I slapped a hand over his mouth and his eyes widened.

"What?" He mumbled against my hand.

I made a shushing gesture against my mouth.

"Listen," I mouthed.

He grew quiet and we both heard the sound of someone coming upstairs.

"Take her and get into the closet or…just fucking hide," he hissed, rolling out of bed.

"What about you?" I whispered as he tiptoed to the bedroom door.

"I'll be fine," he mouthed back, slipping from the room.

I watched in horror as he left the room. I wanted to run after him, to stop him from whatever he was going to do, but Mia was my top priority.

I grabbed her into my arms and she startled awake. I immediately put my hand over her mouth so that she wouldn't scream. Her mouth opened beneath my hand, like she was going to bite me, but when she saw that it was me she relaxed.

I carried her into the closet and eased the door closed just as I heard the person top the stairs.

The closet was large and I carried her all the way into the back, sitting her on the floor behind a box filled with blankets.

"Mia, listen to mommy…I need you to be *very* quiet. Do you hear me?" I waited for her to nod. "Whatever you do, don't make a sound."

She nodded again.

"I love you. I'll be right back, I promise."

Before I could talk myself out of leaving her I eased out of the closet and tiptoed into the bathroom.

I heard the sound of whoever was in the house rummaging through a room a few doors down. They were close, too close for comfort, and I needed a weapon. I refused to be defenseless.

I remembered seeing a heavy-duty flashlight in one of the bathroom drawers, but I couldn't remember which one.

With my heart beating unsteadily I rummaged through the drawers as quietly as I could.

I found the flashlight in the third drawer I checked, and I held it tightly in my hand.

I eased the drawer closed, taking a deep breath before I passed out.

"Mia, come out, come out, where ever you are."

Todd.

He laughed manically, and I knew then that he was truly off his rocker.

I started to ease out of the bathroom but I caught sight of his shadow approaching the room, so I quickly ducked back inside, holding my breath.

"Mia, I just want to play. Don't you want to play with your daddy?"

I held the flashlight so tight in my hands that my fingers started to go numb.

I heard his feet shuffling against the carpet and I pressed my back against the wall, praying he didn't glance in the bathroom and see my reflection.

"Mia, where are you?" He called. Clucking his tongue, he said, "It's not very nice to hide from your daddy."

In the reflection of the mirror I saw him bend down and peer under the bed.

He reached under it and when he pulled his arm out I saw that he was clutching one of her many stuff animals. He held the panda tightly in his hands, gritting his teeth as he stood.

"I know you're here, you little brat!" He yelled, his voice echoing off of the high ceilings. "Where are you?"

With another cry he stripped off the bed covers and threw them on the floor.

"Arden! I know you're here too! You whore!"

I pressed a shaking hand over my mouth.

"Did you *really* think I wouldn't know about your transgressions? You belong to me, and only me." He spun around the room, looking for any sign of us. When he wasn't looking towards the bathroom I eased down behind the counter, squatting on the floor.

I couldn't see him from this vantage point, but I hoped that meant he couldn't see me either.

I had counted to thirty in my head when he finally crossed the threshold into the bathroom.

I was shaking like a leaf, but I knew I had to do something.

I jumped up, taking him by surprise.

"Arden!" He made to grab for me, but by some miracle I was faster. My arm had reared back with the flashlight and I brought it down on his face.

His nose shattered with a satisfying crack and blood spurted all over the bathroom as he stumbled back.

I ran from the bathroom, but my foot stumbled over the stupid stuffed panda and I went tumbling to the floor. My knee sliced with pain and I rolled over in time to see Todd running from the bathroom.

He collapsed on top of me, pinning me to the floor with his weight.

My face stung with a sharp slap from his hand and I whimpered.

"Fucking bitch." He spat blood on my face.

"Get off of me," I cried, struggling against his hold.

When I'd fallen the flashlight had rolled from my grip and I had no idea where it'd gone.

Now, I was completely and utterly defenseless.

"I can't believe you ever thought you could get rid of me." He held my arms above my head.

"You left *me*, remember?" I bucked against him, my face wet with tears.

"Bitch," he shook me, and my head rolled on my neck, "you were still mine. That pretty boy thought he could have you, but he was wrong." Smiling sadistically he made a show of looking around, and said, "And where is he? Because he's certainly not here."

"Look again."

My whole body sagged with relief at the sound of Hayes' voice.

Todd's lips twisted in a smile and he glanced over his shoulder to see that Hayes had emerged from the closet.

I heard the click of a gun and my body froze before I realized that Hayes was the one with the gun.

"If you know what's good for you," Hayes said slowly, like he was speaking to someone stupid, "you'll get off of her."

"You're not going to shoot me." Todd laughed. In the face of a gun the fucker actually laughed.

"Do you really want to tempt the guy with the gun?"

"Have it your way then." Todd stood slowly.

"Hands in the air," Hayes warned him.

Todd chuckled. "What are you? The police?"

"No, but they're on their way and they have even bigger guns."

Todd threw his head back and laughed. Once he was completely standing Hayes directed him to step away from me—which he did, after he managed a good kick to my stomach.

Hayes growled his disapproval, but kept his eyes and the gun trained on Todd.

"Are you okay?" He asked me.

"Yeah," I squeaked, clutching my side and trying to regain my breath.

"Well aren't you two just the sweetest." Todd's voice dripped with false sweetness and then he lunged toward Hayes.

I screamed, crying out like I was the one that had been hurt.

The gun went off with a loud pop and I was sure my heart had stopped with it.

"HAYES!" I yelled out as he stumbled back.

Todd fell to the ground, clutching the bloody area of his groin, and I sobbed in relief that Hayes wasn't the one hurt.

Todd bellowed on the ground, crying out in pain.

"Oh shut up," Hayes groaned, pushing a piece of hair from his eyes before reaching down to help me up.

"Ow," I mumbled, holding onto my ribs.

"Do you think they're broken?" Hayes asked me, keeping his eyes on Todd in case he decided to lunge for us again.

"No," I breathed out through the pain, "just sore."

"Momma! Momma!" Mia cried from inside the closet.

The pain I felt was momentarily washed away by a burst of adrenaline.

I ran past Hayes and into the open closet. Mia was still hiding behind the box and I pushed it out of the way, dropping to my knees, and wrapping my arms around her.

Her tears wet my shoulder and she clutched at me like she was terrified I might be ripped away at any second.

"Is da bad man gone?" She sniffled, her little hands clinging to my shirt like it was the only thing holding her up.

"He will be," I promised. "It's over this time. He'll never bother us again."

Outside I heard the sound of sirens and I breathed a sigh of relief.

Mia sobbed against me. "I twas so scared momma."

"I know, baby girl, but you did good. You kept quiet just like I asked."

She hiccupped and I pushed her back slightly so I could dry her face with my hands.

"The police are here and they're going to arrest the bad man," I promised her. "You'll never see him again."

She continued to shake in my arms and I picked her up, carrying her out of the closet.

Todd still clutched the injured area on his upper thigh; sweat beading on his top lip.

Hayes kept the gun trained on him, just in case, and I held Mia's head against my shoulder so she wouldn't see it. I was sure the sound of the gunshot had traumatized her enough.

Downstairs we heard the front door being busted open.

"We're up here!" Hayes called.

Feet pounded on the steps and a moment later at least five cops burst into the room, guns aimed at the ready.

It was like something you'd see in a movie or a TV show, only this was very much real.

The officers grabbed Todd and handcuffed him roughly.

"Hey, careful, I've been shot," Todd whined.

"Oh, shut up." Officer Myers shook him a bit before pushing him forward. "Anyone that kidnaps a little girl and breaks into a house to…I don't even want to know…deserves a lot worse than what you got."

Todd growled and started shouting out obscenities, his eyes roaming around crazily. It seemed that he'd only now realized he was actually being arrested and there was no way he was getting out of this.

The officers escorted him from the room and a paramedic came into the room to look all of us over.

Mia flinched away from the paramedic and tears stung my eyes. My poor baby girl had been through more than most adults. I was beyond worried about her well-being, but I kept comforting myself with the fact that kids were resilient.

"Sweetie," the paramedic coaxed, "I need to make sure you're okay. Do you want your mommy to hold your hand while I check you?" He kept his voice as calm and even as possible.

Mia nodded against my shoulder and I set her down on the bed. I didn't move from her side as he checked her over.

"All good." He smiled at her and with a flourish produced a sticker from his pocket. It was a pink glittery unicorn. "That's for you."

"Tank you," she said, and quickly scurried back into my arms.

Several officers returned then, taking our report of the account for their records.

Mia clung to me tightly, like a little monkey.

Hayes smoothed his hand down her back, trying to comfort her.

"What the hell is going on?" Greg asked, strolling into the bedroom.

Hayes rolled his eyes. "I was doing your job, that's what. Thank God Trace insisted I get a gun license and learn to shoot, it sure came in handy tonight." He glanced down at the bloodstain on the carpet from Todd's injury.

"Ah, hell," Greg groaned, tugging at the strands of his hair.

Casey appeared in the doorway behind him with his shirt on backwards and wearing two different shoes. "We heard sirens."

"Really?" Hayes said sarcastically. "I must've missed that."

"So…he showed up here?" Greg asked, staring around the room nervously.

"Obviously…and just so you know, if Mia wasn't here right now I'd call you some pretty colorful names but I'm trying to be a grownup."

"I'll let you pity punch me later," Greg mumbled.

"We're heading out now," one of the officers spoke, tossing a thumb over his shoulder. "That's all we need from you, but once this thing heads to court you'll both need to testify."

"Of course," Hayes sighed. "I'll walk you out. You two, come with me." He eyed his bodyguards.

Everyone filed out of the room and it was just Mia and me.

"I don't wanna be in hwere," she confessed, looking up at me with wide blue eyes.

"I don't blame you, baby girl. I don't want to be in here either."

I stood and carried her into Hayes' room. She scurried up the bed and under the covers.

"Can I watch a mwovie?" She asked, drawing the blankets up to her chin.

"Yeah, sweetie," I said, rummaging through the DVDs in the bedroom. There were a few of Mia's movies in here so I held them aloft and let her pick. I wasn't surprised when she chose The Little Mermaid.

The movie had just started when I heard Hayes top the stairs.

"We're in your room!" I called, knowing he'd check the guestroom first and freak when he didn't see us.

Stepping into the room he leveled me with a look. "*Our* room."

I shook my head. "Nope, your house, your room." I climbed into the middle of the bed beside Mia.

She watched the TV like the movie was the most fascinating thing she'd ever seen. I hoped the movie helped to ease the thoughts that were no doubt plaguing her. I brushed her hair away from her forehead and kissed the skin there.

Hayes looked down at me sternly before getting in the bed.

"I want you guys to stay here."

"Hayes," I mumbled. "You have to be kidding. After everything you want us to *stay?*"

"I'm serious," he said adamantly. "The thought of staying in this house without my girls…it makes me sad. I love having you both here. I thought I was content by myself, but this short time with you guys has shown me how empty this place was. Now that it's filled with laughter and love I don't want to see it barren again."

"You really have a way with words," I told him.

He chuckled. "Maybe I was Shakespeare in another life."

I patted his chest mockingly. "That's cute that you think that, but no."

Laughter rumbled in his chest. "It doesn't feel like I should be able to laugh right now," he admitted, "not after everything we've been through."

"It's over," I whispered. "We can't dwell on it forever." I glanced over at Mia and was surprised to find that she'd fallen asleep. I sent up a silent prayer that she wouldn't have any nightmares, but I doubted that would be enough to keep the demons away. Rolling back towards Hayes, I said, "We were supposed to leave for Disney in two days."

"I know," he winced, "I guess I should cancel that."

I shook my head. "I think the opposite. It would probably be good for Mia to get away from here for a while—instead of surprising her I think we should just tell her though. I wouldn't want to scare her."

He nodded and a small smile graced his lips. "Sounds good. We'll tell her in the morning."

I rolled over onto my other side then and snuggled close to Mia. I wasn't at all surprised when his body wound around mine.

Neither of us were perfect, and everything we'd been through was enough to tear us apart, but we were both fighters and nothing would ever bring us down.

# EPILOGUE
### TWO YEARS LATER

A lot can happen in two years.

People get married.

Babies make appearances.

And others, well they end up in jail rotting for the rest of their days—good riddance Todd, nobody will miss you.

On this particular day, we were gathering together to celebrate a wedding.

My wedding.

To Hayes.

Hayes and I were getting married.

*Finally.*

Our relationship had roared like a fire from the very start and I knew Hayes would've married me when we'd only been dating officially for six months, but I didn't want that. I wanted to take things slow after everything we'd been through.

And now the day had arrived where I was going to make that man my husband.

I clutched the bouquet tightly in my hands.

"Breathe," Sadie whispered, blowing out her own breath in an effort to get me to copy her movements.

Her body was swathed in a pale blue fabric that accentuated her ever-growing baby bump. She'd become Mrs. Ezra Collins only a year ago, and Ezra hadn't wasted any time with getting her pregnant. Sadie was thrilled though, positively glowing, and couldn't wait for the arrival of her baby boy, Everett, the latest Willow Creek baby.

"Are you okay?" She asked me. "You're not going to pass out, right?"

"I'm good," I assured her with a smile.

"Okay. I'm going to go take my seat."

Hayes and I had opted to keep our wedding small and not have any bridesmaids or groomsmen.

The only person that would be up there with us was Mia.

She strolled up to me and smiled before taking my hand.

She was no longer my baby anymore. She'd grown into an intelligent six-year-old who constantly blew my mind. Sometimes she still had night terrors, left over effects from her kidnapping and the break in, but other than that she was fine. We still took her to see a counselor every week, just in case. I never wanted to look back and wonder if I could've done more for her.

"Ready, mommy?" She asked, beaming up at me with a wide, toothy smile. Her red hair curled down her back and she wore a dress in her favorite color, purple.

"I'm definitely ready, baby girl."

I heard the music start up and knew that was my cue.

Together Mia and I rounded the corner and stepped into the ballroom.

Hayes stood at the end of the aisle, looking the best he ever had.

He wore husband well.

Hayes grinned at me and butterflies assaulted my stomach.

I'd once thought that fluttery, jittery feeling would go away, but I'd been wrong. It only intensified as I fell more in love with him.

When I reached the end of the aisle and stood in front of him with Mia at my side I thought I might burst.

"You look beautiful." He mouthed.

"You're not bad yourself." I mouthed back.

He chuckled and ducked his head.

"Shall we begin?" The minister asked.

"Um, no actually," Hayes cleared his throat.

I stared at him in confusion.

"There's something I need to say first."

My confusion only deepened when he got down on his knees.

He grabbed Mia's hands and held them in his own. His were so large that hers completely disappeared.

"I have some vows for you first," he spoke to Mia. "I may not be your real daddy, but I vow to be one in all the ways that matter. I vow to be a shoulder for you to cry on when you're sad. I vow to hold you in my arms and hug you whenever you need it. I vow to protect you always, in any way you may need. I vow to hunt down any guy that thinks he can date you—you're going to be single for life Mia, just accept it. But most importantly, I vow to love you with all my heart and take care of you always."

By this point tears flowed freely down my cheeks. I glanced out at our friends and family and saw that nearly all of them were crying as well. My mom and Hayes' mom both had a tissue pressed to their faces, wiping away smudges of mascara. Even Jessica, Hayes' older sister, was tearing up. She and I had worked through things. We certainly weren't best friends, but things were civil between us.

"I love you." Mia said and wrapped her arms around his neck.

Hayes hugged her back fiercely and kissed her cheek before standing.

Willow, Maddox and Emma's daughter who was nearly two now, let out a squeal that broke the emotional bubble that had formed around all of us.

Everyone laughed at her outburst and the minister cleared his throat to gain everyone's attention.

In what seemed like seconds we were both saying, "I do," and slipping rings onto each other's fingers.

"I now pronounce you husband and wife. You may kiss your bride."

Hayes wasted no time in taking my face between his hands and kissing me deeply.

"Woohoo! Get some!" Maddox yelled and Hayes laughed against my mouth.

Placing one last tender kiss on my lips he pulled away, murmuring, "Wife."

"Daddy," I replied back.

His eyes narrowed in confusion. "Are you trying to be kinky, because I'm not sure I'm into that."

I laughed and shook my head. "No."

His mouth parted in shock and his eyes widened. "Are you saying…?" He prompted, one of his hands moving to cover my flat stomach.

By now everyone was staring at us in confusion, trying to figure out what we were saying.

"I'm pregnant. I just found out yesterday and I wanted to surprise you."

Hayes thrust his hands into the air and turned to our family and friends. "I'm going to be a daddy again!"

I laughed, pleased that he was so happy with this unexpected news.

Everyone burst into excited chatter and shouts of congratulations.

"I'm going to be a big sister?" Mia asked, her eyes filled with wonder and delight.

"That's right." I squeezed her shoulder lovingly.

Hayes leaned forward to kiss me again and reached down for Mia's hand.

"Girls," he smiled crookedly, "I can say, without a doubt, this is the best day of my life."

I stretched up on my toes—still too short to reach his ear even in my heels, and whispered, "And it's just getting started."

# BONUS CONTENT

**Interviewer:** Thank you for taking the time to sit down and talk to us today. I hear congratulations are in order, wedding and a baby?

**HAYES:** <chuckles and rubs mouth> That's right. We work fast. <winks at Arden>

**ARDEN:** We're very excited. <smiles and takes Hayes' hand>

**INTERVIEWER:** I must ask how this will affect your upcoming tour? <raises a brow>

**HAYES:** It won't affect it at all. The tour starts next month and will be over well before the baby arrives.

**ARDEN:** Their fans have nothing to worry about, I promise. <laughs>

**Interviewer:** There has been a rumor going around that you're adopting your wife's daughter from her previous marriage, is there any validity in that, Hayes?

**HAYES:** Mia is already my daughter in all the ways that count, so yes, I'm adopting her.

**INTERVIEWER:  Any other big plans?**

**ARDEN:** <shrugs and glances at Hayes> Not that I know of.

**HAYES:** <tapping his chin in thought> We're getting a puppy.

**ARDEN:** <eyes widen> We *are*? This is the first I'm hearing of this.

**HAYES:** <shrugs> Every family needs a dog. It's a fact of life. We already have a cat, a kid, and a baby on the way, a dog will complete the circle.

**ARDEN:** Or if you're talking to Maddox, then you need a hedgehog.

**HAYES:** Well, Maddox is weird.

**ARDEN:** So…I guess we're getting a dog.

**HAYES:**  A Siberian Husky named Wolfe, because…why not?

**ARDEN:** <shakes head> Only you.

**HAYES:** But you love me. <grins>

**ARDEN:** <kisses his cheek> I do.

**INTERVIEWER:**  That's all we have time for today. <stands and extends hand>

**HAYES:** <too busy kissing Arden to notice the interviewer is still there>

**INTERVIEWER:**  Ahem.

**HAYES:** <glances up> Dude, just let yourself out. I need to make love to my wife now.

**INTERVIEWER:**  <scurries away and mumbles> I don't get paid enough for this.

# BONUS CONTENT

*Today we have the privilege of sitting down with all of the guys from Willow Creek answering YOUR fan submitted questions.*

Interviewer: Thanks for taking time out of your busy schedules to sit down with us and answer some fan questions.

**MADDOX:** <places Sonic on his shoulder> Of course. We love our fans.

**MATHIAS:** I'm only here because I'm getting paid.

**MADDOX:** <glares at Mathais>

**MATHIAS:** And because I love our fans.

**EZRA & HAYES:** <laughing hysterically>

**Interviewer:** Okay then…let's just jump right in. The first fan submitted question we have is…If you weren't in the band, what would your job be?

**MADDOX:** I'd be a hedgehog breeder, obviously…ooh, or a professional knitter. <pauses> *Are* there professional knitters?

**MATHIAS:** <shakes head> Dude, you are so weird. <takes a deep breath> Uh, if I wasn't in the band I'd probably do something with children. Maybe be a social worker.

**MADDOX:** Aw, look at you being all sweet and talking about helping kids.

**MATHIAS:** Shut up.

**EZRA:** <chuckles> With those two around it's hard to get a word in. I'd say I'd be a teacher.

**HAYES:** I'd be an ice cream truck driver. Who doesn't want to eat ice cream all day?

**INTERVIEWER:** Next question. What's your favorite song?

**MADDOX:** The first song Emma and I ever wrote together. Not that I'm biased or anything.

**MATHIAS:** #Ican'teven by The Neighborhood.

**EZRA:** Anything by Hozier. The guy is a genius.

**HAYES:** The only song I've heard recently that isn't one of ours is the My Little Pony theme song since Mia is on a My Little Pony kick, but I have to agree with the lyrics. Friendship *is* magic.

**MADDOX:** <laughs> Love you, Hayes, you big softie.

**HAYES:** <snaps fingers at Maddox> You just wait until Willow gets a little bit older and that song is all you hear.

**INTERVIEWER:** Next question. If you had a choice between being Batman, a Ninja Turtle, or Bananaman, who would you be?

**MADDOX:** Batman.

**MATHIAS:** Batman.

**EZRA:** Ninja Turtle

**HAYES:** Bananaman. I like bananas.

**INTERVIEWER:** What's been the hardest adjustment with fame?

**MADDOX:** Having people monitor your every move.

**MATHIAS:** The paparazzi, and they've only gotten worse now that we have kids. They always want a picture of them and that's not cool. Let them be kids.

**EZRA:** I'd say for me the hardest adjustment has been the fact that you always have to be *on*. You know what I mean? Everybody has bad days, but when you're in the public eye it's like you can't have them or everyone labels you as an asshole.

**MADDOX:** Ezzie-poo, no one could ever think you were an asshole.

**EZRA:** <laughs> Thanks dude.

**HAYES:** Being in the public eye is just *hard*. People always want something from you and it can be exhausting. I'm not saying I don't love it, because I do, but it has its drawbacks. It's just part of the territory though, and if you can't accept it then you shouldn't have pursued fame.

**INTERVIEWER:** What's a food or object you can't live without?

**MADDOX:** Besides my wife and child? I'd say Sonic, my knitting supplies, and my drumsticks.

**MATHIAS:** You were supposed to pick one.

**MADDOX:** I'm feeling rebellious today.

**MATHIAS:** <shakes head> Not including Remy and Liam, I can't live without Shiloh and Percy. <grumbles> The Demon Cat has grown on me.

**MADDOX:** <points an accusing finger> You chose *two* not one!

**MATHIAS:** <mimics Maddox> I'm feeling rebellious today.

This Bonus Material contains eight brand new scenes PLUS previously released bonus material from my website. I have accumulated it all in the order in which fits the timeline of the main four books the best, therefore the POVs jump around, and since these are scenes, not a novella, they don't merge together. Regardless, I hope you will enjoy seeing more of the Willow Creek family. I had so much fun going back to this world.

—Micalea

I was high.

Not *that* kind of high.

I was high on the good stuff. The *real* stuff.

Love.

Apparently love also turned me into a sappy idiot, but maybe I was already that before Emma.

*Nah.*

Band practice was going good. I was floating on a cloud. The new music we'd been working on was some of the best I'd ever written—thanks to my new muse.

"Stop, stop, stop." Mathias stopped singing and signaled his hands for a time-out. "This sounds love sick as fuck." He dipped his head back at me, narrowing his eyes in a glare where I sat behind my drum set.

I pointed at him with a drumstick. "I am love sick and girls dig this shit. It'll be a hit. Trust me."

He rolled his eyes.

If he wasn't my twin brother I might hate the guy sometimes.

"Fine." Mathias waved his hand, signaling for all of us to get back to it. "We'll take it from the top."

I began playing, and like always my hands sort of took over and my mind wandered.

Of course my mind was filled with images of last night. How could it not be?

I'd had sex before, sure, but never like that. I always thought the people that said it was different with someone special were only lying to make you wait. I'd been wrong. With Emma I'd finally had an emotional connection to someone and it had made the sex a hundred—no, a thousand—times better.

I heard a sudden war cry and I looked up in wonder, only to be pelted in the head two seconds later with a drumstick.

My drumsticks dropped from my hands and I reached up to rub my forehead.

*That hurt.*

Everyone else had stopped playing too and I looked up to see the reason for the flying drumstick standing in the open doorway of the guesthouse.

I'd never seen Emma mad—she was always sweet as pie—but if looks could kill I'd be dead right now.

Her blonde hair was a wild tangled mess around her head and her hands were fisted at her sides. She was red in the face and I knew, knew deep down in my gut that she'd finally figured out the truth.

*You should've told her*, my conscience shouted at me.

It was right. I should have. I'd tried. But I was always too scared of losing her.

But the look on her face told me I'd already lost her.

"Emma, I can explain—"

Almost immediately she cuts me off. "Explain, what?" She spread her arms out. "That you lied to me? That you used me? Did you laugh at me behind my back? Did you even care about me at *all*?" Her voice cracks and with it the first fissure in my heart appears.

"Emma," I stood up, and my stool fell to the ground behind me, "I love you. Stop this."

*I have to fix this.*

"Stop what? Stop telling the truth? You lied to me, Maddox!" Tears clog her eyes and my throat feels heavy. *I've ruined everything.* "I have never felt so betrayed in all my life, not even the day my dad walked out on us and didn't even say goodbye."

It would've hurt more if she'd slapped me. "I never meant to hurt you," I whispered.

*Can't she see that? I wanted something real. Something not impeded by my band's fast growing fame. I wanted to hold on to my freedom for a moment longer. It was a breath of fresh air to fall in love with someone I knew didn't want me for my money. She just wanted me.*

"But you did hurt me!" She screamed and her face grew red. "Even if this was some stupid game to you, you still owed me the truth!" *A game? She thinks this was a* game? *She couldn't be more wrong.* I finally managed to get my feet moving and I moved toward her. I stopped in front of her and she shoved the magazine she held into my chest. I hold it, but I don't look at it. I already know it's bound to be the culprit of how she found out. "*This* is not how I deserved to find out." Her voice quieted from her previous shouting and her shoulders sagged with defeat. She looked sad. So fucking sad and I hated myself for putting that look on her face. "I'm a human being, I have feelings, and seeing the truth laid out to me in a magazine isn't fair." She choked on a breath, and it took all of my willpower not to reach out and take her into my arms. I would have, but I knew she'd only shove me away.

I cleared my throat. "Guys, can you give us a minute?" I hated how shaky my voice sounded, but I couldn't help it.

They mumbled a few words and reluctantly headed upstairs.

The words I wanted to say, *needed* to say, tumbled over in my mind but I couldn't seem to voice any of them. We stared at each other with only a few feet between us, but it felt like a whole ocean.

"I never tried to play you."

*Good going dumbass, you couldn't have said anything better than that?*

"Then what do you call this?" She spread her arms out wide. "This whole thing between us is a lie."

I winced. It felt like she'd slammed a knife straight into my heart and turned the blade. *A lie?* How could she possibly think this was a lie? Especially after last night?

"God, Emma," I growled, the hurt I felt seeping into my words, "it wasn't like that."

"Then tell me what it was like!" She yelled, poking her finger into my chest.

I clenched my teeth and then words came tumbling out of my mouth.

"I wanted something for myself, okay? Because I'm a selfish fucking prick. The last year has been insane as our band has grown in popularity. *Everyone* wants something from us. And I was sick and tired of feeling used." I felt tears pooling in my eyes and I hoped she could see them—so she would know how much this was killing me. "And then I met you and you didn't know who I was and…I felt like me again. I wasn't Maddox Wade the drummer from Willow Creek—I was just Maddox. I *craved* that."

"So, what? You only liked me because I didn't know who you were?" She looked sickened by her own words—no, tortured.

"No!" The word ripped out of my mouth immediately and I

clutched at the short strands of my hair. I felt panicked. I didn't see how I was ever going to make her understand. Any way I tried to explain I looked like a bad guy. Maybe I was. But I'd never intended for it to be that way. "You're making this sound so much worse than it is!"

"*I'm* making this worse than what it is?" She seemed shocked that I'd suggest such a thing. "*You're* the one that hid your identity from me. I don't even know you!"

*She doesn't even know me? She's one of the only people that truly knows me.*

"Yes, you do." I said *fuck it* and took several steps to close the distance between us. I took her face between my hands and before I could even relish in the feel of her soft skin and warm cheeks she flinched. *Flinched*. Like I'd hurt her. My hands fell to my sides and my heart broke a tiny bit more. "You know me better than anyone, Em." I tried to plead with her. "I've shared things with you that most people don't know about me. I know you don't believe it right now, but you are special to me, and I love you. That isn't a lie."

"Then why couldn't you tell me the truth? Did you think it would matter that much to me? Did you think I'd try to use you?" She rambled, completely flummoxed.

"No!" I cried and my hands flew into the air. "Jesus Christ, that's not what I thought at all! I tried to tell you so many times, I really did, I swear. But I never could. I just…the words would never come out right and…" I paused and inhaled a breath, trying to gather my racing thoughts. "I was scared," I confessed. She started to speak, but I cut her off. I needed to get these words out. "I was scared to death that if you knew who I really was that my fame might push you away, and the last thing I want to do is live a life without you in it." Sincerity poured out of every word I spoke, but when her face crumpled I knew it'd done no good.

Tears fell down her face in a river.

"Congratulations, Maddox," she sneered the words, looking at me like I was the most despicable thing she'd ever laid her eyes on, "now you'll get to find out what your life is like without me."

She turned, her hair whipping over her shoulder, and started for the door.

"Emma!" I yelled after her. "Please, stop!"

By some miracle she did, and I allowed myself to feel the tiniest bit of relief.

She turned slowly to look at me over her shoulder. My hands clenched into fists at my sides while I warred with whether or not to stay where I was or go to her. I decided to stay where I was, afraid of making her run away.

I finally found the strength to speak, but my voice was barely a whisper. "Loving you is my greatest adventure. Nothing else means anything without you."

Shutters came down over her eyes and I felt the last refuges of hope leave me.

"Then I guess you can live a life full of emptiness."

"Emma!" I started after her.

"Don't follow me!" She yelled, so full of anger. You have no right to follow me! Just leave me alone! You've done enough damage! …If you follow me I'll kidnap your hedgehog!"

If this situation wasn't so serious I might've laughed at that last bit.

But I was too hurt and upset to find anything funny at the moment. "*Emma.*" My voice cracked. "Don't do this."

My body gave out then and I fell to my knees.

Begging.

Pleading.

*Please stay.*

*Don't leave me.*

*I love you.*

"Too late." She opened the door and left.

As it swung shut I yelled her name one last time. "Emma!"

The guys came rushing down the stairs just as I stood and Ezra and Hayes grabbed me when I started to run after her.

"Don't do it," Ezra said, shaking me when I tried to wiggle out of their hold on me, "she's upset, within reason, give her a chance to cool off. You owe it to her."

"You really fucked this up," Hayes added.

Mathias watched me with narrowed eyes from the corner of the room with his arms crossed over his chest. I kept waiting for him to say some smart-ass comment, but he didn't. He was very obviously thinking about something, though.

"I know," I finally said. "*I know.*"

What I didn't know was how I could ever make this right—was there even a way?

# BONUS CONTENT

## MADDOX AND EMMA
### # TWO
#### VALENTINE'S DAY SCENE
##### ORIGINALY WRITTEN FOR THE BLOG PRISONER'S OF PRINT

EMMA

I gazed out the two-story window at the L.A. skyline. Every day I woke up here it never ceased to amaze me that I was living here, with the guy of my dreams, writing songs for a living. How did I get so lucky?

He stepped up behind me, wrapping his arms around my body and pulling me against his solid chest. He nuzzled his head into the crook of my neck and kissed the tender skin behind my ear, making me giggle.

"Happy Valentine's Day," he murmured.

I smiled. Last year we didn't get to spend Valentine's together since he was here in L.A. and I was still in school. "Happy Valentine's Day, Maddox."

"I have big plans for today." He nipped my shoulder and pulled away, sauntering over to the kitchen.

"I told you I didn't want to do anything," I warned him.

"I think you'll enjoy this," he grinned. He opened the refrigerator and grabbed the bottle of orange juice. "Go get dressed and then we'll go."

I sighed. I knew there was no point in arguing with Maddox. He always got his way.

***

"I can't believe you blindfolded me," I growled, sitting back against the plush leather seat of the car.

He clucked his tongue. "I don't want to ruin the surprise."

Maddox and his surprises.

A moment later I smiled when a Willow Creek song came on the radio.

I used to only listen to classical music, but dating a famous drummer had expanded my palate when it came to music. I was extremely proud of him and the other guys, for living their dreams and doing what they loved. I knew the fame weighed heavily on their shoulders—it had been completely unexpected for them. But that made me love all of them that much more, because they were so incredibly humble. They were in it for the music, nothing else.

The car lurched to a stop and my body jolted forward.

"Geez, Maddox, give a girl some warning." I rubbed my chest, sure that I was going to have a seatbelt shaped bruise later.

He merely chuckled, said he was sorry, and got out of the car.

I began to panic.

He wasn't going to leave me in here by myself, was he?

Just when I was ready to freak out, the door on my side opened and a cool breeze swam inside the car. I felt him reach over my body to undo the belt, and then he grabbed my arm, helping me out.

I wrapped my arms around his side and held on tight.

The last thing I wanted to do was trip and fall on my face.

"Can I take this off now?" I asked, reaching up with one hand for the blindfold.

"No." He took my hand, wrapping my arm back around his body.

I sighed, letting him guide me around.

"Hold on," he said a few minutes later. He pried my arms off of his chest and kissed the side of my forehead.

His body heat disappeared.

"Maddox?"

I heard a door open.

"Maddox?" I asked again. "I'm going to take the blindfold off!" I warned.

"So dramatic," he sighed, reappearing at my side. "I had to prop the door open."

"I was scared you were going to leave me here," I mumbled, letting him help me into the building.

"That doesn't sound like a very fun Valentine's Day," he chuckled warmly, "and I'm pretty sure you'd kick my ass if I did that."

"You're right," I nodded.

A few minutes passed and I couldn't figure out where he'd brought me. Nothing felt familiar.

"Alright, you're going to sit down now." He helped me down and my butt landed on a plush pillow. "Keep the blindfold on," he warned.

I wanted to roll my eyes, but it would've been pointless since he couldn't even see my irritation.

"*Now* you can take it off."

I ripped that sucker off and looked around in awe. "Maddox," I gasped.

We were sitting in the center of a large stage, to my left were the seats, and to my right instruments were set up—the drum set boasting the Willow Creek logo on the front.

"I don't understand," I whispered, my eyes now zeroing in on what was in front of me. Pillows and blankets were laid around, and little tea lights had been lit. I could see a bag sitting beside him, and figured he'd packed us a lunch.

He smiled crookedly. "You know how I told you we had a concert coming up in L.A.?"

I nodded, waiting for him to get to the point.

"They've agreed to let us sing our song," he grinned triumphantly.

"Seriously?" My jaw unhinged. Not too long ago I'd been terrified to sing in front of ten people, but since I started songwriting with Maddox fulltime I'd gotten over that fear. It also probably helped that they played our duet on the radio quite a bit. Once you hear yourself singing on the radio, singing in front of people doesn't seem so bad anymore since millions of people have already heard it.

"Seriously," he nodded.

"But Mathias is the singer." I still couldn't believe what he was telling me.

Mathias—his twin brother—was the lead singer of Willow Creek, so the record label had been hesitant to include Maddox's and my song on the soundtrack, but they finally relented and now it was a hit.

"And he can step out of the spotlight for three minutes for us to sing our song." He cupped my cheek, his fingers tangling in my messy hair.

"I can't believe this," I breathed. "Is this real life?"

He pulled me into his arms and I straddled his waist. He pressed his lips softly to mine. "Was *that* real?"

I nodded, wrapping my arms around his neck. "This was the best surprise ever...although I was really hoping we were going to jump out of a plane again."

He threw his head back and laughed a deep, throaty laugh. "My little adrenaline junkie," he murmured.

And then he sealed his lips over mine, and we made that stage ours.

# BONUS CONTENT

## MATHIAS AND REMY

### # ONE
### VISITING HOPE'S GRAVE

MATHIAS

I was so fucking jittery that Remy reached over and placed her hand on my knee, forcing me to keep still. I felt like I was about to crawl out of my damn skin. I'd never been the nervous type, but right now I felt like I was about to blow chunks.

I gazed out the round plane window at the rapidly changing landscape. Green grass gave way for desert sands.

Arizona.

The place Remy had ended up after she moved in high school.

The place where she'd lost our daughter.

Fucking hell, even months later it made me sick to think of her going through that by herself. At first, I wanted to be mad at her for keeping my daughter a secret from me, but after I thought it through I understood why she did it. If the situation was reversed I would've done the same thing. Secrets suck, but sometimes you have to keep them to protect the ones you love.

"Are you this nervous because my parents are meeting us at

the airport?" There was a teasing glint in her eyes.

I glanced at her small bump—a complete surprise, but a blessing nonetheless—and the ring on her finger. "Your parents are the least of my problems."

She laughed and I watched the way her neck arched and her white-blonde hair fell around her like a silky curtain.

My wife was fucking hot.

"Then what has you so upset?" She asked once she'd recovered. My teeth snapped together and I glared out the window. "*Mathias*," she prompted.

My lip furrowed. "I'm scared," I admitted. "I'm scared to see her grave," I whispered so softly I was surprised she could hear me.

"Don't be scared." She took my hand. "It'll be okay. This is hard for me too, you know? I've only been there twice...the first time to bury her, and then again on what would've been her first birthday. I feel horrible that I never went back, but I couldn't," tears shimmered in her eyes, "it's too painful. But we'll be there together this time. We're not alone."

I nodded at her words. *Not alone.*

I took a deep breath. I could do this.

Much too soon our plane touched down at the airport. We only had carry-on luggage since we weren't staying long, and I set down both of our bags from the overhead compartment. I took Remy's hand in mine and we each wheeled our bags.

Out in the terminal two bodyguards met us and Remy turned

on her phone to check her messages. "They're here, but I need to stop at a bathroom first. If I don't pee soon…" She let me fill in the gaps.

I scanned the signs. "Restrooms that way." I guided her in that direction. She cried out in relief when we reached the entrance and left me with the bags.

The guards formed a flank around me, and I wore a baseball cap low over my eyes to hide my face, but neither detracted from the curious glances.

It didn't take long for the whispers to spread and the cameras to come out.

Was this how fucking zoo animals felt?

I could almost deal with this better if people would actually speak to me, instead they acted like I was dangerous and they couldn't get too close.

When Remy emerged from the bathroom I couldn't get out of their fast enough.

And that was why I preferred to use the band's private plane. You could usually avoid all this shit.

The guards kept the growing crowd at bay as we headed for the exit. I kept a close hold on Remy, afraid of her or the baby getting hurt.

When we stepped out into the sunshine I allowed myself to inhale the tiniest bit of relief.

It was short-lived, though, when I noticed Remy's parent's

and brother waiting outside a Ford SUV.

"Oh, great," I muttered, "your brother's here too. A whole fucking family reunion. Fantastic."

"Be nice." Remy smacked my chest.

"I will be if they're nice. Otherwise, no promises."

She rolled her eyes. "You're all impossible."

We finally reached them and stopped across from them.

No one said anything, but around us the crowd grew louder and people called out my name. Remy's too.

"Hey mom, dad, Robert." She waved awkwardly. Remy hadn't always been on the best of terms with her family, and I knew even though she wasn't really showing it she was even more scared than me.

"Remy," her mom was the first to break their silence, "I missed you." She stepped forward to hug Remy and then me. It was awkward as fuck but I'd give her credit for trying.

Meanwhile, Remy's dad and brother looked at me like they wanted to flay me alive.

*Be the bigger man, Mathias*, I told myself.

"Nice to see you guys." I held out my hand. Her father and brother looked at my hand like it was the grossest thing they'd ever seen. "Tough crowd," I muttered, and stuck my hands in my pockets.

Remy sighed beside. "Dad, Robert, be nice. Mathias is my husband, and that's not changing."

Her father's lips curled in distaste. The feeling was mutual but I was able to mask my revulsion to him.

"Shall we go then?" Her mom asked, trying to break the tension.

Without saying a word Remy's dad turned and headed for the driver's side. He didn't even say anything to *her*.

I started after him, about to tell him what a prick he was and he needed to pull the lead pipe up his ass out, but Remy gripped my arm and held on.

"No, don't do it. He isn't worth it. Let it go."

"No one should disrespect you like that," I spat through my teeth. "I can handle people treating me like shit, but not you."

"I'm okay, Mathias. I'm a big girl," she said in a calming voice.

I let out a breath. "Fine. Just get in the car. I promise not to do anything stupid."

I loaded our bags into the car and climbed inside. Of course fucking Robert had taken the window seat and I wasn't about to force my pregnant wife into the middle, so I took the seat between. Nice and cozy beside Robert.

"Hi." I grinned at him—although I'm sure I looked more like a shark showing my teeth.

He huffed and looked out the window.

Remy took my hand and gave me a look that said I needed to watch it. I knew this was her family and she wanted us to get along, even if they hadn't always been the best to *her*, but this was fucking hard. I hated willingly surrounding myself with a bunch of pricks, even if they were my wife's family.

The drive to her parents place was the worst thirty minutes of my life—and *that* was saying something.

"We should've rented our own fucking car," I told Remy as soon as we were out of earshot of her family and safely hidden in the guestroom.

"Stop cussing around the baby," she scolded, pointing at her stomach. "We'll be fine. It's only a few days."

I scrubbed my hands roughly down over my face. It would not be fucking fine. I was going to strangle her brother and her father. Her mother was okay, for the moment.

"They're going to expect us back downstairs for dinner," she warned, "so pull yourself together."

"I am together," I grumbled, "just trying to tell myself all the reasons murder is wrong."

Her fist connected lightly with my stomach. "*Stop it.*" She sat down on the bed and tucked her hair behind her ears. "You know this is hard for me too, but it's the right thing to do."

"I'm not saying we should've flown to Arizona and not seen them, but I am saying we could've stayed in a hotel." I held up my hands innocently. "It would've saved us a lot of headache."

She frowned. "True, but I think we need to face this head on."

"If I punch your brother during dinner, don't say I didn't warn you." I pointed a finger at her. "The dude keeps giving me this weird look and it's freaking me the fuck out."

"*Mathias*," she hissed, pointing at her stomach again. "The *baby*."

I slapped a hand over my mouth and then let it fall. "Just admit it, Rem, the baby's first word will not be *mom* or *dad*. It's going to be *fuck*, because I *fucking* love saying the word *fuck*."

She breathed out a heavy breath. "Should we just go ahead and name the kid Fuck Wade?"

My lips twitched with the threat of a smile. "Come on, Rem, we don't want him or her to get made fun of."

She rolled her eyes, but I could tell she was trying not to smile.

I took a moment to look around the room. Bland beige walls, dark wood furniture, and pastel yellow bedspread.

"Something tells me this is *not* how your room looked when you lived here."

She smiled. "What tipped you off?"

"It's too boring for you."

Her smile grew into a grin.

"Dinner!" Her mom called.

I closed my eyes. I wasn't ready for this.

The bed squeaked as Remy stood and I opened my eyes to find her standing in front of me. She placed her hands on my cheeks and looked into my eyes.

"We're doing this for Hope," she whispered, "nothing else matters."

*Hope.* My daughter. The daughter that never even took her first breath. The daughter I didn't get the chance to hold.

I nodded. "For Hope," I echoed.

She kissed me, and I tried to deepen the kiss, but she pulled back and shook her head at me. "Nice try, Wade."

I grinned. "You'll let me into your pants later, Mrs. *Wade.*"

She winked. "Only if you're a good boy."

The woman was trying to bargain with sex and dammit if it wasn't working.

I followed her out of the room and down the steps. Her parents and brother were already seated at the dining room table. Remy and I took the last two empty seats on the end.

"This looks delicious," I commented, nodding my head at Remy's mom.

"Thank you, Mathias." She smiled back. It wasn't a big smile, but I'd take it.

We grew quiet as we all piled food on our plates, but I knew the reprieve wouldn't last for long.

Remy's dad shoved a forkful of food in his mouth, chewed and swallowed, and then gave me a death glare. "So, *Mathias,*" he said my name like it left a sour taste in his mouth, "you're in a band...how *interesting.*" I knew interesting was the last thing he thought of it.

"Yes, I'm in a band," I nodded, "a highly successful band. One in which I've traveled the world, had our music featured on TV shows, and even won a Grammy."

His upper lip curled. "Regardless, you weren't good enough for my daughter as a teenager and you aren't good enough now."

My fists clenched beneath the table and the muscle in my jaw ticked.

"*Dad*," Remy scolded, "you can't talk to him like that."

Her dad swung his glare to her. "It's my house, I can talk to him any way I want."

"He's also my *husband*," she countered, "and you *will* respect that, or we'll leave."

"Then leave," he said simply.

Remy's mom paled. "He doesn't mean that, honey," she said to Remy.

Remy stood and threw her napkin down on the plate. "Yeah, yeah he does. Come on, Mathias, we're leaving."

"Rem?" I said hesitantly. I wanted to leave as much her, but this was her family.

"*We're leaving*," she repeated through clenched teeth and stormed out of the room.

I cleared my throat and looked at the three people sitting at the table. "Well, um, it was nice seeing you."

And then I got the hell out of dodge. No way was I willingly staying around her psycho father. I didn't think the man would *ever* accept me. He'd wanted Remy to end up with some rich stuck up prep school type boy, and I was definitely not that. Rich? Yes. But none of the other.

Remy had already called for a cab by the time I met her upstairs.

"Are you sure you want to leave?" I asked, standing in the doorway to the room.

She wheeled her bag over to the door. "Yes, absolutely. I should've listened to you from the beginning and we should've stayed at a hotel and *maybe* had dinner with them or something— but look how that turned out." She laughed humorlessly. She tore at her hair. "I can't believe I let my mom talk me into this. She said dad would be fine, and why the *fuck* is Robert here?" She seethed.

"Baby," I mouthed and nodded at her stomach.

"Fuck," she cursed again. She slapped a hand over her mouth. "Do you see what these people do to me?"

I could see her becoming distressed, so I reached out and wrapped her in my arms. "Shh, it's okay," I soothed.

She blubbered into my shirt, "Why do I keep hoping it'll be different?"

"Because they're your family and you love them despite themselves."

She sniffled. "Why are you so smart?"

I snorted. "I'm far from smart, Rem," I took her face in my

hands, "it's just the truth."

She nodded and wiped at her eyes. "Let's get out of here. This kind of stress isn't good for the baby."

Her words spurned me into action and I grabbed up our bags.

We didn't linger another minute.

We waited out on the front porch for the cab, and before it could arrive the door opened behind us and Remy's mother appeared, easing the door closed behind her.

"I want you both to know I'm sorry about this. I know I haven't always been the nicest to you," she addressed me, "but I've accepted that the two of you are pretty perfect for each other. I wish your father and brother could see that." She turned to Remy. "I'd love to have lunch with you guys before you leave. Just me," she added hastily.

Remy looked to me for approval—it was unusual for her to defer to me since she was such a ball-buster, but after this disaster I guessed she felt she owed me.

I nodded. "Yeah, sounds good."

"Great." Her mom smiled. "Remy, you can text me and let me know when and where to meet you guys."

Remy nodded and hugged her mom, and then—because what the hell—I hugged her too.

Her mom slipped back inside with one last apologetic smile.

Thankfully, before anyone else could appear, the cab arrived.

I loaded our suitcases in and instructed the driver to the nearest town. While he drove I googled nearby hotels, and when I found the nicest I called to make a reservation. They weren't very accommodating until I dropped my name. Figured.

We arrived at the hotel and I tipped the driver before leading Remy inside.

We checked in and headed up to our suite on the top floor.

Once inside Remy sunk down on the couch and let out a groan. "I feel like I could sleep for days."

"What happened to the sexy times you promised me?" I jested.

She gave me the finger and I grinned.

I *loved* riling her up.

I moved into the small kitchen and opened the refrigerator. It was freshly stocked with water and beer. I grabbed two water bottles—one for each of us—since beer wasn't my thing and Remy obviously couldn't drink.

I sat down and placed her feet in my lap before handing her the bottle of water.

She took a greedy sip and I set mine on the coffee table. I pulled her shoes off and dropped them on the floor, then massaged the soles of her feet with my thumb.

She let out a moan. "That feels good."

"You know what would feel better?" I waggled my brows.

She threw a pillow at me.

"A pillow fight?" I questioned. "That could be interesting, but not what I had in mind."

She shook her head. "You're incorrigible."

"I have the hots for my wife, is that such a bad thing?"

She smiled at me. "No, but your pregnant wife is exhausted after dealing with her psychotic family."

I nodded. "Thank God you're not crazy. I mean, you are, but not *that* crazy."

She laughed and rubbed her hand over her stomach. "Thanks."

I winked. "Why don't I run you a hot bath and order room service since we didn't get to really eat?"

Her pale blue eyes twinkled—God, I hoped our baby had Remy's eyes, they were so unique and always full of mischief. "Mathias Wade, big bad rock star, you're going to make me a bubble bath?"

I puffed out my chest. "Yes."

She grinned and then sobered. "That sounds wonderful."

I smiled. I loved making my wife happy.

A lot of people didn't see me as the dotting husband, but when it came to Remy I'd do anything for that woman.

I lifted her feet off my lap and made my way into the spacious bedroom.

The bathroom was attached, and pretty big as well. A large white porcelain tub sat in the middle of the space in front of a tinted window. It had one of those little tray things across it, and on it sat a bottle of soap, shampoo and conditioner, bubble bath, and bath salts. *Perfect.*

I made sure the water was warm, not hot, and added the bubble bath and salts. The room immediately smelled like a spa.

When the tub was full I turned off the water and went to get Remy. She was half-asleep on the couch and looked cute as hell.

I touched her cheek and she jolted awake, blinking up at me with wide eyes.

"Your bath is ready."

She yawned and nodded.

I helped her up and led her into the bathroom. Her large smile when she saw the bathtub made my whole fucking day.

As much as I wanted to stay and watch her get naked, and join her in the bath, I knew that would only lead to sex and this wasn't about that. I wanted her to relax.

I closed the bathroom door and found the room service menu. I ordered a bit of this and that, since we hadn't discussed anything, and settled onto the couch to watch TV while I waited.

Unfortunately, the quiet time let my mind wander too much and all I could think about was tomorrow and seeing Hope's grave. I knew I needed to go there—Remy too—to heal, but it was going to be so fucking hard.

I rubbed a hand over my face.

I hoped I didn't have a complete and utter breakdown.

Up until now, I had never really let myself accept the fact that I had a daughter.

I mean, I knew she existed if even for only the briefest moment, but I'd never seen her. Or held her. I didn't know what she looked like—although, I'd asked Remy often enough that I should have a good mental picture, but it wasn't the same as seeing her with my own two eyes.

Every time I thought of Remy in that hospital finding out that Hope was stillborn I felt a piece of my heart break. I didn't know how Remy had coped. She said that things were bad for a while, but my gut told me she wasn't letting on just how bad it was.

The doorbell for the suite rang and I hopped up to grab the room service. I tipped the guy and laid the food out on the table myself. I didn't want the guy to linger in case Remy appeared in a towel—or worse, naked.

"Rem, the food is here!" I called.

A few minutes later she joined me.

I wanted to voice my worries about tomorrow to her, but she'd heard them enough. There was nothing left that she could say to me.

We ate quickly—both of us starved—and ended up crashing in bed afterwards.

My sleep was fitful and restless, and by the time I woke up in the morning I felt like I hadn't slept at all.

Remy and I went about our morning as usual. Showering. Getting dressed. Eating breakfast.

And then…and then it was time to go.

I stood by the door of the suite, waiting for Remy to be ready. I was jumpy and nervous. A stranger might think I was on drugs with how twitchy and sweaty I was. It felt like the collar of my shirt was trying to suffocate me. I needed fresh air.

"Ready!" Remy chimed a moment before I was about to run out of the room and all the way out of the hotel.

A cab was waiting for us outside and we slipped inside.

Remy gave the address for the cemetery and I rubbed my sweaty palms on my jeans.

I wasn't ready.

"I can't do this," I told her in a desperate whisper. "I'm going to be sick."

She took my hand. "You *can* do this and you're *not* going to be sick. You need this. We *both* need this."

I nodded. She was right. I inhaled a shaky breath. I'd never felt this close to losing my mind before.

The ride to the cemetery felt never-ending, but short at the same time. It was hard to explain.

When the cab stopped I handed the guy a wad of cash and muttered, "Wait here."

He nodded eagerly—happy to accommodate thanks to the extra money.

I slid out of the car and held my hand out to Remy. She took it and I helped her from the car.

Both of us were quiet as we stepped through the wrought iron archway that led into the cemetery. The grass was surprisingly green, so green in fact that I wondered if it had been spray-painted.

The whole place had this eerie quietness to it—like it existed in a separate plane from the real world.

We wandered past grave after grave. I'd never contemplated how many dead people there were before, but now I wondered.

"It's this way," Remy's hold on my hand tightened as we veered off the pathway and into the too perfect grass. I wondered if her heart was racing as fast as mine. I felt like the organ was about to fall out of my chest and roll around on the ground.

It was a hot summer day, and the sun beat down on us. It seemed unfair that the sky was so happy when I was so shaken.

"It's this one," she said as she stopped.

Maybe it was some weird as fuck sixth sense, but somehow I'd already known it was hers before we even got there. Like some cosmic force was pulling me to this spot—maybe my daughter had been leading me here. It could have been her way of saying, "Hi, Daddy."

My throat closed up and my hand slipped from Remy's. I dropped to my knees, a shaky breath passing through my lips, and ran the tips of my fingers of the indented letters that formed her name.

**Hope Wade**

A splash of water hit the stone, and for a second I stupidly thought it had started to rain, but then I realized that it came from *me*. I was *crying*.

My whole body began to tremble with the force of my tears. I'd never let this kind of emotion loose before. It was dangerous.

I felt Remy's hand press softly against my shoulder—her way of reminding me that she was there.

I swallowed thickly gazing at the stone. "It never really seemed real before," I confessed softly. I lifted my head to Remy and she stroked her fingers over my cheek and then my lips.

"I wish it wasn't," she murmured.

My head dropped back down to the grave.

I wet my lips with my tongue and opened my mouth. The soft notes of a lullaby filled the air. This was the only chance I had to sing to my baby girl. I wanted her to know that even though she was gone, and I never met her, it didn't change the love I felt for her. The love of a parent for their child is eternal.

When I finished the song I touched my fingers to the cool stone of her grave one last time and whispered, "Daddy loves you." *So fucking much.*

I stood and hastily wiped the tears away on the back of my hands. "How did two fuck-ups like us get lucky enough to have a second chance?" I asked her, and rested my hands on her bump. I couldn't wait to feel the baby kick.

"I don't know. I guess maybe it was fate." She smiled up at me, her eyes glossy with unshed tears as I stroked her stomach.

"Or maybe," I kissed her forehead, cheeks, and her lips,  "it was Hope."

# BONUS CONTENT
## EZRA AND SADIE
### # ONE

She went on a date with Hayes.

*Hayes.*

Of all people why the *fuck* would she go on a date with him.

I knew it wasn't fair for me to be pissed off. Sadie wasn't mine. I'd made it abundantly clear that I didn't want a relationship with her. She was my best friend, and losing her because of the prick of a fiancé she had, sucked enough. I couldn't lose her because we fooled around and it didn't work out. I *needed* her in my life, and to keep her there we had to keep things strictly platonic.

But why did that have to suck so bad?

She'd been gone an hour already and in that time had I done anything productive?

Hell no.

I'd paced the floors like a mad man and when I got sick of that I mowed the front yard—exciting times here for Ezra Collins.

I was pacing again now. I was probably close to wearing a hole in my floors, which wouldn't be half bad since repairing it would give me something to do.

I sat down on the couch, and tried to stay there, but a minute later I was up and pacing again.

*When is she going to be back?*

I shoved my fingers through my unruly hair and let out a loud groan.

This was torture.

And I was fucking pathetic pining for a girl I refused to let myself have.

What was wrong with me?

My hands grew jittery which only added to my irritation. I acted like a juiced up meathead.

"Snap out of it, Ezra," I scolded myself.

Great, now I was talking to myself. Even better.

Time seemed to move at a snail's pace and when I heard Hayes' truck pull into the drive I ran to the window and damn near pressed my whole face against it.

I watched as Hayes said something to her and laughed.

She laughed too at whatever he said, which only made my blood boil even more. I was about to go into Hulk mode and smash some shit.

Hayes nodded and said something else, then leaned over and kissed her cheek.

Kissed. Her. Cheek.

I saw fucking red.

I stormed away from the window and down the hall.

I needed to get a grip. Sadie had the right to go on dates with whomever she wanted to. It was none of my business. I was only her friend.

*Just her friend.*

*Just her friend.*

*Just.*

*Her.*

*Friend.*

If I said it enough it would eventually *mean* something more to me, right?

The door opened and I turned to see her back to me as she closed it.

Something in me snapped and it was like I was having an out of body experience.

I stormed forward and when she turned around I was *right there.*

She jumped and her hand flew to her heart. "You have got to stop sneaking up on me like that."

"Sadie?" I swallowed past the lump in my throat. I had no idea what I was going to say, my brain was filled with too many words to begin picking them apart and forming sentences.

"What?" She looked at me curiously. Sadie had always read me well and she probably wondered what had me so frazzled.

I couldn't stand it a second longer. "Fuck it," I cried, throwing my hands in the air.

I closed the space between us in seconds and cupped the back of her neck as I pushed her back into the wall.

And then I kissed her.

I.

Kissed.

Her.

I'd thought about kissing her so many times—too many times—but I'd sworn to myself I'd never act on it. Apparently I wasn't very good at following my own rules.

My lips were rough against hers. I should've probably been more gentle, but in the back of my mind I knew this would be the first and last time I ever did this and I wanted to make it count. Her mouth opened beneath mine, and she let out the tiniest fucking whimper I'd ever heard and it only spurned me on more. Her hands wandered over my chest and I grabbed them, pinning them above her head. I used my hips to pin her in place and I hoped to God she didn't feel the hard-on I was sporting—but who the hell was I kidding, she *had* to.

I angled my lips down over hers, claiming what wasn't mine to take.

I'd had plenty of kisses over the years. Sweet kisses. Passionate kisses. Every kiss in between. But none of them compared to this. I didn't know what made it different.

No, I did know.

*Sadie.*

Her fingers twitched in my grasp, desperate to touch me, but I wouldn't let her. I was afraid of what would happen if her hands were left to wander—of how far I might let this go.

"Finally," I murmured, pulling her bottom lip between my teeth and letting it go.

She let out the breathiest fucking moan and her hips bucked against mine.

She wanted this as bad as me.

I chuckled at her eagerness and deepened the kiss again. I needed to feel her mouth against mine as long as possible. My brain grew foggy from the heat we were generating. I didn't feel in control of myself. My tongue stroked against hers one last time and then I retreated before we could go up in flames. I let go of her hands and they fell to my shoulders. Her browns eyes were dazed and she sported a goofy smile.

My hand shook as I reached up to touch her cheek reverently. "I've wanted to do that for so long. You have no idea," I confessed. I silently cursed myself. I should've kept that to myself, but it seemed our kiss had sent all reasonable thought out the window.

"Why now?" She whispered, leaning into my touch.

Anger took over again.

"Because," I ground out, "seeing you with Hayes…" I looked away from her, trying to talk myself off of this very dangerous ledge. "It was even worse than seeing you with Braden. At least I had a legitimate reason to hate him, but Hayes? I couldn't hate that guy if I tried, and that made it a thousand times worse."

"What do we do now?" She asked with a small smile and wonder in her eyes.

Shutters came down over my own eyes. This was why I'd never kissed her before. I knew it would come with expectations—ones I couldn't fulfill. I couldn't ruin our friendship. I didn't want to lose the best thing I had in my life.

"It was only a kiss," I muttered roughly, and tried to pull away but her arms only tightened around my neck, refusing to let me get away that easily.

"No, don't you dare say that." Hurt shimmered in her eyes.

"Sadie—"

"Please, stop," she leaned her head against my chest, and I heard her sniffle, "please don't take it back."

I closed my eyes, warring within myself. I was damned if I did, damned if I didn't. "I wasn't going to," I whispered, stroking my fingers through her soft wavy hair.

I swallowed thickly. I'd never felt so torn up inside before. Torn between what I wanted and what was right.

"Why won't you let this—let *us* happen?" She peered up at me as she asked the question.

"You're my best friend. What if things didn't work out between us? I can't lose you."

I'd already lost her once to her dipshit of a fiancé and it had fucking *hurt* not having her in my life all those months. I'd never known it was possible to miss someone as much as I missed her.

She bristled with anger. "And I'm not worth the risk," she stated. Her lips pursed and she let out a humorless laugh. Shaking her head, she stepped around me and stormed upstairs.

I watched her go. I didn't know what to say, or do, to make this better. I couldn't risk our friendship. *I wouldn't.*

HAYES

I watched her across the dance floor like a complete and utter stalker.

I'd been with lots of woman—not tooting my own horn or anything, but it was true—and none of them had ever lingered in my mind the way Arden did and I'd only *kissed* her. One measly kiss at that while the whole group of us were on vacation. There was something different about her. *Special.*

She picked up a flute of champagne and breezed over to an empty table. Kicking off her shoes she rubbed at her feet before resting them on a chair.

A hand clamped down on my shoulder and I'm sorry to admit that I actually jumped in surprise.

"Are you gonna look all night or make a move?"

I looked over at my band mate, and friend, Mathias.

"I don't know what you're talking about." I played dumb.

He smirked and raised a single brow. "Your little crush on the redhead is blatantly obvious."

"It is?" Fuck. I practically admitted to it.

He chuckled and stuffed his hands in his pockets. "Oh yeah. We've all been taking bets."

"You have?" I glared at him.

He nodded, looking out at the dance floor. "You bet. We're all happily settled down. It's your turn."

I swallowed past the lump in my throat and my gaze fell to the gorgeous redhead once more. She wore a pale purple bridesmaid dress and it only accentuated the creaminess of her pale skin. Even from across the yard I could see the smattering of freckles across her nose and shoulders.

"You're wasting time, man," Mathias warned, "get to it. The night will be over before you know it."

He walked off then, leaving me to my own musings.

The normal me would be all over Arden in three seconds flat, because I'm a shameless flirt. But Arden was different. She was sweet, beautiful, *normal*. But she was also a single mom, and I knew that made her wary of men. I also argued with myself, that just because she was a mom it didn't mean she couldn't have some fun.

"Fuck it," I muttered, and strode over to her table. I pulled out the empty chair beside her and sat down. I hadn't had any interaction with her since I escorted her down the aisle since we were paired up.

She looked up when I plopped down and raised a brow. "Hayes, can I help you?"

"You looked lonely."

"Well, I'm not." She raised her glass of champagne to her lips.

"*I* was lonely," I amended.

She laughed. "I doubt that."

I shrugged and tapped my fingers on the tabletop. "Think what you want."

She pursed her lips but said no more. We both grew silent—for once I was at a loss for words. I loved and hated how this woman managed to steal them from me. I shifted in my seat and loosened my tie before undoing the top two buttons on my white dress shirt. When I looked over I saw that Arden was staring at the small amount of chest that had been revealed.

My lips lifted in a crooked smile. "Like what you see?"

She jumped and spilled her champagne on the table. "Oh my God," she muttered, her cheeks turning red as she hastened to clean up the mess.

"Leave it," I put my hand over hers to still it, "someone will be by to clean it up."

Whiskey colored eyes framed by the darkest lashes flashed up to mine. "Do you always have someone to clean up your messes?"

I flashed her an amused smile. "One, it's not *my* mess. Two, it's a wedding there are other people that's job it is to clean up."

If it was possible her cheeks reddened even more.

"Dance with me." I didn't know what made me say the words, but I was suddenly desperate to find any excuse to have her in my arms and dancing seemed to be the best option.

"No." She turned away from me and crossed her arms over her chest, which only served to push up her tits. I'm a guy, so I ogled them shamelessly.

"Dance with me," I said again.

She huffed and glared up at me. "You're awfully persistent."

"It's just a dance, Arden." I leaned forward in my chair, the action moving me closer to her. "Say what you want, but you're attracted to me."

She snorted. "I am, but so is half the female population."

My grin nearly split my face. "Are you saying I'm man candy?"

"You *were* on GQ," she reasoned, "isn't that answer enough?"

"So, because I'm man candy and other women find me attractive, you won't dance with me?" I tipped the chair on its two back legs. "I have to say, Arden, your reasoning isn't very sound. You should be jumping at the chance if I'm such a hot commodity." I waved my hand to encompass the rest of the wedding guests. "I could just as easily asked any of the other single women here, but I asked *you*."

"Oh my God, do you ever shut up?"

I pretended to think about it. "Only if you dance with me."

She grabbed my hand and stood. "Then giddyup cowboy, let's dance."

I smirked and let the fiery redhead haul me onto the dance floor.

It was a faster song, but I didn't let that keep me from gluing her body to mine.

"I don't think we need to dance this close," she groaned, her chin practically resting on my chest.

"Yes we do," I grasped her waist, "all the cool kids are doing it."

She rolled her pretty eyes at me. "You're something else, you know that?"

"I know," I smiled down at her, "it's why you like me." She sighed. "Come on, admit it," I pestered, "you *like* me."

"What is this? Grade-school?" She huffed.

"That's practically an admission."

"Practically." She laughed.

"Ah, there it is." I grinned.

"What?" She wrinkled her nose.

"Your laugh. It's beautiful."

She blushed again, but this time instead of tomato red it was more a flushed pink color.

Sobering, I said, "I know you think I'm a player, and I was, I'll admit, but that's not me anymore. I'd like to get to know you more."

She shifted awkwardly in my arms and looked around, like she was seeking escape.

"Arden?" She forced her eyes to mine. "I get that you're protective of your heart, you have to be, and you have Mia to think about, but I'm not a bad guy."

"I know that," she said quickly.

"Then why do you act like you can't get away from me fast enough?"

Her eyes shifted uneasily to mine. "BecauseIlikeyou."

"Um, can you repeat that?" I turned my ear towards her. "I didn't quite catch it."

"Because I like you." She stared straight at my chest when she said it.

I grinned. "Knew it."

"Shut up." She giggled.

The song blended into another and we continued to dance.

As the night wore on we ate, drank, danced, talked, laughed, and did it all again.

Hours later we stumbled into my hotel room. We were both buzzed from the drinks, but nowhere near drunk.

I tossed my tux jacket on the hotel chair and unbuttoned my dress shirt, laying it on top of the jacket.

Arden turned away from the hotel window and her jaw dropped. "Where'd your shirt go?"

"I was hot," I complained.

"You are hot." She paled. "Did I say that out loud?"

I nodded, grinning like an idiot.

"Oops." She pressed a hand to her mouth. "I take it back."

"Too late." I winked and sat down on the love seat. I hadn't bothered getting a big room since I was only staying the one night. I hadn't wanted to risk driving home since I lived an hour away. I still hadn't figured out how I convinced Arden to come with me.

I patted the empty space beside me and she sunk down onto the couch.

I turned on the TV, but at this time of the morning there was nothing worthwhile on, just a bunch of infomercials. I was ten seconds away from buying a vacuum I didn't need—damn those people were convincing—when Arden began to wiggle.

"What's wrong?" I asked her.

"This dress," she wiggled again, "I swear to God I think it's suffocating me."

I chuckled. "Let me help you. Turn around." I swirled my finger through the air.

"I don't have anything to wear." She frowned.

"I have a shirt you can wear."

"Oh, okay." She turned around and peeked at me over her shoulder. "I really need to get out of this dress."

"I can tell." I chuckled and unzipped the dress. It fell off her torso in a puddle of fabric and she wasn't wearing a fucking bra. All the blood in brain went south.

"Um, Arden," I cleared my throat.

"Yeah?" She hesitated.

"I have a boner. Ignore it."

She busted out in uncontrollable laughter. "I can't ignore it *now*."

I frowned and looked down. "Yeah, I guess it's a bit hard to ignore."

"Hard indeed," she quipped.

"Stop it," I scolded and stood to find my bag. I'd dropped it by the bed earlier in the day. I didn't have much in it so it only took me seconds to get the shirt. I handed it to Arden and she slipped it on. I'll admit, I got an excellent shot of side boob before she could tug it down. Once it was covering her torso she stood and let the dress fall all the way off. She picked up the dress and laid it on the chair along with my shirt and jacket.

When she turned back around we stared at each other for a moment and then someone—I wasn't sure who—made a move for the other and suddenly we were all over each other. It was like the sexual tension had been an elastic band snapped back and suddenly someone let it go and here we were.

My hands were all over her the same way hers were on me. Our mouths collided and I swore sparks flew. My whole body was tingling and that had never happened before.

My tongue caressed hers and she let out a breathy moan.

*Fuck yes.*

I dug my fingertips into her hips and then I lifted her up so her legs wound around my waist. Her center pressed right into my aching cock and I damn near exploded.

Holy shit this woman was going to make me lose my mind.

We collapsed on the bed and somehow she ended up on top, grinding her hips into mine. Her eyes were closed and she tilted her head back, her hair falling behind her like a curtain.

The way she kept rolling her hips...

"Arden," my voice was hoarse, "what are we doing?"

I didn't want to pressure her into anything she didn't want and things were moving fast. If she wanted to stop I didn't want things to go any further.

She opened those brilliant whiskey colored eyes and her lips quirked into a half smile. "I've decided that I'm an adult, and therefore, it's perfectly reasonable to have mind-blowing sex with the hottest man on the planet. I can have fun for a night."

My hands flexed against her hips. "It'll be more than a night."

She smiled sadly. "We both know that can't happen."

"We'll see about that," I growled, and flipped her so she was on the bottom now. I kissed her neck, licking the sensitive skin there, and smiling in approval when she began to make the most delicious little noises.

She smoothed her hands over my chest. "It's not fair that you're hot and have a perfect body like this." She counted my abs by sliding her finger down and pursed her pouty pink lips.

I chuckled. "Is that a compliment?"

"I suppose."

"I think you're wearing too many clothes." I kissed her jaw.

"Same amount as you." Her voice was breathless.

"I've thought about this so many times in the last few weeks. You have no idea," I told her. Maybe it wasn't the best thing to admit, but I wanted her to know that I actually fucking cared about her. I'd gotten to know her and what wasn't there to like?

"Me too."

I paused and pulled back, looking down into her eyes. "What?"

She smiled like she'd been caught—which I guessed she had. "I said I liked you, don't act so surprised."

"You're a mystifying creature," I told her, gliding my hand down her neck, toying with the collar of her shirt.

She glared up at me. All fire. "Shut up and kiss me."

I was more than happy to oblige. We became a tangled mess of legs, arms, and tongues. Breathless whispers lingered in the air.

I lifted the thin cotton shirt off her body like I was revealing a present. She was all pale skin, perky breasts, and perfect pink nipples. I was in fucking heaven. I took her breast in my mouth, swirling my tongue around her nipple. She let out a moan and her fingers tightened in the longer strands of my hair. My dick twitched and I nearly came like an over-excited teenage boy. Arden completely unraveled me.

I kissed the soft flesh of her stomach and moved lower to the skin above her thong.

"Oh God, yes, please." Her hips undulated and she urged me closer.

I didn't know if it was the small amount of alcohol in her system, or if this was just Arden in bed, but I really fucking liked how responsive she was.

I chuckled and kissed her inner thigh. "You want my mouth on that pussy?"

"Yes, please, yes." She begged, jerking against me.

I smiled and kissed her opposite thigh. "Say 'please.'"

"Please."

"Say 'Hayes you are a sex god.'"

She peered down at me with hooded eyes. "Prove it."

I really fucking liked this uninhibited side of Arden.

Without another word I hooked my fingers into the small string she called underwear and slid it down her legs where it landed on the floor. I stared at her for a moment, not moving, and that was when her fingers moved to her center and slid inside.

"If you don't help me out I'll have to take care of business myself."

I'm pretty sure I squeaked. Yes, *squeaked*.

This woman was a devil wrapped in the package of an angel.

I moved her hand out of the way and stroked my tongue against her sensitive flesh.

"That feels so good." Her whole body was practically vibrating.

I added a finger and then two. Her moans and cries grew in volume. So much so that I wouldn't have been surprised if the whole hotel floor heard her. Arden was so quiet and sweet that I hadn't expected her to be so vocal in bed.

"I'm gonna come." Her voice took on a raspy edge. "Oh my God, don't stop. Yes. Yes. Right there. Yeeeees." Her legs shook against me when her orgasm hit.

While she came down from her high I got rid of the last of my clothes and rolled the condom on.

Arden lifted onto her elbows a bit and squinted. "Is that…is that a *piercing?*" She stared at my cock.

I smirked. "Yes."

"Holy shit." I suppressed my laugh. "Did that hurt?" She sat up fully and reached out, rubbing her thumb over the head.

"Yeah, of course. But the pleasure it brings me *and* you, was worth it."

"That…that makes it better for both of us?" She swallowed thickly, eyes wide and lips parted.

"Hell yes."

She gasped and I took her hips in my hands, pulling her until her ass hung off the bed and I held her. She was so wet that I slid in all the way in one smooth, hard thrust.

"Mmm," she moaned, "that feels good." Her eyes glazed over.

I lowered and took her delectable mouth in mine. I kissed her the way I fucked her. First hard. Then slow. Then fast. Then hard again.

Her fingernails dug into my ass and I wouldn't be surprised if there were scratches there and down my back in the morning.

"Oh my *God*, you're right, that does feel good," she said, referring to the piercing.

I wanted to say I told you so, but I was too busy sucking on her breast, so sue me. She had the most perfect fucking tits ever. Actually, everything about her was perfect.

I reached between us and touched my fingers to her clit—that's it—and she went off like a rocket.

I couldn't wait any longer and I came with her. We collapsed in each other's arms. Both sweaty and satisfied.

She started kissing me and in no time I was ready to go again. That woman would be the death of me. She was on top this time, and when we came, she laid splattered across my chest, unable to move.

"Weddings turn me into a whore," she mumbled into my shoulder.

I chuckled, jostling her in the process. "That so? You do this often?"

"Well, no," she blinked her eyes sleepily, "this is a first."

"Then I don't think that's a valid observation," I told her.

"Mhmm, you're right." She couldn't keep her eyes open any longer and flopped off of me onto the right side of the bed where she was completely out seconds later.

I stayed up and watched her. I couldn't help it. She was so beautiful, with her red—freshly fucked—hair fanned around her, bruised lips, and sleepy breaths. I'd grown to care about her and I didn't want this to end here. This wasn't a one-night stand for me, but I knew she thought that's all this was—all *I* could ever want. My reputation as a ladies man was really coming back to bite me in the ass. I hated the fucking tabloids and how they insisted on making us all out to be man-whores. Just because I had a healthy sex life it didn't mean I dipped my stick in every pair of legs that opened up.

When I couldn't keep my eyes open any longer I pulled the sheets over us and drew her body against mine. Her heart beat so fast beneath her rib cage, fluttering almost.

I smiled and pressed a kiss to her neck. She made a soft sound in her sleep, but didn't wake.

I buried my head in the crook of her neck and was out like a light.

When I woke up in the morning she was gone. Only a small down feather lingered on her pillow, telling the story that someone had been here.

I picked up the small white tuft and held it between my fingers, turning it this way and that.

"Until next time, Little Bird."

# BONUS CONTENT
## MADDOX AND EMMA
### #THREE
#### AFTER MADDOX AND EMMA'S WEDDING

EMMA

"Where are you taking me?"

Maddox glanced over at me from behind the wheel of his beloved sports car, and said nothing.

"You know surprises make me uncomfortable when it comes to your ideas. You usually get me arrested."

"That was *one* time." He held up a single finger and wiggled it around. "You're never going to let me live that down." He shook his head, a small smile dancing on his lips.

"Come on, where are we going?" I continued to badger him. "This *is* our wedding night. I think I have the right to know whether or not you're taking me somewhere…" I ran my hand up his thigh and he shuddered. "*Nice.* Or," I took my hand away, "if you're planning to take me into the middle of the woods and murder me. And the way it's looking right now," I glanced outside the car at the setting, "I'd bet that you're gonna kill me. This is  looking very horror movie-ish."

He laughed under his breath. "Oh, Em. If only you knew what I had planned for you." He tossed a wink in my direction and continued to drive.

"Ugh," I groaned, crossing my arms over my chest, "you're such a tease! Just tell me!"

"Nuh-huh, I've been planning this surprise for a while now and I won't let your pouting disrupt it."

"I'm not pouting."

With his eyes still on the road he reached over and plucked my bottom lip between his thumb and index finger. "You're pouting, Emma. And if you think this adorable pouty lip is going to make me cave, you're wrong. But," his voice lowered and he flashed his stormy gray eyes in my direction, "I do plan on biting it later as punishment."

I snapped my teeth together. "I have teeth too and I'm pretty sure there's a certain appendage of yours that you wouldn't appreciate *me* biting."

He chuckled and rubbed a hand over the stubble on his jaw. "I know you think you sound really menacing right now, but all you're doing is turning me on. Nice try, Em."

"You're impossible," I grouched. "This is our wedding night," I reminded him, "and you're dragging me to the middle of nowhere."

He sighed. "Don't make me pull out the duct tape. We're almost there."

"Fine." I sat back and settled my hands over my non-existent baby bump. I couldn't believe that in less than a year we were going to be parents. It was scary and exciting all at the same time. And while I might be currently bitching at him, I knew there was no one else on the planet that I would want to go on this journey with.

A few minutes later Maddox turned into the driveway of an old Victorian style home.

"Maddox," I started, "you didn't do what I think you did, did you?"

He smirked. "You'll see."

He parked the car and slipped out, jogging around to get my door and helping me with the bottom of my dress so that it didn't drag through the dirt.

We walked up the rickety porch steps and stopped in front of the old front door. The paint on the siding was peeling and there were holes in the porch floor, but to me it was beautiful.

Maddox produced a key from his pocket and unlocked the front door.

"Welcome home, Em." He whispered the words and reached out to wipe my cheek where a tear had escaped.

"You…you bought us a house…an old house…but…"

"Yeah, yeah," he rubbed the back of his head, smiling sheepishly, "I wanted to build a new house, but you wanted this. You wanted an old home with character. Something that held a thousand memories and had room for the memories we'd make."

I laughed, wiping away another tear. "So, you do listen when I talk."

"Always," he chuckled, "even when I don't want to."

"This is our house?" I was still in shock.

"This is our *home*," he corrected. "I made up my mind a few months ago that I was going to agree with you, but before I could tell you I saw this house go on the market and I knew it was perfect for us. So, I bought it, and then I didn't tell you because I wanted it to be a surprise." He ducked his head and shrugged. "And then we were both surprised with the news of the baby, and I know renovating now with a baby on the way isn't ideal, but I think we can do it."

"I *know* we can." I reached out and wrapped my arms around his shoulders. "I love you," I kissed his jaw, "don't ever doubt that. This is the best gift you could've ever given me. And yeah, it needs work, but that's what I wanted. Just…Maddox, just imagine it when it's done and we bring the baby home from the hospital. And when he or she learns to ride their bike…and playing in the yard…can you see it?"

He grinned. "I can see it all."

He took my face between his hands and kissed me passionately.

When no air was left in my lungs he plucked my legs up and pulled me into his arms, carrying me over the threshold.

He set my feet down on the ground, but kept his arm around my waist.

The home was in bad shape, that was for sure, but I could see the potential.

More importantly, I could see our future, and it was beautiful.

EMMA

"We do not need a new car." I glared across the kitchen island at my husband.

Around us, workers hustled about trying to finish all the remodels before the baby arrived. We still had months before baby W.C. (Willow Creek) made his or her appearance, but that wasn't a lot of time to finish everything that needed to be done.

"Yes, we do." He countered, crossing his muscular arms over his chest.

"You just bought me that expensive SUV a few months ago, remember?"

"I do, but I'm just not sure it's the safest vehicle for my daughter."

"The baby could be a boy you know," I argued. Maddox was convinced the baby was a girl, while I had no inkling either way. I was still so surprised there was actually a baby inside me that I hadn't even thought about what its gender might be. I didn't care either way.

"Girl," he smiled slowly, "it's definitely a girl."

I rolled my eyes.

"Anyway," he swaggered towards me, grabbing me by the waist

and pulling me into his arms, "we need a minivan."

"We do *not* need a minivan," I argued.

"Yes, we do. I plan on having lots more babies, therefore we need a minivan to haul them around in…complete with an *I Heart Hedgehogs* bumper sticker."

I snorted. "Seriously."

"Hells yeah. I already bought one."

I narrowed my eyes.

"The sticker," he back peddled, "I bought the *sticker* not the minivan." Lowering one of his arms from around me, he glanced at his watch. "But the dealership will be closing soon so we better get a move on."

"Maddox," I whined, "the vehicles we have are enough."

"No, no." He shook his head. "We only have one suitable vehicle. Mine's a sports car, that's not gonna work."

I sighed and quirked a brow. "Are you really going to drive a minivan?"

He grinned, knowing he was inevitably going to win this argument. "Of course. Every dad needs a babymobile."

I laughed and smiled up at him. "Okay, okay. We'll get one."

"Yes!" He fist bumped the air, nearly hitting me in the face in the process. "You won't regret this, Em." He kissed me soundly and bound for the door.

***

Two hours later I did, in fact, regret caving to Maddox's pleas for a minivan.

"George," he said to the car salesman, "I can't decide whether or not we need the single DVD player or dual…" He tapped his lips like he was about to make the biggest decision of his life.

"Em, which do you think?"

"I don't care."

That was my standard response.

"Let's go with dual," he decided, "we're going to have more kids and we'll need them both down the road."

I rolled my eyes—which I'd been doing non stop for the last hour and a half.

"What kind of exterior color would you like?" George asked, inputting everything into the computer.

"Em?" Maddox prompted.

"Orange."

"It doesn't come in orange," George responded.

"Ignore her," Maddox waved a hand, "she doesn't even like orange. She's just cranky."

Yeah, I was cranky. I didn't want to be here and, maybe it was irrational, but I was upset that Maddox kept referring to the baby as a girl. It had me worried that if the baby was a boy he might not be happy.

"That pearl white looks nice," Maddox waved a hand towards the computer, "let's go with that."

"That's our most popular color." George pushed his glasses further up his nose.

"Interior color?"

"Em?" Maddox asked. "What color interior would you prefer?"

"As long as it's easy to clean, I'm happy."

Maddox grinned. "You said that without grimacing at me. I'm proud of you." He patted my head.

I snapped my teeth at him and he merely laughed.

"We'll go with the chestnut interior," Maddox told him.

"Excellent." George nodded, clicking a few things on the computer screen.

He asked several more questions before giving us the total with everything we wanted.

"That's a lot cheaper than my car." Maddox laughed, writing out a check for the full amount.

"We have one on a lot a few towns over and we can have it here within the hour."

"Perfect." Maddox grinned and handed over the check.

George left to grab more paperwork and Maddox glanced at me, noting my slumped form and frown.

"Em," he groaned, "What's wrong? I know you're not acting like this just because of the minivan."

I frowned, twisting my wedding band around on my finger.

"Emma." He grabbed my chin, forcing me to look at him. His soft silvery gray eyes instantly sent a flood of calm through me. "Talk to me."

"It's just…you keep talking about the baby being a girl and it has me worried."

"Worried?" His face twisted in confusion. "Why?"

"It's just that…well, we won't know for a little longer whether or not it's a boy or a girl and I'm scared you'll be sad if the baby is a boy." I tugged my bottom lip between my teeth and looked down.

He was quiet for a moment and then a second later his laughter echoed around the dealership.

"Shh," I scolded him, slapping my hand over his mouth.

He continued to laugh, grabbing my hand and holding it in his.

"Oh, Em, you're hilarious." He wiped tears from his eyes with his freehand. "How could you ever think I'd be upset whether or not the baby is a boy or girl? I love this baby so much already and I'll be happy either way. Yeah, I'm convinced it's a girl, but I'll be just as happy to have a son. At the end of the day all that matters is that we have a healthy baby." He cupped my cheek, staring into my eyes. He swiped his thumb over my bottom lip. "I'm sorry if I upset you."

I shook my head. "No, I'm sorry. I was being silly."

He cracked a smile. "I should've been more sensitive to your feelings. I'm sure your emotions are all over the place." He lowered his hand to the tiny bump of my stomach. "Just know that I love baby W.C. very much…girl *or* boy."

I wrapped my arms around his neck and gave him a chaste kiss on the lips. "I love you even if you drive me nuts."

He chuckled. "I love you too. More than you'll ever know."

"I'm really looking forward to seeing you drive this minivan. Don't be surprised if I don't point and laugh."

"Puh-lease," He exaggerated, "I'm a DILF."

"We're not putting a hedgehog sticker on it, though," I warned him.

He cackled. "We'll see about that."

George returned then and cleared his throat, clearly flustered.

With a wink Maddox turned away from me and signed everything George handed him.

From there we waited in the lobby for Maddox's 'babymobile' to show up.

When it pulled into the lot he ran outside like an excited kid on Christmas.

He slapped his hand against the back before running to the driver's side and all but pushing the guy that had brought it out of his way.

He climbed behind the wheel and honked the horn, waving me forward.

With a shake of my head I stepped outside and into the cool fall air.

My mouth fell open when I saw that he'd already stuck the *I Heart Hedgehogs* sticker onto the back.

Jerk.

I slid into the passenger seat while a grinning Maddox fiddled with the radio.

Moments later a Willow Creek song flooded the car and he tapped his hands against the steering wheel in time with the beat.

Putting the car in drive, he turned to me. "Ready, Em?"

"You bet."

I was always ready when it came to Maddox and the many adventures he led me on.

Instead of jumping out of planes our next adventure included bottles, dirty diapers, and lots of crying.

But we'd conquer it together.

REMY

I clutched my stomach as another contraction rocked through my body.

"Remy," Mathias growled, "I swear to fucking God if you've been in labor this whole time I'm going to shake you as soon as the baby is out."

I held onto the back of one of the kitchen chairs and tried to straighten my spine while hiding my grimace of pain.

"I'm not in labor," I said adamantly, even though I most definitely was.

I'd talked to the doctor on the phone earlier and he'd told me not to come in until my contractions were closer together—and they were definitely starting to get there.

"You're such a fucking liar," he growled, pacing away from me and tugging on his hair. "Come on, Rem, let's just go to the hospital. Let's not fuck this up before it even starts. I mean, I don't know how to deliver a baby."

I snorted. "But you definitely knew how to put one in me."

He grinned at that, but quickly sobered.

"Should I grab the baby bag?" He asked me.

"We don't need to go—ow!" I clutched my abdomen again,

breathing through the pain. "Scratch that," I hissed, "we do need to go."

"I fucking knew it!" He yelled, throwing his hands in the air and ran from the room, no doubt to grab the duffel bag full of clothes for the baby and us. He'd insisted we have a bag packed when I was only five months pregnant. Mathias had nearly driven me nuts through my pregnancy. He'd been crazily overprotective, going so far as to not even let me pick up my cat. Like, seriously?!

Mathias returned to the kitchen a moment later with the duffel bag slung over his shoulder.

"How do you feel?" He asked.

"Like a bowling ball is trying to force its way out of my vagina," I responded.

He chuckled a bit at that.

"Do I…uh…need to carry you?" He asked.

I rolled my eyes and shoved at his chest so he'd get out of my way.

"I can walk on my own, thank you very much."

"Sorry," he mumbled, "I wasn't sure."

He hovered behind me as I made my way to the garage.

Every time I looked over my shoulder at him he had this terrified expression like he thought any time I was going to squat and our son was going to come sailing out.

If only childbirth was that easy.

Once in the garage Mathias hurried around me and opened the passenger door of his Range Rover. He offered me his hand and I accepted it, letting him help me into the car.

"Oh God," I doubled over in pain, "hurry."

Mathias paled and threw the duffel bag into the back of the car before running around and sliding into the driver's seat.

He sped down the driveway and fiddled with the buttons on the steering wheel—connecting to his Bluetooth and letting his family and friends know that the baby was on his way.

"It hurts," I whimpered.

Mathias glanced at me with worry filled eyes.

He knew it was bad if I was confessing how much pain I was in.

He offered me his hand and I squeezed it.

"I'm scared." A tear fell down my cheek. "What if—"

"No," he shook his head adamantly, "Liam isn't Hope. Everything will be fine this time Remy."

"But—"

"No," he growled, reaching up with our joined hands to wipe away my tears.

"I love you," I whispered. "So much. You know that, don't you?"

He smiled. "I know, Rem. But it's good to hear."

***

# CONTINUED IN MATHIAS' POV

I fucking hated hospitals.

I hated the smell.

I hated the color—so fucking bland.

But most of all I hated how helpless hospitals made me feel.

My leg bounced up and down restlessly while a nurse hurried around the room getting everything set up.

In the corner of the room was a tiny little bed thing just waiting for the arrival of my son.

*My son.*

I'd never thought about having kids.

Hell, I'd never even thought about having a *wife*.

Remy had always been it for me, and for a long time I believed I was destined to be alone and without her. An asshole like me didn't deserve love.

But then by some sort of miracle Remy came back into town.

From the moment I saw her at the bar that day I knew she'd be mine again.

There was no one else for me and I knew I was it for her.

We were a perfect fucking match.

We'd been through a lot to get to this moment—through hell and back basically, but for the first time ever in my life I could say I was happy.

I was also scared shitless.

I had no fucking idea what it took to be a dad.

I was terrified of fucking this up and having a screwed up kid like I'd been.

"What are you thinking about?"

Remy's soft voice interrupted my thoughts.

"Nothing," I lied.

She snorted. "The fact that you think I believe that is cute. Now, spill it, Wade."

I shook my head, fighting a smile. That woman.

"I don't want to fuck this up," I admitted, rubbing my thumb over her hand.

"What?" Her blonde brows furrowed together. "The delivery? You just stand there and let me yell at you. It's not that difficult."

I chuckled. "No, Rem. I'm talking about everything that comes after. I don't want to fuck it up like my parents did."

"Mathias," she softened, "that would never happen. Look at how much you love Collin and he's not even your kid. You've got this," she squeezed my hand, "don't worry."

"It's just…this is a kid, Remy. I don't want to screw it up."

She laughed. "We're going to mess up and make mistakes. There's no rulebook for perfect parenting. All that matters is that he knows we love him."

"I love him already." I moved my hands to her stomach and felt Liam push against my hand with a solid kick. I grinned. "That's my boy."

She smiled and put her hand over mine. "Everything will be okay. You'll see."

"Alright, guys, the doctor is on his way now. It's time to get this show on the road."

I glanced at Remy with horror filled eyes.

It was happening.

Like, now.

My son was about to enter the world and irrevocably change my life.

My heart pounded in my chest.

The doctor entered the room and I stood, standing by Remy's side and holding her hand.

"We've got this," Remy said, squeezing my hand.

Despite her words I saw the fear in her eyes and I knew she was thinking of Hope.

"Yes, we do." I kissed the side of her forehead.

"Alright, you're going to have to start pushing now." The doctor instructed.

Remy's hold on my hand tightened and her face turned red as she pushed with all her strength.

I lowered and whispered words of encouragement in her ear.

*You can do this.*

*You're so strong, baby.*

*I'm so proud of you.*

*I love you.*

And then, my son was here, letting out the loudest war cry I'd ever heard.

Remy broke down into tears.

"We did it." She breathed a sigh of relief.

"No, Rem, *you* did it. That was all you."

She sobbed, smiling through her tears as our son's cries echoed around us.

It felt so good to hear him.

He sounded so healthy and strong.

"Would you like to cut the umbilical cord?" The nurse asked me.

"Uh…yeah." My hands shook as she handed me the scissors.

"It's okay. You won't hurt him." She assured me.

I nodded and cut where she instructed me, all the while Liam continued to wail—reminding us that he was *alive*.

Once he was separated they laid him on Remy's chest and his little mouth opened and closed.

"He's so beautiful," Remy sobbed, tracing her fingers over his lips. "He looks just like you." She laughed.

"Fuck, Rem." I wiped away my tears—I couldn't believe I was crying, but watching your child come into the world would get to the best of them. "He's amazing." I rubbed my hand over his tiny head and the tuft of dark brown hair there. "He's fucking perfect." I touched his hand and his little fingers wiggled at my touch. "Thank you," I kissed her, "thank you for giving me him."

She laughed. "Well, you did help."

I smiled against her lips and kissed her again. "And don't you forget it."

The nurse took him away then to clean him up and get his weight and all that.

Hours later I lay in the bed with Remy, gazing down at our perfect son in her arms.

A knock on the hospital room door had us both looking up.

"You guys can come in," I called, knowing full well it was my family at the door.

Immediately, my twin brother came bounding into the room.

"Let me see my nephew!" He cried.

"Shut the fuck up," I glared at him, "he's sleeping."

Maddox shook his head, fighting a smile. "Still not curbing the cussing, I see."

"Some habits die hard," I shrugged.

My mom and dad came forward and oohing and ahhing over the baby.

He was pretty fucking cute so I expected no less.

Emma, my brother's wife, stood at his side gazing at the baby with a look of awe.

Ezra and Sadie stood at the end of the bed and Hayes hovered in the back, glancing over the tops of everyone's heads to see the baby.

Liam yawned, and blinked his open, gazing around sleepily.

He also might've been a little bit milk drunk.

"Hey, Liam," I rubbed his cheek, "meet everyone." He let out a small little cry. "And everyone, meet Liam Maxwell Wade. Something tells me this one is going to make waves."

# BONUS CONTENT
## HAYES AND ARDEN
### # TWO
#### HAYES, ARDEN, AND MIA GO TO DISNEY AFTER EVENTS IN TAKE A CHANCE

ARDEN

"I see Mickey! I see Mickey!" Mia chanted from Hayes arms, trying to wiggle her way out of them.

You wouldn't believe that only a few days before her psycho father had kidnapped her. Kids were resilient, but I still worried about what this had done to her. As soon as we got home I was going to look for a therapist that specialized in working with kids. I didn't want to do nothing and have this affect her later on. Nip it in the bud was my current mindset.

Hayes set her down and grabbed her hand before she could run off.

"Mama! That's Mickey!" Mia pointed, like I hadn't figured it out by this point.

"I know, baby girl." I smiled down at her. Her red hair was braided down her back—courtesy of Hayes. He'd let me sleep in and when I finally woke up I found Mia already dressed with her hair done.

We finally reached Mickey and Hayes let Mia go so she could run straight at the mouse. She wrapped her arms around his legs and squeezed tight.

I heard her say, "I love you, Mickey."

Hayes took a picture and I handed her the autograph book we bought when we entered the park. "Do you want Mickey to sign it?" I bent to her level.

She nodded and held out the notebook to him while I dug around in my purse for the Disney pen we'd also been suckered into buying.

Once Mia had Mickey's signature she was a happy camper and let Hayes pick her up again. He ended up sticking her on his shoulders and she giggled happily. God I loved that sound and I loved it even more that the man I loved made my daughter happy. After how things ended with her father I'd been scared to love again, and even more scared that a man wouldn't be able to love my daughter as much as I did. But then Hayes came along and single-handedly bulldozed all of my preconceived notions.

"Can we ride that?" Mia tapped the top of his head and pointed at the Dumbo ride.

"You betcha."

Hayes set her down again—something told me he was going to be doing *a lot* of that—and I pointed in the direction of a store.

"While you guys are doing that, there's something I need to get?"

Hayes grinned. He already knew what I was up to.

"Take your time. We'll be in line for an hour."

I rolled my eyes. "Yeah, right, rock star."

He chuckled.

The four guards with us split up, two going with him and Mia, and two with me.

Sadly, I was kind of getting used to always being surrounded by guards. They'd become more like shadows now and I barely noticed them. As weird as it was to have them around, I welcomed the extra set of eyes. Mia wasn't going to be let out of my sight until she went to college—and even then I might find an excuse to enroll so I could check on her.

I stepped into the busy store and searched the racks of princess dresses.

Mia's obsession with the *Little Mermaid* hadn't waned, and I figured it had something to do with their matching red hair. I finally found Ariel's outfit and snagged one, along with the matching crown. Mia was going to lose it. I spotted stuffed animals of Flounder and Sebastian, and decided to get those too. Mia deserved to be spoiled after everything, plus the trip was for her birthday.

I paid for my items and with my bags in hand went to find Mia and Hayes.

Surprise, surprise. They'd gotten to jump the line and were waiting for me.

"Mama, it was so fun!" Mia cried energetically.

"That's awesome," I told her, crouching down with my bags in hand. "I got you something."

"What? What?" She chirped excitedly.

"Close your eyes."

She pursed her lips but did as I asked.

I pulled the dress out of the bag and said, "You can open them now."

She did and gasped. "Dis is for me?" She grasped the shimmery fabric meant to mimic a mermaid's tail.

"Just for you, baby girl."

She gasped again. "Dank you, Mama."

"You're welcome." I kissed her plump pink cheek. My love for that little girl far exceeded anything I'd ever thought it was possible to feel for another human being. Becoming a parent taught you so many things about life and love.

"Can I puts it on?" She batted her long lashes at me.

"Sure," I shrugged, "we'll find a bathroom."

We gathered up our bags and went in search of a restroom

"Mama, I wanna wear my dress," she whined, tugging on my hand and dragging me into the restroom.

I shook my head and closed us into the handicap stall.

"Baby girl," I warned, "slow down."

"I need my princess dress," she explained.

I took the dress out of the bag and tore off the tag before helping her into it. I hoped it didn't make her itchy, because it would be a nightmare having to wait again to get her out of it.

I pulled the crown out of the bag and took the price tag off of it as well.

"You gots me a crown too?" Her mouth parted in an O shape.

I nodded.

"Can you take my bwaid out?" She asked, already turning around for me to do so.

"Sure, sweetie."

I let the braid out and fluffed her hair before setting the crown on her head.

"Am I a real princess now, Mama?" She asked.

I tapped her nose with my finger and hugged her to me. "You were already a princess."

I let her go and stuffed her clothes into the bag before taking her hand and leading her out of the bathroom.

Hayes and the guards were waiting outside for us. Poor Hayes was surrounded by a group of teenage girls and was signing autographs. He did it all with a smile on his face.

When he saw us he signed the last piece of paper and pointed at us. "Sorry, ladies, my family is here. I have to go."

They thanked him and went on their way.

He mock-gasped when he saw Mia. "Look, Arden! It's a *real* princess."

"No, it's just me! Mia!" She giggled and ran up to him. "See?" She removed the crown.

Hayes clapped a hand over his chest. "Oh look at that! You're right." He took her hand. "Where to next?"

"The castle!" Mia pointed to Cinderella's castle in the distance.

"You got it."

I took her other hand and together the three of us started for the castle. I smiled up at Hayes and he smiled back. Happiness surged in my chest. I was with the man I loved and I had the best little girl anyone could ask for. I didn't know what the future held for us, and the possibilities used to scare me, but not anymore. I was ready for anything. Love had made me stronger, when I'd spent years thinking it weakened me. I guessed all it took was finding the right kind of love.

# BONUS CONTENT
## A WILLOW CREEK CHRISTMAS
### EZRA AND SADIE
#### # TWO

**SADIE**

"It's beginning to look a lot like Christmas!" I sing-songed, dancing around the front yard of Ezra's parents' house. Little white puffs of snow fell from the sky and I stuck out my tongue trying to catch one lone flake.

Ezra's arms wound around my waist and he pulled me against his solid chest, lifting my feet off the ground and spinning me around.

I laughed merrily. I'd never been happier in my life than when I was with Ezra. He was the one person that completed me. I hated that it'd taken both of us so long to realize we were perfect for each other, but we were together now and that's what mattered.

He put me down and I spun around, throwing my arms around his neck. His cheeks were flushed from the cold and his curly black hair stuck out from beneath a beanie.

"I love you." I stroked my fingers over the scruff on his cheeks.

"I love you too." He ducked his head down, gliding his lips over mine.

"Hey! Ezzie-poo get in here!"

Ezra pulled away from me with a chuckle and we both glanced towards the now open front door. Maddox, Ezra's band mate and foster brother, stood in the doorway. His wife, Emma, who was also my best friend, stood at his side and it looked like she was scolding him for interrupting us. Maddox laughed at her and wrapped his arm around her, pulling her as much against his side as he could with her now rounded in stomach in the way.

Ezra took my hand and helped guide me up the icy walkway to the front door.

"Hayes has probably eaten all the cookies already." Maddox grumbled, looking forlorn.

"I'm baking more!" Ezra's mom called out, having heard him.

"Yes!" Maddox fist-pumped the air.

Ezra shook his head, laughing under his breath.

"Don't worry," Maddox continued, "mom wouldn't let us start decorating without you."

We followed him and Emma into the spacious family room area where the biggest Christmas tree I'd ever seen stood in the corner.

The four guys—Ezra, Maddox, Mathias, and Hayes—had gone and cut it down yesterday. They'd thought they were so manly for cutting it down themselves. All of us girls had watched them from the safety of the warm car, laughing our asses off at them. They were rock stars, and definitely not mountain men. Mathias had stood back, grumbling and telling them what to do, while Hayes and Maddox tried to saw it down. Ezra had just stood and looked at the tree.

Today was Christmas Eve, and as per the Collins family tradition it was time to decorate the tree.

My family had always put our tree up on December first, but I wasn't going to argue with another family's tradition. Besides, Ezra and I had already decorated our own small tree at our house.

Bins and boxes of ornaments were scattered all over the family room and everyone else was already there.

I smiled and waved at Arden and Hayes. Little Mia sat in Hayes' lap with a Minnie Mouse headband stuck on her head.

Mathias and Remy sat on the other end of the couch, cooing at their tiny son Liam.

It was crazy to see how much all of our lives had changed in such a short amount of time. We'd grown up so much.

Ezra shrugged out of his coat and I did the same with mine. He gathered both in his arms and went to hang them.

I crouched down on the floor and began sorting through the bins.

Maddox was already going to town adding ornaments to the tree like an excited little kid.

Ezra returned and sat down beside me. He leaned over and kissed the side of my forehead and a happy sigh escaped my lips.

"Is there a theme for the tree?" I asked him, holding a blue ornament and a silver one.

"Nah," he shook his head, "mom's always let us do whatever we want. It's always a mess, but she says she loves it."

I laughed, leaning my head on his shoulder. "Yeah, I see the *mess*." I pointed at Maddox. He now had a handful of silver and gold tinsel and was tossing it haphazardly at the tree.

A chunk of it fell off and landed on Emma's head. She pretended to glare at him, but soon couldn't hold in her laughter. She picked it off her head and tossed it at Maddox's chest.

"Oh, is that how you're gonna play?" He grinned at his wife and grabbed a whole new handful.

"Bring it, Wade!" She goaded him.

He threw the tinsel at her and it exploded in a shower of silver and gold, landing on her, the floor, and the chair a few feet behind her.

Before I could blink tinsel was being tossed by everyone. Even little Mia was joining in on the fun. Baby Liam didn't seem to like all the noise and started crying, so naturally Mathias escaped the madness, but not Remy. Her laughter echoed as loud as the rest of us.

Maddox helped Emma to stand, and the two of them began to dance around to the Christmas music playing while the tinsel still fluttered through the air.

When there was no more tinsel to throw we all collapsed on the floor, our stomachs hurting from laughing so much.

"You're a glitter monster." Ezra chortled, picking off a piece of gold tinsel stuck to my lip.

I grinned up at him. "That's the best kind of monster. Grrr." I made a slashing motion with my hand before breaking out into more giggles.

"Oh. My. God."

We all turned to see Mrs. Collins standing in the large archway with a plate of cookies looking horrified.

"Maddox, what have you done?" She pressed her lips together, suppressing a laugh.

Maddox opened his mouth in surprise. "Me? Why do you assume it's me?" He defended.

She narrowed her eyes on him. "Because it's always you."

"True," he shrugged, "I can't argue with that."

"Pick up this mess and then you can all have cookies."

Maddox grumbled, "Holding the cookies hostage is all kinds of cruel."

Mrs. Collins couldn't suppress her laugh this time. "Just get it cleaned up."

Even with all of us it still took a good thirty minutes to get all the tinsel picked up and then put on the tree.

Mathias came back, minus Liam who'd fallen asleep.

Ezra grabbed a stepladder from the garage to make adding ornaments to the top of the tree easier.

Hayes lifted Mia onto his shoulders and handed her ornaments to stick in places. Her giggles filled the room and Arden watched the two of them with so much love in her eyes. I was so happy she'd found love for her and her daughter in Hayes.

Ezra handed me a red ornament and looked around until I found a bare spot for it. I wasn't like the others, piling ornaments in any place and over top of each other. I wanted to make sure every part of the tree had a sprinkling of decorations.

When I placed the red one Ezra handed me another, this time silver.

His parents came back into the room and passed out cookies before the two of them helped add ornaments too.

With so many of us trying to decorate the tree we kept getting in each other's way, but no one minded. It was nice to have all of us together doing something.

"Why don't you put this one up there?" Ezra pointed and held out a microphone shaped ornament.

"Sure." I took it and he grabbed me around my waist, lifting me up so I could place the ornament.

There were only a few more ornaments left and I let the others put them on.

We all stood back, admiring the tree. It was a bit of a mess, with ornaments all colors of the rainbow, lights galore, and tinsel raining down. Sprinkled between the round ornaments were ones in different shapes, like the microphone. I noticed a drum kit ornament, a bass, and an electric guitar. There was even a willow tree. Each of those ornaments held a special memory. So while the tree might not be perfect to some, it was perfect for us; The Willow Creek Family.

"Wait," Ezra said suddenly, "I think we're missing one."

"We are?" I looked at him with a confused lilt to my brow.

He nodded and proceeded to rummage through one of the bins. He found what he was looking for and handed the tissue wrapped ornament to me.

"Will you put it on?" He shifted nervously from foot to foot.

"Yeah, of course." I smiled and turned towards the tree, unwrapping the tissue paper from the ornament. Whatever it was must have been important to be wrapped so carefully.

I heard a collective gasp from behind me.

"Wha?" I started to turn around just as the tissue paper fell from the ornament onto the floor. Only it wasn't an ornament. Instead, a large diamond ring dangled from a thick piece of red fabric. The diamond swayed back and forth, glittering as the light hit it. The center diamond was huge and then the outside of it was surrounded by smaller diamonds. It almost looked like a flower. It was the most beautiful ring I'd ever seen.

*Did this mean what I thought it meant?*

"Ezra?" Tears clogged my throat as I turned around.

He was crouched behind me down on one knee. His Adam's apple bobbed nervously and his lips lifted into a half smile.

I pressed a hand to my mouth, stifling my gasp.

"Ezra," I breathed again, tears falling freely from my eyes now.

He took my other hand in his, the one that held the ring, and it dangled between our now joined hands.

"I had this whole speech planned out," he chuckled, "but right now, I can't think of anything else, except that I love you, and all I want this Christmas is for you to say you'll be my wife." He cleared his throat and smiled at me. His own eyes were shimmering with tears and love. So much love. "Will you marry me?"

I didn't hesitate. Not even for one second. "Yes! God, yes! A thousand times yes!"

Ezra's grin was so large it took up his whole face. He stood up then and took my face in his hands. He kissed me deeply, and so passionately that my toes curled.

Around us our family cheered and cat-called.

I laughed into his kiss and wiped away my tears—the happiest tears I'd ever cried.

He took the ring from my hand and untied to ribbon before sliding the ring onto the finger it belonged and the one it would never leave.

"I love you." I hugged him to me, kissing him again quickly.

"I love you too." He pressed his forehead to mine and his breath fanned across my lips. "Best Christmas Ever?"

"Ever," I concurred, and my smile was impossible to wipe off.

This last year had been insane. But everything happened for a reason and it had all been leading to moments like this for each of us. I couldn't wait to see what the next year brought us, and the next, and all the ones after that, and I was even happier knowing that in one of those years I'd soon be calling Ezra my husband.

# BONUS CONTENT
## MADDOX AND EMMA
### # FIVE

EMMA

I wiggled uncomfortably in my seat and clutched my round, basketball-sized stomach.

"Are you okay?" Sadie leaned over to ask me.

I nodded. "Yeah, fine."

My teeth gnashed together and I fought a groan.

"Emma…?" She prompted. "Are you in labor?"

My lip quivered. "Maybe."

She eyed the guys on stage. My doctor had not been pleased with me when I insisted on traveling at nine months pregnant, but the baby wasn't due for another two weeks and I'd wanted to be here for Maddox. The guys had a big concert in L.A. and they'd been preparing for it all month. I wanted to see their hard work pay off. Of course baby Willow would want to try to make her appearance in the middle of a concert. She was already as free-spirited as the two of us.

"*Emma*," Sadie scolded, and grabbed my hand, "we should go. You need to get to a hospital."

"No." I shook my head adamantly. I didn't want to ruin the concert for all of these people.

Sadie signaled to our bodyguards. "Hey Thing One and

Thing Two, she's in labor," she pointed at me, "one of you call for an ambulance, and the other get Maddox off that stage." When both of the big men stared at her with a blank face she added, "*Now.*"

"Yes, ma'am!"

I felt a cramp or something like it, claw at my abdomen and I nearly screamed. It wouldn't have mattered if I had. No one would've heard me with all the other screaming going on.

"We need to get you two backstage," the one guard said. I didn't know either of their names, since they weren't our regular guards. "The ambulance is going to pull up the emergency exit at the back of the building."

I nodded and tried to stand, but the pain became too great.

Sadie managed to grab me and keep me from falling. One of the guards picked me up and I wrapped my arms around his neck as he started to carry me away.

On stage the sound of the drums ceased, and with it all of the music.

"Emma!" I heard Maddox call out worriedly. "Em?"

Well, he knew something was up now.

Into the microphone, he spoke, "L.A., you guys have been great, but I've got to go. My wife is being carried out of here and something tells me we're about to have a baby."

I expected the crowd to boo the guys, but surprisingly they cheered.

The guard carried me around the partitions and behind the stage. Sadie and the other guard hurried to keep up.

"Em? Em? Em?" Maddox's worried voice echoed around the stage area. I couldn't see him yet, though.

We finally made it around a stack of large black storage cases and there he was.

"Emma," he cried in relief.

The guard set me down gently and I fell into Maddox's arms. "Are you okay?" He asked, looking me over.

"The baby's coming," I said at the same time my water broke and water cascaded down my legs, drenching my jeans.

"Oh shit." Maddox's eyes fell to the wetness.

"I'm scared." I held tightly to his hand.

We were in L.A., all the way across the country from our home, and doctor, and everything. This wasn't how I'd imagined having my first baby. My mom wasn't even here.

"It'll be okay, Em." He tried to soothe me, but his words fell on deaf ears.

"No, it won't," I sobbed, suddenly overcome by a waterfall of tears.

Maddox picked me up then and the guards led the way. Sadie trailed behind us.

"Shh, shh," Maddox murmured, "it's okay. Don't be worried, or upset. Just think about the fact that we're going to meet our daughter soon. That's all that matters. Shh, I'm here."

I sniffled into his shirt. I knew he was right. This was meant to be a happy moment in our lives—the happiest—and I couldn't let the fact that nothing was going according to plan ruin it.

We reached the back door and one of the guards opened it so we could step outside into a long tunnel. Maddox adjusted his grip on me and I felt his shoulders flex with tension. I knew it wasn't because I was heavy—though that was probably true—but because he was nervous. The big, tough, funny rock star was nervous. That was new.

When we exited the tunnel into a back alleyway I could hear the ringing sound of sirens in the distance.

Another contraction rocked through my body and I cried out.

"*Em*," Maddox choked. He sounded so helpless. I guessed he was.

I breathed through the pain and prayed that the ambulance would get there faster. The pressure I felt was insane.

"I think I need to push," I confessed, looking up at him—behind him the stars of the night sky were hidden by a thick coating of smog.

He paled. "W-what do you mean?"

"I can feel the baby," I cried, my fingers digging into his shoulders. "She's right there."

His eyes widened. "Oh hell, this isn't good. Emma," he said hesitantly, "I'm going to sit you down and I'm going to look, okay?"

I nodded weakly. The urge to push was so strong and sweat had broken out all over my body. I should've known I'd been in labor all day, but I'd had false labor pains a few weeks before and nothing came of it so I dismissed it from my mind.

Maddox lowered me to the ground and then had one of the guards hold me steady while he whipped off his shirt and laid it on the ground.

Sadie took my hand and gave it a slight squeeze. "It's okay," she tried to reassure me.

Maddox helped lower me to the ground and he undid my pants before pulling them off.

His Adam's apple bobbed and he looked *scared*.

"She's right *there*." His voice cracked. "I can see her head."

"I really need to push," I sobbed, the sound of the sirens growing closer.

*Please get here in time.*

"Em," his hands fell to my knees, "you're going to have to push, okay?"

"Not here!" I cried out just as another contraction hit me. Labor hurt like a bitch. I breathed through the pain and added, "I can't have our baby in an *alley*."

"You're going to have to." He forced me to spread my legs more. "Sadie, you stay here with me. You two, go find something for me to clean my hands and blankets. Lots of blankets. Oh, and scissors—but sterilize them."

The two guards took off at their instructions and Sadie looked at Maddox in awe. "How do you know all this?" She asked.

"Some special on TV about emergencies." To me, he said, "Emma, look at me. Just breathe. It's going to be okay."

"I'm so scared," I told him. This wasn't how you were supposed to have a baby. Not in a dirty, cold, alleyway while a concert was going on. What if something bad happened? What if she was stillborn like Mathias and Remy's daughter? *Oh God*.

"It's okay to be scared, but I'm going to take care of you. Both of you." His gray eyes were sincere. I knew I could believe him—trust him—but this was our *baby* and that worry wasn't going away easily.

One of the guards came bursting through the door with a bottle of Germ-X. "Will this work?"

"It's going to have to. With L.A. traffic that ambulance is probably a good ten minutes away." Maddox took the bottle and squirted some on his hands. "Show time, Em. You can do this. Remember that."

I nodded. "Sadie?" I asked weakly. "Will you come here?"

"Of course?" She dropped down beside me and took my outstretched hand. She smoothed my damp hair away from my forehead. "You're going to get to see your beautiful baby girl in a few minutes."

I took a deep breath. "I *have* to push."

"You can push," Maddox said, helping to hold my legs open.

More tears leaked from my eyes as I pushed.

With a cry, I collapsed back and Sadie caught my shoulders before my head hit the ground. She maneuvered behind me then so I could rest my head in her lap.

"Another one is coming," I warned.

"Push when you're ready," Maddox said, with a look of awe on his face. "She has blonde hair like you," he whispered.

"You can see her hair?" I cried softly.

He nodded, smiling. "Yeah, yeah I can."

I sat up a bit. "I have to push again."

I felt like the whole lower half of my body was about to burst. But I kept pushing.

And pushing.

And—

A cry, but not mine.

No, that cry belonged entirely to my daughter.

*My daughter.*

Willow Elise Wade.

Maddox choked on a sob and held up our daughter for me to see.

She was covered in all kinds of goo, but she was still the most beautiful thing I'd ever seen.

"She's beautiful, Em," Maddox cried, a sob shaking his body. "She has your nose and my lips."

Our daughter cried out again, like she knew he was talking about her, and wrapped her tiny fingers around one of his.

"Wow," he breathed.

"Let me hold her," I pleaded, reaching out.

Maddox laid her on my chest and she looked up at me with the biggest, blue eyes I'd ever seen. He was right about the tuft of blond hair she had. It wasn't much, but it was there. I took her tiny hand in mine, marveling at her little fingernails. Everything about her was small.

The door flew open again and this time Maddox's three band members came tumbling out.

"Whoa!" Hayes shouted, slapping a hand over his eyes. "I did not need see to see *that*."

"Holy fucking shit, is that the baby?" Mathias asked.

I nodded. "This is Willow."

Willow let out a loud cry then, like she was yelling at the world, "Here I am."

Behind us the ambulance finally arrived.

"A bit late, huh?" Ezra chuckled, moving over to Sadie.

The paramedics hurried over to us and took the baby from me, wrapping her in a foil looking blanket. They then went to work checking me over and loading me onto the stretcher. As I was being wheeled away the two guards finally appeared with blankets.

"We won't be needing those now." Maddox chuckled, following along beside me.

I was lifted into the back of the ambulance and Maddox climbed in beside me.

"Where's my baby?" I asked, panic clawing at my chest. "Where's Willow?"

"Right here." One of the paramedics appeared with her. "She appears to be doing just fine so we can let you hold her."

I took her into my arms and cuddled her warm body against my breast.

I stroked my finger over her plump pink cheek. "I'm never letting you go."

Maddox leaned forward and wrapped his arms around both of us. He kissed my forehead and then the top of Willow's. "I'm never letting *either* of you go."

1039

# BONUS CONTENT

## EZRA AND SADIE
### # THREE
### THEIR WEDDING

SADIE

This was supposed to be the happiest day of my life and *everything* was going wrong.

"What is *that*?" I cried, tears streaming down my face. "Is that an *ice* sculpture? I didn't order a damn ice sculpture!" I shouted at the poor wedding assistant.

I clutched at my chest. I could feel a panic attack coming on.

*Nothing* was going right with this wedding.

All my life I'd dreamed about my wedding, and now my perfect plans were headed straight for the shitter.

"Calm down," Emma cajoled me, bouncing baby Willow on her hip, "everything will work out."

"No, no it won't," I shook my head.

First the bridesmaid's dresses arrived in the wrong color.

Then the wrong flowers showed up.

And the latest disaster was an ice sculpture showing up when I hadn't even ordered one—and this wasn't just *any* ice sculpture, oh no, this one was in the shape of a monkey.

"What's next? I said to Emma. "I know the shit-fest can't be over yet."

As if conjured by my words, Lisa, the wedding planner, came running towards me in her black stiletto heels. I'd never seen anyone run around in heels the way this woman did.

"We have a problem." She looked at me dejectedly and glanced down at the iPad permanently glued to her hand.

"What is it *now*?" I asked.

She looked like she'd swallowed something sour. "I can't seem to locate your wedding dress."

I stared right at her, opened my mouth, and let out the most blood-curdling scream anyone had ever heard.

Baby Willow joined in with her own war cry.

"Whoa, what's going on?" Ezra asked, appearing around a corner into the ballroom. He was half-dressed already, in a pair of black tuxedo pants, but instead of his dress shirt he was wearing a white wife-beater for the moment.

"Everything is going wrong." I sobbed, pressing my fists to my eyes to dam back the tears. Thank God my makeup hadn't been done yet.

I felt Ezra's strong, warm arms wrap around me and I took comfort in the feel of them.

"Her dress is missing," Lisa informed him, "on top of everything else."

Ezra cursed. "Where could it be?"

"It's probably misplaced or the dry-cleaner hasn't delivered it yet, like I requested."

"Why don't you hunt that down and get one of your minions to get *that* out of here." He motioned to the ice sculpture.

She nodded and took off running again. I was beginning to think the woman didn't know how to walk.

"I'll never understand why weddings are so stressful." We all turned to find Maddox sitting in one of the chairs near the altar, knitting with his hedgehog on his shoulder—yes, I allowed him to bring the hedgehog to the wedding. I wasn't a total bridezilla.

We ignored him and Ezra smoothed his hands down my robe-covered arms. He bent, peering into my eyes. "It'll be okay, Sadie. Take a deep breath. Stop stressing. Just go get ready. I can handle this."

"No, you can't," I argued. "I need to make sure everything is right. I need—"

"Hey, hey," he hushed me, "the only thing you need to do is get ready. Do you trust me?" He waited for me to nod. "I'll make sure this is perfect for us. Believe me. We've both been waiting too long for this day, I won't let it be ruined."

I nodded and swallowed thickly. God I loved this man.

He kissed me quickly and smacked my butt, ushering me in the direction of the room I was to get ready in.

"Don't come out of there until it's time to meet me at the altar," he warned, wagging his finger at me when I looked over my shoulder at him.

I smiled. "You better be there."

He grinned crookedly. "You know I will. Otherwise my best friend will beat my ass." He winked.

I laughed. "You know I will."

Emma hurried to join me and once we were inside the room I closed the door.

Remy and Arden were already in chairs having makeup applied. Liam sat on the floor with an explosion of blocks. He picked one up in his small fist and hit it against the floor.

"No," Mia, Arden's daughter, admonished, "that's not what you do with them. You build things. See?" She pointed to the castle she built.

Liam took one look at her castle and threw his block at it. Her building crumbled to the ground and we all froze, waiting for her to get upset, but instead she began to giggle.

"I like your idea better," she told him, rubbing the brown hair on his head.

He let out a load of gibberish and drooled all over himself.

"Bride, you need to get over here." A makeup artist called me over.

I smiled at the kids one last time as Emma set down Willow to join them.

I closed my eyes and let the makeup artist do her job. It was hard to let go of all my worries in regards to the wedding, but even without Ezra's help it was out of my control. Things were going to happen as they were meant to.

An hour or so later Lisa poked her head in the door, smiling widely. "I have your dress," she sing-songed. "I've already looked it over myself and it's perfect."

She stepped fully into the room then and stood in front of me, unzipping the bag so I could see for myself.

I gasped. It was just as beautiful as I remembered. I hadn't seen it in weeks since it had been receiving final alterations and being repaired.

Tears clogged my eyes and I looked to Emma beside me, reaching for her hand and squeezing it.

"I'm getting married," I said, like it wasn't obvious already.

She smiled back. "Yes, you are."

Lisa hung up the dress on the rack. "I have a few last minute things to take care of, but I promise you everything will be perfect."

I nodded. I wasn't sure I believed her, but I was okay now. All that mattered was the fact that I was marrying Ezra. The rest was just icing on the cake.

Since my makeup was done, they moved on to my hair.

With each passing minute, my heart raced faster.

I glanced at my phone, reading the time.

In one hour I'd be walking down the aisle.

In one hour I would say I do.

In one hour I would become Mrs. Collins.

"How are you feeling?" Emma asked, changing into her bridesmaid dress. Luckily the dresses were the right color—a pale shade of pink—since the designer had made a rush delivery so we got them on time.

"Excited," I said honestly, "and a little nervous."

My fears about the wedding being a complete disaster were now trumped by my fears of tripping over my dress and taking out all the guests.

"That's normal," Emma said, turning so Remy could zip up her dress.

I took a deep breath as the hair stylist put the final touches on my hair and added a diamond clip.

"My throat feels dry," I gasped, looking around for water.

"Here you go," Arden rushed to my side, her red hair flying behind her like a scarlet curtain. She held out a mini bottle of water to me, the cap already off.

"Thank you," I told her, relief evident in my voice.

I gulped down the water like my throat was as dry as the Sahara desert.

"I think I'm sweating," I muttered, "*am* I sweating?" I addressed everyone in the room.

Emma laughed at me. "You're fine, sweetie. *Chill.*"

I nodded.

*There's nothing to freak out about Sadie. Get it together.*

"It's time to get in your dress," Emma said softly, like she was afraid I might break apart at the words.

I fanned my hands over my face, trying to cool down.

"Yeah, yeah," I muttered, "I know."

*Forty-five minutes now.*

I stood and looked at my finished hair and makeup.

"Whoa," I gasped at my reflection.

My hair was pulled back into an elegant up-do, accented with the diamond piece, and my makeup was done in shades of pink and gold that complimented my olive-toned skin. My lips shimmered with a pale pink gloss.

"You look beautiful." Emma appeared behind me and I saw her smile in the reflection of the mirror. "Ezra's going to cry when he sees you."

"You think so?" I asked.

"I know so." She nodded.

I turned away from my reflection and with a giddy laugh, I said, "Dress time."

The girls helped me into my dress and as soon as it was zipped I couldn't get to the floor-length mirror fast enough.

As soon as I saw this dress on a mannequin in a shop window in New York City I knew it had to be mine. It hadn't disappointed when

I tried it on and I bought it on the spot. It wasn't a princess ball gown explosion of tulle and taffeta like someone might expect of me. In fact, it was pretty simple. Elegant. Timeless. It had three-quarter sleeves in a lace design that expanded over the chest and back, down to my waist, where it then feathered out with tulle hanging down in sheets. It was perfect for our winter wedding—Christmas Eve to be exact. The sentimental fools that Ezra and I were, we decided to get married on Christmas Eve, exactly a year after he proposed.

I twirled in front of the mirror and let out a girlish giggle. Rubbing my hands down the front of the dress I couldn't stop grinning at my reflection.

"Twenty minutes," Remy spoke, breaking me from my trance.

I turned around to face my friends.

No.

My *family*.

Tears shimmered in my eyes.

Emma.

Remy.

Arden.

These girls and their guys were everything to me. When Emma's summer fling turned out to be a drummer in a famous band I never imagined the following years would play out the way they did. I never thought I would fall in love with Ezra—even if I lusted after the guy like a crazy fangirl before I even met him—but I did, and we had a rough road to get to here, but I was thankful for that now, even if I wasn't at the time. As rocky as our beginning was, our foundation was solid now. I trusted that we could make it through anything together. And not just the two of us, but *all* of us.

Somehow, along the way, we'd become the Willow Creek family

and it was the greatest family on the planet—in my humble opinion.

"Come here you guys," I held out my arms and sniffled, "I need a hug."

"Don't ruin your makeup," Remy warned as the girls all came in for a group hug.

I hugged them tight.

"I'm so lucky to have you guys," I mumbled into Arden's shirt.

"*We're* lucky to have you," she said.

"We're lucky to have *each other*," Emma added.

I took a deep breath—I'd been doing that a lot today—and Lisa came barreling into the room like the ever-ready bunny.

"T-minus five minutes. *Five*." She held up a hand and wiggled her fingers. "Get in position ladies."

Ezra's mom poked her head through the door along with his dad. "We're here for the kids."

Since Emma, Remy, and Arden were all in the wedding party Ezra's parents had volunteered to let the three children sit with them through the ceremony.

Emma went over and picked up Willow, along with a purple diaper bag. She kissed the little girl on the cheek before handing her over to Ezra's dad.

Remy stepped up next with Liam, showering the little boy with kisses. The media always tried to portray Mathias and Remy as hard and unfeeling, but they couldn't be farther from the truth. If they would only stop and notice how foolish they were in it came to their son they wouldn't make such rude comments.

When Remy was done kissing Liam she handed the toddler over to Ezra's mom.

Mia wasn't joining them since she was our flower girl.

As if conjured from my thoughts, Lisa grabbed the white basket from the corner of the room and handed it to Mia. Mia's face lit up and she beamed at the pale pink petals.

"Two minutes," Lisa warned, "get lined up *now*." She shooed us out of the room.

We lined up in the hallway and the girls took the arms of their guys.

Behind me Lisa fussed with my dress, flattening it where it stuck up and making sure everything lay the way it was supposed to.

"Hey, sweetie." My dad stepped out of a room and offered me his elbow. "You ready to knock 'em dead."

I stood on my tiptoes and kissed his cheek. "You betcha."

The music began to play, signaling the wedding party.

The six people in front of me began to move forward.

I watched them disappear around the corner into the ballroom.

Then the music changed.

*Ready or not, here I come.*

"Showtime, kiddo." My dad reached over with his free hand and patted the hand I used to vice-grip his arm.

I nodded and together we moved forward.

When we rounded the corner I gasped.

The ballroom ceilings were draped with an elegant gold fabric, the aisle was free of footprints, the flowers were in place. Absolutely everything was perfect, but my eyes didn't linger on the décor for long. Instead, my eyes sought out the deep brown of Ezra's and stopped there. He looked like sex on a stick in his tux. Seriously, the guy could wear formal attire like nobody else. I watched as his eyes filled with tears when he looked at me. My own began to fill as well.

This was it.

We were minutes away from the moment the last three-hundred and sixty-five days had been leading to.

My dad and I reached the end of the aisle and Ezra held out his hand to me.

"I love you," my dad said, his throat clogged with emotion. He kissed my cheek and placed my hand in Ezra's before going to join my mom.

Ezra broke out into a wide grin and clasped both of my hands in his.

"You're beautiful," he mouthed.

"You have a nice ass," I mouthed back.

He threw his head back and laughed. Sobering, he shook his head while everyone else shifted in their seats, wondering what was so funny.

"I said he had a nice ass." I shrugged and they all joined in laughing. "It's true."

The preacher cleared his throat, his cheeks tinted pink. "Shall we begin?"

"Absolutely." Ezra grinned, rubbing his fingers over my knuckles.

The man began speaking and Ezra spoke when he needed to. In no time at all it was my turn.

When the words, "I do," passed through my lips I practically mauled Ezra with my mouth.

*Mine. Mine. Mine.* I said silently with each kiss.

The preacher cleared his throat again and we broke apart. That's when I noticed our family and friends laughing.

"We'll get to that part in a moment." The preacher glared at me like I was the unholy-ist thing he'd ever encountered.

"Oh, right. My bad."

He shook his head. "The *ring*."

Emma handed me Ezra's ring and slipped the thick black ring with silver stripe accent onto his finger.

*My husband.*

Holy shit I *loved* the sound of that.

"You're mine now, Collins," I warned him. "You're stuck with me until the end of time."

"I can handle that." He smiled at me and his eyes sparkled with happiness.

"*Now* you may kiss the—"

I threw my arms around Ezra's neck and kissed him like he was my personal oxygen.

"*Bride.*"

When we broke apart the preacher announced us to everyone as, "Mr. and Mrs. Collins."

The two of us made our way down the aisle to the cheers of our friends and families.

When we reached the end, I looked up at him and smiled. "I love you, *husband*."

"I love you, *wife*." He bent to kiss me again. He straightened and pushed his unruly black hair from his eyes. His hands settled on my waist and he pulled me against him where I rested my hands on his chest. "We've been best friends, lovers, and now we're husband and wife. What's next?"

I pursed my lips. "Parents?"

He grinned. "Are you gonna let me put a baby in you tonight, Mrs. Collins?" He raised a brow.

I pretended to think. "Depends…will several screaming orgasms be involved?"

His smile widened. "Always."

"Then I accept."

It was safe to say I was ready for whatever life threw at us next—even parenthood—because I knew that Ezra and I could handle anything.

We were unstoppable together.

# BONUS CONTENT

## MATHIAS AND REMY
### # THREE
#### FAMILY VACATION WHEN LIAM IS NINE
#### FIRST TIME LIAM EVER GETS ON A SURFBOARD

REMY

I never thought I was the kind of person that got the fairytale ending. I always viewed myself as the ugly step-sister who would never be happy. But then I got a second chance and I finally believed in miracles, fairytales, the whole shebang.

Now, as I watched my husband chase our son around the beach—their laughter music to my ears—I couldn't help but smile.

Dreams did come true, even when you weren't hoping for them.

My son, Liam—who was just shy of his tenth birthday—picked up a pile of sand and lobbed it at Mathias. Mathias feigned that he was mad and ran at Liam. Liam tried to run away, but Mathias was faster and caught him, tossing him over his shoulder. Liam's laughter turned to hiccups and Mathias set him down. Both of them came running at me, spraying sand all over me in the process.

I brushed off the sand as they plopped on either side of me.

"You two," I admonished.

They both grinned, and once again I was struck by how much the two of them looked alike.

"You know you love us." Mathias leaned over to kiss my cheek.

I rolled my eyes. It was true, I did.

"Mom? Dad?" Liam said and the two of us turned to look at him. "Can I do that?" He pointed to where a surf instructor was working with several people, their ages varying from older to younger.

Mathias and I exchanged a look and I shrugged.

"Sure," Mathias answered him, "I'll do it too."

"Mom, do you want to do it?" Liam asked. My sweet boy always tried to include me in everything. I'd miss those days when they stopped, because I knew they would eventually.

I shook my head. "No, but I'll watch you guys."

Mathias leaned over and kissed me quickly, which earned an, "Ew," from Liam.

I laughed and watched as they went over to join the others. Mathias spoke to the instructor, who then pointed at a hut a ways down the beach.

I watched Mathias and Liam start in that direction, mockingly shoving one another.

Watching Mathias be a dad had been one of the most gratifying things in my life. When Mathias loved, he loved completely.

When they came back, each was carrying a surfboard, but Liam was struggling with his. Mathias tried to help him, but he was determined to do it on his own. That was Liam, he was a stubborn and hard-headed as his father.

They set their boards down in the sand and listened to everything the instructor said.

Liam's eyes lit up when he stepped on the board, and when the instructor finally led them into the water he was positively beaming.

I stood and dusted the sand off my body and went to stand by the water's edge so I could get a better look.

Liam paddled out, his small arms working over time. He sat up on the board and grinned up at his dad beside him.

A small wave came and Mathias urged Liam to try to catch it.

Liam appeared apprehensive, but after only a moment he laid down flat and with a determined look back at me, he went for it.

I watched in awe from the shore as Liam stood up on his board, riding the small wave. He wobbled back and forth, but he *did* it. His grin lit up his whole face before he jumped off the board into the water.

When he surfaced he let out a cry of joy. "Mom! Dad! Did you see that? I did it!" He pushed his wet hair out of his eyes. "I actually did it!"

He got back on the board and paddled towards shore. When he was close he hopped off and carried the board out.

"That was the best!" He cried enthusiastically, wrapping his arms around my waist and hugging. "I felt like a superhero!"

"You are a superhero," Mathias said, emerging from the water. He ruffled our son's hair and smiled down at him. "Good job." He held out his fist for a bump and they pounded it out. *Boys.*

With his eyes glowing, Liam grinned up at us. "I'm going to be a surfer when I grow up."

Mathias' lips twitched in amusement. "Is that so?"

Liam nodded his head eagerly. "I am," he said, resolute.

Mathias' eyes glowed with pride. "Then you better get back out there. Practice makes perfect, right?"

"Right." Liam nodded eagerly and ran back into the water. He nearly tripped over the board, and glanced back at us with a sheepish grin.

I shook my head and looked up at Mathias when he wrapped his arm around me.

"We're in trouble with that one," Mathias remarked.

I laughed. "It's your fault. He's just like you."

Mathias' lips quirked. "Of course he is. I'm awesome."

"You keep telling yourself that," I jested, leaning into him.

He hugged me tighter against his side and kissed the side of my head. "I love you, Rem," he murmured, "and I love our life, even if we had one hell of a bumpy ride to get here."

"Me too," I agreed.

It wasn't easy, but our story belonged to us, and it was my favorite.

1059

# BONUS CONTENT
## INTERVIEW
### THE GUYS

The guys are here to answer your twitter submitted questions. We thank them for taking time out of their busy schedules to answer their fans questions.

@hannahpacket To Matthias and Maddox: Who is the better looking twin?

MADDOX: Me. Obviously.

MATHIAS: We're identical, dip shit. You can't be better looking.

@wracine Ezra, how did you feel when Maddox and Mathias came to live with you? And what's up with you and Maddox's bromance lol?

EZRA: It was cool. They were my friends so it didn't bother me. I knew they had it rough and to be completely honest I worried about them a lot, so it was a relief to have them live with us. <chuckles> The bromance. <rubs jaw> I've known Maddox forever and we've always been close so I guess it naturally evolved into a bromance. I'm not as close to Mathias because he's kind of a dick. No offense.

MATHIAS: None taken. I am a dick.

@sjc_aust Most embarrassing moment on stage/ while on tour?

EZRA: Maddox wins this one.

HAYES: <laughing>  Yep, you answer this one. <claps Maddox on the shoulder>

MADDOX: <groaning> I tripped over a stage wire, fell face first, and rolled off the stage into the pit. I'm pretty sure it has been viewed over ten million times on You Tube. I'm not kidding. There's even a Vine of when I rolled of the stage.

@whatislife Maddox, what made you so obsessed with hedgehogs and why that animal?

MADDOX: I saw a documentary on Animal Planet about hedgehogs and thought they were cool. I mean, they have quills. So I got one and decided they were the best pet ever—because they are.

@budgiesaurus Ezra, have you ever straightened your hair?

EZRA: That'd be a NO. I'm not putting something that hot close to my scalp. Girls are nuts for using those.

@whatislife Hayes, do you feel separated from the band in a way since you didn't grow up together?

HAYES: Yeah, of course. I mean, these guys have known each other since they were practically in diapers and they didn't find me until high school when they needed a guitar player. Don't get me wrong, we're all friends, but they have a different kind of bond.

@ldkoke Hayes what would you surprise Mia for a Breakfast Birthday?

HAYES: Mickey Mouse pancakes. She loves those.

The lovely ladies of Willow Creek are here to answer your questions. We thank them for taking the time to do this. We know their just as busy as their guys.

@budgiesaurus Arden, which name do you like better? Hayes or Josh? :P

ARDEN: It doesn't really matter to me, but Hayes I guess, since that's how I know him best.

@run-naked-in-the-street Remy, why do you always wear red lipstick?

REMY: It's empowering.

@wracine Emma, what did you think of Maddox after that adventurous first date of jumping into the pond? Lol

Emma: I was so mad at him and sort of embarrassed since it was my first date. Obviously he ended up winning me over. He's pretty charming.

@sjc_aust If your man was magically turned into an animal what would it be and why?

EMMA: Maddox would be a hedgehog. No doubt about it.

REMY: I think Mathias would be a great white shark. Or an alligator. Something mean with a lot of teeth. He likes to bite.

SADIE: <giggles> A poodle. They have the same hair.

ARDEN: I'm not sure. Anything that eats a lot.

# Author's Note

Being inside these characters again has been beyond amazing. I had so much fun getting back into the Willow Creek series and I hope you all enjoy hearing from them again. The last few months have been so sad for me. I spent so long with these characters, back to back. Normally, when I write a series I take a "break" and write something different in between each book. But not with this series. The characters were too loud and couldn't be quieted. I had to write, and write, and write some more. I get to hold on to them a little bit longer with the kids series, which is great. It's not quite the same, though. And while I love all my books and characters there's just something extra special about this one. Maybe it's the way so many people fell in love and connected with them or maybe it's just *them*. Whatever it is, I know these characters will always have a special place in my heart.

You know, when I first started Last To Know, I proclaimed on an almost daily basis that *no one* was going to like these books. They were far too funny, sweet, and *different* for a rock star series. When people think rock star books they think of sex, drugs, fights, everything that Willow Creek is not. I wanted my rock star series to be the complete opposite of that. I wanted it to be fun, and focused on family. And of course I had to go and throw a hedgehog in there, which made me think that people would find Maddox weird—because what kind of rock star has a pet *hedgehog*. And then…and then people *loved* it. You loved the hedgehog. You loved Maddox. You saw yourselves in bookworm Emma. Then, the best part of all, you wanted more. I received all kinds of messages, proclaiming your love for Maddox and Emma and how you couldn't wait to hear from Mathias.

This is the part where I let you in on a little secret...I *hated* Mathias before I started writing Last To Know. When I was in the planning stages (in my mind. I don't plan on paper) I couldn't stand Mathias. He was too moody and rude. At that point in time his book was going to be book 3 and Ezra and Sadie were going to be book 2. But since Maddox and Mathias are identical twins it meant I needed to use the same male model for those book covers. I could have done the shoot for Last To Know and Never Too Late separately, but I decided to do them together because I was afraid if I didn't, "the guy will move." ←That's what I told my cover designer/photographer. Well, it turns out that my plan to do the shoots for Maddox and Mathias' books at the same time was a good one since the model ended up joining the military a short time later and moved away. Since I had the photos for Mathias' book I decided to move his story up to 2nd in the series, and as I began delving further into Last To Know, Mathias began speaking even more, preparing me for his story. And you guys, the more he spoke the more I fell in love with him. So much so that I couldn't wait to finish Last To Know because I wanted to start his book. When I finally started Never Too Late I fell head over heels in love with Mathias. I couldn't believe that I was able to love a character I had originally hated so much. But you see, Mathias had so much *depth*. He wasn't an asshole just to be an asshole. He'd been hurt. Devastatingly hurt. His pain ripped me apart and I fell a little more in love with him because he made me *feel*. No joke. Mathias Wade made me *cry* FOUR times while writing Never Too Late and I *never* cry when I write. But his pain, and love, and *heart* that he tried so hard to hide were so beautiful and whenever he let it shine, or revealed a piece of his heart, I cried. Not just a tear. I mean, I *cried*. Because of all that Mathias has become one of my all time favorite characters I've ever written. Who am I kidding? He's number one. I know some people

1068

don't like him, and that's okay. Not everyone can see the beauty in his character, and I guess since I wrote him I probably see it more than anyone else. Mathias is another reason this series is special to me, but if I'm completely honest there's an unlimited number of reasons why it's special. All books contain magic, but some have a little more, and for me this one has that little extra sprinkle.

Now, I know I just sang Mathias' praises for *way* too long, but I also have some mad love for Maddox, Ezra, and Hayes.

Maddox, the goofball, is impossible not to love. That boy made me laugh out loud so many times while writing. I honestly thought that no one would find the things he said funny, but you guys did. (Let's face it, I doubt everything when it comes to my writing) Ezra, sweet-sweet Ezra. Ezra's character was so sweet and his love for his family and foster brothers/best friends always warmed my heart. Ezra is the kind of character that's there for everyone. He's a fixer. And Hayes, oh Hayes. Hayes is pretty absent from the first two books and that's because he wouldn't talk to me. I had no idea what his personality was like and so I kept him hidden until he decided to speak to me—because I didn't want to write him one way, only for him to act completely different in the later books. Hayes ended up playing a bigger role in In Your Heart and boy did I fall in love with him. Funnily enough, his popular quote in that book, "I am a mist. I do not exist," is one where I was nearly asleep and bolted upright in bed and had to email myself at like two in the morning. I said to myself, "That's so stupid. You'll never keep that in the book." But I did and it's the quote I hear about the most, which is awesome. Then in Take A Chance Hayes' scenes with Mia stole my heart. That boy is the definition of swoon-worthy.

I feel like this "Author's Note" has turned into a rambling mess, so hopefully you guys are okay with that.

I hope you guys know how much it means to me that you guys love this series and support my books. Every message, like, comment, share, review, means so incredibly much to me. I tear up at your messages all the time. Sometimes I have to ask myself when did this become my life? I remember being happy to have sold *ten* books in *one* month, and now there are so many of you that read my books. I'm so incredibly blessed to be able to live my dream and every day I thank you guys for this. Seriously, it's all thanks to you. Pat yourselves on the back. You guys have not only read my books, but so many of you have shared them with your friends, who then share it, and then they share it, and...you get the idea. Word of mouth is truly an author's best asset and it means so much to me that you guys would spread the word.

Before I get any mushier I'm going to end this. I love you guys. So much.

XOXO

Micalea